PHILIP ROTH

PHILIP ROTH

THE AMERICAN TRILOGY 1997–2000

American Pastoral
I Married a Communist
The Human Stain

THE LIBRARY OF AMERICA

American Pastoral copyright © 1997 by Philip Roth. *I Married a Communist*
copyright © 1998 by Philip Roth. *The Human Stain* copyright ©
2000 by Philip Roth. Published by special arrangement with
Houghton Mifflin Harcourt Publishing Company.

The paper used in this publication meets the
minimum requirements of the American National Standard for
Information Sciences–Permanence of Paper for Printed
Library Materials, ANSI Z39.48–1984.

Distributed to the trade in the United States
by Penguin Group (USA) Inc.
and in Canada by Penguin Group Canada Ltd.

Library of Congress Control Number: 2011923051
ISBN: 978-1-59853-103-9

———

First Printing
The Library of America—220

Manufactured in the United States of America

ROSS MILLER
WROTE THE CHRONOLOGY AND NOTES
FOR THIS VOLUME

Contents

AMERICAN PASTORAL

To J. G.

Dream when the day is thru,
Dream and they might come true,
Things never are as bad as they seem,
So dream, dream, dream.
—JOHNNY MERCER,
from "Dream," popular song of the 1940s

the rare occurrence of the expected . . .
—WILLIAM CARLOS WILLIAMS,
from "At Kenneth Burke's Place," 1946

Dream with the day a little.
Dream and the... bright ones, bright...
Things never seem bad as they seem...
So dream, dream, dream.
—ODYSSEY ...

... a citizen of both countries of the...

... the two countries of his invention ...
—WILLIAM CARLOS WILLIAMS,
Paterson, Book Three

I
Paradise
Remembered

1

THE Swede. During the war years, when I was still a grade school boy, this was a magical name in our Newark neighborhood, even to adults just a generation removed from the city's old Prince Street ghetto and not yet so flawlessly Americanized as to be bowled over by the prowess of a high school athlete. The name was magical; so was the anomalous face. Of the few fair-complexioned Jewish students in our preponderantly Jewish public high school, none possessed anything remotely like the steep-jawed, insentient Viking mask of this blue-eyed blond born into our tribe as Seymour Irving Levov.

The Swede starred as end in football, center in basketball, and first baseman in baseball. Only the basketball team was ever any good—twice winning the city championship while he was its leading scorer—but as long as the Swede excelled, the fate of our sports teams didn't matter much to a student body whose elders, largely undereducated and overburdened, venerated academic achievement above all else. Physical aggression, even camouflaged by athletic uniforms and official rules and intended to do no harm to Jews, was not a traditional source of pleasure in our community—advanced degrees were. Nonetheless, through the Swede, the neighborhood entered into a fantasy about itself and about the world, the fantasy of sports fans everywhere: almost like Gentiles (as they imagined Gentiles), our families could forget the way things actually work and make an athletic performance the repository of all their hopes. Primarily, they could forget the war.

The elevation of Swede Levov into the household Apollo of the Weequahic Jews can best be explained, I think, by the war against the Germans and the Japanese and the fears that it fostered. With the Swede indomitable on the playing field, the meaningless surface of life provided a bizarre, delusionary kind of sustenance, the happy release into a Swedian innocence, for those who lived in dread of never seeing their sons or their brothers or their husbands again.

And how did this affect him—the glorification, the sanctification, of every hook shot he sank, every pass he leaped up and caught, every line drive he rifled for a double down the left-field line? Is this what made him that staid and stone-faced boy? Or was the mature-seeming sobriety the outward manifestation of an arduous inward struggle to keep in check the narcissism that an entire community was ladling with love? The high school cheerleaders had a cheer for the Swede. Unlike the other cheers, meant to inspire the whole team or to galvanize the spectators, this was a rhythmic, foot-stomping tribute to the Swede alone, enthusiasm for his perfection undiluted and unabashed. The cheer rocked the gym at basketball games every time he took a rebound or scored a point, swept through our side of City Stadium at football games any time he gained a yard or intercepted a pass. Even at the sparsely attended home baseball games up at Irvington Park, where there was no cheerleading squad eagerly kneeling at the sidelines, you could hear it thinly chanted by the handful of Weequahic stalwarts in the wooden stands not only when the Swede came up to bat but when he made no more than a routine putout at first base. It was a cheer that consisted of eight syllables, three of them his name, and it went, Bah bah-*bah!* Bah bah bah . . . bah-*bah!* and the tempo, at football games particularly, accelerated with each repetition until, at the peak of frenzied adoration, an explosion of skirt-billowing cartwheels was ecstatically discharged and the orange gym bloomers of ten sturdy little cheerleaders flickered like fireworks before our marveling eyes . . . and not for love of you or me but of the wonderful Swede. "Swede Levov! It rhymes with . . . 'The Love'! . . . Swede Levov! It rhymes with . . . 'The Love'! . . . Swede Levov! It rhymes with . . . 'The Love'!"

Yes, everywhere he looked, people were in love with him. The candy store owners we boys pestered called the rest of us "Hey-you-no!" or "Kid-cut-it-out!"; him they called, respectfully, "Swede." Parents smiled and benignly addressed him as "Seymour." The chattering girls he passed on the street would ostentatiously swoon, and the bravest would holler after him, "Come back, come back, Levov of my life!" And he let it happen, walked about the neighborhood in possession of all that love, looking as though he didn't feel a thing. Contrary to whatever daydreams the rest of us may have had about the enhancing effect on ourselves of total, uncritical, idolatrous adulation, the love thrust upon the Swede seemed actually to *deprive* him of feeling. In this boy embraced as a symbol of hope by so many—as the embodiment of the strength, the resolve, the emboldened valor that would prevail to return our high school's servicemen home unscathed from Midway, Salerno, Cherbourg, the Solomons, the Aleutians, Tarawa— there appeared to be not a drop of wit or irony to interfere with his golden gift for responsibility.

But wit or irony is like a hitch in his swing for a kid like the Swede, irony being a human consolation and beside the point if you're getting your way as a god. Either there was a whole side to his personality that he was suppressing or that was as yet asleep or, more likely, there wasn't. His aloofness, his seeming passivity as the desired object of all this asexual lovemaking, made him appear, if not divine, a distinguished cut above the more primordial humanity of just about everybody else at the school. He was fettered to history, an *instrument* of history, esteemed with a passion that might never have been if he'd broken the Weequahic basketball record—by scoring twenty-seven points against Barringer—on a day other than the sad, sad day in 1943 when fifty-eight Flying Fortresses were shot down by Luftwaffe fighter planes, two fell victim to flak, and five more crashed after crossing the English coast on their way back from bombing Germany.

The Swede's younger brother was my classmate, Jerry Levov, a scrawny, small-headed, oddly overflexible boy built along the lines of a licorice stick, something of a mathematical wizard, and the January 1950 valedictorian. Though Jerry never really had a friendship with anyone, in his imperious, irascible way, he took an interest in me over the years, and that was how I wound up, from the age of ten, regularly getting beaten by him at Ping-Pong in the finished basement of the Levovs' one-family house, on the corner of Wyndmoor and Keer—the word "finished" indicating that it was paneled in knotty pine, domesticated, and not, as Jerry seemed to think, that the basement was the perfect place for finishing off another kid.

The explosiveness of Jerry's aggression at a Ping-Pong table exceeded his brother's in any sport. A Ping-Pong ball is, brilliantly, sized and shaped so that it cannot take out your eye. I would not otherwise have played in Jerry Levov's basement. If it weren't for the opportunity to tell people that I knew my way around Swede Levov's house, nobody could have got me down into that basement, defenseless but for a small wooden paddle. Nothing that weighs as little as a Ping-Pong ball can be lethal, yet when Jerry whacked that thing murder couldn't have been far from his mind. It never occurred to me that this violent display might have something to do with what it was like for him to be the kid brother of Swede Levov. Since I couldn't imagine anything better than being the Swede's brother—short of being the Swede himself—I failed to understand that for Jerry it might be difficult to imagine anything worse.

The Swede's bedroom—which I never dared enter but would pause to gaze into when I used the toilet outside Jerry's room —was tucked under the eaves at the back of the house. With its slanted ceiling and dormer windows and Weequahic pennants on the walls, it looked like what I thought of as a real boy's room. From the two windows that opened out over the back lawn you could see the roof of the Levovs' garage, where the Swede as a grade school kid practiced hitting in the wintertime by swinging at a baseball taped to a cord hung from a rafter—an idea he might have got from a baseball novel by John R. Tunis called *The Kid from Tomkinsville*. I came to that book and to other of Tunis's baseball books—*Iron Duke, The Duke Decides, Champion's Choice, Keystone Kids, Rookie of the Year*—by spotting them on the built-in shelf beside the Swede's bed, all lined up alphabetically between two solid bronze bookends that had been a bar mitzvah gift, miniaturized replicas of Rodin's "The Thinker." Immediately I went to the library to borrow all the Tunis books I could find and started with *The Kid from Tomkinsville*, a grim, gripping book to a boy, simply written, stiff in places but direct and dignified, about the Kid, Roy Tucker, a clean-cut young pitcher from the rural Connecticut hills whose father dies when he is four and whose mother dies when he is sixteen and who helps his grandmother make ends meet by working the family farm during the day and working at night in town at "MacKenzie's drugstore on the corner of South Main."

The book, published in 1940, had black-and-white drawings

that, with just a little expressionistic distortion and just enough anatomical skill, cannily pictorialize the hardness of the Kid's life, back before the game of baseball was illuminated with a million statistics, back when it was about the mysteries of earthly fate, when major leaguers looked less like big healthy kids and more like lean and hungry workingmen. The drawings seemed conceived out of the dark austerities of Depression America. Every ten pages or so, to succinctly depict a dramatic physical moment in the story—"He was able to put a little steam in it," "It was over the fence," "Razzle limped to the dugout"—there is a blackish, ink-heavy rendering of a scrawny, shadow-faced ballplayer starkly silhouetted on a blank page, isolated, like the world's most lonesome soul, from both nature and man, or set in a stippled simulation of ballpark grass, dragging beneath him the skinny statuette of a wormlike shadow. He is unglamorous even in a baseball uniform; if he is the pitcher, his gloved hand looks like a paw; and what image after image makes graphically clear is that playing up in the majors, heroic though it may seem, is yet another form of backbreaking, unremunerative labor.

The Kid from Tomkinsville could as well have been called The Lamb from Tomkinsville, even The Lamb from Tomkinsville Led to the Slaughter. In the Kid's career as the spark-plug newcomer to a last-place Brooklyn Dodger club, each triumph is rewarded with a punishing disappointment or a crushing accident. The staunch attachment that develops between the lonely, homesick Kid and the Dodgers' veteran catcher, Dave Leonard, who successfully teaches him the ways of the big leagues and who, "with his steady brown eyes behind the plate," shepherds him through a no-hitter, comes brutally undone six weeks into the season, when the old-timer is dropped overnight from the club's roster. "Here was a speed they didn't often mention in baseball: the speed with which a player rises—and goes down." Then, after the Kid wins his fifteenth consecutive game—a rookie record that no pitcher in either league has ever exceeded—he's accidentally knocked off his feet in the shower by boisterous teammates who are horsing around after the great victory, and the elbow injury sustained in the fall leaves him unable ever to pitch again. He rides the bench for the rest of the year, pinch-hitting because of his strength at the plate, and then, over the snowy winter—back home in Connecticut spending days on the farm and evenings at the drugstore, well known now but really Grandma's boy all over again—he works diligently by himself on Dave Leonard's directive to keep his swing level ("A tendency to keep his right shoulder down, to swing up, was his worst fault"), suspending a ball from a string out in the barn and whacking at it on cold winter mornings with "his beloved bat" until he has worked himself into a sweat. " 'Crack . . .' The clean sweet sound of a bat squarely meeting a ball." By the next season he is ready to return to the Dodgers as a speedy right fielder, bats .325 in the second spot, and leads his team down to the wire as a contender. On the last day of the season, in a game against the Giants, who are in first place by only half a game, the Kid kindles the Dodgers' hitting attack, and in the bottom of the fourteenth—with two down, two men on, and the Dodgers ahead on a run scored by the Kid with his audacious, characteristically muscular baserunning—he makes the final game-saving play, a running catch smack up against the right center-field wall. That tremendous daredevil feat sends the Dodgers into the World Series and leaves him "writhing in agony on the green turf of deep right center." Tunis concludes like this: "Dusk descended upon a mass of players, on a huge crowd pouring onto the field, on a couple of men carrying an inert form through the mob on a stretcher. . . . There was a clap of thunder. Rain descended upon the Polo Grounds." Descended, descended, a clap of thunder, and thus ends the boys' Book of Job.

I was ten and I had never read anything like it. The cruelty of life. The injustice of it. I could not believe it. The reprehensible member of the Dodgers is Razzle Nugent, a great pitcher but a drunk and a hothead, a violent bully fiercely jealous of the Kid. And yet it is not Razzle carried off "inert" on a stretcher but the best of them all, the farm orphan called the Kid, modest, serious, chaste, loyal, naive, undiscourageable, hard-working, soft-spoken, courageous, a brilliant athlete, a beautiful, austere boy. Needless to say, I thought of the Swede and the Kid as one and wondered how the Swede could bear to read this book that had left me near tears and unable to sleep. Had I had the courage to address him, I would have asked if he thought the ending meant the Kid was finished or whether it meant the possibility of yet another comeback. The word "inert" terrified me. Was the Kid *killed* by the last catch of the year? Did the Swede know? Did he care? Did it occur to him that if disaster could strike down the Kid from Tomkinsville, it could come and strike the great Swede down too? Or was a book about a sweet star savagely and unjustly punished—a book about a greatly gifted innocent whose worst fault is a tendency to keep his right shoulder down and swing up but whom the thundering heavens destroy nonetheless—simply a book between those "Thinker" bookends up on his shelf?

Keer Avenue was where the rich Jews lived—or rich they seemed to most of the families who rented apartments in the two-, three-, and four-family dwellings with the brick stoops integral to our after-school sporting life: the crap games, the blackjack, and the stoopball, endless until the cheap rubber ball hurled mercilessly against the steps went pop and split at the seam. Here, on this grid of locust-tree-lined streets into which the Lyons farm had been partitioned during the boom years of the early twenties, the first postimmigrant generation of Newark's Jews had regrouped into a community that took its inspiration more from the mainstream of American life than from the Polish shtetl their Yiddish-speaking parents had re-created around Prince Street in the impoverished Third Ward. The Keer Avenue Jews, with their finished basements, their screened-in porches, their flagstone front steps, seemed to be at the forefront, laying claim like audacious pioneers to the normalizing American amenities. And at the vanguard of the vanguard were the Levovs, who had bestowed upon us our very own Swede, a boy as close to a goy as we were going to get.

The Levovs themselves, Lou and Sylvia, were parents neither more nor less recognizably American than my own Jersey-born Jewish mother and father, no more or less refined, well spoken, or cultivated. And that to me was a big surprise. Other than the one-family Keer Avenue house, there was no division between us like the one between the peasants and the aristocracy I was learning about at school. Mrs. Levov was, like my own mother, a tidy housekeeper, impeccably well mannered, a nice-looking woman tremendously considerate of everyone's feelings, with a way of making her sons feel important—one of the many women of that era who never dreamed of being free of the great domestic enterprise centered on the children. From their mother both Levov boys had inherited the long bones and fair hair, though since her hair was redder, frizzier, and her skin still youthfully freckled, she looked less startlingly Aryan than they did, less vivid a genetic oddity among the faces in our streets.

The father was no more than five seven or eight—a spidery man even more agitated than the father whose anxieties were shaping my own. Mr. Levov was one of those slum-reared Jewish fathers whose rough-hewn, undereducated perspective goaded a whole generation of striving, college-educated Jewish sons: a father for whom everything is an unshakable duty, for whom there is a right way and a wrong way and nothing in between, a father whose compound of ambitions, biases, and beliefs is so unruffled by careful thinking that he isn't as easy to escape from as he seems. Limited men with limitless energy; men quick to be friendly and quick to be fed up; men for whom the most serious thing in life is *to keep going despite everything.* And we were their sons. It was our job to love them.

The way it fell out, my father was a chiropodist whose office was for years our living room and who made enough money for our family to get by on but no more, while Mr. Levov got rich manufacturing ladies' gloves. His own father—Swede Levov's grandfather—had come to Newark from the old country in the 1890s and found work fleshing sheepskins fresh from the lime vat, the lone Jew alongside the roughest of Newark's Slav, Irish, and Italian immigrants in the Nuttman Street tannery of the patent-leather tycoon T. P. Howell, then *the* name in the city's oldest and biggest industry, the tanning and manufacture of leather goods. The most important thing in making leather is water—skins spinning in big drums of water, drums spewing out befouled water, pipes gushing with cool and hot water, hundreds of thousands of gallons of water. If there's soft water, good water, you can make beer and you can make leather, and Newark made both—big breweries, big tanneries, and, for the immigrant, lots of wet, smelly, crushing work.

The son Lou—Swede Levov's father—went to work in the tannery after leaving school at fourteen to help support the family of nine and became adept not only at dyeing buckskin by laying on the clay dye with a flat, stiff brush but also at sorting and grading skins. The tannery that stank of both the slaughterhouse and the chemical plant from the soaking of flesh and the cooking of flesh and the dehairing and pickling and degreasing of hides, where round the clock in the summertime the blowers drying the thousands and thousands of hanging skins raised the temperature in the low-ceilinged dry room to a hundred and twenty degrees, where the vast vat rooms were dark as caves and flooded with swill, where brutish workingmen, heavily aproned, armed with hooks and staves, dragging and pushing overloaded wagons, wringing and hanging waterlogged skins, were driven like animals through the laborious storm that was a twelve-hour shift—a filthy, stinking place awash with water dyed red and black and blue and green, with hunks of skin all over the floor, everywhere pits of grease, hills of salt, barrels of solvent—this was Lou Levov's high school and college. What was amazing was not how tough he turned out. What was amazing was how civil he could sometimes still manage to be.

From Howell & Co. he graduated in his early twenties to found, with two of his brothers, a small handbag outfit specializing in alligator skins contracted from R. G. Salomon, Newark's king of cordovan leather and leader in the tanning of alligator; for a time the business looked as if it might flourish, but after the crash the company went under, bankrupting the three hustling, audacious Levovs. Newark Maid Leatherware started up a few years later, with Lou Levov, now on his own, buying seconds in leather goods—imperfect handbags, gloves, and belts —and selling them out of a pushcart on weekends and door-to-door at night. Down Neck—the semi-peninsular protuberance that is easternmost Newark, where each fresh wave of immigrants first settled, the lowlands bounded to the north and east by the Passaic River and to the south by the salt marshes —there were Italians who'd been glovers in the old country and they began doing piecework for him in their homes. Out of the skins he supplied they cut and sewed ladies' gloves that he peddled around the state. By the time the war broke out, he had a collective of Italian families cutting and stitching kid gloves in a small loft on West Market Street. It was a marginal business, no real money, until, in 1942, the bonanza: a black, lined sheepskin dress glove, ordered by the Women's Army Corps. He leased the old umbrella factory, a smoke-darkened brick pile fifty years old and four stories high on Central Avenue and 2nd Street, and very shortly purchased it outright, leasing the top floor to a zipper company. Newark Maid began pumping out gloves, and every two or three days the truck backed up and took them away.

A cause for jubilation even greater than the government contract was the Bamberger account. Newark Maid cracked Bamberger's, and then became the major manufacturer of their fine ladies' gloves, because of an unlikely encounter between Lou Levov and Louis Bamberger. At a ceremonial dinner for Meyer Ellenstein, a city commissioner since 1933 and the only Jew ever to be mayor of Newark, some higher-up from Bam's, hearing that Swede Levov's father was present, came over to congratulate him on his boy's selection by the *Newark News* as an all-county center in basketball. Alert to the opportunity of a lifetime—the opportunity to cut through all obstructions and go right to the top—Lou Levov brazenly talked his way into an introduction, right there at the Ellenstein dinner, to the legendary L. Bamberger himself, founder of Newark's most prestigious department store and the philanthropist who'd given the city its museum, a powerful personage as meaningful to local Jews as Bernard Baruch was meaningful to Jews around the country for his close association with FDR. According to the gossip that permeated the neighborhood, although Bamberger barely did more than shake Lou Levov's hand and quiz him (about the Swede) for a couple of minutes at most, Lou Levov had dared to say to his face, "Mr. Bamberger, we've got the quality, we've got the price—why can't we sell you people gloves?" And before the month was out, Bam's had placed an order with Newark Maid, its first, for five hundred dozen pairs.

By the end of the war, Newark Maid had established itself—in no small part because of Swede Levov's athletic achievement—as one of the most respected names in ladies' gloves south of Gloversville, New York, the center of the glove trade, where Lou Levov shipped his hides by rail, through Fultonville, to be tanned by the best glove tannery in the business. Little more than a decade later, with the opening of a factory in Puerto

Rico in 1958, the Swede would himself become the young president of the company, commuting every morning down to Central Avenue from his home some thirty-odd miles west of Newark, out past the suburbs—a short-range pioneer living on a hundred-acre farm on a back road in the sparsely habitated hills beyond Morristown, in wealthy, rural Old Rimrock, New Jersey, a long way from the tannery floor where Grandfather Levov had begun in America, paring away from the true skin the rubbery flesh that had ghoulishly swelled to twice its thickness in the great lime vats.

The day after graduating Weequahic in June '45, the Swede had joined the Marine Corps, eager to be in on the fighting that ended the war. It was rumored that his parents were beside themselves and did everything to talk him out of the marines and get him into the navy. Even if he surmounted the notorious Marine Corps anti-Semitism, did he imagine himself surviving the invasion of Japan? But the Swede would not be dissuaded from meeting the manly, patriotic challenge—secretly set for himself just after Pearl Harbor—of going off to fight as one of the toughest of the tough should the country still be at war when he graduated high school. He was just finishing up his boot training at Parris Island, South Carolina—where the scuttlebutt was that the marines were to hit the Japanese beaches on March 1, 1946—when the atomic bomb was dropped on Hiroshima. As a result, the Swede got to spend the rest of his hitch as a "recreation specialist" right there on Parris Island. He ran the calisthenic drill for his battalion for half an hour before breakfast every morning, arranged for the boxing smokers to entertain the recruits a couple of nights a week, and the bulk of the time played for the base team against armed forces teams throughout the South, basketball all winter long, baseball all summer long. He was stationed down in South Carolina about a year when he became engaged to an Irish Catholic girl whose father, a marine major and a one-time Purdue football coach, had procured him the cushy job as drill instructor in order to keep him at Parris Island to play ball. Several months before the Swede's discharge, his own father made a trip to Parris Island, stayed for a full week, near the base at the hotel in Beaufort, and departed only when the engagement to Miss Dunleavy had been broken off. The Swede returned home in '47 to enroll at Upsala College, in East Orange, at twenty unencumbered by a Gentile wife and all the more glamorously heroic for having made his mark as a Jewish marine—a drill instructor no less, and at arguably the cruelest military training camp anywhere in the world. Marines are made at boot camp, and Seymour Irving Levov had helped to make them.

We knew all this because the mystique of the Swede lived on in the corridors and classrooms of the high school, where I was by then a student. I remember two or three times one spring trekking out with friends to Viking Field in East Orange to watch the Upsala baseball team play a Saturday home game. Their star cleanup hitter and first baseman was the Swede. Three home runs one day against Muhlenberg. Whenever we saw a man in the stands wearing a suit and a hat we would whisper to one another, "A scout, a scout!" I was away at college when I heard from a schoolyard pal still living in the neighborhood that the Swede had been offered a contract with a Double A Giant farm club but had turned it down to join his father's company instead. Later I learned through my parents about the Swede's marriage to Miss New Jersey. Before competing at Atlantic City for the 1949 Miss America title, she had been Miss Union County, and before that Spring Queen at Upsala. From Elizabeth. A shiksa. Dawn Dwyer. He'd done it.

One night in the summer of 1985, while visiting New York, I went out to see the Mets play the Astros, and while circling the stadium with my friends, looking for the gate to our seats, I saw the Swede, thirty-six years older than when I'd watched him play ball for Upsala. He wore a white shirt, a striped tie, and a charcoal-gray summer suit, and he was still terrifically handsome. The golden hair was a shade or two darker but not any thinner; no longer was it cut short but fell rather fully over his ears and down to his collar. In this suit that fit him so exquisitely he seemed even taller and leaner than I remembered him in the uniform of one sport or another. The woman with us noticed him first. "*Who* is that? That's—that's . . . Is that John Lindsay?" she asked. "No," I said. "My God. You know who that is? It's Swede Levov." I told my friends, "That's the Swede!"

A skinny, fair-haired boy of about seven or eight was walking alongside the Swede, a kid under a Mets cap pounding away at a first baseman's mitt that dangled, as had the Swede's, from his left hand. The two, clearly a father and his son, were laughing about something together when I approached and introduced myself. "I knew your brother at Weequahic."

"You're Zuckerman?" he replied, vigorously shaking my hand. "The author?"

"I'm Zuckerman the author."

"Sure, you were Jerry's great pal."

"I don't think Jerry had great pals. He was too brilliant for pals. He just used to beat my pants off at Ping-Pong down in your basement. Beating me at Ping-Pong was very important to Jerry."

"So you're the guy. My mother says, 'And he was such a nice, quiet child when he came to the house.' You know who this is?" the Swede said to the boy. "The guy who wrote those books. Nathan Zuckerman."

Mystified, the boy shrugged and muttered, "Hi."

"This is my son Chris."

"These are friends," I said, sweeping an arm out to introduce the three people with me. "And this man," I said to them, "is the greatest athlete in the history of Weequahic High. A real artist in three sports. Played first base like Hernandez—thinking. A line-drive doubles hitter. Do you know that?" I said to his son. "Your dad was our Hernandez."

"Hernandez's a lefty," he replied.

"Well, that's the only difference," I said to the little literalist, and put out my hand again to his father. "Nice to see you, Swede."

"You bet. Take it easy, Skip."

"Remember me to your brother," I said.

He laughed, we parted, and someone was saying to me, "Well, well, the greatest athlete in the history of Weequahic High called you 'Skip.'"

"I know. I can't believe it." And I did feel almost as wonderfully singled out as I had the one time before, at the age of ten, when the Swede had got so personal as to recognize me by the playground nickname I'd acquired because of two grades I skipped in grade school.

Midway through the first inning, the woman with us turned to me and said, "You should have seen your face—you might as well have told us he was Zeus. I saw just what you looked like as a boy."

The following letter reached me by way of my publisher a couple of weeks before Memorial Day, 1995.

Dear Skip Zuckerman:

I apologize for any inconvenience this letter may cause you. You may not remember our meeting at Shea Stadium. I was with my oldest son (now a first-year college student) and you were out with some friends to see the Mets. That was ten years ago, the era of Carter-Gooden-Hernandez, when you could still watch the Mets. You can't anymore.

I am writing to ask if we might meet sometime to talk. I'd be delighted to take you to dinner in New York if you would permit me.

I'm taking the liberty of proposing a meeting because of something I have been thinking about since my father died last year. He was ninety-six. He was his feisty, combative self right down to the end. That made it all the harder to see him go, despite his advanced age.

I would like to talk about him and his life. I have been trying to write a tribute to him, to be published privately for friends, family, and business associates. Most everybody thought of my father as indestructible, a thick-skinned man on a short fuse. That was far from the truth. Not everyone knew how much he suffered because of the shocks that befell his loved ones.

Please be assured that I will understand if you haven't time to respond.

Sincerely,
Seymour "Swede" Levov, WHS 1945

Had anyone else asked if he could talk to me about a tribute he was writing to his father, I would have wished him luck and kept my nose out of it. But there were compelling reasons for my getting off a note to the Swede—within the hour—to say that I was at his disposal. The first was *Swede Levov wants to meet me.* Ridiculously, perhaps, at the onset of old age, I had only to see his signature at the foot of the letter to be swamped by memories of him, both on and off the field, that were some fifty years old and yet still captivating. I remembered going up every day to the playing field to watch football practice the year that the Swede first agreed to join the team. He was already a high-scoring hook-shot artist on the basketball court, but no one knew he could be just as magical on the football field until the coach pressed him into duty as an end and our losing team, though still at the bottom of the city league, was putting up one, two, even three touchdowns a game, all scored on passes to the Swede. Fifty or sixty kids gathered along the sidelines at practice to watch the Swede—in a battered leather helmet and the brown jersey numbered, in orange, 11—working out with the varsity against the JVs. The varsity quarterback, Lefty Leventhal, ran pass play after pass play ("Lev-en-*thal* to Le-*vov!* Lev-en-*thal* to Le-*vov!*" was an anapest that could always get us going back in the heyday of the Swede), and the task of the JV squad, playing defense, was to stop Swede Levov from scoring every time. I'm over sixty, not exactly someone with the outlook on life that he'd had as a boy, and yet the boy's beguilement has never wholly evaporated, for to this day I haven't forgotten the Swede, after being smothered by tacklers, climbing slowly to his feet, shaking himself off, casting an upward, remonstrative glance at the darkening fall sky, sighing ruefully, and then trotting undamaged back to the huddle. When he scored, that was one kind of glory, and when he got tackled and piled on hard, and just stood up and shook it off, that was another kind of glory, even in a scrimmage.

And then one day I shared in that glory. I was ten, never before touched by greatness, and would have been as beneath the Swede's attention as anyone else along the sidelines had it not been for Jerry Levov. Jerry had recently taken me on board as a friend; though I was hard put to believe it, the Swede must have noticed me around their house. And so late on a fall afternoon in 1943, when he got slammed to the ground by the whole of the JV team after catching a short Leventhal bullet and the coach abruptly blew the whistle signaling that was it for the day, the Swede, tentatively flexing an elbow while half running and half limping off the field, spotted me among the other kids, and called over, "Basketball was never like this, Skip."

The god (himself all of sixteen) had carried me up into

athletes' heaven. The adored had acknowledged the adoring. Of course, with athletes as with movie idols, each worshiper imagines that he or she has a secret, personal link, but this was one forged openly by the most unostentatious of stars and before a hushed congregation of competitive kids—an amazing experience, and I was thrilled. I blushed, I was thrilled, I probably thought of nothing else for the rest of the week. The mock jock self-pity, the manly generosity, the princely graciousness, the athlete's self-pleasure so abundant that a portion can be freely given to the crowd—this munificence not only overwhelmed me and wafted through me because it had come wrapped in my nickname but became fixed in my mind as an embodiment of something grander even than his talent for sports: the talent for "being himself," the capacity to be this strange engulfing force and yet to have a voice and a smile unsullied by even a flicker of superiority—the natural modesty of someone for whom there were no obstacles, who appeared never to have to struggle to clear a space for himself. I don't imagine I'm the only grown man who was a Jewish kid aspiring to be an all-American kid during the patriotic war years—when our entire neighborhood's wartime hope seemed to converge in the marvelous body of the Swede—who's carried with him through life recollections of this gifted boy's unsurpassable style.

The Jewishness that he wore so lightly as one of the tall, blond athletic winners must have spoken to us too—in our idolizing the Swede and his unconscious oneness with America, I suppose there was a tinge of shame and self-rejection. Conflicting Jewish desires awakened by the sight of him were simultaneously becalmed by him; the contradiction in Jews who want to fit in and want to stand out, who insist they are different and insist they are no different, resolved itself in the triumphant spectacle of this Swede who was actually only another of our neighborhood Seymours whose forebears had been Solomons and Sauls and who would themselves beget Stephens who would in turn beget Shawns. Where was the Jew in him? You couldn't find it and yet you knew it was there. Where was the irrationality in him? Where was the crybaby in him? Where were the wayward temptations? No guile. No artifice. No mischief. All that he had eliminated to achieve his perfection. No striving, no ambivalence, no doubleness—just the style, the natural physical refinement of a star.

Only . . . what did he do for subjectivity? What *was* the Swede's subjectivity? There had to be a substratum, but its composition was unimaginable.

That was the second reason I answered his letter—the substratum. What sort of mental existence had been his? What, if anything, had ever threatened to destabilize the Swede's trajectory? No one gets through unmarked by brooding, grief, confusion, and loss. Even those who had it all as kids sooner or later get the average share of misery, if not sometimes more. There had to have been consciousness and there had to have been blight. Yet I could not picture the form taken by either, could not desimplify him even now: in the residuum of adolescent imagination I was still convinced that for the Swede it had to have been pain-free all the way.

But what had he been alluding to in that careful, courteous letter when, speaking of the late father, a man not as thick-skinned as people thought, he wrote, "Not everyone knew how much he suffered because of the shocks that befell his loved ones"? No, the Swede had suffered a shock. And it was suffering the shock that he wanted to talk about. It wasn't the father's life, it was his own that he wanted revealed.

I was wrong.

We met at an Italian restaurant in the West Forties where the Swede had for years been taking his family whenever they came over to New York for a Broadway show or to watch the Knicks at the Garden, and I understood right off that I wasn't going to get anywhere near the substratum. Everybody at Vincent's knew him by name—Vincent himself, Vincent's wife, Louie the maitre d', Carlo the bartender, Billy our waiter, everybody knew Mr. Levov and everybody asked after the missus and the boys. It turned out that when his parents were alive he used to bring them to celebrate an anniversary or a birthday at Vincent's. No, I thought, he's invited me here to reveal only that he is as admired on West 49th Street as he was on Chancellor Avenue.

Vincent's is one of those oldish Italian restaurants tucked into the midtown West Side streets between Madison Square

Garden and the Plaza, small restaurants three tables wide and four chandeliers deep, with decor and menus that have changed hardly at all since before arugula was discovered. There was a ballgame on the TV set by the small bar, and a customer every once in a while would get up, go look for a minute, ask the bartender the score, ask how Mattingly was doing, and head back to his meal. The chairs were upholstered in electric-turquoise plastic, the floor was tiled in speckled salmon, one wall was mirrored, the chandeliers were fake brass, and for decoration there was a five-foot-tall bright red pepper grinder standing in one corner like a Giacometti (a gift, said the Swede, to Vincent from his hometown in Italy); counterbalancing it in the opposite corner, on a stand like statuary, stood a stout jeroboam of Barolo. A table piled with jars of Vincent's Marinara Sauce was just across from the bowl of free after-dinner mints beside Mrs. Vincent's register; on the dessert cart was the napoleon, the tiramisù, the layer cake, the apple tart, and the sugared strawberries; and behind our table, on the wall, were the autographed photographs ("Best regards to Vincent and Anne") of Sammy Davis, Jr., Joe Namath, Liza Minnelli, Kaye Ballard, Gene Kelly, Jack Carter, Phil Rizzuto, and Johnny and Joanna Carson. There should have been one of the Swede, of course, and there would have been if we were still fighting the Germans and the Japanese and across the street were Weequahic High.

Our waiter, Billy, a small, heavyset bald man with a boxer's flattened nose, didn't have to ask what the Swede wanted to eat. For over thirty years the Swede had been ordering from Billy the house specialty, ziti à la Vincent, preceded by clams posillipo. "Best baked ziti in New York," the Swede told me, but I ordered my own old-fashioned favorite, the chicken cacciatore, "off the bone" at Billy's suggestion. While writing up our order, Billy told the Swede that Tony Bennett had been in the evening before. For a man with Billy's compact build, a man you might have imagined lugging around a weightier burden all his life than a plate of ziti, Billy's voice—high-pitched and intense, taut from some distress too long endured—was unexpected and a real treat. "See where your friend is sitting? See his chair, Mr. Levov? Tony Bennett sat in that chair." To me he said, "You know what Tony Bennett says when people come up to his table and introduce themselves to him? He says, 'Nice to see you.' And you're in his seat."

That ended the entertainment. It was work from there on out.

He had brought photographs of his three boys to show me, and from the appetizer through to dessert virtually all conversation was about eighteen-year-old Chris, sixteen-year-old Steve, and fourteen-year-old Kent. Which boy was better at lacrosse than at baseball but was being pressured by a coach . . . which was as good at soccer as at football but couldn't decide . . . which was the diving champion who had also broken school records in butterfly and backstroke. All three were hardworking students, A's and B's; one was "into" the sciences, another was more "community-minded," while the third . . . etc. There was one photograph of the boys with their mother, a good-looking fortyish blonde, advertising manager for a Morris County weekly. But she hadn't begun her career, the Swede was quick to add, until their youngest had entered second grade. The boys were lucky to have a mom who still put staying at home and raising kids ahead of . . .

I was impressed, as the meal wore on, by how assured he seemed of everything commonplace he said, and how everything he said was suffused by his good nature. I kept waiting for him to lay bare something more than this pointed unobjectionableness, but all that rose to the surface was more surface. What he has instead of a being, I thought, is blandness—the guy's radiant with it. He has devised for himself an incognito, and the incognito has become him. Several times during the meal I didn't think I was going to make it, didn't think I'd get to dessert if he was going to keep praising his family and praising his family . . . until I began to wonder if it wasn't that he was incognito but that he was mad.

Something was on top of him that had called a halt to him. Something had turned him into a human platitude. Something had warned him: You must not run counter to anything.

The Swede, some six or seven years my senior, was close to seventy, and yet he was no less splendid-looking for the crevices at the corners of his eyes and, beneath the promontory of cheekbones, a little more hollowing out than classic standards of ruggedness required. I chalked up the gauntness to a regimen of serious jogging or tennis, until near the end of the meal I found out that he'd had prostate surgery during the winter and was only beginning to regain the weight he'd lost. I don't know if it was learning that he'd suffered an affliction or his confessing to one that most surprised me. I even wondered if it might not be his recent experience of the surgery and its aftereffects that was feeding my sense of someone who was not mentally sound.

At one point I interrupted and, trying not to appear in any way desperate, asked about the business, what it was like these days running a factory in Newark. That's how I discovered that Newark Maid hadn't been in Newark since the early seventies. Virtually the whole industry had moved offshore: the unions had made it more and more difficult for a manufacturer to make any money, you could hardly find people to do that kind of piecework anymore, or to do it the way you wanted it done, and elsewhere there was an availability of workers who could be trained nearly to the standards that had obtained in the glove industry forty and fifty years ago. His family had kept their operation going in Newark for quite a long time; out of duty to long-standing employees, most of whom were black, the Swede had hung on for some six years after the '67 riots, held on in the face of industry-wide economic realities and his father's imprecations as long as he possibly could, but when he was unable to stop the erosion of the workmanship, which had deteriorated steadily since the riots, he'd given up, managing to get out more or less unharmed by the city's collapse. All the Newark Maid factory had suffered in the four days of rioting were some broken windows, though fifty yards from the gate to his loading dock, out on West Market, two other buildings had been gutted by fire and abandoned.

"Taxes, corruption, and race. My old man's litany. Anybody at all, people from all over the country who couldn't care less about the fate of Newark, made no difference to him—whether it was down in Miami Beach at the condo, on a cruise ship in the Caribbean, they'd get an earful about his beloved old Newark, butchered to death by taxes, corruption, and race. My father was one of those Prince Street guys who loved that city all his life. What happened to Newark broke his heart.

"It's the worst city in the world, Skip," the Swede was telling me. "Used to be the city where they manufactured everything. Now it's the car-theft capital of the world. Did you know that? Not the most gruesome of the gruesome developments but it's awful enough. The thieves live mostly in our old neighborhood. Black kids. Forty cars stolen in Newark every twenty-four hours. That's the statistic. Something, isn't it? And they're murder weapons—once they're stolen, they're flying missiles. The target is anybody in the street—old people, toddlers, doesn't matter. Out in front of our factory was the Indianapolis Speedway to them. That's another reason we left. Four, five kids drooping out the windows, eighty miles an hour—right on Central Avenue. When my father bought the factory, there were trolley cars on Central Avenue. Further down were the auto showrooms. Central Cadillac. LaSalle. There was a factory where somebody was making something in every side street. Now there's a liquor store in every street—a liquor store, a pizza stand, and a seedy storefront church. Everything else in ruins or boarded up. But when my father bought the factory, a stone's throw away Kiler made watercoolers, Fortgang made fire alarms, Lasky made corsets, Robbins made pillows, Honig made pen points—Christ, I *sound* like my father. But he was right—'The joint's jumpin',' he used to say. The major industry now is car theft. Sit at a light in Newark, anywhere in Newark, and all you're doing is looking around you. Bergen near Lyons is where I got rammed. Remember Henry's, 'the Sweet Shop,' next to the Park Theater? Well, right there, where Henry's used to be. Took my first high school date to Henry's for a soda. In a booth there. Arlene Danziger. Took her for a black-and-white soda after the movie. But a black-and-white doesn't mean a soda anymore on Bergen Street. It means the worst kind of hatred in the world. A car coming the wrong way on a one-way street and they ram me. Four kids drooping out the windows. Two of them get out, laughing, joking, and point a gun at my head. I hand over the keys and one of them takes off in my car. Right in front of what used to be Henry's. It's something horrible. They ram cop cars in broad daylight. Front-end collisions. To explode the air bags. Doughnuting. Heard of doughnuting? Doing doughnuts? You haven't heard about this? This is what they steal the cars for. Top speed, they slam on the brakes, yank the emergency brake, twist the steering wheel, and the car starts spinning. Wheeling the car in circles at tremendous speeds. Killing pedestrians means nothing to them. Killing motorists means nothing to them. Killing *themselves* means nothing to them. The skid marks are enough to frighten you. They killed a woman right out in front of our place, same week my car was stolen. Doing a doughnut. I witnessed this. I was leaving for the day. Tremendous speed. The car groaning. Ungodly screeching. It was terrifying. It made my blood run cold. Just driving her own car out of 2nd Street, and this woman, young black woman, gets it. Mother of three kids. Two days later it's one of my own employees. A black guy. But they don't care, black, white doesn't matter to them. They'll kill anyone. Fellow named Clark Tyler, my shipping guy—all he's doing is pulling out of our lot to go home. Twelve hours of surgery, four months in a hospital. Permanent disability. Head injuries, internal injuries, broken pelvis, broken shoulder, fractured spine. A high-speed chase, crazy kid in a stolen car and the cops are chasing him, and the kid plows right into him, crushes the driver's-side door, and that's it for Clark. Eighty miles an hour down Central Avenue. The car thief is twelve years old. To see over the wheel he has to roll up the floor mats to sit on. Six months in Jamesburg and he's back behind the wheel of another stolen car. No, that was it for me, too. My car's robbed at gunpoint, they cripple Clark, the woman gets killed—that week did it. That was enough."

Newark Maid manufactured now exclusively in Puerto Rico. For a while, after leaving Newark, he'd contracted with the Communist government in Czechoslovakia and divided the work between his own factory in Ponce, Puerto Rico, and a Czech glove factory in Brno. However, when a plant that suited him went up for sale in Aguadilla, Puerto Rico, over near Mayagüez, he'd bailed out on the Czechs, whose bureaucracy had been irritating from the start, and unified his manufacturing operation by purchasing a second Puerto Rico facility, another good-sized factory, moved in the machinery, started a training program, and hired an additional three hundred people. By the eighties, though, even Puerto Rico began to grow expensive and about everybody but Newark Maid fled to wherever in the Far East the labor force was abundant and cheap, to the Philippines first, then Korea and Taiwan, and now to China. Even baseball gloves, the most American glove of all, which used to be made by friends of his father's, the Denkerts up in Johnstown, New York, for a long time now had been manufactured in Korea. When the first guy left Gloversville, New York, in '52 or '53 and went to the Philippines to make gloves, they laughed at him, as though he were going to the moon. But when he died, around 1978, he had a factory there with four thousand workers and the whole industry had gone essentially from Gloversville to the Philippines. Up in Gloversville, when the Second World War began, there must have been ninety glove factories, big and small. Today there isn't a one—all of them out of business or importers from abroad, "people who don't know a fourchette from a thumb," the Swede said. "They're business people, they know if they need a hundred thousand pair of this and two hundred thousand pair of that in so many colors and so many sizes, but they don't know the details on how to get it done." "What's a fourchette?" I asked. "The part of the glove between the fingers. Those small oblong pieces between the fingers, they're die-cut along with the thumbs—those are the fourchettes. Today you've got a lot of underqualified people, probably don't know half what I knew when I was five, and they're making some pretty big decisions. A guy buying deerskin, which can run up to maybe three dollars and fifty cents a foot for a garment grade, he's buying this fine garment-grade deerskin to cut a little palm patch to go on a pair of ski gloves. I talked to him just the other day. A novelty part, runs about five inches by one inch, and he pays three fifty a foot where he could have paid a dollar fifty a foot and come out a long, long ways ahead. You multiply this over a large order, you're talking a hundred-thousand-dollar mistake, and he never knew it. He could have put a hundred grand in his pocket."

The Swede found himself hanging on in P.R., he explained, the way he had hung on in Newark, in large part because he had trained a lot of good people to do the intricate work of making a glove carefully and meticulously, people who could give him what Newark Maid had demanded in quality going back to his father's days; but also, he had to admit, staying on because his family so much enjoyed the vacation home he'd built some fifteen years ago on the Caribbean coast, not very far from the Ponce plant. The life the kids lived there they just loved . . . and off he went again, Kent, Chris, Steve, water-skiing, sailing, scuba diving, catamaraning . . . and though it was clear from all he had just been telling me that this guy could be engaging if he wanted to be, he didn't appear to have any judgment at all as to what was and wasn't interesting about his world. Or, for reasons I couldn't understand, he didn't want his world to be interesting. I would have given anything to get him back to Kiler, Fortgang, Lasky, Robbins, and Honig, back to the fourchettes and the details of how to get a good glove done, even back to the guy who'd paid three fifty a foot for the wrong grade of deerskin for a novelty part, but once he was off and running there was no civil way I could find to shift his focus for a second time from the achievements of his boys on land and sea.

While we waited for dessert, the Swede let pass that he was in-dulging himself in a fattening zabaglione on top of the ziti only because, after having had his prostate removed a couple of months back, he was still some ten pounds underweight.

"The operation went okay?"

"Just fine," he replied.

"A couple friends of mine," I said, "didn't emerge from that surgery as they'd hoped to. That operation can be a real catas-trophe for a man, even if they get the cancer out."

"Yes, that happens, I know."

"One wound up impotent," I said. "The other's impotent and incontinent. Fellows my age. It's been rough for them. Desolating. It can leave you in diapers."

The person I had referred to as "the other" was me. I'd had the surgery in Boston, and—except for confiding in a Boston friend who had helped me through the ordeal till I was back on my feet—when I returned to the house where I live alone, two and a half hours west of Boston, in the Berkshires, I had thought it best to keep to myself both the fact that I'd had cancer and the ways it had left me impaired.

"Well," said the Swede, "I got off easy, I guess."

"I'd say you did." I replied amiably enough, thinking that this big jeroboam of self-contentment really was in possession

of all he ever had wanted. To respect everything one is supposed to respect; to protest nothing; never to be inconve-
nienced by self-distrust; never to be enmeshed in obsession,
tortured by incapacity, poisoned by resentment, driven by
anger . . . life just unraveling for the Swede like a fluffy ball
of yarn.

This line of thinking brought me back to his letter, his request for professional advice about the tribute to his father
that he was trying to write. I wasn't myself going to bring up
the tribute, and yet the puzzle remained not only as to why *he*
didn't but as to why, if he didn't, he had written me about it in
the first place. I could only conclude—given what I now knew
of this life neither overly rich in contrasts nor troubled too
much by contradiction—that the letter and its contents had to
do with the operation, with something uncharacteristic that
arose in him afterward, some surprising new emotion that had
come to the fore. Yes, I thought, the letter grew out of Swede
Levov's belated discovery of what it means to be not healthy
but sick, to be not strong but weak; what it means to not look
great—what physical shame is, what humiliation is, what the
gruesome is, what extinction is, what it is like to ask "Why?"
Betrayed all at once by a wonderful body that had furnished
him only with assurance and had constituted the bulk of his
advantage over others, he had momentarily lost his equilibrium
and had clutched at me, of all people, as a means of grasping
his dead father and calling up the father's power to protect him.
For a moment his nerve was shattered, and this man who, as
far as I could tell, used himself mainly to conceal himself had
been transformed into an impulsive, devitalized being in dire
need of a blessing. Death had burst into the dream of his life
(as, for the second time in ten years, it had burst into mine),
and the things that disquiet men our age disquieted even him.

I wondered if he was willing any longer to recall the sickbed
vulnerability that had made certain inevitabilities as real for
him as the exterior of his family's life, to remember the shadow
that had insinuated itself like a virulent icing between the layers and layers of contentment. Yet he'd showed up for our dinner date. Did that mean the unendurable wasn't blotted out,
the safeguards weren't back in place, the emergency wasn't
yet over? Or was showing up and going blithely on about

everything that *was* endurable his way of purging the last of his fears? The more I thought about this simple-seeming soul sitting across from me eating zabaglione and exuding sincerity, the farther from him my thinking carried me. The man within the man was scarcely perceptible to me. I could not make sense of him. I couldn't imagine him at all, having come down with my own strain of the Swede's disorder: the inability to draw conclusions about anything but exteriors. Rooting around trying to figure this guy out is ridiculous, I told myself. This is the jar you cannot open. This guy cannot be cracked by thinking. That's the mystery of his mystery. It's like trying to get something out of Michelangelo's David.

I'd given him my number in my letter—why hadn't he called to break the date if he was no longer deformed by the prospect of death? Once it was all back to how it had always been, once he'd recovered that special luminosity that had never failed to win whatever he wanted, what use did he have for me? No, his letter, I thought, cannot be the whole story—if it were, he wouldn't have come. Something remains of the rash urge to change things. Something that overtook him in the hospital is still there. An unexamined existence no longer serves his needs. He wants something recorded. That's why he's turned to me: to record what might otherwise be forgotten. Omitted and forgotten. What could it be?

Or maybe he was just a happy man. Happy people exist too. Why shouldn't they? All the scattershot speculation about the Swede's motives was only my professional impatience, my trying to imbue Swede Levov with something like the tendentious meaning Tolstoy assigned to Ivan Ilych, so belittled by the author in the uncharitable story in which he sets out to heartlessly expose, in clinical terms, what it is to be ordinary. Ivan Ilych is the well-placed high-court official who leads "a decorous life approved of by society" and who on his deathbed, in the depths of his unceasing agony and terror, thinks, "'Maybe I did not live as I ought to have done.'" Ivan Ilych's life, writes Tolstoy, summarizing, right at the outset, his judgment of the presiding judge with the delightful St. Petersburg house and a handsome salary of three thousand rubles a year and friends all of good social position, *had been most simple and most ordinary and therefore most terrible*. Maybe so. Maybe in Russia in 1886.

But in Old Rimrock, New Jersey, in 1995, when the Ivan Ilyches come trooping back to lunch at the clubhouse after their morning round of golf and start to crow, "It doesn't get any better than this," they may be a lot closer to the truth than Leo Tolstoy ever was.

Swede Levov's life, for all I knew, had been most simple and most ordinary and therefore just great, right in the American grain.

"Is Jerry gay?" I suddenly asked.

"My brother?" The Swede laughed. "You're kidding."

Maybe I was and had asked the question out of mischief, to alleviate the boredom. Yet I did happen to be remembering that line the Swede had written me about how much his father "suffered because of the shocks that befell his loved ones," which led me to wondering again what he'd been alluding to, which spontaneously reminded me of the humiliation Jerry had brought upon himself in our junior year of high school when he attempted to win the heart of a strikingly unexceptional girl in our class who you wouldn't have thought required a production to get her to kiss you.

As a Valentine present, Jerry made a coat for her out of hamster skins, a hundred and seventy-five hamster skins that he cured in the sun and then sewed together with a curved sewing needle pilfered from his father's factory, where the idea dawned on him. The high school biology department had been given a gift of some three hundred hamsters for the purpose of dissection, and Jerry diligently finagled to collect the skins from the biology students; his oddness and his genius made credible the story he told about "a scientific experiment" he was conducting at home. He finagled next to find out the girl's height, he designed a pattern, and then, after he got most of the stink out of the hides—or thought he had—by drying them in the sun on the roof of his garage, he meticulously sewed the skins together, finishing the coat off with a silk lining made out of a section of a white parachute, an imperfect parachute his brother had sent home to him as a memento from the marine air base in Cherry Point, North Carolina, where the Parris Island team won the last game of the season for the Marine Corps baseball championship. The only person Jerry told about the coat was me, the Ping-Pong stooge. He was going to send it to the girl in a Bamberger's coat box of his mother's, wrapped in lavender tissue paper and tied with velvet ribbon. But when the coat was finished, it was so stiff—because of the idiotic way he'd dried the skins, his father would later explain—that he couldn't get it to fold up in the box.

Across from the Swede in Vincent's restaurant, I suddenly recalled seeing it in the basement: this big thing sitting on the floor with sleeves. Today, I was thinking, it would win all kinds of prizes at the Whitney Museum, but back in Newark in 1949 nobody knew dick about what great art was and Jerry and I racked our brains trying to figure out what he could do to get the coat into the box. He was set on that box because she would think, when she began to open it, that it contained an expensive coat from Bam's. I was thinking of what she would think when she saw that *wasn't* what it contained; I was thinking that surely it didn't take such hard work to gain the attention of a chubby girl with bad skin and no boyfriend. But I cooperated with Jerry because he had a cyclonic personality you either fled or yielded to and because he was Swede Levov's brother and I was in Swede Levov's house and everywhere you looked were Swede Levov's trophies. Eventually Jerry tore the entire coat apart and resewed it so that the stitching lay straight across the chest, creating a hinge of sorts where the coat could be bent and placed in the box. I helped him—it was like sewing a suit of armor. Atop the coat he placed a heart that he cut out of cardboard and painted his name on in Gothic letters, and the package was sent parcel post. It had taken him three months to transform an improbable idea into nutty reality. Brief by human standards.

She screamed when she opened the box. "She had a fit," her girlfriends said. Jerry's father also had a fit. "This is what you do with the parachute your brother sent you? You cut it up? You cut up a parachute?" Jerry was too humiliated to tell him that it was to get the girl to fall into his arms and kiss him the way Lana Turner kissed Clark Gable. I happened to be there when his father went after him for curing the skins in the midday sun. "A skin must be preserved *properly*. Properly! And properly is not in the sun—you must dry a skin in the shade. You don't want them sunburned, damn it! Can I teach you once and for all, Jerome, how to preserve a skin?" And that he proceeded to do, in a boil at first, barely able to contain his frustration with his own son's ineptitude as a leather worker, explaining to both of us what they had taught the traders to do to the sheepskins in Ethiopia before they shipped them to Newark Maid to be contracted out to the tanner. "You can salt it, but salt's expensive. Especially in Africa, very, very expensive. And they steal the salt there. These people don't have salt. You have to put poison into the salt over there so they won't steal it. Other way is to pack the skin up, various ways, either on a board or on a frame, you tie it, and make little cuts, tie it up and dry it in the shade. *In the shade*, boys. That's what we call flint-dried skin. Sprinkle a little flint on it, keeps it from deteriorating, prevents the bugs from entering—" Much to my own relief, the outrage had given way surprisingly fast to a patient, if tedious, pedagogical assault, which seemed to gall Jerry even more than being blown down by his father's huffing and puffing. It could well have been that very day when Jerry swore to himself never to go near his father's business.

To deal with malodorous skins, Jerry had doused the coat with his mother's perfume, but by the time the coat was delivered by the postman it had begun to stink as it had intermittently all along, and the girl was so revolted when she opened the box, so insulted and horrified, that she never spoke to Jerry again. According to the other girls, she thought he had gone out and hunted and killed all those tiny beasts and then sent them to her because of her blemished skin. Jerry was in a rage when he got the news and, in the midst of our next Ping-Pong game, cursed her and called all girls fucking idiots. If he hadn't before had the courage to ask anyone out on a date, he never tried after that and was one of only three boys who didn't show up at the senior prom. The other two were what we identified as "sissies." And that was why I now asked the Swede a question about Jerry that I would never have dreamed of asking in 1949, when I had no clear idea what a homosexual was and couldn't imagine that anybody I knew could be one. At the time I thought Jerry was Jerry, a genius, with obsessive naiveté and colossal innocence about girls. In those days, that explained it all. Maybe it still does. But I was really looking to see what, if anything, could roil the innocence of this regal Swede—and to prevent myself from being so rude as to fall asleep on him—so I asked him, "Is Jerry gay?"

"As a kid there was always something secretive about Jerry," I said. "There were never any girls, never close friends, always something about him, even *besides* his brains, that set him apart. . . ."

The Swede nodded, looking at me as though he understood my deeper meaning as no human being ever had before, and because of this probing stare that I would swear saw nothing, all this giving that gave nothing and gave away nothing, I had no idea where his thoughts might be or if he even had "thoughts." When, momentarily, I stopped speaking, I sensed that my words, rather than falling into the net of the other person's awareness, got linked up with nothing in his brain, went in there and vanished. Something about the harmless eyes—the promise they made that he could never do anything other than what was right—was becoming annoying to me, which has to be why I next brought up his letter instead of keeping my mouth shut until the bill came and I could get away from him for another fifty years so that when 2045 rolled around I might actually look forward to seeing him again.

You fight your superficiality, your shallowness, so as to try to come at people without unreal expectations, without an overload of bias or hope or arrogance, as untanklike as you can be, sans cannon and machine guns and steel plating half a foot thick; you come at them unmenacingly on your own ten toes instead of tearing up the turf with your caterpillar treads, take them on with an open mind, as equals, man to man, as we used to say, and yet you never fail to get them wrong. You might as well have the *brain* of a tank. You get them wrong before you meet them, while you're anticipating meeting them; you get them wrong while you're with them; and then you go home to tell somebody else about the meeting and you get them all wrong again. Since the same generally goes for them with you, the whole thing is really a dazzling illusion empty of all perception, an astonishing farce of misperception. And yet what are we to do about this terribly significant business of *other people*, which gets bled of the significance we think it has and takes on instead a significance that is ludicrous, so ill-equipped are we all to envision one another's interior workings and invisible aims? Is everyone to go off and lock the door and sit secluded like the lonely writers do, in a soundproof cell, summoning people out of words and then proposing that these word people are closer to the real thing than the real people that we mangle with our ignorance every day? The fact remains that getting people right is not what living is all about anyway. It's getting them wrong that is living, getting them wrong and wrong and wrong and then, on careful reconsideration, getting them wrong again. That's how we know we're alive: we're wrong. Maybe the best thing would be to forget being right or wrong about people and just go along for the ride. But if you can do that—well, lucky you.

"When you wrote me about your father, and the shocks he'd suffered, it occurred to me that maybe Jerry had been the shock. Your old man wouldn't have been any better than mine at coming to grips with a queer son."

The Swede smiled the smile that refused to be superior, that was meant to reassure me that nothing in him ever could or would want to resist me, that signaled to me that, adored as he was, he was no better than me, even perhaps a bit of a nobody beside me. "Well, fortunately for my father, he didn't have to. Jerry was the-son-the-doctor. He couldn't have been prouder of anyone than he was of Jerry."

"Jerry's a physician?"

"In Miami. Cardiac surgeon. Million bucks a year."

"Married? Jerry married?"

The smile again. The vulnerability in that smile was the surprising element—the vulnerability of our record-breaking muscle-man faced with all the crudeness it takes to stay alive. The smile's refusal to recognize, let alone to sanction in himself, the savage obstinacy that seven decades of surviving requires of a man. As though anyone over ten believes you can subjugate with a smile, even one that kind and warm, all the things that are out to get you, with a smile hold it all together when the strong arm of the unforeseen comes crashing down on your head. Once again I began to think that he might be mentally unsound, that this smile could perhaps be an indication of derangement. There was no sham in it—and that was the worst

of it. The smile wasn't insincere. He wasn't imitating anything.
This caricature was *it*, arrived at spontaneously after a lifetime
of working himself deeper and deeper into . . . what? The
idea of himself neighborhood stardom had wreathed him in—
had that mummified the Swede as a boy forever? It was as
though he had abolished from his world everything that didn't
suit him—not only deceit, violence, mockery, and ruthlessness
but anything remotely coarse-grained, any threat of contingency, that dreadful harbinger of helplessness. Not for a second
did he stop trying to make his relation to me appear as simple
and sincere as his seeming relationship to himself.

Unless, unless, he was just a mature man, as devious as the
next mature man. Unless what was awakened by the cancer
surgery—and what had momentarily managed to penetrate a
lifelong comfy take on things—the hundred percent recovery
had all but extinguished. Unless he was not a character with no
character to reveal but a character with none that he wished to
reveal—just a sensible man who understands that if you regard
highly your privacy and the well-being of your loved ones, the
last person to take into your confidence is a working novelist.
Give the novelist, instead of your life story, the brazen refusal
of the gorgeous smile, blast him with the stun gun of your
prince-of-blandness smile, then polish off the zabaglione and
get the hell back to Old Rimrock, New Jersey, where your life
is your business and not his.

"Jerry's been married four times," said the Swede, smiling.
"Family record."

"And you?" I had already figured, from the ages of his three
boys, that the fortyish blonde with the golf clubs was more
than likely a second wife and perhaps a third. Yet divorce didn't
fit my picture of someone who so refused to register life's irrational element. If there had been a divorce, it had to have been
initiated by Miss New Jersey. Or she had died. Or being married to someone who had to keep the achievement looking
perfect, someone devoted heart and soul to the illusion of stability, had led her to suicide. Maybe *that* was the shock that
had befallen . . . Perversely, my attempts to come up with
the missing piece that would make the Swede whole and coherent kept identifying him with disorders of which there was
no trace on his beautifully aging paragon's face. I could not

decide if that blankness of his was like snow covering something or snow covering nothing.

"Me? Two wives, that's my limit. I'm a piker next to my brother. His new one's in her thirties. Half his age. Jerry's the doctor who marries the nurse. All four, nurses. They revere the ground Dr. Levov walks on. Four wives, six kids. *That* drove my dad a little nuts. But Jerry's a big guy, a gruff guy, the high-and-mighty prima donna surgeon—got a whole *hospital* by the short hairs—and so even my dad fell in line. Had to. Would have lost him otherwise. My kid brother doesn't screw around. Dad kicked and screamed through each divorce, wanted to shoot Jerry a hundred times over, but as soon as Jerry remarried, the new wife, in my father's eyes, was more of a princess than the wife before. 'She's a doll, she's a sweetheart, she's my girl. . . .' Anybody said anything about any of Jerry's wives, my father would have murdered him. Jerry's kids he outright adored. Five girls, one boy. My dad loved the boy, but the girls, they were the apple of his eye. There's nothing he wouldn't do for those kids. For any of our kids. When he had everybody around him, all of us, all the kids, my old man was in heaven. Ninety-six and never sick a day in his life. After the stroke, for the six months before he died, that was the worst. But he had a good run. Had a good life. A real fighter. A force of nature. Unstoppable guy." A light, floating tone to the words when he goes off on the subject of his father, the voice resonant with amorous reverence, disclosing unashamedly that nothing had permeated more of his life than his father's expectations.

"The suffering?"

"Could have been a lot worse," the Swede said. "Just the six months, and even then he didn't know half the time what was going on. He just slipped away one night . . . and we lost him."

By "suffering" I had meant that suffering he had referred to in his letter, provoked in his father by the shocks "that befell his loved ones." But even if I had thought to bring his letter with me and had rattled it in his face, the Swede would have eluded his own writing as effortlessly as he'd shaken off his tacklers on that Saturday fifty years before, at City Stadium, against South Side, our weakest rival, and set a state record by scoring four times on consecutive pass plays. Of course, I thought, of course—my urge to discover a substratum, my continuing suspicion that more was there than what I was looking at, aroused in him the fear that I might go ahead and tell him that he wasn't what he wanted us to believe he was. . . . But then I thought, Why bestow on him all this thinking? Why the appetite to know this guy? Ravenous because once upon a time he said to you and to you alone, "Basketball was never like this, Skip"? Why clutch at him? What's the matter with you? There's nothing here but what you're looking at. He's all about being looked at. He always was. He is not faking all this virginity. You're craving depths that don't exist. This guy is the embodiment of nothing.

I was wrong. Never more mistaken about anyone in my life.

2

Let's remember the energy. Americans were governing not only themselves but some two hundred million people in Italy, Austria, Germany, and Japan. The war-crimes trials were cleansing the earth of its devils once and for all. Atomic power was ours alone. Rationing was ending, price controls were being lifted; in an explosion of self-assertion, auto workers, coal workers, transit workers, maritime workers, steel workers—laborers by the millions demanded more and went on strike for it. And playing Sunday morning softball on the Chancellor Avenue field and pickup basketball on the asphalt courts behind the school were all the boys who had come back alive, neighbors, cousins, older brothers, their pockets full of separation pay, the GI Bill inviting them to break out in ways they could not have imagined possible before the war. Our class started high school six months after the unconditional surrender of the Japanese, during the greatest moment of collective inebriation in American history. And the upsurge of energy was contagious. Around us nothing was lifeless. Sacrifice and constraint were over. The Depression had disappeared. Everything was in motion. The lid was off. Americans were to start over again, en masse, everyone in it together.

If that wasn't sufficiently inspiring—the miraculous conclusion of this towering event, the clock of history reset and a whole people's aims limited no longer by the past—there was the neighborhood, the communal determination that we, the children, should escape poverty, ignorance, disease, social injury and intimidation—escape, above all, insignificance. You must not come to nothing! *Make something of yourselves!*

Despite the undercurrent of anxiety—a sense communicated daily that hardship was a persistent menace that only persistent diligence could hope to keep at bay; despite a generalized mistrust of the Gentile world; despite the fear of being battered that clung to many families because of the Depression—ours was not a neighborhood steeped in darkness. The place was bright with industriousness. There was a big belief in life and we were steered relentlessly in the direction of success: a better existence was going to be ours. The goal was to *have* goals, the aim to *have* aims. This edict came entangled often in hysteria, the embattled hysteria of those whom experience had taught how little antagonism it takes to wreck a life beyond repair. Yet it was this edict—emotionally overloaded as it was by the uncertainty in our elders, by their awareness of all that was in league against them—that made the neighborhood a cohesive place. A whole community perpetually imploring us not to be immoderate and screw up, imploring us to grasp opportunity, exploit our advantages, remember *what matters.*

The shift was not slight between the generations and there was plenty to argue about: the ideas of the world they wouldn't give up; the rules they worshiped, for us rendered all but toothless by the passage of just a couple of decades of American time; those uncertainties that were theirs and not ours. The question of how free of them we might dare to be was ongoing, an internal debate, ambivalent and exasperated. What was most cramping in their point of view a few of us did find the audacity to strain against, but the intergenerational conflict never looked like it would twenty years later. The neighborhood was never a field of battle strewn with the bodies of the misunderstood. There was plenty of haranguing to ensure obedience; the adolescent capacity for upheaval was held in check by a thousand requirements, stipulations, prohibitions—restraints that proved insuperable. One was our own highly realistic appraisal of what was most in our interest, another the pervasive rectitude of the era, whose taboos we'd taken between our teeth at birth; not least was the enacted ideology of parental self-sacrifice that bled us of wanton rebelliousness and sent underground almost every indecent urge.

It would have taken a lot more courage—or foolishness—than most of us could muster to disappoint their passionate, unflagging illusions about our perfectibility and roam very far from the permissible. Their reasons for asking us to be both law-abiding and superior were not reasons we could find the conscience to discount, and so control that was close to absolute was ceded to adults who were striving and improving themselves through us. Mild forms of scarring may have resulted from this arrangement but few cases of psychosis were reported, at least at the time. The weight of all that expectation was not necessarily killing, thank God. Of course there were families where it might have helped if the parents had eased up a little on the brake, but mostly the friction between generations was just sufficient to give us purchase to move forward.

Am I wrong to think that we delighted in living there? No delusions are more familar than those inspired in the elderly by nostalgia, but am I completely mistaken to think that living as well-born children in Renaissance Florence could not have held a candle to growing up within aromatic range of Tabachnik's pickle barrels? Am I mistaken to think that even back then, in the vivid present, the fullness of life stirred our emotions to an extraordinary extent? Has anywhere since so engrossed you in its ocean of details? The *detail*, the immensity of the detail, the force of the detail, the weight of the detail—the rich endlessness of detail surrounding you in your young life like the six feet of dirt that'll be packed on your grave when you're dead.

Perhaps by definition a neighborhood is the place to which a child spontaneously gives undivided attention; that's the unfiltered way meaning comes to children, just flowing off the surface of things. Nonetheless, fifty years later, I ask you: has the immersion ever again been so complete as it was in those streets, where every block, every backyard, every house, every *floor* of every house—the walls, ceilings, doors, and windows of every last friend's family apartment—came to be so absolutely individualized? Were we ever again to be such keen recording instruments of the microscopic surface of things close at hand, of the minutest gradations of social position conveyed by linoleum and oilcloth, by yahrzeit candles and cooking smells, by Ronson table lighters and venetian blinds? About one another, we knew who had what kind of lunch in the bag in his locker and who ordered what on his hot dog at Syd's; we knew one another's every physical attribute—who walked pigeon-toed and who had breasts, who smelled of hair oil and who oversalivated when he spoke; we knew who among us was belligerent and who was friendly, who was smart and who was dumb; we knew whose mother had the accent and whose father had the mustache, whose mother worked and whose father was dead; somehow we even dimly grasped how every family's different set of circumstances set each family a distinctive difficult human problem.

And, of course, there was the mandatory turbulence born of need, appetite, fantasy, longing, and the fear of disgrace. With only adolescent introspection to light the way, each of us, hopelessly pubescent, alone and in secret, attempted to regulate it—and in an era when chastity was still ascendant, a national cause to be embraced by the young like freedom and democracy.

It's astonishing that everything so immediately visible in our lives as classmates we still remember so precisely. The intensity of feeling that we have seeing one another today is also astonishing. But most astonishing is that we are nearing the age that our grandparents were when we first went off to be freshmen at the annex on February 1, 1946. What is astonishing is that we, who had no idea how anything was going to turn out, now know exactly what happened. That the results are in for the class of January 1950—the unanswerable questions answered, the future revealed—is that not astonishing? To have lived—and in this country, and in our time, and as who we were. Astonishing.

This is the speech I didn't give at my forty-fifth high school reunion, a speech to myself masked as a speech to them. I began to compose it only *after* the reunion, in the dark, in bed, groping to understand what had hit me. The tone—too ruminative for a country club ballroom and the sort of good time people were looking for there—didn't seem at all ill-conceived between three and six A.M., as I tried, in my overstimulated state, to comprehend the union underlying the reunion, the common experience that had joined us as kids. Despite gradations of privation and privilege, despite the array of anxieties fostered by an impressively nuanced miscellany of family quarrels— quarrels that, fortunately, promised more unhappiness than they always delivered—something powerful united us. And united us not merely in where we came from but in where we were going and how we would get there. We had new means and new ends, new allegiances and new aims, new innards—a new *ease*, somewhat less agitation in facing down the exclusions the goyim still wished to preserve. And out of what context did these transformations arise—out of what historical drama, acted unsuspectingly by its little protagonists, played out in classrooms and kitchens looking nothing at all like the great theater of life? Just what collided with what to produce the spark in us?

I was still awake and all stirred up, formulating these questions and their answers in my bed—blurry, insomniac shadows of these questions and their answers—some eight hours after I'd driven back from New Jersey, where, on a sunny Sunday late in October, at a country club in a Jewish suburb far from the futility prevailing in the streets of our crime-ridden, drug-infested childhood home, the reunion that began at eleven in the morning went ebulliently on all afternoon long. It was held in a ballroom just at the edge of the country club's golf course for a group of elderly adults who, as Weequahic kids of the thirties and forties, would have thought a niblick (which was what in those days they called the nine iron) was a hunk of schmaltz herring. Now I couldn't sleep—the last thing I could remember was the parking valet bringing my car around to the steps of the portico, and the reunion's commander in chief, Selma Bresloff, kindly asking if I'd had a good time, and my telling her, "It's like going out to your old outfit after Iwo Jima."

Around three A.M., I left my bed and went to my desk, my head vibrant with the static of unelaborated thought. I wound up working there until six, by which time I had got the reunion speech to read as it appears above. Only after I had built to the emotional peroration culminating in the word "astonishing" was I at last sufficiently unastonished by the force of my feelings to be able to put together a couple of hours of sleep—or something resembling sleep, for, even half out of it, I was a biography in perpetual motion, memory to the marrow of my bones.

Yes, even from as benign a celebration as a high school reunion it's not so simple to instantaneously resume existence back behind the blindfold of continuity and routine. Perhaps if I were thirty or forty, the reunion would have faded sweetly away in the three hours it took me to drive home. But there is no easy mastery of such events at sixty-two, and only a year beyond cancer surgery. Instead of recapturing time past, I'd been captured by it in the present, so that passing seemingly out of the world of time I was, in fact, rocketing through to its secret core.

For the hours we were all together, doing nothing more than hugging, kissing, kibitzing, laughing, hovering over one another recollecting the dilemmas and disasters that hadn't in the long run made a damn bit of difference, crying out, "Look who's here!" and "Oh, it's been a long time" and "You remember me? I remember you," asking each other, "Didn't we once . . . ," "Were you the kid who . . . ," commanding one another—with those three poignant words I heard people repeat all afternoon as they were drawn and tugged into numerous conversations at once—"Don't go away!" . . . and, of course, dancing, cheek-to-cheek dancing our outdated dance steps to a "one-man band," a bearded boy in a tuxedo, his brow encircled with a red bandanna (a boy born at least two full decades after we'd marched together out of the school auditorium to the rousing recessional tempo of *Iolanthe*), accompanying himself on a synthesizer as he imitated Nat "King" Cole, Frankie Laine, and Sinatra—for those few hours time, the chain of time, the whole damn drift of everything called time, had seemed as easy to understand as the dimensions of the doughnut you effortlessly down with your morning coffee. The one-man band in the bandanna played "Mule Train" while I thought, The Angel of Time is passing over us and breathing with each breath all that we've lived through—the Angel of Time unmistakably as present in the ballroom of the Cedar Hill Country Club as that kid doing "Mule Train" like Frankie Laine. Sometimes I found myself looking at everyone as though it were still 1950, as though "1995" were merely the futuristic theme of a senior prom that we'd all come to in humorous papier-mâché masks of ourselves as we might look at the close of the twentieth century. That afternoon time had been invented for the mystification of no one but us.

Inside the commemorative mug presented by Selma to each of us as we were departing were half a dozen little *rugelach* in an orange tissue-paper sack, neatly enclosed in orange cellophane and tied shut with striped curling ribbon of orange and brown, the school colors. The *rugelach*, as fresh as any I'd ever snacked on at home after school—back then baked by the recipe broker of her mahjongg club, my mother—were a gift from one of our class members, a Teaneck baker. Within five minutes of leaving the reunion, I'd undone the double wrapping and eaten all six *rugelach*, each a snail of sugar-dusted pastry dough, the cinnamon-lined chambers microscopically studded with midget raisins and chopped walnuts. By rapidly devouring mouthful after mouthful of these crumbs whose floury richness—blended of butter and sour cream and vanilla and cream cheese and egg yolk and sugar—I'd loved since childhood, perhaps I'd find vanishing from Nathan what, according to Proust, vanished from Marcel the instant he recognized "the savour of the little *madeleine*": the apprehensiveness of death. "A mere taste," Proust writes, and "the word 'death' . . . [has] . . .

no meaning for him." So, greedily I ate, gluttonously, refusing to curtail for a moment this wolfish intake of saturated fat but, in the end, having nothing like Marcel's luck.

Let's speak further of death and of the desire—understandably in the aging a desperate desire—to forestall death, to resist it, to resort to whatever means are necessary to see death with anything, anything, *anything* but clarity:

One of the boys up from Florida—according to the reunion booklet we each received at the door, twenty-six out of a graduating class of a hundred and seventy-six were now living in Florida . . . a good sign, meant we still had more people in Florida (six more) than we had who were dead; and all afternoon, by the way, it was not in my mind alone that the men were tagged the boys and the women the girls—told me that on the way to Livingston from Newark Airport, where his plane had landed and he'd rented a car, he'd twice had to pull up at service stations and get the key to the restroom, so wracked was he by trepidation. This was Mendy Gurlik, in 1950 voted the handsomest boy in the class, in 1950 a broad-shouldered, long-lashed beauty, our most important jitterbugger, who loved to go around saying to people, "Solid, Jackson!" Having once been invited by his older brother to a colored whorehouse on Augusta Street, where the pimps hung out, virtually around the corner from his father's Branford Place liquor store—a whorehouse where, he eventually confessed, he'd sat fully clothed, waiting in an outer hallway, flipping through a *Mechanix Illustrated* that he'd found on a table there, while his brother was the one who "did it"—Mendy was the closest the class had to a delinquent. It was Mendy Gurlik (now Garr) who'd taken me with him to the Adams Theater to hear Illinois Jacquet, Buddy Johnson, and "Newark's own" Sarah Vaughan; who'd got the tickets and taken me with him to hear Mr. B., Billy Eckstine, in concert at the Mosque; who, in '49, had got tickets for us to the Miss Sepia America Beauty Contest at Laurel Garden. It was Mendy who, some three or four times, took me to watch, broadcasting in the flesh, Bill Cook, the smooth late-night Negro disc jockey of the Jersey station WAAT. *Musical Caravan*, Bill Cook's show, I ordinarily listened to in my darkened bedroom on Saturday nights. The opening theme was Ellington's "Caravan," very exotic, very sophisticated, Afro-Oriental rhythms, a belly-dancing beat—just by itself it was worth tuning in for; "Caravan," in the Duke's very own rendition, made me feel nicely illicit even while tucked up between my mother's freshly laundered sheets. First the tom-tom opening, then winding curvaceously up out of the casbah that great smoky trombone, and then the insinuating, snake-charming flute. Mendy called it "boner music."

To get to WAAT, and Bill Cook's studio, we took the 14 bus downtown, and only minutes after we'd settled quietly like churchgoers in the row of chairs outside his glass-enclosed booth, Bill Cook would come out from behind the microphone to greet us. With a "race record" spinning on the turntable—for listeners still unadventurously at home—Cookie would cordially shake the hands of the two tall, skinny white sharpies, all done up in their one-button-roll suits from the American Shop and their shirts from the Custom Shoppe, with the spread collars. (The clothes on my back were on loan from Mendy for the night.) "And what might I play for you gentlemen?" Cookie graciously inquired of us in a voice whose mellow resonance Mendy would imitate whenever we talked on the phone. I asked for the melodious stuff, "Miss" Dinah Washington, "Miss" Savannah Churchill—and how arresting that was back then, the salacious chivalry of the dj's "Miss"—while Mendy's taste, spicier, racially far more authoritative, was for musicians like the lowdown saloon piano player Roosevelt Sykes, for Ivory Joe Hunter ("*When* . . . I lost my *bay-bee* . . . I *aahll* . . . *most* lost my *mind*"), and for a quartet that Mendy seemed to me to take excessive pride in calling "the *Ray*-O-Vacs," emphasizing the first syllable exactly as did the black kid from South Side, Melvyn Smith, who delivered for Mendy's father's store after school. (Mendy and his brother did the Saturday deliveries.) Mendy boldly accompanied Melvyn Smith one night to hear live bebop at the lounge over the bowling alley on Beacon Street, Lloyd's Manor, a place to which few whites other than a musician's reckless Desdemona would venture. It was Mendy Gurlik who first took me down to the Radio Record Shack on Market Street, where we picked out bargains from the 19-cent bin and could listen to the record in a booth before we bought it. During the war, when, to keep up morale on the home front, there'd be dances one night a week during July and August at the Chancellor Avenue playground, Mendy used to scramble through the high-spirited crowd—neighborhood parents and schoolkids and little kids up late who ran gleefully round and round the painted white bases where we played our perpetual summer softball game—dispensing for whoever cared to listen a less conventional brand of musical pleasure than the Glenn Miller–Tommy Dorsey–inspired arrangements that most everybody else liked dancing to beneath the dim floodlights back of the school. Regardless of the dance tune the band up on the flag-festooned bandstand happened to be playing, Mendy would race around most of the evening singing, "Cal*don*ia, Cal*don*ia, what makes your big head so *hard?* Rocks!" He sang it, as he blissfully proclaimed, "free of charge," just as nuttily as Louis Jordan and his Tympany Five did on the record he obliged all the Daredevils to listen to whenever, for whatever refractory purpose (to play dollar-limit seven-card stud, to examine for the millionth time the drawings in his Tillie the Toiler "hot book," on rare occasions to hold a circle jerk), we entered his nefarious bedroom when nobody else was home.

And here now was Mendy in 1995, the Weequahic boy with the biggest talent for being less than a dignified model child, a personality halfway between mildly repellent shallowness and audacious, enviable deviance, flirting back then with indignity in a way that hovered continuously between the alluring and the offensive. Here was Dapper, Dirty, Daffy Mendy Gurlik, not in prison (where I was certain he'd wind up when he'd urge us to sit in a circle on the floor of his bedroom, some four or five Daredevils with our pants pulled down, competing to win the couple of bucks in the pot by being the one to "shoot" first), not in hell (where I was sure he'd be consigned after being stabbed to death at Lloyd's Manor by a colored guy "high on reefer"—whatever that meant), but simply a retired restaurateur—owner of three steakhouses called Garr's Grill in suburban Long Island—at no place more disreputable than his high school class's forty-fifth reunion.

"You shouldn't worry, Mend—you still got your build, your looks. You're amazing. You look great."

He did, too: well tanned, slender, a tall narrow-faced jogger wearing black alligator boots and a black silk shirt beneath a green cashmere jacket. Only the head of brimming silver-white hair looked suspiciously not quite his own but as though it had had an earlier life as the end of a skunk.

"I take care of myself—that isn't my point. I called Mutty"— Marty "Mutty" Sheffer, star sidearm pitcher of the Daredevils, the team we three played on in the playground softball league, and, according to the biographical listing in the reunion booklet, a "Financial Consultant" and, too (unlikely as it seemed when I remembered that, paralyzingly shy of girls, babyfaced Mutty had made pitching pennies his major adolescent diversion), progenitor of "Children 36, 34, 31. Grandchildren 2, 1" —"I told Mutty," Mendy said, "that if he didn't sit next to me I wasn't coming. I had to deal with the real goons in my business. Dealt with the fucking Mob. But this I could not deal with from day one. Not twice, Skip, *three* times I had to stop the car to take a crap."

"Well," I said, "after years and years of painting ourselves opaque, this carries us straight back to when we were sure we were transparent."

"Is that it?"

"Maybe. Who knows."

"Twenty kids dead in our class." He showed me at the back of the booklet the page headed "In Memoriam." "Eleven of the guys dead," Mendy said. "*Two* from the Daredevils. Bert Bergman. Utty Orenstein." Utty was Mutty's battery mate, Bert played second base. "Prostate cancer. The both of them. And both in the last three years. I get the blood test. I get it every six months since I heard about Utty. You get the test?"

"I get it." Of course, I didn't any longer because I no longer had a prostate.

"How often?"

"Every year."

"Not enough," he told me. "Every six months."

"Okay. I'll do that."

"You been all right though?" he asked, taking hold of me by the shoulders.

"I'm in good shape," I said.

"Hey, I taught you to jerk off, you know that?"

"That you did, Mendel. Anywhere from ninety to a hundred

twenty days before I would have happened upon it myself. You're the one who got me going."

"I'm the guy," he said, laughing loudly, "who taught Skip Zuckerman to jerk off. My claim to fame," and we embraced, the bald first baseman and white-haired left fielder of the dwindling Daredevil Athletic Club. The torso I could feel through his clothes attested to just how well he did take care of himself.

"I'm still at it," Mendy said happily. "Fifty years later. A Daredevil record."

"Don't be so sure," I said. "Check with Mutty."

"I heard you had a heart attack," he said.

"No, just a bypass. Years ago."

"The fucking bypass. They stick that tube down your throat, don't they?"

"They do."

"I saw my brother-in-law with the tube down his throat. That's all I need," Mendy said. "I didn't want to be here in the worst fucking way, but Mutty keeps calling and saying, 'You're not going to live forever,' and I keep telling him, 'I *am*, Mutt. I have to!' Then I'm schmuck enough to come, and the first thing I see when I open up this booklet is obituaries."

When Mendy went off to get a drink and find Mutty, I looked for his name in the booklet: "Retired Restaurateur. Children 36, 33, 28. Grandchildren 14, 12, 9, 5, 5, 3." I wondered if the six grandchildren, including what appeared to be a set of twins, were what made Mendy so fearful of death or if there were other reasons, like reveling still in whores and sharp clothes. I should have asked him.

I should have asked people a lot of things that afternoon. But later, though regretting that I hadn't, I understood that to have gotten answers to any of my questions beginning "Whatever happened to . . ." would not have told me why I had the uncanny sense that what goes on *behind* what we see is what I was seeing. It didn't take more than one of the girls' saying to the photographer, the instant before he snapped the class photo, "Be sure and leave the wrinkles out," didn't take more than laughing along with everyone else at the nicely timed wisecrack, to feel that Destiny, the most ancient enigma of the civilized world—and our first composition topic in freshman

Greek and Roman Mythology, where I wrote "the Fates are three goddesses, called the Moerae, Clotho who spins, Lachesis who determines its length, and Atropos who cuts the thread of life"—Destiny had become perfectly understandable while everything unenigmatic, such as standing for the photograph in the third row back, with my one arm on the shoulder of Marshall Goldstein ("Children 39, 37. Grandchildren 8, 6") and my other on the shoulder of Stanley Wernikoff ("Children 39, 38. Grandchildren 5, 2, 8 mo."), had become inexplicable.

A young NYU film student named Jordan Wasser, the grandson of fullback Milton Wasserberger, had come along with Milt to make a documentary of our reunion for one of his classes; from time to time, as I floated around the room documenting the event in my own outdated way, I overheard Jordan interviewing somebody on camera. "It was like no other school," sixty-three-year-old Marilyn Koplik was telling him. "The kids were great, we had good teachers, the worst crime we could commit was chewing gum. . . ." "Best school around," said sixty-three-year-old George Kirschenbaum, "best teachers, best kids. . . ." "Mind for mind," said sixty-three-year-old Leon Gutman, "this is the smartest group of people I've ever worked with. . . ." "School was just different in those days," said sixty-three-year-old Rona Siegler, and to the next question Rona replied with a laugh—a laugh without much delight in it—"Nineteen fifty? It was just a couple of years ago, Jordan."

"I always tell people," somebody was saying to me, "when they ask if I went to school with you, how you wrote that paper for me in Wallach's class. On *Red Badge of Courage.*" "But I didn't." "You did." "What could I know about *Red Badge of Courage*? I didn't even read it till college." "No. You wrote a paper for me on *Red Badge of Courage*. I got an A plus. I handed it in a week late and Wallach said to me, 'It was worth waiting for.'"

The person telling me this, a small, dour man with a close-clipped white beard, a brutal scar beneath one eye, and two hearing aids, was one of the few I saw that afternoon on whom time had done a job and then some; on him time had worked overtime. He walked with a limp and spoke to me leaning on a cane. His breathing was heavy. I did not recognize him, not when I looked squarely at him from six inches away and not even after I read on his name tag that he was Ira Posner. Who was Ira Posner? And why would I have done him that favor, especially when I couldn't have? Did I write the paper for Ira without bothering to read the book? "Your father meant a lot to me," Ira said. "Did he?" I asked. "In the few moments I spent with him in my life I felt better about myself than the entire life I spent with my own father." "I didn't know that." "My own father was a very marginal person in my life." "What did he do? Remind me." "He scraped floors for a living. Spent his whole life scraping floors. Your father was always pushing you to get the best grades. My father's idea of setting me up in business was buying me a shoeshine kit so I could give quarter shines at a newsstand. That's what he got me for graduation. Dumb fuck. I really suffered in that family. A really benighted family. I lived in a dark place with those people. You get shunted aside by your father, Nathan, you wind up a touchy fellow. I had a brother we had to put in an institution. You didn't know that. Nobody did. We weren't allowed even to mention his name. Eddie. Four years older than me. He would go into wild rages and bite his hands until they would bleed. He would scream like a coyote until my parents quieted him down. At school they asked if I had brothers or sisters and I wrote 'None.' While I was at college, my parents signed some permission form for the nuthouse and they gave Eddie a lobotomy and he went into a coma and died. Can you imagine? Tells me to shine shoes on Market Street outside the courthouse—that is a father's advice to a son." "So what'd you do instead?" "I'm a psychiatrist. It's your father I got my inspiration from. He was a physician." "Not exactly. He wore a white coat but he was a chiropodist." "Whenever I came with the guys to your house, your mother always put out a bowl of fruit and your father always said to me, 'What is your idea on this subject, Ira? What is your idea on that subject, Ira?' Peaches. Plums. Nectarines. Grapes. I never saw an apple in my house. My mother is ninety-seven. I got her in a home now. She sits there crying in a chair all day long but I honestly don't believe she's any more depressed than she was when I was a kid. I assume your father is dead." "Yes. Yours?" "Mine couldn't wait to die. Failure went to his head in a really big way." And still I had no idea who Ira was or what he was talking about, because, as much as I was remembering that day of all that had once happened, far more was so beyond recall that it might never have happened, regardless of how many Ira Posners stood face to face with me attesting otherwise. As best I could tell, when Ira was in my house being inspired by my father I could as well not have been born. I had run out of the power to remember even faintly my father's asking Ira what he thought while Ira was eating a piece of our fruit. It was one of those things that get torn out of you and thrust into oblivion just because they didn't matter enough. And yet what I had missed completely took root in Ira and changed his life.

So you don't have to look much further than Ira and me to see why we go through life with a generalized sense that every-body is wrong except us. And since we don't just forget things because they don't matter but also forget things because they matter too much—because each of us remembers and forgets in a pattern whose labyrinthine windings are an identification mark no less distinctive than a fingerprint—it's no wonder that the shards of reality one person will cherish as a biography can seem to someone else who, say, happened to have eaten some ten thousand dinners at the very same kitchen table, to be a willful excursion into mythomania. But then nobody really bothers to send in their fifty bucks for a forty-fifth high school reunion so as to turn up and stage a protest against the other guy's sense of the-way-it-was; the truly important thing, the supreme delight of the afternoon, is simply finding that you haven't yet made it onto the "In Memoriam" page.

"How long is your father dead?" Ira asked me. "Nineteen sixty-nine. Twenty-six years. A long time," I replied. "To whom? To him? I don't think so. To the dead," said Ira, "it's a drop in the bucket." Just then, from directly behind me, I heard Mendy Gurlik saying to someone, "Whoja jerk off over?" "Lorraine," a second man replied. "Sure. Everyone did. Me too. Who else?" said Mendy. "Diane." "Right. Diane. Absolutely. Who else?" "Selma." "Selma? I didn't realize that," Mendy said. "I'm surprised to hear that. No, I never wanted to fuck Selma. Too short. For me it was always twirlers. Watch 'em practicing up on the field after school and then go home and beat off. The pancake makeup. Cocoa-colored pancake makeup. On their legs. Drove me nuts. You notice something? The guys on the whole don't look too bad, a lot of them work out, but the girls, you know . . . no, a forty-fifth reunion is not the best place to come looking for ass." "True, true," said the other man, who spoke softly and seemed not to have found in the occasion quite the nostalgic license that Mendy had, "time has not been kind to the women." "You know who's dead? Bert and Utty," Mendy said. "Prostate cancer. Went to the spine. Spread. Ate 'em up. Both of them. Thank God I get the test. You get the test?" "What test?" the other fellow asked. "Shit, you don't get the test?" "Skip," said Mendy, pulling me away from Ira, "Meisner doesn't get the test."

Now Meisner was Mr. Meisner, Abe Meisner, a short, swarthy, heavyset man with stooped shoulders and a jutting head, proprietor of Meisner's Cleaners—"5 Hour Cleaning Service" —situated on Chancellor between the shoe repair shop, where the Italian radio station was always playing while you waited on the seat behind the swinging half-door for Ralph to fix your heels, and the beauty salon, Roline's, from which my mother once brought home the copy of *Silver Screen* where I read an article that stunned me called "George Raft Is a Lonely Man." Mrs. Meisner, a short, indestructible earthling like her husband, worked with him in the store and one year also sold war bonds and stamps with my mother in a booth right out on Chancellor Avenue. Alan, their son, had gone through school with me, beginning with kindergarten, skipping the same grades I did all through grade school. Alan Meisner and I used to be thrown into a room together by our teacher and, as though we were George S. Kaufman and Moss Hart, told to turn something out whenever a play was needed at assembly for a national holiday. For a couple of seasons right after the war Mr. Meisner—through some miracle—got to be the dry cleaner for the Newark Bears, the Yankees' Triple A farm team, and one summer day, and a great day it was, I was enlisted by Alan to help him carry the Bears' freshly dry-cleaned away uniforms, via three buses, to the Ruppert Stadium clubhouse all the way down on Wilson Avenue.

"Alan. Jesus," I said, "you are your old man." "Who else's old man should I be?" he replied, and, taking my face between his hands, gave me a kiss. "Al," Mendy said, "tell Skippy what you heard Schrimmer telling his wife. Schrimmer's got a new wife, Skip. Six feet tall. Three years ago he went to a psychiatrist. He was depressed. The psychiatrist said to him, 'What do you think when I ask you to imagine your wife's body.' 'I think I should slit my throat,' Schrim said. So he divorces her and marries the shiksa secretary. Six feet tall. Thirty-five. Legs to the ceiling. Al, tell Skip what she said, the *langer loksh*." "She said to Schrim," said Alan, the two of us grinning as we clutched each other's diminished biceps, "she said, 'Why are they all Mutty and Utty and Dutty and Tutty? If his name is Charles, why is he called Tutty?' 'I shouldn't have brought you,' Schrim said to her. 'I knew I shouldn't. I can't explain it,' Schrim said to her, '*nobody* can. It's *beyond* explanation. *It just is*.' "

And what was Alan now? Raised by a dry cleaner, worked after school for a dry cleaner, himself a dead ringer for a dry cleaner, he was a superior court judge in Pasadena. In his father's pocket-sized dry-cleaning shop there had been a rotogravure picture of FDR framed on the wall above the pressing machine, beside an autographed photo of Mayor Meyer Ellenstein. I remembered these photographs when Alan told me that he had twice been a member of Republican delegations to the presidential convention. When Mendy asked if Alan could get him tickets to the Rose Bowl, Alan Meisner, with whom I used to travel to Brooklyn to see Dodger Sunday doubleheaders the year that Robinson broke in, with whom I'd start out at eight A.M. on a bus from our corner, take it downtown to Penn Station, switch to the tubes to New York, in New York switch to the subway to Brooklyn, all to get to Ebbets Field and eat our sandwiches from our lunch bags before batting practice began—Alan Meisner, who, once the ballgame got under way, drove everybody around us crazy with his vocally unmodulated play-by-play of both ends of the doubleheader—this same Alan Meisner took a pocket diary out of his jacket and carefully inscribed a note to himself. I saw what he'd written from over his shoulder: "R.B. tix for Mendy G."

Meaningless? Unspectacular? Nothing very enormous going on there? Well, what you make of it would depend on where you grew up and how life got opened up to you. Alan Meisner could not be said to have risen out of nothing; however, remembering him as a little hick obliviously yapping away nonstop in his seat at Ebbets Field, remembering him delivering the dry cleaning through our streets late on a winter afternoon, hatless and in a snow-laden pea jacket, one could easily imagine him destined for something less than the Tournament of Roses.

Only after strudel and coffee had capped off a chicken dinner that, what with barely anyone able to stay seated very long in one place to eat it, had required nearly all afternoon to get through; after the kids from Maple got up on the bandstand and sang the Maple Avenue School song; after classmate upon classmate had taken the microphone to say "It's been a great life" or "I'm proud of all of you"; after people had just about finished tapping one another on the shoulder and falling into one another's arms; after the ten-member reunion committee stood on the dance floor and held hands while the one-man band played Bob Hope's theme song, "Thanks for the Memory," and we applauded in appreciation of all their hard work; after Marvin Lieb, whose father sold my father our Pontiac and offered each of us kids a big cigar to smoke whenever we came to get Marvin from the house, told me about his alimony miseries —"A guy takes a leak with more forethought than I gave to my two marriages"—and Julius Pincus, who'd always been the kindest kid and who now, because of tremors resulting from taking the cyclosporin essential to the long-term survival of his transplant, had had to give up his optometry practice, told me ruefully how he'd come by his new kidney—"If a little fourteen-year-old girl didn't die of a brain hemorrhage last October, I would be dead today"—and after Schrimmer's tall young wife had said to me, "You're the class writer, maybe you can explain it. Why are they all called Utty, Dutty, Mutty, and Tutty?"; only after I had shocked Shelly Minskoff, another Daredevil, with a nod of the head when he asked, "Is it true what you said at the mike, you don't have kids or anything like that?," only after Shelly had taken my hand in his and said, "Poor Skip," only then did I discover that Jerry Levov, having arrived late, was among us.

3

I HADN'T even thought to look for him. I knew from the Swede that Jerry lived in Florida, but even more to the point, he'd always been such an isolated kid, so little engaged by anything other than his own abstruse interests, that it didn't seem likely he'd have any more desire now than he'd had then to endure the wisdom of his classmates. But only minutes after Shelly Minskoff had bid me good-bye, Jerry came bounding over, a big man in a double-breasted blue blazer like my own, but with a chest like a large birdcage, and bald except for a ropelike strand of white hair draped across the crown of his skull. His body had really achieved a strange form: despite the majestic upper torso that had replaced the rolling-pin chest of the gawky boy, he locomoted himself on the same ladderlike legs that had made his the silliest gait in the school, legs no heavier or any shapelier than Olive Oyl's in the *Popeye* comic strip. The face I recognized immediately, from those afternoons when my own face was target for its focused animosity, when I used to see it weaving wildly above the Ping-Pong table, crimson with belligerence and lethal intention—yes, the core of that face I could never forget, long-limbed Jerry's knotted little face, the determined mask of the prowling beast that won't let you be until you're driven from your lair, the ferret face that declares, "Don't talk to me about compromise! I know nothing of compromise!" Now in that face was the obstinacy of a *lifetime* of smashing the ball back at the other guy's gullet. I could imagine that Jerry had made himself important to people by means different from his brother's.

"I didn't expect to see you here," Jerry said.

"I didn't expect to see you."

"I wouldn't have thought this was a big enough stage for you," he said, laughing. "I was sure you'd find the sentimentality repellent."

"Exactly what I was thinking about you."

"You're somebody who has banished all superfluous sentiments from his life. No asinine longings to be home again. No

patience for the nonessential. Only time for what's indispensable. After all, what they sit around calling the 'past' at these
things isn't a fragment of a fragment of the past. It's the past
undetonated—nothing is really brought back, nothing. It's
nostalgia. It's bullshit."

These few sentences telling me what I was, what *everything*
was, would have accounted not merely for four wives but for
eight, ten, sixteen of them. Everyone's narcissism is strong at a
reunion, but this was an outpouring of another magnitude.
Jerry's body may have been divided between the skinny kid
and the large man but not the character—he had the character
of one big unified thing, coldly accustomed to being listened
to. What an evolution this was, the eccentric boy elaborated
into a savagely sure-of-himself man. The original unwieldy impulses appeared to have been brought into a crude harmony
with the enormous intelligence and willfulness; the effect was
not only of somebody who called the shots and would never
dream of doing what he was told but of somebody you could
count on to churn things up. It seemed truer even than it had
been when we were boys that if Jerry got an idea in his head,
however improbable, something big would come of it. I could
see why I had been infatuated with him as a kid, understood
for the first time that my fascination had been not solely with
his being the Swede's brother but with the Swede's brother's
being so decisively odd, his masculinity so imperfectly socialized compared with the masculinity of the three-letterman.

"Why *did* you come?" Jerry asked.

About the cancer scare of the year before, and the impact on
urogenital function of the ensuing prostate surgery, I said nothing directly. Or rather, said everything that was necessary—and
perhaps not merely for myself—when I replied, "Because I'm
sixty-two. I figured that of all the forms of bullshit-nostalgia
available, this was the one least likely to be without unsettling
surprises."

He enjoyed that. "You like unsettling surprises."

"Might as well. Why did you come?"

"I happened to be up here. At the end of the week I had to
be up here, so I came." Smiling at me, he said, "I don't think
they were expecting their writer to be so laconic. I don't
think they were expecting quite so *much* modesty." Keeping in

mind what I took to be the spirit of the occasion, when I'd been called up to the microphone near the end of the meal by the MC (Erwin Levine, Children 43, 41, 38, 31. Grandchildren 9, 8, 3, 1, 6 weeks), I'd said only, "I'm Nathan Zuckerman. I was vice president of our class in 4B and a member of the prom committee. I have neither child nor grandchild but I did, ten years ago, have a quintuple bypass operation of which I am proud. Thank you." That was the history I gave them, as much as was called for, medical or otherwise—enough to be a little amusing and sit down.

"What were you expecting?" I asked Jerry.

"That. Exactly that. Unassuming. The Weequahic Everyman. What else? Always behave contrary to their expectations. You even as a kid. Always found a practical method to guarantee your freedom."

"I'd say that was a better description of you, Jer."

"No, no. I found the *impractical* method. Rashness personified, Little Sir Hothead—just went nuts and started screaming when I couldn't have it my way. You were the one with the big outlook on things. You were more theoretical than the rest of us. Even back then you had to hook up everything with your thoughts. Sizing up the situation, drawing conclusions. You kept a sharp watch over yourself. All the crazy stuff contained inside. A sensible boy. No, not like me at all."

"Well, we both had a big investment in being right," I said.

"Yeah, being wrong," Jerry said, "was unendurable to me. Absolutely unendurable."

"And it's easier now?"

"Don't have to worry about it. The operating room turns you into somebody who's never wrong. Much like writing."

"Writing turns you into somebody who's always wrong. The illusion that you may get it right someday is the perversity that draws you on. What else could? As pathological phenomena go, it doesn't *completely* wreck your life."

"How is your life? Where are you? I read somewhere, on the back of some book, you were living in England with an aristocrat."

"I live in New England now, without an aristocrat."

"So who instead?"

"No one instead."

"Can't be. What do you do for somebody to eat dinner with?"

"I go without dinner."

"For now. The Wisdom of the Bypass. But my experience is that personal philosophies have a shelf life of about two weeks. Things'll change."

"Look, this is where life has left me. Rarely see anyone. Where I live in western Massachusetts, a tiny place in the hills there, I talk to the guy who runs the general store and to the lady at the post office. The postmistress. That's it."

"What's the name of the town?"

"You wouldn't know it. Up in the woods. About ten miles from a college town called Athena. I met a famous writer there when I was just starting out. Nobody mentions him much anymore, his sense of virtue is too narrow for readers now, but he was revered back then. Lived like a hermit. Reclusion looked awfully austere to a kid. He maintained it solved his problems. Now it solves mine."

"What's the problem?"

"Certain problems having been taken out of my life—that's the problem. At the store the Red Sox, at the post office the weather—that's it, my social discourse. Whether we deserve the weather. When I come to pick up my mail and the sun is shining outside, the postmistress tells me, 'We don't deserve this weather.' Can't argue with that."

"And pussy?"

"Over. Live without dinner, live without pussy."

"Who are you, Socrates? I don't buy it. Purely the writer. The single-minded writer. Nothing more."

"Nothing more all along and I could have saved myself a lot of wear and tear. That's all I've had anyway to keep the shit at bay."

"What's 'the shit'?"

"The picture we have of one another. Layers and layers of misunderstanding. The picture we have of *ourselves.* Useless. Presumptuous. Completely cocked-up. Only we go ahead and we *live* by these pictures. 'That's what she is, that's what he is, this is what I am. This is what happened, this is *why* it happened—' Enough. You know who I saw a couple of months ago? Your brother. Did he tell you?"

"No, he didn't."

"He wrote me a letter and invited me to dinner in New York. A nice letter. Out of the blue. I drove down to meet him. He was composing a tribute to your old man. In the letter he asked for my help. I was curious about what he had in mind. I was curious about him writing me to announce that he wanted to write something. To you he's just a brother—to me he's still 'the Swede.' You carry those guys around with you forever. I *had* to drive down. But at dinner he never mentioned the tribute. We just uttered the pleasantries. At some place called Vincent's. That was it. As always, he looked terrific."

"He's dead."

"Your brother's dead?"

"Died Wednesday. Funeral two days ago. Friday. That's why I was in Jersey. Watched my big brother die."

"Of what? *How?*"

"Cancer."

"But he'd had prostate surgery. He told me they got it out."

Impatiently Jerry said, "What else was he going to tell you?"

"He was thin, that was all."

"That wasn't all."

So, the Swede too. What, astoundingly to Mendy Gurlik, was decimating the Daredevils right up the middle; what, astoundingly to me, had, a year earlier, made of me "purely a writer"; what, in the wake of all the other isolating losses, in the wake of everything gone and everyone gone, had stripped me down into someone whose aging powers had now but a single and unswerving aim, a man who would be seeking his solace, like it or not, nowhere but in sentences, had managed the most astounding thing of all by carrying off the indestructible hero of the wartime Weequahic section, our neighborhood talisman, the legendary Swede.

"Did he know," I asked, "when I saw him, that he was in trouble?"

"He had his hopes, but sure he knew. Metastasized. All through him."

"I'm sorry to hear it."

"His *fiftieth* was coming up next month. You know what he said at the hospital on Tuesday? To me and his kids the day before he died? Most of the time he was incoherent, but twice he said, so we could understand him, 'Going to get to my fiftieth.' He'd heard everyone from his class was asking, 'Will the Swede be there?' and he didn't want to let them down. He was very stoical. He was a very nice, simple, stoical guy. Not a humorous guy. Not a passionate guy. Just a sweetheart whose fate it was to get himself fucked over by some real crazies. In one way he could be conceived as completely banal and conventional. An absence of negative values and nothing more. Bred to be dumb, built for convention, and so on. That ordinary decent life that they all want to live, and that's it. The social norms, and that's it. Benign, and that's it. But what he was trying to do was to survive, keeping his group intact. He was trying to get through with his platoon intact. It was a war for him, finally. There was a noble side to this guy. Some excruciating renunciations went on in that life. He got caught in a war he didn't start, and he fought to keep it all together, and he went down. Banal, conventional—maybe, maybe not. People could think that. I don't want to get into judging. My brother was the best you're going to get in this country, by a long shot."

I was wondering while he spoke if this had been Jerry's estimate of the Swede while he was alive, if there wasn't perhaps a touch of mourner's rethinking here, remorse for a harsher Jerry-like view he might once have held of the handsome older brother, sound, well adjusted, quiet, normal, somebody everybody looked up to, the neighborhood hero to whom the smaller Levov had been endlessly compared while himself evolving into something slightly ersatz. This kindly unjudging judgment of the Swede could well have been a new development in Jerry, compassion just a few hours old. That can happen when people die—the argument with them drops away and people so flawed while they were drawing breath that at times they were all but unbearable now assert themselves in the most appealing way, and what was least to your liking the day before yesterday becomes in the limousine behind the hearse a cause not only for sympathetic amusement but for admiration. In which estimate lies the greater reality—the uncharitable one permitted us before the funeral, forged, without any claptrap, in the skirmish of daily life, or the one that suffuses us with sadness at the family gathering afterward—even an outsider can't judge. The sight of a coffin going into the ground can effect a great change of heart—all at once you find you are not so disappointed in this person who is dead—but what the sight of a coffin does for the mind in its search for the truth, this I don't profess to know.

"My father," Jerry said, "was one impossible bastard. Overbearing. Omnipresent. I don't know how people worked for him. When they moved to Central Avenue, the first thing he had the movers move was his desk, and the first place he put it was not in the glass-enclosed office but dead center in the middle of the factory floor, so he could keep his eye on everybody. You can't imagine the noise out there, the sewing machines whining, the clicking machines pounding, hundreds of machines going all at once, and right in the middle his desk and his telephone and the great man himself. The owner of the glove factory, but he would always sweep his own floors, especially around the cutters, where they cut the leather, because he wanted to see from the size of the scraps who was losing money for him. I told him early on to fuck off, but Seymour wasn't built like me. He had a big, generous nature and with that they really raked him over the coals, all the impossible ones. Unsatisfiable father, unsatisfiable wives, and the little murderer herself, the monster daughter. The monster *Merry*. The solid thing he once was. At Newark Maid he was an absolute, unequivocal success. Charmed a lot of people into giving their all for Newark Maid. Very adroit businessman. Knew how to cut a glove, knew how to cut a deal. Had an in on Seventh Avenue with the fashion people. The designers there would tell the guy anything. That's how he stayed abreast of the pack. In New York, he was always stopping into the department stores, shopping the competition, looking for something unique about the other guy's product, always in the stores taking a look at the leather, stretching the glove, doing everything just the way my old man taught him. Did most of the selling himself. Handled all the big house accounts. The lady buyers went nuts for Seymour. You can imagine. He'd come over to New York, take these tough Jewish broads out to dinner— buyers who could make or break you—wine and dine them, and they'd fall head over heels for the guy. Instead of him buttering them up, by the end of the evening they'd be buttering him up. Come Christmastime they'd be sending my brother the theater tickets and the case of Scotch rather than the other way around. He knew how to get the confidence of these people just by being himself. He'd find out a buyer's favorite charity, get a ticket to the annual dinner at the Waldorf-Astoria, show up like a movie star in his tuxedo, on the spot make a fat donation to cancer, muscular dystrophy, whatever it was, United Jewish Appeal—next thing Newark Maid had the account. Knew all the stuff: what colors are going to be next season's colors, whether the length is going to be up or down. Attractive, responsible, hardworking guy. A couple of unpleasant strikes in the sixties, a lot of tension. But his employees are out on the picket line and they see him pull up in the car and the women who sew the gloves start falling all over themselves apologizing for not being at the machines. They were more loyal to my brother than they were to their union. Everybody loved him, a perfectly decent person who could have escaped stupid guilt forever. No reason for him to know anything about anything except gloves. Instead he is plagued with shame and uncertainty and pain for the rest of his life. The incessant questioning of a conscious adulthood was never something that obstructed my brother. He got the meaning for his life some other way. I don't mean he was simple. Some people thought he was simple because all his life he was so kind. But Seymour was never that simple. Simple is *never* that simple. Still, the self-questioning did take some time to reach him. And if there's anything worse than self-questioning coming too early in life, it's self-questioning coming too late. His life was blown up by that bomb. The real victim of that bombing was him."

"What bomb?"

"Little Merry's darling bomb."

"I don't know what 'Merry's darling bomb' is."

"Meredith Levov. Seymour's daughter. The 'Rimrock Bomber' was Seymour's daughter. The high school kid who blew up the post office and killed the doctor. The kid who stopped the war in Vietnam by blowing up somebody out mailing a letter at five A.M. A doctor on his way to the hospital. Charming child," he said in a voice that was all contempt and still didn't seem to contain the load of contempt and hatred that he felt. "Brought the war home to Lyndon Johnson by blowing up the post office in the general store. Place is so small the post office is in the general store—just a window at the back of the general store and a couple rows of those boxes with the locks, and that's the whole post office. Get your stamps right in there with the Rinso and the Lifebuoy and the Lux. Quaint Americana. Seymour was into quaint Americana. But the kid wasn't. He took the kid out of real time and she put him right back in. My brother thought he could take his family out of human confusion and into Old Rimrock, and she put them right back in. Somehow she plants a bomb back behind the post office window, and when it goes off it takes out the general store too. And takes out the guy, this doctor, who's just stopping by the collection box to drop off his mail. Good-bye, Americana; hello, real time."

"This passed me by. I had no idea."

"That was '68, back when the wild behavior was still new. People suddenly forced to make sense of madness. All that public display. The dropping of inhibitions. Authority powerless. The kids going crazy. Intimidating everybody. The adults don't know what to make of it, they don't know what to do. Is this an act? Is the 'revolution' real? Is it a game? Is it cops and robbers? What's going on here? Kids turning the country upside down and so the adults start going crazy too. But Seymour wasn't one of them. He was one of the people who knew his way. He understood that something was going wrong, but he was no Ho-Chi-Minhite like his darling fat girl. Just a liberal sweetheart of a father. The philosopher-king of ordinary life. Brought her up with all the modern ideas of being rational with your children. Everything permissible, everything forgivable, and she hated it. People don't like to admit how much they resent other people's children, but this kid made it easy for you. She was miserable, self-righteous—little shit was no good from the time she was born. Look, I've got kids, kids galore—I know what kids are like growing up. The black hole of self-absorption is bottomless. But it's one thing to get fat, it's one thing to let your hair grow long, it's one thing to listen to rock-and-roll music too loud, but it's another to jump the line and throw a bomb. That crime could never be made right. There was no way back for my brother from that bomb. That bomb detonated his life. His perfect life was over. Just what she had in mind. That's why they had it in for him, the daughter and her friends. He was so in love with his own good luck, and they hated him for it. Once we were all up at his place for Thanksgiving, the Dwyer mother, Dawn's kid brother Danny, Danny's wife, all the Levovs, our kids, everybody, and Seymour got up to make a toast and he said, 'I'm not a religious man, but when I look around this table, I know that something is shining down on me.' It was him they were really out to get. And they did it. They got him. The bomb might as well have gone off in their living room. The violence done to his life was awful. Horrible. Never in his life had occasion to ask himself, 'Why are things the way they are?' Why should he bother, when the way they were was always perfect? Why are things the way they are? The question to which there is no answer, and up till then he was so blessed he didn't even know the question existed."

Had Jerry ever before been so full of his brother's life and his brother's story? It did not strike me that all the despotic determination concentrated in that strange head could ever have allowed him to divide his attention into very many parts. Not that death ordinarily impinges upon the majesty of self-obsession; generally it intensifies it: "What about me? What if this happens to me?"

"He told you it was horrible?"

"Once. Only once," Jerry replied. "No, Seymour just took it and took it. You could stay on this guy and stay on this guy and he'd just keep making the effort," Jerry said bitterly. "Poor son of a bitch, that was his fate—built for bearing burdens and taking shit," and with his saying this, I remembered those scrimmage pileups from which the Swede would extricate himself, always still clutching the ball, and how seriously I'd fallen in love with him on that late-autumn afternoon long ago when he'd transformed my ten-year-old existence by selecting me to enter the fantasy of Swede Levov's life—when for a moment it had seemed that I, too, had been called to great things and that nothing in the world could ever obstruct my way now that our god's benign countenance had shed its light on me alone. "Basketball was never like this, Skip." How captivatingly that innocence spoke to my own. The significance he had given me. It was everything a boy could have wanted in 1943.

"Never caved in. He could be tough. Remember, when we

were kids, he joined the marines to fight the Japs? Well, he *was* a goddamn marine. Caved in only once, down in Florida," Jerry said. "It just got to be too much for him. He'd brought the whole family down to visit us, the boys and the second superbly selfish Mrs. Levov. That was two years ago. We all went to this stone-crab place. Twelve of us for dinner. Lots of noise, the kids all showing off and laughing. Seymour loved it. The whole handsome family there, life just the way it's supposed to be. But when the pie and coffee came he got up from the table, and when he didn't come back right away I went out and found him. In the car. In tears. Shaking with sobs. I'd never seen him like that. My brother the rock. He said, 'I miss my daughter.' I said, 'Where is she?' I knew he always knew where she was. He'd been going to see her in hiding for years. I believe he saw her frequently. He said, 'She's dead, Jerry.' I didn't believe him at first. It was to throw me off the track, I thought. I thought he must have just seen her somewhere. I thought, He's still going to wherever she is and treating this killer like his own child—this killer who is now in her forties while everybody she killed is still killed. But then he threw his arms around me and he just let go, and I thought, Is it true, the family's fucking monster's really dead? But why is he crying if she's dead? If he had half a brain, he would have realized that it was just too extraordinary to have a child like that—if he had half a brain, he would have been enraged by this kid and estranged from this kid long ago. Long ago he would have torn her out of his guts and let go. The angry kid who gets nuttier and nuttier—and the sanctified cause to hang her craziness on. Crying like that—for her? No, I couldn't buy it. I said to him, 'I don't know whether you're lying to me or you're telling me the truth. But if you're telling me the truth, that she's dead, it's the best news I ever heard. Nobody else is going to say this to you. Everybody else is going to commiserate. But I grew up with you. I talk straight to you. The best thing for you is for her to be dead. She did not belong to you. She did not belong to anything that you were. She did not belong to anything anyone is. *You* played ball—there was a field of play. She was not on the field of play. She was nowhere near it. Simple as that. She was out of bounds, a freak of nature, *way* out of bounds. You are to stop your mourning for her. You've kept this wound open for twenty-five years. And twenty-five years is enough. It's driven you mad. Keep it open any longer and it's going to kill you. She's dead? Good! Let her go. Otherwise it will rot in your gut and take your life too.' That's what I told him. I thought I could let the rage out of him. But he just cried. He couldn't let it go. I said this guy was going to get killed from this thing, and he did."

Jerry said it and it happened. It is Jerry's theory that the Swede is nice, that is to say passive, that is to say trying always to do the right thing, a socially controlled character who doesn't burst out, doesn't yield to rage ever. Will not have the angry quality as his liability, so doesn't get it as an asset either. According to this theory, it's the no-rage that kills him in the end. Whereas aggression is cleansing or curing.

It would seem that what kept Jerry going, without uncertainty or remorse and unflaggingly devoted to his own take on things, was that he had a special talent for rage and another special talent for not looking back. Doesn't look back at all, I thought. He's unseared by memory. To him, all looking back is bullshit-nostalgia, including even the Swede's looking back, twenty-five years later, at his daughter before that bomb went off, looking back and helplessly weeping for all that went up in that explosion. Righteous anger at the daughter? No doubt that would have helped. Incontestable that nothing is more uplifting in all of life than righteous anger. But given the circumstances, wasn't it asking a lot, asking the Swede to overstep the limits that made him identifiably the Swede? People must have been doing that to him all his life, assuming that because he was once upon a time this mythic character the Swede he had no limits. I'd done something like that in Vincent's restaurant, childishly expecting to be wowed by his godliness, only to be confronted by an utterly ordinary humanness. One price you pay for being taken for a god is the unabated dreaminess of your acolytes.

"You know Seymour's 'fatal attraction'? Fatally attracted to his duty," Jerry said. "Fatally attracted to responsibility. He could have played ball anywhere he wanted, but he went to Upsala because my father wanted him near home. Giants offered him a Double A contract, might have played one day with Willie Mays—instead he went down to Central Avenue to work for Newark Maid. My father started him off at a tannery. Puts him for six months working in a tannery on Frelinghuysen Avenue. Up six mornings a week at five A.M. You know what a tannery is? A tannery is a shithole. Remember those days in the summer? A strong wind from the east and the tanning stench wafts over Weequahic Park and covers the whole neighborhood. Well, he gets out of the tannery, Seymour does, strong as an ox, and my father sits him down at a sewing machine for another six months and Seymour doesn't let out a peep. Just masters the fucking machine. Give him the pieces of a glove and he can close it up better than the sewers and in half the time. He could have married any beauty he wanted. Instead he marries the bee-yoo-ti-full Miss Dwyer. You should have seen them. Knockout couple. The two of them all smiles on their outward trip into the USA. She's post-Catholic, he's post-Jewish, together they're going to go out there to Old Rimrock to raise little post-toasties. Instead they get that fucking kid."

"What was wrong with Miss Dwyer?"

"No house they lived in was right. No amount of money in the bank was enough. He set her up in the cattle business. That didn't work. He set her up in the nursery tree business. That didn't work. He took her to Switzerland for the world's best face-lift. Not even into her fifties, still in her forties, but that's what the woman wants, so they schlep to Geneva for a face-lift from the guy who did Princess Grace. He would have been better off spending his life in Double A ball. He would have been better off knocking up some waitress down there in Phoenix and playing first base for the Mudhens. That fucking kid! She stuttered, you know. So to pay everybody back for her stuttering, she set off the bomb. He took her to speech therapists. He took her to clinics, to psychiatrists. There wasn't enough he could do for her. And the reward? Boom! Why does this girl hate her father? This great father, this truly great father. Good-looking, kind, providing, thinks about nothing really but them, his family—why does she take off after him? That our own ridiculous father should have produced such a *brilliant* father—and that he should then produce *her*? Somebody tell me what caused it. The genetic need to separate? For that she has to run from Seymour Levov to Che Guevara? No, no. What is the poison that caused it, that caused this poor guy to be placed outside his life for the rest of his life? He kept peering in from outside at his own life. The struggle of his life was to bury this thing. But could he? How? How could a big, sweet, agreeable putz like my brother be expected to deal with this bomb? One day life started laughing at him and it never let up."

That was as far as we got, as much of an earful as I was to hear from Jerry—anything more I wanted to know, I'd have to make up—because just then a small, gray-haired woman in a brown pantsuit came up to introduce herself, and Jerry, not a man equipped by nature to stand around more than five seconds while someone else was getting a third party's attention, shot me a mock salute and disappeared, and when I went looking for him later, I heard that he'd had to leave, to catch a Newark plane back to Miami.

After I'd already written about his brother—which is what I would do in the months to come: think about the Swede for six, eight, sometimes ten hours at a stretch, exchange my solitude for his, inhabit this person least like myself, disappear into him, day and night try to take the measure of a person of apparent blankness and innocence and simplicity, chart his collapse, make of him, as time wore on, the most important figure of my life—just before I set about to alter names and disguise the most glaring marks of identification, I had the amateur's impulse to send Jerry a copy of the manuscript to ask what he thought. It was an impulse I quashed: I hadn't been writing and publishing for nearly forty years not to know by now to quash it. "That's not my brother," he'd tell me, "not in any way. You've misrepresented him. My brother couldn't think like that, didn't talk like that," etc.

Yes, by this time Jerry might well have recovered the objectivity that had deserted him directly after the funeral, and with it the old resentment that helped make him the doctor at the hospital everybody was afraid to talk to because he was never wrong. Also, unlike most people whose dear one winds up as a model for the life-drawing class, Jerry Levov would probably be amused rather than outraged by my failure to grasp the Swede's tragedy the way he did. A strong possibility: Jerry's flipping derisively through my pages and giving me, item by item, the bad news. "The wife was nothing like this, the kid was nothing like this—got even my father wrong. I won't talk about what you do with me. But missing my father, man, that's missing the side of a barn. Lou Levov was a brute, man. This guy is a pushover. He's *charming*. He's *conciliatory*. No, we had something over us light-years away from that. We had a sword. Dad on the rampage—laid down the law and that was it. No, nothing bears the slightest resemblance to . . . here, for instance, giving my brother a mind, awareness. This guy responds with consciousness to his loss. But my brother is a guy who had cognitive *problems*—this is nowhere *like* the mind he had. This is the mind he *didn't* have. Christ, you even give him a mistress. Perfectly misjudged, Zuck. Absolutely off. How could a big man like you fuck up like this?"

Well, Jerry wouldn't have gotten much of an argument from me had that turned out to be his reaction. I had gone out to Newark and located the abandoned Newark Maid factory on a barren stretch of lower Central Avenue. I went out to the Weequahic section to look at their house, now in disrepair, and to look at Keer Avenue, a street where it didn't seem like a good idea to get out of the car and walk up the driveway to the garage where the Swede used to practice his swing in the wintertime. Three black kids were sitting on the front steps eyeing me in the car. I explained to them, "A friend of mine used to live here." When I got no answer, I added, "Back in the forties." And then I drove away. I drove to Morristown to look at Merry's high school and then on west to Old Rimrock, where I found the big stone house up on Arcady Hill Road where the Seymour Levovs once had lived as a happy young family; later, down in the village, I drank a cup of coffee at the counter of the new general store (McPherson's) that had replaced the old general store (Hamlin's) whose post office the teenage Levov daughter had blown up "to bring the war home to America." I went to Elizabeth, where the Swede's beautiful Dawn was born and raised, and walked around her pleasant neighborhood, the residential Elmora section; I drove by her family's church, St. Genevieve's, and then headed due east to her father's neighborhood, the old port on the Elizabeth River, where the Cuban immigrants and their offspring replaced, back in the sixties, the last of the Irish immigrants and their offspring. I was able to get the New Jersey Miss America Pageant office to dig up a glossy photo of Mary Dawn Dwyer, age twenty-two, being crowned Miss New Jersey in May of 1949. I found another picture of her—in a 1961 number of a Morris County weekly—standing primly before her fireplace mantel in a blazer, a skirt, and a turtleneck sweater, a picture captioned, "Mrs. Levov, the former Miss New Jersey of 1949, loves living in a 170-year-old home, an environment which she says reflects the values of her family." At the Newark Public Library I scanned microfilmed sports pages of the *Newark News* (expired 1972), looking for accounts and box scores of games in which the Swede had shined for Weequahic High (in extremis 1995) and Upsala College (expired 1995). For the first time in fifty years I reread the baseball books of John R. Tunis and at one point even began to think of my book about the Swede as *The Kid from Keer Avenue*, calling it after Tunis's 1940 story for boys about the Tomkinsville, Connecticut, orphan whose only fault, as a major leaguer, is a tendency to keep his right shoulder down and his swing up, but a fault, alas, that is provocation enough for the gods to destroy him.

Yet despite these efforts and more to uncover what I could about the Swede and his world, I would have been willing to admit that my Swede was not the primary Swede. Of course I was working with traces; of course essentials of what he was to Jerry were gone, expunged from my portrait, things I was ignorant of or I didn't want; of course the Swede was concentrated differently in my pages from how he'd been concentrated in the flesh. But whether that meant I'd imagined an outright fantastical creature, lacking entirely the unique substantiality of the real thing; whether that meant my conception of the Swede was any more fallacious than the conception held by Jerry (which he wasn't likely to see as in any way fallacious); whether the Swede and his family came to life in me any less truthfully than in his brother—well, who knows? Who *can* know? When it comes to illuminating someone with the Swede's opacity, to understanding those regular guys everybody likes and who go about more or less incognito, it's up for grabs, it seems to me, as to whose guess is more rigorous than whose.

"You don't remember me, do you?" asked the woman who had sent Jerry scurrying. Smiling warmly, she had taken my two hands in hers. Beneath the short-cropped hair, her head looked imposingly well made, large and durable, its angular mass like the antique stone head of a Roman sovereign. Though the broad planes of her face were deeply scored as if with an engraving stylus, the skin beneath the rosy makeup looked to be seriously wrinkled only around the mouth, which, after nearly six hours of exchanging kisses, had lost most of its lipstick; otherwise there was an almost girlish softness to her flesh, indicating that perhaps she hadn't partaken of every last one of the varied forms of suffering available to a woman over a lifetime.

"Don't look at my name tag. Who was I?"

"You tell me," I said.

"Joyce. Joy Helpern. I had a pink angora sweater. Originally my cousin's. Estelle's. She was three years ahead of us. She's dead, Nathan—in the ground. My beautiful cousin, Estelle, who smoked and dated older guys. In high school she was dating a guy who shaved twice a day. Her parents had the dress and corset shop on Chancellor. Grossman's. My mother worked there. You took me on a class hayride. Believe it or not, I used to be Joy Helpern."

Joy: a bright little girl with curly reddish hair, freckles, a round face, a girl with a provocative chubbiness that did not go unobserved by Mr. Roscoe, our stout, red-nosed Spanish teacher who on the mornings when Joy came to school in a sweater was always asking her to stand at her desk to recite her homework. Mr. Roscoe called her Dimples. Amazing what you could get away with back in those days when it didn't seem to me anybody got away with anything.

Because of an association of words not entirely implausible, Joy's figure had continued to tantalize me, no less than it had Mr. Roscoe, long after I last saw her springing up Chancellor Avenue to school in that odd but stirring pair of unclasped galoshes obviously outgrown by her older brother and handed down to Joy like her beautiful cousin's angora sweater. Whenever a couple of famous lines from John Keats happened, for whatever reason, to fall into my head, I'd invariably remember the full, plump feel of her beneath me, the wonderful buoyancy of her that my adolescent boy's exquisite radar sensed even through my mackinaw on that hayride. The lines are from

"Ode on Melancholy": ". . . him whose strenuous tongue /
Can burst Joy's grape against his palate fine."

"I remember that hayride, Joy Helpern. You weren't as kind
on that hayride as you might have been."

"And now I look like Spencer Tracy," she said, breaking into
laughter. "Now that I'm no longer frightened it's much too
late. I used to be shy—I'm not shy anymore. Oh, Nathan,
aging," she cried, as we embraced each other, "aging, aging—it
is so very strange. You wanted to touch my bare breasts."

"I would have settled for that."

"Yes," she said. "They were new then."

"You were fourteen and they were about one."

"There's *always* been a thirteen-year difference. Back then I
was thirteen years older than they were and now they're about
thirteen years older than I am. But we certainly did kiss, didn't
we, darling?"

"Kissed and kissed and kissed."

"I had practiced. All that afternoon I practiced kissing."

"On whom?"

"My fingers. I *should* have let you undo my bra. Undo it
now if you'd like to."

"I'm afraid I haven't the daring anymore to undo a brassiere
in front of the class."

"What a surprise. Just when I'm ready, Nathan's grown up."

We bantered back and forth, our arms tight around each
other, and leaning backwards from the waist so each could see
clearly what had happened to the other's face and figure, the
external shape that half a century of living had bestowed.

Yes, the overwhelming spell that we continue to cast on one
another, right down to the end, with the body's surface, which
turns out to be, as I suspected on that hayride, about as serious
a thing as there is in life. The body, from which one cannot
strip oneself however one tries, from which one is not to be
freed this side of death. Earlier, looking at Alan Meisner I was
looking at his father, and looking now at Joy I was looking at
her mother, the stout seamstress with her stockings rolled
down to her knees in the back room of Grossman's Dress Shop
on Chancellor Avenue. . . . But who I was thinking of was
the Swede, the Swede and the tyranny that his body held over
him, the powerful, the gorgeous, the lonely Swede, whom life

had never made shrewd, who did not want to pass through life as a beautiful boy and a stellar first baseman, who wanted instead to be a serious person for whom others came before himself and not a baby for whose needs alone the wide, wide world of satisfactions had been organized. He wanted to have been born something more than a physical wonder. As if for one person that gift isn't enough. The Swede wanted what he took to be a higher calling, and his bad luck was to have found one. The responsibility of the school hero follows him through life. Noblesse oblige. You're the hero, so then you have to behave in a certain way—there is a prescription for it. You have to be modest, you have to be forbearing, you have to be deferential, you have to be understanding. And it all began—this heroically idealistic maneuver, this strategic, strange spiritual desire to be a bulwark of duty and ethical obligation—because of the war, because of all the terrible uncertainties bred by the war, because of how strongly an emotional community whose beloved sons were far away facing death had been drawn to a lean and muscular, austere boy whose talent it was to be able to catch anything anybody threw anywhere near him. It all began for the Swede—as what doesn't?—in a circumstantial absurdity.

And ended in another one. A bomb.

When we'd met at Vincent's, perhaps he insisted on how well his three boys had turned out because he assumed I knew about the bomb, about the daughter, the Rimrock Bomber, and had judged him harshly, as some people must have. Such a sensational thing, in his life certainly—even twenty-seven years later, how could anybody not know or have forgotten? Maybe that explains why he couldn't stop himself, even had he wanted to, from going interminably on and on to me about the myriad nonviolent accomplishments of Chris, Steve, and Kent. Maybe that explains what he had wanted to talk about in the first place. "The shocks" that had befallen his father's loved ones was the daughter—*she* was "the shocks" that had befallen them all. *This* was what he had summoned me to talk about—had wanted me to help him *write* about. And I missed it—I, whose vanity is that he is never naive, was more naive by far than the guy I was talking to. Sitting there at Vincent's getting the shallowest bead I could on the Swede when the story he had to tell me was this one, the revelation of the interior life that was unknown and unknowable, the story that is tragic and awful and impossible to ignore, the ultimate reunion story, and I missed it entirely.

The father was the cover. The burning subject was the daughter. How much of that was he aware of? All of it. He was aware of everything—I had that wrong too. The unconscious one was me. He knew he was dying, and this terrible thing that had happened to him—that over the years he'd been partially able to bury, that somewhere along the way he had somewhat overcome—came back at him worse than ever. He'd put it aside as best he could, new wife, new kids—the three terrific boys; he sure seemed to me to have put it aside the night in 1985 I saw him at Shea Stadium with young Chris. The Swede had got up off the ground and he'd done it—a second marriage, a second shot at a unified life controlled by good sense and the classic restraints, once again convention shaping everything, large and small, and serving as barrier against the improbabilities—a second shot at being the traditional devoted husband and father, pledging allegiance all over again to the standard rules and regulations that are the heart of family order. He had the talent for it, had what it took to avoid anything disjointed, anything special, anything improper, anything difficult to assess or understand. And yet not even the Swede, blessed with all the attributes of a monumental ordinariness, could shed that girl the way Jerry the Ripper had told him to, could go all the way and shed completely the frantic possessiveness, the paternal assertiveness, the obsessive love for the lost daughter, shed every trace of that girl and that past and shake off forever the hysteria of "my child." If only he could have just let her fade away. But not even the Swede was that great.

He had learned the worst lesson that life can teach—that it makes no sense. And when that happens the happiness is never spontaneous again. It is artificial and, even then, bought at the price of an obstinate estrangement from oneself and one's history. The nice gentle man with his mild way of dealing with conflict and contradiction, the confident ex-athlete sensible and resourceful in any struggle with an adversary who is fair, comes up against the adversary who is not fair—the evil ineradicable from human dealings—and he is finished. He whose natural nobility was to be exactly what he seemed to be has taken in far too much suffering to be naively whole again. Never again will the Swede be content in the trusting old Swedian way that, for the sake of his second wife and their three boys—for the sake of *their* naive wholeness—he ruthlessly goes on pretending to be. Stoically he suppresses his horror. He learns to live behind a mask. A lifetime experiment in endurance. A performance over a ruin. Swede Levov lives a double life.

And now he is dying and what sustained him in a double life can sustain him no longer, and that horror mercifully half submerged, two-thirds submerged, even at times nine-tenths submerged, comes back distilled despite the heroic creation of that second marriage and the fathering of the wonderful boys; in the final months of the cancer, it's back worse than ever; *she's* back worse than ever, the first child who was the cancellation of everything, and one night in bed when he cannot sleep, when every effort fails to control his runaway thoughts, he is so depleted by his anguish he thinks, "There's this guy who was in my brother's class, and he's a writer, and maybe if I told him. . . ." But what would happen if he told the writer? He doesn't even know. "I'll write him a letter. I know he writes about fathers, about sons, so I'll write him about my father—can he turn that down? Maybe he'll respond to that." The hook to which I am to be the eye. But I come because he is the Swede. No other hook is necessary. He is the hook.

Yes, the story was back worse than ever, and he thought, "If I can give it to a pro . . . ," but when he got me there he couldn't deliver. Once he got my attention he didn't want it. He thought better of it. And he was right. It was none of my business. What good would it have done him? None at all. You go to someone and you think, "I'll tell him this." But why? The impulse is that the telling is going to relieve you. And that's why you feel awful later—you've relieved yourself, and if it truly is tragic and awful, it's not better, it's worse—the exhibitionism inherent to a confession has only made the misery worse. The Swede realized this. He was nothing like the chump I was imagining, and he had figured this out simply enough. He realized that there was nothing to be had through me. He certainly didn't want to cry in front of me the way he had with his brother. I wasn't his brother. I wasn't anyone—that's what he saw when he saw me. So he just blabbered deliberately on about the boys and went home and, the story untold, he died. And I missed it. He turned to me, of all people, and he was conscious of everything and I missed everything.

And now Chris, Steve, Kent, and their mother would be at the Rimrock house, perhaps along with the Swede's old mother, with Mrs. Levov. The mother must be ninety. Sitting shiva at ninety for her beloved Seymour. And the daughter, Meredith, Merry . . . obviously hadn't attended the funeral, not with that outsized uncle around who hated her guts, that vindictive uncle who might even take it upon himself to turn her in. But with Jerry now gone, she dares to leave her hideout to join in the mourning, makes her way to Old Rimrock, perhaps in disguise, and there, alongside her half-brothers and her stepmother and Grandma Levov, weeps her heart out over her father's death. . . . But no, she was dead too. If the Swede had been telling Jerry the truth, the daughter in hiding had died—perhaps in hiding she had been murdered or had even taken her own life. Anything might have occurred—and "anything" wasn't supposed to occur, not to him.

The brutality of the destruction of this indestructible man. Whatever Happened to Swede Levov. Surely not what befell the Kid from Tomkinsville. Even as boys we must have known that it couldn't have been as easy for him as it looked, that a part of it was a mystique, but who could have imagined that his life would come apart in this horrible way? A sliver off the comet of the American chaos had come loose and spun all the way out to Old Rimrock and him. His great looks, his larger-than-lifeness, his glory, our sense of his having been exempted from all self-doubt by his heroic role—that all these manly properties had precipitated a political murder made me think of the compelling story not of John R. Tunis's sacrificial Tomkinsville Kid but of Kennedy, John F. Kennedy, only a decade the Swede's senior and another privileged son of fortune, another man of glamour exuding American meaning, assassinated while still in his mid-forties just five years before the Swede's daughter violently protested the Kennedy-Johnson war and blew up her father's life. I thought, But of course. He is our Kennedy.

Meanwhile Joy was telling me things about her life that I'd never known as a single-minded kid searching the neighborhood for a grape to burst—Joy was tossing into this agitated pot of memory called "the reunion" yet more stuff no one knew at the time, that no one *had* to know back when all our storytelling about ourselves was still eloquently naive. Joy was telling me about how her father had died of a heart attack when she was nine and the family was living in Brooklyn; about how she and her mother and Harold, her older brother, had moved from Brooklyn to the Newark haven of Grossman's Dress Shop; about how, in the attic space above the shop, she and her mother slept in the double bed in their one big room while Harold slept in the kitchen, on a sofa he made up each night and unmade each morning so they could eat breakfast there before going to school. She asked if I remembered Harold, now a retired pharmacist in Scotch Plains, and told me how just the week before she'd gone out to the cemetery in Brooklyn to visit her father's grave—as frequently as once a month she went out there, all the way to Brooklyn, she said, surprised herself by how much this graveyard now mattered to her. "What do you do at the cemetery?" "I unabashedly talk to him," Joy said. "When I was ten it wasn't nearly as bad as it is now. I thought then it was odd that people had two parents. Our threesome seemed right." "Well, all this," I told her, as we stood there just swaying together to the one-man band closing the day down singing, "Dream . . . when you're feelin' blue, . . . dream . . . that's the thing to do"—"all this I did not know," I told her, "on the harvest moon hayride in October 1948."

"I didn't want you to know. I didn't want anybody to know. I didn't want anybody to find out Harold slept in the kitchen. That's why I wouldn't let you undo my bra. I didn't want you to be my boyfriend and come to pick me up and see where my brother had to sleep. It had nothing to do with you, sweetheart."

"Well, I feel better for being told that. I wish you'd told me sooner."

"I wish I had," she said, and first we were laughing and then, unexpectedly, Joy began to cry and, perhaps because of that damn song, "Dream," which we used to dance to with the

lights turned down in somebody or other's basement back
when the Pied Pipers still had Jo Stafford and used to sing it
the way it's supposed to be sung—in locked harmony, to that
catatonic forties beat, with the ethereal tinkle of the xylophone
hollowly sounding behind them—or perhaps because Alan
Meisner had become a Republican and second baseman Bert
Bergman had become a corpse and Ira Posner, instead of shining shoes at the newsstand outside the Essex County courthouse, had escaped his Dostoyevskian family and become a
psychiatrist, because Julius Pincus had disabling tremors from
the drug that prevented the rejection from his body of the
fourteen-year-old girl's kidney keeping him alive and because
Mendy Gurlik was still a horny seventeen-year-old kid and because Joy's brother, Harold, had slept for ten years in a kitchen
and because Schrimmer had married a woman nearly half his
age who had a body that didn't make him want to slit his throat
but to whom he now had to explain every single thing about
the past, or perhaps because I seemed alone in having wound
up with no children, grandchildren, or, in Minskoff's words,
"anything like that," or perhaps because after all these years of
separation this reuniting of perfect strangers had all gone on a
little too long, a load of unruly emotion began sliding around
in me, too, and there I was thinking again of the Swede, of the
notorious significance that an outlaw daughter had thrust on
him and his family during the Vietnam War. A man whose dis-
contents were barely known to himself, awakening in middle
age to the horror of self-reflection. All that normalcy interrupted by murder. All the small problems any family expects to
encounter exaggerated by something so impossible ever to
reconcile. The disruption of the anticipated American future
that was simply to have unrolled out of the solid American
past, out of each generation's getting smarter—smarter for knowing the inadequacies and limitations of the generations before
—out of each new generation's breaking away from the paro-
chialism a little further, out of the desire to go the limit in
America with your rights, forming yourself as an ideal person
who gets rid of the traditional Jewish habits and attitudes, who
frees himself of the pre-America insecurities and the old, con-
straining obsessions so as to live unapologetically as an equal
among equals.

And then the loss of the daughter, the fourth American generation, a daughter on the run who was to have been the perfected image of himself as he had been the perfected image of his father, and his father the perfected image of his father's father . . . the angry, rebarbative spitting-out daughter with no interest whatever in being the next successful Levov, flushing him out of hiding as if he were a fugitive—initiating the Swede into the displacement of another America entirely, the daughter and the decade blasting to smithereens his particular form of utopian thinking, the plague America infiltrating the Swede's castle and there infecting everyone. The daughter who transports him out of the longed-for American pastoral and into everything that is its antithesis and its enemy, into the fury, the violence, and the desperation of the counterpastoral —into the indigenous American berserk.

The old intergenerational give-and-take of the country-that-used-to-be, when everyone knew his role and took the rules dead seriously, the acculturating back-and-forth that all of us here grew up with, the ritual postimmigrant struggle for success turning pathological in, of all places, the gentleman farmer's castle of our superordinary Swede. A guy stacked like a deck of cards for things to unfold entirely differently. In no way prepared for what is going to hit him. How could he, with all his carefully calibrated goodness, have known that the stakes of living obediently were so high? Obedience is embraced to *lower* the stakes. A beautiful wife. A beautiful house. Runs his business like a charm. Handles his handful of an old man well enough. He was really living it out, his version of paradise. This is how successful people live. They're good citizens. They feel lucky. They feel grateful. God is smiling down on them. There are problems, they adjust. And then everything changes and it becomes impossible. Nothing is smiling down on anybody. And who can adjust then? Here is someone not set up for life's working out poorly, let alone for the impossible. But who is set up for the impossible that is going to happen? Who is set up for tragedy and the incomprehensibility of suffering? Nobody. The tragedy of the man not set up for tragedy—that is every man's tragedy.

He kept peering in from outside at his own life. The struggle of his life was to bury this thing. But how could he?

Never in his life had occasion to ask himself, "Why are things the way they are?" Why should he bother, when the way they were was always perfect? Why are things the way they are? The question to which there is no answer, and up till then he was so blessed he didn't even know the question existed.

After all the effervescent strain of resuscitating our class's mid-century innocence—together a hundred aging people recklessly turning back the clock to a time when time's passing was a matter of indifference—with the afternoon's exhilarations finally coming to an end, I began to contemplate the very thing that must have baffled the Swede till the moment he died: how had he become history's plaything? History, American history, the stuff you read about in books and study in school, had made its way out to tranquil, untrafficked Old Rimrock, New Jersey, to countryside where it had not put in an appearance that was notable since Washington's army twice wintered in the highlands adjacent to Morristown. History, which had made no drastic impingement on the daily life of the local populace since the Revolutionary War, wended its way back out to these cloistered hills and, improbably, with all its predictable unforeseenness, broke helter-skelter into the orderly household of the Seymour Levovs and left the place in a shambles. People think of history in the long term, but history, in fact, is a very sudden thing.

In earnest, right then and there, while swaying with Joy to that out-of-date music, I began to try to work out for myself what exactly had shaped a destiny unlike any imagined for the famous Weequahic three-letterman back when this music and its sentimental exhortation was right to the point, when the Swede, his neighborhood, his city, and his country were in their exuberant heyday, at the peak of confidence, inflated with every illusion born of hope. With Joy Helpern once again close in my arms and quietly sobbing to hear the old pop tune enjoining all of us sixty-odd-year-olds, "Dream . . . and they might come true," I lifted the Swede up onto the stage. That evening at Vincent's, for a thousand different excellent reasons, he could not bring himself to ask me to do this. For all I know he had no intention of asking me to do this. To get me to write his story may not have been why he was there at all. Maybe it was only why I was there.

Basketball was never like this.

He'd invoked in me, when I was a boy—as he did in hundreds of other boys—the strongest fantasy I had of being someone else. But to wish oneself into another's glory, as boy or as man, is an impossibility, untenable on psychological grounds if you are not a writer, and on aesthetic grounds if you are. To embrace your hero in his destruction, however—to let your hero's life occur within you when everything is trying to diminish him, to imagine yourself into his bad luck, to implicate yourself not in his mindless ascendancy, when he is the fixed point of your adulation, but in the bewilderment of his tragic fall—well, that's worth thinking about.

So then . . . I am out there on the floor with Joy, and I am thinking of the Swede and of what happened to his country in a mere twenty-five years, between the triumphant days at wartime Weequahic High and the explosion of his daughter's bomb in 1968, of that mysterious, troubling, extraordinary historical transition. I am thinking of the sixties and of the disorder occasioned by the Vietnam War, of how certain families lost their kids and certain families didn't and how the Seymour Levovs were one of those that did—families full of tolerance and kindly, well-intentioned liberal goodwill, and theirs were the kids who went on a rampage, or went to jail, or disappeared underground, or fled to Sweden or Canada. I am thinking of the Swede's great fall and of how he must have imagined that it was founded on some failure of his own responsibility. There is where it must begin. It doesn't matter if he was the cause of anything. He makes himself responsible anyway. He has been doing that all his life, making himself unnaturally responsible, keeping under control not just himself but whatever else threatens to be uncontrollable, giving his all to keep his world together. Yes, the cause of the disaster has for him to be a transgression. How else would the Swede explain it to himself? It has to be a transgression, a single transgression, even if it is only he who identifies it as a transgression. The disaster that befalls him begins in a failure of his responsibility, *as he imagines it*.

But what could that have been?

Dispelling the aura of the dinner at Vincent's, when I'd rushed to conclude the most thoughtless conclusion—that simple *was* that simple—I lifted onto my stage the boy we were all going to follow into America, our point man into the next immersion, at home here the way the Wasps were at home here, an American not by sheer striving, not by being a Jew who invents a famous vaccine or a Jew on the Supreme Court, not by being the most brilliant or the most eminent or the best. Instead—by virtue of his isomorphism to the Wasp world —he does it the ordinary way, the natural way, the regular American-guy way. To the honeysweet strains of "Dream," I pulled away from myself, pulled away from the reunion, and I dreamed . . . I dreamed a realistic chronicle. I began gazing into his life—not his life as a god or a demigod in whose triumphs one could exult as a boy but his life as another assailable man—and inexplicably, which is to say lo and behold, I found him in Deal, New Jersey, at the seaside cottage, the summer his daughter was eleven, back when she couldn't stay out of his lap or stop calling him by cute pet names, couldn't "resist," as she put it, examining with the tip of her finger the close way his ears were fitted to his skull. Wrapped in a towel, she would run through the house and out to the clothesline to fetch a dry bathing suit, shouting as she went, "Nobody look!" and several evenings she had barged into the bathroom where he was bathing and, when she saw him, cried out, "Oh, pardonnez-moi—j'ai pensé que—" "Scram," he told her, "get-outahere-moi." Driving alone with him back from the beach one day that summer, dopily sun-drunk, lolling against his bare shoulder, she had turned up her face and, half innocently, half audaciously, precociously playing the grown-up girl, said, "Daddy, kiss me the way you k-k-kiss umumumother." Sun-drunk himself, voluptuously fatigued from rolling all morning with her in the heavy surf, he had looked down to see that one of the shoulder straps of her swimsuit had dropped over her arm, and there was her nipple, the hard red bee bite that was her nipple. "N-n-no," he said—and stunned them both. "And fix your suit," he added feebly. Soundlessly she obeyed. "I'm sorry, cookie—" "Oh, I deserve it," she said, trying with all her might to hold back her tears and be his chirpingly charming pal again. "It's the same at school. It's the same with my friends. I get started with something and I can't stop. I just get c-c-carried awuh-awuh-awuh-awuh—"

It was a while since he'd seen her turn white like that or seen her face contorted like that. She fought for the word longer than, on that particular day, he could possibly bear. "Awuh-awuh—" And yet he knew better than anyone what not to do when, as Merry put it, she "started phumphing to beat the band." He was the parent she could always rely on not to jump all over her every time she opened her mouth. "Cool it," he would tell Dawn, "relax, lay off her," but Dawn could not help herself. Merry began to stutter badly and Dawn's hands were clasped at her waist and her eyes fixed on the child's lips, eyes that said, "I know you can do it!" while saying, "I know that you can't!" Merry's stuttering just killed her mother, and that killed Merry. "I'm not the problem—Mother is!" And so was the teacher the problem when she tried to spare Merry by not calling on her. So was everybody the problem when they started feeling sorry for her. And when she was fluent suddenly and free of stuttering, the problem was the compliments. She resented terribly being praised for fluency, and as soon as she was praised she lost it completely—sometimes, Merry would say, to the point that she was afraid "I'm going to short out my whole *system*." Amazing how this child could summon up the strength to joke about it—his precious lighthearted jokester! If only it were within Dawn's power to become a little light-hearted about it herself. But it was the Swede alone who could always manage to be close to perfect with her, though even he had all he could do not to cry out in exasperation, "If you dare the gods and are fluent, what terrible thing do you think will happen?" The exasperation never surfaced: he did not wring his hands like her mother, when she was in trouble he did not watch her lips or mouth her words with her like her mother, he did not turn her, every time she spoke, into the most important person not merely in the room but in the entire world—he did everything he could not to make her stigma into Merry's way of being Einstein. Instead his eyes assured her that he would do all he could to help but that when she was with him she must stutter freely if she needed to. And yet he had said to her, "N-n-no." He had done what Dawn would rather die than do—he had made fun of her.

"Awuh-awuh-awuh—"

"Oh, cookie," he said, and at just the moment when he had

understood that the summer's mutual, seemingly harmless playacting—the two of them nibbling at an intimacy too enjoyable to swear off and yet not in any way to be taken seriously, to be much concerned with, to be given an excessive significance, something utterly uncarnal that would fade away once the vacation was over and she was in school all day and he had returned to work, nothing that they couldn't easily find their way back from—just when he had come to understand that the summer romance required some readjusting all around, he lost his vaunted sense of proportion, drew her to him with one arm, and kissed her stammering mouth with the passion that she had been asking him for all month long while knowing only obscurely what she was asking for.

Was he supposed to feel that way? It happened before he could think. She was only eleven. Momentarily it was frightening. This was not anything he had ever worried about for a second, this was a taboo that you didn't even think of as a taboo, something you are prohibited from doing that felt absolutely natural not to do, you just proceeded effortlessly—and then, however momentary, *this*. Never in his entire life, not as a son, a husband, a father, even as an employer, had he given way to anything so alien to the emotional rules by which he was governed, and later he wondered if this strange parental misstep was not the lapse from responsibility for which he paid for the rest of his life. The kiss bore no resemblance to anything serious, was not an imitation of anything, had never been repeated, had itself lasted five seconds . . . ten at most . . . but after the disaster, when he went obsessively searching for the origins of their suffering, it was that anomalous moment—when she was eleven and he was thirty-six and the two of them, all stirred up by the strong sea and the hot sun, were heading happily home alone from the beach—that he remembered.

But then he also wondered if after that day he had perhaps withdrawn from her too radically, become physically distant more than was necessary. He had only meant to let her know she needn't be concerned that he would lose his equilibrium again, needn't worry about her *own* natural-enough infatuation, and the result may well have been that having exaggerated the implications of that kiss, having overestimated what constituted provocation, he went on to alter a perfectly harmless spontaneous bond, only to exacerbate a stuttering child's burden of self-doubt. And all he had ever meant was to help her, to help her heal!

What then was the wound? What could have wounded Merry? The indelible imperfection itself or those who had fostered in her the imperfection? But by doing what? What had they done other than to love her and look after her and encourage her, give her the support and guidance and independence that seemed reasonable to them—and still the undisclosed Merry had become tainted! Twisted! Crazed! By what? Thousands upon thousands of young people stuttered—they didn't all grow up to set off bombs! What went wrong with Merry? What did he do to her that was so wrong? The kiss? That kiss? So beastly? How could a kiss make someone into a criminal? The aftermath of the kiss? The withdrawal? Was that the beastliness? But it wasn't as though he'd never held her or touched her or kissed her again—he *loved* her. She *knew* that.

Once the inexplicable had begun, the torment of self-examination never ended. However lame the answers, he never ran out of the questions, he who before had nothing of consequence really to ask himself. After the bomb, he could never again take life as it came or trust that his life wasn't something very different from what he perceived. He found himself recalling his own happy childhood, the success that had been his boyhood, as though that were the cause of their blight. All the triumphs, when he probed them, seemed superficial; even more astonishing, his very virtues came to seem vices. There was no longer any innocence in what he remembered of his past. He saw that everything you say says either more than you wanted it to say or less than you wanted it to say; and everything you do does either more than you wanted it to do or less than you wanted it to do. What you said and did made a difference, all right, but not the difference you intended.

The Swede as he had always known himself—well-meaning, well-behaved, well-ordered Seymour Levov—evaporated, leaving only self-examination in his place. He couldn't disentangle himself from the idea that he was responsible any more than he could resort to the devilishly tempting idea that everything was accidental. He had been admitted into a mystery more bewildering even than Merry's stuttering: there was no fluency anywhere. It was *all* stuttering. In bed at night, he pictured the whole of his life as a stuttering mouth and a grimacing face— the whole of his life without cause or sense and completely bungled. He no longer had any conception of order. There was no order. None. He envisioned his life as a stutterer's thought, wildly out of his control.

Merry's other great love that year, aside from her father, was Audrey Hepburn. Before Audrey Hepburn there had been astronomy and before astronomy, the 4-H Club, and along the way, a bit distressingly to her father, there was even a Catholic phase. Her grandmother Dwyer took her to pray at St. Genevieve's whenever Merry was visiting down in Elizabeth. Little by little, Catholic trinkets made their way into her room —and as long as he could think of them as trinkets, as long as she wasn't going overboard, everything was okay. First there was the palm frond bent into the shape of the cross that Grandma had given her after Palm Sunday. That was all right. Any kid might want that up on the wall. Then came the candle, in thick glass, about a foot tall, the Eternal Candle; on its label was a picture of the Sacred Heart of Jesus and a prayer that began, "O Sacred Heart of Jesus who said, 'Ask and you shall receive.'" That wasn't so great, but as she didn't seem to be lighting and burning it, as it just seemed to sit there on her dresser for decoration, there was no sense making a fuss. Then, to hang over the bed, came the picture of Jesus, in profile, praying, which really wasn't all right, though still he said nothing to her, nothing to Dawn, nothing to Grandma Dwyer, told himself, "It's harmless, it's a picture, to her a pretty picture of a nice man. What difference does it make?"

What did it was the statue, the plaster statue of the Blessed Mother, a smaller version of the big ones on the breakfront in Grandma Dwyer's dining room and on the dressing table in Grandma Dwyer's bedroom. The statue was what led him to sit her down and ask if she would be willing to take the pictures and the palm frond off the wall and put them away in her closet, along with the statue and the Eternal Candle, when Grandma and Grandpa Levov came to visit. Quietly he explained that though her room was her room and she had the right to hang anything there she wanted, Grandma and Grandpa Levov were Jews, and so, of course, was he, and, rightly or wrongly, Jews don't, etc., etc. And because she was a sweet girl who wanted to please people, and to please her daddy most of all, she was careful to be sure that nothing Grandma Dwyer had given her was anywhere to be seen when next the Swede's parents visited Old Rimrock. And then one day everything Catholic came down off the wall and off her dresser for good. She was a perfectionist who did things passionately, lived intensely in the new interest, and then the passion was suddenly spent and everything, including the passion, got thrown into a box and she moved on.

Now it was Audrey Hepburn. Every newspaper and magazine she could get hold of she combed for the film star's photograph or name. Even movie timetables—"Breakfast at Tiffany's, 2, 4, 6, 8, 10"—were clipped from the newspaper after dinner and pasted in her Audrey Hepburn scrapbook. For months she went in and out of pretending to be gaminish instead of herself, daintily walking to her room like a wood sprite, smiling with meaningfully coy eyes into every reflecting surface, laughing what they call an "infectious" laugh whenever her father said a word. She bought the soundtrack from *Breakfast at Tiffany's* and played it in her bedroom for hours. He could hear her in there singing "Moon River" in the charming way that Audrey Hepburn did, and absolutely fluently—and so, however ostentatious and singularly self-conscious was the shameless playacting, nobody in the house ever indicated that it was tiresome, let alone ludicrous, an improbable dream of purification that had taken possession of her. If Audrey Hepburn could help her shut down just a little of the stuttering, then let her go on ludicrously pretending, a girl blessed with golden hair and a logical mind and a high IQ and an adultlike sense of humor even about herself, blessed with long, slender limbs and a wealthy family and her own brand of dogged persistence—with everything except fluency. Security, health, love, every advantage imaginable—missing only was the ability to order a hamburger without humiliating herself.

How hard she tried! Two afternoons she went to ballet class after school and two afternoons Dawn drove her to Morristown to see a speech therapist. On Saturday she got up early, made her own breakfast, and then bicycled the five hilly miles into Old Rimrock village to the tiny office of the local circuit-riding psychiatrist, who had a slant that made the Swede furious when he began to see Merry's struggle getting worse rather than better. The psychiatrist got Merry thinking that the stutter was a choice she made, a way of being special that she had chosen and then locked into when she realized how well it worked. The psychiatrist asked her, "How do you think your father would feel about you if you didn't stutter? How do you think your mother would feel?" He asked her, "Is there anything good that stuttering brings you?" The Swede did not understand how it was going to help the child to make her feel responsible for something she simply could not do, and so he went to see the man. And by the time he left he wanted to kill him.

It seemed that the etiology of Merry's problem had largely to do with her having such good-looking and successful parents. As best the Swede could follow what he was hearing, her parental good fortune was just too much for Merry, and so, to withdraw from the competition with her mother, to get her mother to hover over and focus on her and eventually climb the walls—and, in addition, to win the father away from the beautiful mother—she chose to stigmatize herself with a severe stutter, thereby manipulating everyone from a point of seeming weakness. "But Merry is made miserable by her stutter," the Swede reminded him. "That's why we brought her to see you." "The benefits may far outweigh the penalties." For the moment, the Swede couldn't understand what the doctor was explaining and replied, "But, no, no—watching her stutter is *killing* my wife." "Maybe, for Merry, that's one of the benefits. She is an extremely bright and manipulative child. If she weren't, you wouldn't be so angry with me because I'm telling you that stuttering can be an extremely manipulative, an extremely useful, if not even a vindictive type of behavior." He hates me, thought the Swede. It's all because of the way I look. Hates me because of the way Dawn looks. He's obsessed with our looks. That's why he hates us—we're not short and ugly like him! "It's difficult," the psychiatrist said, "for a daughter to grow up the daughter of somebody who had so much attention for what sometimes seems to the daughter to be such a silly thing. It's tough, on top of the natural competition between mother and daughter, to have people asking a little girl,

'Do you want to grow up to be Miss New Jersey just like your mommy?'" "But nobody asks her that. Who asks her that? We never have. We never talk about it, it never comes up. Why would it? My wife isn't Miss New Jersey—my wife is her *mother*." "But people ask her that, Mr. Levov." "Well, for God's sake, people ask children all sorts of things that don't mean anything—that is not the *problem* here." "But you do see how a child who has reason to feel she doesn't quite measure up to Mother, that she couldn't come close, might choose to adopt—" "She hasn't *adopted* anything. Look, I think that perhaps you put an unfair burden on my daughter by making her see this as a 'choice.' She *has* no choice. It's perfect hell for her when she stutters." "That isn't always what she tells me. Last Saturday, I asked her point-blank, 'Merry, why do you stutter?' and she told me, 'It's just easier to stutter.'" "But you know what she meant by that. It's obvious what she meant by that. She means she doesn't have to go through all that she has to go through when she tries *not* to stutter." "I happen to think she was telling me something more than that. I think that Merry may even feel that if she doesn't stutter, then, oh boy, people are really going to find the real problem with her, particularly in a highly pressured perfectionist family where they tend to place an unrealistically high value on her every utterance. 'If I don't stutter, then my mother is really going to read me the riot act, then she's going to find out my *real* secrets.'" "Who said we're a highly pressured perfectionist family? Jesus. We're an ordinary family. Are you quoting Merry? That's what she told you, about her mother? That she was going to read her *the riot act*?" "Not in so many words." "Because it's not *true*," the Swede said. "That's not the cause. Sometimes I just think it's because her brain is so quick, it's so much quicker than her tongue—" Oh, the pitying way he is looking at me and my pathetic explanation. Superior bastard. Cold, heartless bastard. *Stupid* bastard. That's the worst of it—the stupidity. And all of it is because he looks the way he looks and I look the way I look and Dawn looks the way she looks and . . . "We frequently see fathers who can't accept, who refuse to believe—" Oh, these people are completely useless! They only make things worse! Whose idea was this fucking psychiatrist! "I'm not *not* accepting anything, damn it. I brought her here," the Swede said, "in the first place. I do everything any professional has told me to do to help support her efforts to stop. I just want to know from you what good it is doing my daughter, with her grimacing and her tics and her leg twitches and her banging on the table and turning white in the face, with all of that difficulty, to be told that, on top of everything else, she's doing all this to *manipulate* her mother and father." "Well, who is in charge when she is banging on the table and turning white? Who is in control there?" "*She* certainly isn't!" said the Swede angrily. "You find me taking a very uncharitable view toward her," replied the doctor. "Well . . . in a way, as her father, yes. It never seems to occur to you that there might be some *physiological* basis for this." "No, I didn't say that. Mr. Levov, I can give you organic theories if you want them. But that isn't the way I have found I can be most effective."

Her stuttering diary. When she sat at the kitchen table after dinner writing the day's entry in her stuttering diary, that's when he most wanted to murder the psychiatrist who had finally to inform him—one of the fathers "who can't accept, who refuse to believe"—that she would stop stuttering only when stuttering was no longer necessary for her, when she wanted to "relate" to the world in a different way—in short, when she found a more valuable replacement for the manipulativeness. The stuttering diary was a red three-ring notebook in which, at the suggestion of her speech therapist, Merry kept a record of when she stuttered. Could she have been any more the dedicated enemy of her stuttering than when she sat there scrupulously recalling and recording how the stuttering fluctuated throughout the day, in what context it was least likely to occur, when it was most likely to occur and with whom? And could anything have been more heartbreaking for him than reading that notebook on the Friday evening she rushed off to the movies with her friends and happened to leave it open on the table? "When do I stutter? When somebody asks me something that requires an unexpected, unrehearsed response, that's when I'm likely to stutter. When people are looking at me. People who know I stutter, particularly when *they're* looking at me. Though sometimes it's worse with people who don't know me. . . ." On she went, page after page in her strikingly neat handwriting—and all she seemed to be saying was that she stuttered in all situations. She had written, "Even when I'm doing fine, I can't stop thinking, 'How soon is it going to be before he knows I'm a stutterer? How soon is it going to be before I start stuttering and screw this up?'" Yet, despite every disappointment, she sat where her parents could see her and worked on her stuttering diary every night, weekends included. She worked with her therapist on the different "strategies" to be used with strangers, store clerks, people with whom she had relatively safe conversations; they worked on strategies to be used with the people who were closer to her—teachers, girl-friends, boys, finally her grandparents, her father, her mother. She recorded the strategies in the diary. She listed in the diary what topics she could expect to talk about with different people, wrote down the points she would try to make, anticipating when she was most likely to stutter and getting herself thoroughly prepared. How could she bear the hardship of all that self-consciousness? The planning required of her to make the spontaneous unspontaneous, the persistence with which she refused to shrink from these tedious tasks—was that what the arrogant son of a bitch had meant by "a vindictive exercise"? It was unflagging commitment the likes of which the Swede had never known, not even in himself that fall they turned him into a football player and, reluctant as he was to go banging heads in a sport whose violence he never really liked, he did it, excelled at it, "for the good of the school."

But none of what she diligently worked at did Merry an ounce of good. In the quiet, safe cocoon of her speech therapist's office, taken out of her world, she was said to be terrifically at home with herself, to speak flawlessly, make jokes, imitate people, sing. But outside again, she saw it coming, started to go around it, would do anything, *anything*, to avoid the next word beginning with a *b*—and soon she was sputtering all over the place, and what a field day that psychiatrist had the next Saturday with the letter *b* and "what it unconsciously signified to her." Or what *m* or *c* or *g* "unconsciously signified." And yet nothing of what he surmised meant a goddamn thing. None of his great ideas disposed of a single one of her difficulties. Nothing anybody said meant anything or, in the end, made any sense. The psychiatrist didn't help, the speech therapist's strategies didn't help, the stuttering diary didn't help, he didn't help, Dawn didn't help, not even the light, crisp enunciation of Audrey Hepburn made the slightest dent. She was simply in the hands of something she could not get out of.

And then it was too late: like some innocent in a fairy story who has been tricked into drinking the noxious potion, the grasshopper child who used to scramble delightedly up and down the furniture and across every available lap in her black leotard all at once shot up, broke out, grew stout—she thickened across the back and the neck, stopped brushing her teeth and combing her hair; she ate almost nothing she was served at home but at school and out alone ate virtually all the time, cheeseburgers with French fries, pizza, BLTs, fried onion rings, vanilla milk shakes, root beer floats, ice cream with fudge sauce, and cake of any kind, so that almost overnight she became large, a large, loping, slovenly sixteen-year-old, nearly six feet tall, nicknamed by her schoolmates Ho Chi Levov.

And the impediment became the machete with which to mow all the bastard liars down. "You f-f-fucking madman! You heartless mi-mi-mi-miserable m-monster!" she snarled at Lyndon Johnson whenever his face appeared on the seven o'clock news. Into the televised face of Humphrey, the vice president, she cried, "You prick, sh-sh-shut your lying m-m-mouth, you c-c-coward, you f-f-f-f-filthy fucking collaborator!" When her father, as a member of the ad hoc group calling itself New Jersey Businessmen Against the War, went down to Washington with the steering committee to visit their senator, Merry refused his invitation to come along. "But," said the Swede, who had never belonged to a political group before and would not have joined this one and volunteered for the steering committee and paid a thousand dollars toward their protest ad in the *Newark News* had he not hoped his conspicuous involvement might deflect a little of her anger away from him, "this is your chance to say what's on your mind to Senator Case. You can confront him directly. Isn't that what you want?" "Merry," said her petite mother to the large glowering girl, "you might be able to influence Senator Case—" "C-c-c-c-c-c-case!" erupted Merry and, to the astonishment of her parents, proceeded to spit on the tiled kitchen floor.

She was on the phone now all the time, the child who formerly had to run through her telephone "strategy" just to be sure that when she picked up the phone she could get out the word "Hello" in under thirty seconds. She had conquered the anguishing stutter all right, but not as her parents and her therapist had hoped. No, Merry concluded that what was deforming her life wasn't the stuttering but the futile effort to overturn it. The crazy effort. The ridiculous significance she had given to that stutter to meet the Rimrock expectations of the very parents and teachers and friends who had caused her to so overestimate something as secondary as the way she talked. Not what she said but how she said it was all that bothered them. And all she really had to do to be free of it was to not give a shit about how it made them so miserable when she had to pronounce the letter *b*. Yes, she cut herself away from caring about the abyss that opened up under everybody's feet when she started stuttering; her stuttering was no longer going to be the center of her existence—and she'd make damn sure that it wasn't going to be the center of theirs. Vehemently she renounced the appearance and the allegiances of the good little girl who had tried so hard to be adorable and lovable like all the other good little Rimrock girls—renounced her meaningless manners, her petty social concerns, her family's "bourgeois" values. She had wasted enough time on the cause of herself. "I'm not going to spend my whole life wrestling day and night with a fucking stutter when kids are b-b-b-being b-b-b-b-b-bu-bu-bu roasted alive by Lyndon B-b-b-baines b-b-b-bu-bu-burn-'em-up Johnson!"

All her energy came right to the surface now, unimpeded, the force of resistance that had previously been employed otherwise; and by no longer bothering with the ancient obstruction, she experienced not only her full freedom for the first time in her life but the exhilarating power of total self-certainty. A brand-new Merry had begun, one who'd found, in opposing the "v-v-v-vile" war, a difficulty to fight that was worthy, at last, of her truly stupendous strength. North Vietnam she called the Democratic Republic of Vietnam, a country she spoke of with such patriotic feeling that, according to Dawn, one would have thought she'd been born not at the Newark Beth Israel but at the Beth Israel in Hanoi. "'The Democratic Republic of Vietnam'—if I hear that from her one more time, Seymour, I swear, I'll go out of my mind!" He tried to convince her that perhaps it wasn't as bad as it sounded. "Merry has a credo, Dawn, Merry has a political position. There may not be much subtlety in it, she may not yet be its best spokesman, but there is some thought behind it, there's certainly a lot of emotion behind it, there's a lot of *compassion* behind it. . . ."

But there was now no conversation she had with her daughter that did not drive Dawn, if not out of her mind, out of the house and into the barn. The Swede would overhear Merry fighting with her every time the two of them were alone together for two minutes. "Some people," Dawn says, "would be perfectly *happy* to have parents who are contented middle-class people." "I'm sorry I'm not brainwashed enough to be one of them," Merry replies. "You're a sixteen-year-old girl," Dawn says, "and I can tell you what to do and I *will* tell you what to do." "Just because I'm sixteen doesn't make me a g-g-girl! I do what I w-w-want!" "You're not antiwar," Dawn says, "you're anti *everything*." "And what are you, Mom? You're pro c-c-c-cow!"

Night after night now Dawn went to bed in tears. "What is she? What is this?" she asked the Swede. "If someone simply defies your authority, what can you do? Seymour, I'm totally puzzled. How did this happen?" "It happens," he told her. "She's a kid with a strong will. With an idea. With a cause." "Where did this *come* from? It's inexplicable. Am I a bad mother? Is that it?" "You are a good mother. You are a wonderful mother. That is not it." "I don't know why she's turned against me like this. I don't have any sense of what I did to her or even what she perceives I did to her. I don't know what's happened. Who *is* she? Where did *she* come from? I cannot control her. I cannot *recognize* her. I thought she was smart. She's not smart at all. She's become *stupid*, Seymour; she gets more and more stupid each time we talk." "No, it's just a very crude kind of aggression. It's not very well worked out. But she is still smart. She's very smart. This is what teenagers are like. There are these very turbulent sorts of changes. It has nothing to do with you or me. They just amorphously object to everything." "It's all from the stuttering, isn't it?" "We're doing everything we can for her stutter. We always have." "She's angry because she stutters. She doesn't make friends," Dawn said, "because she stutters." "She's always had friends. She has many friends. Besides, she was on top of her stuttering. Stuttering is not the explanation." "Yes, it is. You never get on top of your stutter," Dawn said, "you're in constant fear." "That's not an explanation, Dawnie, for what is going on." "She's sixteen—is *that* the explanation?" asked Dawn. "Well, if it is," he said, "and maybe an awful lot of it is, we'll do the best we can until she stops being sixteen." "And? When she's not sixteen anymore, she'll be seventeen." "At seventeen she won't be the same. At eighteen she won't be the same. Things change. She'll discover new interests. She'll have college—academic pursuits. We can work this out. The important thing is to keep talking with her." "I can't. I can't talk to her. Now she's even jealous of the cows. It's too maddening." "Then I'll keep talking to her. The important thing is not to abandon her and not to capitulate to her, and to keep talking even if you have to say the same thing over and over and over. It doesn't matter if it all seems hopeless. You can't expect what you say to have an immediate impact." "It's what she says *back* that has the *impact*!" "It doesn't matter what she says back. We have to keep saying to her what we have to say to her, even if saying it seems interminable. We must draw the line. If we don't draw the line, then surely she's not going to obey. If we do draw the line, there's at least a fifty percent chance that she will." "And if she still doesn't?" "All we can do, Dawn, is to continue to be reasonable and continue to be firm and not lose hope or patience, and the day will come when she will outgrow all this objecting to everything." "She doesn't *want* to outgrow it." "Now. Today. But there is tomorrow. There's a bond between us all and it's tremendous. As long as we don't let her go, as long as we keep talking, tomorrow will come. Of course she's maddening. She's unrecognizable to me, too. But if you don't allow her to exhaust your patience and if you keep talking to her and you don't give up on her, she will eventually become herself again."

And so, hopeless as it seemed, he talked, he listened, he was reasonable; endless as the struggle seemed, he remained patient, and whenever he saw her going too far he drew the line. No matter how much it might openly enrage her to answer him, no matter how sarcastic and caustic and elusive and dishonest her answers might be, he continued to question her about her political activities, about her after-school whereabouts, about her new friends; with a gentle persistence that infuriated her, he asked about her Saturday trips into New York. She could shout all she wanted at home—she was still just a kid from Old Rimrock, and the thought of whom she might meet in New York alarmed him.

Conversation #1 about New York. "What do you do when you go to New York? Who do you see in New York?" "What do I do? I go see New York. That's what I do." "What do you do, Merry?" "I do what everyone else does. I window-shop. What else would a girl do?" "You're involved with political people in New York." "I don't know what you're talking about. Everything is political. Brushing your *teeth* is political." "You're involved with people who are against the war in Vietnam. Isn't that who you go to see? Yes or no?" "They're people, yes. They're people with ideas, and some of them don't b-b-b-believe in the war. Most of them don't b-b-b-believe in the war." "Well, I don't happen to believe in the war myself." "So what's your problem?" "Who are these people? How old are they? What do they do for a living? Are they students?" "Why do you want to know?" "Because I'd like to know what you're doing. You're alone in New York on Saturdays. Not everyone's parents would allow a sixteen-year-old girl to go that far." "I go in . . . I, you know, there are people and dogs and streets . . ." "You come home with all this Communist material. You come home with all these books and pamphlets and magazines." "I'm trying to *learn*. You taught me to *learn*, didn't you? Not just to study, but to *learn*. C-c-c-communist . . ." "It *is* Communist. It says on the page that it's Communist." "C-c-c-communists have ideas that aren't always about C-communism." "For instance." "About poverty. About war. About injustice. They have all kinds of ideas. Just b-b-because you're Jewish doesn't mean you just have ideas about Judaism. Well, the same holds for C-c-communism."

Conversation #12 about New York. "Where do you eat your meals in New York?" "Not at Vincent's, thank God." "Where then?" "Where everybody else eats their meals. Restaurants. Cafeterias. People's apartments." "Who are the people who live in these apartments?" "Friends of mine." "Where did you meet them?" "I met some here, I met some in the city—" "Here? Where?" "At the high school. Sh-sh-sh-sherry, for instance." "I never met Sherry." "Sh-sh-sh-sherry is the one, do you remember, who played the violin in all the class plays? And she goes into New York b-because she takes music lessons." "Is she involved with politics too?" "Daddy, everything is political. How can she not be involved if she has a b-b-b-brain?" "Merry, I don't want you to get into trouble. You're angry about the war. A lot of people are angry about the war. But there are some people who are angry about the war who don't have any limits. Do you know what the limits are?" "Limits. That's all you think about. Not going to the extreme. Well, sometimes you have to fucking go to the extreme. What do you think war is? War is an extreme. It isn't life out here in little Rimrock. Nothing is too extreme out here." "You don't like it out here anymore. Would you want to live in New York? Would you like that?" "Of c-c-c-course." "Suppose when you graduate from high school you were to go to college in New York. Would you like that?" "I don't know if I'm going to go to college. Look at the administration of those colleges. Look what they do to their students who are against the war. How can I want to be going to college? Higher education. It's what I call lower education. Maybe I'll go to college, maybe I won't. I wouldn't start p-planning now."

Conversation #18 about New York, after she fails to return home on a Saturday night. "You're never to do that again. You're never to stay over with people who we don't know. Who are these people?" "Never say never." "Who are the people you stayed with?" "They're friends of Sh-sherry's. From the music school." "I don't believe you." "Why? You can't b-b-b-believe that I might have friends? That people might like me— you don't b-b-b-believe that? That people might put me up for the night—you don't b-b-b-believe that? What *do* you b-b-b-b-b-b-believe in?" "You're sixteen years old. You're to come home. You cannot stay over in New York City." "Stop reminding me of how old I am. We all have an age." "When you went off yesterday we expected you back at six o'clock. At seven o'clock at night you phoned to say you're staying over. We said you weren't. You insisted. You said you had a place to stay. So I let you do it." "You let me. Sure." "But you can't do it again. If you do it again, you will never be allowed to go into New York by yourself." "Says who?" "Your father." "We'll see." "I'll

make a deal with you." "What's the deal, *Father?*" "If you ever
go into New York again and you find it's getting late and you
have to stay somewhere, you stay with the Umanoffs." "The
Umanoffs?" "They like you, you like them, they've known you
all your life. They have a very nice apartment." "Well, the people I stayed with have a very nice apartment too." "Who are
they?" "I told you, they're Sh-sherry's friends." "Who are they?"
"Bill and Melissa." "And who are Bill and Melissa?" "They're
p-p-p-people. Like everyone else." "What do they do for a living? How old are they?" "Melissa's twenty-two. And Bill is
nineteen." "Are they students?" "They were students. Now
they organize people for the betterment of the Vietnamese."
"Where do they live?" "What are you going to do, come and
get me?" "I'd like to know where they live. There are all sorts
of neighborhoods in New York. Some are good, some aren't."
"They live in a perfectly fine neighborhood and a perfectly fine
b-b-b-b-building." "Where?" "They live up in Morningside
Heights." "Are they Columbia students?" "They were." "How
many people stay in this apartment?" "I don't see why I have
to answer all these questions." "Because you're my daughter
and you are sixteen years old." "So for the rest of my life, because I'm your daughter—" "No, when you are eighteen and
graduate high school, you can do whatever you want." "So the
difference we're talking about here is two years." "That's right."
"And what's the b-big thing that's going to happen in two
years?" "You will be an independent person who can support
herself." "I can support myself now if I w-w-w-w-wanted to."
"I don't want you to stay with Bill and Melissa." "W-w-w-
why?" "It's my responsibility to look after you. I want you to
stay with the Umanoffs. If you can agree to do that, then you
can go to New York and stay over. Otherwise you won't be
permitted to go there at all. The choice is yours." "I'm in there
to stay with the people I want to stay with." "Then you're not
going to New York." "We'll see." "There is no 'we'll see.'
You're not going and that's the end of it." "I'd like to see you
stop me." "Think about it. If you can't agree to stay with
the Umanoffs, then you can't go to New York." "What about
the war—" "My responsibility is to you and not to the war."
"Oh, I know your responsibility is not to the war—that's why
I have to go to New York. B-b-b-because people there do feel

responsible. They feel responsible when America b-blows up
Vietnamese villages. They feel responsible when America is
b-blowing little b-babies to b-b-b-bits. B-but you don't, and
neither does Mother. You don't care enough to let it upset a
single day of yours. You don't care enough to make *you* spend
another night somewhere. You don't stay up at night worrying
about it. You don't really care, Daddy, one way or the other."

Conversations #24, 25, and 26 about New York. "I can't
have these conversations, Daddy. I won't! I refuse to! Who
talks to their parents like this!" "If you are underage and you
go away for the day and don't come home at night, then you
damn well talk to your parents like this." "B-b-but you drive
me c-c-c-crazy, this kind of sensible parent, trying to be understanding! I don't want to be understood—I want to be f-f-f-
free!" "Would you like it better if I were a senseless parent
trying not to understand you?" "I would! I think I would!
Why don't you fucking t-t-try it for a change and let me fucking see!"

Conversation #29 about New York. "No, you can't disrupt
our family life until you are of age. Then do whatever you
want. So long as you're under eighteen—" "All you can think
about, all you can talk about, all you c-c-care about is the well-
being of this f-fucking l-l-little f-f-family!" "Isn't that all you
think about? Isn't that what you are angry about?" "N-n-no!
N-n-never!" "Yes, Merry. You are angry about the families in
Vietnam. You are angry about their being destroyed. Those
are families too. Those are families just like ours that would
like to have the right to have lives like our family has. Isn't that
what you yourself want for them? What Bill and Melissa want
for them? That they might be able to have secure and peaceful
lives like ours?" "To have to live out here in the privileged
middle of nowhere? No, I don't think that's what B-b-bill and
Melissa want for them. It's not what I want for them." "Don't
you? Then think again. I think that to have this privileged mid-
dle-of-nowhere kind of life would make them quite content,
frankly." "They just want to go to b-bed at night, in their own
country, leading their own lives, and without thinking they're
going to get b-b-blown to b-b-b-b-bits in their sleep. B-b-
blown to b-b-b-b-bits all for the sake of the privileged people

of New Jersey leading their p-p-peaceful, s-s-secure, acquisitive, meaningless l-l-l-little bloodsucking lives!"

Conversation #30 about New York, after Merry returns from staying overnight with the Umanoffs. "Oh, they're oh-so-liberal, B-b-b-b-Barry and Marcia. With their little comfortable b-b-bourgeois life." "They are professors, they are serious academics who are against the war. Did they have any people there?" "Oh, some English professor against the war, some sociology professor against the war. At least he involves his family against the war. They all march tugu-tugu-tugu-together. That's what I call a family. Not these fucking c-c-c-cows." "So it went all right there." "No. I want to go with my friends. I don't want to go to the Umanoffs at eight o'clock. Whatever is happening is happening *after* eight o'clock! If I wanted to be with your friends after eight o'clock at night, I could stay here in Rimrock. I want to be with my friends after eight o'clock!" "Nonetheless it worked out. We compromised. You didn't get to be with your friends after eight o'clock but you got to spend the day with your friends, which is a lot better than nothing at all. I feel much better about what you have agreed to do. You should too. Are you going to go in next Saturday?" "I don't plan these things y-years in advance." "If you're going in next Saturday, then you're to phone the Umanoffs beforehand and let them know you're coming."

Conversation #34 about New York, after Merry fails to show up at the Umanoffs for the night. "Okay, that's it. You made an agreement and you broke it. You're not leaving this house on a Saturday again." "I'm under house arrest." "Indefinitely." "What is it that you're so afraid of? What is it that you think I'm going to do? I'm hanging out with f-friends. We discuss the war and other important things. I don't know why you want to know so much. You don't ask me a z-z-z-z-zillion fucking questions every time I go down to Hamlin's s-s-store. What are you so afraid of? You're just a b-b-b-b-bundle of fear. You just can't keep hiding out here in the woods. Don't go spewing your fear all over me and making me as fearful as you and Mom are. All you can deal with is c-cows. C-cows and trees. Well, there's something besides c-c-c-c-cows and trees. There are people. People with real pain. Why don't you say it?

Are you afraid I'm going to get laid? Is that what you're afraid of? I'm not that moronic to get knocked up. What have I ever done in my life that's irresponsible?" "You broke the agreement. That's the end of it." "This is not a corporation. This isn't b-b-b-b-b-b-b-business, Daddy. House arrest. Every day in this house is like being under house arrest." "I don't like you very much when you act like this." "Daddy, shut up. I don't like you either. I never d-d-did."

Conversation #44 about New York. The next Saturday. "I'm not driving you to the train. You're not leaving the house." "What are you going to do? B-barricade me in? How you going to stop me? You going to tie me to my high chair? Is that how you treat your daughter? I can't b-b-believe my own father would threaten me with physical force." "I'm not threatening you with physical force." "Then how are you going to keep me in the house? I'm not just one of Mom's dumb c-c-c-c-cows! I'm not going to live here forever and ever and ever. Mr. C-cool, Calm, and Collected. What is it that you're so afraid of? What is it you're so afraid of people for? Haven't you ever heard that New York is one of the world's great cultural centers? People come from the whole world to experience New York. You always wanted me to experience everything else. Why can't I experience New York? Better than this d-dump here. What are you so angry about? That I might have a real idea of my own? Something that you didn't come up with first? Something that isn't one of your well-thought-out plans for the family and how things should go? All I'm doing is taking a fucking train into the city. Millions of men and women do it every day to go to work. Fall in with the wrong people. God forbid I should ever get another point of view. You married an Irish Catholic. What did your family think about your falling in with the wrong people? She married a J-j-j-j-jew. What did her family think about her falling in with the wrong people? How much worse can I do? Maybe hang out with a guy with an Afro—is that what you're afraid of? I don't think so, *Daddy*. Why don't you worry about something that matters, like the war, instead of whether or not your overprivileged little girl takes a train into the b-big city b-by herself?"

Conversation #53 about New York. "You still won't tell me

what kind of horrible fucking fate is going to b-b-befall me if I take a fucking train to the city. They have apartments and roofs in New York too. They have locks and doors too. A lock isn't something that is unique to Old Rimrock, New Jersey. Ever think of that, Seymour-Levov-it-rhymes-with-the-love? You think everything that is f-foreign to you is b-bad. Did you ever think that there are some things that are f-foreign to you that are good? And that as your daughter I would have some instinct to go with the right people at the right time? You're always so sure I'm going to fuck up in some way. If you had any confidence in me, you'd think that I might hang out with the right people. You don't give me any credit." "Merry, you know what I'm talking about. You're involving yourself with political radicals." "Radicals. B-b-because they don't agree with y-y-y-you they're radical." "These are people who have very extreme political ideas—" "That's the only thing that gets anything done is to have strong ideas, Daddy." "But you are only sixteen years old, and they are much older and more sophisticated than you." "Good. So maybe I'll learn something. Extreme is b-b-b-blowing up a little country for some misunderstood notions about freedom. That is extreme. B-b-b-blowing off b-b-boys' legs and b-balls, that is extreme, Daddy. Taking a b-bus or a train into New York and spending a night in a locked, secure apartment—I don't see what's so extreme about that. I think people sleep somewhere every night if they can. T-t-tell me what's so extreme about that. Do you think war is b-bad? Eww—extreme idea, Daddy. It's not the idea that's extreme—it's the fact that someone might care enough about something to try to make it different. You think that's extreme? That's *your* problem. It might mean more to someone to try to save other people's lives than to finish a d-d-d-d-d-d-degree at Columbia—that's extreme? No, the other is extreme." "You talking about Bill and Melissa?" "Yeah. She dropped out because there are things that are more important to her than a d-d-d-degree. To stop the killing is more important to her than the letters B-b-b.A. on a piece of paper. You call that extreme? No, I think extreme is to continue on with life as usual when this kind of craziness is going on, when people are b-being exploited left, right, and center, and you can just go on and get into your suit and tie every day and go to work. As if nothing is happening. That is extreme. That is extreme s-s-s-stupidity, that is what that is."

Conversation #59 about New York. "Who are they?" "They went to Columbia. They dropped out. I *told* you all this. They live on Morningside Heights." "That doesn't tell me enough, Merry. There are drugs, there are violent people, it is a dangerous city. Merry, you can wind up in a lot of trouble. You can wind up getting raped." "B-because I didn't listen to my daddy?" "That's not impossible." "Girls wind up getting raped whether they listen to their daddies or not. Sometimes the daddies do the raping. Rapists have ch-ch-chil-dren too. That's what makes them daddies." "Tell Bill and Melissa to come here and spend the weekend with us." "Oh, they'd really like to stay out here." "Look, how would you like to go away to school in September? To prep school for your last two years. Maybe you've had enough of living at home and living with us here." "Always planning. Always trying to figure out the most reasonable course." "What else should I do? Not plan? I'm a man. I'm a husband. I'm a father. I run a business." "I run a b-b-b-business, therefore I am." "There are all kinds of schools. There are schools with all kinds of interesting people, with all kinds of freedom. . . . You talk to your faculty adviser, I'll make inquiries too—and if you're sick and tired of living with us, you can go away to school. I understand that there isn't much for you to do out here anymore. Let's all of us think seriously about your going away to school."

Conversation #67 about New York. "You can be as active in the antiwar movement as you like here in Morristown and here in Old Rimrock. You can organize people here against the war, in your school—" "Daddy, I want to do it my w-way." "Listen to me. Please listen to me. The people here in Old Rimrock are not antiwar. To the contrary. You want to be in opposition? Be in opposition here." "You can't do anything about it here. What am I going to do, march around the general store?" "You can organize here." "Rimrockians Against the War? That's going to make a b-big difference. Morristown High Against the War." "That's right. Bring the war home. Isn't that the slogan? So do it—bring the war home to your town. You like to be unpopular? You'll be plenty unpopular, I can assure you." "I'm not looking to be unpopular." "Well, you will be. Because it's an unpopular position here. If you oppose the war here with all your strength, believe me, you will make an impact. Why don't you educate people here about the war? This is part of America too, you know." "A minute part." "These people are Americans, Merry. You can be actively against the war right here in the village. You don't have to go to New York." "Yeah, I can be against the war in our living room." "You can be against the war at the Community Club." "All twenty people." "Morristown is the county seat. Go into Morristown on Saturdays. There are people there who are against the war. Judge Fontane is against the war, you know that. Mr. Avery is against the war. They signed the ad with me. The old judge went to Washington with me. People around here weren't very happy to see my name there, you know. But that's my position. You can organize a march in Morristown. You can work on the march." "And the Morristown High School paper is going to cover it. That'll get the troops out of Vietnam." "I understand you're quite vocal about the war at Morristown High already. Why do you even bother if you don't think it matters? You do think it matters. Everyone's point of view in America matters in terms of this war. Start in your hometown, Merry. That's the way to end the war." "Revolutions don't b-b-begin in the countryside." "We're not talking about revolution." "*You're* not talking about revolution."

And that was the last conversation they ever had to have about New York. It worked. Interminable, but he was patient and reasonable and firm and it worked. As far as he knew, she did not go to New York again. She took his advice and stayed at home, and, after turning their living room into a battlefield, after turning Morristown High into a battlefield, she went out one day and blew up the post office, destroying right along with it Dr. Fred Conlon and the village's general store, a small wooden building with a community bulletin board out front and a single old Sunoco pump and the metal pole on which Russ Hamlin—who, with his wife, owned the store and ran the post office—had raised the American flag every morning since Warren Gamaliel Harding was president of the United States.

II
The Fall

4

A TINY, bone-white girl who looked half Merry's age but claimed to be some six years older, a Miss Rita Cohen, came to the Swede four months after Merry's disappearance. She was dressed like Dr. King's successor, Ralph Abernathy, in freedom-rider overalls and ugly big shoes, and a bush of wiry hair emphatically framed her bland baby face. He should have recognized immediately who she was—for the four months he had been waiting for just such a person—but she was so tiny, so young, so ineffectual-looking that he could barely believe she was at the University of Pennsylvania's Wharton School of Business and Finance (doing a thesis on the leather industry in Newark, New Jersey), let alone the provocateur who was Merry's mentor in world revolution.

On the day she showed up at the factory, the Swede had not known that Rita Cohen had undertaken some fancy footwork —in and out through the basement door beneath the loading dock—so as to elude the surveillance team the FBI had assigned to observe from Central Avenue the arrival and departure of everyone visiting his office.

Three, four times a year someone either called or wrote to ask permission to see the plant. In the old days, Lou Levov, busy as he might be, always made time for the Newark school classes, or Boy Scout troops, or visiting notables chaperoned by a functionary from City Hall or the Chamber of Commerce. Though the Swede didn't get nearly the pleasure his father did from being an authority on the glove trade, though he wouldn't claim his father's authority on anything pertaining to the leather industry—pertaining to anything else, either—occasionally he did assist a student by answering questions over the phone or, if the student struck him as especially serious, by offering a brief tour.

Of course, had he known beforehand that this student was no student but his fugitive daughter's emissary, he would never have arranged their meeting to take place at the factory. Why Rita hadn't explained to the Swede whose emissary she was, said nothing about Merry until the tour had been concluded, was undoubtedly so she could size up the Swede first; or maybe she said nothing for so long the better to enjoy toying with him. Maybe she just enjoyed the power. Maybe she was just another politician and the enjoyment of power lay behind much of what she did.

Because the Swede's desk was separated from the making department by glass partitions, he and the women at the machines could command a clear view of one another. He had instituted this arrangement so as to wrest relief from the mechanical racket while maintaining access between himself and the floor. His father had refused to be confined to any office, glass-enclosed or otherwise: just planted his desk in the middle of the making room's two hundred sewing machines—royalty right at the heart of the overcrowded hive, the swarm around him whining its buzz-saw bee buzz while he talked to his customers and his contractors on the phone and simultaneously plowed through his paperwork. Only from out on the floor, he claimed, could he distinguish within the contrapuntal din the sound of a Singer on the fritz and with his screwdriver be over the machine before the girl had even alerted her forelady to the trouble. Vicky, Newark Maid's elderly black forelady, so testified (with her brand of wry admiration) at his retirement banquet. While everything was running without a hitch, Lou was impatient, fidgety—in a word, said Vicky, the insufferable boss—but when a cutter came around to complain about the foreman, when the foreman came around to complain about a cutter, when skins arrived months late or in damaged condition or were of poor quality, when he discovered a lining contractor cheating him on the yield or a shipping clerk robbing him blind, when he determined that the glove slitter with the red Corvette and the sunglasses was, on the side, a bookie running a numbers game among the employees, then he was in his element and in his inimitable way set out to make things right —so that when they *were* right, said the next-to-last speaker, the proud son, introducing his father in the longest, most laudatory of the evening's jocular encomiums, "he could begin driving himself—and the rest of us—nuts with worrying again. But then, always expecting the worst, he was never disappointed for long. Never caught off guard either. All of which goes to show that, like everything else at Newark Maid, worrying *works*. Ladies and gentlemen, the man who has been my lifelong teacher—and not just in the art of worrying—the man who has made of my life a lifelong education, a difficult education sometimes but always a profitable one, who explained to me when I was a boy of five the secret of making a product perfect—'You work at it,' he told me—ladies and gentlemen, a man who has worked at it and succeeded at it since the day he went off to begin tanning hides at the age of fourteen, the glover's glover, who knows more about the glove business than anybody else alive, Mr. Newark Maid, my father, Lou Levov." "Look," began Mr. Newark Maid, "don't let anybody kid you tonight. I enjoy working, I enjoy the glove business, I enjoy the challenge, I don't like the idea of retiring, I think it's the first step to the grave. But none of that bothers me for one big reason—because I am the luckiest man in the world. And lucky because of one word. The biggest little word there is: family. If I was being pushed out by a competitor, I wouldn't be standing here smiling—you know me, I would be standing here shouting. But who I am being pushed out by is my own beloved son. I have been blessed with the most wonderful family a man could want: a wonderful wife, two wonderful boys, wonderful grandchildren. . . ."

The Swede had Vicky bring a sheepskin into the office and he gave it to the Wharton girl to feel.

"This has been pickled but it hasn't been tanned," he told her. "It's a hair sheepskin. Doesn't have wool like a domestic sheep but hair."

"What happens to the hair?" she asked him. "Does it get used?"

"Good question. The hair is used to make carpet. Up in Amsterdam, New York. Bigelow. Mohawk. But the primary value is the skins. The hair is a by-product, and how you get the hair off the skin and all the rest of it is another story entirely. Before synthetics came along, the hair mostly went into cheap carpets. There's a company that brokered all the hair from the tanneries to the carpetmakers, but you don't want to go into that," he said, observing how before they'd really even begun she'd filled with notes the top sheet of a fresh yellow legal pad. "Though if you do," he added, touched by—and attracted by—her thoroughness, "because I suppose it does all sort of tie together, I could send you to talk to those people. I think the family is still around. It's a niche that not many people know about. It's interesting. It's *all* interesting. You've settled on an interesting subject, young lady."

"I think I have," she said, warmly smiling over at him.

"Anyway, this skin"—he'd taken it back from her and was stroking it with the side of a thumb as you might stroke the cat to get the purr going—"is called a cabretta in the industry's terminology. Small sheep. Little sheep. They only live twenty or thirty degrees north and south of the equator. They're sort of on a semiwild grazing basis—families in an African village will each own four or five sheep, and they'll all be flocked together and put out in the bush. What you were holding in your hand isn't raw anymore. We buy them in what's called the pickled stage. The hair's been removed and the preprocessing has been done to preserve them to get here. We used to bring them in raw—huge bales tied with rope and so on, skins just dried in the air. I actually have a ship's manifest—it's somewhere here, I can find it for you if you want to see it—a copy of a ship's manifest from 1790, in which skins were landed in Boston similar to what we were bringing in up to last year. And from the same ports in Africa."

It could have been his father talking to her. For all he knew, every word of every sentence uttered by him he had heard from his father's mouth before he'd finished grade school, and then two or three thousand times again during the decades they'd run the business together. Trade talk was a tradition in glove families going back hundreds of years—in the best of them, the father passed the secrets on to the son along with all the history and all the lore. It was true in the tanneries, where the tanning process is like cooking and the recipes are handed down from the father to the son, and it was true in the glove shops and it was true on the cutting-room floor. The old Italian cutters would train their sons and no one else, and those sons accepted the tutorial from their fathers as he had accepted the tutorial from his. Beginning when he was a kid of five and extending into his maturity, the father as the authority was unopposed: accepting his authority was one and the same with extracting from him the wisdom that had made Newark Maid manufacturer of the country's best ladies' glove. The Swede quickly came to love in the same wholehearted way the very things his father did and, at the factory, to think more or less as he did. And to sound as he did—if not on every last subject, then whenever a conversation came around to leather or Newark or gloves.

Not since Merry had disappeared had he felt anything like this loquacious. Right up to that morning, all he'd been wanting was to weep or to hide; but because there was Dawn to nurse and a business to tend to and his parents to prop up, because everybody else was paralyzed by disbelief and shattered to the core, neither inclination had as yet eroded the protective front he provided the family and presented to the world. But now words were sweeping him on, buoying him up, his *father's* words released by the sight of this tiny girl studiously taking them down. She was nearly as small, he thought, as the kids from Merry's third-grade class, who'd been bused the thirty-eight miles from their rural schoolhouse one day back in the late fifties so that Merry's daddy could show them how he made gloves, show them especially Merry's magical spot, the laying-off table, where, at the end of the making process, the men shaped and pressed each and every glove by pulling it carefully down over steam-heated brass hands veneered in chrome. The hands were dangerously hot and they were shiny and they stuck straight up from the table in a row, thin-looking as hands that had been flattened in a mangle and then amputated, beautifully amputated hands afloat in space like the souls of the dead. As a little girl, Merry was captivated by their enigma, called them "the pancake hands." Merry as a little girl saying to her classmates, "You want to make five dollars a dozen," which was what glovemakers were always saying and what she'd been hearing since she was born—five dollars a dozen, that was what you shot for, regardless. Merry whispering to the teacher, "People cheating on piece rates is always a problem. My daddy had to fire one man. He was stealing time," and the Swede telling her, "Honey, let Daddy conduct the tour, okay?" Merry as a little girl reveling in the dazzling idea of stealing *time*. Merry flitting from floor to floor, so proud and proprietary, flaunting her familiarity with all the employees, unaware as yet of the desecration of dignity inherent to the ruthless exploitation of the worker by the profit-hungry boss who unjustly owns the means of production.

No wonder he felt so untamed, craving to spill over with talk. Momentarily it was *then* again—nothing blown up, nothing ruined. As a family they still flew the flight of the immigrant rocket, the upward, unbroken immigrant trajectory from slave-driven great-grandfather to self-driven grandfather to self-confident, accomplished, independent father to the highest high flier of them all, the fourth-generation child for whom America was to be heaven itself. No wonder he couldn't shut up. It was impossible to shut up. The Swede was giving in to the ordinary human wish to live once again in the past—to spend a self-deluding, harmless few moments back in the wholesome striving of the past, when the family endured by a truth in no way grounded in abetting destruction but rather in eluding and outlasting destruction, overcoming its mysterious inroads by creating the utopia of a rational existence.

He heard her asking, "How many come in a shipment?"

"How many skins? A couple of thousand dozen skins."

"A bale is how many?"

He liked finding that she was interested in every last detail. Yes, talking to this attentive student up from Wharton, he was suddenly able to like something as he had not been able to like anything, to bear anything, even to understand anything he'd come up against for four lifeless months. He'd felt himself instead to be perishing of everything. "Oh, a hundred and twenty skins," he replied.

She continued taking notes as she asked, "They come right to your shipping department?"

"They come to the tannery. The tannery is a contractor. We buy the material and then we give it to them, and we give them the process to use and then they convert it into leather for us. My grandfather and my father worked in the tannery right here in Newark. So did I, for six months, when I started in the business. Ever been inside a tannery?"

"Not yet."

"Well, you've got to go to a tannery if you're going to write about leather. I'll set that up for you if you'd like that. They're primitive places. The technology has improved things, but what you'll see isn't that different from what you would have seen hundreds of years ago. Awful work. Said to be the oldest industry of which relics have been found anywhere. Six-thousand-year-old relics of tanning found somewhere—Turkey, I believe. First clothing was just skins that were tanned by smoking them. I told you it was an interesting subject once you get into it. My father is the leather scholar. He's who you should be talking to, but he's living in Florida now. Start my father off about gloves and he'll talk for two days running. That's typical, by the way. Glovemen love the trade and everything about it. Tell me, have you ever seen anything manufactured, Miss Cohen?"

"I can't say I have."

"Never seen anything made?"

"Saw my mother make a cake when I was a kid."

He laughed. She had made him laugh. A feisty innocent, eager to learn. His daughter was easily a foot taller than Rita Cohen, fair where she was dark, but otherwise Rita Cohen, homely little thing though she was, had begun to remind him of Merry before her repugnance set in and she began to become their enemy. The good-natured intelligence that would just waft out of her and into the house when she came home from school overbrimming with what she'd learned in class. How she remembered everything. Everything neatly taken down in her notebook and memorized overnight.

"I'll tell you what we're going to do. We're going to bring you right through the whole process. Come on. We're going to make you a pair of gloves and you're going to watch them being made from start to finish. What size do you wear?"

"I don't know. Small."

He'd gotten up from the desk and come around and taken hold of her hand. "Very small. I'm guessing you're a four." He'd already got from the top drawer of his desk a measuring tape with a D ring at one end, and now he put it around her hand, threaded the other end through the D ring, and pulled the tape around her palm. "We'll see what kind of guesser I am. Close your hand." She made a fist, causing the hand to slightly expand, and he read the size in French inches. "Four it is. In a ladies' size that's as small as they come. Anything smaller is a child's. Come on. I'll show you how it's done."

He felt as though he'd stepped right back into the mouth of the past as they started, side by side, up the wooden steps of the old stairwell. He heard himself telling her (while simultaneously hearing his father telling her), "You always sort your skins at the northern side of the factory, where there's no direct sunlight. That way you can really study the skins for quality. Where the sunlight comes in you can't see. The cutting room and the sorting, always on the northern side. Sorting at the top. The second floor the cutting. And the first floor, where you came, the making. Bottom floor finishing and shipping. We're going to work our way from the top down."

That they did. And he was happy. He could not help himself. It was not right. It was not real. Something must be done to stop this. But she was busy taking notes, and he could not stop—a girl who knew the value of hard work and paying attention, and interested in the right things, interested in the preparation of leather and the manufacture of gloves, and to stop himself was impossible.

When someone is suffering as the Swede was suffering, asking him to be undeluded by a momentary uplifting, however dubious its rationale, is asking an awful lot.

In the cutting room, there were twenty-five men at work, about six to a table, and the Swede led her over to the oldest of them, whom he introduced as "the Master," a small, bald fellow with a hearing aid who continued working at a rectangular piece of leather—"That's the piece the glove is made from," said the Swede, "called a trank"—working at it with a ruler and shears all the time that the Swede was telling her just who this Master was. With a light heart. Still floating free. Doing nothing to stop it. Letting his father's patter flow.

The cutting room was where the Swede had got inspired to follow his father into gloves, the place where he believed he'd grown from a boy into a man. The cutting room, up high and full of light, had been his favorite spot in the factory since he was just a kid and the old European cutters came to work identically dressed in three-piece suits, starched white shirts, ties, suspenders, and cuff links. Each cutter would carefully remove the suit coat and hang it in the closet, but no one in the Swede's memory had ever removed the tie, and only a very few descended to the informality of removing the vest, let alone turning up shirtsleeves, before donning a fresh white apron and getting down to the first skin, unrolling it from the dampened muslin cloth and beginning the work of stretching. The wall of big windows to the north illuminated the hardwood cutting tables with the cool, even light you needed for grading and matching and cutting skins. The polished smoothness of the table's rounded edge, worked smooth over the years from all the animal skins stretched across it and pulled to length, was so provocative to the boy that he always had to restrain himself from rushing to press the concavity of his cheek against the convexity of the wood—restrained himself until he was alone. There was a blurry line of footprints worn into the wood floor where the men stood all day at the cutting tables, and when no one else was up there he liked to go and stand with his shoes where the floor was worn away. Watching the cutters work, he knew that they were the elite and that they knew it and the boss knew it. Though they considered themselves to be men more aristocratic than anyone around, including the boss, a cutter's working hand was proudly calloused from cutting with his big, heavy shears. Beneath those white shirts were arms and chests and shoulders full of a workingman's strength —powerful they had to be, to pull and pull on leather all their lives, to squeeze out of every skin every inch of leather there was.

A lot of licking went on, a lot of saliva went into every glove, but, as his father joked, "The customer never knows it." The cutter would spit into the dry inking material in which he rubbed the brush for the stencil that numbered the pieces he cut from each trank. Having cut a pair of gloves, he would touch his finger to his tongue so as to wet the numbered pieces, to stick them together before they were rubber-banded for the sewing forelady and the sewers. What the boy never got over were those first German cutters employed by Newark Maid, who used to keep a schooner of beer beside them and sip from it, they said, "to keep the whistle wet" and their saliva flowing. Quickly enough Lou Levov had done away with the beer, but the saliva? No. Nobody could want to do away with the saliva. That was part and parcel of all that they loved, the son and heir no less than the founding father.

"Harry can cut a glove as good as any of them." Harry, the

Master, stood directly beside the Swede, indifferent to his boss's words and doing his work. "He's only been forty-one years with Newark Maid but he works at it. The cutter has to visualize how the skin is going to realize itself into the maximum number of gloves. Then he has to cut it. Takes great skill to cut a glove right. Table cutting is an art. No two skins are alike. The skins all come in different according to each animal's diet and age, every one different as far as stretchability goes, and the skill involved in making every glove come out like every other is amazing. Same thing with the sewing. Kind of work people don't want to do anymore. You can't just take a sewer who knows how to run a traditional sewing machine, or knows how to sew dresses, and start her here on gloves. She has to go through a three- or four-month training process, has to have finger dexterity, has to have patience, and it's six months before she's proficient and reaches even eighty percent efficiency. Glove sewing is a tremendously complicated procedure. If you want to make a better glove, you have to spend money and train workers. Takes a lot of hard work and attention, all the twists and turns where the finger crotches are sewn —it's very hard. In the days when my father first opened a glove shop, the people were in it for life—Harry's the last of them. This cutting room is one of the last in this hemisphere. Our production is still always full. We still have people here who know what they're doing. Nobody cuts gloves this way anymore, not in this country, where hardly anybody's left to cut them, and not anywhere else either, except maybe in a little family-run shop in Naples or Grenoble. These were people, the people who worked here, who were in it for life. They were born into the glove industry and they died in the glove industry. Today we're constantly retraining people. Today our economy is such that people take a job here and if something comes along for another fifty cents an hour, they're gone."

She wrote all this down.

"When I first came into the business and my father sent me up here to learn how to cut, all I did was stand right here at the cutting table and watch this guy. I learned this business in the old-fashioned way. From the ground up. My father started me literally sweeping the floors. Went through every single department, getting a feel for each operation and why it was being done. From Harry I learned how to cut a glove. I wouldn't say I was a proficient glove cutter. If I cut two, three pairs a day it was a lot, but I learned the rudimentary principles —right, Harry? A demanding teacher, this fellow. When he shows you how to do something, he goes all the way. Learning from Harry almost made me yearn for my old man. First day I came up here Harry set me straight—he told me that down where he lived boys would come to his door and say, 'Could you teach me to be a glove cutter?' and he would tell them, 'You've got to pay me fifteen thousand first, because that's how much time and leather you're going to destroy till you get to the point where you can make the minimum wage.' I watched him for a full two months before he let me anywhere near a hide. An average table cutter will cut three, three and a half dozen a day. A good, fast table cutter will cut five dozen a day. Harry was cutting five and a half dozen a day. 'You think I'm good?' he told me. 'You should have seen my dad.' Then he told me about his father and the tall man from Barnum and Bailey. Remember, Harry?" Harry nodded. "When the Barnum and Bailey circus came to Newark . . . this is 1917, 1918?" Harry nodded again without stopping his work. "Well, they came to town and they had a tall man, approaching nine feet or so, and Harry's father saw him one day in the street, walking along the street, at Broad and Market, and he got so excited he ran over to the tall man and he took his shoelace off his own shoe, measured the guy's hand right out there on the street, and he went home and made up a perfect size-seventeen pair of gloves. Harry's father cut it and his mom sewed it, and they went over to the circus and gave the gloves to the tall man, and the whole family got free seats, and a big story about Harry's dad ran in the *Newark News* the next day."

Harry corrected him. "The *Star-Eagle*."

"Right, before it merged with the *Ledger*."

"Wonderful," the girl said, laughing. "Your father must have been very skilled."

"Couldn't speak a word of English," Harry told her.

"He couldn't? Well, that just goes to show, you don't have to know English," she said, "to cut a perfect pair of gloves for a man nine feet tall."

Harry didn't laugh but the Swede did, laughed and put his

arm around her. "This is Rita. We're going to make her a dress glove, size four. Black or brown, honey?"

"Brown?"

From a wrapped-up bundle of hides dampening beside Harry, he picked one out in a pale shade of brown. "This is a tough color to get," the Swede told her. "British tan. You can see, there's all sorts of variation in the color—see how light it is there, how dark it is down there? Okay. This is sheepskin. What you saw in my office was pickled. This has been tanned. This is leather. But you can still see the animal. If you were to look at the animal," he said, "here it is—the head, the butt, the front legs, the hind legs, and here's the back, where the leather is harder and thicker, as it is over our own backbones. . . ."

Honey. He began calling her honey up in the cutting room and he could not stop, and this even before he understood that by standing beside her he was as close to Merry as he had been since the general store blew up and his honey disappeared. This is a French ruler, it's about an inch longer than an American ruler. . . . This is called a spud knife, dull, beveled to an edge but not sharp. . . . Now he's pulling the trank down like that, to the length again—Harry likes to bet you that he'll pull it right down to the pattern without even touching the pattern, but I don't bet him because I don't like losing. . . . This is called a fourchette. . . . See, all meticulously done. . . . He's going to cut yours and give it to me so we can take it down to the making department. . . . This is called the slitter, honey. Only mechanical process in the whole thing. A press and a die, and the slitter will take about four tranks at a time. . . .

"Wow. This is an elaborate process," said Rita.

"That it is. Hard really to make money in the glove business because it's so labor-intensive—a time-consuming process, many operations to be coordinated. Most of the glove businesses have been family businesses. From father to son. Very traditional business. A product is a product to most manufacturers. The guy who makes them doesn't know anything about them. The glove business isn't like that. This business has a long, long history."

"Do other people feel the romance of the glove business the

way you do, Mr. Levov? You really are mad for this place and all the processes. I guess that's what makes you a happy man."

"Am I?" he asked, and felt as though he were going to be dissected, cut into by a knife, opened up and all his misery revealed. "I guess I am."

"Are you the last of the Mohicans?"

"No, most of them, I believe, in this business have that same feeling for the tradition, that same love. Because it does require a love and a legacy to motivate somebody to stay in a business like this. You have to have strong ties to it to be able to stick it out. Come on," he said, having managed momentarily to quash everything that was shadowing him and menacing him, succeeded still to be able to speak with great precision despite her telling him he was a happy man. "Let's go back to the making room."

This is the silking, that's a story in itself, but this is what she's going to do first. . . . This is called a piqué machine, it sews the finest stitch, called piqué, requires far more skill than the other stitches. . . . This is called a polishing machine and that is called a stretcher and you are called honey and I am called Daddy and this is called living and the other is called dying and this is called madness and this is called mourning and this is called hell, pure hell, and you have to have strong ties to be able to stick it out, this is called trying-to-go-on-as-though-nothing-has-happened and this is called paying-the-full-price-but-in-God's-name-for-what, this is called wanting-to-be-dead-and-wanting-to-find-her-and-to-kill-her-and-to-save-her-from-whatever-she-is-going-through-wherever-on-earth-she-may-be-at-this-moment, this unbridled outpouring is called blotting-out-everything *and it does not work, I am half insane, the shattering force of that bomb is too great.* . . . And then they were back at his office again, waiting for Rita's gloves to come from the finishing department, and he was repeating to her a favorite observation of his father's, one that his father had read somewhere and always used to impress visitors, and he heard himself repeating it, word for word, as his own. If only he could get her to stay and not go, if he could keep on talking about gloves to her, about gloves, about skins, about his horrible riddle, implore her, beg her, *Don't leave me alone*

with this horrible riddle. . . . "Monkeys, gorillas, they have
brains and we have a brain, but they don't have this thing, the
thumb. They can't move it opposite the way we do. The inner
digit on the hand of man, that might be the distinguishing
physical feature between ourselves and the rest of the animals.
And the glove protects that inner digit. The ladies' glove, the
welder's glove, the rubber glove, the baseball glove, et cetera.
This is the root of humanity, this opposable thumb. It enables
us to make tools and build cities and everything else. More
than the brain. Maybe some other animals have bigger brains
in proportion to their bodies than we have. I don't know. But
the hand itself is an intricate thing. It moves. There is no other
part of a human being that is clothed that is such a complex
moving structure. . . ." And that was when Vicky popped in
the door with the size-four finished gloves. "Here's your pair
of gloves," Vicky said, and gave them to the boss, who looked
them over and then leaned across the desk to show them to
the girl. "See the seams? The width of the sewing at the edge
of the leather—that's where the quality workmanship is. This
margin is probably about a thirty-second of an inch between
the stitching and the edge. And that requires a high skill level,
far higher than normal. If a glove is not well sewn, this edge
might come to an eighth of an inch. It also will not be straight.
Look at how straight these seams are. This is why a Newark
Maid glove is a good glove, Rita. Because of the straight seams.
Because of the fine leather. It's well tanned. It's soft. It's pli-
able. Smells like the inside of a new car. I love good leather, I
love fine gloves, and I was brought up on the idea of making
the best glove possible. It's in my blood, and nothing gives me
greater pleasure"—he clutched at his own effusiveness the way
a sick person clutches at any sign of health, no matter how
minute—"than giving you these lovely gloves. Here," he said,
"with our compliments," and, smiling, he presented the gloves
to the girl, who excitedly pulled them onto her little hands—
"Slowly, slowly . . . always draw on a pair of gloves by the
fingers," he told her, "afterward the thumb, then draw the
wrist down in place . . . always the first time draw them on
slowly"—and she looked up and, smiling back at him with the
pleasure that any child takes in receiving a gift, showed him
with her hands in the air how beautiful the gloves looked, how

beautifully they fit. "Close your hand, make a fist," the Swede said. "Feel how the glove expands where your hand expands and nicely adjusts to your size? That's what the cutter does when he does his job right—no stretch left in the length, he's pulled that all out at the table because you don't want the fingers to stretch, but an exactly measured amount of hidden stretch left in the width. That stretch in the width is a precise calculation."

"Yes, yes, it's wonderful, absolutely perfect," she told him, opening and closing her hands in turn. "God bless the precise calculators of this world," she said, laughing, "who leave stretch hidden in the width," and only after Vicky had shut the door to his glass-enclosed office and headed back into the racket of the making department did Rita add, very softly, "She wants her Audrey Hepburn scrapbook."

The next morning the Swede met Rita at the Newark airport parking lot to give her the scrapbook. From his office he had first driven to Branch Brook Park, miles in the opposite direction from the airport, where he'd got out of the car to take a solitary walk. He strolled along where the Japanese cherry trees were blooming. For a while he sat on a bench, watching the old people with their dogs. Then, back in the car, he just began to drive—through Italian north Newark and on up to Belleville, making right turns for half an hour until he determined that he was not being followed. Rita had warned him not to make his way to their rendezvous otherwise.

The second week, at the airport parking lot, he handed over the ballet slippers and the leotard Merry had last worn at age fourteen. Three days after that it was her stuttering diary.

"Surely," he said, having decided that now, with the diary in his hands, the time had come to repeat the words his wife had spoken to him before each of his meetings with Rita, meetings in which he had scrupulously done nothing other than what Rita asked and deliberately asked nothing of her in return— "surely you can now tell me something about Merry. If not where she is, how she is."

"I surely cannot," Rita said sourly.

"I'd like to speak with her."

"Well, she wouldn't like to speak with you."

"But if she wants these things . . . why else would she want these things?"

"Because they're hers."

"So are we hers, Miss."

"Not to hear her tell it."

"I can't believe that."

"She hates you."

"Does she?" he asked lightly.

"She thinks you ought to be shot."

"Yes, that too?"

"What do you pay the workers in your factory in Ponce, Puerto Rico? What do you pay the workers who stitch gloves for you in Hong Kong and Taiwan? What do you pay the women going blind in the Philippines hand-stitching designs to satisfy the ladies shopping at Bonwit's? You're nothing but a shitty little capitalist who exploits the brown and yellow people of the world and lives in luxury behind the nigger-proof security gates of his mansion."

Till now the Swede had been civil and soft-spoken with Rita no matter how menacing she was determined to be. Rita was all they had, she was indispensable, and though he did not expect to change her any by keeping his emotions to himself, each time he steeled himself to show no desperation. Taunting him was the project she had set herself; imposing her will on this conservatively dressed success story six feet three inches tall and worth millions clearly provided her with one of life's great moments. But then it was all great moments these days. They had Merry, sixteen-year-old stuttering Merry. They had a live human being and her family to play with. Rita was no longer an ordinary wavering mortal, let alone a novice in life, but a creature in clandestine harmony with the brutal way of the world, entitled, in the name of historical justice, to be just as sinister as the capitalist oppressor Swede Levov.

The *unreality* of being in the hands of this child! This loathsome kid with a head full of fantasies about "the working class"! This tiny being who took up not even as much space in the car as the Levov sheepdog, pretending that she was striding on the world stage! This utterly insignificant *pebble*! What was the whole sick enterprise other than angry, infantile egoism thinly disguised as identification with the oppressed? Her weighty responsibility to the workers of the world! Egoistic pathology bristled out of her like the hair that nuttily proclaimed, "I go wherever I want, as far as I want—all that matters is what I want!" Yes, the nonsensical hair constituted half of their revolutionary ideology, about as sound a justification for her actions as the other half—the exaggerated jargon about changing the world. She was twenty-two years old, no more than five feet tall, and off on a reckless adventure with a very potent thing way beyond her comprehension called power. Not the least need of thought. Thought just paled away beside their ignorance. They were omniscient without even thinking. No wonder his tremendous effort to hide his agitation was thwarted momentarily by uncontrollable rage, and sharply he said to her—as though he were not joined to her maniacally uncompromising mission in the most unimaginable way, as though it could matter to him that she enjoyed thinking the worst of him—"You have no idea what you're talking about! American firms make gloves in the Philippines and Hong Kong and Taiwan and India and Pakistan and all over the place—but not mine! I own two factories. *Two.* One of my factories you visited in Newark. You saw how unhappy my employees were. That's why they've worked for us for forty years, because they're exploited so miserably. The factory in Puerto Rico employs two hundred and sixty people, Miss Cohen—people we have trained, trained from scratch, people we trust, people who before we came to Ponce had barely enough work to go around. We furnish employment where there was a shortage of employment, we have taught needle skills to Caribbean people who had few if any of these skills. You know nothing. You know nothing about anything—you didn't even know what a factory *was* till I showed you one!"

"I know what a plantation is, Mr. Legree—I mean, Mr. Levov. I know what it means to run a plantation. You take good care of your niggers. Of course you do. It's called paternal capitalism. You own 'em, you sleep with 'em, and when you're finished with 'em you toss 'em out. Lynch 'em only when necessary. Use them for your sport and use them for your profit—"

"Please, I haven't two minutes' interest in childish clichés. You don't know what a factory is, you don't know what manufacturing is, you don't know what capital is, you don't know what labor is, you haven't the faintest idea what it is to be employed or what it is to be unemployed. You have no idea what *work* is. You've never held a job in your life, and if you even cared to find one, you wouldn't last a single day, not as a worker, not as a manager, not as an owner. Enough nonsense. I want you to tell me where my daughter is. That is all I want to hear from you. She needs help, she needs serious help, not ridiculous clichés. I want you to tell me where I can find her!"

"Merry never wants to see you again. *Or* that mother."

"You don't know anything about Merry's mother."

"Lady Dawn? Lady Dawn of the Manor? I know all there is to know about Lady Dawn. So ashamed of her class origins she has to make her daughter into a debutante."

"Merry shoveled cowshit from the time she was six. You don't know what you're talking about. Merry was in the 4-H Club. Merry rode tractors. Merry—"

"Fake. All fake. The daughter of the beauty queen and the captain of the football team—what kind of nightmare is that for a girl with a soul? The little shirtwaist dresses, the little shoes, the little this and the little that. Always playing with her hair. You think she wanted to fix Merry's hair because she loved her and the way she looked or because she was disgusted with her, disgusted she couldn't have a baby beauty queen that could grow up in her own image to become Miss Rimrock? Merry has to have dancing lessons. Merry has to have tennis lessons. I'm surprised she didn't get a nose job."

"You don't know what you are talking about."

"Why do you think Merry had the hots for Audrey Hepburn? Because she thought that was the best chance she had with that vain little mother of hers. Miss Vanity of 1949. Hard to believe you could fit so much vanity into that cutesy figure. Oh, but it does, it fits, all right. Just doesn't leave much room for Merry, does it?"

"You don't know what you're saying."

"No imagination for somebody who isn't beautiful and lovable and desirable. None. The frivolous, trivial beauty-queen mentality and no imagination for her own daughter. 'I don't want to see anything messy, I don't want to see anything dark.'

But the world isn't like that, Dawnie dear—it *is* messy, it *is* dark. It's *hideous*!"

"Merry's mother works a farm all day. She works with animals all day, she works with farm machinery all day, she works from six A.M. to—"

"Fake. Fake. Fake. She works a farm like a fucking upper-class—"

"You don't know anything about any of this. Where is my daughter? Where is she? The conversation is pointless. Where is Merry?"

"You don't remember the 'Now You Are a Woman Party'? To celebrate her first menstruation."

"We're not talking about any party. What party?"

"We're talking about the humiliation of a daughter by her beauty-queen mother. We're talking about a mother who completely colonized her daughter's self-image. We're talking about a mother who didn't have an inch of feeling for her daughter—who has about as much depth as those gloves you make. A whole family and all you really fucking care about is skin. Ectoderm. Surface. But what's underneath, you don't have a clue. You think that was real affection she had for that stuttering girl? She tolerated that stuttering girl, but you can't tell the difference between affection and tolerance because you're too stupid yourself. Another one of your fucking fairy tales. A menstruation party. A party for it! Jesus!"

"You mean—*no*, that wasn't that. The party? You mean when she took all her friends to Whitehouse for dinner? That was her twelfth birthday. What is this 'Now You Are a Woman' crap? It was a *birthday* party. Nothing to do with menstruating. *Nothing*. Who told you this? Merry didn't tell you this. I remember that party. *She* remembers that party. It was a simple birthday party. We took all those girls down to that restaurant in Whitehouse. They had a wonderful time. We had ten twelve-year-old girls. This is all cracked. Somebody is dead. My daughter is being accused of murder."

Rita was laughing. "Mr. Law-abiding New Jersey Fucking Citizen, a little bit of fake affection looks just like love to him."

"But what you are describing never *happened*. What you are saying never *happened*. It wouldn't have mattered if it did, but *it did not*."

"Don't you know what's made Merry Merry? Sixteen years of living in a household where she was hated by that mother."

"For what? Tell me. Hated her for *what*?"

"Because she was everything Lady Dawn wasn't. Her mother hated her, Swede. It's a shame you're so late in finding out. Hated her for not being petite, for not being able to have her hair pulled back in that oh-so-spiffy country way. Merry was hated with that hatred that seeps into you like toxin. Lady Dawn couldn't have done a better job if she'd slipped poison into her a meal at a time. Lady Dawn would look at her with that look of hatred and Merry was turned into a piece of shit."

"There was no look of hatred. Something may have gone wrong . . . but that wasn't it. That wasn't hatred. I know what she's talking about. What you're calling hatred was her mother's anxiety. I know the look. But it was about the stuttering. My God, it wasn't *hatred*. It was the *opposite*. It was concern. It was distress. It was *helplessness*."

"Still protecting that wife of yours," said Rita, laughing at him again. "Incredible incomprehension. Simply incredible. You know why else she hated her? She hated her because she's your daughter. It's all fine and well for Miss New Jersey to marry a Jew. But to raise a Jew? That's a whole other bag of tricks. You have a shiksa wife, Swede, but you didn't get a shiksa daughter. Miss New Jersey is a bitch, Swede. Merry would have been better off sucking the cows if she wanted a little milk and nurturance. At least the cows have maternal feelings."

He had allowed her to talk, he had allowed himself to listen, only because he wanted to know; if something had gone wrong, of course he wanted to know. What *is* the grudge? What *is* the grievance? That was the central mystery: how did Merry get to be who she is? But none of this explained anything. This could not be what it was all about. This could not be what lay behind the blowing up of the building. No. A desperate man was giving himself over to a treacherous girl not because she could possibly begin to know what went wrong but because there was no one else to give himself over to. He felt less like someone looking for an answer than like someone mimicking someone who was looking for an answer. This whole exchange had been a ridiculous mistake. To expect this kid to talk to him truthfully. She couldn't insult him enough.

Everything about their lives transformed absolutely by *her* hatred. *Here* was the hater—this insurrectionist child!

"Where is she?"

"Why do you want to know where she is?"

"I want to see her," he said.

"Why?"

"She's my daughter. Somebody is dead. My daughter is being accused of murder."

"You're really stuck on that, aren't you? Do you know how many Vietnamese have been killed in the few minutes we've had the luxury to talk about whether or not Dawnie loves her daughter? It's all relative, Swede. Death is all relative."

"Where is she?"

"Your daughter is safe. Your daughter is loved. Your daughter is fighting for what she believes in. Your daughter is finally having an experience of the world."

"Where is she, damn you!"

"She's not a possession, you know—she's not property. She's not powerless anymore. You don't own Merry the way you own your Old Rimrock house and your Deal house and your Florida condo and your Newark factory and your Puerto Rico factory and your Puerto Rican workers and all your Mercedes and all your Jeeps and all your beautiful handmade suits. You know what I've come to realize about you kindly rich liberals who own the world? Nothing is further from your understanding than the nature of reality."

No one begins like this, the Swede thought. This can't be what she is. This bullying infant, this obnoxious, stubborn, angry bullying infant cannot be my daughter's protector. She is her jailer. Merry with all her intelligence under the spell of this childlike cruelty and meanness. There's more human sense in one page of the stuttering diary than in all the sadistic idealism in this reckless child's head. Oh, to crush that hairy, tough little skull of hers—right now, between his two strong hands, to squeeze it and squeeze it until all the vicious ideas came streaming from her nose!

How does a child get to be like this? Can anyone be utterly without thoughtfulness? The answer is yes. His only contact with his daughter was this child who did not know anything and would say anything and more than likely do anything—resort to anything to excite herself. Her opinions were all stimuli: the goal was excitement.

"The paragon," Rita said, speaking to him out of the side of her mouth, as though that would make it all the easier to wreck his life. "The cherished and triumphant paragon who is in actuality the criminal. The great Swede Levov, all-American capitalist criminal."

She was some clever child crackpot gorging herself on an escapade entirely her own, a reprehensible child lunatic who'd never laid eyes on Merry except in the paper; some "politicized" crazy was what she was—the streets of New York were full of them—a criminally insane Jewish kid who'd picked up her facts about their lives from the newspapers and the TV and from the school friends of Merry's who were all out peddling the same quotation: "Quaint Old Rimrock is in for a big surprise." From the sound of it, Merry had gone around school the day before the bombing telling that to four hundred kids. That was the evidence against her, all these kids on TV claiming they heard her say it—that hearsay and her disappearance were the whole of the evidence. The post office had been blown up, and the general store along with it, but nobody had seen her anywhere near it, nobody had seen her do the thing, nobody would have even thought of her as the bomber if she hadn't disappeared. "She's been tricked!" For days Dawn went around the house crying, "She's been abducted! She's been tricked! She's somewhere right now being brainwashed! Why does everybody say she did it? Nobody's had any *contact* with her. She is not connected with it in any way *at all*. How can they believe this of a *child*? Dynamite? What does Merry have to do with dynamite? No! It isn't true! Nobody knows a *thing*!"

He should have informed the FBI of Rita Cohen's visit the day she'd come to ask for the scrapbook—at the very least should have demanded proof from her of Merry's existence. And he should have taken into his confidence someone other than Dawn, formulated strategy with a person less likely to kill herself if he proceeded other than as her desperation demanded. Answering the needs of a wife incoherent with grief, in no condition to think or act except out of hysteria, was an inexcusable error. He should have heeded his mistrust and contacted immediately the agents who had interviewed him and Dawn at the house the day after the bombing. He should have picked up the phone the moment he understood who Rita Cohen was, even while she was seated in his office. But instead he had driven directly home from the office and, because he could never calculate a decision free of its emotional impact on those who claimed his love; because seeing them suffer was his greatest hardship; because ignoring their importuning and defying their expectations, even when they would not argue reasonably or to the point, seemed to him an illegitimate use of his superior strength; because he could not disillusion anyone about the kind of selfless son, husband, and father he was; because he had come so highly *recommended* to everyone, he sat across from Dawn at the kitchen table, watching her deliver a long, sob-wracked, half-demented speech, a plea to tell the FBI nothing.

Dawn begged him to do whatever the girl wanted: it remained possible for Merry to go unapprehended if only they kept her out of sight until the destruction of the store—and the death of Dr. Conlon—had been forgotten. If only they hid her somewhere, provided for her, maybe even in another country, until this war-mad witch-hunt was over and a new time had begun; then she could be treated fairly for something she never, never could have done. "She's been *tricked*!" and he believed this himself—what else *could* a father believe?—until he heard it, day after day, a hundred times a day, from Dawn.

So he'd turned over the Audrey Hepburn scrapbook, the leotard, the ballet slippers, the stuttering book; and now he was to meet Rita Cohen at a room in the New York Hilton, this time bearing five thousand dollars in unmarked twenties and tens. And just as he'd known to call the FBI when she asked for the scrapbook, he now understood that if he acceded any further to her malicious daring there'd be no bottom to it, there would only be misery on a scale incomprehensible to all of them. With the scrapbook, the leotard, the ballet slippers, and the stuttering book he had been craftily set up; now for the disastrous payoff.

But Dawn was convinced that if he traveled over to Manhattan, got himself lost in the crowds, then, at the appointed afternoon hour, certain he wasn't being tailed, made his way to the hotel, Merry herself would be there waiting for him—an

absurd fairy-tale hope for which there wasn't a shred of justification, but which he didn't have the heart to oppose, not when
he saw his wife shedding another layer of sanity whenever the
telephone rang.

For the first time she was got up in a skirt and blouse, gaudily
floral bargain-basement stuff, and wearing high-heeled pumps;
when she unsteadily crossed the carpet in them, she looked
tinier even than she had in her work boots. The hairdo was as
aboriginal as before but her face, ordinarily a little pot, soulless
and unadorned, had been emblazoned with lipstick and painted
with eye shadow, her cheekbones highlighted with pink grease.
She looked like a third grader who had ransacked her mother's
room, except that the cosmetics caused her expressionlessness
to seem even more frighteningly psychopathic than when her
face was just unhumanly empty of color.

"I have the money," he said, standing in the hotel room
doorway towering above her and knowing that what he was
doing was as wrong as it could be. "I have the money," he repeated, and prepared himself for the retort about the sweat
and blood of the workers from whom he had stolen it.

"Oh, hi. Do come in," the girl said. *I'd like you to meet my
parents. Mom and Dad, this is Seymour.* An act for the factory,
an act for the hotel. "Please, do come in. Do make yourself at
home."

He had the money packed into his briefcase, not just the five
thousand in the tens and twenties she'd asked for but five
thousand more in fifties. A total of ten thousand dollars—and
with no idea why. What good would any of it do Merry? Merry
wouldn't see a penny of it. Still, he said yet again—summoning
all his strength so as not to lose hold—"I've brought the
money you requested." He was trying hard to continue to exist as himself despite the unlikeliness of everything.

She had moved onto the bedspread and, with her legs
crossed at the ankle and two pillows propped up behind her
head, began lightly to sing: "Oh Lydia, oh Lydia, my encyclo-
pid-e-a, oh Lydia, the tattooed lady . . ."

It was one of the old, silly songs he'd taught his little daughter once they saw that singing, she could always be fluent.

"Come to fuck Rita Cohen, have you?"

"I've come," he said, "to deliver the money."

"Let's f-f-f-fuck, D-d-d-dad."

"If you have any feeling for what everyone is going through—"

"Come off it, Swede. What do you know about 'feeling'?"

"Why are you treating us like this?"

"Boo-hoo. Tell me another. You came here to fuck me. Ask anybody. Why does a middle-aged capitalist dog come to a hotel room to meet a young piece of ass? To fuck her. Say it, just say, 'I came to fuck you. To fuck you good.' Say it, Swede."

"I don't want to say any such thing. Stop all this, please."

"I'm twenty-two years old. I do everything. I do it all. Say it, Swede."

Could this lead to Merry, this onslaught of sneering and mockery? She could not insult him enough. Was she impersonating someone, acting from a script prepared beforehand? Or was he dealing with a person who could not be dealt with because she was mad? She was like a gang member. Was she the gang *leader*, this tiny white-faced thug? In a gang the authority is given to the one who is most ruthless. Is she the most ruthless or are there others who are worse, those others who are holding Merry captive right now? Maybe she is the most intelligent. Their actress. Maybe she is the most corrupt. Their budding whore. Maybe this is all a *game* to them, middle-class kids out on a spree.

"Don't I suit you?" she asked. "No crude desires in a big guy like you? Come on, I'm not such a frightening person. You can't have met your match in little me. Look at you. Like a naughty boy. A child in terror of being disgraced. Isn't there anything else in there except your famous purity? I bet there is. I bet you've got yourself quite a pillar in there," she said. "The pillar of society."

"What is the aim of all this talk? Will you tell me?"

"The aim? Sure. To introduce you to reality. That's the aim."

"And how much ruthlessness is necessary?"

"To introduce you to reality? To get you to admire reality? To get you to partake of reality? To get you out there on the frontiers of reality? It ain't gonna be no picnic, jocko."

He had braced himself not to become entangled in her loathing for him, not to be affronted by anything she said. He was prepared for the verbal violence and prepared, this time, not to react. She was not unintelligent and she was not afraid to say anything—he knew that much. But what he had not counted on was lust, an urge—he had not counted on being assailed by something *other* than the verbal violence. Despite the repugnance inspired by the sickly whiteness of her flesh, by the comically childish makeup and the cheap cotton clothes, half reclining on the bed was a young woman half reclining on a bed, and the Swede himself, the superman of certainties, was one of the people whom he could not deal with.

"Poor thing," she said scornfully. "Little Rimrock rich boy. All locked up like that. Let's fuck, D-d-d-daddy. I'll take you to see your daughter. We'll wash your prick and zip up your fly and I'll take you to where she is."

"Do I know you will? How do I know you will?"

"Wait. See how things turn out. The worst is you get your-self some twenty-two-year-old gash. Come on, Dad. Come on over to the bed, D-d-d—"

"Stop this! My daughter has nothing to do with *any* of this! My daughter has nothing to do with *you*! You little shit—you're not fit to wipe my daughter's *shoes*! My daughter had nothing to do with that bombing. You know that!"

"Calm down, Swede. Calm down, lover boy. If you want to see your daughter as much as you say, you'll just calm down and come on over here and give Rita Cohen a nice big fuck. First the fuck, then the dough."

She had raised her knees toward her chest and now, with either foot planted on the bed, she let her legs fall open. The floral skirt was gathered up by her hips and she wore no underwear.

"There," she said softly. "Put it right there. Attack there. It's all permissible, baby."

"Miss Cohen . . ." He did not know what to reach for in his estimable strongbox of reactions—this boiling up of some-thing so visceral in with the rhetorical was not the attack he had prepared himself for. She'd brought to the hotel a stick of dynamite to throw. This was it. To blow *him* up.

"What is it, dear?" she replied. "You must speak up like a big boy if you wish to be heard."

"What does this display have to do with what has happened?"

"Everything," she said. "You'll be surprised by what a very clear picture of things you're going to get from this display." She edged her two hands down onto her pubic hair. "Look at it," she told him and, by rolling the labia lips outward with her fingers, exposed to him the membranous tissue veined and mottled and waxy with the moist tulip sheen of flayed flesh. He looked away.

"It's a jungle down there," she said. "Nothing in its place. Nothing on the left side like anything on the right side. How many extras are there? Nobody knows. Too many to count. There are glands down there. There's another hole. There are flaps. Don't you see what this has to do with what happened? Take a look. Take a good long look."

"Miss Cohen," he said, fixing on her eyes, the one mark of beauty she was blessed with—a child's eyes, he discovered, a *good* child's eyes that had nothing in common with what she was up to, "my daughter is missing. Someone is dead."

"You don't get the point. You don't get the point about anything. Look at it. Describe it to me. Have I got it wrong? What do you see? Do you see anything? No, you don't see anything. You don't see anything because you don't look at anything."

"This makes no sense," he said. "You are subjugating no one by this. Only yourself."

"You know what size it is? Let's see what kind of guesser you are. It's small. I'm guessing that it's a size four. In a ladies' size that's as small as cunts come. Anything smaller is a child's. Let's see how you'll fit into a teeny size four. Let's see if a size four doesn't provide just the nicest, warmest, snuggest fuck you've ever dreamed of fucking. You love good leather, you love fine gloves—stick it in. But slowly, slowly. Always the first time stick it in slowly."

"Why don't you stop right now?"

"Okay, if that's your decision, that you're such a brave man you won't even *look* at it, shut your eyes and step right up and smell it. Step right up and take a whiff. The swamp. It *sucks* you in. Smell it, Swede. You know what a glove smells like. It smells like the inside of a new car. Well, this is what life smells like. Smell this. Smell the inside of a brand-new pussy."

Her dark child's eyes. Full of excitement and fun. Full of audacity. Full of unreasonableness. Full of oddness. Full of *Rita*. And only half of it was performance. To agitate. To infuriate. To arouse. She was in an altered state. The imp of upheaval. The genie of disaster. As though in being his tormentor and wrecking his family she had found the malicious meaning for her own existence. Kid Mayhem.

"Your physical restraint is amazing," she said. "Isn't there *anything* that can get you off dead center? I didn't believe there were any left like you. Any other man would have been overcome by his hard-on hours ago. You *are* a throwback. *Taste it*."

"You're not a woman. This does not make you a woman in any way. This makes you a *travesty* of a woman. This is loathsome." Rapidly firing back at her like a soldier under attack.

"And a man who won't look, what's he a travesty of?" she asked him. "Isn't it just human *nature* to look? What about a man always averting his eyes because it's all too steeped in reality for him? Because nothing is in harmony with the world as he knows it? *Thinks* he knows it. *Taste* it! Of *course* it's loathsome, you great big Boy Scout—I'm *depraved*!" and merrily laughing off his refusal to lower his gaze by so much as an inch, she cried, "*Here!*"

She must have reached inside herself with her hand, her hand must have disappeared inside her, because a moment later it was the whole of her hand that she was extending upward to him. The tips of her fingers bore the smell of her right up to him. That he could not shut out, the fecund smell released from within.

"This'll unlock the mystery. You want to know what this has to do with what happened?" she said. "This'll tell you."

There was so much emotion in him, so much uncertainty, so much inclination and counterinclination, he was bursting so with impulse and counterimpulse that he could no longer tell which of them had drawn the line that he would not pass over. All his thinking seemed to be taking place in a foreign language, but still he knew enough not to pass over the line. He would not pick her up and hurl her against the window. He would not pick her up and throw her onto the floor. He would not pick her up for any reason. All the strength left in him would be marshaled to keep him paralyzed at the foot of the bed. He would not go near her.

The hand she'd offered him she now carried slowly up to her face, making loony, comical little circles in the air as she approached her mouth. Then, one by one, she slipped each finger between her lips to cleanse it. "You know what it tastes like? Want me to tell you? It tastes like your d-d-d-daughter."

Here he bolted the room. With all his strength.

That was it. Ten, twelve minutes and it was over. By the time the FBI responded to his phone call and got to the hotel, she was gone, as was the briefcase he had abandoned. He'd bolted not from the childlike cruelty and meanness, not even from the vicious provocation, but from something that he could no longer name.

Faced with something he could not name, he had done everything wrong.

Five years pass. In vain, the Rimrock Bomber's father waits for Rita to reappear at his office. He did not take her photograph, did not save her fingerprints—no, whenever they met, for those few minutes, she, a child, was boss. And now she's disappeared. With an agent and a sketch artist to assist him, he is asked to construct a picture of Rita for the FBI, while alone he studies the daily paper and the weekly newsmagazines, searching for the real thing. He waits for Rita's picture to turn up. She is bound to be there. Bombs are going off everywhere. In Boulder, Colorado, bombs destroy a Selective Service office and the ROTC headquarters at the University of Colorado. In Michigan there are explosions at the university and dynamite attacks on a police headquarters and the draft board. In Wisconsin a bomb destroys a National Guard armory; a small plane flies over and drops two jars filled with gunpowder on an ammunition plant. College buildings are attacked with bombs at the University of Wisconsin. In Chicago a bomb destroys the memorial statue to the policemen killed in the Haymarket riots. In New Haven someone firebombs the home of the judge in the trial of nineteen Black Panthers accused of planning to destroy department stores, the police station, and the

New Haven Railroad. Buildings are bombed at universities in Oregon, Missouri, and Texas. A Pittsburgh shopping mall, a Washington nightclub, a Maryland courtroom—all bombed. In New York there are a series of explosions—at the United Fruit Line pier, at the Marine Midland Bank, at Manufacturers Trust, at General Motors, at the Manhattan headquarters of Mobil Oil, IBM, and General Telephone and Electronics. A downtown Manhattan Selective Service center is bombed. The criminal courts building is bombed. Three Molotov cocktails go off in a Manhattan high school. Bombs explode in safe-deposit boxes in banks in eight cities. She has to have set off one of them. They'll find Rita, catch her red-handed—catch the whole bunch of them—and she will lead them to Merry.

In his pajamas, in their kitchen, he sits watching every night for her soot-covered face at the window. He sits alone in the kitchen, waiting for his enemy, Rita Cohen, to return.

A TWA jet is bombed in Las Vegas. A bomb goes off on the *Queen Elizabeth*. A bomb goes off in the Pentagon—in a women's restroom on the fourth floor of an air force area of the Pentagon! The bomber leaves a note: "Today we attacked the Pentagon, the center of the American military command. We are reacting at a time when growing U.S. air and naval shelling are being carried out against the Vietnamese; while U.S. mines and warships are used to block the harbors of the Democratic Republic of Vietnam; while plans for even more escalation are being made in Washington." *The Democratic Republic of Vietnam—if I hear that from her once again, Seymour, I swear, I'll go out of my mind.* It's their daughter! Merry has bombed the Pentagon.

"D-d-dad!" Above the noise of the sewing machines he hears her crying for him in his office. "D-d-d-daddy!"

Two years after her disappearance, there is a bomb blast in the most elegant Greek Revival house on the most peaceful residential street in Greenwich Village—three explosions and a fire destroy the old four-story brick townhouse. The house is owned by a prosperous New York couple who are on vacation in the Caribbean. After the explosion, two dazed young women stumble, bruised and lacerated, out of the building. One of them, who is naked, is described as being between sixteen and eighteen. The two are sheltered by a neighbor. She gives them clothes to wear, but while the neighbor rushes off to the bombed-out building to see what more she can do, the two young women disappear. One is the twenty-five-year-old daughter of the owners of the townhouse, a member of a violent revolutionary faction of the Students for a Democratic Society called the Weathermen. The other is unidentified. The other is Rita. The other is *Merry*. They've roped her into this too!

He waits all night in the kitchen for his daughter and the girl Weatherman. It is safe now—the surveillance of the house, of the factory, the monitoring of the phones, were dropped more than a year before. It's okay now to show up. He defrosts some soup to feed them. He thinks back to when she had begun to lean toward the sciences. Because of Dawn's cattle, she thought she'd be a vet. It was the stuttering, too, that sent her into the sciences, because when she was focused and concentrated on one of her science projects, doing close work, the stuttering always abated a little. No parent in the world could have seen the connection to a bomb. Everyone would have missed it, not just him. Her interest in science was totally innocent. *Everything* was.

The body of a young man found in the rubble of the burned-out house is identified the next day as that of a one-time Columbia student, a veteran of violent antiwar demonstrations, the founder of a radical SDS splinter group, the Mad Dogs. The following day the second young woman who fled the bomb scene is identified: another radical activist but not Merry—the twenty-six-year-old daughter of a left-wing New York lawyer. Even worse is news of another corpse discovered in the rubble at the Village townhouse: the torso of a young woman. "The body of the second victim of the blast was not immediately identified and Dr. Elliott Gross, associate medical examiner, said, 'It will take some time before we have any idea who she is.'"

Alone at the kitchen table, her father knows who she is. Sixty sticks of dynamite, thirty blasting caps, a cache of homemade bombs—twelve-inch pipes packed with dynamite—are found only twenty feet from the body. It was a pipe packed with dynamite that blew up Hamlin's. She was putting the components of a new bomb together, did something wrong, and blew up the townhouse. First Hamlin's, now herself. She did do it, gave the quaint town its big surprise—and this is the result. "Dr. Gross confirmed that the torso had a number of puncture wounds, caused by nails, giving credence to the report from the police source that the bombs were apparently being wrapped to act more as antipersonnel weapons than just as explosive devices."

The next day more explosions are reported in Manhattan: three midtown buildings bombed simultaneously at about one-forty A.M. The torso's not hers! Merry is alive! Hers is not the body skewered by nails and blown apart! "As a result of the telephoned warning police arrived at the building at 1:20 and evacuated 24 janitors and other workers before the explosion occurred." The midtown bomber and the Rimrock Bomber *must* be one and the same. Had she known enough to telephone before her first bomb was set to go off, no one would have been killed and she would not be wanted for murder. So at least she has learned something, at least she is alive and there is reason to be sitting every night in the kitchen waiting to see her at the window with Rita.

He reads about the parents of the two young women who are missing and wanted for questioning in the townhouse explosion. The mother and father of one of them appeal to their daughter on television to disclose how many people were in the building when it exploded. "If there were no others," the mother says, "the search could be called off until the surrounding walls are removed. I believe in you," the mother tells the missing daughter, who, with SDS comrades, used the house as a bomb factory, "and know that you would not wish to add more sorrow to this tragedy. Please, please telephone or wire or have someone call for you with this information. There is nothing else that we need to know except that you are safe, and nothing we need to say except that we love you and want desperately to help."

The very words spoken to the press and television by the father of the Rimrock Bomber when *she* disappeared. *We love you and want to help.* "Asked if he had been 'communicating well' with his daughter, the father of the townhouse bomber replied," and no less truthfully or miserably than the father of the

Rimrock Bomber answering a similar question, "'As parents, we'd have to say no, not in recent years.'" His daughter is quoted by him as fighting for what Merry too—in her dinnertable outbursts decrying her selfish mother and father and their bourgeois life—proclaimed as the motive for her own struggle: "To change the system and give power to the 90 percent of the people who have no economic or political control now."

The father of the other missing girl is said by the police investigator to be "very uncommunicative." He says only, "I have no knowledge concerning her whereabouts." And the father of the Rimrock Bomber believes him, understands his uncommunicativeness all too well, knows better than any other father in America the burden of anguish concealed by the emotionless formulation "I have no knowledge concerning her whereabouts." If it hadn't happened to him, he would probably have marveled at the tight-lipped façade. But he knows the truth is that the missing girl's parents are drowning exactly as he is, drowning day and night in inadequate explanations.

A third body is found in the townhouse rubble, the body of an adult male. Then, a week later, a statement appears in the paper, attributed to the mother of the second missing girl, that dissipates his compassion for both sets of parents. Asked about her daughter, the mother says, "We know she is safe."

Their daughter has killed three people and they know she is safe, while about his daughter, who has not been proved by anyone to have killed anybody—about his daughter, who is being used by radical little thugs just like these privileged townhouse bombers, who has been framed, who is *innocent*—he knows nothing. What has he got to do with them? *His* daughter *didn't* do it. She no more set off the bomb at Hamlin's than she set off the bomb in the Pentagon. Since '68 thousands of bombs have been exploded in America, and his daughter has had nothing to do with a single one of them. How does he know? Because Dawn knows. Because Dawn knows for sure. Because if their daughter had been going to do it, she would never have gone around school telling kids that the town of Old Rimrock was in for a big surprise. Their daughter was too smart for that. If she had been going to do it, she would have said nothing.

*

Five years pass, five years searching for an explanation, going back over everything, over the circumstances that shaped her, the people and the events that influenced her, and none of it adequate to begin to explain the bombing until he remembers the Buddhist monks, the self-immolation of the Buddhist monks. . . . Of course she was just ten then, maybe eleven years old, and in the years between then and now a million things had happened to her, to them, to the world. Though she had been terrified for weeks afterward, crying about what had appeared on television that night, talking about it, awakened from her sleep by dreaming about it, it hardly stopped her in her tracks. And yet when he remembers her sitting there and seeing that monk going up in flames—as unprepared as the rest of the country for what she was seeing, a kid half watching the news with her mother and father one night after dinner—he is sure he has unearthed the reason for what happened.

It was back in '62 or '63, around the time of Kennedy's assassination, before the war in Vietnam had begun in earnest, when, as far as everybody knew, America was merely at the periphery of whatever was going haywire over there. The monk who did it was in his seventies, thin, with a shaved head and wearing a saffron robe. Cross-legged and straight-backed on an empty city street somewhere in South Vietnam, gracefully seated like that in front of a crowd of monks who had gathered to witness the event as though to observe a religious ritual, the monk had upended a large plastic canister, poured the gasoline or the kerosene, whatever it was, out of the canister and over himself and drenched the asphalt around him. Then he struck the match, and a nimbus of ragged flames came roiling out of him.

There is sometimes a performer in a circus, advertised as the fire eater, who makes flames seemingly shoot out of his mouth, and there on the street of some city in South Vietnam, this shaven-headed monk somehow made it look as though flames, instead of assaulting him from without, were shooting forward into the air from within him, not just from his mouth, however, but in an instantaneous eruption from his scalp and his face and his chest and his lap and his legs and his feet. Because he remained perfectly upright, indicating in no way that he could feel himself to be on fire, because he did not so much as move a muscle, let alone cry out, it at first looked very much like a circus stunt, as though what was being consumed were not the monk but the air, the monk setting the air on fire while no harm at all befell him. His posture remained exemplary, the posture of someone altogether elsewhere leading another life entirely, a servant of selfless contemplation, meditative, serene, a mere link in the chain of being untouched by what happened to be happening to him within view of the entire world. No screaming, no writhing, just his calmness at the heart of the flames—no pain registering on anyone on camera, only on Merry and the Swede and Dawn, horrified together in their living room. Out of nowhere and into their home, the nimbus of flames, the upright monk, and the sudden liquefaction before he keels over; into their home all those other monks, seated along the curbstone impassively looking on, a few with their hands pressed together before them in the Asian gesture of peace and unity; into their home on Arcady Hill Road the charred and blackened corpse on its back in that empty street.

That was what had done it. Into their home the monk came to stay, the Buddhist monk calmly sitting out his burning up as though he were a man both fully alert and anesthetized. The television transmitting the immolation *must* have done it. If their set had happened to be tuned to another channel or turned off or broken, if they had all been out together as a family for the evening, Merry would never have seen what she shouldn't have seen and would never have done what she shouldn't have done. What other explanation was there? "These gentle p-p-people," she said, while the Swede gathered her into his lap, a lanky eleven-year-old girl, held her to him, rocking and rocking her in his arms, "these gentle p-p-p-people. . . ." At first she was so frightened she couldn't even cry—she could get out of her just those three words. Only later, a moment after going to bed, when she got up and with a yelp ran from her room down the corridor and into their room and asked, as she hadn't since she was five, to get into bed with them, was she able to let everything out of her, everything awful that she was thinking. All the lights remained on in their bedroom and they let her go on and on, sitting up between them in their bed and talking until there were no words left inside her to panic or terrorize her. When she fell asleep, sometime after three, it was with their lights all still burning—she would not let him turn them off—but she had at least by then talked herself out enough and cried herself out enough to succumb to her exhaustion. "Do you have to m-m-melt yourself down in fire to bring p-p-people to their s-senses? Does anybody care? Does anybody have a conscience? Doesn't anybody in this w-world have a conscience left?" Every time "conscience" crossed her lips she began to cry.

What could they tell her? How could they answer her? Yes, some people have a conscience, many people have a conscience, but unfortunately there are people who don't have a con-science, that is true. You are lucky, Merry, you have a very well-developed conscience. It's admirable for someone your age to have such a conscience. We're proud of having a daugh-ter who has so much conscience and who cares so much about the well-being of others and who is able to sympathize with the sufferings of others. . . .

She couldn't sleep alone in her room for a week. The Swede carefully read the papers in order to be able to explain to her why the monk had done what he did. It had to do with the South Vietnamese president, General Diem, it had to do with corruption, with elections, with complex regional and political conflicts, it had to do with something about Buddhism itself. . . . But for her it had only to do with the extremes to which gentle people have to resort in a world where the great major-ity are without an ounce of conscience.

Just when she seemed to have gotten over the self-immola-tion of that elderly Buddhist monk on that street in South Vietnam and began to be able to sleep in her own room and without a light on and without awakening screaming two and three times a night, it happened again, another monk in Vietnam set himself on fire, then a third, then a fourth . . . and once that started up he found that he couldn't keep her away from the television set. If she missed a self-immolation on the evening news, she got up early to see it on the morning news before she left for school. They did not know how to stop her. What was she doing by watching and watching as though she intended never to stop watching? He wanted her to be not up-set, but not to be not upset like this. Was she simply trying to

make sense of it? To master her fear of it? Was she trying to figure out what it was like to be able to do something like that to
yourself? Was she imagining herself as one of those monks?
Was she watching because she was still appalled or was she
watching now because she was excited? What was starting to
unsettle him, to frighten him, was the idea that Merry was less
horrified now than curious, and soon he himself became obsessed, though not, like her, by the self-immolators in Vietnam
but by the change of demeanor in his eleven-year-old. That
she'd always wanted to know things had made him tremendously proud of her from the time she was small, but did he really want her to want to know so much about something like
this?

Is it a sin to take your own life? How can the others stand by
and just watch? Why don't they stop him? Why don't they put
out the flames? They stand by and let it be televised. They
want it televised. Where has *their* morality gone? What about
the morality of the television crews who are doing the filming?
. . . Were these the questions she was asking herself? Were
they a necessary part of her intellectual development? He
didn't know. She watched in total silence, as still as the monk
at the center of the flames, and afterward she would say nothing; even if he spoke to her, questioned her, she just sat transfixed before that set for minutes on end, her gaze focused
somewhere else than on the flickering screen, focused inward
—inward where the coherence and the certainty were supposed
to be, where everything she did not know was initiating a gigantic upheaval, where nothing that registered would ever fade
away. . . .

Though he didn't know how to stop her, he did try to find
ways to divert her attention, to make her forget this madness
that was going on halfway around the world for reasons having
nothing to do with her or her family—he took her at night to
drive golf balls with him, he took her to a couple of Yankee
games, he took her and Dawn for a quick trip down to the factory in Puerto Rico and a week of vacation in Ponce by the
beach, and then, one day, she did forget, but not because of
anything he had done. It had to do with the immolations—they
stopped. There were five, six, seven immolations and then
there were no more, and shortly thereafter Merry did become

herself again, thinking again about things immediate to her daily life and more appropriate to her years.

When this South Vietnamese president, Diem, the man against whom the martyred Buddhist monks had been directing their protest—when some months later he was assassinated (according to a CBS Sunday morning show, assassinated by the USA, by the CIA, who had propped him up in power in the first place), the news seemed to pass Merry by, and the Swede didn't convey it to her. By then this place called Vietnam no longer even existed for Merry, if it ever had except as an alien, unimaginable backdrop for a ghastly TV spectacle that had embedded itself in her impressionable mind when she was eleven years old.

She never spoke again of the martyrdom of the Buddhist monks, even after she became so committed to her own political protest. The fate of those monks back in 1963 appeared to have nothing whatsoever to do with what galvanized into expression, in 1968, a newly hatched vehemence against capitalist America's imperialist involvement in a peasant war of national liberation . . . and yet her father spent days and nights trying to convince himself that no other explanation existed, that nothing else sufficiently awful had ever happened to her, nothing causal even remotely large enough or shocking enough to explain how his daughter could be the bomber.

Five years pass. Angela Davis, a black philosophy professor of about Rita Cohen's age—born in Alabama in 1944, eight years before the birth in New Jersey of the Rimrock Bomber—a Communist professor at UCLA who is against the war, is tried in San Francisco for kidnapping, murder, and conspiracy. She is charged with supplying guns used in an armed attempt to free three black San Quentin convicts during their trial. A shotgun that killed the trial judge is said to have been purchased by her only days before the courthouse battle. For two months she lived underground, dodging the FBI, until she was apprehended in New York and extradited to California. All around the world, as far away as France and Algeria and the Soviet Union, her supporters claim that she is the victim of a political frame-up. Everywhere she is transported by the police as a prisoner, blacks and whites are waiting in the nearby streets, holding up placards for the TV cameras and shouting, "Free Angela! End political repression! End racism! End the war!"

Her hair reminds the Swede of Rita Cohen. Every time he sees that bush encircling her head he is reminded of what he should have done that afternoon in the hotel. He should not have let her get away from him, no matter what.

Now he watches the news to see Angela Davis. He reads everything he can about her. He knows that Angela Davis can get him to his daughter. He remembers how, when Merry was still at home, he went into her room one Saturday when she was off in New York, opened the bottom drawer of the dresser and, seated at her desk, read through everything in there, all that political stuff, the pamphlets, the paperbacks, the mimeographed booklets with the satiric cartoons. There was a copy of *The Communist Manifesto*. Where did she get that? Not in Old Rimrock. Who was supplying her with all this literature? Bill and Melissa. These weren't just diatribes against the war— they were written by people wanting to overthrow capitalism and the U.S. government, people screaming for violence and revolution. It was awful for him to come upon passages that, being the good student she was, she had neatly underlined, but he could not stop reading . . . and now he believes he can remember something in that drawer written by Angela Davis. There was no way of his knowing for sure because the FBI had confiscated it all, put all those publications into evidence bags, sealed them, and removed them from the house. They had dusted her room, looking for a solid set of fingerprints that they could use to match up with anything incriminating. They collected the household phone bills to trace Merry's calls. They searched her room for hiding places: pried up floorboards from beneath her rug, removed wainscoting from the walls, took the globe off the ceiling light—they went through the clothes in her closet, looking for things hidden in the sleeves. After the bombing, the state police stopped all traffic on Arcady Hill Road, closed off the area, and twelve FBI agents spent sixteen hours combing the house from the attic to the basement; when finally, in the kitchen, they searched the dustbag of the vacuum cleaner for "papers," Dawn had let out a scream. And all because of Merry's reading Karl Marx and Angela Davis!

Yes, now he remembers clearly sitting at Merry's desk trying to read Angela Davis himself, working at it, wondering how his child did it, thinking, Reading this stuff is like deep-sea diving. It's like being in an Aqua-Lung with the window right up against your face and the air in your mouth and no place to go, no place to move, no place to put a crowbar and escape. It's like reading those tiny pamphlets and illustrated holy cards about the saints that the old lady Dwyer used to give her in Elizabeth. Luckily the child outgrew them, but for a while, whenever she misplaced her fountain pen, she'd pray to St. Anthony, and whenever she thought she hadn't studied enough for a test, she prayed to St. Jude, and whenever her mother made her spend a Saturday morning cleaning up her messy room, she prayed to St. Joseph, the patron saint of laborers. Once when she was nine and some diehards down at Cape May reported that the Virgin Mary appeared to their children in their barbecue and people flocked in from miles around and kept vigil in their yard, Merry was fascinated, perhaps less by the mystery of the Virgin's appearance in New Jersey than by a child's having been singled out to see her. "I wish I could see that," she told her father, and she told him about how apparitions of the Virgin Mary had appeared to three shepherd children in Fátima, in Portugal, and he nodded and held his tongue, though when her grandfather got wind of the Cape May vision from his granddaughter, he said to her, "I guess next they'll see her at the Dairy Queen," a remark Merry repeated down in Elizabeth. Grandma Dwyer then prayed to St. Anne to help Merry stay Catholic despite her upbringing, but in a couple of years saints and prayer had disappeared from Merry's life; she stopped wearing the Miraculous Medal, with the impression on it of the Blessed Virgin, which she had sworn to Grandma Dwyer to wear "perpetually" without even taking it off to bathe. She outgrew the saints just as she would have outgrown the Communism. And she *would* have outgrown it—Merry outgrew everything. It was merely a matter of months. Maybe weeks and the stuff in that drawer would have been completely forgotten. All she had to do was wait. If only she could have waited. That was Merry's story in a nutshell. She was impatient. She was always impatient. Maybe it was the stuttering that made her impatient, I don't know. But

whatever it was she was passionate about, she was passionate
for a year, she did it in a year, and then she got rid of it overnight. Another year and she would have been ready for college.
And by then she would have found something new to hate and
new to love, something new to be intense about, and that
would have been that.

At the kitchen table one night Angela Davis appears to the
Swede, as Our Lady of Fátima did to those children in Portugal,
as the Blessed Virgin did down in Cape May. He thinks, Angela
Davis can get me to her—and there she is. Alone in the kitchen
at night the Swede begins to have heart-to-heart talks with
Angela Davis, at first about the war, then about everything important to both of them. As he envisions her, she has long
lashes and wears large hoop earrings and is more beautiful even
than she looks on television. Her legs are long and she wears
colorful minidresses to expose them. The hair is extraordinary.
She peers defiantly out of it like a porcupine. The hair says,
"Do not approach if you don't like pain."

He tells her whatever she wants to hear, and whatever she
tells him he believes. He has to. She praises his daughter,
whom she calls "a soldier of freedom, a pioneer in the great
struggle against repression." He should take pride in her political boldness, she says. The antiwar movement is an anti-
imperialist movement, and by lodging a protest in the only
way America understands, Merry, at sixteen, is in the forefront
of the movement, a Joan of Arc of the movement. His daughter
is the spearhead of the popular resistance to a fascist government and its terrorist suppression of dissent. What she did was
criminal only inasmuch as it is defined as criminal by a state
that is itself criminal and will commit ruthless aggression anywhere in the world to preserve the unequal distribution of
wealth and the oppressive institutions of class domination. The
disobedience of oppressive laws, she explains to him, including
violent disobedience, goes back to abolitionism—his daughter
is one with John Brown!

Merry's was not a criminal act but a political act in the power
struggle between the counterrevolutionary fascists and the
forces of resistance—blacks, Chicanos, Puerto Ricans, Indians,
draft resisters, antiwar activists, heroic white kids like Merry
herself, working, either by legal means or by what Angela calls

extralegal means, to overthrow the capitalist-inspired police state. And he should not fear for her fugitive life—Merry is not alone, she is part of an army of eighty thousand radical young people who have gone underground the better to fight the social wrongs fostered by an oppressive politico-economic order. Angela tells him that everything he has heard about Communism is a lie. He must go to Cuba if he wants to see a social order that has abolished racial injustice and the exploitation of labor and is in harmony with the needs and aspirations of its people.

Obediently he listens. She tells him that imperialism is a weapon used by wealthy whites to pay black workers less for their work, and that's when he seizes the opportunity to tell her about the black forelady, Vicky, thirty years with Newark Maid, a tiny woman of impressive wit, stamina, and honesty, with twin sons, Newark Rutgers graduates, Donny and Blaine, both of them now in medical school. He tells her how Vicky alone stayed with him in the building, round the clock, during the '67 riots. On the radio, the mayor's office was advising everyone to get out of the city immediately, but he had stayed, because he thought that by being there he could perhaps protect the building from the vandals and also for the reason that people stay when a hurricane hits, because they cannot leave behind the things they cherish. For something like that reason, Vicky stayed.

In order to appease any rioters who might be heading from South Orange Avenue with their torches, Vicky had made signs and stuck them where they would be visible, in Newark Maid's first-floor windows, big white cardboard signs in black ink: "Most of this factory's employees are NEGROES." Two nights later every window with a sign displayed in it was shot out by a band of white guys, either vigilantes from north Newark or, as Vicky suspected, Newark cops in an unmarked car. They shot the windows out and drove away, and that was the total damage done to the Newark Maid factory during the days and nights when Newark was on fire. And he tells this to St. Angela.

A platoon of the young National Guardsmen who were on Bergen Street to seal off the riot zone had camped out back by the Newark Maid loading dock on the second day of fighting, and when he and Vicky went down with hot coffee, Vicky talked to each of them—uniformed kids, in helmets and boots, conspicuously armed with knives and rifles and bayonets, white country boys up from south Jersey who were scared out of their wits. Vicky told them, "Think before you shoot into somebody's window! These aren't 'snipers'! These are people! These are good people! Think!" The Saturday afternoon the tank sat out in front of the factory—and the Swede, seeing it there, could at last phone Dawn to tell her, "We'll make it"— Vicky had gone up and knocked on the lid with her fists until they opened up. "Don't go nuts!" she shouted at the soldiers inside. "Don't go crazy! People have to live here when you're gone! This place is their *home*!" There'd been a lot of criticism afterward of Governor Hughes for sending in tanks, but not from the Swede—those tanks put a stop to what could have been total disaster. Though this he does not say to Angela.

For the two worst, most terrifying days, Friday and Saturday, July 14 and 15, 1967, while he kept in touch with the state police on a walkie-talkie and with his father on the phone, Vicky would not desert him. She told him, "This is mine too. You just own it." He tells Angela how he knew the way things worked between Vicky and his family, knew it was an old and lasting relationship, knew how close they all were, but he had never properly understood that her devotion to Newark Maid was no less than his. He tells Angela how, after the riots, after living under siege with Vicky at his side, he was determined to stand alone and not leave Newark and abandon his black employees. He does not, of course, tell her that he wouldn't have hesitated—and wouldn't still—to pick up and move were it not for his fear that, if he should join the exodus of businesses not yet burned down, Merry would at last have her airtight case against him. *Victimizing black people and the working class and the poor solely for self-gain, out of filthy greed!*

In the idealistic slogans there was no reality, not a drop of it, and yet what else could he do? He could not provide his daughter with the justification for doing something crazy. So he stayed in Newark, and after the riots Merry did something crazier than crazy. The Newark riots, then the Vietnam War; the city, then the entire country, and that took care of the Seymour Levovs of Arcady Hill Road. First the one colossal

blow—seven months later, in February '68, the devastation of
the next. The factory under siege, the daughter at large, and
that took care of their future.

On top of everything else, after the sniper fire ended and the
flames were extinguished and twenty-one Newarkers were
counted dead by gunfire and the National Guard was withdrawn and Merry had disappeared, the quality of the Newark
Maid line began to fall off because of negligence and indifference on the part of his employees, a marked decline in workmanship that had the effect of sabotage even if he couldn't call
it that. He does not tell Angela, for all that he is tempted to,
about the struggle his decision to stay on in Newark has precipitated between himself and his own father; might only antagonize her against Lou Levov and deter her from leading
them to Merry.

"What we've got now," his father argued each time he flew
up from Florida to plead with his son to get the hell out before
a second riot destroyed the rest of the city, "is that every step
of the way we're no longer making one step, we're making
two, three, and four steps. Every step of the way you have got
to go back a step to get it cut again, to get it stitched again,
and nobody is doing a day's work and nobody is doing it right.
A whole business is going down the drain because of that son
of a bitch LeRoi Jones, that Peek-A-Boo-Boopy-Do, whatever
the hell he calls himself in that goddamn hat. I built this with
my *hands*! With my blood! They think somebody gave it to me?
Who? Who gave it to me? Who gave me anything, ever?
Nobody! What I have I built! With work—w-o-r-k! But they
took that city and now they are going to take that business and
everything that I built up a day at a time, an *inch* at a time, and
they are going to leave it *all* in ruins! And that'll do 'em a
world of good! They burn down their own houses—that'll
show whitey! Don't fix 'em up—burn 'em down. Oh, that'll do
wonders for a man's black pride—a totally ruined city to live
in! A great city turned into a total nowhere! They're just going
to love living in that! And *I* hired 'em! How's that for a laugh?
I hired 'em! 'You're nuts, Levov'—this is what my friends in the
steam room used to tell me—'What are you hiring schvartzes
for? You won't get gloves, Levov, you'll get dreck.' But I hired
'em, treated them like human beings, kissed Vicky's ass for

twenty-five years, bought all the girls a Thanksgiving turkey every goddamn Thanksgiving, came in every morning with my tongue hanging out of my mouth so I could lick their asses with it. 'How is everybody,' I said, 'how are we all, my time is yours, I don't want you complaining to anybody but me, here at this desk isn't just a boss, here is your ally, your buddy, your friend.' And the party I gave for Vicky's twins when they graduated? And what a jerk-off I was. *Am.* To this day! I'm by the pool and my wonderful friends look up from the paper and they tell me they ought to take the schvartzes and line 'em up and shoot 'em, and I'm the one who has to remind them that's what Hitler did to the Jews. And you know what they tell me, as an answer? 'How can you compare schvartzes to Jews?' They are telling me to shoot the schvartzes and I am hollering no, and meanwhile I'm the one whose business they are ruining because they cannot make a glove that fits. Bad cutting, the stretch is wrong—the glove won't even go *on.* Careless people, careless, and it is inexcusable. One operation goes wrong, the whole operation is spoiled all the way through, and, still, when I am arguing with these fascist bastards, Seymour, Jewish men, men of my age who have seen what I've seen, who should know better *a million times over*, when I am arguing with them, *I am arguing against what I should be arguing for!*" "Well, sometimes you wind up doing that," the Swede said. "Why? Tell me why!" "I suppose out of conscience." "*Conscience?* Where is *theirs*, the schvartzes' conscience? Where is *their* conscience after working for me for twenty-five years?"

Whatever it cost him to deny his father relief from his suffering, stubbornly to defy the truth of what his father was saying, the Swede could not submit to the old man's arguments, for the simple reason that if Merry were to learn—and she would, through Rita Cohen, if Rita Cohen actually had anything to do with her—that Newark Maid had fled the Central Avenue factory she would be all too delighted to think, "He did it! He's as rotten as the rest! My own father! Everything justified by the profit principle! Everything! Newark's just a black colony for my own father. Exploit it and exploit it and then, when there's trouble, fuck it!"

These thoughts and thoughts even stupider—engendered in her by the likes of *The Communist Manifesto*—would surely foreclose any chance of ever seeing her again. Despite all that he could tell Angela Davis that might favorably influence her about his refusal to desert Newark and his black employees, he knows that the personal complications of that decision could not begin to conform to the utter otherworldliness of the ideal of St. Angela, and so he decides instead to explain to a vision that he is one of two white trustees (this is not true—the father of a friend is the trustee) of an antipoverty organization that meets regularly in Newark to promote the city's comeback, which (also not true—how could it be?) he still believes in. He tells Angela that he attends evening meetings all over Newark despite his wife's fears. He is trying to do everything he can for the liberation of her people. He reminds himself to repeat these words to her every night: the liberation of the people, America's black colonies, the inhumanity of the society, embattled humanity.

He does not tell Angela that his daughter is childishly boasting, lying in order to impress her, that his daughter knows nothing about dynamite or revolution, that these are just words to her and she blurts them out to make herself feel powerful despite her speech impediment. No, Angela is the person who knows Merry's whereabouts, and if Angela has come to him like this, it's no mere friendly visit. Why would Angela Davis drop out of nowhere into the Levovs' Old Rimrock kitchen at midnight every single night if she weren't the revolutionary leader assigned to looking after his daughter's well-being? What's in it for her otherwise—why else would she keep coming back?

So he says to her *yes*, his daughter *is* a soldier of freedom, yes, he *is* proud, yes, everything he has heard about Communism *is* a lie, yes, the United States *is* concerned solely with making the world safe for business and keeping the have-nots from encroaching on the haves—yes, the United States is responsible for oppression *everywhere*. Everything is justified by her cause, Huey Newton's cause, Bobby Seale's cause, George Jackson's cause, Merry Levov's cause. Meanwhile he mentions Angela's name to no one, certainly not to Vicky, who thinks Angela Davis is a troublemaker and who says as much to the girls at work. Alone then and in secret he prays—ardently prays to God, to Jesus, to anyone, to the Blessed Virgin, to St. Anthony, St.

Jude, St. Anne, St. Joseph—for Angela's acquittal. And when it
happens he is jubilant. She is free! But he does not send her
the letter that he sits up writing in the kitchen that night, nor
does he some weeks later when Angela, in New York, behind a
four-sided shield of bulletproof glass and before fifteen thousand exultant supporters, demands the freedom of political
prisoners deprived of due process and unjustly imprisoned.
Free the Rimrock Bomber! Free my daughter! Free her, please!
cries the Swede. "I think it's about time," Angela says, "for all
of us to begin to teach the rulers of this country a few lessons,"
and yes, cries the Swede, yes, it *is* about time, a socialist revolution in the United States of America! But nonetheless he remains alone at his kitchen table because he still cannot do
anything that he should do or believe anything that he should
believe or even know any longer what it is he does believe. Did
she do it or didn't she do it? He should have fucked Rita
Cohen, if only to find out—fucked the conniving little sexual
terrorist until she was his slave! Until she took him to the hideout where they made the bombs! *If you want to see your daughter as much as you say, you'll just calm down and come over here
and give Rita Cohen a nice big fuck.* He should have looked at
her cunt and tasted it and fucked her. Is that what any father
would have done? If he would do anything for Merry, why not
that? Why did he run?

And this is just a part of what is meant by "Five years pass." A
very tiny part. Everything he reads or sees or hears has a single
significance. Nothing is impersonally perceived. For one whole
year he cannot go into the village without seeing where the
general store used to be. To buy a newspaper or a quart of milk
or a tank of gas he has to drive almost clear into Morristown,
and so does everybody else in Old Rimrock. The same to buy
a stamp. Basically the village is one street. Going east there is
the new Presbyterian church, a white pseudocolonial building
that doesn't look like much of anything and that replaced the
old Presbyterian church that burned to the ground in the
twenties. Just a little ways from the church are The Oaks, a
pair of two-hundred-year-old oak trees that are the town's
pride. Some thirty yards beyond The Oaks is the old blacksmith
shop that was converted, just before Pearl Harbor, into the

Home Shop, where local women go to buy wallpaper and lampshades and decorative knicknacks and to get advice from Mrs. Fowler about interior decorating. Down at the far end of the street is the auto-repair garage run by Perry Hamlin, a hard-drinking cousin of Russ Hamlin's who also canes chairs, and then beyond that, encompassing some five hundred acres, is the rolling terrain of the dairy farm owned and worked by Paul Hamlin, who is Perry's younger brother. Hills like these where Hamlins have farmed now for close to two hundred years run northeast to southwest, in a thirty- or forty-mile-wide swath, crossing north Jersey at around Old Rimrock, a range of small hills that continue up into New York to become the Catskills and from there all the way up to Maine.

Diagonally across from where the store used to be is the yellow-stuccoed six-room schoolhouse. Before they sent her to the Montessori school and then on to Morristown High, Merry had been a pupil there for the first four grades. Every kid who goes there now sees every day where the store used to be, as do their teachers, as do their parents when they drive into the village. The Community Club meets at the school, they hold their chicken suppers there, people vote there, and everybody who drives up there and sees where the store used to be thinks about the explosion and the good man it killed, thinks about the girl who set off the explosion, and, with varying degrees of sympathy or of contempt, thinks about her family. Some people are overly friendly; others, he knows, try their best to avoid running into him. He receives anti-Semitic mail. It is so vile it sickens him for days on end. He overhears things. Dawn overhears things. "Lived here all my life. Never saw anything like this before." "What can you expect? They have no business being out here to begin with." "I thought they were nice people, but you never know." An editorial from the local paper, recording the tragedy and commemorating Dr. Conlon, is thumbtacked to the Community Club bulletin board and hangs there, right out by the street. There is no way that the Swede can take it down, much as he would like to, for Dawn's sake at least. You would think that what with exposure to the rain and the wind and the sun and the snow the thing would rot away in a matter of weeks, but it not only remains intact but is almost completely legible for one whole year. The editorial is called "Dr. Fred." "We live in a society where violence is be-coming all too prevalent . . . we do not know why and we may never understand . . . the anger that all of us feel . . . our hearts go out to the victim and his family, to the Hamlins, and to an entire community that is trying to understand and to cope with what has happened . . . a remarkable man and a wonderful physician who touched all our lives . . . a special fund in memory of 'Doctor Fred' . . . to contribute to this memorial, which will help indigent local families in time of medical need . . . in this time of grief, we must rededicate ourselves, in his memory. . . ." Alongside the editorial is an article headlined "Distance Heals All Wounds," which begins, "We'd all just as soon forget . . ." and continues, ". . . that soothing distance will come quicker to some than others. . . . The Rev. Peter Baliston of the First Congregational Church, in his sermon, sought to find some good in all the tragedy . . . will bring the community closer together in a shared sorrow. . . . The Rev. James Viering of St. Patrick's Church gave an impassioned homily. . . ." Beside that article is a third clip-ping, one that has no business being there, but he cannot tear that one down any more than he can go ahead and tear down the others, so it, too, hangs there for a year. It is the interview with Edgar Bartley—both the interview and the picture of Edgar from the paper, showing him standing in front of his family's house with a shovel and his dog and behind him the path to the house freshly cleared of snow. Edgar Bartley is the boy from Old Rimrock who'd taken Merry to the movies in Morristown some two years before the bombing. He was a year ahead of her at the high school, a boy as tall as Merry and, as the Swede remembered him, nice enough looking though terrifically shy and a bit of an oddball. The newspaper story de-scribes him as Merry's boyfriend at the time of the bombing, though as far as her parents knew, Merry's date with Edgar Bartley two years earlier was the one and only date she'd ever had with him or with anyone. Whatever, someone has under-lined in black all the quotations attributed to Edgar. Maybe a friend of his did it as a joke, a high school joke. Maybe the arti-cle with the photograph was hung there as a joke in the first place. Joke or not, there it remains, month after month, and the Swede cannot get rid of it. "It doesn't seem real. . . . I never thought she would do something like this. . . . I knew her as a very nice girl. I never heard her say anything vicious. I'm sure something snapped. . . . I hope they find her so that she can get the help that she needs. . . . I always thought of Old Rimrock as a place where nothing can happen to you. But now I'm like everybody, I'm looking over my shoulder. It's going to take time before things return to normal. . . . I'm just moving on. I have to. I have to forget about it. Like nothing happened. But it's very sad."

The only solace the Swede can take from the Community Club bulletin board is that no one has posted there the clipping whose headline reads "Suspected Bomber Is Described as Bright, Gifted but with 'Stubborn Streak.'" That one he *would* have torn down. He would have had to go there in the middle of the night and just do it. This one article is no worse, probably, than any of the others that were appearing then, not just in their local weekly but in the New York papers—the *Times*, the *Daily News*, the *Daily Mirror*, the *Post*; in the Jersey dailies—the *Newark News*, the *Newark Star-Ledger*, the *Morristown Record*, the *Bergen Record*, the *Trenton Times*, the *Paterson News*; in the nearby Pennsylvania papers—the *Philadelphia Inquirer*, the *Philadelphia Bulletin*, and the *Easton Express*; and in *Time* and *Newsweek*. Most of the papers and the wire services dropped the story after the first week, but the *Newark News* and the *Morristown Record* in particular wouldn't let up—the *News* had three star reporters on the case, and both papers were churning out their stories about the Rimrock Bomber every single day for weeks. The *Record*, with its local orientation, couldn't stop reminding its readers that the Rimrock bombing was the most shattering disaster in Morris County since the September 12, 1940, Hercules Powder Company explosion, some twelve miles away in Kenvil, when fifty-two people were killed and three hundred injured. There had been a murder of a minister and a choirmaster in the late twenties, down in Middlesex County, in a lane just outside New Brunswick, and in the Morris village of Brookside there had been a murder by an inmate who had walked off the grounds of the Greystone mental asylum, visited his uncle in Brookside, and split the man's head open with an ax—and these stories, too, are dug up and rehashed. And, of course, the Lindbergh kidnapping down in Hopewell, New Jersey, the abduction and murder of the infant son of Charles A. Lindbergh, the famous transatlantic aviator—that, too, the papers luridly recall, reprinting details over thirty years old about the ransom, the baby's battered corpse, the Flemington trial, reprinting newspaper excerpts from April 1936 about the electrocution of the convicted kidnapper-murderer, an immigrant carpenter named Bruno Hauptmann. Day after day, Merry Levov is mentioned in the context of the region's slender history of atrocities—her name several times appearing right alongside Hauptmann's—and yet nothing of what's written wounds him as savagely as the story about her "stubborn streak" in the local weekly. There is something concealed there—yet implicit—a degree of provincial smugness, of simplemindedness, of sheer stupidity, that is so enraging to him that he could not have borne to see it hanging up for everybody to read and to shake their heads over at the Community Club bulletin board. Whatever Merry may or may not have done, he could not have allowed her life to be on display like that just outside the school.

SUSPECTED BOMBER IS DESCRIBED AS BRIGHT, GIFTED BUT WITH "STUBBORN STREAK"

To her teachers at Old Rimrock Community School, Meredith "Merry" Levov, who allegedly bombed Hamlin's General Store and killed Old Rimrock's Dr. Fred Conlon, was known as a multi-talented child, an excellent student and somebody who never challenged authority. People looking to her childhood for some clue about her alleged violent act remained stymied when they remembered her as a cooperative girl full of energy.

"We are in disbelief," ORCS Principal Eileen Morrow said about the suspected bomber. "It is hard to understand why this happened."

As a student at the six-room elementary school, Principal Morrow said, Merry Levov was "very helpful and never in trouble."

"She's not the kind of person who would do that," Mrs. Morrow said. "At least not when we knew her here."

At ORCS, Merry Levov had a straight A average and was involved in school activities, Mrs. Morrow said, and was well liked by both students and faculty.

"She was hard-working and enthusiastic and set very high standards for herself," Mrs. Morrow said. "Her teachers respected her as a quality student and her peers admired her."

At ORCS Merry Levov was a talented art student and a leader in team sports, particularly kickball. "She was just a normal kid growing up," Mrs. Morrow said. "This is something we would never have dreamt could happen," the principal said. "Unfortunately, nobody can see the future."

Mrs. Morrow said that Meredith associated with "model students" at the school, though she did show a "stubborn streak," for example, sometimes refusing to do school assignments which she thought unnecessary.

Others remembered the alleged bomber's stubborn streak, when she went on to become a student at Morristown High School. Sally Curren, a 16-year-old classmate, described Meredith as someone with an attitude she described as "arrogant and superior to everybody else."

But 16-year-old Barbara Turner said Meredith "seemed nice enough, though she had her beliefs."

Though Morristown High students asked about Merry had many different impressions, all the students who knew her agreed that she "talked a lot about the Vietnam war." Some students remembered her "lashing out in anger" if somebody else opposed her way of thinking about the presence of American troops in Vietnam.

According to her homeroom teacher, Mr. William Paxman, Meredith had been "working hard and doing well, A's or B's" and had expressed a strong interest in attending his alma mater, Penn State.

"If you mention her family, people say, 'What a nice family,'" Mr. Paxman said. "We just can't believe this has happened."

The only ominous note about her activities came from one of the alleged bomber's teachers who has been interviewed by agents from the FBI. "They told me, 'We have received a great deal of information about Miss Levov.'"

For a year there is "where the store used to be." Then construction begins on a new store, and month after month he watches it going up. One day a big red, white, and blue banner appears—"Greatly Expanded! New! New! New! McPherson's Store!"—announcing the grand opening on the Fourth of July. He has to sit Dawn down and tell her they are going to shop at the new store like everyone else and, though for a while it will not be easy for them, eventually. . . . But it is never easy. He cannot go into the new store without remembering the old store, even though the Russ Hamlins have retired and the new store is owned by a young couple from Easton who care nothing about the past and who, in addition to an expanded general store, have put in a bakery that turns out delicious cakes and pies as well as bread and rolls baked fresh every day. At the back of the store, alongside the post office window, there is now a little counter where you can buy a cup of coffee and a fresh bun and sit and chat with your neighbor or read your paper if you want to. McPherson's is a tremendous improvement over Hamlin's, and soon everybody around seems to have forgotten their blown-up old-fashioned country store, except for the local Hamlins and for the Levovs. Dawn cannot go near the new place, simply refuses to go in there, while the Swede makes it his business, on Saturday mornings, to sit at the counter with his paper and a cup of coffee, despite what anybody who sees him there may be thinking. He buys his Sunday paper there too. He buys his stamps there. He could bring stamps home from his office, could do all the family mailing in Newark, but he prefers to patronize the post office window at McPherson's and to linger there musing over the weather with young Beth McPherson the way he used to enjoy the same moment with Mary Hamlin, Russ's wife.

That is the outer life. To the best of his ability, it is conducted just as it used to be. But now it is accompanied by an inner life, a gruesome inner life of tyrannical obsessions, stifled inclinations, superstitious expectations, horrible imaginings, fantasy conversations, unanswerable questions. Sleeplessness and self-castigation night after night. Enormous loneliness. Unflagging remorse, even for that kiss when she was eleven and he was thirty-six and the two of them, in their wet bathing suits, were driving home together from the Deal beach. Could *that* have done it? Could *anything* have done it? Could *nothing* have done it?

Kiss me the way you k-k-kiss umumumother.

And in the everyday world, nothing to be done but respectably carry on the huge pretense of living as himself, with all the shame of masquerading as the ideal man.

5

Sept. 1, 1973

Dear Mr. Levov,

Merry is working in the old dog and cat hospital on New Jersey Railroad Avenue in the Ironbound Section of Newark, 115 N.J. Railroad Avenue, five minutes from Penn Station. She is there every day. If you wait outside you can catch her leaving work and heading home just after four P.M. She doesn't know I'm writing this letter to you. I am at the breaking point and can't go on. I want to go away but I can leave her to no one. You have to take over. Though I warn you that if you tell her that it was from me that you discovered her whereabouts, you will be doing her serious harm. She is an incredible spirit. She has changed everything for me. I got into this over my head because I couldn't ever resist her power. That is too much to get into here. You must believe me when I tell you that I never said anything or did anything other than what Merry demanded me to say and to do. She is an overwhelming force. You and I were in the same boat. I lied to her only once. That was about what happened at the hotel. If I had told her that you refused to make love with me she would have refused to take the money. She would have been back begging on the streets. I would never have made you suffer so if I hadn't the strength of my love for Merry to help me. To you that will sound crazy. I am telling you it is so. Your daughter is divine. You cannot be in the presence of such suffering without succumbing to its holy power. You don't know what a nobody I was before I met Merry. I was headed for oblivion. But I can't take any more. YOU MUST NOT MENTION ME TO MERRY EXCEPT AS SOMEONE WHO TORMENTED YOU EXACTLY AS I DID. DO NOT MENTION THIS LETTER IF YOU CARE ABOUT MERRY'S SURVIVAL. You must take every precaution before getting to the hospital. She could not survive the FBI. Her name is Mary Stoltz. She must be allowed to fulfill her destiny. We can only stand as witnesses to the anguish that sanctifies her.

The Disciple Who Calls Herself "Rita Cohen"

He could never root out the unexpected thing. The unexpected thing would be waiting there unseen, for the rest of his life ripening, ready to explode, just a millimeter behind everything else. The unexpected thing was the other *side* of everything else. He had already parted with everything, then remade everything, and now, when everything appeared to be back under his control, he was being incited to part with everything again. And if that should happen, the unexpected thing becoming the only thing . . .

Thing, thing, thing, thing—but what other word was tolerable? They could not be forever in bondage to this fucking thing! For five years he had been waiting for just such a letter —it had to come. Every night in bed he begged God to deliver it the following morning. And then, in this amazing transitional year, 1973, the year of Dawn's miracle, during these months when Dawn was giving herself over to designing the new house, he had begun to dread what he might find in the morning's mail or hear each time he picked up the phone. How could he allow the unexpected thing back into their lives now that Dawn had ruled out of their lives forever the improbability of what had happened? Leading his wife back to herself had been like flying them through a five-year storm. He had fulfilled every demand. To disentangle her from her horror, there wasn't anything he had omitted to do. Life had returned to something like its recognizable proportions. Now tear the letter up and throw it away. Pretend it never arrived.

Because Dawn had twice been hospitalized in a clinic near Princeton for suicidal depression, he had come to accept that the damage was permanent and that she would be able to function only under the care of psychiatrists and by taking sedatives and an antidepressant medication—that she would be in and out of psychiatric hospitals and that he would be visiting her in those places for the rest of their lives. He imagined that once or twice a year he would find himself sitting at the side of her bed in a room where there were no locks on the door. There would be flowers he'd sent her in a vase on the writing desk; on a windowsill, the ivy plants he'd brought from her study, thinking it might help her to care for something; on the bedside table framed photographs of himself and Merry and

Dawn's parents and brother. At the side of the bed he himself would be holding her hand while she sat propped up against the pillows in her Levi's and a big turtleneck sweater and wept. "I'm frightened, Seymour. I'm frightened all the time." He would sit patiently there beside her whenever she began to tremble and he would tell her to just breathe, slowly breathe in and out and think of the most pleasant place on earth that she knew of, imagine herself in the most wonderfully calming place in the entire world, a tropical beach, a beautiful mountain, a holiday landscape from her childhood . . . and he would do this even when the trembling was brought on by a tirade aimed at him. Sitting up on the bed, with her arms crossed in front of her as though to warm herself, she would hide the whole of her body inside the sweater—turn the sweater into a tent by extending the turtleneck up over her chin, stretching the back under her buttocks, and drawing the front across her bent knees, down over her legs, and beneath her feet. Often she sat tented like that all the time he was there. "You know when I was in Princeton last? I do! I was invited by the governor. To his mansion. Here, to Princeton, to his mansion. I had dinner at the governor's mansion. I was twenty-two—in an evening gown and scared to death. His chauffeur drove me from Elizabeth and I danced in my crown with the governor of New Jersey—so how did *this* happen? How have I wound up *here*? You, that's how! You wouldn't leave me alone! *Had* to have me! *Had* to marry me! I just wanted to become a teacher! That's what I *wanted*. I *had* the job. I had it *waiting*. To teach kids music in the Elizabeth system, and to be left alone by boys, and that was it. I never wanted to be Miss America! I never wanted to marry *anyone*! But you wouldn't let me *breathe* —you wouldn't let me out of your *sight*. All I ever wanted was my college education and that job. I should never have left Elizabeth! Never! Do you know what Miss New Jersey did for my life? It ruined it. I only went after the damn scholarship so Danny could go to college and my father wouldn't have to pay. Do you think if my father didn't have the heart attack I would have entered for Miss Union County? No! I just wanted to win the money so Danny could go to college without the burden on my dad! I didn't do it for boys to go traipsing after me everywhere—I was trying to help out at home! But then you arrived. You! Those hands! Those shoulders! Towering over me with your *jaw*! This huge animal I couldn't get rid of! You wouldn't leave me be! Every time I looked up, there was my boyfriend, gaga because I was a ridiculous beauty queen! You were like some *kid*! You had to make me into a *princess*. Well, look where I have wound up! In a madhouse! Your princess is in a *madhouse*!"

For years to come she would be wondering how what happened to her could have happened to her and blaming him for it, and he would be bringing her food she liked, fruit and candy and cookies, in the hope that she might eat something aside from bread and water, and bringing her magazines in the hope that she might be able to concentrate on reading for even just half an hour a day, and bringing clothes that she could wear around the hospital grounds to accommodate to the weather when the seasons changed. At nine o'clock every evening, he would put away in her dresser whatever he'd brought for her, and he would hold her and kiss her good-bye, hold her and tell her he'd be seeing her the next night after work, and then he would drive the hour in the dark back to Old Rimrock remembering the terror in her face when, fifteen minutes before visiting hours were to end, the nurse put her head in the door to kindly tell Mr. Levov that it was almost time for him to go.

The next night she'd be angry all over again. He had swayed her from her real ambitions. He and the Miss America Pageant had put her off her program. On she went and he couldn't stop her. Didn't try. What did any of what she said have to do with why she was suffering? Everybody knew that what had broken her was quite enough in itself and that what she said had no bearing on anything. That first time she was in the hospital, he simply listened and nodded, and strange as it was to hear her going angrily on about an adventure that at the time he was certain she couldn't have enjoyed more, he sometimes wondered if it wasn't better for her to identify what had happened to her in 1949, not what had happened to her in 1968, as the problem at hand. "All through high school people were telling me, 'You should be Miss America.' I thought it was ridiculous. Based on what should I be Miss America? I was a clerk in a dry-goods store after school and in the summer, and people would come up to my cash register and say, 'You should be Miss

America.' I couldn't stand it. I couldn't stand when people said
I should do things because of the way that I looked. But when
I got a call from the Union County pageant to come to that
tea, what could I do? I was a baby. I thought this was a way for
me to kick in a little money so my father wouldn't have to
work so hard. So I filled out the application and I went, and after all the other girls left, that woman put her arm around me
and she told all her neighbors, 'I want you to know that you've
just spent the afternoon with the next Miss America.' I thought,
'This is all so silly. Why do people keep saying these things to
me? I don't want to be doing this.' And when I won Miss
Union County, people were already saying to me, 'We'll see
you in Atlantic City'—people who know what they're talking
about saying I'm going to win this thing, so how could I back
out? I couldn't. The whole front page of the *Elizabeth Journal*
was about me winning Miss Union County. I was mortified. I
was. I thought somehow I could keep it all a secret and just
win the money. I was a *baby*! I was sure *at least* I wasn't going
to win Miss New Jersey, I was *positive*. I looked around and
there was this sea of good-looking girls and they all knew what
to do, and I didn't know anything. They knew how to use hair
rollers and put false eyelashes on, and I couldn't roll my hair
right until I was halfway through my Miss New Jersey year. I
thought, 'Oh, my God, look at their makeup,' and they had
beautiful wardrobes and I had a prom dress and borrowed
clothes, and so I was convinced there was no way I could *ever*
win. I was so *introverted*. I was so *unpolished*. But I won *again*.
And then they were coaching me on how to sit and how to
stand, even how to *listen*—they sent me to a model agency to
learn how to *walk*. They didn't like the way I walked. I didn't
care how I walked—I *walked*! I walked well enough to become
Miss New Jersey, didn't I? If I don't walk well enough to become Miss America, the hell with it! But you have to *glide*.
No! I will walk the way I walk! Don't swing your arms too
much, but don't hold them stiffly at your side. All these little
tricks of the trade to make me so self-conscious I could barely
move! To land not on your heels but on the balls of your feet—
this is the kind of thing I went through. If I can just drop out
of this thing! How can I back out of this thing? Leave me
alone! All of you leave me alone! I never wanted this in the first

place! Do you see why I married you? *Now* do you understand?
One reason only! I wanted something that seemed normal! So
desperately after that year, I wanted something *normal*! How I
wish it had never happened! *None of it!* They put you up on a
pedestal, which I didn't ask for, and then they rip you off it so
damn fast it can *blind* you! And I did not ask for *any* of it! I
had nothing in common with those other girls. I hated them
and they hated me. Those tall girls with their big feet! None of
them gifted. All of them so *chummy*! I was a serious music student! All I wanted was to be left alone and not to have that
goddamn crown sparkling like crazy up on top of my head! I
never wanted *any* of it! *Never!*"

It was a great help to him, driving home after one of those
visits, to remember her as the girl she had really been back
then, who, as he recalled it, was nothing like the girl she portrayed as herself in those tirades. During the week in September
of 1949 leading up to the Miss America Pageant, when she
called Newark every night from the Dennis Hotel to tell him
about what happened to her that day as a Miss America contestant, what radiated from her voice was sheer *delight* in being
herself. He'd never heard her like that before—it was almost
frightening, this undisguised exulting in being where she was
and who she was and what she was. Suddenly life existed rapturously and for Dawn Dwyer alone. The surprise of this new
and uncharacteristic immoderation even made him wonder if,
when the week was over, she could ever again be content with
Seymour Levov. And suppose she should win. What chance
would he have against all the men who set their sights on marrying Miss America? Actors would be after her. Millionaires
would be after her. They'd flock to her—the new life opening up
to her could attract a host of powerful new suitors and wind up
excluding him. Nonetheless, as the current suitor, he was spellbound by the prospect of Dawn's winning; the more real a possibility it was, the more reasons he had to flush and perspire.

They would talk long distance for as long as an hour at a
time—she was too excited to sleep, even though she had been
on the go since breakfast, which she'd eaten in the dining room
with her chaperone, just the two of them at the table, the
chaperone a large local woman in a small hat, Dawn wearing
her Miss New Jersey sash pinned to her suit and, on her hands,

white kid gloves, tremendously expensive gloves, a present to her from Newark Maid, where the Swede was beginning his training to take over the business. All the girls wore the same style of white kid glove, four-button in length, up over the wrist. Dawn alone had got hers for nothing, along with a second pair of gloves—opera length, in black, Newark Maid's formal, sixteen-button kid glove (a small fortune at Saks), the table-cut workmanship as expert as anything from Italy or France —and, in addition, a third pair of gloves, above the elbow, custom made to match her evening gown. The Swede had asked Dawn for a yard of fabric the same as her gown, and a friend of the family's who did fabric gloves made them for Dawn as a courtesy to Newark Maid. Three times a day, seated across from the chaperones in the small hats, the girls, with their beautiful, nicely combed hair and neat, nice dresses and four-button gloves, attempted to have a meal, something of each course, at least, between giving autographs to all the people in the dining room who came over to gawk and to say where they were from. Because Dawn was Miss New Jersey and the hotel guests were *in* New Jersey, she was the most popular girl by far, and so she had to say a kind word to everyone and smile and sign autographs and still try to get something to eat. "This is what you have to do," she told him on the phone, "this is why they give you the free room."

When she arrived at the train station, they'd put her in a little convertible, a Nash Rambler, that had her name and her state on it, and her chaperone was in the convertible too. Dawn's chaperone was the wife of a local real-estate dealer, and everywhere Dawn went the chaperone was sure to go—in the car with her when she got in, and out of the car with her when she got out. "She does not leave my side, Seymour. You don't see a man the whole time except the judges. You can't even *talk* to one. A few boyfriends are here. Some are even fiancés. But what's the sense? The girls aren't allowed to see them. There's a book of rules so long I can hardly read through it. 'Members of the male sex are not permitted to talk to contestants except in the presence of their hostesses. At no time is a contestant permitted to enter a cocktail lounge or partake of an intoxicating beverage. Other rules include no padding—'" The Swede laughed. "Uh-oh." "Let me finish, Seymour—it just goes on and on. 'No one is permitted an interview with a contestant without her hostess present to protect her interests. . . .'"

Not just Dawn but all the girls got the little Nash Rambler convertibles—though not to keep. You got to keep it only if you became Miss America. Then it would be the car from which you waved to the capacity crowd when you were driven around the edge of the field at the most famous of college football games. The pageant was pushing the Rambler because American Motors was one of the sponsors.

There had been a box of Fralinger's Original saltwater taffy in the room when she arrived, and a bouquet of roses; everybody got both, compliments of the hotel, but Dawn's roses never opened, and the rooms the girls got—at least the girls put up at Dawn's hotel—were small, ugly, and at the back. But the hotel itself, as Dawn excitedly described it, at Boardwalk and Michigan Avenue, was one of the swanky ones where every afternoon they had a proper tea with little sandwiches and croquet was played on the lawn by the paying guests, who rightly enough got the big, beautiful rooms and the ocean views. Every night she'd come back exhausted to the ugly back room with the faded wallpaper, check to see if the roses had opened, and then phone to answer his questions about her chances.

She was one of four or five girls whose photographs kept appearing in the papers, and everybody said that one of these girls had to win—the New Jersey pageant people were sure they had a winner, especially when the photographs of her popped up every morning. "I hate to let them down," she told him. "You're not going to. You're going to win," he told her. "No, this girl from Texas is going to win. I know it. She's so pretty. She has a round face. She has a dimple. Not a beauty but very, very cute. And a great figure. I'm scared to death of her. She's from some tacky little town in Texas and she tap-dances and she's the one." "Is she in the papers with you?" "Always. She's one of the four or five *always*. I'm there because it's Atlantic City and I'm Miss New Jersey and the people on the boardwalk see me in my sash and they go nuts, but that happens to Miss New Jersey *every* year. And she *never* wins. But Miss Texas is there in those papers, Seymour, because she's going to win."

Earl Wilson, the famous syndicated newspaper columnist, was one of the ten judges, and when he heard that Dawn was from Elizabeth he was reported to have said to someone at the float parade, in which Dawn had ridden along the boardwalk with two other girls on the float of her hotel, that Elizabeth's longtime mayor, Joe Brophy, was one of his friends. Earl Wilson told someone who told someone who then told Dawn's chaperone. Earl Wilson and Joe Brophy were old friends—that was all Earl Wilson said, or was able to say in public, but Dawn's chaperone was sure he'd said it because after he'd seen Dawn in her evening gown on the float she'd become his candidate. "Okay," said the Swede, "one down, nine to go. You're on your way, Miss America."

All she talked about with her chaperone was who they thought her closest competition was; apparently this was all any of the girls talked about with their chaperones and all they wound up talking about when they called home, even if, among themselves, they pretended to love one another. The southern girls in particular, Dawn told him, could really lay it on: "Oh, you're just so wonderful, your hair's so wonderful. . . ." The veneration of hair took some getting used to for a girl as down-to-earth as Dawn; you might almost think, from listening to the conversation among the other girls, that life's possibilities resided in hair—not in the hands of your destiny but in the hands of your hair.

Together with the chaperones, they visited the Steel Pier and had a fish dinner at Captain Starn's famous seafood restaurant and yacht bar, and a steak dinner at Jack Guischard's Steak House, and the third morning they had their picture taken together in front of Convention Hall, where a pageant official told them the picture was one they would treasure for the rest of their lives, that the friendships they were making would last the rest of their lives, that they would keep up with one another for the rest of their lives, that when the time arrived they would name their children after one another—and meanwhile, when the papers came out in the morning, the girls said to their chaperones, "Oh God, I'm not in this. Oh God, this one looks like she's going to win."

Every day there were rehearsals and every night for a week they gave a show. Year after year people visited Atlantic City just for the Miss America contest and bought tickets for the nightly show and came all dressed up to see the girls on the stage individually exhibiting their talent and performing as an ensemble in costumed musical numbers. The one other girl who played piano played "Clair de Lune" for her solo performance and so Dawn had to herself the much flashier number, the currently popular hit "Till the End of Time," a danceable arrangement of a Chopin polonaise. "I'm in *show* business. I don't stop all day. You don't have a moment. Because New Jersey's host state there's all this focus on me, and I don't want to let everybody down, I really don't, I couldn't bear it—" "You won't, Dawnie. Earl Wilson's in your pocket, and he's the most famous of all the judges. I feel it. I know it. You're going to win."

But he was wrong. Miss Arizona won. Dawn didn't make it even into the top ten. In those days the girls waited backstage while the winners were announced. There was row after row of mirrors and tables lined up alphabetically by state, and Dawn was right in the middle of everyone when the announcement was made, so she had to start smiling to beat the band and clapping like crazy because she had lost and then, to make matters worse, had to rush back onstage and march around with the other losers, singing along with MC Bob Russell the Miss America song of that era: "Every flower, every rose, stands up on her tippy toes . . . when Miss America marches by!" while a girl just as short and slight and dark as she was—little Jacque Mercer from Arizona, who won the swimsuit competition but who Dawn never figured would win it all—took the crowd at Convention Hall by storm. Afterward, at the farewell ball, though it was for Dawn a terrific letdown, she wasn't nearly as depressed as most of the others. The same thing she had been told by the New Jersey pageant people they'd been told by *their* state pageant people: "You're going to make it. You're going to be Miss America." So the ball, she told him, was the saddest sight she'd ever seen. "You have to go and smile and it's awful," she said. "They have these people from the Coast Guard or wherever they're from—Annapolis. They have fancy white uniforms and braid and ribbons. I guess they're considered safe enough for us to dance with. So they dance with you with their chin tucked in, and the evening's over, and you go home."

Still, for months afterward the superstimulating adventure refused to die; even while she was being Miss New Jersey and going around snipping ribbons and waving at people and opening department stores and auto showrooms, she wondered aloud if anything so wonderfully unforeseen as that week in Atlantic City would ever happen to her again. She kept beside her bed the 1949 Official Yearbook of the Miss America Pageant, a booklet prepared by the pageant that was sold all week at Atlantic City: individual photos of the girls, four to a page, each with a tiny outline drawing of her state and a capsule biography. Where Miss New Jersey's photoportrait appeared—smiling demurely, Dawn in her evening gown with the matching twelve-button fabric gloves—the corner of the page had been neatly turned back. "Mary Dawn Dwyer, 22 year old Elizabeth, N.J. brunette, carries New Jersey's hopes in this year's Pageant. A graduate of Upsala College, East Orange, N.J., where she majored in music education, Mary Dawn has the ambition of becoming a high school music teacher. She is 5-2½ and blue-eyed, and her hobbies are swimming, square dancing, and cooking. (*Left above*)" Reluctant to give up excitement such as she'd never known before, she talked on and on about the fairy tale it had been for a kid from Hillside Road, a plumber's daughter from Hillside Road, to have been up in front of all those people, competing for the title of Miss America. She almost couldn't believe the courage she'd shown. "Oh, that ramp, Seymour. That's a long ramp, a long runway, it's a long way to go just smiling. . . ."

In 1969, when the invitation arrived in Old Rimrock for the twentieth reunion of the Miss America contestants of her year, Dawn was back in the hospital for the second time since Merry's disappearance. It was May. The psychiatrists were as nice as they were the first time, and the room was as pleasant, and the rolling landscape as pretty, and the walks were even prettier, with tulips around the bungalows where the patients lived, the huge fields green this time around, beautiful, beautiful views—and because this *was* the second time in two years, and because the place *was* beautiful, and because when he arrived directly from Newark in the early evening, after they had just cut the grass, there was a smell in the air as fresh and sharp as the smell of chives, it was all a thousand times worse. And so he did not show Dawn the invitation for the 1949 reunion.

Things were bad enough—the things she was saying to him were bizarre enough; the relentless crying about her shame, her mortification, the futility of her life was all quite sad enough —without any more of the Miss New Jersey business.

And then the change occurred. Something made her decide to want to be free of the unexpected, improbable thing. She was not going to be deprived of her life.

The heroic renewal began with the face-lift at the Geneva clinic she'd read about in *Vogue*. Before going to bed he'd see her at her bathroom mirror drawing the crest of her cheekbones back between her index fingers while simultaneously drawing the skin at her jawline back and upward with her thumbs, firmly tugging the loose flesh until she had eradicated even the natural creases of her face, until she was staring at a face that looked like the polished kernel of a face. And though it was clear to her husband that she had indeed begun to age like a woman in her mid-fifties at only forty-five, the remedy suggested in *Vogue* in no way addressed anything that mattered; so remote was it from the disaster that had befallen them he saw no reason to argue with her, thinking she knew the truth better than anyone, however much she might prefer to imagine herself another prematurely aging reader of *Vogue* rather than the mother of the Rimrock Bomber. But because she had run out of psychiatrists to see and medications to try and because she was terrified at the prospect of electric shock therapy should she have to be hospitalized a third time, the day came when he took her to Geneva. They were met at the airport by the liveried chauffeur and the limousine, and she booked herself into Dr. LaPlante's clinic.

In their suite of rooms the Swede slept in the bed beside hers. The night after the operation, when she could not stop vomiting, he was there to clean her up and to comfort her. During the next several days, when she wept from the pain, he sat at her bedside and, as he had night after night at the psychiatric clinic, held her hand, certain that this grotesque surgery, this meaningless, futile ordeal, was ushering in the final stage of her downfall as a recognizable human being: far from assisting at his wife's recovery, he understood himself to be acting as the unwitting accomplice to her mutilation. He looked at her head buried in bandages and felt he might as well be witnessing the preparation for burial of her corpse.

He was totally wrong. As it was to turn out, only a few days before the letter from Rita Cohen reached his office, he happened to pass Dawn's desk and to see there a brief handwritten letter beside an envelope addressed to the plastic surgeon in Geneva: "Dear Dr. LaPlante: A year has passed since you did my face. I do not feel that when I last saw you I understood what you have given me. That you would spend five hours of your time for my beauty fills me with awe. How can I thank you enough? I feel it's taken me these full twelve months to recover from the surgery. I believe, as you said, that my system was more beaten down than I had realized. Now it is as if I have been given a new life. Both from within and from the outside. When I meet old friends I have not seen for a while, they are puzzled as to what happened to me. I don't tell them. It is quite wonderful, dear doctor, and without you it would never have been possible. Much love and thank you, Dawn Levov."

Almost immediately after the reconstitution of her face to its former pert, heart-shaped pre-explosion perfection, she decided to build a small contemporary house on a ten-acre lot the other side of Rimrock ridge and to sell the big old house, the outbuildings, and their hundred-odd acres. (Dawn's beef cattle and the farm machinery had been sold off in '69, the year after Merry became a fugitive from justice; by then it was clear that the business was too demanding for Dawn to continue to run on her own, and so he took an ad in one of the monthly cattle magazines and within only weeks had got rid of the baler, the kicker, the rake, the livestock—everything, the works.) When he overheard her telling the architect, their neighbor Bill Orcutt, that she had always hated their house, the Swede was as stunned as if she were telling Orcutt she had always hated her husband. He went for a long walk, needed to walk almost the five miles down into the village to keep reminding himself that it was the *house* she said she'd always hated. But even her meaning no more than that left him so miserable it took all his considerable powers of suppression to turn himself around and head home for lunch, where Dawn and Orcutt were to review with him Orcutt's first set of sketches.

Hated their old stone house, the beloved first and only house? How could she? He had been dreaming about that house since he was sixteen years old and, riding with the baseball team to a game against Whippany—sitting there on the school bus in his uniform, idly rubbing his fingers around the deep pocket of his mitt as they drove along the narrow roads curving westward through the rural Jersey hills—he saw a large stone house with black shutters set on a rise back of some trees. A little girl was on a swing suspended from a low branch of one of those big trees, swinging herself high into the air, just as happy, he imagined, as a kid can be. It was the first house built of stone he'd ever seen, and to a city boy it was an architectural marvel. The random design of the stones *said* "House" to him as not even the brick house on Keer Avenue did, despite the finished basement where he'd taught Jerry Ping-Pong and checkers; despite the screened-in back porch where he'd lie in the dark on the old sofa and listen on hot nights to the Giant games; despite the garage where as a boy he would use a roll of black tape to affix a ball to the end of a rope hanging from a cross beam, where, all winter long, assuming his tall, erect, no-nonsense stance, he would duteously spend half an hour swinging at it with his bat after he came home from basketball practice, so as not to lose his timing; despite the bedroom under the eaves, with the two dormer windows, where the year before high school he'd put himself to sleep reading and re-reading *The Kid from Tomkinsville*—"A gray-haired man in a dingy shirt and a blue baseball cap well down over his eyes shoved an armful of clothes at the Kid and indicated his locker. 'Fifty-six. In the back row, there.' The lockers were plain wooden stalls about six feet high with a shelf one or two feet from the top. The front of his locker was open and along the edge at the top was pasted: 'TUCKER. NO. 56.' There was his uniform with the word 'DODGERS' in blue across the front and the number 56 on the back of the shirt. . . ."

The stone house was not only engagingly ingenious-looking to his eyes—all that irregularity regularized, a jigsaw puzzle fitted patiently together into this square, solid thing to make a beautiful shelter—but it looked indestructible, an impregnable house that could never burn to the ground and that had probably been standing there since the country began. Primitive stones, rudimentary stones of the sort that you would see scattered about among the trees if you took a walk along the paths in Weequahic Park, and out there they were a house. He couldn't get over it.

At school he'd find himself thinking about which girl in each of his classes to marry and take to live with him in that house. After the ride with the team to Whippany, he had only to hear someone saying "stone"—even saying "west"—and he would imagine himself going home after work to that house back of the trees and seeing his daughter there, his little daughter high up in the air on the swing he'd built for her. Though he was only a high school sophomore, he could imagine a daughter of his own running to kiss him, see her flinging herself at him, see himself carrying her on his shoulders into that house and straight on through to the kitchen, where standing by the stove in her apron, preparing their dinner, would be the child's adoring mother, who would be whichever Weequahic girl had shimmied down in the seat in front of him at the Roosevelt movie theater just the Friday before, her hair hanging over the back of her chair, within stroking distance, had he dared. All of his life he had this ability to imagine himself completely. Everything always added up to something whole. How could it not when he felt *himself* to add up, add up exactly to one?

Then he saw Dawn at Upsala. She'd be crossing the common to Old Main where the day students hung out between classes; she'd be standing under the eucalyptus trees talking with a couple of the girls who lived in Kenbrook Hall. Once he followed her down Prospect Street toward the Brick Church bus station when suddenly she stopped in front of the window at Best & Co. After she went inside the store, he went up to the window to look at the mannequin in a long "New Look" skirt and imagined Dawn Dwyer in a fitting room trying the skirt on over her slip. She was so lovely that it made him extraordinarily shy even to glance her way, as though glancing were itself touching or clinging, as though if she knew (and how could she not?) that he was uncontrollably looking her way, she'd do what any sensible, self-possessed girl would do, disdain him as a beast of prey. He'd been a U.S. Marine, he'd been engaged to a girl in South Carolina, at his family's request had broken off the engagement, and it was years since he'd thought about that stone house with the black shutters and the swing out front. Sensationally handsome as he was, fresh from the service and a glamorous campus athletic star however determinedly he worked at containing conceit and resisting the role, it took him a full semester to approach Dawn for a date, not only because nakedly confronting her beauty gave him a bad conscience and made him feel shamefully voyeuristic but because once he approached her there'd be no way to prevent her from looking right through him and into his mind and seeing for herself how he pictured her: there at the stove of the stone house's kitchen when he came trundling in with their daughter, Merry, on his back—"Merry" because of the joy she took in the swing he'd built her. At night he played continuously on his phonograph a song popular that year called "Peg o' My Heart." A line in the song went, "It's your Irish heart I'm after," and every time he saw Dawn Dwyer on the paths at Upsala, tiny and exquisite, he went around the rest of the day unaware that he was whistling that damn song nonstop. He would find himself whistling it even during a ballgame, while swinging a couple of bats in the on-deck circle, waiting his turn at the plate. He lived under two skies then—the Dawn Dwyer sky and the natural sky overhead.

But still he didn't immediately approach her, for fear that she'd see what he was thinking and laugh at his intoxication with her, this ex-marine's presumptuous innocence about the Upsala Spring Queen. She would think that his imagining, before they were even *introduced*, that she was especially intended to satisfy Seymour Levov's yearnings meant that he was still a child, vain and spoiled, when in fact what it meant to the Swede was that he was fully charged up with purpose long, long before anyone else he knew, with a grown man's aims and ambitions, someone who excitedly foresaw, in perfect detail, the outcome of his story. He had come home from the service at twenty in a rage to be "mature." If he was a child, it was only insofar as he found himself looking ahead into responsible manhood with the longing of a kid gazing into a candy-store window.

Understanding all too well why she wanted to sell the old house, he acceded to her wish without even trying to make her understand that the reason she wanted to go—because Merry was still there, in every room, Merry at age one, five, ten—was the reason he wanted to stay, a reason no less important than hers. But as she might not survive their staying—and he, it still seemed, could endure anything, however brutally it flew in the face of his own inclinations—he agreed to abandon the house he loved, not least for the memories it held of his fugitive child. He agreed to move into a brand-new house, open everywhere to the sun, full of light, just big enough for the two of them, with only a small extra room for guests out over the garage. A modern dream house—"luxuriously austere" was how Orcutt described it back to Dawn after sounding her out on what she had in mind—with electric baseboard heating (instead of the insufferable forced hot air that gave her sinusitis) and built-in Shaker-like furniture (instead of those dreary period pieces) and recessed ceiling lighting (instead of the million standing lamps beneath the gloomy oak beams) and large, clear casement windows throughout (instead of those mullioned old sashes that were always sticking), and with a basement as technologically up-to-date as a nuclear submarine (instead of that dank, cavernous cellar where her husband took guests to see the wine he had "laid down" for drinking in his old age, reminding them as they shuffled between the mildewed stone walls to be on guard against the low-slung cast-iron drainage pipes: "Your head, be careful, watch it there . . ."). He understood everything, all of it, understood just how awful it was for her, and so what could he do but accede? "Property is a responsibility," she said. "With no machinery and no cattle, you grow up a lot of grass. You're going to have to keep this mowed two or three times a year to keep it down. You have to have it bush-hogged—you can't just let things grow up into woods. You've got to keep them mowed and it's just ridiculously expensive and it's crazy for you to keep laying that money out year after year. There's keeping the barns from falling down—there's a *responsibility* you have with land. You just can't let it go. The best thing to do, the *only* thing to do," she told him, "is to move."

Okay. They'd move. But why did she have to tell Orcutt

she'd hated that house "from the day we found it"? That she was there only because her husband had "dragged" her there when she was too young to have any idea what it would be like trying to run a huge, antiquated, dark barn of a place in which something was always leaking or rotting or in need of repair? The reason she first went into cattle, she told him, was to get out of that terrible house.

And if that was true? To find this out so late in the game! It was like discovering an infidelity—all these years she had been unfaithful to the house. How could he have gone around dopily believing he was making her happy when there was no justification for his feelings, when they were absurd, when, year in, year out, she was seething with hatred for their house? How he had loved the providing. Had he only been given the opportunity to provide for *more* than the three of them. If only there had been more children in that big house, if only Merry had been raised among brothers and sisters whom she loved and who loved her, this thing might never have happened to them. But Dawn wanted from life something other than to be the slavish mom to half a dozen kids and the nursemaid to a two-hundred-year-old house—she wanted to raise beef cattle. Because of her being introduced, no matter where they went, as "a former Miss New Jersey," she was sure that even though she had a bachelor's degree people were always dismissing her as a bathing beauty, a mindless china doll, capable of doing nothing more productive for society than standing around looking pretty. It did not matter how many times she patiently explained to them, when they brought up her title, that she had entered at the local Union County level only because her father had the heart attack, and money was tight, and her brother Danny was graduating St. Mary's, and she thought that if she won—and she believed she had a chance not because of having been Upsala Spring Queen but because she was a music-education major who played classical piano—she could use the scholarship money that went with the title for Danny's college tuition, thereby unburdening . . .

But it didn't matter what she said or how much she said or how often she mentioned the piano: nobody believed her. Nobody really believed that she never wanted to look better than everybody else. They only thought that there are lots of

other ways to get a scholarship than to go walking around
Atlantic City in high heels and a bathing suit. She was always
telling people her serious reasons for becoming Miss New
Jersey and nobody even listened. They smiled. To them she
couldn't have serious reasons. They didn't want her to have serious reasons. All she could have for them was that face. Then
they could go away saying, "Oh her, she's nothing but a face,"
and pretend they weren't jealous or intimidated by her looks.
"Thank God," Dawn would mutter to him, "I didn't win Miss
Congeniality. If they think Miss New Jersey has to be dumb,
imagine if I'd won the booby prize. Though," she'd then add
wistfully, "it would have been nice to bring home the thousand
dollars."

After Merry was born, when they first began going to Deal
in the summer, people used to stare at Dawn in her bathing
suit. Of course she never wore the white Catalina one-piece
suit that she'd worn on the runway in Atlantic City, with the
logo, just below the hip, of the traditional swim girl in her
bathing cap. He loved that bathing suit, it fit her so marvelously, but after Atlantic City she never put it on again. They
stared at her no matter what style or color suit she wore, and
sometimes they would come up and snap her picture and ask
for an autograph. More disturbing, however, than the staring
and the photographs was their *suspiciousness* of her. "For some
strange reason," she said, "the women always think that because I'm a former whatever I want their husbands." And probably, the Swede thought, what made it so frightening for them
is that they believed Dawn could get their husbands—they'd
noticed how men looked at her and how attentive they were to
her wherever she went. He'd noticed it himself but never worried, not about a wife as proper as Dawn who'd been brought
up as strictly as she was. But all of this so rankled Dawn that
first she gave up going to the beach club in a bathing suit, any
bathing suit; then, much as she loved the surf, she gave up going to the beach club at all and whenever she wanted to swim
drove the four miles down to Avon, where, as a child, she used
to vacation with her family for a week in the summertime. On
the beach at Avon she was just a simple, petite Irish girl with
her hair pulled back about whom nobody cared one way or
another.

She went to Avon to get away from her beauty, but Dawn couldn't get away from it any more than she could openly flaunt it. You have to enjoy power, have a certain ruthlessness, to accept the beauty and not mourn the fact that it overshadows everything else. As with any exaggerated trait that sets you apart and makes you exceptional—and enviable, and hateable —to accept your beauty, to accept its effect on others, to play with it, to make the best of it, you're well advised to develop a sense of humor. Dawn was not a stick, she had spirit and she had spunk, and she could be cutting in a very humorous way, but that wasn't quite the inward humor it took to do the job and make her free. Only after she was married and no longer a virgin did she discover the place where it was okay for her to be as beautiful as she was, and that place, to the profit of both husband and wife, was with the Swede, in bed.

They used to call Avon the Irish Riviera. The Jews without much money went to Bradley Beach, and the Irish without much money went next door to Avon, a seaside town all of ten blocks long. The swell Irish—who had the money, the judges, the builders, the fancy surgeons—went to Spring Lake, beyond the imposing manorial gates just south of Belmar (another resort town, which was more or less a mixture of everybody). Dawn used to get taken to stay in Spring Lake by her mother's sister Peg, who'd married Ned Mahoney, a lawyer from Jersey City. If you were an Irish lawyer in that town, her father told her, and you played ball with City Hall, Mayor "I-am-the-law" Hague took care of you. Since Uncle Ned, a smooth talker, a golfer, and good-looking, had been on the Hudson County gravy train from the day he graduated John Marshall and signed on across the street with a powerful firm right there in Journal Square, and since he seemed to love pretty Mary Dawn best of all his nieces and nephews, every summer after the child had spent her week in the Avon rooming house with her mother and father and Danny, she went on by herself to spend the next week with Ned and Peg and all the Mahoney kids at the huge old Essex and Sussex Hotel right on the oceanfront at Spring Lake, where every morning in the airy dining room overlooking the sea she ate French toast with Vermont maple syrup. The starched white napkin that covered her lap was big enough to wrap around her waist like a sarong, and the sparkling silverware weighed a ton. On Sunday, they all went together to St. Catherine's, the most gorgeous church the little girl had ever seen. You got there by crossing a bridge—the loveliest bridge she had ever seen, narrow and humpbacked and made of wood—that spanned the lake back of the hotel. Sometimes when she was unhappy at the swim club she'd drive beyond Avon into Spring Lake and remember how Spring Lake used to materialize out of nowhere every summer, magically full blown, Mary Dawn's Brigadoon. She remembered how she dreamed of getting married in St. Catherine's, of being a bride there in a white dress, marrying a rich lawyer like her Uncle Ned and living in one of those grand summer houses whose big verandas overlooked the lake and the bridges and the dome of the church while only minutes from the booming Atlantic. She could have done it, too, could have had it just by snapping her fingers. But her choice was to fall in love with and marry Seymour Levov of Newark instead of any one of those dozens and dozens of smitten Catholic boys she'd met through her Mahoney cousins, the smart, rowdy boys from Holy Cross and Boston College, and so her life was not in Spring Lake but down in Deal and up in Old Rimrock with Mr. Levov. "Well, that's the way it happened," her mother would say sadly to whoever would listen. "Could have had a wonderful life there just like Peg's. Better than Peg's. St. Catherine's and St. Margaret's are there. St. Catherine's is right by the lake there. Beautiful building. Just beautiful. But Mary Dawn's the rebel in the family—always was. Always did just what she wanted, and from the time she marched off to be in that contest, fitting in like everybody else is apparently not something she wanted."

Dawn went to Avon strictly to swim. She still hated lying on the beach to take the sun, still resented having been made to expose her fair skin to the sun every day by the New Jersey pageant people—on the runway, they told her, her white swimsuit would look striking against a deep tan. As a young mother she tried to get as far as she could from everything that marked her as "a former whatever" and that aroused insane contempt in other women and made her feel unhappy and like a freak. She even gave away to charity all the clothes the pageant director (who had his own idea of what kind of girl should be presented by New Jersey to the Miss America judges) had picked out for her at the designers' showrooms in New York during Dawn's daylong buying trip for Atlantic City. The Swede thought she'd looked great in those gowns and he hated to see them go, but at least, at his urging, she kept the state crown so that someday she could show it to their grandchildren.

And then, after Merry started at nursery school, Dawn set out to prove to the world of women, for neither the first time nor the last, that she was impressive for something more than what she looked like. She decided to raise cattle. That idea, too, went back to her childhood—way back to her grandfather, her mother's father, who as a twenty-year-old from County Kerry came to the port in the 1880s, married, settled in south Elizabeth close to St. Mary's, and proceeded to father eleven children. His living he earned at first as a hand on the docks, but he bought a couple of cows to provide milk for the family, wound up selling the surplus to the big shots on West Jersey Street—the Moores from Moore Paint, Admiral "Bull" Halsey's family, Nicholas Murray Butler the Nobel Prize winner—and soon became one of the first independent milkmen in Elizabeth. He had about thirty cows on Murray Street, and though he didn't own much property, it didn't matter—in those days you could let them graze anywhere. All his sons went into the business and stayed in it until after the war, when the big supermarkets came along and knocked out the little man. Dawn's father, Jim Dwyer, had worked for her mother's family, and that was how Dawn's parents had met. When he was still only a kid, before refrigeration, Jim Dwyer used to go out on the milk truck at twelve o'clock at night and stay out till morning delivering milk off the back of the truck. But he hated it. Too tough a life. The heck with that, he finally said, and took up plumbing. Dawn, as a small child, loved to visit the cows, and when she was about six or seven, she was taught by one of her cousins how to milk them, and that thrill—squirting the milk out of those udders, the animals just standing there eating hay and letting her tug to her heart's content—she never forgot.

With beef cattle, however, she wouldn't need the manpower to milk and she could run the operation almost entirely by herself. The Simmental, which made a lot of milk but was a beef animal as well, still weren't a registered breed in the United

States at that time, so she could get in on the ground floor. Crossbreeding—Simmental to polled Hereford—was what interested her, the genetic vigor, the hybrid vigor, the sheer growth that results from crossbreeding. She studied the books, took the magazines, the catalogs started coming in the mail, and at night she would call him over to where she was paging through a catalog and say, "Isn't that a good-looking heifer? Have to go out and take a look at her." Pretty soon they were traveling together to shows and sales. She loved the auctions. "This reminds me just a little too much," she whispered to the Swede, "of Atlantic City. It's the Miss America Pageant for cows." She wore a tag identifying herself—"Dawn Levov, Arcady Breeders," which was the name of her company, taken from their Old Rimrock address, Box 62, Arcady Hill Road—and found it very hard to resist buying a nice cow.

A cow or a bull would be led into the ring and paraded around and the show sponsors would give the background of the animal, the sire and the dam and what they did, what the potential was, and then the people would bid, and though Dawn bought carefully, her pleasure just in raising her hand and topping the previous bid was serious pleasure. Much as he wanted more children, not more cows, he had to admit that she was never so fascinating to him, not even when he first saw her at Upsala, as in those moments at the auctions when her beauty came enticingly cloaked in the excitement of bidding and buying. Before Count arrived—the champion bull she bought at birth for ten thousand dollars, which her husband, who was a hundred percent behind her, still had to tell her was an awful lot of money—his accountant would look at her figures for Arcady Breeders at the end of each year and tell the Swede, "This is ridiculous, you can't go on this way." But they really couldn't take a beating as long as it was mostly her own time she put into it, and so he told the accountant, "Don't worry, she'll make some money." He wouldn't have dreamed of stopping her, even if eventually she didn't make a cent, because, as he said to himself when he watched her and the dog out with the herd, "These are her friends."

She worked like hell, all by herself, keeping track of the calving, getting the calves drinking out of a plastic bottle with a nipple if they didn't get the idea of sucking, tending to the mothers' feeding before she put them back in the herd. For the fencing she had to hire a man, but she was out there with him baling hay, the eighteen hundred, two thousand bales that saw them through the winter, and when Count was on in years and got lost one winter day she was heroic in hunting him down, for three days combed the woods for him before she found him where he had got himself onto a little island out in the swamp. Getting him back to the barn was ghastly. Dawn weighed a hundred and three pounds and was five feet two inches tall, and Count weighed about twenty-five hundred pounds, a very long, very beautiful animal with big brown spots around either eye, sire of the most sought-after calves. Dawn kept all the bull calves, breeding for other cattle owners, who would keep these bulls in their herds; the heifers she didn't sell often, but when she did, people wanted them. Count's progeny won year after year at the national shows and the investment returned itself many times over. But then Count got stranded out in the swamp because he had thrown his stifle out; it was icy and he must have got his foot caught in a hole, between roots, and when he saw that to get off this little island he had to get through wet mud, he just quit, and it was three days before Dawn could find him anywhere. Then, with the dog and Merry, she went out with a halter and tried to get him out but he hurt too much and didn't want to get up. So they came back later with some pills, loaded him up with cortisone and different things and sat there with him for another few hours in the rain, and then they tried again to move him. They had to get him through roots and stones and deep muck, and he'd walk a bit and stop, walk a bit and stop, and the dog got behind him and she'd bark and so he'd walk another couple of steps, and that was the way it went for hours. They had him on a rope and he'd take his head, this great big head, all curly with those beautiful eyes, and he'd pull the rope and just swing the two of them, Dawn and Merry together—boom! So then they'd get themselves up and start all over again. They had some grain and he'd eat a little and then he'd come a little farther, but all together it took four hours to get him out of the woods. Ordinarily he led very well, but he hurt so that they had to get him home almost piece by piece. Seeing his petite wife—a woman who could, if she'd wanted to, have been just a pretty face—and his small daughter drenched and covered with mud when they emerged with the bull on the rain-soaked field back of the barn was something the Swede never forgot. "This is right," he thought. "She is happy. We have Merry and that's enough." He was not a religious man but at that moment he offered up thanks, saying aloud, "Something is shining down on me."

To get the bull to the barn took Dawn and Merry nearly another hour, and there he just lay down in the hay for four days. They got the vet, and the vet said, "You're not going to get him any better. I can make him more comfortable, that's all I can do for you." Dawn brought him water to drink in buckets and food to eat, and one day (as Merry used to tell the story to whoever came to the house) he decided, "Hey, I'm all right," and he got up and he wandered out and he took it easy and that's when he fell in love with the old mare and they became inseparable. The day they had to ship Count—send him to the butcher—Dawn was in tears and kept saying, "I can't do this," and he kept saying, "You've got to do this," and so they did it. Magically (Merry's word) the night before Count left he bred a perfect little heifer, his parting shot. She got the brown spots around the eyes—"He th-th-th-threw brown eyes all around him"—but after that, though the bulls were well bred, never again was there an animal to compare with the Count.

So did it matter finally that she told people she hated the house? He was now far and away the stronger partner, she was now far and away the weaker; he was the fortunate, doubtlessly undeserving recipient of so much—what the hell, to whatever demand she made on him, he acceded. If he could bear something and Dawn couldn't, he didn't understand how he could do anything *but* accede. That was the only way the Swede knew for a man to go about being a man, especially one as lucky as himself. From the very beginning it had been a far greater strain for him to bear her disappointments than to bear his own; her disappointments seemed to dangerously rob him of himself—once he had absorbed her disappointments it became impossible for him to do nothing about them. Half measures wouldn't suffice. His effort to arrive at what she wanted always had to be wholehearted; never was he free of his quiet wholeheartedness. Not even when everything was on top of him, not even when giving everyone what they needed from him at the factory and everyone what they needed from him at home—dealing promptly with the suppliers' screw-ups, with the union's exactions, with the buyers' complaints; contending with an uncertain marketplace and all the overseas headaches; attending, on demand, to the importuning of a stuttering child, an independent-minded wife, a putatively retired, easily riled-up father—did it occur to him that this relentlessly impersonal use of himself might one day wear him down. He did not think like that any more than the ground under his feet thought like that. He seemed never to understand or, even in a moment of fatigue, to admit that his limitations were not entirely loathsome and that he was not himself a one-hundred-and-seventy-year-old stone house, its weight borne imperturbably by beams carved of oak—that he was something more transitory and mysterious.

It wasn't this house she hated anyway; what she hated were memories she couldn't shake loose from, all of them associated with the house, memories that of course he shared. Merry as a grade school kid lying on the floor of the study next to Dawn's desk, drawing pictures of Count while Dawn did the accounts for the farm. Merry emulating her mother's concentration, enjoying working with the same discipline, silently delighting to feel an equal in a common pursuit, and in some preliminary way offering them a glimpse of herself as the adult—yes, of the adult friend to them that she would someday be. Memories particularly of when they weren't being what parents are nine-tenths of the time—the taskmasters, the examples, the moral authorities, the nags of pick-that-up and you're-going-to-be-late, keepers of the diary of her duties and routines—memories, rather, of when they found one another afresh, beyond the tensions between parental mastery and inept childish uncertainty, of those moments of respite in a family's life when they could reach one another in calm.

The early mornings in the bathroom shaving while Dawn went to wake Merry up—he could not imagine a better start to the morning than catching a glimpse of that ritual. There was never an alarm clock in Merry's life—Dawn was her alarm clock. Before six o'clock Dawn was already out in the barn, but at promptly six-thirty she stopped tending the herd, came back

in the house, and went up to the child's room, where, as she
sat at the edge of the bed, daybreak's comforting observance
began. Without a word it began—Dawn simply stroking Merry's
sleeping head, a pantomime that could go on for two full minutes. Next, almost singing the whispered words, Dawn lightly
inquired, "A sign of life?" Merry responded not by opening
her eyes but by moving a little finger. "Another sign, please?"
On the game went—Merry playing along by wrinkling her
nose, by moistening her lips, by sighing just audibly—till eventually she was up out of bed ready to go. It was a game embodying a loss, for Merry the state of being completely
protected, for Dawn the project of completely protecting what
once had seemed completely protectable. Waking The Baby: it
continued until the baby was nearly twelve, the one rite of infancy that Dawn could not resist indulging, that neither one of
them ever appeared eager to outgrow.

How he loved to sight them doing together what mothers
and daughters do. To a father's eye, one seemed to amplify the
other. In bathing suits rushing out of the surf together and
racing each other to the towels—the wife now a little past her
robust moment and the daughter edging up to the beginning
of hers. A delineation of life's cyclical nature that left him feeling afterward as though he had a spacious understanding of
the whole female sex. Merry, with her growing curiosity about
the trappings of womanhood, putting on Dawn's jewelry while,
beside her at the mirror, Dawn helped her preen. Merry confiding in Dawn about her fears of ostracism—of other kids ignoring her, of her girlfriends ganging up on her. In those quiet
moments from which he was excluded (daughter relying on
mother, Dawn and Merry emotionally one inside the other
like those Russian dolls), Merry appeared more poignantly
than ever not a small replica of his wife, or of himself, but an
independent little being—something similar, a version of them,
yet distinctive and new—for which he had the most passionate
affinity.

It wasn't the house Dawn hated—what she hated, he knew,
was that the motive for having the house (for making the beds,
for setting the table, for laundering the curtains, for organizing
the holidays, for apportioning her energies and differentiating
her duties by the day of the week) had been destroyed right

along with Hamlin's store; the tangible daily fullness, the smooth regularity that was once the underpinning of all of their lives survived in her only as an illusion, as a mockingly inaccessible, bigger-than-life-size fantasy, real for every last Old Rimrock family but hers. He knew this not just because of the million memories but also because in the top drawer of his office desk he still kept handy a ten-year-old copy of a local weekly, the *Denville-Randolph Courier*, featuring on the first page the article about Dawn and her cattle business. She had consented to be interviewed only if the journalist promised not to mention her having been Miss New Jersey of 1949. The journalist agreed and the piece was titled "Old Rimrock Woman Feels Lucky to Love What She's Doing," and concluded with a paragraph that, simple as it was, made him proud of her whenever he went back to read it: "'People are lucky if they get to do what they love and are good at it,' Mrs. Levov declared."

The *Courier* story testified just how much she had loved the house, as well as everything else about their lives. Beneath a photograph of her standing before the pewter plates lined up on the fireplace mantel—in her white turtleneck shirt and cream-colored blazer, with her hair styled in a pageboy and her two delicate hands in front of her, the fingers decorously intertwined, looking sweet though a bit plain—the caption read, "Mrs. Levov, the former Miss New Jersey of 1949, loves living in a 170-year-old home, an environment which she says reflects the values of her family." When Dawn called the paper in a fury about mentioning Miss New Jersey, the journalist answered that he had kept to his promise not to mention it in the article; it was the editor who had put it in the caption.

No, she had not hated the house, of course she hadn't—and that didn't matter anyway. All that mattered now was the restoration of her well-being; the foolish remarks she might make to this one or that one were of no consequence beside the recovery taking hold. Maybe what was agitating him was that the self-adjustments on which she was building a recovery were not regenerative for him or entirely admirable to him, were even something of an affront to him. He could not tell people —certainly couldn't convince himself—that he hated the things he'd loved. . . .

He was back to it. But he couldn't help it, not when he remembered how at seven Merry would eat herself sick with the
raw batter while baking two dozen tollhouse cookies, and a
week later they'd still be finding batter all over the place, even
up on top of the refrigerator. So how could he hate the refrigerator? How could he let his emotions be reshaped, imagine
himself being rescued, as Dawn did, by their leaving it behind
for an all-but-silent new IceTemp, the Rolls-Royce of refrigerators? He for one could not say he hated the kitchen in which
Merry used to bake her cookies and melt her cheese sandwiches
and make her baked ziti, even if the cupboards weren't stainless
steel or the counters Italian marble. He could not say he hated
the cellar where she used to go to play hide-and-seek with her
screaming friends, even if sometimes it spooked even him a little
to be down there in the wintertime with those scuttling mice.
He could not say he hated the massive fireplace adorned with
the antique iron kettle that was all at once insufferably corny in
Dawn's estimation, not when he remembered how, early every
January, he would chop up the Christmas tree and set it afire
there, the whole thing in one go, so that the explosive blaze of
the bone-dry branches, the great whoosh and the loud crackling and the dancing shadows, cavorting devils climbing to the
ceiling from the four walls, would transport Merry into a delir-
ium of terrified delight. He could not say he hated the ball-
and-claw-foot bathtub where he used to give her baths, just
because decades of indelible mineral stains from the well water
streaked the enamel and encircled the drain. He could not
even hate the toilet whose handle required all that jiggling to
get the thing to stop gushing, not when he remembered her
kneeling beside it and throwing up while he knelt next to her,
holding her sick little forehead.

Nor could he say he hated his daughter for what she had
done—if he could! If only, instead of living chaotically in the
world where she wasn't and in the world where she once was
and in the world where she might now be, he could come to
hate her enough not to care anything about her world, then *or*
now. If only he could be back thinking like everybody else,
once again the totally natural man instead of this riven charlatan of sincerity, an artless outer Swede and a tormented inner
Swede, a visible stable Swede and a concealed beleaguered Swede,

an easygoing, smiling sham Swede enshrouding the Swede buried alive. If only he could even faintly reconstitute the undivided oneness of existence that had made for his straightforward physical confidence and freedom before he became the father of an alleged murderer. If only he could be as unknowing as some people perceived him to be—if only he could be as perfectly simple as the legend of Swede Levov concocted by the hero-worshiping kids of his day. If only *he* could say, "I hate this house!" and be Weequahic's Swede Levov again. If he could say, "I hate that child! I never want to see her again!" and then go ahead, disown her, forevermore despise and reject her and the vision for which she was willing, if not to kill, then to cruelly abandon her own family, a vision having nothing whatsoever to do with "ideals" but with dishonesty, criminality, megalomania, and insanity. Blind antagonism and an infantile desire to menace—*those* were her ideals. In search always of something to hate. Yes, it went way, way beyond her stuttering. That violent hatred of America was a disease unto itself. And he loved America. Loved being an *American*. But back then he hadn't dared begin to explain to her why he did, for fear of unleashing the demon, insult. They lived in dread of Merry's stuttering tongue. And by then he had no influence anyway. Dawn had no influence. His parents had no influence. In what way was she "his" any longer if she hadn't even been his then, certainly not his if to drive her into her frightening blitzkrieg mentality it required no more than for her own father to begin to explain why his affections happened to be for the country where he'd been born and raised. Stuttering, sputtering little bitch! Who the fuck did she think she was?

Imagine the vileness with which she would have assaulted him for revealing to her that just reciting the names of the forty-eight states used to thrill him back when he was a little kid. The truth of it was that even the road maps used to give him a kick when they gave them away free at the gas station. So did the offhand way he had got his nickname. The first day of high school, down in the gym for their first class, and him just jerking around with the basketball while the other kids were still all over the place getting into their sneakers. From fifteen feet out he dropped in two hook shots—swish! swish!— just to get started. And then that easygoing way that Henry

"Doc" Ward, the popular young phys ed teacher and wrestling coach fresh from Montclair State, laughingly called from his office doorway—called out to this lanky blond fourteen-year-old with the brilliant blue gaze and the easy, effortless style whom he'd never seen in his gym before—"Where'd you learn that, Swede?" Because the name differentiated Seymour Levov from Seymour Munzer and Seymour Wishnow, who were also on the class roll, it stuck all through gym his freshman year; then other teachers and coaches took it up, then kids in the school, and afterward, as long as Weequahic remained the old Jewish Weequahic and people there still cared about the past, Doc Ward was known as the guy who'd christened Swede Levov. It just stuck. Simple as that, an old American nickname, proclaimed by a gym teacher, bequeathed in a gym, a name that made him mythic in a way that Seymour would never have done, mythic not only during his school years but to his schoolmates, in memory, for the rest of their days. He carried it with him like an invisible passport, all the while wandering deeper and deeper into an American's life, forthrightly evolving into a large, smooth, optimistic American such as his conspicuously raw forebears—including the obstinate father whose American claim was not inconsiderable—couldn't have dreamed of as one of their own.

The way his father talked to people, that got him too, the American way his father said to the guy at the pump, "Fill 'er up, Mac. Check the front end, will ya, Chief?" The excitement of their trips in the DeSoto. The tiny, musty tourist cabins they stopped at overnight while meandering up through the scenic back roads of New York State to see Niagara Falls. The trip to Washington when Jerry was a brat all the way. His first liberty home from the marines, the pilgrimage to Hyde Park with the folks and Jerry to stand together as a family looking at FDR's grave. Fresh from boot camp and there at Roosevelt's grave, he felt that something meaningful was happening; hardened and richly tanned from training through the hottest months on a parade ground where the temperature rose some days to a hundred twenty degrees, he stood silent, proudly wearing his new summer uniform, the shirt starched, the khaki pants sleekly pocketless over the rear and perfectly pressed, the tie pulled taut, cap centered on his close-shaven head, black leather

dress shoes spit-shined, agleam, and the belt—the belt that
made him feel most like a marine, that tightly woven khaki
fabric belt with the metal buckle—girding a waist that had
seen him through some ten thousand sit-ups as a raw Parris
Island recruit. Who was she to sneer at all this, to reject all this,
to hate all this and set out to destroy it? The war, winning the
war—did she hate that too? The neighbors, out in the street,
crying and hugging on V-J Day, blowing car horns and marching up and down front lawns loudly banging kitchen pots. He
was still at Parris Island then, but his mother had described it
to him in a three-page letter. The celebration party at the playground back of the school that night, everyone they knew,
family friends, school friends, the neighborhood butcher, the
grocer, the pharmacist, the tailor, even the bookie from the
candy store, all in ecstasy, long lines of staid middle-aged people
madly mimicking Carmen Miranda and dancing the conga,
one-two-three *kick*, one-two-three *kick*, until after two A.M.
The war. Winning that war. Victory, victory, victory had come!
No more death and war!

    His last months of high school, he'd read the paper every
night, following the marines across the Pacific. He saw the
photographs in *Life*—photographs that haunted his sleep—of
the crumpled bodies of dead marines killed on Peleliu, an island in a chain called the Palaus. At a place called Bloody Nose
Ridge, Japs ferreted in old phosphate mines, who were themselves to be burned to a crisp by the flamethrowers, had cut
down hundreds and hundreds of young marines, eighteen-
year-olds, nineteen-year-olds, boys barely older than he was.
He had a map up in his room with pins sticking out of it, pins
he had inserted to mark where the marines, closing in on
Japan, had assaulted from the sea a tiny atoll or an island chain
where the Japs, dug into coral fortresses, poured forth ferocious mortar and rifle fire. Okinawa was invaded on April 1,
1945, Easter Sunday of his senior year and just two days after
he'd hit a double and a home run in a losing game against
West Side. The Sixth Marine Division overran Yontan, one of
the two island air bases, within three hours of wading ashore.
Took the Motobu Peninsula in thirteen days. Just off the
Okinawa beach, two kamikaze pilots attacked the flagship carrier *Bunker Hill* on May 14—the day after the Swede went

four for four against Irvington High, a single, a triple, and two doubles—plunging their planes, packed with bombs, into the flight deck jammed with American planes all gassed up to take off and laden with ammunition. The blaze climbed a thousand feet into the sky, and in the explosive firestorm that raged for eight hours, four hundred sailors and aviators died. Marines of the Sixth Division captured Sugar Loaf Hill, May 14, 1945— three more doubles for the Swede in a winning game against East Side—maybe the worst, most savage single day of fighting in marine history. Maybe the worst in human history. The caves and tunnels that honeycombed Sugar Loaf Hill at the southern end of the island, where the Japs had fortified and hidden their army, were blasted with flamethrowers and then sealed with grenades and demolition charges. Hand-to-hand fighting went on day and night. Jap riflemen and machine gunners, chained to their positions and unable to retreat, fought until they died. The day the Swede graduated from Weequahic High, June 22—having racked up the record number of doubles in a single season by a Newark City League player—the Sixth Marine Division raised the American flag over Okinawa's second air base, Kadena, and the final staging area for the invasion of Japan was secured. From April 1, 1945, to June 21, 1945—coinciding, give or take a few days, with the Swede's last and best season as a high school first baseman—an island some fifty miles long and about ten miles wide had been occupied by American forces at the cost of 15,000 American lives. The Japanese dead, military and civilian, numbered 141,000. To conquer the Japanese homeland to the north and end the war meant the number of dead on each side could run ten, twenty, thirty times as great. And still the Swede went out and, to be a part of the final assault on Japan, joined the U.S. Marines, who on Okinawa, as on Tarawa, Iwo Jima, Guam, and Guadalcanal, had absorbed casualties that were stupefying.

The marines. Being a marine. Boot camp. Knocked us around every which way, called us all kinds of names, physically and mentally murdered us for three months, and it was the best experience I ever had in my life. Took it on as a challenge and I did it. My name became "Ee-oh." That's the way the southern drill instructors pronounced Levov, dropping the *L* and the two *v*'s—all consonants overboard—and lengthening

out the two vowels. "Ee-oh!" Like a donkey braying. "Ee-oh!"
"Yes, sir!" Major Dunleavy, the athletic director, big guy, Purdue
football coach, stops the platoon one day and the hefty sergeant we called Sea Bag shouts for Private Ee-oh and out I run
with my helmet on, and my heart was pounding because I
thought my mother had died. I was just a week away from being assigned to Camp Lejeune, up in North Carolina, for advanced weaponry training, but Major Dunleavy pulled the
plug on that and so I never got to fire a BAR. And that was why
I'd joined the marines—wanted more than anything to fire the
BAR from flat on my belly with the barrel elevated on a mount.
Eighteen years old and that was the Marine Corps to me, the
rapid-firing, air-cooled .30 caliber machine gun. What a patriotic kid that innocent kid was. Wanted to fire the tank killer,
the hand-held bazooka rocket, wanted to prove to myself I
wasn't scared and could do that stuff. Grenades, flamethrowers,
crawling under barbed wire, blowing up bunkers, attacking
caves. Wanted to hit the beach in a duck. Wanted to help win
the war. But Major Dunleavy had got a letter from his friend in
Newark, what an athlete this Levov was, glowing letter about
how wonderful I was, and so they reassigned me and made me
a drill instructor to keep me on the island to play ball—by then
they'd dropped the atomic bomb and the war was over anyway.
"You're in my unit, Swede. Glad to have you." A great break,
really. Once my hair grew in, I was a human being again. Instead
of being called "shithead" all the time or "shithead-move-
your-ass," suddenly I was a DI the recruits called Sir. What the
DI called the recruits was You People! Hit the deck, You
People! On your feet, You People! Double time, You People,
double time *hup*! Great, great experience for a kid from Keer
Avenue. Guys I would never have met in my life. Accents from
all over the place. The Midwest. New England. Some farm
boys from Texas and the Deep South I couldn't even understand. But got to know them. Got to like them. Hard boys,
poor boys, lots of high school athletes. Used to live with the
boxers. Lived with the recreation gang. Another Jewish guy,
Manny Rabinowitz from Altoona. Toughest Jewish guy I ever
met in my life. What a fighter. A great friend. Didn't even finish
high school. Never had a friend like that before or since. Never
laughed so hard in my life as I did with Manny. Manny was

money in the bank for me. Nobody ever gave us any Jewboy shit. A little back in boot camp, but that was it. When Manny fought, the guys would bet their cigarettes on him. Buddy Falcone and Manny Rabinowitz were always the two winners for us whenever we fought another base. After the fight with Manny the other guy would say that nobody had ever hit him as hard in his life. Manny ran the entertainment with me, the boxing smokers. The duo—the Jewish leathernecks. Manny got the wiseguy recruit who made all the trouble and weighed a hundred and forty-five pounds to fight somebody a hundred and sixty pounds who he could be sure would beat the shit out of him. "Always pick a redhead, Ee-oh," Manny said, "he'll give you the best fight in the world. Redhead'll never quit." Manny the scientist. Manny going up to Norfolk to fight a sailor, a middleweight contender before the war, and whipping him. Exercising the battalion before breakfast. Marching the recruits down to the pool every night to teach them to swim. We practically threw them in—the old-fashioned way of teaching swimming, but you had to swim to be a marine. Always had to be ready to do ten more push-ups than any of the recruits. They'd challenge me, but I was in shape. Getting on the bus going to play ball. The long distances we flew. Bob Collins on the team, the big St. John's guy. My teammate. Terrific athlete. Boozer. With Bob C. got drunk for the first time in my life, talked for two hours nonstop about playing ball for Weequahic and then threw up all over the deck. Irish guys, Italian guys, Slovaks, Poles, tough little bastards from Pennsylvania, kids who'd run away from fathers who worked in the mines and beat them with belt buckles and with their fists—these were the guys I lived with and ate with and slept alongside. Even an Indian guy, a Cherokee, a third baseman. Called him Piss Cutter, the same as the name for our caps. Don't ask me why. Not all of them decent people but on the whole all right. Good guys. Lots of organized grabass. Played against Fort Benning. Cherry Point, North Carolina, the marine air base. Beat them. Beat Charleston Navy Yard. We had a couple of boys who could throw that ball. One pitcher went on to the Tigers. Went down to Rome, Georgia, to play ball, over to Waycross, Georgia, to an army base. Called the army guys doggies. Beat *them*. Beat everybody. Saw the South. Saw

things I never saw. Saw the life the Negroes live. Met every
kind of Gentile you can think of. Met beautiful southern girls.
Met common whores. Used a condom. Skinned 'er back and
squeezed 'er down. Saw Savannah. Saw New Orleans. Sat in a
rundown slopchute in Mobile, Alabama, where I was damn
glad the shore patrol was just outside the door. Playing basketball and baseball with the Twenty-second Regiment. Got to be
a United States Marine. Got to wear the emblem with the anchor and the globe. "No pitcher in there, Ee-oh, poke it outta
here, Ee-oh—" Got to be Ee-oh to guys from Maine, New
Hampshire, Louisiana, Virginia, Mississippi, Ohio—guys without an education from all over America calling me Ee-oh and
nothing more. Just plain Ee-oh to them. Loved that.
Discharged June 2, 1947. Got to marry a beautiful girl named
Dwyer. Got to run a business my father built, a man whose
own father couldn't speak English. Got to live in the prettiest
spot in the world. Hate America? Why, he lived in America the
way he lived inside his own skin. All the pleasures of his younger
years were American pleasures, all that success and happiness
had been American, and he need no longer keep his mouth
shut about it just to defuse her ignorant hatred. The loneliness
he would feel as a man without all his American feelings. The
longing he would feel if he had to live in another country. Yes,
everything that gave meaning to his accomplishments had
been American. Everything he loved was here.

For her, being an American was loathing America, but loving America was something he could not let go of any more
than he could have let go of loving his father and his mother,
any more than he could have let go of his decency. How could
she "hate" this country when she had no *conception* of this
country? How could a child of his be so blind as to revile the
"rotten system" that had given her own family every opportunity to succeed? To revile her "capitalist" parents as though
their wealth were the product of anything other than the un-
stinting industry of three generations. The men of three generations, including even himself, slogging through the slime
and stink of a tannery. The family that started out in a tannery,
at one with, side by side with, the lowest of the low—now to
her "capitalist dogs." There wasn't much difference, *and she
knew it*, between hating America and hating them. He loved

the America she hated and blamed for everything that was imperfect in life and wanted violently to overturn, he loved the "bourgeois values" she hated and ridiculed and wanted to subvert, he loved the mother she hated and had all but murdered by doing what she did. Ignorant little fucking bitch! The price they had paid! Why *shouldn't* he tear up this Rita Cohen letter? Rita Cohen! They were back! The sadistic mischief-makers with their bottomless talent for antagonism who had extorted the money from him, who, for the fun of it, had extracted from him the Audrey Hepburn scrapbook, the stuttering diary, and the ballet shoes, these delinquent young brutes calling themselves "revolutionaries" who had so viciously played with his hopes five years back had decided the time had again rolled around to laugh at Swede Levov.

We can only stand as witnesses to the anguish that sanctifies her. The Disciple Who Calls Herself "Rita Cohen." They were laughing at him. They *had* to be laughing. Because the only thing worse than its all being a wicked joke was its *not* being a wicked joke. *Your daughter is divine.* My daughter is anything and everything but. She is all too frail and misguided and wounded—she's hopeless! Why did you tell her that you slept with me? And tell me that it was *she* who wanted you to. You say these things because you hate us. And you hate us because we *don't* do such things. You hate us not because we're reckless but because we're prudent and sane and industrious and agree to abide by the law. You hate us because we haven't failed. Because we've worked hard and honestly to become the best in the business and because of that we have prospered, so you envy us and you hate us and want to destroy us. And so you used her. A sixteen-year-old kid with a stutter. No, nothing small about you people. Made her into a "revolutionary" full of great thoughts and high-minded ideals. Sons of bitches. You *enjoy* the spectacle of our devastation. Cowardly bastards. It isn't clichés that enslaved her, it's *you* who enslaved her in the loftiest of the shallow clichés—and that resentful kid, with her stutterer's hatred of injustice, had no protection at all. You got her to believe she was at one with the downtrodden people—and made her into your patsy, your stooge. And Dr. Fred Conlon, as a result, is dead. That was who you killed to stop the war: the chief of staff up at the hospital in Dover, the guy who in a small community hospital established a coronary care unit of eight beds. That was *his* crime.

Instead of exploding in the middle of the night when the village was empty, the bomb, either as planned or by mistake, went off at five A.M., an hour before Hamlin's store opened for the day and the moment that Fred Conlon turned away from having dropped into the mailbox envelopes containing checks for household bills that he'd paid at his desk the evening before. He was on his way to the hospital. A chunk of metal flying out of the store struck him at the back of the skull.

Dawn was under sedation and couldn't see anyone, but the Swede had gone to Russ and Mary Hamlin's house and expressed his sympathy about the store, told the Hamlins how much the store had meant to Dawn and him, how it was no less a part of their lives than it was of everyone else's in the community; then he went to the wake—in the coffin Conlon looked fine, fit, just as affable as ever—and the following week, with their doctor already arranging for Dawn's hospitalization, the Swede went alone to visit Conlon's widow. How he managed to get to that woman's house for tea is another story— another *book*—but he did it, he did it, and heroically she served him tea while he extended his family's condolences in the words that he had revised in his mind five hundred times but that, when spoken, were still no good, even more hollow than those he'd uttered to Russ and Mary Hamlin: "deep and sincere regrets . . . the agony of your family . . . my wife would like you to know. . . ." After listening to everything he had to say, Mrs. Conlon quietly replied, displaying an outlook so calm and kind and compassionate that the Swede wanted to disappear, to hide like a child, while at the same time the urge was nearly overpowering to throw himself at her feet and to remain there forever, begging for her forgiveness. "You are good parents and you raised your daughter the way you thought best," she said to him. "It was not your fault and I don't hold anything against you. You didn't go out and buy the dynamite. You didn't make the bomb. You didn't plant the bomb. You had nothing to do with the bomb. If, as it appears, your daughter turns out to be the one who is responsible, I will hold no one responsible but her. I feel badly for you and your family, Mr. Levov. I have lost a husband, my children have lost a father. But you have lost something even greater. You are parents who have lost a child. There is not a day that goes by that you won't be in my thoughts and in my prayers." The Swede had known Fred Conlon only slightly, from cocktail parties and charity events where they found themselves equally bored. Mainly he knew him by reputation, a man who cared about his family and the hospital with the same devotion—a hard worker, a good guy. Under him, the hospital had begun to plan a building program, the first since its construction, and in addition to the new coronary care unit, during his steward-ship there had been a long-overdue modernization of emer-gency room facilities. But who gives a shit about the emergency room of a community hospital out in the sticks? Who gives a shit about a rural general store whose owner has been running it since 1921? We're talking about *humanity*! When has there ever been progress for humanity without a few small mishaps and mistakes? The people are angry and they have spoken! Violence will be met by violence, regardless of consequences, until the people are liberated! Fascist America down one post office, facility completely destroyed.

Except, as it happened, Hamlin's was not an official U.S. post *office* nor were the Hamlins U.S. postal employees—theirs was merely a postal *station* contracted, for *x* number of dollars, to handle a little postal business on the side. Hamlin's was no more a government installation than the office where your ac-countant makes out your tax forms. But that is a mere techni-cality to world revolutionaries. Facility destroyed! Eleven hundred Old Rimrock residents forced, for a full year and a half, to drive five miles to buy their stamps and to get packages weighed and to send anything registered or special delivery. That'll show Lyndon Johnson who's boss.

They were laughing at him. *Life* was laughing at him.

Mrs. Conlon had said, "You are as much the victims of this tragedy as we are. The difference is that for us, though recovery will take time, we will survive as a family. We will survive as a loving family. We will survive with our memories intact and with our memories to sustain us. It will not be any easier for us than it will be for you to make sense of something so senseless. But we are the same family we were when Fred was here, and we will survive."

The clarity and force with which she implied that the Swede and his family would *not* survive made him wonder, in the weeks that followed, if her kindness and her compassion were so all-encompassing as he had wanted at first to believe.

He never went to see her again.

He told his secretary that he was going over to New York, to the Czech mission, where he'd already had preliminary discussions about a trip to Czechoslovakia later in the fall. In New York he had examined specimen gloves as well as shoes, belts, pocketbooks, and wallets manufactured in Czechoslovakia, and now the Czechs were working up plans for him to visit factories in Brno and Bratislava so he could see the glove setup firsthand and examine a more extensive sample of their work while it was in production and when it came off the floor. There was no longer any question that in Czechoslovakia leather apparel could be more cheaply made than in Newark or Puerto Rico—and probably better made, too. The workmanship that had begun falling off in the Newark plant since the riots had continued to deteriorate, especially once Vicky retired as making room forelady. Even granting that what he'd seen at the Czech mission might not be representative of day-to-day production, it had been impressive enough. Back in the thirties the Czechs had flooded the American market with fine gloves, over the years excellent Czech cutters had been employed by Newark Maid, and the machinist who for thirty years had been employed full-time tending Newark Maid's sewing machines, keeping those workhorses running—replacing worn-out shafts, levers, throat plates, bobbins, endlessly adjusting each machine's timing and tension—was a Czech, a wonderful worker, expert with every glove machine on earth, able to fix anything. Even though the Swede had assured his father he had no intention of signing over any aspect of their operation to a Communist government until he'd returned with a thorough report, he was confident that pulling out of Newark wasn't far down the line.

Dawn by this time had her new face and had begun the startling comeback, and as for Merry . . . well, Merry dear, Merry darling, my precious one-and-only Merry-child, how can I possibly remain on Central Avenue struggling to keep my production up, taking the beating we're taking there from black people who care nothing any longer about the quality of my product—people who are careless, people who've got me over a barrel because they know there's nobody trainable left in Newark to replace them—for fear that if I leave Central Avenue you will call me a racist and never see me again? I have waited so long to see *you* again, your mother has waited, Grandpa and Grandma have waited, we have all been waiting twenty-four hours a day every day of every year for five years to see you or to hear from you or somehow to get some word of you, and we can postpone our lives no longer. It's 1973. Mother is a new woman. If we are ever again going to live, now is when we must begin.

Nonetheless, he was waiting not for the pleasant consul at the Czech mission to welcome him with a glass of slivovitz (as his father or his wife would think if they happened to phone the office) but across from the dog and cat hospital on New Jersey Railroad Avenue, a ten-minute car ride from the Newark Maid factory.

Ten minutes away. And for years? In Newark, for years? Merry was living in the one place in the world he would never have guessed had he been given a thousand guesses. Was he deficient in intelligence, or was she so provocative, so perverse, so insane he still could not imagine *anything* she might do? Was he deficient also in imagination? What father wouldn't be? It was preposterous. His daughter was living in Newark, working across the Pennsylvania Railroad tracks, and not at the end of the Ironbound where the Portuguese were reclaiming the poor Down Neck streets but here at the Ironbound's westernmost edge, in the shadow of the railroad viaduct that closed off Railroad Avenue all along the western side of the street. That grim fortification was the city's Chinese wall, brownstone boulders piled twenty feet high, strung out for more than a mile and intersected only by half a dozen foul underpasses. Along this forsaken street, as ominous now as any street in any ruined city in America, was a reptilian length of unguarded wall barren even of graffiti. But for the wilted weeds that managed to jut forth in wiry clumps where the mortar was cracked and washed away, the viaduct wall was barren of everything except the affirmation of a weary industrial city's prolonged and triumphant struggle to monumentalize its ugliness.

On the east side of the street, the dark old factories—Civil War factories, foundries, brassworks, heavy-industrial plants blackened from the chimneys pumping smoke for a hundred years—were windowless now, the sunlight sealed out with brick and mortar, their exits and entrances plugged with cinderblock. These were the factories where people had lost fingers and arms and got their feet crushed and their faces scalded, where children once labored in the heat and the cold, the nineteenth-century factories that churned up people and churned out goods and now were unpierceable, airtight tombs. It was Newark that was entombed there, a city that was not going to stir again. The pyramids of Newark: as huge and dark and hideously impermeable as a great dynasty's burial edifice has every historical right to be.

The rioters hadn't crossed beneath the elevated railroad tracks—if they had, these factories, the whole block of them, would be burned-out rubble like the West Market Street factories back of Newark Maid.

His father used to tell him, "Brownstone and brick. There was the business. Brownstone quarried right here. Know that? Out by Belleville, north along the river. This city's got everything. What a business that must have been. The guy who sold Newark brownstone and brick—*he* was sittin' pretty."

On Saturday mornings, the Swede would drive Down Neck alongside his father to pick up the week's finished gloves from the Italian families paid to do piecework in their homes. As the car bounced along the streets paved with bricks, past one poor little frame house after another, the massive railroad viaduct remained brokenly within view. It would not go away. This was the Swede's first encounter with the manmade sublime that divides and dwarfs, and in the beginning it was frightening to him, a child susceptible to his environment even then, with a proclivity to be embraced by it and to embrace it in return. Six or seven years old. Maybe five, maybe Jerry hadn't even been born yet. The dwarfing stones causing the city to be even more gigantic for him than it already was. The manmade horizon, the brutal cut in the body of the giant city—it felt as though they were entering the shadow world of hell, when all the boy was seeing was the railroad's answer to the populist crusade to hoist the tracks above the grade crossings so as to end the crashes and the pedestrian carnage. "Brownstone and brick," said his father admiringly. "*There* was a guy whose worries were over."

That had all taken place before they'd moved to Keer Avenue, when they were living across from the synagogue in a three-family house at the poor end of Wainwright Street. His father didn't have even a loft then but got his skins from a fellow who was also Down Neck and who trafficked out of his garage in whatever the workers could carry from the tanneries hidden within their big rubber boots or wrapped around them beneath their overalls. The hide man was himself a tannery worker, a big, gruff Pole with tattoos up and down his massive arms, and the Swede had vague memories of his father's standing at the garage's one window holding the finished hides up to the light and searching them for defects, then stretching them over his knee before making his selection. "Feel this," he'd say to the Swede once they were safely back in the car, and the child would crease a delicate kidskin as he'd seen his father do, finger the fineness appreciatively, the velvet texture of the skin's close, tight grain. "*That's* leather," his father told him. "What makes kidskin so delicate, Seymour?" "I don't know." "Well, what is a kid?" "A baby goat." "Right. And what does he eat?" "Milk?" "Right. And because all the animal has eaten is milk, that's what makes the grain smooth and beautiful. Look at the pores of this skin with a magnifying glass and they're so fine you can't even see 'em. But the kid starts eating grass, that skin's a different story. The goat eats grass and the skin is like sandpaper. The finest glove leather for a formal glove is what, Seymour?" "Kid." "That's my boy. But it's not only the kid, son, it's the tanning. You've got to know your tannery. It's like a good cook and a bad cook. You get a good piece of meat and a bad cook can spoil it for you. How come someone makes a wonderful cake and the other doesn't? One is moist and nice and the other is dry. Same thing in leather. I worked in the tannery. It's the chemicals, it's the time, it's the temperature. That's where the difference comes in. That, and not buying second-rate skins to begin with. Cost as much to tan a bad skin as a good skin. Cost more to tan a bad one—you work harder at it. Beautiful, beautiful," he said, "wonderful stuff," once again lovingly kneading the kidskin between his fingertips. "You know how you get it like this, Seymour?" "How, Daddy?" "You work at it."

There were eight, ten, twelve immigrant families scattered throughout Down Neck to whom Lou Levov distributed the skins along with his own patterns, people from Naples who had been glovers in the old country and the best of whom wound up working at Newark Maid's first home when he could come up with the rent for the small loft on West Market Street on the top floor of the chair factory. The old Italian grandfather or the father did the cutting on the kitchen table, with the French rule, the shears, and the spud knife he'd brought from Italy. The grandmother or the mother did the sewing, and the daughters did the laying off—ironing the glove—in the old-fashioned way, with irons heated up in a box set atop the kitchen's potbellied stove. The women worked on antique Singers, nineteenth-century machines that Lou Levov, who'd learned to reassemble them, had bought for a song and then repaired himself; at least once a week, he'd have to drive all the way Down Neck at night and spend an hour getting a machine running right again. Otherwise, both day and night, he was all over Jersey peddling the gloves the Italians had made for him, selling them at first out of the trunk of the car, right on a main downtown street, and, in time, directly to apparel shops and department stores that were Newark Maid's first solid accounts. It was in a tiny kitchen not half a mile from where the Swede was now standing that the boy had seen a pair of gloves cut by the oldest of the old Neapolitan artisans. He believed that he could remember sitting in his father's lap while Lou Levov sampled a glass of the family's homemade wine and across from them a cutter said to be a hundred years old who was supposed to have made gloves for the queen of Italy smoothed the ends of a trank with half a dozen twists of his knife's dull blade. "Watch him, Seymour. See how small the skin is? The most difficult thing in the world to cut a kidskin efficiently. Because it's so small. But watch what he does. You're watching a genius and you're watching an artist. The Italian cutter, son, is always more artistic in his outlook. And this is the master of them all." Sometimes hot meatballs would be frying in a pan, and he remembered how one of the Italian cutters, who always purred "Che bellezza . . ." and called him Piccirell', sweet little thing, when he stroked the Swede's blond head, taught him how to dip the crisp Italian bread in a pot of tomato sauce. No matter how tiny the yard out back, there were tomato plants growing, and a grapevine and a pear tree, and in every household there was always a grandfather. It was he who had made the wine and to whom Lou Levov uttered, in a Neapolitan dialect and with what he took to be the appropriate gesture, his repertoire's one complete Italian sentence, " 'Na mano lava 'nad"—One hand washes the other—when he laid out on the oilcloth the dollar bills for the week's piecework. Then the boy and his father got up from the table with the finished lot and left for home, where Sylvia Levov would examine each glove, with a stretcher meticulously examine each seam of each finger and each thumb of every glove. "A pair of gloves," his father told the Swede, "are supposed to match perfectly—the grain of the leather, the color, the shading, everything. The first thing she looks to see is if the gloves match." While his mother worked she taught the boy about all the mistakes that can occur in the making of a glove, mistakes she had been taught to recognize as her husband's wife. A skipped stitch can turn into an open seam, but you can't see it, she told the child, without putting the stretcher into the glove and tensioning the seam. There are stitch holes that aren't supposed to be there but are because the sewer stitched wrong and then just tried to go on. There is something called butcher cuts that occur if the animal was cut too deeply when it was flayed. Even after the leather is shaved they're there, and though they don't necessarily break when you stress the glove with the stretcher, they could break if someone put the glove on. In every batch they brought up from Down Neck his father found at least one glove where the thumb didn't match the palm. This drove him wild. "See that? See, the cutter is trying to make his quota out of a skin, and he can't get a thumb out of the same hide as the trank, so he cheats —he takes the next skin and cuts the thumb, and it doesn't match, and it's no goddamn good to me at all. See here? Twisted fingers. This is what Mario was showing you this morning. When you're cutting a fourchette or a thumb or any-thing, you got to pull it straight. If you don't pull it straight, you're going to have a problem. If he pulled that fourchette crookedly on the bias, then when it's sewn together the finger is going to corkscrew just like this. That's what your mother is looking for. Because remember *and don't forget*—a Levov makes a glove that is *perfect*." Whenever his mother found something wrong she gave the glove to the Swede, who stuck a pin where the defect was, through the stitch and never through leather. "Holes in leather stay," his father warned him. "It's not like fabric, where the holes disappear. Always through the stitch, always!" After the boy and his mother had inspected the gloves in a lot, his mother used special thread to tack the gloves together, thread that breaks easily, his father explained, so that when the buyer pulls them apart the knots sewn on each side won't tear through the leather. After the gloves were tacked, the Swede's mother tissued them—laid a pair down on a sheet of tissue paper, folded the paper over, then over again so that each pair was protected together. A dozen pairs, counted out loud for her by the Swede, went into a box. It wasn't a fancy box back in the early days, just a plain brown box with a size scale on the end showing the sizes. The fancy black box with the gold trim and the name Newark Maid stamped in gold came along only when his father landed the breakthrough Bamberger's account and, afterward, the account with Macy's Little Accessory Shop. A distinctive, attractive box with the company name and a gold and black woven label in every glove made all the difference not only to the shop but to the knowledgeable upscale customer.

Every Saturday when they drove Down Neck to collect that week's finished gloves, they'd bring along the gloves the Swede had marked with a pin where his mother had discovered a defect. If a glove bristled with three pins or more, his father would have to warn the family who had made it that if they wanted to work for Newark Maid, sloppiness would not be tolerated. "Lou Levov doesn't sell a table-cut glove unless it is a *perfect* table-cut glove," he told them. "I'm not here to play games. I'm here like you are—I'm here to make money. 'Na mano lava 'nad, *and don't forget it*."

"What is calfskin, Seymour?" "The skin from young calves." "What kind of grain?" "It has a tight, even grain. Very smooth. Glossy." "What's it used for?" "Mostly for men's gloves. It's heavy." "What is Cape?" "The skin of the South African haired sheep." "Cabretta?" "Not the wool-type sheep but the hair-type sheep." "From where?" "South America. Brazil." "That's part of the answer. The animals live a little north and south of the equator. Anywhere around the world. Southern India. Northern Brazil. A band across Africa—" "We got ours from *Brazil*." "Right. That's true. You're right. I'm only telling you they come from other countries too. So you'll know. What's the key operation in preparing the skin?" "Stretching." "And never forget it. In this business, a sixteenth of an inch makes all the difference in the world. Stretching! Stretching is a hundred percent right. How many parts in a pair of gloves?" "Ten, twelve if there's a binding." "Name 'em." "Six fourchettes, two thumbs, two tranks." "The unit of measurement in the glove trade?" "Buttons." "What's a one-button glove?" "A one-button glove is one inch long if you measure from the base of the thumb to the top." "Approximately one inch long. What is silking?" "The three rows of stitching on the back of the glove. If you don't do the end pulling, all the silking is going to come right out." "Excellent. I didn't even ask you about end pulling. Excellent. What's the most difficult seam to make on a glove?" "Full piqué." "Why? Take your time, son—it's difficult. Tell me why." The prixseam. The gauge seam. Single draw points. Spear points. Buckskin. Mocha. English does. Soaking. Dehairing. Pickling. Sorting. Taxing. The grain finish. The velvet finish. Pasted linings. Skeleton linings. Seamless knitted wool. Cut-and-sewed knitted wool. . . .

As they drove back and forth Down Neck, it never stopped. Every Saturday morning from the time he was six until he was nine and Newark Maid became a company with its own loft.

The dog and cat hospital was located on the corner in a small, decrepit brick building next door to an empty lot, a tire dump, patchy with weeds nearly as tall as he was, the twisted wreckage of a wire-mesh fence lying at the edge of the sidewalk where he waited for his daughter . . . who lived in Newark . . . and for how long . . . and where, in what kind of quarters in this city? No, he did not lack imagination any longer—the imagining of the abhorrent was now effortless, even though it was impossible still to envisage how she had got herself from

Old Rimrock to here. There was no delusion that he could any longer clutch at to soften whatever surprise was next.

This place where she worked certainly didn't make it look as if she continued to believe her calling was to change the course of American history. The building's rusted fire escape would just come down, just come loose from its moorings and crash onto the street, if anyone stepped on it—a fire escape whose function was not to save lives in the event of a fire but to use-lessly hang there testifying to the immense loneliness inherent to living. For him it was stripped of any other meaning—no meaning could make better use of that building. Yes, alone we are, deeply alone, and always, in store for us, a layer of loneli-ness even deeper. There is nothing we can do to dispose of that. No, loneliness shouldn't surprise us, as astonishing to ex-perience as it may be. You can try turning yourself inside out, but all you are then is inside out and lonely instead of inside in and lonely. My stupid, stupid Merry dear, stupider even than your stupid father, not even blowing up buildings helps. It's lonely if there are buildings and it's lonely if there are no build-ings. There is no protest to be lodged against loneliness—not all the bombing campaigns in history have made a dent in it. The most lethal of manmade explosives can't touch it. Stand in awe not of Communism, my idiot child, but of ordinary, every-day loneliness. On May Day go out and march with your friends to its greater glory, the superpower of superpowers, the force that overwhelms all. Put your money on it, bet on it, worship it—bow down in submission not to Karl Marx, my stuttering, angry, idiot child, not to Ho Chi Minh and Mao Tse-tung—bow down to the great god Loneliness!

I'm lonesome, she used to say to him when she was a tiny girl, and he could never figure out where she had picked up that word. Lonesome. As sad a word as you could hear out of a two-year-old's mouth. But she had learned to say so much so soon, had talked so easily at first, so *intelligently*—maybe *that* was what lay behind the stutter, all those words she uncannily knew before other kids could pronounce their own names, the emotional overload of a vocabulary that included even "I'm lonesome."

He was the one she could talk to. "Daddy, let's have a con-versation." More often than not, the conversations were about

Mother. She would tell him that Mother had too much say about her clothes, too much say about her hair. Mother wanted to dress her more adultlike than the other kids. Merry wanted long hair like Patti, and Mother wanted it cut. "Mother would really be happy if I had to wear a uniform the way she did at St. Genevieve's." "Mother's conservative, that's all. But you do like shopping with her." "The best part of shopping with Mother is that you get a nice little lunch, which is fun. And sometimes it's fun picking out clothes. But still, Mother has too much s-s-s-s-say." At lunch in school she never ate what Mother gave her. "Baloney on white bread is disgusting. Liverwurst is disgusting. Tuna in the lunch bag gets all wet. The only thing that I like is Virginia ham, but with the crusts *off*. I like hot s-s-soup." But when she took hot soup to school she was always breaking the thermos. If not the first week, the second. Dawn got her special breakproof ones, but even those she could break. That was the extent of her destructiveness.

After school, when she baked with her friend Patti, Merry would always have to crack the eggs because Patti said cracking eggs made her sick. Merry thought this was silly, and so one afternoon she cracked the egg right in front of her and Patti threw up. *And that was her destructiveness—breaking a thermos and cracking an egg.* And getting rid of whatever her mother gave her for lunch. Never complained about it, just wouldn't eat it. And when Dawn began suspecting what was up and asked her what she had for lunch, Merry might have thrown it out without checking. "You're sometimes a troublesome child," Dawn told her. "I'm not. I'm not that t-t-t-troublesome if you don't ask what I had for lunch." Exasperated, her mother said, "It isn't always easy being you, is it, Merry?" "I think it's easier being me, Mom, than maybe it is being n-n-near me." To her father she confided, "I didn't think the fruit was that ex-ex-citing, so I threw that out too." "And the milk you threw out." "The milk was a little bit warm, Dad." But there was always a dime at the bottom of the lunch bag for ice cream, and so that's what she would have. Didn't like mustard. That was another complaint in the years before she began to complain about capitalism. "What kid does?" she asked him. The answer was Patti. Patti would eat sandwiches with mustard and processed cheese; Merry, as she confided to her father in their conversations, didn't understand that "*at all.*" Melted cheese sandwiches were what Merry preferred to everything else. Melted Muenster cheese and white bread. After school she'd bring Patti home with her, and because Merry had thrown out her lunch, they made melted cheese sandwiches. Sometimes they would just melt cheese on a piece of foil. She was sure that she could survive on melted cheese alone, she told her father, if she ever had to. That was probably the most irresponsible thing the child had ever done—after school with Patti melting cheese on pieces of foil and gobbling it down—until she blew up the general store. She couldn't even bring herself to say how much Patti got on her nerves, for fear of hurting Patti's feelings. "The problem is when somebody comes over to your house, after a while you get s-s-s-sick of them." But always she acted with Dawn as though she wanted Patti to stay longer. *Mom, can Patti stay for dinner? Mom, can Patti stay overnight? Mom, can Patti wear my boots? Mom, can you drive me and Patti to the village?*

In fifth grade she gave her mother a Mother's Day gift. On a doily in school they were asked to write something they would do for their mothers, and Merry wrote that she would prepare dinner every Friday night, a fairly generous offer for a ten-year-old but one she made good on and kept up largely because that way she could be sure that one night a week they got baked ziti; also, if you made dinner you didn't have to clean up. With Dawn's help she would sometimes make lasagna or stuffed shells, but the baked ziti she made by herself. Sometimes on Friday it would be macaroni and cheese but mostly it was baked ziti. The important thing, she told her father, was to see that the cheese melted, though it was equally important to be sure that the top zitis got hard and crunchy. He was the one who cleaned up when she cooked the baked ziti, and there was always a lot to clean up. But he loved it. "Cooking is fun and cleaning up is not," she confided in him, but that was not his experience when Merry was cooking. When he heard from a Bloomingdale's buyer that a restaurant on West 49th Street had the best baked ziti in New York, he began to take the family to Vincent's once a month. They'd go to Radio City or to a Broadway musical, and then to Vincent's. Merry loved Vincent's. And a young waiter named Billy loved her, as it turned out, because of a kid brother he had at home who also stuttered. He told Merry about the TV stars and the movie stars who showed up at Vincent's to eat. "See where your dad is sitting? See his chair, signorina? Danny Thomas sat in that chair last night. You know what Danny Thomas says when people come up to his table and introduce themselves to him?" "I d-d-don't," said the signorina. "He says, 'Nice to see you.'" And on Monday, at school, she repeated to Patti whatever Billy at Vincent's in New York had told her the day before. Had there ever been a happier child? A less destructive child? A little signorina any more loved by her mother and father?

No.

A black woman in tight yellow slacks, a woman colossal as a dray horse through the hindquarters, tottered up to him on her high-heeled shoes, extending a tiny scrap of paper in one hand. Her face was badly scarred. He knew she had come to inform him that his daughter was dead. That was what was written on the paper. It was a note from Rita Cohen. "Sir," she said, "can you tell me where the Salvation Army is?" "Is there one?" he asked. She did not look as though she thought there was. But she replied, "I believe so, yeah." She held up the piece of paper. "Says so. Do you know where it is, sir?" Anything beginning with sir or ending with sir usually means "I want money," and so he reached into his pocket, passed her some bills, and she lurched away, disappeared down into the underpass on those ill-fitting shoes, and after that he saw no one.

He waited for forty more minutes and would have waited another forty, have waited there until it grew dark, might well have remained long after that, a man in a seven-hundred-dollar custom-made suit with his back against a lamppost like a vagrant in threadbare rags, a man who from all appearances had meetings to attend and business to transact and social obligations to fulfill, self-consciously loitering on a blighted street near the railroad station, maybe a rich out-of-towner under the mistaken impression that he'd landed in the red-light district, pretending to stare aimlessly into space while his head is full of secrets and his heart is (as it was) thumping away. On the chance that, horribly enough, Rita Cohen was telling the truth and always had been, he might well have stood vigil there all night long and through to the next morning, thinking to catch Merry *coming* to work. But, mercifully, if that is the word, in only forty minutes she appeared, a figure tall and female but one he might never have taken for his daughter had he not been told to look for her there.

Again imagination had failed him. He felt as though he had no control over muscles that he'd mastered at the age of two— he wouldn't have been surprised if everything, not excluding his blood, had come gushing from him onto the pavement. This was too much to battle with. This was too much to bring home to Dawn's new face. Not even electrically operated skylights over a modern kitchen whose heart was a state-of-the-art cooking island would enable her to find her way back from this. Eighteen hundred nights at the mercy of a murderer's father's imagination still hadn't prepared him for her incognito. It had not required this to elude the FBI. How she got to this was too horrible for him to contemplate. But to run from his own child? In fear? There was her *soul* to cherish. "Life!" he instructed himself. "I cannot let her go! Our life!" And by then Merry had seen him, and had it even been possible for him, he did not fall to pieces and run, because it was now too late to run.

And to what would he have run anyway? To that Swede who did it all so effortlessly? To that Swede blessedly oblivious of himself and his thoughts? To the Swede Levov who once upon a time . . . He might as well turn for help to that hefty black woman with the scarred face, expect to find himself by asking her, "Madam, do you know where it is that I am? Have you any idea where I went?"

Merry had seen him. How could she miss him? How could she have missed him even on a street where there was life and not death, where there was a throng of the striving and the harried and the driven and the decisive and not this malignant void? There was her handsome, utterly recognizable six-foot-three father, the handsomest father a girl could have. She raced across the street, this frightful creature, and like the carefree child he used to enjoy envisioning back when he was himself a carefree child—the girl running from her swing outside the stone house—she threw herself upon his chest, her arms encircling his neck. From beneath the veil she wore across the lower half of her face—obscuring her mouth and her chin, a sheer veil that was the ragged foot off an old nylon stocking—she said to the man she had come to detest, "Daddy! Daddy!" faultlessly, just like any other child, and looking like a person whose tragedy was that she'd never been anyone's child.

They are crying intensely, the dependable father whose center is the source of all order, who could not overlook or sanction the smallest sign of chaos—for whom keeping chaos far at bay had been intuition's chosen path to certainty, the rigorous daily given of life—and the daughter who is chaos itself.

6

SHE had become a Jain. Her father didn't know what that meant until, in her unhampered, chantlike speech—the unimpeded speech with which she would have spoken at home had she ever been able to master a stutter while living within her parents' safekeeping—she patiently told him. The Jains were a relatively small Indian religious sect—that he could accept as fact. But whether Merry's practices were typical or of her own devising he could not be certain, even if she contended that every last thing she now did was an expression of religious belief. She wore the veil to do no harm to the microscopic organisms that dwell in the air we breathe. She did not bathe because she revered all life, including the vermin. She did not wash, she said, so as "to do no harm to the water." She did not walk about after dark, even in her own room, for fear of crushing some living object beneath her feet. There are souls, she explained, imprisoned in every form of matter; the lower the form of life, the greater is the pain to the soul imprisoned there. The only way ever to become free of matter and to arrive at what she described as "self-sufficient bliss for all eternity" was to become what she reverentially called "a perfected soul." One achieves this perfection only through the rigors of asceticism and self-denial and through the doctrine of *ahimsa* or nonviolence.

The five "vows" she'd taken were typewritten on index cards and taped to the wall above a narrow pallet of dirty foam rubber on the unswept floor. That was where she slept, and given that there was nothing but the pallet in one corner of the room and a rag pile—her clothing—in the other, that must be where she sat to eat whatever it was she survived on. Very, very little, from the look of her; from the look of her she could have been not fifty minutes east of Old Rimrock but in Delhi or Calcutta, near starvation not as a devout purified by her ascetic practices but as the despised of the lowest caste, miserably moving about on an untouchable's emaciated limbs.

The room was tiny, claustrophobically smaller even than the cell in the juveniles' prison where, when he could not sleep, he would imagine visiting her after she was apprehended. They had reached her room by walking from the dog and cat hospital down toward the station, then turning west through an underpass that led to McCarter Highway, an underpass no more than a hundred and fifty feet long but of the kind that causes drivers to hit the lock button on the door. There were no lights overhead, and the walkways were strewn with broken pieces of furniture, with beer cans, bottles, lumps of things that were unidentifiable. There were license plates underfoot. The place hadn't been cleaned in ten years. Maybe it had never been cleaned. Every step he took, bits of glass crunched beneath his shoes. There was a bar stool upright in the middle of the walkway. It had got there from where? Who had brought it? There was a twisted pair of men's pants. Filthy. Who was the man? What had happened to him? The Swede would not have been surprised to see an arm or a leg. A garbage sack blocked their way. Dark plastic. Knotted shut. What was in it? It was large enough for a dead body. And there were bodies, too, that were living, people shifting around in the filth, dangerous-looking people back in the dark. And above the blackened rafters, the thudding of a train—the noise of the trains rolling into the station heard from beneath their wheels. Five, six hundred trains a day rolling overhead.

To get where Merry rented a room just off McCarter Highway, you had to make it through an underpass not just as dangerous as any in Newark but as dangerous as any underpass in the world.

They were walking because she would not drive with him. "I only walk, Daddy, I do not go in motor vehicles," and so he had left his car out on Railroad Avenue for whoever came along to steal it, and walked beside her the ten minutes it took to reach her room, a walk that would have brought him to tears within the first ten steps had he not continued to recite to himself, "This is life! This is our life! I cannot let her go," had he not taken her hand in his and, as they traversed together that horrible underpass, reminded himself, "This is her hand. Merry's hand. Nothing matters but her hand." Would have brought him to tears because when she was six and seven years old she'd loved to play marines, either him yelling at her or her yelling at him, " 'Ten*shun!* Stand at ease! Rest!"; she loved to march with him—"Forward *march!* To the left flank *march!* To the rear *march!* Right oblique *march!*"; loved to do marine calisthenics with him—"You People, hit the deck!"; she loved to call the ground "the deck," to call their bathroom "the head," to call her bed "the rack" and Dawn's food "the chow"; but most of all she loved to count Parris Island cadence for him as she started out across the pasture—mounted up on his shoulders—to find Momma's cows. "By yo leh, rah, leh, rah, leh, rah yo leh. Leh, rah, yo leh. . . ." And without stuttering. When they played marines, she did not stutter over a single word.

The room was on the ground floor of a house that a hundred years ago might have been a boardinghouse, not a bad one either, a respectable boardinghouse, brownstone below the parlor floor, neat brickwork above, curved railings of cast iron leading up the brick steps to the double doorway. But the old boardinghouse was now a wreck marooned on a narrow street where there were only two other houses left. Incredibly, two of the old Newark plane trees were left as well. The house was tucked between abandoned warehouses and overgrown lots studded with chunks of rusted iron junk, mechanical debris scattered amid the weeds.

From over the door of the house, the pediment was gone, ripped out; the cornices had been ripped out too, carefully stolen and taken away to be sold in some New York antiques store. All over Newark, the oldest buildings were missing ornamental stone cornices—cornices from as high up as four stories plucked off in broad daylight with a cherry picker, with a hundred-thousand-dollar piece of equipment; but the cop is asleep or paid off and nobody stops whoever it is, from whatever agency that has a cherry picker, who is making a little cash on the side. The turkey frieze that ran around the old Essex produce market on Washington and Linden, the frieze with the terra-cotta turkeys and the huge cornucopias overflowing with fruit—stolen. Building caught fire and the frieze disappeared overnight. The big Negro churches (Bethany Baptist closed down, boarded up, looted, bulldozed; Wycliffe Presbyterian disastrously gutted by fire)—cornices stolen. Aluminum drainpipes even from occupied buildings, from standing buildings —stolen. Gutters, leaders, drainpipes—stolen. Everything was gone that anybody could get to. Just reach up and take it.

Copper tubing in boarded-up factories, pull it out and sell it. Anyplace where the windows are gone and boarded up tells people immediately, "Come in and strip it. Whatever's left, strip it, steal it, sell it." Stripping stuff—that's the food chain. Drive by a place where a sign says this house is for sale, and there's nothing there, there's nothing to sell. Everything stolen by gangs in cars, stolen by the men who roam a city with shopping carts, stolen by thieves working alone. The people are desperate and they take anything. They "go junkin'" the way a shark goes fishing.

"If there's one brick still on top of the other," cried his father, "the idea gets into their heads that the *mortar* might be useful, so they'll push them apart and take *that*. Why not? The mortar! Seymour, this city isn't a city—it's a carcass! Get out!"

The street where Merry lived was paved with bricks. There couldn't be more than a dozen of these brick streets intact in the entire city. The last of the cobblestone streets, a pretty old cobblestone street, had been stolen about three weeks after the riots. While the rubble still reeked of smoke where the devastation was the worst, a developer from the suburbs had arrived with a crew around one A.M., three trucks and some twenty men moving stealthily, and during the night, without a cop to bother them, they'd dug up the cobblestones from the narrow side street that cut diagonally back of Newark Maid and carted them all away. The street was gone when the Swede showed up for work the next morning.

"Now they're stealing streets?" his father asked. "Newark can't even hold on to its streets? Seymour, get the hell out!" His father's had become the voice of reason.

Merry's street was just a couple of hundred feet long, squeezed into the triangle between McCarter—where, as always, the heavy truck traffic barreled by night and day—and the ruins of Mulberry Street. Mulberry the Swede could recall as a Chinatown slum as long ago as the 1930s, back when the Newark Levovs, Jerry, Seymour, Momma, Poppa, used to file up the narrow stairwell to one of the family restaurants for a chow mein dinner on a Sunday afternoon and, later, driving home to Keer Avenue, his father would tell the boys unbelievable stories about the Mulberry Street "tong wars" of old.

Of old. Stories of old. There were no longer stories of old.

There was nothing. There was a mattress, discolored and water-logged, like a cartoon-strip drunk slumped against a pole. The pole still held up a sign telling you what corner you were on. And that's all there was.

Above and beyond the roofline of her house, he could see the skyline of commercial Newark half a mile away and those three familiar, comforting words, the most reassuring words in the English language, cascading down the elegantly ornate cliff that was once the focal point of a buzzing downtown—ten stories high the huge, white stark letters heralding fiscal confidence and institutional permanence, civic progress and opportunity and pride, indestructible letters that you could read from the seat of your jetliner descending from the north toward the international airport: FIRST FIDELITY BANK.

That's what was left, that lie. First. *Last.* LAST FIDELITY BANK. From down on the earth where his daughter now lived at the corner of Columbia and Green—where his daughter lived even worse than her greenhorn great-grandparents had, fresh from steerage, in their Prince Street tenement—you could see a mammoth signboard designed for concealing the truth. A sign in which only a madman could believe. A sign in a fairy tale.

Three generations. All of them growing. The working. The saving. The success. Three generations in raptures over America. Three generations of becoming one with a people. And now with the fourth it had all come to nothing. The total vandalization of their world.

Her room had no window, only a narrow transom over the door that opened onto the unlit hallway, a twenty-foot-long urinal whose decaying plaster walls he wanted to smash apart with his fists the moment he entered the house and smelled it. The hallway led out to the street through a door that had neither lock nor handle, nor glass in the double frame. Nowhere in her room could he see a faucet or a radiator. He could not imagine what the toilet was like or where it might be and wondered if the hallway was it for her as well as for the bums who wandered in off the highway or down from Mulberry Street. She would have lived better than this, far better, if she were one of Dawn's cattle, in the shed where the herd gathered in the worst weather with the proximity of one another's carcasses to warm them, and the rugged coats they grew in winter, and

Merry's mother, even in the sleet, even on an icy, wintry day, up before six carrying hay bales to feed them. He thought of the cattle not at all unhappy out there in the winter and he thought of those two they called the "derelicts," Dawn's retired giant, Count, and the old mare Sally, each of them in human years comparable to seventy or seventy-five, who found each other when they were both over the hill and then became inseparable—one would go and the other would follow, doing all the things together that would keep them well and happy. It was fascinating to watch their routine and the wonderful life they had. Remembering how when it was sunny they would stretch out in the sun to warm their hides, he thought, If only she had become an animal.

It was beyond understanding, not only how Merry could be living in this hovel like a pariah, not only how Merry could be a fugitive wanted for murder, but how he and Dawn could have been the source of it all. How could their innocent foibles add up to this human being? Had none of this happened, had she stayed at home, finished high school, gone to college, there would have been problems, of course, big problems; she was precocious in her rebellion and there would have been problems even without a war in Vietnam. She might have wallowed a long while in the pleasures of resistance and the challenge of discovering how unrestrained she could be. But she would have been at home. At home you flip out a little and that's it. You do not have the pleasure of the *unadulterated* pleasure, you don't get to the point where you flip out a little so many times that finally you decide it's such a great, great kick, why not flip out a lot? At home there is no opportunity to douse yourself in this squalor. At home you can't live where the disorder is. At home you can't live where nothing is reined in. At home there is that tremendous discrepancy between the way she imagines the world to be and the way the world is for her. Well, no longer is there that dissonance to disturb her equilibrium. Here are her Rimrockian fantasies, and the culmination is horrifying.

Their disaster had been tragically shaped by time—they did not have enough time with her. When she's your ward, when she's there, you can do it. If you have contact with your child steadily over time, then the stuff that is off—the mistakes in judgment that are made on both sides—is somehow, through that steady, patient contact, made better and better, until at last, inch by inch, day by day and inch by inch, there is remediation, there are the ordinary satisfactions of parental patience rewarded, of things working out. . . . But this. Where was the remediation for *this*? Could he bring Dawn here to see her, Dawn in her bright, tight new face and Merry sitting cross-legged on the pallet in her tattered sweatshirt and ill-shapen trousers and black plastic shower clogs, meekly composed behind that nauseating veil? How broad her shoulder bones were. Like his. But hanging off those bones there was nothing. What he saw sitting before him was not a daughter, a woman, or a girl; what he saw, in a scarecrow's clothes, stick-skinny as a scarecrow, was the scantiest farmyard emblem of life, a travestied mock-up of a human being, so meager a likeness to a Levov it could have fooled only a bird. How could he bring Dawn here? Driving Dawn down McCarter Highway, turning off McCarter and into this street, the warehouses, the rubble, the garbage, the debris . . . Dawn seeing this room, smelling this room, her hands touching the walls of this room, let alone the unwashed flesh, the brutally cropped, bedraggled hair . . .

He kneeled down to read the index cards positioned just about where she once used to venerate, over her Old Rimrock bed, magazine photos of Audrey Hepburn.

I renounce all killing of living beings, whether subtle or gross, whether movable or immovable.

I renounce all vices of lying speech arising from anger, or greed, or fear, or mirth.

I renounce all taking of anything not given, either in a village, or a town, or a wood, either of little or much, or small or great, or living or lifeless things.

I renounce all sexual pleasures, either with gods, or men, or animals.

I renounce all attachments, whether little or much, small or great, living or lifeless; neither shall I myself form such attachments, nor cause others to do so, nor consent to their doing so.

As a businessman the Swede was astute, and if need be, beneath the genial surface of the man's man—capitalizing on the genial surface—he could be as artfully calculating as the deal required. But he could not see how even the coldest calculation could help him here. Neither could all the fathering talent in the world collected and gathered up and mobilized in one man. He read through her five vows again, considered them as seriously as he could, all the while bewildering himself with the thought, For purity—in the name of purity.

Why? Because she'd killed someone, or because she would have needed purity whether she'd never killed a fly? Did it have to do with him? That foolish kiss? That was ten years behind them, and besides, it had been nothing, had come to nothing, did not appear to have meant anything much to her even at the time. Could something as meaningless, as commonplace, as ephemeral, as understandable, as forgivable, as innocent . . . No! How could he be asked again and again to take seriously things that were not serious? Yet that was the predicament that Merry had forced on him all the way back when she was blasting away at the dinner table about the immorality of their bourgeois life. How could anybody take that childish ranting seriously? He had done as well as any parent could have—he had listened and listened when it was all he could do not to get up from dinner and walk away until she'd spewed herself out; he had nodded and agreed to as much as he could even marginally agree to, and when he opposed her—say, about the moral efficacy of the profit motive—always it was with restraint, with all the patient reasonableness he could muster. And this was not easy for him, given that it was the profit motive to which a child requiring tens of thousands of dollars' worth of orthodontia, psychiatry, and speech therapy—not to mention ballet lessons and riding lessons and tennis lessons, all of which, growing up, she at one time or another was convinced she could not survive without—might be thought to owe if not a certain allegiance then at least a minuscule portion of gratitude. Perhaps the *mistake* was to have tried so hard to take seriously what was in no way serious; perhaps what he should have done, instead of listening so intently, so *respectfully*, to her ignorant raving was to reach over the table and whack her across the mouth.

But what would that have taught her about the profit motive—what would it have taught her about him? Yet if he had, *if*, then the veiled mouth could be taken seriously. He could now berate himself, "Yes, I did it to her, I did it with my outbursts, my temper." But it seemed as though he had done whatever had been done to her because he could not *abide* a temper, had not wanted one or dared to have one. He had done it by kissing her. But that couldn't be. *None of this could possibly be.*

Yet it was. Here we are. Here *she* is, imprisoned in this rat hole with these "vows."

She was better off steeped in contempt. If he had to choose between angry, fat Merry stuttering with Communist outrage and *this* Merry, veiled, placid, dirty, infinitely compassionate, this raggedly attired scarecrow Merry . . . But why have to choose either? Why must she always be enslaving herself to the handiest empty-headed idea? From the moment she had become old enough to think for herself she had been tyrannized instead by the thinking of crackpots. What had he done to produce a daughter who, after excelling for years at school, refused to think for herself—a daughter who had to be either violently against everything in sight or pathetically *for* everything, right down to the microorganisms in the air we breathe? Why did a girl as smart as she was *strive* to let other people do her thinking for her? Why was it beyond her to strive—as he had every day of his life—to be all that one is, to be true to *that*? "But the one who doesn't think for himself is *you*!" she'd told him when he'd suggested that she might be parroting the clichés of others. "*You're* the living example of the person who *never* thinks for himself!" "Am I really?" he said, laughing. "Yes! You're the most conformist man I ever met! All you do is what's expec-expec-expected of you!" "That's terrible too?" "It's not *thinking*, D-d-dad! It isn't! It's being a s-s-stupid aut-aut-aut-aut-aut-automaton! A r-r-r-r-robot!" "Well," he replied, believing that it was all a phase, a bad-tempered phase she would outgrow, "I guess you're just stuck with a comformist father— better luck next time," and pretended that he had not been terrified by the sight of her distended, pulsating, frothing lips hammering "r-r-r-r-robot" into his face with the ferocity of a lunatic riveter. A phase, he thought, and felt comforted, and never once considered that thinking "a phase" might be a not bad example of not thinking for yourself.

Fantasy and magic. Always pretending to be somebody else. What began benignly enough when she was playing at Audrey Hepburn had evolved in only a decade into this outlandish myth of selflessness. First the selfless nonsense of the People, now the selfless nonsense of the Perfected Soul. What next, Grandma Dwyer's Cross? Back to the selfless nonsense of the Eternal Candle and the Sacred Heart? Always a grandiose un-reality, the remotest abstraction around—*never* self-seeking, not in a million years. The lying, inhuman horror of all this selflessness.

Yes, he had liked his daughter better when she was as self-seeking as everyone else rather than blessed with flawless speech and monstrous altruism.

"How long have you been here?" he asked her.

"Where?"

"This room. This street. In Newark. How long have you been in Newark?"

"I came six months ago."

"You've been . . ." Because there was everything to say, to ask, to demand to know, he could say no more. Six months. In Newark six months. There was no here and now for the Swede, there were just two inflammatory words matter-of-factly spoken: six months.

He stood over her, facing her, his power pinned to the wall, rocking almost imperceptibly back on the heels of his shoes, as though in this way he might manage to take leave of her *through* the wall, then rocking forward onto his toes, as though at any moment to grab her, to whisk her up into his arms and out. He couldn't return home to sleep in perfect safety in the Old Rimrock house knowing that she was in those rags in that veil on that mat, looking like the loneliest person on earth, sleeping only inches from a hallway that sooner or later had to catch up with her.

This girl was mad by the time she was fifteen, and kindly and stupidly he had tolerated that madness, crediting her with nothing worse than a point of view he didn't like but that she would surely outgrow along with her rebellious adolescence. And now look what she looked like. The ugliest daughter ever born of two attractive parents. I renounce this! I renounce that! I renounce everything! *That* couldn't be it, could it? All of it to renounce his looks and Dawn's? All of it because the mother was once Miss New Jersey? Is life this belittling? It can't be. I won't have it!

"How long have you been a Jain?"

"One year."

"How did you find out about all this?"

"Studying religions."

"How much do you weigh, Meredith?"

"More than enough, Daddy."

Her eye sockets were huge. Half an inch above the veil, big, big dark eye sockets, and inches above the eye sockets the hair, which no longer streamed down her back but seemed just to have happened onto her head, still blond like his but long and thick no longer because of a haircut that was itself an act of violence. Who'd done it? She or someone else? And with what? She could not, in keeping with her five vows, have renounced any attachment as savagely as she had renounced her once-beautiful hair.

"But you don't look as though you eat *anything*," and despite his intention to state this to her unemotionally, he as good as moaned—unbidden a voice emerged from the Swede wretchedly laced with all his dismay. "What do you *eat*?"

"I destroy plant life. I am insufficiently compassionate as yet to refuse to do that."

"You mean you eat vegetables. Is that what you mean? What is wrong with that? How could you refuse to do that? Why *should* you?"

"It is an issue of personal sanctity. It is a matter of reverence for life. I am bound to harm no living being, neither man, nor animal, nor plant."

"But you would *die* if you did that. How can you be 'bound' to that? You would eat nothing."

"You ask a profound question. You are a very intelligent man, Daddy. You ask, 'If you respect life in all forms, how can you live?' The answer is you cannot. The traditional way by which a Jain holy man ends his life is by *salla khana*—self-starvation. Ritual death by *salla khana* is the price paid for perfection by the perfect Jain."

"I cannot believe this is you. I have to tell you what I think."

"Of course you do."

"I cannot believe, clever as you are, that you know what you are saying or what you are doing here or why. I cannot believe that you are telling me that a point will come when you will decide that you will not even destroy plant life, and that you won't eat anything, and that you will just doom yourself to death. For whom, Merry? For what?"

"It's all right. It's all right, Daddy. I can believe that you can't believe that you know what I'm saying or what I'm doing or why."

She addressed him as though *he* were the child and *she* were the parent, with nothing but sympathetic understanding, with that loving tolerance that he once had so disastrously extended to her. And it galled him. The condescension of a lunatic. Yet he neither bolted for the door nor leaped to do what had to be done. He remained the reasonable father. The reasonable father of someone mad. Do something! Anything! In the name of everything reasonable, stop being reasonable. This child needs a hospital. She could not be in any greater peril if she were adrift on a plank in the middle of the sea. She's gone over the edge of the ship—how that happened is not the question now. She must be rescued immediately!

"Tell me where you studied religions."

"In libraries. Nobody looks for you there. I was in libraries often, and so I read. I read a lot."

"You read a lot when you were a little girl."

"I did? I like to read."

"That's where you became a member of this religion. In a library."

"Yes."

"And church? Do you go to some sort of a church?"

"There is no church at the center. There is no god at the center. God is at the center of the Judeo-Christian tradition. And God may say, 'Take life.' And it is then not just permissible but obligatory. That's all over the Old Testament. There are examples even in the New Testament. In Judaism and Christianity the position is taken that life belongs to God. Life isn't sacred, God is sacred. But at the center for us is not a belief in the sovereignty of God but a belief in the sanctity of life."

The monotonous chant of the indoctrinated, ideologically armored from head to foot—the monotonous, spellbound chant of those whose turbulence can be caged only within the suffocating straitjacket of the most supercoherent of dreams. What was missing from her unstuttered words was not the sanctity of life—missing was the sound of life.

"How many of you are there?" he asked, working fiercely to adjust to clarifications with which she was only further bewildering him.

"Three million."

Three million people like her? It could not be. In rooms like this one? Locked away in three million terrible rooms? "Where are they, Merry?"

"In India."

"I'm not asking you about India. I don't care about India. We do not live in India. In America, how many of you are there?"

"I don't know. It's unimportant."

"I would think very few."

"I don't know."

"Merry, are you the only one?"

"My spiritual exploration I undertook on my own."

"I do not understand. Merry, I do not understand. How did you get from Lyndon Johnson to this? How do you get from point A to point Z, where there is no point of contact *at all*? Merry, it does not hang together."

"There is a point of contact. I assure you there is. It all hangs together. You just don't see it."

"Do *you?*"

"Yes."

"Tell it to me then. I want you to tell it to me so that I can understand what has *happened* to you."

"There is a logic, Daddy. You mustn't raise your voice. I will explain. It all links up. I have given it much thought. It goes like this. *Ahimsa*, the Jain concept of nonviolence, appealed to Mahatma Gandhi. He was not a Jain. He was Hindu. But when he was looking in India for a group that was genuinely Indian and not Western and that could point to charitable works as impressive as those the Christian missionaries had produced, he landed on the Jains. We are a small group. We are not Hindus but our beliefs are akin to Hindus'. We are a religion founded in the sixth century B.C. Mahatma Gandhi took from us this notion of *ahimsa*, nonviolence. We are the core of truth that created Mahatma Gandhi. And Mahatma Gandhi, in his nonviolence, is the core of truth that created Martin Luther King. And Martin Luther King is the core of truth that created the civil rights movement. And, at the end of his life, when he was moving beyond the civil rights movement to a larger vision, when he was opposing the war in Vietnam . . ."

Without stuttering. Speech that once would have impelled her to grimace and turn white and bang on the table—would have made of her an embattled speaker attacked by the words and obstinately attacking them back—delivered now patiently, graciously, still in that monotonous chant but edged with the gentlest tone of spiritual urgency. Everything she could not achieve with a speech therapist and a psychiatrist and a stuttering diary she had beautifully realized by going mad. Subjecting herself to isolation and squalor and terrible danger, she had attained control, mental and physical, over every sound she uttered. An intelligence no longer impeded by the blight of stuttering.

And intelligence was what he was hearing, Merry's quick, sharp, studious brain, the logical mind she'd had since earliest childhood. And hearing it opened him up to pain such as he had never before imagined. The intelligence was intact and yet she was mad, her logic a brand of logic bereft totally of the power to reason with which it had already entwined itself by the time she was ten. It was absurd—this being reasonable with her was *his* madness. Sitting there trying to act as though he were respectful of her religion when her religion consisted of an absolute failure to understand what life is and is not. The two of them acting as if he had come there to be educated. Being *lectured*, by her!

". . . we do not understand salvation as in any way the union of the human soul with something beyond itself. The spirit of Jain piety lives in founder Mahavira's saying, 'O man,

thou art thine own friend. Why seekest thou for a friend beyond thyself?' "

"Merry, did you do it? I must ask you this now. Did you
do it?"

It was the question he had expected to ask her first, once
they had reached her room and before everything else that was
horrible began painfully to be sifted through and scrutinized.
He thought he had waited because he did not want her to
think that his first consideration was anything other than at
long last seeing her and seeing to her, attending to her well-
being; but now that he had asked, he knew that he hadn't already asked because he could not bear to hear an answer.

"Do what, Daddy?"

"Did you bomb the post office?"

"Yes."

"You intended to blow up Hamlin's too?"

"There was no other way to do it."

"Except not to do it. Merry, you must tell me now who
made you do it?"

"Lyndon Johnson."

"That will not do. No! Answer me. Who talked you *into* it?
Who brainwashed you? Who did you do it *for*?"

There had to be forces outside. The prayer went, "Lead me
not into temptation." If people were not led by others, why
was that the famous prayer that it was? A child who had been
blessed with every privilege could not have done this on her
own. Blessed with love. Blessed with a loving and ethical and
prosperous family. Who had enlisted her and lured her into this?

"How strongly you still crave the idea," she said, "of your
innocent offspring."

"Who was it? Don't protect them. Who is responsible?"

"Daddy, you can detest me alone. It's all right."

"You are telling me you did it all on your own. Knowing
that Hamlin's would be destroyed too. That's what you are
saying."

"Yes. I am the abomination. Abhor *me*."

He remembered then something she had written in the sixth
or seventh grade, before she'd gone on to Morristown High.
The students in her class at her Montessori school were asked

ten questions about their "philosophy," one a week. The first
week the teacher asked, "Why are we here?" Instead of writing
as the other kids did—here to do good, here to make the world
a better place, etc.—Merry answered with her own question:
"Why are apes here?" But the teacher found this an inadequate
response and told her to go home and think about the question more seriously—"Expand on this," the teacher said. So
Merry went home and did as she was told and the next day
handed in an additional sentence: "Why are kangaroos here?"
It was at this point that Merry was first informed by a teacher
that she had a "stubborn streak." The final question assigned
to the class was "What is life?" Merry's answer was something
her father and mother chuckled over together that night.
According to Merry, while the other students labored busily
away with their phony deep thoughts, she—after an hour of
thinking at her desk—wrote a single, unplatitudinous declarative sentence: "Life is just a short period of time in which you
are alive." "You know," said the Swede, "it's smarter than it
sounds. She's a kid—how has she figured out that life is short?
She is somethin', our precocious daughter. This girl is going to
Harvard." But once again the teacher didn't agree, and she
wrote beside Merry's answer, "Is that *all*?" Yes, the Swede
thought now, that is all. Thank God, that is all; even that is
unendurable.

The truth was that he had known all along: without a
tempter's assistance, everything angry inside her had broken
into the open. She was unintimidated, she was *unintimidat-
able*, this child who had written for her teacher not, like the
other kids, that life was a beautiful gift and a great opportunity
and a noble endeavor and a blessing from God but that it was
just a short period of time in which you were alive. Yes, the intention had been all her own. That had to be. Her antagonism
had been intent on murder and nothing less. Otherwise this
mad repose would not be the result.

He tried to let reason rise once again to the surface. How
hard he tried. What does a reasonable man say next? If, after
being battered and once again brought nearly to tears by what
he'd just heard uttered so matter-of-factly—everything incredible uttered so matter-of-factly—a man could hold on and be

reasonable, what does he go ahead to say? What does a reason-able, responsible father say if he is able still to feel intact as a father?

"Merry, may I tell you what I think? I think you are terrified of being punished for what you've done. I think that rather than evade your punishment you have taken it into your own hands. I don't believe that's a difficult conclusion to reach, honey. I don't believe I'm the only person in the world who, seeing you here, seeing you here looking like this, would come up with that idea. You're a good girl and so you want to do pen-ance. But this is not penance. Not even the state would punish you like this. I have to say these things, Merry. I have to tell you truthfully what this looks like to me."

"Of course you do."

"Just look at what you've done to yourself—you are going to *die* if you keep this up. Another year of this and you *will* die—from self-starvation, from malnutrition, from *filth*. You cannot go back and forth every day under those railroad tracks. That underpass is a home for derelicts—for derelicts who do not play by your rules. Their world is a ruthless world, Merry, a terrible world—a *violent* world."

"They won't harm me. They know that I love them."

The words sickened him, the flagrant childishness, the senti-mental grandiosity of the self-deception. What does she see in the hopeless scurryings of these wretched people that could justify such an idea? Derelicts and love? To be a derelict living in an underpass is to have clobbered out of you a hundred times over the minutest *susceptibility* to love. This was awful. Now that her speech is finally cleared of the stuttering, all that comes through is this junk. What he had dreamed about—that his wonderful, gifted child would one day stop stuttering—had come to pass. She had mastered miraculously the agitated stut-tering only to reveal, at the eye of the storm that was her erupted personality, this insane clarity and calm. What a great revenge to take: This is what you wanted, Daddy? Well, here it is.

Her being able successfully to explain and to talk was now the worst thing of all.

The harshness he felt but didn't want her to hear was in his voice nonetheless when he said, "You will meet a violent end,

Meredith. Keep trying them out twice a day, keep it up and you'll find out just how much they know about your love. Their hunger, Merry, is not for love. Somebody will kill you!"

"But only to be reborn."

"I doubt that, honey. I seriously doubt that."

"Will you concede that my guess is as good as yours, Dad?"

"Won't you at least take off that mask while we're talking? So I can see you?"

"See me stutter, do you mean?"

"Well, I don't know if wearing that is what accounts for the disappearance of your stutter or not. You tell me that it has. You tell me that the stutter was only your way of doing no violence to the air and the things that live in the air . . . is that correct? Have I understood what you were saying?"

"Yes."

"Well . . . even if I were to concede that, I have to tell you I think you might eventually have a better life *with* your stutter. I don't minimize the hardship it was for you. But if it turns out you had to carry things to this extreme to be rid of that damn thing . . . then I really do wonder . . . well, if it's the best trade-off imaginable."

"You can't explain away what I've done by motives, Daddy. I certainly wouldn't explain away what *you've* done by motives."

"But I *do* have motives. *Everyone* has motives."

"You cannot reduce the journey of a soul to that kind of psychology. It is not worthy of you."

"Then *you* explain it. Explain it to me, *please*. How do you explain that when you took all this . . . what looks to me like misery and nothing more, that when you did that, took upon yourself real suffering, which is all this is, suffering that you have *chosen*, Merry, real suffering and nothing more or less than suffering"—his voice was wavering but on he went, reasonable, reasonable, responsible, responsible—"*then*, only *then*—do you see what I'm saying?—the stutter vanished?"

"I've told you. I am done with craving and selfhood."

"Sweet, sweet child and girl." He sat down amid the filth of the floor, helpless to do anything other than try to his utmost not to lose control.

In the tiny room, where they now sat no more than an arm's length from each other, there was no light other than what fell through the dirty transom. She lived without light. Why? Had she renounced the vice of electricity too? She lived without light, she lived without everything. This was how their life had worked out: she lived in Newark with nothing, he lived in Old Rimrock with everything except her. Was his good fortune to blame for that too? The revenge of the have-nots upon those who have and own. All the self-styled have-nots, the playacting Rita Cohens seeking to associate themselves with their parents' worst enemies, modeling themselves on whatever was most loathsome to those who most loved them.

There used to be a slogan she'd crayoned in two colors on a piece of cardboard, a handmade poster that she'd hung over her desk, replacing his Weequahic football pennant; the poster had hung there undisturbed all during the year before her disappearance. Till it went up, she had always coyly coveted the Weequahic pennant because the Swede's high school sweetheart had taken it to sewing class in 1943 and stitched into the felt along the bottom edge of the orange and brown triangle, in thick white thread, "To All-City Levov, XXXX, Arlene." The poster was the only thing he had dared to remove from her room and destroy, and even doing that much had taken three months; appropriating the property of another, adult or child, was simply repugnant to him. But three months after the bombing he marched up the stairs and into her room and tore the poster down. It read: "We are against everything that is good and decent in honky America. We will loot and burn and destroy. We are the incubation of your mother's nightmares." In large square letters the attribution: "WEATHERMEN MOTTO." And because he was a tolerant man he'd tolerated that too. "Honky" in his daughter's hand. Hanging there for a year in his own home, each red letter shadowed heavily in black.

And because even though he hadn't liked it one bit he did not believe it was his right blah-blah blah-blah blah, because—out of regard for her property and her personal freedom—he couldn't even pull down an awful poster, because he was not capable of even that much righteous violence, now the hideous realization of the nightmare had come along to test even further the limits of his enlightened tolerance. She thinks if she raises a hand she'll swat and kill an innocent mite that is innocently floating by her—so in touch is she with the environment

that any and every move she makes will have the most stupen-
dously dire consequences—and he thinks that if he removes a
hateful and disgusting poster that she has put up, he'll do damage to her integrity, to her psyche, to her First Amendment
rights. No, he wasn't a Jain, thought the Swede, but he might
as well have been—he was just as pathetically and naively nonviolent. The idiocy of the uprightness of the goals he had set.

"Who is Rita Cohen?" he asked.

"I don't know. Who is she?"

"The girl who came to me in your behalf. In '68. After you
disappeared. She came to my office."

"Nobody has ever come to you in my behalf, no one I have
ever sent."

"Yes, a short little girl. Very pale. Her hair in an Afro. Dark
hair. I gave her your ballet slippers and your Audrey Hepburn
scrapbook and your diary. Is she the person who put you up to
this? Is she the person who made the bomb? You used to talk
to somebody on the phone when you were still at home—those
secret conversations you had." The secret conversations that,
like the poster, he had also "respected." If only he had torn
down that poster and pulled the plug on her phone and locked
her up then and there! "Was that the person?" he asked her
now. "Tell me the truth, please."

"I only speak the truth."

"I gave her ten thousand dollars for you. I gave her cash.
Did you or did you not get that money?"

Her laugh was kindly. "Ten thousand dollars? Not yet,
Daddy."

"Then I must have an answer from you. Who is the Rita
Cohen who told me where I could find you? Is this the Melissa
from New York?"

"You found me," she replied, "because you have been looking. I never expected not to be found by you. You sought me
out because you *must* seek me."

"Did you come to Newark to help me find you? Is that why
you came here?"

But she replied, "No."

"Then *why* did you come? What were you thinking? *Were*
you thinking? You know where the office is. You know how
very close it is. Where's the logic, Merry? This close and . . ."

"I got a ride, and here I was, you see."

"Like that. Coincidence. No logic. No logic anywhere."

"The world is not a place on which I have influence or wish to have any. I relinquish all influence over everything. As to what constitutes a coincidence, you and I, Daddy—"

"Do you 'relinquish all influence'?" he cried. "*Do* you, '*all* influence'?" The most maddening conversation of his life. The know-it-all-ism of her absurdly innocent, profoundly insane, unstuttering solemnity, the awful candor of the room and of the street outside, the awful candor of *everything* outside him that was so powerfully controlling him. "You have an influence over *me*," he shouted, "you are influencing *me*! You who will not kill a mite are killing *me*! What you sit there calling 'coincidence' *is* influence—your powerlessness is power over *me*, goddamn it! Over your mother, over your grandfather, over your grandmother, over everyone who loves you—wearing that veil is bullshit, Merry, complete and absolute *bullshit*! You are the most powerful person in the world!"

There was no solace to be found in thinking, This is *not* my life, this is the *dream* of my life. That was not going to make him any less miserable. Nor was the rage with his daughter, nor was the rage with the little criminal whom he had allowed to be cast as their savior. A cunning and malicious crook who suckered him without half trying. Took him for all she could get in four ten-minute visits. The viciousness. The audacity. The unshatterable nerves. God alone knew where such kids came from.

Then he remembered that one of them came from his house. Rita Cohen merely came from somebody else's house. They were brought up in houses like his own. They were raised by parents like him. And so many were girls, girls whose political identity was total, who were no less aggressive and militant, no less drawn to "armed action" than the boys. There is something terrifyingly pure about their violence and the thirst for self-transformation. They renounce their roots to take as their models the revolutionaries whose conviction is enacted most ruthlessly. They manufacture like unstoppable machines the abhorrence that propels their steely idealism. Their rage is combustible. They are willing to do anything they can imagine to make history change. The draft isn't even hanging over their heads; they sign on freely and fearlessly to terrorize against the war, competent to rob at gunpoint, equipped in every way to maim and kill with explosives, undeterred by fear or doubt or inner contradiction—girls in hiding, dangerous girls, attackers, implacably extremist, completely unsociable. He read the names of girls in the papers who were wanted by the authorities for crimes allegedly stemming from antiwar activities, girls that he imagined Merry knew, girls with whose lives he imagined his daughter's to be now interlinked: Bernardine, Patricia, Judith, Cathlyn, Susan, Linda. . . . His father, after foolishly watching a TV news special about the police hunt for the underground Weathermen, among them Mark Rudd and Katherine Boudin and Jane Alpert—all in their twenties, Jewish, middle class, college-educated, violent in behalf of the antiwar cause, committed to revolutionary change and determined to overturn the United States government—went around saying, "I remember when Jewish kids were home doing their homework. What happened? What the hell happened to our smart Jewish kids? If, God forbid, their parents are no longer oppressed for a while, they run where they think they can find oppression. Can't live without it. Once Jews ran away from oppression; now they run away from no-oppression. Once they ran away from being poor; now they run away from being rich. It's crazy. They have parents they can't hate anymore because their parents are so good to them, so they hate America instead." But Rita Cohen was a case unto herself: a vicious slut and a common crook.

Then how is he to explain her letter, if that is all she is? What happened to our smart Jewish kids? They *are* crazy. Something is *driving* them crazy. Something has set them against everything. Something is leading them into disaster. These are not the smart Jewish children intent on getting ahead by doing what they are told better than anyone else does. They only feel at home doing better than anyone else as they are *not* told. Distrust is the madness to which they have been called.

And here on the floor is the result in one of its more heartbreaking forms: the religious conversion. If you fail to bring the world into subjection, then subject yourself to the world.

"I *love* you," he was telling Merry, "you *know* I would look for you. You are my *child*. But how could I find you in a million years, wearing that mask and weighing eighty-eight pounds and living the way you live? How could anyone have found you, even here? Where *were* you?" he cried, as angry as the angriest father ever betrayed by a daughter or a son, so angry he feared that his head was about to spew out his brains just as Kennedy's did when he was shot. "Where have you *been*? Answer me!"

So she told him where she'd been.

And how did he listen? Wondering: If there was some point in their lives *before* she took the wrong path, where and when was it? Thinking: There was no such point, there was never any controlling Merry however many years she managed to deceive them, to seem safely theirs and under their sway. Thinking: Futile, every last thing he had ever done. The preparations, the practice, the obedience; the uncompromising dedication to the essential, to the things that matter most; the systematic system building, the patient scrutiny of every problem, large or small; no drifting, no laxity, no laziness; faithfully meeting every obligation, addressing energetically every situation's demands . . . a list as long as the U.S. Constitution, his articles of faith—and all of it futility. The systemization of futility is all it had ever been. All he had ever restrained by his responsibility was himself.

Thinking: She is not in my power and she never was. She is in the power of something that does not give a shit. Something demented. We all are. Their elders are not responsible for this. They are themselves not responsible for this. Something else is.

Yes, at the age of forty-six, in 1973, almost three-quarters of the way through the century that with no regard for the niceties of burial had strewn the corpses of mutilated children and their mutilated parents everywhere, the Swede found out that we are all in the power of something demented. It's just a matter of time, honky. We all are!

He heard them laughing, the Weathermen, the Panthers, the angry ragtag army of the violent Uncorrupted who called him a criminal and hated his guts because he was one of those who own and have. *The Swede finally found out!* They were delirious with joy, delighted having destroyed his once-pampered daughter and ruined his privileged life, shepherding him at long last to their truth, to the truth as they knew it to be for every Vietnamese man, woman, child, and tot, for every colonized black in America, for everyone everywhere who had been fucked over by the capitalists and their insatiable greed. The something that's demented, honky, is American history! It's the American empire! It's Chase Manhattan and General Motors and Standard Oil and Newark Maid Leatherware! Welcome aboard, capitalist dog! Welcome to the fucked-over-by-America human race!

She told him that for the first seventy-two hours after the bombing she had been hidden in the Morristown home of Sheila Salzman, her speech therapist. Safely she made her way to Sheila's house, was taken in, and lived hidden away in an anteroom to Sheila's office during the day and in the office itself at night. Then her underground wandering began. In just two months she had fifteen aliases and moved every four or five days. But in Indianapolis, where she was befriended by a movement minister who knew only that she was an antiwar activist gone underground, she took a name from a tombstone in a cemetery, the name of a baby born within a year of herself who had died in infancy. She applied for a duplicate birth certificate in the baby's name, which was how she became Mary Stoltz. After that, she obtained a library card, a Social Security number, and when she turned seventeen, a driver's license. For nearly a year, Mary Stoltz washed dishes in the kitchen of an old people's home—a job she got through the minister—until one morning he reached her on the pay phone and said that she was to leave work immediately and meet him at the Greyhound station. There he gave her a ticket to Chicago, told her to stay two days, then to buy a ticket for Oregon—north of Portland was a commune where she could find sanctuary. He gave her the commune's address and some money to buy clothes, food, and the tickets, and she left for Chicago, where she was raped on the night she arrived. Held captive and raped and robbed. Just seventeen.

In the kitchen of a dive not as friendly as the kitchen at the old people's home, she washed dishes to earn the money to get to Oregon. There was no minister to advise her in Chicago and she was afraid that if she tried to make contact with the underground she would do something wrong and be apprehended. She was too frightened even to use a pay phone to call the Indianapolis minister. She was raped again (in the fourth rooming house where she went to live) but this time she wasn't robbed, and so after six weeks as a dishwasher she had put together enough money to head for the commune.

In Chicago the loneliness had been so all-enveloping, she felt it as a current coursing through her. There wasn't a day, on some days not an hour, when she did not set out to phone Old Rimrock. But instead, before remembering her childhood room could completely undo her, she would find a diner or a luncheonette and sit on a stool at the counter and order a BLT and a vanilla milk shake. Saying the familiar words, watching the bacon curl on the grill, watching for her toast to pop up, carefully removing the toothpicks when she was served, eating the layered sandwich between sips of the shake, concentrating on crunching the tasteless fibers from the lettuce, extracting the smoke-scented fat from the brittle bacon and the flowery juices from the soft tomato, swilling everything in with the mash of the mayonnaised toast, grinding patiently away with her jaws and her teeth, thoughtfully pulverizing every mouthful into a silage to settle her down—concentrating on her BLT as fixedly as her mother's livestock focusing on the fodder at the trough—gave her the courage to go on alone. She would eat the sandwich and drink the shake and remember how she got there and go on. By the time she left Chicago she had discovered she no longer needed a home; she would never again come close to succumbing to the yearning for a family and a home.

In Oregon she was involved in two bombings.

Instead of stopping her, killing Fred Conlon had only inspired her; after Fred Conlon, instead of her being crippled by conscience, she was delivered from all residual fear and compunction. The horror of having killed, if only inadvertently, an innocent man, a man as good as any she would ever hope to know, had not taught her anything about that most fundamental prohibition, which, stupefyingly enough, she had failed to learn to observe from being raised by Dawn and him. Killing Conlon only confirmed her ardor as an idealistic revolutionary who did not shrink from adopting any means, however ruthless, to attack the evil system. She had proved that being in opposition to everything decent in honky America wasn't just so much hip graffiti emblazoned on her bedroom wall.

He said, "You planted the bombs."

"I did."

"At Hamlin's and in Oregon you planted the bombs."

"Yes."

"Was anyone killed in Oregon?"

"Yes."

"Who?"

"People."

"People," he repeated. "How many people, Merry?"

"Three," she said.

There was plenty to eat at the commune. They grew a lot of their own food and so there was no need, as there had been when she first got to Chicago, to scavenge for wilted produce outside supermarkets at night. At the commune she began to sleep with a woman she fell in love with, the wife of a weaver whose loom Merry learned to operate when she was not working with the bombs. Assembling bombs had become her specialty after she'd successfully planted her second and third. She loved the patience and the precision required to safely wire the dynamite to the blasting cap and the blasting cap to the Woolworth's alarm clock. That's when the stuttering first began to disappear. She never stuttered when she was with the dynamite.

Then something happened between the woman and her husband, a violent argument that necessitated Merry's leaving the commune to restore peace.

It was while hiding in eastern Idaho, where she worked in the potato fields, that she decided to flee to Cuba. At night in the farm camp barracks she began to study Spanish. Living in the camp with the other laborers, she felt even more passionately committed to her beliefs, though the men were frightening when they were drunk and again there were sexual incidents. She believed that in Cuba she could live among workers without having to worry about their violence. In Cuba she could be Merry Levov and not Mary Stoltz.

She had concluded by this time that there could never be a revolution in America to uproot the forces of racism and reaction and greed. Urban guerrilla warfare was futile against a thermonuclear superstate that would stop at nothing to defend the profit principle. Since she could not help to bring about a revolution in America, her only hope was to give herself to the revolution that was. That would mark the end of her exile and the true beginning of her life.

The next year was devoted to finding her way to Cuba, to Fidel, who had emancipated the proletariat and who had eradicated injustice with socialism. But in Florida she had her first close brush with the FBI. There was a park in Miami full of Dominican refugees. It was a good place to practice Spanish and soon she found herself teaching the boys there how to speak English. Affectionately they called her La Farfulla, the stutterer, which did not prevent them from mischievously stuttering when they repeated the English words she taught them. In Spanish her own speech was flawless. Another reason to flee to the arms of the world revolution.

One day, Merry told her father, she noticed a youngish black bum, new to the park, watching her tutoring her boys. She knew immediately what that meant. A thousand times before she'd thought it was the FBI and a thousand times she'd been wrong—in Oregon, in Idaho, in Kentucky, in Maryland, the FBI watching her at the stores where she clerked; watching in the diners and the cafeterias where she washed dishes; watching on the shabby streets where she lived; watching in the libraries where she hid out to read the newspapers and to study the revolutionary thinkers, to master Marx, Marcuse, Malcolm X, and Frantz Fanon, a French theorist whose sentences, litanized at bedtime like a supplication, had sustained her in much the same way as the ritual sacrament of the vanilla milk shake and the BLT. *It must be constantly borne in mind that the committed Algerian woman learns both her role as "a woman alone in the street" and her revolutionary mission instinctively. The Algerian woman is not a secret agent. It is without apprenticeship, without briefing, without fuss, that she goes out into the street with three grenades in her handbag. She does not have the sensation of playing a role. There is no character to imitate. On the contrary, there is an intense dramatization, a continuity between the woman and the revolutionary. The Algerian woman rises directly to the level of tragedy.*

Thinking: And the New Jersey girl descends to the level of idiocy. The New Jersey girl we sent to Montessori school because she was so bright, the New Jersey girl who at Morristown

High got only A's and B's—the New Jersey girl rises directly to the level of disgraceful playacting. The New Jersey girl rises to the level of psychosis.

Everywhere, in every city where she went to hide, she thought she saw the FBI—but it was in Miami that she was finally discovered while stuttering away on a park bench trying to teach her boys to speak English. Yet how could she not teach them? How could she turn away from those who had been born to nothing, condemned to nothing, who appeared even to themselves to be human trash? On the second day when she came to the park and found the same young black bum pretending to be asleep on a bench beneath a blanket of newspapers, she turned back to the street and began to run and she did not stop until she saw a blind woman begging in the street, a large black woman with a dog. The woman was jiggling a cup and saying softly, "Blind, blind, blind." On the pavement at her feet lay a ragged wool coat inside which Merry realized she could hide. But she couldn't just take it from her; instead she asked the woman if she could help her beg, and the woman said sure, and Merry asked if she could wear the woman's dark glasses and her coat, and the woman said, "Anything, honey," and so Merry stood in the sun in Miami in that heavy old coat, wearing the dark glasses, shaking the cup for her while the woman chanted "Blind, blind, blind." That night she hid out alone beneath a bridge, but the next day she went back to beg with the black woman, once again disguised by the coat and the glasses, and eventually she moved in with her and her dog and took care of her.

That was when she began to study religions. Bunice, the black woman, sang to her in the mornings when they awoke in the bed where they slept, she and Merry and the dog. But when Bunice got cancer and died, that was the worst: the clinics, the ward, the funeral at which she was the only mourner, losing the person she'd loved most in the world . . . that was the hardest it ever was.

During the months while Bunice was dying she found in the library the books that led her to leave behind forever the Judeo-Christian tradition and find her way to the supreme ethical imperative of *ahimsa*, the systematic reverence for life and the commitment to harm no living being.

Her father was no longer wondering at what point he had lost control over her life, no longer thinking that everything he had ever done had been futile and that she was in the power of something demented. He was thinking instead that Mary Stoltz was not his daughter, for the simple reason that his daughter could not have absorbed so much pain. She was a kid from Old Rimrock, a privileged kid from paradise. She could not have worked potato fields and slept under bridges and for five years gone about in terror of arrest. She could never have slept with the blind woman and her dog. Indianapolis, Chicago, Portland, Idaho, Kentucky, Maryland, Florida—never could Merry have lived alone in all those places, an isolated vagabond washing dishes and hiding out from the police and befriending the destitute on park benches. And never would she have wound up in Newark. No. Living for six months ten minutes away, walking to the Ironbound through that underpass, wearing that veil and walking all alone, every morning and every night, past all those derelicts and through all that filth—no! The story was a lie, its purpose to destroy their villain, who was him. The story was a caricature, a sensational caricature, and she was an actress, this girl was a professional, hired and charged with tormenting him because he was everything they were not. They wanted to kill him off with the story of a pariah exiled in the very country where her family had triumphantly rooted itself in every possible way, and so he refused to be convinced by anything she had said. He thought, The rape? The bombs? A sitting duck for every madman? That was more than hardship. That was hell. Merry couldn't survive *any* of it. She could not have survived killing four people. She could not have murdered in cold blood and survived.

And then he realized that she hadn't survived. Whatever the truth might be, whatever had truly befallen her, her determination to leave behind her, in ruin, her parents' contemptible life had driven her to the disaster of destroying herself.

Of course this all could have happened to her. Things happen like this every day all over the face of the earth. He had no idea how people behaved.

"You're not my daughter. You are not Merry."

"If you wish to believe that I am not, that may be just as well. That may be for the best."

"Why don't you ask me about your mother, Meredith? Should I ask you? Where was your mother born? What is her maiden name? What is her father's name?"

"I don't want to talk about my mother."

"Because you know nothing about her. Or about me. Or about the person you pretend to be. Tell me about the house at the shore. Tell me the name of your first-grade teacher. Who was your second-grade teacher? Tell me why you are pretending to be my daughter!"

"If I answer the questions, you will suffer even more. I don't know how much suffering you want."

"Oh, don't worry about my suffering, young lady—just answer the questions. Why are you pretending to be my daughter? Who are you? Who is 'Rita Cohen'? What are you two up to? Where is my daughter? I will turn this matter over to the police unless you tell me now what is going on here and where my daughter is."

"Nothing I'm doing is actionable, Daddy."

The awful legalism. Not only the awful Jainism, but this shit too. "No," he said, "*now* it isn't—now it's just horrible! What about what you *did* do!"

"I killed four people," she replied, as innocently as she might once have told him, "I baked tollhouse cookies this afternoon."

"No!" he shouted. The Jainism, the legalism, the egregious innocence, all of it desperation, all of it to distance herself from the four who are dead. "This will not do! You are not an Algerian woman! You are not from Algeria and you are not from India! You are an American girl from Old Rimrock, New Jersey! A very, very screwed-up American girl! Four people? No!" And now *he* refused to believe it, now it was he for whom the guilt made no sense and could not be. She had been much too blessed for this to be true. So had he. He could never father a child who killed four people. Everything life had provided her, everything life offered her, everything life demanded of her, everything that had happened to her from the day she was born made that *impossible*. Killing people? It was not one of their problems. Mercifully life had omitted that from their lives. Killing people was as far as you could get from all that had been given to the Levovs to do. No, she was not, she could not, be his. "If you are so big on not lying or taking anything, small or great—all that crap, Merry, completely meaningless crap—I beg you to tell me the truth!"

"The truth is simple. Here is the truth. You must be done with craving and selfhood."

"Merry," he cried, "Merry, Merry," and, the unbridled unchecked in him, powerless *not* to attack, with all his manly brawn he fell upon her huddled there on the grimy pallet. "It isn't you! You could not have done it!" She put up no resistance as he tore from her face the veil cut from the end of a stocking. Where the heel should be was her chin. Nothing is more fetid than something where your foot has been, and she puts her mouth up against it. We loved her, she loved us—and as a result she wears her face in a stocking. "*Now* speak!" he commanded her.

But she wouldn't. He pried her mouth open, disregarding a guideline he had never before overstepped—the injunction against violence. It was the end of all understanding. There was no way for understanding to be there anymore, even though he knew violence to be inhuman and futile, and understanding—talking sense to each other for however long it took to bring about accord—all there was that could achieve a lasting result. The father who could never use force on his child, for whom force was the embodiment of moral bankruptcy, pried open her mouth and with his fingers took hold of her tongue. One of her front teeth was missing, one of her beautiful teeth. That *proved* it wasn't Merry. The years of braces, the retainer, the night brace, all those contraptions to perfect her bite, to save her gums, to beautify her smile—*this could not be the same girl*.

"Speak!" he demanded, and at last the true smell of her reached him, the lowest human smell there is, excluding only the stench of the rotting living and the rotting dead. Strangely, though she had told him she did not wash so as to do no harm to the water, he had smelled nothing before—neither when they'd embraced on the street nor sitting in the dimness across from her pallet—nothing other than a sourish, nauseatingly unfamiliar something that he ascribed to the piss-soaked building. But what he smelled now, while pulling open her mouth, was a human being and not a building, a mad human being who grubs about for pleasure in its own shit. Her foulness had reached him. She is disgusting. His daughter is a human mess stinking of human waste. Her smell is the smell of everything organic breaking down. It is the smell of no coherence. It is the smell of all she's become. She could do it, and she did do it, and this reverence for life is the final obscenity.

He tried to locate a muscle in his head somewhere to plug the opening at the top of his throat, something to stop him up and prevent their sliding still further into the filth, but there was no such muscle. A spasm of gastric secretions and undigested food started up the intestinal piping and, in a bitter, acidic stream, surged sickeningly onto his tongue, and when he cried out, "*Who are you!*" it was spewed with his words onto her face.

Even in the dimness of that room, once he was over her he knew very well who she was. It was not necessary for her to speak with her face unprotected to inform him that the inexplicable had forever displaced whatever he once thought he knew. If she was no longer branded as Merry Levov by her stutter, she was marked unmistakably by the eyes. Within the chiseled-out, oversized eye sockets, the eyes were his. The tallness was his and the eyes were his. She was all his. The tooth she was missing had been pulled or knocked out.

She looked not at him when he retreated to the door but anxiously all around her narrow room, as though in his frenzy he had battered most brutally the harmless microorganisms that dwelled with her in her solitude.

Four people. Little wonder that she had vanished. Little wonder that he had. This was his daughter, and she was unknowable. This murderer is mine. His vomit was on her face, a face that, but for the eyes, was now most unlike her mother's or her father's. The veil was off, but behind the veil there was another veil. Isn't there always?

"Come with me," he begged.

"You go, Daddy. Go."

"Merry, you are asking me to do something that is excruciatingly painful. You asking me to leave you. I just found you. Please," he begged her, "come with me. Come home."

"Daddy, let me be."

"But I must see you. I cannot leave you here. I must see you!"

"You've seen me. Please go now. If you love me, Daddy, you'll let me be."

The most perfect girl of all, one's daughter, had been raped.

All he could think of was the two times she had been raped. Four people blown up by her—so grotesque, so out of scale, it was unimaginable. It had to be. To see the faces, to hear the names, to learn that one was a mother of three, the second just married, the third about to retire. . . . Did *she* know what or who they were . . . care who they were . . . ? He could not imagine any of it. Wouldn't. Only the rape was imaginable. Imagine the rape and the rest is blocked out: their faces remain out of sight, their spectacles, their hairdos, their families, their jobs, their birth dates, their addresses, their blameless innocence.

Not one Fred Conlon—four Fred Conlons.

The rape. The rape obscured everything else. Concentrate on the rape.

What *were* the details? Who were these men? Was it somebody who was part of that life, somebody who was against the war and on the run like her, was it somebody she knew or was it a stranger, a bum, an addict, a madman who'd followed her home and into the hallway with a knife? What went on? Had they held her down and threatened her with a knife? Had they beaten her? What did they make her do? Were there no people to help her? Just what did they make her do? He would kill them. She had to tell him who they were. I want to find out who those people are. I want to know where it happened. I want to know when it happened. We're going to go back and find those people and I'm going to kill them!

Now that he could not stop imagining the rapes, there was no relief, not for one second, from the desire to go out and kill somebody. With all the walls he'd built up, she gets raped. All of that protection and he could not prevent her from getting raped. Tell me everything about it! I'm going to kill them!

But it was too late. It had happened. He could do nothing

to make it not happen. For it to not happen, he would have had to kill them before it happened—and how could he manage that? Swede Levov? Off the playing field, when had Swede Levov laid a hand on anyone? Nothing so repelled this muscular man as the use of force.

The places she was in. The people. How did she survive without people? That place she was in now. Were all her places like that or even worse? All right, she should not have done what she did, should never have done it, yet to think of how she'd had to live. . . .

He was sitting at his desk. He had to get some relief from seeing what he did not want to see. The factory was empty. There was only the night watchman who'd come on duty with his dogs. He was down in the parking lot, patrolling the perimeter of the double-thick chain-link fence, a fence topped off, after the riots, with supplemental scrolls of razor ribbon that were to admonish the boss each and every morning he pulled in and parked his car, "Leave! Leave! Leave!" He was sitting alone in the last factory left in the worst city in the world. And it was worse even than sitting there during the riots, Springfield Avenue in flames, South Orange Avenue in flames, Bergen Street under attack, sirens going off, weapons firing, snipers from rooftops blasting the street lights, looting crowds crazed in the street, kids carrying off radios and lamps and television sets, men toting armfuls of clothing, women pushing baby carriages heavily loaded with cartons of liquor and cases of beer, people pushing pieces of new furniture right down the center of the street, stealing sofas, cribs, kitchen tables, stealing washers and dryers and ovens—stealing not in the shadows but out in the open. Their strength is tremendous, their teamwork is flawless. The shattering of the glass windows is thrilling. The not paying for things is intoxicating. The American appetite for ownership is dazzling to behold. *This* is shoplifting. Everything free that everyone craves, a wanton free-for-all free of charge, everyone uncontrollable with thinking, Here it is! Let it come! In Newark's burning Mardi Gras streets, a force is released that feels redemptive, something purifying is happening, something spiritual and revolutionary perceptible to all. The surreal vision of household appliances out under the stars and agleam in the glow of the flames incinerating the Central Ward promises the liberation of all mankind. Yes, here it is, let it come, yes, the magnificent opportunity, one of human history's rare transmogrifying moments: the old ways of suffering are burning blessedly away in the flames, never again to be resurrected, instead to be superseded, within only hours, by suffering that will be so gruesome, so monstrous, so unrelenting and abundant, that its abatement will take the next five hundred years. The fire this time—and next? After the fire? Nothing. Nothing in Newark ever again.

And all the while the Swede is there in the factory with Vicky, waiting with just Vicky beside him for his place to go up, waiting for police with pistols, for soldiers with submachine guns, waiting for protection from the Newark police, the state police, the National Guard—from *someone*—before they burn to the ground the business built by his father, entrusted to him by his father . . . and that wasn't as bad as this. A police car opens fire into the bar across the street, out his window he sees a woman go down, buckle and go down, shot dead right on the street, a woman killed in front of his eyes . . . and not even that was as bad as this. People screaming, shouting, firemen pinned to the ground by gunfire so they cannot fight the flames; explosions, the sound suddenly of bongo drums, in the middle of the night a volley of pistol shots blowing out every one of the street-level windows displaying Vicky's signs . . . and this is worse by far. And then they left, everyone, fled the smoldering rubble—manufacturers, retailers, the banks, the shop owners, the corporations, the department stores; in the South Ward, on the residential blocks, there are two moving vans per day on every street throughout the next year, homeowners fleeing, deserting the modest houses they treasure for whatever they can get . . . but he stays on, refuses to leave, Newark Maid remains behind, and that did not prevent her from getting raped. Not even during the worst of it does he abandon his factory to the vandals; he does not abandon his workers afterward, does not turn his back on these people, and *still* his daughter is raped.

Hanging on the wall directly back of his desk, framed and under glass, there is a letter from the Governor's Select Commission on Civil Disorder thanking Mr. Seymour I. Levov for his testimony as an eyewitness to the riots, praising him for

his courage, for his devotion to Newark, an official letter signed
by ten distinguished citizens, two of them Catholic bishops,
two of them ex-governors of the state; and on the wall alongside that, also framed and under glass, an article that six months
earlier appeared in the *Star-Ledger*, with his photograph and
the headline, "Glove Firm Lauded for Staying in Newark"—
and still she is raped.

The rape was in his bloodstream and he would never get it
out. The odor of it was in his bloodstream, the look of it, the
legs and the arms and the hair and the clothing. There were
the sounds—the thud, her cries, the careening in a tiny enclosure. The horrible bark of a man coming. His grunting. Her
whimpering. The stupendousness of the rape blotted out everything. All unsuspectingly, she had stepped out of her doorway
and they had grabbed her from behind and thrown her down
and there her body for them to do with as they wished.
Only some cloth covered her body and they tore it off. There
was nothing between her body and their hands. Inside her
body. Filling the inside of her body. The tremendous force
with which they did it. The tearing force. They knocked out
her tooth. One of them was insane. He sat over her and let
loose a stream of shit. They were all over her. These men. They
were speaking a foreign language. Laughing. Whatever they
felt the urge to do, they did. One waited behind the other. She
saw him waiting. There was nothing she could do.

And nothing he could do. The man grows crazier and crazier
to do something just when there is nothing left for him to do.

Her body in the crib. Her body in the bassinet. Her body
when she starts to stand on his stomach. The belly showing
between her dungarees and her shirt while she hangs upside
down from him when he comes home from work. Her body
when she leaves the earth and leaps into his arms. The abandon
of her body flying into his arms, granting him a father's permission to touch. The unquestioning adoration of him that is
in that leaping body, a body seemingly all finished, a perfected
creation in miniature, with all of the miniature's charm. A body
that looks quickly put on after having just been freshly ironed
—no folds anywhere. The naive freedom with which she dis-
closes it. The tenderness this evokes. Her bare feet padded like
a little animal's feet. New and unworn, her uncorrupted paws.

Her grasping toes. The stalky legs. Utilitarian legs. Firm. The most muscular part of her. Her sorbet-colored underpants. At the great divide, her baby tuchas, the gravity-defying behind, improbably belonging to the upper Merry and not as yet to the lower. No fat. Not an ounce anywhere. The cleft, as though an awl had made it—that beautifully beveled joining that will petal outward, evolving in the cycle of time into a woman's origami-folded cunt. The implausible belly button. The geometric torso. The anatomical precision of the rib cage. The pliancy of her spine. The bony ridges of her back like keys on a small xylophone. The lovely dormancy of the invisible bosom before the swell begins. All the turbulent wanting-to-become blessedly, blessedly dormant. Yet in the neck somehow is the woman to be, there in that building block of a neck ornamented with down. The face. That's the glory. The face that she will not carry with her and that is yet the fingerprint of the future. The marker that will disappear and yet be there fifty years later. How little of her story is revealed in his child's face. Its youngness is all he can see. So very new in the cycle. With nothing as yet totally defined, time is so powerfully present in her face. The skull is soft. The flare of the unstructured nose is the whole nose. The color of her eyes. The white, white whiteness. The limpid blue. Eyes unclouded. It's *all* unclouded, but the eyes particularly, windows, washed windows with nothing yet of the revelation of what's within. The history in her brow of the embryo. The dried apricots that are her ears. Delicious. If once you started eating them you'd never stop. The little ears always older than she is. The ears that were never just four years old and yet hadn't really changed since she was fourteen months. The preternatural fineness of her hair. The *health* of it. More reddish, more like his mother's than his then, still touched with fire then. The smell of the whole day in her hair. The carefreeness, the abandon of that body in his arms. The catlike abandon to the all-powerful father, the reassuring giant. It is so, it is true—in the abandon of her body to him, she excites an instinct for reassurance that is so abundant that it must be close to what Dawn says she felt when she was lactating. What he feels when his daughter leaves the earth to leap into his arms is the absoluteness of their intimacy. And built into it always is the knowledge that he is not going too far, that he cannot, that it is an enormous freedom and an enormous pleasure, the equivalent of her breast-feeding bond with Dawn. It's true. It's undeniable. He was wonderful at it and so was she. So wonderful. How did all this happen to this wonderful kid? She stuttered. So what? What was the big deal? How did all this happen to this perfectly normal child? Unless this is the sort of thing that *does* happen to the wonderful, perfectly normal kids. The nuts don't do these things—the normal kids do. You protect her and protect her—and she is unprotectable. If you don't protect her it's unendurable, if you *do* protect her it's unendurable. It's all unendurable. The awfulness of her terrible autonomy. The worst of the world had taken his child. If only that beautifully chiseled body had never been born.

He calls his brother. It is the wrong brother from whom to seek consolation, but what can he do? When it comes to consolation, it is always the wrong brother, the wrong father, the wrong mother, the wrong wife, which is why one must be content to console oneself and be strong and go on in life consoling others. But he needs some relief from this rape, needs the rape taken out of his heart, where it is stabbing him to death, *he cannot put up with it*, and so he calls the only brother he has. If he had another brother he would call him. But for a brother he has only Jerry and Jerry has only him. For a daughter he has only Merry. For a father she has only him. There is no way around any of this. Nothing else can be made to come true.

It is half past five on a Friday afternoon. Jerry is in the office seeing postoperative patients. But he can talk, he says. The patients can wait. "What is it? What's wrong with you?"

He has only to hear Jerry's voice, the impatience in it, the acerbic cocksuredness in it, to think, He's no good to me. "I found her. I just came from Merry. I found her in Newark. She's here. In a room. I saw her. What this girl has been through, what she looks like, where she lives—you can't imagine it. You cannot begin to imagine it." He proceeds to recount her story, not breaking down, trying to repeat what she said to him about where she had been, how she had lived, and what had become of her, trying to get it into his head, his own head, trying to find in his head the room for it all when he could not even find enough room for that room in which she lived. He comes closest to crying when he tells his brother that she had twice been raped.

"Are you done?" asks Jerry.

"What?"

"If you're done, if that's it, tell me what you are going to do now. What are you going to do, Seymour?"

"I don't know what there is to do. She did it. She blew up Hamlin's. She killed Conlon." He cannot tell him about Oregon and the other three. "She did it on her own."

"Well, sure she did it. Jesus. Who did we think did it? Where is she now, in that room?"

"Yes. It's awful."

"Then go back to the room and get her."

"I can't. She won't let me. She wants me to leave her alone."

"*Fuck* what she wants. Get back in your fucking car and get over there and drag her out of that fucking room by her hair. Sedate her. Tie her up. But get her. Listen to me. You're paralyzed. I'm not the one who thinks holding his family together is the most important thing in existence—you are. Get back in that car and get her!"

"That won't work. I can't drag her. There's more to this than you understand. Once you get beyond the point of forcing somebody back into their house—then what? There's bravado about it—but then what? It's complicated, too complicated. It won't work your way."

"That's *just* the way it works."

"She killed three other people. She has killed four people."

"*Fuck* the four people. What's the matter with you? You're acceding to her the way you acceded to your father, the way you have acceded to everything in your life."

"She was raped. She's crazy, she's gone crazy. You just look at her and you know it. *Twice* she was raped."

"What did you think was going to happen? You sound surprised. Of course she got raped. Either get off your ass and do something or she's going to get raped for a third time. Do you love her or don't you love her?"

"How can you ask that?"

"You force me to."

"Please, not now, don't tear me down, don't undermine me. I love my daughter. I never loved anything more in the world."

"As a thing."

"What? What is that?"

"As a thing—you loved her as a fucking thing. The way you love your wife. Oh, if someday you could become conscious of why you are doing what you are doing. Do you know why? Do you have any idea? Because you're afraid of creating a bad scene! You're afraid of letting the beast out of the bag!"

"What are you talking about? What beast? What beast?" No, he is not expecting perfect consolation, but this attack—why is he launching this attack without even the pretext of consoling? Why, when he has just explained to Jerry how everything has turned out thousands and thousands of times worse than the worst they'd expected?

"What are you? Do you know? What you are is you're always trying to smooth everything over. What you are is always trying to be moderate. What you are is never telling the truth if you think it's going to hurt somebody's feelings. What you are is you're always compromising. What you are is always complacent. What you are is always trying to find the bright side of things. The one with the manners. The one who abides everything patiently. The one with the ultimate decorum. The boy who never breaks the code. Whatever society dictates, you do. Decorum. Decorum is what you spit in the *face* of. Well, your daughter spit in it for you, didn't she? Four people? Quite a critique she has made of decorum."

If he hangs up, he will be alone in that hallway behind the man who is waiting behind the man who is down on the stairs tearing at Merry, he will be seeing everything he does not want to see, knowing everything he cannot stand to know. He cannot sit there imagining the rest of that story. If he hangs up, he will never know what Jerry has to say after he says all this stuff that he for some reason wants to say about the beast. What beast? All his relations with people are like this—it isn't an attack on me, it is Jerry. Nobody can control him. He was born like this. I knew that before I called him. I've known it all my life. We do not live the same way. A brother who isn't a brother. I panicked. I am in a panic. This is panic. I called the worst person to call in the world. This is a guy who wields a knife for a living. Remedies what is ailing with a knife. Cuts out what is rotting with a knife. I am on the ropes, I am dealing with something that nobody can deal with, and for him it's business as usual—he just keeps coming at me with his knife.

"I'm not the renegade," the Swede says. "I'm not the renegade—you are."

"No, you're not the renegade. You're the one who does everything right."

"I don't follow this. You say that like an insult." Angrily he says, "What the hell is wrong with doing things right?"

"Nothing. Nothing. Except that's what your daughter has been blasting away at all her life. You don't reveal yourself to people, Seymour. You keep yourself a secret. Nobody knows what you are. You certainly never let *her* know who you are. That's what she's been blasting away at—that façade. All your fucking *norms*. Take a good look at what she did to your *norms*."

"I don't know what you want from me. You've always been too smart for me. Is this your response? Is this it?"

"You win the trophy. You always make the right move. You're loved by everybody. You marry Miss New Jersey, for God's sake. There's thinking for you. Why did you marry her? For the appearance. Why do you do everything? For the appearance!"

"I loved her! I opposed my own father I loved her so much!"

Jerry is laughing. "Is that what you believe? You really think you stood up to him? You married her because you couldn't get out of it. Dad raked her over the coals in his office and you sat there and didn't say shit. Well, isn't that true?"

"My daughter is in that room, Jerry. What is this all about?"

But Jerry does not hear him. He hears only himself. Why is this Jerry's grand occasion to tell his brother the truth? Why does someone, in the midst of your worst suffering, decide the time has come to drive home, disguised in the form of character analysis, all the contempt they have been harboring for you for all these years? What in your suffering makes their superiority so fulsome, so capacious, makes the expression of it so enjoyable? Why this occasion for launching his protest at living in the shadow of me? Why, if he had to tell me all this, couldn't he have told it to me when I was feeling my oats? Why does he even believe he's in my shadow? Miami's biggest cardiac surgeon! The heart victim's savior, Dr. Levov!

"Dad? He fucking let you slide through—don't you know that? If Dad had said, 'Look, you'll never get my approval for this, never, I am not having grandchildren half this and half that,' then you would have had to make a choice. But you *never* had to make a choice. *Never.* Because he let you slide through. Everybody has always let you slide through. And that is why, to this day, nobody knows who you are. You are unrevealed— that is the story, Seymour, *unrevealed.* That is why your own daughter decided to blow you away. You are never straight about anything and she hated you for it. You keep yourself a secret. You don't choose *ever.*"

"Why are you saying this? What do you want me to choose? What are we talking about?"

"You think you know what a man is? You have no *idea* what a man is. You think you know what a daughter is? You have no *idea* what a daughter is. You think you know what this country is? You have no *idea* what this country is. You have a false image of *everything.* All you know is what a fucking glove is. This country is *frightening.* Of course she was raped. What kind of company do you think she was keeping? Of course out there she was going to get raped. This isn't Old Rimrock, old buddy —she's out there, old buddy, in the USA. She enters that world, that loopy world out there, with what's going on out there—what do you *expect?* A kid from Rimrock, New Jersey, *of course* she doesn't know how to behave out there, *of course* the shit hits the fan. What could she know? She's like a wild child out there in the world. She can't get enough of it—she's *still* acting up. A room off McCarter Highway. And why not? Who wouldn't? You prepare her for life milking the cows? For what kind of life? Unnatural, all artificial, all of it. Those *assumptions* you live with. You're still in your old man's dream-world, Seymour, still up there with Lou Levov in glove heaven. A household tyrannized by gloves, bludgeoned by gloves, the only thing in life—ladies' gloves! Does he still tell the great one about the woman who sells the gloves washing her hands in a sink between each color? Oh where oh where is that out-moded America, that decorous America where a woman had twenty-five pairs of gloves? Your kid blows your norms to kingdom come, Seymour, and you still think you know what life is!"

Life is just a short period of time in which we are alive. Meredith Levov, 1964.

"You wanted Miss America? Well, you've got her, with a vengeance—she's your daughter! You wanted to be a real American jock, a real American marine, a real American hotshot with a beautiful Gentile babe on your arm? You longed to belong like everybody else to the United States of America? Well, you do now, big boy, thanks to your daughter. The reality of this place is right up in your kisser now. With the help of your daughter you're as deep in the shit as a man can get, the real American crazy shit. America amok! America amuck! Goddamn it, Seymour, goddamn you, if you were a father who loved his daughter," thunders Jerry into the phone—and the hell with the convalescent patients waiting in the corridor for him to check out their new valves and new arteries, to tell how grateful they are to him for their new lease on life, Jerry shouts away, shouts all he wants if it's shouting he wants to do, and the hell with the rules of the hospital. He is one of the surgeons who shouts: if you disagree with him he shouts, if you cross him he shouts, if you just stand there and do nothing he shouts. He does not do what hospitals tell him to do or fathers expect him to do or wives want him to do, he does what *he* wants to do, does as he pleases, tells people just who and what he is every minute of the day so that *nothing* about him is a secret, not his opinions, his frustrations, his urges, neither his appetite nor his hatred. In the sphere of the will, he is unequivocating, uncompromising; he is king. He does not spend time regretting what he has or has not done or justifying to others how loathsome he can be. The message is simple: You will take me as I come—there is no choice. He cannot endure swallowing anything. He just lets loose.

And these two are brothers, the same parents' sons, one for whom the aggression's been bred out, the other for whom the aggression's been bred in.

"If you were a father who loved his daughter," Jerry shouts at the Swede, "you would never have left her in that room! You would never have let her out of your sight!"

The Swede is in tears at his desk. It is as though Jerry has been waiting all his life for this phone call. That something's grotesquely out of whack has made him furious with his older brother, and now there is nothing he will not say. All his life, thinks the Swede, waiting to lay into me with these terrible things. People are infallible: they pick up on what you want and then they don't give it to you.

"I didn't *want* to leave her," says the Swede. "You don't understand. You don't want to understand. That isn't why I left her. It *killed* me to leave her! You don't understand me, you won't. Why do you say I don't love her? This is terrible. Horrible." He suddenly sees his vomit on her face and he cries out, "Everything is horrible!"

"*Now* you're getting it. Right! My brother is developing the beginning of a point of view. A point of view of his own instead of everybody else's point of view. Taking something other than the party line. Good. Now we're getting somewhere. Thinking becoming just a little untranquilized. Everything is horrible. And so what are you going to do about it? Nothing. Look, do you want me to come up there and get her? Do you want me to get her, yes or no?"

"No."

"Then why did you call me?"

"I don't know. To help me."

"Nobody can help you."

"You're a hard man. You are a hard man with me."

"Yeah, I don't come off looking very good. I never do. Ask our father if I do. You're the one who always comes off looking good. And look where it's got you. Refusing to give offense. Blaming yourself. Tolerant respect for every position. Sure, it's 'liberal'—I know, a liberal father. But what does that mean? What is at the *center* of it? Always holding things together. And look where the fuck it's got you!"

"I didn't make the war in Vietnam. I didn't make the television war. I didn't make Lyndon Johnson Lyndon Johnson. You forget where this begins. Why she threw the bomb. That fucking *war.*"

"No, you didn't make the war. You made the angriest kid in America. Ever since she was a kid, every word she *spoke* was a bomb."

"I gave her all I could, everything, everything, I gave everything. I swear to you I gave everything." And now he is crying easily, there is no line between him and his crying, and an amazing new experience it is—he is crying as though crying like this has been the great aim of his life, as though all along crying like this was his most deeply held ambition, and now he has achieved it, now that he remembers everything he gave and everything she took, all the spontaneous giving and taking that had filled their lives and that one day, inexplicably (despite whatever Jerry might say, despite all the blame that it is his pleasure now to heap upon the Swede), quite inexplicably, became repugnant to her. "You talk about what I'm dealing with as though *anybody* could deal with it. But *nobody* could deal with it. Nobody! Nobody has the weapons for this. You think I'm inept? You think I'm inadequate? If I'm inadequate, where are you going to get people who *are* adequate . . . if I'm . . . do you understand what I'm saying? What am I supposed to be? What are other people if I am inadequate?"

"Oh, I understand you."

Crying easily was always about as difficult for the Swede as losing his balance when he walked or deliberately being a bad influence on somebody; crying easily was something he sometimes almost envied in other people. But whatever chunks and fragments remain of the big manly barrier against crying, his brother's response to his pain demolishes. "If what you are telling me is what I was . . ." he begins, ". . . wasn't, wasn't enough, then, then . . . I'm telling *you*—I'm telling you that what *anybody* is *is not enough*."

"You got it! Exactly! We are *not* enough. We are *none* of us enough! Including even the man who does everything right! Doing things right," Jerry says with disgust, "going around in this world doing things right. Look, are you going to break with appearances and pit your will against your daughter's or aren't you? Out on the *field* you did it. That's how you scored, remember? You pitted your will against the other guy's and you *scored*. Pretend it's a game if that helps. It doesn't help. For the typical male activity you're there, the man of action, but this isn't the typical male activity. Okay. Can't see yourself doing that. Can only see yourself playing ball and making gloves and marrying Miss America. Out there with Miss America, dumbing down and dulling out. Out there playing at being Wasps, a little Mick girl from the Elizabeth docks and a Jewboy from Weequahic High. The cows. Cow society. Colonial old America. And you thought all that façade was going to come without cost. Genteel and innocent. *But that costs, too, Seymour. I* would have thrown a bomb. *I* would become a Jain and live in Newark. That Wasp bullshit! I didn't know just how entirely muffled you were internally. But this is how muffled you are. Our old man really swaddled you but good. What do you want, Seymour? You want to bail out? That's all right too. Anybody else would have bailed out a long time ago. Go ahead, bail out. Admit her contempt for your life and bail out. Admit that there is something very personal about you that she hates and bail the fuck out and never see the bitch again. Admit that she's a monster, Seymour. Even a monster has to be from somewhere—even a monster needs parents. But parents don't need monsters. Bail out! But if you are *not* going to bail out, if that is what you are calling to tell me, then for Christ's sake go in there and get her. *I'll* go in and get her. How about that? Last chance. Last offer. You want me to come, I'll clear out the office and get on a plane and I'll come. And I'll go in there, and, I assure you, I'll get her off the McCarter Highway, the little shit, the selfish little fucking shit, playing her fucking games with you! She won't play them with me, I assure you. Do you want that or not?"

"I don't want that." These things Jerry thinks he knows that he doesn't know. His idea that things are connected. But there *is* no connection. How we lived and what she did? Where she was raised and what she did? It's as disconnected as everything else—it's all a part of the same mess! *He* is the one who knows nothing. Jerry rants. Jerry thinks he can escape the bewilderment by ranting, shouting, but everything he shouts is wrong. None of this is true. Causes, clear answers, who there is to blame. Reasons. But there are no reasons. She is obliged to be as she is. We all are. Reasons are in books. Could how we lived as a family ever have come back as this bizarre horror? It couldn't. It hasn't. Jerry tries to rationalize it but you can't. This is all something else, something he knows absolutely nothing about. No one does. It is not rational. It is chaos. It is chaos from start to finish. "I don't want that," the Swede tells him. "I can't have that."

"Too brutal for you. In this world, too brutal. The daughter's a murderer but this is too brutal. A drill instructor in the Marine Corps but this is too brutal. Okay, Big Swede, gentle giant. I got a waiting room full of patients. You're on your own."

III
Paradise Lost

7

I T was the summer of the Watergate hearings. The Levovs had spent nearly every night on the back porch watching the replay of the day's session on Channel 13. Before the farm equipment and the cattle had been sold off, it was from there, on warm evenings, that they looked out onto Dawn's herd grazing along the rim of the hill. Up a ways from the house was a field of eighteen acres, and some years they'd have the cows up there all summer and forget them. But if they were merely out of sight nearby, and Merry, in her pajamas, wanted to see them before she went to bed, Dawn would call out, "*Here*boy, *Here*boy," the kind of thing people had been calling to them for thousands of years, and they'd sound off in return and start up the hill and out from the swamp, come out of wherever they were, bellowing their response as they trudged toward the sound of Dawn's voice. "Aren't they beautiful, our girls?" Dawn would ask her daughter, and the next day Merry and Dawn would be out at sunrise getting them all together again, and he'd hear Dawn say, "Okay, we're going to cross the road," and Merry would open the gate and just with a stick and the dog, Apu the Australian sheepdog, mother and tiny daughter would move some twelve or fifteen or eighteen beasts, each weighing about two thousand pounds. Merry, Apu, and Dawn, sometimes the vet, and the boy down the road to help with the fencing and the haying when an extra hand was needed. *I've got Merry to help me hay. If there's a stray calf, Merry gets after it. Seymour goes in there and those two cows will be very unpleasant, they'll paw the grass, they'll shake their heads at him—but Merry goes in, well, they know her, and they just tell her what they want. They know her and they know exactly what she's going to do with them.*

How could she ever say to him, "I don't want to talk about my mother"? What in God's name had her mother done? What crime had her mother committed? The crime of being gentle master to these compliant cows?

During this last week, while his parents had been with them, up from Florida for the annual late-summer visit, Dawn hadn't even worried about keeping the two of them entertained. Whenever she returned from the new building site or drove back from the architect's office, they were seated before the set with the father-in-law in the role of assistant counsel to the committee. Her in-laws watched the proceedings all day and then saw the whole thing over again at night. In what time he had left to himself during the day, the Swede's father composed letters to the committee members which he read to everyone at dinner. "Dear Senator Weicker: You're surprised at what was going on in Tricky Dicky's White House? Don't be a shnook. Harry Truman had him figured out in 1948 when he called him Tricky Dicky." "Dear Senator Gurney: Nixon equals Typhoid Mary. Everything he touches he poisons, you included." "Dear Senator Baker: You want to know WHY? Because they're a bunch of common criminals, that's WHY!" "Dear Mr. Dash:" he wrote to the committee's New York counsel, "I applaud you. God bless you. You make me proud to be an American and a Jew."

His greatest contempt he reserved for a relatively insignificant figure, a lawyer named Kalmbach, who'd arranged for large illegal contributions to sift into the Watergate operation, and whose disgrace could not be profound enough to suit the old man. "Dear Mr. Kalmbach: If you were a Jew and did what you did the whole world would say, 'See those Jews, real money-grubbers.' But who is the money-grubber, my dear Mr. Country Club? Who is the thief and the cheat? Who is the American and who is the gangster? Your smooth talk never fooled me, Mr. Country Club Kalmbach. Your golf never fooled me. Your manners never fooled me. Your clean hands I always knew were dirty. And now the whole world knows. You should be ashamed."

"You think I'll get an answer from the son of a bitch? I ought to publish these in a book. I ought to find somebody to print 'em up and just distribute them free so people could know what an ordinary American feels when these sons of bitches . . . look, look at that one, *look* at him." Ehrlichman, Nixon's former chief of staff, had appeared on the screen.

"He makes me nauseous," the Swede's mother said. "Him and that Tricia."

"Please, she's unimportant," her husband said. "This is a real fascist—the whole bunch of 'em, Von Ehrlichman, Von Haldeman, Von Kalmbach—"

"She still makes me nauseous," his wife said. "You'd think she was a princess, the way they carry on about her."

"These so-called patriots," Lou Levov said to Dawn, "would take this country and make Nazi Germany out of it. You know the book *It Can't Happen Here?* There's a wonderful book, I forget the author, but the idea couldn't be more up-to-the-moment. These people have taken us to the edge of something terrible. *Look* at that son of a bitch."

"I don't know which one I hate more," his wife said, "him or the other one."

"They're the same thing," the old man told her, "they're interchangeable, the whole bunch of them."

Merry's legacy. That his father might have been no less incensed if she were there, sitting with them all in front of the set, the Swede recognized, but now that she was gone who better was there to hate for what had become of her than these Watergate bastards?

It was during the Vietnam War that Lou Levov had begun mailing Merry copies of the letters he sent to President Johnson, letters that he had written to influence Merry's behavior more than the president's. Seeing his teenage granddaughter as enraged with the war as he could get when things started to go too wrong with the business, the old man became so distressed that he would take his son aside and say, "Why does she care? Where does she even get this stuff? Who feeds it to her? What's the difference to her anyway? Does she carry on like this at school? She can't do this at school, she could harm her chances at school. She can harm her chances for college. In public people won't put up with it, they'll chop her head off, she's only a child. . . ." To control, if he could, not so much Merry's opinions as the ferocity with which she sputtered them out, he would ostentatiously ally himself with her by sending articles clipped from the Florida papers and inscribed in the margins with his own antiwar slogans. When he was visiting he would read aloud to her from the portfolio of his Johnson letters that he carried around the house under his arm—in his effort to save her from herself, tagging after the child as though *he* were the child. "We've got to nip this in the bud," he confided to his son. "This won't do, not at all."

"Well," he'd say—after reading to Merry yet another plea to the president reminding him what a great country America was, what a great president FDR had been, how much his own family owed to this country and what a personal disappointment it was to him and his loved ones that American boys were halfway around the world fighting somebody else's battle when they ought to be at home with their loved ones—"well, what do you think of your grandfather?"

"J-j-johnson's a war criminal," she'd say. "He's not going to s-s-s-stop the w-w-war, Grandpa, because you tell him to."

"He's also a man trying to do his job, you know."

"He's an imperialist dog."

"Well, that is one opinion."

"There's no d-d-d-difference between him and Hitler."

"You're exaggerating, sweetheart. I don't say Johnson didn't let us down. But you forget what Hitler did to the Jews, Merry dear. You weren't born then, so you don't remember."

"He did nothing that Johnson isn't doing to the Vietnamese."

"The Vietnamese aren't being put into concentration camps."

"Vietnam is one *b-b-big* camp! The 'American boys' aren't the issue. That's like saying, 'Get the storm troopers out of Auschwitz in time for Chris-chris-chris-*christ*mas.'"

"I *gotta* be political with the guy, sweetheart. I can't write the guy and call him a murderer and expect that he's going to listen. Right, Seymour?"

"I don't think that would help," the Swede said.

"Merry, we all feel the way you do," her grandfather told her. "Do you understand that? Believe me, I know what it is to read the newspaper and start to go nuts. Father Coughlin, that son of a bitch. The hero Charles Lindbergh—pro-Nazi, pro-Hitler, and a so-called national hero in this country. Mr. Gerald L. K. Smith. The great Senator Bilbo. Sure we have bastards in this country—homegrown and plenty of 'em. Nobody denies that. Mr. Rankin. Mr. Dies. Mr. Dies and his committee. Mr. J. Parnell Thomas from New Jersey. Isolationist, bigoted, know-nothing fascists right there in the U.S. Congress, crooks like J. Parnell Thomas, crooks who wound up in jail and their salaries were paid for by the U.S. taxpayer. Awful people. The worst. Mr. McCarran. Mr. Jenner. Mr. Mundt. The Goebbels from Wisconsin, the Honorable Mr. McCarthy, may he burn in hell. His sidekick Mr. Cohn. A disgrace. A *Jew* and a disgrace! There have always been sons of bitches here just like there are in every country, and they have been voted into office by all those geniuses out there who have the right to vote. And what about the newspapers? Mr. Hearst. Mr. McCormick. Mr. Westbrook Pegler. Real fascist, reactionary dogs. And I have hated their guts. Ask your father. Haven't I, Seymour—hated them?"

"You have."

"Honey, we live in a democracy. Thank God for that. You don't have to go around getting angry with your family. You can write letters. You can vote. You can get up on a soapbox and make a speech. Christ, you can do what your father did— you can join the marines."

"Oh, Grandpa—the marines are the *prob-prob-prob—*"

"Then damn it, Merry, join the *other* side," he said, momentarily losing his grip. "How's that? You can join *their* marines if you want to. It's been done. That's true. Look at history. When you're old enough you can go over and fight for the other army if you want it. I don't recommend it. People don't like it, and I think you're smart enough to understand why they don't. 'Traitor' isn't a pleasant thing to be called. But it's been done. It's an option. Look at Benedict Arnold. Look at him. He did it. He went over to the other side, as far as I remember. From school. And I suppose I respect him. He had guts. He stood up for what he believed in. He risked his own life for what he believed in. But he happened to be wrong, Merry, in my estimation. He went over to the other side in the Revolutionary War and, as far as I'm concerned, the man was dead wrong. Now you don't happen to be wrong. You happen to be *right*. This family is one hundred percent against this goddamn Vietnam thing. You don't have to rebel against your family *because your family is not in disagreement with you*. You are not the only person around here against this war. We are against it. Bobby Kennedy is against it—"

"*Now*," said Merry, with disgust.

"Okay, now. Now is better than not now, isn't it? Be realistic,

Merry—it doesn't help anything not to be. Bobby Kennedy is against it. Senator Eugene McCarthy is against it. Senator Javits is against it, and he's a Republican. Senator Frank Church is against it. Senator Wayne Morse is against it. And how he is. I admire that man. I've written him to tell him and I have gotten the courtesy of a hand-signed reply. Senator Fulbright, of course, is against it. It's Fulbright who, admittedly, introduced the Tonkin Gulf resolu—"

"F-f-f-ful—"

"Nobody is saying—"

"Dad," said the Swede, "let Merry finish."

"I'm sorry, honey," said Lou Levov. "Finish."

"Ful-ful-fulbright is a racist."

"Is he? What are you talking about? Senator William Fulbright from Arkansas? Come on with that stuff. I think there's where you've got your facts wrong, my friend." She had slandered one of his heroes who'd stood up to Joe McCarthy, and to prevent himself from lashing out at her about Fulbright took a supreme effort of will. "But now just let *me* finish what I was saying. What *was* I saying? Where was I? Where the hell was I, Seymour?"

"Your point," the Swede said, acting evenhandedly as the moderator for these two dynamos, a role he preferred to being the adversary of either, "is that both of you are against the war and want it to stop. There's no reason for you to argue on that issue—I believe *that's* your point. Merry feels it's all gone beyond writing letters to the president. She feels that's futile. You feel that, futile or not, it's something within your power to do and you're going to do it, at least to continue to put yourself on record."

"Exactly!" the old man cried. "Here, listen to what I tell him here. 'I am a lifetime Democrat.' Merry, listen—'I am a lifetime Democrat—'"

But nothing he told the president ended the war, nor did anything he told Merry nip the catastrophe in the bud. Yet alone in the family he had seen it coming. "I saw it coming. I saw it clear as day. I saw it. I knew it. I sensed it. I fought it. She was out of control. Something was wrong. I could smell it. I told you. 'Something has to be done about that child. Something is going wrong with that child.' And it went in one ear and out the other. I got, 'Dad, take it easy.' I got, 'Dad, don't exaggerate. Dad, it's a phase. Lou, leave her alone, don't argue with her.' 'No, I will *not* leave her alone. This is my grand-daughter. I *refuse* to leave her alone. I refuse to lose a grand-daughter by leaving her alone. Something is *haywire* with that child.' And you looked at me like I was nuts. All of you. Only I wasn't nuts. I was *right*. With a *vengeance* I was right!"

There were no messages for him when he got home. He had been praying for a message from Mary Stoltz.

"Nothing?" he said to Dawn, who was in the kitchen pre-paring a salad out of greens she'd pulled from the garden.

"Nope."

He poured a drink for himself and his father and carried the glasses out to the back porch, where the set was still on.

"You going to make a steak, darling?" his mother asked him.

"Steak, corn, salad, and Merry's big beefsteak tomatoes." He'd meant Dawn's tomatoes but did not correct himself once it was out.

"No one makes a steak like you," she said, after the first shock of his words had worn off.

"Good, Ma."

"My big boy. Who could want a better son?" she said, and when he embraced her she went to pieces for the first time that week. "I'm sorry. I was remembering the phone calls."

"I understand," he said.

"She was a little girl. You'd call, you'd put her on, and she'd say, 'Hi, Grandma! Guess what?' 'I don't know, honey—what?' And she'd tell me."

"Come on, you've been terrific so far. You can keep it up. Come on. Buck up."

"I was looking at the snapshots, when she was a baby . . ."

"Don't look at them," he said. "Try not to look at them. You can do it, Ma. You have to."

"Oh, darling, you're so brave, you're such an inspiration, it's such a tonic when we come to see you. I love you so."

"Good, Ma. I love you. But you mustn't lose control in front of Dawn."

"Yes, yes, whatever you say."

"That's my girl."

His father, continuing to watch the television set—and after having miraculously contained himself for ten full days—said to him, "No news."

"No news," the Swede replied.

"Nothing."

"Nothing."

"O-kay," his father said, feigning fatalism, "o-kay—if that's the way it is, that's the way it is," and went back to watching TV.

"Do you still think she's in Canada, Seymour?" his mother asked.

"I never thought she was in Canada."

"But that's where the boys went . . ."

"Look, why don't we save this discussion? There's nothing wrong with asking questions but Dawn will be in and out—"

"I'm sorry, you're right," his mother replied. "I'm terribly sorry."

"Not that the situation has changed, Mother. Everything is exactly the same."

"Seymour . . ." She hesitated. "Darling, one question. If she gave herself up now, what would happen? Your father says—"

"Why are you bothering him with that?" his father said. "He told you about Dawn. Learn to control yourself."

"*Me* control myself?"

"Mother, you must stop thinking these thoughts. She is gone. She may never want to see us again."

"*Why?*" his father erupted. "Of course she wants to see us again. This I refuse to believe!"

"Now who's controlling himself?" his mother asked.

"Of course she wants to see us again. The problem is *she can't.*"

"Lou dear," his mother said, "there are children, even in ordinary families, who grow up and go away and that's the end of it."

"But not at *sixteen*. For Christ's sake, not under these circumstances. What are you talking about 'ordinary' families? *We* are an ordinary family. This is a child who needs help. This is a child who is in trouble and we are not a family who walks out on a child in trouble!"

"She's twenty years old, Dad. Twenty-one."

"Twenty-one," his mother said, "last January."

"Well, she's not a child," the Swede told them. "All I'm saying is that you must not set yourself up for disappointment, neither of you."

"Well, I don't," his father said. "I have more sense than that. I assure you I don't."

"Well, you mustn't. I seriously doubt that we will ever see her again."

The only thing worse than their never seeing her again would be their seeing her as he had left her on the floor of that room. Over these last few years, he had been moving them in the direction, if not of total resignation, of adaptation, of a realistic appraisal of the future. How could he now tell them what had happened to Merry, find words to describe it to them that would not destroy them? They haven't the faintest picture in their mind of what they'd see if they were to see her. Why does anyone have to know? What is so indispensable about any of them knowing?

"You got reason to say that, son, that we'll never see her?"

"The five years. The time that's gone by. That's reason enough."

"Seymour, sometimes I'm walking on the street, and I'm behind someone, a girl who's walking in front of me, and if she's tall—"

He took his mother's hands in his. "You think it's Merry."

"Yes."

"That happens to all of us."

"I can't stop it."

"I understand."

"And every time the phone rings," she said.

"I know."

"I tell her," his father said, "that she wouldn't do it with a phone call anyway."

"And why not?" she said to her husband. "Why not phone us? That's the safest thing she could possibly do, to phone us."

"Ma, none of this speculation means anything. Why not try to keep it to a minimum tonight? I know you can't help having these thoughts. You can't be free of it, none of us can be. But you have to try. You can't make happen what you want to happen just by thinking about it. Try to free yourself from a little of it."

"Whatever you say, darling," his mother replied. "I feel better now, just talking about it. I can't keep it inside me all the time."

"I know. But we can't start whispering around Dawn."

It was never difficult, as it was with his restless father—who spent so much of life in a transitional state between compassion and antagonism, between comprehension and blindness, between gentle intimacy and violent irritation—to know what to make of his mother. He had never feared battling with her, never uncertainly wondered what side she was on or worried what she might be inflamed by next. Unlike her husband, she was a big industry of nothing other than family love. Hers was a simple personality for whom the well-being of the boys was everything. Talking to her he'd felt, since earliest boyhood, as though he were stepping directly into her heart. With his father, to whose heart he had easy enough access, he had first to collide with that skull, the skull of a brawler, to split it open as bloodlessly as he could to get at whatever was inside.

It was astonishing how small a woman she had become. But what hadn't been consumed by osteoporosis had, in the last five years, been destroyed by Merry. Now the vivacious mother of his youth, who well into middle age was being complimented on her youthful vigor, was an old lady, her spine twisted and bent, a hurt and puzzled expression embedded in the creases of her face. Now, when she did not realize people were watching her, tears would rise in her eyes, eyes bearing that look both long accustomed to living with pain and startled to have been in so much pain so long. Yet all his boyhood recollections (which, however hard to credit, he knew to be genuine; even the ruthlessly unillusioned Jerry would, if asked, have to corroborate them) were of his mother towering over the rest of them, a healthy, tall reddish blonde with a wonderful laugh, who adored being the woman in that masculine household. As a small child he had not found it nearly so odd and amazing as he did looking at her now to think that you could recognize people as easily by their laugh as by their face. Hers, back when she had something to laugh about, was light and like a bird in flight, rising, rising, and then, delightfully, if you were her child, rising yet again. He didn't even have to be in the same room to know where his mother was—he'd hear her laughing and could pinpoint her on the map of the house that was not so much *in* his brain as it *was* his brain (his cerebral cortex divided not into frontal lobes, parietal lobes, temporal lobes, and occipital lobes but into the downstairs, the upstairs, and the basement—the living room, the dining room, the kitchen, etc.).

What had been oppressing her when she arrived from Florida the week before was the letter she was carrying secreted in her purse, a letter addressed by Lou Levov to the second wife Jerry had left, from whom he had only recently separated. Sylvia Levov had been given a stack of letters to mail by her husband, but that one she simply could not send. Instead she had dared to go off alone and open it, and now she had brought the contents north with her to show Seymour. "You know what would happen with Jerry if Susan ever got this? You know the rampage Jerry would go on? He is not a boy without a temper. He never was. He's not you, dear, he is not a diplomat. But your father has to stick his nose in everywhere, and what the results will be means nothing to him, so long as he's got his nose in the wrong place. All he has to do is send her this, and put Jerry in the wrong like this, and there will be hell to pay with your brother—unmitigated hell."

The letter, two pages long, began, "Dear Susie, The check enclosed is for you and for nobody else's information. It is found money. Put it somewhere where nobody knows about it. I'll say nothing and you say nothing. I want you to know that I have not forgotten you in my will. This money is yours to do whatever you want with. The children I'll take care of separately. But if you decide to invest it, *and I strongly hope you do*, my suggestion is gold stocks. The dollar isn't going to be worth a thing. I myself have just put ten thousand into three gold stocks. I will give you the names. Bennington Mines. Castworp Development. Schley-Waiggen Mineral Corp. Solid investments. I got the names from the Barrington Newsletter that has never steered me wrong yet."

Stapled to the letter—stapled so that when she opened the letter the enclosure didn't just flutter away to get lost under the sofa—there was a check made out to Susan R. Levov for seventy-five hundred dollars. A check for twice that amount had gone off to her the day after she had called, sobbing and screaming for help, to say that Jerry had left her that morning for the new nurse in his office. The position of new nurse in the office was one that she had herself occupied before Jerry began the affair with her that ended in his divorcing his first wife. According to the Swede's mother, after Jerry found out about the check for fifteen thousand he proceeded over the phone to call his father "every name in the book," and that night, for the first time in his life, Lou Levov had chest pain that necessitated her calling their doctor at two A.M.

And now, four months later, he was at it again. "Seymour, what should I do? He goes around screaming, 'A second divorce, a second broken family, *more* grandchildren in a broken home, three more wonderful children without parental guidance.' *You* know how he goes on. It's on and on, it's over and over, till I think I'm going out of my mind. 'Where did my son get so good at getting divorced? Who in the history of this entire family has ever been divorced? No one!' I cannot take it anymore, dear. He screams at me, 'Why doesn't your son just go to a whorehouse? Marry a whore out of a whorehouse and get it over with!' He'll get in another fight with Jerry, and Jerry doesn't pull his punches. Jerry doesn't have your considerateness. He never did. When they had that fight about the coat, when Jerry made that coat out of the hamsters—do you remember? Maybe you were in the service by then. Hamster skins Jerry got somewhere, I think at school, and made them into a coat for some girl. He thought he was doing her a favor. But she received this thing, I think by mail, in a box, all wrapped up and it smelled to high heaven, and the girl burst into tears, and her mother telephoned, and your father was fit to be tied. He was mortified. And they had an argument, he and Jerry, and it scared me to death. A fifteen-year-old boy and he screamed so at his own father, his 'rights,' his 'rights,' you could have heard him on Broad and Market about his 'rights.' Jerry does not back down. He doesn't know the meaning of 'back down.' But now he won't be shouting at a man who is forty-five, he will be shouting at a man who is *seventy*-five, and with angina, and this time it won't be indigestion afterwards. There won't be a headache. This time there will be a full-scale heart attack." "There won't be a heart attack. Mother, calm down." "Did I do the wrong thing? I never touched another person's mail in my life. But how could I let him send this to

Susan? Because she won't keep it to herself. She'll do what she did the last time. She'll use it against Jerry—she'll tell him. And this time Jerry *will* kill him." "Jerry won't kill him. He doesn't want to kill him and he won't. Mail it, Momma. You still have the envelope?" "Yes." "It isn't torn? You didn't tear it?" "I'm ashamed to tell you—it's not torn, I used steam. But I don't want him to drop *dead*." "He won't. He hasn't yet. You stay out of it, Ma. Mail Susan the envelope with the check, with the letter. And when Jerry calls, you just go out and take a walk." "And when he gets chest pains again?" "If he gets chest pains again, you'll call the doctor again. You just stay out of it. You cannot intervene to protect him from himself. It's too late in the day for that." "Oh, thank goodness I have you. You're the only one I can turn to. All your own troubles, all you've gone through, and you're the only one in this family who says things to me that are not completely insane."

"Dawn's holding up?" his father asked.

"She's doing fine."

"She looks like a million bucks," his father said. "That girl looks like herself again. Getting rid of those cows was the smartest thing you ever did. I never liked 'em. I never saw why she needed them. Thank God for that face-lift. I was against it but I was wrong. Dead wrong. I got to admit it. That guy did a wonderful job. Thank God our Dawn doesn't look anymore like all that she went through."

"He did do a great job," the Swede said. "Erased all that suffering. He gave her back her face." No longer does she have to look in the mirror at the record of her misery. It had been a brilliant stroke: she had got the thing out from directly in front of her.

"But she's waiting. I see it, Seymour. A mother sees such things. Maybe you erase the suffering from the face, but you can't remove the memory inside. Under that face, the poor thing is waiting."

"Dawn's not a poor thing, Ma. She's a fighter. She's fine. She's made tremendous strides." True—all the while he has been stoically enduring it she has made tremendous strides by find-ing it *unendurable*, by being devastated by it, destroyed by it, and then by denuding herself of it. She doesn't resist the blows the way he does; she *receives* the blows, falls apart, and when she gets herself up again, decides to make herself over. Nothing that isn't admirable in that—abandon first the face assaulted by the child, abandon next the house assaulted by the child. This is her life, after all, and she will get the original Dawn up and going again if it's the last thing she does. "Ma, let's stop this. Come on outside with me while I start the coals."

"No," his mother said, looking ready to cry again. "Thank you, darling. I'll stay here with Daddy and watch the television."

"You watched it all day. Come outside and help me."

"No, thank you, dear."

"She's waiting for them to get Nixon on," his father said. "When they get Nixon on and drive a stake through his heart, your mother will be in seventh heaven."

"And you won't?" she said. "He can't sleep," she told the Swede, "because of that *mamzer*. He's up in the middle of the night writing him letters. Some I have to censor myself, I have to physically stop him, the language is so filthy."

"That skunk!" the Swede's father said bitterly. "That miserable fascist dog!" and out of him, with terrifying force, poured a tirade of abuse, vitriol about the president of the United States that, absent the stuttering that never failed to impart to her abhorrence the exterminating adamance of a machine gun, Merry herself couldn't have topped in her heyday. Nixon liberates him to say anything—as Johnson liberated Merry. It is as though in his uncensored hatred of Nixon, Lou Levov is merely mimicking his granddaughter's vituperous loathing of LBJ. Get Nixon. Get the bastard in some way. Get Nixon and all will be well. If we can just tar and feather Nixon, America will be America again, without everything loathsome and lawless that's crept in, without all this violence and malice and madness and hate. Put him in a cage, cage the crook, and we'll have our great country back the way it was!

Dawn ran in from the kitchen to see what was wrong, and soon they were all in tears, holding one another, huddled together and weeping on that big old back porch as though the bomb had been planted right under the house and the porch was all that was left of the place. And there was nothing the Swede could do to stop them or to stop himself.

The family had never seemed so wrecked as this. Despite all that he had summoned up to lessen the aftershock of the day's horror and to prevent *himself* from cracking—despite the resolve with which he had rearmed himself after hurrying through the underpass and finding his car still there, undamaged, where he had left it on that grim Down Neck street; despite the resolve with which he had for a *second* time rearmed himself after Jerry pummeled him on the phone; despite the resolve he'd had to summon up a *third* time, beneath the razor ribbon of his parking lot fence, with the key to his car in his hand; despite the self-watchfulness, despite the painstaking impersonation of impregnability, despite the elaborate false front of self-certainty with which he was determined to protect those he loved from the four she had killed—he had merely to misspeak, to say "Merry's big beefsteak tomatoes" instead of "Dawn's," for them to sense that something unsurpassingly awful had happened.

In addition to the Levovs there were six guests for dinner that evening. The first to arrive were Bill and Jessie Orcutt, Dawn's architect and his wife, who'd been friendly enough neighbors a few miles down the road all these years, in Orcutt's old family house, and became acquaintances and then dinner guests when Bill Orcutt began designing the new Levov home. Orcutt's family had long been the prominent legal family in Morris County, lawyers, judges, state senators. As president of the local landmarks society, already established as the historical con- science of a new conservationist generation, Orcutt had been a leader in the losing battle to keep Interstate 287 from cutting through the historical center of Morristown and a victorious opponent of the jetport that would have destroyed the Great Swamp, just west of Chatham, and with it much of the county's wildlife. He was trying now to keep Lake Hopatcong from devastation by pollutants. Orcutt's bumper sticker read, "Morris Green, Quiet, and Clean," and he'd good-naturedly slapped one on the Swede's car the first time they met. "Need all the help we can get," he said, "to keep the modern ills at bay." Once he learned that his new neighbors were originally city kids to whom the rural Morris Highlands was an unknown landscape, he vol- unteered to take them on a county tour, one that, as it turned out, went on all one day and would have extended into the next had not the Swede lied and said he and Dawn and the baby had to be in Elizabeth, at his in-laws', Sunday morning.

Dawn had said no to the tour right off. Something in Orcutt's proprietary manner had irritated her at that first meeting, something she found gratingly egotistical in his expansive courtesy, causing her to believe that to this young country squire with the charming manners she was nothing but laughable lace-curtain Irish, a girl who'd somehow got down the knack of aping her betters so as now to come ludicrously barging into his privileged backyard. The confidence, that's what unstrung her, that great confidence. Sure she'd been Miss New Jersey, but the Swede had seen her on a few occasions with these rich Ivy League guys in their shetland sweaters. Her affronted defensiveness always came as a surprise. She didn't seem ever to feel deficient in confidence until she met them and felt the class sting. "I'm sorry," she'd say, "I know it's just my Irish resentment, but I don't like being looked down on." And as much as this resentment of hers had always secretly attracted him—in the face of hostility, he thought proudly, my wife is no pushover—it perturbed and disappointed him as well; he preferred to think of Dawn as a young woman of great beauty and accomplishment who was too *renowned* to have to feel resentful. "The only difference between them and us"—by "them" she meant Protestants—"is, on our side, a little more liquor. And not much at that. 'My new Celtic neighbor. *And* her Hebrew husband.' I can hear him already with the other nobs. I'm sorry—if you can do it that's fine with me, but I for one cannot revere his contempt for our embarrassing origins."

The mainspring of Orcutt's character—and this she was sure of without having even to speak to him—was knowing all too well just how far back he and his manners reached into the genteel past, and so she stayed at home the day of the tour, perfectly content to be alone with the baby.

Her husband and Orcutt, promptly at eight, headed diagonally to the northwest corner of the county and then, backtracking, followed the southward meandering spine of the old iron mines, Orcutt all the while recounting the glory days of the nineteenth century, when iron was king, millions of tons pulled from this very ground; starting from Hibernia and

Boonton down to Morristown, the towns and villages had been thick with rolling mills, nail and spike factories, foundries and forging shops. Orcutt showed him the site of the old mill in Boonton where axles, wheels, and rails were manufactured for the original Morris and Essex Railroad. He showed him the powder company plant in Kenvil that made dynamite for the mines and then, for the First World War, made TNT and more or less paved the way for the government to build the arsenal up at Picatinny, where they'd manufactured the big shells for the Second World War. It was at the Kenvil plant that there'd been the munitions explosion in 1940—fifty-two killed, carelessness the culprit, though at first foreign agents, spies, were suspected. He drove him partway along the western course of the old Morris Canal, where barges had carried the anthracite in from Phillipsburg to fuel the Morris foundries. With a little smile, Orcutt added—to the Swede's surprise—that directly across the Delaware from Phillipsburg was Easton, and "Easton," he said, "was where the whorehouse was for young men from Old Rimrock."

The eastern terminus of the Morris Canal had been Jersey City and Newark. The Swede knew of the Newark end of the canal from when he was a boy and his father would remind him, if they were downtown and anywhere near Raymond Boulevard, that until as recently as the year the Swede was born a real canal ran up by High Street, near where the Jewish Y was, and down through to where there was now this wide city thoroughfare, Raymond Boulevard, leading traffic from Broad Street under Penn Station and out old Passaic Avenue onto the Skyway.

In the Swede's young mind, the "Morris" in Morris Canal never connected with Morris County—a place that seemed as remote as Nebraska then—but with his father's enterprising oldest brother, Morris. In 1918, at the age of twenty-four, already the owner of a shoe store he ran with his young wife—a cubbyhole Down Neck on Ferry Street, amid all the poor Poles and Italians and Irish, and the family's greatest achievement until the wartime contract with the WACs put Newark Maid on the map—Morris had perished virtually overnight in the influenza epidemic. Even on his tour of the county that day, every time Orcutt mentioned the Morris Canal, the Swede thought first of the dead uncle he had never known, a beloved brother who was much missed by his father and for whom the child had come to believe the canal beneath Raymond Boulevard was named. Even when his father bought the Central Avenue factory (no more than a hundred yards from the very spot where the canal had turned north toward Belleville, a factory that virtually backed on the city subway built beneath the old canal route), he persisted in associating the name of the canal with the story of the struggles of their family rather than with the grander history of the state.

After going around Washington's Morristown headquarters —where he politely pretended he hadn't already seen the muskets and the cannonballs and the old eyeglasses as a Newark fourth grader—he and Orcutt drove southwest a ways, out of Morristown to a church cemetery dating back to the American Revolution. Soldiers killed in the war were buried there, as well as twenty-seven soldiers, buried in a common grave, who were victims of the smallpox epidemic that swept the encampments in the countryside in the spring of 1777. Out among those old, old tombstones, Orcutt was no less historically edifying than he'd been all morning on the road, so that at the dinner table that evening, when Dawn asked where Mr. Orcutt had taken him, the Swede laughed. "I got my money's worth all right. The guy's a walking encyclopedia. I never felt so ignorant in my life." "How boring was it?" Dawn asked. "Why, not at all," the Swede told her. "We had a good time. He's a good guy. Very nice. More there than you think when you first meet him. Much more to Orcutt than the old school tie." He was thinking particularly of the Easton whorehouse but said instead, "Family goes back to the Revolution." "Doesn't that come as a surprise," Dawn replied. "The guy knows everything," he said, feigning indifference to her sarcasm. "For instance, that old graveyard where we were, it's at the top of the tallest hill around, so the rain that falls on the northern roof of the old church there finds its way north to the Passaic River and eventually to Newark Bay, and the rain that falls on the southern side finds its way south to a branch of the Raritan, which eventually goes to New Brunswick." "I don't believe that," said Dawn. "Well, it's true." "I refuse to believe it. *Not* to New Brunswick." "Oh, don't be a kid, Dawn. It's interesting *geologically.*" Deliberately he added, "Very interesting," to let her know he was having no part of the Irish resentment. It was beneath him and happened also to be beneath her.

In bed that night, he thought that when Merry got to be a schoolgirl he'd inveigle Orcutt into taking her along on this very same trip so she could learn firsthand the history of the county where she was growing up. He wanted her to see where, at the turn of the century, a railroad line used to run up into Morristown from Whitehouse to carry the peaches from the orchards in Hunterdon County. Thirty miles of railroad line just to transport peaches. Among the well-to-do there was a peach craze then in the big cities and they'd ship them from Morristown into New York. The Peach Special. Wasn't that something? On a good day seventy cars of peaches hauled from the Hunterdon orchards. Two million peach trees down there before a blight carried them all away. But he could himself tell her about that train and the trees and the blight when the time came, take her on his own to show her where the tracks used to be. It wouldn't require Orcutt to do it for him.

"The first Morris County Orcutt," Orcutt told him at the cemetery, pointing to a brown weathered gravestone decorated at the top with the carving of a winged angel, a gravestone set close up to the back wall of the church. "Thomas. Protestant immigrant from northern Ireland. Arrived 1774. Age of twenty. Enlisted in a local militia outfit. A private. January 2, 1777, fought at Second Trenton. Battle that set the stage for Washington's victory at Princeton the next day."

"Didn't know that," the Swede said.

"Wound up at the logistical base at Morristown. Commissary support for the Continental artillery train. After the war bought a Morristown ironworks. Destroyed by a flash flood, 1795. Two flash floods, '94 *and* '95. Big supporter of Jefferson. Political appointment from Governor Bloomfield saved his life. Surrogate of Morris County. Master in chancery. Eventually county clerk. There he is. The sturdy, fecund patriarch."

"Interesting," said the Swede—interesting at just the moment he found it all about as deadly as it could get. How it *was* interesting was that he'd never met anybody like this before.

"Over here," said Orcutt, leading him some twenty feet on to another old brownish stone with an angel carved at the top, this one with an indecipherable rhyme of four lines inscribed near the bottom. "His son William. Ten sons. One died in his thirties but the rest lived long lives. Spread out all over Morris County. None of them farmers. Justices of the peace. Sheriffs. Freeholders. Postmasters. Orcutts everywhere, even into Warren and up into Sussex. William was the prosperous one. Turnpike development. Banking. New Jersey presidential elector in 1828. Pledged to Andrew Jackson. Rode the Jackson victory to a big judicial appointment. State's highest judicial body. Never a member of the bar. That didn't matter then. Died a much-respected judge. See, on the stone? 'A virtuous and useful citizen.' It's *his* son—over here, this one here—his son George who clerked for August Findley and became a partner. Findley was a state legislator. Slavery issue drove him into the Republican Party. . . ."

As the Swede told Dawn, whether she wanted to hear it or not—no, because she did *not* want to hear it—"It was a lesson in American history. John Quincy Adams. Andrew Jackson. Abraham Lincoln. Woodrow Wilson. His grandfather was a classmate of Woodrow Wilson's. At Princeton. He told me the class. I forget it now. Eighteen seventy-nine? I'm full of dates, Dawnie. He told me *everything*. And all we were doing was walking around a cemetery out back of a church at the top of a hill. It was something. It was *school*."

But once was enough. He'd paid all the attention he could, never stopped trying to keep straight in his mind the progress of the Orcutts through almost two centuries—though each time Orcutt had said "Morris" as in Morris County, the Swede had thought "Morris" as in Morris Levov. He couldn't remember ever in his life feeling more like his father—not like his father's son but like his *father*—than he did marching around the graves of those Orcutts. His family couldn't compete with Orcutt's when it came to ancestors—they would have run out of ancestors in about two minutes. As soon as you got back earlier than Newark, back to the old country, no one knew anything. Earlier than Newark, they didn't know their names or anything about them, how anyone made a living, let alone whom they'd voted for. But Orcutt could spin out ancestors forever. Every rung into America for the Levovs there was another rung to attain; this guy was *there*.

Is that why Orcutt had laid it on a little thick? Was it to make clear what Dawn accused him of making clear simply by the way he smiled at you—just who he was and just who you weren't? No, that was thinking not too much like Dawn but *way* too much like his father. Jewish resentment could be just as bad as the Irish resentment. It could be worse. They hadn't moved out here to get caught up in that stuff. He was no Ivy Leaguer himself. He'd been educated, like Dawn, at lowly Upsala in East Orange, and thought "Ivy League" was a name for a kind of clothes before he knew it had anything to do with a university. Little by little the picture came into focus, of course—a world of Gentile wealth where the buildings were covered with ivy and the people had money and dressed in a certain style. Didn't admit Jews, didn't know Jews, probably didn't like Jews all that much. Maybe they didn't like Irish Catholics—he'd take Dawn's word for it. Maybe they looked down on them, too. But Orcutt was Orcutt. He had to be judged according to his own values and not the values of "the Ivy League." As long as he's fair and respectful to me, I'll be fair and respectful to him.

All it came down to, in his mind, was that the guy could get boring on the subject of the past. The Swede wasn't going to take it to mean more until somebody proved otherwise. They weren't out there to get all worked up about neighbors across the hill whose house they couldn't even see—they were out there because, as he liked to joke to his mother, "I want to own the things that money can't buy." Everybody else who was picking up and leaving Newark was headed for one of the cozy suburban streets in Maplewood or South Orange, while they, by comparison, were out on the frontier. During the two years when he was down in South Carolina with the marines, it used to thrill him to think, "This is the Old South. I am below the Mason-Dixon line. I am Down South!" Well, he couldn't commute from Down South but he could skip Maplewood and South Orange, leapfrog the South Mountain Reservation, and just keep going, get as far out west in New Jersey as he could while still being able to make it every day to Central Avenue in an hour. Why not? A hundred acres of America. Land first cleared not for agriculture but to furnish timber for those old iron forges that consumed a thousand acres of timber a year. (The real-estate lady turned out to know almost as much local history as Bill Orcutt and was no less generous in ladling it out to a potential buyer from the streets of Newark.) A barn, a millpond, a millstream, the foundation remains of a gristmill that had supplied grain for Washington's troops. Back on the property somewhere, an abandoned iron mine. Just after the Revolution, the original house, a wood structure, and the sawmill had burned down and the house was replaced by this one—according to a date engraved on a stone over the cellar door and carved into a corner beam in the front room, built in 1786, its exterior walls constructed of stones collected from the fireplaces of the Revolutionary army's former campsites in the local hills. A house of stone such as he had always dreamed of, with a gambrel roof no less, and, in what used to be the kitchen and was now the dining room, a fireplace unlike any he'd ever seen, large enough for roasting an ox, fitted out with an oven door and a crane to swing an iron kettle around over the fire; a nineteen-inch-high lintel beam extending seventeen feet across the whole width of the room. Four smaller fireplaces in other rooms, all working, with the original chimneypieces, the wooden carving and moulding barely visible beneath coats and coats of a hundred and sixty-odd years of paint but waiting there to be restored and revealed. A central hallway ten feet wide. A staircase with newel posts and railings carved of pale-striped tiger maple—according to the real-estate lady, tiger maple a rarity in these parts at that time. Two rooms to either side of the staircase both upstairs and downstairs, making in all eight rooms, plus the kitchen, plus the big back porch. . . . Why the hell shouldn't it be his? Why shouldn't he own it? "I don't want to live next door to anybody. I've done that. I grew up doing that. I don't want to see the stoop out the window—I want to see the *land*. I want to see the streams running everywhere. I want to see the cows and the horses. You drive down the road, there's a *falls* there. We don't *have* to live like everybody else—we can live any way we want to now. We did it. Nobody stopped us. They couldn't. We're married. We can go anywhere, we can do anything. Dawnie, we're free!"

Moreover, getting to be free had not been painless, what with the pressure from his father to buy in the Newstead development in suburban South Orange, to buy a modern house

with everything in it brand new instead of a decrepit "mauso-
leum." "You'll never heat it," predicted Lou Levov the Saturday he first laid eyes on the huge, vacant old stone house with
the For Sale sign, a house on a hilly country road out in the
middle of nowhere, eleven miles west of the nearest train stop,
the Lackawanna station in Morristown, where the screen-door-
green cars with the yellowish cane seats took people all the way
into New York. Because it came with the hundred acres and
with a collapsing barn and a fallen-down gristmill, because it
had been vacant and up for sale for almost a year, it was going
for about half the price of things that sat on just a two-acre lot
in Newstead. "Heat this place, cost you a fortune, and you'll
still freeze to death. When it snows out here, Seymour, how
are you going to get to the train? On these roads, you're not.
What the hell does he need all that ground for anyway?" Lou
Levov demanded of the Swede's mother, who was standing
between the two men in her coat and trying her best to stay
out of the discussion by studying the tops of the roadside trees.
(Or so the Swede thought; later he learned that, in vain, she
had been looking down the road for street lights.) "What are
you going to do with all the ground," his father asked him,
"feed the starving Armenians? You know what? You're dream-
ing. I wonder if you even know where this is. Let's be candid
with each other about this—this is a narrow, bigoted area. The
Klan thrived out here in the twenties. Did you know that? The
Ku Klux Klan. People had crosses burned on their property
out here." "Dad, the Ku Klux Klan doesn't exist anymore."
"Oh, doesn't it? This is rock-ribbed Republican New Jersey,
Seymour. It is Republican out here from top to bottom." "Dad,
Eisenhower is president—the whole *country* is Republican.
Eisenhower's the president and Roosevelt is dead." "Yeah, and
this place was Republican when Roosevelt was *living*. Republican
during the New Deal. Think about that. Why did they hate
Roosevelt out here, Seymour?" "I don't know why. Because he
was a Democrat." "No, they didn't like Roosevelt because they
didn't like the Jews and the Italians and the Irish—that's why
they moved out here to begin with. They didn't like Roosevelt
because he accommodated himself to these new Americans.
He understood what they needed and he tried to help them.
But not these bastards. They wouldn't give a Jew the time of

day. I'm talking to you, son, about bigots. Not about the goose step even—just about hate. And this is where the haters live, out here."

The answer was Newstead. In Newstead he would not have the headache of a hundred acres. In Newstead it would be rock-ribbed Democrat. In Newstead he could live with his family among young Jewish couples, the baby could grow up with Jewish friends, and the commute door-to-door to Newark Maid, taking South Orange Avenue straight in, was half an hour tops. . . . "Dad, I drive to Morristown in fifteen minutes." "Not if it snows you don't. Not if you obey the traffic laws you don't." "The 8:28 express gets me to Broad Street 8:56. I walk to Central Avenue and I'm at work six minutes after nine." "And if it snows? You still haven't answered me. If the train breaks down?" "Stockbrokers take this train to work. Lawyers, businessmen who go into Manhattan. Wealthy people. It's not the milk train—it doesn't break down. On the early-morning trains they've got their own parlor car, for God's sake. It's not the sticks." "You could have fooled me," his father replied.

But the Swede, rather like some frontiersman of old, would not be turned back. What was impractical and ill-advised to his father was an act of bravery to him. Next to marrying Dawn Dwyer, buying that house and the hundred acres and moving out to Old Rimrock was the most daring thing he had ever done. What was Mars to his father was *America* to him—he was settling Revolutionary New Jersey as if for the first time. Out in Old Rimrock, all of America lay at their door. That was an idea he loved. Jewish resentment, Irish resentment—the hell with it. A husband and wife each just twenty-five years of age, a baby of less than a year—it had been *courageous* of them to head out to Old Rimrock. He'd already heard tell of more than a few strong, intelligent, talented guys in the leatherware business beaten down by their fathers, and he wasn't going to let it happen to him. He'd fallen in love with the same business as his old man had, he'd taken his birthright, and now he was moving beyond it to damn well live where he wanted.

No, we are not going to have *anybody's* resentment. We are thirty-five miles out *beyond* that resentment. He wasn't saying it was always easy to blend across religious borders. He wasn't saying there wasn't prejudice—he'd faced it as a recruit in the

Marine Corps, in boot camp on a couple of occasions faced it head-on and faced it down. She'd had her own brush with blatant anti-Semitism at the pageant in Atlantic City when her chaperone referred distastefully to 1945, when Bess Myerson became Miss America, as "the year the Jewish girl won." She'd heard plenty of casual cracks about Jews as a kid, but Atlantic City was the real world and it shocked her. She wouldn't repeat it at the time because she was fearful that he would turn against her for remaining politely silent and failing to tell the stupid woman where to get off, especially when her chaperone added, "I grant she was good-looking, but it was a great embarrassment to the pageant nonetheless." Not that it mattered one way or the other anymore. Dawn was a mere contestant, twenty-two years old—what could she have said or done? His point was that they both were aware, from firsthand experience, that these prejudices existed. In a community as civilized as Old Rimrock, however, differences of religion did not have to be as hard to deal with as Dawn was making them. If she could marry a Jew, she could surely be a friendly neighbor to a Protestant—sure as hell could if her husband could. The Protestants are just another denomination. Maybe they were rare where she grew up—they were rare where he grew up too —but they happen not to be rare in America. Let's face it, they *are* America. But if you do not assert the superiority of the Catholic way the way your mother does, and I do not assert the superiority of the Jewish way the way my father does, I'm sure we'll find plenty of people out here who won't assert the superiority of the Protestant way the way their fathers and mothers did. Nobody dominates anybody anymore. That's what the war was about. Our parents are not attuned to the possibilities, to the realities of the postwar world, where people can live in harmony, all sorts of people side by side no matter what their origins. This is a new generation and there is no need for that resentment stuff from anybody, them *or* us. And the upper class is nothing to be frightened of either. You know what you're going to find once you know them? That they are just other people who want to get along. Let's be intelligent about all this.

As it worked out, he never had to make a case as thorough as this to get Dawn to lay off about Orcutt, since Orcutt was never much in their lives after the sightseeing trip that Dawn kept referring to as "The Orcutt Family Cemetery Tour." Nothing like a social life developed back then between the Orcutts and the Levovs, not even a casual friendship, though the Swede did show up Saturday mornings at the pasture back of Orcutt's house for the weekly touch-football game with Orcutt's local friends and some other fellows like the Swede, ex-GIs from around Essex County trickling out with new families to the wide-open spaces.

Among them was an optician named Bucky Robinson, a short, muscular, pigeon-toed guy with a round angelic face, who'd been second-string quarterback for Hillside High, Weequahic's traditional Thanksgiving Day rival, when Swede was finishing high school. The first week Bucky showed up, the Swede overheard him telling Orcutt about Swede Levov's senior year, enumerating on his fingers, "all-city end in football; all-city, all-county center in basketball; all-city, all-county, all-state first baseman in baseball. . . ." Though ordinarily the Swede would have found this awe of him, so nakedly demonstrated, not at all to his liking in an environment where he only wished to inspire neighborly goodwill, where being just another of the guys who showed up to play ball was fine with him, he seemed not to mind that Orcutt was the one standing there enduring the excess of Bucky's enthusiasm. He had no quarrel with Orcutt and no reason to have any, yet seeing everything he would ordinarily prefer to hide behind a modest demeanor being revealed so passionately to Orcutt by Bucky was more pleasurable than he might have imagined, almost like the satisfaction of a desire he personally knew nothing about—a desire for revenge.

When, for several weeks running, Bucky and the Swede wound up together on the same team, the newcomer couldn't believe his good fortune: while to everybody else the new neighbor was Seymour, Bucky at every opportunity called him Swede. It did not matter who else might be in the clear, wildly waving his arms in the air—the Swede was the receiver Bucky saw. "Big Swede, way to go!" he'd shout whenever the Swede came back to the huddle having gathered in yet another Robinson pass—Big Swede, which nobody but Jerry had called him since high school. And with Jerry it was always sardonic.

One day Bucky hitched a ride with the Swede to a local garage where his car was being repaired and, as they were driving along, announced surprisingly that he was Jewish too and that he and his wife had recently become members of a Morristown temple. Out here, he said, they were more and more involving themselves with the Morristown Jewish community. "It can be very sustaining in a Gentile town," Bucky told the Swede, "to know you have Jewish friends nearby." Though not enormous, Morristown's was an established Jewish community, went back to before the Civil War, and included quite a few of the town's influential people, among them a trustee at Morristown Memorial Hospital—through whose insistence the first Jewish doctors had, two years back, finally been invited to join the hospital staff—and the owner of the town's best department store. Successful Jewish families had been living in the big stucco houses on Western Avenue for fifty years now, though on the whole this wasn't an area known to be terribly friendly toward Jews. As a child Bucky had been taken by his family up to Mt. Freedom, the resort town in the nearby hills, where they would stay for a week each summer at Lieberman's Hotel and where Bucky first fell in love with the beauty and serenity of the Morris countryside. Up at Mt. Freedom, needless to say, it was great for Jews: ten, eleven large hotels that were all Jewish, a summer turnover in the tens of thousands that was entirely Jewish—the vacationers themselves jokingly referred to the place as "Mt. Friedman." If you lived in an apartment in Newark or Passaic or Jersey City, a week in Mt. Freedom was heaven. And as for Morristown, although solidly Gentile, it was nonetheless a cosmopolitan community of lawyers, doctors, and stockbrokers where Bucky and his wife loved going to the movies at the Community, loved the shops, which were excellent, loved the beautiful old buildings and where there were the Jewish shopkeepers with their neon signs up and down Speedwell Avenue. But did the Swede know that before the war there'd been a swastika scrawled on the golf-course sign at the edge of Mt. Freedom? Did he know that the Klan held meetings in Boonton and Dover, rural people, working-class people, members of the Klan? Did he know that crosses were burned on people's lawns not five miles from the Morristown green?

From that day on, Bucky kept trying to land the Swede, who would have been a considerable catch, and to haul him in for the Morristown Jewish community, to get him, if not to join the temple outright, at least to play evening basketball in the Interchurch League for the team the temple fielded. Robinson's mission irritated the Swede in just the way his mother had when, some months after Dawn became pregnant, she'd astonished him by asking if Dawn was going to convert before the baby was born. "A man to whom practicing Judaism means nothing, Mother, doesn't ask his wife to convert." He had never been so stern with her in his life, and, to his dismay, she had walked away near tears, and it had taken numerous hugs throughout the day to get her to understand that he wasn't "angry" with her—he had only been making clear that he was a grown man with the prerogatives of a grown man. Now with Dawn he talked about Robinson—talked a lot about him as they lay in bed at night. "I didn't come out here for that stuff. I never got that stuff anyway. I used to go on the High Holidays with my father, and I just never understood what they were getting at. Even seeing my father there never made sense. It wasn't him, it wasn't like him—he was bending to something that he didn't have to, something he didn't even understand. He was just bending to this because of my grandfather. I never understood what any of that stuff had to do with his being a man. What the glove factory had to do with his being a man anybody could understand—just about everything. My father knew what he was talking about when he was talking about gloves. But when he started about that stuff? You should have heard him. If he'd known as little about leather as he knew about God, the family would have wound up in the poorhouse." "Oh, but Bucky Robinson isn't talking about God, Seymour. He wants to be your friend," she said, "that's all." "I guess. But I never was interested in that stuff, Dawnie, back for as long as I can remember. I never understood it. Does anybody? I don't know what they're talking about. I go into those synagogues and it's all foreign to me. It always has been. When I had to go to Hebrew school as a kid, all the time I was in that room I couldn't wait to get out on the ball field. I used to think, 'If I sit in this room any longer, I'm going to get sick.' There was something unhealthy about those places. Anywhere near any of those places and I knew it wasn't where I wanted to be. The factory was a place I wanted to be from the time I was a boy. The ball field was a place I wanted to be from the time I started kindergarten. That this is a place where I want to be I knew the moment I laid eyes on it. Why shouldn't I be where I want to be? Why shouldn't I be with *who* I want to be? Isn't that what this country's all about? I want to be where I want to be and I don't want to be where I don't want to be. That's what being an American is—isn't it? I'm with you, I'm with the baby, I'm at the factory during the day, the rest of the time I'm out here, and that's everywhere in this world I *ever* want to be. We own a piece of America, Dawn. I couldn't be happier if I tried. I did it, darling, I did it—I did what I set out to do!"

For a while, the Swede stopped showing up at the touch-football games just to avoid having to deflect Bucky Robinson on the subject of his temple. With Robinson he did not feel like his father—he felt like Orcutt. . . .

No, no. You know whom he really felt like? Not during the hour or two a week he happened to be on the receiving end of a Bucky Robinson pass, but whom he felt like all the rest of the time? He couldn't tell anybody, of course: he was twenty-six and a new father and people would have laughed at the childishness of it. He laughed at it himself. It was one of those kid things you keep in your mind no matter how old you get, but whom he felt like out in Old Rimrock was Johnny Appleseed. Who cares about Bill Orcutt? Woodrow Wilson knew Orcutt's grandfather? Thomas Jefferson knew his grandfather's uncle? Good for Bill Orcutt. Johnny Appleseed, that's the man for me. Wasn't a Jew, wasn't an Irish Catholic, wasn't a Protestant Christian—nope, Johnny Appleseed was just a happy American. Big. Ruddy. Happy. No brains probably, but didn't need 'em—a great walker was all Johnny Appleseed needed to be. All physical joy. Had a big stride and a bag of seeds and a huge, spontaneous affection for the landscape, and everywhere he went he scattered the seeds. What a story that was. Going everywhere, walking everywhere. The Swede had loved that story all his life. Who wrote it? Nobody, as far as he could remember. They'd just studied it in grade school. Johnny Appleseed, out there everywhere planting apple trees. That bag of seeds. I loved that bag. Though maybe it was his hat—did he keep the

seeds in his hat? Didn't matter. "Who told him to do it?"
Merry asked him when she got old enough for bedtime stories
—though still baby enough, should he try to tell any other
story, like the one about the train that used to carry only
peaches, to cry, "Johnny! I want Johnny!" "Who told him?
Nobody told him, sweetheart. You don't have to tell Johnny
Appleseed to plant trees. He just takes it on himself." "Who is
his wife?" "Dawn. Dawn Appleseed. That's who his wife is."
"Does he have a child?" "Sure he has a child. And you know
what her name is?" "What?" "Merry Appleseed!" "Does she
plant apple seeds in a hat?" "Sure she does. She doesn't plant
them in the hat, honey, she stores them in the hat—and then
she throws them. Far as she can, she casts them out. And everywhere she throws the seed, wherever it lands on the ground,
do you know what happens?" "What?" "An apple tree grows
up, right there." And every time he walked into Old Rimrock
village he could not restrain himself—first thing on the weekend he pulled on his boots and walked the five hilly miles into
the village and the five hilly miles back, early in the morning
walked all that way just to get the Saturday paper, and he could
not help himself—he thought, "Johnny Appleseed!" The pleasure of it. The pure, buoyant unrestrained pleasure of striding.
He didn't care if he played ball ever again—he just wanted to
step out and stride. It seemed somehow that the ballplaying
had cleared the way to *allow* him to do this, to stride in an
hour down to the village, pick up the Lackawanna edition of
the *Newark News* at the general store with the single Sunoco
pump out front and the produce out on the steps in boxes and
burlap bags. It was the only store down there in the fifties and
hadn't changed since the Hamlin son, Russ, took it over from
his father after World War I—they sold washboards and tubs,
there was a sign up outside for Frostie, a soft drink, another
nailed to the clapboards for Fleischmann's Yeast, another for
Pittsburgh Paint Products, even one out front that said "Syracuse
Plows," hanging there from when the store sold farm equipment
too. Russ Hamlin could remember from earliest boyhood a
wheelwright shop perched across the way, could still recall
watching wagon wheels rolled down a ramp to be cooled in
the stream; remembered, too, when there was a distillery out
back, one of many in the region that had made the famous

local applejack and had shut down only with the passage of the Volstead Act. Clear at the back of the store there was one window that was the U.S. post office—one window was it, and thirty or so of those boxes with the combination locks. Hamlin's general store, with the post office inside, and outside the bulletin board and the flagpole and the gas pump—that's what had served the old farming community as its meeting place since the days of Warren Gamaliel Harding, when Russ became proprietor. Diagonally across the street, alongside where there'd been the wheelwright shop, was the six-room schoolhouse that would be the Levovs' daughter's first school. Kids sat on the steps of the store. Your girl would meet you there. A meeting place, a greeting place. The Swede loved it. The familiar old *Newark News* he picked up had a special section out here, the second section, called "Along the Lackawanna." Even that pleased him, and not just reading through it at home for the local Morris news but merely carrying it home in his hand. The word "Lackawanna" was pleasing to him in and of itself. From the front counter he'd pick up the paper with "Levov" scrawled at the top in Mary Hamlin's hand, charge a quart of milk if they needed it, a loaf of bread, a dozen fresh-laid eggs from Paul Hamlin's farm up the road, say "See ya, Russell" to the owner, and then he'd turn and stride all the way back, past the white pasture fences he loved, the rolling hay fields he loved, the corn fields, the turnip fields, the barns, the horses, the cows, the ponds, the streams, the springs, the falls, the watercress, the scouring rushes, the meadows, the acres and acres of woods he loved with all of a new country dweller's puppy love for nature, until he reached the century-old maple trees he loved and the substantial old stone house he loved—pretending, as he went along, to throw the apple seed everywhere.

Once, from an upstairs window, Dawn saw him approaching the house from the foot of their hill while he was doing just that, flinging out one arm, flinging it out not as though he were throwing a ball or swinging a bat but as though he were pulling handfuls of seed from the grocery bag and throwing them with all his strength across the face of the historic land that was now no less his than it was William Orcutt's. "What are you practicing out there?" she said, laughing at him when he burst into the bedroom looking, from all that exercise, handsome as hell, big, carnal, ruddy as Johnny Appleseed himself, someone to whom something marvelous was happening. When people raise their glasses and toast a youngster, when they say to him, "May you have health and good fortune!" the picture that they have in mind—or that they should have in mind—is of the earthy human specimen, the very image of unrestricted virility, who burst so happily into that bedroom and found there, all alone, a little magnificent beast, his young wife, stripped of all maidenly constraints and purely, blissfully his. "Seymour, what *are* you doing down at Hamlin's—taking ballet lessons?" Easily, so easily, with those large protecting hands of his he raised the hundred and three pounds of her up from the floor where she stood barefoot in her nightgown, and using all his considerable strength, he held her to him as though he were holding together, binding together, into one unshatterable entity, the wonderful new irreproachable existence of husband and father Seymour Levov, Arcady Hill Road, Old Rimrock, New Jersey, USA. What he had been doing out on the road—which, as though it were a shameful or superficial endeavor, he could not bring himself openly to confess even to Dawn—was making love to his life.

About the intensity of his physical intimacy with his young wife he was actually more discreet. Together they were rather prudish around people, and no one would have guessed at the secret that was their sexual life. Before Dawn he had never slept with anybody he'd dated—he'd slept with two whores while he was in the Marine Corps, but that didn't count really, and so only after they were married did they discover how passionate he could be. He had tremendous stamina and tremendous strength, and her smallness next to his largeness, the way he could lift her up, the bigness of his body in bed with her seemed to excite them both. She said that when he would fall asleep after making love she felt as though she were sleeping with a mountain. It thrilled her sometimes to think she was sleeping beside an enormous rock. When she was lying under him, he would plunge in and out of her very hard but at the same time holding himself at a distance so she would not be crushed, and because of his stamina and strength he could keep this up for a long time without getting tired. With one arm he could pick her up and turn her around on her knees or he could sit her on his lap and move easily under the weight of her hundred and three pounds. For months and months following their marriage, she would begin to cry after she had reached her orgasm. She would come and she would cry and he didn't know what to make of it. "What's the matter?" he asked her. "I don't know." "Do I hurt you?" "No. I don't know where it comes from. It's almost as if the sperm, when you shoot it into my body, sets off the tears." "But I don't hurt you." "No." "Does it please you, Dawnie? Do you like it?" "I love it. There's something about it . . . it just gets to a place that nothing else gets to. And that's the place where the tears are. You reach a part of me that nothing else ever reaches." "Okay. As long as I don't hurt you." "No, no. It's just strange . . . it's just strange . . . it's just strange not being alone," she said. She stopped crying only when he went down on her for the first time. "You don't cry this way," he said. "It was so different," she said. "How? Why?" "I guess . . . I don't know. I guess I'm alone again." "Do you want me not to do it again?" "Oh, no," she laughed, "absolutely not." "Okay." "Seymour . . . how did you know how to do that? Did you ever do that before?" "Never." "Why did you then? Tell me." But he couldn't explain things as well as she could and so he didn't try. He was just overtaken by the desire to do something more, and so he lifted her buttocks in one hand and raised her body into his mouth. To stick his face there and just go. Go to where he had never been before. Ecstatically complicitous, he and Dawn. He had no reason to believe she would ever do it for him, of course, and then one Sunday morning she just did it. He didn't know what to think. His little Dawn put her beautiful little mouth around his cock. He was stunned. They both were. It was taboo for both of them. From then on, it just went on for years and years. It never stopped. "There's something so touching about you," she whispered to him, "when you get to the point where you're out of control." So touching to her, she told him, this very restrained, good, polite, well-brought-up man, a man always so in charge of his strength, who had *mastered* his tremendous strength and had no violence in him, when he got past the point of no return, beyond the point of anyone's being embarrassed about anything, when he was beyond the point of being able to judge her or to think that somehow she was a bad girl for wanting it as much as she wanted it from him then, when *he* just wanted it, those last three or four minutes that would culminate in the screaming orgasm. . . . "It makes me feel so extremely feminine," she told him, "it makes me feel extremely powerful . . . it makes me feel *both*." When she got out of bed after they made love and she looked wildly disheveled, flushed and with her hair all over the place and her eye makeup smudged and her lips swollen, and she went off into the bathroom to pee, he would follow her there and lift her off the seat after she had wiped herself and look at the two of them together in the bathroom mirror, and she would be taken aback as much as he was, not simply by how beautiful she looked, how beautiful the fucking *allowed* her to look, but how *other* she looked. The social face was gone —there was Dawn! But all this was a secret from others and had to be. Particularly from the child. Sometimes after Dawn had been all day on her feet with the cows, he would pull his chair up to hers after dinner and he would rub her feet, and Merry would make a face and say, "Oh, Daddy, that's disgusting." But that was the only truly demonstrative thing they ever did in front of her. Otherwise there was just the usual affectionate stuff around the house that kids expect to see from parents and would miss if it didn't go on. The life they led together behind their bedroom door was a secret about which their daughter knew no more than anyone else. And on it went, on and on for years; it never stopped until the bomb went off and Dawn wound up in the hospital. After she came out was when it began stopping.

Orcutt had married the granddaughter of one of his grandfather's law partners at Orcutt, Findley, the Morristown firm that he had been expected to join. After graduating from Princeton, he had declined, however, to accept a place at Harvard Law School—Princeton and Harvard Law had for over a hundred years constituted the education of an Orcutt boy—and breaking with the traditions of the world he'd been born to, he moved to a lower Manhattan studio to become an abstract painter and a new man. Only after three depressive years feverishly painting behind the dirty windows over the truck traffic on Hudson Street did he marry Jessie and come back to Jersey to begin architecture studies at Princeton. He never relinquished entirely his dream of an artistic calling, and though his architectural work—mostly on the restoration of the eighteenth- and nineteenth-century houses out in their moneyed quarter of Morris County and, from Somerset and Hunterdon counties all the way down through Bucks County in Pennsylvania, the converting of old barns into elegant rustic homes—kept him happily occupied, every three or four years there was an exhibition of his at a Morristown frame shop that the Levovs, always flattered to be invited to the opening, faithfully attended.

The Swede was never so uncomfortable in any social situation as he was standing in front of Orcutt's paintings, which were said by the flier you got at the door to be influenced by Chinese calligraphy but looked like nothing much to him, not even Chinese. Right from the beginning Dawn had found them "thought-provoking"—to her they showed a most unlikely side to Bill Orcutt, a sensitivity she'd never seen a single indicator of before—but the thought the exhibition most provoked in the Swede was how long he should continue pretending to look at one of the canvases before moving on to pretend to be looking at another one. All he really had any inclination to do was to lean forward and read the titles pasted up on the wall beside each painting, thinking they might help, but when he did—despite Dawn's telling him not to, pulling his jacket and whispering, "Forget those, look at the *brushwork*"—he was only more disheartened than when he did look at the brushwork. *Composition #16*, *Picture #6*, *Meditation #11*, *Untitled #12* . . . and what was there on the canvas but a band of long gray smears so pale across a white background that it looked as though Orcutt had tried not to paint the painting but to rub it out? Consulting the description of the exhibition in the flier, written and signed by the young couple who owned the frame shop, didn't do any good either. "Orcutt's calligraphy is so intense the shapes dissolve. Then, in the glow of its own energy, the brush stroke dissolves itself. . . ." Why on earth would a guy like Orcutt, no stranger to the natural world and the great historical drama of this country—and a helluva tennis player—why on earth did he want to paint pictures of nothing? Since the Swede had to figure the guy wasn't a phony—why would someone as well educated and as self-confident as Orcutt devote all this effort to being a phony?—he could for a while put the confusion down to his own ignorance about art. Intermittently the Swede might continue to think, "There's something wrong with this guy. There is some big dissatisfaction there. This Orcutt does not have what he wants," but then the Swede would read something like that flier and realize that he didn't know what he was talking about. "Two decades after the Greenwich Village years, Orcutt's ambition remains lofty: to create," the flier concluded, "a personal expression of universal themes that include the enduring moral dilemmas which define the human condition."

It never occurred to the Swede, reading the flier, that enough could not be claimed for the paintings just because they *were* so hollow, that you had to say they were pictures of everything *because* they were pictures of nothing—that all those words were merely another way of saying Orcutt was talentless and, however earnestly he might try, could never hammer out for himself an artistic prerogative or, for that matter, any but the prerogative whose rigid definitions had swaddled him at birth. It did not occur to the Swede that he was right, that this guy who seemed so at one with himself, so perfectly attuned to the place where he lived and the people around him, might be inadvertently divulging that to be *out* of tune was, in fact, a secret and long-standing desire he hadn't the remotest idea of how to achieve except by oddly striving to paint paintings that looked like they didn't look like anything. Apparently the best he could do with his craving to be otherwise was this stuff. Sad. Anyway, it didn't matter how sad it was or what the Swede did or did not ask or understand or know about the painter once one of those calligraphic paintings expressing the universal themes that define the human condition made its way onto the Levov living room wall a month after Dawn returned from Geneva with her new face. And that's when things got a little sad for the Swede.

It was a band of brown streaks and not gray ones that Orcutt had been trying to rub out of *Meditation #27*, and the background was purplish rather than white. The dark colors, according to Dawn, signaled a revolution of the painter's formal means. That's what she told him, and the Swede, not knowing quite how to respond and with no interest in what "formal means" meant, settled lamely on "Interesting." They didn't have any art hanging on the walls when he was a kid, let alone "modern" art—art hadn't existed in his house any more than it did in Dawn's. The Dwyers had religious pictures, which might even be what accounted for Dawn's having all of a sudden become a connoisseur of "formal means": a secret embarrassment about growing up where, aside from the framed photos of Dawn and her kid brother, the only pictures were pictures of the Virgin Mary and of Jesus' heart. These tasteful people have modern art on the wall, *we're* going to have modern art on the wall. Formal means on the wall. However much Dawn might deny it, wasn't there something of that going on here? Irish *envy*?

She'd bought the painting right out of Orcutt's studio for exactly half as much as it had cost them to buy Count when he was a baby bull. The Swede told himself, "Forget the dough, write it off—you can't compare a bull to a painting," and in this way managed to control his disappointment when he saw *Meditation #27* go up on the very spot where once there had been the portrait of Merry that he'd loved, a painstakingly perfect if somewhat overly pinkish likeness of the glowing child in blond bangs she had been at six. It had been painted in oils for them by a jovial old gent down in New Hope who wore a smock and a beret in his studio there—he'd taken the time to serve them mulled wine and tell them about his apprenticeship copying paintings in the Louvre—and who'd come to the house six times for Merry to sit for him at the piano, and wanted only two thousand smackers for the painting *and* the gilt frame. But as the Swede was told, since Orcutt hadn't asked for the additional thirty percent it would have cost had they purchased #27 from the frame shop, the five grand was a bargain.

His father's comment, when he saw the new painting, was "How much the guy charge you for that?" With reluctance Dawn replied, "Five thousand dollars." "Awful lot of money for a first coat. What's it going to be?" "*Going* to be?" Dawn had replied sourly. "Well, it ain't finished . . . I hope it ain't. . . . Is it?" "That it isn't 'finished,'" said Dawn, "is the idea, Lou." "Yeah?" He looked again. "Well, if the guy ever wants to finish it, I can tell him how." "Dad," said the Swede, to forestall further criticism, "Dawn bought it because she likes it," and though he also could have told the guy how to finish it (probably in words close to those his father had in mind), he was more than willing to hang anything Dawn bought from Orcutt *just because she had bought it*. Irish envy or no Irish envy, the painting was another sign that the desire to live had become stronger in her than the wish to die that had put her into the psychiatric clinic twice. "So the picture is shit," he told his father later. "The thing is, *she wanted it*. The thing is she *wants* again. Please," he warned him, feeling himself—strangely, given the slightness of the provocation—at the edge of anger, "no more about that picture." And Lou Levov being Lou Levov, the next time he visited Old Rimrock the first thing he did was to walk up to the picture and say loudly, "You know something? I like that thing. I'm gettin' used to it and I actually like it. Look," he said to his wife, "look at how the guy didn't finish it. See that? Where it's blurry? He did that on purpose. That's art."

In the back of Orcutt's van was his large cardboard model of the new Levov house, ready to unveil to the guests after dinner. Sketches and blueprints had been piling up in Dawn's study for weeks now, among them a diagram prepared by Orcutt charting how sunlight would angle into the windows on the first day of each month of the year. "A flood of sunlight," said Dawn. "Light!" she exclaimed. "Light!" And if not with the brutal directness that could truly test to the limit his understanding of her suffering and of the panacea she'd devised, by implication she was damning yet again the stone house he loved and, too, the old maple trees he loved, the giant trees that shaded the house against the summer heat and every autumn ceremoniously cloaked the lawn in a golden wreath at whose heart he'd hung Merry's swing once upon a time.

The Swede couldn't get over those trees in the first years out in Old Rimrock. *I own those trees.* It was more astonishing to him that he owned trees than that he owned factories, more astonishing that he owned trees than that a child of the Chancellor Avenue playing field and the unbucolic Weequahic streets should own this stately old stone house in the hills where Washington had twice made his winter camp during the

Revolutionary War. It was *puzzling* to own trees—they were not owned the way a business is owned or even a house is owned. If anything, they were held in trust. In trust. Yes, for all of posterity, beginning with Merry and *her* kids.

To protect against ice storms and high winds, he had cables installed in each of the big maples, four cables forming a rough parallelogram against the sky where the heavy branches opened dramatically out some fifty feet up. The lightning rods that snaked from the trunk to the topmost point of each tree he arranged to have inspected annually, just to be on the safe side. Twice a year, the trees were sprayed against insects, every third year they were fertilized, and regularly an arborist came around to prune out the deadwood and check the overall health of the private park beyond their door. Merry's trees. Merry's family's trees.

In the fall—just as he had always planned it—he'd be sure to get home from work before the sun went down, and there she would be—just as he had planned it—swinging high up over the fallen leaves encircling the maple by the front door, their largest tree, from which he'd first suspended that swing for her when she was only two. Up she would swing, nearly into the leaves of the branches that spread just beyond the panes of their bedroom windows . . . and, though to him those precious moments at the end of each day had symbolized the realization of his every hope, to her they had meant not a goddamn thing. She turned out to love the trees no more than Dawn had loved the house. What *she* worried about was Algeria. *She* loved Algeria. The kid in that swing, the kid in that tree. The kid in that tree who was now on the floor of that room.

The Orcutts had come early so that Bill and Dawn would have time together to go over the problem of the link that was to join the one-story house to the two-story garage. Orcutt had been away in New York for a couple of days, and Dawn was impatient to get this, their last problem, resolved after weeks of thinking and rethinking how to create a harmonious relationship between the very different buildings. Even if the garage was more or less disguised as a barn, Dawn didn't want it too close, overwhelming the distinctiveness of the house, but she was afraid that a link twenty-four feet long, which was Orcutt's proposal, might impart the look of a motel. They ruminated together almost daily, not only over the dimensions but now over whether the effect should perhaps be that of a greenhouse rather than of the simple passageway first planned. Whenever Dawn felt that Orcutt was trying to impose on her, however graciously, a solution that had more to do with some old-fashioned architectural aesthetic of his own than with the rigorous modernity she had in mind for their new home, she could be quite peeved, and she even wondered, on those few occasions when she was outright furious with him, if it hadn't been a mistake to turn to someone who, though he had considerable authority with the local contractors—guaranteeing a first-class construction job—and an excellent professional reputation, was "essentially a restorer of antiques." Years had passed since she'd been intimidated by the snobbery that, fresh from Elizabeth and the family home (and the pictures on the wall and the statue in the hallway), she'd taken to be more or less Orcutt's whole story. Now his credentials as county gentry were what she was most cutting about when the two of them were at odds. The angry disdain disappeared, however, when Orcutt came back to her, usually within twenty-four hours, having alighted on—in Dawn's words—"a perfectly elegant plan," whether it was for the location of the washer-dryer or a bathroom skylight or the stairway to the guest room above the garage.

Orcutt had brought with him, along with the large one-sixteenth-inch scale model out in the van, samples of a new transparent plastic material he wanted her to consider for the walls and the roof of the link. He'd gone into the kitchen to show it to her. And there the two of them remained, the resourceful architect and the exacting client, debating all over again—while Dawn cleaned the lettuce, sliced the tomatoes, shucked the two dozen ears of corn the Orcutts had brought over in a bag from their garden—the pros and cons of a transparent link rather than the board-and-batten enclosure Orcutt had first proposed to unify it with the exterior of the garage. And meanwhile on the back terrace that looked out toward the hill where, in another time, on an evening like this one, Dawn's herd would be silhouetted against the flamboyance of the late-summer sunset, the Swede prepared the barbecue coals. Keeping him company were his father and Jessie Orcutt, who rarely these days was seen out socializing with Bill but who, according to Dawn, was going through what had wearily been described—by Orcutt, phoning to ask if they wouldn't mind his wife's coming along with him for dinner—as "the calm that heralds the manic upswing."

The Orcutts had three boys and two girls, all grown now, living and working at jobs in New York, five kids to whom Jessie, from all reports, had been a conscientious mother. It was after they'd gone that the heavy drinking began, at first only to lift her spirits, then to suppress her misery, and in the end for its own sake. Yet back when the two couples had first met, it was Jessie's *soundness* that had impressed the Swede: so fresh, so outdoorsy, so cheerily at one with life, not the least bit false or insipid . . . or that's how she'd struck the Swede, if not his wife.

Jessie was a Philadelphia heiress, a finishing-school girl, who always during the day, and sometimes in the evening, wore her mud-spattered jodhpurs and who generally had her hair arranged in flossy flaxen braids. What with those braids and her pure, round, unblemished face—behind which, said Dawn, if you bit into it, you'd find not a brain but a McIntosh apple—she could have passed for a Minnesota farm girl well into her forties, except on those days when her hair was worn up and she could look as much like a young boy as like a young girl. The Swede would never have imagined that there was anything missing from Jessie's endowment to prevent her from sailing right on through into old age as the laudable mother and lively wife who could make a party for everyone's children out of raking the leaves and whose Fourth of July picnics, held on the lawn of the old Orcutt estate, were a treasured tradition among her friends and neighbors. Her character struck the Swede back then as a compound in which you'd find just about everything *toxic* to desperation and dread. At the core of her he could imagine a nucleus of confidence plaited just as neatly and tightly as her braided hair.

Yet hers was another life broken cleanly in two. Now the hair was a ganglion of iron-gray hemp always in need of brushing, and Jessie was a haggard old woman at fifty-four, an undernourished drunk hiding the bulge of a drunk's belly beneath her shapeless sack dresses. All she could ever find to talk about —on the occasions when she managed to leave the house and go out among people—was the "fun" she'd had back before she'd ever had a drink, a husband, a child, or a single thought in her head, before she'd been enlivened (as she certainly had looked to him to be) by the stupendous satisfactions of being a dependable person.

That people were manifold creatures didn't come as a surprise to the Swede, even if it was a bit of a shock to realize it anew when someone let you down. What was astonishing to him was how people seemed to run out of their own being, run out of whatever the stuff was that made them who they were and, drained of themselves, turn into the sort of people they would once have felt sorry for. It was as though while their lives were rich and full they were secretly sick of themselves and couldn't wait to dispose of their sanity and their health and all sense of proportion so as to get down to that other self, the *true* self, who was a wholly deluded fuckup. It was as though being in tune with life was an accident that might sometimes befall the fortunate young but was otherwise something for which human beings lacked any real affinity. How odd. And how odd it made him seem to himself to think that he who had always felt blessed to be numbered among the countless unembattled normal ones might, in fact, be the abnormality, a stranger from real life *because* of his being so sturdily rooted.

"We had a place outside Paoli," Jessie was telling his father. "We always raised animals. When I was seven I got the most wonderful thing. Somebody gave me a pony and a cart. And after that there was nothing to stop me. I just loved horses. I've ridden all my life. Showed and hunted. Was involved in a drag down there in school in Virginia. When I went to school in Virginia I was the whip."

"Wait a minute," said Mr. Levov. "Whoa. I don't know what a drag and a whip is. Slow down, Mrs. Orcutt. You got a guy from Newark here."

She pursed her lips—when he called her "Mrs. Orcutt"— seemingly for his having addressed her as though he were her social inferior, which, the Swede knew, was in part why his father *had* called her "Mrs. Orcutt." But she was "Mrs. Orcutt" to Lou Levov also because of the distancing disdain he had for the drink in her glass, her third Scotch and water in under an hour, and the cigarette—her fourth—burning down between the fingers of her trembling hand. He was amazed by her lack of control—by *anyone's* lack of control but particularly by the lack of control of the goy who drank. Drink was the devil that lurked in the goy—"Big-shot goyim," his father said, "the presidents of companies, and they're like Indians with firewater."

" 'Jessie,' " she said, " 'Jessie,' please," her grin painfully artificial, disguising, by the Swede's estimate, about ten percent of the agony she now felt at having decided against staying alone at home with her dogs and her TV tray and her own J&B and, in a ridiculous eruption of hope, opting instead for going out like a wife with her husband. At home there was a phone next to the J&B; she could reach over her glass and pick it up and dial, and even if only half dressed, she could tell the people she knew, without having to face the terror of facing them, how much she liked them. Months might go by without one of Jessie's phone calls, and then she'd phone three times after they were already in bed for the night. "Seymour, I'm calling to tell you how much I like you." "Well, Jessie, thank you. I like you too." "Do you?" "Of course I do. You know that." "Yes, I like you, Seymour. I always liked you. Did you know I liked you?" "Yes, I did." "I always admired you. So does Bill. We've always admired you and liked you. We like Dawn." "Well, we like you, Jessie." The night after the bombing, around midnight, after Merry's photograph had been on television and everybody in America knew that the day before she had said to somebody at school that Old Rimrock was in for a big surprise, Jessie tried to walk the three miles to their house to see the Levovs but on the unpaved country road, alone in the dark, had twisted her ankle and, two hours later, still lying there, was nearly run over by a pickup truck.

"Okay, my friend Jessie, fill me in. What is a drag and a whip?" You couldn't say his father didn't try to get along with people for all that he really couldn't. If she was a guest of his children, then she was his friend, regardless of how repelled he might be by the cigarettes, by the whiskey, by the unkempt hair and the rundown shoes and the burlap tent concealing the ill-used body—by all the privilege she had squandered and the disgrace she had made of her life.

"A drag is a hunt and it's not with a fox. It's over a line that's laid by a man on a horse ahead of you . . . that has a scent in a bag. It's to make the *effect* of a hunt. The hounds go after it. There are huge, huge fences, and it's done in a sort of a course. It's a lot of fun. You go very fast. Huge, huge, thick brush fences. Eight, ten feet wide with bars on top. Quite exciting. Down there there's a lot of steeplechasing and a lot of good riders and everybody gets out there and bombs through those places and it's fun."

It appeared to the Swede to be as much her confoundment with her predicament—a tipsy woman, out at a party, blabbing uncontrollably—as his father's genial I'm-just-a-dope inquiry that drew her disastrously on, each slurred word unsuccessfully stimulating her mouth to try to produce one that rang clear as a bell. Clear as the "Daddy!" that had pealed out perfectly from behind the veil of his daughter the Jain.

He knew what his father was thinking without bothering to look up from where he was using the tongs to make a pyramid of the reddest coals. Fun, his father was thinking, what *is* it with them and fun? What is this fun? What is so much *fun*? His father was wondering, as he had ever since his son had bought the house and the hundred acres forty miles west of Keer Avenue, Why does he want to live with these people? Forget the drinking. Sober's just as bad. They would bore me to death in two minutes.

Dawn had one brief against them, his father had another.

"Anyway," Jessie was saying, trying, with the cigarette-holding hand, to stir into being some sort of conclusion, "that was why I went to school with my horse."

"You went to school with a horse?"

Again she impatiently pursed her lips, probably because this father, who thought he was helping her out with his questions, was driving her even more rapidly than usual to whatever collapse was in store. "Yes. We both got on the train at the same time," she told him. "Wasn't I *lucky*?" she asked, and to the surprise of both Levov men, as though she weren't at all in serious straits—as though that was just a laughable illusion that disgustingly self-satisfied sober people persisted in having about drunks—laid a flirtatious hand on the side of Lou Levov's head.

"I'm sorry, I don't understand how you got on the train with a horse. How big was this horse?"

"In those days horses were on horsecars."

"Ah-hah," said Mr. Levov, as though his lifelong bewilderment at the pleasures of Gentiles had at last been put to rest. He took her hand from where it lay on his hair and, as though to squeeze into her everything he knew about life's purpose that she would seem to have forgotten, held it firmly between his own hands. Meanwhile, under the impetus of that force which, by failing to size up the situation, would lead her into humiliation before the night was through, Jessie went waveringly on.

"They were all leaving with the polo circuit and they were all going down south in the winter train. The train stopped in Philadelphia. So I put my horse in with them. I put my horse in the car two cars up from where I was bunked in, waved good-bye to the family, and it was great."

"How old were you?"

"I was thirteen. I didn't feel homesick at all, and it was just great, great, great"—here she began to cry—"fun."

Thirteen, his father was thinking, a *pisherke*, and you waved good-bye to the family? What was the matter? Was something the matter with them? What the hell were you waving good-bye to your family for at thirteen? No wonder you're *shicker* now.

But what he said was "That's all right, let it all out. Why not? You're among friends." Unsavory as the job must have seemed to him, it had to be done, and so he removed the glass from her one hand, discarded for her the freshly lit cigarette in the other, and took her into his arms, which was perhaps all she had been asking for all along.

"I see where I have to be a father again," he said to her softly, and she could say nothing, she could only weep and let herself be rocked by the Swede's father, whom, on the one other occasion she had met him in her life—when, some fifteen years back, they had gone to picnic on the Orcutts' lawn for Fourth of July—she had tried to interest in skeet shooting, yet another of those diversions that had long defied Lou Levov's Jewish comprehension. For "fun" pulling a trigger and shooting with a gun. They're meshugeh.

That was the day when, on the way back home, they'd passed a handmade sign on the road by the Congregational church that said "Tent Sale" and Merry had begged the Swede, in her fervent way, to stop and buy one for her.

If Jessie could cry on his father's shoulder over waving goodbye to her family at the age of thirteen, about being shipped off alone at thirteen with nothing but a horse, why shouldn't that memory of his—"Daddy, *stop*, they're selling t-t-t-*tents*!" —bring the Swede to the edge of tears about his daughter the Jain when she was six?

Figuring that Orcutt ought to know what was happening to Jessie and needing time to collect himself, feeling suddenly the full weight of the situation he was so strenuously working to obliterate from his thinking at least until the guests went home—the situation he was in as the father of a daughter who had killed not just one person more or less accidentally but, in the name of truth and justice, three more people quite indifferently, a daughter who, having repudiated everything she had ever learned from him and her mother, had now gone on to disown virtually the whole of civilized existence, beginning with cleanliness and ending with reason—the Swede left his father temporarily to tend alone to Jessie and went around, by way of the back of the house, to the rear kitchen door to get Orcutt. Through the door's glass panes he could see a stack of papers on the table, a new batch of Orcutt's drawings, probably of the troublesome link, and then, by the sink, he saw Orcutt himself.

Orcutt had on his raspberry-colored linen pants and, hanging clear of the pants, a loose-fitting Hawaiian shirt decorated with a colorful array of tropical flora best described in a word favored by Sylvia Levov for everything distasteful to her in wearing apparel: "loud." Dawn maintained that the outfit was just part of that superconfident Orcutt façade by which, as a young newcomer to Old Rimrock, she had once been so ridiculously intimidated. According to Dawn's interpretation— which, when she told it to him, struck the Swede as not without a tinge still of the old resentment—the message of the Hawaiian summer shirts was simply this: I am William Orcutt III and I can wear what other people around here wouldn't dare to wear. "The grander you believe you are in the great world of Morris County," said Dawn, "the more flamboyant you think you can be. The Hawaiian shirt," she said, smiling her mocking smile, "is Wasp extremism—Wasp motley. That's what I've learned living out here—even the William Orcutt the Thirds have their little pale moments of exuberance."

Just the year before, the Swede's father had made a similar observation. "I've noticed this about the rich goyim in the summertime. Comes the summer, and these reserved, correct people wear the most incredible costumes." The Swede had laughed. "It's a form of privilege," he said, repeating Dawn's line. "Is it?" asked Lou Levov, laughing along with him. "Maybe it is," Lou concluded. "Still, I got to hand it to this goy: you have to have guts to wear those pants and those shirts."

Certainly, seeing Orcutt dressed like that down in the village, a burly guy, big and substantial-looking, you would not have imagined—if you were the Swede—his paintings having that rubbed-out look as their distinctive feature. A person as unsophisticated about abstract art as the Swede was said to be by Dawn might easily have imagined the guy who went everywhere in those shirts as painting pictures like the famous one of Firpo knocking Dempsey out of the ring in the second round at the old Polo Grounds. But then artistic creation obviously was not achieved in any way or for any of the reasons Swede Levov could understand. According to the Swede's interpretation, all of the guy's effervescence seemed rather to go into wearing those shirts—all his flamboyance, his boldness, his defiance, and perhaps, too, his disappointment and his despair.

Well, perhaps not *all*, the Swede discovered as he stood peering in through the kitchen door from the big granite step outside. Why he hadn't just opened the door and gone straight ahead into his own kitchen to say that Jessie was in serious need of her husband was because of the way that Orcutt was leaning over Dawn while Dawn was leaning over the sink, shucking the corn. In the first instant it looked to the Swede—despite the fact that Dawn needed no such instruction—as though Orcutt were showing Dawn *how* to shuck corn, bending over her from behind and, with his hands on hers, helping her get the knack of cleanly removing the husk and the silk. But if he was only helping her learn to shuck corn, why, beneath the florid expanse of Hawaiian shirt, were his hips and his buttocks moving like that? Why was his cheek pressed against hers like that? And why was Dawn saying—if the Swede was correctly reading her lips—"Not here, not here . . ."? Why *not* shuck the corn here? The kitchen was as good a place as any. No, it took a moment to figure out that, one, they were not merely shucking corn together and, two, not all of the effervescence, flamboyance, boldness, defiance, disappointment, and despair nibbling at the edges of the old-line durability was necessarily sated by wearing those shirts.

So *this* was why she was always losing her patience with Orcutt—to put me off the track! Making cracks about his blood-lessness, his breeding, his empty warmth, putting him down like that *whenever we are about to get into bed*. Sure she talks that way—she has to, she's in love with him. The unfaithful-ness to the house was never unfaithfulness to the house—it was unfaithfulness. "The poor wife doesn't drink for no reason. Always holding everything back. So busy being so polite," Dawn said, "so Princeton," Dawn said, "so *unerring*. He works so hard to be one-dimensional. That Wasp blandness. Living completely off what they once were. The man is simply not *there* half the time."

Well, Orcutt was there now, right there. What the Swede be-lieved he'd seen, before quickly turning back to the terrace and the steak on the fire, was Orcutt putting himself exactly where he intended to be, while telling Dawn exactly where he was. "There! There! There! There!" And he did not appear to be holding anything back.

8

A T dinner—outdoors, on the back terrace, with darkness coming on so gradually that the evening seemed to the Swede stalled, stopped, suspended, provoking in him a distressing sense of nothing more to follow, of nothing ever to happen again, of having entered a coffin carved out of time from which he would never be extricated—there were also the Umanoffs, Marcia and Barry, and the Salzmans, Sheila and Shelly. Only a few hours had passed since the Swede learned that it was Sheila Salzman, the speech therapist, who had hidden Merry after the bombing. The Salzmans had not told him. And if only they had—called when she showed up there, done their duty to him then . . . He could not complete the thought. If he were to contemplate head-on all that would not have happened had Merry never been permitted to become a fugitive from justice . . . Couldn't complete that thought either. He sat at dinner, eternally inert—immobilized, ineffectual, inert, estranged from those expansive blessings of openness and vigor conferred on him by his hyperoptimism. A lifetime's agility as a businessman, as an athlete, as a U.S. Marine, had in no way conditioned him for being a captive confined to a futureless box where he was not to think about what had become of his daughter, was not to think about how the Salzmans had assisted her, was not to think about . . . about what had become of his wife. He was supposed to get through dinner not thinking about the only things he could think about. He was supposed to do this forever. However much he might crave to get out, he was to remain stopped dead in the moment in that box. Otherwise the world would explode.

Barry Umanoff, once the Swede's teammate and closest high school friend, was a law professor at Columbia, and whenever the folks flew up from Florida Barry and his wife were invited for dinner. Seeing Barry always made his father happy, in part because Barry, the son of an immigrant tailor, had evolved into a university professor but also because Lou Levov—wrongly, though the Swede pretended not to care—credited Barry

Umanoff with getting Seymour to lay down his baseball glove and enter the business. Every summer Lou reminded Barry— "Counselor" as he'd been calling him since high school—of the good deed Barry had done for the Levov family by the example of his professional seriousness, and Barry would say that, if he'd been one-hundredth the ballplayer the Swede was, nobody would have gotten him near a law school.

It was Barry and Marcia Umanoff with whom Merry had stayed overnight a couple of times in New York before the Swede finally forbade her going into New York at all, and it was Barry from whom the Swede had sought legal advice after Merry's disappearance from Old Rimrock. Barry took him to meet Schevitz, the Manhattan litigator. When the Swede asked Schevitz to level with him—what was the worst that could be laid on his daughter if she was apprehended and found guilty? —he was told, "Seven to ten years." "But," said Schevitz, "if it's done in the passion of the antiwar movement, if it's done accidentally, if everything was done to try to prevent anyone from getting hurt . . . And do we know she did it alone? We don't. Do we even know she did it? We don't. No significant political history, a lot of rhetoric, a lot of violent rhetoric, but is this a kid who, on her own, would kill someone deliberately? How do we know she made the bomb or set the bomb? To make a bomb you have to be fairly sophisticated—could this kid light a match?" "She was excellent in science," the Swede said. "For her chemistry project she got an A." "Did she make a bomb for her chemistry project?" "No, of course not—no." "Then we don't know, do we, whether she could light a match or not. It might have been all rhetoric to her. We don't know what she did and we don't know what she meant to do. We don't know anything and neither does anyone else. She could have won the Westinghouse Science Prize and we wouldn't know. What can be proved? Probably very little. The worst, since you ask me, is seven to ten. But let's assume she's treated as a juvenile. Under juvenile law she gets two to three, and even if she pleads guilty to something, the record is sealed and nobody can get at it. Look, it all depends on her role in the homicide. It doesn't have to be too bad. If the kid will come in, even if she did have something to do with it, we might get her off with practically nothing." And until a few hours ago—when he'd learned that on the Oregon commune making bombs was her specialty, when from her own unstuttering mouth he heard that it was not a single possibly accidental death for which she was responsible but the coldhearted murder of four people—Schevitz's words were sometimes all he had to keep him from giving up hope. This man did not deal in fairy tales. You could see that as soon as you walked into his office. Schevitz was somebody who liked to be proved right, somebody whose wish to prevail was his *vocation*. Barry had made it clear beforehand that Schevitz was not a guy interested in making people feel good. He was not addressing the Swede's yearnings when he said, *If the kid will come in we might get her off.* But this was back when they thought they could find a jury that would believe she didn't know how to light a match. This was before five o'clock that afternoon.

Barry's wife, Marcia, a literature professor in New York, was, by even the Swede's generous estimate, "a difficult person," a militant nonconformist of staggering self-certainty much given to sarcasm and calculatedly apocalyptic pronouncements designed to bring discomfort to the lords of the earth. There was nothing she did or said that didn't make clear where she stood. She had barely to move a muscle—swallow while you were speaking, tap with a fingernail on the arm of her chair, even nod her head as if she were in total agreement—to inform you that nothing you were saying was correct. To encompass all her convictions she dressed in large block-printed caftans—an extensive woman, for whom a disheveled appearance was less a protest against convention than a sign that she was a thinker who got right to the point. No nonsense, no commonplace stood between her and the harshest truths.

Yet Barry enjoyed her. Since they couldn't have been more dissimilar, perhaps theirs was one of those so-called attractions of opposites. In Barry, there was such thoughtfulness and kindly concern—ever since he was a kid, and the poorest kid the Swede had known, he'd been a diligent, upright gentleman, a solid catcher in baseball, eventually the class valedictorian, who, after his stint in the service, went to NYU on the GI Bill. That's where he met and married Marcia Schwartz. It was hard for the Swede to understand how a strongly built, not unhandsome guy like Barry could free himself at the age of twenty-two from the desire to be with anybody else in this world but Marcia Schwartz, already so opinionated as a college girl that the Swede had to battle in her presence to stay awake. Yet Barry liked her. Sat there and listened to her. Didn't at all seem to care that she was a slob, dressed even in college like somebody's grandmother, and with those buoyant eyes, unnervingly enlarged by the heavy spectacles. Dawn's opposite in every way. For Marcia to have spawned a self-styled revolutionary— yes, had Merry been raised within earshot of Marcia's mouth . . . but Dawn? Pretty, petite, unpolitical Dawn—why *Dawn*? Where do you look for the cause? Where is the explanation for this mismatch? Was it nothing more than a trick played by their genes? During the March on the Pentagon, the march to stop the war in Vietnam, Marcia Umanoff had been thrown into a paddy wagon with some twenty other women and, very much to her liking, locked up overnight in a D.C. jail, where she didn't stop talking protest talk till they were all let out in the morning. If Merry had been *her* daughter, things *would* make sense. If only Merry had fought a war of words, fought the world with words alone, like this strident yenta. Then Merry's would be not a story that begins and ends with a bomb but another story entirely. But a bomb. A bomb. A bomb tells the whole fucking story.

Hard to grasp Barry's marrying that woman. Maybe it had to do with his family's being so poor. Who knows? Her animus, her superior airs, the sense she gave of being unclean, everything intolerable to the Swede in a friend, let alone in a mate— well, those were the very characteristics that seemed to enliven Barry's appreciation of his wife. It was a puzzle, it truly was, how one perfectly reasonable man could adore what a second perfectly reasonable man couldn't abide for half an hour. But just because it was a puzzle, the Swede tried his best to restrain his aversion and neutralize his judgment and see Marcia Umanoff as simply an oddball from another world, the academic world, the intellectual world, where always to be antagonizing people and challenging whatever they said was apparently looked on with admiration. What it was they got out of being so negative was beyond him; it seemed to him far more productive when everybody grew up and got over that. Still, that didn't mean that Marcia was really out to needle people and work them over just because she was so often needling people and working them over. He couldn't call her vicious once he'd recognized that this was the way she was accustomed to socializing in Manhattan; moreover, he couldn't believe that Barry Umanoff—who at one time was closer to him than his own kid brother—could marry someone vicious. As usual, the Swede's default reaction to not being able to fathom cause and effect (as opposed to his father's reflexive suspiciousness) was to fall back on a lifelong strategy and become tolerant and charitable. And so he was content to chalk up Marcia as "difficult," allowing at worst, "Well, let's just say she's no bargain."

But Dawn loathed her. Loathed her because she knew herself to be loathed by Marcia for having been Miss New Jersey. Dawn couldn't stand people who made that story the whole of her story, and Marcia was especially exasperating because the pleasure of explaining Dawn by a story that had never explained her—and hardly explained her now—was so smugly exhibited. When they'd all first met, Dawn told the Umanoffs about her father's heart attack and how no money was coming into the house and how she realized that the door to college was about to be slammed shut on her brother . . . the whole scholarship story, but none of it made Miss New Jersey seem like anything but a joke to Marcia Umanoff. Marcia barely bothered to hide the fact that when she looked at Dawn Levov she saw no one there, that she thought Dawn pretentious for raising cows, thought she was doing it for the image—it wasn't a serious operation Dawn ran twelve, fourteen hours a day, seven days a week; as far as Marcia was concerned it was a pretty *House and Garden* fantasy contrived by a rich, silly woman who lived, not in stinky-smelling New Jersey, no, no, who lived *in the country*. Dawn loathed Marcia because of her undisguised superiority to the Levovs' wealth, to their taste, to the rural way of life they loved, and loathed her beyond loathing because she was convinced that privately Marcia was altogether pleased about what Merry was alleged to have done.

The privileged place in Marcia's feelings went to the Vietnamese—the North Vietnamese. She never for a moment compromised her political convictions or her compassionate comprehension of international affairs, not even when she saw from six inches away the misery that had befallen her husband's

oldest friend. And this was what led Dawn to make the accusations that the Swede knew to be false, not because he could
swear to Marcia's honorableness but because for him the pro-
bity of Barry Umanoff was beyond question. "I will not have
her in this house! A *pig* has more humanity in her than that
woman does! I don't care how many degrees she has—she is
callous and she is *blind*! She is the most blind, self-involved,
narrow-minded, obnoxious so-called intelligent person I have
ever met in my life and I will not have her in my house!" "Well,
I can't very well ask Barry to come by himself." "Then Barry
can't come." "Barry has to come. I want Barry to come. My
father gets a terrific boot out of seeing Barry here. He *expects*
to see Barry here. It's Barry, Dawn, who got me to Schevitz."
"But that woman took Merry *in*. Don't you see? That's where
Merry went! To New York—to them! That's who gave her a
hiding place! Somebody did, somebody *had* to. A real bomb
thrower in her house—that *excited* her. She hid her from us,
hid Merry from her parents when she needed her parents most.
Marcia Umanoff is the one who sent her underground!"
"Merry didn't want to stay there even before. She stayed exactly twice at Barry's. That was it. The third time she never
showed up. You don't remember. She went somewhere else to
stay and never showed up at the Umanoffs' again." "Marcia is
the *one*, Seymour. Who else has her connections? Wonderful
Father This One, wonderful Father That One, pouring blood
on the draft records. So cozy she is with her war-resister priests,
so buddy-buddy—but they're not priests, Seymour! Priests are
not great forward-thinking liberals. Otherwise they don't *become* priests. It's just that that's not what priests are supposed
to *do*—no more than they're supposed to stop praying for the
boys who go over there. What *she* likes about these priests is
that these *aren't* priests. She doesn't love them because they
are in the Church, she loves them because they are doing
something that, in her estimation, *taints* the Church. Because
they are doing something *outside* the Church, outside the regular *role* of the priest. That these priests are an affront to what
people like me grew up with, *that's* what she likes. That's what
this fat bitch likes about *everything*. I hate her. I hate her guts!"
"Fine. Fine with me. Hate her all you want," he said, "but not

for something she hasn't done. She didn't do it, Dawn. You are driving yourself crazy with something that cannot be true."

And it wasn't true. It wasn't Marcia who had taken Merry in. Marcia *was* all talk—always had been: senseless, ostentatious talk, words with the sole purpose of scandalously exhibiting themselves, uncompromising, quarrelsome words expressing little more than Marcia's intellectual vanity and her odd belief that all her posturing added up to an independent mind. It was Sheila Salzman who'd taken Merry in, the Morristown speech therapist, the pretty, kindly, soft-spoken young woman who for a while had given Merry so much hope and confidence, the teacher who provided Merry all those "strategies" to outwit her impediment and replaced Audrey Hepburn as her heroine. In the months when Dawn was on sedatives and was in and out of the hospital; in the months before Sheila and the Swede would back off from ignoring the whole responsible orientation of their lives; in the months before these two well-ordered, well-behaved people could bring themselves to stop endangering their precious stability, Sheila Salzman had been Swede Levov's mistress, the first and last.

Mistress. A most un-Swede-like acquisition, incongruous, implausible, even ridiculous. "Mistress" does not quite make sense in the untarnished context of that life—and yet, for the four months after Merry disappeared, that is what Sheila was to him.

At dinner the conversation was about Watergate and about *Deep Throat*. Except for the Swede's parents and the Orcutts, everybody at the table had been to see the X-rated movie starring a young porno actress named Linda Lovelace. The picture was no longer playing only in the adult houses but had become a sensation in neighborhood theaters all over Jersey. What surprised him, Shelly Salzman was saying, was that the electorate who overwhelmingly chose as president and vice president Republican politicians hypocritically pretending to deep moral piety should make a hit out of a movie that so graphically caricatured acts of oral sex.

"Maybe it's not the same people," said Dawn, "who are going to the movie."

"It's McGovernites?" Marcia Umanoff asked her.

"At this table it is," answered Dawn, already inflamed at the outset of dinner by this woman she could not bear.

"Please," said the Swede's father, "what these two things have got to do with each other is a mystery to me. I don't know why you people pay good money to go to that trash in the first place. It's pure trash—am I right, Counselor?" He looked to Barry for support.

"It's a kind of trash," Barry said.

"Then why do you let it into your lives?"

"It leaks in, Mr. Levov," Bill Orcutt said to him pleasantly, "whether we like it or not. Whatever is out there leaks in. It pours in. It's not the same out there anymore, in case you haven't heard."

"Oh, I heard, sir. I come from the late city of Newark. I heard more than I want to hear. Look, the Irish ran the city, the Italians ran the city, now let the colored run the city. That's not my point. I got nothing against that. It's the colored people's turn to reach into the till? I wasn't born yesterday. In Newark corruption is the name of the game. What is new, number one, is race; number two, taxes. Add *that* to the corruption, *there's* your problem. Seven dollars and seventy-six cents. That is the tax rate in the city of Newark. I don't care how big you are or how small you are, I'm here to tell you that you cannot run a business with those kind of taxes. General Electric already moved out in 1953. GE, Westinghouse, Breyer's down on Raymond Boulevard, Celluloid, all left the city. Every one of them big employers, and *before* the riots, *before* the racial hatred, they got out. Race is just the icing on the cake. Streets aren't cleaned. Burned-out cars nobody takes away. People in abandoned buildings. *Fires* in abandoned buildings. Unemployment. Filth. Poverty. More filth. More poverty. Schooling nonexistent. Schools a disaster. On every street corner dropouts. Dropouts doing nothing. Dropouts dealing drugs. Dropouts looking for trouble. The projects—don't get me started on the projects. Police on the take. Every kind of disease known to man. As far back as the summer of '64 I told my son, 'Seymour, get out.' 'Get out,' I said, but he won't listen. Paterson goes up, Elizabeth goes up, Jersey City goes up. You got to be blind in both eyes not to see what is next. And I told this to Seymour. 'Newark is the next Watts,' I told him. 'You heard it here first. The summer of '67.' I predicted it in those very words. Didn't I, Seymour? Called it practically to the *day*."

"That is true," the Swede acknowledged.

"Manufacturing is finished in Newark. *Newark* is finished. The riots were just as bad if not worse in Washington, in Los Angeles, in Detroit. But, mark my words, Newark will be the city that never comes back. It can't. And gloves? In America? Kaput. Also finished. Only my son hangs on. Five more years and outside of the government contracts there won't be a pair of gloves made in America. Not in Puerto Rico either. They're already in the Philippines, the big boys. It will be India, it'll be Indonesia, Pakistan, Bangladesh—you'll see, every place around the world making gloves except here. The union alone didn't break us, however. Sure, the union didn't understand, but some of the manufacturers didn't understand either—'I wouldn't pay the sons of bitches another five cents,' and here the guy is driving a Cadillac and sitting in Florida in the winter. No, a lot of the manufacturers didn't think straight. But the unions never understood the competition from overseas, and there is no doubt in my mind that the union speeded up the demise of the glove industry by being tough and making it so that people couldn't make money. The union rate on piecework ran a lot of people out of business or offshore. In the thirties our competition was heavy from Czechoslovakia, from Austria, from Italy. The war came along and saved us. Government contracts. Seventy-seven million pairs of gloves purchased by the quartermaster. The glove man got rich. But then the war ended, and I tell you, as far back as that, even in the good days, it was already the beginning of the end. Our downfall was that we could never compete with overseas. We hastened it because there wasn't some good judgment on either side. But it could not be saved regardless. The only thing that could have stopped it—and I was not for this, I don't think you can stop world trade and I don't think you should try—but the only thing that could have stopped it is if we put up trade barriers, making it not just five percent duties but thirty percent, forty percent—"

"Lou," said his wife, "what does any of this have to do with this movie?"

"This movie? These goddamn movies? Well, of course, they're not new either, you know. We had a pinochle club, this is years ago . . . you remember, the Friday Night Club? And we had a guy in the electrical business. You remember him, Seymour, Abe Sacks?"

"Sure," the Swede said.

"Well, I hate to tell you but he had all these kind of movies right in his house. Sure they existed. On Mulberry Street, where we used to go with the kids to eat Chinks, was a saloon where you could go in and buy whatever filth you wanted. And you know something? I watched five minutes and I went back in the kitchen and, to his credit, so did my dear friend, he's dead now, a wonderful fella, my mind is going, the glove cutter, what the hell was his name—"

"Al Haberman," said his wife.

"Right. The two of us just played gin for an hour, until there was this hullabaloo in the living room where they were show-ing the movie, and what happened was the whole damn movie, the camera, the whole what-do-you-call-it caught fire. I couldn't have been happier. That is thirty, forty years ago, and to this day I remember sitting with Al Haberman playing cards while the rest of them were drooling like idiots in the living room."

He was by now telling this to Orcutt, directing his remarks solely at him. As though, despite the evidence of the drunken woman Lou Levov was sitting next to, despite the incontro-vertible evidence of so much of Jewish lore, the anarchy of a highborn Gentile remained essentially unimaginable to him, and Orcutt, therefore, of everyone at the table, could best ap-preciate the platitude he was getting at. They're supposed to be the dependable ones in control of themselves. Aren't they? They marked the territory. Didn't they? They made the rules, the very rules that the rest of us who came here have agreed to follow. Could Orcutt fail to admire him for sitting in that kitchen, sitting there patiently playing gin until at last the forces of good overcame the forces of evil and that dirty movie went up in smoke back in 1935?

"Well, I'm sorry to say, Mr. Levov, that you can't keep it out any longer just by playing cards," Orcutt told him. "That was a way to keep it out that doesn't exist any longer."

"Keep what out?" Lou Levov asked.

"What you're talking about," said Orcutt. "The permissiveness. Abnormality cloaked as ideology. The perpetual protest. Time was you could step away from it, you could make a stand against it. As you point out, you could even just play cards against it. But these days it's getting harder and harder to find relief. The grotesque is supplanting everything commonplace that people love about this country. Today, to be what they call 'repressed' is a source of shame to people—as not to be repressed used to be."

"That is true, that is true. Let me tell you about Al Haberman. You want to talk about the old-style world and what used to be, let's talk about Al. A wonderful fella, Al, a handsome fella. Got rich cutting gloves. You could in those days. A husband and a wife who had any ambition could get a few skins and make some gloves. Ended up in a small room, two men cutting, a couple of women sewing, they could make the gloves, they could press them and ship them. They made money, they were their own bosses, they could work sixty hours a week. Way, way back when Henry Ford was paying the unheard-of sum of a dollar a day, a fine table cutter would make five dollars a day. But look, in those days it was nothing for an ordinary woman to own twenty, twenty-five pair of gloves. Quite common. A woman used to have a glove wardrobe, different gloves for every outfit—different colors, different styles, different lengths. A woman wouldn't go outside without a pair in any weather. In those days it wasn't unusual for a woman to spend two, three hours at the glove counter and try on thirty pair of gloves, and the lady behind the desk had a sink and she would wash her hands between each color. In a fine ladies' glove, we had quarter sizes into the fours and up to eight and a half. Glove cutting is a wonderful trade—was, anyway. Everything now is 'was.' A cutter like Al always had a shirt and a tie on. In those days a cutter never worked without a shirt and a tie. You could work at seventy-five and eighty years old too. They could start in the way Al did, at fifteen, or even younger, and they could go to eighty. Seventy was a spring chicken. And they could work at their leisure, Saturday and Sunday. These people could work constantly. Money to send their kids to school. Money to fix up their homes nicely. Al could take a piece of leather, say to me, for a gag, 'What do you want, Lou, eight and nine-sixteenths?' And just snip it off without a ruler, measuring it perfectly with just his eye. The cutter was the prima donna. But all that pride of craftsmanship is gone, of course. Of the actual table cutters who could cut a sixteen-button white glove, I think Al Haberman may have been the last guy in America who could do it. The long glove, of course, vanished. Another 'was.' There was the eight-button glove which became very popular, silk-lined, but that was gone by '65. We were already taking gloves that were longer, chopping off the tops, making shorties, and using the top to make another glove. From this point where the thumb seam is, every inch on out they used to put a button, so we still talk, in terms of length, of buttons. Thank God in 1960 Jackie Kennedy walked out there with a little glove to the wrist, and a glove to the elbow, and a glove above the elbow, and a pillbox hat, and all of a sudden gloves were in style again. First Lady of the glove industry. Wore a size six and a half. People in the glove industry were praying to that lady. She herself stocked up in Paris, but so what? That woman put the ladies' fine leather glove back on the map. But when they assassinated Kennedy and Jacqueline Kennedy left the White House, that and the miniskirt was the end of the ladies' fashion glove. The assassination of John F. Kennedy and the arrival of the miniskirt, and together that was the death knell for the ladies' dress glove. Till then it was a twelve-month, year-round business. There was a time when a woman would not go out unless she wore a pair of gloves, even in the spring and the summer. Now the glove is for cold weather or for driving or for sports—"

"Lou," his wife said, "nobody is talking about—"

"Let me finish, please. Don't interrupt me, please. Al Haberman was a great reader. No schooling but he loved to read. His favorite author was Sir Walter Scott. And Sir Walter Scott, in one of his classic books, gets an argument going between the glovemaker and the shoemaker about who is the better craftsman, and the glovemaker wins the argument. You know what he says? 'All you do,' he tells the shoemaker, 'is make a mitten for the foot. You don't have to articulate around each toe.' But Sir Walter Scott was the son of a glover, so it makes sense he would win the argument. You didn't know Sir Walter Scott was the son of a glover? You know who else, aside from

Sir Walter and my two sons? William Shakespeare. Father was a glover who couldn't read and write his own name. You know what Romeo says to Juliet when she's up on the balcony? Everybody knows 'Romeo, Romeo, where are you, Romeo'— that *she* says. But what does Romeo say? I started in a tannery when I was thirteen, but I can answer for you because of my friend Al Haberman, who since has passed away, unfortunately. Seventy-three years old, he came out of his house, slipped on the ice, and broke his neck. Terrible. He told me this. Romeo says, 'See the way she leans her cheek on her hand? I only wish I was the glove on that hand so that I could touch that cheek.' Shakespeare. Most famous author in history."

"Lou dear," Sylvia Levov said again softly, "what does this have to do with what everybody is talking about?"

"*Please*," he said, and impatiently, with one hand, without even looking at her, waved away her objection. "And McGovern," he went on, "this is an idea I don't follow at all. What does McGovern have to do with that lousy movie? I voted for McGovern. I campaigned in the whole condominium for McGovern. You should hear what I put up with from Jewish people, how Nixon was this for Israel and that for Israel, and I reminded them, in case they forgot, that Harry Truman had him pegged for Tricky Dicky back in 1948, and now look, the reward they're reaping, my good friends who voted for Mr. Von Nixon and his storm troopers. Let me tell you who goes to those movies: riffraff, bums, and kids without adult supervision. Why my son takes his lovely wife to such a movie is something I'll go to my grave not understanding."

"To see," said Marcia, "how the other half lives."

"My daughter-in-law is a lady. She has no interest in those things."

"Lou," his wife said to him, "maybe not everybody sees it your way."

"I cannot believe that. These are intelligent, educated people."

"You put too much stock in intelligence," Marcia teased him. "It doesn't annihilate human nature."

"That's human nature, those movies? Tell me, what do you tell to children about that movie when they ask? That it's good, wholesome fun?"

"You don't have to tell them a thing," Marcia said. "They don't ask. These days they just go."

And what puzzled him, of course, was that what was happening these days did not seem to displease her, a professor, a *Jewish* professor—with *children*.

"I wouldn't say children are going," Shelly Salzman put in, as much, seemingly, to disrupt the unpromising dialogue as to give comfort to the Swede's father. "I would say adolescents."

"And, Dr. Salzman, *you* approve of this?"

Shelly smiled at the title Lou Levov insisted on using with him after all these years. Shelly was a pale, plump, round-shouldered man in a bow tie and a seersucker jacket, a hard-working family doctor who could not keep the kindness out of his voice. The pallor and the posture, the old-fashioned steel-rimmed glasses, the hairless crown of his head, the wiry white curls above his ears—this unstudied lack of luster had made the Swede feel particularly sorry for him during the months of the love affair with Sheila Salzman. . . . Yet he, nice Dr. Salzman, had harbored Merry in his house, hidden her not only from the FBI but from him, her father, the person she'd needed most in the world.

And I was the one, the Swede was thinking, guilty over *my* secret—even as Shelly was gently saying to the Swede's father, "My approval or disapproval is beside the point of whether they go to those movies or not."

When Dawn had first proposed going for a face-lift to the clinic of a Geneva doctor she had read about in *Vogue*—a doctor they didn't know, a procedure they knew nothing about—the Swede had quietly contacted Shelly Salzman and went off to see him alone in his office. Their own family doctor was a man the Swede respected, a cautious and thorough elderly man who would have counseled the Swede and answered his questions and tried, on the Swede's behalf, to dissuade Dawn from the idea, but instead the Swede had called Shelly and asked if he might come over to talk about a family problem. Only when he got to Shelly's office did he understand that he had gone there to confess, four years after the fact, to having had the affair with Sheila in the aftermath of Merry's disappearance. When Shelly smiled and asked, "How can I help you?" the Swede found himself on the brink of saying, "By forgiving me." Throughout the conversation, every time the Swede spoke he had to quash the impulse to tell Shelly everything, to say, "I'm not here because of the face-lift. I'm here because I did what I should never have done. I betrayed my wife, I betrayed you, I betrayed myself." But saying this would be a betrayal of Sheila, would it not? He could no more justify his taking it solely upon himself to confess to her husband than he could had she taken it upon herself to confess to his wife. However much he might yearn to be rid of a secret that stained and oppressed him, and imagine that a confession might unburden him, did he have the right to free himself at Sheila's expense? At Shelly's expense? At Dawn's expense? No, there was such a thing as ethical stability. No, he could not be so ruthlessly self-regarding. A cheap stunt, a treacherous stunt, and one that probably wouldn't pay off in long-term relief—yet each time the Swede opened his mouth to speak, he needed desperately to say to this kindly man, "I was the lover of your wife," to seek from Shelly Salzman the magical restitution of equilibrium that Dawn must be hoping she'd find in Geneva. But instead he only told Shelly how against the face-lift he was, only enumerated his reasons against it, and then, to his surprise, listened to Shelly telling him that Dawn had perhaps begun to entertain a potentially promising idea. "If she thinks this will help her start over again," Shelly said, "why not give her the opportunity? Why not give this woman *every* opportunity? There's nothing wrong with it, Seymour. This is life—not a life sentence but life. Nothing immoral about having a face-lift. Nothing frivolous about a woman wanting one. She found the idea in *Vogue* magazine? That shouldn't throw you off. She only found what she was looking for. You don't know how many women come to me who've been through a terrible trauma and they want to talk about something or other, and what turns out to be on their mind is just this, plastic surgery. And without *Vogue* magazine. The emotional and psychological implications can turn out to be something. The relief they get, those that get relief, is not to be minimized. I can't say I know how it happens, I'm not saying it always happens, but I've seen it happen again and again, women who've lost their husbands, who've been seriously ill . . . You don't look like you believe me." But the Swede knew what he looked like: like a man with

"Sheila" written all over his face. "I know," said Shelly, "it seems like a purely physical way of dealing with something profoundly emotional, but for many people it's a wonderful survival strategy. And Dawn may be one of them. I don't think you want to be puritanical about this. If Dawn feels strongly about a face-lift, and if you were to go along with her, if you were to support her . . ." Later that same day Shelly phoned the Swede at the factory—he'd made some inquiries about Dr. LaPlante. "We've got people as good as him here, I'm sure, but if you want to go to Switzerland and get away and let her recuperate there, why not? This LaPlante is tops." "Shelly, thanks, it's awfully kind of you," said the Swede, disliking himself more than ever in the light of Shelly's generosity . . . and yet this was the same guy who, with his co-conspirator wife, had provided Merry a hiding place not only from the FBI but from her father and mother. A fact about as fantastic as a fact could be. What kind of mask is everyone wearing? I thought these people were on my side. But the mask is all that's on my side—that's it! For four months I wore the mask myself, with him, with my wife, and I could not stand it. I went there to tell him that. I went to tell him that I had betrayed him, and only didn't so as not to compound the betrayal, and never once did he let on how cruelly he'd betrayed me.

"My approval or disapproval," Shelly had been saying to Lou Levov, "is beside the point of whether they go to those movies or not."

"But you are a physician," the Swede's father insisted, "a respected person, an ethical person, a responsible person—"

"Lou," said his wife, "maybe, dear, you're monopolizing the conversation."

"Let me finish, *please*." To the table at large, he asked, "Am I? Am I monopolizing the conversation?"

"Absolutely not," said Marcia, throwing an arm good-naturedly across his back. "It's delightful to hear your delusions."

"I don't know what that means," he told her.

"It means social conditions may have altered in America since you were taking the kids to eat at the Chinks and Al Haberman was cutting gloves in a shirt and a tie."

"Really?" Dawn said to her. "They've altered? Nobody told

us," and, to contain herself, got up and left for the kitchen. Waiting there for Dawn's instructions were a couple of local high school girls who helped to do the serving and the cleaning up whenever the Levovs had dinner guests.

Marcia was to one side of Lou Levov, Jessie Orcutt to the other. Jessie's new glass of Scotch, which she must have managed to pour for herself in the kitchen, he had picked up from her place and moved out of her reach only minutes into the cold cucumber soup. When she then made a move to leave the table, he would not allow her to get up. "Just sit," he told her. "Sit and eat. You don't need that. You need food. Eat your dinner." Each time she so much as shifted in her chair, he laid a hand firmly on hers to remind her she was going nowhere.

A dozen candles burned in two tall ceramic candelabra, and to the Swede, who sat flanked by his mother and by Sheila Salzman, everyone's eyes—deceptively enough, even Marcia's eyes—appeared blessed in that light with spiritual understanding, with kindly lucidity, alive with all the meaning one so craves to find in one's friends. Sheila, like Barry, was on hand every year at Labor Day because of what she had come to mean to his folks. On the phone to Florida the Swede almost never got through a conversation without his father's asking, "And how is that lovely Sheila, that lovely woman, how is she doing?" "She is such a dignified woman," his mother said, "such a refined person. Isn't she Jewish, darling? Your father says no. He insists she isn't."

Why this disagreement should persist for years he could not understand exactly, but the subject of fair-haired Sheila Salzman's religious origins had proved indispensable to his parents' lives. To Dawn, who'd been trying for decades to be as tolerant of the Swede's imperfect parents as he was of her imperfect mother, this was their most inexplicable preoccupation—their most enraging as well (particularly as Dawn knew that, for her adolescent daughter, Sheila had something Dawn didn't have, that somehow Merry had come to trust the speech therapist in a way she no longer trusted her mother). "Are there no Jewish blonds in the world other than you?" Dawn asked him. "It hasn't anything to do with her appearance," the Swede explained, "it has to do with Merry." "What does her being Jewish have

to do with Merry?" "I don't know. She was the speech therapist. They're in awe of her," the Swede said, "because of all she
did for Merry." "She wasn't the child's mother by any chance—
or was she?" "They know that, darling," calmly answered the
Swede, "but because of the speech therapy, they've made her
into some kind of magician."

And so had he, not so much while she was Merry's therapist
—when he had merely found her composure a curious stimulus
to sexual imaginings—but after Merry disappeared and grief
absconded with his wife.

Thrown violently off his own narrow perch, he felt an intan-
gible need open hugely within him, a need with no bottom to
it, and he yielded to a solution so foreign to him that he did
not even recognize how improbable it was. In the quiet,
thoughtful woman, who had once made Merry less strange to
herself by teaching her how to overcome her word phobias
and to control the elaborate circumlocutionary devices that,
paradoxically, only increased her child's sense of being out of
control, was someone he found himself wanting to incorporate
into himself. The man who had lived correctly within marriage
for almost twenty years was determined to be senselessly, wor-
shipfully in love. It was three months before he could begin to
understand that this was no way around anything, and it was
Sheila who had to tell him. He hadn't gotten a romantic mistress—he'd gotten a candid mistress. She sensibly told him
what all his adoration of her meant, told him that he was no
more himself with her than Dawn was Dawn at the psychiatric
clinic, explained to him that he was out to sabotage everything
—but he was in such a state that he went on anyway telling her
how, when they ran away together to Ponce, she could learn
Spanish and teach techniques of speech therapy at the university there, and he could operate the business from his Ponce
plant and they could live in a modern hacienda up in the hills,
among the palms, above the Caribbean. . . .

What she did not tell him about was Merry in her house—
after the bombing, Merry hiding in her house. She told him
everything except that. The candor stopped just where it should
have begun.

Was everyone's brain as unreliable as his? Was he the only
one unable to see what people were up to? Did everyone slip

around the way he did, in and out, in and out, a hundred different times a day go from being smart to being smart enough, to being as dumb as the next guy, to being the dumbest bastard who ever lived? Was it stupidity deforming him, the simpleton son of a simpleton father, or was life just one big deception that everyone was on to except him?

This sense of inadequacy he might once have described to *her*; he could talk to Sheila, talk about his doubts, his bewilderment—all the serenity in her allowed for that, this magician of a woman who had given Merry the great opportunity that Merry had thrown away, who had supplanted with "a wonderful floating feeling," according to Merry, half at least of her stutterer's frustration, the lucid woman whose profession was to give sufferers a second chance, the mistress who knew everything, including how to harbor a murderer.

Sheila had been with Merry and she had told him nothing.

All the trust between them, like all the happiness he'd ever known (like the killing of Fred Conlon—like *everything*), had been an accident.

She'd been with Merry and said nothing.

And said nothing now. The eagerness with which others spoke seemed, under the peculiar intensity of her gaze, to strike her as a branch of pathology. Why would anyone say *that*? She herself was to say nothing all evening, nothing about Linda Lovelace or Richard Nixon or H. R. Haldeman and John Ehrlichman, her advantage over other people being that her head was not filled by what filled everybody else's head. This way of hers, of lying in wait behind herself, the Swede had once taken to be a mark of her superiority. Now he thought, "Icy bitch. *Why?*" Once she had said to him, "The influence you allow others to have on you, it's absolute. Nothing so captivates you as another person's needs." And he had said, "I think you are describing Sheila Salzman," and, as always, he was wrong.

He thought she was omniscient and all she was was cold.

Whirling about inside him now was a frenzied distrust of everyone. The excision of certain assurances, the *last* assurances, made him feel as though he had gone in one day from being five to being one hundred. It would give him comfort, he thought, it would help him right then if, of all things, he knew that resting out in the pasture beyond their dinner table was Dawn's herd, with Count, the big bull, protecting them. If Dawn still had Count, if only Count. . . . A relief-filled, real-ityless moment passed before he realized that of course it would be a comfort to have Count roaming the dark pasture among the cows, because then Merry would be roaming among the guests, here, Merry, in her circus pajamas, leaning up against the back of her father's chair, whispering into her father's ear. *Mrs. Orcutt drinks whiskey. Mrs. Umanoff has BO. Dr. Salzman is bald.* A mischievous intelligence that was ut-terly harmless—back then unanarchic and childish and well within bounds.

Meanwhile he heard himself saying, "Dad, take some more steak," in what he knew was a hopeless effort—a good son's effort—to get his self-abandoned father to be, if not tranquil, less insistently chagrined over the inadequacies of the non-Jewish human race.

"I'll tell you who I'll take some steak for—for this young lady." Spearing a slice from the platter that one of the serving girls was holding beside him, he dumped it onto Jessie's plate; he had taken Jessie on as a full-scale project. "Now pick up your knife and fork and eat," he told her, "you could use some red meat. Sit up straight," and, as though she believed he could well resort to violence if she did otherwise, Jessie Orcutt drunkenly mumbled, "I was going to," but began to fiddle with the meat in such a clumsy way that the Swede feared his father was going to start cutting her food for her. All that crude energy that, try as it might, could not remake the trou-bled world.

"But this is serious business, this children business." Having gotten Jessie taking nourishment, he was in a state again about *Deep Throat*. "If that isn't serious, what is anymore?"

"Dad," said the Swede, "what Shelly is saying is not that it's not serious. He agrees it's serious. He's saying that once you've made your case to an adolescent child, you've made your case and you can't then take these kids and lock them up in their rooms and throw away the key."

His daughter was an insane murderer hiding on the floor of a room in Newark, his wife had a lover who dry-humped her over the sink in their family kitchen, his ex-mistress had knowingly

brought disaster upon his house, and he was trying to propi-
tiate his father with on-the-one-hand-this and on-the-other-
hand-that.

"You'd be surprised," Shelly told the old man, "how much
the kids today have learned to take in their stride."

"But degrading things should *not* be taken in their stride! I
say *lock* them in their rooms if they take this in their stride!
I remember when kids used to be at home doing their homework and not out seeing movies like this. This is the morality
of a country that we're talking about. Well, isn't it? Am I nuts?
It is an affront to decency and to decent people."

"And what," Marcia asked him, "is so inexhaustibly interesting about decency?"

The question so surprised him that it left him looking a little
frantically around the table for somebody with an opinion
learned enough to subdue this woman.

It turned out to be Orcutt, that great friend of the family.
Bill Orcutt was coming to Lou Levov's aid. "And what is wrong
with decency?" Orcutt asked, smiling broadly at Marcia.

The Swede could not look at him. On top of all the things
he could not think about there were two people—Sheila and
Orcutt—he could not look at. Did Dawn consider Bill Orcutt
handsome? He never thought so. Round face, snout nose, pucker-
ing lower lip . . . piggy-looking bastard. Must be something
else that drove her to that frenzy over the kitchen sink. What?
The easy assurance? Was that what got her going? The comfort
taken by Bill Orcutt in being Bill Orcutt, his contentment in
being Bill Orcutt? Was it because he wouldn't dream of slighting you even if both you and he knew that you weren't up to
snuff? Was it his appropriateness that got her going like that, the
flawless appropriateness, how very appropriately he played his
role as steward of the Morris County past? Was it the sense he
exuded of never having had to grub for anything or take shit
from anyone or be at a loss as to how to behave even when the
wife on his arm was a hopeless drunk? Was it because he'd entered the world expecting things not even a Weequahic three-
letterman begins to expect, that none of us begin to expect,
that the rest of us, if we even get those things by working our
asses off for them, still never feel entitled to? Was that why
she was in heat over the sink—because of his inbred sense of

entitlement? Or was it the laudable environmentalism? Or was it the great art? Or was it simply his cock? Is that it, Dawn dear? I want an answer! I want it tonight! *Is it just his cock?*

The Swede could not stop imagining the particulars of Orcutt fucking his wife any more than he could stop imagining the particulars of the rapists fucking his daughter. Tonight the imagining would not let him be.

"Decency?" Marcia said to Orcutt, foxily smiling back at him. "Much overvalued, wouldn't you say, the seductions of decency and civility and convention? Not the richest response to life I can think of."

"So what *do* you recommend for 'richness'?" Orcutt asked her. "The high road of transgression?"

The patrician architect was amused by the literature professor and the menacing figure she tried to cut in order to appall the squares. Amused he was. Amused! But the Swede could not turn the dinner party into a battle for his wife. Things were bad enough without colliding with Orcutt in front of his parents. All he had to do was to not listen to him. Yet each time that Orcutt spoke, every word antagonized him, convulsed him with spite and hatred and sinister thoughts; and when Orcutt wasn't speaking, the Swede was constantly looking down the table to see what in God's name there was in that face that could so excite his wife.

"Well," Marcia was saying, "without transgression there isn't very much knowledge, is there?"

"My God," cried Lou Levov, "*that's* one I never heard before. Excuse me, Professor, but where the hell do you get that idea?"

"The Bible," said Marcia, deliciously, "for a start."

"The *Bible? Which* Bible?"

"The one that begins with Adam and Eve. Isn't that what they tell us in Genesis? Isn't that what the Garden of Eden story is telling us?"

"What? Telling us *what?*"

"Without transgression there is no knowledge."

"Well, that ain't what they taught me," he replied, "about the Garden of Eden. But then I never got past eighth grade."

"What *did* they teach you, Lou?"

"That when God above tells you not to do something, you

damn well don't do it—that's what. Do it and you pay the piper. Do it and you will suffer from it for the rest of your days."

"Obey the good Lord above," said Marcia, "and all the terrible things will vanish."

"Well . . . yes," he replied, though without conviction, realizing that he was being mocked. "Look, we are way off the subject—we are not talking about the Bible. Forget the Bible. This is no place to talk about the Bible. We are talking about a movie where a grown woman, from all reports, goes in front of a movie camera, and for money, openly, for millions and millions of people to see, children, everyone, does everything she can think of that is degrading. *That's* what we're talking about."

"Degrading to whom?" Marcia asked him.

"To *her*, for God's sake. Number one, *her*. She has made herself into the scum of the earth. You can't tell me you are in favor of *that*."

"Oh, she hasn't made herself into the scum of anything, Lou."

"To the contrary," said Orcutt, laughing. "She has eaten of the Tree of Knowledge."

"*And*," announced Marcia, "made herself into a superstar. The highest of the high. I think Miss Lovelace is having the time of her life."

"Adolf Hitler had the time of his life, Professor, shoveling Jews into the furnace. That does not make it *right*. This is a woman who is poisoning young minds, poisoning the country, and in the bargain she *is* making herself the scum of the earth —period!"

There was nothing inactive in Lou Levov when he argued, and it looked as though just observing the phenomenon of an opinionated old man, fettered still to his fantasy of the world, was all that was prompting Marcia to persist. To bait and bite and draw blood. Her sport. The Swede wanted to kill her. Leave him alone! Leave him alone and he'll shut up! It's no big deal getting him to say more and more and more—so stop it!

But this problem that he had long ago learned to circumnavigate, in part by subduing his own personality, seemingly subjugating it to his father's while maneuvering around Lou where he could—this problem of the father, of maintaining filial love against the onslaught of an unrelenting father—was not a problem that she'd had decades of experience integrating into her life. Jerry just told their father to fuck off; Dawn was driven almost crazy by him; and Sylvia Levov stoically and impatiently endured him, her only successful form of resistance being to freeze him out and live with the isolation—and see more of herself evaporating year by year. But Marcia took him on as the fool that he was for still believing in the power of his indignation to convert the corruptions of the present into the corruptions of the past.

"So what would you want her to be instead, Lou? A cocktail waitress?" Marcia asked.

"Why not? That's a job."

"Not much of one," Marcia replied. "Not one that would interest anyone here."

"Oh?" said Lou Levov. "They'd prefer what she does instead?"

"I don't know," said Marcia. "We'll have to poll the girls. Which would you prefer," she said to Sheila, "cocktail waitress or porn star?"

But Sheila was not about to be engulfed in Marcia's mockery, and with eyes that seemed to stare past it and right on through to the egotism, she gave her unequivocal reply. The Swede remembered that after Sheila had first met Marcia and Barry Umanoff here, at the Old Rimrock house, he had asked her, "How can he love this person?" and instead of answering him as Dawn did, "Because he's a ball-less wonder," Sheila had replied. "By the end of a dinner party, everybody is probably thinking that about somebody. Sometimes everybody is thinking that about everybody." "Do you?" he'd asked her. "I think that about couples all the time," she'd said.

The wise woman. And yet this wise woman had harbored a murderer.

"What about Dawn?" Marcia asked. "Cocktail waitress or porno actress?"

Smiling sweetly, exhibiting her best Catholic schoolgirl posture—the girl who makes the nuns happy by sitting at her desk without slouching—Dawn said, "Up yours, Marcia."

"What kind of conversation is this?" Lou Levov asked.

"A dinner conversation," Sylvia Levov replied.

"And what makes *you* so blasé?" he asked her.

"I'm not blasé. I'm listening."

Now Bill Orcutt said, "Nobody's polled you, Marcia. Which would you prefer, assuming you had the choice?"

She laughed merrily at the slighting innuendo. "Oh, they've got big fat mamas in dirty movies. They, too, appear in the dreams of men. And not only for comic relief. Listen, you folks are too hard on Linda. Why is it that if a girl takes off her clothes in Atlantic City it's for a scholarship and makes her an American goddess, but if she takes off her clothes in a sex flick it's for filthy money and makes her a whore? Why is that? Why? All right—nobody knows. But seriously, folks, I love this word 'scholarship.' A hooker comes to a hotel room. The guy asks her how much she gets. She says, 'Well, if you want blank I get a three-hundred-dollar scholarship. And if you want blank-blank I get a five-hundred-dollar scholarship. And if you want blank-blank-blank—'"

"Marcia," said Dawn, "try as you will, you can't get under my skin tonight."

"Can't I?"

"Not tonight."

There was a beautiful floral arrangement at the center of the table. "From Dawn's garden," Lou Levov had told them all proudly as they were sitting down to eat. There were also large platters of the beefsteak tomatoes, sliced thickly, dressed in oil and vinegar, and encircled by slices of red onion fresh from the garden. And there were two wooden buckets—old feed buckets that they'd picked up at a junk shop in Clinton for a dollar apiece—each lined gaily with a red bandanna and brimming with the ears of corn that Orcutt had helped her shuck. Cradled in wicker baskets near either end of the table were freshly baked loaves of French bread, those new baguettes from McPherson's, reheated in the oven and pleasant to tear apart with your hands. And there was good strong Burgundy wine, half a dozen bottles of the Swede's best Pommard, four of them open on the table, bottles that five years back he had laid down for drinking in 1973—according to his wine register, Pommards laid down in his cellar just one month to the day before Merry killed Dr. Conlon. Yes, earlier in the evening he had found 1/3/68 inscribed, in his handwriting, in the spiral notebook he used for recording the details of each new purchase . . . "1/3/68" he had written, with no idea that on 2/3/68 his daughter would go ahead and outrage all of America, except perhaps for Professor Marcia Umanoff.

The two high school kids who were doing the serving emerged from the kitchen every few minutes, silently offering around the steaks he'd cooked, arranged on pewter platters, all carved up and running with blood. The Swede's set of carving knives were from Hoffritz, the best German stainless steel. He'd gone over to New York to buy the set and the big carving block for their first Thanksgiving in the Old Rimrock house. He once had cared about all that stuff. Loved to hone the blade on the long conical file before he went after the bird. Loved the sound of it. The sad inventory of his domestic bounty. Wanted his family to have the best. Wanted his family to have everything.

"Please," said Lou Levov, "can I get an answer about the effect of this on the children? You are all way, way off the topic. Haven't we seen enough tragedy with the young children? Pornography. Drugs. The violence."

"Divorce," Marcia threw in to help him out.

"Professor, don't get me started on divorce. You understand French?" he asked her.

"I do if I have to," she said, laughing.

"Well, I got a son down in Florida, Seymour's brother, whose *spécialité* is divorce. *I* thought his *spécialité* was cardiac surgery. But no, it's divorce. I thought I sent him to medical school—I thought that's where all the bills were coming from. But no, it was divorce school. That's what he's got the diploma in—divorce. Has there ever been a more terrible thing for a child than the specter of divorce? I don't think so. And where will it end? What is the limit? *You* didn't all grow up in this kind of world. Neither did I. We grew up in an era when it was a different place, when the feeling for community, home, family, parents, work . . . well, it was different. The changes are beyond conception. I sometimes think that more has changed since 1945 than in all the years of history there have ever been. I don't know what to make of the end of so many things. The lack of feeling for individuals that a person sees in that movie,

the lack of feeling for places like what is going on in Newark—
how did this happen? You don't have to revere your family, you
don't have to revere your country, you don't have to revere
where you live, but you have to know you *have* them, you have
to know that you are *part* of them. Because if you don't, you
are just out there on your own and I feel for you. I honestly
do. Am I right, Mr. Orcutt, or am I wrong?"

"To wonder where the limit is?" Orcutt replied.

"Well, yes," said Lou Levov, who, the Swede observed—and
not for the first time—had spoken of children and violence
without any sense that the subject intersected with the life of
his immediate family. Merry had been used for somebody else's
evil purposes—that was the story to which it was crucial for
them all to remain anchored. He kept such a sharp watch over
each and every one of them to be certain that nobody wavered
for a moment in their belief in that story. No one in this family
was going to fall into doubt about Merry's absolute innocence,
not so long as he was alive.

Among the many things the Swede could not think about
from within the confines of his box was what would happen to
his father when he learned that the death toll was four.

"You're right," Bill Orcutt was saying to Lou Levov, "to
wonder where the limit is. I think everybody here is wondering
where the limit is and worrying where the limit is every time
they look at the papers. Except the professor of transgression.
But then we're all stifled by convention—we're not great outlaws like William Burroughs and the Marquis de Sade and the
holy saint Jean Genet. The Let Every Man Do Whatever He
Wishes School of Literature. The brilliant school of Civilization
Is Oppression and Morality Is Worse."

And he did not blush. "Morality" without batting an eye.
"Transgression" as though he were a stranger to it, as though
it were not he of all the men here—William III, latest in that
long line of Orcutts advertised in their graveyard as virtuous
men—who had transgressed to the utmost by violating the
unity of a family already half destroyed.

His wife had a lover. And it was for the lover that she'd undergone the rigors of a face-lift, to woo and win *him*. Yes, now
he understood the gushing letter profusely thanking the plastic
surgeon for spending "the five hours of your time for my

beauty," thanking him as if the Swede had not paid twelve thousand dollars for those five hours, plus five thousand more for the clinic suite where they had spent the two nights. *It is quite wonderful, dear doctor. It is as though I have been given a new life. Both from within and from the outside.* In Geneva he had sat up with her all night, held her hand through the nausea and the pain, and all of it for the sake of somebody else. It was for the sake of somebody else that she was building the house. The two of them were designing the house for each other.

To run away to Ponce to live with Sheila after Merry disappeared—no, Sheila had made him come to his senses and recover his rectitude and go back to his wife and as much of their life as remained intact, to the wife even a mistress knew he could not wound, let alone desert, in such a crisis. Yet these other two were going to pull it off. He knew it the moment he saw them in the kitchen. Their pact. Orcutt dumps Jessie and she dumps me and the house is for them. She thinks our catastrophe is over and so she is going to bury the past and start anew—face, house, husband, all new. *Try as you will, you can't get under my skin tonight. Not tonight.*

They are the outlaws. Orcutt, said Dawn to her husband, lived completely off what his family once was—well, she was living off what she'd just become. Dawn and Orcutt: two predators.

The outlaws are everywhere. They're inside the gates.

9

HE had a phone call. One of the girls came out of the kitchen to tell him. She whispered, "It's from I *think* Czechoslovakia."

He took the call in Dawn's downstairs study, where Orcutt had already moved the large cardboard model of the new house. After leaving Jessie on the terrace with the Swede and his parents and the drinks, Orcutt must have gone back to the van to get the model and carried it into Dawn's study and set it up on her desk before proceeding into the kitchen to help her shuck the corn.

Rita Cohen was on the line. She knew about Czechoslovakia because "they" were following him: they'd followed him earlier in the summer to the Czech consulate; they'd followed him that afternoon to the animal hospital; they'd followed him to Merry's room, where Merry had told him there was no such person as Rita Cohen.

"How can you do this to your own daughter?" she asked.

"I've done nothing to my daughter. I went to see my daughter. You wrote and told me where she was."

"You told her about the hotel. You told her we didn't fuck."

"I did not mention any hotel. I don't know what this is all about."

"You are lying to me. You told your daughter you did not fuck me. I warned you about that. I warned you in the letter."

Directly in front of the Swede sat the model of the house. He could see now what he had not been able to envision from Dawn's explanations—exactly how the long shed roof let the light into the main hallway through the high row of windows running the length of the front wall. Yes, now he saw how the sun would arc through the southern sky and the light would wash—and how happy it seemed to make her just to say "wash" after "light"—wash over the white walls, thus changing everything for everyone.

The cardboard roof was detachable, and when he lifted it up he could look right into the rooms. All the interior walls were in place, there were doors and closets, in the kitchen there

were cabinets, a refrigerator, a dishwasher, a range. Orcutt ha
gone so far as to install in the living room tiny pieces of furni
ture also fashioned out of cardboard, a library table by th
western wall of windows, a sofa, end tables, an ottoman, tw
club chairs, a coffee table in front of a raised fireplace hear
that extended the width of the room. In the bedroom, acro
from the bay window, where there were the built-in drawers-
Shaker drawers, Dawn called them—was the large bed, awaitir
its two occupants. On the wall to either side of the headboa
were built-in shelves for books. Orcutt had made some boo
and put them on the shelves, miniaturized books fashione
out of cardboard. They even had titles on them. He was goo
at all this. Better at this, thought the Swede, than at the pair
ing. Yes, wouldn't life be so much less futile if we could do it
the scale of one-sixteenth inch to a foot? The only thing mis
ing from the bedroom was a cardboard cock with Orcut
name on it. Orcutt should have made a sixteenth-inch sca
model of Dawn on her stomach, with her ass in the air an
from behind, his cock going in. It would have been nice f
the Swede to have found that, too, while he stood over h
desk, looking down at Dawn's cardboard dreaming and a
sorbing the fury of Rita Cohen.

What does Rita Cohen have to do with Jainism? What do
one thing have to do with the other? No, Merry, it does *n*
hang together. What does any of this ranting have to do wi
you, who will not even do harm to *water*? *Nothing* han
together—*none* of it is linked up. It is only in your head that
is linked up. Nowhere else is there any logic.

She's been tracking Merry, trailing her, tracing her, b
they're not connected and they never were! There's the logi

"You've gone too far. You *go* too far. You think you are ru
ning the show, D-d-daddy? You are not running *anything*!"

But whether he was or wasn't running the show no long
mattered, because if Merry and Rita Cohen *were* connected,
any way, if Merry had lied to him about not knowing Ri
Cohen, then she might as easily have been lying about bei
taken in by Sheila after the bombing. If that was so, wh
Dawn and Orcutt ran off to live in this cardboard house,
and Sheila could run off to Puerto Rico after all. And if, as

result, his father dropped dead, well, they'd just have to bury him. That's what they'd do: bury him deep in the ground.

(He was all at once remembering the death of his grandfather —what it did to his father. The Swede was a little kid, seven years old. His grandfather had been rushed to the hospital the evening before, and his father and his uncles sat at the old man's bedside all night long. When his father arrived home it was seven-thirty in the morning. The Swede's grandfather had died. His father got out of the car, went as far as the front steps of the house, and then just sat himself down. The Swede watched him from behind the living room curtains. His father did not move, even when the Swede's mother came out to comfort him. He sat without moving for over an hour, all the time leaning forward, his elbows on his knees and his face invisible in his hands. There was such a load of tears inside his head that he had to hold it like that in his two strong hands to prevent it from tumbling off of him. When he was able to raise the head up again, he got back in the car and drove to work.)

Is Merry lying? Is Merry brainwashed? Is Merry a lesbian? Is Rita the girlfriend? Is Merry running the whole insane thing? Are they out to do nothing but torture me? Is that the game, the entire game, to torture and torment me?

No, Merry's not lying—Merry is *right*. Rita Cohen does not exist. If Merry believes it, I believe it. He did not have to listen to somebody who did not exist. The drama she'd constructed did not exist. Her hateful accusations did not exist. Her authority did not exist, her power. If she did not exist, she could not *have* any power. Could Merry have these religious beliefs *and* Rita Cohen? You had only to listen to Rita Cohen howling into the phone to know that she was someone to whom there was no sacred form of life on earth *or* in heaven. What does she have to do with self-starvation and Mahatma Gandhi and Martin Luther King? She does not exist because she does not fit in. These are not even her words. These are not a young girl's words. There are no *grounds* for these words. This is an imitation of someone. Someone has been telling her what to do and what to say. From the beginning this has all been an act. She's an act; she did not arrive at this by herself. Someone is behind her, someone corrupt and cynical and distorted who

sets these kids to do these things, who strips a Rita Cohen and
a Merry Levov of everything good that was their inheritance
and lures them into this *act*.

"*You* are going to take her back to all your dopey pleasure?
Take her from her holiness into that shallow, soulless excuse
for a life? Yours is the lowest species on this earth—don't you
know that *yet*? Are you really able to believe that *you*, with your
conception of life, you basking unpunished in the crime of
your wealth, have anything whatsoever to offer *this woman*?
Just exactly what? A life of bad faith lived to the hilt, that's
what, the ultimate in bloodsucking propriety! Don't you know
who this woman *is*? Don't you realize what this woman has
become? Don't you have any inkling of what she is in *communion* with?" The perennial indictment of the middle class, from
somebody who did not exist; the celebration of his daughter's
degradation and the excoriation of his class: Guilty!—according
to somebody who did not exist. "*You* are going to take her
away from *me*? You, who felt *sick* when you saw her? Sick because she refuses to be captured in your shitty little moral universe? Tell me, Swede—how did you get so smart?"

He hung up. Dawn has Orcutt, I have Sheila, Merry has
Rita or she doesn't have Rita—*Can Rita stay for dinner? Can
Rita stay overnight? Can Rita wear my boots? Mom, can you
drive me and Rita to the village?*—and my father drops dead. If
it has to be, it has to be. He got over *his* father's dying, I'll get
over *my* father's dying. I'll get over everything. I do not care
what meaning it has or what meaning it doesn't have, whether
it fits or whether it doesn't fit—they are not dealing with me
anymore. *I* don't exist. They are dealing now with an irresponsible person; they are dealing with someone who does not care.
Can Rita and I blow up the post office? Yes. Whatever you want,
dear. And whoever dies, dies.

Madness and provocation. Nothing recognizable. Nothing
plausible. No context in which it hangs together. *He* no longer
hangs together. Even his capacity for suffering no longer exists.

A great idea takes hold of him: his capacity for suffering no
longer exists.

But that idea, however great, did not make it out of the room
with him. Never should have hung up—never. She'd make him

pay a huge price for that. Six foot three, forty-six years old, a multimillion-dollar business, and broken for a second time by a ruthless, pint-sized slut. This is his enemy and she *does* exist. But where did she come from? Why does she write me, phone, strike out at me—what does she have to do with my poor broken girl? Nothing!

Once again she leaves him soaked with sweat, his head a ringing globe of pain; the entire length of his body is suffused with a fatigue so extreme that it feels like the onset of death, and yet his enemy evinces little more substance than a mythical monster. Not a shadow enemy exactly, *not* nothing—but what then? A courier. Yes. Does her number on him, indicts him, exploits him, eludes him, resists him, brings him to a total bewildered standstill by saying whatever mad words come into her head, encircles him in her lunatic clichés and is in and out like a courier. But a courier from whom? From where?

He knows nothing about her. Except that she expresses perfectly the stupidity of her kind. Except that he is still her villain, that her hatred of him is resolute. Except that she's now twenty-seven. Not a kid anymore. A woman. But grotesquely fixed in her position. Behaves like a mechanism of human parts, like a loudspeaker, human parts assembled as a loudspeaker designed to produce shattering sound, a sound that is disruptive and maddening. After five years the change is only in the direction of more of the same sound. The deterioration of Merry comes as Jainism; the deterioration of Rita Cohen comes as *more*. He knows nothing about her except that she needs more than ever to be in charge—to be more and more and more *unexpected*. He knows he is dealing with an unbending destroyer, with something big in someone very small. Five years have passed. Rita is back. Something is up. Something unimaginable is about to happen again.

He would never get across the line that was tonight. Ever since leaving Merry in that cell, behind that veil, he has known that he's no longer a man who can endlessly forestall being crushed.

I am done with craving and selfhood. Thanks to you.

Someone opened the study door. "Are you all right?" It was Sheila Salzman.

"What do you want?"

She pulled the door shut behind her and came into the room. "You looked ill at dinner. Now you look even worse."

Over Dawn's desk was a framed photograph of Count. All the blue ribbons Count won were pinned to the wall on either side of the picture. It was the same picture of Count that used to appear in Dawn's annual ad in the Simmental breeder's magazine. Merry had been the one to choose the slogan for the ad from the three Dawn had proposed to them in the kitchen after dinner one night. COUNT CAN DO WONDERFUL THINGS FOR YOUR HERD. IF EVER THERE WAS A BULL TO USE, IT'S COUNT. A BULL UPON WHICH A HERD CAN BE BUILT. Merry at first argued for a suggestion of her own—YOU CAN COUNT ON COUNT—but after Dawn and the Swede each made the case against it, Merry chose A BULL UPON WHICH A HERD CAN BE BUILT, and that became the slogan for Arcady Breeders for as long as Count was Dawn's stylish superstar.

On the desk there used to be a snapshot of Merry, age thirteen, standing at the head of their long-bodied prize bull, the Golden Certified Meat Sire, holding him by a leather lead shank clipped into his nose ring. As a 4-H kid she'd been taught how to lead and walk and wash and handle a bull, first a yearling, but then the big boys, and Dawn had taught her how to show Count—to hold her hand up on the strap so that his head was up and to keep a bit of tension on the lead and move it a little with her hand, first so as to show Count off to advantage but also to be in communication with him so that he'd listen a little more than he might if her hand was slack and down at her side. Even though Count wasn't difficult or arrogant, Dawn taught Merry never to trust him. He could sometimes have a strong attitude, even with Merry and Dawn, the two people he was most used to in the world. In just that photograph—a picture he'd loved in the same way he'd loved the picture that had appeared on page one of the *Denver-Randolph Courier* of Dawn in her blazer at the fireplace mantel —he could see all that Dawn had patiently taught Merry and all that Merry had eagerly learned from her. But it was gone, as was the sentimental memento of Dawn's childhood, a photograph of the charming wooden bridge down at Spring Lake that led across the lake to St. Catherine's, a picture taken in the spring sunshine, with the azaleas in bloom at either end of the bridge and, resplendent in the background, the weathered copper dome of the grand church itself, where, as a kid, she had liked to imagine herself a bride in a white bridal gown. All there was on Dawn's desk now was Orcutt's cardboard model.

"Is this the new house?" Sheila asked him.

"You bitch."

She did not move; she looked directly back at him but did not speak or move. He could take Count's picture off the wall and bludgeon her over the head with it and she would *still* be unruffled, still somehow deprive him of a heartfelt response. Five years earlier, for four months, they had been lovers. Why tell him the truth now if she was able to withhold it from him even then?

"Leave me alone," he said.

But when she turned to do as he gruffly requested, he grabbed her arm and swung her flat against the closed door. "You took her in." The force of the rage was in no way concealed by the whisper that rasped up from his throat. Her skull was locked between his hands. Her head had been held in his powerful grip before but never, never like this. "You took her in!"

"Yes."

"You never told me!"

She did not answer.

"I could kill you!" he said, and, immediately upon saying it, let her go.

"You've seen her," Sheila said. Her hands neatly folded before her. That nonsensical calm, only moments after he had threatened to kill her. All that ridiculous self-control. Always that ridiculous, careful, self-controlled thinking.

"You know everything," he snarled.

"I know what you've been through. What can be done for her?"

"By *you*? Why did you let her go? She went to your house. She'd blown up a building. You knew all about it—why didn't you call me, get in touch with me?"

"I didn't know about it. I found out later that night. But when she came to me she was just beside herself. She was upset and I didn't know why. I thought something had happened at home."

"But you knew within the next few hours. How long w_s she with you? Two days, three days?"

"Three. She left on the third day."

"So you knew what happened."

"I found out later. I couldn't believe it, but—"

"It was on television."

"But she was in my house by then. I had already promis_d her that I would help her. And that there was no problem s_e could tell me that I couldn't keep to myself. She asked me _o trust her. That was before I watched the news. How coul_ _ betray her then? I'd been her therapist, she'd been my clie_t. I'd always wanted to do what was in her best interest. Wh_t was the alternative? For her to get arrested?"

"Call me. That was the alternative. Call her father. If you h_d gotten to me right there and then, and said, 'She's safe, do__t worry about her,' and then not let her out of your sight—"

"She was a big girl. How can you not let her out of yo_r sight?"

"You lock her in the house and keep her there."

"She's not an animal. She's not like a cat or a bird that y_u can keep in a cage. She was going to do whatever she was g__ ing to do. We had a trust, Seymour, and violating her trust _t that point . . . I wanted her to know that there was someo__ in this world she could trust."

"*At that moment, trust was not what she needed! S_e needed me!*"

"But I was sure that your house was where they'd be loo_ ing. What good was calling you? I couldn't drive her out he__ I even started thinking they would know she would be at _y house. All of a sudden it seemed like it was the most obvio_s place for her to be. I started thinking *my* phone was bugge__ How could I call you?"

"You could have somehow made contact."

"When she first came she was agitated, something had go__ wrong, she was just yelling about the war and her family__ thought something terrible had happened at home. Somethi__ terrible had happened to *her*. She wasn't the same, Seymo__ Something very wrong had happened to that girl. She was tal__ ing as if she hated you so. I couldn't imagine . . . but som_ times you start to believe the worst about people. I thi__ maybe that's what I was trying to figure out when we were together."

"What? What are you talking about?"

"Could there really be something wrong? Could there really be something that she was subjected to that could lead her to something like that? I was confused too. I want you to know that I never really believed it and I didn't want to believe it. But of course I had to wonder. Anyone would have."

"And? And? Having had an affair with me—what the hell did you find out, having had your little affair with me?"

"That you're kind and compassionate. That you do just about everything you can to be an intelligent, decent person. Just as I would have imagined before she'd blown up that building. Seymour, believe me, please, I just wanted her to be safe. So I took her in. And got her showered and clean. And gave her a place to sleep. I really had no idea—"

"She blew up a building, Sheila! Somebody was killed! It was all over the goddamn television!"

"But I didn't know until I turned on the TV."

"So at six o'clock at night you knew. She was there for three days. And you do not contact me."

"What good would it have done to contact you?"

"I'm her father."

"You're her father and she blew up a building. What good was it going to do bringing her back to you?"

"Don't you grasp what I'm saying? She's my daughter!"

"She's a very strong girl."

"Strong enough to look after herself in the world? No!"

"Turning her over to you wasn't going to help any. She wasn't going to sit and eat her peas and mind her business. You don't go from blowing up a building to—"

"It was your duty to tell me that she came to your house."

"I just thought that would make it easier for them to find her. She'd come so far, she'd gotten so much stronger, I thought that she could make it on her own. She *is* a strong girl, Seymour."

"She's a crazy girl."

"She's troubled."

"Oh, Christ! The father plays no role with the troubled daughter?"

"I'm sure he played plenty of a role. That was why
couldn't . . . I just thought something terrible had happen
at home."

"Something terrible happened at the general store."

"But you should have seen her—she'd gotten so fat."

"I should have *seen* her? Where do you think she'd been?
was your responsibility to get in touch with her parents! N
to let the child run off into nowhere! She never needed n
more. She never needed her father more. And you're tellir
me she never needed him less. You made a terrible error.
hope you know it. A terrible, terrible error."

"What could you have done for her then? What could an
one have done for her then?"

"I deserved to know. I had a right to know. She's a minc
She's my daughter. You had an obligation to get to me."

"My first obligation was to her. She was my client."

"She was no longer your client."

"She had been my client. A very special client. She'd con
so far. My first obligation was to her. How could I violate h
confidence? The damage had already been done."

"I don't believe you are saying any of this."

"It's the law."

"What's the law?"

"That you don't betray your client's confidence."

"There's another law, idiot—a law against committing mu
der! She was a fugitive from justice!"

"Don't talk about her like that. Of course she ran. What el
could she do? I thought that maybe she would turn herself i
But that she would do it in her own time. In her own way."

"And me? And her mother?"

"Well, it killed me to see you."

"You saw me for four months. It killed you every day?"

"Each time I thought that maybe it would make a differen
if I let you know. But I didn't see what difference it wou
really make. It wouldn't change anything. You were already
broken."

"You are an inhuman bitch."

"There was nothing else I could do. She asked me not
tell. She asked me to trust her."

"I don't understand how you could be so shortsighted.

don't understand how you could be so taken in by a girl who was so obviously crazy."

"I know it's difficult to face. The whole thing is impossible to understand. But to try to pin it on me, to try to act like anything I could have done would have made a difference—it wouldn't have made a difference in her life, it wouldn't have made a difference in your life. She was running. There was no bringing her back there. She wasn't the same girl that she'd been. Something had gone wrong. I saw no point in bringing her back. She'd gotten so fat."

"Stop that! What difference did *that* make!"

"I just thought she was so fat and so angry that something very bad must have gone on at home."

"That it was my fault."

"I didn't think that. We all have homes. That's where everything always goes wrong."

"So you took it on yourself to let this sixteen-year-old who had killed somebody run off into the night. Alone. Unprotected. Knowing God knows what could happen to her."

"You're talking about her as if she were a defenseless girl."

"She *is* a defenseless girl. She was *always* a defenseless girl."

"Once she'd blown up the building there's nothing that could have been done, Seymour. I would have betrayed her confidence and what difference would it have made?"

"I would have been with my daughter! I could have protected her from what has happened to her! You don't know what has happened to her. You didn't see her the way I saw her today. She's completely crazy. I saw her today, Sheila. She's not fat anymore—she's a stick, a stick wearing a rag. She's in a room in Newark in the most awful situation imaginable. I cannot describe to you how she lives. If you had only told me, it would all be different!"

"We wouldn't have had an affair—that's all that would have been different. Of course I knew that you might be hurt."

"By what?"

"By my having seen her. But to bring it all up again? I didn't know where she was. I didn't have any more information on her. That's the whole thing. She wasn't crazy. She was upset. She was angry. But she wasn't crazy."

"It's not crazy to blow up the general store? It's not crazy to make a bomb, to plant a bomb in the post office of the general store?"

"I'm saying that at my house she wasn't crazy."

"She'd already *been* crazy. You *knew* she'd been crazy. What if she went on to kill somebody else? Isn't that a bit of a responsibility? She did, you know. She did, Sheila. She killed three more people. What do you think of that?"

"Don't say things just to torture me."

"I'm telling you something! She killed three more people! You could have prevented that!"

"You're torturing me. You're trying to torture me."

"She killed three more people!" And that was when he pulled Count's picture off the wall and hurled it at her feet. But that did not faze her—that seemed only to bring her under her own control again. Acting the role of herself, without rage, without even a reaction, dignified, silent, she turned and left the room.

"What can be *done* for her?" he was growling, and all the while, down on his knees, carefully gathering together the shattered fragments of the glass and dumping them into Dawn's waste-basket. "What can be done for her? What can be done for *anyone*? *Nothing* can be done. She was sixteen. Sixteen years old and completely crazy. She was a minor. She was my daughter. She blew up a building. She was a lunatic. You had no *right* to let her go!"

Without its glass, the picture of the immovable Count he hung again over the desk, and then, as though listening to people unabatedly chattering on about something or other were the task assigned him by the forces of destiny, he returned from the savagery of where he'd been to the solid and orderly ludicrousness of a dinner party. That's what was left to hold him together—a dinner party. All there was for him to cling to as the entire enterprise of his life continued careering toward destruction—a dinner party.

To the candlelit terrace he duteously returned, while bearing within him everything that he could not understand.

Dishes had been cleared, the salad eaten, and dessert served, fresh strawberry-rhubarb pie from McPherson's. The Swede saw that the guests had rearranged themselves for the last course.

rcutt, hiding still the vicious shit that he was behind the
awaiian shirt and the raspberry trousers, had moved across
e table and sat talking with the Umanoffs, all of them amiable
d laughing together now that *Deep Throat* was off the
enda. *Deep Throat* had never been the real subject anyway.
oiling away beneath *Deep Throat* was the far more disgusting
d transgressive subject of Merry, of Sheila, of Shelly, of
rcutt and Dawn, of wantonness and betrayal and deception,
treachery and disunity among neighbors and friends, the
bject of cruelty. The mockery of human integrity, every ethi-
l obligation destroyed—that was the subject here tonight!

The Swede's mother had come around to sit beside Dawn,
o was talking with the Salzmans, and his father and Jessie
re nowhere to be seen.

Dawn asked, "Important?"

"The Czech guy. The consul. The information I wanted.
here's my dad?"

He waited for her to say "Dead," but after she looked around
e mouthed only "Don't know" and turned back to Shelly
d Sheila.

"Daddy left with Mrs. Orcutt," his mother whispered. "They
nt somewhere together. I think in the house."

Orcutt came up to him. They were the same size, both big
n, but the Swede had always been the stronger, going back
their twenties, to when Merry was born and the Levovs
oved out to Old Rimrock from their apartment on Elizabeth
enue in Newark and the newcomer had showed up for the
turday morning touch-football games back of Orcutt's
use. Out there just for the fun of it, to enjoy the fresh air
d the feel of the ball and the camaraderie, to make some new
ends, the Swede had not the slightest inclination to appear
owy or superior, except when he simply had no choice: when
rcutt, who off the field had never been other than kind and
nsiderate, began to use his hands more recklessly than the
ede considered sportsmanlike—in a way that the Swede
nsidered cheap and irritating, for a pickup game the worst
rt of behavior even if Orcutt's team did happen to have fallen
hind. After it had occurred for two weeks in a row, he deed the third week to do what he of course could have done
any time—to dump him. And so, near the end of the game,

with a single, swift maneuver—employing the other person's weight to do the damage—he managed at once to catch a long pass from Bucky Robinson and to make sure Orcutt was sprawled in the grass at his feet, before he pranced away to pile on the score. Pranced away and thought, of all things, "I don't like being looked down on," the words that Dawn had used to decline joining The Orcutt Family Cemetery Tour. He had not realized, not till he was speeding alone toward the goal line, how much Dawn's assailability had gotten to him nor how unsettled he was by the remotest likelihood (a likelihood that, to her face, he had dismissed) of his wife's being ridiculed out here for growing up in Elizabeth the daughter of an Irish plumber. When, after scoring, he turned around and saw Orcutt still on the ground, he thought, "Two hundred years of Morris County history, flat on its ass—that'll teach you to look down on Dawn Levov. Next time you'll play the whole *game* on your ass," before trotting back up the field to see if Orcutt was all right.

The Swede knew that once he got him on the floor of the terrace he would have no difficulty in slamming Orcutt's head against the flagstones as many times as might be required to get him into that cemetery with his distinguished clan. Yes, something is wrong with this guy, there always was, and the Swede had known it all along—knew it from those terrible paintings, knew it from the reckless use of his hands in a back-yard pickup game, knew it even at the cemetery, when for one solid hour Orcutt got to goyishly regale a Jewish sightseer. . . . Yes, big dissatisfaction there right from the start. Dawn said it was art, modern art, when all the time, baldly displayed on their living room wall, was William Orcutt's dissatisfaction. But now he has my wife. Instead of that misfortune Jessie, he's got revamped and revitalized Miss New Jersey of 1949. Got it made, got it *all* now, the greedy, thieving son of a bitch.

"Your father's a good man," Orcutt said. "Jessie doesn't usually get all this attention when she goes out. It's why she doesn't go out. He's a very generous man. He doesn't hold anything back, does he? Nothing left undisclosed. You get the whole person. Unguarded. Unashamed. Works himself up. It's wonderful. An amazing person, really. A huge presence. Always himself. Coming from where I do, you have to envy all that."

Oh, I'll bet you do, you son of a bitch. Laugh at us, you fucker. Just keep laughing.

"Where are they?" the Swede asked.

"He told her there's only one way to eat a fresh piece of pie. That's sitting at a kitchen table with a nice cold glass of milk. I guess they're in the kitchen with the milk. Jessie's learning a lot more about making a glove than she may ever need to know, but that's all right too. No harm in that. I hope you didn't mind that I couldn't leave her home."

"We wouldn't want you to leave her home."

"You're all very understanding."

"I was looking at the model of your house," the Swede told him, "in Dawn's study." But what he was looking at was a mole on the left side of Orcutt's face, a dark mole buried in the crease that ran from his nose to the corner of his mouth. Along with the snout nose Orcutt had an ugly mole. Does she find the mole appealing? Does she kiss the mole? Doesn't she ever find this guy just a wee bit fat in the face? Or, when it comes to an upper-class Old Rimrock boy, is she as unmindful of his looks, as unperturbed, as professionally detached as the whore-house ladies over in Easton?

"Uh-oh," said Orcutt, amiably feigning how uncertain he was. Uses his hands when he plays football, wears those shirts, paints those paintings, fucks his neighbor's wife, and manages through it all to maintain himself as the ever-reasonable un-knowable man. All façade and subterfuge. *He works so hard*, Dawn said, *at being one-dimensional*. Up top the gentleman, underneath the rat. Drink the devil that lurks in his wife; lust and rivalry the devils lurking in him. Sealed and civilized and predatory. To reinforce the genealogical aggression—the over-powering by origins—the aggression of scrupulous manners. The humane environmentalist and the calculating predator, protecting what he has by birthright and taking surreptitiously what he doesn't have. The civilized savagery of William Orcutt. His civilized form of animal behavior. I prefer the cows. "It's supposed to be seen *after* dinner—with the spiel," Orcutt said. "Did it make any sense without the spiel?" he asked. "I wouldn't think so."

But of course—being unknowable is the *goal*. Then you move instrumentally through life, appropriating the beautiful wives. In the kitchen he should have hit those two over the head with a skillet.

"It did. A lot," the Swede said. And then, as he could never stop himself from doing with Orcutt, he added, "It's interesting. I get the idea now about the light. I get the idea of the light washing over those walls. That's going to be something to see. I think you're going to be very happy in it."

Orcutt laughed. "You, you mean."

But the Swede had not heard his own error. He hadn't heard it because of the huge thought that had just come at him: what he should have done and failed to do.

He should have overpowered her. He should not have left her there. Jerry was right. Drive to Newark. Leave immediately. Take Barry. The two of them could subdue her and bring her back in the car to Old Rimrock. And if Rita Cohen is there? I'll kill her. If she is anywhere near my daughter, I'll pour gasoline all over that hair and set the little cunt on fire. Destroying my daughter. Showing me her pussy. Destroying my child. *There's the meaning—they are destroying her for the pleasure of destroying* her. Take Sheila. Take Sheila. Calm down. Take Sheila to Newark. Merry listens to Sheila. Sheila will talk to her and get her out of that room.

"—leave it to our visiting intellectual to get everything wrong. The complacent rudeness with which she plays the old French game of beating up on the bourgeoisie. . . ." Orcutt was confiding to the Swede his amusement with Marcia's posturing. "It's to her credit, I suppose, that she doesn't defer to the regulation dinner-party discipline of not saying anything about anything. But still it's amazing, constantly amazes me, how emptiness always goes with cleverness. She hasn't the faintest idea, really, of what she's talking about. Know what my father used to say? 'All brains and no intelligence. The smarter the stupider.' Applies."

Not Dawn? No. Dawn wanted nothing further to do with their catastrophe. She was just biding her time with him until the house was built. Go and do it yourself. *Get back in the fucking car and get her. Do you love her or don't you love her? You're acceding to her the way you acceded to your father, the way you have acceded to everything in your life. You're afraid of letting the beast out of the bag. Quite a critique she has made of decorum.*

ou keep yourself a secret. You don't choose ever! But how could
 bring Merry home, now, tonight, in that veil, with his father
 re? If his father were to see her, he'd expire on the spot. To
here else then? Where would he take her? Could the two of
em go live in Puerto Rico? Dawn wouldn't care where he
 ent. As long as she had her Orcutt. He had to get her before
 again set foot in that underpass. Forget Rita Cohen. Forget
 at inhuman idiot Sheila Salzman. Forget Orcutt. He does
 t matter. Find a place for Merry to live where there is not
 at underpass. That's *all* that matters. Start with the under-
 ss. Save her from getting herself killed in the underpass.
 fore the morning, before she has even left her room—*start*
 ere.

He had been cracking up in the only way he knew how,
 ich is not really cracking up at all but sinking, all evening
 ng being unmade by steadily sinking under the weight. A
 an who never goes full out and explodes, who only sinks . . .
 t now it was clear what to do. Go get her out of there before
 wn.

After Dawn. After Dawn life was inconceivable. There was
 thing he could do without Dawn. But she wanted Orcutt.
 hat Wasp blandness," she'd said, all but yawning to make
 r point. But that blandness had terrific glamour for a little
 sh Catholic girl. The mother of Merry Levov needs nothing
 ss than William Orcutt III. The cuckolded husband under-
 nds. Of course. Understands everything now. Who will get
 r back to the dream of where she has always wanted to go?
 r. America. Teamed up with Orcutt she'll be back on the
 ck. Spring Lake, Atlantic City, now Mr. America. Rid of the
 in of our child, the stain on her credentials, rid of the stain
 the destruction of the store, she can begin to resume the
 contaminated life. But I was stopped at the general store.
 d she knows it. Knows that I am allowed in no farther. I'm
 no use anymore. This is as far as she goes with me.

He brought a chair around, sat himself down between his
 fe and his mother, and, even as Dawn spoke, took her hand
 his. There are a hundred different ways to hold someone's
 nd. There are the ways you hold a child's hand, the ways
 u hold a friend's hand, the ways you hold an elderly parent's
 nd, the ways you hold the hands of the departing and of the

dying and of the dead. He held Dawn's hand the way a man holds the hand of a woman he adores, with all that excitement passing into his grip, as though pressure on the palm of the hand effects a transference of souls, as though the interlinking of fingers symbolizes every intimacy. He held Dawn's hand as though he possessed no information about the condition of his life.

But then he thought: She wants to be back with me, too. But she can't because it's all too awful. What else can she do? She must think she's poison. She gave birth to a murderer. She *has* to put on a new crown.

He should have listened to his father and never married her. He had defied him, just that one time, but that was all it had taken—that did it. His father had said, "There are hundreds and thousands of lovely Jewish girls, but you have to find *her*. You found one down in South Carolina, Dunleavy, and finally you saw the light and got rid of her. So now you come home and find Dwyer up here. *Why*, Seymour?" The Swede could not say to him, "The girl in South Carolina was beautiful, but not half as beautiful as Dawn." He could not say to him, "The authority of beauty is a very irrational thing." He was twenty-three years old and could only say, "I'm in love with her."

" 'In love,' what does that mean? What is 'in love' going to do for you when you have a child? How are you going to raise a child? As a Catholic? As a Jew? No, you are going to raise a child who won't be one thing or the other—all because you are 'in love.' "

His father was right. That was what happened. They raised a child who was neither Catholic nor Jew, who instead was first a stutterer, then a killer, then a Jain. He had tried all his life never to do the wrong thing, and that was what he had done. All the wrongness that he had locked away in himself, that he had buried as deep as a man could bury it, had come out anyway, because a girl was beautiful. The most serious thing in his life, seemingly from the time he was *born*, was to prevent the suffering of those he loved, to be kind to people, a kind person through and through. That was why he had brought Dawn to meet secretly with his father at the factory office—to try to resolve the religious impasse and avoid making either of them unhappy. The meeting had been suggested by his father: face to face, between "the girl," as Lou Levov charitably referred to her around the Swede, and "the ogre," as the girl called him. Dawn hadn't been afraid; to the Swede's astonishment she agreed. "I walked out on that runway in a bathing suit, didn't I? It wasn't easy, in case you didn't know. Twenty-five thousand people. It's not a very dignified feeling, in a bright white bathing suit and bright white high heels, being looked at by twenty-five thousand people. I appeared in a *parade* in a bathing suit. In Camden. Fourth of July. I had to. I hated that day. My father almost died. But I did it. I taped the back of that damn bathing suit to my skin, Seymour, so it wouldn't ride up on me—masking tape on my own behind. I felt like a *freak*. But I took the job of Miss New Jersey and so I did the work. A very tiring job. Every town in the state. Fifty dollars an appearance. But if you work hard, the money adds up, so I did it. Working hard at something totally different that scared me to death—but I did it. The Christmas I broke the news to my parents about Miss Union County—you think that was fun? *But I did it.* And if I could do all that, I can do this, because this isn't being a silly girl on a float, this is my *life*, my entire *future*. This is for *keeps*! But you'll be there, won't you? I cannot go there by myself. You *have* to be there!"

She was so incredibly gutsy there was no choice but to say, "Where else would I be?" On the way down to the factory, he warned her not to mention rosary beads or the cross or heaven and to stay away from Jesus as much as possible. "If he asks if there are any crosses hanging in the house, say no." "But that's a lie. I can't say no." "Then say one." "That's a lie." "Dawnie, it won't help anything if you say three. One is just the same as three. It gets your point over. Say it. For me. Say one." "We'll see." "And you don't have to mention the other stuff." "What other stuff?" "The Virgin Mary." "That is not *stuff*." "The statues. Okay? Just forget it. If he asks, 'Do you have any statues?' just tell him no, just tell him, 'We don't have statues, we don't have pictures, the one cross and that's it.'" Religious ornaments, he explained, statues like those in her dining room and her mother's bedroom, pictures like those her mother had on the walls were sore subjects with his father. He wasn't defending his father's position. He was just explaining that the man had been brought up a certain way, and that's the way he

was, and there was nothing anybody could do about it, so wh
stir him up?

Opposing the father is no picnic and not opposing the fath
is no picnic—that's what he was discovering.

Anti-Semitism was another sore subject. Watch out wh
you say about Jews. Best to say nothing about Jews. And st:
away from priests, don't talk about priests. "Don't tell him th
story about your father and the priests when he was a caddie
the country club as a kid." "Why would I ever tell him that
"I don't know, but don't go near it." "*Why?*" "I don't *know*
just *don't*."

But he knew why. Because if she told him that the first tin
her father realized priests had genitals was in the locker roo
when he used to caddie on weekends, that up until then l
didn't even think they were *anatomically* sexual, his own fath
might very well be tempted to ask her, "You know what the
do with the foreskins of the little Jewish boys after the circun
cision?" And she would have to say, "I don't know, Mr. Levo
What *do* they do with the foreskins?" and Mr. Levov wou
reply—the joke was one of his favorites—"They send them t
Ireland. They wait till they got enough of them, they colle
them all together, then they send them to Ireland and the
make priests out of them."

It was a conversation the Swede would never forget, and nc
so much because of what his father said—all that he'd expecte
It was Dawn who made it an unforgettable exchange. He
truthfulness, how she had not seriously fudged about her pa
ents or about anything that he knew was important to her—he
courage was what was unforgettable.

She was more than a full foot shorter than her fiancé and
according to one of the judges who'd confided in Danny Dwye
after the pageant, had failed to be in the top ten in Atlanti
City only because without her high heels she measured five foc
two and a half, in a year when half a dozen other girls equall
talented and pretty were positively statuesque. This petitenes
(which may or may not have disqualified her from a seriou
shot at runner-up—it hardly explained to the Swede's satisfac
tion why Miss Arizona should walk off winner of the whol
shebang at only five *three*) had simply deepened the Swede

votion to Dawn. In a youngster as innately dutiful as the
Swede—and a handsome boy always making the extra effort
not to be mistaken for the owner of his startling good looks—
Dawn's being only five foot two quickened in him a manly
urge to shield and to shelter. Up until that drawn-out, draining
negotiation between Dawn and his father, he'd had no idea he
was in love with a girl as strong as this. He even wondered if he
wanted to be in love with a girl as strong as this.

Aside from the number of crosses in her house, the only
other thing she lied about outright was the baptism, an issue on
which she finally appeared to capitulate, but only after three
solid hours of negotiations during which it seemed to the
Swede that, amazingly enough, his *father* had yielded on that
issue almost right off the bat. Not until later did he realize that
his father had deliberately let the negotiation string out until
the twenty-two-year-old girl was at the end of her strength and
then, shifting by a hundred and eighty degrees his position on
baptism, wrapped up the deal giving her only Christmas Eve,
Christmas Day, and the Easter bonnet.

But after Merry was born, Dawn got the child baptized anyway. She could have performed the baptism herself or got her
mother to do it but she wanted the real thing, and so she got a
priest and some godparents and took the baby to the church,
and until Lou Levov happened to come upon the baptismal
certificate in a dresser in the unused back bedroom of the Old
Rimrock house, no one ever knew—only the Swede, whom
Dawn told in the evening, after the freshly baptized baby had
been put to bed cleansed of original sin and bound for heaven.
By the time the baptismal certificate was unearthed, Merry was
a family treasure six years old, and the uproar was short-lived.
Though that didn't mean that the Swede's father could shake
the conviction that what lay behind Merry's difficulties all along
was the secret baptism: that, and the Christmas tree, and the
Easter bonnet, enough for that poor kid *never* to know who
she was. That and her grandma Dwyer—she didn't help either.
Seven years after Merry was born, Dawn's father had the second heart attack, dropped dead while installing a furnace, and
from then on there was no dragging Grandma Dwyer out of
St. Genevieve's. Every time she could get her hands on Merry,
she spirited the child off to church, and God alone knew what

they pumped into her there. The Swede, far more confident with his father—about this, about everything, really, than he'd been before becoming a father himself—would tell him, "Dad, Merry takes it all with a grain of salt. It's just Grandma to her, and what Grandma does. Going to church with Dawn's mother doesn't mean a thing to Merry either way." But his father wasn't buying it. "She kneels, doesn't she? They're up there doing all that stuff, and Merry is kneeling—right?" "Well, sure, I guess so, sure, she kneels. But it doesn't *mean* anything to her." "Yeah? Well it does to me—it means plenty!"

Lou Levov backed off—that is, with his son—from attributing Merry's screaming to the baptism. But alone with his wife he wasn't so cautious, and when he was riled up about "some Catholic crap" the Dwyer woman had inflicted on his granddaughter, he wondered aloud if it wasn't the secret baptism that all along lay behind the screaming that scared the hell out of the whole family during Merry's first year. Perhaps everything bad that *ever* happened to Merry, not excluding the *worst* thing that happened to her, had originated then and there.

She entered the world screaming and the screaming did not stop. The child opened her mouth so wide to scream that she broke the tiny blood vessels in her cheeks. At first the doctor figured it was colic, but when it went on for three months, another explanation was needed and Dawn took her for all kinds of tests, to all kinds of doctors—and Merry never disappointed you, she screamed there too. At one point Dawn even had to wring some urine out of the diaper to take it to the doctor for a test. They had happy-go-lucky Myra as their housekeeper then, a large, cheery bartender's daughter from Morristown's Little Dublin, and though she would pick up Merry and nestle her into that pillowy, plentiful bosom of hers and coo and coo at her as sweetly as though she were her own, if Merry was already off and screaming, Myra got results no better than Dawn's. There was nothing Dawn didn't try to outwit whatever mechanism triggered the screaming. When she took Merry with her to the supermarket, she made elaborate preparations beforehand, as though to *hypnotize* the child into a state of calm. Just to go out shopping, she would give her a bath and a nap, put her in nice clean clothes, get her all set in the car, wheel her around the store in the shopping cart—and everything might be going fine, until somebody came along and leaned over the cart and said, "Oh, what a cute baby," and that would be it: inconsolable for the next twenty-four hours. At dinnertime, Dawn would tell the Swede, "All that hard work for nothing. I'm going crazier and crazier. I'd stand on my *head* if it helped —but *nothing* helps." The home movie of Merry's first birthday showed everybody singing "Happy Birthday" and Merry, in her high chair, screaming. But only weeks later, for no apparent reason, the fury of the screaming began to ebb, then the frequency, and by the time she was one and a half, everything was wonderful and remained wonderful and went on being wonderful until the stuttering.

What had gone wrong for Merry was what her Jewish grandfather had known would go wrong from the morning of the meeting on Central Avenue. The Swede had sat in a chair in the corner of the office, well out of the line of fire; whenever Dawn said the name Jesus, he looked miserably through the glass at the hundred and twenty women working at the sewing machines on the floor—the rest of the time he looked at his feet. Lou Levov sat iron-faced at his desk, not his favorite desk, out amid the clamorous activity of the making department, but at the desk he rarely ever used, tucked away for the sake of quiet within the glass enclosure. And Dawn didn't cry, didn't go to pieces, and lied, really, hardly at all—just held her ground throughout, all sixty-two and a half inches of her. Dawn— whose only preparation for such a grilling was the Miss New Jersey prepageant interview, heavily weighted in the scoring, when she stood before five seated judges and answered questions about her biography—was sensational.

Here's the opening of the inquisition that the Swede never forgot:

WHAT IS YOUR FULL NAME, MISS DWYER?

Mary Dawn Dwyer.

DO YOU WEAR A CROSS AROUND YOUR NECK, MARY DAWN?

I have. In high school I did for a while.

SO YOU THINK OF YOURSELF AS A RELIGIOUS PERSON.

No. That isn't why I wore it. I wore it because I'd been to a retreat and when I got home I just started wearing a cross. It wasn't a huge religious symbol. It was just a sign really of having been to this weekend retreat, where I made a lot of friends. It was much more that than a sign of being a devout Catholic.

ANY CROSSES IN YOUR HOUSE? HANGING UP?

Only one.

IS YOUR MOTHER DEVOUT?

Well, she goes to church.

HOW OFTEN?

Often. Every Sunday. Without fail. And then there'll be times during Lent when they'll go every day.

AND WHAT DOES SHE GET OUT OF IT?

Get out of it? I don't know if I understand. She gets comfort. There's a comfort about being in a church. When my grandmother died she went to church a lot. When someone dies or someone is sick, it helps give you some kind of comfort. Something to do. You start saying your rosary for special intentions—

ROSARIES ARE THE BEADS?

Yes, sir.

AND YOUR MOTHER DOES THAT?

Well, sure.

I SEE. AND YOUR FATHER'S LIKE THAT TOO?

Like what?

DEVOUT.

Yes. Yes, he is. Going to church makes him feel like a good man. That he's doing his duty. My father is very conventional in terms of morality. He grew up with a much more extreme Catholic upbringing than I did. He's a workingman. He's a plumber. Oil heating. In his view the Church is a big powerful thing that makes you do what's right. He's someone who's very caught up in issues of right and wrong and being punished for doing wrong and the prohibitions against sex.

I WOULDN'T DISAGREE WITH THAT.

I don't think you would. You and my father aren't that different, when you come down to it.

EXCEPT THAT HE IS CATHOLIC. HE IS A DEVOUT CATHOLIC AND I AM A JEW. THAT'S NO SMALL DIFFERENCE.

Well, maybe it's not such a big difference either.

IT IS.

Yes, sir.

WHAT ABOUT JESUS AND MARY?

What about them?

WHAT DO YOU THINK ABOUT THEM?

As individuals? I don't think in terms of them as individuals. I do remember being little and telling my mother that I loved her more than anybody else, and she told me that wasn't right, I had to love God more.

GOD OR JESUS?

I think it was God. Maybe it was Jesus. But I didn't like it. I wanted to love her the most. Other than that, I can't remember any specific examples of Jesus as a person or an individual. The only time for me the people are real is when you do the Stations of the Cross on Good Friday and you follow Jesus up the hill to his crucifixion. That's a time when he becomes a real figure. And, of course, Jesus in the manger.

JESUS IN THE MANGER. WHAT DO YOU THINK ABOUT JESUS IN THE MANGER?

What do I think about it? I like little baby Jesus in the manger.

WHY?

Well, there's always something so pleasant and comforting about the scene. And important. This moment of humility. There's all that straw and little animals around, all cuddled up. It's just a nice, warming scene. You never imagine it as cold and windy out there. There's always some candles. Everyone's just adoring this little baby.

THAT'S ALL. EVERYBODY IS JUST ADORING THIS LITTLE BABY.

Yes. I don't see anything wrong with that.

AND WHAT ABOUT JEWS? LET'S GET DOWN TO BRASS TACKS, MARY DAWN. WHAT DO YOUR PARENTS SAY ABOUT JEWS?

(*Pause.*) Well, I don't hear much about Jews at home.

WHAT DO YOUR PARENTS SAY ABOUT JEWS? I WOULD LIKE AN ANSWER.

I think what's more remarkable than what I think you're getting at is that my mother might be aware that she doesn't like people for being Jewish but she doesn't realize that there are people who might not like her for being Catholic. One thing I didn't like, I remember, was that on Hillside Road one of my friends was Jewish, and I remember that I didn't like that I was going to go to heaven and she wasn't.

WHY WASN'T SHE GOING TO HEAVEN?

If you weren't Christian, you weren't going to heaven. It seemed very sad to me that Charlotte Waxman wasn't going to be up in heaven with me.

WHAT DOES YOUR MOTHER HAVE AGAINST JEWS, MARY DAWN?

Could you just call me Dawn, please?

WHAT DOES YOUR MOTHER HAVE AGAINST JEWS, DAWN?

Well, it isn't that Jews are Jews. It's that you're non-Catholics. To my parents you're just lumped with the Protestants.

WHAT DOES YOUR MOTHER HAVE AGAINST JEWS? ANSWER ME.

Well, the usual things you hear.

I DON'T HEAR THEM, DAWN. YOU'RE GOING TO HAVE TO TELL ME.

Well, mostly about being pushy. (*Pause.*) And materialistic. (*Pause.*) The term "Jewish lightning" would be used.

JEWISH LIGHT?

Jewish lightning.

WHAT DOES THAT MEAN?

You don't know what Jewish lightning is?

NOT YET.

When a fire is set for insurance purposes. There's lightning. You never heard that?

NO, THAT'S A NEW ONE ON ME.

You're shocked. I didn't mean to.

YES, I AM SHOCKED ALL RIGHT. BUT WE MIGHT AS WELL GET THIS OUT IN THE OPEN, DAWN. THAT IS WHAT WE ARE HERE FOR.

It wouldn't be all Jews. It would be New York Jews.

WHAT ABOUT NEW JERSEY JEWS?

(*Pause.*) Well, yes, I think they're probably a variant of New York Jews.

I SEE. TO JEWS IN UTAH IT DOESN'T APPLY, JEWISH LIGHT-NING. JEWS IN MONTANA. IS THAT RIGHT? IT DOESN'T APPLY TO JEWS IN MONTANA.

I don't know.

AND WHAT ABOUT YOUR FATHER AND JEWS? LET'S GET IT OUT IN THE OPEN AND SPARE EVERYBODY A LOT OF SUFFERING LATER ON.

Mr. Levov, even though those things are said, most of the time nothing is said. My family doesn't say very much about anything. Two or three times a year we go out to a restaurant, my father and my mother, my younger brother and me, and I'm always surprised when I look around and see all the other families talking away amongst themselves. We just sit there and eat.

YOU ARE CHANGING THE SUBJECT.

I'm sorry. I don't mean this as a way to excuse it, because I don't like it, but I'm only trying to say that it isn't even something they strongly feel. There's no real anger or hatred behind it. What I'm pointing out is that on rare occasions he uses the word "Jew" in a derogatory fashion. It isn't really an issue one way or another, but every once in a while something will come up. That is true.

AND HOW WOULD THEY FEEL ABOUT YOU MARRYING A JEW?

They feel about the same way you feel about your son marrying a Catholic. One of my cousins married a Jew. They might tease about it but it wasn't a big scandal. She was a little older, so everybody was glad, in a way, she found somebody.

SHE WAS SO OLD EVEN A JEW WOULD DO. HOW OLD WAS SHE, A HUNDRED?

She was thirty. But nobody was brought to tears. It's not a big deal until somebody wants to insult somebody.

AND THEN?

Well, then you might want to get in a snide remark if you were angry at the person. I don't think the issue of marrying a Jew is a huge deal necessarily.

UNTIL THE ISSUE OF WHAT TO RAISE THE KIDS AS.

Well, yes.

SO HOW WOULD YOU RESOLVE THIS ISSUE WITH YOUR PARENTS?

I'd have to resolve the issue with myself.

WHAT DOES THAT MEAN?

I would like my child baptized.

YOU WOULD LIKE THAT.

You can be as liberal as you want, Mr. Levov, but not when it comes to baptism.

WHAT IS BAPTISM? WHAT IS SO IMPORTANT ABOUT THAT?

Well, it's technically washing away original sin. But what it does, it gets the child into heaven if they die. Otherwise, if they die before they're baptized, they just go into limbo.

WELL, WE WOULDN'T WANT THAT. LET ME ASK YOU SOME-
THING ELSE. SUPPOSE I SAY OKAY, YOU CAN BAPTIZE THE
CHILD. WHAT ELSE WOULD YOU WANT?

I guess when the time came, I'd want my children to make
their first communion. There are the sacraments, you see—

SO ALL YOU WANT IS THE BAPTISM, SO IF THE KID DIES IT
GETS INTO HEAVEN AS FAR AS YOU'RE CONCERNED, AND THE
FIRST COMMUNION. EXPLAIN TO ME WHAT THAT IS.

It's the first time we take the Eucharist.

AND WHAT IS THAT?

This is my body, this is my blood—

THIS IS ABOUT JESUS?

Yes. You don't know that? You know, when everybody kneels.
"This is my body, eat of it. This is my blood, drink of it." And
then you say "My Lord and my God" and eat the body of
Christ.

I CAN'T GO THAT FAR. I'M SORRY, I CANNOT GO THAT FAR.

Well, as long as there's baptism, we'll worry about the rest
later. Why don't we leave it up to the child when the time
comes?

I'D RATHER NOT LEAVE IT UP TO A CHILD, DAWN. I'D RATHER
MAKE THE DECISION MYSELF. I DON'T WANT TO LEAVE IT UP
TO A CHILD TO DECIDE TO EAT JESUS. I HAVE THE HIGHEST
RESPECT FOR WHATEVER YOU DO, BUT MY GRANDCHILD IS
NOT GOING TO EAT JESUS. I'M SORRY. THAT IS OUT OF THE
QUESTION. HERE'S WHAT I'LL DO FOR YOU. I'LL GIVE YOU THE
BAPTISM. THAT'S ALL I CAN DO FOR YOU.

That's *all*?

AND I'LL GIVE YOU CHRISTMAS.

Easter?

EASTER. SHE WANTS EASTER, SEYMOUR. TO ME YOU KNOW
WHAT EASTER IS, DAWN DEAR? EASTER IS A HUGE TARGET FOR
DELIVERIES. HUGE, HUGE PRESSURES TO GET GLOVES IN STOCK
FOR PEOPLE TO BUY THEIR EASTER OUTFITS. I'LL TELL YOU A
STORY. EVERY NEW YEAR'S EVE, IN THE AFTERNOON, WE'D
CLEAN UP ALL THE ORDERS FOR THE YEAR, SEND EVERYBODY
HOME, AND WITH MY FORELADY AND MY FOREMAN I'D POP A
BOTTLE OF CHAMPAGNE, AND BEFORE WE'D FINISHED TAKING
THE FIRST SIP WE WOULD GET A CALL FROM A STORE DOWN IN
WILMINGTON, IN DELAWARE, A CALL FROM THE BUYER THERE

FOR A HUNDRED DOZEN LITTLE WHITE SHORT LEATHER
GLOVES. FOR TWENTY YEARS OR MORE WE KNEW THAT CALL
WAS GOING TO COME FOR THE HUNDRED DOZEN AS WE WERE
TOASTING IN THE NEW YEAR, AND THOSE WERE GLOVES THAT
WERE FOR EASTER.

That was your tradition.

IT WAS, YOUNG LADY. NOW TELL ME, WHAT IS EASTER
ANYWAY?

He rises.

WHO?

Jesus. Jesus rises.

MISS, YOU MAKE IT AWFULLY HARD FOR ME. I THOUGHT
THAT'S WHEN YOU HAVE THE PARADE.

We do have the parade.

WELL, ALL RIGHT, I'LL GIVE YOU THE PARADE. HOW'S THAT?

We have ham on Easter.

YOU WANT A HAM ON EASTER, YOU CAN HAVE A HAM ON
EASTER. WHAT ELSE?

We go to church in an Easter bonnet.

AND IN A PAIR OF GOOD WHITE GLOVES, I HOPE.

Yes.

YOU WANT TO GO TO CHURCH ON EASTER AND TAKE MY
GRANDCHILD WITH YOU?

Yes. We'll be what my mother calls once-a-year Catholics.

IS THAT IT? ONCE A YEAR? (*Claps his hands together.*) LET'S
SHAKE ON THAT. ONCE A YEAR. YOU'VE GOT A DEAL!

Well, it would be twice a year. Easter and Christmas.

WHAT ARE YOU GOING TO DO CHRISTMAS?

When the child's small we can just go to the Mass where
they sing all the Christmas carols. You have to be there when they
sing all the Christmas carols. Otherwise it's not worth it. You
hear the Christmas carols on the radio, but in church they
won't give you the Christmas carols until Jesus is born.

I DON'T CARE ABOUT THAT. THOSE CAROLS DON'T INTER-
EST ME ONE WAY OR THE OTHER. HOW MANY DAYS IS THIS GO-
ING TO GO ON AT CHRISTMAS?

Well, there's Christmas Eve. There's Midnight Mass. Midnight Mass is a High Mass—

I DON'T KNOW WHAT THAT MEANS. I DON'T WANT TO. I'LL
GIVE YOU CHRISTMAS EVE AND I'LL GIVE YOU CHRISTMAS DAY

AND I'LL GIVE YOU EASTER. BUT I'M NOT GIVING YOU THE
STUFF WHERE THEY EAT HIM.

Catechism. What about catechism?

I CAN'T GIVE YOU THAT.

Do you know what it is?

I DON'T HAVE TO KNOW WHAT IT IS. THAT'S AS FAR AS I GO.
I THINK THIS IS A GENEROUS OFFER. MY SON WILL TELL YOU,
HE KNOWS ME—I AM MEETING YOU MORE THAN HALFWAY.
WHAT IS CATECHISM?

Where you go to school and learn about Jesus.

ABSOLUTELY NOT. ALL RIGHT? IS IT CLEAR? SHOULD WE
SHAKE? SHOULD WE WRITE THIS DOWN? CAN I TRUST YOU OR
SHOULD WE WRITE THIS DOWN?

This is scaring me, Mr. Levov.

YOU'RE SCARED?

Yes. (*Near tears.*) I don't think I can fight this fight.

I ADMIRE YOU FIGHTING THIS FIGHT.

Mr. Levov, we'll work it out later.

LATER NEVER WORKS. WE WORK IT OUT NOW OR NEVER. WE
STILL WANT TO TALK ABOUT BAR MITZVAH LESSONS.

If it's a boy and he's going to be bar mitzvahed, then he has
to be baptized. And then he can decide.

DECIDE WHAT?

After he grows up, he can decide which he likes better.

NO, HE'S NOT GOING TO DECIDE ANYTHING. YOU AND I ARE
GOING TO DECIDE RIGHT HERE.

But why don't we just wait and we'll see?

WE WILL NOT SEE.

(*To the Swede.*) I can't have this conversation anymore with
your father. He's too tough. I can only lose. We can't negotiate
like this, Seymour. I don't want a bar mitzvah.

YOU DON'T WANT A BAR MITZVAH?

With the Torah and all that?

THAT'S RIGHT.

No.

NO? THEN I DON'T THINK WE CAN REACH AN AGREEMENT.

Then we won't have any children. I love your son. We just
won't have children.

AND I'LL NEVER BE A GRANDFATHER. IS THAT THE DEAL?

You have another son.

NO, NO, THAT WON'T DO. NO HARD FEELINGS BUT I THINK
MAYBE EVERYBODY SHOULD JUST GO THEIR OWN WAY.

Can't we wait and see what happens? Mr. Levov, it's all a lot
of years away. Why can't we just let him or her decide what
they want?

ABSOLUTELY NOT. I'M NOT LETTING SOME CHILD MAKE
THESE KIND OF DECISIONS. HOW THE HELL CAN HE DECIDE?
WHAT DOES HE KNOW? WE'RE ADULTS. THE CHILD IS NOT AN
ADULT. (*Stands at his desk.*) MISS DWYER, YOU ARE PRETTY AS A
PICTURE. I CONGRATULATE YOU ON HOW FAR YOU'VE COME.
NOT EVERY GIRL REACHES YOUR HEIGHTS. YOUR PARENTS
MUST BE VERY PROUD. I THANK YOU FOR COMING TO MY OF-
FICE. THANK YOU AND GOOD-BYE.

No. I'm not leaving. I'm not going to go. I'm not a picture,
Mr. Levov. I'm myself. I'm Mary Dawn Dwyer of Elizabeth,
New Jersey. I'm twenty-two years old. I love your son. That is
why I'm here. I love Seymour. I love him. Let's go on, please.

So the deal was cut, the youngsters were married, Merry was
born and secretly baptized, and until Dawn's father died of the
second heart attack in 1959, both families got together every
year for Thanksgiving dinner up in Old Rimrock, and to everyone's surprise—except maybe Dawn's—Lou Levov and Jim
Dwyer would wind up spending the whole time swapping stories about what life had been like when they were boys. Two
great memories meet, and it is futile to try to contain them.
They are on to something even more serious than Judaism and
Catholicism—they are on to Newark and Elizabeth—and all
day long nobody can tear them apart. "All immigrants down at
the port." Jim Dwyer always began with the port. "Worked at
Singer's. That was the big one down there. There was the ship-
building industry down there too, of course. But everyone in
Elizabeth worked at Singer's at one time or another. Some
maybe out on Newark Avenue, at the Burry Biscuit Cookie
Company. People either making sewing machines or making
cookies. But mostly it was at Singer's, see, right at the port,
down at the end, right by the river. Biggest hirer in the community," Dwyer said. "Sure, all the immigrants, when they
come over, could get a job at Singer's. That was the biggest
thing around. That and Standard Oil. Standard Oil out in

Linden. The Bayway section. Right at the edge of what they called then Greater Elizabeth. . . . The mayor? Joe Brophy. Sure. He owned the coal company and he was also the mayor of the city. Then Jim Kirk took over. . . . Oh, sure, Mayor Hague. Quite a character. Ned, my brother-in-law, can tell you all about Frank Hague. He's the Jersey City expert. If you voted the right way in that town, you had a job. All I know is the ballpark. Jersey City had a great ballpark. Roosevelt Stadium. Beautiful. And they never got Hague, as you know, never put him away. Winds up with a place at the shore, right next to Asbury Park. A beautiful place he has. . . . The thing is, see, Elizabeth is a great sports town, but without having the great sports facilities. A baseball park where you could charge fifty cents or something to get in, never had that. We had open fields, we had Brophy Field, Mattano Park, Warananco Park, all public facilities, and still we had great teams and great players. Mickey McDermott pitched for St. Patrick's Elizabeth. Newcombe, the colored fella, an Elizabeth boy. Lives in Colonia now but an Elizabeth boy, pitched for Jefferson. . . . Swimming in the Arthur Kill, that was it. Sure. Close as I ever got to a vacation. Went twice a year to Asbury Park on the excursion. That was the vacation. Did my swimming in the Arthur Kill, underneath the Goethals Bridge. Bareback, you know. I'd come home with grease in my hair and my mother would say, 'You are swimming in the Arthur Kill again.' And I'd say, 'Elizabeth River? You think I'm crazy?' And all the while my hair is sticking up greasy, you know. . . ."

It was not quite so easy as this for the two mothers-in-law to find common ground and hit it off, for though Dorothy Dwyer could be a bit loquacious herself at Thanksgiving—just about as loquacious as she was nervous—her subject always was church. "St. Patrick's, that was the original one down there, at the port, and that was Jim's parish. The Germans started St. Michael's parish and the Polish had St. Adalbert's, at Third Street and East Jersey Street, and St. Patrick's is right behind Jackson Park, around the corner. St. Mary's is up in south Elizabeth, in the West End section, and that's where my parents started. They had the milk business there on Murray Street. St. Patrick's, Sacred Heart in north Elizabeth, Blessed Sacrament, Immaculate Conception Church, all Irish. And St. Catherine's.

That's up in Westminster. Well, it's on the city line. Actually it's in Hillside, but the school across the street is in Elizabeth. And then our church, St. Genevieve's. St. Genevieve's, when it started, was a missionary church, you see, just a part of St. Catherine's. Just a wooden church. It's a big, beautiful church now. But the building that stands now—and I remember when I first went in it—"

That was as trying as it ever got: Dorothy Dwyer prattling on about Elizabeth as though this were the Middle Ages and beyond the fields tilled by the peasants the only points of demarcation were the spires of the parish churches on the horizon. Dorothy Dwyer prattling on about St. Gen's and St. Patrick's and St. Catherine's while Sylvia Levov sat across from her too polite to do anything other than nod and smile but her face as white as a sheet. Just sat there and endured it, and good manners got her through. So all in all, it was never anywhere near as bad as everybody had been expecting. And it was never but once a year that they were brought together anyway, and that was on the neutral, dereligionized ground of Thanksgiving, when everybody gets to eat the same thing, nobody sneaking off to eat funny stuff—no kugel, no gefilte fish, no bitter herbs, just one colossal turkey for two hundred and fifty million people —one colossal turkey feeds all. A moratorium on funny foods and funny ways and religious exclusivity, a moratorium on the three-thousand-year-old nostalgia of the Jews, a moratorium on Christ and the cross and the crucifixion for the Christians, when everyone in New Jersey and elsewhere can be more passive about their irrationalities than they are the rest of the year. A moratorium on all the grievances and resentments, and not only for the Dwyers and the Levovs but for everyone in America who is suspicious of everyone else. It is the American pastoral par excellence and it lasts twenty-four hours.

"It was wonderful. The Presidential Suite. Three bedrooms and a living room. That's what you got in those days for having been a Miss New Jersey. The U.S. Line. I guess it wasn't booked, so we got on board and they just gave it to us."

Dawn was telling the Salzmans about their trip abroad to look at the Simmentals in Switzerland.

"I'd never been to Europe before, and all the way over

everybody was telling me, 'There's nothing like France, just wait until we come into Le Havre in the morning and you smell France. You'll love it.' So I waited, and early in the morning Seymour was still in bed and I knew we had docked and so I raced on deck and I sniffed," Dawn said, laughing, "and it was just garlic and onions all over the place."

She had raced out of the cabin with Merry while he was still in bed, but in the story she was on deck alone, astonished to find that France didn't smell like one big flower.

"The train to Paris. It was sublime. You see miles and miles of woods, but every tree is in line. They plant their forests in a line. We had a wonderful time, didn't we, darling?"

"We did," said the Swede.

"We walked around with great big bread sticks sticking out of our pockets. They practically said, 'Hey, look at us, a couple of rubes from New Jersey.' We were probably just the kind of Americans they laugh at. But who cared? We walked around, nibbling at the tops of them, looking at everything, the Louvre, the garden of the Tuileries—it was just wonderful. We stayed at the Crillon. The greatest treat of the whole trip. I loved it. Then we got on the night train, the Orient Express to Zurich, and the porter didn't get us up on time. Remember, Seymour?"

Yes, he remembered. Merry wound up on the platform in her pajamas.

"It was absolutely horrendous. The train had already started up. I had to get all our things and throw them all out the window—you know, that's the way people get out of the train there—and we ran out half dressed. They never woke us up. It was ghastly," Dawn said, again laughing happily at the recollection of the scene. "There we were, Seymour and me and our suitcases, wearing our underwear. So, anyway"—for a moment she was laughing too hard to go on—"we got to Zurich, and we went to wonderful restaurants—smelled of delicious croissants and good pâtés—and *pâtisseries* everywhere. Things like that. Oh, it was so good. All of the papers were on canes, they were hung up on racks, so you take your paper down and sit and have your breakfast and it was wonderful. So from there we took a car and we went down to Zug, the center of the Simmentals, and then we went to Lucerne, which was beautiful, absolutely beautiful, and then we went to the Beau Rivage in Lausanne. Remember the Beau Rivage?" she asked her husband, her hand still firmly held in his.

And he did remember it. Never had forgotten it. Coincidentally enough, had himself been thinking of the Beau Rivage just that afternoon, on the drive back to Old Rimrock from Central Avenue. Merry at afternoon tea, with the band playing, before she'd been raped. She had danced with the headwaiter, his six-year-old child, before she'd killed four people. Mademoiselle Merry. On his own, on their last afternoon at the Beau Rivage, the Swede had gone down to the jewelry shop off the lobby, and while Merry and Dawn were out walking on the promenade to take a last look together at the boats on Lake Geneva and the Alps out across the way, he had bought Dawn a diamond necklace. He had a vision of her wearing the diamond necklace along with the crown she kept in a hatbox at the top of her closet, the silver crown with the double row of rhinestones that she had worn as Miss New Jersey. Since he couldn't even get her to wear the crown to show to Merry—"No, no, it's just too silly a thing," Dawn told him; "to her I'm 'Mom,' which is perfectly fine"—he'd never get her to put it on with the new necklace. Knowing Dawn and her sense of herself as well as he did, he realized that even to cajole her into trying them on, the necklace and the crown together, in the bedroom, just modeling them there for him alone, would be impossible. She was never more stubborn about anything than about not being an ex–beauty queen. "It's not a beauty pageant," she was already telling people back then who persisted in asking about her year as Miss New Jersey. "Most people involved with the pageant will fight with anyone who says they were in a beauty pageant, and I'm one of them. Your only prize for winning at any level is a *scholarship*." And yet it was with the crown in her hair, the crown not of a scholarship winner but of a beauty queen, that he had imagined her wearing that necklace when he caught sight of it in the window of the shop at the Beau Rivage.

In one of their photograph albums there was a series of pictures he used to like to look at back when they were first married and even on occasion to show to people. They always made him so proud of her, these glossy photos taken in 1949–50, when she'd held down the fifty-two-week-a-year job that the head man over at the Miss New Jersey Scholarship Pageant liked to describe as serving as the state's official "hostess"—the job of accommodating as many cities and towns and groups as possible for every kind of event, working like a dog, really, and receiving in compensation the $500 cash scholarship, a pageant trophy, and the fifty bucks for each personal appearance. There was, of course, a picture of her at the Miss New Jersey coronation on the night of Saturday, May 21, 1949, Dawn in a strapless evening gown of silk, stiff and scalloped at the top, very tight to the waist, and below, to the floor, a full, voluptuous skirt, thickly embroidered with flowers and sparkling with beads. And on her head her crown. "You don't feel ridiculous in your evening gown wearing a crown," she told him, "but you definitely feel ridiculous in your clothes and your crown. Little girls always asking if you're a princess. People coming up and asking if the crown is diamonds. In just a suit and wearing that thing, Seymour, you feel absolutely *silly*." But she hardly looked silly—wearing her very simple, tailored clothes and that crown, she looked stunning. There was a picture of her in a suit and her crown—and her Miss New Jersey sash, pinned at the waist with a brooch—at an agricultural fair with some farmers, another of her in her crown and the sash at a manufacturer's convention with some businessmen, and one of her in that strapless silk evening gown and her crown at the governor's Princeton mansion, Drumthwacket, dancing with the governor of New Jersey, Alfred E. Driscoll. Then there were the pictures of her at parades and ribbon cuttings and charity fund-raisers around the state, pictures of her assisting at the crowning in local pageants, pictures of her opening the department stores and the auto showrooms—"That's Dawnie. The beefy guy owns the place." There were a couple of her visiting schools where, seated at the piano in the auditorium, she generally played the popularized Chopin polonaise that she'd performed to become Miss New Jersey, leaving out clots and clots of black notes to get it in at two and a half minutes so she wouldn't be disqualified by the stopwatch at the state level. And in all of those pictures, whatever clothes she might be wearing that were appropriate to the event, she would always have the crown set in her hair, making her look, as much to her husband as to the little girls who came up to ask, like a princess—more like a princess was supposed to look than any of a whole string of European princesses whose photographs he'd seen in *Life*.

Then there were the pictures taken at Atlantic City, at the Miss America Pageant in September, pictures of her in her swimsuit and in evening wear, which made him wonder how she ever could have lost. She told him, "When you're out on that runway you can't imagine how ridiculous you feel in that swimsuit and your high heels, and you know that when you walk a ways the back end is going to ride up, and you can't reach behind you and pull it down. . . ." But she hadn't been ridiculous at all: he never looked at the swimsuit pictures that he didn't say aloud, "Oh, she was beautiful." And the crowd had been with her; at Atlantic City most of the audience was naturally rooting for Miss New Jersey, but during the parade of states Dawn had received a spontaneous ovation that bespoke more than local pride. The pageant wasn't on TV back then, it was still for the folks jammed into Convention Hall, so afterward, when the Swede, who'd sat in the hall beside Dawn's brother, called to tell his parents that Dawn hadn't won, he could still say of her reception, without exaggerating, "She brought the house down."

Certainly, of the five other former Miss New Jerseys at their wedding, none could compare to Dawn in any way. Together they constituted a kind of sorority, these former Miss New Jerseys, and for a while there in the fifties they all attended one another's weddings, so that he must have met up with at least ten girls who had won the state crown and probably twice as many who'd become friends of this or that bride during the days of rehearsal for the state competition, girls who'd gotten as far as being Miss Shore Resort and Miss Central Coast and Miss Columbus Day and Miss Northern Lights, and there wasn't a one who could rival his wife in any category—talent, intelligence, personality, poise. If he should ever happen to remark to someone that why Dawn hadn't become Miss America was something he would never understand, Dawn always begged him not to go around saying that, because it gave the impression that her having not become Miss America was something she was embittered about when, in many ways, losing had been a relief. Just getting through without humiliating herself and her family had been a relief. Sure, after all the buildup the New Jersey people had given her she was surprised and a little let down not to have made the Court of Honor or even the top ten, but that, too, might have been a blessing in disguise. And though losing would not be a relief for a competitor like him, not a blessing of any kind, he nonetheless admired Dawn's graciousness—gracious was how the folks over at the pageant liked to describe all the girls who lost—even if he couldn't understand it.

Losing allowed her, for one thing, to begin to restore the relations with her father that had nearly been ruined because of her persisting at something he so strongly disapproved of. "I don't care what they're giving away," Mr. Dwyer said when she tried to explain about the pageant scholarship money. "The whole damn thing," he told her, "is about being ogled. Those girls are there to be ogled. The more money they give for it, the worse it is. The answer is *no*."

That Mr. Dwyer agreed finally to come down to Atlantic City had been due to the persuasive skills of Dawn's favorite aunt, Peg, her mother's sister, the schoolteacher who'd married rich Uncle Ned and taken Dawn as a kid to the hotel in Spring Lake. "It would make any father uncomfortable seeing his baby up there," Peg had told her brother-in-law in that gentle, diplomatic way Dawn always admired and wanted to emulate. "It brings certain images to mind that a father would just as soon not have associated with his daughter. I'd feel that way if it were my daughter," she told him, "and I don't have what it is that fathers naturally feel for their daughters. It would bother me, of course it would. I would think that what you feel is the case with a lot of dads. They're really proud, their buttons are popping and all that, but at the same time, 'Oh, my God, that's my baby up there.' But Jim, this is so clean and beyond reproach there is just nothing to worry about. The trashy ones get sifted out early—they go on to work the truckers' convention. These are just ordinary kids from small towns, decent, sweet girls whose fathers own the grocery store and don't belong to the country club. They get them up to look like debutantes but there is nothing big in their backgrounds. They're just good kids who go home and settle down and marry the boy next door. And the judges are serious people. Jim, this is for Miss

America. If it were compromising to the girls, they wouldn't allow it. It is an *honor*. Dawn wants you there to share in that honor. She will not be very happy if you are not there, Jimmy. She will be crushed, especially if you are the *only* father who isn't there." "Peggy, it's beneath her. It's beneath all of us. I'm not going." So that's when she laid into him about his responsibility not merely to Dawn but to the nation. "You wouldn't come when she won at the local level. You wouldn't come when she won at the state level. Are you now telling me that you are not going to come if she wins at the national level? If she is awarded Miss America and you're not there to walk up on the stage and hug your daughter with pride, what will they think? They'll think, 'A great tradition, a part of the American heritage, and her father isn't there. Photographs of Miss America with her family, and her father isn't in a one of them.' Tell me, how's that going to go down the next day?"

And so he humbled himself and he did it—against his better judgment, consented to come for the big night to Atlantic City with the rest of Dawn's relatives, and it was a disaster. When Dawn saw him waiting there in his Sunday suit in the lobby with her mother and her aunts and her uncles and her cousins, every last Dwyer in Union *and* Essex *and* Hudson counties, all she was allowed to do by her chaperone was to shake his hand, and he was fit to be tied. But that was a pageant rule, in case anybody who was watching might not know it was her father and see some kind of embrace and think something untoward was going on. It was all so that absolutely *nothing* smacked of impropriety, but Jim Dwyer, who had only recently recovered from the first heart attack and so was on edge anyway, had misunderstood, thinking that now she was such a big shot she had dared to rebuff her own dad, actually given her father the cold shoulder, and in public, before the entire public.

Of course, for the week that she was in Atlantic City under the watchful eye of the pageant, she had not been allowed to see the Swede *at all*, not in the company of her chaperone, not even in a public place, and so, until the very last night, he'd just stayed up in Newark and had to be content, like her family, to talk to her on the phone. But Dawn's sincerity in recounting to her father this hardship—of her being deprived, for a whole week, of the company of her Jewish beau—did not much impress him when, back in Elizabeth, she attempted to assuage his grudge at what he remembered for many years afterward as "the snub."

"That was just an Old World hotel that was the most wonderful place," Dawn was telling the Salzmans. "Huge place. Glorious. Right on the water. Something you see in a movie. Big rooms overlooking Lake Geneva. We loved that. I'm boring you," she suddenly said.

"No, no," they replied in unison.

Sheila pretended to be listening intently to every word Dawn spoke. She had to be pretending. Not even she could have recovered so completely from the eruption in Dawn's study. If she had—well, it would be hard then to say what sort of woman she was. She was nothing like the one he had imagined. And that was not because she had been passing herself off with him as something else or somebody else but because he had understood her no better than he was able to understand anyone. How to penetrate to the interior of people was some skill or capacity he did not possess. He just did not have the combination to that lock. Everybody who flashed the signs of goodness he took to be good. Everybody who flashed the signs of loyalty he took to be loyal. Everybody who flashed the signs of intelligence he took to be intelligent. And so he had failed to see into his daughter, failed to see into his wife, failed to see into his one and only mistress—probably had never even begun to see into himself. What was *he*, stripped of all the signs he flashed? People were standing up everywhere, shouting "This is me! This is me!" Every time you looked at them they stood up and told you who they were, and the truth of it was that they had no more idea of who or what they were than he had. *They* believed their flashing signs too. They ought to be standing up and shouting, "This *isn't* me! This *isn't* me!" They would if they had any decency. "This *isn't* me!" Then you might know how to proceed through the flashing bullshit of this world.

Sheila Salzman may or may not have been listening to Dawn's every word, but Shelly Salzman surely was. The kindly doctor wasn't merely acting like the kindly doctor but appeared to have fallen somewhat under Dawn's spell—the spell of that alluring surface whose underside, as she presented it to people, was as charmingly straightforward as it could be. Yes, after all she'd been through, she looked and she behaved as though nothing had happened. For him there was this two-sidedness to everything: side by side, the way it had been and the way it was now. But Dawn made it sound as though the way it had been was *still* the way it was. After the tragic detour their lives had taken, she'd managed in the last year to arrive back at being herself, apparently just by not thinking about certain things. And arrived back not merely at Dawn with her face-lift and her petite gallantry and her breakdowns and her cattle and her decisions to change her life but back at the Dawn of Hillside Road, Elizabeth, New Jersey. A gate, some sort of psychological gate, had been installed in her brain, a mighty gate past which nothing harmful could travel. She locked the gate, and that was that. Miraculous, or so he'd thought, until he'd learned that the gate had a name. The William Orcutt III Gate.

Yes, if you'd missed her back in the forties, here once again was Mary Dawn Dwyer of Elizabeth's Elmora section, an up-and-coming Irish looker from a working-class family that was starting to do okay, respectable parishioners at St. Genevieve's, the classiest Catholic church in town—miles uptown from the church by the docks where her father and his brothers had been altar boys. Once again she was in possession of that power she'd had even as a twenty-year-old to stir up interest in whatever she said, somehow to touch you *inwardly*, which was not often true of the contestants who *won* at Atlantic City. But she could do that, lay bare something juvenile even in adults, by nothing more than venting ordinary lively enthusiasms through that flagrantly perfect, strikingly executed heart-shaped face. Maybe, until she spoke and revealed her attitudes as not so different from any decent person's, people were frightened of her for looking like that. Discovering that she was not at all a goddess, had no interest in pretending to be one—discovering in her almost an excess of *no* pretense—made even more riveting the brilliant darkness of her hair, the angular mask not much bigger than a cat's, and the eyes, the big pale eyes almost alarmingly keen and vulnerable. From the message in those eyes one would never have believed that this girl was going to grow up to be a shrewd businesswoman resolutely determined

about turning a profit as a cattle breeder. What excited the
Swede's tenderness always was that she who wasn't at all frail
nonetheless looked so delicate and frail. This always impressed
him: how strong she was (once was) and how vulnerable her
kind of beauty caused her to appear, even to him, her husband,
long after one might imagine that married life had dulled the
infatuation.

And how plain Sheila looked sitting alongside her, purportedly listening to her, plain and proper, sensible, dignified, and
dreary. So dreary. Everything in her severely withheld. Hidden.
There was nothing hearty in Sheila. There was lots in Dawn.
There once was in him. That once described everything there
was in him. It was not easy to understand how he could ever
have found in this prim, severe, hidden whatever-she-was a
woman more magnetic than Dawn. How pathetic he must have
been, how depleted, a broken, helpless creature escaping from
everything that had collapsed, running in the headlong way
that someone in trouble will take flight in order to make a bad
thing worse. Almost all there was to attract him was that Sheila
was someone else. Her clarity, her candor, her equilibrium, her
perfect self-control were at first almost beside the point. Shrinking from such a blinding catastrophe—disconnected as he'd
never been before from his ready-made life; notorious and disgraced as he'd never been before—he turned in a daze to the
one woman other than his wife whom he knew even remotely
in a personal way. That was how he got there, seeking asylum,
hounded—the forlorn reason for a straight arrow so assertively
uxorious, so intensely and spotlessly monogamous, hurling
himself at such an extraordinary moment into a situation he
would have thought he hated, the shameful fiasco of being
untrue. But amorousness had little to do with his clutching.
He could not offer the passionate love that Dawn drew from
him. Lust was far too natural a task for someone suddenly so
misshapen—the father of someone gruesomely misbegotten.
He was there for the illusion. He lay atop Sheila like a person
taking cover, digging in, a big male body in hiding, a man disappearing: because she was somebody else, maybe he could be
somebody else too.

But that she *was* someone else was what made it all wrong.
Alongside Dawn, Sheila was a well-groomed impersonal

thinking-machine, a human needle threaded with a brain, no-body he could want to touch, let alone sleep with. Dawn was the woman who had inspired the feat for which even his rec-ord-breaking athletic career had barely fortified him: vaulting his father. The feat of standing up to his father. And how she had inspired it was by looking as spectacular as she looked and yet talking like everyone else.

Was it bigger, more important, worthier things that inclined others to a lifelong mate? Or at the heart of everyone's mar-riage was there something irrational and unworthy and odd?

Sheila would know. She knew it all. Yes, she'd have an answer to that one too. . . . She'd come so far, Sheila had said, she'd gotten so much stronger I thought that she could make it on her own. She's a strong girl, Seymour. *She's a crazy girl. She's crazy!* She's troubled. *And the father plays no role with the trou-bled daughter?* I'm sure he played plenty of a role. I just thought something terrible had happened at home. . . .

Oh, he wanted his wife back—it was impossible to exagger-ate the extent to which he wanted her back, the wife so serious about being a serious mother, the woman so fiercely disinclined to be thought spoiled or vain or frivolously nostalgic for her once-glamorous eminence that she would not wear even as a joke for her family the crown in the hatbox at the top of her closet. His endurance had run out—he wanted that Dawn back *right now.*

"What were the farms like?" Sheila asked her. "In Zug. You were going to tell us about the farms." This interest of Sheila's in figuring it all out—how could he have wanted *anything* to do with her? These deep thinkers were the only people he could not stand to be around for long, these people who'd never manufactured anything or seen anything manufactured, who did not know what things were made of or how a com-pany worked, who, aside from a house or a car, had never sold anything and didn't know how to sell anything, who'd never hired a worker, fired a worker, trained a worker, been fleeced by a worker—people who knew nothing of the intricacies or the risks of building a business or running a factory but who nonetheless imagined that they knew everything worth know-ing. All that *awareness,* all that introspective Sheila-like gazing into every nook and cranny of one's soul went repellently against the grain of life as he had known it. To his way of thinking it was simple: you had only to carry out your duties strenuously and unflaggingly like a Levov and orderliness became a natural condition, daily living a simple story tangibly unfolding, a deeply unagitating story, the fluctuations predictable, the combat containable, the surprises satisfying, the continuous motion an undulation carrying you along with the utmost faith that tidal waves occur only off the coast of countries thousands and thousands of miles away—or so it all had seemed to him *once upon a time*, back when the union of beautiful mother and strong father and bright, bubbly child rivaled the trinity of the three bears.

"I got lost, yes. Oh, lots and lots of farms," said Dawn, gratified just by the thought of all those farms. "They showed us their best cows. Wonderful warm barns. We were there in the early spring when they haven't been out to pasture yet. They're living under the house and the chalet is on top. Porcelain stoves, very ornate . . ." *I don't understand how you could be so shortsighted. So taken in by a girl who was obviously crazy.* She was running. There was no bringing her back there. She wasn't the same girl that she'd been. Something had gone wrong. She'd gotten so fat. I just thought she was so fat and so angry that something very bad must have gone on at home. *That it was my fault.* I didn't think that. We all have homes. That's where everything always goes wrong. ". . . and they gave us wine that they made, little things to eat, and so friendly," Dawn said. "When we went back the second time it was fall. The cows live up in the mountains all summer and they milk them and the cow that made the most milk all summer would be the first one to come down with a great bell on her neck. That was the number-one cow. They put flowers on her horns and had great celebrations. When they come down from the high mountain pastures they come down in a line, the leading cow the first one." *What if she went on to kill somebody else? Isn't that a bit of a responsibility? She did, you know. She killed three more people. What do you think of that?* Don't say these things just to torture me. *I'm telling you something! She killed three more people! You could have prevented that!* You're torturing me. You're trying to torture me. *She killed three more people!* "And all the people, all the children, the girls and the women who had been milking all summer would come in beautiful clothes, all dressed in Swiss outfits, and a band, music, a big fiesta down in the square. And then the cows would all go in for the winter in the barns under the houses. Very clean and very nice. Oh, that was an occasion, seeing that. Seymour took lots of pictures of all their cows so we could put them on the projector."

"Seymour took pictures?" his mother asked. "I thought you couldn't take a picture if it killed you," and she leaned over and kissed him. "My wonderful son," whispered Sylvia Levov, in her eyes adoring admiration shining for her firstborn boy.

"Well, he did back then, the wonderful son. He was a Leica man back then," Dawn was saying. "You took good pictures, didn't you, dear?"

Yes, he had. That was him all right. That was the wonderful son himself who had taken the pictures, who had bought Merry the Swiss girl's outfit, who had bought Dawn the jewelry in Lausanne, and who had told his brother and Sheila that Merry killed four people. Who had bought for the family, as a memento of Zug, of the gloriously Switzerlandish state of their lives, the ceramic candelabra, now half encased with candle drippings, and who had told his brother and Sheila that Merry killed four people. Who had been a Leica man and told those two—the two he could least trust in the world and over whom he had no control—what Merry had done.

"Where else did you go?" Sheila asked Dawn, careful to give no indication that in the car she would tell Shelly, and Shelly would say, "My God, my God"; because he was such a mild and decent person, he might even cry. But when they got home, the instant they were home, the first thing he would do would be to call the police. Once before he had harbored this murderer. For three days. That had been frightening, awful, brutally nerve-racking. But only one was dead, and bad as it was, you could wrap your mind around that number—and as his wife had insisted, as idiotically, he had agreed, they had no alternative; the girl was her client, a promise had been made, professional conscience wouldn't allow . . . But four people. This was too much. This was unacceptable. Four innocent people, to kill them off—no, this was barbarism, gruesome, depraved, this was evil, and they certainly did have an alternative: the law. Obligation to the law. They knew where she was.

They could be prosecuted for keeping a secret like this. No, it was not going to spin any farther out of Shelly's control. The Swede saw it all. Shelly would phone the police—he had to. "Four people. She's in Newark. Seymour Levov knows the address. He was there. He was with her there today." Shelly was exactly as Lou Levov had described him—"a physician, a respected person, an ethical person, a responsible person"—and he would not allow his wife to become accessory to the murder of four people by this wretched, loathsome girl, another homicidal savior of the world's oppressed. Insane terroristic behavior coupled with that bogus ideology—she had done the worst thing that anyone can do. That would be Shelly's interpretation and what could the Swede do to change it? How could he get Shelly to see it otherwise when *he* could no longer see it otherwise? Take him aside immediately, the Swede thought, tell him, explain to Shelly now, say whatever has to be said to stop him from taking action, to stop him from thinking that turning her in is his duty as a law-abiding citizen, that it's a way of protecting innocent lives—tell him, "She was used. She was malleable. She was a compassionate child. She was a wonderful child. She was *only* a child, and she got herself in with the wrong people. She could never have masterminded anything like that on her own. She just hated the war. We all did. We all felt angry and impotent. But she was a kid, a confused adolescent, a high-strung girl. She was too young to have had any real experience, and she got herself caught up in something that she did not understand. She was attempting to save lives. I'm not trying to give a political excuse for her, because there is no political excuse—there is no justification, none. But you can't just look at the appalling effect of what she did. She had her reasons, which were very strong for her, and the reasons don't matter now—she has changed her philosophy and the war is over. None of us really know all that happened and none of us can really know why. There is more behind it, much, much more than we can understand. She was wrong, of course —she made a tragic, terrible, ghastly mistake. There's no defense of her to be made. But she's not a risk to anyone anymore. She is now a skinny, pathetic wreck of a girl who wouldn't hurt a fly. She's quiet, she's harmless. She's not a hardened criminal, Shelly. She is a broken creature who did something terrible and who regrets it to the bottom of her soul. What good will it do to call the police? Of course justice must be served, but she is no longer a danger. There is no need for you to get involved. We don't have to call the police to protect anyone. And there's no need for vengeance. Vengeance has been taken on her, believe me. I know she's guilty. The question is not if she's guilty. The question is what is to be done now. Leave her to me. I will look after her. She won't do anything—I'll see to that. I'll see that she is taken care of, that she is given help. Shelly, give me a chance to bring her back to human life—*don't call the police!*"

But he knew what Shelly would think: Sheila had done enough for that family. They both had. That family was in real trouble now, but there was no more help from Dr. Salzman. This wasn't a face-lift. Four people were dead. That girl should get the electric chair. Yes, the number four would transform even Shelly into an outraged citizen ready to pull the switch. He would go ahead and turn her in because she was a little bitch who deserved it.

"That second time? Oh, we went everywhere," Dawn was saying. "It doesn't really matter in Europe where you go, everywhere you go there are things that are beautiful, and we sort of followed that path."

But the police knew. From Jerry. It's inevitable. Jerry has already called the FBI. Jerry. To give Jerry her address. To tell Jerry. To tell anyone. To sit here so battered as to overlook the implications of disclosing what Merry had done! Battered, doing nothing—holding Dawn's hand, thinking back again to Atlantic City, to the Beau Rivage, to Merry dancing with the headwaiter—mindless of the consequences of his reckless disclosure, bereft of his lifelong talent for being Swede Levov, instead floating free of the battering ram that is this world, dreaming, dreaming, helplessly dreaming, while down in Florida the hotheaded brother who thought the worst of him and wasn't a brother to him at all, who'd been antagonized from the beginning by all the Swede had been blessed with, by that impossible perfection they'd both had to contend with, the inflamed and willful and ruthless brother who never did anything halfway, who would like nothing better than a reckoning—yes, a final reckoning for all the world to see. . . .

He'd turned her in. Not his brother, not Shelly Salzman,

but *he*, he was the one who'd done it. What would it have taken to keep my mouth shut? What did I expect to get by opening it? Relief? Childish relief? Their reaction? I was after something so ridiculous as their *reaction*? By opening his mouth he had made things as bad as they could be—by retelling to them what Merry had told him, the Swede had done it: turned her in for killing four people. Now he had planted his own bomb. Without wanting to, without knowing what he was doing, without even being importuned, he had yielded—he had done what he should do and he had done what he shouldn't do: he had turned her in.

It would have taken another day entirely to keep his mouth shut—a different day, the abolition of this day. Lead me not into this day! Seeing so much so fast. And how stoical he had always been in his ability not to see, how prodigious had been his powers to regularize. But in the three extra killings he had been confronted by something impossible to regularize, even for him. Being told it was horrible enough, but only by retelling it had he understood how horrible. One plus three. Four. And the instrument of this unblinding is Merry. The daughter has made her father see. And perhaps this was all she had ever wanted to do. She has given him sight, the sight to see clear through to that which will never be regularized, to see what you can't see and don't see and won't see until three is added to one to get four.

He had seen how improbable it is that we should come from one another and how improbable it is that we do come from one another. Birth, succession, the generations, history—utterly improbable.

He had seen that we *don't* come from one another, that it only appears that we come from one another.

He had seen the way that it is, seen out beyond the number four to all there is that cannot be bounded. The order is minute. He had thought most of it was order and only a little of it was disorder. He'd had it backwards. He had made his fantasy and Merry had unmade it for him. It was not the specific war that she'd had in mind, but it was a war, nonetheless, that she brought home to America—home into her very own house.

And just then they heard his father scream: "No!" They heard Lou Levov screaming, "Oh my God! *No!*" The girls in

the kitchen were screaming. The Swede understood instantaneously what was happening. Merry had appeared in her veil!
And told her grandfather that the death toll was four! She'd
taken the train up from Newark and walked the five miles from
the village. She'd come on her own! Now everyone knew!

The thought of her walking the length of that underpass
one more time had terrified him all through dinner—in her
rags and sandals walking alone through that filth and darkness
among the underpass derelicts who understood that she loved
them. However, while he had been at the table formulating no
solution, she had been nowhere near the underpass but—he all
at once envisioned it—already back in the countryside, here in
the lovely Morris County countryside that had been tamed
over the centuries by ten American generations, back walking
the hilly roads that were edged now, in September, with the
red and burnt orange of devil's paintbrush, with a matted pro-
fusion of asters and goldenrod and Queen Anne's lace, an
entangled bumper crop of white and blue and pink and wine-
colored flowers artistically topping their workaday stems, all
the flowers she had learned to identify and classify as a 4-H
Club project and then on their walks together had taught him,
a city boy, to recognize—"See, Dad, how there's a n-notch at
the tip of the petal?"—chicory, cinquefoil, pasture thistle, wild
pinks, joe-pye weed, the last vestiges of yellow-flowered wild
mustard sturdily spilling over from the fields, clover, yarrow,
wild sunflowers, stringy alfalfa escaped from an adjacent farm
and sporting its simple lavender blossom, the bladder campion
with its clusters of white-petaled flowers and the distended little
sac back of the petals that she loved to pop loudly in the palm
of her hand, the erect mullein whose tonguelike velvety leaves
she plucked and wore inside her sneakers—so as to be like the
first settlers, who, according to her history teacher, used mullein leaves for insoles—the milkweed whose exquisitely made
pods she would carefully tear open as a kid so she could blow
into the air the silky seed-bearing down, thus feeling herself at
one with nature, imagining that she was the everlasting wind.
Indian Brook flowing rapidly on her left, crossed by little
bridges, dammed up for swimming holes along the way and
opening into the strong trout stream where she'd fished with
her father—Indian Brook crossing under the road, flowing

eastward from the mountain where it arises. On her left the
pussy willows, the swamp maples, the marsh plants; on her
right the walnut trees nearing fruition, only weeks from dropping the nuts whose husks when she pulled them apart would
darkly stain her fingers and pleasantly stink them up with an
acid pungency. On her right the black cherry, the field plants,
the mowed fields. Up on the hills the dogwood trees; beyond
them the woodlands—the maples, the oaks, and the locusts,
abundant and tall and straight. She used to collect their bean-
pods in the fall. She used to collect everything, catalog everything, explain to him everything, examine with the pocket
magnifying glass he'd given her every chameleonlike crab spi-
der that she brought home to hold briefly captive in a moist-
ened mason jar, feeding it on dead houseflies until she released
it back onto the goldenrod or the Queen Anne's lace ("Watch
what happens now, Dad") where it resumed adjusting its color
to ambush its prey. Walking northwest into a horizon still
thinly alive with light, walking up through the twilight call of
the thrushes: up past the white pasture fences she hated, up
past the hay fields, the corn fields, the turnip fields she hated,
up past the barns, the horses, the cows, the ponds, the streams,
the springs, the falls, the watercress, the scouring rushes ("The
pioneers used them, Mom, to scrub their pots and pans"), the
meadows, the acres and acres of woods she hated, up from
the village, tracing her father's high-spirited, happy Johnny
Appleseed walk until, just as the first few stars appeared, she
reached the century-old maple trees that she hated and the
substantial old stone house, imprinted with her being, that
she hated, the house in which there lived the substantial family,
also imprinted with her being, that she also hated.

At an hour, in a season, through a landscape that for so long
now has been bound up with the idea of solace, of beauty and
sweetness and pleasure and peace, the ex-terrorist had come,
quite on her own, back from Newark to all that she hated and
did not want, to a coherent, harmonious world that she despised and that she, with her embattled youthful mischief, the
strangest and most unlikely attacker, had turned upside down.
Come back from Newark and immediately, *immediately* confessed to her father's father what her great idealism had caused
her to do.

"Four people, Grandpa," she'd told him, and his heart could not bear it. Divorce was bad enough in a family, but *murder*, and the murder not merely of one but of one plus three? The murder of *four*?

"No!" exclaimed Grandpa to this veiled intruder reeking of feces who claimed to be their beloved Merry, "*No!*" and his heart gave up, gave out, and he died.

There was blood on Lou Levov's face. He was standing beside the kitchen table clutching his temple and unable to speak, the once-imposing father, the giant of the family of six-footers at five foot seven, speckled now with blood and, but for his pot-belly, looking barely like himself. His face was vacant of everything except the struggle not to weep. He appeared helpless to prevent even that. He could not prevent anything. He never could, though only now did he look prepared to believe that manufacturing a superb ladies' dress glove in quarter sizes did not guarantee the making of a life that would fit to perfection everyone he loved. Far from it. You think you can protect a family and you cannot protect even yourself. There seemed to be nothing left of the man who could not be diverted from his task, who neglected no one in his crusade against disorder, against the abiding problem of human error and insufficiency —nothing to be seen, in the place where he stood, of that eager, unbending stalk of a man who, just thirty minutes earlier, would jut his head forward to engage even his allies. The combatant had borne all the disappointment he could. Nothing blunt remained within him for bludgeoning deviancy to death. What should be did not exist. Deviancy prevailed. You can't stop it. Improbably, what was not supposed to happen had happened and what was supposed to happen had not happened.

The old system that made order doesn't work anymore. All that was left was his fear and astonishment, but now concealed by nothing.

At the table was Jessie Orcutt, seated before a half-empty dessert plate and an untouched glass of milk and holding in her hand a fork whose tines were tipped red with blood. She had stabbed at him with it. The girl at the sink was telling them this. The other girl had run screaming out of the house, so there was just the one still in the kitchen to recount the story as best she could through her tears. Because Mrs. Orcutt would not eat, the girl said, Mr. Levov had started to feed Mrs. Orcutt the pie himself, a bite at a time. He was explaining to her how much better it was for her to drink milk instead of Scotch whiskey, how much better for herself, how much better for her husband, how much better for her children. Soon she would be having grandchildren and it would be better for them. With each bite she swallowed he said, "Yes, Jessie good girl, Jessie very good girl," and told her how much better it would be for everybody in the world, even for Mr. Levov and his wife, if Jessie gave up drinking. After he had fed her almost all of one whole slice of the strawberry-rhubarb pie, she had said, "*I* feed Jessie," and he was so happy, so pleased with her, he laughed and handed over the fork, and she had gone right for his eye.

It turned out she'd missed it by no more than an inch. "Not bad," Marcia said to everyone in the kitchen, "for somebody as drunk as this babe is." Meanwhile Orcutt, appalled by a scene exceeding any previously contrived by his wife to humiliate her civic-minded, adulterous mate, who looked not at all invincible, not at all important to himself or anyone else, who looked just as silly as he had the morning the Swede had dumped him in the midst of their friendly football game—Orcutt tenderly lifted Jessie up from the chair and to her feet. She showed no remorse, none, seemed to have been stripped of all receptors and all transmitters, without a single cell to notify her that she had overstepped a boundary fundamental to civilized life.

"One drink less," Marcia was saying to the Swede's father, whose wife was already dabbing at the tiny wounds in his face with a damp napkin, "and you'd be blind, Lou." And then this large, unimpeded social critic in a caftan could not help herself. Marcia sank into Jessie's empty chair, in front of the brimming glass of milk, and with her face in her hands, she began to laugh at their obtuseness to the flimsiness of the whole contraption, to laugh and laugh and laugh at them all, pillars of a society that, much to her delight, was going rapidly under—to laugh and to relish, as some people, historically, always seem to do, how far the rampant disorder had spread, enjoying enormously the assailability, the frailty, the enfeeblement of supposedly robust things.

Yes, the breach had been pounded in their fortification, even out here in secure Old Rimrock, and now that it was opened it would not be closed again. They'll never recover. Everything is against them, everyone and everything that does not like their life. All the voices from without, condemning and rejecting their life!

And what is wrong with their life? What on earth is less reprehensible than the life of the Levovs?

I MARRIED A COMMUNIST

To my friend and editor
VERONICA GENG
1941–1997

Many songs have I heard in my native land—
Songs of joy and sorrow.
But one of them was deeply engraved in my memory:
It's the song of the common worker.

> Ekh, lift up the cudgel,
> Heave-ho!
> Pull harder together,
> Heave-ho!

—"Dubinushka," a Russian folksong.
*In the 1940s performed and recorded,
in Russian, by the Soviet Army Chorus
and Band.*

1

IRA RINGOLD's older brother, Murray, was my first high school English teacher, and it was through him that I hooked up with Ira. In 1946 Murray was just back from the army, where he'd served with the 17th Airborne Division at the Battle of the Bulge; in March 1945, he'd made the famous jump across the Rhine that signaled the beginning of the end of the European war. He was, in those days, a crusty, brash, baldheaded guy, not as tall as Ira but rangy and athletic, who hovered over our heads in a perpetual state of awareness. He was altogether natural in his manner and posture while in his speech verbally copious and intellectually almost menacing. His passion was to explain, to clarify, to make us understand, with the result that every last subject we talked about he broke down into its principal elements no less meticulously than he diagrammed sentences on the blackboard. His special talent was for dramatizing inquiry, for casting a strong narrative spell even when he was being strictly analytic and scrutinizing aloud, in his clear-cut way, what we read and wrote.

Along with the brawn and the conspicuous braininess, Mr. Ringold brought with him into the classroom a charge of visceral spontaneity that was a revelation to tamed, respectablized kids who were yet to comprehend that obeying a teacher's rules of decorum had nothing to do with mental development. There was more importance than perhaps even he imagined in his winning predilection for heaving a blackboard eraser in your direction when the answer you gave didn't hit the mark. Or maybe there wasn't. Maybe Mr. Ringold knew very well that what boys like me needed to learn was not only how to express themselves with precision and acquire a more discerning response to words, but how to be rambunctious without being stupid, how not to be too well concealed or too well behaved, how to begin to release the masculine intensities from the institutional rectitude that intimidated the bright kids the most.

You felt, in the sexual sense, the power of a male high school teacher like Murray Ringold—masculine authority uncorrected by piety—and you felt, in the priestly sense, the vocation of a male high school teacher like Murray Ringold, who wasn't lost in the amorphous American aspiration to make it big, who—unlike the school's women teachers—could have chosen to be almost anything else and chose instead, for his life's work, to be ours. All he wanted all day long was to deal with young people he could influence, and his biggest kick in life he got from their response.

Not that the impression his bold classroom style left on my sense of freedom was apparent at the time; no kid thought that way about school or teachers or himself. An incipient craving for social independence, however, had to have been nourished somewhat by Murray's example, and I told him this when, in July 1997, for the first time since I graduated from high school in 1950, I ran into Murray, now ninety years old but in every discernible way still the teacher whose task is realistically, without self-parody or inflating dramatics, to personify for his students the maverick dictum "I don't give a good goddamn," to teach them that you don't have to be Al Capone to transgress —you just have to *think*. "In human society," Mr. Ringold taught us, "thinking's the greatest transgression of all." "Criti-cal think-ing," Mr. Ringold said, using his knuckles to rap out each of the syllables on his desktop, "—there is the ultimate subversion." I told Murray that hearing this early on from a manly guy like him—seeing it *demonstrated* by him—provided the most valuable clue to growing up that I had clutched at, albeit half comprehendingly, as a provincial, protected, high-minded high school kid yearning to be rational and of consequence and free.

Murray, in turn, told me everything that, as a youngster, I didn't know and couldn't have known about his brother's private life, a grave misfortune replete with farce over which Murray would sometimes find himself brooding even though Ira was dead now more than thirty years. "Thousands and thousands of Americans destroyed in those years, political casualties, historical casualties, because of their beliefs," Murray said. "But I don't remember anybody else being brought down quite the way that Ira was. It wasn't on the great American battlefield he would himself have chosen for his destruction.

Maybe, despite ideology, politics, and history, a genuine catastrophe is always personal bathos at the core. Life can't be impugned for any failure to trivialize people. You have to take your hat off to life for the techniques at its disposal to strip a man of his significance and empty him totally of his pride."

Murray also told me, when I asked, how he had been stripped of *his* significance. I knew the general story but little of the details because I began my own army stint—and wasn't around Newark again for years—after I graduated college in 1954, and Murray's political ordeal didn't get under way until May 1955. We started with Murray's story, and it was only at the end of the afternoon, when I asked if he'd like to stay for dinner, that he seemed to feel, in unison with me, that our relations had shifted to a more intimate plane and that it wouldn't be incorrect if he went on to speak openly about his brother's.

Out near where I live in western New England, a small college called Athena runs a series of weeklong summer programs for elderly people, and Murray was enrolled as a student, at ninety, for the course grandly entitled "Shakespeare at the Millennium." That's how I'd run into him in town on the Sunday he arrived—having failed to recognize him, I was fortunate that he recognized me—and how we came to spend our six evenings together. That's how the past turned up this time, in the shape of a very old man whose talent was to give his troubles not one second more thought than they warranted and who still couldn't waste his time talking other than to a serious point. A palpable obstinacy lent his personality its flinty fullness, and this despite time's radical pruning of his old athletic physique. Looking at Murray while he spoke in that familiarly unhidden, scrupulous way of his, I thought, There it is—human life. There is endurance.

In '55, almost four years after Ira was blacklisted from radio for being a Communist, Murray had been dismissed from his teaching job by the Board of Education for refusing to cooperate with the House Un-American Activities Committee when it had come through Newark for four days of hearings. He was reinstated, but only after a six-year legal struggle that ended in a 5–4 decision by the state supreme court, reinstated with back pay, minus the amount of money he had earned supporting his family those six years as a vacuum salesman.

"When you don't know what else to do," Murray said with a smile, "you sell vacuum cleaners. Door to door. Kirby vacuum cleaners. You spill a full ashtray onto the carpet and then you vacuum it up for them. You vacuum the house for them. That's how you sell the thing. Vacuumed half the houses in New Jersey in my day. Look, I had a lot of well-wishers, Nathan. I had a wife whose medical expenses were constant, and we had a child, but I was getting a pretty good amount of business and I sold a lot of people vacuum cleaners. And despite her scoliosis problems, Doris went back to work. She went back to the lab at the hospital. Did the blood work. Eventually ran the lab. In those days there was no separation between the technical stuff and the medical arts, and Doris did it all: drew the blood, stained the slides. Very patient, very thorough with a microscope. Well trained. Observant. Accurate. Knowledgeable. She used to come home from the Beth Israel, just across the street from us, and cook dinner in her lab coat. Ours was the only family I ever knew of whose salad dressing was served in laboratory flasks. The Erlenmeyer flask. We stirred our coffee with pipettes. All our glassware was from the lab. When we were on our uppers, Doris made ends meet. Together we were able to tackle it."

"And they came after you because you were Ira's brother?" I asked. "That's what I always assumed."

"I can't say for sure. Ira thought so. Maybe they came after me because I never behaved the way a teacher was supposed to behave. Maybe they would have come after me even without Ira. I started out as a firebrand, Nathan. I burned with zeal to establish the dignity of my profession. That may be what rankled them more than anything else. The personal indignity that you had to undergo as a teacher when I first started teaching—you wouldn't believe it. Being treated like children. Whatever the superiors told you, that was law. Unquestioned. You will get here at this time, you will sign the time book on time. You will spend so many hours in school. And you will be called on for afternoon and evening assignments, even though that wasn't part of your contract. All kinds of chicken-shit stuff. You felt denigrated.

"I threw myself into organizing our union. I moved quickly into committee leadership, executive board positions. I was outspoken—at times, I admit, pretty glib. I thought I knew all the answers. But I was interested in teachers' getting respect—respect, and proper emoluments for their labors, and so forth. Teachers had problems with pay, working conditions, benefits . . .

"The superintendent of schools was no friend of mine. I had been prominent in the move to deny him promotion to the superintendency. I supported another man, and he lost. So because I made no bones about my opposition to this son of a bitch, he hated my guts, and in '55 the ax fell and I was called downtown to the Federal Building, to a meeting of the House Un-American Activities Committee. To testify. Chairman was a Representative Walter. Two more members of the committee came with him. Three of them up from Washington, with their lawyer. They were investigating Communist influence in everything in the city of Newark but primarily investigating what they called 'the infiltration of the party' into labor and education. There had been a sweep of these hearings throughout the country—Detroit, Chicago. We knew it was coming. It was inevitable. They knocked us teachers off in one day, the last day, a Thursday in May.

"I testified for five minutes. 'Have you now or have you ever been . . . ?' I refused to answer. Well, why won't you? they said. You got nothing to hide. Why don't you come clean? We just want information. That's all we're here for. We write legislation. We're not a punitive body. And so forth. But as I understood the Bill of Rights, my political beliefs were none of their business, and that's what I told them—'It's none of your business.'

"Earlier in the week they'd gone after the United Electrical Workers, Ira's old union back in Chicago. On Monday evening, a thousand UE members came over on chartered buses from New York to picket the Robert Treat Hotel, where the committee staff members were staying. The *Star-Ledger* described the picketers' appearance as 'an invasion of forces hostile to the congressional inquiry.' Not a legal demonstration as guaranteed by rights laid down in the Constitution but an *invasion*, like Hitler's of Poland and Czechoslovakia. One of the committee congressmen pointed out to the press—and without a trace of embarrassment at the un-Americanness lurking in his observation—that a lot of the demonstrators were chanting in Spanish, evidence to him that they didn't know the meaning of the signs they were carrying, that they were ignorant 'dupes' of the Communist Party. He took heart from the fact that they had been kept under surveillance by the 'subversives squad' of the Newark police. After the bus caravan passed through Hudson County on the way back to New York, some big cop there was quoted as saying, 'If I knew they were Reds, I'd of locked all thousand of them up.' That was the local atmosphere, and that was what had been appearing in the press, by the time I got to be questioned, the first to be called up on Thursday.

"Near the end of my five minutes, in the face of my refusal to cooperate, the chairman said that he was disappointed that a man of my education and understanding should be unwilling to help the security of this country by telling the committee what it wanted to know. I took that silently. The only hostile remark I made was when one of those bastards closed off by telling me, 'Sir, I question your loyalty.' I told him, 'And I question yours.' And the chairman told me that if I continued to 'slur' any member of the committee, he would have me ejected. 'We don't have to sit here,' he told me, 'and take your bunk and listen to your slurs.' 'Neither do I,' I said, 'have to sit here and listen to *your* slurs, Mr. Chairman.' That was as bad as it got. My lawyer whispered to me to cut it out, and that was the end of my appearance. I was excused.

"But as I got up to leave my chair, one of the congressmen called after me, I suppose to provoke me into contempt—'How can you be paid by the taxpayers' money when you are obligated by your damnable Communist oath to teach the Soviet line? How in God's name can you be a free agent and teach what the Communists dictate? Why don't you get out of the party and reverse your tracks? I plead with you—return to the American way of life!'

"But I didn't take the bait, didn't tell him that what I taught had nothing to do with the dictates of anything other than composition and literature, though, in the end, it didn't seem to matter what I said or didn't say: that evening, in the Sports Final edition, there was my kisser on the front page of the *Newark News*, over the caption 'Red Probe Witness Balky' and the line '"Won't take your bunk," HUAC tells Newark teacher.'

"Now, one of the committee members was a congressman from New York State, Bryden Grant. You remember the Grants, Bryden and Katrina. Americans everywhere remember the Grants. Well, the Ringolds were the Rosenbergs to the Grants. This society pretty boy, this vicious nothing, all but destroyed our family. And did you ever know why? Because one night Grant and his wife were at a party that Ira and Eve were giving on West Eleventh Street and Ira went after Grant the way only Ira could go after somebody. Grant was a pal of Wernher von Braun's, or Ira thought so, and Ira laid into him but good. Grant was—to the naked eye, that is—an effete upper-class guy of the sort who set Ira's teeth on edge. The wife wrote those popular romances that the ladies devoured and Grant was then still a columnist for the *Journal-American*. To Ira, Grant was the incarnation of pampered privilege. He couldn't stand him. Grant's every gesture made him sick and his politics he abhorred.

"Well, there was a big, loud scene, Ira shouting and calling Grant names, and for the rest of his life Ira maintained that a Grant vendetta against us began that night. Ira had a way of presenting himself without camouflage. Comes just as he is, holding nothing back, without a single plea. That was his magnetism for you, but it's also what made him repellent to his enemies. And Grant was one of his enemies. The whole squabble took three minutes, but according to Ira, three minutes that sealed his fate and mine. He'd humiliated a descendant of Ulysses S. Grant and a graduate of Harvard and an employee of William Randolph Hearst's, not to mention the husband of the author of *Eloise and Abelard*, the biggest bestseller of 1938, and *The Passion of Galileo*, the biggest bestseller of 1942—and that was it for us. We were finished: by publicly insulting Bryden Grant, Ira had challenged not only the husband's impeccable credentials but the wife's inextinguishable need to be right.

"Now, I'm not sure that explains everything—though not because Grant was any less reckless in the use of power than the rest of Nixon's gang. Before he went to Congress, he wrote that column for the *Journal-American*, a gossip column three times a week about Broadway and Hollywood, with a dollop of Eleanor Roosevelt–defiling thrown in. That's how Grant's

public service career began. That's what qualified him so highly
for a seat on the Un-American Activities Committee. He was a
gossip columnist before it became the big business it is today.
He was in there at the start, in the heyday of the great pioneers.
There was Cholly Knickerbocker and Winchell and Ed Sullivan
and Earl Wilson. There was Damon Runyon, there was Bob
Considine, there was Hedda Hopper—and Bryden Grant was
the *snob* of the mob, not the street fighter, not the lowlife, not
the fast-talking insider who hung out at Sardi's or the Brown
Derby or Stillman's Gym, but the blueblood to the rabble who
hung out at the Racquet Club.

"Grant began with a column called 'Grant's Grapevine,' and,
if you remember, he nearly ended as Nixon's White House chief
of staff. Congressman Grant was a great favorite of Nixon's.
Sat as Nixon did on the Un-American Activities Committee.
Did a lot of President Nixon's arm-twisting in the House. I
remember when the new Nixon administration floated Grant's
name back in '68 for chief of staff. Too bad they let it drop. The
worst decision Nixon ever made. If only Nixon had found the
political advantage in appointing, instead of Haldeman, this
Brahmin hack to head the Watergate cover-up operation,
Grant's career might have ended behind bars. Bryden Grant in
jail, in a cell between Mitchell's and Ehrlichman's. Grant's
Tomb. But it was never to be.

"You can hear Nixon singing Grant's praises on the White
House tapes. It's there in the transcripts. 'Bryden's heart is in
the right place,' the president tells Haldeman. 'And he's tough.
He'll do anything. I mean anything.' He tells Haldeman Grant's
motto for how to handle the administration's enemies: 'Destroy them in the press.' And then, admiringly—an epicurean
of the perfect smear, of the vilification that burns with a hard,
gemlike flame—the president adds: 'Bryden's got the killer instinct. Nobody does a more beautiful job.'

"Congressman Grant died in his sleep, a rich and powerful
old statesman, still greatly esteemed in Staatsburg, New York,
where they named the high school football field after him.

"During the hearing I watched Bryden Grant, trying to believe that there was more to him than a politician with a personal vendetta finding in the national obsession the means to
settle a score. In the name of reason, you search for some higher

motive, you look for some deeper meaning—it was still my wont in those days to try to be reasonable about the unreasonable and to look for complexity in simple things. I would make demands upon my intelligence where none were really necessary. I would think, He *cannot* be as petty and vapid as he seems. That can't be more than one-tenth of the story. There must be more to him than that.

"But why? Pettiness and vapidity can come on the grand scale too. What could be more *unwavering* than pettiness and vapidity? Do pettiness and vapidity get in the way of being cunning and tough? Do pettiness and vapidity vitiate the aim of being an important personage? You don't need a developed view of life to be fond of power. You don't need a developed view of life to *rise* to power. A developed view of life may, in fact, be the worst impediment, while *not* having a developed view the most splendid advantage. You didn't have to summon up misfortunes from his patrician childhood to make sense of Congressman Grant. This is the guy, after all, who took over the congressional seat of Hamilton Fish, the original Roosevelt hater. A Hudson River aristocrat like FDR. Fish went to Harvard just after FDR. Envied him, hated him, and, because Fish's district included Hyde Park, wound up FDR's congressman. A terrific isolationist and stupid as they come. Fish, back in the thirties, was the first upper-crust ignoramus to serve as chairman of the precursor of that pernicious committee. The prototypical self-righteous, flag-waving, narrow-minded patrician son of a bitch—that was Hamilton Fish. And when they redistricted the old fool's district in '52, Bryden Grant was his boy.

"After the hearing, Grant left the dais where the three committee members and their lawyer were seated and made a beeline for my chair. He was the one who'd said to me, 'I question your loyalty.' But now he smiled graciously—as only Bryden Grant could, as though he had invented the gracious smile—and he put out his hand and so, loathsome as it was to me, I shook it. The hand of unreason, and reasonably, civilly, the way fighters touch gloves before a fight, I shook it, and my daughter, Lorraine, was appalled with me for days afterward.

"Grant said, 'Mr. Ringold, I traveled up here today to help you clear your name. I wish you could have been more cooperative. You don't make it easy, even for those of us who are sympathetic. I want you to know that I wasn't scheduled to represent the committee in Newark. But I knew you were to be a witness and so I asked to come because I didn't think it would be much help to you if my friend and colleague Donald Jackson were to show up instead.'

"Jackson was the guy who had taken Nixon's seat on the committee. Donald L. Jackson of California. A dazzling thinker, given to public statements like, 'It seems to me that the time has come to be an American or not an American.' It was Jackson and Velde who led the manhunt to root out Communist subversives in the Protestant clergy. That was a pressing national issue for these guys. After Nixon's departure from the committee, Grant was considered the committee's intellectual spearhead who drew their profound conclusions for them—and, sad to say, more than likely he was.

"He said to me, 'I thought that perhaps I could help you more than the honorable gentleman from California. Despite your performance here today, I still think I can. I want you to know that if, after a good night's sleep, you decide you want to clear your name—'

"That was when Lorraine erupted. She was all of fourteen. She and Doris had been sitting behind me, and throughout the session Lorraine had been fuming even more audibly than her mother. Fuming and squirming, barely able to contain the agitation in her fourteen-year-old frame. 'Clear his name of *what*?' Lorraine said to Congressman Grant. 'What did my father *do*? Grant smiled at her benignly. He was very good-looking, with all that silver hair, and he was fit, and his suits were the most expensive Tripler's made, and his manners couldn't have affronted anyone's mother. He had that nicely blended voice, respectful, at once soft and manly, and he said to Lorraine, 'You're a loyal daughter.' But Lorraine wouldn't quit. And neither Doris nor I tried to stop her right off. 'Clear his name? *He* doesn't have to clear his name—it's not dirty,' she told Grant. 'You're the one who's dirtying his name.' 'Miss Ringold, you are off the issue. Your father has a history,' Grant said. 'History?' Lorraine said. 'What history? What's his history?' Again he smiled. 'Miss Ringold,' he said, 'you're a very nice young lady—' 'Whether I'm nice has nothing to do with it. What is his history? What did he do? What is it that he has to clear? Tell me what my father did.' 'Your father will have to tell us what he did.' 'My father has already spoken,' she said, 'and you are twisting everything he says into a pack of lies just to make him look bad. His name *is* clean. He can go to bed at night. I don't know how you can, sir. My father served his country as well as the rest of them. He knows about loyalty and fighting and what's American. This is how you treat people who've served their country? Is that what he fought for—so you could sit here and try to blacken his name? Try to sling mud all over him? That's what America is? That's what you call loyalty? What have *you* done for America? Gossip columns? That's so American? My father has principles, and they're decent American principles, and you have no business trying to destroy him. He goes to school, he teaches children, he works as hard as he can. You should have a *million* teachers like him. Is that the problem? He's too good? Is that why you have to tell lies about him? *Leave my father alone!*'

"When Grant still wouldn't reply, Lorraine cried, 'What's the matter? You had so much to say when you were up there on the stand—and now you're Mr. Dumbmouth? Your little lips sealed shut—' Right there I put my hand on hers and I said, 'That's enough.' And then she got angry with me. 'No, it's *not* enough. It's not going to be enough until they stop treating you like this. Aren't you going to say *anything*, Mr. Grant? Is this what America is—nobody says anything in front of fourteen-year-olds? Just because I don't vote—is that the problem? Well, I'd certainly never vote for you or any of your lousy friends!' And she burst into tears, and that was when Grant said to me, 'You know where to reach me,' and he smiled at the three of us and left for Washington.

"That's the way it goes. They fuck you and then they tell you, 'You were lucky you got fucked by me and not by the honorable gentleman from California.'

"I never did get in touch with him. The fact was that my political beliefs were pretty localized. They were never inflated like Ira's. I was never interested like he was in the fate of the world. I was more interested, from a professional point of view, in the fate of the community. My concern was not even so much political as economic and I would say sociological, in terms of working conditions, in terms of the status of teachers in the city of Newark. The next day the mayor, Mayor Carlin, told the press that people like me should not be teaching our children, and the Board of Education put me on trial for conduct unbecoming a teacher. The superintendent saw this was his warrant for getting rid of me. I didn't answer the questions of a responsible government agency, so ipso facto I was unfit. I told the Board of Education that my political beliefs were not relevant to my being an English teacher in the Newark school system. There were only three grounds for dismissal: insubordination, incompetence, and moral turpitude. I argued that none of these applied. Former students came down to the board hearing to testify that I had never tried to indoctrinate anybody, in class or anywhere else. Nobody in the school system had ever heard me attempt to indoctrinate anyone into anything other than respect for the English language—none of the parents, none of the students, none of my colleagues. My former army captain, he testified for me. Came up from Fort Bragg. That was impressive.

"I enjoyed selling vacuum cleaners. There were people who crossed the street when they saw me coming, even people who may have felt ashamed doing it but who didn't want to be contaminated, but that didn't bother me. I had a lot of support within the teachers' union and a lot of support outside. Contributions came in, we had Doris's salary, and I sold my vacuum cleaners. I met people in all lines of work and I made contact with the real world beyond teaching. You know, I was a professional, a schoolteacher, reading books, teaching Shakespeare, making you kids diagram sentences and memorize poetry and appreciate literature, and I thought no other kind of life was worth living. But I went out selling vacuum cleaners and I acquired a great deal of admiration for a lot of people I met, and I am still grateful for it. I think I have a better outlook on life because of it."

"Suppose you hadn't been reinstated by the court. Would you still have a better outlook?"

"If I had lost? I think I would have made a fair living. I think I would have survived intact. I might have had some regrets. But I don't think I would have been affected temperamentally. In an open society, as bad as it can get, there's an escape. To lose your job and have the newspapers calling you a traitor—

these are very unpleasant things. But it's still not the situation that is total, which is totalitarianism. I wasn't put in jail and I wasn't tortured. My child wasn't denied anything. My livelihood was taken away from me and some people stopped talking to me, but other people admired me. My wife admired me. My daughter admired me. Many of my ex-students admired me. Openly said so. And I could put up a legal fight. I had free movement, I could give interviews, raise money, hire a lawyer, make courtroom challenges. Which I did. Of course you can become so depressed and miserable that you give yourself a heart attack. But you can find alternatives, which I also did.

"Now, if the *union* had failed, that would have affected me. But we didn't. We fought and eventually we won. We equalized the pay of men and women. We equalized the pay of secondary and elementary school teachers. We made sure that all after-school activities were, first, voluntary and, then, paid for. We fought to get more sick leave. We argued for five days off for any purpose whatsoever that the individual chose. We achieved promotion by examination—as opposed to favoritism—which meant that all minorities had a fair chance. We attracted blacks to the union, and as they increased in numbers, they moved into leadership positions. But that was years ago. Now the union is a big disappointment to me. Just become a money-grubbing organization. Pay, that's all. What to do to educate the kids is the last thing on anybody's mind. Big disappointment."

"How awful was it for those six years?" I asked him. "What did it take out of you?"

"I don't think it took anything out of me. I really don't think so. You do a helluva lot of not sleeping at night, of course. Many nights I had a hard time sleeping. You're thinking of all kinds of things—how do you do this, and what are you going to do next, whom do you call on, and so forth. I was always redoing what had happened and projecting what would happen. But then the morning comes, and you get up and you do what you have to do."

"And how did Ira take this happening to you?"

"Oh, it distressed him. I'd go as far as to say it ruined him had he not already been ruined by everything else. I was confident all along that I was going to win, and I told this to him.

They had no legal reasons for firing me. He kept saying, 'You're kiddin' yourself. They don't need legal reasons.' He knew of too many guys who had been fired, period. Eventually I won, but he felt responsible for what I went through. He carried it around with him for the rest of his life. About you, too, you know. About what happened to you."

"Me?" I said. "Nothing happened to me. I was a kid."

"Oh, something happened to you."

Of course it should not be too surprising to find out that your life story has included an event, something important, that you have known nothing about—your life story is in and of itself something that you know very little about.

"If you remember," Murray said, "when you graduated from college you didn't get a Fulbright. That was because of my brother."

In 1953–54, my last year at Chicago, I'd applied for a Fulbright to do graduate work in literature at Oxford and been turned down. I had been near the top of my class, had enthusiastic recommendations, and, as I now remembered it—for the first time, probably, since it happened—was shocked not only at being turned down but because a Fulbright to study literature in England went to a fellow student who was well below me in class standing.

"This true, Murray? I just thought it was screwy, unfair. The fickleness of fate. I didn't know what to think. I wuz robbed, I thought—and then I got drafted. How do you know this is so?"

"The agent told Ira. The FBI. He was on Ira for years. Stopping around to visit him. Coming around to try to get him to name names. Told him that's how he could clear himself. They had you down for Ira's nephew."

"His nephew? How come his nephew?"

"Don't ask me. The FBI didn't always get everything right. Maybe they didn't always want to get everything right. The guy told Ira, 'You know your nephew who applied for a Fulbright? The kid in Chicago? He didn't get it because of your being a Communist.'"

"You think that was true."

"No doubt about it."

All the while I was listening to Murray—and looking at the needle of a man he'd become and thinking of this physique as the materialization of all that coherence of his, as the consequence of a lifelong indifference to everything other than liberty in its most austere sense . . . thinking that Murray was an essentialist, that his character wasn't contingent, that wherever he'd found himself, even selling vacuum cleaners, he'd managed to find his dignity . . . thinking that Murray (whom I didn't love or have to; with whom there was just the contract, teacher and student) was Ira (whom I did love) in a more mental, sensible, matter-of-fact version, Ira with a practical, clear, well-defined social goal, Ira without the heroically exaggerated ambitions, without that passionate, overheated relationship to everything, Ira unblurred by impulse and the argument with everything—I had a picture in my mind of Murray's unclothed upper torso, still blessed (when he was already forty-one) with all the signs of youth and strength. The picture I had was of Murray Ringold as I had seen him late one Tuesday afternoon in the fall of 1948, leaning out the window and removing the screens from the second-floor apartment where he lived with his wife and daughter on Lehigh Avenue.

Taking down the screens, putting up the screens, clearing the snow, salting the ice, sweeping the sidewalk, clipping the hedge, washing the car, collecting and burning the leaves, twice daily from October through March descending to the cellar and tending the furnace that heated your flat—stoking the fire, banking the fire, shoveling the ashes, lugging ashes up the stairs in buckets and out to the garbage: a tenant, a renter, had to be fit to get all his chores done before and after going to work, vigilant and diligent and fit, just as the wives had to be fit to lean from their open back windows while rooted to the floor of the apartment and, whatever the temperature—up there like seamen at work in the rigging—to hang the wet clothes out on the clothesline, to peg them with the clothespins an item at a time, feeding the line out until all the waterlogged family wash was hung and the line was full and flapping in the air of industrial Newark, and then to haul the line in again to remove the laundry item by item, remove it all and fold it into the laundry basket to carry into the kitchen when the clothes were dry and ready to be ironed. To keep a family going, there was primarily money to be made and food to be prepared and discipline to be imposed, but there were also these heavy, awkward, sailorlike activities, the climbing, the hoisting, the hauling, the dragging, the cranking in, the reeling out—all the stuff that would tick by me as, on my bicycle, I traversed the two miles from my house to the library: tick, tock, tick, the metronome of daily neighborhood life, the old American-city chain of being.

Across the street from Mr. Ringold's Lehigh Avenue house was the Beth Israel Hospital, where I knew Mrs. Ringold had worked as a lab assistant before their daughter was born, and around the corner was the Osborne Terrace branch library, where I used to bicycle for a weekly supply of books. The hospital, the library, and, as represented by my teacher, the school: the neighborhood's institutional nexus was all reassuringly present for me in virtually that one square block. Yes, the everyday workability of neighborhood life was in full swing on that afternoon in 1948 when I saw Mr. Ringold hanging out over the sill undoing a screen from the front window.

As I braked to descend the steep Lehigh Avenue hill, I watched him thread a rope through one of the screen's corner hooks and then, after calling down "Here she comes," lower it along the face of the two-and-a-half-story building to a man in the garden, who undid the rope and set the screen onto a pile stacked against the brick stoop. I was struck by the way Mr. Ringold performed an act that was both athletic and practical. To perform that act as gracefully as he did, you had to be very strong.

When I got to the house I saw that the man in the garden was a giant wearing glasses. It was Ira. It was the brother who had come to our high school, to "Auditorium," to portray Abe Lincoln. He'd appeared on the stage in costume and, standing all alone, delivered Lincoln's Gettysburg Address and then the Second Inaugural, concluding with what Mr. Ringold, the orator's brother, later told us was as noble and beautiful a sentence as any American president, as any American *writer*, had ever written (a long, chugging locomotive of a sentence, its tail end a string of weighty cabooses, that he then made us diagram and analyze and discuss for an entire class period): "With malice toward none, with charity for all, with firmness in the right as God gives us to see the right, let us strive on to finish the work we are in, to bind up the nation's wounds, to care for him who shall have borne the battle and for his widow and his orphan, to do all which may achieve and cherish a just and lasting peace among ourselves and with all nations." For the rest of the program, Abraham Lincoln removed his stovepipe hat and debated the pro-slavery senator Stephen A. Douglas, whose lines (the most insidiously anti-Negro of which a group of students—we members of an extracurricular discussion group called the Contemporary Club—loudly booed) were read by Murray Ringold, who had arranged for Iron Rinn to visit the school.

As if it weren't disorienting enough to see Mr. Ringold out in public without a shirt and tie—without even an undershirt—Iron Rinn wasn't wearing any more than a prizefighter. Shorts, sneakers, that was it—all but naked, not only the biggest man I'd ever seen up close but the most famous. Iron Rinn was heard on network radio every Thursday night on *The Free and the Brave*—a popular weekly dramatization of inspiring episodes out of American history—impersonating people like Nathan Hale and Orville Wright and Wild Bill Hickok and Jack London. In real life, he was married to Eve Frame, the leading lady of the weekly repertory playhouse for "serious" drama called *The American Radio Theater*. My mother knew everything about Iron Rinn and Eve Frame through the magazines she read at the beauty parlor. She would never have bought any of these magazines—she disapproved of them, as did my father, who wished his family to be exemplary—but she read them under the dryer, and then she saw all the fashion magazines when she went off on Saturday afternoons to help her friend Mrs. Svirsky, who, with her husband, had a dress shop on Bergen Street right next door to Mrs. Unterberg's millinery shop, where my mother also occasionally helped out on Saturdays and during the pre-Easter rush.

One night after we had listened to *The American Radio Theater*, which we'd done since I could remember, my mother told us about Eve Frame's wedding to Iron Rinn and all the stage and radio personalities who were guests. Eve Frame had worn a two-piece wool suit of dusty pink, sleeves trimmed with double rings of matching fox fur, and, on her head, the sort of hat that no one in the world wore more charmingly than she did. My mother called it "a veiled come-hither hat," a style that Eve Frame had apparently made famous opposite the silent-film matinee idol Carlton Pennington in *My Darling, Come Hither*, where she played to perfection a spoiled young socialite. It was a veiled come-hither hat that she was well known for wearing when she stood before the microphone, script in hand, performing on *The American Radio Theater*, though she had also been photographed before a radio microphone in slouch-brimmed felts, in pillboxes, in Panama straw hats, and once, when she was a guest on *The Bob Hope Show*, my mother remembered, in a black straw saucer seductively veiled with gossamer silk thread. My mother told us that Eve Frame was six years older than Iron Rinn, that her hair grew an inch a month and she lightened its color for the Broadway stage, that her daughter, Sylphid, was a harpist, a Juilliard graduate, and the offspring of Eve Frame's marriage to Carlton Pennington.

"Who cares?" my father said. "Nathan does," my mother replied defensively. "Iron Rinn is Mr. Ringold's brother. Mr. Ringold is his *idol*."

My parents had seen Eve Frame in silent movies when she was a beautiful girl. And she was still beautiful; I knew because, four years earlier, for my eleventh birthday, I had been taken to see my first Broadway play—*The Late George Apley* by John P. Marquand—and Eve Frame was in it, and afterward my father, whose memories of Eve Frame as a young silent-film actress were still apparently amorously tinged, had said, "That woman speaks the King's English like nobody's business," and my mother, who may or may not have grasped what was fueling his praise, had said, "Yes, but she's let herself go. She speaks beautifully, and she did the part beautifully, and she looked adorable in that short pageboy, but the extra pounds are not becoming on a little thing like Eve Frame, certainly not in a fitted white piqué summer dress, full skirt or no full skirt."

A discussion as to whether or not Eve Frame was Jewish invariably occurred among the women in my mother's mahjong club when it was my mother's turn to have them for their weekly game, and particularly after the evening a few months later when I had been a guest of Ira's at Eve Frame's dinner table. The starstruck world round the starstruck boy couldn't stop talking about the fact that people said her real name was Fromkin. Chava Fromkin. There were Fromkins in Brooklyn who were supposed to be the family she had disowned when she went to Hollywood and changed her name.

"Who cares?" my serious-minded father would say whenever the subject came up and he happened to be passing through the living room, where the mahjong game was in progress. "They all change their names in Hollywood. That woman opens her mouth and it's an elocution lesson. She gets up on that stage and portrays a lady, you *know* it's a lady."

"They say she's from Flatbush," Mrs. Unterberg, who owned the millinery shop, would routinely put in. "They say that her father is a kosher butcher."

"They say Cary Grant is Jewish," my father reminded the ladies. "The fascists used to say that *Roosevelt* was Jewish. People say everything. That's not what I'm concerned with. I'm concerned with her *acting*, which in my book is superlative."

"Well," said Mrs. Svirsky, who with her husband owned the dress shop, "Ruth Tunick's brother-in-law is married to a Fromkin, a Newark Fromkin. And she has relatives in Brooklyn, and they swear their cousin is Eve Frame."

"What does Nathan say?" asked Mrs. Kaufman, a housewife and a girlhood friend of my mother's.

"He doesn't," my mother replied. I had trained her to say that I didn't. How? Easy. When she had asked, on behalf of the ladies, if I knew whether Eve Frame of *The American Radio Theater* was, in actuality, Chava Fromkin of Brooklyn, I had told her, "Religion is the opiate of the people! Those things don't matter—I don't care. I don't know and I don't care!"

"What is it like there? What did she wear?" Mrs. Unterberg asked my mother.

"What did she serve?" Mrs. Kaufman asked.

"How was her hair done?" Mrs. Unterberg asked.

"Is he really six six? What does Nathan say? Does he wear a size sixteen shoe? Some people say that's just publicity."

"And his skin is as pockmarked as it looks in the pictures?"

"What does Nathan say about the daughter? What kind of name is Sylphid?" asked Mrs. Schessel, whose husband was a chiropodist, like my father.

"That's her real name?" asked Mrs. Svirsky.

"It's not Jewish," said Mrs. Kaufman. " 'Sylvia' is Jewish. I think it's French."

"But the father wasn't French," said Mrs. Schessel. "The father is Carlton Pennington. She acted with him in all those films. She eloped with him in that movie. Where he was the older baron."

"Is that the one where she wore the hat?"

"Nobody in the world," said Mrs. Unterberg, "looks like that woman in a hat. Put Eve Frame in a snug little beret, in a small floral dinner hat, in a crocheted straw baby doll, in a veiled big black cartwheel—put her in *anything*, put her in a Tyrolean brown felt with a feather, put her in a white jersey turban, put her in a fur-lined parka *hood*, and the woman is gorgeous, regardless."

"In one picture she wore—I'll never forget it," said Mrs. Svirsky, "—a gold-embroidered white evening suit with a white ermine muff. I never saw such elegance in my life. There was a play—which was it? We went to see it together, girls. She wore a burgundy wool dress, full at the bodice and the skirt, and the most enchanting scrollwork embroidery—"

"Yes! And that matching veiled hat. Tall burgundy felt," said Mrs. Unterberg, "with a crushed veil."

"Remember her in ruffles in whatever that other play was?" said Mrs. Svirsky. "No one wears ruffles the way she does. White *double* ruffles on a black cocktail dress!"

"But the name *Sylphid*," asked Mrs. Schessel yet again. "Sylphid comes from *what*?"

"Nathan knows. Ask Nathan," Mrs. Svirsky said. "Is Nathan here?"

"He's doing his homework," my mother said.

"Ask him. What kind of name is Sylphid?"

"I'll ask him later," said my mother.

But she knew enough not to—even though secretly, ever since I had entered the enchanted circle, I was bursting to talk about all of it to everyone. What do they wear? What do they eat? What do they say *while* they eat? What is it *like* there? It is spectacular.

The Tuesday that I first met Ira, out in front of Mr. Ringold's house, was Tuesday, October 12, 1948. Had the World Series not just ended on Monday, I might, timorously, out of deference to my teacher's privacy, have speeded on by the house where he was taking down the screens with his brother and, without even waving or shouting hello, turned left at the corner onto Osborne Terrace. As it happened, however, the day before I had listened to the Indians beat the old Boston Braves in the final game of the Series from the floor of Mr. Ringold's office. He had brought a radio with him that morning, and after school those whose families didn't yet own a television set —the vast majority of us—were invited to spill directly out of his eighth-period English class and down the hall to crowd into the English department chairman's little office to hear the game, which was already under way at Braves Field.

Courtesy, then, necessitated that I slow way, way down and call out to him, "Mr. Ringold—thanks for yesterday." Courtesy necessitated that I nod and smile at the giant in his yard. And—with a dry mouth, stiffly—stop and introduce myself. And respond a little daffily when he startled me by saying, "How ya' doin', buddy," by replying that on the afternoon he'd appeared at Auditorium, I'd been one of the boys who had booed Stephen A. Douglas when he announced into Lincoln's face, "I am opposed to negro citizenship in any and every form. [Boo.] I believe this government was made on a white basis. [Boo.] I believe it was made for white men [Boo], for the benefit of white men [Boo], and their posterity for ever. [Boo.] I am in favor of confining citizenship to white men . . . instead of conferring it upon Negroes, Indians, and other inferior races. [Boo. Boo. Boo.]"

Something rooted deeper than mere courtesy (ambition, the ambition to be admired for my moral conviction) prompted me to break through the shyness and tell him, tell the trinity of Iras, all three of him—the patriot martyr of the podium Abraham Lincoln, the natural, hardy American of the airwaves Iron Rinn, and the redeemed roughneck from Newark's First Ward Ira Ringold—that it was I who had instigated the booing.

Mr. Ringold came down the stairs from the second-floor flat, sweating heavily, wearing just khaki trousers and a pair of moccasins. Right behind him came Mrs. Ringold, who, before retreating back upstairs, set out a tray with a pitcher of ice water and three glasses. And so it was—four-thirty P.M., October 12, 1948, a blazing hot autumn day and the most astonishing afternoon of my young life—that I tipped my bike onto its side and sat on the steps of my English teacher's stoop with Eve Frame's husband, Iron Rinn of *The Free and the Brave*, discussing a World Series in which Bob Feller had lost two games—unbelievable—and Larry Doby, the pioneering black player in the American League, whom we all admired, but not the way we admired Jackie Robinson, had gone seven for twenty-two.

Then we were talking about boxing: Louis knocking out Jersey Joe Walcott when Walcott was way ahead on points; Tony Zale regaining the middleweight title from Rocky Graziano right in Newark, at Ruppert Stadium in June, crushing him with a left in the third round, and then losing it to a Frenchman, Marcel Cerdan, over in Jersey City a couple of weeks back, in September . . . And then from talking to me about Tony Zale one minute, Iron Rinn was talking to me about Winston Churchill the next, about a speech that Churchill had made a few days earlier that had him boiling, a speech advising the United States not to destroy its atomic bomb reserve because the atomic bomb was all that prevented the Communists from dominating the world. He talked about Winston Churchill the way he talked about Leo Durocher and Marcel Cerdan. He called Churchill a reactionary bastard and a warmonger with no more hesitation than he called Durocher a loudmouth and Cerdan a bum. He talked about Churchill as though Churchill ran the gas station out on Lyons Avenue. It wasn't how we talked about Winston Churchill in my house. It was closer to how we talked about Hitler. In his conversation, as in his brother's, there was no invisible line of propriety observed and there were no conventional taboos. You could stir together anything and everything: sports, politics, history, literature, reckless opinionating, polemical quotation, idealistic sentiment, moral rectitude . . . There was something marvelously bracing about it, a different and dangerous world, demanding, straightforward, aggressive, freed from the need to please. And freed from school. Iron Rinn wasn't just a radio star. He was some-

body outside the classroom who was not afraid to say anything.

I had just finished reading about somebody else who wasn't
afraid to say anything—Thomas Paine—and the book I'd read,
a historical novel by Howard Fast called *Citizen Tom Paine*,
was one of the collection in my bicycle basket that I was returning to the library. While Ira was denouncing Churchill to
me, Mr. Ringold had stepped over to where the books had
tumbled from the basket onto the pavement at the foot of the
stoop and was looking at their spines to see what I was reading.
Half the books were about baseball and were by John R. Tunis,
and the other half were about American history and were by
Howard Fast. My idealism (and my idea of a man) was being
constructed along parallel lines, one fed by novels about baseball champions who won their games the hard way, suffering
adversity and humiliation and many defeats as they struggled
toward victory, and the other by novels about heroic Americans who fought against tyranny and injustice, champions of
liberty for America and for all mankind. Heroic suffering. That
was my specialty.

Citizen Tom Paine was not so much a novel plotted in the
familiar manner as a sustained linking of highly charged rhetorical flourishes tracing the contradictions of an unsavory man
with a smoldering intellect and the purest social ideals, a writer
and a revolutionary. "He was the most hated—and perhaps by
a few the most loved—man in all the world." "A mind that
burned itself as few minds in all human history." "To feel on
his own soul the whip laid on the back of millions." "His
thoughts and ideas were closer to those of the average working
man than Jefferson's could ever be." That was Paine as Fast
portrayed him, savagely single-minded and unsociable, an epic,
folkloric belligerent—unkempt, dirty, wearing a beggar's clothes,
bearing a musket in the unruly streets of wartime Philadelphia,
a bitter, caustic man, often drunk, frequenting brothels, hunted
by assassins, and friendless. He did it all alone: "My only friend
is the revolution." By the time I had finished the book, there
seemed to me no way other than Paine's for a man to live and
die if he was intent on demanding, in behalf of human freedom
—demanding both from remote rulers and from the coarse
mob—the transformation of society.

He did it all alone. There was nothing about Paine that could have been more appealing, however unsentimentally Fast depicted an isolation born of defiant independence and personal misery. For Paine had ended his days alone as well, old, sick, wretched, and alone, ostracized, betrayed—despised beyond everything for having written in his last testament, *The Age of Reason*, "I do not believe in the creed professed by the Jewish church, by the Roman church, by the Greek church, by the Turkish church, by the Protestant church, nor by any church that I know of. My own mind is my own church." Reading about him had made me feel bold and angry and, above all, free to fight for what I believed in.

Citizen Tom Paine was the very book that Mr. Ringold had picked out of my bicycle basket to bring back to where we were sitting.

"You know this one?" he asked his brother.

Iron Rinn took my library book in Abe Lincoln's enormous hands and began flipping through the opening pages. "Nope. Never read Fast," he said. "I should. Wonderful man. Guts. He was with Wallace from day one. I catch his column whenever I see the *Worker*, but I don't have the time for novels anymore. In Iran I did, in the service read Steinbeck, Upton Sinclair, Jack London, Caldwell . . ."

"If you're going to read him, this is Fast at his best," Mr. Ringold said. "Am I right, Nathan?"

"This book is great," I answered.

"You ever read *Common Sense*?" Iron Rinn asked me. "Ever read Paine's writings?"

"No," I said.

"Read 'em," Iron Rinn told me while still leafing through my book.

"There's a lot of Paine's writing quoted by Howard Fast," I said.

Looking up, Iron Rinn said, " 'The strength of the many is revolution, but curiously enough mankind has gone through several thousand years of slavery without realizing that fact.' "

"That's in the book," I said.

"I should hope so."

"You know what the genius of Paine was?" Mr. Ringold

asked me. "It was the genius of all those men. Jefferson. Madison. Know what it was?"

"No," I said.

"You do know what it was," he said.

"To defy the English."

"A lot of people did that. No. It was to articulate the cause *in* English. The revolution was totally improvised, totally disorganized. Isn't that the sense you get from this book, Nathan? Well, these guys had to find a language for their revolution. To find the words for a great purpose."

"Paine said," I told Mr. Ringold, "'I wrote a little book because I wanted men to see what they were shooting at.'"

"And that he did," Mr. Ringold said.

"Here," said Iron Rinn, pointing to some lines in the book. "On George III. Listen. 'I should suffer the misery of devils, were I to make a whore of my soul by swearing allegiance to one whose character is that of a sottish, stupid, stubborn, worthless, brutish man.'"

Both quotations from Paine that Iron Rinn had recited—employing his *The Free and the Brave* people-bound, in-the-rough voice—were among the dozen or so that I had myself written down and memorized.

"You like that line," Mr. Ringold said to me.

"Yes. I like 'a whore of my soul.'"

"Why?" he asked me.

I was beginning to perspire profusely from the sun on my face, from the excitement of meeting Iron Rinn, and now from being on the spot, having to answer Mr. Ringold as though I were in class while I was sitting between two shirtless brothers well over six feet tall, two big, natural men exuding the sort of forceful, intelligent manliness to which I aspired. Men who could talk about baseball and boxing talking about books. And talking about books as though something were at stake in a book. Not opening up a book to worship it or to be elevated by it or to lose yourself to the world around you. No, *boxing* with the book.

"Because," I said, "you don't ordinarily think of your soul as a whore."

"What's he *mean*, 'a whore of my soul'?"

"Selling it," I replied. "Selling his soul."

"Right. Do you see how much stronger it is to write 'I should suffer the misery of devils, were I to make a *whore* of my soul' rather than 'were I to *sell* my soul'?"

"Yes, I do."

"Why is that stronger?"

"Because in 'whore' he personifies it."

"Yeah—what else?"

"Well, the word 'whore' . . . it's not a conventional word, you don't hear it in public. People don't go around writing 'whore' or, in public, saying 'whore.'"

"Why don't they?"

"Shame. Embarrassment. Propriety."

"Propriety. Good. Right. So this is audacious, then."

"Yes."

"And *that's* what you like about Paine, isn't it? His audacity?"

"I think so. Yes."

"And now you know *why* you like what you like. You're way ahead of the game, Nathan. And you know it because you looked at one word he used, just one word, and you thought about that word he used, and you asked yourself some questions about that word he used, until you saw right through that word, saw through it as through a magnifying glass, to one of the sources of this great writer's power. He is audacious. Thomas Paine is audacious. But is that enough? That is only a part of the formula. Audacity must have a purpose, otherwise it's cheap and facile and vulgar. Why is Thomas Paine audacious?"

"In behalf," I said, "of his convictions."

"Hey, that's my boy," Iron Rinn suddenly announced. "That's my boy who booed Mr. Douglas!"

So it was that I wound up five nights later as Iron Rinn's backstage guest at a rally held in downtown Newark, at the Mosque, the city's biggest theater, for Henry Wallace, the presidential candidate of the newly formed Progressive Party. Wallace had been in Roosevelt's cabinet as secretary of agriculture for seven years before becoming his vice president during Roosevelt's third term. In '44 he'd been dropped from the ticket and replaced by Truman, in whose cabinet he served briefly as secretary of commerce. In '46, the president fired Wallace for sounding off in favor of cooperation with Stalin and friendship with the Soviet Union at just the point when the Soviet Union had begun to be perceived by Truman and the Democrats not only as an ideological enemy but as a serious threat to peace whose expansion into Europe and elsewhere had to be contained by the West.

This division within the Democratic Party—between the anti-Soviet majority led by the president and the "progressive" Soviet sympathizers led by Wallace and opposed to the Truman Doctrine and the Marshall Plan—was reflected in the split within my own household between father and son. My father, who had admired Wallace when he was FDR's protégé, was against the Wallace candidacy for the reason Americans traditionally choose not to support third-party candidates—in this case, because it would draw the votes of the left wing of the Democratic Party away from Truman and make all but certain the election of Governor Thomas E. Dewey of New York, the Republican candidate. The Wallace people were talking about their party polling some six or seven million votes, a percentage of the popular vote vastly greater than had ever gone to any American third party.

"Your man is only going to deny the Democrats the White House," my father told me. "And if we get the Republicans, that will mean the suffering in this country that it has always meant. You weren't around for Hoover and Harding and Coolidge. You don't know firsthand about the heartlessness of the Republican Party. You despise big business, Nathan? You despise what you and Henry Wallace call 'the Big Boys from Wall Street'? Well, you don't know what it is when the party of big business has its foot in the face of ordinary people. I do. I know poverty and I know hardship in ways you and your brother have been spared, thank God."

My father had been born in the Newark slums and become a chiropodist only by going to school at night while working by day on a bakery truck; and all his life, even after he had made a few bucks and we had moved into a house of our own, he continued to identify with the interests of what he called ordinary people and what I had taken to calling—along with Henry Wallace—"the common man." I was terrifically disappointed to hear my father flatly refuse to vote for the candidate who, as I tried to convince him, supported his own New Deal principles. Wallace wanted a national health program, protection for unions, benefits for workers; he was opposed to Taft-Hartley and the persecution of labor; he was opposed to the Mundt-Nixon bill and the persecution of political radicals. The Mundt-Nixon bill, if passed, would require the registration with the government of all Communists and "Communist-front" organizations. Wallace had said that Mundt-Nixon was the first step to a police state, an effort to frighten the American people into silence; he called it "the most subversive" bill ever introduced in Congress. The Progressive Party supported the freedom of ideas to compete in what Wallace called "the marketplace of thoughts." Most impressive to me was that, campaigning in the South, Wallace had refused to address any audience that was segregated —the first presidential candidate ever to have that degree of courage and integrity.

"The Democrats," I told my father, "will never do anything to end segregation. They will never outlaw lynching and the poll tax and Jim Crow. They never have and they never will."

"I do not agree with you, Nathan," he told me. "You watch Harry Truman. Harry Truman has got a civil rights plank in his platform, and you watch and see what he does now that he's rid of those southern bigots."

Not only had Wallace bolted from the Democratic Party that year, but so had the "bigots" my father spoke of, the southern Democrats, who had formed their own party, the States' Rights Party—the "Dixiecrats." They were running for president Governor Strom Thurmond of South Carolina, a rabid segregationist. The Dixiecrats were also going to draw away votes, southern votes, that routinely went to the Democratic Party, which was another reason Dewey was favored to defeat Truman in a landslide.

Every night over dinner in the kitchen, I did everything I could to persuade my father to vote for Henry Wallace and the restoration of the New Deal, and every night he tried to get me to understand the necessity for compromise in an election like this one. But as I had taken as my hero Thomas Paine, the most uncompromising patriot in American history, at the mere sound of the first *syllable* of the word "compromise," I jumped up from my chair and told him and my mother and my ten-year-old brother (who, whenever I got going, liked to repeat to me, in an exaggeratedly exasperated voice, "A vote for Wallace is a vote for *Dewey*") that I could never again eat at that table if my father was present.

One night at dinner my father tried another tack—to educate me further about the Republicans' contempt for every value of economic equality and political justice that I held dear—but I would have none of it: the two major political parties were equally without conscience when it came to the Negro's rights, equally indifferent to the injustices inherent to the capitalist system, equally blind to the catastrophic consequences for all of mankind of our country's deliberate provocation of the peace-loving Russian people. Close to tears, and meaning every word, I told my father, "I'm really surprised at you," as though it were he who was the uncompromising son.

But a greater surprise was coming. Late on Saturday afternoon he told me that he would rather I didn't go down to the Mosque that evening to attend the Wallace rally. If I still wanted to after we had spoken, he wouldn't try to stop me, but he at least wanted me to hear him out before I made my decision final. When I'd come home on Tuesday from the library and triumphantly announced at dinner that I had been invited to be a guest of Iron Rinn, the radio actor, at the Wallace rally downtown, I was obviously so thrilled at meeting Rinn, so beside myself with the personal interest he'd shown in me, that my mother had simply forbidden my father from raising his reservations about the rally. But now he wanted me to listen to what he felt he had a duty, as a parent, to discuss, and without my flying off the handle.

My father was taking me as seriously as the Ringolds were, but not with Ira's political fearlessness, with Murray's literary ingenuity, above all, with their seeming absence of concern for my decorum, for whether I would or would not be a good boy. The Ringolds were the one-two punch promising to initiate me into the big show, into my beginning to understand what it takes to be a man on the larger scale. The Ringolds compelled me to respond at a level of rigor that felt appropriate to who I now was. Be a good boy wasn't the issue with them. The sole issue was my convictions. But then, their responsibility wasn't a father's, which is to steer his son away from the pitfalls.

The father has to worry about the pitfalls in a way the teacher doesn't. He has to worry about his son's conduct, he has to worry about socializing his little Tom Paine. But once little Tom Paine has been let into the company of men and the father is still educating him as a boy, the father is finished. Sure, he's worrying about the pitfalls—if he wasn't, it would be wrong. But he's finished anyway. Little Tom Paine has no choice but to write him off, to betray the father and go boldly forth to step straight into life's very first pit. And then, all on his own —providing real unity to his existence—to step from pit to pit for the rest of his days, until the grave, which, if it has nothing else to recommend it, is at least the last pit into which one can fall.

"Hear me out," my father said, "and then you make up your own mind. I respect your independence, son. You want to wear a Wallace button to school? Wear it. It's a free country. But you have to have all the facts. You can't make an informed decision without facts."

Why had Mrs. Roosevelt, the great president's revered widow, withheld her endorsement and turned against Henry Wallace? Why had Harold Ickes, Roosevelt's trusted and loyal secretary of interior, a great man in his own right, withheld his endorsement and turned against Henry Wallace? Why had the CIO, as ambitious a labor organization as this country had ever known, withdrawn its money and its support from Henry Wallace? Because of the Communist infiltration into the Wallace campaign. My father didn't want me to go to the rally because of the Communists who had all but taken over the Progressive Party. He told me that Henry Wallace was either too naive to know it or—what was, unfortunately, probably closer to the truth—too dishonest to admit it, but Communists, particularly from among Communist-dominated unions already expelled from the CIO—

"Red-baiter!" I shouted, and I left the house. I took the 14 bus and went to the rally. I met Paul Robeson. He reached out to shake my hand after Ira introduced me as the kid at the high school he'd told him about. "Here he is, Paul, the boy who led the booing of Stephen A. Douglas." Paul Robeson, the Negro actor and singer, cochairman of the Wallace for President

Committee, who only a few months earlier at a Washington demonstration against the Mundt-Nixon bill had sung "Ol' Man River" to a crowd of five thousand protesters at the foot of the Washington Monument, who'd been fearless before the Senate Judiciary Committee, telling them (when asked at their hearings on Mundt-Nixon if he would comply with the bill if it was passed), "I would violate the law," then answering no less forthrightly (when asked what the Communist Party stood for), "For complete equality of the Negro people"—Paul Robeson took my hand in his and said, "Don't lose your courage, young man."

Standing backstage with the performers and speakers at the Mosque—enveloped simultaneously in two exotic new worlds, the leftist milieu and the world of "the wings"—was as thrilling as it would have been to sit down in the dugout with the players at a major league game. From the wings I heard Ira do Abraham Lincoln again, this time tearing into not Stephen A. Douglas but the warmongers in both political parties: "Supporting reactionary regimes all over the world, arming Western Europe against Russia, militarizing America . . ." I saw Henry Wallace himself, stood no more than twenty feet away from him before he went onto the stage to address the crowd, and then stood almost at his side when Ira went up to whisper something to him at the gala reception after the rally. I stared at the presidential candidate, a Republican farmer's son from Iowa as American-looking and American-sounding as any American I had ever seen, a politician against high prices, against big business, against segregation and discrimination, against appeasing dictators like Francisco Franco and Chiang Kai-shek, and I remembered what Fast had written of Paine: "His thoughts and ideas were closer to those of the average working man than Jefferson's could ever be." And in 1954—six years after that night at the Mosque when the candidate of the common man, the candidate of the people and the people's party, raised gooseflesh all over me by clenching his fist and crying out from the lectern, "We are in the midst of a fierce attack upon our freedom"—I got turned down for a Fulbright scholarship.

I did not and could not have made a scrap of difference, and yet the zealotry to defeat Communism reached even me.

*

Iron Rinn had been born in Newark two decades before me, in 1913, a poor boy from a hard neighborhood—and from a cruel family—who briefly attended Barringer High, where he failed every subject but gym. He had bad eyesight and useless glasses and could barely read what was in the lesson books, let alone what the teacher wrote on the blackboard. He couldn't see and he couldn't learn and one day, as he explained it, "I just didn't wake up to go to school."

Murray and Ira's father was someone Ira refused even to discuss. In the months after the Wallace rally, the most Ira ever told me was this: "My father I couldn't talk to. He never paid the slightest bit of attention to his two sons. He didn't do this on purpose. It was the nature of the beast." Ira's mother, a beloved woman in his memory, died when he was seven, and her replacement he described as "the stepmother you hear about in the fairy tales. A real bitch." He quit high school after a year and a half and, a few weeks later, left the house forever at fifteen and found a job digging ditches in Newark. Till the war broke out, while the country was in the Depression, he drifted round and round, first in New Jersey and then all over America, taking whatever work he could get, mostly jobs requiring a strong back. Immediately after Pearl Harbor, he enlisted in the army. He couldn't see the eye chart, but a long line of guys were waiting for the examination, and so Ira went around up close to the chart, memorized as much of it as he could, then got back in line, and that was how he passed the physical. When Ira came out of the army in 1945, he spent a year in Calumet City, Illinois, where he shared a room with the closest buddy he'd made in the service, a Communist steelworker, Johnny O'Day. They'd been soldier stevedores together on the docks in Iran, unloading lend-lease equipment that was shipped by rail through Teheran to the Soviet Union; because of Ira's strength on the job, O'Day had nicknamed his friend "Iron Man Ira." In the evenings, O'Day had taught the Iron Man how to read a book and how to write a letter and gave him an education in Marxism.

O'Day was a gray-haired guy some ten years older than Ira —"How he ever got into the service at his age," Ira said, "I still don't know." A six-footer skinny as a telephone pole, but the toughest son of a bitch he'd ever met. O'Day carried in his gear a light punching bag that he used for his timing; so quick and strong was he that, "if forced to," he could lick two or three guys together. And O'Day was brilliant. "I knew nothing about politics. I knew nothing about political action," Ira said. "I didn't know one political philosophy or one social philosophy from another. But this guy talked a lot to me," he said. "He talked about the workingman. About things in general in the United States. The harm our government was doing to the workers. And he backed up what he said with facts. And a nonconformist? O'Day was so nonconformist that everything he did he did not do by the book. Yeah, O'Day did a lot for me, I know that."

Like Ira, O'Day was unmarried. "Entangling alliances," he told Ira, "is something I don't want any part of at no time. I regard kids as hostages to the malevolent." Though he had but a year's education more than Ira, on his own O'Day had "skilled himself," as he put it, "in verbal and written polemics" by slavishly copying passage after passage out of all sorts of books and, with the aid of a grade school grammar, analyzing the structure of the sentences. It was O'Day who gave Ira the pocket dictionary that Ira claimed remade his life. "I had a dictionary I read at night," Ira told me, "the way you would read a novel. I had somebody send me a *Roget's Thesaurus*. After unloading ships all day, I would work every night to improve my vocabulary."

He discovered reading. "One day—it must have been one of the worst mistakes the army ever made—they sent us a complete library. What an error," he said, laughing. "I probably read every book they had in that library eventually. They built a Quonset hut to house the books, and they made shelves, and they told the guys, 'You want a book, you come in here and get one.'" It was O'Day who told him—who still told him—which books to get.

Early on, Ira showed me three sheets of paper titled "Some Concrete Suggestions for Ringold's Utilization" that O'Day had prepared when they were in Iran together. "One: Always keep a dictionary at hand—a good one with plenty of antonyms and synonyms—even when you write a note to the milkman. And use it. Don't make wild passes at spelling and exact shades of meaning as you have been accustomed to doing. Two:

Double-space everything you write in order to permit interpolation of afterthoughts and corrections. I don't give a damn if it does violate good usage insofar as personal correspondence is involved; it makes for accurate expression. Three: Don't run your thoughts together in a solid page of typing. Every time you treat a new thought or elaborate what you're already talking about, indent for a new paragraph. It may add up to jerkiness, but it will be much more readable. Four: Avoid clichés. Even if you have to drag it in by the tail, express something you've read or heard quoted in other than the original words. One of your sentences from the other night at the library session in point of demonstration: 'I stated briefly some of the ills of the present regime . . .' You've read that, Iron Man, and it isn't yours; it's somebody else's. It sounds as if it came out of a can. Suppose you expressed the same idea something like this: 'I build my argument about the effect of landed proprietorship and the dominance of foreign capital on what I have witnessed here in Iran.'"

There were twenty points in all, and the reason Ira showed them to me was to assist with *my* writing—not with my high school radio plays but with my journal, intended to be "political" where I was beginning to put down my "thoughts" when I remembered to. I'd begun keeping my journal in imitation of Ira, who'd begun keeping his in imitation of Johnny O'Day. The three of us used the same brand of notebook: a dime pad from Woolworth's, fifty-two lined pages about four inches by three inches, stitched at the top and bound between mottled brown cardboard covers.

When an O'Day letter mentioned a book, any book, Ira got a copy and so did I; I'd go right to the library and take it out. "I've been reading Bowers's *Young Jefferson* recently," O'Day wrote, "along with other treatments of early American history, and the Committees of Correspondence in that period were the principal agency by which the revolutionary-minded colonists developed their understanding and coordinated their plans." That's how I came to read *Young Jefferson* while in high school. O'Day wrote, "A couple of weeks ago I bought the twelfth edition of *Bartlett's Quotations*, allegedly for my reference library, actually for the enjoyment I get from browsing," and so I went downtown to the main library, to sit among the reference books browsing in *Bartlett* the way I imagined O'Day did, my journal beside me, skimming each page for the wisdom that would expedite my maturing and make me somebody to reckon with. "I buy the *Cominform* (official organ published in Bucharest) regularly," O'Day wrote, but the *Cominform*—abbreviated name of the Communist Information Bureau—I knew I wouldn't find in any local library, and prudence cautioned me not to go looking.

My radio plays were in dialogue and susceptible less to O'Day's Concrete Suggestions than to conversations Ira had with O'Day that he repeated to me, or, rather, acted out word for word, as though he and O'Day were together there before my eyes. The radio plays were colored, too, by the workingman's argot that continued to crop up in Ira's speech long after he'd come to New York and become a radio actor, and their convictions were strongly influenced by those long letters O'Day was writing to Ira, which Ira often read aloud at my request.

My subject was the lot of the common man, the ordinary Joe—the man that the radio writer Norman Corwin had lauded as "the little guy" in *On a Note of Triumph*, a sixty-minute play that was transmitted over CBS radio the evening the war ended in Europe (and then again, at popular request, eight days later) and that buoyantly entangled me in those salvationist literary aspirations that endeavor to redress the world's wrongs through writing. I wouldn't care to judge today if something I loved as much as I loved *On a Note of Triumph* was or was not art; it provided me with my first sense of the conjuring *power* of art and helped strengthen my first ideas as to what I wanted and expected a literary artist's language to do: enshrine the struggles of the embattled. (And taught me, contrary to what my teachers insisted, that I could begin a sentence with "And.")

The form of the Corwin play was loose, plotless—"experimental," I informed my chiropodist father and homemaking mother. It was written in the high colloquial, alliterative style that may have derived in part from Clifford Odets and in part from Maxwell Anderson, from the effort by American playwrights of the twenties and thirties to forge a recognizable native idiom for the stage, naturalistic yet with lyrical coloration and serious undertones, a poeticized vernacular that, in Norman Corwin's case, combined the rhythms of ordinary speech with a faint literary stiltedness to make for a tone that struck me, at twelve, as democratic in spirit and heroic in scope, the verbal counterpart of a WPA mural. Whitman claimed America for the roughs, Norman Corwin claimed it for the little man—who turned out to be nothing less than the Americans who had fought the patriotic war and were coming back to an adoring nation. The little man was nothing less than Americans themselves! Corwin's "little guy" was American for "proletariat," and, as I now understand it, the revolution fought and won by America's working class was, in fact, World War II, the something large that we were all, however small, a part of, the revolution that confirmed the reality of the myth of a national character to be partaken of by all.

Including me. I was a Jewish child, no two ways about that, but I didn't care to partake of the Jewish character. I didn't even know, clearly, what it was. I didn't much want to. I wanted to partake of the national character. Nothing had seemed to come more naturally to my American-born parents, nothing came more naturally to me, and no method could have seemed to me any more profound than participating through the tongue that Norman Corwin spoke, a linguistic distillation of the excited feelings of community that the war had aroused, the high demotic poetry that was the liturgy of World War II.

History had been scaled down and personalized, America had been scaled down and personalized: for me, that was the enchantment not only of Norman Corwin but of the times. You flood into history and history floods into you. You flood into America and America floods into you. And all by virtue of being alive in New Jersey and twelve years old and sitting by the radio in 1945. Back when popular culture was sufficiently connected to the last century to be susceptible still to a little language, there was a swooning side to all of it for me.

It can at last be said without jinxing the campaign:
Somehow the decadent democracies, the bungling bolsheviks, the saps and softies,
Were tougher in the end than the brownshirt bully-boys, and smarter too:

For without whipping a priest, burning a book or slugging a Jew,
    without corraling a girl in a brothel, or bleeding a child for
    plasma,
Far-flung ordinary men, unspectacular but free, rousing out of
    their habits and their homes, got up early one morning, flexed
    their muscles, learned (as amateurs) the manual of arms, and
    set out across perilous plains and oceans to whop the beje-
    sus out of the professionals.
This they did.
For confirmation, see the last communiqué, bearing the mark
    of the Allied High Command.
Clip it out of the morning paper and hand it over to your chil-
    dren for safe keeping.

When *On a Note of Triumph* appeared in book form, I
bought a copy immediately (making it the first hardcover I'd
ever owned outright rather than borrowed on my library card),
and over several weeks I memorized the sixty-five pages of
free-verse-like paragraphs in which the text was arranged, rel-
ishing particularly the lines that took playful liberties with everyday street-corner English ("There's a hot time in the old town
of Dnepropetrovsky tonight") or that joined unlikely proper
nouns so as to produce what seemed to me to be surprising
and stirring ironies ("the mighty warrior lays down his Samurai
sword before a grocery clerk from Baltimore"). At the conclusion of a great war effort that had provided a splendid stimulus
for fundamental feelings of patriotism to grow strong in someone my age—almost nine when the war began and halfway to
thirteen when it came to a close—the mere citing, on the radio,
of American cities and states ("through the nippy night air of
New Hampshire," "from Egypt to the Oklahoma prairie town,"
"And the reasons for mourning in Denmark are the same as
they are in Ohio") had every ounce of the intended apotheo-
sizing effect.

So they've given up.
They're finally done in, and the rat is dead in an alley back of
    the Wilhelmstrasse.
Take a bow, G.I.,
Take a bow, little guy.
The superman of tomorrow lies at the feet of you common
    men of this afternoon.

This was the panegyric with which the play opened. (On the radio there'd been an unflinching voice not unlike Iron Rinn's assertively identifying our hero for the praise due him. It was the determined, compassionately gruff, slightly hectoring halftime voice of the high school coach—the coach who also teaches English—the voice of the common man's collective conscience.) And this was Corwin's coda, a prayer whose grounding in the present made it seem to me—already an affirmed atheist—wholly secular and unchurchy while at the same time mightier and more daring than any prayer I had ever heard recited in school at the beginning of the day or had read, translated in the prayer book at the synagogue, when I was alongside my father at High Holiday services.

> Lord God of trajectory and blast . . .
> Lord God of fresh bread and tranquil mornings . . .
> Lord God of the topcoat and the living wage . . .
> Measure out new liberties . . .
> Post proofs that brotherhood . . .
> Sit at the treaty table and convoy the hopes of little peoples
>   through expected straits . . .

Tens of millions of American families had sat beside their radios and, complex as this stuff was compared to what they were used to hearing, listened to what had aroused in me, and, I innocently assumed, in them, a stream of transforming, self-abandoning emotion such as I, for one, had never before experienced as a consequence of anything coming out of a radio. The power of that broadcast! There, amazingly, was *soul* coming out of a radio. The Spirit of the Common Man had inspired an immense mélange of populist adoration, an effusion of words bubbling straight up from the American heart into the American mouth, an hour-long homage to the paradoxical superiority of what Corwin insisted on identifying as absolutely ordinary American mankind: "far-flung ordinary men, unspectacular but free."

Corwin modernized Tom Paine for me by democratizing the risk, making it a question not of one just wild man but a collective of all the little just men pulling together. Worthiness and the people were one. *Greatness* and the people were one. A thrilling idea. And how Corwin labored to force it, at least imaginatively, to come true.

After the war, for the first time, Ira consciously entered the class struggle. He'd been up to his neck in it his entire life, he told me, without any idea what was going on. Out in Chicago, he worked for forty-five dollars a week in a record factory that the United Electrical Workers had organized under a contract so solid they even had union hiring. O'Day meanwhile returned to his job on a rigging gang at Inland Steel in Indiana Harbor. Time and again O'Day dreamed about quitting and, at night in their room, would pour his frustration out to Ira. "If I could have full time for six months and no handcuffs, the party could really be built here in the harbor. There's plenty of good people, but what's needed is a guy who can spend *all* his time at organizing. I ain't that good at organizing, that is true. You have to be something of a hand holder with timid Bolsheviks, and I lean more to bopping their heads. And what's the difference anyway? The party here is too broke to support a full-timer. Every dime that can be scraped up is going for defense of our leadership, and for the press, and a dozen other things that won't wait. I was broke after my last check, but I got by on jaw-bone for a while. But taxes, the damn car, one thing and another . . . Iron Man, I can't handle it—I *have* to go to work."

I loved when Ira repeated the lingo that rough union guys used among themselves, even guys like Johnny O'Day, whose sentence structure wasn't quite so simple as the average workingman's but who knew the power of their diction and who, despite the potentially corrupting influence of the thesaurus, wielded it effectively all his life. "I have to take it on the slow bell for a while . . . All this with management poising the ax . . . As soon as we pull the pin . . . As soon as the boys hit the bricks . . . If they move to force the acceptance of their yellow-dog contract, it looks like blood on the bricks. . . ."

I loved when Ira explained the workings of his own union, the UE, and described the people at the record factory where he'd worked. "It was a solid union, progressively led, controlled by the rank and file." *Rank and file*—three little words that thrilled me, as did the idea of hard work, tenacious courage, and a just cause to fuse the two. "Of the hundred and fifty members on each shift, a hundred or so attended the biweekly shop meetings. Although most of the work is hourly paid," Ira told me, "there's no whip swinging at that factory. Y'understand? If a boss has something to tell you, he's courteous about it. Even for serious offenses, the offender's called into the office together with his steward. That makes a big difference."

Ira would tell me all that transpired at an ordinary union meeting—"routine business like proposals for a new contract, the problem of absenteeism, a parking-lot beef, discussion of the looming war" (he meant war between the Soviet Union and the United States), "racism, the wages-causes-prices myth" —going on and on not just because I was, at fifteen and sixteen, eager to learn all that a workingman did, how he talked and acted and thought, but because even after he cleared out of Calumet City to go to New York to work in radio and was solidly established as Iron Rinn on *The Free and the Brave*, Ira continued to speak of the record plant and the union meetings in the charismatic tongue of his fellow workers, talked as though he still went off to work there every morning. Every night, rather, for after a short while he had got himself put on the night shift so that he could have his days for "missionary work," by which, I eventually learned, he meant proselytizing for the Communist Party.

O'Day had recruited Ira into the party when they were on the docks in Iran. Just as I, anything but orphaned, was the perfect target for Ira's tutorials, the orphaned Ira was the perfect target for O'Day's.

It was for his union's Washington-Lincoln birthday fund-raiser his first February out in Chicago that somebody got the idea to turn Ira, a wiry man, knobbily jointed, with dark, coarse Indian-like hair and a floppy, big-footed gait, into Abe Lincoln: put whiskers on him, decked him out in a stovepipe hat, high button shoes, and an old-fashioned, ill-fitting black suit, and sent him up to the lectern to read from the Lincoln-Douglas debates one of Lincoln's most telling condemnations of slavery. He got such a big hand for giving to the word "slavery" a strong working-class, political slant—and enjoyed himself so much doing it—that he continued right on with the only thing he remembered by heart from his nine and a half years of schooling, the Gettysburg Address. He brought the house down with the finale, that sentence as gloriously resolute as any sounded in heaven or uttered on earth since the world began. Raising and wiggling one of those huge hairy-knuckled, superflexible hands of his, plunging the longest of his inordinately long fingers right into the eyeball of his union audience each of the three times, he dramatically dropped his voice and rasped "the people."

"Everybody thought I got carried away by emotion," Ira told me. "That that's what fired me up. But it wasn't emotions. It was the first time I ever felt carried away by *intellect*. I understood for the first time in my life what the hell I was talking about. I understood what this country is all about."

After that night, on his weekends, on holidays, he traveled the Chicago area for the CIO, as far as Galesburg and Springfield, out to authentic Lincoln country, portraying Abraham Lincoln for CIO conventions, cultural programs, parades, and picnics. He went on the UE radio show, where, even if nobody could see him standing two inches taller even than Lincoln, he did a bang-up job bringing Lincoln to the masses by speaking every word so that it made good plain sense. People began to take their kids along when Ira Ringold was to appear on the platform, and afterward, when whole families came up to shake his hand, the kids would ask to sit on his knee and tell him what they wanted for Christmas. Not so strangely, the unions he performed for were by and large locals that either broke with the CIO or were expelled when CIO president Philip Murray began in 1947 to rid member unions of Communist leadership and Communist membership.

But by '48 Ira was a rising radio star in New York, newly married to one of the country's most revered radio actresses and, for the moment, safely protected from the crusade that would annihilate forever, and not only from the labor movement, a pro-Soviet, pro-Stalin political presence in America.

How did he get from the record factory to a network drama show? Why did he leave Chicago and O'Day in the first place? It could never have occurred to me at that time that it had anything to do with the Communist Party, mainly because I never knew back then that he was a member of the Communist Party.

What I understood was that the radio writer Arthur Sokolow, visiting Chicago, happened to catch Ira's Lincoln act in a union hall on the West Side one night. Ira had already met Sokolow in the army. He'd come to Iran, as a GI, with the *This Is the Army* show. A lot of left-wing guys were touring with the show, and late one evening Ira had gone off with a few of them for a bull session during which, as Ira remembered it, they'd discussed "all the political stuff in the world." Among the group was Sokolow, whom Ira came quickly to admire as someone who was always battling for a cause. Because Sokolow had begun life, in Detroit, as a Jewish street kid fighting off the Poles, he was also completely recognizable, and Ira felt at once a kinship he'd never wholly had with the rootless Irishman O'Day.

By the time Sokolow, now a civilian writing *The Free and the Brave*, happened to turn up in Chicago, Ira was onstage for a full hour as Lincoln, not only reciting or reading from speeches and documents but responding to audience questions about current political controversies in the guise of Abraham Lincoln, with Lincoln's high-pitched country twang and his awkward giant's gestures and his droll, plainspoken way. Lincoln supporting price controls. Lincoln condemning the Smith Act. Lincoln defending workers' rights. Lincoln vilifying Mississippi's Senator Bilbo. The union membership loved their stalwart autodidact's irresistible ventriloquism, his mishmash of Ringoldisms, O'Dayisms, Marxisms, and Lincolnisms ("Pour it on!" they shouted at bearded, black-haired Ira. "Give 'em hell, Abe!"), and so did Sokolow, who brought Ira to the attention of another Jewish ex-GI, a New York soap opera producer with left-leaning sympathies. It was the introduction to the producer that led to the audition that landed Ira the part of the scrappy super of a Brooklyn tenement on one of daytime radio's soap operas.

The salary was fifty-five dollars a week. Not much, even in 1948, but steady work and more money than he made at the record plant. And, almost immediately, he began doing other jobs as well, getting jobs everywhere, jumping into waiting taxis and rushing from studio to studio, from one daytime show to another, as many as six different shows a day, always playing characters with working-class roots, tough-talking guys truncated from their politics, as he explained it to me, in order to make their anger permissible: "the proletariat Americanized for the radio by cutting off their balls and their brains." It was all this work that propelled him, within months, onto Sokolow's prestigious weekly hour-long show, *The Free and the Brave*, as a leading player.

Out in the Midwest, there had begun to be physical difficulties for Ira to cope with, and these, too, furnished a motive for him to try his luck back east in a new line of work. He was plagued by muscle pain, soreness so bad that several times a week—when he didn't have to just endure the pain and go off to play Lincoln or do his missionary work—he'd head right home, soak for half an hour in a tub of steaming water down the hall from his room, and then get into bed with a book, his dictionary, his notepad, and whatever was around to eat. A couple of bad beatings he'd taken in the army seemed to him the cause of this problem. From the worst of the beatings—he'd been pounced on by a gang from the port who had him down for a "nigger lover"—he'd wound up in the hospital for three days.

They'd begun baiting him when he started to pal around with a couple of Negro soldiers from the segregated unit stationed at the riverfront three miles away. O'Day was by then running a group that met at the Quonset hut library and under his tutelage discussed politics and books. Barely anybody on the base paid attention to the library or to the nine or ten GIs who drifted over there after chow a couple of nights a week to talk about *Looking Backward* by Bellamy or *The Republic* by Plato or *The Prince* by Machiavelli, until the two Negroes from the segregated unit joined the group.

At first Ira tried to reason with the men in his outfit who called him nigger lover. "Why do you make derogatory remarks about colored people? All I hear from you guys about the Negro is derogatory remarks. And you aren't only anti-Negro. You're anti-labor, you're anti-liberal, and you're anti-brains. You're anti every goddamn thing that's in your interest. How can people give their three or four years to the army, see friends die, get wounded, have their lives disrupted, and yet not know why it happened and what it's all about? All you know is that Hitler started something. All you know is that the draft board got you. You know what I say? You guys would duplicate the very actions of the Germans if you were in their place. It might take a little longer because of the democratic element in our society, but eventually we would be completely fascist, dictator and all, because of people spouting the shit you guys spout. The discrimination of the top officers who run this port is bad enough, but *you* people, from poor families, guys without two nickels to rub together, guys who are nothing but fodder for the assembly line, for the sweatshop, for the coal mines, who the system *pisses* on—low wages, high prices, astronomical profits—and you turn out to be a bunch of vociferous, bigoted Red-baiting bastards who don't know . . ." Then he'd tell them all they didn't know.

Heated discussions that changed nothing, that, because of his temper, Ira admitted, made things only worse. "I would lose a good deal of what I wanted to impress them with because in the beginning I was too emotional. Later I learned how to cool down with these kind of people, and I believe that I impressed a few of them with some facts. But it is very difficult to talk to such men because of the deeply ingrained ideas they have. To explain to them the psychological reasons for segregation, the economic reasons for segregation, the psychological reasons for the use of their beloved word 'nigger'—they are beyond grasping such things They say nigger because a nigger *is* a nigger—I'd explain and explain to them, and that's what they'd answer me. I pounded home about education of children and our personal responsibility, and still, for all my goddamn explaining, they beat the shit out of me so bad I thought I was going to die."

His reputation as a nigger lover turned truly dangerous for Ira when he wrote a letter to *Stars and Stripes* complaining about the segregated units in the army and demanding integration. "That's when I used my dictionary and *Roget's Thesaurus*. I would devour those two books and try to put 'em to practical use by writing. Writing a letter for me was like building a scaffold. Probably I would have been criticized by somebody who knew the English language. My grammar was God knows what. But I wrote it anyway because this is what I felt I should do. I was so goddamn angry, see? Y'understand? I wanted to tell people that this was *wrong*."

After the letter was published, he was working one day up in the loading basket, above the hold of the ship, when the guys operating the basket threatened to drop him into the hold unless he shut up worrying about niggers. Repeatedly they dropped him ten, fifteen, twenty feet, promising next time to let go and break every bone in his body, but, scared as he was, he wouldn't say what they wanted to hear, and in the end they let him out. Then the following morning someone in the mess hall called him a Jew bastard. A nigger-loving Jew bastard. "A southern hillbilly with a big mouth," Ira told me. "Always made remarks in the mess hall about Jews, about Negroes. This one morning I'm sitting there near the end of the meal—there weren't that many guys left in the place—and he started to yap off about niggers and Jews. I'm still boiling from the incident the day before on the ship, and so I couldn't take it anymore, and I took off my glasses and I gave 'em to a guy I was sitting with, the only guy who'd still sit with me. By then I'd walk in the mess hall, two hundred guys sitting there, and because of my politics I'd be totally ostracized. Anyway, I went at that son of a bitch. He was a private and I was a sergeant. From one end of that mess hall to the other I kicked the shit out of him. Then the first sergeant comes up to me and says, 'You want to press charges against this guy? A private attacking a noncommissioned officer?' I quickly said to myself, I'll probably be damned if I do and damned if I don't. Right? But from that moment on, nobody ever made an anti-Semitic remark when I was in the vicinity. That didn't mean they'd ever let up about niggers. Niggers this and niggers that, a hundred times a day. This hillbilly tried again with me that same night. We were washing off our mess kits. You know the stinking little knives they have there? He came at me with that knife. Again I had him, I put him away, but I didn't do anything more about it."

Hours later Ira got ambushed in the dark and wound up in the hospital. As best he could diagnose the pains that began to develop while he was working at the record factory, they were from the damage caused by that savage beating. Now he was always pulling a muscle or spraining a joint—his ankle, his wrist, his knee, his neck—and as often as not from doing virtually nothing, no more than stepping off the bus coming home or reaching across the counter for the sugar bowl in the diner where he went to eat.

And this is why, however unlikely it seemed that anything would materialize from it, when something was said about a radio audition, Ira leaped at the chance.

Maybe there were more machinations than I knew of behind Ira's move to New York and his overnight radio triumph, but I didn't think so back then. I didn't have to. Here was the guy to take my education beyond Norman Corwin, to tell me, for one thing, about the GIs that Corwin didn't talk about, GIs not so nice or, for that matter, so antifascist as the heroes of *On a Note of Triumph*, the GIs who went overseas thinking about niggers and kikes and who came home thinking about niggers and kikes. Here was an impassioned man, someone rough and scarred by experience, bringing with him firsthand evidence of all the brutish American stuff that Corwin left out. It didn't require Communist connections to explain Ira's overnight radio triumph to me. I just thought, This guy is wonderful. He *is* an iron man.

2

THAT night in '48 at the Henry Wallace rally in Newark, I'd also met Eve Frame. She was with Ira and with her daughter, Sylphid, the harpist. I saw nothing of what Sylphid felt for her mother, didn't know about their struggle until Murray began to tell me of all that had passed me by as a kid, everything about Ira's marriage that I didn't or couldn't understand or that Ira had kept from me during those two years when I got to see him every couple of months, either when he came to visit Murray or when I visited him at the cabin—which Ira called his "shack"—in the hamlet of Zinc Town, in northwest New Jersey.

Ira retreated to Zinc Town to live not so much close to nature as close to the bone, to live life in the raw, swimming in the mud pond right into November, tramping the woods on snowshoes in coldest winter, or, on rainy days, meandering around in his Jersey car—a used '39 Chevy coupe—talking to the local dairy farmers and the old zinc miners, whom he tried to get to understand how they were being screwed by the system. He had a fireplace out there where he liked to cook his hot dogs and beans over the coals, even to brew his coffee, all so as to remind himself, after he'd become Iron Rinn and a bit enlarded with money and fame, that he was still nothing more than a "working stiff," a simple man with simple tastes and expectations who during the thirties had ridden the rails and who had got incredibly lucky. About owning the Zinc Town shack, he used to say, "Keeps me in practice being poor. Just in case."

The shack furnished an antidote to West Eleventh Street and an asylum from West Eleventh Street, the place where you go to sweat out the bad vapors. It was also a link to the earliest vagabond days, when he was surviving among strangers for the first time and every day was hard and uncertain and, as it would always be for Ira, a battle. After leaving home at fifteen and digging ditches for a year in Newark, Ira had taken jobs in the northwesternmost corner of Jersey, sweeping up in various factories, working sometimes as a farmhand, as a watchman, as a handyman, and then, for two and a half years, until he was nearly nineteen and headed west, sucking air in shafts twelve hundred feet down in the Sussex zinc mines. After the blasting, with the place still smoky and reeking sickeningly of dynamite powder and gas, Ira worked with a pick and a shovel alongside the Mexicans as the lowest of the low, as what they called a mucker.

In those years, the Sussex mines were unorganized and as profitable for the New Jersey Zinc Company, and as unpleasant for New Jersey Zinc's workers, as zinc mines anywhere in the world. The ore got smelted into metallic zinc down on Passaic Avenue in Newark and also processed into zinc oxide for paint, and though by the time Ira bought his shack in the late forties Jersey zinc was losing ground to foreign competition and the mines were already headed for extinction, it was still that first big immersion in brute life—eight hours underground loading the shattered rock and ore into rail cars, eight hours of enduring the awful headaches and swallowing the red and brown dust and shitting in the pails of sawdust . . . and all for forty-two cents an hour—that lured him back to the remote Sussex hills. The Zinc Town shack was the radio actor's openly sentimental expression of solidarity with the dispensable, coarse nobody he'd once been—as he described himself, "a brainless human tool if ever there was one." Another person, having achieved success, might have wanted to abolish those gruesome memories for good, but without the history of his unimportance made somehow tangible, Ira would have felt himself unreal and badly deprived.

I hadn't even known that when he came over to Newark—when, after I got out of my last class, we took our hikes through Weequahic Park, circling the lake and ending up at our neighborhood's dining simulacrum to Coney Island's Nathan's, a place called Millman's, for a hot dog with "the works"—he wasn't visiting Lehigh Avenue solely to see his brother. On those after-school afternoons, when Ira told me about his years as a soldier and what he'd learned in Iran, about O'Day and what O'Day taught him, about his own recent former life as a factory worker and a union man, and his experiences as a kid shoveling muck in the mines, he was seeking refuge from a household where, from the day he arrived, he'd found himself unwelcome and unwanted by Sylphid and more and more at odds with Eve Frame because of her unforeseen contempt for Jews.

Not all Jews, Murray explained—not the accomplished Jews at the top whom she'd met in Hollywood and on Broadway and in the radio business, not, by and large, the directors and the actors and the writers and the musicians she'd worked with, many of whom were regularly to be seen at the salon she'd made of her West Eleventh Street house. Her contempt was for the garden-variety, the standard-issue Jew she saw shopping in the department stores, for run-of-the-mill people with New York accents who worked behind counters or who tended their own little shops in Manhattan, for the Jews who drove taxis, for the Jewish families she saw talking and walking together in Central Park. What drove her to distraction on the streets were the Jewish ladies who loved her, who recognized her, who came up to her and asked for her autograph. These women were her old Broadway audience, and she despised them. Elderly Jewish women particularly she could not pass without a groan of disgust. "Look at those faces!" she'd say with a shudder. "Look at those hideous faces!"

"It was a sickness," Murray said, "that aversion she had for the Jew who was insufficiently disguised. She could go along parallel to life for a long time. Not *in* life—parallel to life. She could be quite convincing in that ultracivilized, ladylike role she'd chosen. The soft voice. The precise locution. Back in the twenties, English Genteel was a style that a lot of American girls worked up for themselves when they wanted to become actresses. And with Eve Frame, who was herself starting out in Hollywood then, it took, it hardened. English Genteel hardened into a form like layers of wax—only burning right in the middle was the wick, this flaming wick that wasn't very genteel at all. She knew all the moves, the benign smile, the dramatic reserve, all the delicate gestures. But then she'd veer off that parallel course of hers, the thing that looked so much like life, and there'd be an episode that could leave you spinning."

"And I never saw any of this," I said. "She was always kind and considerate to me, sympathetic, trying to make me feel comfortable—which wasn't easy. I was an excitable kid and she had a lot of the movie star clinging to her, even in those radio days."

I was thinking again, as I spoke, of that night at the Mosque. She'd said to me—who was finding it impossible to know what to say to her—that she didn't know what to say to Paul Robeson, that in his presence she was tongue-tied. "Are you as in awe of him as I am?" she whispered, as though *both* of us were fifteen years old. "He is the most beautiful man I have ever seen. It's shameful—I cannot stop looking at him."

I knew how she felt because I hadn't been able to stop looking at *her*, looking as though if I looked long enough, a *meaning* might emerge. Looking not only because of the delicacy of her gestures and the dignity of her bearing and the indeterminate elegance of *her* beauty—a beauty hovering between the darkly exotic and the softly demure and shifting continuously in its proportions, a type of beauty that must have been spellbinding at its height—but because of something visibly aquiver in her despite all the restraint, a volatility that at the time I associated with the sheer exaltation that must come of being Eve Frame.

"Do you remember the day I met Ira?" I asked him. "You two were working together, taking the screens down on Lehigh Avenue. What was he doing at your place? It was in October '48, a few weeks before the election."

"Oh, that was a bad day. That day I remember very well. He was in a bad way, and he came to Newark that morning to stay with Doris and me. He slept on the couch for two nights. It was the first time that happened. Nathan, that marriage was a mismatch from the start. He'd already pulled something like it before, except at the other end of the social spectrum. You couldn't miss it. The enormous difference in temperament and interests. Anybody could see it."

"Ira couldn't?"

"See? Ira? Well, to be generous about it, for one thing, he was in love with her. They met and he fell for her, and the first thing he did, he went out and bought her a fancy Easter parade hat that she would never have worn because her taste in clothes was all Dior. But he didn't know what Dior was, and he bought her this big ridiculous expensive hat and had it delivered to her house after their first date. Lovestruck and starstruck. He was dazzled by her. She *was* dazzling—and dazzlement has a logic all its own.

"What did she see in him, the big rube who hits New York and lands a job in a soap opera? Well, it's not a great riddle. After a short apprenticeship, he is not a simple rube, he is a star on *The Free and the Brave*, so there's that. Ira took on those heroes that he played. *I* never bought it, but the average listener believed in him as their embodiment. He had an aura of heroic purity. He believed in himself, and so he steps into the room, and bingo. He shows up at some party, and there she is. There is this lonely actress in her forties, three times divorced, and there's this new face, this new guy, this *tree*, and she's needy, and she's famous, and she surrenders to him. Isn't that what happens? Every woman has her temptations, and surrendering is Eve's. Outwardly, a pure, gangling giant with huge hands who'd been a factory worker, who'd been a stevedore, who was now an actor. Pretty appealing, those guys. It's hard to believe something that raw can be tender too. Tender rawness, the goodness of a big rough guy—all that stuff. Irresistible to her. How could a giant be anything *else* to her? There's something exotic to her about the amount of harsh life he's exposed himself to. She felt that he'd really lived and, after he heard her story, he felt that *she'd* really lived.

"When they meet, Sylphid's away in France for the summer with her father, and Ira doesn't get to see that stuff firsthand. And so these strong, if *sui generis*, maternal urges of hers Ira gets instead, and they have this idyll together all summer long. The guy never had a mother after the age of seven, and he's starved for the attentive, refined care that she lavishes on him, and they're living alone in the house, without the daughter, and ever since he came to New York he's been living, like a good member of the proletariat, in some dump on the Lower East Side. He hangs out in cheap places and eats in cheap restaurants, and suddenly these two are isolated together on West Eleventh Street, and it's summer in Manhattan and it's great, it's life as paradise. Sylphid's picture is all around the house, Sylphid as a little girl in her pinafore, and he finds it wonderful that Eve's so devoted. She tells the story of her horrible experiences with marriage and men, she tells him about Hollywood and the tyrannical directors and the philistine producers, the terrible, terrible tawdriness, and it's *Othello* in reverse: "'twas strange, 'twas passing strange; 'twas pitiful, 'twas wondrous pitiful'—he loved her for the dangers *she* had passed. Ira's mystified, enchanted, and he's *needed*. He's big and he's physical, and so he rushes in. A woman with pathos. A beautiful woman with pathos and a story to tell. A spiritual woman with décolletage. Who better to activate his protective mechanism?

"He even takes her to Newark to meet us. We have a drink at our house, and then we all go down to Elizabeth Avenue to the Tavern, and she behaves well. Nothing inexplicable. It seemed so surprisingly easy to know what to make of her. That evening he first brought Eve to our place and we went out for dinner, I didn't see anything wrong myself. It's only fair to say that it's not Ira alone who couldn't figure this out. He doesn't know who she is because, to be honest, *nobody* would have right off. Nobody could have. In society, Eve was invisible behind the disguise of all that civility. And so, though others might proceed slowly, because of his nature, Ira, as I said, rushes right in.

"What registered on me right off weren't her inadequacies but his. She struck me as too smart for him, too polished for him, certainly too cultivated. I thought, Here is a movie star with a mind. Turned out she'd been reading conscientiously since she was a kid. I don't think there was a novel on my shelves that she couldn't talk about with familiarity. It even sounded that night as though her inmost pleasure in life were reading books. She remembered the complicated plots of nineteenth-century novels—I would teach the books and I still couldn't remember them.

"Sure, she was showing her best side. Sure, like everyone else on first meeting, like all of us, she was keeping a prudent watch over her worst side. But a best side was there, she *had* one. It looked real and it was unostentatious, and in someone so renowned, that made it very winning. Sure, I saw—I couldn't help but see—that this was by no means a necessary union of souls. The two of them were more than likely without any affinity at all. But I was dazzled myself that first night by what I took to be her quiet substance on top of the looks.

"Don't forget the effect of fame. Doris and I had grown up on those silent films of hers. She was always cast with older men, tall men, often white-haired men, and she was a girlish, daughterly-looking thing—*granddaughterly*-looking thing— and the men were always wanting to kiss her and she was always saying no. Took no more than that in those days to heat things up in a movie house. A movie of hers, maybe her first, was called *Cigarette Girl*. Eve's the cigarette girl, working in a nightclub, and at the end of the movie, as I remember, there's a charity event to which she's taken by the nightclub's owner. It's held at the Fifth Avenue mansion of a rich, stuffy dowager, and the cigarette girl is dressed up in a nurse's uniform and the men are asked to bid to kiss her—money that will go to the Red Cross. Each time one man tops another's bid, Eve covers her mouth and giggles behind her hand like a geisha. The bidding goes higher and higher, and the stout society ladies looking on are aghast. But when a distinguished banker with a black mustache—Carlton Pennington—bids the astronomical sum of one thousand dollars and steps up to plant the kiss we've all been waiting to see, the ladies surge madly forward to watch. At the finale, instead of the kiss at the heart of the screen, there are their big corseted society behinds obscuring everything.

"Quite something that was in 1924. Quite something *Eve* was. The radiant smile, the hopeless shrug, the acting they did in those days with their eyes—she'd mastered it all as just a kid. She could do defeated, she could display temper, she could do crying with her hand to her forehead; she could do the funny pratfalls too. When Eve Frame was happy, she would do a run with a little skip in it. Skipping with happiness. Very charming. She played either the poor cigarette girl or the poor laundress who meets the swell, or she played the spoiled rich girl who is swept off her feet by the trolley conductor. Movies about crossing class barriers. Street scenes of the immigrant poor with all their crude energy and then dinner scenes of the privileged American rich with all their strictures and taboos. Baby Dreiser. You couldn't watch those things today. You could barely watch them then, if not for her.

"Doris and Eve and I were the same age. She'd started out in Hollywood when she was seventeen, and then, still back before the war, she was on Broadway. Doris and I had seen her from up in the balcony in some of those plays, and she was good, you know. The plays weren't so wonderful, but as a stage actress she had a direct way about her, unlike what had made her popular as the girlish silent-film star. On the stage she had a talent for making things that weren't very intelligent seem intelligent, and things that weren't serious seem somewhat serious. Strange, her perfect equilibrium on the stage. As a human being she wound up exaggerating everything, and yet as a stage actress she was all moderation and tact, nothing exaggerated. And then, after the war, we'd hear her on the radio because Lorraine liked to listen, and even on those *American Radio Theater* shows, she brought an air of tastefulness to some pretty awful stuff. To have her in our living room looking through my bookshelves, to talk to her about Meredith and Dickens and Thackeray—well, what is a woman with her experience and her interests doing with my brother?

"That night I never figured on their getting married. Though his vanity was clearly flattered and he was excited and proud as hell of her over lobster thermidor at the Tavern. The toniest restaurant Jews ate at in Newark, and there, escorting Eve Frame, the epitome of theatrical class, is the onetime roughneck from Newark's Factory Street, and not an ounce of uncertainty in him. Did you know that Ira was once a busboy at the Tavern? One of his menial jobs after he quit school. Lasted about a month. Too big to be rushing with those loaded trays through the kitchen door. They fired him after he broke his thousandth dish, and that's when he headed up to Sussex County to the zinc mines. So—nearly twenty years pass and he's back at the Tavern, a radio star himself and showing off that night for his brother and sister-in-law. The master of life exulting in his own existence.

"The owner of the Tavern, Teiger, Sam Teiger, spots Eve and comes over to the table with a bottle of champagne, and Ira invites him to have a drink with us and regales him with the story of his thirty days as a Tavern busboy in 1929, and, now that his life hasn't come to nothing, everybody enjoys the comedy of his mishaps and the irony that Ira should ever have got back here. We all enjoy his sporting spirit about his old wounds. Teiger goes to his office and returns with a camera and he takes a picture of the four of us eating our dinner, and afterward it hangs in the Tavern foyer, along with the photo-graphs of all the other notables who've ever dined there. No reason that picture wouldn't have hung there till the Tavern closed for business after the '67 riots had Ira not been black-listed sixteen years earlier. I understand they took it down then overnight, as though his life *had* come to nothing.

"To go back to when their idyll first began—he heads home at night to this room he rented, but gradually enough he doesn't, and then he's at her place, and they're not kids, and the woman hasn't been up to much lately, and it's passionate and wonderful, locked up alone in that West Eleventh Street house like a pair of sex criminals tethered to the bed. All the spontaneous intrigue of that at the onset of middle age. Let-ting go and falling into the affair. It's Eve's release, her libera-tion, her emancipation. Her *salvation*. Ira's given her a new script, if she wants it. At forty-one, she thought it was all over and instead she's been saved. 'Well,' she says to him, 'so much for the patiently nurtured desire to keep things in perspective.'

"She says things to him nobody's ever said to him before. She calls their affair 'our exceedingly, achingly sweet and strange thing.' She tells him, 'It keeps dissolving me.' She tells him, 'In the middle of a conversation with someone, I'm suddenly not there.' She calls him '*mon prince*.' She quotes Emily Dick-inson. For Ira Ringold, Emily Dickinson. 'With thee, in the Desert / With thee in the thirst / With thee in the Tamarind wood / Leopard breathes—at last!'

"Well, it feels to Ira like the love of his life. And with the love of your life you don't think about the particulars. If you find such a thing, you don't throw it away. They decide to get married, and that's what Eve tells Sylphid when she gets back from France. Mommy's getting married again but this time to a wonderful man. Sylphid's supposed to buy that. Sylphid, from the *old* script.

"Eve Frame was the big world to Ira. And why shouldn't she have been? He was no baby, he'd been in a lot of rough places and knew how to be rough himself. But Broadway? Holly-wood? Greenwich Village? All brand-new to him. Ira wasn't the brightest guy around when it came to personal affairs. He'd taught himself a lot. He and O'Day had brought him a long, long way from Factory Street. But that was all political stuff.

And that was not sharp thinking either. It wasn't 'thinking' at all. The pseudoscientific Marxist lexicon, the utopian cant that went with it—dish that stuff out to someone as unschooled and ill educated as Ira, indoctrinate an adult who is not too skilled in brainwork with the intellectual glamour of Big Sweeping Ideas, inculcate a man of limited intelligence, an excitable type who is as angry as Ira . . . But that's a subject all its own, the connection between embitterment and not thinking.

"You're asking me about how he wound up in Newark that day you two met. Ira wasn't prone to going at life in ways that were conducive to solving the problems of a marriage. And it was early days, it was only a matter of months since the wedding to the star of stage, screen, and radio and his moving into that townhouse of hers. How could I tell him it was a mistake? The guy wasn't without vanity, after all. He was not without conceit, my brother. Wasn't without *scale* either. There was a theatrical instinct in Ira, an immodest attitude toward himself. Don't think he minded becoming someone of enhanced importance. That's an adaptation people seem able to implement in about seventy-two hours, and generally the effect is invigorating. Everything all at once filled with possibility, everything in motion, everything *imminent*—Ira in the drama in every sense of the word. He has pulled off a great big act of control over the story that was his life. He is all at once awash in the narcissistic illusion that he has been sprung from the realities of pain and loss, that his life is *not* futility—that it's anything *but*. No longer walking in the valley of the shadow of his limitations. No longer the excluded giant consigned to be the strange one forever. Barges in with that brash courage—and there he is. Out of the grips of obscurity. And proud of his transformation. The exhilaration of it. The naive dream—he's in it! The new Ira, the worldly Ira. A big guy with a big life. Watch out.

"Besides, I already *had* told him it was a mistake—and after that we didn't talk for six weeks, and then only because I went to New York and explained to him I was wrong and begged him not to hold it against me did I get the guy back. He would have shot me down for good if I'd tried it a second time. And a complete falling-out—that would have been awful for both of us. I'd been taking care of Ira since he was born. I was seven years old, I used to push him down Factory Street in his baby carriage. After our mother died, when my father remarried and a stepmother came into the house, if I hadn't been around, Ira would have wound up in reform school. We had a wonderful mother. And she didn't have such a good time of it, either. She was married to our father. That was no picnic."

"What was your father like?" I asked.

"We don't want to go into that."

"That's what Ira used to say."

"That's the only thing there is to say. We had a father who . . . well, much later in life I learned what made him tick. But by then it was too late. Anyway, I was luckier than my brother. When our mother died, after those awful months in the hospital, I was already in high school. Then I got a scholarship to the University of Newark. I was on my way. But Ira was still a kid. A tough kid. A crude kid. Full of mistrust.

"Do you know about the canary funeral in the old First Ward, when one of the local shoemakers buried his pet canary? This'll show you how tough Ira was—and how tough he wasn't. It was in 1920. I was thirteen and Ira was seven, and on Boyden Street, a couple streets away from our tenement, there was a cobbler, Russomanno, Emidio Russomanno, a poor-looking old guy, small, with big ears and a gaunt face and a white chin beard and, on his back, a threadbare suit a hundred years old. For company in his shop Russomanno kept a pet canary. The canary was named Jimmy and Jimmy lived a long time and then Jimmy ate something he shouldn't have and died.

"Russomanno was devastated, so he hired a parade band, rented a hearse and two coaches drawn by horses, and after the canary was laid out for viewing on a bench in the cobbler shop —beautifully exhibited with flowers, candles, and a crucifix— there was a funeral procession through the streets of the whole district, past Del Guercio's grocery store, where they had clams outside in bushel baskets and an American flag in the window, past Melillo's fruit and vegetable stand, past Giordano's bakery, past Mascellino's bakery, past Arre's Italian Tasty Crust Bakery. It went past Biondi's butcher shop and De Lucca's harness shop and De Carlo's garage and D'Innocenzio's coffee store and Parisi's shoe store and Nole's bicycle shop and Celentano's *latteria* and Grande's pool hall and Basso's barbershop and

Esposito's barbershop and the bootblack stand with the two scarred old dining chairs that the customers had to step up high, onto a platform, to get to.

"Gone now for forty years. City knocked down that whole Italian neighborhood in '53 to make way for low-rent high-rise housing. In '94, they blew the high-rises up on national TV. By then nobody'd been living in them for about twenty years. Uninhabitable. Now there's nothing there at all. St. Lucy's and that's it. That's all that's standing. The parish church, but no parish and no parishioners.

"Nicodemi's Café on Seventh Avenue and Café Roma on Seventh Avenue and D'Auria's bank on Seventh Avenue. That was the bank where, before the second war broke out, they extended credit to Mussolini. When Mussolini took Ethiopia, the priest rang the church bells for half an hour. Here in America, in Newark's First Ward.

"The macaroni factory and the decoration factory and the monument shop and the marionette playhouse and the movie theater and the bocce alleys and the icehouse and the print shop and the clubhouses and the restaurants. Past the mobster Ritchie Boiardo's hangout, the Victory Café. In the thirties, when Boiardo got out of jail, he built the Vittorio Castle on the corner of Eighth and Summer. Show-business people used to travel from New York to dine at the Castle. The Castle is where Joe DiMaggio ate when he came to Newark. The Castle is where DiMaggio and his girlfriend held their engagement party. It's from the Castle that Boiardo lorded it over the First Ward. Ritchie Boiardo ruled the Italians in the First Ward and Longy Zwillman ruled the Jews in the Third Ward, and these two gangsters were always at war.

"Past the dozens of neighborhood saloons the procession wound from east to west, north up one street and south down the next, all the way to the Clifton Avenue Municipal Bathhouse—the First Ward's most extravagant lump of architecture after the church and the cathedral, the massive old public bathhouse where my mother used to take us for our baths as babies. My father went there too. Shower free and a penny for the towel.

"The canary was placed in a small white coffin with four pallbearers to carry it. A huge crowd assembled, maybe as many as ten thousand people stretched out along the procession route. People were squeezed together on the fire escapes and up on the roofs. Whole families were hanging out of their tenement windows to watch.

"Russomanno rode in the carriage behind the coffin, Emidio Russomanno weeping while everybody else in the First Ward was laughing. Some people were laughing so hard they wound up hurling themselves to the ground. They couldn't stand up from laughing so hard. Even the pallbearers were laughing. It was infectious. The guy driving the hearse was laughing. Out of respect for the mourner, people on the sidewalk tried to hold it in until Russomanno's carriage had passed by, but it was just too hilarious for most of them, particularly for the kids.

"Ours was a tiny neighborhood swarming with kids: kids in the alleys, kids crowding the stoops, kids pouring out of the tenements and stampeding from Clifton Avenue down to Broad Street. All day long and, during the summertime, through half the night you could hear these kids shouting to one another, 'Guahl-yo! Guahl-yo!' Everywhere you looked, bands of kids, battalions of kids—pitching pennies, playing cards, rolling dice, shooting pool, licking ices, playing ball, making bonfires, frightening girls. Only the nuns with rulers could control these kids. Thousands and thousands of boys there were, all under ten years old. Ira was one of them. Thousands and thousands of scrappy little Italian kids, the children of the Italians who laid the railroad tracks and paved the streets and dug the sewers, the children of peddlers and factory workers and rag pickers and saloon keepers. Kids called Giuseppe and Rodolfo and Raffaele and Gaetano, and the one Jewish kid called Ira.

"Well, the Italians were having the time of their lives. They'd never seen anything like that canary's funeral. They never saw anything like it again. Sure, there were funeral processions before that, and there were bands playing funeral dirges and mourners surging through the streets. There were the feast days all year round with processions for all those saints they brought over with them from Italy, hundreds and hundreds of people venerating their society's special saint by dressing up and bearing the saint's embroidered flag and carrying candles the size of tire irons. And there was St. Lucy's *presepio* for Christmas, a replica of a Neapolitan village depicting the birth of

Jesus, a hundred Italian figurines planted in it along with Mary, Joseph, and the Bambino. There were the Italian bagpipes parading with a plaster Bambino and, behind the Bambino, the people in the procession singing Italian Christmas carols. And the vendors out along the streets selling eel for Christmas Eve dinner. People turned out in droves for the religious stuff, and they stuck dollar bills all over the robe of the plaster statue of whatever saint it was and threw flower petals out their windows like ticker tape. They even released birds from cages, doves that flew crazily above the crowd from one telephone pole to the next. On a saint's day the doves must have been wishing they'd never seen the outside of a birdcage.

"On the feast of Saint Michael, the Italians would dress up a couple of little girls as angels. From the fire escapes on either side of the street, they'd swing them over the crowd from ropes the girls were harnessed to. Little skinny girls in white gowns with haloes and wings attached, and the crowd would go silent with awe when they appeared in the air, chanting some prayer, and when the girls had finished being angels, the crowd went nuts. That's when they would set the doves free and that's when the fireworks would explode and somebody would wind up in the hospital with a couple of fingers blown off.

"So, lively spectacle was nothing new to the Italians in the First Ward. Funny characters, old-country carrying on, noise and fights, colorful stunts—nothing new. Funerals certainly weren't new. During the flu epidemic, so many people died that the coffins had to be lined up on the street. Nineteen eighteen. The funeral parlors couldn't handle the business. Behind the coffins, processions from St. Lucy's wended the couple miles to Holy Sepulcher Cemetery all day long. There were tiny coffins for the babies. You had to wait your turn to bury your baby—you had to wait for your neighbors to bury theirs first. Unforgettable terror for a kid. And yet two years after the flu epidemic, that funeral for Jimmy the canary . . . well, that topped 'em all.

"Everybody there that day was in stitches. Except for one person. Ira was the only one in Newark who wasn't in on the joke. I couldn't explain it to him. I tried, but he couldn't understand. Why? Maybe because he was stupid, or maybe because he wasn't stupid. Maybe he simply was not born with the mentality of the carnival—maybe utopianists aren't. Or maybe it was because our mother had died a few months earlier and we'd had our own funeral that Ira had wanted no part of. He wanted to be out on the street instead, kicking a ball around. He begged me not to make him change out of his overalls and go to the cemetery. He tried hiding in a closet. But he came along with us anyway. My father saw to that. At the cemetery he stood there watching us bury her, but he refused to take my hand or let me put my arm around him. He just scowled at the rabbi. Glowered at him. Refused to be touched or comforted by anyone. Didn't cry either, not a tear. He was too angry for tears.

"But when the canary died, everybody at the funeral was laughing away except Ira. Ira knew Jimmy only from walking by the cobbler's shop on the way to school and looking in the window at his cage. I don't believe he'd ever stepped inside the shop, and yet, aside from Russomanno, he was the only one around who was in tears.

"When *I* started to laugh—because it *was* funny, Nathan, *very* funny—Ira lost control completely. That was the first time I saw that happen to Ira. He started swinging his fists and screaming at me. He was a big kid even then, and I couldn't rein him in, and suddenly he was swinging at a couple of kids next to us who were also laughing themselves sick, and when I reached down to try to pluck him up and save him from being slaughtered by a whole slew of kids, one of his fists caught me on the nose. He broke my nose at the bridge, a seven-year-old. I was bleeding, the damn thing was obviously broken, and so Ira ran away.

"We didn't find him till the next day. He'd slept back of the brewery on Clifton Avenue. It wasn't the first time. In the yard, under the loading dock. My father found him there in the morning. He dragged him by the scruff of the neck all the way to school and into the room where Ira's class was already in session. When the kids saw Ira, wearing those filthy overalls he'd slept in all night and being flung into the room by his old man, they began to go 'Boo-hoo,' and that was Ira's nickname for months afterward. Boo-hoo Ringold. The Jewboy who cried at the canary funeral.

"Luckily, Ira was always bigger than the others his age, and he was strong, and he could play ball. Ira would have been a star athlete if it hadn't been for his eyes. What respect he got in that neighborhood he got from playing ball. But the fights? From then on he was in fights all the time. That's when his extremism began.

"It was a blessing, you know, that we didn't grow up in the Third Ward with the poor Jews. Growing up in the First Ward, Ira was always a loudmouth kike outsider to the Italians, and so, however big and strong and belligerent he was, Boiardo could never perceive him as local talent auditioning for the Mob. But in the Third Ward, among the Jews, it might have been different. There Ira wouldn't have been the official outcast among the kids. If only because of his size, he would probably have come to Longy Zwillman's attention. From what I understand, Longy, who was ten years older than Ira, was a lot like Ira growing up: furious, a big, menacing boy who also quit school, who was fearless in a street fight, and who had the commanding looks along with something of a brain. In bootlegging, in gambling, in vending machines, on the docks, in the labor movement, in the building trades—Longy eventually made it big. But even at the top, when he was teamed up with Bugsy Siegel and Lansky and Lucky Luciano, his closest intimates were the friends he'd grown up with in the streets, Third Ward Jewish boys like himself, whom it took little to provoke. Niggy Rutkin, his hit man. Sam Katz, his bodyguard. George Goldstein, his accountant. Billy Tiplitz, his numbers man. Doc Stacher, his adding machine. Abe Lew, Longy's cousin, ran the retail clerks' union for Longy. Christ, Meyer Ellenstein, another street kid from the Third Ward ghetto—when he was mayor of Newark, Ellenstein all but ran the city for Longy.

"Ira could have wound up one of Longy's henchmen, loyally doing one of their jobs. He was ripe for recruitment. There would have been nothing aberrant in it: crime was what those boys were bred for. It was the next logical step. Had that violence in them that you need as a business tactic in the rackets to inspire fear and gain the competitive edge. Ira could have started off down at Port Newark, unloading the bootleg whiskey from Canada out of the speedboats and into Longy's trucks, and he could have ended up, like Longy, with a millionaire's mansion in West Orange and a rope around his neck.

"It's so fickle, isn't it, who you wind up, how you wind up? It's only because of a tiny accident of geography that the opportunity to string along with Longy never came Ira's way. The opportunity to launch a successful career by using a black-jack on Longy's competitors, by putting the squeeze on Longy's customers, by supervising the gaming tables at Longy's casinos. The opportunity to conclude it by testifying for two hours in front of the Kefauver committee before going home to hang himself. When Ira met someone tougher and smarter than him who was going to be the big influence, he was already in the army, and so it wasn't a Newark gangster but a Communist steelworker who worked the transformation on him. Ira's Longy Zwillman was Johnny O'Day."

"Why didn't I tell him, that first time he stayed over with us, to can the marriage and get out? Because that marriage, that woman, that beautiful house, all those books, records, the paintings on the wall, that life she had full of accomplished people, polished, interesting, educated people—it was everything he'd never known. Forget that he was now somebody himself. The guy had a *home*. He never had that before, and he was by then thirty-five. Thirty-five and he wasn't living in a room anymore, wasn't eating in cafeterias anymore, wasn't sleeping with waitresses and barmaids and worse—women, some of them, who couldn't write their names.

"After his discharge, when he first got to Calumet City to live with O'Day, Ira had an affair with a nineteen-year-old stripper. Girl named Donna Jones. Ira met her in the laundro-mat. Thought at first she was a local high school kid, and for a while she didn't bother to set him straight. Petite, scrappy, brassy, tough. At least the surface was tough. And she's a little pleasure factory. The kid has her hand on her pussy all the time.

"Donna's from Michigan, a resort town on the lake called Benton Harbor. In Benton Harbor, Donna used to work sum-mers at a hotel on the lakefront. Sixteen, a chambermaid, and she gets knocked up by one of the customers over from Chi-cago. Which one she doesn't know. Carries the baby to term, gives it up for adoption, leaves town in disgrace, and winds up stripping in one of those Cal City joints.

"When he wasn't out being Abe Lincoln for the union on

Sundays, Ira used to borrow O'Day's car to take Donna over to Benton Harbor to visit her mother. The mother worked in a little factory that manufactured candy and fudge, stuff they sold to the vacationers on Benton Harbor's main street. Resort sweets. The fudge was famous, shipped fudge all over the Middle West. Ira starts talking to the guy who runs the candy factory, he sees how they make the stuff, and pretty soon he's writing to me about marrying Donna and moving back with her to her hometown, living in a bungalow on the lake and using what's left of his separation pay to buy into this guy's business. There was also the thousand bucks he'd won shooting craps on the troopship coming home—all of it could go into the candy business. That Christmas he mailed Lorraine a gift box of fudge. Sixteen different flavors: chocolate coconut, peanut butter, pistachio, mint chocolate chip, rocky road . . . all fresh and creamy, direct from the Fudge Kitchen in Benton Harbor, Michigan. Tell me, what could be further from being a raving Red hell-bent on overthrowing the American system than being a guy in Michigan who gift-wraps fudge to mail out to your old auntie for the holiday season? 'Goodies Made by the Lake'—that's the slogan on the box. Not 'Workers of the World Unite' but 'Goodies Made by the Lake.' If only Ira had married Donna Jones, *that* would have been the slogan he lived by.

"It was O'Day, not me, who talked him out of Donna. Not because a nineteen-year-old featured at the Cal City Kit Kat Klub as 'Miss Shalimar, Recommended for Good Eating by Duncan Hines' might in any way be a bad risk as a wife and mother; not because the missing Mr. Jones, Donna's father, was a drunk who used to beat his wife and kids; not because the Benton Harbor Joneses were ignorant rednecks and not a family somebody back from four years in the service should be wanting to take on as a lasting responsibility—which is what I politely tried to tell him. But to Ira everything that was a guaranteed recipe for domestic disaster constituted the argument *for* Donna. The lure of the underdog. The struggle of the disinherited up from the bottom was an *irresistible* lure. You drink deep, you drink dregs: humanity to Ira was synonymous with hardship and calamity. Toward hardship, even its disreputable forms, the kinship was unbreakable. It took O'Day to undo the all-around aphrodisiac that was Donna Jones and the sixteen flavors of fudge. It was O'Day who tore into him for personalizing his politics, and O'Day didn't do it with my 'bourgeois' reasoning. O'Day didn't apologize for presuming to criticize Ira's shortcomings. O'Day never apologized for anything. O'Day set people straight.

"O'Day gave Ira what he called 'a refresher course in matrimony as it pertains to the world revolution,' based on his own encounter with marriage before the war. 'Is this what you came out with me to the Calumet for? To prepare to run a candy factory or to run a revolution? This is no time for ridiculous aberrations! This is it, boy! This is life or death for working conditions as we've known them for the past ten years! All the factions and groups are coming together right here in Lake County. *You* see that. If we can hold this pitch, if nobody jumps ship, then damn it, Iron Man, in a year, two at most, the mills will be ours!'

"So, some eight months on, Ira told Donna it was all off, and she swallowed some pills and tried to kill herself a little. About a month later—Donna's by then back at the Kit Kat and got herself a new guy—her long-lost drunken father turns up with one of Donna's brothers at Ira's door saying he's going to teach Ira a lesson for what he did to his daughter. Ira's in the doorway fighting the two of them off, and the father pulls a knife and O'Day takes one swing and breaks the bastard's jaw and grabs the knife . . . That was the *first* family Ira was going to marry into.

"From such a farce it's not always a short way back, but by '48 the putative savior of little Donna has become Iron Rinn of *The Free and the Brave* and is up and ready for his next big mistake. You should have heard him when he learned Eve was pregnant. A child. A family of his own. And not with an ex-stripper whom his brother had disapproved of but with a re-nowned actress whom American radioland adored. It was the greatest thing ever to come his way. That solid foothold he'd never had before. He could hardly believe it. Two years—and this! The man wasn't impermanent anymore."

"She was pregnant? When was that?"

"After they were married. It didn't last but ten weeks. That's why he'd stayed with me and how you two met. She'd decided to abort."

We were sitting out back, on the deck, looking toward the pond and, in the distance, to the mountain range in the west. I live here by myself and the house is small, a room where I write and eat my meals—a workroom with a bathroom and a kitchen alcove off at one end, a stone fireplace at right angles to a wall of books, and a row of five twelve-over-twelve sash windows looking onto the broad hay field and a protective squadron of old maples that separates me from the dirt road. The other room is where I sleep, a nice-sized rustic-looking room with a single bed, a dresser, a wood-burning stove, exposed old beams upright in the four corners, more bookshelves, an easy chair where I do my reading, a small writing desk, and, in the west wall, a sliding glass door that opens onto the deck where Murray and I were each drinking a martini before dinner. I'd bought the house, winterized it—it had been somebody's summer cottage—and come here when I was sixty to live alone, by and large apart from people. That was four years ago. Though it isn't always desirable living as austerely as this, without the varied activities that ordinarily go to make up a human existence, I believe I made the least harmful choice. But my seclusion is not the story here. It is not a story in any way. I came here because I don't want a story any longer. I've had my story.

I wondered if Murray had as yet recognized my house as an upgraded replica of the two-room shack on the Jersey side of the Delaware Water Gap that was Ira's beloved retreat and the spot where I happened to have got my first taste of rural America when I went up, in the summers of '49 and '50, to spend a week with him. I'd loved my first time living alone with Ira in that shack, and I thought of his place immediately when I was shown this house. Though I had been looking for something larger and more conventionally a house, I bought it right off. The rooms were about the same size as Ira's and similarly situated. The long oval pond was about the same dimensions as his and about the same distance from the back door. And though my place was much brighter—over time, his stained pine-board walls had gone almost black, the beamed ceilings were low (ridiculously low for him), and the windows were small and not that plentiful—mine was tucked away on a dirt road as his was, and, if from the outside it didn't have that dark, drooping ramshackle look that proclaimed, "Hermit here—back off," the owner's state of mind was discernible in the absence of anything like a path across the hay field that led to the bolted front door. There was a narrow dirt drive that swung up and around to the workroom side of the house, to an open shed where, in the winter, I parked my car; a tumbledown wooden structure that predated the cottage, the shed could have been lifted right off Ira's overgrown eight acres.

How did the idea of Ira's shack maintain its hold so long? Well, it's the earliest images—of independence and freedom, particularly—that do live obstinately on, despite the blessing and the bludgeoning of life's fullness. And the idea of the shack, after all, isn't Ira's. It has a history. It was Rousseau's. It was Thoreau's. The palliative of the primitive hut. The place where you are stripped back to essentials, to which you return —even if it happens not to be where you came from—to decontaminate and absolve yourself of the striving. The place where you disrobe, molt it all, the uniforms you've worn and the costumes you've gotten into, where you shed your batteredness and your resentment, your appeasement of the world and your defiance of the world, your manipulation of the world and its manhandling of you. The aging man leaves and goes into the woods—Eastern philosophical thought abounds with that motif, Taoist thought, Hindu thought, Chinese thought. The "forest dweller," the last stage on life's way. Think of those Chinese paintings of the old man under the mountain, the old Chinese man all alone under the mountain, receding from the agitation of the autobiographical. He has entered vigorously into competition with life; now, becalmed, he enters into competition with death, drawn down into austerity, the final business.

The martinis were Murray's idea. A good though not a great idea, since a drink at the end of a summer's day with somebody I enjoyed, talk with a person like Murray, made me remember the pleasures of companionship. I'd enjoyed a lot of people, had not been an indifferent participant in life, had not backed away from it . . .

But the story is Ira's. Why it was impossible for *him*.

"He'd wanted a boy," Murray said. "Was dying to name it after his friend, Johnny O'Day Ringold. Doris and I had Lorraine, our daughter, and whenever he stayed over on the couch, Lorraine could always lift his spirits. Lorraine used to like to watch Ira sleep. Liked standing in the doorway watching Lemuel Gulliver sleep. He got attached to that little girl with those black bangs of hers. And she to him. When he came to the house, she'd get him to play with her Russian nested dolls. He'd given them to her for a birthday. You know, a traditional Russian woman in a babushka, the one replica nestles inside the other, till you get down to the nut-sized doll at the core. They'd make up stories about each of the dolls and how hard these little people worked in Russia. Then he'd nestle the whole thing in one of those hands of his so that you couldn't even see it. Just disappear whole inside those spatulate fingers—such long, peculiar fingers, the fingers Paganini must have had. Lorraine loved it when he did that: the biggest nesting doll of them all was this enormous uncle.

"For Lorraine's next birthday he bought her the album of the Soviet Army Chorus and Band performing Russian songs. More than a hundred men in that chorus, another hundred in the band. The basses' portentous rumblings—terrific sound. She and Ira would have a great time with those records. The singing was in Russian, and they'd listen together, and Ira would pretend to be the bass soloist, mouthing the incomprehensible words and making dramatic 'Russian' gestures, and, when the refrain came, Lorraine would mouth the incomprehensible words of the chorus. My kid knew how to be a comedian.

"There was one song she especially loved. It was beautiful too, a stirring, mournful, hymnlike folksong called 'Dubinushka,' a simple song sung with a balalaika in the background. The words to 'Dubinushka' were printed in English on the inside of the album cover, and she learned them by heart and went around the house singing them for months.

Many songs have I heard in my native land—
Songs of joy and sorrow.
But one of them was deeply engraved in my memory:
It's the song of the common worker.

That was the solo part. But what she liked best to sing was the choral refrain. Because it had 'heave-ho' in it.

> Ekh, lift up the cudgel,
> Heave-ho!
> Pull harder together,
> Heave-ho!

When Lorraine was by herself in her room, she'd line up all the hollow dolls and put on the 'Dubinushka' record, and she'd sing tragically 'Heave-ho! Heave-ho!' while pushing the dolls this way and that way all over the floor."

"Stop a minute. Murray, wait," I said, and I got up and went from the deck into the house, into my bedroom, where I had my CD player and my old phonograph. Most of my records were boxed and stored in a closet, but I knew in which box to find what I was looking for. I took out the album Ira had given to *me* back in 1948, and removed the record on which "Dubinushka" was performed by the Soviet Army Chorus and Band. I pushed the rpm switch to 78, dusted the record, and put it on the turntable. I placed the needle into the margin just before the record's last band, turned the volume up loud enough so that Murray could hear the music through the open doors separating my bedroom from the deck, and went out to rejoin him.

In the dark we listened, though now neither I to him nor he to me but both of us to "Dubinushka." It was just as Murray had described it: beautiful, a stirring, mournful, hymnlike folksong. Except for the crackle off the worn surface of the old record—a cyclical sound not unlike some familiar, natural night noise of the summer countryside—the song seemed to be traveling to us from a remote historical past. It wasn't at all like lying on my deck listening on the radio to the Saturday night concerts live from Tanglewood. "Heave-ho! Heave-ho!" was out of a distant place and time, a spectral residue of those rapturous revolutionary days when everyone craving for change programmatically, naively—madly, unforgivably—underestimates how mankind mangles its noblest ideas and turns them into tragic farce. Heave-ho! Heave-ho! As though human wiliness, weakness, stupidity, and corruption didn't stand a chance against the collective, against the might of the people pulling together to renew their lives and abolish injustice. Heave-ho.

When "Dubinushka" was over, Murray was silent and I began to hear once again everything I had filtered out while listening to him talk: the snores, twangs, and trills of the frogs, the rails in Blue Swamp, the reedy marsh just east of my house, *kuck*-ing and *kek*-ing and *ki-tic*-ing away, and the wrens there chattering their accompaniment. And the loons, the crying and the laughing of the manic-depressive loons. Every few minutes there was the whinny of a distant screech owl, and, continuously throughout, the western New England string ensemble of crickets sawed away at cricket Bartók. A raccoon twittered in the nearby woods, and, as time wore on, I even thought I was hearing the beavers gnawing on a tree back where the woodland tributaries feed my pond. Some deer, fooled by the silence, must have prowled too close to the house, for all at once—the deer having sensed our presence—their Morse code of flight is swiftly sounded: the snorting, the in-place thud, the stamping, hooves pounding, the bounding away. Their bodies barge gracefully into the thicket of scrub, and then, subaudibly, they race for their lives. Only Murray's murmurous breathing is heard, the eloquence of an old man evenly expirating.

Close to half an hour must have passed before he spoke. The arm of the phonograph hadn't returned to the starting position, and now I could hear the needle, too, whirring atop the label. I didn't go in to fix it and interrupt whatever it was that had quieted my storyteller and created the intensity of his silence. I wondered how long it would be before he said something, if perhaps he wouldn't speak at all but just get up and ask to be driven back to the dormitory—if whatever thoughts had been set loose in him would require a full night's sleep to subdue.

But, softly laughing, Murray said at last, "That hit me."

"Did it? Why?"

"I miss my girl."

"Where is she?"

"Lorraine is dead."

"When did that happen?"

"Lorraine died twenty-six years ago. Nineteen seventy-one.

Died at thirty, leaving two kids and a husband. Meningitis, and overnight she was dead."

"And Doris is dead."

"Doris? Sure."

I went into the bedroom to lift the needle and return it to its rest. "Want to hear more?" I called to Murray.

He laughed heartily this time and said, "Trying to see how much I can take? Your idea of my strength, Nathan, is just a little too grand. I've met my match in 'Dubinushka.'"

"I doubt that," I said, going back outside and sitting in my chair. "You were telling me—?"

"I was telling you . . . I was telling you . . . Yes. That when Ira got booted off the air, Lorraine was desolate. She was only nine or ten, but she was up in arms. After Ira got fired for being a Communist, she wouldn't salute the flag."

"The American flag? Where?"

"At school," Murray said. "Where else do you salute the flag? The teacher tried to protect her, took her to one side and said you have to salute the flag. But this child wouldn't do it. A lot of anger. The real Ringold anger. She loved her uncle. She took after him."

"What happened?"

"I had a long talk with her and she got back to saluting the flag."

"What did you tell her?"

"I told her I loved my brother, too. I didn't think it was right either. I told her I thought as she did, that it was dead wrong to fire a person for his political beliefs. I believed in freedom of thought. *Absolute* freedom of thought. But I told her you don't go looking for that kind of fight. It's not an important issue. What are you achieving? What are you winning? I told her, Don't pick a fight you know you can't win, one that isn't even worth winning. I told her what I used to try to tell my brother about the problem of impassioned speech—tried from the time he was a little kid, for all the good it did him. It's not being angry that's important, it's being angry about the right things. I told her, Look at it from the Darwinian perspective. Anger is to make you effective. That's its survival function. That's why it's given to you. If it makes you ineffective, drop it like a hot potato."

As my teacher some fifty years earlier, Murray Ringold used

to play things up, make a show out of the lesson, dozens of tricks to get us to stay alert. Teaching was a passionate occupation for him, and he was an exciting guy. But now, though by no means an old man who'd run out of juice, he no longer found it necessary to tear himself apart to make clear his meaning, but had brought himself close to being totally dispassionate. His tone was more or less unvaried, mild—no attempt to lead you (or mislead you) by being overtly expressive with his voice or his face or his hands, not even when singing "Heave-ho. Heave-ho."

His skull looked so fragile and small now. Yet within it were cradled ninety years of the past. There was a great deal in there. All the dead were there, for one thing, their deeds and their misdeeds converging with all the unanswerable questions, those things about which you can never be sure . . . to produce for him an exacting task: to reckon fairly, to tell this story without too much error.

Time, we know, goes very fast near the end, but Murray had been near the end so long that, when he spoke as he did, patiently, to the point, with a certain blandness—only intermittently pausing to wholeheartedly sip that martini—I had the feeling that time had dissolved for him, that it ran neither quickly nor slowly, that he was no longer living in time but exclusively within his own skin. As though that active, effortful, outgoing life as a conscientious teacher and citizen and family man had been a long battle to reach a state of ardorlessness. Aging into decrepitude was not unendurable and neither was the unfathomability of oblivion; neither was everything's coming down to nothing. It had *all* been endurable, even despising, without remission, the despicable.

In Murray Ringold, I thought, human dissatisfaction has met its match. He has outlived dissatisfaction. This is what remains after the passing of everything, the disciplined sadness of stoicism. This is the cooling. For so long it's so hot, everything in life is so intense, and then little by little it goes away, and then comes the cooling, and then come the ashes. The man who first taught me how you box with a book is back now to demonstrate how you box with old age.

And an amazing, noble skill it is, for nothing teaches you less about old age than having lived a robust life.

3

"THE reason Ira came to see me," Murray continued, "and to stay overnight with us the day before you two met was because of what he'd heard that morning."

"She'd told him about wanting the abortion."

"No, she'd already told him that the night before, told him that she was going to Camden for an abortion. There was a doctor in Camden whom a lot of rich people went to back when abortion was a dodgy business. Her decision didn't come as a total surprise. For weeks she'd been back and forth, uncertain what to do. She was forty-one years old—she was older than Ira. Her face didn't show it, but Eve Frame wasn't a kid. She was concerned to be having a baby at her age. Ira understood that, but he couldn't accept it and refused to believe that her being forty-one was something to stand in their way. He wasn't that cautious, you know. He had that all-out steamrolling side, and so he tried and tried to convince her that they had nothing to worry about.

"He thought he *had* convinced her. But a new issue emerged —work. It had been hard enough to tend a career and a child the first time around, with Sylphid, the daughter. Eve was only eighteen when Sylphid was born—she was a starlet then out in Hollywood. She was married to that actor, Pennington. Big name when I was young. Carlton Pennington, the silent-film hero with a profile molded precisely to classical specifications. Tall, slender, graceful man with hair as dark and sleek as a raven and a dark mustache. Elegant to the marrow of his bones. Member in good standing of both the social aristocracy and the aristocracy of eros—his acting capitalizes on the interplay of both. A fairy-tale prince—and a carnal powerhouse—in one, guaranteed to drive you to ecstasy in a silver-plated Pierce-Arrow.

"Studio arranged the wedding. She and Pennington had made such a hit together, and she was so enamored of him, that the studio decided they ought to get married. And once they were married, that they ought to have a child. All this was to squelch the rumors that Pennington was gay. Which, of course, he was.

"In order to marry Pennington there was a first husband to be gotten rid of. Pennington was the second husband. The first was a fellow named Mueller, whom she'd run away with when she was sixteen. An uneducated roughneck just back from five years in the navy, a big, burly German-American boy who'd grown up the son of a bartender in Kearny, near Newark. Crude background. Crude guy. A sort of Ira without the idealism. She met him at a neighborhood theater group. He wanted to be an actor and she wanted to be an actress. He was living in a boarding house and she was in high school and still living at home, and they ran off together to Hollywood. That's how Eve wound up in California, eloped as a kid with the bartender's boy. Within the year she was a star, and, so as to get rid of Mueller, who was nothing, her studio paid him off. Mueller did appear in a few silent films—as part of the payoff —and he even had a couple of roles as a tough in the first talkies, but his connection to Eve was all but erased from the record books. Until much later on, that is. We'll get back to Mueller. The point is that she marries Pennington, a coup for everyone: there's the studio wedding, there's the little baby, and then the twelve years with Pennington living the life of a nun.

"She used to take Sylphid to see Pennington in Europe even after she married Ira. Pennington's dead now, but he lived on the French Riviera after the war. He had a villa up in the hills back of St. Tropez. Drunk every night, on the prowl, a bitter ex-somebody ranting and raving about the Jews who run Hollywood who ruined his career. She'd take Sylphid over to France to see Pennington, and they'd all go out for dinner in St. Tropez and he'd drink a couple bottles of wine and be staring all through dinner at some waiter, and then he'd send Sylphid and Eve back to their hotel. The next morning they'd go to Pennington's for breakfast and the waiter would be at the table in a bathrobe and they'd all have fresh figs together. Eve would return to Ira in tears, saying the man was fat and drunk and there was always some eighteen-year-old sleeping there, a waiter, or a beach bum, or a street cleaner, and she could never go to France again. But back she went—for good or bad, she took Sylphid to St. Tropez two or three times a year to see her father. It couldn't have been easy on the kid.

"After Pennington, Eve marries a real estate speculator, this guy Freedman, who she claimed spent everything she had and all but got her to sign over the house. So when Ira shows up on the radio scene in New York, naturally she falls for him. The noble rail-splitter, outgoing, unpolluted, a great big walking conscience yapping away about justice and equality for all. Ira and his ideals had attracted all sorts, from Donna Jones to Eve Frame, and everything problematic in between. Women in distress were crazy about him. The vitality. The energy. The Samson-like revolutionary giant. The luggish sort of chivalry he had. And Ira smelled good. Do you remember that? A natural smell of his. Lorraine used to say, 'Uncle Ira smells like maple syrup.' He did. He smelled like sap.

"In the beginning, the fact that Eve would deliver up her daughter to Pennington used to drive Ira nuts. I think he felt that it wasn't only to give Sylphid a chance to see Pennington —that there was still something about Pennington that Eve found attractive. And maybe she did. Maybe it was Pennington's queerness. Maybe it was that wellborn background. Pennington was old California money. That's the money he lived on in France. Some of the jewelry that Sylphid wore was Spanish jewelry collected by her father's family. Ira would say to me, 'His daughter is in the house with him, in one room, and he's in another room with a sailor. She should *protect* her daughter from this stuff. She shouldn't drag her over to France to have her witness stuff like that. Why doesn't she protect her daughter?'

"I know my brother—I know what he wants to say. He wants to say, I forbid you to go ever again. I told him, 'You're not the girl's father. You can't forbid her kid to do anything.' I said, 'If you want to leave the marriage because of this, leave it because of this. Otherwise, stay and live with it.'

"It was the first shot I'd had at even hinting at what I'd been wanting to say all along. Having a fling with her was one thing. A movie star—why not? But marriage? Glaringly wrong in every way. This woman has no contact with politics and especially not with Communism. Knows her way around the complicated plots of the Victorian novelists, can rattle off the names of the people in Trollope, but completely unknowing about society and the workaday doings of anything. The woman is dressed by Dior. Fabulous clothes. Owns a thousand little hats with little veils. Shoes and handbags made out of reptiles. Spends lots of money on clothes. While Ira is a guy who spends four ninety-nine for a pair of shoes. He finds one of her bills for an eight-hundred-dollar dress. Doesn't even know what this means. He goes to her closet and looks at the dress and tries to figure out how it can cost so much. As a Communist, he should be irritated by her from the first second. So what explains this marriage with her and not with a comrade? In the party, couldn't he have found somebody who supported him, who was together with him in the fight?

"Doris always excused him and made allowances for him, came to Ira's defense every time I started in. 'Yes,' Doris said, 'here is a Communist, a big revolutionary, a party member with his kind of zeal, and he suddenly falls in love with an unthinking actress in this year's ladylike waspy-waist jackets and long skirts, who is famous and beautiful, who is steeped like a teabag in aristocratic pretensions, and it contradicts his entire moral standard—but this is love.' 'Is it?' I would ask her. 'Looks like credulity and confusion to me. Ira has no intuition about emotional questions. The lack of emotional intuition goes along with his being the kind of flat-footed radical he is. Those people are not very psychologically attuned.' But Doris's rebuttal is to justify him by nothing less than the annihilating power of love. 'Love,' says Doris, 'love is not something that is logical. Vanity is not something that is logical. *Ira* is not something that is logical. Each of us in this world has his own vanity, and therefore his own tailor-made blindness. Eve Frame is Ira's.'

"Even at his funeral, where there weren't twenty people, Doris stood up and made a speech on this very subject, a woman who dreaded speaking in public. She said he was a Communist with a weakness for life; he was an impassioned Communist who was not, however, made to live in the closed enclave of the party, and that was what subverted and destroyed him. He was not perfect from the Communist point of view—thank God. The personal he could not renounce. The personal kept bursting out of Ira, militant and single-minded though he would try to be. It's one thing to have your party allegiance and it's also one thing to be who you are and not able to restrain yourself. There was no side of himself that he could suppress. Ira lived everything personally, Doris said, to the hilt, including his contradictions.

"Well, maybe yes, maybe no. The contradictions were indisputable. The personal openness and the Communist secrecy. The home life and the party. The need for a child, the desire for a family—should a party member with his aspirations care about having a child like that? Even to one's contradictions one might impose a limit. A guy from the streets marries an *artiste*? A guy in his thirties marries a woman in her forties with a big adult baby who is still living at home? The incompatibilities were endless. But then, that was the challenge. With Ira, the more that's wrong, the more to correct.

"I told him, 'Ira, the situation with Pennington is *un*correctable. The only way to correct it is by not being there.' I told him more or less what O'Day had been telling him back with Donna. 'This is not politics—this is private life. You can't bring to private life the ideology that you bring to the great world. You cannot change her. What you've got, you've got; if it is insufferable, then leave. This is a woman who married a homosexual, lived twelve years untouched by a homosexual husband, and who continues her involvement with him even though he behaves in front of their daughter in a way that she considers detrimental to her daughter's well-being. She must consider it even more detrimental for Sylphid not to see her father at all. She's caught in a dilemma, probably there *is* no right thing for her to do—so let it be, don't bother her about it, let it go.'

"Then I asked, 'Tell me, are other things insufferable? Other things you want to go in and change? Because if there are, forget it. You cannot change *anything*.'

"But change was what Ira lived for. *Why* he lived. Why he lived *strenuously*. It is the essence of the man that he treats everything as a challenge to his will. He must always make the effort. He must change everything. For him that was the purpose of being in the world. Everything he wanted to change was here.

"But as soon as you want passionately what is beyond your control, you are primed to be thwarted—you are preparing to be brought to your knees.

"'Tell me,' I said to Ira, 'if you were to put all the insufferable things in a column and draw a line under them and add them up, do they add up to "Totally Insufferable"? Because if they do, then even if you only got there the day before yesterday, even if this marriage is still brand-new, you must go. Because your tendency, when you make a mistake, is not to go. Your tendency is to correct things in that vehement way that the people in this family like to correct things. That's a worry to me right now.'

"He had already told me about Eve's third marriage, the marriage after Pennington, to Freedman, and so I said to him, 'Sounds like one disaster after another. And you are going to do what, exactly—undo the disasters? The Great Emancipator off the stage as well as on? Is that why you seek her out in the first place? You're going to show her that you're a bigger and better man than the great Hollywood star? You're going to show her that a Jew isn't a rapacious capitalist like Freedman but a justice-making machine like you?'

"Doris and I had been to dinner there already. I had seen the Pennington-Frame family in action, and so I unloaded about that too. I unloaded everything. 'That daughter is a time bomb, Ira. Resentful, sullen, baleful—a person narrowly focused on exhibiting herself who otherwise is not there. She is a strong-willed person used to getting what she wants, and you, Ira Ringold, are in her way. Sure, you are strong-willed too, and bigger and older and a man. But you will not be able to make your will known. Where the daughter is concerned, you can have no moral authority *because* you are bigger and older and a man. That is going to be a source of frustration to a tycoon in the moral-authority racket like you. In you, the daughter is going to discover the meaning of a word that she could never have begun to learn from her mother: resistance. You are a six-foot six-inch hindrance, a hazard to her tyranny over the star who is mom.'

"I used strong language. I was an intense fellow myself in those days. I would get unsettled by the irrational, particularly when it emanated from my brother. I was more vehement than I should have been, but I didn't really overstate the case. I saw it right off, out of the gate, the night we went there for dinner. I would have thought you couldn't miss it, but Ira gets indignant. 'How do you know all this? How do you know all these things? Because you're so smart,' he says, 'or because I'm so dumb?' 'Ira,' I told him, 'there is a family of two living in that house, not a family of three, a family of two that has no concrete human relationships except each with the other. There is a family living in that house that can't find the right scale for *anything*. The mother in that house is being emotionally blackmailed by the daughter. You will not live happily as the protector of someone who is being emotionally blackmailed. Nothing is clearer in that household than the reversal of authority. Sylphid is the one wielding the whip. Nothing is clearer than that the daughter bears a rankling grudge against the mother. Nothing is clearer than that the daughter has got it in for the mother for some unpardonable crime. Nothing is clearer than how uncurbed the two of them are with their overwrought emotions. There is certainly no pleasure between those two. There will never be anything resembling a decent, modest state of accord between so frightened a mother and this overweening, unweaned child.'

"'Ira, the relationship between a mother and a daughter or a mother and a son isn't all that complicated. I have a daughter,' I told him, 'I know about daughters. It's one thing to be with your daughter because you're infatuated with her, because you're in love; it's another to be with her because you're terrified of her. Ira, the daughter's rage at her mother's remarrying will doom your household from the start. "Every unhappy family is unhappy in its own way." I am simply describing to you the way that family is unhappy.'

"That's when he lit into me. 'Look, I don't live on Lehigh Avenue,' he told me. 'I love your Doris, she's a wonderful wife and a wonderful mother, but I'm not myself interested in the bourgeois Jewish marriage with the two sets of dishes. I never lived inside the bourgeois conventions and I have no intention of starting now. You actually propose that I give up a woman I love, a talented, wonderful human being—whose life, by the way, hasn't been a bed of roses either—give her up and run away because of this kid who plays the harp? That to you is the great problem in my life? The problem in my life is that union I belong to, Murray, moving that goddamn actors' union from where it is stuck to where it belongs. The problem in my life is the writer for my show. My problem isn't being a hindrance to

Eve's kid—I'm a hindrance to Artie Sokolow, *that's* the problem. I sit down with this guy before he turns in the script, and I go over it with him, and if I don't like my lines, Murray, I tell him so. I won't *do* the goddamn lines if I don't like 'em. I sit down and I fight with him till he gives me something to say that gets across a message that is socially useful—'

"Leave it to Ira to aggressively miss the point. His mind moved, all right, but not with clarity. It moved only with force. 'I don't care,' I told him, 'if you're strutting the stage and telling people how to write their scripts. I'm talking about something else. I'm not talking about conventional or unconventional or bourgeois or bohemian. I'm talking about a household where the mother is a pathetic carpet for the daughter to stomp on. It's crazy that you, the son of our father, who grew up in our house, won't recognize how explosive domestic arrangements can be, how ruinous to people. The enervating bickering. The daily desperation. The hour-by-hour negotiation. This is a household that is completely out of whack—'

"Well, it wasn't hard for Ira to say 'Fuck off' and never see you again. He didn't modulate. There's first gear and then suddenly there's fifth gear, and he's gone. I couldn't stop, I wouldn't stop, and so he tells me to go fuck myself and he leaves. Six weeks later I wrote him a letter he didn't answer. Then I made phone calls he wouldn't answer. In the end I went to New York and I corralled the guy and I apologized. 'You were right, I was wrong. It's none of my business. We miss you. We want you to come over. You want to bring Eve, bring her—you don't want to, don't. Lorraine misses you. She loves you and she doesn't know what happened. Doris misses you . . .' Et cetera. I wanted to say, 'You've got your eye on the wrong menace. The menace to you is not imperialist capitalism. The menace to you isn't your public actions, the menace to you is your private life. It always was and it always will be.'

"There were nights I couldn't sleep. I'd say to Doris, 'Why doesn't he *leave*? Why can't he *leave*?' And do you know what Doris would answer? 'Because he's like everybody—you only realize things when they're over. Why don't you leave *me*? All the human stuff that makes it hard for anybody to be with anybody else—don't we have it? We have arguments. We have disagreements. We have what everybody has—the little this and

the little that, the little insults that pile up, the little temptations that pile up. Don't you think I know that there are
women who are attracted to you? Teachers at school, women
in the union, powerfully attracted to my husband? Don't you
think I know you had a year, after you got back from the war,
when you didn't know why you were still with me, when you
asked yourself every day, "Why don't I leave her?" But you
didn't. Because by and large people don't. Everyone's dissatis-
fied, but by and large *not* leaving is what people do. Especially
people who've been left themselves, like you and your brother.
Come through what you two came through and you value
stability very highly. Probably overvalue it. The hardest thing
in the world is to cut the knot of your life and leave. People
make ten thousand adjustments to even the most pathological
behavior. Why, emotionally, is a man of his type reciprocally
connected to a woman of her type? The usual reason: their
flaws fit. Ira cannot leave that marriage any more than he can
leave the Communist Party.'

"Anyway, the baby. Johnny O'Day Ringold. Eve told Ira
that when she had Sylphid out in Hollywood, it was different
for her than it was for Pennington. When Pennington went off
every day to work in a movie, everybody accepted it; when *she*
went off every day to work in a movie, the baby was left with a
governess, and so Eve was a bad mother, a neglectful mother,
a selfish mother, and everybody was unhappy, including her.
She told him she couldn't go through that again. It had been
too hard on her and too hard on Sylphid. She told Ira that in
many ways that strain was what had ruined *her* Hollywood
career.

"But Ira said she wasn't in movies anymore, she was in radio.
She was at the top of radio. She didn't go off every day to a
studio—she went off two days a week. It wasn't the same at all.
And Ira Ringold wasn't Carlton Pennington. He wouldn't
leave her in the lurch with the kid. They wouldn't need any
governess. The hell with that. He'd raise their Johnny O'Day
himself if he had to. Once Ira got something between his teeth,
he wasn't about to let go. And Eve wasn't somebody who
could take the barrage. People went after her and she collapsed.
And so he believed he'd convinced her on this score, too. Finally she said to him he was right, it wasn't at all the same, and

she said okay, they'd have the baby, and he was euphoric, in seventh heaven—you should have heard him.

"But then that night before he came over to Newark, the night before you two met, she broke down and said she couldn't go through with it. She told him how wretched she felt denying him something he wanted so much, but she couldn't live through it all again. This went on for hours, and what could he do? What good was it going to do anybody—her, or him, or little Johnny—for this to be the backdrop to their family life? He was miserable, and they were up till three or four that night, but it was over as far as he was concerned. He was a persistent guy, but he couldn't tie her to her bed and keep her there for seven more months in order to have a child. If she didn't want it, she didn't want it. And so he told her he'd go with her down to Camden to the abortion doctor. She wouldn't be alone."

Listening to Murray, I couldn't help but be overtaken by memories of being with Ira, memories I didn't even know I continued to have, memories of how I used to gorge myself on his words and on his adult convictions, solid memories of the two of us walking in Weequahic Park and his telling me about the impoverished kids he'd seen in Iran—pronounced by Ira "Eye-ran."

"When I got to Iran," Ira told me, "the natives there suffered from every type of illness you can think of. Being Moslem, they used to wash their hands before and after defecating—but they did it in the river, the river that was in front of us, so to speak. They washed their hands in the same water they urinated in. Their living conditions were terrible, Nathan. The place was run by sheiks. And not romantic sheiks. These guys were like the dictator of the tribe. Y'understand? The army gave them money so the natives would work for us, and we gave the natives rations of rice and tea. That was it. Rice and tea. Those living conditions—I had never seen anything like it. I'd grubbed for work in the Depression, I hadn't been brought up at the Ritz—but this was something else. When we had to defecate, for instance, we defecated into GI pails—iron buckets, that's what they were. And somebody had to empty them out, and so we emptied them out in the garbage dump. And who do you think was there?"

All at once Ira couldn't go on, couldn't speak. He couldn't walk. It would always alarm me when this happened to him. And because he knew that, he'd tap the air with his hand, signaling me to be still, to wait him out, he'd be all right.

Things that were not to his liking he could not discuss with equilibrium. His whole manly bearing could be altered almost beyond recognition by anything that involved human degradation, and, perhaps because of his own shattered development as a boy, that involved particularly the suffering and degradation of children. When he said to me, "And who do you think was there?" I knew who was there because of the way he began to breathe. "Ahhh . . . ahhh . . . ahhh." Gasping like someone about to die. When he was emotionally intact enough to resume the walk, I asked as though I didn't know, "Who, Ira? Who was there?"

"The kids. They lived there. And they would pick through the garbage dump for food—"

This time when he stopped speaking my alarm got the better of me; fearful that he might get stuck, be so overwhelmed—not only by his emotions but by an immense loneliness that seemed suddenly to strip him of his strength—that he'd never find the way back to being the brave, angry hero I adored, I knew I had to do something, anything I could, and so I tried at least to complete his thought for him. I said, "And it was awful."

He patted my back and we started walking again.

"To me it was," he finally replied. "To my army buddies it mattered not. I never heard anybody comment on it. I never saw anybody—from my own America—deploring the situation. I was really pissed. But there was nothing I could do about it. In the army there's no democracy. Y'understand? You don't go telling anybody higher up. And this had been going on for God knows how long. This is what world history *is*. That's how people live." Then he erupted, "This is how people *make* them live!"

We took trips around Newark together so that Ira could show me the non-Jewish neighborhoods I didn't really know—the First Ward, where he'd been brought up and where the poor

Italians lived; Down Neck, where the poor Irish and the poor
Poles lived—and Ira all the while explaining to me that, contrary to what I might have heard growing up, these were not
simply goyim but "working people like working people all over
this country, diligent, poor, powerless, struggling every goddamn day to live a decent and dignified life."

We went into Newark's Third Ward, where the Negroes had
come to occupy the streets and houses of the old Jewish immigrant slum. Ira spoke to everyone he saw, men and women,
boys and girls, asked what they did and how they lived and
what they thought about maybe changing "the crappy system
and the whole damn pattern of ignorant cruelty" that deprived
them of their equality. He'd sit down on a bench outside a
Negro barbershop on shabby Spruce Street, around the corner
from where my father had been raised in a Belmont Avenue
tenement, say to the men congregated on the sidewalk, "I'm
ever a guy to butt into other people's conversations," and begin
talking to them about their equality, and to me he never looked
more like the elongated Abraham Lincoln who is cast in bronze
at the foot of the broad stairway leading up to Newark's Essex
County Courthouse, Gutzon Borglum's locally famous Lincoln,
seated and waiting welcomingly on a marble bench before the
courthouse, in his sociable posture and by his gaunt bearded
face revealing that he is wise and grave and fatherly and judi-
cious and good. Out in front of that Spruce Street barbershop
—with Ira declaiming, when someone asked his opinion, that
"a Negro has the right to eat any damn place he feels like paying the check!"—I realized that I'd never before imagined, let
alone seen, a white person being so easygoing and at home
with Negroes.

"What most people mistake for Negro sullenness and stupidity—you know what that is, Nathan? It's a protective shell.
But when they meet somebody who is free of race prejudice—you see what happens, they don't *need* that shell. They
got their share of psychos, sure, but you tell me who doesn't."

When Ira one day discovered outside the barbershop a very
old, bitter black man who liked nothing better than to vent
his spleen in vehement discussion about the beastliness of
humanity—"Everything we know of has developed not out of
the tyranny of tyrants but out of the tyranny of mankind's

greed, ignorance, brutality, and hatred. The tyrant of evil is *Everyman!*"—we went back several times more, and people gathered round to hear Ira going at it with this impressive malcontent who was always neatly dressed in a dark suit and a tie and who all the other men respectfully called "Mr. Prescott": Ira proselytizing one on one, one Negro at a time, the Lincoln-Douglas debates in a strange new form.

"Are you still convinced," Ira asked him, graciously, "that the working class will go along for the crumbs from the imperialist's table?" "I am, sir! The mass of men of *whatever* color is and always will be mindless, torpid, wicked, and stupid. If ever they should become less impoverished, they will be even *more* mindless, torpid, wicked, and stupid!" "Well, I've been thinking about that, Mr. Prescott, and I'm convinced that you are in error. The simple fact that there aren't enough crumbs to keep the working class fed and docile refutes that theory. All you gentlemen here are underestimating the proximity of industrial collapse. It's true that most of our working people would stick with Truman and the Marshall Plan if they were sure it would keep them employed. But the contradiction is this: the channeling of the bulk of production to war materiel, both for the American forces and for those of the puppet governments, *is impoverishing American workers.*"

Even in the face of Mr. Prescott's seemingly hard-won misanthropy, Ira tried to insert some reason and hope into the discussion, plant if not in Mr. Prescott then in the sidewalk audience an awareness of the transformations that could be effected in men's lives through concerted political action. For me it was, as Wordsworth describes the days of the French Revolution, "very Heaven": "Bliss was it in that dawn to be alive, / But to be young was very Heaven!" The two of us, white and surrounded by some ten or twelve black men, and there was nothing for us to worry about and nothing for any of them to fear: it was not we who were their oppressors or they who were our enemies—the oppressor-enemy by which we were all appalled was the way the society was organized and run.

It was after the first visit to Spruce Street that he treated me to cheesecake at the Weequahic Diner and, while we ate, told me about the Negroes he'd worked with in Chicago.

"This plant was in the heart of Chicago's black belt," he

said. "About ninety-five percent of the employees were colored, and there is where the esprit I was telling you about enters in. It's the only place I've ever been where a Negro is on an absolutely equal footing with everybody else. So the whites don't feel guilty and the Negroes don't feel mad all the time. Y'understand? Promotions based solely on seniority—no finagling about it."

"What are Negroes like when you work with them?"

"As far as I can determine, there was no suspicion of us whites. First off, the colored people knew that any white the UE sent to this plant was either a Communist or a pretty faithful fellow traveler. So they weren't inhibited. They knew that we were as free from race prejudice as an adult in this time and society can be. When you saw a paper being read, about two to one it was the *Daily Worker*. The *Chicago Defender* and the *Racing Form* were about neck and neck for second place. Hearst and McCormick strictly ruled off the track."

"But what are Negroes actually like? Personally."

"Well, buddy, there are some ugly types, if that's what you're asking me. That has a basis in actuality. But that's a small minority, and an El ride through the Negro ghettos is enough to indicate to anyone with an open mind what warps people into these shapes. The characteristic I was most aware of among the Negro people is their warm friendliness. And, at our record factory, the love of music. At our factory, there were speakers all over the place, amplifiers, and anybody who wanted a special tune played—and this is all on working time—just had to request it. The guys would sing, jive—not uncommon for a guy to grab a girl and dance. About a third of the employees were Negro girls. Nice girls. We'd smoke, read, brew coffee, argue at the top of our voices, and the work went right along without a hitch or a break."

"Did you have Negro friends?"

"Sure. Sure I did. There was a big guy named Earl Something-or-Other who I took a liking to right away because he looked like Paul Robeson. It didn't take me long to discover that he was about the same kind of tramp working stiff as me. Earl would ride the streetcar and El as far as I did, and we made a point to take the same ones, the way guys do, to have somebody to chew the fat with. Right up to the plant gates,

Earl and me would talk and laugh the same as we did on the job. But once inside, where there were whites he doesn't know, Earl clams right up and just says 'So long' when I get off the El. That's it. Y'understand?"

In the pages of the small brown notebooks that Ira had brought back from the war, interspersed among his observations and the statements of belief, were the names and stateside addresses of about every politically like-minded soldier he had met in the service. He had begun to track these men down, sending letters all over the country and visiting the guys who lived in New York and Jersey. One day we took a ride up to suburban Maplewood, just west of Newark, to visit former sergeant Erwin Goldstine, who in Iran had been as far to the left as Johnny O'Day—"a very well developed Marxist," Ira called him—but who, back home, we discovered, had married into a family that owned a Newark mattress factory and now, a father of three, had become an adherent of everything he had once opposed. About Taft-Hartley, about race relations, about price controls, he did not even argue with Ira. He just laughed.

Goldstine's wife and his kids were away with the in-laws for the afternoon, and we sat together in his kitchen drinking soda while Goldstine, a wiry little guy with the haughty, knowing air of a street-corner sharpie, laughed and sneered at everything Ira said. His explanation for his turnabout? "Didn't know shit from shinola. Didn't know what I was talking about." To me Goldstine said, "Kid, don't listen to him. You live in America. It's the greatest country in the world and it's the greatest system in the world. Sure, people get shit on. You think they don't get shit on in the Soviet Union? He tells you capitalism is a dog-eat-dog system. What is life if not a dog-eat-dog system? This is a system that is in tune with life. And because it is, it works. Look, everything the Communists say about capitalism is true, and everything the capitalists say about Communism is true. The difference is, our system works because it's based on the truth about people's selfishness, and theirs doesn't because it's based on a fairy tale about people's *brotherhood*. It's such a crazy fairy tale they've got to take people and put them in Siberia in order to get them to believe it. In order to get them to believe in their brotherhood, they've got to control people's every thought or shoot 'em. And meanwhile in America, in

Europe, the Communists go on with this fairy tale even when they know what is really there. Sure, for a while you don't know. But what don't you know? You know human beings. So you know everything. You know that this fairy tale cannot be possible. If you are a very young man I suppose it's okay. Twenty, twenty-one, twenty-two, okay. But after that? No reason that a person with an average intelligence can take this story, this fairy tale of Communism, and swallow it. 'We will do something that will be wonderful . . .' But we know what our brother is, don't we? He's a shit. And we know what our friend is, don't we? He's a semi-shit. And *we* are semi-shits. So how can it be wonderful? Not even cynicism, not even skepticism, just ordinary powers of human observation tell us *that is not possible.*

"You want to come down to my capitalist factory and watch a mattress being made the way a capitalist makes a mattress? You come down and you'll talk to real working guys. This guy's a radio star. You're not talking to a workingman, you're talking to a radio star. Come on, Ira, you're a star like Jack Benny— what the hell do you know about work? The kid comes to my factory and he'll see how we manufacture a mattress, he'll see the care we take, he'll see how I have to stand over the whole operation every step of the way to see they don't fuck up my mattress. He'll see what it is to be the evil owner of the means of production. It's to work your ass off twenty-four hours a day. The workers go home at five o'clock—I don't. I'm there till midnight every night. I come home and I don't sleep 'cause I'm doing the books in my head and then I'm there again at six in the morning to open the place up. Don't let him fill you full of Communist ideas, kid. They're all lies. Make money. Money's not a lie. Money's the democratic way to keep score. Make your money—then, if you still have to, *then* make your points about the brotherhood of man."

Ira leaned back in his chair, raised his arms so that his huge hands were interlaced behind his neck, and, his contempt undisguised, said—though not to our host but, so as to gall him to the utmost, pointedly to me—"You know one of life's best feelings? Maybe *the* best? Not being afraid. The mercenary schmuck whose house we are in—you know what his story is?

He is afraid. That's the simple fact of it. In World War II Erwin Goldstine was not afraid. But now the war is over, and Erwin Goldstine is afraid of his wife, afraid of his father-in-law, afraid of the bill collector—he is afraid of everything. You look with your big eyes into the capitalist shop window, you want and you want, you grab and you grab, you take and you take, you acquire and you own and you accumulate, and there is the end of your convictions and the beginning of your fear. There is nothing that I have that I can't give up. Y'understand? Nothing has come my way that I'm tied and bound to like a mercenary is. How I ever got from my father's miserable house on Factory Street to being this character Iron Rinn, how Ira Ringold, with one and a half years of high school behind him, got to meeting the people I meet and knowing the people I know and having the comforts I have now as a card-carrying member of the privileged class—that is all so unbelievable that losing everything overnight would not seem so strange to me. Y'understand? Y'understand me? I can go back to the Midwest. I can work in the mills. And if I have to, I will. Anything but to become a rabbit like this guy. That's what you now are politically," he said, looking at last at Goldstine—"not a man, a rabbit, a rabbit of no consequence."

"Full of shit in Iran and full of shit still, Iron Man." Then, again to me—I was the sounding board, the straight man, the fuse on the bomb—Goldstine said, "Nobody could ever listen to anything he says. Nobody could ever take him seriously. The guy's a joke. He can't think. Never could. Doesn't know anything, doesn't see anything, doesn't learn anything. The Communists get a dummy like Ira and they use him. Mankind at its stupidest doesn't come any stupider." Then, turning to Ira, he said, "Get out of my house, you dumb Communist prick."

My heart was already wildly thumping before I even saw the pistol that Goldstine had drawn out of a kitchen cabinet drawer, out of the drawer right behind him where the silverware was stored. Up close, I'd never seen a pistol before, except tucked safely away in the hip holster of a Newark cop. It wasn't because Goldstine was small that the pistol looked big. It *was* big, improbably big, black, and well made, molded, machined—eloquent with possibility.

Though Goldstine was standing and pointing the pistol at Ira's forehead, even up on his feet he wasn't much taller than Ira was seated.

"I'm scared of you, Ira," Goldstine said to him. "I've always been scared of you. You're a wild man, Ira. I'm not going to wait for you to do to me what you did to Butts. Remember Butts? Remember little Butts? Get up and get out, Iron Man. Take Kid Asslick with you. Asslick, didn't the Iron Man ever tell you about Butts?" Goldstine said to me. "He tried to kill Butts. He tried to drown Butts. He dragged Butts out of the mess hall—didn't you tell the kid, Ira, about you in Iran, about the rages and the tantrums in Iran? Guy weighing a hundred and twenty pounds comes at the Iron Man here with a mess kit knife, a very dangerous weapon, you see, and the Iron Man picks him up and carries him out of the mess hall and drags him down to the docks, and he holds him upside down over the water, holds him by his feet, and he says, 'Swim, hillbilly.' Butts is crying, 'No, no, I can't,' and the Iron Man says, 'Can't you?' and drops him in. Headfirst over the side of the dock into the Shatt-al-Arab. River's thirty feet deep. Butts goes straight down. Then Ira turns and he is screaming at *us*. 'Leave the redneck bastard alone! Get out of here! Nobody go near that water!' 'He's drowning, Iron Man.' 'Let him,' Ira says, 'stay back! I know what I'm doing! Let him go down!' Somebody jumps in the water to try and get at Butts, and so Ira jumps in after him, lands on him, starts pummeling this guy's head and gouging his eyes and holding *him* under. You didn't tell the kid about Butts? How come? Didn't you tell him about Garwych, either? About Solak? About Becker? Get up. Get up and get out, you crazy fucking homicidal nut."

But Ira didn't move. Except for his eyes. His eyes were like birds that wanted to fly out of his face. They were twitching and blinking in a way I'd never before seen, while along the entire length of him he looked as though he'd ossified, assumed a tautness as terrifying as the flapping of his eyes.

"No, Erwin," he said, "not with a sidearm in my face. Only ways to get me out are pull the trigger or call the cops."

I couldn't have said which of them was more frightening. Why didn't Ira do what Goldstine wanted—why didn't the *two* of us get up and go? Who was crazier, the mattress manufacturer with the loaded pistol or the giant daring him to fire it? What was happening here? We were in a sunny kitchen in Maplewood, New Jersey, drinking Royal Crown from the bottle. We were all three of us Jews. Ira had come by to say hello to an old army buddy. What was *wrong* with these guys?

It was when I began to tremble that Ira ceased to look deformed by whatever antirational thought he was thinking. Across the table from him he saw my teeth chattering all on their own, my hands uncontrollably shaking all on their own, and he came to his senses and slowly rose from his chair. He raised his arms over his head the way they do when the bank robbers in the movies shout "It's a stickup!"

"All over, Nathan. Quarrel called on account of darkness." But despite the easygoing way he managed to say that, despite the surrender that was implicit in his mockingly raised arms, as we left the house through the kitchen door and made our way down the driveway to Murray's car, Goldstine continued after us, his pistol only inches from Ira's skull.

In a sort of trance state Ira drove us through the quiet Maplewood streets, past all the pleasant one-family houses where there lived the ex-Newark Jews who'd lately acquired their first homes and their first lawns and their first country club affiliations. Not the sort of people or the sort of neighborhood where you would expect to find a pistol in with the dinnerware.

Only when we crossed the Irvington line and were heading into Newark did Ira come around and ask, "You okay?"

I was miserable, though less frightened now than humiliated and ashamed. Clearing my throat so as to be sure to speak in an unbroken voice, I said, "I pissed in my pants."

"Did you?"

"I thought he was going to kill you."

"You were brave. You were very brave. You were fine."

"Walking down the driveway, I pissed in my pants!" I said angrily. "Goddamnit! Shit!"

"It's *my* fault. The whole thing. Exposing you to that putz. Pulling a gun! A *gun*!"

"Why did he *do* that?"

"Butts didn't drown," Ira suddenly said. "*Nobody* drowned. Nobody was *going* to drown."

"Did you throw him in?"

"Sure. Sure I threw him in. This was the hillbilly who called me a kike. I told you that story."

"I remember." But what he'd told me was only a part of that story. "That's the night they waylaid you. They beat you up."

"Yeah. They beat me, all right. After they fished the son of a bitch out."

He let me off at my house, where no one was at home and I was able to drop my damp clothing into the hamper and take a shower and calm down. I had the shakes again in the shower, not so much because I was remembering sitting at the kitchen table with Goldstine pointing his pistol at Ira's forehead or remembering Ira's eyes looking like they wanted to fly out of his head, but because I was thinking, A loaded pistol in with the forks and the knives? In Maplewood, New Jersey? Why? Because of Garwych, that's why! Because of Solak! Because of Becker!

All the questions I hadn't dared to ask him in the car, I started asking aloud alone in the shower. "What did you do to them, Ira?"

My father, unlike my mother, didn't see Ira as a means of social advancement for me and was always perplexed and bothered by his calling me: what is this grown man's interest in this kid? He thought something complicated, if not downright sinister, was going on. "Where do you go with him?" my father asked me.

His suspiciousness erupted vehemently one night when he found me at my desk reading a copy of the *Daily Worker*. "I don't want the Hearst papers in my house," my father told me, "and I don't want *that* paper in my house. One is the mirror image of the other. If this man is giving you the *Daily Worker*—" "What 'man'?" "Your actor friend. *Rinn*, as he calls himself." "He doesn't give me the *Daily Worker*. I bought it downtown. I bought it myself. Is there a law against that?" "Who told you to buy it? Did he tell you go out and buy it?" "He doesn't tell me to do anything." "I hope that's true." "I don't lie! It is!"

It was. I'd remembered Ira saying that there was a column in the *Worker* by Howard Fast, but it was on my own that I had bought the paper, across from Proctor's movie theater at a

Market Street newsstand, ostensibly to read Howard Fast but also out of simple, dogged curiosity. "Are you going to confiscate it?" I asked my father. "No—you're out of luck. I'm not going to make you a martyr to the First Amendment. I only hope that after you've read it and studied and thought about it, you have the good sense to know that it's a sheet of lies and to confiscate it yourself."

Toward the end of the school year, when Ira invited me to spend a week up at the shack with him that summer, my father said I wasn't going unless Ira had a talk with him first.

"Why?" I demanded to know.

"I want to ask him some questions."

"What are you, the House Un-American Activities Committee? Why are you making such a big thing out of this?"

"Because in my eyes *you* are a big thing. What's his telephone number in New York?"

"You *can't* ask him questions. About what?"

"You have your right as an American to buy and read the *Daily Worker*? I have a right as an American to ask anybody anything I want. If he doesn't want to answer me, that's *his* right."

"And if he doesn't want to answer, what's he supposed to do, take the Fifth Amendment?"

"No. He can tell me to go jump in the lake. I just explained it to you: that's how we do it in the USA. I don't say that's going to work for you in the Soviet Union with the secret police, but here that's all it ordinarily takes for a fellow citizen to leave you alone about your political ideas."

"*Do* they leave you alone?" I asked bitterly. "Does Congressman Dies leave you alone? Does Congressman Rankin leave you alone? Maybe you better explain it to *them*."

I had to sit there—he told me I had to—and listen to him while he asked Ira, on the phone, to come over to his office for a talk. Iron Rinn and Eve Frame were the biggest things ever to enter the Zuckerman household from the outside world, yet it was clear from my father's tone that this didn't throw him at all.

"He said *yes*?" I asked when my father hung up.

"He said he'd be there if Nathan would be there. You're going to be there."

"Oh, no I'm not."

"Yep," my father said, "you are. You are if you want me even to begin to consider your going up there to visit. What are you afraid of, an open discussion of ideas? It's going to be democracy in action, next Wednesday, after school, at three-thirty in my office. You be on time, son."

What was I afraid of? My father's anger. Ira's temper. What if because of how my father attacked him Ira picked him up bodily the way he picked up Butts and carried him down to the lake at Weequahic Park and threw him in? If a fight broke out, if Ira threw a lethal punch . . .

My father's chiropody office was on the ground floor of a three-family house at the bottom of Hawthorne Avenue, a modest dwelling in need of a face-lift near the rundown edge of our otherwise plainly pedestrian neighborhood. I was there early, feeling sick to my stomach. Ira, looking serious and not at all enraged (as yet), arrived promptly at three-thirty. My father asked him to be seated.

"Mr. Ringold, my son Nathan is not a run-of-the-mill boy. He is an older son who is an excellent student and who, I believe, is advanced and mature beyond his years. We are very proud of him. I want to give him all the latitude I can. I try not to stand in his way in life, as some fathers do. But because I honestly happen to think that for him the sky is the limit, I don't want anything to happen to him. If anything should happen to this boy . . ."

My father's voice grew husky and he abruptly stopped talking. I was terrified that Ira was going to laugh at him, to mock him the way he'd mocked Goldstine. I knew that my father was choked up not merely because of me and my promise but because his two youngest brothers, the first members of that large, poor family of his who were targeted to go to a real college and become real doctors, had both died of illnesses in their late teens. Studio portrait photos of them rested next to each other in twin frames on our dining room sideboard. I should have explained to Ira about Sam and Sidney, I thought.

"I have to ask you a question, Mr. Ringold, that I don't want to ask you. I don't consider another person's beliefs—religious, political, or otherwise—my business. I respect your privacy. I can assure you that whatever you say here will not go beyond this room. But I want to know whether you are a Communist, and I want my son to know whether you are a Communist. I'm not asking if you ever have been a Communist. I don't care about the past. I care about right now. I have to tell you that back before Roosevelt I was so disgusted with the way things were going in this country, and with the anti-Semitism and anti-Negro prejudice in this country, and with how the Republicans scorned the unfortunate in this country, and with how the greed of big business was milking the people of this country to death, that one day, right here in Newark—and this will come as a shock to my son, who thinks his father, a lifelong Democrat, is to the right of Franco—but one day . . . Well, Nathan," he said, looking now at me, "they had their headquarters—you know where the Robert Treat Hotel is? Right down the street. Upstairs. Thirty-eight Park Place. They had offices up there. One was the office of the Communist Party. I never even told this to your mother. She would have killed me. She was my girlfriend then—this must be 1930. Well, one time, one day, I was angry. Something had happened, I don't even remember what it was any longer, but I read something in the papers and I remember that I went up there, and nobody was there. The door was locked. They had gone to lunch. I rattled the door handle. That's as close as I got to the Communist Party. I rattled the door and said, 'Let me in.' You didn't know that, did you, son?"

"No," I said.

"Well, now you do. Luckily, that door was locked. And in the next election Franklin Roosevelt became the president, and the kind of capitalism that sent me down to the Communist Party office began to get an overhaul the likes of which this country had never seen. A great man saved this country's capitalism from the capitalists and saved patriotic people like me from Communism. Saved all of us from the dictatorial regime that *results* from Communism. Let me tell you something that shook me—the death of Masaryk. Did that bother you, Mr. Ringold, as much as it bothered me? I always admired Masaryk in Czechoslovakia, ever since I first heard his name and what he was doing for his people. I always thought of him as the Czech Roosevelt. I don't know how to account for his murder. Do you, Mr. Ringold? I was troubled by it. I couldn't believe the Communists could kill a man like that. But they did . . . Sir, I don't want to get started having a political argument. I'm going to ask you one single question, and I'd like you to answer so that my son and I know where we stand. Are you a member of the Communist Party?"

"No, Doctor, I'm not."

"Now I want my son to ask you. Nathan, I want you to ask Mr. Ringold if he is now a member of the Communist Party."

To put such a question to somebody went against my every political principle. But because my father wanted me to and because my father had asked Ira already to no ill effect and because of Sam and Sidney, my father's dead younger brothers, I did it.

"Are you, Ira?" I asked him.

"Nope. No, sir."

"You don't go to meetings of the Communist Party?" my father asked.

"I do not."

"You don't plan, up where you want Nathan to visit you—what's the name of the place?"

"Zinc Town. Zinc Town, New Jersey."

"You don't plan up there to take him to any such meetings?"

"No, Doctor, I don't. I plan on taking him swimming and hiking and fishing."

"I'm glad to hear that," said my father. "I believe you, sir."

"May I now ask *you* a question, Dr. Zuckerman?" Ira asked, smiling at my father in that droll sidewise way he smiled when he was playing Abraham Lincoln. "Why do you have me down for a Red in the first place?"

"The Progressive Party, Mr. Ringold."

"Do you have Henry Wallace down for a Red? The former vice president to Mr. Roosevelt? Do you think Mr. Roosevelt would choose a Red for vice president of the United States of America?"

"It's not as simple as that," my father replied. "I wish it were. But what's going on in the world is not simple at all."

"Dr. Zuckerman," said Ira, changing tactics, "you wonder what I'm doing with Nathan? I envy him—that's what I'm doing with him. I envy that he has a father like you. I envy that he has a teacher like my brother. I envy that he has good eyes and can read without glasses a foot thick and isn't an idiot who's going to quit school so as to go out and dig ditches. I've got nothing hidden and nothing to hide, Doctor. Except that I wouldn't mind a son like him myself someday. Maybe the world today isn't simple, but this sure is: I get a kick out of talking to your boy. Not every kid in Newark takes as his hero Tom Paine."

Here my father stood up and extended his hand to Ira. "I *am* a father, Mr. Ringold—to *two* boys, to Nathan and to Henry, his younger brother, who is also somebody to crow about. And my responsibilities as a father . . . well, that's all that this has been about."

Ira took my father's ordinary-sized hand in his huge one and pumped it once very hard, so hard—with such sincerity and warmth—that oil, or at least water, a pure geyser of something, might as a result have come gushing from my father's mouth. "Dr. Zuckerman," Ira said, "you don't want your son stolen from you, and nobody here is going to steal him."

Whereupon I had to make a superhuman effort not to start to bawl. I had to pretend to myself that my whole aim in life was not to cry, never to cry, at the sight of two men affectionately shaking hands—and I barely managed to succeed. They'd done it! Without shouting! Without bloodshed! Without the motivating, distorting rage! Magnificently they had pulled it off—though largely because Ira was not telling us the truth.

I'll insert this here and not return to the subject of the wound inflicted on my father's face. I count on the reader to remember it when that seems appropriate.

Ira and I left my father's office together, and to celebrate—purportedly to celebrate my upcoming summer visit to Zinc Town but also, complicitously, to celebrate our victory over my dad—we went to Stosh's, a few blocks away, to have one of Stosh's overstuffed ham sandwiches. I ate so much with Ira at four-fifteen that when I got home, at five of six, I had no appetite and sat at my place at the table while everybody else ate my mother's dinner—and it was then that I observed in my father's face the wound. I had planted it there earlier by going out the door of his office with Ira and not staying behind to talk a little to him until the next patient showed up.

At first I tried to think that maybe I was guiltily imagining that wound because of having felt, not necessarily contemptuous of him, but certainly superior leaving, virtually arm in arm, with Iron Rinn of *The Free and the Brave.* My father didn't want his son stolen from him, and though, strictly speaking, nobody had stolen anybody, the man was no fool and knew that he had lost and, Communist or no Communist, the six-foot six-inch intruder had won. I saw in my father's face a look of resigned disappointment, his kind gray eyes softened by—distressfully subdued by—something midway between melancholy and futility. It was a look that would never be entirely forgotten by me when I was alone with Ira, or, later, with Leo Glucksman, Johnny O'Day, or whomever. Just by taking instruction from these men, I seemed to myself somehow to be selling my father short. His face with that look on it was always looming up, superimposed on the face of the man who was then educating me in life's possibilities. His face bearing the wound of betrayal.

The moment when you first recognize that your father is vulnerable to others is bad enough, but when you understand that he's vulnerable to *you*, still needs you more than you any longer think you need him, when you realize that you might actually be able to frighten him, even to *quash* him if you wanted to—well, the idea is at such cross-purposes with routine filial inclinations that it does not even begin to make sense. All the laboring he had gone through to get to be a chiropodist, a provider, a protector, and I was now running off with another man. It is, morally as well as emotionally, a more dangerous game than one knows at the time, getting all those extra fathers like a pretty girl gets beaux. But that was what I was doing. Always making myself eminently adoptable, I discovered the sense of betrayal that comes of trying to find a surrogate father even though you love your own. It isn't that I ever denounced my father to Ira or anyone else for a cheap advantage—it was enough just, by exercising my freedom, to dump the man I loved for somebody else. If only I had hated him, it would have been easy.

In my third year at Chicago, I brought a girl home with me at Thanksgiving break. She was a gentle girl, mannerly and clever, and I remember the pleasure my parents took in talking to her. One evening, while my mother stayed in the living room entertaining my aunt, who had eaten dinner with us, my father came out to the corner drugstore with the girl and me, and sitting in a booth together we all three ate ice cream sundaes. At one point I went over to buy something like a tube of shaving cream at the pharmacy counter, and when I got back to the table, I saw my father leaning toward the girl. He was holding her hand, and I overheard him telling her, "We lost Nathan when he was sixteen. Sixteen and he left us." By which he meant that I had left *him*. Years later he would use the same words with my wives. "Sixteen and he left us." By which he meant that all my mistakes in life had flowed from that precipitate departure of mine.

He was right, too. If it weren't for my mistakes I'd still be at home sitting on the front stoop.

It was about two weeks later that Ira went as far as he could toward telling the truth. He was in Newark one Saturday to see his brother, and he and I met downtown for lunch, at a bar and grill near City Hall where, for seventy-five cents—"six bits" to Ira—they served charcoal-broiled steak sandwiches with grilled onions, pickles, home fries, cole slaw, and ketchup. For dessert we each ordered apple pie with a rubbery slice of American cheese, a combination that Ira had introduced me to and that I assumed to be the manly way you ate a piece of pie in a "bar and grill."

Then Ira opened a package he was carrying and presented me with a record album called *The Soviet Army Chorus and Band in a Program of Favorites*. Conducted by Boris Alexandrov. Featuring Artur Eisen and Alexei Sergeyev, basses, and Nikolai Abramov, tenor. On the cover of the album was a picture ("Photograph courtesy SOVFOTO") of the conductor, the band, and the chorus, some two hundred men, all wearing Russian military dress uniforms and performing in the great marble Hall of the People. The hall of the Russian working people.

"Ever hear them?"

"Never," I said.

"Take it home and listen. It's yours."

"Thanks, Ira. This is great."

But it was awful. How could I take this album home, and, at home, how could I *listen*?

Instead of driving back to the neighborhood with Ira after lunch, I told him I had to go over to the public library, the main branch on Washington Street, to work on a history paper. Outside the bar and grill I thanked him again for lunch and the present, and he got into his station wagon and drove back to Murray's on Lehigh Avenue while I proceeded down Broad Street in the direction of Military Park and the big main library. I walked past Market Street and all the way to the park, as if my destination were indeed the library, but then, instead of turning left at Rector Street, I ducked off to the right and took a back way along the river to reach Pennsylvania Station.

I asked a newsdealer in the station to change a dollar for me. I took the four quarters over to the storage area and I put one of them into the coin slot of the smallest of the lockers, and into the locker I shoved the record album. After slamming the door shut, I nonchalantly deposited the locker key in my trouser pocket, and proceeded *then* to the library, where I had nothing to do except to sit for several hours in the reference room worrying about where I was going to hide the key.

My father was around the house all weekend, but on Monday he went back to his office, and on Monday afternoons my mother went up to Irvington to visit her sister, and so after my last class I jumped on a 14 bus across the street from school, took it to the end of the line, to Penn Station, removed the record album from the locker, put it in the Bamberger's shopping bag I had folded up inside my notebook that morning and taken with me to school. At home I hid the record album in a small windowless bin in the basement where my mother stored our set of glass Passover dishes in grocery cartons. Come the spring and Passover, when she removed the dishes for us to use that week, I'd have to find another hiding place, but for the time being the album's explosive potential was defused.

Not until I got to college was I able to play the records on a phonograph, and by then Ira and I were already drifting apart. Which didn't mean that when I heard the Soviet Army Chorus singing "Wait for Your Soldier" and "To an Army Man" and

"A Soldier's Farewell"—and, yes, "Dubinushka"—the vision of equality and justice for working people all over the world wasn't reawakened in me. In my dormitory room, I felt proud for having had the guts not to ditch that album—even if I still hadn't guts enough to understand that, with the album, Ira had been trying to tell me: "Yes, I'm a Communist. Of course I'm a Communist. But not a bad Communist, not a Communist who would kill Masaryk or anyone else. I am a beautiful, heartfelt Communist who loves the people and who loves these songs!"

"What happened that next morning?" I asked Murray. "Why did Ira come to Newark that day?"

"Well, Ira slept late that morning. He'd been up with Eve about the abortion till four, and around ten A.M. he was still asleep when he was awakened by someone shouting downstairs. He was in the master bedroom on the second floor on West Eleventh Street, and the voice was coming from the foot of the staircase. It was Sylphid . . .

"Did I mention that the first thing to drive Ira wild was Sylphid telling Eve that she wasn't coming to their wedding? Eve told Ira that Sylphid was doing some kind of program with a flutist and that the Sunday of the wedding was the only day the other girl could rehearse. He himself doesn't particularly care if Sylphid's coming to the wedding but Eve does, and she's crying about it and she's very distraught, and this upsets him. Constantly she gives the daughter the instruments and the power to hurt her—and then she's hurt, but this is the first time he sees it, and he's infuriated. 'Her mother's *wedding*,' Ira said. 'How can she not come to her mother's wedding if that's what her mother wants? *Tell* her she's coming. Don't ask her —*tell* her!' 'I *can't* tell her,' Eve says, 'this is her professional life, this is her music—' 'Okay, *I'll* tell her,' Ira says.

"The upshot was that Eve talked to the girl, and God knows what she said, or promised, or how she begged, but Sylphid showed up at the wedding, in those clothes of hers. A scarf in her hair. She had kinky hair, so she wears these Greek scarves, rakishly as she thought, and they drive her mother crazy. Wears peasant blouses that make her look enormous. Sheer blouses with Greek embroidery on them. Hoop earrings. Lots of bracelets. When she walks, she clinks. You hear her coming. Embroidered schmattas and lots of jewelry. Wore the Greek sandals that you could buy in Greenwich Village. The thongs that tie up to her knees and that dig in and leave marks, and this also makes Eve miserable. But at least the daughter was there, however she looked, and Eve was happy, and so Ira was happy.

"At the end of August, when both their shows were off the air, they married and went up to Cape Cod for a long weekend, and then they got back to Eve's place and Sylphid has disappeared. No note, nothing. They call her friends, they call her father in France, thinking maybe she decided to go back to him. They call the police. On the fourth day Sylphid finally checks in. She's on the Upper West Side with some old teacher she'd had at Juilliard. She'd been staying with her; Sylphid acts as though she didn't know when they were getting back, and that explains why she didn't bother to call from Ninety-sixth Street.

"That evening they all eat dinner together and the silence is awful. It doesn't help the mother any to watch the daughter eat. Sylphid's weight makes Eve frantic on a good night—and this night is not good.

"When she finished each course, Sylphid always cleaned her plate the same way. Ira'd been around army mess halls, crummy diners—lapses of etiquette didn't bother him all that much. But Eve was refinement itself, and watching Sylphid cleaning up was, as Sylphid well knew, a torment for her mother.

"Sylphid would take the side of her index finger, you see, and she'd run it around the edge of the empty plate so as to get all the gravy and the leavings. She'd lick everything off the finger and then she'd do it again and again until her finger squeaked against the plate. Well, on the night that Sylphid decided to come home after her disappearance, she started cleaning her plate that way of hers at dinner, and Eve, who was screwed pretty tight on an ordinary evening, came undone. Could not keep that smile of the ideal mother plastered serenely across her face one second more. 'Stop it!' she screams. 'Stop it! You are twenty-three years old! Stop it, please!'

"Suddenly Sylphid is up on her feet and clubbing at her mother's head—going after her with her fists. Ira leaps up, and

that's when Sylphid screams at Eve, 'You kike bitch!' and Ira
sinks back into his chair. 'No,' he says. 'No. That won't do. I
live here now. I am your mother's husband, and you cannot
strike her in my presence. You cannot strike her, period. I forbid it. And you cannot use that word, not in my hearing.
Never. *Never in my hearing.* Never use that filthy word *again!*'

"Ira gets up and he leaves the house and he takes one of his
calming-down hikes—from the Village walks all the way up to
Harlem and back. Tries everything so as not to outright explode. Tells himself all the reasons why the daughter is upset.
Our stepmother and our father. Remembers how they treated
him. Remembers everything he hated about them. Everything
awful that he swore he would never be in life. But what's he to
do? The kid takes a swing at her mother, calls her a kike, a kike
bitch—what is Ira going to do?

"He gets home around midnight and he does *nothing.* He
goes to bed, gets in bed with the brand-new wife, and, amazingly, that's it. In the morning he sits down at breakfast with
the brand-new wife and with the brand-new stepdaughter and
he explains that they are all going to live together in peace and
harmony, and that to do this they must have respect for one
another. He tries to explain everything reasonably, the way
nothing was ever explained to him when he was a kid. He's still
appalled by what he saw and heard, furious about it, yet he is
trying his damnedest to believe that Sylphid isn't really an anti-
Semite in the true Anti-Defamation League sense of the word.
Which more than likely was the case: Sylphid's insistence upon
ego-justice for Sylphid was so extensive, so exclusive, so *automatic,* that a grand historical hostility of even the simplest, most
undemanding sort, like hating Jews, could never have taken
root in her—there was no room in her. Anti-Semitism was too
theoretical for her anyway. The people Sylphid could not endure she could not endure for a good, tangible reason. There
was nothing impersonal about it: they stood in her way and
blocked her view; they affronted the regal sense of dominance,
her *droit de fille.* The whole incident, Ira rightly surmises,
hasn't to do with hating Jews. About Jews, about Negroes,
about any group that presents a knotty social problem—as
opposed to somebody posing an immediate private problem
—she does not care one way or the other. She is concerned at

that moment only with him. Consequently, she allows to break out into the open a malicious epithet that she instinctively gauges to be so repugnant, so foul and disgusting and out of bounds, as to cause him to walk out the door and never again set foot in her house. 'Kike bitch' is her protest not against the existence of Jews—or even against the existence of her Jewish mother—but against the existence of *him*.

"But having figured all this out overnight, Ira goes ahead—cagily he thinks—not to ask Sylphid for an apology due him, let alone to take the hint and disappear, but to offer *her* an apology. This is how the shrewdie is going to tame her, by offering an apology for his being an interloper. For his being a stranger, an outsider, for his being not her own father but an unknown quantity whom she doesn't have any reason in the world to like or to trust. He tells her that since he's another human being, and human beings don't have a great record going for them, there's probably every reason to *dislike* him and *distrust* him. He says, 'I know the last guy wasn't so hot. But why don't you try me out? My name isn't Jumbo Freedman. I'm a different person from a different outfit with a different serial number. Why not give me a chance, Sylphid? How about giving me ninety days?'

"Then he explains to Sylphid Jumbo Freedman's rapacity—how it stems from *America's* corruption. 'It's a dirty game, American business. It's an insider's game,' he tells her, 'and Jumbo was the classic insider. Jumbo isn't even a speculator in real estate, which would be bad enough. He is a stalking horse for the speculator. He gets a piece of the deal and he doesn't even put down a dime. Now, basically, in America big money is made through secrets. Y'understand? Transactions that are deep underground. Sure, everybody's supposed to play by the same rules. Sure, there is the pretense to virtue, the pretense that everybody is playing fair. Look, Sylphid—do you know the difference between a speculator and an investor? An investor holds the real estate and has the risk involved; he rides the gains or suffers the loss. A speculator trades. Trades land like sardines. Fortunes are made this way. Now, before the Crash occurred, people had speculated with money they had got through taking out the value of the property, extracting from the banks the amortized value in terms of cash. What happened was that when all of these loans were called, they lost their land. The land went back to the banks. Enter the Jumbo Freedmans of the world. For the banks to raise some cash on this worthless paper they were holding, they had to sell it at an enormous discount, a penny on a dollar . . .'

"Ira the educator, the Marxist economist, Ira the star pupil of Johnny O'Day. Well, Eve is elated, a new woman, everything is wonderful again. A real man for herself, a real father for her daughter. At last a father who does what a father is supposed to do!

" 'Now, the illegal part of this, Sylphid, the way it is a fixed deal,' Ira explains, 'the collusion involved . . .'

"When the lecture is finally over, Eve gets up and goes over and takes Sylphid's hand and she says, 'I love you.' But not once. Uh-uh. It's 'I love you I love you I love you I love you I love you—' She keeps holding tight to the kid's hand and saying 'I love you.' Each repetition is more heartfelt than the last. She's a performer—she can convince herself when something is heartfelt. 'I love you I love you I love you'—and does Ira think to himself, Go? Does Ira think to himself, This woman is under assault, this woman is up against something I know a little something about: this is a family at war and *nothing* I do is going to work.

"No. He thinks that the Iron Man who has beaten back every disadvantage to get to where he's gotten is not going to be defeated by a twenty-three-year-old. The guy is tenderized by sentiment: he's madly in love with Eve Frame, he's never known a woman like her, he wants to have a child by her. He wants to have a home and a family and a future. He wants to eat dinner the way people do—not alone at some counter somewhere, pouring sugar into his coffee out of a grimy canister, but around a nice table with a family of his own. Just because a twenty-three-year-old throws a temper tantrum, is he going to deny himself everything he has ever dreamed of? Fight the bastards. *Educate* the bastards. *Change* them. If anybody can make things work and straighten people out, it's Ira and his persistence.

"And things do calm down. No fisticuffs. No explosions. Sylphid appears to be getting the message. Sometimes at the dinner table she even tries for two minutes to listen to what Ira is saying. And he thinks, It was the shock of my arrival. That's all it was. Because he's Ira, because he doesn't give in, because he doesn't quit, because he explains everything to everybody sixty-two times, he believes he's got it licked. Ira demands respect from Sylphid for her mother and he believes he's going to get it. But that is just the demand that Sylphid cannot forgive. As long as she can boss her mother around she can have everything she wants, which makes Ira an obstacle right off. Ira shouted, Ira yelled, but he was the first man in Eve's life who ever treated her decently. And that's what Sylphid couldn't take.

"Sylphid was beginning to play professionally, and she was subbing as second harpist in the orchestra at Radio City Music Hall. She was called pretty regularly, once or twice a week, and she'd also got a job playing at a fancy restaurant in the East Sixties on Friday night. Ira would drive her from the Village up to the restaurant with her harp and then go and pick her and the harp up when she finished. He had the station wagon, and he'd pull up in front of the house and go inside and have to carry it down the stairs. The harp is in its felt cover, and Ira puts one hand on the column and one hand in the sound hole at the back and he lifts it up, lays the harp on a mattress they keep in the station wagon, and drives Sylphid and the harp uptown to the restaurant. At the restaurant he takes the harp out of the car and, big radio star that he is, he carries it inside. At ten-thirty, when the restaurant is finished serving dinner and Sylphid's ready to come back to the Village, he goes around to pick her up and the whole operation is repeated. Every Friday. He hated the physical imposition that it was—those things weigh about eighty pounds—but he did it. I remember that in the hospital, when he had cracked up, he said to me, 'She married me to carry her daughter's harp! That's why the woman married me! To haul that fucking harp!'

"On those Friday night trips, Ira found he could talk to Sylphid in ways he couldn't when Eve was around. He'd ask her about being a movie star's child. He'd say to her, 'When you were a little girl, when did it dawn on you that something was up, that this wasn't the way everyone grew up?' She told him it was when the tour buses went up and down their street in Beverly Hills. She said she never saw her parents' movies until she was a teenager. Her parents were trying to keep her normal and so they downplayed those movies around the house. Even the rich kid's life in Beverly Hills with the other movie stars' kids seemed normal enough until the tour buses stopped in front of her house and she could hear the tour guide saying, 'This is Carlton Pennington's house, where he lives with his wife, Eve Frame.'

"She told him about the production that birthday parties were for the movie stars' kids—clowns, magicians, ponies, puppet shows, and every child attended by a nanny in a white nurse's uniform. At the dining table, behind every child would be a nanny. The Penningtons had their own screening room and they ran movies. Kids would come over. Fifteen, twenty kids. And the nannies came for that too and they all sat at the back. At the movies Sylphid had to be dressed to the nines.

"She told him about her *mother's* clothes, how alarming her mother's clothes were to a little kid like her. She told him about all the girdles and the bras and the corsets and the waist cinchers and the stockings and the impossible shoes—all that stuff they wore in those days. Sylphid thought how could she possibly ever pull it off. Not in a million years. The hairdos. The slips. The heavy perfume. She remembered wondering how this was all going to happen to her.

"She even told him about her father, just a few things, but enough for Ira to realize how adoring of him she'd been as a child. He had a boat, a boat called the *Sylphid*, docked off the coast of Santa Monica. On Sundays, they sailed to Catalina, her father at the helm. The two of them rode horses together. In those days there was a bridle path that went up Rodeo Drive and down to Sunset Boulevard. Her father used to play polo behind the Beverly Hills Hotel and then go riding alone with Sylphid along the bridle path. One Christmas her father had presents for her dropped from a Piper Cub by one of the stuntmen from the studio. Swooped low over the back lawn and dropped them. Her father, she told him, had his shirts made in London. His suits and his shoes were made in London. Back then, no one in Beverly Hills walked around without ties and suits, but he was the best dressed of them all. To Sylphid, there had been no father more handsome, more delightful, more charming in all of Hollywood. And then, when she was twelve, her mother divorced him, and Sylphid found out about his escapades.

"She told Ira all this stuff on those Friday nights, and in Newark he told it to me, and I was supposed to come away thinking that I had been dead wrong, that Ira would make this kid his pal yet. It was still the beginning of all of them living together, and all the conversations were to try to make some contact with Sylphid, to make peace with her and so on. And it seemed to work—something like intimacy began to develop. He even started going in at night when Sylphid was practicing. He'd ask her, 'How the hell do you play that thing? I gotta tell you, every time I see anybody playing a harp—' And Sylphid would say, 'You think of Harpo Marx,' and they'd both laugh because that was true. 'Where does the sound come from?' he asked her. 'Why are the strings different colors? How can you remember which pedal is which? Don't your fingers hurt?' He asked a hundred questions to show he was interested, and she answered them and explained how the harp worked and showed him her calluses, and things were looking up, things were definitely beginning to look good.

"But then that morning after Eve said that she could not have the baby, and she wept and she wept, and he thought, Okay, that's it, and agreed to take her to the doctor in Camden—that morning he hears Sylphid at the bottom of the stairs. She is giving it to her mother, really laying into her, and Ira jumps out of bed to open the bedroom door, and that's when he hears what Sylphid is saying. This time she's not calling Eve a kike bitch. It's worse than that. Bad enough to send my brother straight back to Newark. And that's how you came to meet him. It puts him on our couch for two nights.

"That morning, that moment, was when Ira realized that it wasn't true that Eve felt she was too old to have a child with him. The alarm sounds and he realizes that it wasn't true that Eve was worried about the effect of a new baby on her career. He realizes that Eve had wanted the baby too, no less than he did, that it had been no easy thing to decide to abort the child of a man she loved, *especially* at the age of forty-one. This is a woman whose deepest sense is her sense of incapacity, and to experience the incapacity of not being generous enough to do this, of not being big enough to do this, of not being *free* enough to do this—*that* was why she had been crying so hard.

"That morning he realizes that the abortion wasn't Eve's decision—it was Sylphid's. That morning he realizes that it wasn't his baby to decide what to do with—it was Sylphid's baby to decide what to do with. The abortion was Eve evading the wrath of her daughter. Yes, the alarm sounds, but still not loud enough for Ira to clear out.

"Yes, all kinds of elemental things percolated up from Sylphid that had nothing to do with playing the harp. What he hears Sylphid saying to her mother is, 'If you ever, ever try that again, I'll strangle the little idiot in its crib!' "

4

THE townhouse on West Eleventh Street where Ira lived with Eve Frame and Sylphid, its urbanity, its beauty, its comfort, its low-key aura of luxurious intimacy, the quiet aesthetic harmony of its thousand details—the warm habitation as a rich work of art—altered my conception of life as much as the University of Chicago would when I enrolled there a year and a half later. I had only to walk through the door to feel ten years older and freed from family conventions that, admittedly, I'd grown up adhering to mostly with pleasure and without much effort. Because of Ira's presence, because of the lumbering, easygoing way he strode around the place in baggy corduroy pants and old loafers and checked flannel shirts too short in the sleeves, I didn't feel intimidated by an atmosphere, unknown to me, of wealth and privilege; because of those folksy powers of appropriation that contributed so much to Ira's appeal—at home both on Newark's black Spruce Street and in Eve's salon—I quickly got the idea of how cozily comfortable, how *domesticized*, high living could be. High culture as well. It was like penetrating a foreign language and discovering that, despite the alienating exoticism of its sounds, the foreigners fluently speaking it are saying no more than what you've been hearing in English all your life.

Those hundreds and hundreds of serious books lining the library shelves—poetry, novels, plays, volumes of history, books about archeology, antiquity, music, costume, dance, art, mythology—the classical records filed six feet high in cabinets to either side of the record player, those paintings and drawings and engravings on the walls, the artifacts arranged along the fireplace mantel and crowding the tabletops—statuettes, enamel boxes, bits of precious stone, ornate little dishes, antique astronomical devices, unusual objects sculpted of glass and silver and gold, some recognizably representational, others odd and abstract—were not decoration, not ornamental bric-a-brac, but possessions bound up with pleasurable living and, at the same time, with *morality*, with mankind's aspiration to achieve significance through connoisseurship and thought. In such an environment, roaming from room to room looking for the evening paper, sitting and eating an apple in front of the fire could in themselves be part of a great enterprise. Or so it seemed to a kid whose own house, though clean, orderly, and comfortable enough, had never awakened in him or in anybody else ruminations on the ideal human condition. My house— with its library of the *Information Please Almanac* and nine or ten other books that had come into our possession as gifts for convalescing family members—seemed by comparison shabby and bleak, a colorless hovel. I could not have believed back then that there was anything on West Eleventh Street that anyone would ever want to flee. It looked to me like the luxury liner of havens, the *last* place where you would have to worry about having your equilibrium disturbed. At its heart, upright and massively elegant on the library's oriental rug, utterly grace-ful in its substantiality and visible the instant you turned from the entryway into the living room, was that symbol, reaching back to civilization's enlightened beginnings, of the spiritually rarefied realm of existence, the gorgeous instrument whose shape alone embodies an admonishment to every defect of coarseness and crudeness in man's mundane nature . . . that stately instrument of transcendence, Sylphid's gold-leafed Lyon and Healy harp.

"That library was to the rear of the living room and up a step," Murray was remembering. "There were sliding oak doors that closed the one room off from the other, but when Sylphid practiced Eve liked to listen, and so the doors were left open and the sound of that instrument carried through the house. Eve, who'd started Sylphid on the harp out in Beverly Hills when she was seven, couldn't get enough of it, but Ira could make no sense of classical music—never listened to anything, as far as I know, except the popular stuff on the radio and the Soviet Army Chorus—and so at night, when he preferred to be sitting around downstairs in the living room with Eve, talk-ing, reading the paper, a husband at home and so forth, he kept retreating to his study. Sylphid would be plucking away and Eve would be doing her needlepoint in front of the fire, and when she'd look up, he'd be gone, upstairs writing letters to O'Day.

"But after what she'd been through in that third marriage, the fourth, when it got going, was still pretty wonderful. When she met Ira, she was coming out of a bad divorce and recovering from a nervous breakdown. The third husband, Jumbo Freedman, was a sex clown from the sound of it, expert at entertaining them in the bedroom. Had a high old time of it altogether till she came home early from a rehearsal one day and found him in his upstairs office with a couple of tootsies. But he was everything Pennington wasn't. She has an affair with him out in California, obviously very passionate, certainly for a woman twelve years with Carlton Pennington, and in the end Freedman leaves his wife and she leaves Pennington, and she, Freedman, and Sylphid decamp for the East. She buys that house on West Eleventh Street and Freedman moves in, sets up his office in what became Ira's study, and starts trading property in New York as well as in L.A. and Chicago. For a while he is buying and selling Times Square property, and so he meets the big theatrical producers, and they all start to socialize together, and soon enough Eve Frame is on Broadway. Drawing room comedies, thrillers, all starring the one-time silent-screen beauty. One after another is a hit. Eve is making money hand over fist, and Jumbo sees that it's well spent.

"Being Eve, she goes along with this guy's extravagance, acquiescing to his wild ways, is even caught up in the wild ways. Sometimes when Eve would start to cry out of nowhere and Ira would ask her why, she would tell him, 'The things he made me do—what I had to do . . .' After she wrote that book and her marriage to Ira was all over the papers, Ira got a letter from some woman in Cincinnati. Said that if he was interested in a little book of his own, he might want to come out to Ohio for a talk. She'd been a nightclub entertainer back in the thirties, a singer, a girlfriend of Jumbo's. She said Ira might like to see some photographs Jumbo had taken. Maybe she and Ira could collaborate on a memoir of their own—he'd supply the words, she, for a price, would fork over the pictures. At the time Ira was so hell-bent on getting his revenge that he wrote the woman back, sent her a check for a hundred dollars. She claimed to have two dozen, and so he sent her the hundred bucks she was asking for just in order to see one."

"Did he get it?"

"She was true to her word. She sent him one, all right, by return mail. But because I wasn't going to allow my brother to further distort people's idea of what his life had meant, I took it from him and destroyed it. Stupid. Sentimental, priggish, stupid, and not very farsighted of me, either. Circulating the picture would have been benevolent compared to what happened."

"He wanted to disgrace Eve with the picture."

"Look, once upon a time all Ira thought about was how to alleviate the effects of human cruelty. Everything was funneled through that. But after that book of hers came out, all he thought about was how to inflict it. They stripped him of his job, his domestic life, his name, his reputation, and when he realized he'd lost all of that, lost the status and no longer had to live up to it, he shed Iron Rinn, he shed *The Free and the Brave*, he shed the Communist Party. He even stopped talking so much. All that endless outraged rhetoric. Going on and on when what this huge man really wanted to do was to lash out. The talk was the way to blunt those desires.

"What do you think the Abe Lincoln act was about? Putting on that stovepipe hat. Mouthing Lincoln's words. But everything that ever tamed him, all the civilizing accommodations, he shed, and he was stripped right back to the Ira who'd dug ditches in Newark. Back to the Ira who'd mined zinc up in the Jersey hills. He reclaimed his earliest experience, when his tutor was the shovel. He made contact with the Ira before all the moral correction took place, before he'd been to Miss Frame's Finishing School and taken all those etiquette lessons. Before he went to finishing school with *you*, Nathan, acting out the drive to father and showing you what a good, nonviolent man he could be. Before he went to finishing school with *me*. Before he went to finishing school with *O'Day*, the finishing school of Marx and Engels. The finishing school of political action. Because O'Day was the first Eve, really, and Eve just another version of O'Day, dragging him up out of the Newark ditch and into the world of light.

"Ira knew his own nature. He knew that he was physically way out of scale and that this made him a dangerous man. He had the rage in him, and the violence, and standing six and a half feet tall, he had the means. He knew he needed his Ira-tamers—knew he needed all his teachers, knew he needed a kid like you, knew that he hungered for a kid like you, who'd got all he'd never got and was the admiring son. But after *I Married a Communist* appeared, he shed the finishing school education, and he reclaimed the Ira you never saw, who beat the shit out of guys in the army, the Ira who, as a boy starting out on his own, used the shovel he dug with to protect himself against those Italian guys. Wielded his work tool as a weapon. His whole life was a struggle not to pick up that shovel. But after her book, Ira set out to become his own uncorrected first self."

"And did he?"

"Ira never shirked a man-sized job, however onerous. The ditch-digger made his impact on her. He put her in touch with what she had done. 'Okay, I'll educate her,' he told me, 'without the dirty picture.'"

"And he did it."

"He did it, all right. Enlightenment through the shovel."

Early in 1949, some ten weeks after Henry Wallace was so badly defeated—and, I now know, after her abortion—Eve Frame threw a big party (preceded by a smaller dinner party) to try to cheer Ira up, and he called our house to invite me to come. I had seen him only once again in Newark after the Wallace rally at the Mosque, and until I got the astonishing phone call ("Ira Ringold, buddy. How's my boy?") I'd begun to believe that I'd never see him again. After the second time that we'd met —and gone off for our first walk ever in Weequahic Park, where I learned about "Eye-ran"—I'd mailed to him in New York a carbon copy of my radio play *The Stooge of Torquemada*. As the weeks went by and there was no response from him, I realized the mistake I'd made in giving to a professional radio actor a play of mine, even one that I considered my best. I was sure that now that he'd seen how little talent I had, I'd killed any interest he might have had in me. Then, while I was doing my homework one night, the phone rang and my mother came running into my room. "Nathan—dear, it's Mr. Iron Rinn!"

He and Eve Frame were having people to dinner, and among

them would be Arthur Sokolow, whom he'd given my script to read. Ira thought I might like to meet him. My mother made me go to Bergen Street the next afternoon to buy a pair of black dress shoes, and I took my one suit to the tailor shop on Chancellor Avenue to have Schapiro lengthen the sleeves and the trousers. And then early one Saturday evening, I popped a Sen-Sen in my mouth and, my heart beating as though I were intent on crossing the state line to commit murder, I went out to Chancellor Avenue and boarded a bus to New York.

My companion at the dinner table was Sylphid. All the traps laid for me—the eight pieces of cutlery, the four differently shaped drinking glasses, the large appetizer called an artichoke, the serving dishes presented from behind my back and over my shoulder by a solemn black woman in a maid's uniform, the finger bowl, the enigma of the finger bowl—everything that made me feel like a very small boy instead of a large one, Sylphid all but nullified with a sardonic wisecrack, a cynical explanation, even just with a smirk or with a roll of her eyes, helping me gradually to understand that there wasn't as much at stake as all the pomp suggested. I thought she was splendid, in her satire particularly.

"My mother," Sylphid said, "likes to make everything a strain the way it was when she grew up in Buckingham Palace. She makes the most of every opportunity to turn everyday life into a joke." Sylphid kept it up throughout the meal, dropped into my ear remarks rife with the worldliness of someone who'd grown up in Beverly Hills—next door to Jimmy Durante—and then in Greenwich Village, America's Paris. Even when she teased me I felt relieved, as if my mishap might not lie but one course away. "Don't worry too much about doing the right thing, Nathan. You'll look a lot less comical doing the wrong thing."

I also took heart from watching Ira. He ate the same way here as he did at the hot dog stand across from Weequahic Park; he talked the same way too. He alone among the men at the table was without a tie and a dress shirt and a jacket, and though he didn't lack for ordinary table manners, it was clear from watching him spear and swallow his food that the subtleties of Eve's kitchen were not overscrupulously assessed by his palate. He did not seem to draw any line between conduct permissible at a hot dog stand and in a splendid Manhattan dining room, neither conduct nor conversation. Even here, where the silver candelabra were lit with ten tall candles and bowls of white flowers illuminated the sideboard, everything made him hot under the collar—on this night, only a couple of months after the crushing Wallace defeat (the Progressive Party had received little more than a million votes nationwide, about a sixth of what it had anticipated), even something seemingly as uncontroversial as Election Day.

"I'll tell you one thing," he announced to the table, and everyone else's voice faded while his, strong and natural, charged with protest and barbed with contempt for the stupidity of his fellow Americans, promptly commanded, *You just listen to me.* "I think this darling country of ours doesn't understand politics. Where else in the world, in a democratic nation, do people go to work on Election Day? Where else are the schools still open? If you're young and you're growing up and you say, 'Hey, it's Election Day, don't we have a day off?' your father and mother say, 'No, it's Election Day, that's all,' and what are you left to think? How important can Election Day be if I have to go to school? How can it be important if the stores and everything else are open? Where the hell are your values, you son of a bitch?"

By "son of a bitch" he was alluding to nobody present at the table. He was addressing everyone in his life he had ever had to fight.

Here Eve Frame put her finger to her lips to get him to rein himself in. "Darling," she said in a voice so soft it was barely audible. "Well, what's more important," he loudly replied, "to stay home on Columbus Day? You close the schools up because of a shitty holiday, but you don't close them up because of Election Day?" "But nobody's arguing the point," Eve said with a smile, "so why be angry?" "Look, I get angry," he said to her, "I always got angry, I hope to my dying day I *stay* angry. I get in trouble because I get angry. I get in trouble because I won't shut up. I get very angry with my darling country when Mr. Truman tells people, and they believe him, that Communism is the big problem in this country. Not the racism. Not the inequities. That's not the problem. The Communists are the problem. The forty thousand or sixty thousand or a hundred thousand Communists. They're going to overthrow the government of a country of a hundred and fifty million people. Don't insult my intelligence. I'll tell you what's going to overthrow the whole goddamn place—the way we treat the colored people. The way we treat the working people. It's not going to be the Communists who overthrow this country. This country is going to overthrow itself by treating people like animals!"

Seated across from me was Arthur Sokolow, the radio writer, another of those assertive, self-educated Jewish boys whose old neighborhood allegiances (and illiterate immigrant fathers) strongly determined their brusque, emotional style as men, young guys only recently back from a war in which they'd discovered Europe and politics, in which they'd first really discovered America through the soldiers they had to live alongside, in which they'd begun, without formal assistance but with a gigantic naive faith in the transforming power of art, to read the fifty or sixty opening pages of the novels of Dostoyevsky. Until the blacklist destroyed his career, Arthur Sokolow, though not as eminent a writer as Corwin, was certainly in the ranks of the other radio writers I most admired: Arch Oboler, who wrote *Lights Out*, Himan Brown, who wrote *Inner Sanctum*, Paul Rhymer, who wrote *Vic and Sade*, Carlton E. Morse, who wrote *I Love a Mystery*, and William N. Robson, who'd done a lot of war radio from which I also drew for my own plays. Arthur Sokolow's prizewinning radio dramas (as well as two Broadway plays) were marked by their intense hatred of corrupt authority as represented by a grossly hypocritical father. I kept fearing throughout dinner that Sokolow, a short, wide tank of a man, a defiant pile driver who'd once been a Detroit high school fullback, was going to point at me and denounce me to everyone at the table as a plagiarist because of all I had stolen from Norman Corwin.

Following dinner, the men were invited up to Ira's second-floor study for cigars while the women went to Eve's room to freshen up before the after-dinner guests began to arrive. Ira's study overlooked the floodlit statuary in the rear garden, and on the three walls of bookshelves he kept all his Lincoln books, the political library he'd carried home in three duffel bags from the war, and the library he'd since accumulated browsing in the secondhand bookshops on Fourth Avenue. After passing around the cigars and advising his guests to take whatever they liked from the whiskey cart, Ira got his copy of my radio play out of the top drawer of the massive mahogany desk—the one where I imagined he kept up his correspondence with O'Day—and began to read aloud the play's opening speech. And to read it not to denounce me for plagiarism. Rather, he began by telling his friends, including Arthur Sokolow, "You know what gives me hope for this country?" and he pointed at me, all aglow and tremulously waiting to be seen through. "I got more faith in a kid like this than in all those so-called mature people in our darling country who went into the voting booth pre-pared to vote for Henry Wallace, and all of a sudden they saw a big picture of Dewey in front of their eyes—and I'm talking about people in my own *family*—so they pulled down Harry Truman's lever. Harry Truman, who is going to lead this coun-try into World War III, and that's their enlightened choice! The Marshall Plan, that is their choice. All they can think is to bypass the United Nations and to hem in the Soviet Union and to destroy the Soviet Union while siphoning off into their Marshall Plan hundreds and hundreds of millions of dollars that could go to raising the standard of living for the poor in this country. But tell me, who is going to hem in Mr. Truman when he drops his atomic bombs on the streets of Moscow and Leningrad? You think they won't drop atomic bombs on innocent Russian children? To preserve our wonderful democ-racy they won't do that? Tell me another one. Listen to this kid here. Still in high school and he knows more about what's wrong with this country than every one of our darling country-men in the voting booth."

Nobody laughed or even smiled. Arthur Sokolow was backed against the bookcases, quietly paging through a book he'd taken down from Ira's Lincoln collection, and the rest of the men stood smoking their cigars and sipping their whiskey and act-ing as though my view of America were what they'd gone out with their wives to hear that night. Only much later did I real-ize that the collective seriousness with which my introduction was received signified nothing more than how accustomed they were to the agitations of their overbearing host.

"Listen," said Ira, "just listen to this. Play about a Catholic

family in a small town and the local bigots." Whereupon Iron
Rinn launched into my lines: Iron Rinn inside the skin, inside
the *voice-box*, of an ordinary, good-natured, Christian American
of the kind I'd had in mind and knew absolutely nothing about.

"'I'm Bill Smith,'" Ira began, plunking down into his high-
backed leather chair and throwing his legs up onto his desktop.
"'I'm Bob Jones. I'm Harry Campbell. My name doesn't
matter. It's not a name that bothers anyone. I'm white and Protestant, and so you don't have to worry about me. I get along
with you, I don't bother you, I don't annoy you. I don't even
hate you. I quietly earn my living in a nice little town. Center-
ville. Middletown. Okay Falls. Forget the name of the town.
Could be anywhere. Let's *call* it Anywhere. Many people here
in Anywhere give lip service to the fight against discrimination.
They talk about the need to wreck the fences that keep minorities in social concentration camps. But too many carry on
their fight in abstract terms. They think and speak of justice
and decency and right, about Americanism, the Brotherhood
of Man, and the Constitution and the Declaration of Independence. All this is fine, but it shows they are really unaware of
the what and why of racial, religious, and national discrimination. Take this town, take Anywhere, take what happened here
last year when a Catholic family right around the corner from
me found that zealous Protestantism can be just as cruel as
Torquemada was. You remember Torquemada. The hatchet man
for Ferdinand and Isabella. Ran the Inquisition for the king
and queen of Spain. Guy who expelled the Jews from Spain for
Ferdinand and Isabella back in 1492. Yeah, you heard right,
pal—1492. There was Columbus, sure, there was the *Niña*,
the *Pinta*, and the *Santa María*—and then there was Torquemada. There's always Torquemada. Maybe there always will
be . . . Well, here's what happened right here in Anywhere,
USA, under the Stars and Stripes, where all men are created
equal, and not in 1492 . . .'"

Ira flipped through the pages. "And it goes on like that
. . . and here, the ending. This is the end. The narrator again.
A fifteen-year-old kid has the courage to write this, y'understand? Tell me the network that would have the courage to put
it on. Tell me the sponsor who in the year 1949 would stand up
to Commandant Wood and his committee, who would stand

up to Commandant Hoover and his storm-trooper brutes, who would stand up to the American Legion and the Catholic War Veterans and the VFW and the DAR and all our darling patriots, who wouldn't give a shit if they called him a goddamn Red bastard and threatened to boycott his precious product. Tell me who would have the courage to do that because it is the right thing to do. Nobody! Because they don't give any more of a shit about freedom of speech than the guys I was with in the army gave a shit about it. They didn't talk to me. Did I ever tell you that? I walked into the mess hall, y'understand, two hundred and some-odd men, nobody said hello, nobody said anything because of the stuff I was saying and the letters I was writing to *Stars and Stripes*. Those guys gave you the distinct impression that World War II was being fought to spite them. Contrary to what some people may think about our darling boys, they didn't have the slightest notion, didn't know what the hell they were there for, didn't give a shit about fascism, about Hitler—what did they care? Get them to understand the social problems of Negroes? Get them to understand the devious ways capitalism endeavors to weaken labor? Get them to understand why when we bomb Frankfurt the I. G. Farben plants are not touched? Maybe I am myself handicapped by my lack of education, but the picayune minds of 'our boys' make me violently sick! 'It all comes to this,'" he suddenly read from my script. "'If you want a moral, here it is: The man who swallows the guff about racial, religious, and national groups is a sap. He hurts himself, his family, his union, his community, his state, and his country. He's the stooge of Torquemada.' Written," Ira said, angrily tossing the script down on his desk, "by a fifteen-year-old kid!"

There must have been another fifty people who showed up after dinner. Despite the extraordinary stature Ira had imposed on me up in his study, I would never have had the courage to stay and mingle with everybody pressed into the living room had it not been for Sylphid's again coming to my rescue. There were actors and actresses, directors, writers, poets, there were lawyers and literary agents and theatrical producers, there was Arthur Sokolow, and there was Sylphid, who not only called all the guests by their given names but knew in caricatured detail their every flaw. She was a reckless, entertaining talker, a great hater with the talent of a chef for filleting, rolling, and roasting a hunk of meat, and I, whose aim was to be radio's bold, uncompromising teller of the truth, was in awe of how she did nothing to rationalize, let alone to hide, her amused contempt. That one is the vainest man in New York . . . that one's need to be superior . . . that one's insincerity . . . that one hasn't the faintest idea . . . that one got so drunk . . . that one's talent is so minute, so infinitesimal . . . that one is so embittered . . . that one is so depraved . . . what's most laughable about that lunatic is her grandiosity . . .

How delicious to belittle people—and to watch them being belittled. Especially for a boy whose every impulse at that party was to revere. Worried as I was about getting home late, I couldn't deprive myself of this first-class education in the pleasures of spite. I'd never met anyone like Sylphid: so young and yet so richly antagonistic, so worldly-wise and yet, costumed in something long and gaudy as if she were a fortuneteller, so patently oddballish. So happy-go-lucky about being repelled by *everything*. I'd had no idea how very tame and inhibited I was, how eager to please, until I saw how eager Sylphid was to antagonize, no idea how much freedom there was to enjoy once egoism unleashed itself from the restraint of social fear. There was the fascination: her formidability. I saw that Sylphid was fearless, unafraid to cultivate within herself the threat that she could be to others.

The two people she announced herself least able to endure were a couple whose Saturday morning radio show happened to be a favorite of my mother's. The program, called *Van Tassel and Grant*, emanated from the Hudson River farmhouse, up in Dutchess County, New York, of the popular novelist Katrina Van Tassel Grant and her husband, the *Journal-American* columnist and entertainment critic Bryden Grant. Katrina was an alarmingly thin six-footer with long dark ringlets that once must have been thought alluring and a bearing that suggested that she did not lack for a sense of the influence she brought to bear on America through her novels. The little I knew about her up until that night—that dinnertime in the Grant house was reserved for discussion with her four handsome children of their obligations to society, that her friends in traditional old

Staatsburg (where her ancestors, the Van Tassels, first settled, reportedly as local aristocracy, in the seventeenth century, long before the arrival of the English) had impeccable ethical and educational credentials—I had happened to overhear when my mother was tuned in to *Van Tassel and Grant*.

"Impeccable" was a word much favored in Katrina's weekly monologue on her rich and varied record-breaking existence in the bustling city and the bucolic countryside. Not only were *her* sentences infested with "impeccable," but so were my mother's after an hour of listening to Katrina Van Tassel Grant—whom my mother thought "cultivated"—lauding the superiority of whoever was so fortunate as to be brought within the Grants' social purview, whether it was the man who fixed her teeth or the man who fixed her toilet. "An impeccable plumber, Bryden, im*pec*cable," she said, while my mother, like millions of others, listened enraptured to a discussion of the drainage difficulties that afflict the households of even the most wellborn of Americans, and my father, who was solidly in Sylphid's camp, said, "Oh, turn that woman off, will you, please?"

It was Katrina Grant about whom Sylphid had muttered to me, "What's most laughable about that lunatic is her grandiosity"; it was about the husband, Bryden Grant, that she had said, "That one is the vainest man in New York."

"My mother goes to lunch with Katrina and she comes home white with rage. 'That woman is impossible. She tells me about the theater and she tells me about the latest novels and she thinks she knows everything and she knows *nothing*.' And it's true: when they go to lunch, Katrina invariably lectures Mother on the one thing Mother happens to know all about. Mother can't stand Katrina's books. She can't even read them. She bursts out laughing when she tries, and then she tells Katrina how wonderful they are. Mother has a nickname for everyone who frightens her—Katrina's is 'Loony.' 'You should have heard Loony on the O'Neill play,' she tells me. 'She outdid herself.' Then Loony calls at nine the next morning and Mother spends an hour with her on the phone. My mother goes through vehement indignation the way a spendthrift goes through a bankroll, then she turns right around and sucks up to her because of the 'Van' in her name. And because when Bryden drops Mother's name in his column, he calls her 'the

Sarah Bernhardt of the Airwaves.' Poor Mother and her social ambitions. Katrina is *the* most pretentious of all the rich, pretentious river folk up in Staatsburg, and *he's* supposed to be a descendant of Ulysses S. Grant. Here," she said, and in the midst of the party, with guests everywhere so closely huddled together that they looked as though they had all they could do to keep their muzzles out of one another's drinks, Sylphid turned to search the wall of bookcases behind us for a novel by Katrina Van Tassel Grant. To either side of the living room fireplace, bookcases extended from floor to ceiling, rising so high that a library ladder had to be mounted to get to the topmost shelves.

"Here," she said. "*Eloise and Abelard.*" "My mother read that," I said. "Your mother's a shameless hussy," Sylphid replied, rendering me weak in the knees until I realized she was joking. Not just my mother, but nearly half a million Americans had bought it and read it. "Here—open to a page, any page, put a finger down anywhere, and then prepare to be ravished, Nathan of Newark."

I did as she told me, and when Sylphid saw where my finger was pointing she smiled and said, "Oh, you don't have to look very far to find V.T.G. at the top of her talent." Aloud to me Sylphid read, " 'His hands clasped about her waist, drawing her to him, and she felt the powerful muscles of his legs. Her head fell back. Her mouth parted to receive his kiss. One day he would suffer castration as a brutal and vengeful punishment for this passion for Eloise, but for now he was far from mutilated. The harder he grasped, the harder was the pressure on her sensitive areas. How aroused he was, this man whose genius would revamp and revitalize the traditional teaching of Christian theology. Her nipples were drawn hard and sharp, and her gut tightened as she thought, "I am kissing the greatest writer and thinker of the twelfth century!" "Your figure is magnificent," he whispered in her ear, "swelling breasts, small waist! And not even the full satin skirts of your gown can conceal from view your loveliness of hip and thigh." Best known for his solution of the problem of universals and for his original use of dialectics, he knew no less well, even now, at the height of his intellectual fame, how to melt a woman's heart. . . . By morning they were sated. At last it was her chance to say to the canon and master of Notre Dame, "Now teach me, please. Teach me, Pierre! Explain to me your dialectical analysis of the mystery of God and the Trinity." This he did, patiently going into the ins and outs of his rationalistic interpretation of the Trinitarian dogma, and then he took her as a woman for the eleventh time.'

"Eleven times," said Sylphid, hugging herself from the sheer delight of what she'd heard. "That husband of hers doesn't know what *two* is. That little fairy doesn't know what *one* is." And it was a while before she was able to stop laughing—before either of us could. "'Oh, teach me, *please*, Pierre,'" cried Sylphid, and for no reason in the world—other than her happiness—she kissed me loudly on the tip of my nose.

After Sylphid had returned *Eloise and Abelard* to the shelves and we were both more or less sober again, I felt emboldened enough to ask her a question I'd been wanting to ask all evening. One of the questions I'd been wanting to ask. Not "What was it like to grow up in Beverly Hills?"; not "What was it like to live next door to Jimmy Durante?"; not "What was it like having movie star parents?" Because I was afraid of her ridiculing me, I asked only what I considered to be my most serious question.

"What's it like," I said, "to play at Radio City Music Hall?"

"It's a horror. The *conductor's* a horror. 'My dear lady, I know it's *so* difficult to count to four in that bar, but if you *wouldn't* mind, that would be *so* nice.' The more polite he is, the nastier you know he's feeling. If he's really angry, he says, 'My dear *dear* lady.' The 'dear' dripping with venom. 'That's not quite right, dear, that should be done arpeggiated.' And you have your part printed *non*-arpeggiated. You can't go back, without seeming argumentative and wasting time, and say, 'Excuse me, maestro, actually it's printed the other way.' So everybody looks at you, thinking, Don't you know how it's supposed to be done, idiot—he has to tell you? He's the world's worst conductor. All he's conducting is music from the standard repertoire, and still you have to think, Has he never *heard* this piece before? Then there's the band car. At the Music Hall. You know, this platform that moves the band into view. It moves up and backward and forward and down, and every time it moves, it jerks—it's on a hydraulic lift—and you sit and hold on to your harp for dear life even as it's going out of tune. Harpists spend half their time tuning and the other half playing out of tune. I hate all harps."

"Do you really?" I said, laughing away, in part because she was being funny and in part because, imitating the conductor, she'd been laughing too.

"They're impossibly difficult to play. They break down all the time. You *breathe* on a harp," she said, "and it's out of tune. Trying to have a harp in perfect condition makes me *crazy*. Moving it around—it's like moving an aircraft carrier."

"Then why do you play the harp?"

"Because the conductor's right—I *am* stupid. Oboists are smart. Fiddle players are smart. But not harpists. Harpists are dummies, moronic dummies. How smart can you be to pick an instrument that's going to ruin and run your life the way the harp does? There's no way, had I not been seven years old and too stupid to know better, that I would have begun playing the harp, let alone be playing it still. I don't even have conscious memories of life before harp."

"Why did you start so young?"

"Most little girls who start the harp start the harp because Mommy thinks it's such a *lovely* thing for them to do. It looks so pretty and all the music is so damned sweet, and it's played politely in small rooms for polite people who aren't the least bit interested. The column painted in gold leaf—you need sunglasses to look at it. Really refined. It sits there and reminds you of itself all the time. And it's so monstrously big, you can never put it away. *Where* are you going to put it? It's always there, sitting there and mocking you. You can never get away from it. Like my mother."

A young woman still in her coat and carrying a small black case in her hand appeared suddenly beside Sylphid, apologizing in an English accent for arriving late. With her were a stout, dark-haired young man—elegantly turned out and, as though corseted in all his privilege, holding his youthful chubbiness militarily erect—and a virginally sensuous young woman, ripish-looking, just verging on fullness, with a cascade of curling reddish gold hair to offset her fair complexion. Eve Frame rushed up to meet all the newcomers. She embraced the girl carrying the small black case, whose name was Pamela, and was then introduced by Pamela to the glamorous couple, affianced and soon to be married, who were Rosalind Halladay and Ramón Noguera.

Within only minutes Sylphid was in the library, the harp against her knees and cradled on her shoulder while she tuned it, Pamela was out of her coat and was alongside Sylphid fingering the keys of her flute, and, seated beside the two of them, Rosalind tuned a stringed instrument that I assumed was a violin but that I shortly discovered was something slightly larger called a viola. Gradually everybody in the living room turned toward the library, where Eve Frame stood waiting for silence, Eve Frame wearing an outfit I later described to my mother as well as I could and that my mother then told me was a white pleated chiffon gown and capelet with an emerald green chiffon sash. When I described her hairdo as I remembered it, my mother told me it was called a feather cut, with long curls all around and a smooth crown. Even while Eve Frame patiently waited, a faint smile intensifying her loveliness (and her fascination to me), a joyful excitement was evidently mounting within her. When she spoke, when she said, "Something beautiful is about to happen," all her elegant reserve seemed on the brink of being swept away.

It was quite a performance, particularly to an adolescent who in half an hour was going to have to get back on the number 107 Newark bus and return to a household whose intensities no longer left him anything other than frustrated. Eve Frame came and went in less than a minute, but in just the grand way she strode down the step and back into the living room in her white pleated chiffon gown and capelet, she gave the whole evening a new meaning: the adventure for which life is lived was about to unfold.

I don't want to make it seem as though Eve Frame appeared to be playing a role. Far from it: this was her *freedom* being revealed, Eve Frame unimpeded, rapturously unintimidated, in a state of serene exaltation. If anything, it was as if *we* had been assigned by *her* nothing less than the role of our lives—the role of privileged souls whose fondest dream had been made to come true. Reality had fallen victim to artistic wizardry; some store of hidden magic had purified the evening of its mundane social function, purged that glittering half-drunk assemblage of all vile instincts and low-down schemes. And this illusion had been created out of practically nothing: a few perfectly enunciated syllables from the edge of the library step, and all the nonsensical self-seeking of a Manhattan soirée dissolved into a romantic endeavor to flee into aesthetic bliss.

"Sylphid Pennington and the young London flutist Pamela Solomon will play two duets for flute and harp. The first is by Fauré and is called 'Berceuse.' The second is by Franz Doppler, his 'Casilda Fantasie.' The third and final selection will be the lively second movement, the Interlude, from the Sonata for Flute, Viola, and Harp by Debussy. The violist is Rosalind Halladay, who is visiting New York from London. Rosalind is a native of Cornwall, England, and a graduate of London's Guildhall School of Music and Drama. In London, Rosalind Halladay now plays with the orchestra of the Royal Opera House."

The flutist was a mournful-looking girl, long-faced, dark-eyed, and slender, and the more I looked at her and the more enamored I became of her—and the more I looked at Rosalind and the more enamored I became of *her*—the more trenchantly I saw how deficient my friend Sylphid was in anything designed to promote a man's desire. With her square trunk and stout legs and that odd excess of flesh that thickened her a bit like a bison across the upper back, Sylphid looked to me, while playing the harp—and even despite the classical elegance of her hands moving along the strings—like a wrestler wrestling the harp, one of those Japanese sumo wrestlers. Because this was a thought that I was ashamed to be having, it only gathered substance the longer the performance continued.

I couldn't make head or tail of the music. Like Ira, I was deaf to the sound of anything other than the familiar (in my case, to what I heard Saturday mornings on *Make-Believe Ballroom* and Saturday nights on *Your Hit Parade*), but the sight of Sylphid gravely under the spell of the music she was disentangling from those strings and, too, the *passion* of her playing, a concentrated passion that you could see in her eyes—a passion liberated from everything in her that was sardonic and negative—made me wonder what powers might have been hers if, in addition to her musicianship, her face were as alluringly angular as her delicate mother's.

Not until decades later, after Murray Ringold's visit, did I understand that the only way Sylphid could begin to feel at ease in her skin was by hating her mother and playing the harp. Hating her mother's infuriating weakness and producing ethereally enchanting sounds, making with Fauré and Doppler and Debussy all the amorous contact the world would allow.

When I looked at Eve Frame, in the front rank of the spectators, I saw that she was looking at Sylphid with a gaze so needy that you would think that in Sylphid was the genesis of Eve Frame rather than the other way around.

Then everything that had stopped was starting up again. There was the applause, the bravos, the bows, and Sylphid, Pamela, and Rosalind came down from the stage that the library had become and Eve Frame was there to embrace each of them in turn. I was close enough to hear her say to Pamela, "You know what you looked like, my darling? A Hebrew princess!" And to Rosalind, "And you were lovely, absolutely lovely!" And finally to her daughter, "Sylphid, Sylphid," she said, "Sylphid Juliet, never, never have you played more beautifully! Never, darling! The Doppler was especially lovely."

"The Doppler, Mother, is salon garbage," Sylphid said.

"Oh, I love you!" cried Eve. "Your mother loves you so!"

Others started coming up to congratulate the trio of musicians, and the next I knew, Sylphid slipped an arm around my waist and was good-naturedly introducing me to Pamela, to Rosalind, and to Rosalind's fiancé. "This is Nathan of Newark," Sylphid said. "Nathan is a political protégé of the Beast's." Since she said it with a smile, I smiled too, trying to believe that the epithet was harmlessly meant, no more than a family joke about Ira's height.

I looked all around the room for Ira and saw that he wasn't there, but rather than asking to be excused to go and find him, I allowed myself to remain appropriated within Sylphid's grip— and engulfed by the sophistication of her friends. I had never seen anyone as young as Ramón Noguera so well dressed or so smoothly decorous and urbane. As for the dark Pamela and the fair Rosalind, each seemed so pretty to me that I couldn't look openly at either of them for more than a split second at a time, though simultaneously I was unable to forgo the opportunity to stand casually within only inches of their flesh.

Rosalind and Ramón were to be married in three weeks at

the Nogueras' estate just outside Havana. The Nogueras were tobacco growers, Ramón's father having inherited from Ramón's grandfather thousands of farm acres in a region called the Partido, land that would be inherited by Ramón, and in time by the children of Ramón and Rosalind. Ramón was formidably silent—grave with his sense of self-destiny, diligently resolved to act out the position of authority bestowed upon him by the cigar smokers of the world, while Rosalind—who only a few years back had been a poor London music student from a remote corner of rural England but who was now as close to the end of all her fears as she was to the beginning of all that spending—grew more and more vivacious. And loquacious. She told us about Ramón's grandfather, the most renowned and revered of the Nogueras, for some thirty years a provincial governor as well as a vast landowner until he entered the cabinet of President Mendieta (whose chief of staff, I happened to know, was the infamous Fulgencio Batista); she told us about the beauty of the tobacco plantations where, under cloth, they grew the wrapper leaf for the Cuban cigars; and then she told us about the grand Spanish-style wedding that the Nogueras had planned for them. Pamela, a childhood friend, was being flown from New York to Havana, at the expense of the Noguera family, and would be put up at a guesthouse on the estate; and if Sylphid could find the time, said the overbrimming Rosalind, she was welcome to come along with Pamela.

Rosalind spoke with eager innocence, with a joyful blend of pride and accomplishment, about the enormous wealth of the Nogueras while I kept thinking, But what about the Cuban peasants who are the tobacco workers—who flies *them* back and forth from New York to Havana for a family wedding? In what sort of "guesthouses" do *they* live on the beautiful tobacco plantations? What about disease and malnutrition and ignorance among your tobacco workers, Miss Halladay? Instead of obscenely squandering all that money on your Spanish-style wedding, why not begin to compensate the Cuban masses whose land your fiancé's family illegitimately holds?

But I was as close-mouthed as Ramón Noguera, though, internally, nowhere near as emotionally composed as he looked to be, unflinchingly staring straight ahead as if reviewing the troops. Everything Rosalind said appalled me, and yet I could not be socially incorrect enough to tell her so. Nor could I summon up the strength to confront Ramón Noguera with the Progressive Party's assessment of his riches and their source. Nor could I move voluntarily away from Rosalind's English radiance, a young woman both physically lovely and musically gifted who seemed not to understand that by abandoning her ideals for Ramón's allurements—or, if not her ideals, by abandoning mine—by marrying into Cuba's oligarchical, landholding upper class, she was not only fatally compromising the values of an artist but, in my political estimation, trivializing herself with someone far less worthy of her talent—and her reddish gold hair and eminently caressable skin—than, for instance, me.

As it turned out, Ramón had reserved a table at the Stork Club for Pamela, Rosalind, and himself, and when he asked Sylphid to join them, he also, with a certain vacant aplomb, a kind of upper-class analogue to courtesy, turned to extend an invitation to me. "Please, sir," he said, "come as my guest."

"I can't, no—" I said, but then, without explaining—as I knew that I should, that I had to, that I must . . . as I knew *Ira* would—"I don't approve of you or your kind!" but adding instead, "Thanks. Thanks just the same," I turned and, as though I were escaping the plague rather than a marvelous opportunity for a budding writer to see Sherman Billingsley's famous Stork Club and the table where Walter Winchell sat, I rushed away from the temptations being dangled by the first plutocrat I had ever laid eyes on.

Alone I went up to a second-floor guest bedroom, where I was able to find my coat at the bottom of the dozens piled on the twin beds, and there I ran into Arthur Sokolow, who was said by Ira to have read my play. I'd been too shy to say anything to him up in Ira's study after Ira's brief reading, and, occupying himself with browsing through that Lincoln book, he hadn't appeared to have anything to say to me. Several times during the party, however, I'd overheard something he was aggressively telling someone in the living room. "That got me so goddamn mad," I heard him say. "I sat down in a white heat and wrote the piece overnight"; I heard him say, "The possibilities were unlimited. There was an atmosphere of freedom, of willingness to establish new frontiers"; then I heard him laugh and say, "Well, they fed me against the ranking number-one program in radio . . . ," and the impact on me was as though I had encountered the indispensable truth.

I got my strongest picture ever of what I wanted my life to be like when, by deliberately roaming within earshot of him, I listened to Sokolow describing to a couple of women a play he was planning to write for Ira, a one-man show based not on the speeches but on the entire life of Abraham Lincoln, from his birth to his death. "The First Inaugural, the Gettysburg Address, the Second Inaugural—that's not the story. That's the rhetoric. I want Ira up there telling the *story*. Telling how goddamn *difficult* it was: no schooling, the stupid father, the terrific stepmother, the law partners, running against Douglas, losing, that hysterical shopper his wife, the brutal loss of the son—the death of Willie—the condemnation from every side, the daily political assault from the moment the man took office. The savagery of the war, the incompetence of the generals, the Emancipation Proclamation, the victory, the Union preserved and the Negro freed—*then* the assassination that changed this country forever. Wonderful stuff there for an actor. Three hours. No intermission. Leave them speechless in their seats. Leave them grieving for what America might be like today, for the Negro *and* the white man, if he'd served his second term and overseen Reconstruction. I've thought a lot about that man. Killed by an actor. Who else?" He laughed. "Who else would be so vain and so stupid as to kill Abraham Lincoln? Can Ira do three hours up there alone? The oratorical stuff—that we know he can do. Otherwise, together we'll work on it, and he'll get it: a mightily harassed leader full of wit and cunning and intellectual power, a huge creature alternately high-spirited and savagely depressed, and," said Sokolow, laughing again, "not yet apprised of the fact that he is 'Lincoln' of the Memorial."

Now Sokolow merely smiled, and in a voice that surprised me by its gentleness, he said, "Young Mr. Zuckerman. This must be some night for you." I nodded but again found myself tongue-tied, unable to ask if he had any advice for me or any criticism of my play. A well-developed sense of reality (for a fifteen-year-old) told me that Arthur Sokolow hadn't read the play.

As I was stepping out of the bedroom with my coat, I saw Katrina Van Tassel Grant coming toward me from the bathroom. I was a tall boy for my age but, in high-heeled shoes, she towered above me, though perhaps I would have fallen under the spell of her imposingness, felt that she considered herself to be the loftiest example of something or other, even had I been a foot taller. It all happened so spontaneously that I couldn't begin to understand how this person I was supposed to hate—and to hate so effortlessly—could be so impressive up close. A trashy writer as well as a supporter of Franco's and a foe of the USSR, yet where, when I needed it, was my antipathy? When I heard myself saying, "Mrs. Grant? Would you sign your name—for my mother?" I had to wonder who I suddenly was or what sort of hallucination I was having. This was worse than I'd behaved with the Cuban tobacco tycoon.

Smiling at me, Mrs. Grant came up with a suggestion as to who I might indeed be to explain my presence in this grand house. "Aren't you Sylphid's young man?"

I hadn't even to think to lie. "Yes," I said. I didn't know that I looked old enough, but perhaps teenage boys were a specialty of Sylphid's. Or perhaps Mrs. Grant still thought of Sylphid as just a kid. Or maybe she'd seen Sylphid kiss me on the nose, and assumed that kiss had to do with the two of us rather than with Abelard taking Eloise for the eleventh time.

"Are you a musician too?"

"Yes," I said.

"What instrument do you play?"

"The same. The harp."

"Isn't that unusual for a boy?"

"No."

"What shall I write on?" she asked.

"I think in my wallet there's a piece of paper—" But then I remembered that pinned inside my wallet was the Wallace-for-President button that I'd worn to school on my shirt pocket every day for two months and that, after the disastrous election, I had refused to part with. I now flashed it like a police badge whenever I went to get money to pay for something. "I forgot my wallet," I said.

From the beaded bag that she carried in one hand, she extracted a notepad and a silver pen. "What's your mother's name?"

She had asked kindly enough, but I couldn't tell her.

"Don't you remember?" she said with a harmless smile.

"Just *your* name. That's enough. Please."

As she was writing, she said to me, "What is your background, young man?"

I didn't at first understand that she was asking to what subspecies of humanity I belonged. The word "background" was impenetrable—and then it wasn't. I had no intention of being humorous when I replied, "I don't have one."

Now, why had she seemed a greater star to me, a more *frightening* star, than Eve Frame? Especially after Sylphid's dissection of her and her husband, how could I be so overwhelmed by the cravenness of fandom and address her in the tones of a nincompoop?

It was her power, of course, the power of celebrity; it was the power of one who partook of her husband's power as well, for with a few words spoken over the radio or with a remark in his column—with an *ellipsis* in his column—Bryden Grant was able to make and break show-business careers. Hers was the chilling power of someone whom people are always smiling at and thanking and hugging and hating.

But why did *I* kiss her ass? I didn't have a show-business career. What did I have to gain—or to lose? It had taken under a minute for me to abandon every principle and belief and allegiance I had. And I would have continued to if she had not mercifully signed her name and returned to the party. Nothing was required of me except to ignore her, as she was having no trouble ignoring me until I asked for the autograph for my mother. But my mother wasn't somebody who collected autographs, nor had anyone forced me to fawn and lie. It was just the easiest thing to do. It was worse than easy. It was automatic.

"Don't lose your courage," Paul Robeson had warned me backstage at the Mosque. Proudly I shook his hand, and I had lost it, first time out. Pointlessly lost it. I wasn't pulled into police headquarters and beaten with a truncheon. I walked out into the hallway with my coat. That was all it took for little Tom Paine to go off the rails.

I headed down the stairs seething with the self-disgust of someone young enough to think that you had to mean everything you said. I would have given anything to have had the wherewithal to go back and somehow put her in her place—just because of how pathetically I had behaved instead. Soon enough my hero would do that for me, however, and with none of my egregious politeness diluting the rich recklessness of his antagonism. Ira would more than make up for all that I had omitted to say.

I found Ira in the basement kitchen, drying the dishes that were being washed in the double sink by Wondrous, the maid who'd served our dinner, and a girl about my age who turned out to be her daughter, Marva. When I walked in, Wondrous was saying to Ira, "I did not want to waste my vote, Mr. Ringold. I did not want to waste my precious vote."

"Tell her," Ira said to me. "The woman won't believe me. I don't know why. You tell her about the Democratic Party. I don't know how a Negro woman can get it into her head that the Democratic Party is going to stop breaking its promises to the Negro race. I don't know who told her that or why she would believe him. Who told you, Wondrous? I didn't. Damn it, I told you six months ago—they are not going to bring an end to Jim Crow, your weak-kneed liberals of the Democratic Party. They are not and never have been the partners of the Negro people! There was only one party in the election that a Negro could vote for, one party that fights for the underdog, one party dedicated to making the Negro in this country a first-class citizen. And it was not the Democratic Party of Harry Truman!"

"I could not throw away my vote, Mr. Ringold. That's all I would be doing. Throwing it down the drain."

"The Progressive Party nominated more Negro candidates for office than any party in American history—fifty Negro candidates for important national offices on Progressive Party tickets! For offices no Negro has ever been nominated for, let alone held! That's throwing a vote down the drain? Damn it, don't insult your intelligence, and don't insult mine. I get damn angry with the Negro community when I think that you were not alone in not thinking what you were doing."

"I'm sorry, but a man who loses like that man lost cannot do nothing for us. We got to live somehow, too."

"Well, what you *did* was nothing. Worse than nothing. What you did with your vote was to put back in power the people who are going to give you segregation and injustice and lynching and the poll tax for as long as you live. As long as Marva lives. As long as Marva's *children* live. Tell her, Nathan. You met Paul Robeson. He met Paul Robeson, Wondrous. To my mind, the greatest Negro in American history. Paul Robeson shook his hand, and what did he tell you, Nathan? Tell Wondrous what he said to you."

"He said, 'Don't lose your courage.'"

"And that's what you lost, Wondrous. You lost your courage in the voting booth. I am surprised at you."

"Well," she said, "you all can wait if you want, but we got to live somehow."

"You let me down. What's worse, you let Marva down. You let Marva's *children* down. I don't understand it and I never will. No, I do not understand the working people of this country! What I hate with a passion is listening to people who do not know how to vote in their own goddamn interest! I would like to throw this dish, Wondrous!"

"Do what you want, Mr. Ringold. Ain't *my* dish."

"I get so goddamn angry about the Negro community and what they did and did not do for Henry Wallace, what they did not do for *themselves*, that I would really like to break this dish!"

"Good night, Ira," I said, while Ira stood there threatening to break the dinner dish that he was finishing drying. "I have to go home."

Just then, Eve Frame's voice came from the top of the landing: "Come say good night to the Grants, dear."

Ira pretended not to hear and turned again to Wondrous. "Many are the fine words, Wondrous, bantered by men everywhere of a new world—"

"Ira? The Grants are leaving. Come upstairs to say good night."

Suddenly he did throw the dish, just let it fly. Marva cried

"Momma!" when it struck the wall, but Wondrous shrugged— the irrationality of even white people *opposed* to Jim Crow did not surprise her—and she set about picking up the broken pieces as Ira, dishtowel in hand, streaked for the stairs, bounding up them three at a time, and shouting so as to be heard at the top of the landing. "I can't understand, when you have freedom of choice and you live in a country like ours, where supposedly nobody compels you to do anything, how anybody can sit down to dinner with that Nazi son-of-a-bitch killer. How do they do that? Who compels them to sit down with a man whose life's work is to perfect something new to kill people better than what they killed them with before?"

I was right behind him. I didn't know what he was talking about until I saw that he was headed for Bryden Grant, standing in the doorway wearing a Chesterfield overcoat and a silk scarf and holding his hat in one hand. Grant was a square-faced man with a prominent jaw and a head enviably thick with soft silver hair, a solidly constructed fifty-year-old about whom there was, nonetheless—and just because he was so attractive —something a little porous-looking.

Ira hurtled toward Bryden Grant and didn't stop himself until their faces were only inches apart.

"Grant," he said to him. "Grant, right? Isn't that your name? You're a college graduate, Grant. A Harvard man, Grant. A Harvard man and a Hearst newspaperman, and you're a Grant —of the Grants! You are supposed to know something better than the ABCs. I know from the shit you write that your stock-in-trade is to be devoid of convictions, but are you devoid of any convictions about anything?"

"Ira! Stop this!" Eve Frame had her hands to her face, which was drained of color, and then her hands were clutching at Ira's arms. "Bryden," she cried, looking helplessly back over her shoulder while trying to force Ira into the living room, "I'm terribly, terribly—I don't know—"

But Ira easily swept her away and said, "I repeat: are you devoid, Grant, of *any* convictions?"

"This is not your best side, Ira. You are not presenting your best side." Grant spoke with the superiority of one who had learned very young not to stoop to defend himself verbally against a social inferior. "Good night, all," he said to those dozen or so guests still in the house who had gathered in the hallway to see what the commotion was about. "Good night, dear Eve," Grant said, throwing her a kiss, and then, turning to open the door to the street, took his wife by the arm to leave.

"Wernher von Braun!" Ira shouted at him. "A Nazi son-of-a-bitch engineer. A filthy fascist son of a bitch. You sit down with him and you have dinner with him. True or false?"

Grant smiled and, with perfect self-control—his calm tone divulging just the hint of a warning—said to Ira, "This is extremely rash of you, sir."

"You have this Nazi at your house for dinner. True or false? People who work and make things that kill people are bad enough, but this friend of yours was a friend of Hitler's, Grant. Worked for Adolf Hitler. Maybe you never heard about all this because the people he wanted to kill weren't Grants, Grant—they were people like me!"

All this time, Katrina had been glaring at Ira from her husband's side, and it was she who now replied on his behalf. Anyone listening for one morning to *Van Tassel and Grant* might have surmised that Katrina often replied on his behalf. That way he maintained an ominous autocratic demeanor and she got to feed a hunger for supremacy that she did nothing to conceal. While Bryden clearly considered himself more intimidating if he said little and let the authority flow from the inside outward, Katrina's frighteningness—not unlike Ira's—came from her saying it all.

"Nothing you are shouting makes one bit of sense." Katrina Grant's mouth was full-sized and yet—I now noticed—a tiny hole was all that she employed to speak, a hole at the center of her lips the circumference of a cough drop. Through this she extruded the hot little needles that constituted her husband's defense. The spell of the encounter was upon her—this was war—and she did look impressively statuesque, even up against a lug six foot six. "You are an ignorant man, and a naive man, and a rude man, a bullying, simple-minded, arrogant man, you are a boor, and you don't know the facts, you don't know the reality, you don't know what you are talking about, now or ever! You know only what you parrot from the *Daily Worker*!"

"Your dinner guest von Braun," Ira shouted back, "didn't kill enough Americans? Now he wants to work for Americans to kill Russians? Great! Let's kill Commies for Mr. Hearst and Mr. Dies and the National Association of Manufacturers. This Nazi doesn't care who he kills, as long as he gets his paycheck and the veneration of—"

Eve screamed. It was not a scream that seemed theatrical or calculated, but in that hallway full of well-turned-out party-goers—where one man in tights was not, after all, running a rapier through another man in tights—she did seem to have arrived awfully fast at a scream whose pitch was as horrifying as any human note I had ever heard sounded, on or off a stage. Emotionally, Eve Frame did not seem to have to go far to get where she wanted to be.

"Darling," said Katrina, who had stepped forward to take Eve by the shoulders and protectively to embrace her.

"Ah, cut the crap," said Ira, as he started back down the stairs to the kitchen. "Darling's fine."

"She is *not* fine," said Katrina, "nor *should* she be. This house is not a political meeting hall," Katrina called after him, "for political thugs! Must you raise the roof every time you open your rabble-rousing mouth, must you drag into a beautiful, civilized home your Communist—"

He was instantly up out of the stairwell, and shouting, "This is a democracy, Mrs. Grant! My beliefs are my beliefs. If you want to know Ira Ringold's beliefs, all you have to do is ask him. I don't give a damn if you don't like them *or* me. These are my beliefs, and I don't give a damn if *nobody* likes them! But no, your husband draws his salary from a fascist, so anyone comes along daring to say what the fascists don't like to hear, it's 'Communist, Communist, there's a Communist in our civilized home.' But if you had enough flexibility in your think-ing to know that in a democracy the Communist philosophy, *any* philosophy—"

This time when Eve Frame screamed it was a scream with neither a bottom to it nor a top, a scream that signaled a life-threatening state of emergency and that ended effectively all political discourse and, with it, my first big evening out on the town.

5

"THE Jew hatred, this contempt for Jews," I said to Murray. "Yet she married Ira, married Freedman before him . . ."

It was our second session. Before dinner, we had sat out on the deck overlooking the pond, and while we drank our martinis, Murray had told me about the day's lectures down at the college. I shouldn't have been surprised by his mental energy, even by his enthusiasm for the three-hundred-word writing assignment—discuss, from the perspective of a lifetime, any one line in Hamlet's most famous soliloquy—that the professor had given his elderly students. Yet that a man so close to oblivion should be preparing homework for the next day, educating himself for a life that had all but run out—that the puzzle continued to puzzle him, that clarification remained a vital need—more than surprised me: a sense of error settled over me, bordering on shame, for living to myself and keeping everything at such a distance. But then the sense of error vanished. There were no more difficulties I wished to create.

I grilled chicken on the barbecue and we ate dinner outside on the deck. It was well after eight when we finished our meal, but we were only into the second week of July and, though that morning when I went for my mail the postmistress had informed me that we were going to lose forty-nine minutes of sun that month—and that if we didn't have rain soon, we would all have to go to the store for blackberry and raspberry preserves; and that the local roadkill was running four times greater than this time last year; and that there had been another sighting, near somebody's bird feeder at the edge of the woods, of our resident six-foot-tall black bear—there was as yet no end in sight for this day. Night was tucked away behind a straightforward sky proclaiming nothing but permanence. Life without end and without upheaval.

"Was she a Jew? She was," said Murray, "a pathologically embarrassed Jew. Nothing superficial about that embarrassment. Embarrassed that she looked like a Jew—and the cast of Eve Frame's face was subtly quite Jewish, all the physiognomic nuances Rebecca-like, right out of Scott's *Ivanhoe*—embarrassed that her daughter looked like a Jew. When she learned that I spoke Spanish, she told me, 'Everybody thinks Sylphid is Spanish. When we went to Spain, everybody took her for a native.' It was too pathetic even to dispute. Who cared anyway? Ira didn't. Ira had no use for it. Politically opposed. Couldn't stand religion of any kind. At Passover, Doris used to prepare a family seder and Ira wouldn't come near it. Tribal superstition.

"I think when he first met Eve Frame he was so bowled over by her, by everything—fresh to New York, fresh to *The Free and the Brave*, squiring around on his arm *The American Radio Theater*—I think that her being or not being a Jew never came up. What difference did it make to him? But anti-Semitism? That made *all* the difference. Years later he told me how whenever he said the word 'Jew' in public she would try to quiet him down. They'd take the elevator in an apartment building after visiting somebody somewhere and there'd be a woman with a baby in her arms or a baby in a carriage, and Ira wouldn't even notice them, but when they got into the street, Eve would say, 'What a perfectly hideous child.' Ira couldn't figure what was eating her until he realized that the hideous child was always the child of a woman who looked to her grossly Jewish.

"How could he stand five minutes of that crap? Well, he couldn't. But it wasn't the army, Eve Frame was no southern hillbilly, and he wasn't about to take a swing at her. Pummeled her instead with adult education. Ira tried to be an O'Day to Eve, but she was no Ira. The Social and Economic Origins of Anti-Semitism. That was the course. Sat her down in his study and read aloud to her from his books. Read aloud to her from the notepads he'd carried around with him during the war, where he'd put down his observations and thoughts. 'There is nothing superior in being Jewish—and there is nothing inferior or degrading. You are Jewish, and that's it. That's the story.'

"He bought her what was one of his favorite novels back then, a book by Arthur Miller. Ira must have given away dozens of copies of it. Called *Focus*. He gave Eve a copy, then marked it all up for her, so she wouldn't miss the important passages. He explained it to her the way O'Day used to explain books at the base library in Iran. Remember *Focus*, Miller's novel?"

I remembered it well. Ira had given me a copy too, for my

sixteenth birthday, and, like O'Day, explained it to *me*. During my last years of high school, *Focus* took its place, alongside *On a Note of Triumph* and the novels of Howard Fast (and two war novels that he gave me, *The Naked and the Dead* and *The Young Lions*), as a book that affirmed my own political sympathies as well as furnishing a venerated source from which I could take lines for my radio plays.

Focus was published in 1945, the year Ira returned from overseas with his duffel bags full of books and the thousand bucks he'd won on the troopship shooting craps, and three years before the Broadway production of *Death of a Salesman* made Arthur Miller a famous playwright. The book tells of the harshly ironic fate of a Mr. Newman, a personnel officer for a big New York corporation, a cautious, anxiety-ridden conformist in his forties—too cautious to become actively the racial and religious bigot he is secretly in his heart. After Mr. Newman is fitted for his first pair of glasses, he discovers that they set off "the Semitic prominence of his nose" and make him dangerously resemble a Jew. And not just to himself. When his crippled old mother sees her son in his new glasses, she laughs and says, "Why, you almost look like a Jew." When he turns up at work in the glasses, the response to his transformation is not so benign: he is abruptly demoted from his visible position in personnel to a lowly job as a clerk, a job from which Mr. Newman resigns in humiliation. From that moment on, he who himself despises Jews for their looks, their odors, their meanness, their avarice, their bad manners, even for "their sensuous lust for women," is marked as a Jew everywhere he goes. So socially wide-ranging is the animosity he incites that it feels to the reader—or did to me as an adolescent—that it cannot be Newman's face alone that is responsible but that the source of his persecution is a mammoth, spectral incarnation of the extensive anti-Semitism that he was himself too meek to enact. "He had gone all his life bearing this revulsion toward Jews" and now that revulsion, materialized on his Queens street and throughout New York as in a terror-filled nightmare, ostracizes him brutally—in the end, violently—from the neighbors whose acceptance he had courted with his obedient conformism to their ugliest hatreds.

I went into the house and came back with the copy of *Focus*

I probably hadn't opened since I got it from Ira and read it through in one night, then through again twice more, before setting it between the bookends on the bedroom desk where I kept my stash of sacred texts. On the title page Ira had inscribed a message to me. When I gave the book to Murray, he handled it a moment (a relic of his brother) before turning to the inscription to read it aloud:

> Nathan—There are so few times I find anybody to hold an intelligent conversation with. I read lots and believe that what good I get from that must be stimulated and take form in discussion with other people. You are one of those few people. I feel slightly less pessimistic as regards the future because of knowing a young person like you.
>
> Ira, April 1949

My former teacher flipped through *Focus* to see what I had underlined in 1949. He stopped a quarter of the way in and again read aloud to me, this time from one of the printed pages. " 'His face,' " Murray read. " '*He* was not this face. Nobody had a right to dismiss him like that because of his face. Nobody! He was *him*, a human being with a certain definite history and he was not this face which looked like it had grown out of another alien and dirty history.'

"She reads this book at Ira's request. She reads what he underlines for her. She listens to his lecture. And what is the subject of the lecture? The subject is the subject of the book —the *subject* is the Jewish face. Well, as Ira used to say: It's hard to know how much she hears. This was a prejudice that, no matter what she heard, no matter how much she heard, she could not let go of."

"*Focus* didn't help," I said when Murray handed back the book to me.

"Look, they met Arthur Miller at a friend's house. Maybe it was at a party for Wallace, I don't remember. After Eve was introduced to him, she volunteered to Arthur Miller how *gripping* she had found his book. Probably wasn't lying, either. Eve read many books, and with a far wider understanding and appreciation than Ira, who if he didn't find political and social implications in the book, the whole thing was no good. But whatever she learned from reading or from music or art or acting—or from personal experience, from all the tremulous living she'd done—remained apart from where the hatred did its work. She couldn't escape it. Not that she was a person who couldn't make a change. She changed her name, changed husbands, changed from movies to the stage to radio when her professional fortunes altered and a change had to be made, but this was fixed in her.

"I don't mean that things didn't get better the longer Ira hammered away—or didn't look as though they'd gotten better. To avoid those lectures of his, she probably censored herself at least a little. But a change of heart? When she *had* to—to hide the way she felt from her social set, from the prominent *Jews* in her social set, to hide the way she felt from Ira himself —she did it. Indulged him, patiently listened when he was off and running about anti-Semitism in the Catholic Church and the Polish peasantry and in France during the Dreyfus affair. But when she found a face inexcusably Jewish (like the one on my wife, like Doris's), her thoughts weren't Ira's or Arthur Miller's.

"Eve hated Doris. Why? A woman who'd worked in a hospital lab? A former lab technician? A Newark mother and housewife? What threat could she possibly pose to a famous star? How much effort would it have taken to tolerate her? Doris had scoliosis, there was pain as she aged, she had to have an operation to insert a rod and that didn't go very well, and so on and so forth. The fact is that Doris, who to me was pretty as a picture from the day I met her till the day she died, had a deformation of the spine and you noticed it. Her nose was not so straight as Lana Turner's. You noticed *that*. She grew up speaking English the way it was spoken in the Bronx when she was a kid—and Eve could not bear to be in her presence. Couldn't look at her. My wife was too upsetting for her to look at.

"During those three years they were married, we were invited for dinner exactly once. You could see it in Eve's eyes. What Doris wore, what Doris said, what Doris looked like—all repellent to her. Me, Eve was apprehensive of; she didn't care for me for other reasons. I was a schoolteacher from Jersey, a nobody in her world, but she must have seen in me a potential foe and so she was always polite. And charming. The way she was with you, I'm sure. I had to admire the pluck in her: a fragile, high-strung person, easily addled, who'd come as far as she had, a woman of the world—that requires tenacity. To keep trying, to keep surfacing after all she'd been through, after all her career setbacks, to make a success in radio, to create that house, to establish that salon, to entertain all those people . . . Sure, she was wrong for Ira. And he for her. They had no business together. Nonetheless, to take him on, to take on yet another husband, to get a big new life going again, that took *something*.

"If I separated out her marriage to my brother, if I separated out her attitude to my wife, if I tried looking at her separate from that stuff—well, she was a bright, peppy little thing. Separate out all that and she was probably the same bright, peppy little thing who'd gone out to California and taken on being a silent-movie actress at the age of seventeen. She had spirit. You saw it in those silent films. Under all that civility, she masked a lot of spirit—I venture to say, *Jewish* spirit. There was a generous side to her when she could relax, which was not often. When she was relaxed, you felt that there was something in her wanting to do the right thing. She tried to pay attention. But the woman was hog-tied—it wouldn't work. You couldn't establish any sort of independent relationship with her, and she couldn't take any independent interest in you. You couldn't count on her judgment for very long, either, not with Sylphid at her other side.

"Well, after we left that night, she said to Ira, a propos of Doris, 'I hate those wonderful wives, those doormats.' But it wasn't a doormat Eve saw in Doris. She saw a Jewish woman of the sort she could not abide.

"I knew this; it didn't take Ira to clue me in. He felt too compromised to anyway. My kid brother could tell me anything, tell *anybody* anything—had since the day he could talk—but *that* he couldn't tell me until everything was kaput. But he didn't have to for me to know that the woman had got caught in her own impersonation. The anti-Semitism was just a part of the role she was playing, a careless part of what went into playing the role. In the beginning, I would think, it was almost inadvertent. It was unthinking more than malicious. In that way went along with everything else she did. The thing that's happening to her is unobserved by her.

"You're an American who doesn't want to be your parents' child? Fine. You don't want to be associated with Jews? Fine. You don't want anybody to know you were born Jewish, you want to disguise your passage into the world? You want to drop the problem and pretend you're somebody else? Fine. You've come to the right country. But you don't have to hate Jews into the bargain. You don't have to punch your way out of something by punching somebody else in the face. The cheap pleasures of Jew hating aren't necessary. You're convincing as a Gentile without them. That's what a good director would have told her about her performance. He would have told her that the anti-Semitism is overdoing the role. It's no less a deformity than the deformity she was trying to obliterate. He would have told her, 'You're a film star already—you don't need anti-Semitism as a part of your superior baggage.' He would have told her, 'As soon as you do that, you're gilding the lily and you're not convincing at all. It's over the top, you're doing too much. The performance is logically too complete, too airless. You're succumbing to a logic that doesn't obtain in real life like that. Drop it, you don't need it, it'll work much better without it.'

"There is, after all, the aristocracy of art, if it's aristocracy she was after—the aristocracy of the performer to which she could naturally belong. Not only can it accommodate being un-anti-Semitic, it can even accommodate being a Jew.

"But Eve's mistake was Pennington, taking him for her model. She hit California and she changed her name and she was a knockout and got into pictures and then, under the studio's pressure and prodding, with its help, she left Mueller and married this silent-screen star, this rich, polo-playing, upper-class *genuine* aristocrat, and she took her idea of a Gentile from *him*. *He* was her director. That's where she screwed up but good. To take for your model, for your Gentile mentor, another outsider guarantees that the impersonation will not work. Because Pennington is not just an aristocrat. He's also homosexual. He's also anti-Semitic. And she picks up his attitudes. All she's trying to do is get away from where she began, and that is no crime. To launch yourself undisturbed by the past into America—that's your choice. The crime isn't even bringing an anti-Semite close to you. That's your choice too. The crime is being unable to stand up to him, unable to defend against the assault, and taking his attitudes for yours. In America, as I see it, you can allow yourself every freedom but that one.

"In my time, as in yours, the Sandhurst of this sort of thing, the foolproof training ground—if such a thing there is—for Jews de-Jewing themselves, was usually the Ivy League. Remember Robert Cohn in *The Sun Also Rises*? Graduates from Princeton, boxes there, never thinks about the Jewish part of himself, and is still an oddity, at least to Ernest Hemingway. Well, Eve took her degree, not at Princeton, but in Hollywood, under Pennington. She settled on Pennington for his seeming normality. That is, Pennington was such an exaggerated Gentile aristocrat that she, an innocent—that is to say, a Jew— thought of him as not exaggerated but normal. Whereas the Gentile woman would have smelled this out and understood it. The Gentile woman of Eve's intelligence would never have consented to marrying him, studio or no studio; she would have understood at the outset that he was defiant and damaging and spitefully superior to the Jewish outsider.

"The enterprise was flawed from the beginning. She did not have a natural affinity with the common model of what she was interested in, so she impersonated the wrong Gentile. And she was young and she got rigidly fixed in the role, unable to improvise. Once the performance was set, A to Z, she was fearful of pulling any part of it, fearful that the whole act would come undone. There's no self-scrutiny, and so there's no possibility for minor adjustment. She's not the master of the role. The role mastered her. On the stage she would have been able to give a more subtle performance. But then, on the stage she had a level of consciousness that she did not always exhibit in life.

"Now, if you want to be a real American Gentile aristocrat, you would, whether or not you felt it, pretend to great *sympathy* for the Jews. That would be the cunning way to do it. The point about being an intelligent, sophisticated aristocrat is that, unlike everyone else, you force yourself to overcome, or to appear to overcome, the contemptuous reaction to difference. You can still hate 'em in private if you have to. But not to be able to engage Jews easily, with good-spirited ease, would morally compromise a true aristocrat. Good-spirited and easy —that's the way Eleanor Roosevelt did it. That's the way Nelson Rockefeller did it. That's the way Averell Harriman did it. Jews aren't a problem for these people. Why should they be? But they are for Carlton Pennington. And that's whose route she takes and how she became embedded in all those attitudes she didn't need.

"For her, as Pennington's mock-aristocratic young wife, the permissible transgression, the *civilized* transgression, wasn't Judaism and couldn't be; the permissible transgression was homosexuality. Until Ira came along, she was unaware not only of how offensive all the accoutrements of anti-Semitism were but of how damaging they were to *her*. Eve thought, If I hate Jews, how can I possibly be a Jew? How can you hate the thing you are?

"She hated what she was and she hated how she looked. Eve Frame, of all people, hated her looks. Her own beauty was her own ugliness, as though that lovely woman had been born with a big purple blotch spread across her face. The indignation at having been born that way, the outrage of it, never left her. She, like Arthur Miller's Mr. Newman, was not her face either.

"You must be wondering about Freedman. An unsavory character, but Freedman, unlike Doris, wasn't a woman. He was a man, and he was rich, and he offered protection from everything that oppressed Eve as much as or even more than her being a Jew. He ran her finances for her. He was going to make *her* rich.

"Freedman, by the way, had a very large nose. You'd think Eve would flee at the sight of him—a swarthy little Jew, a real estate speculator with a big nose and bowed legs and Adler elevated shoes. The guy even has an accent. He's one of those crinkly-haired Polish Jews, with the orange-reddish hair and the old-country accent and the tough little immigrant's vigor and drive. He's all appetite, a heavyset bon vivant, but large as his belly is, his prick, by all reports, is still larger and visible beyond it. Freedman, you see, is her reaction to Pennington as Pennington was her reaction to Mueller: you marry one exaggeration one time, you marry the antithetical exaggeration the next. Third time round she marries Shylock. Why not? By the end of the twenties silent films were all but over, and despite that diction (or because of it, because it was too elocutionary back then), she never took off in talkies, and now it's 1938, and she was terrified that she would never work again, and so she went to the Jew for what you go to a Jew for—money and business and licentious sex. I suppose for a while he sexually resuscitated her. It's not a complicated symbiosis. It was a transaction. A transaction in which she got taken to the cleaners.

"You have to remember Shylock, you have also to remember *Richard III*. You'd think Lady Anne would run a million miles from Richard, duke of Gloucester. This is the foul monster who murdered her husband. She spits in his face. 'Why dost thou spit at me?' he says. 'Would it were mortal poison,' she says. Yet the next we know, she's wooed and won. 'I'll have her,' Richard says, 'but I will not keep her long.' The erotic power of a foul monster.

"Eve had no idea in the world how to oppose or how to resist, no idea how to conduct herself in a dispute or a disagreement. But everybody every day has to oppose and resist. You don't have to be an Ira, but you have to steady yourself every day. But for Eve, since every conflict is perceived as an assault, a siren is sounded, an air-raid siren, and reason never enters the picture. One second exploding with spite and fury, the next capitulating, caving in. A woman with a superficial kind of delicacy and gentleness but confused by everything, bitter and poisoned by life, by that daughter, by herself, by her insecurity, by her total insecurity from one minute to the next—and Ira falls for her.

"Blind to women, blind to politics, head-over-heels committed to both. Seizes everything with the same overengagement. Why Eve? Why choose Eve? He wants most in this world to be worthy of Lenin and Stalin and Johnny O'Day, and so he entangles himself with her. Responds to the oppressed in all forms, and responds to their oppression in exactly the wrong way. If he weren't my brother, I wonder how seriously I would have taken his hubris. Well, that must be what brothers are for—not to stand on ceremony about the bizarre."

"Pamela," Murray erupted, having had to overcome some

minor impediment—the age of his brain—to get to the name. "Sylphid's best friend was an English girl named Pamela. Played the flute. I never met her. She was only described to me. Once I saw her photograph."

"I met Pamela," I said. "I knew Pamela."

"Attractive?"

"I was fifteen. I wanted something unheard-of to happen to me. That makes every girl attractive."

"A beauty, according to Ira."

"According to Eve Frame," I said, "'a Hebrew princess.' That's what she called Pamela that night I met her."

"What else? She must romantically aggrandize everything. The exaggeration washes away the stain. You had better be a princess if you are a Hebrew woman expecting to be made welcome in the home of Eve Frame. Ira had a fling with the Hebrew princess."

"Did he?"

"Ira fell in love with Pamela and wanted her to run off with him. He used to take her out to Jersey on her day off. In Manhattan she had a small apartment by herself, near Little Italy, a ten-minute walk from West Eleventh Street, but it was dangerous for Ira to show up at her place. You couldn't miss a guy that size on the street, and in those days he was doing his Lincoln all over town, free for schools and so on, and a lot of people in Greenwich Village knew who he was. On the street he was always talking to people, finding out what they did for a living and telling them how they were getting screwed by the system. So on Mondays he took the girl to Zinc Town with him. They'd spend the day and then he'd drive like hell to get back in time for dinner."

"Eve never knew?"

"Never knew. Never found out."

"And I couldn't, as a kid, have imagined it," I said. "Never had Ira down for a lady's man. Didn't go with dressing up in Lincoln's suit. I'm so stuck in my early vision of him, even now I find it unbelievable."

Murray, laughing, said, "That a man has a lot of sides that are unbelievable is, I thought, the subject of your books. About a man, as your fiction tells it, *everything* is believable. Christ, yes, women. Ira's women. A big social conscience and the wide sexual appetite to go with it. A Communist with a conscience and a Communist with a cock.

"When I'd get disgusted about the women, Doris defended that, too. Doris, who you would think, from the life she led, would be the first to condemn it. But she understood him as a sister-in-law in a gentle way. About his weakness for women, she had a surprisingly gentle point of view. Doris was not so ordinary as she looked. She wasn't as ordinary as Eve Frame thought she was. Nor was Doris a saint. Eve's contempt for Doris also had something to do with her forgiving point of view. What does Doris care? He's betraying that prima donna—fine with her. 'A man attracted to women all the time. And women attracted to him. And is this bad?' Doris asked me. 'Isn't this human? Did he kill a woman? Did he take money from a woman? No. So what's so bad?' Some needs my brother knew very well how to take care of. Others he was hopeless about."

"Which were those others?"

"The need to choose your fight. Couldn't do it. Had to fight everything. Had to fight on all fronts, all the time, everyone and everything. Back in that era, there were a lot of angry Jewish guys around like Ira. Angry Jews all over America, fighting something or other. One of the privileges of being American and Jewish was that you could be angry in the world in Ira's way, aggressive about your beliefs and leaving no insult un-avenged. You didn't have to shrug and resign yourself. You didn't have to muffle anything. To be an American with your own inflection wasn't that difficult anymore. Just get out in the open and argue your point. That's one of the biggest things that America gave to the Jews—gave them their anger. Especially our generation, Ira's and mine. Especially after the war. The America we came home to offered us a place to really get pissed off, without the Jewish governor on. Angry Jewish guys in Hollywood. Angry Jewish guys in the garment business. The lawyers, the angry Jewish guys in the courtroom. Everywhere. In the bakery line. At the ballpark. On the ball field. Angry Jewish guys in the Communist Party, guys who could be bel-ligerent and antagonistic. Guys who could throw a punch, too. America was paradise for angry Jews. The shrinking Jew still existed, but you didn't have to be one if you didn't want to.

"My union. My union wasn't the teachers' union—it was the Union of Angry Jews. They organized. Know their motto? Angrier than Thou. That should be your next book. *Angry Jews since World War II.* Sure, there are the affable Jews—the inappropriate-laughing Jews, the I-love-everyone-deeply Jews, the I-was-never-so-moved Jews, the Momma-and-Poppa-were-saints Jews, the I-do-it-all-for-my-gifted-children Jews, the I'm-sitting-here-listening-to-Itzhak-Perlman-and-I'm-crying Jews, the entertaining Jew of perpetual punning, the serial Jewish joker—but I don't think that's a book you'll write."

I was laughing aloud at Murray's taxonomy, and he was too.

But after a moment, his laughter deteriorated into a cough, and he said, "I better settle down. I'm ninety years old. I better get to the point."

"You were telling me about Pamela Solomon."

"Well," Murray said, "she eventually played flute for the Cleveland Symphony Orchestra. I know this because when that plane went down back in the sixties, or maybe it was the seventies—whichever, a dozen members of the Cleveland Symphony on board, and Pamela Solomon listed among the dead. She was a very talented musician, apparently. When she first got to America she was a bit of a bohemian as well. Daughter of a proper, stifling London Jewish family, her father a doctor more English than the English. Pamela couldn't bear her family's propriety, and so she came to America. Attended Juilliard and, fresh from restrained England, fell for unrestrainable Sylphid: the cynicism, the sophistication, the American brashness. She was impressed by Sylphid's luxurious house, impressed by Sylphid's mom, the star. Motherless in America, she wasn't unhappy being gathered under Eve's wing. Though she lived only blocks away, the nights when she was visiting Sylphid she would end up having dinner and sleeping over at the house. In the mornings, down in the kitchen, she wandered around in her nightie, making herself coffee and toast and pretending either that she didn't have genitals or that Ira didn't.

"And Eve buys it, treats delightful young Pamela like her Hebrew princess and nothing more. The English accent washes away the Semitic stigma, and all in all she's so happy Sylphid has such a talented, well-behaved friend, she's so happy Sylphid has *any* friend, that she's deficient in sizing up the implications of Pamela's tuchas moving up and down the stairs inside the little-girl nightie.

"One night Eve and Sylphid went to a concert and Pamela happened to be staying over, and she wound up at home with Ira and they sat in the living room, alone together for the first time, and he asked Pamela about where she came from. His opening gambit with everyone. Pamela gave him a charming comical account of her proper family and the insufferable schools they sent her to. He asked about her job at Radio City. She was third flute-piccolo, a combined job. She was the one who got Sylphid her job subbing there. The girls would jabber together about the orchestra all the time—the politics, and the stupid conductor, and do you believe that tux he's wearing, and why doesn't he get a haircut, and nothing he does with his hands and his stick makes any sense at all. Kid stuff.

"To Ira, that night, she said, 'The principal cellist keeps flirting with me. I'm going out of my mind.' 'How many women in the orchestra?' 'Four.' 'Out of?' 'Seventy-four.' 'And how many of the men make passes at you? Seventy?' 'Uh-huh,' she said, and she laughed. 'Well, no, they don't all have the nerve, but anyone who *has* the nerve,' she told him. 'What do they say to you?' 'Oh—"That dress looks really great." "You always look so beautiful when you come to rehearsal." "I'm playing a concert next week, and I need a flutist." Things like that.' 'And what do you do about it?' 'I can take care of myself.' 'Do you have a boyfriend?' That's when Pamela told him that she had been having an affair for two years with the principal oboist.

"'A single man?' Ira asked her. 'No,' she told him, 'he's married.' 'It never bothers you that he's married?' And Pamela said, 'It's not the formal arrangement of life that interests me.' 'What about his wife?' 'I don't know his wife. I never met her. I never intend to meet her. I don't want to know anything about her particularly. It has nothing to do with his wife, it has nothing to do with his children. He loves his wife and he loves his children.' 'What does it have to do with?' 'It has to do with our pleasure. I do what I want to do for my own pleasure. Don't tell me you still believe in the sanctity of marriage. You think you take a vow and that's it, the two of you are faithful forever?' 'Yes,' he tells her, 'I believe that.' 'You've never—'

'Nope.' 'You're faithful to Eve.' 'Sure.' 'You intend to be faithful for the rest of your life?' 'Depends.' 'On what?' 'On you,' Ira said. Pamela laughs. They both laugh. 'It depends,' she says, 'on my convincing you that it's all right? That you're free to do so? That you're not the bourgeois proprietor of your wife and she's not the bourgeois proprietress of her husband?' 'Yes. Try to convince me.' 'Are you really such a hopelessly typical American that you're enslaved by middle-class American morality?' 'Yes, that's me—the hopelessly typical enslaved American. What are you?' 'What am I? I'm a musician.' 'What does that mean?' 'I'm given a score and I play it. I play what's given to me. I'm a player.'

"Now, Ira figured that he could be being set up by Sylphid, so that first night all he did when Pamela had finished showing off and started upstairs to bed was to take her hand and say, 'You're not a kid, are you? I had you down for a kid.' 'I'm a year older than Sylphid,' she tells him. 'I'm twenty-four. I'm an expatriate. I'll never go back to that idiotic country with its stupid subterranean emotional life. I love being in America. Here I'm free of all that showing-your-feelings-is-taboo crap. You can't imagine what it's like there. Here there's *life*. Here I have my own apartment in Greenwich Village. I work hard and I earn my own way in the world. I do six shows a day, six days a week. I am not a kid. Not in any way, Iron Rinn.'

"The scene went something like that. What there was to enkindle Ira is obvious. She was fresh, young, flirtatious, naive —and not naive, shrewd too. Off on her great American adventure. He admires the way this child of the upper middle class lives outside the bourgeois conventions. The squalid walk-up she lives in. Her coming alone to America. He admires the dexterity with which she adopts all her roles. For Eve she plays the sweet little girl, it's pajama-party stuff with Sylphid, at Radio City she's a flutist, a musician, a professional, and with him it's as though she'd been raised in England by the Fabians, a free, unfettered spirit, highly intelligent and unintimidated by respectable society. In other words, she's a human being— this with this one, that with that one, something else with the other one.

"And all of this is great. Interesting. Impressive. But falling in love? With Ira everything emotional had to be superabundant.

When he found his target, Ira fired. He not only fell for her. That baby he'd wanted to have with Eve? He wanted now to have it with Pamela. But he was afraid of frightening Pamela away, so about this he said nothing right off.

"They just have their antibourgeois fling. She can explain to herself everything that she's doing. 'I'm a friend to Sylphid and I'm a friend to Eve, and I'd do anything for either of them, but, as long as it does them no harm, I don't see where being a friend involves the heroic self-sacrifice of my own inclinations.' She too has an ideology. But Ira is by then thirty-six, and he *wants*. Wants the child, the family, the home. The Communist wants everything that is at the *heart* of bourgeois. Wants to get from Pamela everything he thought he was getting from Eve when he got Sylphid instead.

"Out together at the shack they used to talk a lot about Sylphid. 'What is her gripe?' Ira asks Pamela. Money. Status. Privilege. Harp lessons from birth. Twenty-three and her laundry is done for her, her meals are prepared for her, her bills are paid for her. 'You know the way I was brought up? Left home at fifteen. Dug ditches. I was *never* a kid.' But Pamela explains to him that when Sylphid was only twelve years old, Eve left Sylphid's father for the coarsest savior she could find, an immigrant dynamo with a hard-on who was going to make her rich, and her mother was so intoxicated by him that Sylphid lost her for all those years, and then they moved to New York and Sylphid lost her California friends, and she didn't know anybody and she started to get fat.

"Psychiatric bullshit to Ira. 'Sylphid sees Eve as a movie star who abandoned her to the nannies,' Pamela tells him, 'who dumped her for men and her man craziness, who betrayed her at every turn. Sylphid sees Eve as someone who keeps throwing herself at men so as not to stand on her own two feet.' 'Is Sylphid a lesbian?' 'No. Her motto is, Sex makes you powerless. Look at her mother. She tells me never to get involved with anybody sexually. She hates her mother for giving her up for all these men. Sylphid has a notion of absolute autonomy. She's going to be beholden to no one. She's tough.' 'Tough? Yeah? So how come,' Ira asks, 'she doesn't leave her mother if she's so tough? Why doesn't she go out on her own? You're not making sense. Toughness in a vacuum. Autonomy in a vacuum.

Independence in a vacuum. You want to know the answer to Sylphid? Sylphid is a sadist—*sadist* in a vacuum. Every night this Juilliard graduate rubs her finger through the leavings at the edge of her dinner plate, round and round the edge of her dinner plate till it squeaks, and then, the better to drive her mother round the bend, she puts the finger in her mouth and licks it till it's clean. Sylphid is there because her mother's afraid of her. And Eve will never *stop* being afraid of her because she doesn't want Sylphid to leave her, and that's *why* Sylphid won't leave her—until she finds a still better way to torture her. Sylphid is the one wielding the whip.'

"So, you see, Ira repeated to Pamela that stuff I'd told him at the outset about Sylphid but that he'd refused to take seriously coming from me. He repeated it to his beloved as though he'd figured it out himself. As people will. The two of them had a lot of these conversations. Pamela liked these conversations. They excited her. It made her feel strong to talk freely like that with Ira about Sylphid and Eve.

"One night something peculiar happened with Eve. She and Ira were lying in bed with the lights out, ready for sleep, when she began to weep uncontrollably. Ira said, 'What's the matter?' She wouldn't answer him. 'What are you crying about? What's happened now?' 'Sometimes I think . . . Oh, I can't,' she said. She couldn't speak, and she also couldn't stop crying. He turned the light on. Told her to go ahead and get it out of her system. To say it. 'Sometimes I feel,' she said, 'that *Pamela* should have been my child. Sometimes,' she said, 'it seems more natural.' 'Why Pamela?' 'The easy way we get along. Though maybe that's because she *isn't* my daughter.' 'Maybe it is, maybe it isn't,' he said. 'Her airiness,' Eve said, 'her lightness.' And she started weeping again. Out of guilt, more than likely, for having allowed herself that harmless fairy-tale wish, the wish to have a daughter who didn't remind her every second of her failure.

"By lightness I don't think Eve necessarily meant only physical lightness, the displacement of the fat by the thin. She was pointing to something else, to some kind of excitement in Pamela. *Inner* lightness. I thought she meant that in Pamela she could recognize, almost despite herself, the susceptibility that had once vibrated beneath her own demure surface. Recognized it however childishly Pamela behaved in her presence, however maidenly she acted. After that night, Eve never said anything like this again. It happened only that one time, just when Ira's passion for Pamela, when the illegitimacy of their reckless affair, was generating its greatest heat.

"So, each lays claim to the spirited young flutist as the pleasure-piping dream creature each had failed to obtain: the daughter denied Eve, the wife denied Ira.

" 'So sad. So sad,' Eve tells him. 'So very, very sad.' She holds on to him all that night. Right through to the morning, weeping, sighing, whimpering; all the pain, the confusion, the contradiction, the longing, the delusion, all the incoherence pouring out of her. He never felt sorrier for her—what with the affair with Pamela, he never felt farther from her either. 'Everything's gone all wrong. I tried and I tried,' she says, 'and nothing comes out quite right. I tried with Sylphid's father. I tried with Jumbo. I tried to give her stability and connection and a mother she could look up to. I tried to be a good mother. And then I had to be a good father. And she's had too many fathers. All I thought about was myself.' 'You haven't thought just about yourself,' he says. 'I have. My career. My careers. My acting. I always had to take care of my acting. I tried. She had good schools and good tutors and a good nanny. But maybe I should have just been with her all the time. She's inconsolable. She eats and she eats and she eats. That's her only consolation for something I didn't give her.' 'Maybe,' he says, 'that's just the way she is.' 'But there are plenty of girls who eat too much, and then they lose some weight—they don't just eat and eat and eat. I've tried everything. I've taken her to doctors, to specialists. She just keeps eating. She keeps eating to hate me.' 'Then maybe,' he says, 'if that is true, it's time for her to go out on her own.' 'What does that have to do with anything? Why should she be on her own? She's happy here. This is her house. No matter what other disruption I brought into her life, this is her house, it's always been her house, and it will be her house for as long as she wants. There's no reason that she should leave any sooner than she's ready to.' 'Suppose,' he says, 'her leaving were a way of getting her to stop eating.' 'I don't see how eating and living where she does have anything to do with each other! You're not making any sense! This is my daughter we're talking about!' 'Okay. Okay. But you just expressed a certain amount of disappointment . . .' 'I said she was eating to console herself. If she leaves here, she'll have to console herself *twice* as much. She'll have to console herself that much more. Oh, there's something terribly wrong. I should have stayed with Carlton. He was a homosexual, but he was her father. I just should have stayed with him. I don't know what I was thinking. I would never have met Jumbo, I would have never gotten involved with you, she would have had a father, and she wouldn't always be eating so much.' 'Why didn't you stay with him?' 'I know it seems as though it was selfish, as though it was for me. So that I could find satisfaction and companionship. But really I wanted *him* to be freed. Why should he be confined by family life and with this wife that he couldn't find attractive or interesting? Every time we were together I thought he must be thinking about the next busboy or waiter. I wanted him not to have to lie so much anymore.' 'But he didn't lie about that.' 'Oh, I knew it, and he knew I knew it, and everybody in Hollywood knew it, but he was still always skulking around and planning. Phone calls and disappearing and excuses as to why he was late and why he wasn't at Sylphid's party—I couldn't take another sorry excuse. He didn't care, and yet he continued to lie anyway. I wanted to relieve him of that, I wanted to relieve me of that. It wasn't for my own personal happiness, really. It was more for his.' 'Why didn't you go off by yourself, then? Why did you go off with Jumbo?' 'Well . . . that was an easy way to do it. To not be alone. To make the decision but to not be alone. But I could have stayed. And Sylphid would have had a father, and she wouldn't have known the truth about him, and we wouldn't have had the years with Jumbo, and we wouldn't have these dreadful trips to France that are just a nightmare. I could have stayed, and she could have just had an absent father like everyone else's absent father. So what if he was queer? Yes, some of it was Jumbo, and the passion. But I couldn't take the lies anymore, the false deception. It was fake deceit. Because Carlton *didn't* care, but for some modicum of dignity, of decency, he would pretend to hide it. Oh, I love Sylphid so! I love my daughter. I'd do anything for my daughter. But if it could be lighter and easier and more natural—more *like* a daughter. She's here, and I love her, but every little decision is a struggle, and her power . . . She doesn't treat me like a mother, and it makes it hard to treat her like a daughter. Though I'd do *anything* for her, *anything*.' 'Why don't you let her go away, then?' 'You keep bringing that up! She doesn't *want* to go away. Why do you think the solution is for her to go? The solution is for her to stay. She didn't get enough of me. If she were ready to go, she would have gone by now. She's not ready. She looks mature, but she isn't. I'm her mother. I'm her supporter. I love her. She needs me. I know it doesn't look as if she needs me, but she needs me.' 'But you're so unhappy,' he says. 'You don't understand. It's not me, it's Sylphid I worry about. Me, I'll get through. I always get through.' 'What do you worry about with her?' 'I want her to find a nice man. Somebody she can love and who'll take care of her. She's not dating that much,' Eve says. 'She doesn't date at all,' Ira says. 'That's not true. There was a boy.' 'When? Nine years ago?' 'A lot of men are very interested in her. At the Music Hall. A lot of musicians. She's just taking her time.' 'I don't understand what you're talking about. You have to go to sleep. Close your eyes and try to sleep.' 'I can't. I close my eyes and I think, What is going to happen to her? What is going to happen to me? So much trying and so much trying . . . and so little peace. So little peace of mind. Each day is a new . . . I know it may look like happiness to other people. I know she looks very happy and I know we look very happy together, and we really are very happy together, but each day just gets harder.' 'You look happy together?' 'Well, she loves me. She loves me. I'm her mummy. Of course we look happy together. She's beautiful. She's beautiful.' 'Who is?' he asks her. 'Sylphid. Sylphid is beautiful.' He had thought she was going to say 'Pamela.' 'Look deep into her eyes and her face. The beauty,' Eve says, 'and the strength there. It doesn't come out at you in that superficial look-at-me way. But there's deep beauty there. Very deep. She's a beautiful girl. She's my daughter. She's remarkable. She's a brilliant musician. She's a beautiful girl. She's my daughter.'

"If ever Ira knew it was hopeless, it was that night. He couldn't have seen any more purely how impossible it was. Easier to make America go Communist, easier to bring about the proletarian revolution in New York, on Wall Street, than separate a woman and her daughter who didn't want to be separated.

Yes, he should have just separated *himself*. But he didn't. Why? Finally, Nathan, I have no answer. Ask why anybody makes any tragic mistake. No answer."

"Throughout these months, Ira was becoming more and more isolated in the house. On the nights when he wasn't at a union executive meeting or wasn't at the meeting of his party unit, or they weren't out for the evening together, Eve would be in the living room doing her needlepoint and listening to Sylphid plucking away and Ira'd be upstairs writing to O'Day. And when the harp went silent and he went downstairs to find Eve, she wouldn't be there. She'd be up in Sylphid's room, listening to the record player. The two of them in bed, under the covers, listening to *Così Fan Tutte*. When he'd go up to the top floor and hear the Mozart blaring and see them together in bed, Ira felt as though *he* were the child. An hour or so later Eve would return, still warm from Sylphid's bed, to get in bed with him, and that was more or less the end of conjugal bliss.

"When the explosion comes, Eve is astonished. Sylphid must get an apartment of her own. He says, 'Pamela lives three thousand miles from her family. Sylphid can live three blocks from hers.' But all Eve does is cry. This is unfair. This is horrible. He is trying to drive her daughter out of her life. No, around the corner, he says—she is twenty-four years old, and it's time she stopped going to bed with Mommy. 'She is my daughter! How dare you! I love my daughter! How dare you!' 'Okay,' he says, '*I'll* live around the corner,' and the next morning he finds a floor-through apartment over on Washington Square North, just four blocks away. Puts down a deposit, signs a lease, pays the first month's rent, and comes home and tells her what he's done. 'You're leaving me! You're divorcing me!' No, he says, just going to live around the corner. Now you can lie in bed with her *all* night long. Though if, for variety, you should ever want to lie in bed with me all night long, he says, put on your coat and your hat and come around the corner and I will be delighted to see you. As for dinner, he tells her, who will even notice that I am not there? Just you wait. There is going to be a considerable improvement in Sylphid's outlook on life. 'Why are you *doing* this to me? To make me choose between my daughter and you, to make a mother choose—it's inhuman!' It takes hours more to explain that he is asking her to entertain a solution that would obviate the *need* for a choice, but it's doubtful that Eve ever understood what he was talking about. Comprehension was not the bedrock on which her decisions were based—desperation was. Capitulation was.

"The next night, Eve went up as usual to Sylphid's room, but this time to present her with the proposal she and Ira had agreed to, the proposal that was going to bring peace to their lives. Eve had gone with him that day to look at the apartment he'd leased on Washington Square North. There were French doors and high ceilings and ornamental moldings and parquet floors. There was a fireplace with a carved mantel. Below the rear bedroom was a walled-in garden much like the one on West Eleventh Street. It wasn't Lehigh Avenue, Nathan. Washington Square North, in those days, was as beautiful a street as there was in Manhattan. Eve said, 'It's lovely.' 'It's for Sylphid,' Ira said. He would keep the lease in his name, pay the rent, and Eve, who always made money but was always terrified about money, always losing it to some Freedman or other, Eve wouldn't have to worry about a thing. 'This is the solution,' he said, 'and is it so terrible?' She sat down in the sunlight in one of those front parlor window seats. There was a veil on her hat, one of those veils with the dots on it that she made popular in some film, and she lifted it away from her delectable little face and she began to sob. Their struggle was over. *Her* struggle was over. She jumped to her feet, she hugged him, she kissed him, she began to run from room to room, figuring out where to put the lovely old pieces of furniture that she was going to move from West Eleventh Street for Sylphid. She couldn't have been happier. She was seventeen again. Magical. Enchanting. She was the come-hither girl in the silent film.

"That night she gathered her courage and went upstairs bearing the drawing she'd made, the floor plan of the new apartment, and a list of the pieces from the house that would have gone to Sylphid anyway and so were hers to have forever right now. It took no time at all, of course, for Sylphid to register her objection and for Ira to be racing up the stairs to Sylphid's room. He found them in bed together. But no Mozart this time. Bedlam this time. What he saw was Eve on her back screaming and crying, and Sylphid in her pajamas sitting astride her, also screaming, also crying, her strong harpist's hands pinning Eve's shoulders to the bed. There were bits of paper all over the place—the floor plan for the new apartment —and there, on top of his wife, sat Sylphid, screaming, 'Can't you stand up to *anyone*? Won't you once stand up for your own daughter against him? Won't you be a mother, *ever*? *Ever*?'"

"What did Ira do?" I asked.

"What do you think Ira did? Out of the house, roaming the streets, up to Harlem, back down to the Village, walking for miles, and then, in the middle of the night, he headed for Pamela's on Carmine Street. He tried never to see her there if he could help it, but he rang her doorbell and zoomed up the five flights and told her it was over with Eve. He wanted her to come with him to Zinc Town. He wanted to marry her. He had wanted to marry her all along, he told her, and to have a child with her. You can imagine the impact that made.

"She lived in her one bohemian room—closets without doors, the mattress on the floor, the Modigliani prints, the chianti bottle with the candle, and sheet music all over the place. A tiny walk-up forty feet square and there is that giraffe of a man storming around her, overturning the music stand, knocking over all her 78s, kicking at the bathtub, which is in the kitchen, and telling this well-brought-up English kid with her new Greenwich Village ideology who thought that what they were doing was going to be consequence-free—a big, passionate con-sequence-free adventure with a famous older man—that she was the mother-to-be of his unborn heirs and the woman of his life.

"Overpowering Ira, the outsized, knocking over, crazy, giraffelike Ira, the driven man, with his all or nothing, says to her, 'Pack your clothes, you're coming with me,' and so he learns, sooner than he might have otherwise, that Pamela had been wanting to end things for months. 'End? *Why*?' She couldn't stand the strain anymore. 'Strain? *What* strain?' And so she told him: every time she was with him in Jersey, he wouldn't stop holding her and fondling her and making her sick with anxiety by telling her a thousand times how much he loved her; then he'd sleep with her and she'd come back to New York and go over to see Sylphid, and all Sylphid could talk about was the man she had nicknamed the Beast; Ira and her mother she linked together as Beauty and the Beast. And Pamela had to agree with her, had to laugh about him; she too had to make jokes about the Beast. How could he be so blind to the toll this was taking on her? She couldn't run away with him and she couldn't marry him. She had a job, she had a career, she was a musician who loved her music—and she could never see him again. If he didn't leave her alone . . . And so Ira left her. He got in the car and he drove to the shack, and that's where I went to see him the next day after school.

"He talked, I listened. He didn't let on to me about Pamela; he didn't because he damn well knew my thoughts on adultery. I'd already told him more times than he liked to hear, 'The excitement in marriage *is* the fidelity. If that idea doesn't excite you, you have no business being married.' No, he didn't tell me about Pamela—he told me about Sylphid sitting on Eve. All night, Nathan. At dawn I drove back to school, shaved in the faculty bathroom, met my homeroom class; in the afternoon, after my last class, I got in the car and drove back up again. I didn't want him out there alone at night because I didn't know what he might do next. It wasn't only his home life that he was confronting head-on. That was just a part of it. The political stuff was encroaching—the accusations, the firings, the permanent blacklisting. *That's* what was undermining him. The domestic crisis wasn't yet *the* crisis. Sure, he was at risk on both sides and eventually they'd merge, but for the time being he was able to keep them separate.

"The American Legion already had Ira in their sights for 'pro-Communist sympathies.' His name had been in some Catholic magazine, on some list, as somebody with 'Communistic associations.' His whole show was under suspicion. And there was friction with the party. That was heating up. Stalin and the Jews. The Soviet anti-Semitism was beginning to penetrate the consciousness of even the party blockheads. The rumors were starting to circulate among the Jewish party members, and Ira didn't like what he was hearing. He wanted to know more. About the claims to purity of the Communist Party and the Soviet Union, even Ira Ringold wanted to know more. The sense of betrayal by the party was faintly setting in, though the full moral shock wouldn't come until Khrushchev's revelations. Then everything collapsed for Ira and his pals, the justification for all their effort and all their suffering. Six years later, the heart of their adult biographies went right down the drain. Still, as early as 1950, Ira was causing problems for himself by wanting to know more. Though that stuff he'd never talk about with me. He didn't want me implicated, and he didn't want to hear me sounding off. He knew that if we tangled on the Communist issue, we'd wind up like a lot of other families, not talking again for the rest of our lives.

"We'd already had a lulu of an argument, back in '46, when he was first out in Calumet City rooming with O'Day. I went to visit him and it was not pleasant. Because Ira, when he argued about the things that mattered to him most, would never be finished with you. Especially in those early days after the war, Ira, in a political argument, was extremely disinclined to lose. Not least with me. Uneducated little brother educating the educated big one. He'd be staring straight at me, his finger jabbing straight at me, obstreperous, forcing the issue, overriding everything I said with 'Don't insult my intelligence,' 'That is a goddamn contradiction in terms,' 'I'm not going to stand here and take that shit.' The energy for the fight was astonishing. 'I don't give a damn if nobody knows it except me!' 'If you had any knowledge of what this world is all about . . . !' He could be particularly incendiary putting me in my place as an English teacher. 'What I hate with a passion is please define what the hell you are saying!' There was nothing that was small for Ira in those days. Everything he thought about, because he thought about it, was *big*.

"My first night visiting him out where he lived with O'Day, he told me that the teachers' union should push for the development of 'the people's culture.' That should be its official policy. Why? I knew why. Because it was the official policy of the party. You've got to elevate the cultural understanding of the poor Joe on the street, and instead of classical, old-time, traditional education, you've got to emphasize those things that contribute to a people's culture. The party line, and I thought it was unrealistic in every way. But the *willfulness* in that guy. I was no pushover, I knew how to convince people that I meant business too. But Ira's antagonism was inexhaustible. Ira wouldn't quit. When I got back from Chicago, I didn't hear from him for nearly a year.

"I'll tell you what else was closing in on him. Those muscle pains. That disease he had. They told him it was one thing and then another thing and they never figured out what the hell it was. Polymyositis. Polymyalgia rheumatica. Every doctor gave it another name. That's about all they gave him, aside from Sloan's Liniment and Ben-Gay. His clothes started stinking of every kind of goo they sold for aches and pains. One doctor that I took him to myself, across the street at the Beth Israel, a physician friend of Doris's, listened to his case history, drew blood, examined him thoroughly, and described him to us as hyperinflammatory. The guy had an elaborate theory and he drew us pictures—a failure of inhibition in the cascade that leads to inflammation. He described Ira's joints as quick to develop inflammatory reactions that rapidly escalate. Quick to inflame, slow to extinguish.

"After Ira died, some doctor suggested to me—made a persuasive case to me—that Ira suffered from the disease that they believe Lincoln had. Dressed up in the clothes and got the disease. Marfan's. Marfan's syndrome. Excessive tallness. Big hands and feet. Long, thin extremities. And lots of joint and muscle pain. Marfan's patients frequently kick off the way Ira did. The aorta explodes and they're gone. Anyway, whatever Ira had went undiagnosed, at least in terms of finding a treatment, and by '49, '50, those pains were beginning to be more or less intractable, and he was feeling under political pressure from both ends of the spectrum—from the network and from the party —and the guy had me worried.

"In the First Ward, Nathan, we were not just the only Jewish family on Factory Street. More than likely we were the only family that wasn't Italian between the Lackawanna tracks and the Belleville line. These First Warders came from the mountains, little guys mostly, with big shoulders and huge heads, from the mountains east of Naples, and when they got to Newark somebody put a shovel in their hands and they began to dig and they dug for the rest of their lives. They dug ditches. When Ira quit school, he dug ditches with them. One of those Italians tried to kill him with a shovel. My brother had a big mouth and he had to fight to live in that neighborhood. He had to fight to survive on his own from the time that he was seven years old.

"But all at once he was battling on every front, and I didn't want him to do something stupid or irreparable. I didn't drive out to tell him anything in particular. This wasn't a man you told what to do. I wasn't even there to tell him what I *thought*. What I thought was that to go on living with Eve and her daughter was insane. The night Doris and I went there for dinner, you couldn't miss the strangeness of the link between those two. I remember driving back to Newark that night with Doris and saying over and over, 'There is no room for Ira in that combination.'

"Ira called his utopian dream Communism, Eve called hers Sylphid. The parent's utopia of the perfect child, the actress's utopia of let's pretend, the Jew's utopia of not being Jewish, to name only the grandest of her projects to deodorize life and make it palatable.

"That Ira had no business in that household Sylphid had let him know right off the bat. And Sylphid was right: he *had* no business there, he *didn't* belong there. Sylphid made perfectly clear to him that *de*-utopianizing her mom—giving Mom a dose of life's dung she'd never forget—was her deepest daughterly inclination. Frankly, I didn't think he had any business on the radio, either. Ira was no actor. He had the chutzpah to get up and shoot off his mouth—that he never lacked—but an actor? He did every part the same way. That easygoing crap, as though he were sitting across from you at pinochle. The simple human approach, only it wasn't an approach. It was nothing. The absence of an approach. What did Ira know about acting? He had resolved as a kid to strike out on his own, and everything that urged him on was an accident. There was no plan. He wanted a home with Eve Frame? He wanted a home with the English girl? I realize that's a primary urge in people; in Ira particularly, the urge to have a home was the residue of a very, very old disappointment. But he picked some real beauts to have a home with. Ira asserted himself into New York City with all his intensity, with all that craving for a life of weight and meaning. From the party he got the idea that he was an instrument of history, that history had called him to the capital of the world to set society's wrongs right—and to me the whole thing looked ludicrous. Ira wasn't so much a displaced person as he was a misplaced person, always the wrong size for where he was, in both spirit and physique. But that wasn't a perspective I was about to share with him. My brother's vocation is to be stupendous? Suits me. I just didn't want him to wind up unrecognizable as anything else.

"I'd brought some sandwiches for us to eat that second night, and we ate and he talked and I listened, and it must have been about three in the morning when a New York Yellow Cab pulled up at the shack. It was Eve. Ira'd had the phone off the hook for two days, and when she couldn't stand any more phoning and getting a busy signal, she'd called a taxi and taken it sixty miles into the sticks in the middle of the night. She knocked, I got up and opened the door, and she rushed by me into the room, and there he was. What followed might have been planned by her all the way out in the taxi or might as easily have been improvised. It was right out of those silent pictures she used to act in. A completely screwy performance, pure exaggerated invention, yet so right for her that she would repeat it almost exactly only a few weeks later. A favorite role. The Suppliant.

"She threw herself onto her knees in the middle of the floor and, oblivious to me—or maybe not all that oblivious—she cried, 'I beg you! I implore you! Don't leave me!' The two arms upthrust in the mink coat. The hands trembling in the air. And tears, as though it weren't a marriage at stake but the redemption of mankind. Confirming—if confirmation was necessary—that she absolutely repudiated being a rational human being. I remember thinking, Well, she's cooked her goose this time.

"But I didn't know my brother, didn't know what he couldn't withstand. People down on their knees was what he'd been protesting all his life, but I would have thought that by then he had the wherewithal to distinguish between someone driven to her knees because of social conditions and someone just acting away. There was an emotion he could not quiet in himself when he saw her like that. Or so I thought. The sucker for suffering rushing to the fore—or so I thought—and so I stepped outside and got into the taxi and had a cigarette with the driver until harmony was restored.

"Everything permeated with stupid politics. That's what I was thinking in the taxi. The ideologies that fill people's heads and undermine their observation of life. But it was only driving back to Newark that night that I began to understand how those words applied to the predicament my brother was in with his wife. Ira wasn't *merely* a sucker for her suffering. Sure, he could be swept away by those impulses that most everybody has when somebody they are intimate with starts to cave in; sure, he could arrive at a mistaken idea of what he should do about it. But that isn't what happened. Only driving home did I realize that wasn't *at all* what had happened.

"Remember, Ira belonged to the Communist Party heart and soul. Ira obeyed every one-hundred-eighty-degree shift of policy. Ira swallowed the dialectical justification for Stalin's every villainy. Ira backed Browder when Browder was their American messiah, and when Moscow pulled the plug and expelled Browder, and overnight Browder was a class collaborator and a social imperialist, Ira bought it all—backed Foster and the Foster line that America was on the road to fascism. He managed to squelch his doubts and convince himself that his obedience to every last one of the party's twists and turns was helping to build a just and equitable society in America. His self-conception was of being virtuous. By and large I believe he was—another innocent guy co-opted into a system he didn't understand. Hard to believe that a man who put so much stock in his freedom could let that dogmatizing control his thinking. But my brother abased himself intellectually the same way they all did. Politically gullible. Morally gullible. Wouldn't face it. Shut their minds, the Iras, to the source of what they were selling and celebrating. Here was somebody whose greatest strength was his power to say no. Unafraid to say no and to say it into your face. Yet all he could ever say to the party was yes.

"He had reconciled himself to her because no sponsor or network or advertising agency was going to touch Ira as long as he was married to the Sarah Bernhardt of the Airwaves. That's what he was gambling on, that they couldn't expose him, wouldn't dispose of him, as long as at his side he had radio's royalty. She was going to protect her husband and by extension protect the clique of Communists who ran Ira's show. She threw herself on the floor, she implored him to come home, and what Ira realized was that he damn well better do what she asked, because without her he was sunk. Eve was his front. The bulwark's bulwark.'"

"That's when the deus ex machina appears with her gold tooth. Eve discovered her. Heard about her from some actor who'd heard about her from some dancer. A masseuse. Probably ten, twelve years older than Ira and pushing fifty by then. Had that worn, twilight look about her, the sensuous female rumbling downhill, but her work kept her in shape, kept that big, warm body firm enough. Helgi Pärn. Estonian woman married to an Estonian factory worker. A solid working-class woman who likes her vodka and is a little bit of a prostitute and a little bit of a thief. A large, healthy woman who, when she first shows up, is missing a tooth. And then she comes back and the tooth has been replaced—a gold tooth, a present from a dentist she's massaging. And then she comes back with a dress, a present from a dress manufacturer she's massaging. Over the course of the year she comes back with some costume jewelry, she has a fur coat, she has a watch, soon she's buying stocks, et cetera, et cetera. Helgi is constantly being improved. She jokes about all her improvements. It's just appreciation, she tells Ira. The first time Ira gives her money she says, 'I don't take money, I take presents.' He says, 'I can't go shopping. Here. Buy yourself what you want.'

"She and Ira have the obligatory class-consciousness discussion, he tells her how Marx urged working people like the Pärns to wrest the capital from the bourgeoisie and organize as the ruling class, in control of the means of production, and Helgi's having none of it. She's Estonian, the Russians had occupied Estonia and turned it into a Soviet republic, and so she's *instinctively* anti-Communist. There is only one country for her, the United States of America. Where else could an immigrant farm girl with no education, blah blah blah blah. The improvements are comic to Ira. Ordinarily he is a little short on humor, but not where Helgi is concerned. Maybe he should have married *her*. Maybe this big, good-natured slob who does not recoil from reality was his soulmate. His soulmate the way Donna Jones was his soulmate: because of what was untamed in her. Because of what was wayward.

"He sure did get a kick out of the acquisitive side of her. 'What is it this week, Helgi?' To her it's not whoring, it's not sinister—it's self-improvement. The fulfillment of Helgi's American dream. America is the land of opportunity, and her clients appreciate her, and a girl has to make a living, and so three times a week she came around after dinner, looking like a nurse—starched white dress, white stockings, white shoes—and carrying with her a table that folded in half, a massage table. She sets the table up in his study, in front of his desk, and though he was half a foot too tall for it, he stretched himself out on it, and for a solid hour she massaged him very professionally. Afforded him, with those massages, the only real relief Ira ever got from all that pain.

"Then, still in her white uniform, altogether professionally, she concluded with something that provided more relief. A wonderful outpouring gushed forth from his penis, and momentarily the prison dissolved. In that gush was all the freedom that Ira had left. The lifelong battle to exercise fully his political, civil, and human rights had evolved itself down to coming, for dough, onto this fifty-year-old Estonian woman's gold tooth while, below them in the living room, Eve listened to Sylphid play on her harp.

"Helgi might have been a handsome woman, but the shallowness shone right through. Her English wasn't so hot, and, as I said, there was always a thin stream of vodka gurgling through her veins, and all of this together gave her the aura of somebody pretty thick. Eve nicknamed her. The Peasant. That's what they called her around West Eleventh Street. But Helgi Pärn was no peasant. Shallow maybe, but not thick. Helgi knew that Eve considered her the equivalent of a beast of burden. Eve didn't bother to hide it, didn't think she had to with a lowly masseuse, and the lowly masseuse despised her for it. When Helgi was blowing Ira, and Eve was downstairs in the living room listening to the harp, Helgi used to have fun imitating the dainty, ladylike way that she imagined Eve deigning to suck him off. Behind the blanked-out Baltic mask, there was somebody reckless who knew when to strike out and how to strike out against her dismissive betters. And when she struck out at Eve, she brought the whole thing down. When the vodka was in there, Helgi wasn't about to impose restrictions on herself.

"Revenge," announced Murray. "Nothing so big in people and nothing so small, nothing so audaciously creative in even the most ordinary as the workings of revenge. And nothing so ruthlessly creative in even the most refined of the refined as the workings of betrayal."

I was taken back to Murray Ringold's English class by the sound of that: the teacher summing up for the class, Mr. Ringold recapitulating, intent, before the hour ended, on concisely synthesizing his theme, Mr. Ringold hinting, by his emphatic tone and his careful phrasing, that "revenge and betrayal" might well be the answer to one of his weekly "Twenty Questions."

"In the army I remember getting hold of a copy of Burton's *Anatomy of Melancholy* and reading it every night, reading it for the first time in my life when we were training in England to invade France. I loved that book, Nathan, but it left me puzzled. Do you remember what Burton says about melancholy? Every one of us, he says, has the predisposition for melancholy, but only some of us get the habit of melancholy. How do you get the habit? That's a question that Burton doesn't answer. That book of his doesn't say, and so I had to wonder about it right through the invasion, wonder until from personal experience I found out.

"You get the habit by being betrayed. What does it is betrayal. Think of the tragedies. What brings on the melancholy, the raving, the bloodshed? Othello—betrayed. Hamlet—betrayed. Lear—betrayed. You might even claim that Macbeth is betrayed—by himself—though that's not the same thing. Professionals who've spent their energy teaching masterpieces, the few of us still engrossed by literature's scrutiny of things, have no excuse for finding betrayal anywhere but at the heart of history. History from top to bottom. World history, family history, personal history. It's a very big subject, betrayal. Just think of the Bible. What's that book about? The master story situation of the Bible is betrayal. Adam—betrayed. Esau—betrayed. The Shechemites—betrayed. Judah—betrayed. Joseph

—betrayed. Moses—betrayed. Samson—betrayed. Samuel—betrayed. David—betrayed. Uriah—betrayed. Job—betrayed. Job betrayed by whom? By none other than God himself. And don't forget the betrayal of God. God betrayed. Betrayed by our ancestors at every turn."

6

I N mid-August of 1950, only a few days before I left home for the University of Chicago (left forever, as it developed) to enroll for my first year of college, I went up on the train to spend a week in the Sussex County countryside with Ira, as I had the previous year when Eve and Sylphid were in France visiting Sylphid's father—and when my own father had first to interview Ira before granting his permission for me to go. That second summer, I arrived late in the day at the rural station a curvy five-mile drive from Ira's shack through narrow back lanes and past the dairy herds. Ira was waiting there in the Chevy coupe.

Beside him in the front seat was a woman in a white uniform whom he introduced as Mrs. Pärn. She had come out from New York that day to help him with his neck and his shoulders and was about to return on the next eastbound train. She had a folding table with her, and I remember her going to lift it out of the trunk by herself. That's what I remember—her strength in lifting the table, and that she wore a white uniform and white stockings and that she called him "Mr. Rinn" and he called her "Mrs. Pärn." I didn't notice anything special about her except her strength. I noticed her hardly at all. And after she got out of the car and, lugging her table with her, crossed over to the track where the local would take her as far as Newark, I never saw the woman again. I was seventeen. She seemed to me old and hygienic and of no importance.

In June, a list of 151 people in radio and television with purported connections to "Communist causes" had appeared in a publication called *Red Channels*, and it had set in motion a round of firings that spread panic throughout the broadcasting industry. Ira's name had not been on the list, however, nor had that of anyone else involved with *The Free and the Brave*. I had no idea that Ira had more than likely been spared because of the insulation afforded him by being Eve Frame's husband, and because Eve Frame was herself being protected (by Bryden Grant, an informer for the people running *Red Channels*) from the suspicion that might automatically have fallen on her as the wife of somebody with Ira's reputation. Eve, after all, had attended with Ira more than one political function that, in those days, could have put in question her loyalty to the United States. It didn't require much incriminating evidence—in cases of mistaken identity, it didn't require any—even for someone as unengaged by politics as Eve Frame was, to be labeled a "fronter" and to wind up out of work.

But I wasn't to know Eve's role in shaping Ira's predicament until some fifty years later, when Murray told me about it at my house. My theory at the time for why they didn't go after Ira was that they were afraid of him, afraid of the fight he'd put up, of what looked to me back then to be his indestructibility. I thought the editors of *Red Channels* were afraid that, if provoked, Ira might singlehandedly bring them down. I even had a romantic moment, while Ira was telling me about *Red Channels* over our first meal together, of thinking of the shack on Pickax Hill Road as one of those austere training camps in the Jersey sticks where heavyweights used to go for months before the big fight, the heavyweight here being Ira.

"The standards of patriotism for my profession are about to be set by three policemen from the FBI. Three ex-FBI men, Nathan, that's who's running this *Red Channels* operation. Who should be employed on radio and who shouldn't be employed will be determined by three guys whose favored source of information is the House Un-American Activities Committee. You'll see how courageous the bosses are in the face of this shit. Watch how the profit system holds out against the pressure. Freedom of thought, of speech, due process—screw all that. People are going to be destroyed, buddy. It's not livelihoods that are going to be lost, it's *lives*. People are going to die. They're going to get sick and die, they're going to jump off buildings and die. By the time this is over, the people with names on that list are going to wind up in concentration camps, courtesy of Mr. McCarran's darling Internal Security Act. If we go to war with the Soviet Union—and nothing the right wing in this country wants more than a war—McCarran will take a personal hand in putting us all behind barbed wire."

The list neither shut Ira up nor sent him, like any number of colleagues, running for cover. Only a week after the list was published, the Korean War suddenly broke out, and in a letter to the old *Herald Tribune*, Ira (signing himself defiantly as *The Free and the Brave*'s Iron Rinn) had publicly stated his opposition to what he described as Truman's determination to turn that remote conflict into the long-awaited postwar showdown between the capitalists and the Communists and, by doing so, "maniacally to set the stage for the atomic horror of World War III and the destruction of mankind." It was Ira's first letter to an editor since he'd written from Iran to *Stars and Stripes* about the injustice of troop segregation, and it was more than an inflamed declaration against going to war with Communist North Korea. By implication it was a blatant, calculated act of resistance against *Red Channels* and its goal not simply of purging Communists but of menacing into silent submission the airwaves' liberals and non-Communist left wingers.

Korea was virtually all Ira could talk about during that week up at the shack in August 1950. Almost every evening during my previous visit, Ira and I had stretched out back on rickety beach chairs, surrounded by citronella candles to repel the gnats and mosquitoes—the lemony fragrance of citronella oil would forever after recall Zinc Town to me—and, while I looked up at the stars, Ira had told me all sorts of stories, some new, some old, about his teenage mining days, his Depression days as a homeless hobo, his wartime adventures as a stevedore at the U.S. Army base at Abadan on the Shatt-al-Arab, the river that, down near the Persian Gulf, more or less separates Iran from Iraq. I had never before known anyone whose life was so intimately circumscribed by so much American history, who was personally familiar with so much American geography, who had confronted, face to face, so much American lowlife. I'd never known anyone so immersed in his moment or so defined by it. Or tyrannized by it, so much its avenger and its victim and its tool. To imagine Ira *outside* of his moment was impossible.

For me, on those nights up in the shack, the America that was my inheritance manifested itself in the form of Ira Ringold. What Ira was saying, the not entirely limpid (or unrepetitious) flood of loathing and love, aroused exalted patriotic cravings to know firsthand an America beyond Newark, sparked those same native-son passions that had been kindled in me as a boy

by the war, that had then been fostered in early adolescence by
Howard Fast and Norman Corwin, and that would be sustained a year or two down the line by the novels of Thomas
Wolfe and John Dos Passos. My second year visiting Ira, it
began to get deliciously cold at night up in the Sussex hills at
the tail end of summer, and I would be feeding the roaring
flames in the fireplace with wood that I had split in the hot sun
that morning, while Ira, sipping coffee out of his chipped old
mug and wearing short pants, battered basketball sneakers, and
a washed-out olive T-shirt from his army days—looking like
nothing so much as the Great American Scoutmaster, the big
natural guy who is adored by the boys, who can live off the
land and scare off the bear and make sure your kid doesn't
drown in the lake—would go on about Korea in a voice of
protest and disgust you were unlikely to hear around the fire at
any other campsite in the country.

"I cannot believe that any American citizen who has half a
brain can believe that the North Korean Communist troops
will get into ships and travel six thousand miles and take over
the United States. But this is what people are saying. 'You have
to watch out for the Communist threat. They're going to take
over this country.' Truman is showing the Republicans his muscle
—*that's* what he's up to. That's what this is all about. Showing
his muscle at the expense of innocent Korean people. We're
going in and we're going to bomb those sons of bitches,
y'understand? And all to prop up this fascist of ours Syngman
Rhee. President Wonderful Truman. General Wonderful Mac-
Arthur. The Communists, the Communists. Not the racism in
this country, not the inequities in this country. No, the Communists are the problem! Five thousand Negroes have been
lynched in this country and not one lyncher has been convicted
yet. Is that the fault of the Communists? Ninety Negroes have
been lynched since Truman came to the White House full of
talk about civil rights. Is that the fault of the Communists, or
is it the fault of Truman's attorney general, Mr. Wonderful
Clark, who resorts to the outrageous persecution in an American courtroom of twelve leaders of the Communist Party,
ruthlessly destroys their lives because of their beliefs, but when
it comes to the lynchers refuses to raise a finger! Let's make
war on the Communists, let's send our soldiers to fight the

Communists—and everywhere you go, around the world, the first ones to die in the struggle against fascism are the Communists! The first ones to struggle in behalf of the Negro, in behalf of the worker . . ."

I'd heard it all before, these exact words many times, and by the end of my vacation week I couldn't wait to get out of earshot of him and go home. This time round, staying at the shack wasn't what it had been for me the first summer. With hardly an inkling of how embattled he saw himself on every front, of how compromised he felt his defiant independence to have become—still imagining that my hero was on his way to leading and winning radio's fight against the reactionaries at *Red Channels*—I couldn't understand the fear and desperation, the growing sense of failure and isolation that were feeding Ira's indignant righteousness. "Why do I do the things I do politically? I do things because I think it is *right* to do them. I have to do something, because something has to be *done*. And I don't give a damn if nobody knows it except me. I squirm, Nathan, at the cowardice of my erstwhile associates . . ."

The summer before, even though I wasn't old enough to get a license, Ira had taught me how to drive his car. When I turned seventeen and my father got around to teaching me, I was sure that if I told him that Ira Ringold had beat him to it back in August, it would hurt his feelings, and so with my father I pretended that I didn't know what I was doing and that learning to drive was brand-new to me. Ira's '39 Chevy was black, a two-door coupe, and really good-looking. Ira was so big that he looked like something out of the circus sitting at the wheel of the car, and that second summer, when he sat beside me and let me drive, I felt as though I were driving a monument around, a monument in a mad rage about the Korean War, a battle monument commemorating the battle *against* battling.

The car had been somebody's grandmother's and had only twelve thousand miles on it when Ira bought it in '48. Floor shift, three speeds forward and the reverse on the upper left of the H. Two separate seats in front, with a space behind them just large enough for a small kid to perch uncomfortably. No radio, no heater. To open the vents, you pushed down a little handle and the flaps would come up in front of the windshield, with a screen on them to keep out the bugs. Pretty efficient. No-draft windows with their own crank. Seats upholstered in that mousy gray fuzz that all cars came through with in those days. Running boards. Big trunk. The spare, with the jack, under the floor panel of the trunk. Sort of a pointed grill, and the hood ornament had a piece of glass in it. Real fenders, big and rounded, and the headlights separate, like two torpedoes, right behind that aerodynamic grill. The windshield wipers worked on a vacuum, so that when you stepped on the gas the wipers would slow down.

I can remember the ashtray. Right in the center of the dash, between the two passengers: a nice elongated piece of plastic, hinged at the bottom, that rocked out toward you. To get at the engine, you twisted a handle on the outside. No lock—you could have vandalized that engine in two seconds. Each side of the hood opened independently. The texture of the steering wheel was not slick and shiny but fibrous, and the horn was in the center only. The starter was a little round rubber pedal with a corrugated piece of rubber around its neck. The choke that was needed for a start on a cold day was on the right, and something called the throttle on the left. The throttle had no conceivable use that I understood. On the glove compartment a recessed wind-up clock. The gas-tank cover, smack on the side, to the rear of the passenger-side door, screwed off like a lid. To lock the car, you pressed the button on the driver's window, and when you got out of the car, you pulled the ro-tating handle down and slammed the door. That way, if you were thinking about something else, you could manage to lock the key in the car.

I could go on and on about that car because it was the first place I ever got laid. That second summer out with Ira I met the daughter of the Zinc Town chief of police, and one night I borrowed Ira's car and took her on a date to a drive-in. Her name was Sally Spreen. She was a redhead a couple of years older than me who worked at the general store and was known locally as "easy." I took Sally Spreen out of New Jersey to a drive-in across the Delaware in Pennsylvania. The drive-in speakers in those days hung inside the car window, and it was an Abbott and Costello movie. Loud. We started necking right away. She *was* easy. The funny part (if one can speak of just a part of it being funny) was that my underpants were around my left foot. And my left foot was on the accelerator, and so while I was humping her I was flooding Ira's engine. By the time I came, my underwear had somehow wound itself around the brake pedal and my ankle. Costello is yelling, "Hey, Abbott! Hey, Abbott!," the windows are steaming, the engine is flooded, her father is the chief of the Zinc Town police, and I am tied to the floor of the car.

Driving her home, I didn't know what to say or what to feel or what punishment to expect for having taken her across state lines to have sexual intercourse, and so I found myself explaining to her how American soldiers had no business fighting in Korea. I gave it to her about General MacArthur, as though *he* were her father.

When I got back to the shack, Ira looked up from the book he was reading. "Was she good?"

I didn't know what the answer was. The idea hadn't even occurred to me. "*Anybody* would have been good," I told him, and the two of us burst into laughter.

In the morning, we discovered that in my exalted state of the previous night, I had locked the key inside the car before entering the shack no longer a virgin. Again Ira laughed out loud—but otherwise, during my week at the shack, he was impossible to amuse.

Sometimes Ira invited his nearest neighbor, Raymond Svecz, over to have dinner with us. Ray was a bachelor who lived some two miles down the road, at the edge of an abandoned quarry, a most primeval-looking excavation, an enormous, terrifying manmade chasm whose broken, bottom-of-the-world nothingness gave me the willies even when it was sunlit. Ray lived there by himself in a one-room structure that decades earlier had been a storage shed for mining equipment, as forlorn a human habitat as any I'd ever seen. He had been a POW in Germany during the war and had returned home with what Ira called "mental problems." A year later, back at his job drilling in the zinc mine—in the zinc mine where Ira had himself worked with a shovel as a boy—he'd had his skull injured in an accident. Fourteen hundred feet below the surface of the earth, an overhead rock about the size of a coffin, weighing over a thousand pounds, broke off near a wall he was drilling and, though it didn't crush him, sent him hurtling to the floor, face first. Ray survived, but he never went underground again, and doctors had been rebuilding his skull ever since. Ray was handy, and Ira gave him odd jobs to do, had him weed the vegetable garden and keep it watered when he wasn't around, paid him to repair and paint things at the shack. Most weeks he paid him to do nothing, and when Ira was in residence and saw that Ray wasn't eating properly, he brought him in and fed him. Ray hardly ever spoke. An agreeable sort of dopey fellow, always nodding his head (which was said to look little like the head he'd had before the accident), very polite . . . and even when he was eating with us, Ira's attack against our enemies never stopped.

I should have expected it. I *had* expected it. I had looked forward to it. I would have thought that I couldn't get enough of it. Yet I did. I was starting college the following week, and my education with Ira had ended. With a speed that was incredible, it was over. That innocence was over too. I had walked in the shack on Pickax Hill Road one person, and I was walking out another. Whatever the name of the driving new force that had come to the surface, it had come unbidden, all by itself, and was irreversible. The tearing away from my father, the straining of filial affection prompted by my infatuation with Ira, was now being replicated in my disillusionment with him.

Even when Ira took me to see his favorite local friend, Horace Bixton—who, with his son, Frank, ran a taxidermy business in a half-converted cow barn of two rooms next to the Bixton family farmhouse on a dirt road nearby—all Ira could talk about with Horace was what he'd been talking about nonstop with me. The year before, we'd been out there and I'd had a great time listening, not to Ira going on about Korea and Communism, but to Horace going on about taxidermy. That was *why* Ira had taken me out, to hear Horace go on about taxidermy. "You could write a radio play, Nathan, starring this guy and based on taxidermy alone." Ira's interest in taxidermy was part of a working-class fascination he still had, not so much with nature's beauty, but with man's interfering with nature, with industrialized nature and exploited nature, with nature man-touched, man-worn, man-defaced, and, as it was beginning to look out in the heart of zinc country, man-ruined.

When I walked in the Bixtons' door that first time, the bizarre clutter of the small front room staggered me: tanned skins piled up everywhere; antlers strung from the ceiling, tagged and hanging from bits of wire, back and forth the whole length of the room antlers by the dozens; enormous lacquered fish also hanging from the ceiling, shiny fish with extended sails, shiny fish with elongated swords, one shiny fish with a face like a monkey; animal heads—small, medium, large, and extralarge —mounted on every square inch of wall; a populous flock of ducks and geese and eagles and owls spread across the floor, many with their wings open as if in flight. There were pheasants and wild turkeys, there was a pelican, there was a swan, there was also, scattered furtively among the birds, a skunk, a bobcat, a coyote, and a pair of beavers. In dusty glass cases along the walls were the smaller birds, doves and pigeons, a small alligator as well as coiled snakes, lizards, turtles, rabbits, squirrels, and rodents of every kind, mice, weasels, and other ugly little things I could not name realistically nestled in wilted old natural tableaux. And the dust was everywhere, cloaking fur, feathers, pelts, everything.

Horace, a slight elderly man, himself not much taller than the span of the wings of his vulture, and wearing overalls and a khaki tractor hat, came out from the back to shake my hand, and when he saw my startled expression, he smiled apologetically. "Yeah," he said, "we don't throw much out."

"Horace," Ira said, looking way, way down to this elfin person who, Ira had told me, made his own hard cider and smoked his own meats and knew every bird by its song, "this is Nathan, a young high school writer. I told him what you told me about a good taxidermist: the test of a good taxidermist is to create the illusion of life. He says, 'That's the test of a good writer,' and so I brought him over so you two artistes could chew the fat."

"Well, we take our work seriously," Horace informed me. "We do everything. Fish, birds, mammals. Game heads. All positions, all species."

"Tell him about that beast," Ira said with a laugh, pointing to a tall bird on stalky legs that looked to me like a nightmare rooster.

"That's a cassowary," Horace said. "Big bird from New Guinea. Don't fly. This here was in a circus. A traveling circus sideshow, and it died, and back in '38 they brought it to me and I stuffed it, and the circus never came back for it. That's an oryx," he said, beginning to differentiate his handiwork for me. "That's Cooper's hawk flying. Cape buffalo skull—that's called the European mount, the top half of the skull. These are the antlers of an elk. Huge. A wildebeest—the top of the skull with the fur there . . . ."

We were half an hour making the safari through the front showroom, and when we stepped into the back workroom— "the shop," as Horace called it—there was Frank, a balding man of about forty, a full-scale model of his father, sitting at a bloody table skinning a fox with a knife that, we later learned, Frank himself had made out of a hacksaw blade.

"Different animals, you know, have different smells," Horace explained to me. "You smell the fox?"

I nodded.

"Yep, there's an odor associated with the fox," Horace said. "It's not as pleasant as it might be."

Frank had nearly all of the fox's right hind leg skinned clear down to raw muscle and bone. "That one," said Horace, "is going to be mounted whole. It's going to look like a lifelike fox." The fox, freshly shot, lay there looking like a lifelike fox already, only asleep. We all sat around the table while Frank kept working neatly away. "Frank has very nimble fingers," Horace said with a father's pride. "A lot of people can do the fox and the bear and the deer and the big birds, but my son can do the songbirds, too." Frank's prize homemade tool, Horace said, was a tiny brain spoon, for the small birds, of a kind you could not begin to buy. By the time Ira and I got up to go, Frank, who was deaf and could not speak, had skinned the whole fox so it was down to an emaciated-looking red carcass about the size of a newborn human baby.

"People eat fox?" Ira asked.

"Not normally," said Horace. "But during the Depression we used to try things. Everybody was in the same fix then, you know—no meat. We ate possum, woodchuck, rabbits."

"What was good?" Ira asked.

"It was all good. We was always hungry. During the Depression you ate anything you could get. We ate crow."

"What's crow like?"

"Well, the trouble with crow is you don't know how old the darn things are. One crow, it was like shoe leather. Some of those crows were only really fit for soup. We used to eat squirrel."

"How do you cook a squirrel?"

"Black cast-iron pot. Wife used to trap squirrels. She'd skin 'em, and when she had three, she'd cook 'em in the pot. You just eat 'em like chicken legs."

"Got to bring my little woman over," Ira said, "so's you can give her the recipe."

"One time the wife tried to feed me raccoon. But I knew. She said it was black bear." Horace laughed. "She was a good cook. She died on Groundhog Day. Seven years ago."

"When did you get that in, Horace?" Ira was motioning above Horace's tractor hat to the outthrust head of a wild boar mounted on the wall; it hung between shelves loaded with the wire frames and the frames of burlap impregnated with plaster over which animal skins were stretched and adjusted and sewn back together to create the illusion of life. The boar was every inch a beast, a great beast at that, blackish with a brown throat and a whitish mask of hairs between the eyes and adorning its jowls, and a snout as big and black and hard as a wet black stone. Its jaws were set menacingly open so that you could see the rawness of the mouth's carnivorous interior and the imposing white tusklike teeth. The boar had the illusion of life, all right; so too, as yet, did Frank's fox, whose stink I could hardly stand.

"Boar looks real," Ira said.

"Oh, that's real. The tongue isn't real, though. The tongue is fake. Hunter wanted the original teeth. Usually we use fake ones, because by and by the originals crack. They kind of get brittle and fall apart. But he wanted its real teeth in there so we put its real ones in there."

"How long did that take you, from day one?"

"That would be about three days, twenty hours."

"How much you get to do that boar?"

"Seventy dollars."

"To me that seems cheap," Ira said.

"You're used to New York City prices," Horace told him.

"You get the whole boar or just the head?"

"Usually the whole skull is in there and it's cut off at the back of the neck. We do get on occasion whole bear, black bear—a tiger I did."

"A tiger? Did you? You never told me that." I could see that though Ira was leading Horace on for the benefit of my education as a writer, he also liked questioning him in order to hear him reply in his small, sharp, chirpy voice, a voice that sounded as if it had been whittled out of a piece of wood. "Where was the tiger shot?" Ira asked.

"It's a guy who owns 'em, like pets. One of them died. And they're valuable, the skins, and he wanted this one made into a rug. He called up, and he put it on a stretcher, and Frank got it right in the car and brought it in, the whole thing. Because they didn't know how to skin it or anything."

"And did you know how to do a tiger, or did you have to look it up in a book?"

"A book, Ira? No, Ira, no book. Once you been doing it for a while you can figure out just about any animal."

Ira said to me, "You got any questions you want Horace to answer? Anything you want to know for school?"

Just to be listening, I couldn't have been any happier, and so I mouthed "No."

"Was it fun to skin that tiger, Horace?" Ira asked.

"Yes. I enjoyed it. I got a fellow and I hired him to take a home movie, a movie of the whole process, and I showed it at Thanksgiving that year."

"Before or after dinner?" Ira asked.

Horace smiled. Though there was no irony that I could discern in the practice of taxidermy, the taxidermist himself had a good American sense of fun. "Well, you're eating all day long, aren't you? Everybody remembered that Thanksgiving. In a taxidermy family they're used to things like that, but you can still always come up with a surprise, you know."

And so the talk continued, an amiable, quiet conversation with a little laughter in it that finished up with Horace making me a gift of a deer toe. Ira throughout was as gentle and untroubled as I'd ever seen him with anyone. Except for my nausea from smelling the fox, I couldn't remember ever having been so unagitated myself in Ira's company. Nor had I ever before seen him so serious about something that wasn't world affairs or American politics or the failings of the human race. Talking about cooking crows and making a tiger into a rug and the cost of stuffing a wild boar outside New York City freed him to be unexcitable, at peace, almost unrecognizable as himself.

There was something so winning about those two men's good-humored absorption in each other (particularly with a beautiful animal being relieved of its lovely looks right under their noses) that I had to wonder afterward if this person who didn't have to get all stirred up and go through all that Ira-ish emotion to have a conversation wasn't perhaps the real, if unseen, inactive Ira and the other, the furious radical, an impersonation, an imitation of something, like his Lincoln or the boar's tongue. The respect and fondness that Ira had for Horace Bixton suggested even to me, a boy, that there was a very simple world of simple people and simple satisfactions into which Ira might have drifted, where all his vibrating passions, where all that equipped him (and ill equipped him) for society's onslaught might have been remade and even pacified. Maybe with a son like Frank whose nimble fingers he could be proud of and a wife who knew how to trap and cook a squirrel, maybe by appropriating those sorts of near-at-hand things, by making his own hard cider and smoking his own meats and wearing overalls and a khaki tractor hat and by listening to the songbirds sing . . . And then again, maybe not. Maybe to be, like Horace, without a great enemy would have made life even more impossible for Ira to tolerate than it already was.

The second year we went out to see Horace, there was no laughter in the conversation and Ira did all the talking.

Frank was skinning a deer's head—"Frank," Horace said, "can do deer head with his eyes closed"—while Horace sat hunched over the other end of the worktable "preparing skulls." Laid out before him was an assortment of very small skulls he was repairing with wire and glue. Some science teachers at a school over in Easton wanted a collection of small mammal skulls, and they knew Horace might have what they wanted because, he told me, grinning at the fragile, tiny bones before him, "I don't throw nothin' out."

"Horace," Ira was saying, "can any American citizen who has half a brain believe that the North Korean Communist troops will get into ships and travel six thousand miles and take over the United States? Can you believe that?"

Without looking up from the skull of a muskrat whose loose teeth he was fixing in its jaw with glue, Horace slowly shook his head.

"But this is exactly what people are saying," Ira told him. " 'You have to watch out for the Communist threat—they're going to take over this country.' This Truman is showing the Republicans his muscle—that's what he is up to. That's what this is all about. Showing his muscle at the expense of innocent Koreans. We're going in there and all to prop up this fascist bastard Syngman Rhee. We're going to bomb those sons of bitches, y'understand? President Wonderful Truman. General Wonderful MacArthur . . ."

And, unable to stop myself from being bored by the tireless harangue that was Ira's primal script, I was thinking, spitefully, "Frank doesn't know how lucky he is to be deaf. That muskrat doesn't know how lucky it is to be dead. That deer . . ." Et cetera.

Same thing happened—Syngman Rhee, President Wonderful Truman, General Wonderful MacArthur—when we went by the rock dump out on the highway one morning to say hello to Tommy Minarek, a retired miner, a burly, hearty Slovak who had been working in the mines when Ira first showed up in Zinc Town in 1929 and who had taken a fatherly interest in Ira back then. Now Tommy worked for the town, looking after the rock dump—its one tourist attraction—where, along with serious mineral collectors, families sometimes drove out with their kids to go hunting through the vast dump for chunks of rock to take home and put under an ultraviolet light. Under the light, as Tommy explained to me, the minerals "fluoresce" —glow, that is, with fluorescent red, orange, purple, mustard, blue, cream, and green; some look to be made of black velvet.

Tommy sat on a big flat rock at the entrance to the dump, hatless in all weather, a handsome old fellow with a wide, square face, white hair, hazel eyes, and all his teeth. He charged the adults a quarter to go in and, though the town told him to charge the kids a dime, he always let the kids in free. "People come from all over the world to go in there," Tommy told me. "Some through the years that come every Saturday and Sunday, even wintertime. I make fires for certain people and they give me a few bucks for that. They come every Saturday or Sunday, rain or shine."

On the hood of Tommy's jalopy, parked directly beside the large flat rock where Tommy sat, he had samples of minerals from the collection in his own cellar spread out on a towel for sale, chunky specimens selling for as much as five and six dollars, pickle jars full of smaller specimens for a dollar fifty, and small brown paper bags full of bits and pieces of rock, which went for fifty cents. He kept the fifteen-, twenty-, and twenty-five-dollar stuff in the trunk of the car.

"In the back," he told me, "I got the more valuable things. I can't put 'em out here. I go sometimes across the road to Gary's machine shop, to use the toilet or somethin', and the stuff is out here . . . I had two specimens last fall, in the back, guy put a black thing over 'em, and he's lookin' with a light, and I had two fifty-dollar specimens in the car and he got 'em both."

The year before, I had sat alone with Tommy outside the rock dump, watching him deal with the tourists and the collectors and listening to his spiel (and later I wrote a radio play about that morning called *The Old Miner*). That was the morning after he'd come to have a hot dog dinner with us at the shack. Ira was at me, educating me, all the time when I was up at the shack, and Tommy was brought in as visiting lecturer, to give me the lowdown on the plight of the miner before the union came in.

"Tell Nathan about your dad, Tom. Tell him what happened to your dad."

"My dad died from workin' in the mine. Him and another guy went in a place where two other guys worked every day, in a raise, a vertical hole. Both of them didn't show up that day. It's a ways up, over a hundred feet up. My dad and another guy the boss sent in there, a young guy, a husky guy—was he a beautiful built guy! I went to the hospital and I seen the guy and he wasn't in bed, and my dad was stretched out, didn't even move. I never seen him move. The second day I come in, this other guy was talkin' to another guy, joking, he wasn't even in bed even. My dad was in bed."

Tommy was born in 1880 and started working in the mines in 1902, "May the twenty-fourth," he told me, "1902. That's about the time Thomas Edison was up here, the famous inventor, experimentin'." Though Tommy, despite his years in the mines, was a robust, upright human specimen who hardly looked to be seventy, he had himself to confess that he was not as alert as he'd once been, and every time he got a little befuddled or got stalled in his story, Ira had to get him on the trail again. "I don't think that quick no more," Tommy told us. "I have to follow myself back, starting with the ABCs, you know, and try to hit into it. Get into it somewhere. I'm still alert, but not as good as I was."

"What was the accident?" Ira asked Tommy. "What happened to your dad? Tell Nathan what happened to him."

"The station broke. See, we put a timber in the back of this four-by-four hole at a certain degree—we put one back there, have to dig it out with a pick to make it slantlike, so I wedge this in and I cut it at an angle. One in the front and one over here. And then we put a two-inch plank on there."

Ira interrupted to try to push him ahead, to the good stuff. "So what happened? Tell him how your dad died."

"It collapsed. The vibration collapsed it. The machine and everything went down. Over a hundred feet. He never recovered. His bones were all broke. He died about a year after. We had this old-fashioned stove, and he had his feet right in there, trying to stay warm. Couldn't keep warm."

"Did they have any workmen's compensation? You ask, Nathan, ask the questions. That's what you do if you want to be a writer. Don't be shy. Ask Tommy if he had workmen's compensation."

But I *was* shy. Here, eating hot dogs with me, was a real miner, thirty years in the zinc mines. I couldn't have been any more shy if Tommy Minarek had been Albert Einstein. "Did they?" I asked.

"Give you anything? The company? He didn't get a penny," Tommy said bitterly. "The company was the trouble and the bosses was the trouble. The bosses down there didn't seem to care for their house. You know what I mean? For their territory that they worked in every day. Like me, if I was a boss down there, I would check these planks goin' over where the people walk over the holes. I don't know how deep them holes are, but certain people got killed down there, walkin' on these planks, and the plank broke. Rotten. They never took care of them to check them darn planks. They never did it."

"Didn't you have a union then?" I asked.

"We had no union. My father didn't even get a penny."

I tried to think of what else I ought to know as a writer. "Didn't you have the United Mine Workers down here?" I asked.

"We had it later. In the forties already. It was too late by then," he said, outrage again in his voice. "He was dead, I was retired—and the union didn't help that much anyway. How could they? We had one leader, our local president—he was good, but what could he do? You couldn't do nothin' with a power like that. Look, years before we had a guy tried to organize us. This person went to get water for his house from a spring down the road. Never come back. Nobody ever heard of him anymore. Tryin' to organize the union."

"Ask about the company, Nathan."

"The company store," Tommy said. "I seen people get a white slip."

"Tell him, Tom, what a white slip is."

"You didn't get no pay. The company store got all his money. A white slip. I seen that."

"Owners make a lot of money?" Ira asked.

"The president of the zinc company, the main guy, he's got a big mansion over here, up on the hill alone. Big house up there. I heard one of his friends say, when he died, that he had nine and a half million dollars. That's what he owned."

"And what'd you get to start?" Ira asked him.

"Thirty-two cents an hour. First job I worked in the boiler house. I was twenty-some years old. Then I went down in the mines. Highest I could get was ninety cents because I was like a boss. A headman like. Next to the boss. I did everything."

"Pensions?"

"Nothin'. My father-in-law got a pension. He got eight dollars.

Thirty-some years he worked. Eight dollars a month, that's what he got. I didn't see no pension."

"Tell Nathan how you eat down there."

"We have to eat underground."

"Everybody?" Ira asked.

"The bosses are the only ones who come up twelve o'clock and eat in their washroom. The rest of us, underground."

The next morning, Ira drove me out to the rock dump to sit there with Tommy and learn from him on my own all I could about the evil consequences of the profit motive as it functioned in Zinc Town. "Here's my boy, Tom. Tom's a good man and a good teacher, Nathan."

"I try to be the best," Tommy said.

"He was my teacher down in the mines. Weren't you, Tom?"

"That I was, Gil."

Tommy called Ira Gil. When I had asked, at breakfast that morning, why Tommy called him Gil, Ira laughed and said, "That's what they called me down there. Gil. Never really knew why. Somebody called me that one day, and it just stuck. Mexicans, Russians, Slovaks, all called me Gil."

In 1997, I learned from Murray that Ira had not been telling me the truth. They had called him Gil because up in Zinc Town he had called himself Gil. Gil Stephens.

"I taught Gil how to set the explosives when he was a kid. By then I was a runner, I was the one that drills and sets up everything, the explosives, the timbers and everything. Taught Gil here to drill, and in every one of them you put a stick of dynamite in there, and put a circuit wire through."

"I'm going, Tom. I'll pick him up later. Tell him about the explosives. Educate this city slicker, Mr. Minarek. Tell Nathan about the smell from the explosives and what that does to a man's insides."

Ira drove off, and Tommy said, "The smell? You have to get used to that. I had it once, bad. I was mucking out a pillar, not a pillar, an entrance, a four-by-four entrance. And we drilled and fired it, and we put water on it all night, on that muck, we call it muck, and the next day it smelled like hell. I got a whiff of that good. It bothered me for a while. I was sick. Not as sick as some of the guys, but sick enough."

It was summertime, already hot at nine A.M., but even out at the ugly rock dump, with the big machine shop across the highway where they had the not-so-hygienic toilet Tommy used, it was blue overhead and beautiful, and pretty soon families started driving up in cars to visit. One guy stuck his head out the car window and asked me, "Is this the one where the kids can go in and pick rocks and stuff?"

"Yep," I said, instead of "Yes."

"You got kids here?" Tommy asked him.

He pointed to two in the back seat.

"Right here, sir," Tommy said. "Go in and look around. And when you go out, right here, half a buck a bag here for a miner who mined 'em for thirty years, special rocks for the kids."

An elderly woman drove up in a car full of kids, her grand-children probably, and when she got out, Tommy politely saluted her. "Lady, when you're going out, and you want a nice bag of rocks for the little ones from a miner who mined 'em for thirty years, stop here. Fifty cents a bag. Special rocks for the kids. They fluoresce beautifully."

Getting in the swing of things—getting in the swing of the *joys* of the profit motive as it functioned in Zinc Town—I told her, "He's got the good stuff, lady."

"I'm the only one," he told her, "who makes these bags. These bags are from the good mine. The other is completely different. I don't put no junk in there. There's *real* stuff in there. If you see 'em under light, you'll enjoy what's in there. There's pieces in there only comes from this mine, nowhere else in the world."

"You're in the sun without a hat," she told Tommy. "You don't get hot sitting there like that?"

"Been doing this many years," he told her. "See these ones on my car? These fluoresce different colors. They look ugly but they're nice under light, they got different things in 'em. It's got a lot of different mixtures in."

"This is a fella"—"fella," not "fellow," said I—"who really knows rocks. Thirty years in the mines," I said.

Then a couple pulled up who looked more like city people than any of the other tourists. As soon as they got out of their car, they began to examine Tommy's higher-priced specimens on the hood of the car and to consult together quietly. Tommy whispered to me, "They want my rocks in the worst way. I got

a collection, nobody can touch it. This here's the most extraordinary mineral deposit on this planet—and I got the best
of 'em."

Here I piped up. "This guy's got the best stuff. Thirty years
in the mines. He's got beautiful rocks here. Beautiful rocks."
And they bought four pieces, for a sale totaling fifty-five dollars, and I thought, I'm helpin'. I'm helpin' a real miner.

"If you want any minerals again," I said as they got back
with their purchase into their car, "you come here. This here's
the most extraordinary mineral deposit on this planet."

I was having a fine time of it until, close to noon, Brownie
arrived and the silly gratuitousness of the role I was so enthu-
siastically playing was revealed even to me.

Brownie—Lloyd Brown—was a couple of years older than
me, a skinny, crewcutted, sharp-nosed boy, pale and harmless-
looking in the extreme, particularly in the white shopkeeper's
apron that he wore over a clean white shirt and a clip-on black
bow tie and a pair of fresh dungarees. Because his relation to
himself was so transparently simple, his chagrin when he saw
me with Tommy was plastered all over him and pitiable. Compared with Brownie, I felt like a kid with the most abundant
and frenzied existence, even just sitting quietly beside Tommy
Minarek; compared with Brownie, that's what I *was*.

But if something about my complexity mocked him, something about his simplicity also mocked me. I turned everything
into an adventure, looking always to be altered, while Brownie
lived with a sense of nothing other than hard necessity, had been
so shaped and tamed by constraint as to be able to play only
the role of himself. He was without any craving that wasn't
brewed in Zinc Town. The only thoughts he ever wanted to
think were the thoughts that everybody else in Zinc Town
thought. He wanted life to repeat and repeat itself, and I
wanted to break out. I felt like a freak wanting to be other
than Brownie—perhaps for the very first time but not for the
last. What would it be like to have that passion to break out
vanish from my life? What must it be like to be Brownie? Wasn't
that what the fascination with "the people" was really all about?
What is it like to be them?

"You busy, Tom? I can come back tomorrow."

"Stay here," Tommy said to the boy. "Sit down, Brownie."

Deferentially, Brownie said to me, "I just come here every day on my lunch hour and I talk to him about rocks."

"Sit down, Brownie, my boy. So what you got?"

Brownie laid a worn old satchel at Tommy's feet, and from it he began to extract rock specimens about the size of the ones Tommy was displaying on the hood of his car.

"Black willemite, huh?" Brownie asked.

"No, that's hematite."

"I thought it was a funny-looking willemite. And this?" he asked. "Hendricksite?"

"Yep. Little willemite. There's calcite, too, in there."

"Five bucks for that? Too much?" Brownie asked.

"Somebody may want it," Tommy said.

"You in this business too?" I asked Brownie.

"This was my dad's collection. He was in the mill. Got killed. I'm selling it to get married."

"Nice girl," Tommy told me. "And she's a sweet girl. She's a doll. A Slovak girl. The Musco girl. Nice girl, honest girl, clean girl who uses her head. There's no girls like her anymore. He's gonna live with Mary Musco all his life. I tell Brownie, 'You be good to her, she'll be good to you.' I had a wife like that. Slovak girl. Best in the world. Nobody in the world can take her place."

Brownie held up another specimen. "Bustamite there with that?"

"That's bustamite."

"Got a little willemite crystal on it."

"Yep. There's a little willemite crystal right there."

This went on for close to an hour, until Brownie started packing his specimens back in the satchel to return to the grocery store where he worked.

"He's gonna take my place in Zinc Town," Tommy told me.

"Oh, I don't know," Brownie said. "I won't know as much as you do."

"But you still have to do it." All at once Tommy's voice was fervent, almost anguished, when he spoke. "I want a Zinc Town guy to take over my place here. I want a Zinc Town guy! That's why I'm teaching you here as much as I can. So you can get somewhere. You're the one who's entitled to it. A Zinc

Town person. I don't want to teach somebody else, from out of town."

"Three years ago I started coming here lunchtime, I didn't know anything. And he taught me so much. Right, Tommy? I did pretty good today. Tommy can tell you the mine," Brownie said to me. "He can tell you where in the mine it came from. What level, how deep. He says, 'You gotta hold the rocks in your hand.' Right?"

"Right. You gotta hold the rocks in your hand. You gotta handle that mineral. You gotta see the different matrixes that they come in. If you don't learn that, you're not going to learn Zinc Town minerals. He even knows now, he knows if this is from the other mine or if it's from this mine."

"He taught me that," Brownie said. "I couldn't tell what mine it came from in the beginning. I can tell now."

"So," I said, "you're going to be sitting out here someday."

"I hope so. Like this right here, this is from this mine, right, Tom? And this is from this mine too?"

Because in another year I hoped to go off on a scholarship to the University of Chicago and, after Chicago, become the Norman Corwin of my generation, because I was going everywhere and Brownie was going nowhere—but mostly because Brownie's father had been killed in the mill and my own was alive and well and worrying about me in Newark—I spoke even more fervently than Tommy had to this aproned grocer's assistant whose aspiration in life was to marry Mary Musco and fill Tommy's seat. "Hey, you're good! That's good!"

"And why?" said Tom. "Because he learned right here."

"I learned from this man," Brownie told me proudly.

"I want him to be the next one to take my place."

"Here comes some business, Tom. I gotta run," Brownie said. "Nice to meet you," he said to me.

"Nice to meet *you*," I replied, as though I were the older man and he the child. "When I come back in ten years," I said, "I'll see you out here."

"Oh," said Tom, "he'll be here, all right."

"No, no," Brownie shouted back, for the first time laughing lightheartedly as he headed on foot down the highway. "Tommy'll still be here. Won't you, Tom?"

"We'll see."

In fact, it was Ira who would be out there ten years later. Tommy had educated Ira, too, once Ira was blacklisted from radio and living alone up in the shack and needing a source of income. That was where Ira dropped dead. That's when Ira's aorta gave out, while he was sitting on Tommy's flat rock selling mineral specimens to the tourists and their kids, telling them, "Lady, half a buck a bag here for them when your boys come out, special rocks right from the mine that I mined there for thirty years."

This was how Ira had ended his days—as the overseer at the rock dump whom the local old-timers all called Gil, out there even in the wintertime, making fires for certain people for a few bucks. But I didn't learn this until the night that Murray told me Ira's story there on my deck.

The day before I left that second year, Artie Sokolow and his family drove out to Zinc Town from New York to spend the afternoon with Ira. Ella Sokolow, Artie's wife, was about seven months pregnant, a jolly, dark-haired, freckled-faced woman whose Irish immigrant father, Ira told me, had been a steamfitter up in Albany, one of those big, idealistic union men who are patriotic through and through. "The 'Marseillaise,' 'The Star-Spangled Banner,' the Russian national anthem," Ella laughingly explained that afternoon, "the old man would stand up for all of them."

The Sokolows had twin boys of six, and though the afternoon began happily enough with a game of touch football— refereed in a manner by Ira's neighbor, Ray Svecz—and was followed by a picnic lunch that Ella had brought along from the city and that all of us, including Ray, ate up the slope from the pond, it ended with Artie Sokolow and Ira down by the pond, toe to toe and barking at each other in a way that horrified me.

I had been sitting on the picnic blanket talking to Ella about *My Glorious Brothers*, a book by Howard Fast that she had just finished reading. It was a historical novel set in ancient Judea, about the Maccabees' struggle against Antiochus IV in the second century B.C., and I, too, had read it and even reported on it in school for Ira's brother the second time he was my English teacher.

Ella had been listening to me the way she listened to everyone: taking it all in as if she were being warmed by your words. I must have gone on for close to fifteen minutes, repeating word for word the internationalist-progressive critique I'd written for Mr. Ringold, and all the time Ella gave every indication that what I was saying couldn't have been more interesting. I knew how much Ira admired her as a lifelong radical, and I wanted her to admire me as a radical too. Her background, the physical grandeur of her pregnancy, and certain gestures she made—sweeping gestures with her hands that made her seem to me strikingly uninhibited—all bestowed on Ella Sokolow a heroic authority that I wanted to impress.

"I read Fast and I respect Fast," I'd been telling her, "but I think he lays too much emphasis on the Judeans' fight to return to their past condition, to their worship of tradition and the days of post-Egyptian slavery. There's entirely too much that's merely nationalistic in the book—"

And that was when I heard Ira shout, "You're caving in! Running scared and caving in!"

"If it's not there," Sokolow shot back, "no one knows it's not there!"

"*I* know it's not there!"

The rage in Ira's voice made it impossible for me to go on. All I could think about, suddenly, was the story—which I had refused to believe—that ex-Sergeant Erwin Goldstine had told me in his Maplewood kitchen, about Butts, about the guy in Iran Ira had tried to drown in the Shatt-al-Arab.

I said to Ella, "What's the matter?"

"Just give them room," she said, "and hope they calm down. *You* calm down."

"I just want to know what they're arguing about."

"They're blaming each other for things that have gone wrong. They're arguing over things having to do with the show. Calm down, Nathan. You haven't been around enough angry people. They'll cool off."

But they didn't look it. Ira particularly. He was storming back and forth at the edge of the pond, his long arms lashing out every which way, and each time he turned back to Artie Sokolow, I thought he was going to pounce on him with his fists. "Why do you *make* these goddamn changes!" Ira shouted.

"Keep it in," Sokolow replied, "and we stand to lose more than we gain."

"Bullshit! Let the bastards know we mean business! Just put the fucking thing back in!"

I said to Ella, "Shouldn't we do something?"

"I've heard men arguing all my life," she told me. "Men having one another's carcasses for the sins of omission and commission that they don't seem able to avoid perpetrating. If they were hitting each other it would be something else. But otherwise, your responsibility is to stay away. If you enter where people are already agitated, anything you do will fuel the fire."

"If you say so."

"You've led a very protected life, haven't you?"

"Have I?" I said. "I try not to."

"Best to stay out of it," she told me, "partly out of dignity, to let the guy cool down without your intervention, and partly out of self-defense, and partly because your intervention is only going to make it worse."

Meanwhile, Ira hadn't stopped roaring. "One fucking punch a week—and now we're not even going to get *that* in? So what are we doing on the radio, Arthur? Advancing our careers? A fight is being forced upon us, and you are running! It's the showdown, Artie, and you are gutlessly running away!"

Impotent though I knew I would be if these two powder kegs were to start swinging, I nonetheless jumped up and, with Ray Svecz trailing behind me in his goofy way, ran toward the pond. Last time I'd pissed in my pants. I couldn't let that happen again. With no more idea than Ray had of what could be done to avert a disaster, I ran directly into the fray.

By the time we reached them, Ira had already backed off and was pointedly walking away from Sokolow. It was clear he was still furious with the guy, but it was also evident how hard he was trying to bring himself down. Ray and I caught up with him and then walked along beside him while, intermittently, beneath his breath, Ira carried on a rapid conversation with himself.

The admixture of his absence and his presence so disturbed me that I finally spoke. "What's wrong?" When he didn't seem to hear, I tried to think of what to say that would get his attention. "It's about a script?" All at once he flared up and said, "I'll kill him if he does it again!" And it was not an expression he was using merely for dramatic effect. It was difficult, despite my resistance, not to believe one hundred percent in the meaning of his words.

Butts, I thought. Butts. Garwych. Solak. Becker.

On his face was a look of total fury. Pristine fury. Fury, which along with terror is the primordial power. All that he was had evolved out of that look—also all that he was not. I thought, He's lucky he's not locked up, an alarmingly unexpected conclusion to occur spontaneously to a hero-worshiping kid interlinked for two years with the virtuousness of his hero, and one I dismissed once I was no longer so agitated—and one that I was then to have verified for me by Murray Ringold forty-eight years on.

Eve had made her way out of her past by impersonating Pennington; Ira had made his way out of his by force.

Ella's twin boys, who'd fled from the edge of the pond when the argument flared up, were lying in her arms on the picnic blanket when I returned with Ray. "I think daily living may be harsher than you know," Ella said to me.

"Is this daily living?" I asked.

"Wherever *I've* lived," she said. "Go on. Go on about Howard Fast."

I did my best, but it continued to unsettle me, if not Sokolow's working-class wife, to think of her husband and Ira squaring off.

Ella laughed aloud when I was through. You could hear her naturalness in her laugh as well as all the crap that she had learned to put up with. She laughed the way some people blush: all at once and completely. "Wow," she said. "I'm not sure now *what* I read. My own evaluation of *My Glorious Brothers* is simple. Maybe I don't do enough deep thinking, but I just think, Here's a bunch of rough, tough, and decent guys who believe in the dignity of all men and are willing to die for it."

Artie and Ira had by then cooled off enough to make their way up from the pond to the picnic blanket, where Ira said (trying, apparently, to say something that might ease everybody, himself included, back into the original spirit of the day), "I gotta read it. *My Glorious Brothers.* I gotta get that book."

"It'll put steel in your spine, Ira," Ella said to him, and then, opening wide the big window that was her laugh, she added, "not that I ever thought yours needed any."

Whereupon Sokolow leaned over her and bellowed, "Yes? Whose does? *Just whose does?*"

With that, the Sokolow twins burst into tears, and this in turn caused poor Ray to do the same. Angry herself now for the first time, in something like a mad rage, Ella said, "Christ Almighty, Arthur! Hold yourself together!"

What had lain beneath the afternoon's eruptions I understood more fully that evening when, alone with me in the shack, Ira started in angrily about the lists.

"Lists. Lists of names and accusations and charges. Everybody," Ira said, "has a list. *Red Channels.* Joe McCarthy. The VFW. The HUAC. The American Legion. The Catholic magazines. The Hearst newspapers. Those lists with their sacred numbers—141, 205, 62, 111. Lists of anybody in America who has ever been disgruntled about anything or criticized anything or protested anything—or associated with anybody who has ever criticized or protested anything—all of them now Communists or fronting for Communists or 'helping' Communists or contributing to Communist 'coffers,' or 'infiltrating' labor or government or education or Hollywood or the theater or radio and TV. Lists of 'fifth columnists' busily being compiled in every office and agency in Washington. All the forces of reaction swapping names and mistaking names and linking names together to prove the existence of a mammoth conspiracy *that does not exist.*"

"What about you?" I asked him. "What about *The Free and the Brave*?"

"We've got a lot of progressive-thinking people on our show, sure. And the way they're going to be described to the public now is as actors 'who cunningly sell the Moscow line.' You're going to hear a lot of that—a lot worse than that. 'The dupes of Moscow.'"

"Just the actors?"

"And the director. And the composer. And the writer. Everyone."

"You worried?"

"I can go back to the record factory, buddy. If worse comes to worst, I can always come up here and grease cars at Steve's garage. I've done it before. Besides, you can fight them, you know. You can fight the bastards. Last I heard there was a Constitution in this country, a Bill of Rights *somewhere*. If you look with your big eyes into the capitalist shop window, if you want and you want, if you grab and you grab, if you take and you take, if you acquire and you own and you accumulate, then that is the end of your convictions and the beginning of your fear. But there is nothing that I have that I can't give up. Y'understand? Nothing! How I ever got from my miserable father's shit-eaten house on Factory Street to being this big character Iron Rinn, how Ira Ringold, with one and a half years of high school behind him, got to meeting the people I meet and knowing the people I know and having the comforts I have as a card-carrying member of the comfortable bourgeoisie—that is all so unbelievable that losing everything overnight would not seem so strange to me. Y'understand? Y'understand me? I can go back to Chicago. I can work in the mills. If I have to, I will. But not without standing on my rights as an American! Not without giving the bastards a fight!"

When I was alone and on the train heading back to Newark —Ira had waited at the station in the Chevy to pick up Mrs. Pärn, who, on the day I left, was traveling all the way from New York again to work on those knees of his, aching terribly after our football game of the previous day—I even began to wonder how Eve Frame could stand him, day in and day out. Being married to Ira and his anger couldn't have been much fun. I remembered hearing him deliver virtually the same speech about the capitalist shop window, about his father's miserable house, about his one and a half years of high school, on that afternoon the year before in Erwin Goldstine's kitchen. I remembered variants of that speech being delivered by Ira ten, fifteen times. How could Eve take the sheer repetition, the redundancy of that rhetoric and the attitude of the attacker, the relentless beating from the blunt instrument that was Ira's stump speech?

On that train back to Newark, as I thought of Ira blasting away with his twin apocalyptic prophecies—"The United States of America is about to make atomic war on the Soviet Union! Mark my words! The United States of America is on the road to fascism!"—I didn't know enough to understand why suddenly, so disloyally, when he and people like Artie Sokolow were being most intimidated and threatened, I was so savagely bored by him, why I felt myself to be so much smarter than he. Ready and eager to turn away from him and the irritating, oppressive side of him and to find my inspiration far from Pickax Hill Road.

If you're orphaned as early as Ira was, you fall into the situation that all men must fall into but much, much sooner, which is tricky, because you may either get no education at all or be oversusceptible to enthusiasms and beliefs and ripe for indoctrination. Ira's youthful years were a series of broken connections: a cruel family, frustration in school, headlong immersion in the Depression—an early orphaning that captured the imagination of a boy like me, himself so fixed in a family and a place and its institutions, a boy only just emerging from the emotional incubator; an early orphaning that freed Ira to connect to whatever he wanted but also left him unmoored enough to give himself to something almost right off the bat, to give himself totally and forever. For all the reasons you can think of, Ira was an easy mark for the utopian vision. But for me, who was moored, it was different. If you're *not* orphaned early, if instead you're related intensely to parents for thirteen, fourteen, fifteen years, you grow a prick, lose your innocence, seek your independence, and, if it's not a screwed-up family, are let go, ready to begin to be a man, ready, that is, to choose new allegiances and affiliations, the parents of your adulthood, the chosen parents whom, because you are not asked to acknowledge them with love, you either love or don't, as suits you.

How are they chosen? Through a series of accidents and through lots of will. How do they get to you, and how do you get to them? Who are they? What is it, this genealogy that isn't genetic? In my case they were men to whom I apprenticed myself, from Paine and Fast and Corwin to Murray and Ira and beyond—the men who schooled me, the men I came from. All were remarkable to me in their own way, personalities to contend with, mentors who embodied or espoused powerful ideas and who first taught me to navigate the world and its claims, the adopted parents who also, each in his turn, had to be cast off along with their legacy, had to disappear, thus making way for the orphanhood that is total, which is manhood. When you're out there in this thing all alone.

Leo Glucksman was also an ex-GI, but he had served *after* the war and was now only into his mid-twenties, rosy-cheeked and a little round and looking no older than his first- and second-year college students. Though Leo was still completing his dissertation for a literature Ph.D. at the university, he appeared before us at every session of the class in a three-piece black suit and a crimson bow tie, more formally attired by far than any of the older faculty members. When the weather turned cold he could be seen crossing the quadrangle draped in a black cape that, even on a campus as untypically tolerant of idiosyncrasy and eccentricity—and as understanding of originality and its oddity—as the University of Chicago's was in those days, titillated students whose bright (and amused) "Hi, Professor" Leo would acknowledge by sharply whacking the pavement with the metal tip of the cane he sported. After taking a hasty look late one afternoon at *The Stooge of Torquemada*—which, to kindle Mr. Glucksman's admiration, I'd thought to bring to him, along with the assigned essay on Aristotle's *Poetics*—Leo startled me by dropping it with disgust onto his desk.

His speech was rapid, his tone fierce and unforgiving—no sign in that delivery of the foppishly overdressed boy genius plumply perched back of his bow tie on his cushioned seat. His plumpness and his personality exemplified two very different people. The clothes registered a third person. And his polemic a fourth—not a mannerist but a real adult critic exposing to me the dangers of the tutelage I'd been under with Ira, teaching me to assume a position less rigid in confronting literature. Precisely what I was ready for in my new recruitment phase. Under Leo's guidance I began to be transformed into the

descendant not just of my family but of the past, heir to a culture even grander than my neighborhood's.

"Art as a *weapon*?" he said to me, the word "weapon" rich
with contempt and itself a weapon. "Art as taking the right
stand on everything? Art as the advocate of good things? Who
taught you all this? Who taught you art is slogans? Who taught
you art is in the service of '*the people*'? Art is in the service of
art—otherwise there is no art worthy of *anyone's* attention.
What *is* the motive for writing serious literature, Mr. Zuckerman? To disarm the enemies of price control? The motive for
writing serious literature is *to write serious literature*. You want
to rebel against society? I'll tell you how to do it—write *well*.
You want to embrace a lost cause? Then don't fight in behalf of
the laboring class. They're going to make out fine. They're going
to fill up on Plymouths to their heart's content. The workingman will conquer us all—out of his mindlessness will flow the
slop that is this philistine country's cultural destiny. We'll soon
have something in this country far worse than the government
of the peasants and the workers—we will have the *culture* of
the peasants and the workers. You want a lost cause to fight
for? Then fight for the *word*. Not the high-flown word, not
the inspiring word, not the pro-this and anti-that word, not the
word that advertises to the respectable that you are a wonderful, admirable, compassionate person on the side of the downtrodden and the oppressed. No, for the word that tells the
literate few condemned to live in America that you are on the
side of the word! This play of yours is crap. It's awful. It's infuriating. It is crude, primitive, simple-minded, propagandistic
crap. It *blurs* the world with words. And it reeks to high heaven
of your virtue. Nothing has a more sinister effect on art than
an artist's desire to prove that he's *good*. The terrible temptation of idealism! You must achieve *mastery* over your idealism,
over your virtue as well as over your vice, aesthetic mastery
over everything that drives you to write in the first place—your
outrage, your politics, your grief, your love! Start preaching
and taking positions, start seeing your own perspective as
superior, and you're worthless as an artist, worthless and ludicrous. Why do you write these proclamations? Because you look
around and you're 'shocked'? Because you look around and

you're 'moved'? People give up too easily and fake their feelings. They want to have feelings right away, and so 'shocked' and 'moved' are the easiest. The stupidest. Except for the rare case, Mr. Zuckerman, *shock is always fake*. Proclamations. Art has no *use* for proclamations! Get your lovable shit out of this office, please."

Leo thought better of my Aristotle essay (or, generally, of me), for at my next conference he startled me—no less than he had with his vehemence about my play—by ordering my presence at Orchestra Hall to hear Rafael Kubelik lead the Chicago Symphony Orchestra in Beethoven on Friday night. "Have you ever heard of Raphael Kubelik?" "No." "Beethoven?" "I've heard of him, yes," I said. "Have you ever *heard* him?" "No."

I met Leo on Michigan Avenue, outside Orchestra Hall, half an hour before the performance, my teacher in the cape he'd had made in Rome before being mustered out of the army in '48 and I in the hooded mackinaw bought at Larkey's in Newark to take to college in the icy Middle West. Once we were seated, Leo removed from his briefcase the score for each of the symphonies we were to hear and, throughout the concert, looked not at the orchestra on the stage—which you were supposed to look at, I thought, only occasionally closing your eyes when you were carried away—but rather into his lap, where, with his considerable concentration, he read along in the score while the musicians played first the *Coriolan* Overture and the Fourth Symphony, and after the intermission, the Fifth. Except for the first four notes of the Fifth, I couldn't distinguish one piece from the others.

Following the concert, we took the train back to the South Side and went to his room at International House, a Gothic residence hall on the Midway that was home to most of the university's foreign students. Leo Glucksman, himself the son of a West Side grocer, was slightly better prepared to tolerate their proximity on his hallway—exotic cooking smells and all—than he was that of his fellow Americans. The room he lived in was tinier even than his office cubicle at the college, and he made tea for us by boiling water in a kettle set on a hot plate resting on the floor and squeezed in among the clutter of printed matter piled along the walls. Leo sat at his book-laden desk, his round cheeks lit up by his gooseneck lamp, and I sat in the dark, amid more piles of his books, on the edge of the narrow unmade bed only two feet away.

I felt like a girl, or what I imagined a girl felt like when she wound up alone with an intimidating boy who too obviously liked her breasts. Leo snorted to see me turn timorous, and with that same disgusted sneer with which he had undertaken to demolish my career in radio, he said, "Don't worry, I'm not going to touch you. I just cannot bear that you should be so fucking conventional." And then and there he proceeded to initiate an introduction to Søren Kierkegaard. He wanted me to listen to him read what Kierkegaard, whose name meant no more to me than Raphael Kubelik's, had already surmised in backwater Copenhagen a hundred years ago about "the people"—whom Kierkegaard called "the public," the correct name, Leo informed me, for that abstraction, that "monstrous abstraction," that "all-embracing something which is nothing," that "monstrous nothing," as Kierkegaard wrote, that "abstract and deserted void which is everything and nothing" and which I mawkishly sentimentalized in my script. Kierkegaard hated the public, Leo hated the public, and Leo's purpose in his darkened International House room after that Friday night's concert and the concerts he took me to on the Fridays following was to save my prose from perdition by getting me to hate the public too.

"'Everyone who has read the classical authors,'" read Leo, "'knows how many things a Caesar could try out in order to kill time. In the same way the public keeps a dog to amuse it. That dog is the scum of the literary world. If there is someone superior to the rest, perhaps even a great man, the dog is set on him and the fun begins. The dog goes for him, snapping and tearing at his coat-tails, allowing itself every possible ill-mannered familiarity—until the public tires, and says it may stop. That is my example of how the public levels. Their betters and superiors in strength are mishandled—and the dog remains a dog which even the public despises. . . . The public is un-repentant—it was not really belittling anyone; it just wanted a little amusement.'"

This passage, which meant far more to Leo than it could begin to mean to me, was nonetheless Leo Glucksman's invitation to join him in being "someone superior to the rest," in being, like the Danish philosopher Kierkegaard—and like himself, as he could one day soon envision himself—"a great man." I became Leo's willing student and, through his intercession, Aristotle's willing student, Kierkegaard's willing student, Benedetto Croce's willing student, Thomas Mann's willing student, André Gide's willing student, Joseph Conrad's willing student, Fyodor Dostoyevsky's willing student . . . until soon my attachment to Ira—as to my mother, my father, my brother, even to the place where I'd grown up—was, I believed, thoroughly sundered. When someone is first being educated and his head is becoming transformed into an arsenal armed with books, when he is young and impudent and leaping with joy to discover all the intelligence tucked away on this planet, he is apt to exaggerate the importance of the churning new reality and to deprecate as unimportant everything else. Aided and abetted by the uncompromising Leo Glucksman—by his bile and manias as much as by that perpetually charged-up brain—this is what I did, with all my strength.

Every Friday night, in Leo's room, the spell was cast. All the passion in Leo that was not sexual (and a lot that was but had to be suppressed) he brought to bear on every idea that I had previously been made of, particularly on my virtuous conception of the artistic mission. Leo went at me on those Friday nights as though I were the last student left on earth. It began to seem to me that just about everybody gave me a shot. Educate Nathan. The credo of everybody I dared say hello to.

Occasionally now, looking back, I think of my life as one long speech that I've been listening to. The rhetoric is sometimes original, sometimes pleasurable, sometimes pasteboard crap (the speech of the incognito), sometimes maniacal, sometimes matter-of-fact, and sometimes like the sharp prick of a needle, and I have been hearing it for as long as I can remember: how to think, how not to think; how to behave, how not to behave; whom to loathe and whom to admire; what to embrace and when to escape; what is rapturous, what is murderous, what is laudable, what is shallow, what is sinister, what is shit, and how to remain pure in soul. Talking to me doesn't seem to present an obstacle to anyone. This is perhaps a consequence of my having gone around for years looking as if I needed talking to. But whatever the reason, the book of my life is a book of voices. When I ask myself how I arrived at where I am, the answer surprises me: "Listening."

Can that have been the unseen drama? Was all the rest a masquerade disguising the real no good that I was obstinately up to? Listening to them. Listening to them talk. The utterly wild phenomenon that is. Everyone perceiving experience as something not to have but to have so as to talk about it. Why is that? Why do they want me to hear them and their arias? Where was it decided that this was my use? Or was I from the beginning, by inclination as much as by choice, merely an ear in search of a word?

"Politics is the great generalizer," Leo told me, "and literature the great particularizer, and not only are they in an inverse relationship to each other—they are in an *antagonistic* relationship. To politics, literature is decadent, soft, irrelevant, boring, wrongheaded, dull, something that makes no sense and that really oughtn't to be. Why? Because the particularizing impulse *is* literature. How can you be an artist and renounce the nuance? But how can you be a politician and *allow* the nuance? As an artist the nuance is your *task*. Your task is *not* to simplify. Even should you choose to write in the simplest way, à la Hemingway, the task remains to impart the nuance, to elucidate the complication, to imply the contradiction. Not to erase the contradiction, not to deny the contradiction, but to see where, within the contradiction, lies the tormented human being. To allow for the chaos, to let it in. You *must* let it in. Otherwise you produce propaganda, if not for a political party, a political movement, then stupid propaganda for life itself—for life as it might itself prefer to be publicized. During the first five, six years of the Russian Revolution the revolutionaries cried, 'Free love, there will be free love!' But once they were in power, they couldn't permit it. Because what is free love? Chaos. And they didn't want chaos. That isn't why they made their glorious revolution. They wanted something carefully disciplined, organized, contained, predictable scientifically, if possible. Free love disturbs the organization, their social and political and cultural machine. Art also disturbs the organization. Literature disturbs the organization. Not because it is blatantly for or against, or

even subtly for or against. It disturbs the organization because
it is not general. The intrinsic nature of the particular is to be
particular, and the intrinsic nature of particularity is to fail to
conform. Generalizing suffering: there is Communism. Particularizing suffering: there is literature. In that polarity is the
antagonism. Keeping the particular alive in a simplifying, generalizing world—that's where the battle is joined. You do not
have to write to legitimize Communism, and you do not have
to write to legitimize capitalism. You are out of both. If you
are a writer, you are as unallied to the one as you are to the
other. Yes, you see differences, and of course you see that this
shit is a little better than that shit, or that that shit is a little
better than this shit. Maybe much better. *But you see the shit.*
You are not a government clerk. You are not a militant. You are
not a believer. You are someone who deals in a very different
way with the world and what happens in the world. The militant introduces a faith, a big belief that will change the world,
and the artist introduces a product that has no place in that
world. It's useless. The artist, the serious writer, introduces
into the world something that wasn't there even at the start.
When God made all this stuff in seven days, the birds, the rivers, the human beings, he didn't have ten minutes for literature.
'And then there will be literature. Some people will like it,
some people will be obsessed by it, want to do it . . .' No.
No. He did not say that. If you had asked God then, 'There
will be plumbers?' 'Yes, there will be. Because they will have
houses, they will need plumbers.' 'There will be doctors?' 'Yes.
Because they will get sick, they will need doctors to give them
some pills.' 'And literature?' 'Literature? What are you talking
about? What use does it have? Where does it fit in? Please, I am
creating a universe, not a university. *No literature.*'"

Uncompromising. Tom Paine's irresistible attribute, Ira's, Leo's,
and Johnny O'Day's. Had I gone down to East Chicago to meet
O'Day on my arrival in Chicago—which was what Ira had arranged for me to do—my life as a student, perhaps all life
thereafter, might have fallen under different enticements and
different pressures and I might have set out to abandon the
secure strictures of my background under the passionate tutelage
of a monolith quite different from the University of Chicago.

But the burden of a Chicago education, not to mention the demands being made by Mr. Glucksman's supplemental program to deconventionalize my mind, meant that it wasn't until early December that I was able to take a Saturday morning off and travel by train to meet Ira Ringold's army mentor, the steelworker whom Ira had once described to me as "a Marxist from the belt buckle both ways."

The tracks of the South Shore Line were at Sixty-third and Stony Island, only a fifteen-minute walk from my dormitory. I boarded the orange-painted car and took a seat, the conductor sounded off the names of the dirty towns along the line—"Hegewisch . . . Hammond . . . East Chicago . . . Gary . . . Michigan City . . . *South* Bend"—and I was as stirred up again as if I were listening to *On a Note of Triumph*. Coming as I did from industrial north Jersey, I confronted a not unfamiliar landscape. Looking south to Elizabeth, Linden, and Rahway from the airport, we too had the complex superstructure of refineries off in the distance and the noxious refinery odors and the plumes of fire, up at the top of the towers, burning off the gas from the distilling of petroleum. In Newark we had the big factories and the tiny job shops, we had the grime, we had the smells, we had the crisscrossing rail lines and the lots of steel drums and the hills of scrap metal and the hideous dump sites. We had black smoke rising from high stacks, a lot of smoke coming up everywhere, and the chemical reek and the malt reek and the Secaucus pig-farm reek sweeping over our neighborhood when the wind blew hard. And we had trains like this one that ran up on embankments through the marshes, through bulrushes and swamp grass and open water. We had the dirt and we had the stink, but what we didn't have and couldn't have was Hegewisch, where they'd built the tanks for the war. We didn't have Hammond, where they built the girders for bridges. We didn't have the grain elevators along the shipping canal coming down from Chicago. We didn't have the open-hearth furnaces that lit up the sky when the mills were pouring steel, a red sky that on clear nights I could see, from as far away as my dormitory window, way down in Gary. We didn't have U.S. Steel and Inland Steel and Jones Laughlin and Standard Bridge and Union Carbide and Standard Oil of Indiana. We had what New Jersey had; concentrated here was the power of the Midwest. What they had here was a steelmaking operation, miles and miles of it stretching along the lake through two states and vaster than any other in the world, coke furnaces and oxygen furnaces transforming iron ore into steel, overhead ladles carrying tons of molten steel, hot metal pouring like lava into molds, and amid all this flash and dust and danger and noise, working in temperatures of a hundred degrees, sucking in vapors that could ruin them, men at labor around the clock, men at work that was never finished. This was an America that I was not a native of and never would be and that I possessed as an American nonetheless. While I stared from the train window—took in what looked to me to be mightily up-to-date, modern, the very emblem of the industrial twentieth century, and yet an immense archeological site—no fact of my life seemed more serious than that.

To my right I saw block after block of soot-covered bungalows, the steelworkers' houses, with gazebos and birdbaths in the backyards, and beyond the houses the streets lined with low, ignominious-looking stores where their families shopped, and so strong was the impact on me of the sight of a steelworker's everyday world, its crudity, its austerity, the obdurate world of people who were always strapped, in debt, paying things off—so inspiring was the thought *For the hardest work the barest minimum, for breaking their backs the humblest rewards*—that, needless to say, none of my feelings would have seemed strange to Ira Ringold, while all of them would have appalled Leo Glucksman.

"What about this wife the Iron Man's got?" was almost the first thing O'Day said to me. "Maybe I'd like her if I knew her, but that's an imponderable. Some people I value have intimate friends to whom I'm indifferent. The comfortable bourgeoisie, the circle he now lives in with her . . . I'm not so sure. There's a problem with wives altogether. Most guys who marry are too vulnerable—they've given hostages to reaction in the person of their wives and kids. So it's left to a little coterie of hardened characters on their own to take care of what's got to be taken care of. Sure, all this is a grind, sure, it'd be nice to have a home, to have a soft woman waiting at the end of the day, maybe to have a couple of kids. Even guys who know what it's all about get fed up once in a while. But my immediate responsibility is to the hourly paid workingman, and for him I'm not doing a tithe of the work I should be doing. Whatever the sacrifice, what you have to remember is that movements like these are always upwards, regardless of how the immediate issue turns out."

The immediate issue was that Johnny O'Day had been driven from the union and had lost his job. I met him at a rooming house where he hadn't paid rent in two months; he had a week more to come up with the money or be thrown out. His small room had a window onto some sky and was neatly kept. The mattress of the single bed rested not on a box spring but on metal webbing and was tightly, even beautifully, made up, and the dark green paint on the iron bedstead wasn't chipped or peeling—as it was on the noisy radiator—but was disheartening to look at all the same. Altogether the furnishings were no more meager than those that Leo lived among at International House, and yet the aura of desolation startled me and—until O'Day's quiet, even voice and his peculiarly sharp enunciation began very powerfully to mute the presence of everything except O'Day himself—made me think I ought to get up and go. It was as though whatever wasn't in that room had vanished from the world. The instant he came to the door and let me in and politely invited me to be seated across from him, on one of the room's two bridge chairs, at a table just large enough for his typewriter, I had a sense not so much of everything's having been torn away from O'Day except this existence but, worse, of O'Day's having, almost sinisterly, torn *himself* away from everything that was not this existence.

Now I understood what Ira was doing in the shack. Now I understood the seed of the shack and the stripping back of everything—the aesthetic of the ugly that Eve Frame was to find so insufferable, that left a man lonely and monastic but also unencumbered, free to be bold and unflinching and purposeful. What O'Day's room represented was discipline, that discipline which says that however many desires I have, I can circumscribe myself down to this room. You can risk anything if at the end you know you can tolerate the punishment, and this room was a part of the punishment. There was a firm impression to be taken from this room: the connection between freedom and discipline, the connection between freedom and loneliness, the connection between freedom and punishment. O'Day's room, his cell, was the spiritual essence of Ira's shack. And what was the spiritual essence of O'Day's room? I'd find that out some years later when, on a visit to Zurich, I located the house with the commemorative tablet bearing Lenin's name, and after bribing a janitor with a handful of Swiss marks, was allowed to see the anchorite room where the revolutionary founder of Bolshevism had lived in exile for a year and a half.

O'Day's appearance should have been no surprise. Ira had described him exactly as he still was, a man constructed like a heron: a lean, taut, blade-faced six-footer with close-cut gray hair, eyes that also appeared to have turned gray, a sharp, large knife of a nose, and skin—a *hide*—lined as though he were well beyond his forties. But what Ira hadn't described was how zealotry had bestowed the look of a body that had a man locked up inside serving the severe sentence that was his life. It was the look of a being who has no choice. His story has been made up beforehand. He has no choice about anything. To tear himself from things in behalf of his cause—that's all there is for him to do. And he is not susceptible to others. It isn't just the physique that is a filament of steel, enviably narrow; the ideology, too, is tool-like and contoured like the edgewise silhouette of the heron's fuselage.

I remembered Ira's telling me that O'Day carried a light punching bag in his gear and that in the army he was so quick and strong that, "if forced to," he could lick two or three guys together. I'd been wondering all the way down on the train if there'd be a punching bag in his room. And there was. It wasn't in a corner hanging at head height, as I'd been imagining it and as it would have been if we'd been in a gym. It was on the floor, lying on its side against a closet door, a stout tear-shaped leather bag so old and battered it looked less like leather than like the bleached-out body part of some slaughtered animal—as though to keep in fighting trim O'Day worked with the testicle off a dead hippopotamus. A notion not rational but impossible —because of my initial fear of him—to make go away.

I remembered the words that O'Day had spoken the night that he'd poured out his frustration to Ira about not being able to spend his days "building the party here in the harbor": "I ain't that good at organizing, that is true. You have to be something of a hand holder with timid Bolsheviks, and I lean more to bopping their heads." I remembered because I had gone home and entered those words into my radio play then in progress, a play about a strike in a steel plant, wherein every last drop of the argot of Johnny O'Day emerged inviolate from one Jimmy O'Shea. Once O'Day had written to Ira, "I'm getting to be the official son of a bitch of East Chicago and environs, and that means winding up in Fist City." *Fist City* became the title of my next play. I couldn't help it. I wanted to write about things that seemed important, and the things that seemed important were things I didn't know. And what with the words at my disposal then, I instantly transformed everything into agitprop anyway, thus losing within seconds whatever was important about the important and immediate about the immediate.

O'Day was broke, and the party too broke to hire him as an organizer or to help him financially in any way, and so he was filling his days writing leaflets for mill-gate distribution, using the few dollars secretly contributed by some of his old steelworker buddies to pay for the paper and to rent a mimeograph machine and a staple machine, and then, at the end of each day, himself handing out the leaflets over in Gary. The change he had left he spent on food.

"My case against Inland Steel isn't finished," he told me, going right to the point, leveling with me as though I were an equal, an ally, if not already a comrade, talking to me as though Ira had somehow caused him to think that I was twice my age, a hundred times more independent, a thousand times more courageous. "But it looks as if management and the Red-baiters in the USA-CIO have got me fired and blacklisted for good. In every walk of life, all over this country, the move is on to crush the party. They don't know that it isn't Phil Murray's CIO that decides the great historic issues. Witness China. It's the American worker who will decide the great historic issues. In my occupation there are already more than a hundred unemployed ironworkers in this local union. This is the first time since 1939 that there haven't been more jobs than men, and even the ironworkers, the most obtuse section of the whole wage-earning class, are at last beginning to question the setup. It's coming, it's coming—I assure you it's coming. Still, I got hauled before the executive board of the ironworkers' local and expelled by reason of my membership in the party. These bastards didn't want to expel me, they wanted me to repudiate my membership. The rat press, which is zeroed in on me hereabouts—here," he said, handing me a clipping from beside the typewriter, "yesterday's *Gary Post-Tribune.* The rat press would have made a big thing out of that, and although I'd have retained my working card in the ironmongers', the word would have gone out to the contractors and the gang bosses to blacklist me. It's a closed industry, so expulsion from the union means that I'm deprived of work in my trade. Well, to hell with 'em. I can fight better from the outside anyway. The rat press, the labor fakers, the phony city administrations of Gary and East Chicago regard me as dangerous? Good. They're attempting to keep me from making a living? Fine. I've got nobody dependent on me but me. And I don't depend on friends or women or jobs or any other conventional prop to existence. I get along anyway. If the *Gary Post,*" he said, taking back from me and neatly folding in two the clipping that I hadn't dared to look at while he spoke, "and the *Hammond Times* and the rest of them think that they're going to run us Reds out of Lake County with these kind of tactics, they're playing the wrong number. If they'd left me alone, I would probably have one day soon left under my own power. But now I've got no money to go anywhere and so they are going to have to continue to deal with me. At the mill gates the attitude of the workers when I hand them my leaflets is, on the whole, friendly and interested. They flash me the V, and it's moments like that when the books balance for a while. We got our share of fascist workers, of course. Monday night, the other night, while I was handing out my leaflets at the Gary Big Mill, a fat lug started calling me a traitor and a prick, and I don't know what all else he had in mind. I didn't wait to find out. I hope he likes soup and soft biscuits. Tell that to the Iron Man," he said, smiling for the first time, though in a distressing way, as if forcing a smile were among the more difficult things he had to do. "Tell him I'm still in pretty good shape. Come on, Nathan," he said, and it chagrined me to hear this unemployed steelworker utter my given name (that is, my new college obsessions, my budding superiority, my lapse from political commitment chagrined me) when I had just heard him describe, in the same quiet, even voice, with the same careful enunciation—and with an intimate familiarity that did not seem culled from books—*the great historic issues, China, 1939,* above all describe the harsh, sacrificial selflessness imposed by his mission to *the hourly paid workingman.* "Nathan" spoken in the very voice that had raised gooseflesh on my arms by saying *It's coming, it's coming—I assure you it's coming.* "Let's get something for you to eat," said O'Day.

From the beginning, the difference between O'Day's speech and Ira's was unmistakable to me. Perhaps because there was nothing contradictory in O'Day's aims, because O'Day was living the life he proselytized, because the speech was a pretext for nothing else, because it appeared to rise from the core of the brain that is *experience,* there was a tautened to-the-point quality to what he said, the thinking firmly established, the words themselves seemingly shot through with will, nothing inflated, no waste of energy, but instead, in every utterance, a wily shrewdness and, however utopian the goal, a deep practicality, a sense that he had the mission as much in his hands as in his head; a sense, unlike that communicated by Ira, that it was intelligence and not a lack of intelligence that was availing itself of—and wielding—his ideas. The tang of what I thought of as "the real" permeated his talk. It wasn't difficult to see that the something Ira's speech was a weak imitation of was O'Day's. The tang of the real . . . though also the speech of someone in whom nothing ever laughed. With the result that there was a kind of madness to his singleness of purpose, and that also distinguished him from Ira. In attracting, as Ira did, all the human contingencies that O'Day had banished from life, there was sanity, the sanity of an expansive, disorderly existence.

By the time I got back on the train that evening, the power of O'Day's unrelenting focus had so disoriented me that all I could think about was how I was to tell my parents that three and a half months was enough: I was quitting college to move down to the steel town of East Chicago, Indiana. I wasn't asking them to support me financially. I would find work to support myself, menial work, more than likely—but that was just as well, if not the whole idea. I could no longer justify continuing to accede to bourgeois expectations, theirs *or* mine, not after my visit with Johnny O'Day, who, despite all the softspokenness concealing the passion, came across as the most dynamic person I had ever met, more so even than Ira. The most dynamic, the most unshatterable, the most dangerous.

Dangerous because he didn't care about me the way Ira did and didn't know about me the way Ira did. Ira knew I was somebody else's kid, understood intuitively—and had been told by my father for good measure—and didn't try to take from me my freedom or take me away from where I came from. Ira never tried to indoctrinate me beyond a certain point, nor was he desperate to hold on to me, though all his life he was probably love-hungry enough and love-starved enough to be always yearning for close attachments. He just borrowed me for a while when he came to Newark, occasionally borrowed me to have somebody to talk to when he was lonely visiting Newark or by himself up at the shack, but never took me anywhere near a Communist meeting. That whole other life of his was almost entirely invisible to me. All I got was the rant and the raving and the rhetoric, the window dressing. He was not *just* unrestrained—with me there was tact in Ira. Fanatically obsessive as he was, toward me there was a great decency, a tenderness, and a consciousness of a kind of danger that he was willing to face himself but didn't wish to expose a kid to. With me there was a big-bodied good-naturedness that was the other side of the fury and the rage. Ira saw fit to educate me only to a point. I never saw the zealot whole.

But to Johnny O'Day I wasn't anybody's son he had to protect. To him I was a body to be recruited.

"Don't trifle with the Trotskyites at that university," O'Day had told me at lunch, as though Trotskyites were a problem I'd come to East Chicago to talk over with him. Huddled head to head, we ate hamburgers in the booth of a dark tavern where his credit was still good with the Polish proprietor and where a boy like me, a sucker for manly intimacy, found the situation much to his liking. The little street, not far from the mill, was all taverns except for a grocery on one corner and a church on the other and, right across the way, an open lot that was half scrap heap, half garbage dump. The wind was strong from the east and smelled of sulfur dioxide. Inside, the smell was of smoke and beer.

"I'm unorthodox enough to contend that it's all right to

play with Trotskyites," O'Day said, "as long as you wash your hands afterward. There are people who handle venomous reptiles every day, going so far as to milk them of their poison in order to provide an antidote to it, and few of them are fatally bitten. Precisely because they know the reptiles *are* venomous."

"What's a Trotskyite?" I asked.

"You don't know about the fundamental divergence of Communists and Trotskyites?"

"No."

For the next few hours he told me. The story was replete with terms like "scientific socialism," "neo-fascism," "bourgeois democracy," with names unknown to me like (to begin with) Leon Trotsky, names like Eastman, Lovestone, Zinoviev, Bukharin, with events unknown to me like "the October Revolution" and "the 1937 trials," with formulations beginning "The Marxian precept that the contradictions inherent in a capitalist society . . ." and "Obedient to their fallacious reasoning, Trotskyites conspire to keep the aims from being achieved by . . ." But no matter how abstruse or complicated the story's ins and outs, coming from O'Day every word struck me as pointed and not at all remote, not a subject he was talking about to talk about it, not a subject he was talking about for me to write a term paper about it, but a struggle whose ferocity he had suffered through.

It was nearly three when he relaxed his hold on my attention. His way of having you listen was extraordinary and had much to do with a promise he silently made not to imperil you so long as you concentrated on his every word. I was exhausted, the tavern was all but empty, and yet I had the sense that everything possible was going on around me. I remembered back to that night, as a high school kid, when I'd defied my father and gone off to be Ira's guest at the Wallace rally in Newark, and once again I felt in communion with a quarrel about life that *mattered*, the glorious battle that I had been looking for since I'd turned fourteen.

"Come on," O'Day said, after glancing at his watch, "I'm going to show you the face of the future."

And there we were. There *I* was. There *it* was, the world where I had long secretly dreamed of being a man. The whistle blew, the gates opened wide, and here they came—the workers!

Corwin's far-flung ordinary men, unspectacular but free. The little guy! The common man! The Poles! The Swedes! The Irish! The Croatians! The Italians! The Slovenes! The men who jeopardized their lives making steel, risked being burned or crushed or blown apart, and all for the profit of the ruling class.

I was so excited I couldn't see faces, I couldn't really see bodies. I saw only the crude mass of them heading through the gates for home. The mass of the American masses! Brushing by me, knocking into me—the face, the *force* of the future! The impulse to cry out—in sadness, anger, protest, triumph—was overwhelming, as was the urge to join that mob not quite a menace and not quite a mob, to join the chain, the rush of men in their thick-soled boots, and follow them all home. The noise of them was like the noise of a crowd in an arena before a fight. And the fight? The fight for American equality.

From a pouch slung over his hip, O'Day took a wad of leaflets and thrust them at me. And there, within sight of the mill, this smoking basilica that must have been a mile long, the two of us stood side by side giving a leaflet to any man coming off the seven-to-three shift who stuck out a hand to take one. Their fingers touched mine and my whole life was turned inside out. Everything in America that was against these men was against me too! I took the leafleteer's vow: I would be nothing but the instrument of their will. I would be nothing but rectitude.

Oh yes, you feel the pull with a man like O'Day. Johnny O'Day doesn't take you fifty percent of the way and leave you alone. He takes you all the way. The revolution is going to wipe out this and replace it with that—the un-ironic clarity of the political Casanova. When you're seventeen years old and you meet a guy who has an aggressive stance and who has it all figured out idealistically and all figured out ideologically and who has no family and no relatives and no house—who is without all that stuff that was pulling Ira in twenty different directions, without all those *emotions* pulling Ira in twenty directions, without all that upheaval a man like Ira takes on because of his nature, without the turbulence of wanting to make a revolution that will change the world while also mating with a beautiful actress and acquiring a young mistress and fiddling with an aging whore and longing for a family and struggling with a stepchild and inhabiting an imposing house in the show-business city and a proletarian shack in the backwoods, determined to assert unflaggingly one being in secret and another in public and a third in the interstices between the two, to be Abraham Lincoln and Iron Rinn and Ira Ringold all rolled up into a frenzied, overexcitable group self—who instead is claimed by nothing but his idea, who is responsible to nothing but the idea, who understands almost mathematically what he needs to live an honorable life, then you think as I did, *Here is where I belong!*

Which was probably what Ira had thought on encountering O'Day in Iran. O'Day had viscerally influenced him the same way. Takes you and ties you to the world revolution. Only Ira had wound up with all that other inadvertent, undesigned, unpremeditated stuff, bouncing all those other balls with the same enormous effort to prevail—while all that O'Day had, was, and wanted was nothing other than *the real thing*. Because he wasn't a Jew? Because he was a goy? Because, as Ira had told me, O'Day had been raised in a Catholic orphanage? Was that why he could be so thoroughly, so ruthlessly, so visibly living nothing but the bare, bare bones?

There was none of the softness in him that I knew was inside me. Did he see my softness? I would not let him. My life with its softness squeezed out, here in East Chicago with Johnny O'Day! Down here at the mill gate at seven A.M. and three P.M. and eleven P.M. distributing leaflets after each shift. He will teach me how to write them, what to say and how best to say it so as to move the workingman to action and make of America an equitable society. He will teach me everything. I am someone moving out of the comfortable prison of his human irrelevance and, here at the side of Johnny O'Day, entering the hypercharged medium that is history. A menial job, an impoverished existence, yes, but here at the side of Johnny O'Day, not a meaningless *life*. To the contrary, everything of significance, everything profound and important!

From such emotions you would not imagine that I could ever find my way back. But by midnight I still hadn't phoned my family to tell them my decision. O'Day had given me two thin pamphlets to read on the train to Chicago. One was called *Theory and Practice of the Communist Party*, the first course in a "Marxist Study Series" prepared by the National Education Department of the Communist Party, in which the nature of capitalism, of capitalist exploitation, and of the class struggle were devastatingly exposed in just under fifty pages. O'Day promised that the next time we met, we would discuss what I'd read and he would give me the second course, which "developed on a higher theoretical level," he told me, "the subjects of the first course."

The other pamphlet I took back on the train that day, *Who Owns America?* by James S. Allen, argued—predicted—that "capitalism, even in its most powerful embodiment in America, threatens to reproduce disaster on an ever widening scale." The cover was a cartoon, in blue and white, of a porky-looking fat man in top hat and tails, seated arrogantly atop a swollen moneybag labeled "Profits," his own bloated belly adorned with a dollar sign. Smoking away in the background—and representing the property expropriated unjustly by the rich ruling class from the "principal victims of capitalism," the struggling workers—were the factories of America.

I had read both pamphlets on the train; in my dormitory room I read through them again, hoping to find in their pages the strength to phone home with my news. The final pages of *Who Owns America?* were entitled "Become a Communist!" These I read aloud, as though addressing me were Johnny O'Day himself: "Yes, together we will win our strikes. We will build our unions, we will gather together to fight at every step and stage the forces of reaction, of fascism, of war-making. Together we will seek to build up a great independent political movement that will contest the national election with the parties of the trusts. Not for one moment will we give rest to the usurpers, to the oligarchy which is bringing ruin to the nation. Let no one question your patriotism, your loyalty to the nation. Join the Communist Party. As a Communist, you will be able to fulfill, in the deepest sense of the word, your responsibility as an American."

I thought, Why isn't this reachable? Do it the way you got on that bus and went downtown and attended that Wallace rally. Is your life yours or is it theirs? Have you the courage of your convictions or haven't you? Is this America the kind of America you want to live in or do you intend to go out and revolutionize it? Or are you, like every other "idealistic" college student you know, another selfish, privileged, self-involved hypocrite? What are you afraid of—the hardship, the opprobrium, the danger, or O'Day himself? What are you afraid of if *not* your softness? Don't look to your parents to get you out of this. Don't call home and ask permission to join the Communist Party. Pack your clothes and your books and get back down there and do it! If you don't, is there really any distinction to be made between your capacity for daring to change and Lloyd Brown's, between your audacity and the audacity of Brownie, the grocer's assistant who wants to inherit Tommy Minarek's seat out at the rock dump in Zinc Town? How much does Nathan's failure to renounce his family's expectations and battle his way to genuine freedom differ from Brownie's failure to oppose *his* family's expectations and battle *his* way to freedom? He stays in Zinc Town selling minerals, I stay in college studying Aristotle—and I end up being Brownie with a degree.

At one in the morning I crossed the Midway from my dormitory through a snowstorm—my first Chicago blizzard blowing in—to International House. The Burmese student on desk duty recognized me, and when he unlocked the security door and I said, "Mr. Glucksman," he nodded and, despite the hour, let me through. I went up to Leo's floor and knocked on the door. You could smell curry in the hallway hours after one of the foreign students had cooked up dinner for himself on the hot plate in his room. I was thinking, Some Indian kid comes all the way from Bombay to study in Chicago, and you're afraid to live in Indiana. Stand up and fight against injustice! Turn around, go—the opportunity is yours! Remember the mill gate!

But because I had been pitched so high for so many hours— for so many adolescent *years*, been overcome with all these new ideals and visions of truth—when Leo, in his pajamas, opened his door, I burst into tears and, by doing so, misled him badly. Out of me poured all that I hadn't dared show to Johnny O'Day. The softness, the boyness, all the unworthy un-O'Dayness that was me. Everything nonessential that was me. Why isn't this reachable? I lacked what I suppose Ira also lacked: a heart without dichotomies, a heart like the enviably narrow O'Day's, unequivocal, ready to renounce everyone and everything except the revolution.

"Oh, Nathan," Leo said tenderly. "My dear friend." It was the first time he had called me anything other than "Mr. Zuckerman." He sat me down at his desk and, standing over me just inches away, watched while, still weeping, I undid the buttons of a mackinaw already wet and heavy with snow. Maybe he thought that I was preparing to undo everything. Instead, I began to tell him about the man I had met. I told him that I wanted to move down to East Chicago and to work with O'Day. I had to, for the sake of my conscience. But could I do it without telling my parents? I asked Leo if that was honorable.

"You shit! You whore! Go! Get out of here! You two-faced little cocktease whore!" he said, and shoved me from the room and slammed the door.

I didn't understand. I didn't really understand Beethoven, I was continuing to have trouble with Kierkegaard, and what Leo was shouting and why he was shouting it was also incomprehensible to me. All I'd done was to tell him I was contemplating living alongside a forty-eight-year-old Communist steelworker who, as I described him, looked a little like an aging Montgomery Clift—and Leo, in turn, throws me out.

Not just the Indian student across the hall but nearly all the Indian students and Oriental students and African students on the corridor came out of their rooms to see what the commotion was. Most of them, at this hour, were in their underwear, and what they were looking at was a boy who had only just discovered that heroism was not as easy to come by at seventeen as was a seventeen-year-old's talent for being drawn to heroism and to the moral aspect of just about everything. What they thought they saw was something else altogether. What they thought they saw I myself still couldn't figure out until, at my next humanities class, I realized that Leo Glucksman would henceforth mark me down not merely as nobody superior, let alone nobody destined to be a great man, but as the most callow, culturally backward, comical philistine ever, scandalously, to have been admitted to the University of Chicago. And nothing I said in class or wrote for class during the remainder of the year, none of my lengthy letters explaining myself and apologizing and pointing out that I *hadn't* left the college to join up with O'Day would ever disabuse him.

I sold magazines door to door in Jersey that next summer—not quite the same as distributing handbills at an Indiana steel mill at dawn, dusk, and in the dark of night. Though I was on the phone with Ira a couple of times and we made a plan for me to come out to see him at the shack in August, to my relief he had to cancel at the last minute and then I was back at school. Some weeks later, in the final days of October 1951, I heard that he and Artie Sokolow, as well as the director, the composer, the program's two other leading actors, and the famous announcer Michael J. Michaels, had been fired from *The Free and the Brave*. My father gave me the news on the phone. I didn't regularly see a newspaper, and the news, he told me, had appeared the day before in both Newark papers, as well as in every one of the New York dailies. "Redhot Iron" they had called him in the headline of the *New York Journal-American*, where Bryden Grant was a columnist. The story had broken in "Grant's Grapevine."

I could tell from my father's voice that what he was most worried about was me—about the implications of my having been befriended by Ira—and so indignantly I said to him, "Because they call him a Communist, because they lie and call *everybody* a Communist—" "They can lie and call you one too," he said, "*yes*." "Let them! Just let them!" But no matter how much I shouted at my liberal chiropodist father as though he were the radio executive who had fired Ira and his cohorts, no matter how loudly I claimed that the accusations were as inapplicable to Ira as they would be to me, I knew from having spent just that one afternoon with Johnny O'Day how mistaken I could be. Ira had served over two years with O'Day in Iran. O'Day had been his best friend. When I knew him, he was still getting long letters from O'Day and writing back to him. Then there was Goldstine and all he'd said in his kitchen. Don't let him fill you full of Communist ideas, kid. The Communists get a dummy like Ira and they use him. Get out of my house, you dumb Communist prick . . .

I had willfully refused to put all this together. This and the record album and more.

"Remember that afternoon in my office, Nathan, when he came over from New York? I asked him and you asked him, and what did he tell us?"

"The truth! He told the truth!"

"'Are you a Communist, Mr. Ringold?' I asked him. 'Are you a Communist, Mr. Ringold?' you asked him." With something shocking in his voice I had never heard before, my father cried, "If he lied, if that man lied to my son . . . !"

What I'd heard in his voice was a willingness to kill.

"How can you be in business with somebody who lies to you about something that fundamental? *How?* It wasn't a child's lie," my father said. "It was an adult lie. It was a motivated lie. It was an *unmitigated* lie."

On he went, while I was thinking, Why did Ira bother, why didn't he tell me the truth? I would have gone up to Zinc Town anyway, or tried to. But then, he didn't just lie to me. That wasn't the point. He lied to everyone. If you lie about it to everyone, automatically and all the time, you're doing it deliberately to change your relationship to the truth. Because nobody can improvise it. You tell the truth to this person, you tell the lie to the other person—it won't work. So the lying is part of what happens when he put on that uniform. It was in the nature of his commitment to lie. Telling the truth, particularly to me, never occurred to him; it would have not only put our friendship at risk but put me at risk. There were lots of reasons why he lied, but none that I could explain to my father, even if I had understood them all at the time.

After speaking with my father (and my mother, who said, "I begged Dad not to call you, not to upset you"), I tried to telephone Ira at West Eleventh Street. The phone was busy all evening, and when I dialed again the next morning and got through, Wondrous—the black woman whom Eve used to summon to the dinner table with the little bell that Ira loathed—said to me, "He don't live here no more," and hung up. Because Ira's brother was still very much "my teacher," I restrained myself from phoning Murray Ringold, but I did write to Ira, to Newark, to Lehigh Avenue, in care of Mr. Ringold, and again to the box address up in Zinc Town. I got no answer. I read the clippings my father sent me about him from the papers, crying aloud, "Lies! Lies! Filthy lies!" but then I remembered Johnny O'Day and Erwin Goldstine and I didn't know what to think.

Less than six months later there appeared in America's

bookstores—rushed into publication—*I Married a Communist* by Eve Frame, as told to Bryden Grant. The jacket, front and back, was a replica of the American flag. On the front of the jacket the flag was ripped raggedly open, and within the oval tear was a recent black-and-white photograph of Ira and Eve: Eve looking softly lovely in one of her little hats, with the dotted veil she'd made famous, wearing a fur jacket, and carrying a circular purse—Eve smiling brightly at the camera as she walked arm in arm down West Eleventh Street with her husband. But Ira didn't look at all happy; from beneath his fedora, he stared through his heavy glasses into the camera with a grave and troubled expression. Very nearly at the bull's-eye center of that book jacket proclaiming "*I Married a Communist*, by Eve Frame, as told to Bryden Grant," Ira's head was circled boldly in red.

In the book, Eve claimed that Iron Rinn, "alias Ira Ringold," was "a Communist madman" who had "assaulted and browbeaten" her with his Communist ideas, lecturing her and Sylphid every night at dinner, shouting at them and doing his best to "brainwash" both of them and make them work for the Communist cause. "I don't believe I've ever seen anything so heroic in my life as my young daughter, who loved nothing so much as to sit quietly all day playing her harp, arguing strenuously in defense of American democracy against this Communist madman and his Stalinist, totalitarian lies. I don't believe I've ever seen anything so cruel in my life as this Communist madman using every tactic out of the Soviet concentration camp to bring this brave child to her knees."

On the facing page was a photograph of Sylphid, but not the Sylphid I knew, not the large, sardonic twenty-three-year-old in the gypsy clothes who had hilariously helped me through my dinner that night at the party and who afterward had delighted me by filleting one after another of her mother's friends, but a tiny, round-faced Sylphid with big black eyes, in pigtails and a party dress, smiling at her beautiful mommy over a Beverly Hills birthday cake. Sylphid in a white cotton dress embroidered with little strawberries, its full skirt puffed out with petticoats and cinched by a full sash tied at the back in a bow. Sylphid at forty-two pounds and six years of age, in white anklets and black Mary Janes. Sylphid not as Pennington's child or even Eve's but as God's. The picture achieving what Eve intended at the outset with the misty daydream of a name: the deprofanation of Sylphid, the etherealization from solid to air. Sylphid as saint, perfectly innocent of all the vices and taking up no room in this world whatsoever. Sylphid as everything that antagonism is not.

"Momma, Momma," the brave child cries helplessly to her mother in one climactic scene, "those men up in his study are speaking Russian!"

Russian agents. Russian spies. Russian documents. Secret letters, phone calls, hand-delivered messages pouring into the house day and night from Communists all over the country. Cell meetings in the house and in "the secret Communist hideaway in the remotest wilds of New Jersey." And "in a parlor-floor apartment briefly leased by him in Greenwich Village, on Washington Square North, across from the famous statue of General George Washington—an apartment acquired by Iron Rinn chiefly for the purpose of providing a safe haven for Communists on the run from the FBI."

"Lies!" I cried. "Completely crazy lies!" But how was I to know for sure? How was anyone? What if the startling preface to her book was *true*? Could it possibly be? For years I wouldn't read Eve Frame's book, protecting as long as I could my original relationship to Ira even when I had been progressively abandoning him and his haranguing to a point where I had all but accomplished the rejection of him. But because I didn't want this book to be the awful end to our story, I skipped around and didn't read thoroughly beyond the preface. Nor was I avidly interested in what was written in the papers about the treacherous hypocrisy of the leading actor of *The Free and the Brave*, who'd been personifying all these great American characters despite having cast himself in a more sinister role entirely. Who had, according to Eve's testimony, been personally responsible for submitting every one of Sokolow's scripts to a Russian agent for suggestions and approval. To see somebody I'd loved publicly vilified—why would I want to take part in that? There was no pleasure in it, and there was also nothing I could do about it.

Even putting aside the charge of espionage, accepting that the man who had brought me into the world of men could have lied to our family about being a Communist was no less painful for me than accepting that Alger Hiss or the Rosenbergs could have lied to the nation by denying that they were Communists. I refused to read any of it, as I had earlier refused to believe any of it.

This was how Eve's book began, the preface, the bombshell of an opening page:

Is it right for me to do this? Is it easy for me to do this? Believe me, it is far from easy. It is the most awful and difficult task of my entire life. What is my motive? people will ask. How can I possibly consider it my moral and patriotic duty to inform on a man I loved as much as I loved Iron Rinn?

Because as an American actress I have sworn myself to fight the Communist infiltration of the entertainment industry with every fiber of my being. Because as an American actress I have a solemn responsibility to an American audience that has given me so much love and recognition and happiness, a solemn and unshakable responsibility to reveal and expose the extent of the Communist grip on the broadcasting industry that I came to know through the man I was married to, a man I loved more than any man I have ever known, but a man who was determined to use the weapon of mass culture to tear down the American way of life.

That man was the radio actor Iron Rinn, alias Ira Ringold, card-carrying member of the Communist Party of the United States of America and American ringleader of the underground Communist espionage unit committed to controlling American radio. Iron Rinn, alias Ira Ringold, an American taking his orders from Moscow.

I know why I married this man: out of a woman's love. And why did he marry me? Because he was ordered to by the Communist Party! Iron Rinn never loved me. Iron Rinn exploited me. Iron Rinn married me the better to infiltrate his way into the world of American entertainment. Yes, I married a Machiavellian Communist, a vicious man of enormous cunning who nearly ruined my life, my career, and the life of my beloved child. And all of it to advance Stalin's plan for world domination.

"THE shack. Eve hated it. When they were first lovers, she'd tried fixing it up for him; she hung curtains, bought dishes, glasses, place settings, but there were mice, wasps, spiders got into the place, and she was terrified of them, and it was miles to the general store, and since she didn't drive, a local farmer who smelled of manure had to drive her there to shop. All in all, there was nothing much for her to do in Zinc Town except fend off all the discomforts, and so she started to campaign for them to buy a place in the south of France, where Sylphid's father had a villa, so that Sylphid could be near him in the summers. She said to Ira, 'How can you be so provincial? How will you ever learn anything that isn't screaming about Harry Truman if you won't travel, if you won't go to France to see the French countryside, if you won't go to Italy to see the great paintings, if you won't go anywhere except to New Jersey? You don't listen to music. You won't go to museums. If a book isn't about the working class, you don't read it. How can an actor—' And he would say, 'Look, I'm no actor. I'm a working stiff who earns his living in radio. You *had* a la-di-da husband. You want to go back and try him again? You want a husband like your friend Katrina has, a cultivated Harvard man like Mr. Loony, like Mr. Katrina Van Gossip Grant?'

"Whenever she'd bring up France and buying a vacation house there, Ira got going—it never took much. It wasn't in him casually to dislike somebody like Pennington or Grant. It wasn't in him casually to dislike anything. There was no disagreement that his outrage couldn't make use of. 'I traveled,' he'd tell her. 'I worked on the docks in Iran. Saw enough human degradation in Iran . . .' and so on and so forth.

"The upshot was that Ira wouldn't give up the shack, and that was another source of contention between them. In the beginning the shack was a holdover from his old life and for her a part of his rube charm. After a while she saw the shack as a foothold apart from her, and that also filled her with terror.

"Maybe she loved him and that's what spawned the fear of losing him. Her histrionics never registered on me as love. Eve cloaked herself in the mantle of love, the fantasy of love, but was too weak and vulnerable a person not to be filled with resentment. She was too intimidated by everything to provide love that was sensible and to the point—to provide anything but a caricature of love. That's what Sylphid got. Imagine what it must have meant to be Eve Frame's daughter—*and* Carlton Pennington's daughter—and you begin to understand how Sylphid evolved. A person like that you don't make overnight.

"The whole despised part of Ira, everything disgustingly untamed in him, was also wrapped up for her in that shack, but Ira wouldn't get rid of it. If nothing else, as long as the shack remained a shack, it was Sylphid-proof. Nowhere for her to sleep other than on the daybed in the front room, and the few times each summer she visited for a weekend she was bored and miserable. The pond too muddy for her to swim in, the woods too buggy for her to walk in, and though Eve would endlessly try to keep her entertained, she sulked indoors for a day and a half and then headed back on the train to her harp.

"But that last spring they were together, plans began to be laid to fix the place up. Big renovation to start after Labor Day. Modernizing the kitchen, modernizing the bathroom, large new windows, brand-new floors, new doors that fit, new lighting, blown insulation and a new oil-heating system to properly winterize the place. Paint job inside and out. And a large addition at the back, a whole new room with a huge stone fireplace and with a picture window overlooking the pond and the woods. Ira hired a carpenter, a painter, an electrician, a plumber, Eve made lists and drawings, and all of it was to be ready for Christmas. 'What the hell,' Ira said to me, 'she wants it, let her have it.'

"His coming apart had begun by then, only I didn't realize it. He didn't either. He thought he was being shrewd, you see, thought he could finesse it. But his aches and pains were killing him, and his morale was shot, and the decision wasn't made by what was strong in him but by what was breaking. He thought by making things more to her liking he could minimize the friction and ensure her protecting him against the blacklist. He was afraid now of losing her by losing his temper, and so he began to try to save his political hide by letting all that unreality of hers flow freely over him.

"The fear. The acute fear there was in those days, the disbelief, the anxiety over discovery, the suspense of having one's life and one's livelihood under threat. Was Ira convinced keeping Eve could protect him? Probably not. But what else was there for him to do?

"What happened to his cunning strategy? He hears her calling the new addition 'Sylphid's room,' and that takes care of the cunning strategy. He hears her outside with the excavator saying, 'Sylphid's room this' and 'Sylphid's room that,' and when she comes inside the house, all glowing and happy, Ira's already undergone the transformation. 'Why do you say that?' he asks her. 'Why do you call that Sylphid's room?' 'I did no such thing,' she says. 'You did. I heard you. That's not Sylphid's room.' 'Well, she *is* going to stay there.' 'I thought it was just going to be the big backroom, the new living room.' 'But the daybed. She'll be sleeping there on the new daybed.' 'Will she? When?' 'Why, when she comes here.' 'But she doesn't like it here.' 'But she will when the house is as lovely as it's going to be.' 'Then screw it,' he says. 'The house won't be lovely. The house will be shitty. Fuck the whole project.' 'Why are you doing this to me? Why are you doing this to my daughter? What is *wrong* with you, Ira?' 'It's over. The renovation is off.' 'But *why*?' 'Because I can't stand your daughter and your daughter can't stand me—that is why.' 'How *dare* you say anything against my daughter! I'm getting out of here! I will not stay here! You are persecuting my daughter! I will not have it!' And she picked up the phone and called for the local taxi, and in five minutes she was gone.

"Four hours later he found out to where. He gets a phone call from a real estate woman over in Newton. She asks to speak to Miss Frame, and he tells her Miss Frame isn't around, and she asks if he'll give Miss Frame a message—the two darling farmhouses they saw *are* on the market, either one is perfect for her daughter, and she can show them to her the next weekend.

"What Eve had done, after she left, was to spend the afternoon looking for a summer place in Sussex County to buy for Sylphid.

"That's when Ira phoned me. He said to me, 'I don't believe it. Looking for a house for her up here—I don't *comprehend* it.' 'I do,' I said. 'To bad mothering there is no end. Ira, the time has come to move on to the next improbability.'

"I got in the car and I went up to the shack. I spent the night, and the next morning I brought him to Newark. Eve phoned our house every evening, begging him to come back, but he told her that was it, their marriage was over, and when *The Free and the Brave* returned to the air, he stayed with us and commuted to New York to work.

"I told him, 'You are in the hands of this thing like everybody else. You are going to go down or not go down like everybody else. The woman you are married to is not going to protect you from whatever is in store for you or for the show or for whomever else they decide to destroy. The Red-baiters are on the march. Nobody is going to fool them for long even by living a *quadruple* life. They're going to get you with her or they're going to get you without her, but at least without her you're not going to be encumbered by somebody useless in a crisis.'

"But, as the weeks passed, Ira became less and less convinced that I was right, and so did Doris, and maybe, Nathan, I wasn't right. Maybe if, for his own calculated reasons, he'd gone back to Eve, her aura, her reputation, her connections would have worked together to save him and his career. That is possible. But what was going to save him from the marriage? Every night, after Lorraine had gone to her room, we'd sit in the kitchen, Doris and I going over and over the same ground while Ira listened. We'd gather at the kitchen table with our tea, and Doris would say, 'He's put up with her nonsense for three years now, when there's been no sane reason to put up with it. Why can't he put up with her nonsense for another three years, when at last there *is* a sane reason to put up with it? For whatever motive, good or bad, he has never pushed to completely end the marriage in all this time. Why should he do it now, when being her husband might possibly be helpful to him? If he can salvage some benefit, at least his ridiculous union with those two won't have been in vain.' And I would say, 'If he returns to the ridiculous union, he is going to be destroyed by the ridiculous union. It is more than ridiculous. Half the time he's so miserable, he has to come over here to sleep.' And Doris would say, 'He's going to be more miserable when he's on the blacklist.' 'Ira is going to wind up on the blacklist either way. With his big mouth and his background, Ira is not going to be spared.' And Doris would say, 'How can you be sure everyone is going to get it? The whole thing is so irrational to begin with, so without any rhyme or reason—' And I would say, 'Doris, his name has appeared in fifteen, twenty places already. It's got to happen. It's inevitable. And when it happens, we know whose side she'll stand by. Not his, Sylphid's—to protect Sylphid from what's happening to *him*. I say end the marriage and the marital misery and accept that he is going to wind up on the blacklist wherever he is. If he goes back to her, he's going to fight with her, he's going to battle the daughter, and soon enough she is going to realize why he is there, and that will make it even worse.' 'Eve? Realize anything?' Doris said. 'Reality doesn't seem to make a dent in Miss Frame. Why is reality going to rear its head now?' 'No,' I said, 'the cynical exploitation, the parasitical leeching—it's too demeaning. I don't like it in and of itself, and I don't like it because Ira is not capable of pulling it off. He is open, he is impulsive, he is direct. He is a hothead and he is not going to be able to do it. And when she finds out why he is there, well, she will make things even *more* miserable and confused. She doesn't have to figure it out herself—somebody can do it for her. Her friends the Grants will figure it out. They probably have already. Ira, if you go back there, what are you going to do to change the way you live with her? You're going to have to become a lapdog, Ira. You can do that? *You*?' 'He'll just be shrewd and go his way,' Doris said. 'He *can't* be shrewd and go his way,' I said. 'He'll never be "shrewd" because everything there drives him crazy.' 'Well,' said Doris, 'losing everything he's worked for, being punished in America for what he believes in, his enemies getting the upper hand, that will make Ira even crazier.' 'I don't like it,' I said, and Doris said, 'But you didn't like it from the outset, Murray. Now you're using this to get him to do what you have wanted him to do all along. The hell with exploiting her. Exploit her—that's what she's there for. What is marriage without exploitation? People in marriages get exploited a million times over. One exploits the other's position, one exploits the other's money, one exploits the other's looks. I think he should go back. I think he needs all the protection he can get. Just *because* he is impulsive, *because* he is a hothead. He's in a war, Murray. He's under fire. He needs camouflage. She is his camouflage. Wasn't she Pennington's camouflage because he was a homosexual? Now let her be Ira's because he's a Red. Let her be useful for *something*. No, I don't see the objection. He schlepped the harp, didn't he? He saved her from that kid beating her brains in, didn't he? He did what he could do for her. Now let her do what she can do for him. Now, by luck, through sheer circumstance, those two people can finally do something aside from bitch and moan about Ira and war on each other. They don't even have to be conscious of it. Through no effort on their part, they can be of use to Ira. What's so wrong with that?' 'The man's honor is at stake, that's what,' I said. 'His integrity is at stake. It's all too mortifying. Ira, I argued with you about joining the Communist Party. I argued with you about Stalin and I argued with you about the Soviet Union. I argued with you and it made no difference: you were committed to the Communist Party. Well, this ordeal is part of that commitment. I don't like to think of you groveling. Perhaps the time has come to drop *all* the mortifying lies. The marriage that's a lie and the political party that's a lie. Both are making of you much less than you are.'

"The debate went on for five consecutive nights. And for five nights he was silent. I'd never known him to be so silent. So *calm*. Finally, Doris turned to him and said, 'Ira, this is all we can say. Everything has been discussed. It's your life, your career, your wife, your marriage. It's your radio show. Now it is your decision. It's up to you.' And he said, 'If I can manage to hold on to my position, if I can manage not to be swept aside and thrown into the trash can, then I am doing more for the party than if I sit around and worry about my integrity. I don't worry about being mortified, I worry about being effective. I want to be effective. I'm going back to her.' 'It won't work,' I said. 'It will work,' he told me. 'If it's clear in my mind why I'm there, I will make *sure* it works.'

"That very night, half an hour, forty-five minutes later, the downstairs doorbell rang. She'd hired a cab to drive her to Newark. Her face was drawn, ghostlike. She came racing up the stairs, and when Eve saw Doris with me at the top of the landing, she flashed that smile that an actress is able to flash on the spot—smiled as though Doris were a fan waiting outside the studio door to snap a photograph with her box camera. Then she was by us, and there was Ira, and she was on her knees. Same stunt as that night out at the shack. The Suppliant again. Repeatedly and promiscuously the Suppliant. The aristocratic pretension of stateliness and this kind of perverse, unembarrassable behavior. 'I implore you—don't leave me! I'll do anything!'

"Our little, bright, budding Lorraine had been in her room doing her homework. She had come out into the living room in her pajamas to say good night to everyone when there, in her very own house, was this famous star whom she listened to every week on *The American Radio Theater*, this exalted personage letting life run all over her. All the chaos and rawness of someone's inmost being on exhibit on our living room floor. Ira told Eve to get up, but when he tried to lift her she wrapped her arms around his legs and the howl she let loose made Lorraine's mouth fall open. We'd taken Lorraine to see the stage show at the Roxy, we'd taken her to the Hayden Planetarium, we'd gone up in the car to see Niagara Falls, but as far as spectacles went, this was the pinnacle of her childhood.

"I went and kneeled down beside Eve. Okay, I thought, if what he wants to do is to go back, if this is what he wants more of, he is about to get it, and in spades. 'That's it,' I said to her. 'Come on, let's get up now. Let's go into the kitchen, get you some coffee.' And that was when Eve looked over and saw Doris standing by herself, still holding the magazine she'd been reading. Doris, plain as can be, in her bedroom slippers and her housedress. Her face was blank, as I remember it— stunned, sure, but certainly not mocking. However, just her being there was enough of a challenge to the high drama that was Eve Frame's life for Eve to take aim and fire. 'You! What are *you* staring at, you hideous, twisted little Jew!'

"I have to tell you that I saw it coming; rather, I knew something was coming that wasn't exactly going to advance Eve's cause, and so I wasn't as flabbergasted as my little girl was. Lorraine burst into tears, and Doris said, 'Get her out of the house,' and Ira and I lifted Eve up from the floor and took her into the hallway and down the stairs, and we drove her to Penn Station. Ira sat in the front beside me, and she sat in the back as though she were oblivious to what had happened. All the way to Penn Station she had that smile on her face, the one for the cameras. Underneath the smile there was nothing at all, not her character, not her history, not even her misery. She was just what was stretched across her face. She wasn't even alone. There was no one to *be* alone. Whatever shaming origins she had spent her life escaping had resulted in this: someone from whom life itself had escaped.

"I pulled up in front of Penn Station, we all got out of the car, and stonily, very stonily, Ira said to her, 'Go back to New York.' She said, 'But aren't you coming?' 'Of course not.' 'Why did you come in the car, then? Why do you come to the train with me?' Could that have been why she'd been smiling? Because she believed she'd triumphed and Ira was returning with her to Manhattan?

"This time, the scene wasn't enacted for my little family. This time it was an audience of fifty or so people heading into Penn Station who were brought to a standstill by what they saw. Without a qualm really, this regal presence who endowed the idea of decorum with such tremendous significance threw her two hands up toward the sky and, upon all of downtown Newark, imposed the magnitude of her misery. A woman totally inhibited and under wraps—until she's totally uninhibited. Either inhibited and bound by shame, or uninhibited and shameless. Nothing ever in between. 'You tricked me! I loathe you! I despise you! Both of you! You are the worst people I have ever known!'

"I remember hearing somebody in the crowd then, some guy rushing up who was asking, 'What are they doing, making a movie? Ain't that what's-her-name? Mary Astor?' And I remember thinking that she would never be finished. The movies, the stage, the radio, and now this. The aging actress's last great career—shouting her hatred in the street.

"But after that, nothing happened. Ira returned to the show while staying on with us, and nothing more was said about going back to West Eleventh Street. Helgi came to massage him three times a week, and nothing more happened. Very early on, Eve had tried to call, but I took the phone to tell her that

Ira couldn't speak to her. Would *I* speak to her? Would I at least *listen* to her? I said yes. What else could I do?

"She knows what she did wrong, she says, she knows why Ira is hiding out in Newark: because she had told him about Sylphid's recital. Ira was jealous enough of Sylphid as it was, and he could not reconcile himself to the upcoming recital. But when Eve had decided to tell him about it, she had believed that it was her duty to let him know beforehand everything that a recital entailed. Because it's not just renting a hall, she told me, it's not just showing up and playing a concert—it's a production. It's like a wedding. It's a huge event that consumes a musician's family for months before it happens. Sylphid would herself be preparing for the entire next year. For a performance to qualify as a recital, you have to play at least sixty minutes of music, which is an enormous task. Just choosing the music would be an enormous task, and not for Sylphid alone. There were going to be endless discussions about what Sylphid should begin with and what she should end with and what the chamber piece should be, and Eve had wanted Ira to be prepared so he wouldn't go berserk every time she left him alone to sit down with Sylphid to discuss the program. Eve had wanted him to know beforehand what he, as a family member, was going to have to put up with: there was going to be publicity, frustration, crises—like all other young musicians, Sylphid was going to get cold feet and want to back out. But Eve also wanted Ira to know that it would be worth it in the end, and she wanted me to tell him that. Because a recital was what Sylphid needed to break through. People are stupid, Eve said. They like to see harpists who are tall, blond, and willowy, and Sylphid happened not to be tall, blond, and willowy. But she was an extraordinary musician and the recital was going to prove that once and for all. It was going to be held at Town Hall, and Eve would underwrite it, and Sylphid was to be coached by her old Juilliard teacher, who had agreed to help her prepare, and Eve was going to get every friend she had to attend, and the Grants promised to make certain that the critics were there from all the papers, and Eve had no doubt that Sylphid was going to do wonderfully and get wonderful reviews, and then Eve herself could shop them around to Sol Hurok.

"What was I to say? What difference would it have made if I had reminded her of this, that, or the other thing? She was a selective amnesiac whose forte was to render inconvenient facts inconsequential. To live without remembering was her means of survival. She had it all figured out: the reason Ira was staying with us was because of her having believed it her duty to tell him truthfully about the Town Hall recital and everything it would entail.

"Well, the fact was that when Ira was with us he never mentioned Sylphid's recital. His head was too full of the blacklist for him to be worrying about Sylphid's recital. I doubt that when Eve was telling him about it, it had even registered on him. Following that phone call, I wondered if she had told him about it at all.

"The letter she sent next I marked 'Addressee Unknown' and, with Ira's consent, returned unopened. The second letter I handled the same way. After that, the calls and the letters stopped. It looked for a while as though the disaster were over. Eve and Sylphid were up in Staatsburg on weekends with the Grants. She must have been giving them an earful about Ira—and, perhaps, about me too—and getting an earful about the Communist conspiracy. But still nothing happened, and I began to believe that nothing would happen so long as he remained officially married and the Grants figured there was some remote danger in it for the wife if the husband was exposed in *Red Channels* and fired.

"One Saturday morning, who should turn up on *Van Tassel and Grant* but Sylphid Pennington and her harp. I would think the imprimatur awarded Sylphid by making her the guest of that program that day was a favor to Eve meant to insulate the stepdaughter against any taint of association with the stepfather. Bryden Grant interviewed Sylphid, and she told him her funny stories about being in the orchestra at the Music Hall, and then Sylphid played a few selections for the radio audience, and after that Katrina launched into her weekly monologue on the state of the arts—an extensive fantasy, that Saturday, of the music world's expectations for young Sylphid Pennington's future, of the anticipation already mounting for her debut recital at Town Hall. Katrina explained how after she had arranged for Sylphid to play for Toscanini he had said such-and-such about the young harpist, and after she had arranged for Sylphid to play for Phil Spitalny he had said so-and-so, and there was no famous musical name, high or low, she didn't make use of, and Sylphid had never played for any of them.

"It was bold and spectacular and absolutely in character. Eve could say anything if she felt cornered; Katrina could say anything at any time. Exaggeration, misrepresentation, bald fabrication—that was her talent and skill. As it was her husband's. As it was Joe McCarthy's. The Grants were just Joe McCarthy with a pedigree. With *conviction*. It was a little hard to believe that McCarthy was caught up with his lies the way those two were. 'Tailgunner Joe' could never completely smother his cynicism; McCarthy always looked to me sort of loosely covered in his human shabbiness, whereas the Grants and their shabbiness were one.

"So—nothing happened and nothing happened, and Ira began looking for an apartment of his own in New York . . . and *that's* when something happened—but with Helgi.

"Lorraine got a bang out of this big broad and her gold tooth and her dyed hair swirled up in a helter-skelter blond bun storming into our apartment with her table and speaking in that shrill voice with the Estonian accent. In Lorraine's bedroom, where she massaged Ira, Helgi was always laughing. I remember saying to him once, 'You get along with these people, don't you?' 'Why shouldn't I?' he said. 'There's nothing wrong with them.' That's when I wondered if the greatest mistake any of us ever made was not letting him alone to marry Donna Jones, not letting him alone to earn a livelihood in the American heartland, unrebelliously manufacturing fudge and raising a family with his ex-stripper.

"Well, one morning in October, Eve is by herself and desperate and frightened and she gets it into her head to have Helgi hand-deliver a letter to Ira. She phones her up in the Bronx and tells her, 'Take a taxi to me. I'll give you the money. Then you can carry the letter with you when you go to Newark.'

"Helgi arrives all dressed up, in her fur coat and her fanciest hat and her best outfit, and carrying the massage table. Eve is upstairs writing the letter and Helgi is told to wait in the living room. Helgi sets down the table that goes with her everywhere, and she waits. She waits and she waits, and there's a bar and there's the cabinet with the dainty glasses, and so she finds the key to the cabinet, and she gets a glass and she locates the vodka and she pours herself a drink. And Eve is still upstairs in the bedroom, in her peignoir, writing letter after letter and tearing each one up and starting all over again. Every letter she writes to him is wrong, and with every letter she writes, Helgi pours another drink and smokes another cigarette, and soon Helgi is wandering around the living room and the library and into the hallway and looking at the pictures of Eve when she was a gorgeous young movie star and pictures of Ira and Eve with Bill O'Dwyer, the ex-mayor of New York, and with Impellitteri, the current mayor, and she pours herself another drink, lights another cigarette, and thinks about this woman with all her money and fame and privilege. She thinks about herself and her hard life, and she gets more and more sorry for herself and more and more drunk. Big and strong as she is, she even starts to weep.

"By the time Eve comes down and gives her the letter, Helgi is stretched out on the sofa, in her fur coat and her hat, still smoking and still drinking but now she's not weeping. By now she's worked herself up into an incredible state and she's furious. The boozer's lack of control doesn't begin and end with the booze.

"Helgi says, 'Why do you keep me waiting an hour and a half?' Eve takes one look and says, 'Leave this house.' Helgi doesn't even get off the sofa. She spots the envelope in Eve's hand and she says, 'What do you say in this letter that takes an hour and a half? What do you write him? Do you apologize for what a bad wife you are? Do you apologize that he does not have any physical satisfaction from you? Do you apologize that you don't give him the things a man needs?' 'Shut your mouth, you stupid woman, and leave here immediately!' 'Do you apologize that you never give the man a blow job? Do you apologize that you don't know *how* to? Do you know who gives him a blow job? Helgi gives him a blow job!' 'I am calling the police!' 'Good. The police will arrest you. I will show the police—here, here is how she sucks him off, like the perfect lady, and they will put you in jail for fifty years!'

"When the police come, Helgi's still at it, still going strong —out on West Eleventh Street, telling the world. 'Does the wife give him the blow jobs? No. The Peasant gives him the blow jobs.'

"They take her down to the precinct station, book her—drunk and disorderly conduct, trespassing—and Eve is back in the smoke-filled living room and she's hysterical and she doesn't know what to do next, and then she sees that two of her enamel boxes are missing. She has a beautiful collection of tiny enamel boxes on a side table. Two of them are gone and she calls the police station. 'Check her,' she says, 'there are things missing.' They look in Helgi's handbag. Sure enough, there they are, the two boxes and also Eve Frame's monogrammed silver lighter. It turned out that she'd stolen one from our house too. We never knew where it had gone and I went around saying, 'Where the hell is that lighter?' and then when Helgi wound up at the precinct station, I figured it out.

"I was the one who bailed her out. The phone call she made from the station after they booked her was to our house, to Ira, but I was the one who went there and got her. I drove her up to the Bronx, and on the drive I got the drunken tirade about the rich bitch not pushing her around anymore. Back home, I told Ira the whole story. I told him he'd been waiting all his life for the class war to break out, and guess where it happened? In his living room. He'd explained to Helgi how Marx had urged the proletariat to wrest the wealth from the bourgeoisie, and that was exactly what she'd set out to do.

"The first thing Eve does, after calling the cops about the theft, is to call Katrina. Katrina speeds over from their townhouse, and before the day is out, everything inside Ira's desk finds its way into Katrina's hands and from her hands into Bryden's hands and from there into his column and from there onto the front page of every New York newspaper. In her book Eve would claim that she was the one who broke into the mahogany desk up in Ira's study and found his letters from O'Day and his diary books where he'd recorded the names and serial numbers, the names and home addresses of every Marxist whom he had met in the service. She was much celebrated for this in the patriotic press. But that break-in, I believe, was Eve boasting, performing again, pretending to be the patriots' heroine—Eve boasting and maybe simultaneously protecting the integrity of Katrina Van Tassel Grant, who would not have hesitated to break into anything in order to preserve American democracy but whose husband was then planning his first campaign for the House of Representatives.

"There in 'Grant's Grapevine,' in Ira's writing, are Ira's subversive thoughts, recorded in a secret diary while he was purportedly serving overseas as a loyal sergeant in the U.S. Army. 'The papers and censor and such have distorted the news of Poland, thus creating a wedge between us and Russia. Russia was and is willing to compromise but it has not been presented so by our papers. Churchill directly advocates a total reactionary Poland.' 'Russia requests independence for all colonial peoples. The rest just emphasize self-government plus trusteeships.' 'British cabinet dissolves. Good. Now Churchill's policy of anti-Russia and of status quo may never materialize.'

"That's it. There it is. Dynamite that so terrifies the sponsor and the network that by the end of the week 'Redhot Iron' is finished and so is *The Free and the Brave.* So are some thirty others whose names are down in Ira's diaries. In time, so am I.

"Now, since long before Ira's troubles began my union activities had made me public enemy number one to our superintendent of schools, maybe the school board would have found a way to get me labeled a Communist and fired without the help of Eve's heroism. It was only a matter of time, with or without her assistance, until Ira and his radio program would have gone under, and so maybe nothing that happened to any of us required that she first give that stuff to Katrina. Still, it's instructive to think about what exactly Eve did in falling prey to the Grants and delivering Ira whole to his worst enemies."

Once more, we were together in eighth-period English, with Mr. Ringold perched at the edge of his desk, wearing the tan glen-plaid suit that he'd bought on Broad Street with his army separation pay—at the American Shop's sale for returning GIs —and that, throughout my high school years, he alternated with his other American Shop suit, a gray double-breasted sharkskin. In one hand he would be hefting the blackboard eraser that he wouldn't hesitate to hurl at the head of a student whose answer to a question did not meet his minimum daily requirement for mental alertness, while with the other hand he would regularly cut the air, enumerating dramatically each of the points to be remembered for the test.

"It demonstrates," he told me, "that when you decide to contribute your personal problem to an ideology's agenda, everything that is personal is squeezed out and discarded and all that remains is what is useful to the ideology. In this case, a woman contributes her husband and their marital difficulties to the cause of zealous anti-Communism. Essentially what Eve contributes is an incompatibility that she herself couldn't resolve from day one between Sylphid and Ira. A standard difficulty between stepchild and stepparent, even if somewhat intensified in the Eve Frame household. Everything that Ira was with Eve otherwise—good husband, bad husband, kind man, harsh man, understanding man, stupid man, faithful man, unfaithful man—everything that constitutes marital effort and marital error, everything that is a consequence of marriage's having nothing in common with a dream—is squeezed out, and what is left is what the ideology can make use of.

"Afterward the wife, if she is so inclined (and maybe Eve was and maybe she wasn't), can protest, 'No, no, it wasn't like that. You don't understand. He wasn't only what you are saying he was. He wasn't, with me, at all what you are saying he was. With me he could also be this, he could also be that.' Afterward an informer like Eve may realize that it's not only what she said that's responsible for the bizarre distortion of him that she reads in the press; it's also all that she left out—that she deliberately left out. But by then it's too late. By then the ideology has no time for her because it no longer has a *use* for her. 'This? That?' replies the ideology. 'What do we care about This and That? What do we care about the daughter? She is just more of that flabby mass that is life. Get her out of our way. All we need from you is what advances the righteous cause. Another Communist dragon to be slain! Another example of their treachery!'

"As for Pamela's panicking—"

But it was after eleven, and I reminded Murray, whose course at the college had finished earlier that day—and whose evening's narration seemed to me to have reached its pedagogical crescendo—that he was due to take the bus down to New York the following morning and that perhaps it was time for me to drive him back to the Athena dormitory.

"I could listen and listen," I told him, "but maybe you should get some sleep. In the history of storytelling stamina, you've already taken the title from Scheherazade. We've been sitting out here for six nights."

"I'm fine," he said.

"You're not getting tired? Cold?"

"It's beautiful out here. No, I'm not cold. It's warm, it's lovely. The crickets are counting, the frogs are grunting, the fireflies are inspired, and I haven't had occasion to go on like this since I was running the teachers' union. Look. The moon. It's orange. The perfect setting for peeling back the skin of the years."

"That it is," I said. "You have a choice up on this mountain: either you can lose contact with history, as I sometimes choose to, or mentally you can do what you're doing—by the light of the moon, for hours on end, work to regain possession of it."

"All those antagonisms," Murray said, "and then the torrent of betrayal. Every soul its own betrayal factory. For whatever reason: survival, excitement, advancement, idealism. For the sake of the damage that can be done, the pain that can be inflicted. For the cruelty in it. For the *pleasure* in it. The pleasure of manifesting one's latent power. The pleasure of dominating others, of destroying people who are your enemies. You're surprising them. Isn't that the pleasure of betrayal? The pleasure of tricking somebody. It's a way to pay people back for a feeling of inferiority they arouse in you, of being put down by them, a feeling of frustration in your relationship with them. Their very existence may be humiliating to you, either because you aren't what they are or because they aren't what you are. And so you give them their comeuppance.

"Of course there are those who betray because they have no choice. I read a book by a Russian scientist who, in the Stalin years, betrayed his best friend to the secret police. He was under heavy interrogation, terrible physical torture for six months—at which point he said, 'Look, I cannot resist any longer, so please tell me what you want. Whatever you give me I will sign.'

"He signed whatever they wanted him to sign. He was himself sentenced to life in prison. Without parole. After fourteen years, in the sixties, when things changed, he was released and he wrote this book. He says that he betrayed his best friend for two reasons: because he was not able to resist the torture and because he knew that it didn't matter, that the result of the trial was already established. What he said or didn't say would make no difference. If he didn't say it, another tortured person would. He knew his friend, whom he loved to the end, would despise him, but under brutal torture a normal human being cannot resist. Heroism is a human exception. A person who lives a normal life, which is made up of twenty thousand little compromises every day, is untrained to suddenly not compromise at all, let alone to withstand torture.

"For some people it takes six months of torture to make them weak. And some start off with an advantage: they are already weak. They are people who know only how to give in. With a person like that, you just say, 'Do it,' and they do it. It happens so rapidly they do not even know it is a betrayal. Because they do what they are asked to do, it seems okay. And by the time it sinks in, it's too late: they have betrayed.

"There was an article in the paper not long ago about a man in East Germany who informed on his wife for twenty years. They found documents about him in the files of the East German secret police after the Berlin Wall came down. The wife had a professional position and the police wanted to follow her and the husband was the informer. She didn't know anything about it. She's found out only since they've opened the files. For twenty years it went on. They had kids, they had in-laws, they threw parties, they paid bills, they had operations, they made love, they didn't make love, they went to the seashore in the summertime and bathed in the sea, and all this time he was informing. He was a lawyer. Smart, very well read, even wrote poetry. They gave him a code name, he signed an agreement, and he had weekly meetings with an officer, not at police headquarters but at a special apartment, a private apartment. They told him, 'You are a lawyer, and we need your help,' and he was weak and he signed. He had a father he supported. His father had a terrible enfeebling disease. They told him that if he helped them out they would take good care of his father, whom he loved. It often works that way. Your father is sick, or your mother, or your sister, and they ask you to help and so, keeping uppermost in mind your ill father, you justify the betrayal and sign the agreement.

"To me it seems likely that more acts of personal betrayal were tellingly perpetrated in America in the decade after the war—say, between '46 and '56—than in any other period in our history. This nasty thing that Eve Frame did was typical of lots of nasty things people did in those years, either because they had to or because they felt they had to. Eve's behavior fell well within the routine informer practices of the era. When before had betrayal ever been so destigmatized and rewarded in this country? It was everywhere during those years, the accessible transgression, the *permissible* transgression that any American could commit. Not only does the pleasure of betrayal replace the prohibition, but you transgress without giving up your moral authority. You retain your purity at the same time as you are patriotically betraying—at the same time as you are realizing a satisfaction that verges on the sexual with its ambiguous components of pleasure and weakness, of aggression and shame: the satisfaction of undermining. Undermining sweethearts. Undermining rivals. Undermining friends. Betrayal is in this same zone of perverse and illicit and fragmented pleasure. An interesting, manipulative, underground type of pleasure in which there is much that a human being finds appealing.

"There are even those who have the brilliance of mind to practice the game of betrayal for itself alone. Without any self-interest. Purely to entertain themselves. It's what Coleridge was probably getting at by describing Iago's betrayal of Othello as 'a motiveless malignity.' Generally, however, I would say there is a motive that provokes the vicious energies and brings *out* the malignity.

"The only hitch is that in the halcyon days of the Cold War, turning somebody in to the authorities as a Soviet spy could lead right to the chair. Eve, after all, wasn't turning Ira in to the FBI as a bad husband who fucked his masseuse. Betrayal is an inescapable component of living—who doesn't betray?—but to confuse the most heinous public act of betrayal, treason, with every other form of betrayal was not a good idea in 1951. Treason, unlike adultery, is a capital offense, so reckless exaggeration and thoughtless imprecision and false accusation, even just the seemingly genteel game of naming names—well, the results could be dire in those dark days when our Soviet allies had betrayed us by staying in Eastern Europe and exploding an atomic bomb and our Chinese allies had betrayed us by making a Communist revolution and throwing out Chiang Kai-shek.

Joseph Stalin and Mao Tse-tung: there was the moral excuse for it all.

"The lying. A river of lies. Translating the truth into a lie. Translating one lie into another lie. The *competence* people display in their lying. The *skill*. Carefully sizing up the situation and then, with a calm voice and a straight face, delivering the most productive lie. Should they speak even the *partial* truth, nine times out of ten it's in *behalf* of a lie. Nathan, I've never had a chance to tell this story to anyone this way, at such length. I've never told it before and I won't again. I'd like to tell it right. To the end."

"Why?"

"I'm the only person still living who knows Ira's story, you're the only person still living who cares about it. That's why: because everyone else is dead." Laughing, he said, "My last task. To file Ira's story with Nathan Zuckerman."

"I don't know what I can do with it," I said.

"That's not my responsibility. My responsibility is to tell it to you. You and Ira meant a lot to each other."

"Then go ahead. How did it end?"

"Pamela," he said. "Pamela Solomon. Pamela panicked. When she learned from Sylphid that Eve had broken into Ira's desk. She thought what people seem generally to think when they first get wind of someone else's catastrophe: how does this affect me? So-and-So in my office has a brain tumor? That means I have to take inventory alone. So-and-So from next door went down on that plane? He died in that crash? No. It can't be. He was coming over on Saturday to fix our garbage disposal.

"There was a photograph that Ira had taken of Pamela at the shack. A photograph of her in her bathing suit, by the pond. Pamela was afraid (mistakenly) that the picture was in the desk, along with all the Communist stuff, and that Eve had seen it, or that, if it wasn't there, Ira was going to go to Eve and show it to her, stick it in her face and say, 'Look!' Then what would happen? Eve would be furious and call her a hussy and throw her out of the house. And what would *Sylphid* think of Pamela? What would Sylphid *do*? And what if Pamela was deported? That was the worst possibility of all. Pamela was a foreigner in America—what if her name got dragged into Ira's Communist mess, and it wound up in the papers and she was deported? What if Eve made *sure* she was deported, for trying to steal her husband? Goodbye, bohemia. Back to all that suffocating English propriety.

"Pamela wasn't necessarily wrong in her appraisal of the danger to her of Ira's Communist mess and of the mood of the country. The atmosphere of accusation, threat, and punishment was everywhere. To a foreigner particularly, it looked like a democratic pogrom full of terror. There was enough danger around to justify Pamela's fear. In that political climate, those were reasonable fears. And so, in response to her fears, Pamela brought to bear upon the predicament all her considerable intelligence and commonsense realism. Ira was right to have spotted her for a quick-witted and lucid young woman who knew her mind and did what she wanted.

"Pamela went to Eve and told her that one summer day two years back she'd run into Ira in the Village. He was in the station wagon, on his way to the country, and he told her Eve was already there and asked why she didn't hop in and come out to spend the day. It was so hot and awful that she didn't bother to think things through. 'Okay,' she said, 'I'll go get my bathing suit,' and he waited for her and they drove out to Zinc Town, and when they arrived she discovered that Eve *wasn't* there. She tried to be agreeable and to believe whatever excuse he made and even got into her suit and went for a swim with him. That's when he took the photograph and tried to seduce her. She burst into tears, fought him off, told him what she thought of him and what he was doing to Eve, and then she got the next train back to New York. Because she didn't want to make trouble for herself, she had kept his sexual advances secret. Her fear was that if she didn't, everybody would blame her and think she was a slut just for having got into the car with him. People would call her all kinds of names for letting him take that picture. Nobody would even listen to her side of the story. He would have crushed her with every conceivable lie had she dared expose his treachery by telling the truth. But now that she understood the *scope* of his treachery, she couldn't, in good conscience, remain silent.

"What happens next is that one afternoon, after my last class, I get to my office and there's my brother waiting for me. He's in the corridor, he's signing his autograph for a couple of teachers who've spotted him, and I unlock my door and he comes into the office, and he throws on my desk an envelope with 'Ira' written on it. The return address is the *Daily Worker*. Inside is a second envelope, this one's addressed to 'Iron Rinn.' In Eve's handwriting. It's her blue vellum stationery. The office manager at the *Worker* was a friend of Ira's, and he'd driven all the way out to Zinc Town to deliver it to him.

"It seems that the day after Pamela went to Eve with her story, Eve does the strongest thing she can think of, for the time being the strongest punch she can throw. She gets all dressed up in her lynx jacket and a million-dollar black velvet dream of a dress with white lace trim and her best open-toed black shoes, and she puts on one of her stylish black veiled felt hats, and marches over, not to '21' for lunch with Katrina, but to the *Daily Worker* office. The *Worker* was down on University Place, only a few blocks from West Eleventh Street. Eve takes the elevator to the fifth floor and demands to see the editor. She's led into his office, where she removes the letter from her lynx muff and places it on his desk. 'For the martyred hero of the Bolshevik revolution,' she says, 'for the people's artist and mankind's last best hope,' and turns and walks out. Racked and timorous as she was in the face of any opposition, she could also be impressively imperious when she was tanked up with righteous resentment and having one of her delusionary grande-dame days. She was capable of these transformations—and she didn't go in for half measures, either. At whichever end of the emotional rainbow, the excesses could be persuasive.

"The office manager was given the letter, and he got in his car and he carried it out to Ira. Ira had been living alone in Zinc Town since he'd been fired. Every week he'd drive to New York to confer with lawyers—he was going to sue the network, sue the sponsor, sue *Red Channels*. In the city he'd stop by and visit Artie Sokolow, who'd had his first heart attack and was confined to bed at home on the Upper West Side. Then he'd come to Newark to see us. But by and large Ira was out at the shack, infuriated, brooding, devastated, obsessed, making dinner for his neighbor who'd been in the mining ac-cident, Ray Svecz, eating with him and sounding off about his case to this guy who was fifty-one percent not there.

"It was later on the day that Eve's letter was delivered to

him that Ira shows up at my office, and I read it. It's in my file
with the rest of Ira's papers; I can't do it justice by paraphrasing
it. Three pages long. Scorchingly written. Obviously zipped
off in one draft and perfect. Real bite to it, a ferocious document, and yet very competently done. Under the pressure of
her rage, and on monogrammed blue note paper, Eve was quite
the neo-classicist. I wouldn't have been surprised had that
lambasting of him concluded in a fanfare of heroic couplets.

"Remember Hamlet cursing out Claudius? The passage in
the second act, just after the player-king gives his speech about
Priam's slaughter? It's in the middle of the monologue that
begins 'O what a rogue and peasant slave am I!' 'Bloody, bawdy
villain!' Hamlet says. 'Remorseless, treacherous, lecherous, kind-
less villain! / O! Vengeance!' Well, the gist of Eve's letter is
more or less along those lines: You know what Pamela means
to me, I confided one night to you, and to you alone, all that
Pamela means to me. 'An inferiority complex.' That's what Eve
described as Pamela's problem. A girl with an inferiority complex, far from home and country and family, Eve's ward, Eve's
responsibility to look after and protect, and yet, just as he ugli-
fied everything he had ever laid his hands on, he cunningly
undertook to turn a girl of Pamela Solomon's background into
a striptease artist like Miss Donna Jones. To lure Pamela out to
that isolated hellhole under false pretenses, to salivate like a
pervert over her picture in her bathing suit, to fasten those
gorilla paws of his on her defenseless body—for the sheer
pleasure of it, to turn Pamela into a common whore, and to
humiliate Sylphid and herself in the most sadistic way he could
contrive.

"But this time, she told him, you went too far. I remember
your telling me, she said, how, at the feet of the great O'Day,
you had marveled at Machiavelli's *The Prince*. Now I understand what you learned from *The Prince*. I understand why my
friends have been trying for years to convince me that in every
last thing you say or do, you are, to the letter, a ruthless, depraved Machiavellian who cares not at all for right or wrong
but worships only success. You try to force to have sex with
you this lovely, talented young woman struggling with an inferiority complex. Why didn't you try having sex with me as a
means, perhaps, of expressing love? When we met, you were

living alone on the Lower East Side in the squalid arms of your beloved lumpenproletariat. I gave you a beautiful house full of books and music and art. I provided you with a handsome study of your own and helped you to build up your library. I introduced you to the most interesting, intelligent, talented people in Manhattan, offered you entrée into a social world such as you'd never dreamed of for yourself. As best I could, I tried to give you a family. Yes, I have a demanding daughter. I have a troubled daughter. I know that. Well, life is full of demands. For a responsible adult, life *is* demands . . . On and on in that vein, uphill all the way, philosophical, mature, sensible, wholeheartedly rational—until she ended with the threat:

"Since you may recall that your paragon brother wouldn't allow me to talk to you or to write to you when you were hiding in his house, I went through your comrades to reach you. The Communist Party would appear to have more access to you—and your heart, such as it is—than anyone. You *are* Machiavelli, the quintessential artist of control. Well, my dear Machiavelli, since you don't seem to have understood yet the consequences of anything you have ever done to another human being in order to have your way, it may be time you were taught.

"Nathan, remember the chair in my office, beside my desk —the hot seat? Where you kids sat and sweated while I used to go over your compositions? That's where Ira sat while I went over that letter. I asked, 'Is it true you made a pass at this girl?' 'For six months I had an affair with this girl.' 'You fucked her.' 'Many times, Murray. I thought she was in love with me. I'm astonished that she could do this.' 'Are you now?' 'I was in love with her. I wanted to marry her and have a family with her.' 'Oh, it gets better. You don't think, do you, Ira? You act. You act, and that's it. You shout, you fuck, you act. For six months you fucked her daughter's best friend. Her surrogate daughter. Her *ward.* And now something happened and you're "astonished."' 'I loved her.' 'Speak English. You loved fucking her.' 'You don't understand. She'd come to the shack. I was *mad* for her. I *am* astonished. I am absolutely astonished by what she has done!' 'By what *she* has done.' 'She betrays me to my wife —and then she lies in the process!' 'Yes? So? Where's the astonishing part? You've got a problem here. You've got a big problem with that wife.' 'Do I? What's she going to do? She did it already, with her pals the Grants. I'm fired already. I'm out on my ass. She's making it into a sexual thing, you see, and it wasn't that. Pamela knows that isn't what it was.' 'Well, that's what it is now. You're caught, and your wife is promising *new* consequences. What will those be, do you think?' 'Nothing. There's nothing left. This stupidity,' he said, waving the letter at me, 'a letter hand-delivered by her to the *Worker*. *This* is the consequence. Listen to me. I never did a thing Pamela didn't want. And when she didn't want me anymore, it killed me. I dreamed of a girl like this all my life. It *killed* me. But I did it. I walked down those stairs and out into the street and I left her alone. I never bothered her again.' 'Well,' I said, 'be that as it may, honorable as you were in gentlemanly taking your leave of six months of fancy fucking with your wife's surrogate daughter, you're in a bit of hot water now, my friend.' 'No, it's *Pamela* who's in hot water!' 'Yes? You going to *act* again? You going to act once *again* without thinking? No. I'm not going to let you.'

"And I didn't let him, and he didn't do anything. Now, how much impetus writing this letter gave Eve to rush into the book is hard to say. But if Eve was in search of a motive to really go all out and do the big irrational thing that she'd been born to do, the stuff she got from Pamela couldn't have hurt. You would think that having married a cipher like Mueller, followed by a homosexual like Pennington, followed by a sharpie like Freedman, followed by a Communist like Ira, she'd have fulfilled whatever obligation she had to the forces of unreason. You would think she might have worked off the worst of 'How-could-you-do-this-to-me?' just by going over to the *Worker* in her lynx jacket with the matching muff. But no, it was Eve's destiny always to take her irrationality to greater and greater heights—and this is where the Grants come in again.

"It was the Grants who wrote that book. It was *double* ghostwritten. It was Bryden's name they used on the jacket—'as told to Bryden Grant'—because that was almost as good as having Winchell's name on the jacket, but it's the talent of the pair of them that shines through. What did Eve Frame know about Communism? There were Communists at the Wallace rallies she'd gone to with Ira. There were Communists on *The Free and the Brave*, people who came to their house and had dinner and were at all the soirées. This little unit of people involved with the show was very interested in controlling as much of it as possible. There was the secrecy, the conspiratorial edge— hiring like-minded people, influencing the ideological bias of the script however they could. Ira would sit in his study with Artie Sokolow and try to force into the script every corny party cliché, every so-called progressive sentiment they could get away with, manipulating the script to stick whatever ideological junk they thought of as Communist content into any historical context whatsoever. They imagined they were going to influence public thinking. *The writer must not only observe and describe but participate in the struggle. The non-Marxist writer betrays the objective reality; the Marxist one contributes to its transformation. The party's gift to the writer is the only right and true worldview.* They believed all that. Crapola. Propaganda. But crapola is not forbidden by the Constitution. And the radio in those days was full of it. *Gangbusters. Your FBI.* Kate Smith singing 'God Bless America.' Even your hero Corwin— propagandist for an idealized American democracy. In the end it wasn't so different. They weren't espionage agents, Ira Ringold and Arthur Sokolow. They were publicity agents. There is a distinction. These guys were cheap propagandists, against which the only laws are aesthetic, laws of literary taste.

"Then there was the union, AFTRA, the battle for control of the union. A lot of shouting, terrible infighting, but that was nationwide. In my union, in virtually every union, it was right wingers and left wingers, liberals and Communists struggling for control. Ira was a member of the union executive board, he was on the phone with people, God knows he could shout. Sure, things were said in her presence. And what Ira said, he meant. The party was no debating society to Ira. It was not a discussion club. It wasn't the Civil Liberties Union. What does it mean, 'a revolution'? It means a revolution. He took the rhetoric seriously. You can't call yourself a revolutionary and not be serious in your commitment. It was not something fake. It was something genuine. He took the Soviet Union seriously. At AFTRA, Ira meant business.

"Now, I never saw Ira at most of this stuff. I'm sure *you* never saw Ira at most of this stuff. But Eve never saw *anything* of this stuff. She was oblivious to *all* of it. Actuality wasn't something that mattered to Eve. The woman's mind was rarely on what the people around her were saying. She was a complete stranger to the business of life. It was too coarse for her. Her mind was never on Communism or anti-Communism. Her mind was never on anything present, except when Sylphid was present.

" 'As told to' meant that the whole malevolent story was dreamed up by the Grants. And dreamed up not at all for Eve's sake, and not merely to destroy Ira, much as Katrina and Bryden hated his guts. The consequences for Ira were part of their fun but largely beside the point. The Grants dreamed it all up for Bryden to ride his way into the House on the issue of Communism in broadcasting.

"That writing. That *Journal-American* prose. Plus Katrina's syntax. Plus Katrina's sensibility. *Her* fingerprints are all over the thing. I knew right off that Eve hadn't written it, because Eve couldn't write that badly. Eve was too literate and too well read. Why did she allow the Grants to write her book? Because systematically she made herself the slave of just about everyone. Because what the strong are capable of is appalling, and what the weak are capable of is also appalling. It's all appalling.

"*I Married a Communist* came out in March of '52, when Grant had already announced his candidacy, and then in November, in the Eisenhower landslide, he was swept into the House as representative from New York's Twenty-ninth District. He would have been elected anyway. That radio show of theirs was a big Saturday morning favorite, and for years he had that column, and he had Ham Fish behind him, and he was a Grant, after all, the descendant of a U.S. president. Still, I doubt that Joe McCarthy himself would have traveled up to Dutchess County to appear by his side if it hadn't been for all the big-shot Reds 'Grant's Grapevine' had helped to expose and root out of the networks. Everyone was in Poughkeepsie campaigning for him. Westbrook Pegler was up there. All those Hearst columnists were his pals. All the haters of FDR who'd found in the Communist smear a way to drive the Democrats into the ground. Either Eve had no idea what she was being used for by the Grants or, more likely, she knew but didn't care, because the experience of being an attacker made her feel so strong and brave, striking back at the monsters at last.

"Yet knowing Ira as she did, how could she publish this book and not expect him to do something? This wasn't a three-page letter to Zinc Town. This was a big national best-seller that made a bang. The thing had all the ingredients to become a best-seller: Eve was famous, Grant was famous, Communism was *the* international peril. Ira was himself less famous than either of them, and though the book would guarantee that he would never work in radio again and that his accidental career was over, for the five or six months the book was at the top of the charts, for that season, Ira was conspicuous as he'd never been before. In a single stroke Eve managed to depersonalize her own life while endowing the specter of Communism with a human face—her husband's. I married a Communist, I slept with a Communist, a Communist tormented my child, unsuspectingly America listened to a Communist, disguised as a patriot, on network radio. A wicked two-faced villain, the real names of real stars, a big Cold War backdrop—of course it became a best-seller. Her indictment of Ira was of the sort that could win a large public hearing in the fifties.

"And it didn't hurt to name all the other Jewish Bolsheviks affiliated with Ira's show. The Cold War paranoia had latent anti-Semitism as one of its sources, and so, under the moral guidance of the Grants—who themselves loved the ubiquitous troublemaking left-wing Jew just about as much as Richard Nixon did—Eve could transform a personal prejudice into a political weapon by confirming for Gentile America that, in New York as in Hollywood, in radio as in movies, the Communist under every rock was, nine times out of ten, a Jew to boot.

"But did she imagine that this openly aggressive hothead was going to do nothing in response? This guy who used to have these ferocious arguments at her dinner table, who used to storm around their living room shouting at people, who, after all, *was* a Communist, who knew what it was to take political action, who'd tenaciously gained control of his union, who'd managed to rewrite Sokolow's scripts, to bully a bully like Artie Sokolow—she thought he was now going to take *no* action? Didn't she know him at all? What about the portrait in her book? If he's Machiavelli, then he's Machiavelli. Everybody run for cover.

"I'm really angry, she thinks, I'm angry about Pamela and I'm angry about Helgi and I'm furious about the renovation of the shack and all the other crimes against Sylphid, and I'm going to get the attention of this lecherous, heartless Machiavellian bastard. Well, damn right she got his attention. But surely the obvious thing about getting Ira's attention by sticking a hot poker up his ass in public is that you're going to enrage him. People don't yield to that kind of shit cheerfully. People don't like seeing exposés on the best-seller list that falsely denounce them, and you wouldn't even have to be Ira Ringold to take umbrage. And to take action. Only that never occurs to her. The righteous resentment that fuels her project, the *blameless-ness* that fuels her project can't imagine anybody doing anything to her. All she has done is to settle the score. Ira did all the horrible things—she is merely coming back with her side of the story. She gets last licks, and the only consequences she imagines are consequences she deserves. It has to be that way—what did *she* do?

"That same self-blinding that led to so much pain with Pennington, with Freedman, with Sylphid, with Pamela, with the Grants, even with Helgi Pärn—in the end, that self-blinding was the worm that destroyed her. It's what the high school Shakespeare teacher calls the tragic flaw.

"A great cause had taken possession of Eve: her own. Her cause, presented in the grandiose guise of a selfless battle to save America from the Red tide. Everybody has a failed marriage—she herself has four of them. But she also has the need to be special. A star. She wants to show that she also is important, that she has a brain and that she has the power to fight. Who is this actor Iron Rinn? *I* am the actor! *I* am the one with the name, and I possess the *power* of the name! I am not this weak woman whom you can do anything you want to. I am a star, damn it! Mine isn't an ordinary failed marriage. It's a *star's* failed marriage! I didn't lose my husband because of the horrible trap I'm in with my daughter. I didn't lose my husband because of all those kneeling 'I implore you's.' I didn't lose my husband because of his drunken whore with the gold tooth. It has to be grander than that—and I must be blameless. The refusal to own up to what it is in the human dimension turns it into something melodramatic and false and sellable. I lost my husband to Communism.

"And what that book was really about, actually accomplishing, Eve hadn't the faintest idea. Why was Iron Rinn served up to the public as a dangerous Soviet espionage agent? To get another Republican elected to the House. To get Bryden Grant into the House and put Joe Martin into the speaker's chair.

"Grant was ultimately elected eleven times. A considerable personage in Congress. And Katrina became *the* Republican hostess of Washington, the sovereign of social authority throughout the Eisenhower years. For someone riddled with envy and conceit, no position in the world could have been more rewarding than deciding who sat across from Roy Cohn. In the hierarchical anxieties of the Washington dinner party, Katrina's capacity for rivalry, the sheer cannibal vigor of her taste for supremacy—for awarding and depriving the ruling class itself of their just desserts—found its . . . imperium, I think the word would be. That woman drew up an invitation list with the autocratic sadism of Caligula. *She* knew the enjoyment of humiliating the powerful. *She* sent a tremor or two through that capital. Under Eisenhower and again, later, under Bryden's mentor Nixon, Katrina straddled Washington society like fear itself.

"In '69, when there was that spurt of speculation that Nixon was going to find Grant a place in the White House, the congressman husband and the hostess-novelist wife made the cover of *Life*. No, Grant never got to be Haldeman, but at the end, he too was capsized by Watergate. Threw his lot in with Nixon and, in the face of all the evidence against his leader, defended him on the floor of the House right down to the morning of the resignation. That's what got Grant defeated in '74. But then, he'd been emulating Nixon from the start. Nixon had Alger Hiss, Grant had Iron Rinn. To catapult them into political eminence, each of them had a Soviet spy.

"I saw Katrina on C-SPAN at the Nixon funeral. Grant had died some years before and she's died since. She was my age, maybe a year or two older. But out there at the funeral at Yorba Linda, with the flag waving at half-mast among the palm trees, and Nixon's birthplace in the background, she was still our Katrina, white-haired and wizened but still very much a force for the good, chatting it up with Barbara Bush and Betty Ford and Nancy Reagan. Life seemed never to have forced her to acknowledge, let alone to surrender, a single one of her pretensions. Still wholeheartedly determined to be the national authority in rectitude, stringent in the extreme about the right thing's being done. Saw her talking there to Senator Dole, our other great moral beacon. She didn't look to me to have relinquished one bit the idea that every word she spoke was of the utmost importance. Still oblivious to the introspection of silence. Still the righteous watchdog over everyone else's integrity. And unrepentant. Divinely unrepentant and brandishing that preposterous self-image. For stupidity, you know, there is no cure. The woman is the very embodiment of moral ambition, and the perniciousness of it, and the folly of it.

"All that mattered to the Grants was how to make Ira serve their cause. And what *was* their cause? America? Democracy? If ever patriotism was a pretext for self-seeking, for self-devotion, for self-adoration . . . You know, we learn from Shakespeare that in telling a story you cannot relax your imaginative sympathy for any character. But I am not Shakespeare, and I still despise that hatchet man and his hatchet wife for what they did to my brother—and did so effortlessly, employing Eve the way you do a dog to fetch the paper from the front porch. Remember what Gloucester says of old Lear? 'The king is in high rage.' I came down with a bad case of high rage myself when I spotted Katrina Van Tassel at Yorba Linda. I told myself, She's nothing, nobody, a bit player. In the vast history of twentieth-century ideological malevolence, she's played a clownish walk-on role and no more. But it was still barely endurable for me to watch her.

"But the whole funeral of our thirty-seventh president was barely endurable. The Marine Band and Chorus performing all the songs designed to shut down people's thinking and produce a trance state: 'Hail to the Chief,' 'America,' 'You're a Grand Old Flag,' 'The Battle Hymn of the Republic,' and, to be sure, that most rousing of all those drugs that make everybody momentarily forget everything, the national narcotic, 'The Star-Spangled Banner.' Nothing like the elevating remarks of Billy Graham, a flag-draped casket, and a team of interracial pallbearing servicemen—and the whole thing topped off by 'The Star-Spangled Banner,' followed hard upon by a twenty-one-gun salute and 'Taps'—to induce catalepsy in the multitude.

"Then the realists take command, the connoisseurs of deal making and deal breaking, masters of the most shameless ways of undoing an opponent, those for whom moral concerns must always come last, uttering all the well-known, unreal, sham-ridden cant about everything but the dead man's real passions. Clinton exalting Nixon for his 'remarkable journey' and, under the spell of his own sincerity, expressing hushed gratitude for all the 'wise counsel' Nixon had given him. Governor Pete Wilson assuring everyone that when most people think of Richard Nixon, they think of his 'towering intellect.' Dole and his flood of lachrymose clichés. 'Doctor' Kissinger, high-minded, profound, speaking in his most puffed-up unegoistical mode— and with all the cold authority of that voice dipped in sludge— quotes no less prestigious a tribute than Hamlet's for his murdered father to describe 'our gallant friend.' 'He was a man, take him for all and all, I shall not look upon his like again.' Literature is not a primary reality but a kind of expensive upholstery to a sage himself so plumply upholstered, and so he has no idea of the equivocating context in which Hamlet speaks of the unequaled king. But then who, sitting there under the tremendous pressure of sustaining a straight face while watching the enactment of the Final Cover-up, is going to catch the court Jew in a cultural gaffe when he invokes an inappropriate masterpiece? Who is there to advise him that it's not Hamlet on his father he ought to be quoting but Hamlet on his uncle, Claudius, Hamlet on the conduct of the new king, his father's usurping murderer? Who there at Yorba Linda dares to call out, 'Hey, Doctor—quote *this*: "Foul deeds will rise / Though all the earth o'erwhelm them, to men's eyes"?

"Who? Gerald Ford? Gerald Ford. I don't ever remember seeing Gerald Ford looking so focused before, so charged with intelligence as he clearly was on that hallowed ground. Ronald Reagan snapping the uniformed honor guard his famous salute, that salute of his that was *always* half meshugeh. Bob Hope seated next to James Baker. The Iran-Contra arms dealer Adnan Khashoggi seated next to Donald Nixon. The burglar G. Gordon

Liddy there with his arrogant shaved head. The most disgraced of vice presidents, Spiro Agnew, there with his conscienceless Mob face. The most winning of vice presidents, sparkly Dan Quayle, looking as lucid as a button. The heroic effort made by that poor fellow: always staging intelligence and always failing. All of them mourning platitudinously together in the California sunshine and the lovely breeze: the indicted and the unindicted, the convicted and the unconvicted, and, his towering intellect at last at rest in a star-spangled coffin, no longer grappling and questing for no-holds-barred power, the man who turned a whole country's morale inside out, the generator of an enormous national disaster, the first and only president of the United States of America to have gained from a hand-picked successor a full and unconditional pardon for all the breaking and entering he committed while in office.

"And Van Tassel Grant, adored widow of Bryden, *that* selfless public servant, reveling in her importance and jabbering away. All through the service, the mouth of reckless malice jabbering on and on in her televised grief over our great national loss. Too bad she wasn't born in China instead of the USA. Here she had to settle for being a best-selling novelist and a famous radio personality and a top-drawer Washington hostess. There she could have run Mao's Cultural Revolution.

"In my ninety years I've witnessed two sensationally hilarious funerals, Nathan. Present at the first as a thirteen-year-old, and the second I saw on TV just three years ago, at the age of eighty-seven. Two funerals that have more or less bracketed my conscious life. They aren't mysterious events. They don't require a genius to ferret out their meaning. They are just natural human events that reveal as plainly as Daumier did the unique markings of the species, the thousand and one dualities that twist its nature into the human knot. The first was Mr. Russomanno's funeral for the canary, when the cobbler got hold of a casket and pallbearers and a horse-drawn hearse and majestically buried his beloved Jimmy—and my kid brother broke my nose. The second was when they buried Richard Milhous Nixon with a twenty-one-gun salute. I only wish the Italians from the old First Ward could have been out there at Yorba Linda with Dr. Kissinger and Billy Graham. *They* would have known how to enjoy the spectacle. They would have hurled themselves on the ground with laughter when they heard what those two guys were up to, the indignities to which they descended to dignify that glaringly impure soul.

"And had Ira been alive to hear them, he would have gone nuts all over again at the world getting everything wrong."

8

"ALL his ranting Ira now directed at himself. How could this farce have wrecked his life? Everything to the side of the main thing, all the peripheral stuff of existence that Comrade O'Day had warned him against. Home. Marriage. Family. Mistresses. Adultery. All the bourgeois shit! Why hadn't he lived like O'Day? Why hadn't he gone to prostitutes like O'Day? *Real* prostitutes, trustworthy professionals who understand the rules, and not blabbermouth amateurs like his Estonian masseuse.

"The recriminations started to hound him. He should never have left O'Day, have left the UE shop at the record factory, have come to New York, married Eve Frame, grandiosely conceived of himself as this Mr. Iron Rinn. In Ira's own estimation he should never have done *any* of the living he did once he left the Midwest. He shouldn't have had a human being's appetite for experience or a human being's inability to read the future or a human being's propensity for making mistakes. He shouldn't have allowed himself to pursue a single one of a virile and ambitious man's worldly goals. Being a Communist laborer dwelling alone in a room in East Chicago under a sixty-watt bulb—that was now the ascetic height from which he had fallen into hell.

"The pile-on of humiliation, that was the key to it. It wasn't as though a book had been thrown at him—the book was a bomb that had been thrown at him. McCarthy, you see, would have the two hundred or three hundred or four hundred Communists on his nonexistent lists, but allegorically one person would have to stand for them all. Alger Hiss is the biggest example. Three years after Hiss, Ira became another. What's more, Hiss to the average person was still the State Department and Yalta, stuff far, far away from the ordinary Joe, while Ira's was popular-culture Communism. To the confused popular imagination, this was the democratic Communist. This was Abe Lincoln. It was very easy to grasp: Abe Lincoln as the villainous representative of a foreign power, Abe Lincoln as America's greatest twentieth-century traitor. Ira became the personification of Communism, the personalized Communist for the nation: Iron Rinn was Everyman's Communist traitor in ways that Alger Hiss could never be.

"Here's this giant who was pretty damn strong, in many ways pretty damn insensitive, but the calumny heaped upon him he finally couldn't take. Giants get felled too. He knew he couldn't hide from it and he thought, as time passed, he could never wait it out. He began to think that now that the lid was off there would always be something coming at him from somewhere. The giant couldn't find anything effectual to deal with it, and that's when he caved in.

"I went up and got him, and he lived with us until we couldn't handle the situation anymore, and I put him in the hospital in New York. He sat in that chair for the first month, rubbing his knees and rubbing his elbows and holding his ribs where they ached, but otherwise lifeless, staring into his lap and wishing he were dead. I'd go to see him and he would barely speak. Every once in a while he'd say, 'All I wanted to do . . .' That was it. Never went any further, not out loud. That was all he said to me for weeks. A couple of times he muttered, 'To be like this . . .' 'I never intended . . .' But mostly it was 'All I wanted to do . . .'

"They didn't have much to help mental patients in those days. No pills other than a sedative. Ira wouldn't eat. He sat in that first unit—the Disturbed Unit, they called it—eight beds there and Ira in his robe and pajamas and slippers, looking more like Lincoln with each passing day. Gaunt, exhausted, wearing Abraham Lincoln's mask of sorrow. I would be visiting, sitting beside him holding his hand and thinking, If it weren't for that resemblance, none of this would have happened to him. If only he hadn't been responsible to his looks.

"It was four weeks before they moved him up to the Semi-Disturbed Unit, where the patients got dressed in their clothes, and they had recreational therapy. Some of them went off to play volleyball or to play basketball, though Ira couldn't because of his joint pain. He had been living for over a year with pain that was intractable, and maybe that undid him more than the calumny. Maybe the antagonist who destroyed Ira was physical pain, and the book would not have come close to defeating him if he hadn't been undermined by his health.

"The collapse was total. The hospital was awful. But we couldn't have kept him at the house. He would lie in Lorraine's room cursing himself and crying his heart out: O'Day told him, O'Day warned him, O'Day had known back on the docks in Iran . . . Doris sat beside Lorraine's bed and she held him in her arms and he wailed away. All of the force that was behind those tears. Awful. You don't realize how much plain old misery can be backed up inside a titanically defiant person who's been taking on the world and battling his own nature his whole life. That's what came pouring out of him: the whole damn struggle.

"Sometimes *I* felt terrified. I felt the way I felt in the war when we were under bombardment at the Bulge. Just *because* he was so big and arrogant you had the feeling that there was nothing to be done for him by anyone. I saw that long, gaunt face of his, distorted with desperation, with all that hopelessness, with *failure*, and I was myself in a panic.

"When I would get home from school I'd help him dress; every afternoon I'd force him to shave and I'd insist on his going for a walk with me down Bergen Street. Could any city street in America have been friendlier in those days? But Ira was surrounded by enemies. The marquee on the Park Theater frightened him, the salamis in Kartzman's window frightened him —Schachtman's candy store frightened him, with the newsstand out front. He was sure every paper had his story in it, weeks after the papers had finished having their fun with him. The *Journal-American* ran excerpts from Eve's book. The *Daily Mirror* had his kisser all over the front page. Even the stately *Times* couldn't resist. Ran a human-interest story about the suffering of the Sarah Bernhardt of the Airwaves, took all that crap about Russian espionage completely seriously.

"But that's what happens. Once the human tragedy has been completed, it gets turned over to the journalists to banalize into entertainment. Perhaps it's because the whole irrational frenzy burst right through our door and no newspaper's half-baked insinuating detail passed me by that I think of the McCarthy era as inaugurating the postwar triumph of gossip as the unifying credo of the world's oldest democratic republic. In Gossip We Trust. Gossip as gospel, the national faith. McCarthyism as the beginning not just of serious politics but of serious *everything* as entertainment to amuse the mass audience. McCarthyism as the first postwar flowering of the American unthinking that is now everywhere.

"McCarthy was never in the Communist business; if nobody else knew that, he did. The show-trial aspect of McCarthy's patriotic crusade was merely its theatrical form. Having cameras view it just gave it the false authenticity of real life. McCarthy understood better than any American politician before him that people whose job was to legislate could do far better for themselves by performing; McCarthy understood the entertainment value of disgrace and how to feed the pleasures of paranoia. He took us back to our origins, back to the seventeenth century and the stocks. That's how the country began: moral disgrace as public entertainment. McCarthy was an impresario, and the wilder the views, the more outrageous the charges, the greater the disorientation and the better the all-around fun. *Joe McCarthy's The Free and the Brave*—that was the show in which my brother was to play the biggest role of his life.

"When not just the New York papers but the Jersey papers, too, joined in—well, for Ira that was the killer. They dug up whomever Ira knew out in Sussex County and got them to talk. Farmers, oldsters, local nobodies the radio star had befriended, and they all had a story about Ira coming around to tell them about the evils of capitalism. He had that great geezer pal out in Zinc Town, the taxidermist, and Ira liked to go around and listen to the guy, and the papers went to the taxidermist and the taxidermist gave them an earful. Ira couldn't believe it. But this taxidermist allows how Ira had pulled the wool over his eyes until one day when Ira came in with some young kid and the two of them tried to turn him and his son against the Korean War. Spewing real venom against General Douglas MacArthur. Calling the U.S.A. every bad name in the book.

"The FBI had a field day with him. And with Ira's reputation up there. To stake you out, to ruin you in your community, to go to your neighbors and have them do you in . . . I have to tell you, Ira always suspected that it was the taxidermist who fingered *you*. You were with Ira, weren't you, at the taxidermy shop?"

"I was. Horace Bixton," I said. "Little tiny, humorous fellow. Gave me a deer toe for a present. I sat one morning watching a fox being skinned."

"Well, you paid for that deer toe. Watching 'em skin that fox cost you your Fulbright."

I started to laugh. "Did you say turning his *son* against the war too? The son was stone deaf. The son was deaf and he was dumb. He couldn't hear a goddamn thing."

"This is the McCarthy era—didn't matter. Ira had a neighbor down the road, a zinc miner who'd been in a bad mining accident and who used to work for him. Ira spent a lot of time listening to these guys complain about New Jersey Zinc and trying to turn them around about the system, and this particular guy who was his neighbor, who he used to feed all the time, was the one the taxidermist got to take down the license plate numbers of whoever stopped at Ira's shack."

"I met the guy who'd been in the accident. He ate with us," I said. "Ray. A rock fell on him and crushed his skull. Raymond Svecz. He'd been a POW. Ray used to do odd jobs for Ira."

"I guess Ray did odd jobs for everyone," Murray said. "He'd take down the license plate numbers of Ira's visitors and the taxidermist gave them to the FBI. The plates that turned up most often were mine, and that evidence they also used against me—that I visited my Communist-spy brother so much, sometimes even overnight. Only one guy up there stayed loyal to Ira. Tommy Minarek."

"I met Tommy."

"Charming old guy. Uneducated but an intelligent man. Had backbone. Ira took Lorraine out to the rock dump one day and Tommy gave her some stuff for free and he was all she talked about when she got home. After Tommy saw the news in the papers, he drove over to the shack and he marched straight in. 'If I had the guts,' he said to Ira, 'I woulda been a Communist myself.'

"Tommy was the one who rehabilitated Ira. It was Tommy who brought him out of his brooding and got him back into the world. Tommy had him sit right beside him out at the rock dump where he ran things so that people could see Ira there.

Tommy was somebody the town respected, and so over time, people up there forgave Ira for being a Communist. Not all of them, but most. The two of them sat at the rock dump talking for three, four years together, Tommy teaching Ira all he knew about minerals. Then Tommy had a stroke and died and left his cellar full of rocks to Ira, and Ira took over Tommy's job. And the town let him. Ira sat out there, hyper-inflammatory Ira rubbing his aching joints and muscles, and ran the Zinc Town rock dump till the day *he* died. In the sunshine, a summer day, selling minerals, keeled over dead."

I wondered if Ira ever bled himself of the resolve to be argumentative, contrary, defiant, to be illegitimate when necessary, or if that all still burned on in him while he sold Tommy's specimens out front of the rock dump, across the highway from the machine shop where they had the toilet. Burned on, more than likely; in Ira everything burned on. No one in this world had less talent for frustration than Ira or was worse at controlling his moods. The rage to take action—and selling kids fifty-cent bags of rocks instead. Sitting there till he died, wanting to be something entirely different, believing that by virtue of personal attributes (his size, his animus, the father he'd suffered) he had been *destined* to be something different. Furious to have no outlet for changing the world. The embitterment of that bondage. How he must have choked on it, employing now to destroy himself his inexhaustible capacity never to desist.

"Ira would come back from Bergen Street," Murray said, "from walking past Schachtman's newsstand, a worse wreck than when he'd left the house, and Lorraine couldn't take it. Seeing her great big uncle, with whom she'd sung the song of the common worker, 'Heave-ho, heave-ho'—seeing him humbled like that was too much for her, and so we had to put him into the hospital over in New York.

"He imagined he'd ruined O'Day. He was sure he had ruined everybody whose name and address were in those two little diaries Eve had turned over to Katrina, and he was right. But O'Day was still his idol, and those letters from O'Day that were quoted piecemeal in the papers after they showed up in her book—well, Ira was sure this was the end of O'Day, and the shame of it was awful.

"I tried to contact Johnny O'Day. I'd met the guy. I knew how close they'd been in the army. I remembered when Ira was his sidekick in Calumet City. I didn't like the man, I didn't like his ideas, I didn't like his blend of superiority and cunning, that moral pass he thought he'd been given as a Communist, but I couldn't believe that he was holding Ira responsible for what had happened. I believed that O'Day could take good care of himself, that he was strong and ruthless in his principled Communistic uncaringness, as Ira had turned out not to be. I wasn't wrong, either. Out of desperation, I figured that if anybody could bring Ira around, it would be O'Day.

"But I couldn't get a phone number. He wasn't listed any longer in Gary or Hammond or East Chicago or Calumet City or up in Chicago. When I wrote to the last address Ira had for him, the envelope came back marked 'No such person at this address.' I telephoned every union office in Chicago, I phoned left-wing bookstores, phoned every outfit I could think of, trying to hunt him down. Just when I'd given up, the phone at home rang one night, and it was him.

"What did I want? I told him where Ira was. I told him what Ira was like. I said that if he would be willing to come east on the weekend and go to the hospital and sit with Ira, just sit there with him, I would wire the money for the train and he could stay overnight in Newark with us. I didn't like doing it, but I was trying to entice him, and so I said, 'You mean a lot to Ira. He always wanted to be worthy of O'Day's admiration. I think you might be able to help him.'

"And then, in that quiet, explicit way of his, in the voice of one tough, unreachable son of a bitch with a single overriding relationship to life, he answered me. 'Look, Professor,' he told me, 'your brother tricked me damn good and proper. I always prided myself that I knew who is phony and who ain't. But this time I was fooled. The party, the meetings—all a cover for his personal ambition. Your brother used the party to climb to his professional position, then he betrayed it. If he was a Red with guts, he would have stayed where the fight is, which is not in New York in Greenwich Village. But all Ira ever cared about was everybody thinking what a hero he was. Always impersonating and never the real thing. Because he was tall, that made him Lincoln? Because he spouted "the masses, the masses,

the masses," that made him a revolutionary? He wasn't a revolutionary, he wasn't a Lincoln, he wasn't anything. He wasn't a
man—he impersonates being a man along with everything
else. Impersonates being a *great* man. The guy impersonates
everything. He throws off one disguise and becomes something else. No, your brother isn't as straight as he'd like people
to think. Your brother is not a very committed guy, except
when it comes to the commitment to himself. He's a fake and
he's a dope and he's a traitor. Betrayed his revolutionary comrades and betrayed the working class. Sold out. Bought off.
Totally the creature of the bourgeoisie. Seduced by fame and
money and wealth and power. And pussy, fancy Hollywood
pussy. Doesn't retain a vestige of his revolutionary ideology—
nothing. An opportunistic stooge. Probably an opportunistic
stoolie. You're going to tell me he left that stuff in his desk by
accident? A guy in the party leaves that by accident? Or was
something worked out, Professor, with the FBI? Too bad he's
not in the Soviet Union—they know how to handle traitors. I
don't want to hear from him and I don't want to see him. Because if I ever do see him, tell him to watch out. Tell him that
no matter how thick he butters it with rationalizations, there's
going to be blood on the bricks.'

"That was it. Blood on the bricks. I didn't even try to answer. Who would dare to explain the failure of purity to a militant who was only and always pure? Never in his life had O'Day
been this with this one, and that with that one, and a third
person with somebody else. He does not share in the fickleness
of all creatures. The ideologue is purer than the rest of us because he is the ideologue with everyone. I hung up.

"God knows how long Ira might have languished in the
Semi-Disturbed Unit if it hadn't been for Eve. Visitors weren't
encouraged and he didn't want to see anybody anyway, aside
from me and Doris, but one evening Eve showed up. The doctor wasn't around, the nurse wasn't thinking, and when Eve
announced herself as Ira's wife, the nurse pointed her down
the corridor, and there she was. He was looking emaciated,
still pretty lifeless, hardly talking at all, and so at the sight of
him she started to cry. She said she'd come to say she was sorry
but that just looking at him brought her to tears. She was
sorry, he mustn't hate her, she couldn't live her life knowing he

hated her. Terrible pressures had been exerted on her, he couldn't understand how terrible. She didn't want to do it. She did everything not to do it . . .

"With her face in her hands, she wept and she wept, until at last she told him what we all knew from reading one sentence of that book. She told Ira that the Grants had written it, every word.

"That's when Ira spoke. 'Why did you let them?' he said. 'They forced me to,' Eve told him. 'She threatened me, Ira. Loony. She's a vulgar, terrible woman. A terrible, terrible woman. I still love you. That's what I came to say. Let me say it, please. She couldn't make me stop loving you, ever. You must know that.' 'How did she threaten you?' It was the first time in weeks he was speaking consecutively in sentences. 'It isn't that she threatened only me,' Eve said. 'She did that too. She told me that I'd be finished if I didn't cooperate. She told me that Bryden would see to it that I never worked again. I'd wind up impoverished. When I still said no, told her, No, Katrina, no, I can't do it, I can't, no matter what he's done to me, I love him . . . that's when she said that if I didn't do it, Sylphid's career would be ruined at the start.'

"Well, all at once Ira became himself again. He hit the Semi-Disturbed Unit roof. It was pandemonium. Semi-disturbed is still semi-disturbed, and those guys in that room may have been playing basketball and playing volleyball but they were still a pretty fragile lot and a couple of them went haywire. Ira was shouting at the top of that voice of his, 'You did it for *Sylphid*? You did it for your daughter's *career*?' and Eve began to howl, 'Only *you* matter! Only *you*! What about my child! My child's talent!' One of the inmates is shouting, 'Beat the shit out of her! Beat the shit out of her!' and another one bursts into tears, and by the time the attendants get down the hall, Eve is facedown on the floor, hammering her fists and screaming, 'What about my daughter!'

"They put her in a straitjacket—that's what they used in those days. They didn't gag her, however, and so Eve just let it out, all of it. 'I said to Katrina, "No, you cannot squash that kind of talent." She would destroy *Sylphid*. I couldn't destroy Sylphid. I knew *you* couldn't destroy Sylphid. I was powerless. I was simply powerless! I gave her the least little bit I could. To placate her. Because Sylphid—that talent! It wouldn't be *right*! What mother in the *world* would let her child suffer? What mother would have done any differently, Ira? Answer me! To make my child suffer for the silliness of adults and their ideas and their attitudes? How can you put the blame on me? What choice did I have? You have no idea what I go through. You have no idea what *any* mother would go through if someone says, "I am going to destroy your child's career." You never had children. You don't understand anything *about* parents and children. You had no parents and you have no children, and you don't know what the sacrifice is all about!'

" 'I don't have children?' Ira screamed. They'd gotten her onto a stretcher and were already carrying her away by then, and so Ira ran after them, ran shouting down the hall, '*Why* don't I have children? Because of you! Because of you and your greedy, selfish fucking daughter!'

"They carted her away, something they'd apparently never had to do before with somebody who'd just come by for a visit. They sedated her and they put her in a bed in the Disturbed Unit, locked her up and wouldn't let her out of the hospital until the next morning, when they were able to locate Sylphid, and she turned up to take her mother home. What impulse had brought Eve to the hospital, whether there was any truth at all to what she'd come to say—that she was forced by the Grants to do this ugly thing—whether that was just the new lie, whether even her shame was real, we never knew for sure.

"Maybe it was. It certainly could have been. In those times, anything could have been. People were fighting for their lives. If it *was* true that's what happened, then Katrina was a genius, really, a genius of manipulation. Katrina knew exactly where to get her. Katrina gave Eve her choice of people to betray, and Eve, with her pretense of powerlessness, chose what she had no choice but to choose. One is consigned to be oneself, and no one more so than Eve Frame. She became the instrument of the Grants' will. She was run by those two just like an agent."

"Well, within a matter of days Ira was into the Quiet Unit, and the next week he was out, and then he really became . . .

"Well, maybe," Murray said after a moment's reflection, "he just achieved the old survival clarity he had digging ditches, before all the scaffolding of politics and home and success and fame got erected around him, before he buried the ditchdigger alive and donned Abe Lincoln's hat. Maybe he became himself again, the actor of his own way. Ira wasn't a superior artist brought down. Ira was just brought back to where he began.

"'Revenge.' He said it to me," Murray said, "as plain and calm as that. A thousand convicts, lifers, beating their bars with their spoons couldn't have put it better. 'Revenge.' Between the pleading pathos of defense and the compelling symmetry of revenge, there was no choice. I remember him slowly kneading those joints of his and telling me that he was going to ruin her. I remember him saying, 'Throwing her life into that daughterly toilet. Then throwing mine in with it. That doesn't go down with me. It's not just, Murray. It's degrading to me, Murray. I am her mortal enemy? Okay then, she is mine.'"

"*Did* he ruin her?" I asked.

"You know what happened to Eve Frame."

"I know she died. Of cancer. Didn't she? In the sixties?"

"She died, but not of cancer. Remember that picture I told you about, the photograph Ira got in the mail from one of Freedman's old girlfriends, the picture he was going to use to compromise Eve with? The picture I tore up? I should have let him use it."

"You said that before. Why?"

"Because what Ira was doing with that picture was looking for a way *not* to kill her. His whole life had been looking for a way not to kill somebody. When he got home from Iran, his whole life was an attempt to defuse the violent impulse. That picture—I didn't realize what it was a disguise for, what it meant. When I tore it up, when I prevented him from using *that* as his weapon, he said, 'Okay, you win,' and I went back to Newark stupidly thinking I'd accomplished something, and up in Zinc Town, out in the woods, he starts target shooting. He had knives up there. I drove back to see him the next week and he makes no attempt to hide anything. Too wild with his imaginings to hide anything. He's full of murder talk. 'The smell of gunfire,' he tells me, 'it's an aphrodisiac!' He's absolutely gone. I hadn't even known that he owned a gun. I didn't know what to do. At last I perceived their true affinity, the hopeless interlinking of Ira and Eve as embattled souls: each of them disastrously inclined toward that thing that knows no limits once it gets under way. His recourse to violence was the masculine correlate of her predisposition to hysteria—distinctive gender manifestations of the same waterfall.

"I told him to give me all the weapons he had. Either give them to me right away, or I'd get on the phone and call the police. 'I suffered as much as you did,' I told him. 'I suffered more than you did in that house because I had to face it first. For six years, by myself. You don't know anything. You think I don't know about wanting to pick up a gun and shoot somebody? Everything you want to do to her now I wanted to do when I was *six years old*. And then you came along. I took care of you, Ira. I stood between you and the worst of it for as long as I was at home.

" 'You don't remember this. You were two, I was eight—and you know what happened? I never told you. You had enough humiliation to deal with. We had to move. We weren't living on Factory Street yet. You were a baby and we were living beneath the Lackawanna tracks. On Nassau. Eighteen Nassau Street, backing onto the tracks. Four rooms, no light, lots of noise. Sixteen-fifty a month, the landlord upped it to nineteen, we couldn't pay, and we were evicted.

" 'You know what our father did after we moved out our belongings? You and Momma and I started pushing the stuff over to the two rooms on Factory Street, and he stayed behind in the empty old flat, and he squatted down and he took a crap in the middle of the kitchen. Our kitchen. A pile of his shit right in the middle of where we used to sit at the table and eat. He painted the walls with it. No brush. Didn't need one. Painted the shit on with his hands. Big strokes. Up, down, sidewise. When he finished all the rooms, he washed in the sink, and he left without even closing the door behind him. You know what the kids called me for months after that? Shitwalls. In those days everybody got a nickname. You they called Boo-hoo, me they called Shitwalls. That was our father's legacy to me, his big boy, his oldest son.

" 'I protected you then, Ira, and I'm going to protect you now. I'm not going to let you do it. I found my civilizing path into life, and you found yours, and you are not going back on that now. Let me explain something that you don't appear to understand. Why you became a Communist in the first place. Has that never dawned on you? My civilizing path was books, college, teaching school, yours was O'Day and the party. I never bought your way. I *opposed* your way. But both ways were legitimate and both worked. But what's happened now, you don't understand either. They've told you that they've decided that Communism is not a way out of violence, that it is a program *for* violence. They've criminalized your politics and, in the bargain, criminalized you—and you are going to prove them right. They say you're a criminal, so you load up your gun and strap your knife to your thigh. You say, "God-damn right I am! The smell of gunfire—it's an aphrodisiac!"' Nathan, I talked myself hoarse. But when you are with an enraged homicidal maniac, talking like this doesn't calm him down. It inflames him further. When you are with an enraged homicidal maniac, to start telling a story about childhood, complete with the floor plan of the apartment . . .

"Look," Murray said, "I haven't told you everything about Ira. Ira had already killed somebody. That's why he left Newark and headed for the sticks and worked in the mines when he was a kid. He was on the lam. I got him up to Sussex County, beyond the beyond in those days, but not so far that I couldn't check on him and help him and get him through that thing. I drove him myself and I gave him his new name and I hid him away. Gil Stephens. The first of Ira's new names.

"He worked in the mines till he thought they were after him. Not the cops, the Mob. I told you about Ritchie Boiardo, who ran the rackets in the First Ward. The gangster who owned the restaurant, the Vittorio Castle. Ira got wind that Boiardo's thugs were out looking for him. That's when he started riding the rails."

"What had he done?"

"Ira killed a guy with a shovel. Ira killed a guy when he was sixteen."

Ira killed a guy with a shovel. "Where?" I said. "How? What happened?"

"Ira was working at the Tavern as a busboy. It was a job he'd had for about six weeks when, one night, he finished up swab-bing the floors at two, and he came out alone into the street and set off for the room he rented. He lived on a dinky little street way down by Dreamland Park, where they built the project after the war. He made the turn onto Meeker at Elizabeth Avenue and was headed down the dark street across from Weequahic Park, in the direction of Frelinghuysen Avenue, when a guy emerged from the shadows where Millman's hot dog stand used to be. Out of the shadows there, and he swung at him, aiming at his head, and he caught Ira on the shoulders with a shovel.

"It was one of the Italians from the ditchdigging gang where Ira had worked after he left school. Ira had quit digging ditches to bus tables at the Tavern because of all the trouble he kept having with this guy. It was 1929, the year the Tavern opened. He was going to try to get in on the ground floor and advance from busboy to waiter. That was the goal. I'd helped get him the job. The Italian was drunk and walloped him one, and Ira wrestled the shovel away from him and knocked his teeth out with it. Then he dragged him back of Millman's, back into that pitch-black parking lot. In your day, kids on dates used to park and neck back of Millman's, and that's where Ira beat this guy up.

"Guy's name was Strollo. Strollo was the big Jew hater on the ditchdigging gang. '*Mazzu' crist, giude' maledett*.' Christ killer, no-good Jew . . . that stuff. Strollo specialized in it. Strollo was about ten years older than Ira and not small, a big guy almost Ira's size. Ira beat him on the head until he was unconscious and left him there. He threw down Strollo's shovel and walked back out into the street and started home again, but something in him wasn't finished. Something in Ira was *never* finished. He's sixteen and forceful and full of rage, he's hot and sweaty and worked up and excited—he's *aroused* —and so he turns around and goes back of Millman's and he beats Strollo over the head until the guy is dead."

Millman's was where Ira used to take me for a hot dog after our walks in Weequahic Park. The Tavern was where Ira had taken Eve to have dinner with Murray and Doris the night they all met. That was in 1948. Twenty years earlier he'd killed someone there. The shack up in Zinc Town—that shack meant something else to him that I'd never understood. That was his reformatory. His solitary confinement.

"Where does Boiardo come in?"

"Strollo's brother worked at the Castle, Boiardo's place. Worked in the kitchen. He went to Boiardo and told him what happened. At first nobody connected Ira with the murder because he had already left the ward. But a couple of years later, it's Ira they're looking for. I suspected it was the cops who put Boiardo on to Ira, but I never knew for sure. All I knew was that somebody came to our door asking for my brother. Little Pussy pays me a visit. I grew up with Little Pussy. Little Pussy used to run the dice game in Aqueduct Alley. He ran the ziconette game in the back of Grande's till the cops broke it up. I used to play pool with Little Pussy at Grande's. He got his name because he started out professionally as a cat burglar, sneaking across the rooftops and going in through the windows with his older brother, Big Pussy. In grade school they were already up all night stealing. When they even bothered to come to school, they sat sleeping at their desks and nobody dared to wake them up. Big Pussy died of natural causes, but Little Pussy was bumped off in 1979 in real gangland style: found in his oceanfront apartment in Long Branch, wearing a bathrobe, three bullets from a .32 in his head. The next day Ritchie Boiardo tells one of his cronies, 'Perhaps it was for the best—because he talked too much.'

"Little Pussy wants to know where my brother is. I told him I hadn't seen my brother in years. He tells me, 'The Boot is looking for him.' They called Boiardo 'the Boot' because he made his phone calls from what the First Ward Italians called a 'telephone boot.' 'Why?' I asked. 'Because the Boot protects the neighborhood. Because the Boot helps people in time of need.' This was true. Boiardo used to go around wearing a diamond-studded belt buckle and was held in higher esteem even than the saintly guy who was their parish priest. I got word to Ira about Little Pussy and it was seven years, it was 1938, before we saw him again."

"So it was not because of the Depression that he rode the rails. It was because he was a hunted man."

"Startled to learn this?" Murray asked me. "About somebody you admired the way you admired him?"

"No," I said. "No, I'm not startled. It makes sense."

"That's one reason why he cracked up. That's what he wound

up crying in Lorraine's bed. 'The whole thing failed.' The life shaped to overcome it had all fallen apart. The effort had been futile. He'd been returned to the chaos where it had all begun."

"What's the 'it'?"

"After he came out of the army, Ira wanted people around him whom he couldn't explode in front of. He went looking for them. The violence in him had scared Ira. He lived in fear of it breaking back into existence. So did I. Somebody who showed that propensity for violence so early—what was going to stop him?

"That's why Ira wanted the marriage. That's why Ira wanted that child. That's why that abortion crushed him. That's why he came to stay with us the day he found out what was behind the abortion. And that very next day, he meets you. He meets this boy who was all that he had never been and who had all that he had never had. Ira wasn't recruiting *you*. Maybe your father thought so, but no, you were recruiting *him*. When he came over to Newark that day, the abortion still so raw in him, you were irresistible to Ira. He was the Newark boy with the bad eyes and the cruel household and no education. You were the nurtured Newark boy given everything. You were the guy's Prince Hal. You were Johnny O'Day Ringold—that's what you were all about. That was your job, whether you knew it or not. To help him shield himself against his nature, against all the force in that big body, all the murderous rage. That was *my* job all my life. It's the job of lots of people. Ira was no rarity. Men trying not to be violent? *That's* the 'it.' They're all around. They're everywhere."

"Ira killed the guy with a shovel. What happened after that?" I asked him. "What happened that night?"

"I wasn't teaching in Newark. It was 1929. Weequahic High hadn't been built yet. I was teaching at Irvington High. My first job. I rented a room up by Solondz's lumberyard, near the railroad tracks. It was about four in the morning when Ira turned up. I was on the first floor and he rapped on my window. I went out, took one look at his bloody shoes and his bloody pants and his bloody hands and his bloody face, and I got him into that old Ford I had and we started driving. I didn't know where the hell I was going. Somewhere far from the Newark police. I was thinking about the cops then and not Boiardo."

"He told you what he'd done."

"Yes. You know whom else he told? Eve Frame. Years later. During their courtship. During that summer they were alone together in New York. He was crazy about her and he wanted to marry her but he had to tell her the truth about who he'd been and the worst he'd done. If it frightened her off, then it frightened her off, but he wanted her to know what she would be getting—that he had been a wild man but that the wild man had been obliterated. He said it for the reason that self-reformed people make those confessions: so she could hold him to it. He didn't understand then, he never understood, that a wild man was what Eve needed most.

"Blindly, which was her way, Eve had an insight into herself. She needs the brute. She *demanded* the brute. Who better to protect her? With a brute she was safe. It explains why she can be with Pennington during all those years he was out picking up boys and spending the night with them and coming home through a special side entrance he had built onto his study. Built it at Eve's request, so she wouldn't have to hear him returning from his trysts at four A.M. It explains why she married Freedman. It explains the men she was drawn to. Her romantic life consisted of changing brutes. If a brute came along, she was first in line. She needs the brute to protect her, and she needs the brute to be blameless. Her brutes are the guarantor of her treasured innocence. To drop to her knees before them and beg is of the greatest importance to her. Beauty and submission—that was what she lived by, her key to catastrophe.

"She needs the brute to redeem her purity, while what the brute needs is to be tamed. Who better to domesticate him than the most genteel woman in the world? What better to housebreak him than the dinner parties for his friends and the paneled library for his books and a delicate actress with beautiful diction for his wife? So Ira told Eve about the Italian and the shovel, and she wept for what he had done at sixteen and how he had suffered it and how he had survived it and how he had so bravely transformed himself into a perfect and wonderful man, and they were married.

"Who knows—maybe she thought that an ex-murderer was perfect for still another reason: on a self-confessed wild man and murderer you can safely impose this unimposable presence, Sylphid. An ordinary man would run screaming from that kid. But a brute? He could take it.

"When I first read in the papers that she was writing a book, I thought the worst. You see, Ira had even told her the guy's name. What was to stop this woman who had it in her, when she believed she was cornered, to say anything to anyone—what was to stop her from shouting 'Strollo' from the rooftops? 'Strollo, Strollo—I know who murdered the ditchdigger Strollo!' But when I read the book, nothing about the murder was in there. Either she never told Katrina and Bryden about Ira and Strollo, either there was some restraint in her after all, some sense of what people like the Grants (another couple of Eve's brutes) would do to him with it, or she had forgotten it the way she could conveniently forget any unpleasant fact. I never knew which. Maybe both.

"But Ira was sure it was going to come out. The whole world was going to see him as I saw him that night when I drove him up to Sussex County. Covered with a dead man's blood. With the blood on his face of a man he'd killed. And telling me with a laugh—the cackling laugh of a crazy kid— 'Strollo just took his last strollo.'

"What had begun as an act of self-defense, he had turned into an opportunity to kill someone. He'd lucked into it. Self-defense the instigating event that provides the opportunity to murder. 'Strollo just took his last strollo,' my kid brother tells me. He'd enjoyed it, Nathan.

"'And what did *you* just take, Ira?' I asked him. 'Do you know? You just took the wrong fork in the road. You just made the biggest mistake you've ever made. You just changed everything into something else. And for what? Because the guy attacked you? Well, you beat him up! You beat him silly. You *got* your victory. You spent your rage on beating him to a pulp. But to make the victory *total*, to go back and then *murder* him—for *what*? Because he said something anti-Semitic? That necessitates killing him? The whole weight of Jewish history falls on Ira Ringold's shoulders? Bullshit! You just did something ineradicable, Ira—evil and maniacal and forever rooted in your life. You've done something tonight that can never be made right. You cannot publicly apologize for murder and make everything all right, Ira. *Nothing* can make murder all right. Ever! Murder doesn't just end one life—it ends *two*. Murder ends the human life of the murderer as well! You will never get rid of this secret. You will go to the cemetery with this secret. You will have it with you forever!'

"See, someone commits a crime like murder, I figure the Dostoyevskian reality is going to kick in. A book man, an English teacher, I expect him to manifest the psychological damage that Dostoyevsky writes about. How can you commit an act of murder and not be anguished by it? That makes you a monster, doesn't it? Raskolnikov doesn't kill the old lady and then feel okay about it for the next twenty years. A cold-blooded killer with a mind like Raskolnikov's reflects all his life on his cold-bloodedness. But Ira was not very self-reflective, ever. Ira is an action machine. However that crime contorted Raskolnikov's behavior . . . well, Ira paid the toll in a different way. The penance he paid—how he tried to resurrect his life, his bending backward to stand up straight—was not at all the same.

"Look, I didn't believe he could live with it, and I never believed *I* could live with it. Live with a brother who had gone and committed a murder like that? You would have thought I would either have disowned him or forced him to confess. The idea that I could live with a brother who had murdered somebody and just sit on it, that I could think that I had discharged my obligation to humanity . . . Murder is too big for that. But that is what I did, Nathan. I sat on it.

"But despite my silence, twenty-odd years later, the root at the root of everything was about to be exposed anyway. America was going to see the cold-blooded killer that Ira really was underneath Abraham Lincoln's hat. America was going to find out that he was no fucking good.

"And Boiardo was going to get *his* revenge. Boiardo, by about then, had left Newark for a palazzo stronghold in the Jersey suburbs, but that didn't mean that the Strollos' grievance against Ira Ringold had been forgotten by the Boot's lieutenants holding down the First Ward fort. I was always afraid a goon from the pool hall was going to catch up with Ira, that the Mob would send somebody to do him in, especially after he became Iron Rinn. You know that night he took us all to the Tavern for dinner, and he introduced us to Eve, and Sam Teiger took our picture and hung it up in the foyer there? Did I not like that! What could be worse? How drunk on metamorphosis could he get, the heroic reinvention of himself he called Iron Rinn? Back virtually at the scene of the crime, and he allows his mug to go up on the wall? Maybe *he's* forgotten who he was and what he's done, but Boiardo's going to remember and gun him down.

"But a book did the job instead. In a country where a book hadn't changed a goddamn thing since the publication of *Uncle Tom's Cabin*. A banal show-biz tell-all book, written in hackese by two opportunists exploiting an easy mark named Eve Frame. Ira shakes off Ritchie Boiardo but he couldn't elude the Van Tassel Grants. It's not a goon dispatched by the Boot who does the job on Ira—it's a gossip columnist.

"In all my years with Doris I had never told her about Ira. But the morning I came back from Zinc Town with his gun and his knives I was tempted to. It was about five in the morning when he turned everything over to me. I drove directly to school that morning with that stuff under the front seat of my car. I couldn't teach that day—I couldn't think. I couldn't sleep that night. That was when I nearly told Doris. I'd taken away his gun and his knives, but I knew that wasn't the end of it. Somehow or other, he was going to kill her.

" 'And thus the whirligig of time brings in his revenges.' Line of prose. Recognize it? From the last act of *Twelfth Night*. Feste the clown, to Malvolio, just before Feste sings that lovely song, before he sings, 'A great while ago the world begun, / With hey ho, the wind and the rain,' and the play is over. I couldn't get that line out of my head. 'And thus the whirligig of time brings in his revenges.' Those cryptogrammic *g*'s, the subtlety of their deintensification—those hard *g*'s in 'whirligig' followed by the nasalized *g* of 'brings' followed by the soft *g* of 'revenges.' Those terminal *s*'s . . . 'thus brings his revenges.' The hissing surprise of the plural noun 'reveng*es*.' Guhh. Juhh. Zuhh. Consonants sticking into me like needles. And the pulsating vowels, the rising tide of their pitch—engulfed by that. The low-pitched vowels giving way to the high-pitched vowels.

The bass and tenor vowels giving way to the alto vowels. The assertive lengthening of the vowel *i* just before the rhythm shifts from iambic to trochaic and the prose pounds round the turn for the stretch. Short *i*, short *i*, long *i*. Short *i*, short *i*, short *i*, boom! Revenges. Brings in his revenges. *His* revenges. Sibilated. Hizzzzzuh! Driving back to Newark with Ira's weapons in my car, those ten words, the phonetic webbing, the blanket omniscience . . . I felt I was being asphyxiated inside Shakespeare.

"I went out again that next afternoon, drove up again after school. 'Ira,' I said, 'I couldn't sleep last night, and I couldn't teach the kids all day, because I know that you will not quit until you have brought down on yourself a horror that goes far beyond being blacklisted. Someday the blacklisting is going to end. This country may even make amends to people who were handled like you, but if you go to jail for murder . . . Ira, what are you thinking now?'

"Again it took me half the night to find out, and when finally he told me I said, 'I'm calling the doctors at the hospital, Ira. I'm getting a court order. This time I'm getting you committed for good. I'm going to see that you are confined in a hospital for the mentally ill for the rest of your life.'

"He was going to garotte her. *And* the daughter. He was going to garotte the two of them with the strings off the harp. He had the wire cutter. He meant it. He was going to cut the strings and tie them around their necks and strangle the two of them to death.

"That next morning I came back to Newark with the *wire cutter*. But it was hopeless, I knew that. I went home after school and I told Doris what had happened, and that's when I told her about the murder. I told her, 'I should have let them put him away. I should have turned him over to the police and let the law do what the law does.' I told her that when I left him in the morning, I said, 'Ira, she's got that daughter to live with. There's her punishment, terrible punishment, and it's punishment she brought upon herself.' And Ira laughed. 'Sure, it's terrible punishment,' he said, 'but not terrible enough.'

"In all the years that I had been dealing with my brother, that was the first time I collapsed. Told Doris everything and collapsed. I meant what I said to her. Out of a twisted sense of loyalty, I'd done the wrong thing. I saw my kid brother covered with blood, and I got him in the car and I was twenty-two years old and I did the wrong thing. And now, because the whirligig of time brings in his revenges, Ira was going to kill Eve Frame. The only thing left to do was to go to Eve and tell her to get out of town and take Sylphid with her. But I couldn't. I couldn't go to her and that daughter of hers and say, 'My brother's on the warpath, you better go into hiding.'

"I was defeated. I'd spent a lifetime teaching myself to be reasonable in the face of the unreasonable, teaching what I liked to call vigilant matter-of-factness, teaching myself and teaching my students and teaching my daughter and trying to teach my brother. And I'd failed. Un-Iraing Ira was impossible. Being reasonable in the face of the unreasonable was impossible. I'd already proved this in 1929. Here it was 1952, and I was forty-five years old and it was as though the intervening years had been for nothing. There was my kid brother with all of his power and all of his rage bent once again on murder, and once again I was going to be accessory to the crime. After everything —everything he'd done, everything we'd *all* done—he was going to cross the line again."

"When I told this to Doris, she got in the car and drove up to Zinc Town. Doris took over. She had that kind of authority. When she got back, she said, 'He's not going to murder anybody. Don't think,' she said, 'that I didn't *want* him to murder her. But he's not going to do it.' 'What is he going to do instead?' 'We negotiated a settlement. He's going to call in his chits.' 'What does that mean?' 'He's going to call on some friends.' 'What are you talking about? You don't mean gangsters.' 'I mean journalists. His journalist friends. *They're* going to destroy her. You let Ira alone. I'm in charge of Ira.'

"Why did he listen to Doris and not to me? How did she convince him? Who the hell knows why? Doris had a way with him. Doris had her own kind of savvy, and I turned him over to her."

"Who were the journalists?" I asked.

"Fellow-traveling journalists," Murray said. "There were plenty. Guys who admired him, the culturally authentic man of the people. Ira carried great weight with these people because of his working-class credentials. Because of his battles in the union. They'd been at the house often, for those soirées."

"And they did it?"

"They tore Eve to pieces. They did it, all right. They showed how her whole book was made up. That Ira was never a Communist. That he had nothing to do with Communists. That the Communist plot to infiltrate broadcasting was a bizarre concoction of lies. Which did not shake the confidence of Joe McCarthy or Richard Nixon or Bryden Grant, but it could and would destroy Eve in the New York entertainment world. That was an ultraliberal world. Think of the situation. Every journalist is coming to her, taking down every word she says in their notebooks and writing it up in all the papers. Big spy ring in New York radio. The ringleader her husband. The American Legion takes her up, asks her to address them. An organization called Christian Crusade takes her up, an anti-Communist religious group. They reprint chapters from the book in their monthly magazine. There's a story celebrating her in the *Saturday Evening Post*. The *Reader's Digest* abridges a section of the book, it's the stuff they love, and this, along with the *Post*, puts Ira in every doctor's and dentist's waiting room in America. Everybody wants her to talk to them. Everybody wants to talk to her, but then time passes and there are no more journalists and nobody any longer is buying the book and little by little nobody wants to talk to her.

"In the beginning nobody questions her. They don't question the stature of a well-known actress who looks so delicate and who comes on the scene with this shit in order to sell it. *L'affaire* Frame did not bring out the best thinking in people. The party ordered him to marry her? That was his Communist sacrifice? They took even *that* without questioning it. Anything to empty life of its incongruities, of its meaningless, messy contingencies, and to impose on it instead the simplification that coheres—and misapprehends everything. The party ordered him to do it. Everything is a plot of the party. As if Ira lacked the talent to make that mistake all on his own. As if Ira needed the Comintern to help plan a bad marriage.

"Communist, Communist, Communist, and nobody in America had the least idea of what the hell a Communist was. What do they do, what do they say, what do they look like?

When they're together, do they talk Russian, Chinese, Yiddish, Esperanto? Do they build bombs? Nobody knew, which is why it was so easy to exploit the menace the way Eve's book did. But then Ira's journalists went to work and the pieces begin to appear, in the *Nation*, the *Reporter*, the *New Republic*, tearing her to bits. The public machine she set in motion doesn't always go in the direction one wants. It takes its own direction. The public machine she wanted to destroy Ira begins to turn against her. It has to. This is America. The moment you start this public machine, no other end is possible except a catastrophe for everybody.

"Probably what unhinged her, what weakened her most, occurred at the outset of Ira's counteroffensive, before she even had a chance to figure out what was happening or for somebody else to take her in hand and tell her what not to do in a battle like this one. Bryden Grant got hold of the *Nation* attack, the first attack, when it was still in proof. Why should Grant care what they wrote in the *Nation* any more than he cared what they wrote in *Pravda*? What else would you expect them to write in the *Nation*? But his secretary sent the proof over to Eve, and Eve evidently phoned her lawyer and told him she wanted a judge to serve an injunction on the *Nation* to prevent them from printing the piece: everything in it was malicious and false, lies designed to destroy her name and her career and her reputation. But an injunction was prior restraint, and legally a judge couldn't do that. *After* the thing appeared she could sue for libel, but that wasn't good enough, that would be too late, she would already be ruined, so she went straight to the office of the *Nation* and demanded to see the writer. That was L. J. Podell. The *Nation*'s muckraking hatchet man, Jake Podell. People were frightened of him, and they had reason to be. Podell was still to be preferred to Ira with a shovel in his hands, though not by much.

"She went into Podell's office and there followed the Big Scene, the Academy Award–winning scene. Eve said to Podell the piece was full of lies, it was all vicious lies, and you know what the most vicious lie turned out to be? In that entire piece? Podell identified her as a closet Jew. He wrote that he'd been out to Brooklyn and uncovered the true story. He said that she was Chava Fromkin, born in Brownsville, in Brooklyn, in 1907, grew up on the corner of Hopkinson and Sutter, and that her father was a poor immigrant housepainter, an uneducated Polish Jew who painted houses. He said that nobody in her family had spoken English, not her father, not her mother, not even an older brother and sister. Both of them had been born years before Eve, in the old country. Except for Chava, they all spoke Yiddish.

"Podell even dug up the first husband, Mueller, the bartender's kid from Jersey, the ex-sailor she'd run off with at sixteen. He's still out in California, living on disability, a retired cop with a bad heart, a wife, and two kids, a good old boy with nothing but good things to say about Chava. The beautiful girl she was. The *gutsy* girl she was. A little hellion, believe it or not. How she eloped with him, Mueller said, not because she could possibly love the big idiot that he was back then, but because, as he'd known all along, he was her ticket out of Brooklyn. Knowing this and feeling for her, Mueller never stood in her way, he told Podell, never came back to haunt her for money, even after she made it big. Podell's even got some old snapshots, snapshots that Mueller (for an undisclosed sum) kindly turned over to him. He shows them to her: Chava and Mueller on a wild beach at Malibu, the Pacific big and booming behind them—two handsome, healthy, exhilarated youngsters, robust in their twenties swimsuits, ready and eager to take the big plunge. Snapshots that wound up reprinted in *Confidential* magazine.

"Now, Podell was never really in the business of exposing Jews. He was an indifferent Jew himself, and God knows he was no supporter of Israel's, ever. But here was someone who'd been lying about her background all her life and now she was lying about Ira. Podell had verifying quotations from all sorts of elderly people in Brooklyn, alleged neighbors, alleged relatives, and Eve said that it was all stupid gossip and that if he reported as the truth the things that stupid people make up about someone who is famous, she would sue the magazine right out of existence and sue him personally for every penny he had.

"Somebody there had a camera and came into Podell's office and snapped a picture of the onetime movie star just as she was reminding Podell what she could do to him. Well, any drop of self-mastery still left in her vanishes, the rational outlook, such as it was, evaporates, and she runs down the hall sobbing, and there is the managing editor and he takes her into his office and he sits her down and he says, 'Aren't you Eve Frame? I am a great admirer. What's the trouble? What can I do for you?' And she tells him. 'Oh, my, my,' he says, 'that won't do,' and he calms her down and he asks her what she wants changed in the piece, and she tells him about how she was born in New Bedford, Massachusetts, to an old seafaring family, her great-grandfather and her grandfather captains of a Yankee clipper, and though her own parents had by no means been wealthy, after the death of her father, a patent lawyer, when she was still a little girl, her mother had run a very nice tearoom. The managing editor tells her how glad he is to get the truth. He assures Eve as he sees her into a cab that he will take care that it is printed in the magazine. And Podell, who has been outside the managing editor's office taking down every word Eve says, does just that: puts it in the magazine.

"After she left, Podell went back to the piece and inserted the incident whole—the visit to the office, the Big Scene, the works. Ruthless old battering ram, inordinately fond of that sort of sport, on top of which he especially liked Ira and disliked her. Scrupulously recorded every detail of the New Bedford story and put that in as the conclusion of the piece. The others who did their stories after Podell's picked up on it, and that became another motif in the anti-Eve stories, another reason she turned on Ira, who is not only not a Communist now but himself a proud, observant Jew, et cetera. What they called Ira had almost as little relation to Ira as what she had called Ira. By the time all these savage intellects, with their fidelity to the facts, were finished with the woman, to find anything anywhere of the ugly truth that *was* the story of Ira and Eve, you would have needed a microscope.

"In Manhattan, the ostracism begins. She starts losing friends. People don't come to her parties. Nobody calls her. Nobody wants to talk to her. Nobody believes her any longer. She destroys her husband with lies? What does this say about her human quality? Gradually there's no more work for her. Radio drama is on its last legs, crushed first by the blacklist and then by TV, and Eve's been putting on the weight and television isn't interested.

"I saw her perform just twice on TV. I believe those were the only two times she ever appeared on TV. The first time we watched her, Doris was astounded. Pleasantly so. Doris said, 'You know whom she looks like now that she's built like that? Mrs. Goldberg, from Tremont Avenue in the Bronx.' Remember Molly Goldberg, on *The Goldbergs*? With her husband, Jake, and her children, Rosalie and Samily? Philip Loeb. Remember Philip Loeb? You ever meet him through Ira? Ira brought him to our house. Phil played Papa Jake on *The Goldbergs* for years and years, from the thirties, when the program first started out on radio. In 1950 they fired him from the TV program because his name was on the blacklist. Couldn't get work, couldn't pay his bills, couldn't pay his debts, so in '55 Phil Loeb checked into the Taft Hotel and killed himself with sleeping pills.

"Both parts Eve played were mothers. Awful stuff. On Broadway she'd always been a quiet, tactful, intelligent actress, and now she was sobbing and throwing herself all over the place—acting, unfortunately, much like herself. But by then she must have been mostly on her own, with nobody giving her any guidance. The Grants are down in Washington and haven't the time, and so all she's got is Sylphid.

"And that didn't last either. One Friday night, she and Sylphid appeared together on a TV program that was very popular back then. Called *The Apple and the Tree*. Remember it? Half-hour weekly program about children who had inherited some sort of talent, trait, or profession from a parent. Scientists, people in the arts, in show business, athletes. Lorraine liked to watch it, and sometimes we watched with her. It was an enjoyable program, funny, warm, even interesting sometimes, but pretty light fare, pretty light entertainment. Though not when Sylphid and Eve were the guests. They had to give the public their bowdlerized take on *King Lear*, with Sylphid as Goneril and Regan.

"I remember Doris saying to me, 'She's read and understood all those books. She's read and understood all those roles she's played. Is it so hard for her to come to her senses? What makes someone so experienced so hopelessly foolish? To be in your mid-forties, to be so much in the world, and to be so un-knowing.'

"What interested me was that after publishing and promot-ing *I Married a Communist*, she didn't, even for a second, in passing, own up to the spite. Maybe by then she'd conveniently forgotten the book and all it had done. Maybe this was the pre-Grant, pre-monster version coming out, Eve's story of Ira before it had been properly Van Tasseled. But the about-face she achieved in revisiting her story was still something to see.

"All Eve could talk about on TV was how in love she'd been with Ira, and how happy she'd been with Ira, and how the marriage was destroyed only by his treacherous Communism. She even cried for a moment over all the happiness treacherous Communism had ruined. I remember Doris getting up and walking away from the TV set, then coming back and sitting there stewing. Afterward she said to me, 'Seeing her burst into tears like that on television—it shocked me nearly as much as if she'd been incontinent. Can't she stop crying for two minutes? She's an actress, for God's sake. Can't she try acting her age?'

"So the camera watched the Communist's innocent wife weep, all of TV-land watched the Communist's innocent wife weep, and then the Communist's innocent wife wiped her eyes and, looking nervously to the daughter every two seconds for corroboration—no, for *authorization*—made it clear that every-thing was wonderful between Sylphid and her once again, peace established, bygones bygones, all their old trust and love restored. Now that the Communist had been rooted out, there was no closer family, no family on better terms, this side of *The Swiss Family Robinson*.

"And every time Eve tried smiling at Sylphid with that poorly pasted-on smile, tried looking at her with the most painfully tentative look in her eyes, a look all but pleading with Sylphid to say, 'Yes, Momma, I love you, that's true'—all but blatantly begging her, 'Say it, darling, if only for television'—Sylphid gave the game away by either glowering back at her or conde-scending to her or irritatedly subverting every word Eve had said. There came a point at which even Lorraine couldn't take any more. Suddenly this kid shouted at the TV screen, 'Show some love, the two of you!'

"Sylphid doesn't display a split second's worth of affection for this pathetic woman struggling to hang on. Not a speck of generosity, let alone understanding. Not one conciliatory line. I'm not a kid—I don't speak of love. I don't even speak of happiness, harmony, or friendship. Just of conciliation. What I realized watching that program was that this girl could *never* have loved her mother. Because if you did, even a little, you are able to think about her sometimes as something *other* than your mother. You think of her happiness and her unhappiness. You think of her health. You think of her loneliness. You think of her *craziness*. But this girl has no imagination for any of this. The daughter has no understanding whatsoever of the life of a woman. All she has is her *J'accuse*. All she wants is to put the mother on trial before the whole nation, to make her look terrible in every way. The public grinding of Momma's bones.

"I'll never forget that picture: Eve continually looking to Sylphid as though her whole idea of herself and her worth derived from this daughter who was the most ruthless judge imaginable of her mother's every failing. You should have seen the mockery in Sylphid, deriding her mother with every scornful grimace, spurning her with every smirk, getting her licks in publicly. She's finally got the forum for her anger. Giving her famous mother a ride on TV. Her power is to say, just with her sneer, 'You who were so admired are a stupid woman.' Not very generous stuff. The stuff most kids sort out by the time they're eighteen. Ferociously self-revealing stuff. You feel there's a sexual pleasure in it when it hangs on that late in a person's life. That program made you squirm: the histrionics of the mother's defenselessness no less remarkable than the relentless blackjack of the daughter's malice. But the mask of Eve's face was what was most frightening. The unhappiest mask you could imagine. I knew then that there was nothing left of her. She looked annihilated.

"Finally, the program host mentioned Sylphid's upcoming recital at Town Hall, and Sylphid sat down and played the harp. *There*, that's why Eve agreed to degrade herself like this on TV. Of course—for Sylphid's career. Could there be any better metaphor for their relationship, I thought, than this, than Eve crying in public for all that she's lost while the daughter who doesn't care plays the harp and plugs the recital?

"A couple of years later, the daughter abandons her. When

her mother is sinking and needs her most, Sylphid discovers her independence. At thirty, Sylphid determines that it's not good for a daughter's emotional well-being to live at home intertwined with a middle-aged mother who tucks her in bed every night. Whereas most children leave their parents at eighteen or twenty, live independently of them for fifteen or twenty years and then, in time, reconcile with their aging parents and try to give them a hand, Sylphid prefers to pull it off the other way round. For the best of modern psychological reasons, Sylphid goes to France to live off the father.

"Pennington was already sick by then. A couple of years later he died. Cirrhosis of the liver. Sylphid inherited the villa, the cars, the cats, and the Pennington family fortune. Sylphid gets it all, including Pennington's handsome Italian chauffeur, whom she marries. Yes, Sylphid married. Even begat a son. There's the logic of reality for you. Sylphid Pennington became a mother. Big news in the tabloids here because of an interminable legal wrangle initiated by some well-known French set designer—I forget his name, a onetime long-term lover of Pennington's. He claimed that the chauffeur was a hustler, a fortune hunter, who'd only recently come on the scene, who'd himself been an on-and-off lover of Pennington's, and who'd somehow rigged or doctored the will.

"By the time Sylphid left New York to take up life in France, Eve Frame was a hopeless drunk. Had to sell the house. Died in a drunken stupor in a Manhattan hotel room in 1962, ten years after the book. Forgotten. Fifty-five years old. Two years later, Ira died. Fifty-one. But he lived to see her suffer. And don't think he didn't enjoy it. Don't think he didn't enjoy Sylphid's walking out. 'Where is the lovely daughter we all heard so much about? Where is the daughter to say, "Momma, I'll help you"? Gone!'

"Eve's dying put Ira back in touch with the primary satisfactions, unchained the ditchdigger's pleasure principle. When all the rigging of respectability, when all the social construction that civilizes, is removed from someone who has thrived most of his life on impulse, you have a geyser, don't you? It just starts gushing. Your enemy destroyed—what could be better? Sure, it took a little longer than he hoped and, sure, this time he didn't get to do it himself, to feel the blood spurt up hot in his face, but still and all, I never saw Ira enjoy anything more than her death.

"You know what he said when she died? The same thing he'd said the night he'd murdered the Italian guy and we organized his getaway. He told me, 'Strollo just took his last strollo.' First time he'd uttered that name to me in over thirty years. 'Strollo just took his last strollo,' and then he lets loose the cackling crazy-kid laugh. The just-let-'em-try-to-do-me-in laugh. That defiant laugh I still remembered from 1929."

I helped Murray down the deck's three steps and guided him in the dark along the path to where my car was parked. We were silent as we swung along the curves of the mountain road and past Lake Madamaska and into Athena. When I looked over I saw that his head was back and his eyes were shut. First I thought he was asleep, and then I wondered if he was dead, if, after his having remembered the whole of Ira's story—after his having heard himself *tell* the whole of Ira's story—the will to go on had lost its grip even on this most enduring of men. And then I was recalling him again reading to our high school English class, sitting on the corner of his desk, but without the minatory blackboard eraser, reading scenes to us from *Macbeth*, doing all the voices, not afraid to be dramatic and perform, and myself being impressed by how manly literature seemed in his enactment of it. I remembered hearing Mr. Ringold read the scene at the end of act 4 of *Macbeth* when Macduff learns from Ross that Macbeth has slain Macduff's family, my first encounter with a spiritual state that is aesthetic and overrides everything else.

As Ross he read, "Your castle is surpris'd; your wife and babes / Savagely slaughtered. . . ." Then, after a long silence in which Macduff both comprehends and fails to comprehend, he read as Macduff—quietly, hollowly, almost in his reply like a child himself—"My children too?" "Wife, children, servants," says Mr. Ringold/Ross, "all / That could be found." Mr. Ringold/Macduff is again speechless. So is the class: as a class, the class is by now missing from the room. Everything has vanished except whatever words of disbelief are coming next. Mr. Ringold /Macduff: "My wife kill'd too?" Mr. Ringold/Ross: "I have said." The large clock is ticking toward two-thirty up on the classroom wall. Outside, a 14 bus is grinding up the Chancellor Avenue hill. It is only minutes before the end of eighth period and the long school day. But all that matters—matters more than what happens after school or even in the future—is when Mr. Ringold/Macduff will grasp the incomprehensible. "He has no children," Mr. Ringold says. Whom is he speaking of? Who has no children? Some years later I was taught the standard interpretation, that it is Macbeth to whom Macduff is referring, that Macbeth is the "he" who has no children. But as read by Mr. Ringold, the "he" to whom Macduff is referring is, horribly, Macduff himself. "All my pretty ones? / Did you say all? . . . All? / What, all my pretty chickens and their dam / At one fell swoop?" And now Malcolm speaks, Mr. Ringold /Malcolm, harshly, as though to shake Macduff: "Dispute it like a man." "I shall do so," says Mr. Ringold/Macduff.

Then the simple line that would assert itself, in Murray Ringold's voice, a hundred times, a thousand times, during the remainder of my life: "But I must also feel it as a man." "Ten syllables," Mr. Ringold tells us the next day, "that's all. Ten syllables, five beats, pentameter . . . nine words, the third iambic stress falling perfectly and naturally on the fifth and most important word . . . eight monosyllables and the one word of two syllables a word as common and ordinary and serviceable as any there is in everyday English . . . and yet, all together, and coming where it does, what power! Simple, simple—and like a hammer!

"But I must also feel it as a man," and Mr. Ringold closes the big book of Shakespeare's plays, says to us, as he does at the end of each class, "Be seein' ya," and leaves the room.

By the time we got into Athena, Murray's eyes were open and he was saying, "Here I am with an eminent ex-student and I never let the guy speak. Never asked him about himself."

"Next time."

"Why do you live up there, alone like that? Why don't you have the heart for the world?"

"I prefer it this way," I said.

"No, I watched you listening. I don't think you do. I don't think for a moment the exuberance is gone. You were like that as a kid. That's why I got such a kick out of you—you paid attention. You still do. But what is up here to pay attention to? You should get out from under whatever's the problem. To give in to the temptation to yield isn't smart. At a certain age, that can polish you off like any other disease. Do you really want to whittle it all away before your time has come? Beware the utopia of isolation. Beware the utopia of the shack in the woods, the oasis defense against rage and grief. An impregnable solitude. That's how life ended for Ira, and long before the day he dropped dead."

I parked on one of the college streets and walked with him up the path to the dormitory. It was close to three A.M. and all the rooms were dark. Murray was probably the last of the elderly students to be leaving and the only one who'd be sleeping there that night. I wished I had invited him to stay with me. But I didn't have the heart for that either. To have anyone sleeping anywhere within sound or sight or smell of me would have broken a chain of conditioning that hasn't been that easy to forge.

"I'm going to come down to Jersey and pay you a visit," I said.

"You're going to have to come to Arizona. I don't live in Jersey anymore. Been in Arizona a long time now. I belong to a church book club that the Unitarians run; otherwise it's slim pickins. Not the ideal location if you have a mind, but I also have other problems. Staying tomorrow in New York and the next day I fly to Phoenix. You're going to have to come to Arizona if you want to see me. Only don't dawdle," he said with a smile. "The earth spins very fast, Nathan. Time is not on my side."

As the years pass there is nothing I have less talent for than saying goodbye to somebody I feel a strong attachment to. I don't always realize how strong the attachment is until the moment comes to say goodbye.

"I somehow assumed you were still in Jersey." That was the least dangerous sentiment I could think to express.

"No. I left Newark after Doris got killed. Doris was murdered, Nathan. Across the street from us, back of the hospital. I wouldn't leave the city, you see. I wasn't going to move out of the city where I had lived and taught all my life just because it was now a poor black city full of problems. Even after the riots, when Newark emptied out, we stayed on Lehigh Avenue, the only white family that did stay. Doris, bad spine and all, returned to work at the hospital. I was teaching at South Side. After I was reinstated I went back to Weequahic, where already, by then, teaching was no picnic, and after a couple of years they asked me if I'd take over the English department at South Side, where it was even worse. Nobody could teach these black kids, and so they asked me to. I spent the last ten years there, until I retired. Couldn't teach anybody anything. Barely able to hold down the mayhem, let alone teach. Discipline— that was the whole job. Discipline, patrolling the corridors, bickering until some kid took a swing at you, expulsions. Worst ten years of my life. Worse than when I was fired. I wouldn't say the disenchantment was devastating. I had a feel for the reality of the situation. But the experience was devastating. Brutal. We should have moved, we didn't, and that's the story.

"But all my life, I was one of the firebrands in the Newark system, wasn't I? My old cronies told me I was nuts. They were all in the suburbs by then. But how could I run away? I was interested in respect being shown for these kids. If there's any chance for the improvement of life, where's it going to begin if not in the school? Besides, any time as a teacher I was ever asked to do something that I thought was interesting and worthwhile, I said, 'Yeah, I'd like to do that,' and I threw myself into it. We stayed on Lehigh Avenue and I went down to South Side and I told the teachers in the department, 'We've got to find ways to induce our students to commit themselves,' and so forth.

"I got mugged twice. We should have moved after the first time and we should certainly have moved after that second time. The second time I was just around the corner from the house, four in the afternoon, when three kids surrounded me and pulled a gun. But we didn't move. And one evening, Doris is leaving the hospital, and to get to our house, all she had to do, you remember, was cross the street. Well, she never made it. Somebody hit her over the head. Just about half a mile up from where Ira killed Strollo, somebody cracked her skull open with a brick. For a handbag with nothing in it. You know what I realized? I realized I'd been had. It's not an idea I like, but I've lived with it inside me ever since.

"Had by myself, in case you're wondering. Myself with all my principles. I can't betray my brother, I can't betray my teaching, I can't betray the disadvantaged of Newark. 'Not *me—I'm* not leaving this place. *I'm* not fleeing. My colleagues can do as they see fit—I'm not leaving these black kids.' And so who I betray is my wife. I put the responsibility for my choices onto somebody else. Doris paid the price for my civic virtue. She is the victim of my refusal to— Look, there is no way out of this thing. When you loosen yourself, as I tried to, from all the obvious delusions—religion, ideology, Communism— you're still left with the myth of your own goodness. Which is the final delusion. And the one to which I sacrificed Doris.

"That's enough. Every action produces loss," he said. "It's the entropy of the system."

"What system?" I said.

"The moral system."

Why hadn't he told me about Doris earlier? Was the reticence a kind of heroism or a kind of suffering? This too happened to him. What else is there? We could have sat on my deck for six hundred nights before I heard the entire story of how Murray Ringold, who'd chosen to be nothing more extraordinary than a high school teacher, had failed to elude the turmoil of his time and place and ended up no less a historical casualty than his brother. This was the existence that America had worked out for him—and that he'd worked out for himself by think-ing, by taking *his* revenge on his father by cri-ti-cal think-ing, by being reasonable in the face of no reason. This was what thinking in America had got him. This was what adhering to his convictions had got him, resisting the tyranny of compro-mise. *If there's any chance for the improvement of life, where's it going to begin if not in the school?* Hopelessly entangled in the best of intentions, tangibly, over a lifetime, committed to a constructive course that is now an illusion, to formulations and solutions that will no longer wash.

You control betrayal on one side and you wind up betraying somewhere else. Because it's not a static system. Because it's alive. Because everything that lives is in movement. Because purity is petrifaction. Because purity is a lie. Because unless you're an ascetic paragon like Johnny O'Day and Jesus Christ, you're urged on by five hundred things. Because without the iron pole of righteousness with which the Grants clubbed their way to success, without the big lie of righteousness to tell you why you do what you do, you have to ask yourself, all along the way, "Why *do* I do what I do?" And you have to endure yourself without knowing.

Here, simultaneously, we succumbed to the urge to embrace the other. Holding Murray in my arms I sensed—more than merely sensed—the extent of his decrepitude. It was hard to understand where he had found the strength, for six nights, to revisit so intensely the worst events of his life.

I didn't say anything, thinking that, whatever I said, I would drive home wishing I had been silent. As though I were still his innocent student eager to do good, I was dying to say to him, "You weren't had, Murray. That isn't the proper judgment to be made of your life. You must know that it isn't." But, as I am myself an aging man who knows what unexalted conclusions can be reached when one examines one's history probingly, I didn't.

Having let me hold on to him for close to a minute, Murray suddenly slapped my back. He was laughing at me. "The emotional demands," he said, "of leaving a ninety-year-old."

"Yes. That. And everything else. What happened to Doris. Lorraine's death," I said. "Ira. Everything that happened to Ira."

"Ira and the shovel. All that he imposed on himself," Murray said, "exacted from himself, demanded from himself because of that shovel. The bad ideas and the naive dreams. All *his* romances. His passion was to be someone he didn't know how to be. He never discovered his life, Nathan. He looked for it everywhere—in the zinc mine, in the record factory, in the fudge factory, in the labor union, in radical politics, in radio acting, in rabble-rousing, in proletarian living, in bourgeois living, in marriage, in adultery, in savagery, in civilized society. He couldn't find it anywhere. Eve didn't marry a Communist; she married a man perpetually hungering after his life. That's what enraged him and confused him and that's what ruined him: he could never construct one that fit. The enormous wrongness of this guy's effort. But one's errors always rise to the surface, don't they?"

"It's all error," I said. "Isn't that what you've been telling me? There's only error. *There's* the heart of the world. Nobody finds his life. That *is* life."

"Listen. I don't want to overstep the boundary. I'm not telling you I'm for or against it. I'm asking that when you come down to Phoenix, you'll tell me what it is."

"What what is?"

"*Your* aloneness," he said. "I remember the beginning, this very intense boy so much looking forward to participating in life. Now he's in his middle sixties, a man by himself in the woods. I'm surprised to see you out of the world like this. It's pretty damn monastic, the way you live. All that's missing from your monkhood are the bells to call you to meditation. Sorry, but I *do* have to tell you: you're still a young man by my count, much too young to be up there. What are you warding off? What the hell happened?"

Now I laughed at *him*, a laugh that allowed me to feel substantial again, charged up with my independence of everything, a recluse to be conjured with. "I listened carefully to your story, that's what happened. Goodbye, Mr. Ringold!"

"Be seein' ya."

On the deck, the citronella candle was still burning in its aluminum bucket when I got back, that little pot of fire the only light by which my house was discernible, except for a dim radiance off the orange moon silhouetting the low roof. As I left the car and started toward the house, the elongated wavering of the flame reminded me of the radio dial—no bigger than a watch face and, beneath the tiny black numerals, the color of a ripening banana skin—that was all that could be seen in our dark bedroom when my kid brother and I, contrary to parental directive, stayed up past ten to listen to a favorite program. The two of us in our twin beds and, magisterial on the night table between us, the Philco Jr., the cathedral-shaped table radio we'd inherited when my father bought the Emerson console for the living room. The radio turned as low as it could go, though still with volume enough to act on our ears as the most powerful magnet.

I blew out the candle's scented flame and stretched myself across the chaise on the deck and realized that listening in the black of a summer's night to a barely visible Murray had been something like listening to the bedroom radio when I was a kid ambitious to change the world by having all my untested convictions, masquerading as stories, broadcast nationwide. Murray, the radio: voices from the void controlling everything within, the convolutions of a story floating on air and into the ear so that the drama is perceived well behind the eyes, the cup that is the cranium a cup transformed into a limitless globe of a stage, containing fellow creatures whole. How deep our hearing goes! Think of all it means to *understand* from something that you simply hear. The godlikeness of having an ear! Is it not at least a *semi*divine phenomenon to be hurled into the innermost wrongness of a human existence by virtue of nothing more than sitting in the dark, listening to what is said?

Till dawn I remained out on the deck, lying on the chaise looking up at the stars. My first year alone in this house I taught myself to identify the planets, the great stars, the star clusters, the configuration of antiquity's great constellations, and with the aid of the stargazer's map tucked up in a corner of the second section of the Sunday *New York Times*, I charted their journey's wheeling logic. Soon that was all I cared to look at in that thumping loaf of newsprint and pictures. I'd tear out the small double-columned box called "Sky Watch"—that features, above the elucidating text, a circle encompassing the celestial horizon and that pinpoints the constellations' whereabouts at ten P.M. for the coming week—and chuck out the four pounds of everything else. Soon I was chucking out the daily paper as well; soon I had chucked everything with which I no longer wish to contend, everything but what was needed to live on and to work with. I set out to receive all my fullness from what might once have seemed, even to me, not nearly enough and to inhabit passionately only the parts of speech.

If the weather isn't bad and it's a clear night, I spend fifteen or twenty minutes before bedtime out on the deck looking skyward, or, using a flashlight, I pick my way along the dirt road to the open pasture at the peak of my hill, from where I can see, from above the treeline, the whole heavenly inventory, stars unfurled in every direction, and, just this week, the planets Jupiter in the east and Mars in the west. It is beyond belief and also a fact, a plain and indisputable fact: that we are born, that this is here. I can think of worse ways to end my day.

On the night Murray left I recalled how, as a small child, I'd been told—as a small child unable to sleep because his grandfather had died and he insisted on understanding where the dead man had gone—that Grandpa had been turned into a star. My mother took me out of bed and down into the driveway beside the house and together we looked straight up at the night sky while she explained that one of those stars was my grandfather. Another was my grandmother, and so on. What happens when people die, my mother explained, is that they go up to the sky and live on forever as gleaming stars. I searched the sky and said, "Is he that one?" and she said yes, and we went back inside and I fell asleep.

That explanation made sense then and, of all things, it made sense again on the night when, wide awake from the stimulus of all that narrative engorgement, I lay out of doors till dawn, thinking that Ira was dead, that Eve was dead, that with the exception perhaps of Sylphid off in her villa on the French Riviera, a rich old woman of seventy-two, all the people with a role in Murray's account of the Iron Man's unmaking were now no longer impaled on their moment but dead and free of the traps set for them by their era. Neither the ideas of their era nor the expectations of our species were determining destiny: hydrogen alone was determining destiny. There are no longer mistakes for Eve or Ira to make. There is no betrayal. There is no idealism. There are no falsehoods. There is neither conscience nor its absence. There are no mothers and daughters, no fathers and stepfathers. There are no actors. There is no class struggle. There is no discrimination or lynching or Jim Crow, nor has there ever been. There is no injustice, nor is there justice. There are no utopias. There are no shovels. Contrary to the folklore, except for the constellation Lyra—which happened to perch high in the eastern sky a little west of the Milky Way and southeast of the two Dippers—there are no harps. There is just the furnace of Ira and the furnace of Eve burning at twenty million degrees. There is the furnace of novelist Katrina Van Tassel Grant, the furnace of Congressman Bryden Grant, the furnace of taxidermist Horace Bixton, and of miner Tommy Minarek, and of flutist Pamela Solomon, and of Estonian masseuse Helgi Pärn, and of lab technician Doris Ringold, and of Doris's uncle-loving daughter, Lorraine. There is the furnace of Karl Marx and of Joseph Stalin and of Leon Trotsky and of Paul Robeson and of Johnny O'Day. There is the furnace of Tailgunner Joe McCarthy. What you see from this silent rostrum up on my mountain on a night as splendidly clear as that night Murray left me for good—for the very best of loyal brothers, the ace of English teachers, died in Phoenix two months later—is that universe into which error does not obtrude. You see the inconceivable: the colossal spectacle of no antagonism. You see with your own eyes the vast brain of time, a galaxy of fire set by no human hand.

The stars are indispensable.

THE HUMAN STAIN

For R. M.

OEDIPUS:

What is the rite
of purification? How shall it be done?

CREON:

By banishing a man, or expiation
of blood by blood . . .

—Sophocles, *Oedipus the King*

1

Everyone Knows

IT was in the summer of 1998 that my neighbor Coleman Silk—who, before retiring two years earlier, had been a classics professor at nearby Athena College for some twenty-odd years as well as serving for sixteen more as the dean of faculty —confided to me that, at the age of seventy-one, he was having an affair with a thirty-four-year-old cleaning woman who worked down at the college. Twice a week she also cleaned the rural post office, a small gray clapboard shack that looked as if it might have sheltered an Okie family from the winds of the Dust Bowl back in the 1930s and that, sitting alone and forlorn across from the gas station and the general store, flies its American flag at the junction of the two roads that mark the commercial center of this mountainside town.

Coleman had first seen the woman mopping the post office floor when he went around late one day, a few minutes before closing time, to get his mail—a thin, tall, angular woman with graying blond hair yanked back into a ponytail and the kind of severely sculpted features customarily associated with the church-ruled, hardworking goodwives who suffered through New England's harsh beginnings, stern colonial women locked up within the reigning morality and obedient to it. Her name was Faunia Farley, and whatever miseries she endured she kept concealed behind one of those inexpressive bone faces that hide nothing and bespeak an immense loneliness. Faunia lived in a room at a local dairy farm where she helped with the milking in order to pay her rent. She'd had two years of high school education.

The summer that Coleman took me into his confidence about Faunia Farley and their secret was the summer, fittingly enough, that Bill Clinton's secret emerged in every last mortifying detail—every last *lifelike* detail, the livingness, like the mortification, exuded by the pungency of the specific data. We hadn't had a season like it since somebody stumbled upon the new Miss America nude in an old issue of *Penthouse*, pictures of her

elegantly posed on her knees and on her back that forced the
shamed young woman to relinquish her crown and go on to
become a huge pop star. Ninety-eight in New England was a
summer of exquisite warmth and sunshine, in baseball a summer of mythical battle between a home-run god who was white
and a home-run god who was brown, and in America the summer of an enormous piety binge, a purity binge, when terrorism
—which had replaced communism as the prevailing threat to
the country's security—was succeeded by cocksucking, and a
virile, youthful middle-aged president and a brash, smitten
twenty-one-year-old employee carrying on in the Oval Office
like two teenage kids in a parking lot revived America's oldest
communal passion, historically perhaps its most treacherous
and subversive pleasure: the ecstasy of sanctimony. In the Congress, in the press, and on the networks, the righteous grand-
standing creeps, crazy to blame, deplore, and punish, were
everywhere out moralizing to beat the band: all of them in a
calculated frenzy with what Hawthorne (who, in the 1860s,
lived not many miles from my door) identified in the incipient
country of long ago as "the persecuting spirit"; all of them
eager to enact the astringent rituals of purification that would
excise the erection from the executive branch, thereby making
things cozy and safe enough for Senator Lieberman's ten-year-
old daughter to watch TV with her embarrassed daddy again.
No, if you haven't lived through 1998, you don't know what
sanctimony is. The syndicated conservative newspaper columnist William F. Buckley wrote, "When Abelard did it, it was
possible to prevent its happening again," insinuating that the
president's malfeasance—what Buckley elsewhere called Clinton's
"incontinent carnality"—might best be remedied with nothing
so bloodless as impeachment but, rather, by the twelfth-
century punishment meted out to Canon Abelard by the
knife-wielding associates of Abelard's ecclesiastical colleague,
Canon Fulbert, for Abelard's secret seduction of and marriage
to Fulbert's niece, the virgin Heloise. Unlike Khomeini's
fatwa condemning to death Salman Rushdie, Buckley's wistful
longing for the corrective retribution of castration carried with
it no financial incentive for any prospective perpetrator. It was
prompted by a spirit no less exacting than the ayatollah's,
however, and in behalf of no less exalted ideals.

It was the summer in America when the nausea returned, when the joking didn't stop, when the speculation and the theorizing and the hyperbole didn't stop, when the moral obligation to explain to one's children about adult life was abrogated in favor of maintaining in them every illusion about adult life, when the smallness of people was simply crushing, when some kind of demon had been unleashed in the nation and, on both sides, people wondered "Why are we so crazy?," when men and women alike, upon awakening in the morning, discovered that during the night, in a state of sleep that transported them beyond envy or loathing, they had dreamed of the brazenness of Bill Clinton. I myself dreamed of a mammoth banner, draped dadaistically like a Christo wrapping from one end of the White House to the other and bearing the legend A HUMAN BEING LIVES HERE. It was the summer when—for the billionth time—the jumble, the mayhem, the mess proved itself more subtle than this one's ideology and that one's morality. It was the summer when a president's penis was on everyone's mind, and life, in all its shameless impurity, once again confounded America.

Sometimes on a Saturday, Coleman Silk would give me a ring and invite me to drive over from my side of the mountain after dinner to listen to music, or to play, for a penny a point, a little gin rummy, or to sit in his living room for a couple of hours and sip some cognac and help him get through what was always for him the worst night of the week. By the summer of 1998, he had been alone up here—alone in the large old white clapboard house where he'd raised four children with his wife, Iris—for close to two years, ever since Iris suffered a stroke and died overnight while he was in the midst of battling with the college over a charge of racism brought against him by two students in one of his classes.

Coleman had by then been at Athena almost all his academic life, an outgoing, sharp-witted, forcefully smooth big-city charmer, something of a warrior, something of an operator, hardly the prototypical pedantic professor of Latin and Greek (as witness the Conversational Greek and Latin Club that he started, heretically, as a young instructor). His venerable survey course in ancient Greek literature in translation—known as

GHM, for Gods, Heroes, and Myth—was popular with students precisely because of everything direct, frank, and unacademically forceful in his comportment. "You know how European literature begins?" he'd ask, after having taken the roll at the first class meeting. "With a quarrel. All of European literature springs from a fight." And then he picked up his copy of *The Iliad* and read to the class the opening lines. " 'Divine Muse, sing of the ruinous wrath of Achilles . . . Begin where they first quarreled, Agamemnon the King of men, and great Achilles.' And what are they quarreling about, these two violent, mighty souls? It's as basic as a barroom brawl. They are quarreling over a woman. A girl, really. A girl stolen from her father. A girl abducted in a war. Now, Agamemnon much prefers this girl to his wife, Clytemnestra. 'Clytemnestra is not as good as she is,' he says, 'neither in face nor in figure.' That puts directly enough, does it not, why he doesn't want to give her up? When Achilles demands that Agamemnon return the girl to her father in order to assuage Apollo, the god who is murderously angry about the circumstances surrounding her abduction, Agamemnon refuses: he'll agree only if Achilles gives him *his* girl in exchange. Thus reigniting Achilles. Adrenal Achilles: the most highly flammable of explosive wildmen any writer has ever enjoyed portraying; especially where his prestige and his appetite are concerned, the most hypersensitive killing machine in the history of warfare. Celebrated Achilles: alienated and estranged by a slight to his honor. Great heroic Achilles, who, through the strength of his rage at an insult—the insult of not getting the girl—isolates himself, positions himself defiantly outside the very society whose glorious protector he is and whose need of him is enormous. A quarrel, then, a brutal quarrel over a young girl and her young body and the delights of sexual rapacity: there, for better or worse, in this offense against the phallic entitlement, the phallic *dignity*, of a powerhouse of a warrior prince, is how the great imaginative literature of Europe begins, and that is why, close to three thousand years later, we are going to begin there today . . ."

Coleman was one of a handful of Jews on the Athena faculty when he was hired and perhaps among the first of the Jews permitted to teach in a classics department anywhere in

America; a few years earlier, Athena's solitary Jew had been
E. I. Lonoff, the all-but-forgotten short story writer whom,
back when I was myself a newly published apprentice in trouble
and eagerly seeking the validation of a master, I had once paid
a memorable visit to here. Through the eighties and into the
nineties, Coleman was also the first and only Jew ever to serve
at Athena as dean of faculty; then, in 1995, after retiring as
dean in order to round out his career back in the classroom, he
resumed teaching two of his courses under the aegis of the
combined languages and literature program that had absorbed
the Classics Department and that was run by Professor Delphine Roux. As dean, and with the full support of an ambitious
new president, Coleman had taken an antiquated, backwater,
Sleepy Hollowish college and, not without steamrolling, put
an end to the place as a gentlemen's farm by aggressively en-
couraging the deadwood among the faculty's old guard to seek
early retirement, recruiting ambitious young assistant professors, and revolutionizing the curriculum. It's almost a certainty
that had he retired, without incident, in his own good time, there
would have been the festschrift, there would have been the
institution of the Coleman Silk Lecture Series, there would have
been a classical studies chair established in his name, and perhaps—given his importance to the twentieth-century revital-
ization of the place—the humanities building or even North
Hall, the college's landmark, would have been renamed in his
honor after his death. In the small academic world where he
had lived the bulk of his life, he would have long ceased to be
resented or controversial or even feared, and, instead, officially
glorified forever.

It was about midway into his second semester back as a full-
time professor that Coleman spoke the self-incriminating word
that would cause him voluntarily to sever all ties to the college
—the single self-incriminating word of the many millions spoken aloud in his years of teaching and administering at Athena,
and the word that, as Coleman understood things, directly led
to his wife's death.

The class consisted of fourteen students. Coleman had taken
attendance at the beginning of the first several lectures so as to
learn their names. As there were still two names that failed to

elicit a response by the fifth week into the semester, Coleman, in the sixth week, opened the session by asking, "Does anyone know these people? Do they exist or are they spooks?"

Later that day he was astonished to be called in by his successor, the new dean of faculty, to address the charge of racism brought against him by the two missing students, who turned out to be black, and who, though absent, had quickly learned of the locution in which he'd publicly raised the question of their absence. Coleman told the dean, "I was referring to their possibly ectoplasmic character. Isn't that obvious? These two students had not attended a single class. That's all I knew about them. I was using the word in its customary and primary meaning: 'spook' as a specter or a ghost. I had no idea what color these two students might be. I had known perhaps fifty years ago but had wholly forgotten that 'spooks' is an invidious term sometimes applied to blacks. Otherwise, since I am totally meticulous regarding student sensibilities, I would never have used that word. Consider the context: Do they exist *or* are they spooks? The charge of racism is spurious. It is preposterous. My colleagues know it is preposterous and my students know it is preposterous. The issue, the only issue, is the nonattendance of these two students and their flagrant and inexcusable neglect of work. What's galling is that the charge is not just false—it is spectacularly false." Having said altogether enough in his defense, considering the matter closed, he left for home.

Now, even ordinary deans, I am told, serving as they do in a no man's land between the faculty and the higher administration, invariably make enemies. They don't always grant the salary raises that are requested or the convenient parking places that are so coveted or the larger offices professors believe they are entitled to. Candidates for appointments or promotion, especially in weak departments, are routinely rejected. Departmental petitions for additional faculty positions and secretarial help are almost always turned down, as are requests for reduced teaching loads and for freedom from early morning classes. Funds for travel to academic conferences are regularly denied, et cetera, et cetera. But Coleman had been no ordinary dean, and who he got rid of and how he got rid of them, what he abolished and what he established, and how audaciously he performed his job into the teeth of tremendous resistance succeeded in more than merely slighting or offending a few odd ingrates and malcontents. Under the protection of Pierce Roberts, the handsome young hotshot president with all the hair who came in and appointed him to the deanship—and who told him, "Changes are going to be made, and anybody who's unhappy should just think about leaving or early retirement" —Coleman had overturned everything. When, eight years later, midway through Coleman's tenure, Roberts accepted a prestigious Big Ten presidency, it was on the strength of a reputation for all that had been achieved at Athena in record time—achieved, however, not by the glamorous president who was essentially a fund-raiser, who'd taken none of the hits and moved on from Athena heralded and unscathed, but by his determined dean of faculty.

In the very first month he was appointed dean, Coleman had invited every faculty member in for a talk, including several senior professors who were the scions of the old county families who'd founded and originally endowed the place and who themselves didn't really need the money but gladly accepted their salaries. Each of them was instructed beforehand to bring along his or her c.v., and if someone didn't bring it, because he or she was too grand, Coleman had it in front of him on his desk anyway. And for a full hour he kept them there, sometimes even longer, until, having so persuasively indicated that things at Athena had at long last changed, he had begun to make them sweat. Nor did he hesitate to open the interview by flipping through the c.v. and saying, "For the last eleven years, just what *have* you been doing?" And when they told him, as an overwhelming number of the faculty did, that they'd been publishing regularly in *Athena Notes*, when he'd heard one time too many about the philological, bibliographical, or archaeological scholarly oddment each of them annually culled from an ancient Ph.D. dissertation for "publication" in the mimeographed quarterly bound in gray cardboard that was cataloged nowhere on earth but in the college library, he was reputed to have dared to break the Athena civility code by saying, "In other words, you people recycle your own trash." Not only did he then shut down *Athena Notes* by returning the tiny bequest to the donor—the father-in-law of the editor —but, to encourage early retirement, he forced the deadest of

the deadwood out of the courses they'd been delivering by
rote for the last twenty or thirty years and into freshman English and the history survey and the new freshman orientation
program held during the hot last days of the summer. He
eliminated the ill-named Scholar of the Year Prize and assigned
the thousand dollars elsewhere. For the first time in the college's
history, he made people apply formally, with a detailed project
description, for paid sabbatical leave, which was more often
than not denied. He got rid of the clubby faculty lunchroom,
which boasted the most exquisite of the paneled oak interiors
on the campus, converted it back into the honors seminar
room it was intended to be, and made the faculty eat in the
cafeteria with the students. He insisted on faculty meetings—
never holding them had made the previous dean enormously
popular. Coleman had attendance taken by the faculty secretary so that even the eminences with the three-hour-a-week
schedules were forced onto the campus to show up. He found
a provision in the college constitution that said there were to
be no executive committees, and arguing that those stodgy
impediments to serious change had grown up only by convention and tradition, he abolished them and ruled these faculty
meetings by fiat, using each as an occasion to announce what
he was going to do next that was sure to stir up even more
resentment. Under his leadership, promotion became difficult
—and this, perhaps, was the greatest shock of all: people were
no longer promoted through rank automatically on the basis
of being popular teachers, and they didn't get salary increases
that weren't tied to merit. In short, he brought in competition,
he made the place competitive, which, as an early enemy noted,
"is what Jews do." And whenever an angry ad hoc committee
was formed to go and complain to Pierce Roberts, the president unfailingly backed Coleman.

  In the Roberts years all the bright younger people he recruited loved Coleman because of the room he was making for
them and because of the good people he began hiring out of
graduate programs at Johns Hopkins and Yale and Cornell—
"the revolution of quality," as they themselves liked to describe
it. They prized him for taking the ruling elite out of their little
club and threatening their self-presentation, which never fails
to drive a pompous professor crazy. All the older guys who

were the weakest part of the faculty had survived on the ways that they thought of themselves—the greatest scholar of the year 100 B.C., and so forth—and once those were challenged from above, their confidence eroded and, in a matter of a few years, they had nearly all disappeared. Heady times! But after Pierce Roberts moved on to the big job at Michigan, and Haines, the new president, came in with no particular loyalty to Coleman—and, unlike his predecessor, exhibiting no special tolerance for the brand of bulldozing vanity and autocratic ego that had cleaned the place out in so brief a period—and as the young people Coleman had kept on as well as those he'd recruited began to become the veteran faculty, a reaction against Dean Silk started to set in. How strong it was he had never entirely realized until he counted all the people, department by department, who seemed to be not at all displeased that the word the old dean had chosen to characterize his two seemingly nonexistent students was definable not only by the primary dictionary meaning that he maintained was obviously the one he'd intended but by the pejorative racial meaning that had sent his two black students to lodge their complaint.

I remember clearly that April day two years back when Iris Silk died and the insanity took hold of Coleman. Other than to offer a nod to one or the other of them whenever our paths crossed down at the general store or the post office, I had not really known the Silks or anything much about them before then. I hadn't even known that Coleman had grown up some four or five miles away from me in the tiny Essex County town of East Orange, New Jersey, and that, as a 1944 graduate of East Orange High, he had been some six years ahead of me in my neighboring Newark school. Coleman had made no effort to get to know me, nor had I left New York and moved into a two-room cabin set way back in a field on a rural road high in the Berkshires to meet new people or to join a new community. The invitations I received during my first months out here in 1993—to come to a dinner, to tea, to a cocktail party, to trek to the college down in the valley to deliver a public lecture or, if I preferred, to talk informally to a literature class—I politely declined, and after that both the neighbors and the college let me be to live and do my work on my own.

But then, on that afternoon two years back, having driven directly from making arrangements for Iris's burial, Coleman was at the side of my house, banging on the door and asking to be let in. Though he had something urgent to ask, he couldn't stay seated for more than thirty seconds to clarify what it was. He got up, sat down, got up again, roamed round and round my workroom, speaking loudly and in a rush, even menacingly shaking a fist in the air when—erroneously—he believed emphasis was needed. I had to write something for him—he all but ordered me to. If he wrote the story in all of its absurdity, altering nothing, nobody would believe it, nobody would take it seriously, people would say it was a ludicrous lie, a self-serving exaggeration, they would say that more than his having uttered the word "spooks" in a classroom had to lie behind his downfall. But if *I* wrote it, if a professional writer wrote it . . .

All the restraint had collapsed within him, and so watching him, listening to him—a man I did not know, but clearly someone accomplished and of consequence now completely unhinged—was like being present at a bad highway accident or a fire or a frightening explosion, at a public disaster that mesmerizes as much by its improbability as by its grotesqueness. The way he careened around the room made me think of those familiar chickens that keep on going after having been beheaded. His head had been lopped off, the head encasing the educated brain of the once unassailable faculty dean and classics professor, and what I was witnessing was the amputated rest of him spinning out of control.

I—whose house he had never before entered, whose very voice he had barely heard before—had to put aside whatever else I might be doing and write about how his enemies at Athena, in striking out at him, had instead felled her. Creating their false image of him, calling him everything that he wasn't and could never be, they had not merely misrepresented a professional career conducted with the utmost seriousness and dedication—they had killed his wife of over forty years. Killed her as if they'd taken aim and fired a bullet into her heart. I had to write about this "absurdity," that "absurdity"—I, who then knew nothing about his woes at the college and could not even begin to follow the chronology of the horror that, for five months now, had engulfed him and the late Iris Silk: the punishing immersion in meetings, hearings, and interviews, the documents and letters submitted to college officials, to faculty committees, to a pro bono black lawyer representing the two students . . . the charges, denials, and countercharges, the obtuseness, ignorance, and cynicism, the gross and deliberate misinterpretations, the laborious, repetitious explanations, the prosecutorial questions—and always, perpetually, the pervasive sense of unreality. "Her murder!" Coleman cried, leaning across my desk and hammering on it with his fist. "These people *murdered* Iris!"

The face he showed me, the face he placed no more than a foot from my own, was by now dented and lopsided and—for the face of a well-groomed, youthfully handsome older man —strangely repellent, more than likely distorted from the toxic effect of all the emotion coursing through him. It was, up close, bruised and ruined like a piece of fruit that's been knocked from its stall in the marketplace and kicked to and fro along the ground by the passing shoppers.

There is something fascinating about what moral suffering can do to someone who is in no obvious way a weak or feeble person. It's more insidious even than what physical illness can do, because there is no morphine drip or spinal block or radical surgery to alleviate it. Once you're in its grip, it's as though it will have to kill you for you to be free of it. Its raw realism is like nothing else.

Murdered. For Coleman that alone explained how, out of nowhere, the end could have come to an energetic sixty-four-year-old woman of commanding presence and in perfect health, an abstract painter whose canvases dominated the local art shows and who herself autocratically administered the town artists' association, a poet published in the county newspaper, in her day the college's leading politically active opponent of bomb shelters, of strontium 90, eventually of the Vietnam War, opinionated, unyielding, impolitic, an imperious whirlwind of a woman recognizable a hundred yards away by her great tangled wreath of wiry white hair; so strong a person, apparently, that despite his own formidableness, the dean who reputedly could steamroll anybody, the dean who had done the academically impossible by bringing deliverance to Athena College, could best his own wife at nothing other than tennis.

Once Coleman had come under attack, however—once the racist charge had been taken up for investigation, not only by the new dean of faculty but by the college's small black student organization and by a black activist group from Pittsfield—the outright madness of it blotted out the million difficulties of the Silks' marriage, and that same imperiousness that had for four decades clashed with his own obstinate autonomy and resulted in the unending friction of their lives, Iris placed at the disposal of her husband's cause. Though for years they had not slept in the same bed or been able to endure very much of the other's conversation—or of the other's friends—the Silks were side by side again, waving their fists in the faces of people they hated more profoundly than, in their most insufferable moments, they could manage to hate each other. All they'd had in common as comradely lovers forty years earlier in Greenwich Village—when he was at NYU finishing up his Ph.D. and Iris was an escapee fresh from two nutty anarchist parents in Passaic and modeling for life drawing classes at the Art Students League, armed already with her thicket of important hair, big-featured and voluptuous, already then a theatrical-looking high priestess in folkloric jewelry, the biblical high priestess from before the time of the synagogue—all they'd had in common in those Village days (except for the erotic passion) once again broke wildly out into the open . . . until the morning when she awakened with a ferocious headache and no feeling in one of her arms. Coleman rushed her to the hospital, but by the next day she was dead.

"They meant to kill me and they got her instead." So Coleman told me more than once during that unannounced visit to my house, and then made sure to tell every single person at her funeral the following afternoon. And so he still believed. He was not susceptible to any other explanation. Ever since her death—and since he'd come to recognize that his ordeal wasn't a subject I wished to address in my fiction and he had accepted back from me all the documentation dumped on my desk that day—he had been at work on a book of his own about why he had resigned from Athena, a nonfiction book he was calling *Spooks.*

There's a small FM station over in Springfield that on Saturday nights, from six to midnight, takes a break from the regular classical programming and plays big-band music for the first few hours of the evening and then jazz later on. On my side of the mountain you get nothing but static tuning to that frequency, but on the slope where Coleman lives the reception's fine, and on the occasions when he'd invite me for a Saturday evening drink, all those sugary-sweet dance tunes that kids of our generation heard continuously over the radio and played on the jukeboxes back in the forties could be heard coming from Coleman's house as soon as I stepped out of my car in his driveway. Coleman had it going full blast not just on the living room stereo receiver but on the radio beside his bed, the radio beside the shower, and the radio beside the kitchen bread box. No matter what he might be doing around the house on a Saturday night, until the station signed off at midnight—following a ritual weekly half hour of Benny Goodman—he wasn't out of earshot for a minute.

Oddly, he said, none of the serious stuff he'd been listening to all his adult life put him into emotional motion the way that old swing music now did: "Everything stoical within me unclenches and the wish not to die, never to die, is almost too great to bear. And all this," he explained, "from listening to Vaughn Monroe." Some nights, every line of every song assumed a significance so bizarrely momentous that he'd wind up dancing by himself the shuffling, drifting, repetitious, uninspired, yet wonderfully serviceable, mood-making fox trot that he used to dance with the East Orange High girls on whom he pressed, through his trousers, his first meaningful erections; and while he danced, nothing he was feeling, he told me, was simulated, neither the terror (over extinction) nor the rapture (over "You sigh, the song begins. You speak, and I hear violins"). The teardrops were all spontaneously shed, however astonished he may have been by how little resistance he had to Helen O'Connell and Bob Eberly alternately delivering the verses of "Green Eyes," however much he might marvel at how

Jimmy and Tommy Dorsey were able to transform him into the kind of assailable old man he could never have expected to be. "But let anyone born in 1926," he'd say, "try to stay alone at home on a Saturday night in 1998 and listen to Dick Haymes singing 'Those Little White Lies.' Just have them do that, and then let them tell me afterwards if they have not understood at last the celebrated doctrine of the catharsis effected by tragedy."

Coleman was cleaning up his dinner dishes when I came through a screen door at the side of the house leading into the kitchen. Because he was over the sink and the water was running, and because the radio was loudly playing and he was singing along with the young Frank Sinatra "Everything Happens to Me," he didn't hear me come in. It was a hot night; Coleman wore a pair of denim shorts and sneakers, and that was it. From behind, this man of seventy-one looked to be no more than forty—slender and fit and forty. Coleman was not much over five eight, if that, he was not heavily muscled, and yet there was a lot of strength in him, and a lot of the bounce of the high school athlete was still visible, the quickness, the urge to action that we used to call pep. His tightly coiled, short-clipped hair had turned the color of oatmeal, and so head-on, despite the boyish snub nose, he didn't look quite so youthful as he might have if his hair were still dark. Also, there were crevices carved deeply at either side of his mouth, and in the greenish hazel eyes there was, since Iris's death and his resignation from the college, much, much weariness and spiritual depletion. Coleman had the incongruous, almost puppet-like good looks that you confront in the aging faces of movie actors who were famous on the screen as sparkling children and on whom the juvenile star is indelibly stamped.

All in all, he remained a neat, attractive package of a man even at his age, the small-nosed Jewish type with the facial heft in the jaw, one of those crimped-haired Jews of a light yellowish skin pigmentation who possess something of the ambiguous aura of the pale blacks who are sometimes taken for white. When Coleman Silk was a sailor at the Norfolk naval base down in Virginia at the close of World War II, because his name didn't give him away as a Jew—because it could as easily have been a Negro's name—he'd once been identified, in a brothel, as a nigger trying to pass and been thrown out. "Thrown out of a Norfolk whorehouse for being black, thrown out of Athena College for being white." I'd heard stuff like that from him frequently during these last two years, ravings about black anti-Semitism and about his treacherous, cowardly colleagues that were obviously being mainlined, unmodified, into his book.

"Thrown out of Athena," he told me, "for being a white Jew of the sort those ignorant bastards call the enemy. That's who's made their American misery. That's who stole them out of paradise. And that's who's been holding them back all these years. What is the major source of black suffering on this planet? They know the answer without having to come to class. They know without having to open a book. Without reading they know—without *thinking* they know. Who is responsible? The same evil Old Testament monsters responsible for the suffering of the Germans.

"They killed her, Nathan. And who would have thought that Iris couldn't take it? But strong as she was, *loud* as she was, Iris could *not*. Their brand of stupidity was too much even for a juggernaut like my wife. 'Spooks.' And who here would defend me? Herb Keble? As dean I brought Herb Keble into the college. Did it only months after taking the job. Brought him in not just as the first black in the social sciences but as the first black in anything other than a custodial position. But Herb too has been radicalized by the racism of Jews like me. 'I can't be with you on this, Coleman. I'm going to have to be with them.' This is what he told me when I went to ask for his support. To my face. *I'm going to have to be with them.* Them!

"You should have seen Herb at Iris's funeral. Crushed. Devastated. Somebody died? Herbert didn't intend for anybody to *die*. These shenanigans were so much jockeying for power. To gain a bigger say in how the college is run. They were just exploiting a useful situation. It was a way to prod Haines and the administration into doing what they otherwise would never have done. More blacks on campus. More black students, more black professors. Representation—that was the issue. The only issue. God knows nobody was meant to *die*. Or to resign either. That too took Herbert by surprise. Why should Coleman Silk resign? Nobody was going to fire him. Nobody would dare to fire him. They were doing what they were doing just because they could do it. Their intention was to hold my feet over the flames just a little while longer—why couldn't I have been patient and waited? By the next semester who would have remembered any of it? The incident—*the incident*—provided them with an 'organizing issue' of the sort that was needed at a racially retarded place like Athena. Why did I quit? By the time I quit it was essentially over. What the hell was I *quitting* for?"

On just my previous visit, Coleman had begun waving something in my face from the moment I'd come through the door, yet another document from the hundreds of documents filed in the boxes labeled "Spooks." "Here. One of my gifted colleagues. Writing about one of the two who brought the charges against me—a student who had never attended my class, flunked all but one of the other courses she was taking, and rarely attended *them*. I thought she flunked because she couldn't confront the material, let alone begin to master it, but it turned out that she flunked because she was too intimidated by the racism emanating from her white professors to work up the courage to go to class. The very racism that I had articulated. In one of those meetings, hearings, whatever they were, they asked me, 'What factors, in your judgment, led to this student's failure?' 'What *factors*?' I said. 'Indifference. Arrogance. Apathy. Personal distress. Who knows?' 'But,' they asked me, 'in light of these factors, what positive recommendations did you make to this student?' 'I didn't make any. I'd never laid eyes on her. If I'd had the opportunity, I would have recommended that she leave school.' 'Why?' they asked me. 'Because she didn't belong in school.'

"Let me read from this document. Listen to this. Filed by a colleague of mine supporting Tracy Cummings as someone we should not be too harsh or too quick to judge, certainly not someone we should turn away and reject. Tracy we must nurture, Tracy we must understand—we have to know, this scholar tells us, 'where Tracy's coming from.' Let me read you the last sentences. 'Tracy is from a rather difficult background, in that she separated from her immediate family in tenth grade and lived with relatives. As a result, she was not particularly good at dealing with the realities of a situation. This defect I admit. But she is ready, willing, and able to change her approach to living.

What I have seen coming to birth in her during these last weeks is a realization of the seriousness of her avoidance of reality.' Sentences composed by one Delphine Roux, chairman of Languages and Literature, who teaches, among other things, a course in French classicism. *A realization of the seriousness of her avoidance of reality.* Ah, enough. Enough. This is sickening. This is just too sickening."

That's what I witnessed, more often than not, when I came to keep Coleman company on a Saturday night: a humiliating disgrace that was still eating away at someone who was still fully vital. The great man brought low and suffering still the shame of failure. Something like what you might have seen had you dropped in on Nixon at San Clemente or on Jimmy Carter, down in Georgia, before he began doing penance for his defeat by becoming a carpenter. Something very sad. And yet, despite my sympathy for Coleman's ordeal and for all he had unjustly lost and for the near impossibility of his tearing himself free from his bitterness, there were evenings when, after having sipped only a few drops of his brandy, it required something like a feat of magic for me to stay awake.

But on the night I'm describing, when we had drifted onto the cool screened-in side porch that he used in the summertime as a study, he was as fond of the world as a man can be. He'd pulled a couple of bottles of beer from the refrigerator when we left the kitchen, and we were seated across from each other at either side of the long trestle table that was his desk out there and that was stacked at one end with composition books, some twenty or thirty of them, divided into three piles.

"Well, there it is," said Coleman, now this calm, unoppressed, entirely new being. "That's it. That's *Spooks.* Finished a first draft yesterday, spent all day today reading it through, and every page of it made me sick. The violence in the handwriting was enough to make me despise the author. That I should spend a single quarter of an hour at this, let alone two years . . . Iris died because of *them*? Who will believe it? I hardly believe it myself any longer. To turn this screed into a book, to bleach out the raging misery and turn it into something by a sane human being, would take two years more at least. And what would I then have, aside from two years more of thinking about 'them'? Not that I've given myself over to forgiveness.

Don't get me wrong: I hate the bastards. I hate the fucking bastards the way Gulliver hates the whole human race after he goes and lives with those horses. I hate them with a real biological aversion. Though those horses I always found ridiculous. Didn't you? I used to think of them as the W A S P establishment that ran this place when I first got here."

"You're in good form, Coleman—barely a glimmer of the old madness. Three weeks, a month ago, whenever it was I saw you last, you were still knee-deep in your own blood."

"Because of *this* thing. But I read it and it's shit and I'm over it. I can't do what the pros do. Writing about myself, I can't maneuver the creative remove. Page after page, it is still the raw thing. It's a parody of the self-justifying memoir. The hopelessness of explanation." Smiling, he said, "Kissinger can unload fourteen hundred pages of this stuff every other year, but it's defeated me. Blindly secure though I may seem to be in my narcissistic bubble, I'm no match for him. I quit."

Now, most writers who are brought to a standstill after rereading two years' work—even one year's work, merely *half* a year's work—and finding it hopelessly misguided and bringing down on it the critical guillotine are reduced to a state of suicidal despair from which it can take months to begin to recover. Yet Coleman, by abandoning a draft of a book as bad as the draft he'd finished, had somehow managed to swim free not only from the wreck of the book but from the wreck of his life. Without the book he appeared now to be without the slightest craving to set the record straight; shed of the passion to clear his name and criminalize as murderers his opponents, he was embalmed no longer in injustice. Aside from watching Nelson Mandela, on TV, forgiving his jailers even as he was leaving jail with his last miserable jail meal still being assimilated into his system, I'd never before seen a change of heart transform a martyred being quite so swiftly. I couldn't understand it, and I at first couldn't bring myself to believe in it either.

"Walking away like this, cheerfully saying, 'It's defeated me,' walking away from all this work, from all this loathing—well, how are you going to fill the outrage void?"

"I'm not." He got the cards and a notepad to keep score and we pulled our chairs down to where the trestle table was clear of papers. He shuffled the cards and I cut them and he dealt. And then, in this odd, serene state of contentment brought on by the seeming emancipation from despising everyone at Athena who, deliberately and in bad faith, had misjudged, misused, and besmirched him—had plunged him, for two years, into a misanthropic exertion of Swiftian proportions—he began to rhapsodize about the great bygone days when his cup ranneth over and his considerable talent for conscientiousness was spent garnering and tendering pleasure.

Now that he was no longer grounded in his hate, we were going to talk about women. This *was* a new Coleman. Or perhaps an old Coleman, the oldest adult Coleman there was, the most satisfied Coleman there had ever been. Not Coleman pre-spooks and unmaligned as a racist, but the Coleman contaminated by desire alone.

"I came out of the navy, I got a place in the Village," he began to tell me as he assembled his hand, "and all I had to do was go down into the subway. It was like fishing down there. Go down into the subway and come up with a girl. And then"—he stopped to pick up my discard—"all at once, got my degree, got married, got my job, kids, and that was the end of the fishing."

"Never fished again."

"Almost never. True. Virtually never. As good as never. Hear these songs?" The four radios were playing in the house, and so even out on the road it would have been impossible not to hear them. "After the war, those were the songs," he said. "Four, five years of the songs, the girls, and that fulfilled my every ideal. I found a letter today. Cleaning out that *Spooks* stuff, found a letter from one of the girls. *The* girl. After I got my first appointment, out on Long Island, out at Adelphi, and Iris was pregnant with Jeff, this letter arrived. A girl nearly six feet tall. Iris was a big girl too. But not big like Steena. Iris was substantial. Steena was something else. Steena sent me this letter in 1954 and it turned up today while I was shoveling out the files."

From the back pocket of his shorts, Coleman pulled the original envelope holding Steena's letter. He was still without a T-shirt, which now that we were out of the kitchen and on the porch I couldn't help but take note of—it was a warm July night, but not that warm. He had never struck me before as a man whose considerable vanity extended also to his anatomy. But now there seemed to me to be something more than a mere at-homeness expressed in this exhibition of his body's suntanned surface. On display were the shoulders, arms, and chest of a smallish man still trim and attractive, a belly no longer flat, to be sure, but nothing that had gotten seriously out of hand—altogether the physique of someone who would seem to have been a cunning and wily competitor at sports rather than an overpowering one. And all this had previously been concealed from me, because he was always shirted and also because of his having been so drastically consumed by his rage.

Also previously concealed was the small, Popeye-ish, blue tattoo situated at the top of his right arm, just at the shoulder joining—the words "U.S. Navy" inscribed between the hook-like arms of a shadowy little anchor and running along the hypotenuse of the deltoid muscle. A tiny symbol, if one were needed, of all the million circumstances of the other fellow's life, of that blizzard of details that constitute the confusion of a human biography—a tiny symbol to remind me why our understanding of people must always be at best slightly wrong.

"Kept it? The letter? Still got it?" I said. "Must've been some letter."

"A killing letter. Something had happened to me that I hadn't understood until that letter. I was married, responsibly employed, we were going to have a child, and yet I hadn't understood that the Steenas were over. Got this letter and I realized that the serious things had really begun, the serious life dedicated to serious things. My father owned a saloon off Grove Street in East Orange. You're a Weequahic boy, you don't know East Orange. It was the poor end of town. He was one of those Jewish saloon keepers, they were all over Jersey and, of course, they all had ties to the Reinfelds and to the Mob—they had to have, to survive the Mob. My father wasn't a roughneck but he was rough enough, and he wanted better for me. He dropped dead my last year of high school. I was the only child. The adored one. He wouldn't even let me work in his place when the types there began to entertain me. Everything in life, including the saloon—*beginning* with the saloon —was always pushing me to be a serious student, and, back in those days, studying my high school Latin, taking advanced Latin, taking Greek, which was still part of the old-fashioned curriculum, the saloon keeper's kid couldn't have tried harder to be any *more* serious."

There was some quick by-play between us and Coleman laid down his cards to show me his winning hand. As I started to deal, he resumed the story. I'd never heard it before. I'd never heard anything before other than how he'd come by his hatred for the college.

"Well," he said, "once I'd fulfilled my father's dream and become an ultra-respectable college professor, I thought, as my father did, that the serious life would now never end. That it *could* never end once you had the credentials. But it ended, Nathan. 'Or are they spooks?' and I'm out on my ass. When Roberts was here he liked to tell people that my success as a dean flowed from learning my manners in a saloon. President Roberts with his upper-class pedigree liked that he had this barroom brawler parked just across the hall from him. In front of the old guard particularly, Roberts pretended to enjoy me for my background, though, as we know, Gentiles actually hate those stories about the Jews and their remarkable rise from the slums. Yes, there was a certain amount of mockery in Pierce Roberts, and even then, yes, when I think about it, starting even *then* . . ." But here he reined himself in. Wouldn't go on with it. He was finished with the derangement of being the monarch deposed. The grievance that will never die is hereby declared dead.

Back to Steena. Remembering Steena helps enormously.

"Met her in '48," he said. "I was twenty-two, on the GI Bill at NYU, the navy behind me, and she was eighteen and only a few months in New York. Had some kind of job there and was going to college, too, but at night. Independent girl from Minnesota. Sure-of-herself girl, or seemed so. Danish on one side, Icelandic on the other. Quick. Smart. Pretty. Tall. Marvelously tall. That statuesque recumbency. Never forgotten it. With her for two years. Used to call her Voluptas. Psyche's daughter. The personification to the Romans of sensual pleasure."

Now he put down his cards, picked up the envelope from where he'd dropped it beside the discard pile, and pulled out the letter. A typewritten letter a couple of pages long. "We'd run into each other. I was in from Adelphi, in the city for the day, and there was Steena, about twenty-four, twenty-five by then. We stopped and spoke, and I told her my wife was pregnant, and she told me what she was doing, and then we kissed goodbye, and that was it. About a week later this letter came to me care of the college. It's dated. She dated it. Here— 'August 18, 1954.' 'Dear Coleman,' she says, 'I was very happy to see you in New York. Brief as our meeting was, after I saw you I felt an autumnal sadness, perhaps because the six years since we first met make it wrenchingly obvious how many days of my life are "over." You look very good, and I'm glad you're happy. You were also very gentlemanly. You didn't swoop. Which is the one thing you did (or seemed to do) when I first met you and you rented the basement room on Sullivan Street. Do you remember yourself? You were incredibly good at swooping, almost like birds do when they fly over land or sea and spy something moving, something bursting with life, and dive down—or zero in—and seize upon it. I was astonished, when we met, by your flying energy. I remember being in your room the first time and, when I arrived, I sat in a chair, and you were walking around the room from place to place, occasionally stopping to perch on a stool or the couch. You had a ratty Salvation Army couch where you slept before we chipped in for The Mattress. You offered me a drink, which you handed to me while scrutinizing me with an air of incredible wonder and curiosity, as if it were some kind of miracle that I had hands and could hold a glass, or that I had a mouth which might drink from it, or that I had even materialized at all, in your room, a day after we'd met on the subway. You were talking, asking questions, sometimes answering questions, in a deadly serious and yet hilarious way, and I was trying very hard to talk also but conversation was not coming as easily to me. So there I was staring back at you, absorbing and understanding far more than I expected to understand. But I couldn't find words to speak to fill the space created by the fact that you seemed attracted to me and that I was attracted to you. I kept thinking, "I'm not ready. I just arrived in this city. Not now. But I will be, with a little more time, a few more exchanged notes of conversation, if I can think what I wish to say." ("Ready" for what, I don't know. Not just making love. Ready to *be*.) But then you "swooped," Coleman, nearly halfway across the room, to where I was sitting, and I was flabbergasted but delighted. It was too soon, but it wasn't.' "

He stopped reading when he heard, coming from the radio, the first bars of "Bewitched, Bothered, and Bewildered" being sung by Sinatra. "I've got to dance," Coleman said. "Want to dance?"

I laughed. No, this was not the savage, embittered, embattled avenger of *Spooks*, estranged from life and maddened by it—this was not even another man. This was another *soul*. A boyish soul at that. I got a strong picture then, both from Steena's letter and from Coleman, shirtless, as he was reading it, of what Coleman Silk had once been like. Before becoming a revolutionary dean, before becoming a serious classics professor—and long before becoming Athena's pariah—he had been not only a studious boy but a charming and seductive boy as well. Excited. Mischievous. A bit demonic even, a snub-nosed, goat-footed Pan. Once upon a time, before the serious things took over completely.

"After I hear the rest of the letter," I replied to the invitation to dance. "Read me the rest of Steena's letter."

"Three months out of Minnesota when we met. Just went down into the subway and brought her up with me. Well," he said, "that was 1948 for you," and he turned back to her letter. " 'I was quite taken with you,' " he read, " 'but I was concerned you might find me too young, an uninteresting midwestern bland sort of girl, and besides, you were dating someone "smart and nice and lovely" already, though you added, with a sly smile, "I don't believe she and I will get married." "Why not?" I asked. "I may be getting bored," you answered, thereby ensuring that I would do anything I could think of not to bore you, including dropping out of contact, if necessary, so as to avoid the risk of becoming boring. Well, that's it. That's enough. I shouldn't even bother you. I promise I won't ever again. Take care. Take care. Take care. Take care. Very fondly, Steena.' "

"Well," I said, "that *is* 1948 for you."

"Come. Let's dance."

"But you mustn't sing into my ear."

"Come on. Get up."

What the hell, I thought, we'll both be dead soon enough, and so I got up, and there on the porch Coleman Silk and I began to dance the fox trot together. He led, and, as best I could, I followed. I remembered that day he'd burst into my studio after making burial arrangements for Iris and, out of his mind with grief and rage, told me that I had to write for him the book about all the unbelievable absurdities of his case, culminating in the murder of his wife. One would have thought that never again would this man have a taste for the foolishness of life, that all that was playful in him and lighthearted had been destroyed and lost, right along with the career, the reputation, and the formidable wife. Maybe why it didn't even cross my mind to laugh and let him, if he wanted to, dance around the porch by himself, just laugh and enjoy myself watching him—maybe why I gave him my hand and let him place his arm around my back and push me dreamily around that old bluestone floor was because I had been there that day when her corpse was still warm and seen what he'd looked like.

"I hope nobody from the volunteer fire department drives by," I said.

"Yeah," he said. "We don't want anybody tapping me on the shoulder and asking, 'May I cut in?'"

On we danced. There was nothing overtly carnal in it, but because Coleman was wearing only his denim shorts and my hand rested easily on his warm back as if it were the back of a dog or a horse, it wasn't entirely a mocking act. There was a semi-serious sincerity in his guiding me about on the stone floor, not to mention a thoughtless delight in just being alive, accidentally and clownishly and for no reason alive—the kind of delight you take as a child when you first learn to play a tune with a comb and toilet paper.

It was when we sat down that Coleman told me about the woman. "I'm having an affair, Nathan. I'm having an affair with a thirty-four-year-old woman. I can't tell you what it's done to me."

"We just finished dancing—you don't have to."

"I thought I couldn't take any more of anything. But when this stuff comes back so late in life, out of nowhere, completely unexpected, even unwanted, comes back at you and there's nothing to dilute it with, when you're no longer striving on twenty-two fronts, no longer deep in the daily disorder . . . when it's just *this* . . ."

"And when she's thirty-four."

"And ignitable. An ignitable woman. She's turned sex into a vice again."

" 'La Belle Dame sans Merci hath thee in thrall.' "

"Seems so. I say, 'What is it like for you with somebody seventy-one?' and she tells me, 'It's perfect with somebody seventy-one. He's set in his ways and he can't change. You know what he is. No surprises.' "

"What's made her so wise?"

"Surprises. Thirty-four years of savage surprises have given her wisdom. But it's a very narrow, antisocial wisdom. It's savage, too. It's the wisdom of somebody who expects nothing. That's her wisdom, and that's her dignity, but it's negative wisdom, and that's not the kind that keeps you on course day to day. This is a woman whose life's been trying to grind her down almost for as long as she's had life. Whatever she's learned comes from that."

I thought, He's found somebody he can talk with . . . and then I thought, So have I. The moment a man starts to tell you about sex, he's telling you something about the two of you. Ninety percent of the time it doesn't happen, and probably it's as well it doesn't, though if you can't get a level of candor on sex and you choose to behave instead as if this isn't ever on your mind, the male friendship is incomplete. Most men never find such a friend. It's not common. But when it does happen, when two men find themselves in agreement about this essential part of being a man, unafraid of being judged, shamed, envied, or outdone, confident of not having the confidence betrayed, their human connection can be very strong and an unexpected intimacy results. This probably isn't usual for him, I was thinking, but because he'd come to me in his worst moment, full of the hatred that I'd watched poison him over the months, he feels the freedom of being with someone who's seen you through a terrible illness from the side of your bed. He feels not so much the urge to brag as the enormous relief of not having to keep something so bewilderingly new as his own rebirth totally to himself.

"Where did you find her?" I asked.

"I went to pick up my mail at the end of the day and there she was, mopping the floor. She's the skinny blonde who sometimes cleans out the post office. She's on the regular janitorial staff at Athena. She's a full-time janitor where I was once dean. The woman has nothing. Faunia Farley. That's her name. Faunia has absolutely nothing."

"Why has she nothing?"

"She had a husband. He beat her so badly she ended up in a coma. They had a dairy farm. He ran it so badly it went bankrupt. She had two children. A space heater tipped over, caught fire, and both children were asphyxiated. Aside from the ashes of the two children that she keeps in a canister under her bed, she owns nothing of value except an '83 Chevy. The only time I've seen her come close to crying was when she told me, 'I don't know what to do with the ashes.' Rural disaster has squeezed Faunia dry of even her tears. And she began life a rich, privileged kid. Brought up in a big sprawling house south of Boston. Fireplaces in the five bedrooms, the best antiques, heirloom china—everything old and the best, the family included. She can be surprisingly well spoken if she wants to be. But she's dropped so far down the social ladder from so far up that by now she's a pretty mixed bag of verbal beans. Faunia's been exiled from the entitlement that should have been hers. Declassed. There's a real democratization to her suffering."

"What undid her?"

"A stepfather undid her. Upper-bourgeois evil undid her. There was a divorce when she was five. The prosperous father caught the beautiful mother having an affair. The mother liked money, remarried money, and the rich stepfather wouldn't leave Faunia alone. Fondling her from the day he arrived. Couldn't stay away from her. This blond angelic child, fondling her, fingering her—it's when he tried fucking her that she ran away. She was fourteen. The mother refused to believe her. They took her to a psychiatrist. Faunia told the psychiatrist what happened, and after ten sessions the psychiatrist too sided with the stepfather. 'Takes the side of those who pay him,' Faunia says. 'Just like everyone.' The mother had an affair with the psychiatrist afterward. That is the story, as she reports it, of what launched her into the life of a tough having to make her way on her own. Ran away from home, from high school, went

down south, worked there, came back up this way, got whatever work she could, and at twenty married this farmer, older
than herself, a dairy farmer, a Vietnam vet, thinking that if they
worked hard and raised kids and made the farm work she could
have a stable, ordinary life, even if the guy was on the dumb
side. Especially if he was on the dumb side. She thought she
might be better off being the one with the brains. She thought
that was her advantage. She was wrong. All they had together
was trouble. The farm failed. 'Jerk-off,' she tells me, 'bought
one tractor too many.' And regularly beat her up. Beat her
black and blue. You know what she presents as the high point
of the marriage? The event she calls 'the great warm shit fight.'
One evening they are in the barn after the milking arguing
about something, and a cow next to her takes a big shit, and
Faunia picks up a handful and flings it in Lester's face. He flings
a handful back, and that's how it started. She said to me, 'The
warm shit fight may have been the best time we had together.'
At the end, they were covered with cow shit and roaring with
laughter, and, after washing off with the hose in the barn, they
went up to the house to fuck. But that was carrying a good
thing too far. That wasn't one-hundredth of the fun of the
fight. Fucking Lester wasn't ever fun—according to Faunia, he
didn't know how to do it. 'Too dumb even to fuck right.'
When she tells me that I am the perfect man, I tell her that I
see how that might seem so to her, coming to me after him."

"And fighting the Lesters of life with warm shit since she's
fourteen has made her what at thirty-four," I asked, "aside
from savagely wise? Tough? Shrewd? Enraged? Crazy?"

"The fighting life has made her tough, certainly sexually
tough, but it hasn't made her crazy. At least I don't think so
yet. Enraged? If it's there—and why wouldn't it be?—it's a
furtive rage. Rage without the rage. And, for someone who
seems to have lived entirely without luck, there's no lament in
her—none she shows to me, anyway. But as for shrewd, no.
She says things sometimes that sound shrewd. She says, 'Maybe
you ought to think of me as a companion of equal age who
happens to look younger. I think that's where I'm at.' When I
asked, 'What do you want from me?' she said, 'Some companionship. Maybe some knowledge. Sex. Pleasure. Don't worry.
That's it.' When I told her once she was wise beyond her years,

she told me, 'I'm dumb beyond my years.' She was sure smarter than Lester, but shrewd? No. Something in Faunia is permanently fourteen and as far as you can get from shrewd. She had an affair with her boss, the guy who hired her. Smoky Hollenbeck. *I* hired *him*—guy who runs the college's physical plant. Smoky used to be a football star here. Back in the seventies I knew him as a student. Now he's a civil engineer. He hires Faunia for the custodial staff, and even while he's hiring her, she understands what's on his mind. The guy is attracted to her. He's locked into an unexciting marriage, but he's not angry with her about it—he's not looking at her disdainfully, thinking, Why haven't you settled down, why are you still tramping and whoring around? No bourgeois superiority from Smoky. Smoky is doing all the right things and doing them beautifully—a wife, kids, *five* kids, married as a man can be, a sports hero still around the college, popular and admired in town—but he has a gift: he can also step outside of that. You wouldn't believe it to talk to him. Mr. Athena Square squared, performing in every single way he is supposed to perform. Appears to have bought into the story of himself one hundred percent. You would expect him to think, This stupid bitch with her fucked-up life? Get her the fuck out of my office. But he doesn't. Unlike everyone else in Athena, he is not so caught up in the legend of Smoky that he is incapable of thinking, Yeah, this is a real cunt I'd like to fuck. Or incapable of acting. He fucks her, Nathan. Gets Faunia in bed with him and another of the women from the custodial staff. Fucks 'em together. Goes on for six months. Then a real estate woman, newly divorced, fresh on the local scene, *she* joins the act. Smoky's circus. Smoky's secret three-ring circus. But then, after six months, he drops her—takes Faunia out of the rotation and drops her. I knew nothing about any of this till she told me. And she only told me because one night in bed, her eyes roll back into her head and she calls me by his name. Whispers to me, 'Smoky.' On top of old Smoky. Her being with him in that ménage gave me a better idea of the dame I was dealing with. Upped the ante. Gave me a jolt, actually—this is no amateur. When I ask her how Smoky manages to attract his hordes, she tells me, 'By the force of his prick.' 'Explain,' I say, and she tells me, 'You

know how when a real cunt walks into a room, a man knows
it? Well, the same thing happens the other way round. With
certain people, no matter what the disguise, you understand
what they're there to do.' In bed is the only place where Faunia
is in any way shrewd, Nathan. A spontaneous physical shrewdness plays the leading role in bed—second lead played by
transgressive audacity. In bed nothing escapes Faunia's attention. Her flesh has eyes. Her flesh sees everything. In bed she
is a powerful, coherent, unified being whose pleasure is in
overstepping the boundaries. In bed she is a deep phenomenon.
Maybe that's a gift of the molestation. When we go downstairs
to the kitchen, when I scramble some eggs and we sit there
eating together, she's a kid. Maybe that's a gift of the molestation too. I am in the company of a blank-eyed, distracted, incoherent kid. This happens nowhere else. But whenever we
eat, there it is: me and my kid. Seems to be all the daughter
that's left in her. She can't sit up straight in her chair, she can't
string two sentences together having anything to do with each
other. All the seeming nonchalance about sex and tragedy, all
of that disappears, and I'm sitting there wanting to say to her,
'Pull yourself up to the table, get the sleeve of my bathrobe
out of your plate, try to listen to what I'm saying, and look at
me, damn it, when you speak.'"

"*Do* you say it?"

"Doesn't seem advisable. No, I don't—not as long as I prefer
to preserve the intensity of what *is* there. I think of that canister
under her bed, where she keeps the ashes she doesn't know
what to do with, and I want to say, 'It's two years. It's time to
bury them. If you can't put them in the ground, then go down
to the river and shake out the ashes from the bridge. Let them
float off. Let them go. I'll go do it with you. We'll do it together.' But I am not the father to this daughter—that's not
the role I play here. I'm not her professor. I'm not anyone's
professor. From teaching people, correcting people, advising
and examining and enlightening people, I am retired. I am a
seventy-one-year-old man with a thirty-four-year-old mistress;
this disqualifies me, in the commonwealth of Massachusetts,
from enlightening anyone. I'm taking Viagra, Nathan. *There's*
La Belle Dame sans Merci. I owe all of this turbulence and

happiness to Viagra. Without Viagra none of this would be happening. Without Viagra I would have a picture of the world appropriate to my age and wholly different aims. Without Viagra I would have the dignity of an elderly gentleman free from desire who behaves correctly. I would not be doing something that makes no sense. I would not be doing something unseemly, rash, ill considered, and potentially disastrous for all involved. Without Viagra, I could continue, in my declining years, to develop the broad impersonal perspective of an experienced and educated honorably discharged man who has long ago given up the sensual enjoyment of life. I could continue to draw profound philosophical conclusions and have a steadying moral influence on the young, instead of having put myself back into the perpetual state of emergency that is sexual intoxication. Thanks to Viagra I've come to understand Zeus's amorous transformations. That's what they should have called Viagra. They should have called it Zeus."

Is he astonished to be telling me all this? I think he may be. But he's too enlivened by it all to stop. The impulse is the same one that drove him to dance with me. Yes, I thought, it's no longer writing *Spooks* that's the defiant rebound from humiliation; it's fucking Faunia. But there's even more than that driving him. There's the wish to let the brute out, let that force out—for half an hour, for two hours, for whatever, to be freed into the natural thing. He was married a long time. He had kids. He was the dean at a college. For forty years he was doing what was necessary to do. He was busy, and the natural thing that is the brute was moved into a box. And now that box is opened. Being a dean, being a father, being a husband, being a scholar, a teacher, reading the books, giving the lectures, marking the papers, giving the grades, it's over. At seventy-one you're not the high-spirited, horny brute you were at twenty-six, of course. But the remnants of the brute, the remnants of the natural thing—he is in touch now with the remnants. And he's happy as a result, he's grateful to be in touch with the remnants. He's more than happy—he's thrilled, and he's bound, deeply bound to her already, because of the thrill. It's not family that's doing it—biology has no use for him anymore. It's not family, it's not responsibility, it's not duty, it's not money, it's not a shared philosophy or the love of literature, it's not big discussions of great ideas. No, what binds him to her is the thrill. Tomorrow he develops cancer, and boom. But today he has this thrill.

Why is he telling me? Because to be able to abandon oneself to this freely, someone has to know it. He's free to be abandoned, I thought, because there's nothing at stake. Because there is no future. Because he's seventy-one and she's thirty-four. He's in it not for learning, not for planning, but for adventure; he's in it as she is: for the ride. He's been given a lot of license by those thirty-seven years. An old man and, one last time, the sexual charge. What is more moving for anybody?

"Of course I have to ask," Coleman said, "what she's doing with *me*. What is really going through her mind? An exciting new experience for her, to be with a man as old as her grandfather?"

"I suppose there is that type of woman," I said, "for whom it *is* an exciting experience. There's every other type, why shouldn't there be that type? Look, there is obviously a department somewhere, Coleman, a federal agency that deals with old men, and she comes from that agency."

"As a young guy," Coleman told me, "I was never involved with ugly women. But in the navy I had a friend, Farriello, and ugly women were his specialty. Down at Norfolk, if we went to a dance at a church, if we went at night to the USO, Farriello made a beeline for the ugliest girl. When I laughed at him, he told me I didn't know what I was missing. They're frustrated, he told me. They're not as beautiful, he told me, as the empresses you choose, so they'll do whatever you want. Most men are stupid, he said, because they don't know this. They don't understand that if only you approach the ugliest woman, she is the one who is the most extraordinary. If you can open her up, that is. But if you succeed? If you succeed in opening her up, you don't know what to do first, she is vibrating so. And all because she's ugly. Because she is never chosen. Because she is in the corner when all the other girls dance. And that's what it's like to be an old man. To be like that ugly girl. To be in the corner at the dance."

"So Faunia's your Farriello."

He smiled. "More or less."

"Well, whatever else may be going on," I told him, "thanks to Viagra you're no longer suffering the torture of writing that book."

"I think that's so," Coleman said. "I think that's true. That stupid book. And did I tell you that Faunia can't read? I found this out when we drove up to Vermont one night for dinner. Couldn't read the menu. Tossed it aside. She has a way, when she wants to look properly contemptuous, of lifting just a half of her upper lip, lifting it a hair, and then speaking what's on her mind. Properly contemptuous, she says to the waitress, 'Whatever he has, ditto.'"

"She went to school until she was fourteen. How come she can't read?"

"The ability to read seems to have perished right along with the childhood when she learned how. I asked her how this could happen, but all she did was laugh. 'Easy,' she says. The good liberals down at Athena are trying to encourage her to enter a literacy program, but Faunia's not having it. 'And don't *you* try to teach me. Do anything you want with me, anything,' she told me that night, 'but don't pull that shit. Bad enough having to hear people speak. Start teaching me to read, force me into that, push reading on me, and it'll be you who push me over the edge.' All the way back from Vermont, I was silent, and so was she. Not until we reached the house did we utter a word to each other. 'You're not up to fucking somebody who can't read,' she said. 'You're going to drop me because I'm not a worthy, legitimate person who *reads*. You're going to say to me, "Learn to read or go." 'No,' I told her, 'I'm going to fuck you all the harder because you can't read.' 'Good,' she said, 'we understand each other. I don't do it like those literate girls and I don't want to be done to like them.' 'I'm going to fuck you,' I said, 'for just what you are.' 'That's the ticket,' she says. We were both laughing by then. Faunia's got the laugh of a bar-maid who keeps a baseball bat at her feet in case of trouble, and so she was laughing that laugh of hers, that scrappy, I've-seen-it-all laugh—you know, the coarse, easy laugh of the woman with a past—and by then she's unzipping my fly. But she was right on the money about my having decided to give her up. All the way back from Vermont I was thinking exactly what she said I was thinking. But I'm not going to do that. I'm not going to impose my wonderful virtue on her. Or on myself. That's over. I know these things don't come without a cost. I know that there's no insurance you can buy on this. I know how the thing that's restoring you can wind up killing you. I know that every mistake that a man can make usually has a sexual accelerator. But right now I happen not to care. I wake up in the morning, there's a towel on the floor, there's baby oil on the bedside table. How did all that get there? Then I remember. Got there because I'm alive again. Because I'm back in the tornado. Because this is what it is with a capital isness. I'm not going to give her up, Nathan. I've started to call her Voluptas."

As a result of surgery I had several years ago to remove my prostate—cancer surgery that, though successful, was not without the adverse aftereffects almost unavoidable in such operations because of nerve damage and internal scarring—I've been left incontinent, and so, the first thing I did when I got home from Coleman's was to dispose of the absorbent cotton pad that I wear night and day, slipped inside the crotch of my underwear the way a hot dog lies in a roll. Because of the heat that evening, and because I wasn't going out to a public place or a social gathering, I'd tried to get by with ordinary cotton briefs pulled on over the pad instead of the plastic ones, and the result was that the urine had seeped through to my khaki trousers. I discovered when I got home that the trousers were discolored at the front and that I smelled a little—the pads are treated, but there was, on this occasion, an odor. I'd been so engaged by Coleman and his story that I'd failed to monitor myself. All the while I was there, drinking a beer, dancing with him, attending to the clarity—the predictable rationality and descriptive clarity—with which he worked to make less unsettling to himself this turn that life had taken, I hadn't gone off to check myself, as ordinarily I do during my waking hours, and so, what from time to time now happens to me happened that night.

No, a mishap like this one doesn't throw me as much as it used to when, in the months after the surgery, I was first experimenting with the ways of handling the problem—and when, of course, I was habituated to being a free and easy, dry and odorless adult possessing an adult's mastery of the body's elementary functions, someone who for some sixty years had gone about his everyday business unworried about the status of his underclothes. Yet I do suffer at least a pang of distress when I have to deal with something messier than the ordinary inconvenience that is now a part of my life, and I still despair to think that the contingency that virtually defines the infant state will never be alleviated.

I was also left impotent by the surgery. The drug therapy that was practically brand-new in the summer of 1998 and that had already, in its short time on the market, proved to be something like a miraculous elixir, restoring functional potency to many otherwise healthy, elderly men like Coleman, was of no use to me because of the extensive nerve damage done by the operation. For conditions like mine Viagra could do nothing, though even had it proved helpful, I don't believe I would have taken it.

I want to make clear that it wasn't impotence that led me into a reclusive existence. To the contrary. I'd already been living and writing for some eighteen months in my two-room cabin up here in the Berkshires when, following a routine physical exam, I received a preliminary diagnosis of prostate cancer and, a month later, after the follow-up tests, went to Boston for the prostatectomy. My point is that by moving here I had altered deliberately my relationship to the sexual caterwaul, and not because the exhortations or, for that matter, my erections had been effectively weakened by time, but because I couldn't meet the costs of its clamoring anymore, could no longer marshal the wit, the strength, the patience, the illusion, the irony, the ardor, the egoism, the resilience—or the toughness, or the shrewdness, or the falseness, the dissembling, the dual being, the erotic *professionalism*—to deal with its array of misleading and contradictory meanings. As a result, I was able to lessen a little my postoperative shock at the prospect of permanent impotence by remembering that all the surgery had done was to make me hold to a renunciation to which I had already voluntarily submitted. The operation did no more than to enforce with finality a decision I'd come to on my own, under the pressure of a lifelong experience of entanglements but in a time of full, vigorous, and restless potency, when the venturesome masculine mania to repeat the act—repeat it and repeat it and repeat it—remained undeterred by physiological problems.

It wasn't until Coleman told me about himself and his Voluptas that all the comforting delusions about the serenity achieved through enlightened resignation vanished, and I completely lost my equilibrium. Well into the morning I lay awake, powerless as a lunatic to control my thinking, hypnotized by the other couple and comparing them to my own washed-out state. I lay awake not even trying to prevent myself from mentally reconstructing the "transgressive audacity" Coleman was refusing to relinquish. And my having danced around like a harmless eunuch with this still vital, potent participant in the frenzy struck me now as anything but charming self-satire.

How can one say, "No, this isn't a part of life," since it always is? The contaminant of sex, the redeeming corruption that de-idealizes the species and keeps us everlastingly mindful of the matter we are.

In the middle of the next week, Coleman got the anonymous letter, one sentence long, subject, predicate, and pointed modifiers boldly inscribed in a large hand across a single sheet of white typing paper, the twelve-word message, intended as an indictment, filling the sheet from top to bottom:

> Everyone knows you're
> sexually exploiting an
> abused, illiterate
> woman half your
> age.

The writing on both the envelope and the letter was in red ballpoint ink. Despite the envelope's New York City postmark, Coleman recognized the handwriting immediately as that of the young French woman who'd been his department chair when he'd returned to teaching after stepping down from the deanship and who, later, had been among those most eager to have him exposed as a racist and reprimanded for the insult he had leveled at his absent black students.

In his *Spooks* files, on several of the documents generated by his case, he found samples of handwriting that confirmed his

identification of Professor Delphine Roux, of Languages and
Literature, as the anonymous letter writer. Aside from her having printed rather than written in script the first couple of
words, she hadn't made any effort that Coleman could see to
put him off the trail by falsifying her hand. She might have
begun with that intention but appeared to have abandoned
it or forgotten about it after getting no further than "Everyone knows." On the envelope, the French-born professor
hadn't even bothered to eschew the telltale European sevens
in Coleman's street address and zip code. This laxness, an odd
disregard—in an anonymous letter—for concealing the signs
of one's identity might have been explained by some extreme
emotional state she was in that hadn't allowed her to think
through what she was doing before firing off the letter, except
that it hadn't been posted locally—and hastily—but appeared
from the postmark to have been transported some hundred
and forty miles south before being mailed. Maybe she had
figured that there was nothing distinctive or eccentric enough
in her handwriting for him to be able to recognize it from his
days as dean; maybe she had failed to remember the documents pertaining to his case, the notes of her two interviews
with Tracy Cummings that she had passed on to the faculty
investigating committee along with the final report that bore
her signature. Perhaps she didn't realize that, at Coleman's request, the committee had provided him with a photocopy of
her original notes and all the other data pertinent to the complaint against him. Or maybe she didn't care if he did determine
who out there had uncovered his secret: maybe she wanted both
to taunt him with the menacing aggressiveness of an anonymous indictment and, at the same time, to all but disclose that
the indictment had been brought by someone now far from
powerless.

   The afternoon Coleman called and asked me to come over
to see the anonymous letter, all the samples of Delphine Roux's
handwriting from the *Spooks* files were neatly laid out on the
kitchen table, both the originals and copies of the originals
that he'd already run off and on which he'd circled, in red, every
stroke of the pen that he saw as replicating the strokes in the
anonymous letter. Marked off mainly were letters in isolation

—a *y*, an *s*, an *x*, here a word-ending *e* with a wide loop, here an *e* looking something like an *i* when nestled up against an adjacent *d* but more like a conventionally written *e* when preceding an *r*—and, though the similarities in writing between the letter and the *Spooks* documents were noteworthy, it wasn't until he showed me where his full name appeared on the envelope and where it appeared in her interview notes with Tracy Cummings that it seemed to me indisputable that he had nailed the culprit who'd set out to nail him.

> Everyone knows you're
> sexually exploiting an
> abused, illiterate
> woman half your
> age.

While I held the letter in my hand and as carefully as I could —and as Coleman would have me do—appraised the choice of words and their linear deployment as if they'd been composed not by Delphine Roux but by Emily Dickinson, Coleman explained to me that it was Faunia, out of that savage wisdom of hers, and not he who had sworn them both to the secrecy that Delphine Roux had somehow penetrated and was more or less threatening to expose. "I don't want anybody butting in my life. All I want is a no-pressure bang once a week, on the sly, with a man who's been through it all and is nicely cooled out. Otherwise it's nobody's fucking business."

The nobody Faunia turned out mostly to be referring to was Lester Farley, her ex-husband. Not that she'd been knocked around in her life by this man alone—"How could I be, being out there on my own since I was fourteen?" When she was seventeen, for example, and down in Florida waitressing, the then-boyfriend not only beat her up and trashed her apartment, he stole her vibrator. "That hurt," Faunia said. And always, the provocation was jealousy. She'd looked at another man the wrong way, she'd invited another man to look at *her* the wrong way, she hadn't explained convincingly where she'd been for the previous half hour, she'd spoken the wrong word, used the wrong intonation, signaled, unsubstantially, *she* thought, that she was an untrustworthy two-timing slut—whatever the reason, whoever he might be would be over her swinging his fists and kicking his boots and Faunia would be screaming for her life.

Lester Farley had sent her to the hospital twice in the year before their divorce, and as he was still living somewhere in the hills and, since the bankruptcy, working for the town road crew, and as there was no doubting that he was still crazy, she was as frightened for Coleman, she said, as she was for herself, should he ever discover what was going on. She suspected that why Smoky had so precipitously dumped her was because of some sort of run-in or brush he'd had with Les Farley—because Les, a periodic stalker of his ex-wife, had somehow found out about her and her boss, even though Hollenbeck's trysting places were remarkably well hidden, tucked away in remote corners of old buildings that no one but the boss of the college physical plant could possibly know existed or have access to. Reckless as it might seem for Smoky to be recruiting girlfriends from his own custodial staff and then to be rendezvousing with them right on campus, he was otherwise as meticulous in the management of his sporting life as he was in his work for the college. With the same professional dispatch that could get the campus roads cleared of a blizzard in a matter of hours, he could, if need be, equally expeditiously rid himself of one of his girls.

"So what do I do?" Coleman asked me. "I wasn't against keeping this thing concealed even before I'd heard about the violent ex-husband. I knew that something like this was coming. Forget that I was once the dean where she now cleans the toilets. I'm seventy-one and she's thirty-four. I could count on that alone to do it, I was sure, and so, when she told me that it was nobody's business, I figured, She's taken it out of my hands. I don't even have to broach the subject. Play it like adultery? Fine with me. That's why we went for dinner up in Vermont. That's why if our paths cross at the post office, we don't even bother to say hello."

"Maybe somebody saw you in Vermont. Maybe somebody saw you driving together in your car."

"True—that's probably what happened. That's all that *could* have happened. It might have been Farley himself who saw us.

Christ, Nathan, I hadn't been on a date in almost fifty years—I thought the restaurant . . . I'm an idiot."

"No, it wasn't idiocy. No, no—you just got claustrophobic. Look," I said, "Delphine Roux—I won't pretend I understand why she should care so passionately who you are screwing in your retirement, but since we know that other people don't do well with somebody who fails at being conventional, let's assume that she is one of these other people. But you're not. You're free. A free and independent man. A free and independent *old* man. You lost plenty quitting that place, but what about what you've gained? It's no longer your job to enlighten anyone—you said as much yourself. Nor is this a test of whether you can or cannot rid yourself of every last social inhibition. You may now be retired but you're a man who led virtually the whole of life within the bounds of the communal academic society—if I read you right, this is a most unusual thing for you. Perhaps you never wanted Faunia to have happened. You may even believe that you shouldn't want her to have happened. But the strongest defenses are riddled with weakness, and so in slips the last thing in the world you expected. At seventy-one, there is Faunia; in 1998, there is Viagra; there once again is the all-but-forgotten thing. The enormous comfort. The crude power. The disorienting intensity. Out of nowhere, Coleman Silk's last great fling. For all we know, the last great last-*minute* fling. So the particulars of Faunia Farley's biography form an unlikely contrast to your own. So they don't conform to decency's fantasy blueprint for who should be in bed with a man of your years and your position—if anyone should be. Did what resulted from your speaking the word 'spooks' conform to decency's blueprint? Did Iris's stroke conform to decency's blueprint? Ignore the inanely stupid letter. Why should you let it deter you?"

"*Anonymous* inanely stupid letter," he said. "Who has ever sent me an anonymous letter? Who capable of rational thought sends anyone an anonymous letter?"

"Maybe it's a French thing," I said. "Isn't there a lot of it in Balzac? In Stendhal? Aren't there anonymous letters in *The Red and the Black*?"

"I don't remember."

"Look, for some reason everything you do must have ruthlessness as its explanation, and everything Delphine Roux does must have virtue as its explanation. Isn't mythology full of giants and monsters and snakes? By defining you as a monster, she defines herself as a heroine. This is her slaying of the monster. This is her revenge for your preying on the powerless. She's giving the whole thing mythological status."

From the smile indulgently offered me, I saw that I wasn't making much headway by spinning off, even jokingly, a pre-Homeric interpretation of the anonymous indictment. "You can't find in mythmaking," he told me, "an explanation for her mental processes. She hasn't the imaginative resources for mythmaking. Her métier is the stories that the peasants tell to account for their misery. The evil eye. The casting of spells. I've cast a spell over Faunia. Her métier is folktales full of witches and wizards."

We were enjoying ourselves now, and I realized that in my effort to distract him from his rampaging pique by arguing for the primacy of his pleasure, I had given a boost to his feeling for me—and exposed mine for him. I was gushing and I knew it. I surprised myself with my eagerness to please, felt myself saying too much, explaining too much, overinvolved and overexcited in the way you are when you're a kid and you think you've found a soul mate in the new boy down the street and you feel yourself drawn by the force of the courtship and so act as you don't normally do and a lot more openly than you may even want to. But ever since he had banged on my door the day after Iris's death and proposed that I write *Spooks* for him, I had, without figuring or planning on it, fallen into a serious friendship with Coleman Silk. I wasn't paying attention to his predicament as merely a mental exercise. His difficulties mattered to me, and this despite my determination to concern myself, in whatever time *I* have left, with nothing but the daily demands of work, to be engrossed by nothing but solid work, in search of adventure nowhere else—to have not even a life of my own to care about, let alone somebody else's.

And I realized all this with some disappointment. Abnegation of society, abstention from distraction, a self-imposed separation from every last professional yearning and social delusion and cultural poison and alluring intimacy, a rigorous reclusion such as that practiced by religious devouts who immure themselves in caves or cells or isolated forest huts, is maintained on stuff more obdurate than I am made of. I had lasted alone just five years—five years of reading and writing a few miles up Madamaska Mountain in a pleasant two-room cabin situated between a small pond at the back of my place and, through the scrub across the dirt road, a ten-acre marsh where the migrating Canada geese take shelter each evening and a patient blue heron does its solitary angling all summer long. The secret to living in the rush of the world with a minimum of pain is to get as many people as possible to string along with your delusions; the trick to living alone up here, away from all agitating entanglements, allurements, and expectations, apart especially from one's own intensity, is to organize the silence, to think of its mountaintop plenitude as capital, silence as wealth exponentially increasing. The encircling silence as your chosen source of advantage and your only intimate. The trick is to find sustenance in (Hawthorne again) "the communications of a solitary mind with itself." The secret is to find sustenance in *people* like Hawthorne, in the wisdom of the brilliant deceased.

It took time to face down the difficulties set by this choice, time and heronlike patience to subdue the longings for everything that had vanished, but after five years I'd become so skillful at surgically carving up my days that there was no longer an hour of the eventless existence I'd embraced that didn't have its importance to me. Its necessity. Its excitement even. I no longer indulged the pernicious wish for *something else*, and the last thing I thought I could endure again was the sustained company of *someone else*. The music I play after dinner is not a relief from the silence but something like its substantiation: listening to music for an hour or two every evening doesn't deprive me of the silence—the music is the silence coming true. I swim for thirty minutes in my pond first thing every summer morning, and, for the rest of the year, after my morning of writing—and so long as the snow doesn't make hiking impossible—I'm out on the mountain trails for a couple of hours nearly every afternoon. There has been no recurrence of the cancer that cost me my prostate. Sixty-five, fit, well, working hard—and I know the score. I *have* to know it.

So why, then, having turned the experiment of radical seclusion into a rich, full solitary existence—why, with no warning, should I be lonely? Lonely for what? What's gone is gone. There's no relaxing the rigor, no undoing the renunciations. Lonely for precisely what? Simple: for what I had developed an aversion to. For what I had turned my back on. For life. The entanglement with life.

This was how Coleman became my friend and how I came out from under the stalwartness of living alone in my secluded house and dealing with the cancer blows. Coleman Silk danced me right back into life. First Athena College, then me—here was a man who made things happen. Indeed, the dance that sealed our friendship was also what made his disaster my subject. And made his disguise my subject. And made the proper presentation of his secret my problem to solve. That was how I ceased being able to live apart from the turbulence and intensity that I had fled. I did no more than find a friend, and all the world's malice came rushing in.

Later that afternoon, Coleman took me to meet Faunia at a small dairy farm six miles from his house, where she lived rent-free in exchange for sometimes doing the milking. The dairy operation, a few years old now, had been initiated by two divorced women, college-educated environmentalists, who'd each come from a New England farming family and who had pooled their resources—pooled their young children as well, six children who, as the owners liked to tell their customers, weren't dependent on *Sesame Street* to learn where milk comes from—to take on the almost impossible task of making a living by selling raw milk. It was a unique operation, nothing like what was going on at the big dairy farms, nothing impersonal or factorylike about it, a place that wouldn't seem like a dairy farm to most people these days. It was called Organic Livestock, and it produced and bottled the raw milk that could be found in local general stores and in some of the region's supermarkets and was available, at the farm, for steady customers who purchased three or more gallons a week.

There were just eleven cows, purebred Jerseys, and each had an old-fashioned cow name rather than a numbered ear tag to identify it. Because their milk was not mixed with the milk of the huge herds that are injected with all sorts of chemicals, and because, uncompromised by pasteurization and unshattered by homogenization, the milk took on the tinge, even faintly the flavor, of whatever they were eating season by season—feed that had been grown without the use of herbicides, pesticides, or chemical fertilizers—and because their milk was richer in nutrients than blended milk, it was prized by the people around who tried to keep the family diet to whole rather than processed foods. The farm has a strong following particularly among the numerous people tucked away up here, the retired as well as those raising families, in flight from the pollutants, frustrations, and debasements of a big city. In the local weekly, a letter to the editor will regularly appear from someone who has recently found a better life out along these rural roads, and in reverent tones mention will be made of Organic Livestock milk, not simply as a tasty drink but as the embodiment of a freshening, sweetening country purity that their city-battered idealism requires. Words like "goodness" and "soul" crop up regularly in these published letters, as if downing a glass of Organic Livestock milk were no less a redemptive religious rite than a nutritional blessing. "When we drink Organic Livestock milk, our body, soul, and spirit are getting nourished as a whole. Various organs in our body receive this wholeness and appreciate it in a way we may not perceive." Sentences like that, sentences with which otherwise sensible adults, liberated from whatever vexation had driven them from New York or Hartford or Boston, can spend a pleasant few minutes at the desk pretending that they are seven years old.

Though Coleman probably used, all told, no more than the half cup of milk a day he poured over his morning cereal, he'd signed on with Organic Livestock as a three-gallon-a-week customer. Doing this allowed him to pick up his milk, fresh from the cow, right at the farm—to drive his car in from the road and down the long tractor path to the barn and to walk into the barn and get the milk cold out of the refrigerator. He'd arranged to do this not so as to be able to procure the price break extended to three-gallon customers but because the refrigerator was set just inside the entryway to the barn and only some fifteen feet from the stall where the cows were led in to be milked one at a time, twice a day, and where at 5 P.M. (when he showed up) Faunia, fresh from her duties at the college, would be doing the milking a few times a week.

All he ever did there was watch her work. Even though there was rarely anyone else around at that time, Coleman remained outside the stall looking in and let her get on with the job without having to bother to talk to him. Often they said nothing, because saying nothing intensified their pleasure. She knew he was watching her; knowing she knew, he watched all the harder—and that they weren't able to couple down in the dirt didn't make a scrap of difference. It was enough that they should be alone together somewhere *other* than in his bed, it was enough to have to maintain the matter-of-factness of being separated by unsurpassable social obstacles, to play their roles as farm laborer and retired college professor, to perform consummately at her being a strong, lean working woman of thirty-four, a wordless illiterate, an elemental rustic of muscle and bone who'd just been in the yard with the pitchfork cleaning up from the morning milking, and at his being a thoughtful senior citizen of seventy-one, an accomplished classicist, an amplitudinous brain of a man replete with the vocabularies of two ancient tongues. It was enough to be able to conduct themselves like two people who had nothing whatsoever in common, all the while remembering how they could distill to an orgasmic essence everything about them that was irreconcilable, the human discrepancies that produced all the power. It was enough to feel the thrill of leading a double life.

There was, at first glance, little to raise unduly one's carnal expectations about the gaunt, lanky woman spattered with dirt, wearing shorts and a T-shirt and rubber boots, whom I saw in with the herd that afternoon and whom Coleman identified as his Voluptas. The carnally authoritative-looking creatures were those with the bodies that took up all the space, the creamy-colored cows with the free-swinging, girderlike hips and the barrel-wide paunches and the disproportionately cartoonish milk-swollen udders, the unagitated, slow-moving, strife-free cows, each a fifteen-hundred-pound industry of its own gratification, big-eyed beasts for whom chomping at one extremity from a fodder-filled trough while being sucked dry at the other by not one or two or three but by four pulsating, untiring mechanical mouths—for whom sensual stimulus simultaneously at both ends was their voluptuous due. Each of them deep into a bestial existence blissfully lacking in spiritual depth: to squirt and to chew, to crap and to piss, to graze and to sleep—that was their whole raison d'être. Occasionally (Coleman explained to me) a human arm in a long plastic glove is thrust into the rectum to haul out the manure and then, by feeling with the glove through the rectal wall, guides the other arm in inserting a syringelike breeding gun up the reproductive tract to deposit semen. They propagate, that means, without having to endure the disturbance of the bull, coddled even in breeding and then assisted in delivery—and in what Faunia said could prove to be an emotional process for everyone involved—even on below-zero nights when a blizzard is blowing. The best of carnal everything, including savoring at their leisure mushy, dripping mouthfuls of their own stringy cud. Few courtesans have lived as well, let alone workaday women.

Among those pleasured creatures and the aura they exuded of an opulent, earthy oneness with female abundance, it was Faunia who labored like the beast of burden for all that she seemed, with the cows framing her figure, one of evolution's more pathetic flyweights. Calling them to come out from the open shed where they were reposefully sprawled in a mix of hay and shit—"Let's go, Daisy, don't give me a hard time. C'mon now, Maggie, that's a good girl. Move your ass, Flossie, you old bitch"—grabbing them by the collar and driving and cajoling them through the sludge of the yard and up one step onto the concrete floor of the milking parlor, shoving these cumbersome Daisys and Maggies in toward the trough until they were secure in the stanchion, measuring out and pouring them each their portion of vitamins and feed, disinfecting the teats and wiping them clean and starting the flow with a few jerks of the hand, then attaching to the sterilized teats the suction cups at the end of the milk claw, she was in motion constantly, fixed unwaveringly on each stage of the milking but, in exaggerated contrast to their stubborn docility, moving all the time with a beelike adroitness until the milk was streaming through the clear milk tube into the shining stainless-steel pail, and she at last stood quietly by, watching to make certain that everything was working and that the cow too was standing quietly. Then she was again in motion, massaging the udder to

be sure the cow was milked out, removing the teat cups, pouring out the feed portion for the cow she would be milking
after undoing the milked cow from the stanchion, getting the
grain for the next cow in front of the alternate stanchion, and
then, within the confines of that smallish space, grabbing the
milked cow by the collar again and maneuvering her great bulk
around, backing her up with a push, shoving her with a shoulder, bossily telling her, "Get out, get on out of here, just
get—" and leading her back through the mud to the shed.

Faunia Farley: thin-legged, thin-wristed, thin-armed, with
clearly discernible ribs and shoulder blades that protruded, and
yet when she tensed you saw that her limbs were hard; when
she reached or stretched for something you saw that her breasts
were surprisingly substantial; and when, because of the flies
and the gnats buzzing the herd on this close summer day, she
slapped at her neck or her backside, you saw something of how
frisky she could be, despite the otherwise straight-up style. You
saw that her body was something more than efficiently lean
and severe, that she was a firmly made woman precipitously
poised at the moment when she is no longer ripening but not
yet deteriorating, a woman in the prime of her prime, whose
fistful of white hairs is fundamentally beguiling just because
the sharp Yankee contour of her cheeks and her jaw and the
long unmistakably female neck haven't yet been subject to
the transformations of aging.

"This is my neighbor," Coleman said to her when she took a
moment to wipe the sweat from her face with the crook of her
elbow and to look our way. "This is Nathan."

I hadn't expected composure. I was expecting someone
openly angrier. She acknowledged me with no more than a jerk
of her chin, but it was a gesture from which she got a lot of
mileage. It was a *chin* from which she got a lot of mileage. Keeping it up as she normally did, it gave her—virility. That was in
the response too: something virile and implacable, as well as a
little disreputable, in that dead-on look. The look of someone
for whom both sex and betrayal are as basic as bread. The look
of the runaway and the look that results from the galling
monotony of bad luck. Her hair, the golden blond hair in
the poignant first stage of its unpreventable permutation, was
twisted at the back through an elastic band, but a lock kept

falling toward her eyebrow as she worked, and now, while silently looking our way, she pushed it back with her hand, and
for the first time I noticed in her face a small feature that, perhaps wrongly, because I was searching for a sign, had the effect
of something telling: the convex fullness of the narrow arch of
flesh between the ridge of eyebrow and the upper eyelids. She
was a thin-lipped woman with a straight nose and clear blue
eyes and good teeth and a prominent jaw, and that puff of flesh
just beneath her eyebrows was her only exotic marking, the
only emblem of allure, something swollen with desire. It also
accounted for a lot that was unsettlingly obscure about the
hard flatness of her gaze.

In all, Faunia was not the enticing siren who takes your
breath away but a clean-cut-looking woman about whom one
thinks, As a child she must have been very beautiful. Which
she was: according to Coleman, a golden, beautiful child with
a rich stepfather who wouldn't leave her alone and a spoiled
mother who wouldn't protect her.

We stood there watching while she milked each of the eleven
cows—Daisy, Maggie, Flossie, Bessy, Dolly, Maiden, Sweetheart, Stupid, Emma, Friendly, and Jill—stood there while she
went through the same unvarying routine with every one of
them, and when that was finished and she moved into the white-
washed room with the big sinks and the hoses and the steril-
izing units adjacent to the milking parlor, we watched her
through that doorway mixing up the lye solution and the cleansing agents and, after separating the vacuum line from the pipe-
line and the teat cups from the claw and the two milker pails
from their covers—after disassembling the whole of the milking unit that she'd taken in there with her—setting to work with
a variety of brushes and with sinkful after sinkful of clear water
to scrub every surface of every tube, valve, gasket, plug, plate,
liner, cap, disc, and piston until each was spotlessly clean and
sanitized. Before Coleman took his milk and we got back into
his car to leave, he and I had stood together by the refrigerator
for close to an hour and a half and, aside from the words he
uttered to introduce me to her, nobody human said anything
more. All you could hear was the whirring and the chirping of
the barn swallows who nested there as they whished through
the rafters where the barn opened out behind us, and the pellets

dropping into the cement trough when she shook out the feed pail, and the shuffling clump of the barely lifted hooves on the milking parlor floor as Faunia, shoving and dragging and steering the cows, positioned them into the stanchion, and then the suction noise, the soft deep breathing of the milk pump.

After they were each buried four months later, I would remember that milking session as though it were a theatrical performance in which I had played the part of a walk-on, an extra, which indeed I now am. Night after night, I could not sleep because I couldn't stop being up there on the stage with the two leading actors and the chorus of cows, observing this scene, flawlessly performed by the entire ensemble, of an enamored old man watching at work the cleaning woman–farmhand who is secretly his paramour: a scene of pathos and hypnosis and sexual subjugation in which everything the woman does with those cows, the way she handles them, touches them, services them, talks to them, his greedy fascination appropriates; a scene in which a man taken over by a force so long suppressed in him that it had all but been extinguished revealed, before my eyes, the resurgence of its stupefying power. It was something, I suppose, like watching Aschenbach feverishly watching Tadzio—his sexual longing brought to a boil by the anguishing fact of mortality—except that we weren't in a luxury hotel on the Venice Lido nor were we characters in a novel written in German or even, back then, in one written in English: it was high summer and we were in a barn in the Northeast of our country, in America in the year of America's presidential impeachment, and, as yet, we were no more novelistic than the animals were mythological or stuffed. The light and heat of the day (*that* blessing), the unchanging quiet of each cow's life as it paralleled that of all the others, the enamored old man studying the suppleness of the efficient, energetic woman, the adulation rising in him, his looking as though nothing more stirring had ever before happened to him, and, too, my own willing waiting, my own fascination with their extensive disparity as human types, with the nonuniformity, the variability, the teeming irregularity of sexual arrangements —and with the injunction upon us, human and bovine, the highly differentiated and the all but undifferentiated, to live, not merely to endure but to *live*, to go on taking, giving, feeding, milking, acknowledging wholeheartedly, as the enigma that it is, the pointless meaningfulness of living—all was recorded as real by tens of thousands of minute impressions. The sensory fullness, the copiousness, the abundant—superabundant—detail of life, which is the rhapsody. And Coleman and Faunia, who are now dead, deep in the flow of the unexpected, day by day, minute by minute, themselves details in that superabundance.

Nothing lasts, and yet nothing passes, either. And nothing passes just because nothing lasts.

The trouble with Les Farley began later that night, when Coleman heard something stirring in the bushes outside his house, decided it wasn't a deer or a raccoon, got up from the kitchen table where he and Faunia had just finished their spaghetti dinner, and, from the kitchen door, in the summer evening half-light, caught sight of a man running across the field back of the house and toward the woods. "Hey! You! Stop!" Coleman shouted, but the man neither stopped nor looked back and disappeared quickly into the trees. This wasn't the first time in recent months that Coleman believed he was being watched by someone hiding within inches of the house, but previously it had been later in the evening and too dark for him to know for sure whether he had been alerted by the movements of a peeping Tom or of an animal. And previously he had always been alone. This was the first time Faunia was there, and it was she who, without having to see the man's silhouette cutting across the field, identified the trespasser as her ex-husband.

After the divorce, she told Coleman, Farley had spied on her all the time, but in the months following the death of the two children, when he was accusing her of having killed them by her negligence, he was frighteningly unrelenting. Twice he popped up out of nowhere—once in the parking lot of a supermarket, once when she was at a gas station—and screamed out of the pickup window, "Murdering whore! Murdering bitch! You murdered my kids, you murdering bitch!" There were many mornings when, on her way to the college, she'd look in the rearview mirror and there would be his pickup truck and, back of the windshield, his face with the lips mouthing, "You murdered my kids." Sometimes he'd be on the road behind her when she was driving home from the college. She was then still living in the unburned half of the bungalow-garage where the children had been asphyxiated in the heater fire, and it was out of fear of him that she'd moved from there to a room in Seeley Falls and then, after a foiled suicide attempt, into the room at the dairy farm, where the two owners and their small children were almost always around and the danger was not so great of her being accosted by him. Farley's pickup appeared in her rearview mirror less frequently after the second move, and then, when there was no sign of him for months, she hoped he might be gone for good. But now, Faunia was sure of it, he'd somehow found out about Coleman and, enraged again with everything that had always enraged him about her, he was back at his crazy spying, hiding outside Coleman's house to see what she was doing there. What *they* were doing there.

That night, when Faunia got into her car—the old Chevy that Coleman preferred her to park, out of sight, inside his barn—Coleman decided to follow close behind her in his own car for the six miles until she was safely onto the dirt driveway that led past the cow barn to the farmhouse. And then all the way back to his own house he looked to see if anyone was behind *him*. At home, he walked from the car shed to the house swinging a tire iron in one hand, swinging it in all directions, hoping in that way to keep at bay anyone lurking in the dark.

By the next morning, after eight hours on his bed contending with his worries, Coleman had decided against lodging a complaint with the state police. Because Farley's identity couldn't be positively established, the police would be unable to do anything about him anyway, and should it leak out that Coleman had contacted them, his call would have served only to corroborate the gossip already circulating about the former dean and the Athena janitor. Not that, after his sleepless night, Coleman could resign himself to doing nothing about *everything*: following breakfast, he phoned his lawyer, Nelson Primus, and that afternoon went down to Athena to consult with him about the anonymous letter and there, overriding Primus's suggestion that he forget about it, prevailed on him to write, as follows, to Delphine Roux at the college: "Dear Ms. Roux: I represent Coleman Silk. Several days ago, you sent an anonymous letter to Mr. Silk that is offensive, harassing, and denigrating to

Mr. Silk. The content of your letter reads: 'Everyone knows you're sexually exploiting an abused, illiterate woman half your age.' You have, unfortunately, interjected yourself and become a participant in something that is not your business. In doing that, you have violated Mr. Silk's legal rights and are subject to suit."

A few days later Primus received three curt sentences back from Delphine Roux's lawyer. The middle sentence, flatly denying the charge that Delphine Roux was the author of the anonymous letter, Coleman underlined in red. "None of the assertions in your letter are correct," her lawyer had written to Primus, "and, indeed, they are defamatory."

Immediately Coleman got from Primus the name of a certified documents examiner in Boston, a handwriting analyst who did forensic work for private corporations, U.S. government agencies, and the state, and the next day, he himself drove the three hours to Boston to deliver into the hands of the documents examiner his samples of Delphine Roux's handwriting along with the anonymous letter and its envelope. He received the findings in the mail the next week. "At your request," read the report, "I examined and compared copies of known handwriting of Delphine Roux with a questioned anonymous note and an envelope addressed to Coleman Silk. You asked for a determination of the authorship of the handwriting on the questioned documents. My examination covers handwriting characteristics such as slant, spacing, letter formation, line quality, pressure pattern, proportion, letter height relationship, connections and initials and terminal stroke formation. Based on the documents submitted, it is my professional opinion that the hand that penned all the known standards as Delphine Roux is one and the same hand that penned the questioned anonymous note and envelope. Sincerely, Douglas Gordon, CDE." When Coleman turned the examiner's report over to Nelson Primus, with instructions to forward a copy to Delphine Roux's lawyer, Primus no longer put up an argument, however distressing it was to him to see Coleman nearly as enraged as he'd been back during the crisis with the college.

In all, eight days had passed since the evening he'd seen Farley fleeing into the woods, eight days during which he had determined it would be best if Faunia stayed away and they

communicated by phone. So as not to invite spying on either
of them from any quarter, he didn't go out to the farm to fetch
his raw milk but stayed at home as much as he could and kept
a careful watch there, especially after dark, to determine if
anyone was snooping around. Faunia, in turn, was told to keep
a lookout of her own at the dairy farm and to check her rearview mirror when she drove anywhere. "It's as though we're a
menace to public safety," she told him, laughing her laugh.
"No, public health," he replied—"we're in noncompliance
with the board of health."

By the end of the eight days, when he had been able at least
to confirm Delphine Roux's identification as the letter writer if
not yet Farley's as the trespasser, Coleman decided to decide
that he'd done everything within his power to defend against
all of this disagreeable and provocative meddling. When Faunia
phoned him that afternoon during her lunch break and asked,
"Is the quarantine over?" he at last felt free of enough of his
anxiety—or decided to decide to be—to give the all-clear sign.

As he expected her to show up around seven that evening,
he swallowed a Viagra tablet at six and, after pouring himself a
glass of wine, walked outside with the phone to settle into a
lawn chair and telephone his daughter. He and Iris had reared
four children: two sons now into their forties, both college
professors of science, married and with children and living on
the West Coast, and the twins, Lisa and Mark, unmarried, in
their late thirties, and both living in New York. All but one
of the Silk offspring tried to get up to the Berkshires to see
their father three or four times a year and stayed in touch every
month by phone. The exception was Mark, who'd been at
odds with Coleman all his life and sporadically cut himself off
completely.

Coleman was calling Lisa because he realized that it was
more than a month and maybe even two since he'd spoken to
her. Perhaps he was merely surrendering to a transient feeling
of loneliness that would have passed when Faunia arrived, but
whatever his motive, he could have had no inkling, before the
phone call, of what was in store. Surely the last thing he was
looking for was yet more opposition, least of all from that child
whose voice alone—soft, melodic, girlish still, despite twelve
difficult years as a teacher on the Lower East Side—he could

always depend on to soothe him, to calm him, sometimes to do even more: to infatuate him with this daughter all over again. He was doing probably what most any aging parent will do when, for any of a hundred reasons, he or she looks to a long-distance phone call for a momentary reminder of the old terms of reference. The unbroken, unequivocal history of tenderness between Coleman and Lisa made of her the least affrontable person still close to him.

Some three years earlier—back before the spooks incident —when Lisa was wondering if she hadn't made an enormous mistake by giving up classroom teaching to become a Reading Recovery teacher, Coleman had gone down to New York and stayed several days to see how bad off she was. Iris was alive then, very much alive, but it wasn't Iris's enormous energy Lisa had wanted—it wasn't to be put into motion the way Iris could put you in motion that she wanted—rather, it was the former dean of faculty with his orderly, determined way of untangling a mess. Iris was sure to tell her to forge ahead, leaving Lisa overwhelmed and feeling trapped; with him there was the possibility that, if Lisa made a compelling case against her own persevering, he would tell her that, if she wished, she could cut her losses and quit—which would, in turn, give her the gumption to go on.

He'd not only spent the first night sitting up late in her living room and listening to her woes, but the next day he'd gone to the school to see what it was that was burning her out. And he saw, all right: in the morning, first thing, four back-to-back half-hour sessions, each with a six- or seven-year-old who was among the lowest-achieving students in the first and second grades, and after that, for the rest of the day, forty-five-minute sessions with groups of eight kids whose reading skills were no better than those of the one-on-one kids but for whom there wasn't yet enough trained staff in the intensive program.

"The regular class sizes are too big," Lisa told him, "and so the teachers can't reach these kids. I was a classroom teacher. The kids who are struggling—it's three out of thirty. Three or four. It's not too bad. You have the progress of all the other kids helping you along. Instead of stopping and giving the hopeless kids what they need, teachers just sort of shuffle them through, thinking—or pretending—they are moving with the continuum. They're shuffled to the second grade, the third grade, the fourth grade, and then they seriously fail. But here it's *only* these kids, the ones who can't be reached and don't get reached, and because I'm very emotional about my kids and teaching, it affects my whole being—my whole *world*. And the school, the leadership—Dad, it's not good. You have a principal who doesn't have a vision of what she wants, and you have a mishmash of people doing what they think is best. Which is not necessarily what *is* best. When I came here twelve years ago it was great. The principal was really good. She turned the whole school around. But now we've gone through twenty-one teachers in four years. Which is a lot. We've lost a lot of good people. Two years ago I went into Reading Recovery because I just got burnt out in the classroom. Ten years of *that* day in and day out. I couldn't take any more."

He let her talk, said little, and, because she was but a few years from forty, suppressed easily enough the impulse to take in his arms this battered-by-reality daughter as he imagined she suppressed the same impulse with the six-year-old kid who couldn't read. Lisa had all of Iris's intensity without Iris's authority, and for someone whose life existed only for others—incurable altruism was Lisa's curse—she was, as a teacher, perpetually hovering at the edge of depletion. There was generally a demanding boyfriend as well from whom she could not withhold kindness, and for whom she turned herself inside out, and for whom, unfailingly, her uncontaminated ethical virginity became a great big bore. Lisa was always morally in over her head, but without either the callousness to disappoint the need of another or the strength to disillusion herself about her strength. This was why he knew she would never quit the Reading Recovery program, and also why such paternal pride as he had in her was not only weighted with fear but at times tinged with an impatience bordering on contempt.

"Thirty kids you have to take care of, the different levels that the kids come in at, the different experiences they've had, and you've got to make it all work," she was telling him. "Thirty diverse kids from thirty diverse backgrounds learning thirty diverse ways. That's a lot of management. That's a lot of paperwork. That's a lot of *everything*. But that is still *nothing* compared to *this*. Sure, even with this, even in Reading Recovery,

I have days when I think, Today I was good, but most days I
want to jump out the window. I struggle a lot as to whether
this is the right program for me. Because I'm very intense, in
case you didn't know. I want to do it the right way, and there
is no right way—every kid is different and every kid is hopeless,
and I'm supposed to go in there and make it all work. Of
course everybody always struggles with the kids who can't
learn. What do you do with a kid who can't read? Think of
it—a kid who can't read. It's difficult, Daddy. Your ego gets a
little caught up in it, you know."

Lisa, who contains within her so much concern, whose conscientiousness knows no ambivalence, who wishes to exist only to
assist. Lisa the Undisillusionable, Lisa the Unspeakably Idealistic. Phone Lisa, he told himself, little imagining that he could
ever elicit from this foolishly saintly child of his the tone of
steely displeasure with which she received his call.

"You don't sound like yourself."

"I'm fine," she told him.

"What's wrong, Lisa?"

"Nothing."

"How's summer school? How's teaching?"

"Fine."

"And Josh?" The latest boyfriend.

"Fine."

"How are your kids? What happened to the little one who
couldn't recognize the letter *n*? Did he ever get to level ten?
The kid with all the *n*'s in his name—Hernando."

"Everything's fine."

He then asked lightly, "Would you care to know how I am?"

"I know how you are."

"Do you?"

No answer.

"What's eating you, sweetheart?"

"Nothing." A "nothing," the second one, that meant all too
clearly, *Don't you sweetheart me.*

Something incomprehensible was happening. Who had told
her? *What* had they told her? As a high school kid and then in
college after the war he had pursued the most demanding curriculum; as dean at Athena he had thrived on the difficulties of

a taxing job; as the accused in the spooks incident he had never once weakened in fighting the false accusation against him; even his resignation from the college had been an act not of capitulation but of outraged protest, a deliberate manifestation of his unwavering contempt. But in all his years of holding his own against whatever the task or the setback or the shock, he had never—not even after Iris's death—felt as stripped of all defenses as when Lisa, the embodiment of an almost mockable kindness, gathered up into that one word "nothing" all the harshness of feeling for which she had never before, in the whole of her life, found a deserving object.

And then, even as Lisa's "nothing" was exuding its awful meaning, Coleman saw a pickup truck moving along the black-top road down from the house—rolling at a crawl a couple of yards forward, braking, very slowly rolling again, then braking again . . . Coleman came to his feet, started uncertainly across the mown grass, craning his head to get a look, and then, on the run, began to shout, "You! What are you up to! Hey!" But the pickup quickly increased its speed and was out of sight before Coleman could get near enough to discern anything of use to him about either driver or truck. As he didn't know one make from another and, from where he'd wound up, couldn't even tell if the truck was new or old, all that he came away with was its color, an indeterminate gray.

And now the phone was dead. In running across the lawn, he'd inadvertently touched the off button. That, or Lisa had deliberately broken the connection. When he redialed, a man answered. "Is this Josh?" Coleman asked. "Yes," the man said. "This is Coleman Silk. Lisa's father." After a moment's silence, the man said, "Lisa doesn't want to talk," and hung up.

Mark's doing. It had to be. Could not be anyone else's. Couldn't be this fucking Josh's—who was he? Coleman had no more idea how Mark could have found out about Faunia than how Delphine Roux or anyone else had, but that didn't matter right now—it was Mark who had assailed his twin sister with their father's crime. For crime it would be to that boy. Almost from the time he could speak, Mark couldn't give up the idea that his father was against him: *for* the two older sons because they were older and starred at school and imbibed without complaint their father's intellectual pretensions; *for* Lisa because she was Lisa, the family's little girl, indisputably the child most indulged by her daddy; *against* Mark because everything his twin sister was—adorable, adoring, virtuous, touching, noble to the core—Mark was not and refused to be.

Mark's was probably the most difficult personality it was ever Coleman's lot to try, not to understand—the resentments were all too easy to understand—but to grapple with. The whining and sulking had begun before he was old enough to go off to kindergarten, and the protest against his family and their sense of things started soon after and, despite all attempts at propitiation, solidified over the years into *his* core. At the age of fourteen he vociferously supported Nixon during the impeachment hearings while the rest of them were rooting for the president to be imprisoned for life; at sixteen he became an Orthodox Jew while the rest of them, taking their cue from their anticlerical, atheistic parents, were Jews in little more than name; at twenty he enraged his father by dropping out of Brandeis with two semesters to go, and now, almost into his forties, having taken up and jettisoned a dozen different jobs to which he considered himself superior, he had discovered that he was a narrative poet.

Because of his unshakable enmity for his father, Mark had made himself into whatever his family wasn't—more sadly to the point, into whatever *he* wasn't. A clever boy, well read, with a quick mind and a sharp tongue, he nonetheless could never see his way around Coleman until, at thirty-eight, as a narrative poet on biblical themes, he had come to nurse his great life-organizing aversion with all the arrogance of someone who has succeeded at nothing. A devoted girlfriend, a humorless, high-strung, religiously observant young woman, earned their keep as a dental technician in Manhattan while Mark stayed home in their Brooklyn walk-up and wrote the biblically inspired poems that not even the Jewish magazines would publish, interminable poems about how David had wronged his son Absalom and how Isaac had wronged his son Esau and how Judah had wronged his brother Joseph and about the curse of the prophet Nathan after David sinned with Bathsheba—poems that, in one grandiosely ill-disguised way or another, harked back to the idée fixe on which Markie had staked everything and lost everything.

How could Lisa listen to him? How could Lisa take seriously any charge brought by Markie when she knew what had been driving him all his life? But then Lisa's being generous toward her brother, however misbegotten she found the antagonisms that deformed him, went back almost to their birth as twins. Because it was her nature to be benevolent, and because even as a little schoolgirl she had suffered the troubled conscience of the preferred child, she had always gently indulged her twin brother's grievances and acted as his comforter in family disputes. But must her solicitousness toward the less favored of their twosome extend even to this crazy charge? And what *was* the charge? What harmful act had the father committed, what injury had he inflicted on his children that should put these twins in league with Delphine Roux and Lester Farley? And the other two, his scientist sons—were they and their scruples in on this too? When had he last heard from *them*?

He remembered now that awful hour at the house after Iris's funeral, remembered and was stung all over again by the charges that Mark had brought against his father before the older boys moved in and physically removed him to his old room for the rest of the afternoon. In the days that followed, while the kids were all still around, Coleman was willing to blame Markie's grief and not Mark for what the boy had dared to say, but that didn't mean that he'd forgotten or that he ever would. Markie had begun berating him only minutes after they'd driven back from the cemetery. "The college didn't do it. The blacks didn't do it. Your enemies didn't do it. *You* did it. You killed mother. The way you kill everything! Because you have to be right! Because you won't apologize, because every time you are a hundred percent right, now it's *Mother* who's dead! And it all could have been settled so easily—all of it settled in twenty-four hours if you knew how once in your life to *apologize*. 'I'm sorry that I said "spooks." ' That's all you had to do, great man, just go to those students and say you were sorry, and Mother would not be dead!"

Out on his lawn, Coleman was seized suddenly with the sort of indignation he had not felt since the day following Markie's outburst, when he'd written and submitted his resignation from the college all in an hour's time. He knew that it was not correct to have such feelings toward his children. He knew, from the spooks incident, that indignation on such a scale was a form of madness, and one to which he could succumb. He knew that indignation like this could lead to no orderly and reasoned approach to the problem. He knew as an educator how to educate and as a father how to father and as a man of over seventy that one must regard nothing, particularly within a family, even one containing a grudge-laden son like Mark, as implacably unchangeable. And it wasn't from the spooks incident alone that he knew about what can corrode and warp a man who believes himself to have been grievously wronged. He knew from the wrath of Achilles, the rage of Philoctetes, the fulminations of Medea, the madness of Ajax, the despair of Electra, and the suffering of Prometheus the many horrors that can ensue when the highest degree of indignation is achieved and, in the name of justice, retribution is exacted and a cycle of retaliation begins.

And it was lucky that he knew all this, because it took no less than this, no less than the prophylaxis of the whole of Attic tragedy and Greek epic poetry, to restrain him from phoning on the spot to remind Markie what a little prick he was and always had been.

The head-on confrontation with Farley came some four hours later. As I reconstruct it, Coleman, so as to be certain that no one was spying on the house, was himself in and out the front door and the back door and the kitchen door some six or seven times in the hours after Faunia's arrival. It wasn't until somewhere around ten, when the two of them were standing together inside the kitchen screen door, holding each other before parting for the night, that he was able to rise above all the corroding indignation and to allow the really serious thing in his life—the intoxication with the last fling, what Mann, writing of Aschenbach, called the "late adventure of the feelings" —to reassert itself and take charge of him. As she was about to leave, he at last found himself craving for her as though nothing else mattered—and none of it did, not his daughter, not his sons, not Faunia's ex-husband or Delphine Roux. This is not merely life, he thought, this is the *end* of life. What was unendurable wasn't all this ridiculous antipathy he and Faunia had aroused; what was unendurable was that he was down to the last bucket of days, to the bottom of the bucket, the time if there ever was a time to quit the quarrel, to give up the rebuttal, to undo himself from the conscientiousness with which he had raised the four lively children, persisted in the combative marriage, influenced the recalcitrant colleagues, and guided Athena's mediocre students, as best he could, through a literature some twenty-five hundred years old. It was the time to yield, to let this simple craving be *his* guide. Beyond their accusation. Beyond their indictment. Beyond their judgment. Learn, he told himself, before you die, to live beyond the jurisdiction of their enraging, loathsome, stupid blame.

The encounter with Farley. The encounter that night with Farley, the confrontation with a dairy farmer who had not meant to fail but did, a road crew employee who gave his all to the town no matter how lowly and degrading the task assigned him, a loyal American who'd served his country with not one tour but two, who'd gone back a second time to finish the goddamn job. Re-upped and went back because when he comes home the first time everybody says that he isn't the same person and that they don't recognize him, and he sees that it's true: they're all afraid of him. He comes home to them from jungle warfare and not only is he not appreciated but he is feared, so he might as well go back. He wasn't expecting the hero treatment, but everybody looking at him like that? So he goes back for the second tour, and this time he is geared up. Pissed off. Pumped up. A very aggressive warrior. The first time he wasn't all that gung ho. The first time he was easygoing Les, who didn't know what it meant to feel hopeless. The first time he was the boy from the Berkshires who put a lot of trust in people and had no idea how cheap life could be, didn't know what medication was, didn't feel inferior to anyone, happy-go-lucky Les, no threat to society, tons of friends, fast cars, all that stuff. The first time he'd cut off ears because he was there and it was being done, but that was it. He wasn't one of those who once they were in all that lawlessness couldn't wait to get going, the ones who weren't too well put together or were pretty aggressive to start off with and only needed the slightest opportunity to go ape-shit. One guy in his unit, guy they called Big Man, he wasn't there one or two days when he'd slashed some pregnant woman's belly open. Farley was himself only beginning to get good at it at the end of his first tour. But the second time, in this unit where there are a lot of other guys who'd also come back and who hadn't come back just to kill time or to make a couple extra bucks, this second time, in with these guys who are always looking to be put out in front, ape-shit guys who recognize the horror but know it is the very best moment of their lives, he is ape-shit too. In a firefight, running from danger, blasting with guns, you can't not be frightened, but you can go berserk and get the rush, and so the second time he goes berserk. The second time he fucking wreaks havoc. Living right out there on the edge, full throttle, the excitement and the fear, and there's nothing in civilian life that can match it. Door gunning. They're losing helicopters and they need door gunners. They ask at some point for door gunners and he jumps at it, he volunteers. Up there above the action, and everything looks small from above, and he just guns down *huge*. Whatever moves. Death and destruction, that is what door gunning is all about. With the added attraction that you don't have to be down in the jungle the whole time. But then he comes home and it's not better than the first time, it's worse. Not like the guys in World War II: they had the ship, they got to relax, someone took care of them, asked them how they were. There's no transition. One day he's door gunning in Vietnam, seeing choppers explode, in midair seeing his buddies explode, down so low he smells skin cooking, hears the cries, sees whole villages going up in flames, and the next day he's back in the Berkshires. And now he *really* doesn't belong, and, besides, he's got fears now about things going over his head. He doesn't want to be around other people, he can't laugh or joke, he feels that he is no longer a part of their world, that he has seen and done things so outside what these people know about that he cannot connect to them and they cannot connect to him. They told him he could go home? How could he go home? He doesn't have a helicopter at home. He stays by himself and he drinks, and when he tries the VA they tell him he is just there to get the money while he knows he is there to get the help. Early on, he tried to get government help and all they gave him was some sleeping pills, so fuck the government. Treated him like garbage. You're young, they told him, you'll get over it. So he tries to get over it. Can't deal with the government, so he'll have to do it on his own. Only it isn't easy after two tours to come back and get settled all on his own. He's not calm. He's agitated. He's restless. He's drinking. It doesn't take much to put him into a rage. There are these things going over his head. Still he tries: eventually gets the wife, the home, the kids, the farm. He wants to be alone, but she wants to settle down and farm with him, so he tries to want to settle down too. Stuff he remembers easygoing Les wanting ten, fifteen years back, before Vietnam, he tries to want again. The trouble is, he can't really feel for these folks. He's sitting in the kitchen and he's eating with them and there's nothing. No way he can go from that to this. Yet *still* he tries. A couple times in the middle of the night he wakes up choking her, but it isn't his fault—it's the government's fault. The government did that to him. He thought she was the fucking enemy. What did she think he was going to do? She knew he was going to come out of it. He never hurt her and he never hurt the kids. That was all lies. She never cared about anything except herself. He should have known never to let her go off with those kids. She waited until he was in rehab—that was why she wanted to get him into rehab. She said she wanted him to be better so that they could be together again, and instead she used the whole thing against him to get the kids away from him. The bitch. The cunt. She tricked him. He should have known never to let her go off with those kids. It was partly his own fault because he was so drunk and they could get him to rehab by force, but it would have been better if he'd taken them all out when he said he would. Should have killed her, should have killed the kids, and would have if it hadn't been for rehab. And she knew it, knew he'd have killed them like *that* if she'd ever tried to take them away. He was the father—if anybody was going to raise his kids it was him. If he couldn't take care of them, the kids would be better off dead. She'd had no right to steal his kids. Steals them, then *she* kills them. The payback for what he did in Vietnam. They all said that at rehab —payback this and payback that, but because everyone said it, didn't make it not so. It *was* payback, *all* payback, the death of the kids was payback and the carpenter she was fucking was payback. He didn't know why he hadn't killed him. At first he just smelled the smoke. He was in the bushes down the road watching the two of them in the carpenter's pickup. They were parked in her driveway. She comes downstairs—the apartment she's renting is over a garage back of some bungalow—and she gets in the pickup and there's no light and there's no moon but he knows what's going on. Then he smelled the smoke. The only way he'd survived in Vietnam was that any change, a noise, the smell of an animal, any movement at all in the jungle, and he could detect it before anyone else—alert in the jungle like he was born there. Couldn't see the smoke, couldn't see the flames, couldn't see anything it was so dark, but all of a sudden he could smell the smoke and these things are flying over his head and he began running. They see him coming and they think he is going to steal the kids. They don't know the building is on fire. They think he's gone nuts. But he can smell the smoke and he knows it's coming from the second story and he knows the kids are in there. He knows his wife, stupid bitch cunt, isn't going to do anything because she's in the truck blowing the carpenter. He runs right by them. He doesn't know where he is now, forgets where he is, all he knows is that he's got to get in there and up the stairs, and so he bashes in the side door and he's running up to where the fire is, and that's when he sees the kids on the stairs, huddled there at the top of the stairs, and they're gasping, and that's when he picks them up. They're crumpled together on the stairs and he picks them up and tears out the door. They're alive, he's sure. He doesn't think there's a chance that they're not alive. He just thinks they're scared. Then he looks up and who does he see outside the door, standing there looking, but the carpenter. That's when he lost it. Didn't know what he was doing. That's when he went straight for his throat. Started choking him, and that bitch, instead of going to the kids, worries about him choking the fucking boyfriend. Fucking bitch worries about him killing her boyfriend instead of about her own goddamn kids. And they would have made it. That's why they died. Because she didn't give two shits about the kids. She never did. They weren't dead when he picked them up. They were *warm*. He knows what dead is. Two tours in Vietnam you're not going to tell him what dead is. He can *smell* death when he needs to. He can *taste* death. He knows what death *is*. *They—were—not—dead.*

It was the boyfriend who was going to be fucking dead, until the police, in cahoots with the government, came with their guns, and that's when they put him away. The bitch kills the kids, it's her neglect, and they put *him* away. Jesus Christ, let me be right for a minute! The bitch wasn't paying attention! She never does. Like when he had the hunch they were headed for an ambush. Couldn't say why but he knew they were being set up, and nobody believed him, and he was *right*. Some new dumb officer comes into the company, won't listen to him, and that's how people get killed. That's how people get burned to hell! That's how assholes cause the death of your two best buddies! They don't listen to him! They don't give him credit! He came back alive, didn't he? He came back with all his limbs, he came back with his dick—you know what that took? But she won't listen! Never! She turned her back on him and she turned her back on his kids. He's just a crazy Vietnam vet. But he *knows* things, goddamnit. And she knows *nothing*. But do they put away the stupid bitch? They put *him* away. They shoot him up with stuff. Again they put him in restraints, and they won't let him out of the Northampton VA. And all he did was what they had trained him to do: you see the enemy, you kill the enemy. They train you for a year, then they try to kill you for a year, and when you're just doing what they trained you to do, that is when they fucking put the leather restraints on you and shoot you full of shit. He did what they were training him to do, and while he was doing that, his fucking wife is turning her back on his kids. He should have killed them all when he could. Him especially. The boyfriend. He should have cut their fucking heads off. He doesn't know why he didn't. Better not come fucking near him. If he knows where the fucking boyfriend is, he'll kill him so fast he won't know what hit him, and they won't know he did it because he knows how to do it so no one can hear it. Because that's what the government trained him to do. He is a trained killer thanks to the government of the United States. He did his job. He did what he was told to do. And this is how he fucking gets treated? They get him down in the lockup ward, they put him in the bubble, they send *him* to the fucking bubble! And they won't even cut him a check. For all this he gets fucking twenty percent. Twenty percent. He put his whole family through hell for twenty percent. And even for that he has to grovel. "So, tell me what happened," they say, the little social workers, the little psychologists with their college degrees. "Did you kill anyone when you were in Vietnam?" Was there anyone he *didn't* kill when he was in Vietnam? Wasn't that what he was *supposed* to do when they sent him to Vietnam? Fucking kill gooks. They said everything goes? So everything went. It all relates to the word "kill." Kill gooks! If "Did you kill anyone?" isn't bad enough, they give him a fucking gook psychiatrist, this like Chink shit. He serves his country and he can't even get a doctor who fucking speaks English. All round Northampton they've got Chinese restaurants, they've got Vietnamese restaurants, Korean markets—but him? If you're some Vietnamese, you're some Chink, you make out, you get a restaurant, you get a market, you get a grocery store, you get a family, you get a good education. But they got fuck-all for him. Because they want him dead. They wish he never came back. He is their worst nightmare. He was not *supposed* to come back. And now this college professor. Know where he was when the government sent us in there with one arm tied behind our backs? He was out there leading the fucking protesters. They pay them, when they go to college, to teach, to teach the kids, not to fucking protest the Vietnam War. They didn't give us a fucking chance. They say we lost the war. *We* didn't lose the war, the government lost the war. But when fancy-pants professors felt like it, instead of teaching class some day they go picketing out there against the war, and that is the thanks he gets for serving his country. That is the thanks for the shit he had to put up with day in and day out. He can't get a goddamn night's sleep. He hasn't had a good night's sleep in fucking twenty-six years. And for that, for *that* his wife goes down on some two-bit kike professor? There weren't too many kikes in Vietnam, not that he can remember. They were too busy getting their degrees. Jew bastard. There's something wrong with those Jew bastards. They don't look right. She goes down on *him*? Jesus Christ. Vomit, man. What was it all *for*? She doesn't know what it's like. Never had a hard day in her life. He never hurt her and he never hurt the kids. "Oh, my stepfather was mean to me." Stepfather used to finger her. Should have fucked her, that would have straightened her out a little. The kids would be alive today. His fucking kids would be alive today! He'd be like all the rest of those guys out there, with their families and their nice cars. Instead of locked up in a fucking VA facility. That was the thanks he got: Thorazine. His thanks was the Thorazine shuffle. Just because he thought he was back in the Nam.

This was the Lester Farley who came roaring out of the bushes. This was the man who came upon Coleman and Faunia as they stood just inside the kitchen doorway, who came roaring at them out of the darkness of the bushes at the side of the house. And all of that was just a little of what was inside his head, night after night, all through the spring and now into early summer, hiding for hours on end, cramped, still, living through so much emotion, and waiting there in hiding to see her doing it. Doing what she was doing when her own two kids were suffocating to death in the smoke. This time it wasn't even with a guy her age. Not even Farley's age. This time it wasn't with her boss, the great All-American Hollenbeck. Hollenbeck could give her something in return at least. You could almost respect her for Hollenbeck. But now the woman was so far gone she would do it for nothing with anybody. Now it was with a gray-haired skin-and-bones old man, with a high-and-mighty Jew professor, his yellow Jew face contorted with pleasure and his trembling old hands gripping her head. Who else has a wife sucks off an old Jew? Who else! This time the wanton, murdering, moaning bitch was pumping into her whoring mouth the watery come of a disgusting old Jew, and Rawley and Les Junior were still dead.

Payback. There was no end to it.

It felt like flying, it felt like Nam, felt like the moment in which you go wild. Crazier, suddenly, because she is sucking off that Jew than because she killed the kids, Farley is flying upward, screaming, and the Jew professor is screaming back, the Jew professor is raising a tire iron, and it is only because Farley is unarmed—because that night he'd come there right from fire department drill and without a single one of the guns from his basement full of guns—that he doesn't blow them away. How it happened that he didn't reach for the tire iron and take it from him and end everything that way, he would never know. Beautiful what he could have achieved with that tire iron. "Put it down! I'll open your fuckin' head with it! Fuckin' put it *down*!" And the Jew put it down. Luckily for the Jew, he put it down.

After he made it home that night (never know how he did that either) and right through to the early hours of the morning—when it took five men from the fire department, five buddies of his, to hold him down and get him into restraints and drive him over to Northampton—Lester saw it all, everything, all at once, right there in his own house enduring the heat, enduring the rain, the mud, giant ants, killer bees on his own linoleum floor just beside the kitchen table, being sick with diarrhea, headaches, sick from no food and no water, short of ammo, certain this is his last night, waiting for it to happen, Foster stepping on the booby trap, Quillen drowning, himself almost drowning, freaking out, throwing grenades in every direction and shouting "I don't want to die," the warplanes all mixed up and shooting at them, Drago losing a leg, an arm, his nose, Conrity's burned body sticking to his hands, unable to get a chopper to land, the chopper saying they cannot land because we are under attack and him so fucking angry knowing that he is going to die that he is trying to shoot it down, shoot down our own chopper—the most inhuman night he ever witnessed and it is right there now in his own scumbag house, and the longest night too, his longest night on earth and petrified with every move he makes, guys hollering and shitting and crying, himself unprepared to hear so much crying, guys hit in the face and dying, taking their last breath and dying, Conrity's body all over his hands, Drago bleeding all over the place, Lester trying to shake somebody dead awake and hollering, screaming without stopping, "I don't want to die." No time out from death. No break time from death. No running from death. No letup from death. Battling death right through till morning and everything intense. The fear intense, the anger intense, no helicopter willing to land and the terrible smell of Drago's blood there in his own fucking house. He did not know how bad it could smell. EVERYTHING SO IN-TENSE AND EVERYBODY FAR FROM HOME AND ANGRY ANGRY ANGRY ANGRY RAGE!

Nearly all the way to Northampton—till they couldn't stand

it anymore and gagged him—Farley is digging in late at night and waking up in the morning to find that he's slept in some-one's grave with the maggots. "Please!" he cried. "No more of this! No more!" And so they had no choice but to shut him up.

At the VA hospital, a place to which he could be brought only by force and from which he'd been running for years—fleeing his whole life from the hospital of a government he could not deal with—they put him on the lockup ward, tied him to the bed, rehydrated him, stabilized him, detoxified him, got him off the alcohol, treated him for liver damage, and then, during the six weeks that followed, every morning in his group therapy session he recounted how Rawley and Les Junior had died. He told them all what happened, told them every day what had failed to happen when he saw the suffocated faces of his two little kids and knew for sure that they were dead.

"Numb," he said. "Fuckin' numb. No emotions. Numb to the death of my own kids. My son's eyes are rolled in back of his head and he has no pulse. He has no heartbeat. My son isn't fucking breathing. My son. Little Les. The only son I will ever have. But I did not feel anything. I was acting as if he was a stranger. Same with Rawley. She was a stranger. My little girl. That fucking Vietnam, you caused this! After all these years the war is over, and you caused this! All my feelings are all fucked up. I feel like I've been hit on the side of the head with a two-by-four when nothing is happening. Then something is happening, something fucking *huge*, I don't feel a fucking thing. Numbed out. My kids are dead, but my body is numb and my mind is blank. Vietnam. That's why! I never did cry for my kids. He was five and she was eight. I said to myself, 'Why can't I feel?' I said, 'Why didn't I save them? Why couldn't I save them?' Payback. Payback! I kept thinking about Vietnam. About all the times I think I died. That's how I began to know that I can't die. Because I died already. Because I died already in Vietnam. Because I am a man who fucking *died*."

The group consisted of Vietnam vets like Farley except for two from the Gulf War, crybabies who got a little sand in their eyes in a four-day ground war. A hundred-hour war. A bunch of waiting in the desert. The Vietnam vets were men who, in their postwar lives, had themselves been through the worst—divorce, booze, drugs, crime, the police, jail, the devastating lowness of depression, uncontrollable crying, wanting to scream, wanting to smash something, the hands trembling and the body twitching and the tightness in the face and the sweats from head to toe from reliving the metal flying and the brilliant explosions and the severed limbs, from reliving the killing of the prisoners and the families and the old ladies and the kids—and so, though they nodded their heads about Rawley and Little Les and understood how he couldn't feel for them when he saw them with their eyes rolled back because he himself was dead, they nonetheless agreed, these really ill guys (in that rare moment when any of them could manage to talk about anybody other than themselves wandering around the streets ready to snap and yelling "Why?" at the sky, about anybody else not getting the respect they should receive, about anybody else not being happy until they were dead and buried and forgotten), that Farley had better put it behind him and get on with his life.

Get on with his life. He knows it's shit, but it's all he has. Get on with it. Okay.

He was let out of the hospital late in August determined to do that. And with the help of a support group that he joined, and one guy in particular who walked with a cane and whose name was Louie Borrero, he succeeded at least halfway; it was tough, but with Louie's help he was doing it more or less, was on the wagon for nearly three whole months, right up until November. But then—and not because of something somebody said to him or because of something he saw on TV or because of the approach of another familyless Thanksgiving, but because there was no alternative for Farley, no way to prevent the past from building back up, building up and calling him to action and demanding from him an enormous response—instead of it all being behind him, it was in front of him.

Once again, it *was* his life.

2

Slipping the Punch

WHEN Coleman went down to Athena the next day to ask what could be done to ensure against Farley's ever again trespassing on his property, the lawyer, Nelson Primus, told him what he did not want to hear: that he should consider ending his love affair. He'd first consulted Primus at the outset of the spooks incident and, because of the sound advice Primus had given—and because of a strain of cocky bluntness in the young attorney's manner reminiscent of himself at Primus's age, because of a repugnance in Primus for sentimental nonessentials that he made no effort to disguise behind the regular-guy easy-goingness prevailing among the other lawyers in town—it was Primus to whom he'd brought the Delphine Roux letter.

Primus was in his early thirties, the husband of a young Ph.D.—a philosophy professor whom Coleman had hired some four years earlier—and the father of two small children. In a New England college town like Athena, where most all the professionals were outfitted for work by L. L. Bean, this sleekly good-looking, raven-haired young man, tall, trim, athletically flexible, appeared at his office every morning in crisply tailored suits, gleaming black shoes, and starched white shirts discreetly monogrammed, attire that bespoke not only a sweeping self-confidence and sense of personal significance but a loathing for slovenliness of any kind—and that suggested as well that Nelson Primus was hungry for something more than an office above the Talbots shop across from the green. His wife was teaching here, so for now he was here. But not for long. A young panther in cufflinks and a pinstriped suit—a panther ready to pounce.

"I don't doubt that Farley's psychopathic," Primus told him, measuring each word with staccato exactitude and keeping a sharp watch on Coleman as he spoke. "I'd worry if he were stalking *me*. But did he stalk you before you took up with his ex-wife? He didn't know who you were. The Delphine Roux letter is something else entirely. You wanted me to write to her—against my better judgment I did that for you. You wanted an expert to analyze the handwriting—against my better judgment I got you somebody to analyze the handwriting. You wanted me to send the handwriting analysis to her lawyer —against my better judgment I sent him the results. Even though I wished you'd had it in you to treat a minor nuisance for what it was, I did whatever you instructed me to do. But Lester Farley is no minor nuisance. Delphine Roux can't hold a candle to Farley, not as a psychopath and not as an adversary. Farley's is the world that Faunia only barely managed to survive and that she can't help but bring with her when she comes through your door. Lester Farley works on the road crew, right? We get a restraining order on Farley and your secret is all over your quiet little backwoods town. Soon it's all over *this* town, it's all over the college, and what you started out with is going to bear no resemblance to the malevolent puritanism with which you will be tarred and feathered. I remember the precision with which the local comic weekly failed to understand the ridiculous charge against you and the meaning of your resignation. 'Ex-Dean Leaves College under Racist Cloud.' I remember the caption below your photograph. 'A denigrating epithet used in class forces Professor Silk into retirement.' I remember what it was like for you then, I think I know what it's like now, and I believe I know what it will be like in the future, when the whole county is privy to the sexcapades of the guy who left the college under the racist cloud. I don't mean to imply that what goes on behind your bedroom door is anybody's business but yours. I know it should not be like this. It's 1998. It's years now since Janis Joplin and Norman O. Brown changed everything for the better. But we've got people here in the Berkshires, hicks and college professors alike, who just won't bring their values into line and politely give way to the sexual revolution. Narrow-minded churchgoers, sticklers for propriety, all sorts of retrograde folks eager to expose and punish guys like you. They can heat things up for you, Coleman—and not the way your Viagra does."

Clever boy to come up with the Viagra all on his own. Showing off, but he's helped before, thought Coleman, so don't interrupt, don't put him down, however irritating his being so with-it is. There are no compassionate chinks in his armor? Fine with me. You asked his advice, so hear him out. You don't want to make a mistake for lack of being warned.

"Sure I can get you a restraining order," Primus told him. "But is that going to restrain him? A restraining order is going to inflame him. I got you a handwriting expert, I can get you your restraining order, I can get you a bulletproof vest. But what I can't provide is what you're never going to know as long as you're involved with this woman: a scandal-free, censure-free, Farley-free life. The peace of mind that comes of not being stalked. Or caricatured. Or snubbed. Or misjudged. Is she HIV negative, by the way? Did you have her tested, Coleman? Do you use a condom, Coleman?"

Hip as he imagines himself, he really can't get this old man and sex, can he? Seems utterly anomalous to him. But who can grasp at thirty-two that at seventy-one it's exactly the same? He thinks, How and why does he *do* this? My old-fart virility and the trouble it causes. At thirty-two, thought Coleman, I couldn't have understood it either. Otherwise, however, he speaks with the authority of someone ten or twenty years his senior about the way the world works. And how much experience can he have had, how much exposure to life's difficulties, to speak in such a patronizing manner to a man more than twice his age? Very, very little, if not none.

"Coleman, if you don't," Primus was saying, "does *she* use something? And if she says she does, can you be sure it's so? Even down-and-out cleaning women have been known to shade the truth from time to time, and sometimes even to seek remedy for all the shit they've taken. What happens when Faunia Farley gets pregnant? She may think the way a lot of women have been thinking ever since the act of begetting a bastard was destigmatized by Jim Morrison and The Doors. Faunia might very well want to go ahead and become the mother of a distinguished retired professor's child despite all your patient reasoning to the contrary. Becoming the mother of a distinguished professor's child might be an uplifting change after having been the mother of the children of a deranged total failure. And, once she's pregnant, if she decides that she doesn't want to be a menial anymore, that she wishes never again to work at *anything*, an enlightened court will not hesitate to direct you to support the child *and* the single mother. Now, I can represent you in the paternity suit, and if and when I have to, I will fight to keep your liability down to half your pension. I will do everything in my power to see that something is left in your bank account as you advance into your eighties. Coleman, listen to me: this is a bad deal. In every possible way, it is a bad deal. If you go to your hedonist counselor, he's going to tell you something else, but I am your counselor at law, and I'm going to tell you that it's a *terrible* deal. If I were you, I would not put myself in the path of Lester Farley's wild grievance. If I were you, I would rip up the Faunia contract and get out."

Everything he had to say having been said, Primus got up from behind his desk, a large, well-polished desk conscientiously kept cleared of all papers and files, pointedly bare of everything but the framed photographs of his young professor wife and their two children, a desk whose surface epitomized the unsullied *clean slate* and could only lead Coleman to conclude that there was nothing disorganized standing in the way of this voluble young man, neither weaknesses of character nor extreme views nor rash compulsions nor even the possibility of inadvertent error, nothing ill or well concealed that would ever crop up to prevent him from attaining every professional reward and bourgeois success. There'll be no spooks in Nelson Primus's life, no Faunia Farleys or Lester Farleys, no Markies to despise him or Lisas to desert him. Primus has drawn the line and no incriminating impurity will be permitted to breach it. But didn't I too draw the line and draw it no less rigorously? Was I less vigilant in the pursuit of legitimate goals and of an estimable, even-keeled life? Was I any less confident marching in step behind my own impregnable scruples? Was I any less arrogant? Isn't this the very way I took on the old guard in my first hundred days as Roberts's strongman? Isn't this how I drove them crazy and pushed them out? Was I any less ruthlessly sure of myself? Yet that one word did it. By no means the English language's most inflammatory, most heinous, most horrifying word, and yet word enough to lay bare, for all to see, to judge, to find wanting the truth of who and what I am.

The lawyer who'd not minced a single word—who'd laced virtually every one of them with a cautionary sarcasm that amounted to outright admonishment, whose purpose he would not disguise from his distinguished elderly client with a single circumlocution—came around from behind his desk to escort Coleman out of the office and then, at the doorway, went so far as to accompany him down the stairway and out onto the sunny street. It was largely on behalf of Beth, his wife, that Primus had wanted to be sure to say everything he could to Coleman as tellingly as he could, to say what had to be said no matter how seemingly unkind, in the hope of preventing this once considerable college personage from disgracing himself any further. That spooks incident—coinciding as it did with the sudden death of his wife—had so seriously unhinged Dean Silk that not only had he taken the rash step of resigning (and just when the case against him had all but run its spurious course), but now, two full years later, he remained unable to gauge what was and wasn't in his long-term interest. To Primus, it seemed almost as though Coleman Silk had not been unfairly diminished *enough*, as though, with a doomed man's cunning obtuseness, like someone who falls foul of a god, he was in crazy pursuit of a final, malicious, degrading assault, an ultimate injustice that would validate his aggrievement forever. A guy who'd once enjoyed a lot of power in his small world seemed not merely unable to defend himself against the encroachments of a Delphine Roux and a Lester Farley but, what was equally compromising to his embattled self-image, unable to shield himself against the pitiful sorts of temptations with which the aging male will try to compensate for the loss of a spirited, virile manhood. Primus could tell from Coleman's demeanor that he'd guessed right about the Viagra. Another chemical menace, the young man thought. The guy might as well be smoking crack, for all the good that Viagra is doing him.

Out on the street, the two shook hands. "Coleman," said Primus, whose wife, that very morning, when he'd said that he'd be seeing Dean Silk, had expressed her chagrin about his leavetaking from Athena, again speaking contemptuously of Delphine Roux, whom she despised for her role in the spooks affair—"Coleman," Primus said, "Faunia Farley is not from your world. You got a good look last night at the world that's shaped her, that's quashed her, and that, for reasons you know as well as I do, she'll never escape. Something worse than last night can come of all this, something much worse. You're no longer battling in a world where they are out to destroy you and drive you from your job so as to replace you with one of their own. You're no longer battling a well-mannered gang of elitist egalitarians who hide their ambition behind high-minded ideals. You're battling now in a world where nobody's ruthlessness bothers to cloak itself in humanitarian rhetoric. These are people whose fundamental feeling about life is that they have been fucked over unfairly right down the line. What you suffered because of how your case was handled by the college, awful as that was, is what these people feel every minute of every hour of . . ."

That's enough was by now so clearly written in Coleman's gaze that even Primus realized that it was time to shut up. Throughout the meeting, Coleman had silently listened, suppressing his feelings, trying to keep an open mind and to ignore the too apparent delight Primus took in floridly lecturing on the virtues of prudence a professional man nearly forty years his senior. In an attempt to humor himself, Coleman had been thinking, Being angry with me makes them all feel better—it liberates everyone to tell me I'm wrong. But by the time they were out on the street, it was no longer possible to isolate the argument from the utterance—or to separate himself from the man in charge he'd always been, the man in charge and the man deferred to. For Primus to speak directly to the point to his client had not required quite this much satiric ornamentation. If the purpose was to advise in a persuasive lawyerly fashion, a very *small* amount of mockery would have more effectively done the job. But Primus's sense of himself as brilliant and destined for great things seemed to have got the best of him, thought Coleman, and so the mockery of a ridiculous old fool made potent by a pharmaceutical compound selling for ten dollars a pill had known no bounds.

"You're a vocal master of extraordinary loquaciousness, Nelson. So perspicacious. So fluent. A vocal master of the endless, ostentatiously overelaborate sentence. And so rich with contempt for every last human problem you've never had to face." The impulse was overwhelming to grab the lawyer by the shirt front and slam the insolent son of a bitch through Talbots's window. Instead, drawing back, reining himself in, strategically speaking as softly as he could—yet not nearly so

mindfully as he might have—Coleman said, "I never again want
to hear that self-admiring voice of yours or see your smug
fucking lily-white face."

"'Lily-white'?" Primus said to his wife that evening. "Why 'lily-
white'? One can never hold people to what they lash out with
when they think they've been made use of and deprived of their
dignity. But did I *mean* to seem to be attacking him? Of course
not. It's worse than that. Worse because this old guy has lost
his bearings and I wanted to help him. Worse because the man
is on the brink of carrying a mistake over into a catastrophe
and I wanted to *stop* him. What he took to be an attack on him
was actually a wrong-headed attempt to be taken seriously by
him, to impress him. I failed, Beth, completely mismanaged it.
Maybe because I *was* intimidated. In his slight, little-guy way,
the man is a force. I never knew him as the big dean. I've known
him only as someone in trouble. But you feel the presence.
You see why people were intimidated by him. Somebody's *there*
when he's sitting there. Look, I don't know what it is. It's not
easy to know what to make of somebody you've seen half a
dozen times in your life. Maybe it's primarily something stupid
about me. But whatever caused it, I made every amateurish
mistake in the book. Psychopathology, Viagra, The Doors,
Norman O. Brown, contraception, AIDS. I knew everything
about everything. Particularly if it happened before I was born,
I knew everything that could possibly be known. I should have
been concise, matter-of-fact, unsubjective; instead I was provocative. I wanted to help him and instead I insulted him and
made things worse for him. No, I don't fault him for unloading
on me like that. But, honey, the question remains: why *white*?"

Coleman hadn't been on the Athena campus for two years and
by now no longer went to town at all if he could help it. He
didn't any longer hate each and every member of the Athena
faculty, he just wanted nothing to do with them, fearful that
should he stop to chat, even idly, he'd be incapable of concealing his pain or concealing himself concealing his pain—unable
to prevent himself from standing there seething or, worse,
from coming apart and breaking unstoppably into an overly

articulate version of the wronged man's blues. A few days after his resignation, he'd opened new accounts at the bank and the supermarket up in Blackwell, a depressed mill town on the river some eighteen miles from Athena, and even got a card for the local library there, determined to use it, however meager the collection, rather than to wander ever again through the stacks at Athena. He joined the YMCA in Blackwell, and instead of taking his swim at the Athena college pool at the end of the day or exercising on a mat in the Athena gym as he'd done after work for nearly thirty years, he did his laps a couple of times a week at the less agreeable pool of the Blackwell Y—he even went upstairs to the rundown gym and, for the first time since graduate school, began, at a far slower pace than back in the forties, to work out with the speed bag and to hit the heavy bag. To go north to Blackwell took twice as long as driving down the mountain to Athena, but in Blackwell he was unlikely to run into ex-colleagues, and when he did, it was less self-consciously fraught with feeling for him to nod unsmilingly and go on about his business than it would have been on the pretty old streets of Athena, where there was not a street sign, a bench, a tree, not a monument on the green, that didn't somehow remind him of himself before he was the college racist and everything was different. The string of shops across from the green hadn't even been there until his tenure as dean had brought all sorts of new people to Athena as staff and as students and as parents of students, and so, over time, he'd wound up changing the community no less than he had shaken up the college. The moribund antique shop, the bad restaurant, the subsistence-level grocery store, the provincial liquor store, the hick-town barbershop, the nineteenth-century haberdasher, the understocked bookshop, the genteel tearoom, the dark pharmacy, the depressing tavern, the newspaperless newsdealer, the empty, enigmatic magic shop—all of them had disappeared, to be replaced by establishments where you could eat a decent meal and get a good cup of coffee and have a prescription filled and buy a good bottle of wine and find a book about something other than the Berkshires and also find something other than long underwear to keep you warm in wintertime. The "revolution of quality" that he had once been credited with imposing on the Athena faculty and curriculum, he had, albeit inadvertently, bestowed on Town Street as well. Which only added to the pain and surprise of being the alien he was.

By now, two years down the line, he felt himself besieged not so much by *them*—apart from Delphine Roux, who at Athena cared any longer about Coleman Silk and the spooks incident?—as by weariness with his own barely submerged, easily galvanized bitterness; down in the streets of Athena, he now felt (to begin with) a greater aversion to himself than to those who, out of indifference or cowardice or ambition, had failed to mount the slightest protest in his behalf. Educated people with Ph.D.s, people he had himself hired because he believed that they were capable of thinking reasonably and independently, had turned out to have no inclination to weigh the preposterous evidence against him and reach an appropriate conclusion. Racist: at Athena College, suddenly the most emotionally charged epithet you could be stuck with, and to that emotionalism (and to fear for their personnel files and future promotions) his entire faculty had succumbed. "Racist" spoken with the official-sounding resonance, and every last potential ally had scurried for cover.

Walk up to the campus? It was summer. School was out. After nearly four decades at Athena, after all that had been destroyed and lost, after all that he had gone through to get there, why not? First "spooks," now "lily-white"—who knows what repellent deficiency will be revealed with the next faintly antiquated locution, the next idiom almost charmingly out of time that comes flying from his mouth? How one is revealed or undone by the perfect word. What burns away the camouflage and the covering and the concealment? This, the right word uttered spontaneously, without one's even having to think.

"For the thousandth time: I said spooks because I meant spooks. My father was a saloon keeper, but he insisted on precision in my language, and I have kept the faith with him. Words have meanings—with only a seventh-grade education, even my father knew that much. Back of the bar, he kept two things to help settle arguments among his patrons: a blackjack and a dictionary. My best friend, he told me, the dictionary—and so it is for me today. Because if we look in the dictionary, what do we find as the first meaning of 'spook'? The primary meaning.

'1. *Informal*. a ghost; specter.'" "But Dean Silk, that is not the way it was taken. Let me read to you the *second* dictionary meaning. '2. *Disparaging*. A Negro.' That's the way it was taken—and you can see the logic of that as well: Does anybody know them, or are they blacks whom you don't know?" "Sir, if my intention was to say, 'Does anybody know them, or do you not know them because they are black?' that is what I would have said. 'Does anybody know them, or do none of you know them because these happen to be two black students? Does anybody know them, or are they blacks whom nobody knows?' If I had meant that, I would have said it *just like that*. But how could I know they were black students if I had never laid eyes on them and, other than their names, had no knowledge of them? What I did know, indisputably, was that they were *invisible* students—and the word for invisible, for a ghost, for a specter, is the word that I used in its primary meaning: spook. Look at the adjective 'spooky,' which is the next dictionary entry after 'spook.' Spooky. A word we all remember from childhood, and what does *it* mean? According to the unabridged dictionary: '*Informal*. 1. like or befitting a spook or ghost; suggestive of spooks. 2. eerie; scary. 3. (esp. of horses) nervous; skittish.' Especially of horses. Now, would anyone care to suggest that my two students were being characterized by me as horses as well? No? But why not? While you're at it, why not that, too?"

One last look at Athena, and then let the disgrace be complete.

Silky. Silky Silk. The name by which he had not been known for over fifty years, and yet he all but expected to hear someone shouting, "Hey, Silky!" as though he were back in East Orange, walking up Central Avenue after school—instead of crossing Athena's Town Street and, for the first time since his resignation, starting up the hill to the campus—walking up Central Avenue with his sister, Ernestine, listening to that crazy story she had to tell about what she'd overheard the evening before when Dr. Fensterman, the Jewish doctor, the big surgeon from Mom's hospital down in Newark, had come to call on their parents. While Coleman had been at the gym working out with the track team, Ernestine was home in the

kitchen doing her homework and from there could hear Dr.
Fensterman, seated in the living room with Mom and Dad,
explaining why it was of the utmost importance to him and
Mrs. Fensterman that their son Bertram graduate as class valedictorian. As the Silks knew, it was now Coleman who was first
in their class, with Bert second, though behind Coleman by a
single grade. The one B that Bert had received on his report
card the previous term, a B in physics that by all rights should
have been an A—that B was all that was separating the top two
students in the senior class. Dr. Fensterman explained to Mr.
and Mrs. Silk that Bert wanted to follow his father into medicine, but that to do so it was essential for him to have a perfect
record, and not merely perfect in college but extraordinary
going back to kindergarten. Perhaps the Silks were not aware
of the discriminatory quotas that were designed to keep Jews
out of medical school, especially the medical schools at Harvard and Yale, where Dr. and Mrs. Fensterman were confident
that, were Bert given the opportunity, he could emerge as the
brightest of the brightest. Because of the tiny Jewish quotas in
most medical schools, Dr. Fensterman had had himself to go
down to Alabama for his schooling, and there he'd seen at first
hand all that colored people have to strive against. Dr. Fensterman knew that prejudice in academic institutions against colored students was far worse than it was against Jews. He knew
the kind of obstacles that the Silks themselves had had to
overcome to achieve all that distinguished them as a model
Negro family. He knew the tribulations that Mr. Silk had had
to endure ever since the optical shop went bankrupt in the
Depression. He knew that Mr. Silk was, like himself, a college
graduate, and he knew that in working for the railroad as a
steward—"That's what he called a waiter, Coleman, a 'steward' "
—he was employed at a level in no way commensurate with his
professional training. Mrs. Silk he of course knew from the
hospital. In Dr. Fensterman's estimation, there was no finer
nurse on the hospital staff, no nurse more intelligent, knowledgeable, reliable, or capable than Mrs. Silk—and that included
the nursing supervisor herself. In his estimation, Gladys Silk
should long ago have been appointed the head nurse on the
medical-surgical floor; one of the promises that Dr. Fensterman wanted to make to the Silks was that he was prepared to

do everything he could with the chief of staff to procure that very position for Mrs. Silk upon the retirement of Mrs. Noonan, the current medical-surgical head nurse. Moreover, he was prepared to assist the Silks with an interest-free, nonreturnable "loan" of three thousand dollars, payable in a lump sum when Coleman would be off to college and the family was sure to be incurring additional expenses. And in exchange he asked not so much as they might think. As salutatorian, Coleman would still be the highest-ranking colored student in the 1944 graduating class, not to mention the highest-ranking colored student ever to graduate E. O. With his grade average, Coleman would more than likely be the highest-ranking colored student in the county, even in the state, and his having finished high school as salutatorian rather than as valedictorian would make no difference whatsoever when he enrolled at Howard University. The chances were negligible of his suffering the slightest hardship with a ranking like that. Coleman would lose nothing, while the Silks would have three thousand dollars to put toward the children's college expenses; in addition, with Dr. Fensterman's support and backing, Gladys Silk could very well rise, in just a few years, to become the first colored head nurse on any floor of any hospital in the city of Newark. And from Coleman nothing more was required than his choosing his two weakest subjects and, instead of getting A's on the final exams, getting B's. It would then be up to Bert to get an A in all his subjects—doing that would constitute holding up *his* end of the bargain. And should Bert let everyone down by not working hard enough to get all those A's, then the two boys would finish in a flat-footed tie—or Coleman could even emerge as valedictorian, and Dr. Fensterman would still make good on his promises. Needless to say, the arrangement would be kept confidential by everyone involved.

So delighted was he by what he heard that Coleman broke loose from Ernestine's grasp and burst away up the street, in exuberant delight running up Central to Evergreen and then back, crying aloud, "My two weakest subjects—which are those?" It was as though in attributing to Coleman an academic weakness, Dr. Fensterman had told the most hilarious joke. "What'd they say, Ern? What did Dad say?" "I couldn't hear. He said it too low." "What did Mom say?" "I don't know.

I couldn't hear Mom either. But what they were saying after the doctor left, I heard that." "Tell me! What?" "Daddy said, 'I wanted to kill that man.'" "He did?" "Really. Yes." "And Mom?" "'I just bit my tongue.' That's what Mom said—'I just bit my tongue.'" "But you didn't hear what they said to *him*?" "No." "Well, I'll tell you one thing—I'm not going to do it." "Of course not," Ernestine said. "But suppose Dad told him I would?" "Are you crazy, Coleman?" "Ernie, three thousand dollars is more than Dad makes in a whole year. Ernie, three thousand dollars!" And the thought of Dr. Fensterman handing over to his father a big paper bag stuffed with all that money set him running again, goofily taking the imaginary low hurdles (for successive years now, he had been Essex County high school champ in low hurdles and run second in the hundred-yard dash) up to Evergreen and back. Another triumph—that's what he was thinking. Yet another record-breaking triumph for the great, the incomparable, the one and only Silky Silk! He was class valedictorian, all right, as well as a track star, but as he was also only seventeen, Dr. Fensterman's proposal meant no more to him than that he was of the greatest importance to just about everyone. The larger picture he didn't get yet.

In East Orange, where mostly everyone was white, either poor Italian—and living up at the Orange edge of town or down by Newark's First Ward—or Episcopalian and rich—and living in the big houses out by Upsala or around South Harrison—there were fewer Jews even than there were Negroes, and yet it was the Jews and their kids who these days loomed larger than anyone in Coleman's extracurricular life. First there was Doc Chizner, who had as good as adopted him the year before, when Coleman joined his evening boxing class, and now there was Dr. Fensterman offering three thousand dollars for Coleman to place second academically so as to enable Bert to come in first. Doc Chizner was a dentist who loved boxing. Went to the fights whenever he had a chance—in Jersey at Laurel Garden and at the Meadowbrook Bowl, to New York to the Garden and out to St. Nick's. People would say, "You think you know fights until you sit next to Doc. Sit next to Doc Chizner, and you realize you're not watching the same fight." Doc officiated at amateur fights all over Essex County, including the Golden Gloves in Newark, and to his local classes in boxing Jewish parents from all over the Oranges, from Maplewood, from Irvington—from as far away as the Weequahic section over at Newark's southwest corner—sent their sons to learn how to defend themselves. Coleman had wound up in Doc Chizner's class not because he didn't know how but because his own father had found out that since his second year of high school, after track practice, all on his own—and as often sometimes as three times a week—Coleman had been sneaking down to the Newark Boys Club, below High Street in the Newark slums to Morton Street, and secretly training to be a fighter. Fourteen years old when he began, a hundred and eleven pounds, and he would work out there for two hours, loosen up, spar three rounds, hit the heavy bag, hit the speed bag, skip rope, do his exercises, and then head home to do his homework. A couple of times he even got to spar with Cooper Fulham, who the year before had won the National Championships up in Boston. Coleman's mother was working a shift and a half, even two shifts running at the hospital, his father was waiting tables on the train and hardly at home other than to sleep, his older brother, Walt, was away first at college, then in the army, and so Coleman came and went as he liked, swearing Ernestine to secrecy and making sure not to let his grades slip, in study hall, at night in bed, on the buses back and forth to Newark—two buses each way—plugging away even harder than usual at his schoolwork to be sure nobody found out about Morton Street.

If you wanted to box amateur, the Newark Boys Club was where you went, and if you were good and you were between thirteen and eighteen, you got matched up against guys from the Boys Club in Paterson, in Jersey City, in Butler, from the Ironbound PAL, and so on. There were loads of kids down at the Boys Club, some from Rahway, from Linden, from Elizabeth, a couple from as far away as Morristown, there was a deaf-mute they called Dummy who came from Belleville, but mostly they were from Newark and all of them were colored, though the two guys who ran the club were white. One was a cop in West Side Park, Mac Machrone, and he had a pistol, and he told Coleman that if he ever found out Coleman wasn't doing his roadwork, he'd shoot him. Mac believed in speed, and that's why he believed in Coleman. Speed and pacing and counterpunching. Once he'd taught Coleman how to stand

and how to move and how to throw the punches, once Mac
saw how quickly the boy learned and how smart he was and
how quick his reflexes were, he began to teach him the finer
things. How to move his head. How to slip punches. How to
block punches. How to counter. To teach him the jab, Mac
repeated, "It's like you flick a flea off your nose. Just flick it off
him." He taught Coleman how to win a fight by using only his
jab. Throw the jab, knock the punch down, counter. A jab
comes, you slip it, come over with the right counter. Or you
slip it inside, you come over with a hook. Or you just duck
down, hit him a right to the heart, a left hook to the stomach.
Slight as he was, Coleman would sometimes quickly grab the
jab with both his hands, pull the guy and then hook him to the
stomach, come up, hook him to the head. "Knock the punch
down. Counterpunch. You're a counterpuncher, Silky. That's
what you are, that's all you are." Then they went to Paterson.
His first amateur tournament fight. This kid would throw a jab
and Coleman would lean back, but his feet would be planted
and he could come back and counter the kid with a right, and
he kept catching him like that for the whole fight. The kid kept
doing it, so Coleman kept doing it and won all three rounds.
At the Boys Club, that became Silky Silk's style. When he threw
punches, it was so nobody could say he was standing there
doing nothing. Mostly he would wait for the other guy to
throw, then he'd throw two, three back, and then he'd get out
and wait again. Coleman could hit his opponent more by waiting for him to lead than by leading him. The result was that by
the time Coleman was sixteen, in Essex and Hudson counties
alone, at amateur shows at the armory, at the Knights of Pythias, at exhibitions for the veterans at the veterans hospital, he
must have beaten three guys who were Golden Gloves champs.
As he figured it, he could by then have won 112, 118, 126 . . .
except there was no way he could fight in the Golden Gloves
without its getting in the papers and his family finding out.
And then they found out anyway. He didn't know how. He
didn't have to. They found out because somebody told them.
Simple as that.

They were all sitting down to dinner on a Sunday, after
church, when his father said, "How did you do, Coleman?"

"How did I do at what?"

"Last night. At the Knights of Pythias. How did you do?"

"What's the Knights of Pythias?" Coleman asked.

"Do you think I was born yesterday, son? The Knights of Pythias is where they had the tournament last night. How many fights on the card?"

"Fifteen."

"And how did you do?"

"I won."

"How many fights have you won so far? In tournaments. In exhibitions. How many since you began?"

"Eleven."

"And how many have you lost?"

"So far, none."

"And how much did you get for the watch?"

"What watch?"

"The watch you won at the Lyons Veterans Hospital. The watch the vets gave you for winning the fight. The watch you hocked on Mulberry Street. Down in Newark, Coleman—the watch you hocked in Newark last week."

The man knew everything.

"What do you think I got?" Coleman dared to reply, though not looking up as he spoke—instead looking at the embroidered design on the good Sunday tablecloth.

"You got two dollars, Coleman. When are you planning on turning pro?"

"I don't do it for money," he said, still with his eyes averted. "I don't care about money. I do it for enjoyment. It's not a sport you take up if you don't enjoy it."

"You know, if I were your father, Coleman, you know what I'd tell you now?"

"You are my father," Coleman said.

"Oh, am I?" his father said.

"Well, sure . . ."

"Well—I'm not sure at all. I was thinking that maybe Mac Machrone, at the Newark Boys Club, was your father."

"Come on, Dad. Mac's my trainer."

"I see. So who then is your father, if I may ask?"

"You know. You are. You are, Dad."

"I am? Yes?"

"No!" Coleman shouted. "No, you're not!" And here, at

the very start of Sunday dinner, he ran out of the house and for nearly an hour he did his roadwork, up Central Avenue and over the Orange line, and then through Orange all the way to the West Orange line, and then crossing over on Watchung Avenue to Rosedale Cemetery, and then turning south down Washington to Main, running and throwing punches, sprinting, then just running, then just sprinting, then shadowboxing all the way back to Brick Church Station, and finally sprinting the stretch, sprinting to the house, going back inside to where the family was eating their dessert and where he knew to sit back down at his place, far calmer than when he had bolted, and to wait for his father to resume where he had left off. The father who never lost his temper. The father who had another way of beating you down. With words. With speech. With what he called "the language of Chaucer, Shakespeare, and Dickens." With the English language that no one could ever take away from you and that Mr. Silk richly sounded, always with great fullness and clarity and bravado, as though even in ordinary conversation he were reciting Marc Antony's speech over the body of Caesar. Each of his three children had been given a middle name drawn from Mr. Silk's best-memorized play, in his view English literature's high point and the most educational study of treason ever written: the eldest Silk son was Walter Antony, the second son, Coleman Brutus; Ernestine Calpurnia, their younger sister, took her middle name from Caesar's loyal wife.

Mr. Silk's life in business for himself had come to a bitter end with the closing of the banks. It had taken him quite a time to get over losing the optician's store up in Orange, if he ever did. Poor Daddy, Mother would say, he always wanted to work for himself. He'd attended college in the South, in Georgia where he came from—Mother was from New Jersey—and took farming and animal husbandry. But then he quit and up north, in Trenton, he went to optician's school. Then he was drafted into the army for World War I, then he met Mother, moved with her to East Orange, opened the store, bought the house, then there was the crash, and now he was a waiter on a dining car. But if he couldn't in the dining car, at least at home he was able to speak with all his deliberateness and precision and directness and could wither you with words. He was very fussy about his children's speaking properly. Growing up, they never said, "See the bow-wow." They didn't even say, "See the doggie." They said, "See the Doberman. See the beagle. See the terrier." They learned things had classifications. They learned the power of naming precisely. He was teaching them English all the time. Even the kids who came into the house, his children's friends, had their English corrected by Mr. Silk.

When he was an optician and wore a white medical smock over a ministerial dark suit and was working more or less regular hours, he would sit after dessert and read the newspaper at the dinner table. They all would read from it. Each one of the children, even the baby, even Ernestine, would have to take a turn at the *Newark Evening News*, and not with the funnies. His mother, Coleman's grandmother, had been taught to read by her mistress and after Emancipation had gone to what was then called Georgia State Normal and Industrial School for Colored. His father, Coleman's paternal grandfather, had been a Methodist minister. In the Silk family they had read all the old classics. In the Silk family the children were not taken to prizefights, they were taken to the Metropolitan Museum of Art in New York to see the armor. They were taken to the Hayden Planetarium to learn about the solar system. Regularly they were taken to the Museum of Natural History. And then in 1937, on the Fourth of July, despite the cost, they were all taken by Mr. Silk to the Music Box Theatre on Broadway to see George M. Cohan in *I'd Rather Be Right*. Coleman still remembered what his father told his brother, Uncle Bobby, on the phone the next day. "When the curtain came down on George M. Cohan after all his curtain calls, do you know what the man did? He came out for an hour and sang all his songs. Every one of them. What better introduction could a child have to the theater?"

"If I were your father," Coleman's father resumed, while the boy sat solemnly before his empty plate, "you know what I would tell you now?"

"What?" said Coleman, speaking softly, and not because he was winded from all the roadwork but because he was chastened by having told his own father, who was no longer an optician but a dining car waiter and who would remain a dining car waiter till he died, that he was not his father.

"I would say, 'You won last night? Good. Now you can retire undefeated. You're retired.' That's what I'd say, Coleman."

It was much easier when Coleman spoke to him later, after he had spent the afternoon doing his homework and after his mother had a chance to talk and reason with his father. They were all able to sit more or less peaceably together then in the living room and listen to Coleman describe the glories of boxing and how, given all the resources you had to call on to excel, they exceeded even winning at track.

It was his mother who asked the questions now, and answering her was no problem. Her younger son was wrapped like a gift in every ameliorating dream Gladys Silk had ever had, and the handsomer he became and the smarter he became, the more difficult it was for her to distinguish the child from the dreams. As sensitive and gentle as she could be with the patients at the hospital, she could also be, with the other nurses, even with the doctors, with the white doctors, exacting and stern, imposing on them a code of conduct no less stringent than the one she imposed on herself. She could be that way with Ernestine as well. But never with Coleman. Coleman got what the patients got: her conscientious kindness and care. Coleman got just about anything he wanted. The father leading the way, the mother feeding the love. The old one-two.

"I don't see how you get mad at somebody you don't know. You especially," she said, "with your happy nature."

"You don't get mad. You just concentrate. It's a sport. You warm up before a fight. You shadowbox. You get yourself ready for whatever is going to come at you."

"If you've never seen the opponent before?" asked his father, with all the restraint on his sarcasm he could muster.

"All I mean," Coleman said, "is you don't *have* to get mad."

"But," his mother asked, "what if the other boy is mad?"

"It doesn't matter. It's brains that win, not getting mad. Let him get mad. Who cares? You have to think. It's like a chess game. Like a cat and a mouse. You can lead a guy. Last night, I had this guy, he was about eighteen or nineteen and he was sort of slow. He hit me with a jab on the top of my head. So the next time he did it, I was ready for it, and boom. I came over with the right counter and he didn't know where it came from. I knocked him down. I don't knock guys down, but I knocked this guy down. And I did it because I got him into thinking that he could catch me again with this punch."

"Coleman," his mother said, "I do not like the sound of what I'm hearing."

He stood up to demonstrate for her. "Look. It was a slow punch. You see? I saw his jab was slow and he wasn't catching me. It was nothing that hurt me, Mom. I just was thinking that if he does it again, I'll slip it and bang over with the right. So when he threw it again, I saw it coming because it was so slow, and I was able to counter and catch him. I knocked him down, Mom, but not because I was angry. Because I box better."

"But these Newark boys you fight. They're nothing like the friends you have," and, with affection, she mentioned the names of the two other best-behaved, brightest Negro boys in his year at East Orange High, who were indeed the pals he had lunch with and hung around with at school. "I see these Newark boys on the street. These boys are so *tough*," she said. "Track is so much more civilized than boxing, so much more like you, Coleman. Dear, you run so beautifully."

"It doesn't *matter* how tough they are or how tough they think they are," he told her. "On the street it matters. But not in the ring. In the street this guy could probably have beat me silly. But in the ring? With rules? With gloves? No, no—he couldn't land a punch."

"But what happens when they *do* hit you? It has to hurt you. The impact. It must. And that's so dangerous. Your head. Your *brain*."

"You're rolling with the punch, Mom. That's where they teach you how to roll your head. Like this, see? That reduces the impact. Once, and only once, and only because I was a jerk, only because of my own stupid mistake and because I wasn't used to fighting a southpaw, did I get a little stunned. And it's only like if you bang your head against the wall, you feel a little dizzy or shaky. But then all of a sudden your body comes right back. All you have to do is just hold on to the guy or move away, and then your head clears up. Sometimes, you get hit in the nose, your eyes get a little watery for a second, but that's it. If you know what you're doing, it's not dangerous at all."

With that remark, his father had heard enough. "I've seen

men get hit with a punch that they never saw coming. And when that happens," Mr. Silk said, "their eyes don't get watery—when that happens, it knocks them cold. Even Joe Louis, if you recall, was knocked cold—wasn't he? Am I mistaken? And if Joe Louis can be knocked cold, Coleman, so can you."

"Yeah, but Dad, Schmeling, when he fought Louis that first fight, he saw a weakness. And the weakness was that when Louis threw his jab, instead of coming back—" On his feet again, the boy demonstrated to his parents what he meant. "Instead of coming back, he dropped his left hand—see?—and Schmeling kept coming over—see?—and that's how Schmeling knocked him out. It's all thinking. Really. It *is*, Dad. I swear to you."

"Don't say that. Don't say, 'I swear to you.' "

"I won't, I won't. But see, if he doesn't come back, where he's back in position, if he comes here instead, then the guy's going to come over with his right hand and eventually he's going to catch him. That's what happened that first time. That's exactly what happened."

But Mr. Silk had seen plenty of fights, in the army had seen fights among soldiers staged at night for the troops where fighters were not only knocked out like Joe Louis but so badly cut up nothing could be done to stop the bleeding. On his base he had seen colored fighters who used their heads as their main weapon, who should have had a glove on their heads, tough street fighters, stupid men who butted and butted with their heads until the face of the other fighter was unrecognizable as a face. No, Coleman was to retire undefeated, and if he wanted to box for the enjoyment of it, for the sport, he would do so not at the Newark Boys Club, which to Mr. Silk was for slum kids, for illiterates and hoodlums bound for either the gutter or jail, but right there in East Orange, under the auspices of Doc Chizner, who'd been the dentist for the United Electrical Workers when Mr. Silk was the optician providing the union's members with eyeglasses before he lost the business. Doc Chizner was still a dentist but after hours taught the sons of the Jewish doctors and lawyers and businessmen the basic skills of boxing, and nobody in his classes, you could be sure, ended up hurt or maimed for life. For Coleman's father, the Jews, even audaciously unsavory Jews like Dr. Fensterman, were like Indian scouts, shrewd people showing the outsider his way in, showing the social possibility, showing an intelligent colored family how it might be done.

That was how Coleman got to Doc Chizner and became the colored kid whom all the privileged Jewish kids got to know—probably the only one they would ever know. Quickly Coleman came to be Doc's assistant, teaching these Jewish kids not exactly the fine points of how to economize energy and motion that Mac Machrone had taught his ace student but the basics, which was all they were up to anyway—"I say one, you jab. I say one-one, you double-jab. I say one-two, left jab, right cross. One-two-three, left jab, right cross, left hook." After the other pupils went home—with the occasional one who got a bloody nose packing it in, never to return—Doc Chizner worked alone with Coleman, some nights building up his endurance mainly by doing infighting with him, where you're tugging, you're pulling, you're hitting, and so afterward, by comparison, sparring is kid's play. Doc had Coleman up and out doing his roadwork and his shadowboxing even as the milkman's horse, drawing the wagon, would arrive in the neighborhood with the morning delivery. Coleman would be out there at 5 A.M. in his gray hooded sweatshirt, in the cold, the snow, it made no difference, out there three and a half hours before the first school bell. No one else around, nobody running, long before anybody knew what running was, doing three quick miles, and throwing punches the whole way, stopping only so as not to frighten that big, brown, lumbering old beast when, tucked sinisterly within his monklike cowl, Coleman drew abreast of the milkman and sprinted ahead. He hated the boredom of the running—and he never missed a day.

Some four months before Dr. Fensterman came to the house to make his offer to Coleman's parents, Coleman found himself one Saturday in Doc Chizner's car being driven up to West Point, where Doc was going to referee a match between Army and the University of Pittsburgh. Doc knew the Pitt coach and he wanted the coach to see Coleman fight. Doc was sure that, what with Coleman's grades, the coach could get him a four-year scholarship to Pitt, a bigger scholarship than he could ever get for track, and all he'd have to do was box for the Pitt team.

Now, it wasn't that on the way up Doc told him to tell the

Pitt coach that he was white. He just told Coleman not to mention that he was colored.

"If nothing comes up," Doc said, "you don't bring it up. You're neither one thing or the other. You're Silky Silk. That's enough. That's the deal." Doc's favorite expression: that's the deal. Something else Coleman's father would not allow him to repeat in the house.

"He won't know?" Coleman asked.

"How? How will he know? How the hell is he going to know? Here is the top kid from East Orange High, and he is with Doc Chizner. You know what he's going to think, if he thinks anything?"

"What?"

"You look like you look, you're with me, and so he's going to think that you're one of Doc's boys. He's going to think that you're Jewish."

Coleman never regarded Doc as much of a comedian—nothing like Mac Machrone and his stories about being a Newark cop—but he laughed loudly at that one and then reminded him, "I'm going to Howard. I can't go to Pitt. I've got to go to Howard." For as long as Coleman could remember, his father had been determined to send him, the brightest of the three kids, to a historically black college along with the privileged children of the black professional elite.

"Coleman, box for the guy. That's all. That's the whole deal. Let's see what happens."

Except for educational trips to New York City with his family, Coleman had never been out of Jersey before, and so first he spent a great day walking around West Point pretending he was at West Point because he was going to *go* to West Point, and then he boxed for the Pitt coach against a guy like the guy he'd boxed at the Knights of Pythias—slow, so slow that within seconds Coleman realized that there was no way this guy was going to beat him, even if he was twenty years old and a college boxer. Jesus, Coleman thought at the end of the first round, if I could fight this guy for the rest of my life, I'd be better than Ray Robinson. It wasn't just that Coleman weighed some seven pounds more than when he'd boxed on the amateur card at the Knights of Pythias. It was that something he could not even name made him want to be more damaging than he'd ever dared before, to do something more that day than merely win. Was it because the Pitt coach didn't know he was colored? Could it be because who he really was was entirely his secret? He did love secrets. The secret of nobody's knowing what was going on in your head, thinking whatever you wanted to think with no way of anybody's knowing. All the other kids were always blabbing about themselves. But that wasn't where the power was or the pleasure either. The power and pleasure were to be found in the opposite, in being counterconfessional in the same way you were a counterpuncher, and he knew that with nobody having to tell him and without his having to think about it. That's why he liked shadowboxing and hitting the heavy bag: for the secrecy in it. That's why he liked track, too, but this was even better. Some guys just banged away at the heavy bag. Not Coleman. Coleman *thought*, and the same way that he thought in school or in a race: rule everything else out, let nothing else in, and immerse yourself in the thing, the subject, the competition, the exam—whatever's to be mastered, become that thing. He could do that in biology and he could do it in the dash and he could do it in boxing. And not only did nothing external make any difference, neither did anything internal. If there were people in the fight crowd shouting at him, he could pay no attention to that, and if the guy he was fighting was his best friend, he could pay no attention to that. After the fight there was plenty of time for them to be friends again. He managed to force himself to ignore his feelings, whether of fear, uncertainty, even friendship—to have the feelings but have them separately from himself. When he was shadowboxing, for instance, he wasn't just loosening up. He was also imagining another guy, in his head fighting through a secret fight with another guy. And in the ring, where the other guy was real—stinky, snotty, wet, throwing punches as real as could be—the guy still could have no idea what you were thinking. There wasn't a teacher to ask for the answer to the question. All the answers that you came up with in the ring, you kept to yourself, and when you let the secret out, you let it out through everything *but* your mouth.

So at magic, mythical West Point, where it looked to him that day as though there were more of America in every square inch of the flag flapping on the West Point flagpole than in any

flag he'd ever seen, and where the iron faces of the cadets had
for him the most powerful heroic significance, even here, at
the patriotic center, the marrow of his country's unbreakable
spine, where his sixteen-year-old's fantasy of the place matched
perfectly the official fantasy, where everything he saw made
him feel a frenzy of love not only for himself but for all that
was visible, as if everything in nature were a manifestation of
his own life—the sun, the sky, the mountains, the river, the
trees, just Coleman Brutus "Silky" Silk carried to the millionth
degree—even here nobody knew his secret, and so he went
out there in the first round and, unlike Mac Machrone's undefeated counterpuncher, started hitting this guy with everything
he had. When the guy and he were of the same caliber, he
would have to use his brains, but when the guy was easy and
when Coleman saw that early, he could always be a more aggressive fighter and begin to pound away. And that's what
happened at West Point. Before you turned around, he had
cut the guy's eyes, the guy's nose was bleeding, and he was
knocking him all over the place. And then something happened
that had never happened before. He threw a hook, one that
seemed to go three-quarters of the way into the guy's body. It
went so deep he was astonished, though not half as astonished
as the Pitt guy. Coleman weighed a hundred and twenty-eight
pounds, hardly a young boxer who knocked people out. He
never really planted his feet to throw that one good shot, that
was not his style; and still this punch to the body went so deep
that the guy just folded forward, a college boxer already twenty
years old, and Coleman caught him in what Doc Chizner
called "the labonz." Right in the labonz, and the guy folded
forward, and for a moment Coleman thought the guy was
even going to throw up, and so before he threw up and before
he went down, Coleman set himself to whack him with the
right one more time—all he saw as this white guy was going
down was somebody he wanted to beat the living shit out
of—but suddenly the Pitt coach, who was the referee, called,
"Don't, Silky!" and as Coleman started to throw that last right,
the coach grabbed him and stopped the fight.

"And that kid," said Doc on the drive home, "that kid was a
goddamn good fighter, too. But when they dragged him back
to his corner, they had to tell him the fight was over. This kid

is already back in his corner, and *still* he didn't know what hit him."

Deep in the victory, in the magic, in the ecstasy of that last punch and of the sweet flood of fury that had broken out and into the open and overtaken him no less than its victim, Coleman said—almost as though he were speaking in his sleep rather than aloud in the car as he replayed the fight in his head—"I guess I was too quick for him, Doc."

"Sure, quick. Of course quick. I know you're quick. But also strong. That is the best hook you ever threw, Silky. My boy, you were too *strong* for him."

Was he? Truly strong?

He went to Howard anyway. Had he not, his father would— with words alone, with just the English language—have killed him. Mr. Silk had it all figured out: Coleman was going to Howard to become a doctor, to meet a light-skinned girl there from a good Negro family, to marry and settle down and have children who would in turn go to Howard. At all-Negro Howard, Coleman's tremendous advantages of intellect and of appearance would launch him into the topmost ranks of Negro society, make of him someone people would forever look up to. And yet within his first week at Howard, when he eagerly went off on Saturday with his roommate, a lawyer's son from New Brunswick, to see the Washington Monument, and they stopped in Woolworth's to get a hot dog, he was called a nigger. His first time. And they wouldn't give him the hot dog. Refused a hot dog at Woolworth's in downtown Washington, on the way out called a nigger, and, as a result, unable to divorce himself from his feelings as easily as he did in the ring. At East Orange High the class valedictorian, in the segregated South just another nigger. In the segregated South there were no separate identities, not even for him and his roommate. No such subtleties allowed, and the impact was devastating. Nigger —and it meant *him*.

Of course, even in East Orange he had not escaped the minimally less malevolent forms of exclusion that socially separated his family and the small colored community from the rest of East Orange—everything that flowed from what his father called the country's "Negrophobia." And he knew, too, that working for the Pennsylvania Railroad, his father had to put up with insults in the dining car and, union or no union, prejudicial treatment from the company that were far more humbling than anything Coleman would have known as an East Orange kid who was not only as light-skinned as a Negro could get but a bubbling, enthusiastic, quick-witted boy who happened also to be a star athlete and a straight-A student. He would watch his father do everything he could so as not to explode when he came home from work after something had happened on the job about which, if he wanted to keep the job, he could do nothing but meekly say, "Yes, suh." That Negroes who were lighter were treated better didn't always hold true. "Any time a white deals with you," his father would tell the family, "no matter how well intentioned he may be, there is the presumption of intellectual inferiority. Somehow or other, if not directly by his words then by his facial expression, by his tone of voice, by his impatience, even by the opposite—by his forbearance, by his wonderful display of *humaneness*—he will always talk to you as though you are dumb, and then, if you're not, he will be astonished." "What happened, Dad?" Coleman would ask. But, as much out of pride as disgust, rarely would his father elucidate. To make the pedagogical point was enough. "What happened," Coleman's mother would explain, "is beneath your father even to repeat."

At East Orange High, there were teachers from whom Coleman sensed an unevenness of acceptance, an unevenness of endorsement compared to what they lavished on the smart white kids, but never to the degree that the unevenness was able to block his aims. No matter what the slight or the obstacle, he took it the way he took the low hurdles. If only to feign impregnability, he shrugged things off that Walter, say, could not and would not. Walt played varsity football, got good grades, as a Negro was no less anomalous in his skin color than Coleman, and yet he was always a little angrier about everything. When, for instance, he didn't get invited into a white kid's house but was made to wait outside, when he wasn't asked to the birthday party of a white teammate whom he'd been foolish enough to consider a buddy, Coleman, who shared a bedroom with him, would hear about it for months. When Walt didn't get his A in trigonometry, he went right to the teacher and stood there and, to the man's white face, said, "I think you made a mistake." When the teacher went over his grade book and looked again at Walt's test scores, he came back to Walt and, even while allowing his mistake, had the nerve to say, "I couldn't believe your grades were as high as they were," and only after a remark like that made the change from a B to an A. Coleman wouldn't have dreamed of asking a teacher to change a grade, but then he'd never had to. Maybe because he didn't have Walt's brand of bristling defiance, or maybe because he was lucky, or maybe because he was smarter and excelling academically wasn't the same effort for him that it was for Walt, he got the A in the first place. And when, in the seventh grade, *he* didn't get invited to some white friend's birthday party (and this was somebody who lived just down the block in the corner apartment house, the little white son of the building's super who'd been walking back and forth to school with Coleman since they'd started kindergarten), Coleman didn't take it as rejection by white people—after his initial mystification, he took it as rejection by Dicky Watkin's stupid mother and father. When he taught Doc Chizner's class, he knew there were kids who were repelled by him, who didn't like to be touched by him or to come in contact with his sweat, there was occasionally a kid who dropped out—again, probably because of parents who didn't want him taking boxing instruction, or any instruction, from a colored boy—and yet, unlike Walt, on whom no slight failed to register, Coleman, in the end, could forget it, dismiss it, or decide to appear to. There was the time one of the white runners on the track team was injured seriously in a car crash and guys from the team rushed to offer blood to the family for the transfusions, and Coleman was one of them, yet his was the blood the family didn't take. They thanked him and told him that they had enough, but he knew what the real reason was. No, it wasn't that he didn't know what was going on. He was too smart not to know. He competed against plenty of white Newark guys at track meets, Italians from Barringer, Poles from East Side, Irish from Central, Jews from Weequahic. He saw, he heard—he *overheard*. Coleman knew what was going on. But he also knew what wasn't going on, at the center of his life anyway. The protection of his parents, the protection provided by Walt as his older, six-foot-two-and-a-half-inch brother, his own innate confidence, his bright charm, his running prowess ("the fastest kid in the Oranges"), even his color, which made of him someone that people sometimes couldn't quite figure out—all this combined to mute for Coleman the insults that Walter found intolerable. Then there was the difference of personality: Walt was Walt, vigorously Walt, and Coleman was vigorously not. There was probably no better explanation than that for their different responses.

But "nigger"—directed at *him*? That infuriated him. And yet, unless he wanted to get in serious trouble, there was nothing he could do about it except to keep walking out of the store. This wasn't the amateur boxing card at the Knights of Pythias. This was Woolworth's in Washington, D.C. His fists were useless, his footwork was useless, so was his rage. Forget Walter. How could his *father* have taken this shit? In one form or another taken shit like this in that dining car every single day! Never before, for all his precocious cleverness, had Coleman realized how protected his life had been, nor had he gauged his father's fortitude or realized the powerful force that man was—powerful not merely by virtue of being his father. At last he saw all that his father had been condemned to accept. He saw all his father's defenselessness, too, where before he had been a naïve enough youngster to imagine, from the lordly, austere, sometimes insufferable way Mr. Silk conducted himself, that there was nothing vulnerable there. But because somebody, belatedly, had got around to calling Coleman a nigger to his face, he finally recognized the enormous barrier against the great American menace that his father had been for him.

But that didn't make life better at Howard. Especially when he began to think that there was something of the nigger about him even to the kids in his dorm who had all sorts of new clothes and money in their pockets and in the summertime didn't hang around the hot streets at home but went to "camp" —and not Boy Scout camp out in the Jersey sticks but fancy places where they rode horses and played tennis and acted in plays. What the hell was a "cotillion"? Where was Highland Beach? What were these kids talking about? He was among the very lightest of the light-skinned in the freshman class, lighter even than his tea-colored roommate, but he could have been the blackest, most benighted field hand for all they knew that he didn't. He hated Howard from the day he arrived, within the week hated Washington, and so in early October, when his father dropped dead serving dinner on the Pennsylvania Railroad dining car that was pulling out of 30th Street Station in Philadelphia for Wilmington, and Coleman went home for the funeral, he told his mother he was finished with that college. She pleaded with him to give it a second chance, assured him that there had to be boys from something like his own modest background, scholarship boys like him, to mix with and befriend, but nothing his mother said, however true, could change his mind. Only two people were able to get Coleman to change his mind once he'd made it up, his father and Walt, and even they had to all but break his will to do it. But Walt was in Italy with the U.S. Army, and the father whom Coleman had to placate by doing as he was told was no longer around to sonorously dictate anything.

Of course he wept at the funeral and knew how colossal this thing was that, without warning, had been taken away. When the minister read, along with the biblical stuff, a selection from *Julius Caesar* out of his father's cherished volume of Shakespeare's plays—the oversized book with the floppy leather binding that, when Coleman was a small boy, always reminded him of a cocker spaniel—the son felt his father's majesty as never before: the grandeur of both his rise and his fall, the grandeur that, as a college freshman away for barely a month from the tiny enclosure of his East Orange home, Coleman had begun faintly to discern for what it was.

> Cowards die many times before their deaths;
> The valiant never taste of death but once.
> Of all the wonders that I yet have heard,
> It seems to me most strange that men should fear;
> Seeing that death, a necessary end,
> Will come when it will come.

The word "valiant," as the preacher intoned it, stripped away Coleman's manly effort at sober, stoical self-control and laid bare a child's longing for that man closest to him that he'd never see again, the mammoth, secretly suffering father who talked so easily, so sweepingly, who with just his powers of speech had inadvertently taught Coleman to want to be stupendous.

Coleman wept with the most fundamental and copious of all emotions, reduced helplessly to everything he could not bear. As an adolescent complaining about his father to his friends, he would characterize him with far more scorn than he felt or had the capacity to feel—pretending to an impersonal way of judging his own father was one more method he'd devised to invent and claim impregnability. But to be no longer circumscribed and defined by his father was like finding that all the clocks wherever he looked had stopped, and all the watches, and that there was no way of knowing what time it was. Down to the day he arrived in Washington and entered Howard, it was, like it or not, his father who had been making up Coleman's story for him; now he would have to make it up himself, and the prospect was terrifying. And then it wasn't. Three terrible, terrifying days passed, a terrible week, two terrible weeks, until, out of nowhere, it was exhilarating.

"What can be avoided / Whose end is purposed by the mighty gods?" Lines also from *Julius Caesar*, quoted to him by his father, and yet only with his father in the grave did Coleman at last bother to hear them—and when he did, instantaneously to aggrandize them. *This* had been purposed by the mighty gods! Silky's freedom. The raw I. All the subtlety of being Silky Silk.

At Howard he'd discovered that he wasn't just a nigger to Washington, D.C.—as if that shock weren't strong enough, he discovered at Howard that he was a Negro as well. A Howard Negro at that. Overnight the raw I was part of a we with all of the we's overbearing solidity, and he didn't want anything to do with it or with the next oppressive we that came along either. You finally leave home, the Ur of we, and you find *another* we? Another place that's just like that, the *substitute* for that? Growing up in East Orange, he was of course a Negro, very much of their small community of five thousand or so, but boxing, running, studying, at everything he did concentrating and succeeding, roaming around on his own all over the Oranges and, with or without Doc Chizner, down across the Newark line, he was, without thinking about it, everything else as well. He was Coleman, the greatest of the great *pioneers* of the I.

Then he went off to Washington and, in the first month, he

was a nigger and nothing else and he was a *Negro* and nothing else. No. No. He saw the fate awaiting him, and he wasn't having it. Grasped it intuitively and recoiled spontaneously. You can't let the big they impose its bigotry on you any more than you can let the little they become a we and impose its ethics on you. Not the tyranny of the we and its we-talk and everything that the we wants to pile on your head. Never for him the tyranny of the we that is dying to suck you in, the coercive, inclusive, historical, inescapable moral *we* with its insidious *E pluribus unum*. Neither the they of Woolworth's nor the we of Howard. Instead the raw I with all its agility. *Self-discovery—that* was the punch to the labonz. Singularity. The passionate struggle for singularity. The singular animal. The sliding relationship with everything. Not static but sliding. Self-knowledge but *concealed*. What is as powerful as that?

"Beware the ides of March." Bullshit—beware *nothing*. Free. With both bulwarks gone—the big brother overseas and the father dead—he is repowered and free to be whatever he wants, free to pursue the hugest aim, the confidence right in his bones to be his particular I. Free on a scale unimaginable to his father. As free as his father had been unfree. Free now not only of his father but of all that his father had ever had to endure. The impositions. The humiliations. The obstructions. The wound and the pain and the posturing and the shame—all the inward agonies of failure and defeat. Free instead on the big stage. Free to go ahead and be stupendous. Free to enact the boundless, self-defining drama of the pronouns we, they, and I.

The war was still on, and unless it ended overnight he was going to be drafted anyway. If Walt was in Italy fighting Hitler, why shouldn't he fight the bastard too? It was October of 1944, and he was still a month shy of being eighteen. But he could easily lie about his age—to move his birth date back by a month, from November 12 to October 12, was no problem at all. And dealing as he was with his mother's grief—and with her shock at his quitting college—it didn't immediately occur to him that, if he chose to, he could lie about his race as well. He could play his skin however he wanted, color himself just as he chose. No, that did not dawn on him until he was seated in the federal building in Newark and had all the navy enlistment forms spread out in front of him and, before filling them out, and carefully, with the same meticulous scrutiny that he'd studied for his high school exams—as though whatever he was doing, large or small, was, for however long he concentrated on it, the most important thing in the world—began to read them through. And even then it didn't occur to *him*. It occurred first to his heart, which began banging away like the heart of someone on the brink of committing his first great crime.

In '46, when Coleman came out of the service, Ernestine was already enrolled in the elementary education program at Montclair State Teachers College, Walt was at Montclair State finishing up, and both of them were living at home with their widowed mother. But Coleman, determined to live by himself, on his own, was across the river in New York, enrolled at NYU. He wanted to live in Greenwich Village far more than to go to NYU, wanted to be a poet or a playwright far more than to study for a degree, but the best way he could think to pursue his goals without having to get a job to support himself was by cashing in on the GI Bill. The problem was that as soon as he started taking classes, he wound up getting A's, getting interested, and by the end of his first two years he was on the track for Phi Beta Kappa and a summa cum laude degree in classics. His quick mind and prodigious memory and classroom fluency made his performance at school as outstanding as it had always been, with the result that what he had come to New York wanting most was displaced by his success at what everybody else thought he should do and encouraged him to do and admired him for doing brilliantly. This was beginning to look like a pattern: he kept getting co-opted because of his academic prowess. Sure, he could take it all in and even enjoy it, the pleasure of being conventional unconventionally, but that wasn't really the idea. He had been a whiz at Latin and Greek in high school and gotten the Howard scholarship when what he wanted was to box in the Golden Gloves; now he was no less a whiz in college, while his poetry, when he showed it to his professors, didn't kindle any enthusiasm. At first he kept up his roadwork and his boxing for the fun of it, until one day at the gym he was approached to fight a four-rounder at St. Nick's Arena, offered thirty-five dollars to take the place of a fighter who'd pulled out, and mostly to make up for all he'd missed at the Golden Gloves, he accepted and, to his delight, secretly turned pro.

So there was school, poetry, professional boxing, and there were girls, girls who knew how to walk and how to wear a dress, how to *move* in a dress, girls who conformed to everything he'd been imagining when he'd set out from the separation center in San Francisco for New York—girls who put the streets of Greenwich Village and the crisscrossing walkways of Washington Square to their proper use. There were warm spring afternoons when nothing in triumphant postwar America, let alone in the world of antiquity, could be of more interest to Coleman than the legs of the girl walking in front of him. Nor was he the only one back from the war beset by this fixation. In those days in Greenwich Village there seemed to be no more engrossing off-hours entertainment for NYU's ex-GIs than appraising the legs of the women who passed by the coffeehouses and cafés where they congregated to read the papers and play chess. Who knows why sociologically, but whatever the reason, it was the great American era of aphrodisiacal legs, and once or twice a day at least, Coleman followed a pair of them for block after block so as not to lose sight of the way they moved and how they were shaped and what they looked like at rest while the corner light was changing from red to green. And when he gauged the moment was right—having followed behind long enough to become both verbally poised and insanely ravenous—and quickened his pace so as to catch up, when he spoke and ingratiated himself enough so as to be allowed to fall in step beside her and to ask her name and to make her laugh and to get her to accept a date, he was, whether she knew it or not, proposing the date to her legs.

And the girls, in turn, liked Coleman's legs. Steena Palsson, the eighteen-year-old exile from Minnesota, even wrote a poem about Coleman that mentioned his legs. It was handwritten on a sheet of lined notebook paper, signed "S," then folded in quarters and stuck into his mail slot in the tiled hallway above his basement room. It had been two weeks since they'd first flirted at the subway station, and this was the Monday after the Sunday of their first twenty-four-hour marathon. Coleman had rushed off to his morning class while Steena was

still making up in the bathroom; a few minutes later, she herself
set out for work, but not before leaving him the poem that, in
spite of all the stamina they'd so conscientiously demonstrated
over the previous day, she'd been too shy to hand him directly.
Since Coleman's schedule took him from his classes to the library to his late evening workout in the ring of a rundown
Chinatown gym, he didn't find the poem jutting from the mail
slot until he got back to Sullivan Street at eleven-thirty that
night.

> He has a body.
> He has a beautiful body—
> the muscles on the backs of his legs and the back of his neck.
>
> Also he is bright and brash.
> He's four years older,
> but sometimes I feel he is younger.
>
> He is sweet, still, and romantic,
> though he says he is not romantic.
>
> I am almost dangerous for this man.
>
> How much can I tell
> of what I see in him?
> I wonder what he does
> after he swallows me whole.

Rapidly reading Steena's handwriting by the dim hall light,
he at first mistook "neck" for "negro"—*and the back of his
negro* . . . His negro *what?* Till then he'd been surprised by
how easy it was. What was supposed to be hard and somehow
shaming or destructive was not only easy but without consequences, no price paid at all. But now the sweat was pouring
off him. He kept reading, faster even than before, but the
words formed themselves into no combination that made
sense. His negro WHAT? They had been naked together a
whole day and night, for most of that time never more than
inches apart. Not since he was an infant had anyone other than
himself had so much time to study how he was made. Since
there was nothing about her long pale body that he had not
observed and nothing that she had concealed and nothing
now that he could not picture with a painterlike awareness, a
lover's excited, meticulous connoisseurship, and since he had

spent all day stimulated no less by her presence in his nostrils
than by her legs spread-eagled in his mind's eye, it had to follow that there was nothing about *his* body that *she* had not
microscopically absorbed, nothing about that extensive surface
imprinted with his self-cherishing evolutionary uniqueness,
nothing about his singular configuration as a man, his skin, his
pores, his whiskers, his teeth, his hands, his nose, his ears, his
lips, his tongue, his feet, his balls, his veins, his prick, his arm-
pits, his ass, his tangle of pubic hair, the hair on his head, the
fuzz on his frame, nothing about the way he laughed, slept,
breathed, moved, smelled, nothing about the way he shud-
dered convulsively when he came that she had not registered.
And remembered. And pondered.

Was it the act itself that did it, the absolute intimacy of it,
when you are not just inside the body of the other person but
she is tightly enveloping you? Or was it the physical nakedness?
You take off your clothes and you're in bed with somebody,
and that is indeed where whatever you've concealed, your
particularity, whatever it may be, however encrypted, is going
to be found out, and that's what the shyness is all about and
what *everybody* fears. In that anarchic crazy place, how much of
me is being seen, how much of me is being discovered? *Now I
know who you are. I see clear through to the back of your negro.*

But how, by seeing *what*? What could it have been? Was it
seeable to her, whatever it was, because she was a blond Icelandic Dane from a long line of blond Icelanders and Danes,
Scandinavian-raised, at home, in school, at church, in the
company all her life of nothing but . . . and then Coleman
recognized the word in the poem as a four- and not a five-
letter word. What she'd written wasn't "negro." It was "neck."
Oh, my *neck*! It's only my neck! . . . *the muscles on the backs
of his legs and the back of his neck.*

But what then did this mean: "How much can I tell / of
what I see in him?" What was so ambiguous about what she
saw in him? If she'd written "tell from" instead of "tell of,"
would that have made her meaning clearer? Or would that have
made it less clear? The more he reread that simple stanza, the
more opaque the meaning became—and the more opaque
the meaning, the more certain he was that she distinctly sensed
the problem that Coleman brought to her life. Unless she meant

by "what I see in him" no more than what is colloquially meant
by skeptical people when they ask someone in love, "What can
you possibly see in him?"

And what about "tell"? How much can she tell to *whom*? By
tell does she mean make—"how much can I make," et cetera
—or does she mean reveal, expose? And what about "I am almost dangerous for this man." Is "dangerous for" different
from "dangerous to"? Either way, what's the danger?

Each time he tried to penetrate her meaning, it slipped away.
After two frantic minutes on his feet in the hallway, all he could
be sure of was his fear. And this astonished him—and, as always
with Coleman, his susceptibility, by catching him unprepared,
shamed him as well, triggering an SOS, a ringing signal to self-
vigilance to take up the slack.

Bright and game and beautiful as Steena was, she was only
eighteen years old and fresh to New York from Fergus Falls,
Minnesota, and yet he was now more intimidated by her—and
her almost preposterous, unequivocal goldenness—than by
anybody he had ever faced in the ring. Even on that night in
the Norfolk whorehouse, when the woman who was watching
from the bed as he began to peel off his uniform—a big-titted,
fleshy, mistrustful whore not entirely ugly but certainly no
looker (and maybe herself two thirty-fifths something other than
white)—smiled sourly and said, "You're a black nigger, ain't
you, boy?" and the two goons were summoned to throw him
out, only then had he been as undone as he was by Steena's
poem.

> I wonder what he does
> after he swallows me whole.

Even *that* he could not understand. At the desk in his room,
he battled into the morning with the paradoxical implications
of this final stanza, ferreting out and then renouncing one
complicated formulation after another until, at daybreak, all he
knew for sure was that for Steena, ravishing Steena, not everything he had eradicated from himself had vanished into thin
air.

Dead wrong. Her poem didn't mean anything. It wasn't
even a poem. Under the pressure of her own confusion, fragments of ideas, raw bits of thought, had all chaotically come

tumbling into her head while she was under the shower, and so she'd torn a page from one of his notebooks, scribbled out at his desk whatever words jelled, then jammed the page into the mail slot before rushing off for work. Those lines were just something she'd done—that she'd *had* to do—with the exquisite newness of her bewilderment. A poet? Hardly, she laughed: just somebody leaping through a ring of fire.

They were together in the bed in his room every weekend for over a year, feeding on each other like prisoners in solitary madly downing their daily ration of bread and water. She astonished him—astonished *herself*—with the dance she did one Saturday night, standing at the foot of his foldout sofa bed in her half slip and nothing else. She was getting undressed, and the radio was on—Symphony Sid—and first, to get her moving and in the mood, there was Count Basie and a bunch of jazz musicians jamming on "Lady Be Good," a wild live recording, and following that, more Gershwin, the Artie Shaw rendition of "The Man I Love" that featured Roy Eldridge steaming everything up. Coleman was lying semi-upright on the bed, doing what he most loved to do on a Saturday night after they'd returned from their five bucks' worth of Chianti and spaghetti and cannoli in their favorite Fourteenth Street basement restaurant: watch her take her clothes off. All at once, with no prompting from him—seemingly prompted only by Eldridge's trumpet—she began what Coleman liked to describe as the single most slithery dance ever performed by a Fergus Falls girl after little more than a year in New York City. She could have raised Gershwin himself from the grave with that dance, and with the way she sang the song. Prompted by a colored trumpet player playing it like a black torch song, there to see, plain as day, was all the power of her whiteness. That big white thing. "Some day he'll come along . . . the man I love . . . and he'll be big and strong . . . the man I love." The language was ordinary enough to have been lifted from the most innocent first-grade primer, but when the record was over, Steena put her hands up to hide her face, half meaning, half pretending to cover her shame. But the gesture protected her against nothing, least of all from his enravishment. The gesture merely transported him further. "Where did I find you, Voluptas?" he asked. "*How* did I find you? Who are you?"

It was during this, the headiest of times, that Coleman gave up his evening workout at the Chinatown gym and cut back his early morning five-mile run and, in the end, relinquished in any way taking seriously his having turned pro. He had fought and won a total of four professional bouts, three four-rounders and then, his finale, a six-rounder, all of them Monday night fights at the old St. Nicholas Arena. He never told Steena about the fights, never told anyone at NYU, and certainly never let on to his family. For those first few years of college, that was one more secret, even though at the arena he boxed under the name of Silky Silk and the results from St. Nick's were printed in small type in a box on the sports page of the tabloids the next day. From the first second of the first round of the first thirty-five-dollar four-round fight, he went into the ring as a pro with an attitude different from that of his amateur days. Not that he had ever wanted to lose as an amateur. But as a pro he put out twice as hard, if only to prove to himself that he could stay there if he wanted to. None of the fights went the distance, and in the last fight, the six-rounder—with Beau Jack at the top of the card—and for which he got one hundred dollars, he stopped the guy in two minutes and some-odd seconds and was not even tired when it was over. Walking down the aisle for the six-rounder, Coleman had had to pass the ringside seat of Solly Tabak, the promoter, who was already dangling a contract in front of Coleman to sign away a third of his earnings for the next ten years. Solly slapped him on the behind and, in his meaty whisper, told him, "Feel the nigger out in the first round, see what he's got, Silky, and give the people their money's worth." Coleman nodded at Tabak and smiled but, while climbing into the ring, thought, Fuck you. I'm getting a hundred dollars, and I'm going to let some guy hit me to give the people their money's worth? I'm supposed to give a shit about some jerk-off sitting in the fifteenth row? I'm a hundred and thirty-nine pounds and five foot eight and a half, he's a hundred and forty-five and five foot ten, and I'm supposed to let the guy hit me in the head four, five, ten extra times in order to put on a show? Fuck the show.

After the fight Solly was not happy with Coleman's behavior. It struck him as juvenile. "You could have stopped the nigger in the fourth round instead of the first and gave the people their money's worth. But you didn't. I ask you nicely, and you don't do what I ask you. Why's that, wise guy?"

"Because I don't carry no nigger." That's what he said, the classics major from NYU and valedictorian son of the late optician, dining car waiter, amateur linguist, grammarian, disciplinarian, and student of Shakespeare Clarence Silk. That's how obstinate he was, that's how secretive he was—no matter what he undertook, that's how much he meant business, this colored kid from East Orange High.

He stopped fighting because of Steena. However mistaken he was about the ominous meaning hidden in her poem, he remained convinced that the mysterious forces that made their sexual ardor inexhaustible—that transformed them into lovers so unbridled that Steena, in a neophyte's distillation of self-marveling self-mockery, midwesternly labeled them "two mental cases"—would one day work to dissolve his story of himself right before her eyes. How this would happen he did not know, and how he could forestall it he did not know. But the boxing wasn't going to help. Once she found out about Silky Silk, questions would be raised that would inevitably lead her to stumble on the truth. She knew that he had a mother in East Orange who was a registered nurse and a regular churchgoer, that he had an older brother who'd begun teaching seventh and eighth grades in Asbury Park and a sister finishing up for her teaching certificate from Montclair State, and that once each month the Sunday in his Sullivan Street bed had to be cut short because Coleman was expected in East Orange for dinner. She knew that his father had been an optician—just that, an optician—and even that he'd come originally from Georgia. Coleman was scrupulous in seeing that she had no reason to doubt the truth of whatever she was told by him, and once he'd given up the boxing for good, he didn't even have to lie about that. He didn't lie to Steena about anything. All he did was to follow the instructions that Doc Chizner had given him the day they were driving up to West Point (and that already had gotten him through the navy): if nothing comes up, you don't bring it up.

His decision to invite her to East Orange for Sunday dinner,

like all his other decisions now—even the decision at St. Nick's
to silently say fuck you to Solly Tabak by taking out the other
guy in the first round—was based on nobody's thinking but
his own. It was close to two years since they'd met, Steena was
twenty and he was twenty-four, and he could no longer envision himself walking down Eighth Street, let alone proceeding
through life, without her. Her undriven, conventional daily
demeanor in combination with the intensity of her weekend
abandon—all of it subsumed by a physical incandescence, a
girlish American flashbulb radiance that was practically voo-
dooish in its power—had achieved a startling supremacy over
a will as ruthlessly independent as Coleman's: she had not only
severed him from boxing and the combative filial defiance en-
capsulated in being Silky Silk the undefeated welterweight pro,
but had freed him from the desire for anyone else.

Yet he couldn't tell her he was colored. The words he heard
himself having to speak were going to make everything sound
worse than it was—make *him* sound worse than *he* was. And if
he then left it to her to imagine his family, she was going to
picture people wholly unlike what they were. Because she knew
no Negroes, she would imagine the kind of Negroes she saw in
the movies or knew from the radio or heard about in jokes. He
realized by now that she was not prejudiced and that if only
she were to meet Ernestine and Walt and his mother, she would
recognize right off how conventional they were and how much
they happened to have in common with the tiresome respectability she had herself been all too glad to leave behind in
Fergus Falls. "Don't get me wrong—it's a lovely city," she
hastened to tell him, "it's a beautiful city. It's unusual, Fergus
Falls, because it has the Otter Tail Lake just to the east, and
not far from our house it has the Otter Tail River. And it's, I
suppose, a little more sophisticated than other towns out
there that size, because it's just south and to the east of Fargo-
Moorhead, which is the college town in that section of the
country." Her father owned a hardware supply store and a
small lumberyard. "An irrepressible, gigantic, amazing person,
my father. Huge. Like a slab of ham. He drinks in one night an
entire container of whatever alcohol you have around. I could
never believe it. I still can't. He just keeps going. He gets a big
gash in his calf muscle wrestling with a piece of machinery—he

just leaves it there, he doesn't wash it. They tend to be like this, the Icelanders. Bulldozer types. What's interesting is his personality. Most astonishing person. My father in a conversation takes over the whole room. And he's not the only one. My Palsson grandparents, too. His father is that way. His *mother* is that way." "Icelanders. I didn't even know you call them Icelanders. I didn't even know they were here. I don't know anything about Icelanders at all. When," Coleman asked, "did they come to Minnesota?" She shrugged and laughed. "Good question. I'm going to say after the dinosaurs. That's what it seems like." "And it's him you're escaping?" "I guess. Hard to be the daughter of that sort of feistiness. He kind of submerges you." "And your mother? He submerges her?" "That's the Danish side of the family. That's the Rasmussens. No, she's unsubmergeable. My mother's too practical to be submerged. The characteristics of her family—and I don't think it's peculiar to that family, I think Danes are this way, and they're not too different from Norwegians in this way either—they're interested in objects. *Objects.* Tablecloths. Dishes. Vases. They talk endlessly about how much each object costs. My mother's father is like this too, my grandfather Rasmussen. Her whole family. They don't have any dreams in them. They don't have any unreality. Everything is made up of objects and what they cost and how much you can get them for. She goes into people's houses and examines all the objects and knows where they got half of them and tells them where they could have got them for less. And clothing. Each object of clothing. Same thing. Practicality. A bare-boned practicality about the whole bunch of them. Thrifty. Extremely thrifty. Clean. Extremely clean. She'll notice, when I come home from school, if I have one bit of ink under one fingernail from filling a fountain pen. When she's having guests on a Saturday evening, she sets the table Friday night at about five o'clock. It's there, every glass, every piece of silver. And then she throws a light gossamer thing over it so it won't get dust specks on it. Everything organized perfectly. And a fantastically good cook if you don't like any spices or salt or pepper. Or taste of any kind. So that's my parents. I can't get to the bottom with her particularly. On anything. It's all surface. She's organizing everything and my father's disorganizing everything, and so I got to be eighteen and graduated high school and came here. Since if I'd gone up to Moorhead or North Dakota State, I'd still have to be living at home, I said the heck with college and came to New York. And so here I am. Steena."

That's how she explained who she was and where she came from and why she'd left. For him it was not going to be so simple. *Afterward*, he told himself. Afterward—that's when he could make his explanations and ask her to understand how he could not allow his prospects to be unjustly limited by so arbitrary a designation as race. If she was calm enough to hear him out, he was sure he could make her see why he had chosen to take the future into his own hands rather than to leave it to an unenlightened society to determine his fate—a society in which, more than eighty years after the Emancipation Proclamation, bigots happened to play too large a role to suit him. He would get her to see that far from there being anything wrong with his decision to identify himself as white, it was the most natural thing for someone with his outlook and temperament and skin color to have done. All he'd ever wanted, from earliest childhood on, was to be free: not black, not even white —just on his own and free. He meant to insult no one by his choice, nor was he trying to imitate anyone whom he took to be his superior, nor was he staging some sort of protest against his race or hers. He recognized that to conventional people for whom everything was ready-made and rigidly unalterable what he was doing would never look correct. But to dare to be nothing more than correct had never been his aim. The objective was for his fate to be determined not by the ignorant, hate-filled intentions of a hostile world but, to whatever degree humanly possible, by his own resolve. Why accept a life on any other terms?

This is what he would tell her. And wouldn't it all strike her as nonsense, like one big sales pitch of a pretentious lie? Unless she had first met his family—confronted head-on the fact that he was as much a Negro as they were, and that they were as unlike what she might imagine Negroes to be as he was—these words or any others would seem to her only another form of concealment. Until she sat down to dinner with Ernestine, Walt, and his mother, and they all took a turn over the course of a day at swapping reassuring banalities, whatever explanation he presented to her would sound like so much preening, self-glorifying, self-justifying baloney, high-flown, highfalutin talk whose falseness would shame him in her eyes no less than in his own. No, he couldn't speak this shit either. It was beneath him. If he wanted this girl for good, then it was boldness that was required now and not an elocutionary snow job, à la Clarence Silk.

In the week before the visit, though he didn't prepare anyone else, he readied himself in the same concentrated way he used to prepare mentally for a fight, and when they stepped off the train at the Brick Church Station that Sunday, he even summoned up the phrases that he always chanted semi-mystically in the seconds before the bell sounded: "The task, nothing but the task. At one with the task. Nothing else allowed in." Only then, at the bell, breaking from his corner—or here, starting up the porch stairs to the front door—did he add the ordinary Joe's call to arms: "Go to work."

The Silks had been in their one-family house since 1925, the year before Coleman was born. When they got there, the rest of the street was white, and the small frame house was sold to them by a couple who were mad at the people next door and so were determined to sell it to colored to spite them. But no one in the private houses ran because they'd moved in, and even if the Silks never socialized with their neighbors, everyone was agreeable on that stretch of street leading up toward the Episcopal rectory and church. Agreeable even though the rector, when he arrived some years earlier, had looked around, seen a fair number of Bahamians and Barbadians, who were Church of England—many of them domestics working for East Orange's white rich, many of them island people who knew their place and sat at the back and thought they were accepted—leaned on his pulpit, and, before beginning the sermon on his first Sunday, said, "I see we have some colored families here. We'll have to do something about that." After consulting with the seminary in New York, he had seen to it that various services and Sunday schools for the colored were conducted, outside basic church law, in the colored families' houses. Later, the swimming pool at the high school was shut down by the school superintendent so that the white kids wouldn't have to swim with the colored kids. A big swimming pool, used for swimming classes and a swimming team, a part of the physical education program for years, but since there were objections from some of the white kids' parents who were employers of the black kids' parents—the ones working as maids and housemen and chauffeurs and gardeners and yard-men—the pool was drained and covered over.

Within the four square miles of this residential flyspeck of a Jersey town of not quite seventy thousand people, as through-out the country during Coleman's youth, there existed these rigid distinctions between classes and races sanctified by the church and legitimized by the schools. Yet on the Silks' own modest tree-lined side street ordinary people needed not to be quite so responsible to God and the state as those whose voca-tion it was to maintain a human community, swimming pool and all, untainted by the impurities, and so the neighbors were on the whole friendly with the ultra-respectable, light-skinned Silks—Negroes, to be sure, but, in the words of one tolerant mother of a kindergarten playmate of Coleman's, "people of a very pleasing shade, rather like eggnog"—even to the point of borrowing a tool or a ladder or helping to figure out what was wrong with the car when it wouldn't start. The big apartment house at the corner remained all white until after the war. Then, in late 1945, when colored people began coming in at the Orange end of the street—the families of professional men mainly, of teachers, doctors, and dentists—there was a moving van outside the apartment building every day, and half the white tenants disappeared within months. But things soon settled down, and, though the landlord of the apartment build-ing began renting to colored just in order to keep the place going, the whites who remained in the immediate neighbor-hood stayed around until they had a reason other than Negro-phobia to leave.

Go to work. And he rang the doorbell and pushed open the front door and called, "We're here."

Walt had been unable to make it up that day from Asbury Park but there, coming out of the kitchen and into the hallway, were his mother and Ernestine. And there, in their house, was his girl. She may or may not have been what they were expect-ing. Coleman's mother hadn't asked. Since he'd unilaterally made his decision to join the navy as a white man, she hardly dared ask him anything, for fear of what she might hear. She was prone now, outside the hospital—where she had at last become the first colored head floor nurse of a Newark hospital, and without help from Dr. Fensterman—to let Walt take charge of her life and of the family altogether. No, she hadn't asked anything about the girl, politely declined to know, and encouraged Ernestine not to inquire. Coleman, in turn, hadn't told anyone anything, and so, fair-complexioned as fair could be, and—with her matching blue handbag and pumps, in her cotton floral shirtwaist dress and her little white gloves and pillbox hat—as immaculately trim and correct as any girl alive and young in 1950, here was Steena Palsson, Iceland's and Denmark's American progeny, of the bloodline going back to King Canute and beyond.

He had done it, got it his own way, and no one so much as flinched. Talk about the ability of the species to adapt. Nobody groped for words, nobody went silent, nor did anyone begin jabbering a mile a minute. Commonplaces, yes, cornballisms, you bet—generalities, truisms, clichés aplenty. Steena hadn't been raised along the banks of the Otter Tail River for nothing: if it was hackneyed, she knew how to say it. Chances were that if Coleman had gotten to blindfold the three women before introducing them and to keep them blindfolded throughout the day, their conversation would have had no weightier a meaning than it had while they smilingly looked one another right in the eye. Nor would it have embodied an intention other than the standard one: namely, I won't say anything you can possibly take offense with if you won't say anything I can take offense with. Respectability at any cost—that's where the Palssons and the Silks were one.

The point at which all three got addled was, strangely enough, while discussing Steena's height. True, she was five eleven, nearly three full inches taller than Coleman and six inches taller than either his sister or his mother. But Coleman's father had been six one and Walt was an inch and a half taller than that, so tallness in and of itself was nothing new to the family, even if, with Steena and Coleman, it was the woman who happened to be taller than the man. Yet those three inches of Steena's—the distance, say, from her hairline to her eyebrows —caused a careening conversation about physical anomalies to veer precipitously close to disaster for some fifteen minutes before Coleman smelled something acrid and the women—the three of them—rushed for the kitchen to save the biscuits from going up in flames.

After that, throughout dinner and until it was time for the young couple to return to New York, it was all unflagging rectitude, externally a Sunday like every nice family's dream of total Sunday happiness and, consequently, strikingly in contrast with life, which, as experience had already taught even the youngest of these four, could not for half a minute running be purged of its inherent instability, let alone be beaten down into a predictable essence.

Not until the train carrying Coleman and Steena back to New York pulled into Pennsylvania Station early that evening did Steena break down in tears.

As far as he knew, until then she had been fast asleep with her head on his shoulder all the way from Jersey—virtually from the moment they had boarded at Brick Church Station sleeping off the exhaustion of the afternoon's effort at which she had so excelled.

"Steena—what is wrong?"

"I can't do it!" she cried, and, without another word of explanation, gasping, violently weeping, clutching her bag to her chest—and forgetting her hat, which was in his lap, where he'd been holding it while she slept—she raced alone from the train as though from an attacker and did not phone him or try ever to see him again.

It was four years later, in 1954, that they nearly collided outside Grand Central Station and stopped to take each other's hand and to talk just long enough to stir up the original wonder they'd awakened in each other at twenty-two and eighteen and then to walk on, crushed by the certainty that nothing as statistically spectacular as this chance meeting could possibly happen again. He was married by then, an expectant father, in the city for the day from his job as a classics instructor at Adelphi, and she was working in an ad agency down the street on Lexington Avenue, still single, still pretty, but womanly now, very much a smartly dressed New Yorker and clearly someone with whom the trip to East Orange might have ended on a different note if only it had taken place further down the line.

The way it might have ended—the conclusion against which reality had decisively voted—was all he could think about. Stunned by how little he'd gotten over her and she'd gotten over him, he walked away understanding, as outside his reading in classical Greek drama he'd never had to understand before, how easily life can be one thing rather than another and how accidentally a destiny is made . . . on the other hand, how accidental fate may seem when things can never turn out other than they do. That is, he walked away understanding nothing, knowing he could understand nothing, though with the illusion that he *would* have metaphysically understood something of enormous importance about this stubborn determination of his to become his own man if . . . if only such things were understandable.

The charming two-page letter she sent the next week, care of the college, about how incredibly good he'd been at "swooping" their first time together in his Sullivan Street room— "swooping, almost like birds do when they fly over land or sea and spy something moving, something bursting with life, and dive down . . . and seize upon it"—began, "Dear Coleman, I was very happy to see you in New York. Brief as our meeting was, after I saw you I felt an autumnal sadness, perhaps because the six years since we first met make it wrenchingly obvious how many days of my life are 'over.' You look very good, and I'm glad you're happy . . ." and ended in a languid, floating finale of seven little sentences and a wistful closing that, after numerous rereadings, he took as the measure of her regret for *her* loss, a veiled admission of remorse as well, poignantly signaling to him a subaudible apology: "Well, that's it. That's enough. I shouldn't even bother you. I promise I won't ever again. Take care. Take care. Take care. Take care. Very fondly, Steena."

He never threw the letter away, and when he happened upon it in his files and, in the midst of whatever else he was doing, paused to look it over—having otherwise forgotten it for some five or six years—he thought what he thought out on the street that day after lightly kissing her cheek and saying goodbye to Steena forever: that had she married him—as he'd wanted her to—she would have known everything—as he had wanted her to—and what followed with his family, with hers, with

their own children, would have been different from what it was
with Iris. What happened with his mother and Walt could as
easily never have occurred. Had Steena said fine, he would
have lived another life.

I can't do it. There was wisdom in that, an awful lot of wisdom for a young girl, not the kind one ordinarily has at only
twenty. But that's why he'd fallen for her—because she had the
wisdom that is solid, thinking-for-yourself common sense. If
she hadn't . . . but if she hadn't, she wouldn't have been
Steena, and he wouldn't have wanted her as a wife.

He thought the same useless thoughts—useless to a man of
no great talent like himself, if not to Sophocles: how accidentally a fate is made . . . or how accidental it all may seem
when it is inescapable.

As she first portrayed herself and her origins to Coleman, Iris
Gittelman had grown up willful, clever, furtively rebellious—
secretly plotting, from the second grade on, how to escape her
oppressive surroundings—in a Passaic household rumbling
with hatred for every form of social oppression, particularly the
authority of the rabbis and their impinging lies. Her Yiddish-
speaking father, as she characterized him, was such a thoroughgoing heretical anarchist that he hadn't even had Iris's
two older brothers circumcised, nor had her parents bothered
to acquire a marriage license or to submit to a civil ceremony.
They considered themselves husband and wife, claimed to be
American, even called themselves Jews, these two uneducated
immigrant atheists who spat on the ground when a rabbi
walked by. But they called themselves what they called themselves freely, without asking permission or seeking approval
from what her father contemptuously described as the hypocritical enemies of everything that was natural and good—
namely, officialdom, those illegitimately holding the power.
On the cracking, filth-caked wall over the soda fountain of the
family candy store on Myrtle Avenue—a cluttered shop so small,
she said, "you couldn't bury the five of us there side by side"
—hung two framed pictures, one of Sacco, the other of Van-
zetti, photographs torn from the rotogravure section of the
newspaper. Every August 22—the anniversary of the day in

1927 when Massachusetts executed the two anarchists for murders Iris and her brothers were taught to believe neither man had committed—business was suspended and the family retreated upstairs to the tiny, dim apartment whose lunatic disorder exceeded even the store's, so as to observe a day of fasting. This was a ritual Iris's father had, like a cult leader, dreamed up all on his own, modeling it wackily on the Jewish Day of Atonement. Her father had no real ideas about what he thought of as ideas—all that ran deep was desperate ignorance and the bitter hopelessness of dispossession, the impotent revolutionary hatred. Everything was said with a clenched fist, and everything was a harangue. He knew the names Kropotkin and Bakunin, but nothing of their writings, and the anarchist Yiddish weekly *Freie Arbeiter Stimme*, which he was always carrying around their apartment, he rarely read more than a few words of each night before dropping off to sleep. Her parents, she explained to Coleman—and all this dramatically, scandalously dramatically, in a Bleecker Street café minutes after he had picked her up in Washington Square—her parents were simple people in the grips of a pipe dream that they could not begin to articulate or rationally defend but for which they were zealously willing to sacrifice friends, relatives, business, the good will of neighbors, even their own sanity, even their *children's* sanity. They knew only what they had nothing in common with, which to Iris, the older she got, appeared to be everything. Society as it was constituted—its forces all in constant motion, the intricate underwebbing of interests stretched to its limit, the battle for advantage that is ongoing, the subjugation that is ongoing, the factional collisions and collusions, the shrewd jargon of morality, the benign despot that is convention, the unstable illusion of stability—society as it was made, always has been and *must* be made, was as foreign to them as was King Arthur's court to the Connecticut Yankee. And yet, this wasn't because they'd been bound by the strongest ties to some other time and place and then forcefully set down in a wholly alien world: they were more like people who'd stepped directly into adulthood from the cradle, having had no intervening education in how human beastliness is run and ruled. Iris could not decide, from the time she was a tot, whether she was being raised by crackpots or visionaries, or whether the passionate loathing she was meant to share was a revelation of the awful truth or utterly ridiculous and possibly insane.

All that afternoon she told Coleman folklorishly enchanting stories that made having survived growing up above the Passaic candy store as the daughter of such vividly benighted individualists as Morris and Ethel Gittelman appear to have been a grim adventure not so much out of Russian literature as out of the Russian funny papers, as though the Gittelmans had been the deranged next-door neighbors in a Sunday comic strip called "The Karamazov Kids." It was a strong, brilliant performance for a girl barely nineteen years old who had fled from Jersey across the Hudson—as who among his Village acquaintances wasn't fleeing, and from places as far away as Amarillo? —without any idea of being anything other than free, a new impoverished exotic on the Eighth Street stage, a theatrically big-featured, vivacious dark girl, emotionally a dynamic force and, in the parlance of the moment, "stacked," a student uptown at the Art Students League who partly earned her scholarship there modeling for the life drawing classes, someone whose style was to hide nothing and who appeared to have no more fear of creating a stir in a public place than a belly dancer. Her head of hair was something, a labyrinthine, billowing wreath of spirals and ringlets, fuzzy as twine and large enough for use as Christmas ornamentation. All the disquiet of her childhood seemed to have passed into the convolutions of her sinuous thicket of hair. Her irreversible hair. You could polish pots with it and no more alter its construction than if it were harvested from the inky depths of the sea, some kind of wiry reef-building organism, a dense living onyx hybrid of coral and shrub, perhaps possessing medicinal properties.

For three hours she held Coleman entranced by her comedy, her outrage, her hair, and by her flair for manufacturing excitement, by a frenzied, untrained adolescent intellect and an actressy ability to enkindle herself and believe her every exaggeration that made Coleman—a cunning self-concoction if ever there was one, a product on which no one but he held a patent—feel by comparison like somebody with no conception of himself at all.

But when he got her back to Sullivan Street that evening,

everything changed. It turned out that she had no idea in the world who she was. Once you'd made your way past the hair, all she was was molten. The antithesis of the arrow aimed at life who was twenty-five-year-old Coleman Silk—a self-freedom fighter too, but the agitated version, the *anarchist* version, of someone wanting to find her way.

It wouldn't have fazed her for five minutes to learn that he had been born and raised in a colored family and identified himself as a Negro nearly all his life, nor would she have been burdened in the slightest by keeping that secret for him if it was what he'd asked her to do. A tolerance for the unusual was not one of Iris Gittelman's deficiencies—unusual to her was what most conformed to the standards of legitimacy. To be two men instead of one? To be two colors instead of one? To walk the streets incognito or in disguise, to be neither this nor that but something in between? To be possessed of a double or a triple or a quadruple personality? To her there was nothing frightening about such seeming deformities. Iris's open-mindedness wasn't even a moral quality of the sort liberals and libertarians pride themselves on; it was more on the order of a mania, the cracked antithesis of bigotry. The expectations indispensable to most people, the assumption of meaning, the confidence in authority, the sanctification of coherence and order, struck her as nothing else in life did—as nonsensical, as totally nuts. Why would things happen as they do and history read as it does if inherent to existence was something called normalcy?

And yet, what he told Iris was that he was Jewish, Silk being an Ellis Island attenuation of Silberzweig, imposed on his father by a charitable customs official. He even bore the biblical mark of circumcision, as not many of his East Orange Negro friends did in that era. His mother, working as a nurse at a hospital staffed predominantly by Jewish doctors, was convinced by burgeoning medical opinion of the significant hygienic benefits of circumcision, and so the Silks had arranged for the rite that was traditional among Jews—and that was beginning, back then, to be elected as a post-natal surgical procedure by an increasing number of Gentile parents—to be performed by a doctor on each of their infant boys in the second week of life.

Coleman had been allowing that he was Jewish for several

years now—or letting people think so if they chose to—since
coming to realize that at NYU as in his café hangouts, many
people he knew seemed to have been assuming he was a Jew all
along. What he'd learned in the navy is that all you have to do
is give a pretty good and consistent line about yourself and
nobody ever inquires, because no one's that interested. His
NYU and Village acquaintances could as easily have surmised
—as buddies of his had in the service—that he was of Middle
Eastern descent, but as this was a moment when Jewish self-
infatuation was at a postwar pinnacle among the Washington
Square intellectual avant-garde, when the aggrandizing appetite driving their Jewish mental audacity was beginning to look
to be uncontrollable and an aura of cultural significance emanated as much from their jokes and their family anecdotes, from
their laughter and their clowning and their wisecracks and their
arguments—even from their insults—as from *Commentary*,
Midstream, and the *Partisan Review*, who was he not to go
along for the ride, especially as his high school years assisting
Doc Chizner as a boxing instructor of Essex County Jewish
kids made claiming a New Jersey Jewish boyhood not so laden
with pitfalls as pretending to being a U.S. sailor with Syrian or
Lebanese roots. Taking on the ersatz prestige of an aggressively thinking, self-analytic, irreverent American Jew reveling
in the ironies of the marginal Manhattan existence turned out
to be nothing like so reckless as it might have seemed had he
spent years dreaming up and elaborating the disguise on his
own, and yet, pleasurably enough, it felt spectacularly reckless
—and when he remembered Dr. Fensterman, who'd offered
his family three thousand dollars for Coleman to take a dive on
his final exams so as to make brilliant Bert the class valedictorian, it struck him as spectacularly comical too, a colossal sui
generis score-settling joke. What a great all-encompassing
idea the world had had to turn him into this—what sublimely
earthly mischief! If ever there was a perfect one-of-a-kind creation—and hadn't singularity been his inmost ego-driven ambition all along?—it was this magical convergence into his
father's Fensterman son.

    No longer was he playing at something. With Iris—the
churned-up, untamed, wholly un-Steena-like, non-Jewish Jewish Iris—as the medium through which to make himself anew,

he'd finally got it right. He was no longer trying on and casting off, endlessly practicing and preparing to be. This was it, the solution, the secret to his secret, flavored with just a drop of the ridiculous—the redeeming, reassuring ridiculous, life's little contribution to every human decision.

As a heretofore unknown amalgam of the most unalike of America's historic undesirables, he now made sense.

There was an interlude, however. After Steena and before Iris there was a five-month interlude named Ellie Magee, a petite, shapely colored girl, tawny-skinned, lightly freckled across the nose and cheeks, in appearance not quite over the dividing line between adolescence and womanhood, who worked at the Village Door Shop on Sixth Avenue, excitedly selling shelving units for books and selling doors—doors on legs for desks and doors on legs for beds. The tired old Jewish guy who owned the place said that hiring Ellie had increased his business by fifty percent. "I had nothing going here," he told Coleman. "Eking out a living. But now every guy in the Village wants a door for a desk. People come in, they don't ask for me—they ask for Ellie. They call on the phone, they want to talk to Ellie. This little gal has changed everything." It was true, nobody could resist her, including Coleman, who was struck, first, by her legs up on high heels and then with all her naturalness. Goes out with white NYU guys who are drawn to her, goes out with colored NYU guys who are drawn to her—a sparkling twenty-three-year-old kid, as yet wounded by nothing, who has moved to the Village from Yonkers, where she grew up, and is living the unconventional life with a small *u*, the Village life as advertised. She is a find, and so Coleman goes in to buy a desk he doesn't need and that night takes her for a drink. After Steena and the shock of losing someone he'd so much wanted, he is having a good time again, he's alive again, and all this from the moment they start flirting in the store. Does she think he's a white guy in the store? He doesn't know. Interesting. Then that evening she laughs and, comically squinting at him, says, "What are you anyway?" Right out she spots something and goes ahead and says it. But now the sweat is not pouring off him as it did when he misread Steena's poem. "What am I? Play it any way you like," Coleman says. "Is that the way *you* play it?" she asks. "Of course that's the way I play it," he says. "So white girls think you're white?" "Whatever they think," he says, "I let them think." "And whatever I think?" Ellie asks. "Same deal," Coleman says. That's the little game they play, and that becomes the excitement for them, playing the ambiguity of it. He's not that close to anybody particularly, but the guys he knows from school think he's taking out a colored girl, and her friends all think she's going around with a white guy. There's some real fun in having other people find them important, and most everywhere they go, people do. It's 1951. Guys ask Coleman, "What's she like?" "Hot," he says, drawing the word out while floppily wiggling one hand the way the Italians did back in East Orange. There's a day-to-day, second-to-second kick in all this, a little movie-star magnitude to his life now: he's always in a scene when he's out with Ellie. Nobody on Eighth Street knows what the hell is going on, and he enjoys that. She's got the legs. She laughs all the time. She's a woman in a natural way—full of ease and a lively innocence that's enchanting to him. Something like Steena, except she's not white, with the result that they don't go rushing off to visit his family and they don't go visiting hers. Why should they? They live in the Village. Taking her to East Orange doesn't even occur to him. Maybe it's because he doesn't want to hear the sigh of relief, to be told, even wordlessly, that he's doing the right thing. He thinks about his motivation for bringing Steena home. To be honest with everyone? And what did that achieve? No, no families—not for now anyway.

Meanwhile, he so enjoys being with her that one night the truth just comes bubbling out. Even about his being a boxer, which he could never tell Steena. It's so easy to tell Ellie. That she's not disapproving gives her another boost up in his estimation. She's not conventional—and yet so sound. He is dealing with someone utterly unnarrow-minded. The splendid girl wants to hear it all. And so he talks, and without restraints he is an extraordinary talker, and Ellie is enthralled. He tells her about the navy. He tells her about his family, which turns out to be a family not much different from hers, except that her father, a pharmacist with a drugstore in Harlem, is living, and though he isn't happy about her having moved to the Village, fortunately for Ellie he can't stop himself from adoring her. Coleman tells her about Howard and how he couldn't stand the place. They talk a lot about Howard because that was where her parents had wanted her to go too. And always, whatever they're talking about, he finds he is effortlessly making her laugh. "I'd never seen so many colored people before, not even in south Jersey at the family reunion. Howard University looked to me like just too many Negroes in one place. Of all persuasions, of every stripe, but I just did not want to be around them like that. Did not at all see what it had to do with me. Everything there was just so concentrated that any sort of pride I ever had was diminished. Completely diminished by a concentrated, false environment." "Like a soda that's too sweet," Ellie said. "Well," he told her, "it's not so much that too much has been put in, it's that everything else has been taken out." Talking openly with Ellie, Coleman finds all his relief. True, he's not a hero anymore, but then he's not in any way a villain either. Yes, she's a contender, this one. Her transcendence into independence, her transformation into a Village girl, the way she handles her folks—she seems to have grown up the way you're supposed to be able to.

One evening she takes him around to a tiny Bleecker Street jewelry shop where the white guy who owns it makes beautiful things out of enamel. Just shopping the street, out looking, but when they leave she tells Coleman that the guy is black. "You're wrong," Coleman tells her, "he can't be." "Don't tell me that I'm wrong"—she laughs—"*you're* blind." Another night, near midnight, she takes him to a bar on Hudson Street where painters congregate to drink. "See that one? The smoothie?" she says in a soft voice, inclining her head toward a good-looking white guy in his mid-twenties charming all the girls at the bar. "Him," she says. "*No*," says Coleman, who's the one laughing now. "You're in Greenwich Village, Coleman Silk, the four freest square miles in America. There's one on every other block. You're so vain, you thought you'd dreamed it up yourself." And if *she* knows of three—which she does, positively—there are ten, if not more. "From all over everywhere," she says, "they make straight for Eighth Street. Just like you did from little East Orange." "And," he says, "I don't see it at all." And that too makes them laugh, laugh and laugh and laugh because he is hopeless and cannot see it in others and because Ellie is his guide, pointing them out.

In the beginning, he luxuriates in the solution to his problem. Losing the secret, he feels like a boy again. The boy he'd been before he had the secret. A kind of imp again. He gets from all her naturalness the pleasure and ease of being natural himself. If you're going to be a knight and a hero, you're armored, and what he gets now is the pleasure of being unarmored. "You're a lucky man," Ellie's boss tells him. "A lucky man," he repeats, and means it. With Ellie the secret is no longer operative. It's not only that he can tell her everything and that he does, it's that if and when he wants to, he can now go home. He can deal with his brother, and the other way, he knows, he could never have. His mother and he can go on back and resume being as close and easygoing as they always were. And then he meets Iris, and that's it. It's been fun with Ellie, and it continues to be fun, but some dimension is missing. The whole thing lacks the ambition—it fails to feed that conception of self that's been driving him all his life. Along comes Iris and he's back in the ring. His father had said to him, "Now you can retire undefeated. You're retired." But here he comes roaring out of his corner—he has the secret again. And the *gift* to be secretive again, which is hard to come by. Maybe there *are* a dozen more guys like him hanging around the Village. But not just everybody has that gift. That is, they have it, but in petty ways: they simply lie all the time. They're not secretive in the grand and elaborate way that Coleman is. He's back on the trajectory outward. He's got the elixir of the secret, and it's like being fluent in another language—it's being somewhere that is constantly fresh to you. He's lived without it, it was fine, nothing horrible happened, it wasn't objectionable. It was fun. Innocent fun. But insufficiently everything else. Sure, he'd regained his innocence. Ellie gave him that all right. But what use is innocence? Iris gives more. She raises everything to another pitch. Iris gives him back his life on the scale he wants to live it.

Two years after they met, they decided to get married, and that was when, for this license he'd taken, this freedom he'd sounded, the choices he had dared to make—and could he really have been any more artful or clever in arriving at an actable self big enough to house his ambition and formidable enough to take on the world?—the first large payment was exacted.

Coleman went over to East Orange to see his mother. Mrs. Silk did not know of Iris Gittelman's existence, though she wasn't at all surprised when he told her that he was going to get married and that the girl was white. She wasn't even surprised when he told her that the girl didn't know he was colored. If anyone was surprised, it was Coleman, who, having openly declared his intention, all at once wondered if this entire decision, the most monumental of his life, wasn't based on the least serious thing imaginable: Iris's hair, that sinuous thicket of hair that was far more Negroid than Coleman's—more like Ernestine's hair than his. As a little girl, Ernestine was famous for asking, "Why don't I have blow hair like Mommy?" —meaning, why didn't her hair blow in the breeze, not only like her mother's but like the hair of all the women on the maternal side of the family.

In the face of his mother's anguish, there floated through Coleman the eerie, crazy fear that all that he had ever wanted from Iris Gittelman was the explanation her appearance could provide for the texture of their children's hair.

But how could a motive as bluntly, as dazzlingly utilitarian as that have escaped his attention till now? Because it wasn't in any way true? Seeing his mother suffering like this—inwardly shaken by his own behavior and yet resolved, as Coleman always was, to carry through to the finish—how could this startling idea seem to him anything *other* than true? Even as he remained seated across from his mother in what appeared to be a state of perfect self-control, he had the definite impression that he had just chosen a wife for the stupidest reason in the world and that he was the emptiest of men.

"And she believes your parents are dead, Coleman. That's what you told her."

"That's right."

"You have no brother, you have no sister. There is no Ernestine. There is no Walt."

He nodded.

"And? What else did you tell her?"

"What else do you think I told her?"

"Whatever it suited you to tell her." That was as harsh as she got all afternoon. Her capacity for anger never had been and never would be able to extend to him. The mere sight of him, from the moment of his birth, stimulated feelings against which she had no defenses and that had nothing to do with what he was worthy of. "I'm never going to know my grandchildren," she said.

He had prepared himself. The important thing was to forget about Iris's hair and let her speak, let her find her fluency and, from the soft streaming of her own words, create for him his apologia.

"You're never going to let them see me," she said. "You're never going to let them know who I am. 'Mom,' you'll tell me, 'Ma, you come to the railroad station in New York, and you sit on the bench in the waiting room, and at eleven twenty-five A.M., I'll walk by with my kids in their Sunday best.' That'll be my birthday present five years from now. 'Sit there, Mom, say nothing, and I'll just walk them slowly by.' And you know very well that I will be there. The railroad station. The zoo. Central Park. Wherever you say, of course I'll do it. You tell me the only way I can ever touch my grandchildren is for you to hire me to come over as Mrs. Brown to baby-sit and put them to bed, I'll do it. Tell me to come over as Mrs. Brown to clean your house, I'll do *that*. Sure I'll do what you tell me. I have no choice."

"Don't you?"

"A choice? Yes? What is my choice, Coleman?"

"To disown me."

Almost mockingly, she pretended to give that idea some thought. "I suppose I could be that ruthless with you. Yes, that's possible, I suppose. But where do you think I'm going to find the strength to be that ruthless with myself?"

It was not a moment for him to be recalling his childhood. It was not a moment for him to be admiring her lucidity or her sarcasm or her courage. It was not a moment to allow himself to be subjugated by the all-but-pathological phenomenon of mother love. It was not a moment for him to be hearing all the words that she was not saying but that were sounded more tellingly even than what she did say. It was not a moment to think thoughts other than the thoughts he'd come armed with.

It was certainly not a moment to resort to explanations, to start brilliantly toting up the advantages and the disadvantages and pretend that this was no more than a logical decision. There was no explanation that could begin to address the outrage of what he was doing to her. It was a moment to deepen his focus on what he was there to achieve. If disowning him was a choice foreclosed to her, then taking the blow was all she could do. Speak quietly, say little, forget Iris's hair, and, for however long is required, let her continue to employ her words to absorb into her being the brutality of the most brutal thing he had ever done.

He was murdering her. You don't have to murder your father. The world will do that for you. There are plenty of forces out to get your father. The world will take care of him, as it had indeed taken care of Mr. Silk. Who there is to murder is the mother, and that's what he saw he was doing to her, the boy who'd been loved as he'd been loved by this woman. Murdering her on behalf of his exhilarating notion of freedom! It would have been much easier without her. But only through this test can he be the man he has chosen to be, unalterably separated from what he was handed at birth, free to struggle at being free like any human being would wish to be free. To get that from life, the alternate destiny, on one's own terms, he must do what must be done. Don't most people want to walk out of the fucking lives they've been handed? But they don't, and that's what makes them them, and this was what was making him him. Throw the punch, do the damage, and forever lock the door. You can't do this to a wonderful mother who loves you unconditionally and has made you happy, you can't inflict this pain and then think you can go back on it. It's so awful that all you can do is live with it. Once you've done a thing like this, you have done so much violence it can *never* be undone—which is what Coleman wants. It's like that moment at West Point when the guy was going down. Only the referee could save him from what Coleman had it in him to do. Then as now, he was experiencing the power of it as a fighter. Because that is the test too, to give the brutality of the repudiation its real, unpardonable human meaning, to confront with all the realism and clarity possible the moment when your fate intersects with something enormous. This is his. This man and his mother. This woman and her beloved son. If, in the service of honing himself, he is out to do the hardest thing imaginable, this is it, short of stabbing her. This takes him right to the heart of the matter. This is the major act of his life, and vividly, consciously, he feels its immensity.

"I don't know why I'm not better prepared for this, Coleman. I should be," she said. "You've been giving fair warning almost from the day you got here. You were seriously disinclined even to take the breast. Yes, you were. Now I see why. Even that might delay your escape. There was always something about our family, and I don't mean color—there was something about us that impeded you. You think like a prisoner. You do, Coleman Brutus. You're white as snow and you think like a slave."

It was not a moment to give credence to her intelligence, to take even the most appealing turn of phrase as the embodiment of some special wisdom. It often happened that his mother could say something that made it sound as though she knew more than she did. The rational other side. That was what came of leaving the orating to his father and so seeming by comparison to say what counted.

"Now, I could tell you that there is no escape, that all your attempts to escape will only lead you back to where you began. That's what your father would tell you. And there'd be something in *Julius Caesar* to back him up. But for a young man like you, whom everybody falls for? A good-looking, charming, clever young fellow with your physique, your determination, your shrewdness, with all your wonderful gifts? You with your green eyes and your long dark lashes? Why, this should cause you no trouble at all. I expect coming to see me is about as hard as it's going to get, and look how calmly you're sitting here. And that is because you know what you're doing makes great sense. *I* know it makes sense, because you would not pursue a goal that didn't. Of course you will have disappointments. Of course little is going to turn out as you imagine it, sitting so calmly across from me. Your special destiny will be special all right—but how? Twenty-six years old—you can't begin to know. But wouldn't the same be true if you did nothing? I suppose any profound change in life involves saying 'I don't know you' to someone."

She went on for nearly two hours, a long speech about his autonomy dating back to infancy, expertly taking in the pain by delineating all she was up against and couldn't hope to oppose and would have to endure, during which Coleman did all he could not to notice—in the simplest things, like the thinning of her hair (his mother's hair, not Iris's hair) and the jutting of her head, the swelling of her ankles, the bloating of her belly, the exaggerated splay of her large teeth—how much further along toward her death she'd been drawn since the Sunday three years back when she'd done everything gracious she could to put Steena at her ease. At some point midway through the afternoon, she seemed to Coleman to step up to the very edge of the big change: the point of turning, as the elderly do, into a tiny, misshapen being. The longer she talked, the more he believed he was seeing this happen. He tried not to think about the disease that would kill her, about the funeral they would give her, about the tributes that would be read and the prayers offered up at the side of her grave. But then he tried not to think about her going on living either, of his leaving and her being here and alive, the years passing and her thinking about him and his children and his wife, more years passing and the connection between the two of them only growing stronger for her because of its denial.

Neither his mother's longevity nor her mortality could be allowed to have any bearing on what he was doing, nor could the struggles her family had been through in Lawnside, where she'd been born in a dilapidated shack and lived with her parents and four brothers until her father died when she was seven. Her father's people had been in Lawnside, New Jersey, since 1855. They were runaway slaves, brought north on the Underground Railroad from Maryland and into southwest Jersey by the Quakers. The Negroes first called the place Free Haven. No whites lived there then, and only a handful did now, out on the fringes of a town of a couple of thousand where just about everybody was descended from runaway slaves whom the Haddonfield Quakers had protected—the mayor was descended from them, the fire chief, the police chief, the tax collector, the teachers in the grade school, the kids in the grade school. But the uniqueness of Lawnside as a Negro town had no bearing on anything either. Nor did the uniqueness of

Gouldtown, farther south in Jersey, down by Cape May. That's where her mother's people were from, and that's where the family went to live after the death of her father. Another settlement of colored people, many nearly white, including her own grandmother, everyone somehow related to everyone else. "Way, way back," as she used to explain to Coleman when he was a boy—simplifying and condensing as best she could all the lore she'd ever heard—a slave was owned by a Continental Army soldier who'd been killed in the French and Indian War. The slave looked after the soldier's widow. He did everything, from dawn to dark didn't stop doing what needed to be done. He chopped and hauled the wood, gathered the crops, excavated and built a cabbage house and stowed the cabbages there, stored the pumpkins, buried the apples, turnips, and potatoes in the ground for winter, stacked the rye and wheat in the barn, slaughtered the pig, salted the pork, slaughtered the cow and corned the beef, until one day the widow married him and they had three sons. And those sons married Gouldtown girls whose families reached back to the settlement's origins in the 1600s, families that by the Revolution were all intermarried and thickly intermingled. One or another or all of them, she said, were descendants of the Indian from the large Lenape settlement at Indian Fields who married a Swede—locally Swedes and Finns had superseded the original Dutch settlers —and who had five children with her; one or another or all were descendants of the two mulatto brothers brought from the West Indies on a trading ship that sailed up the river from Greenwich to Bridgeton, where they were indentured to the landowners who had paid their passage and who themselves later paid the passage of two Dutch sisters to come from Holland to become their wives; one or another or all were descendants of the granddaughter of John Fenwick, an English baronet's son, a cavalry officer in Cromwell's Commonwealth army and a member of the Society of Friends who died in New Jersey not that many years after New Cesarea (the province lying between the Hudson and the Delaware that was deeded by the brother of the king of England to two English proprietors) *became* New Jersey. Fenwick died in 1683 and was buried somewhere in the personal colony he purchased, founded, and governed, and which stretched north of Bridgeton to Salem and south and east to the Delaware.

Fenwick's nineteen-year-old granddaughter, Elizabeth Adams, married a colored man, Gould. "That black that hath been the ruin of her" was her grandfather's description of Gould in the will from which he excluded Elizabeth from any share of his estate until such time as "the Lord open her eyes to see her abominable transgression against Him." As the story had it, only one son of the five sons of Gould and Elizabeth survived to maturity, and he was Benjamin Gould, who married a Finn, Ann. Benjamin died in 1777, the year after the signing of the Declaration of Independence across the Delaware in Philadelphia, leaving a daughter, Sarah, and four sons, Anthony, Samuel, Abijah, and Elisha, from whom Gouldtown took its name.

Through his mother, Coleman learned the maze of family history going back to the days of aristocratic John Fenwick, who was to that southwestern region of New Jersey what William Penn was to the part of Pennsylvania that encompassed Philadelphia—and from whom it sometimes seemed all of Gouldtown had descended—and then he heard it again, though never the same in all its details, from great-aunts and great-uncles, from great-*great*-aunts and -uncles, some of them people close to a hundred, when, as children, he, Walt, and Ernestine went with their parents down to Gouldtown for the annual reunion—almost two hundred relatives from southwest Jersey, from Philadelphia, from Atlantic City, from as far off as Boston, eating fried bluefish, stewed chicken, fried chicken, homemade ice cream, sugared peaches, pies, and cakes—eating favorite family dishes and playing baseball and singing songs and reminiscing all day long, telling stories about the women way back spinning and knitting, boiling fat pork and baking huge breads for the men to take to the fields, making the clothes, drawing the water from the well, administering medicines obtained mainly from the woods, herb infusions to treat measles, the syrups of molasses and onions to counter whooping cough. Stories about family women who kept a dairy making fine cheeses, about women who went to the city of Philadelphia to become housekeepers, dressmakers, and schoolteachers, and about women at home of remarkable hospitality.

Stories about the men in the woods, trapping and shooting the winter game for meat, about the farmers plowing the fields, cutting the cordwood and the rails for fences, buying, selling, slaughtering the cattle, and the prosperous ones, the dealers, selling tons of salt hay for packing to the Trenton pottery works, hay cut from the salt marsh they owned along the bay and river shores. Stories about the men who left the woods, the farm, the marsh, and the cedar swamp to serve—some as white soldiers, some as black—in the Civil War. Stories about men who went to sea to become blockade runners and who went to Philadelphia to become undertakers, printers, barbers, electricians, cigar makers, and ministers in the African Methodist Episcopal Church—one who went to Cuba to ride with Teddy Roosevelt and his Rough Riders, and a few men who got in trouble, ran away, and never came back. Stories about family children like themselves, often dressed poorly, without shoes sometimes or coats, asleep on winter nights in the freezing rooms of simple houses, in the heat of summer pitching, loading, and hauling hay with the men, but taught manners by their parents, and catechized in the schoolhouse by the Presbyterians—where they also learned to spell and read—and always eating all they wanted, even in those days, of pork and potatoes and bread and molasses and game, and growing up strong and healthy and honest.

But one no more decides not to become a boxer because of the history of Lawnside's runaway slaves, the abundance of everything at the Gouldtown reunions, and the intricacy of the family's American genealogy—or not to become a teacher of classics because of the history of Lawnside's runaway slaves, the abundance of the Gouldtown reunions, and the intricacy of the family's American genealogy—than one decides not to become anything else for such reasons. Many things vanish out of a family's life. Lawnside is one, Gouldtown another, genealogy a third, and Coleman Silk was a fourth.

Over these last fifty years or more, he was not the first child, either, who'd heard about the harvesting of the salt hay for the Trenton pottery works or eaten fried bluefish and sugared peaches at the Gouldtown reunions and grown up to vanish like this—to vanish, as they used to say in the family, "till all

trace of him was lost." "Lost himself to all his people" was another way they put it.

Ancestor worship—that's how Coleman put it. Honoring
the past was one thing—the idolatry that is ancestor worship
was something else. The hell with that imprisonment.

That night after coming back to the Village from East Orange, Coleman got a call from his brother in Asbury Park that
took things further faster than he had planned. "Don't you
ever come around her," Walt warned him, and his voice was
resonant with something barely suppressed—all the more
frightening for *being* suppressed—that Coleman hadn't heard
since his father's time. There's another force in that family,
pushing him now *all* the way over on the other side. The act
was committed in 1953 by an audacious young man in Greenwich Village, by a specific person in a specific place at a specific
time, but now he will be over on the other side forever. Yet
that, as he discovers, is exactly the point: freedom is dangerous. Freedom is very dangerous. And nothing is on your own
terms for long. "Don't you even *try* to see her. No contact. No
calls. Nothing. Never. Hear me?" Walt said. "*Never.* Don't you
dare ever show your lily-white face around that house again!"

3

What Do You Do with the Kid Who Can't Read?

"IF Clinton had fucked her in the ass, she might have shut her mouth. Bill Clinton is not the man they say he is. Had he turned her over in the Oval Office and fucked her in the ass, none of this would have happened."

"Well, he never dominated her. He played it safe."

"You see, once he got to the White House, he didn't dominate anymore. Couldn't. He didn't dominate Willey either. That's why she got angry with him. Once he became president, he lost his Arkansas ability to dominate women. So long as he was attorney general and governor of an obscure little state, that was perfect for him."

"Sure. Gennifer Flowers."

"What happens in Arkansas? If you fall when you're still back in Arkansas, you don't fall from a very great height."

"Right. And you're expected to be an ass man. There's a tradition."

"But when you get to the White House, you can't dominate. And when you can't dominate, then Miss Willey turns against you, and Miss Monica turns against you. Her loyalty would have been earned by fucking her in the ass. That should be the pact. That should seal you together. But there was no pact."

"Well, she was frightened. She was close to not saying anything, you know. Starr overwhelmed her. Eleven guys in the room with her at that hotel? Hitting on her? It was a gang bang. It was a gang rape that Starr staged there at that hotel."

"Yeah. True. But she was talking to Linda Tripp."

"Oh, right."

"She was talking to everybody. She's part of that dopey culture. Yap, yap, yap. Part of this generation that is proud of its shallowness. The sincere performance is everything. Sincere and empty, totally empty. The sincerity that goes in all directions. The sincerity that is worse than falseness, and the innocence that is worse than corruption. All the rapacity hidden under the sincerity. And under the lingo. This wonderful language they all have—that they appear to *believe*—about their 'lack of self-worth,' all the while what they actually believe is that they're entitled to everything. Their shamelessness they call loving-ness, and the ruthlessness is camouflaged as lost 'self-esteem.' Hitler lacked self-esteem too. That was his problem. It's a con these kids have going. The hyperdramatization of the pettiest emotions. Relationship. My relationship. Clarify my relation-ship. They open their mouths and they send me up the wall. Their whole language is a summation of the stupidity of the last forty years. Closure. *There's* one. My students cannot stay in that place where thinking must occur. Closure! They fix on the conventionalized narrative, with its beginning, middle, and end—every experience, no matter how ambiguous, no matter how knotty or mysterious, must lend itself to this normalizing, conventionalizing, anchorman cliché. Any kid who says 'clo-sure' I flunk. They want closure, there's their closure."

"Well, whatever she is—a total narcissist, a conniving little bitch, the most exhibitionistic Jewish girl in the history of Beverly Hills, utterly corrupted by privilege—he knew it all beforehand. He could read her. If he can't read Monica Lewin-sky, how can he read Saddam Hussein? If he can't read and outfox Monica Lewinsky, the guy *shouldn't* be president. There's *genuine* grounds for impeachment. No, he saw it. He saw it all. I don't think he was hypnotized by her cover story for long. That she was totally corrupt and totally innocent, of course he saw it. The extreme innocence *was* the corruption —it was her corruption and her madness and her cunning. That was her force, that combination. That she had no depth, that was her charm at the end of his day of being commander in chief. The intensity of the shallowness was its appeal. Not to mention the shallowness of the intensity. The stories about her childhood. The boasting about her adorable willfulness: 'See, I was three but I was already a personality.' I'm sure he under-stood that everything he did that didn't conform to her delu-sions was going to be yet another brutal blow to her self-esteem. But what he didn't see was that he had to fuck her in the ass. Why? To shut her up. Strange behavior in our president. It was the first thing she showed him. She stuck it in his face. She offered it to him. And he did nothing about it. I don't get this guy. Had he fucked her in the ass, I doubt she would have talked to Linda Tripp. Because she wouldn't have wanted to talk about that."

"She wanted to talk about the cigar."

"That's different. That's kid stuff. No, he didn't give her regularly something she didn't want to talk about. Something he wanted that she didn't. That's the mistake."

"In the ass is how you create loyalty."

"I don't know if that would have shut her up. I don't know that shutting her up is humanly possible. This isn't Deep Throat. This is Big Mouth."

"Still, you have to admit that this girl has revealed more about America than anybody since Dos Passos. *She* stuck a thermometer up the *country's* ass. Monica's *U.S.A.*"

"The trouble was she was getting from Clinton what she got from all these guys. She wanted something else from him. He's the president, she's a love terrorist. She wanted him to be different from this teacher she had an affair with."

"Yeah, the niceness did him in. Interesting. Not his brutality but his niceness. Playing it not by his rules but by hers. She controls him because he wants it. Has to have it. It's all wrong. You know what Kennedy would have told her when she came around asking for a job? You know what Nixon would have told her? Harry Truman, even Eisenhower would have told it to her. The general who ran World War II, he knew how not to be nice. They would have told her that not only would they not give her a job, but nobody would ever give her a job again as long as she lived. That she wouldn't be able to get a job driving a cab in Horse Springs, New Mexico. *Nothing.* That her father's practice would be sabotaged, and *he'd* be out of work. That her mother would never work again, that her brother would never work again, that nobody in her family would earn another dime, if she so much as dared to open her mouth about the eleven blow jobs. Eleven. Not even a round dozen. I don't think under a dozen in over two years qualifies for the Heisman in debauchery, do you?"

"His caution, his caution did him in. Absolutely. He played it like a lawyer."

"He didn't want to give her any evidence. That's why he wouldn't come."

"There he was right. The moment he came, he was finished. She had the goods. Collected a sample. The smoking come. Had he fucked her in the ass, the nation could have been spared this terrible trauma."

They laughed. There were three of them.

"He never really abandoned himself to it. He had an eye on the door. He had his own system there. She was trying to up the ante."

"Isn't this what the Mafia does? You give somebody something they can't talk about. Then you've got them."

"You involve them in a mutual transgression, and you have a mutual corruption. Sure."

"So his problem is that he's *insufficiently* corrupt."

"Oh, yes. Absolutely. And unsophisticated."

"It's just the opposite of the charge that he's reprehensible. He's insufficiently reprehensible."

"Of course. If you're engaged in that behavior, why draw the line there? Wasn't that fairly artificial?"

"Once you draw the line, you make it clear that you're frightened. And when you're frightened, you're finished. Your destruction is no further than Monica's cell phone."

"He didn't want to lose control, you see. Remember he said, I don't want to be hooked on you, I don't want to be addicted to you? That struck me as true."

"I thought that was a line."

"I don't think so. I think probably the way she remembered it, it sounds like a line, but I think the motivation—no, he didn't want the sexual hook. She was good but she was replaceable."

"Everybody's replaceable."

"But you don't know what his experience was. He wasn't into hookers and that kind of stuff."

"Kennedy was into hookers."

"Oh yeah. The real stuff. This guy Clinton, this is schoolboy stuff."

"I don't think he was a schoolboy when he was down in Arkansas."

"No, the scale was right in Arkansas. Here it was all out of whack. And it must have driven him crazy. President of the United States, he has access to everything, and he can't touch it. This was hell. Especially with that goody two-shoes wife."

"She's goody two-shoes, you think?"

"Oh, sure."

"Her and Vince Foster?"

"Well, she would fall in love with somebody, but she never would have done anything crazy because he was *married*. She could make even adultery boring. She's a real de-transgressor."

"You think she was fucking Foster?"

"Yes. Oh yeah."

"Now the whole world has fallen in love with goody two-shoes. That's exactly what they've fallen in love with."

"Clinton's genius was to give Vince Foster a job in Washington. Put him right there. Make him do his personal bit for the administration. That's genius. There Clinton acted like a good Mafia don and had that on her."

"Yeah. That's okay. But that isn't what he did with Monica. You see, he had only Vernon Jordan to talk to about Monica. Who was probably the best person to talk to. But they couldn't figure that out. Because they thought she was blabbing just to her stupid little California Valley Girls. Okay. So what. But that this Linda Tripp, this Iago, this undercover Iago that Starr had working in the White House—"

At this point, Coleman got up from where he was seated and headed toward the campus. That was all of the chorus Coleman overheard while sitting on a bench on the green, contemplating what move he'd make next. He didn't recognize their voices, and since their backs were to him and their bench was around the other side of the tree from his, he couldn't see their faces. His guess was that they were three young guys, new to the faculty since his time, on the town green drinking bottled water or decaf out of containers, just back from a workout on the town tennis courts, and relaxing together, talking over the day's Clinton news before heading home to their wives and children. To him they sounded sexually savvy and sexually confident in ways he didn't associate with young assistant professors, particularly at Athena. Pretty rough talk, pretty raw for academic banter. Too bad these tough guys hadn't been around in his time. They might have served as a cadre of resistance against . . . No, no. Up on the campus, where not everyone's a tennis buddy, this sort of force tends to get dissipated in jokes when it's not entirely self-suppressed—they would probably have been no more forthcoming than the rest of the faculty when it came to rallying behind him. Anyway, he didn't know them and didn't want to. He knew no one any longer. For two years now, all the while he was writing *Spooks*, he had cut himself off completely from the friends and colleagues and associates of a lifetime, and so not until today—just before noon, following the meeting with Nelson Primus that had ended not merely badly but stunningly badly, with Coleman astounding *himself* by his vituperative words—had he come anywhere near leaving Town Street, as he was doing now, and heading down South Ward and then, at the Civil War monument, climbing the hill to the campus. Chances were there'd be no one he knew for him to bump into, except perhaps whoever might be teaching the retired who came in July to spend a couple of weeks in the college's Elderhostel program, which included visits to the Tanglewood concerts, the Stockbridge galleries, and the Norman Rockwell Museum.

It was these very summer students he saw first when he reached the crest of the hill and emerged from behind the old astronomy building onto the sun-speckled main quadrangle, more kitschily collegiate-looking at that moment than even on the cover of the Athena catalog. They were heading to the cafeteria for lunch, meandering in pairs along one of the tree-lined quadrangle's crisscrossing paths. A procession of twos: husbands and wives together, pairs of husbands and pairs of wives, pairs of widows, pairs of widowers, pairs of rearranged widows and widowers—or so Coleman took them to be—who had teamed up as couples after meeting here in their Elderhostel classes. All were neatly dressed in light summer clothes, a lot of shirts and blouses of bright pastel shades, trousers of white or light khaki, some Brooks Brothers summertime plaid. Most of the men were wearing visored caps, caps of every color, many of them stitched with the logos of professional sports teams. No wheelchairs, no walkers, no crutches, no canes that he could see. Spry people his age, seemingly no less fit than he was, some a bit younger, some obviously older but enjoying what retirement freedom was meant to provide for

those fortunate enough to breathe more or less easily, to am-
bulate more or less painlessly, and to think more or less clearly.
This was where he was supposed to be. Paired off properly.
Appropriately.

Appropriate. The current code word for reining in most any
deviation from the wholesome guidelines and thereby making
everybody "comfortable." Doing not what he was being judged
to be doing but doing instead, he thought, what was deemed
suitable by God only knows which of our moral philosophers.
Barbara Walters? Joyce Brothers? William Bennett? *Dateline
NBC*? If he were around this place as a professor, he could
teach "Appropriate Behavior in Classical Greek Drama," a
course that would be over before it began.

They were on their way to lunch, passing within sight of
North Hall, the ivied, beautifully weathered colonial brick
building where, for over a decade, Coleman Silk, as faculty
dean, had occupied the office across from the president's suite.
The college's architectural marker, the six-sided clock tower of
North Hall, topped by the spire that was topped by the flag—
and that, from down in Athena proper, could be seen the way
the massive European cathedrals are discerned from the approaching roadways by those repairing for the cathedral town
—was tolling noon as he sat on a bench shadowed by the
quadrangle's most famously age-gnarled oak, sat and calmly
tried to consider the coercions of propriety. The *tyranny* of
propriety. It was hard, halfway through 1998, for even him to
believe in American propriety's enduring power, and he was
the one who considered himself tyrannized: the bridle it still is
on public rhetoric, the inspiration it provides for personal
posturing, the persistence just about everywhere of this de-
virilizing pulpit virtue-mongering that H. L. Mencken identified with boobism, that Philip Wylie thought of as Momism,
that the Europeans unhistorically call American puritanism, that
the likes of a Ronald Reagan call America's core values, and
that maintains widespread jurisdiction by masquerading itself
as something else—as *everything* else. As a force, propriety is
protean, a dominatrix in a thousand disguises, infiltrating, if
need be, as civic responsibility, WASP dignity, women's rights,
black pride, ethnic allegiance, or emotion-laden Jewish ethical
sensitivity. It's not as though Marx or Freud or Darwin or

Stalin or Hitler or Mao had never happened—it's as though Sinclair Lewis had not happened. It's, he thought, as though *Babbitt* had never been written. It's as though not even that most basic level of imaginative thought had been admitted into consciousness to cause the slightest disturbance. A century of destruction unlike any other in its extremity befalls and blights the human race—scores of millions of ordinary people condemned to suffer deprivation upon deprivation, atrocity upon atrocity, evil upon evil, half the world or more subjected to pathological sadism as social policy, whole societies organized and fettered by the fear of violent persecution, the degradation of individual life engineered on a scale unknown throughout history, nations broken and enslaved by ideological criminals who rob them of everything, entire populations so demoralized as to be unable to get out of bed in the morning with the minutest desire to face the day . . . all the terrible touchstones presented by this century, and here they are up in arms about Faunia Farley. Here in America either it's Faunia Farley or it's Monica Lewinsky! The luxury of these lives disquieted so by the inappropriate comportment of Clinton and Silk! *This*, in 1998, is the wickedness they have to put up with. *This*, in 1998, is their torture, their torment, and their spiritual death. Their source of greatest moral despair, Faunia blowing me and me fucking Faunia. I'm depraved not simply for having once said the word "spooks" to a class of white students—and said it, mind you, not while standing there reviewing the legacy of slavery, the fulminations of the Black Panthers, the metamorphoses of Malcolm X, the rhetoric of James Baldwin, or the radio popularity of *Amos 'n' Andy*, but while routinely calling the roll. I am depraved not merely because of . . .

All this after less than five minutes sitting on a bench and looking at the pretty building where he had once been dean.

But the mistake had been made. He was back. He was there. He was back on the hill from which they had driven him, and so was his contempt for the friends who hadn't rallied round him and the colleagues who hadn't cared to support him and the enemies who'd disposed so easily of the whole meaning of his professional career. The urge to expose the capricious cruelty of their righteous idiocy flooded him with rage. He was back on the hill in the bondage of his rage and he could feel its intensity driving out all sense and demanding that he take immediate action.

Delphine Roux.

He got up and started for her office. At a certain age, he thought, it is better for one's health not to do what I am about to do. At a certain age, a man's outlook is best tempered by moderation, if not resignation, if not outright capitulation. At a certain age, one should live without either harking too much back to grievances of the past or inviting resistance in the present by embodying a challenge to the pieties that be. Yet to give up playing any but the role socially assigned, in this instance assigned to the respectably retired—at seventy-one, that is surely what is appropriate, and so, for Coleman Silk, as he long ago demonstrated with requisite ruthlessness to his very own mother, that is what is unacceptable.

He was not an embittered anarchist like Iris's crazy father, Gittelman. He was not a firebrand or an agitator in any way. Nor was he a madman. Nor was he a radical or a revolutionary, not even intellectually or philosophically speaking, unless it is revolutionary to believe that disregarding prescriptive society's most restrictive demarcations and asserting independently a free personal choice that is well within the law was something other than a basic human right—unless it is revolutionary, when you've come of age, to refuse to accept automatically the contract drawn up for your signature at birth.

By now he had passed behind North Hall and was headed for the long bowling green of a lawn leading to Barton and the office of Delphine Roux. He had no idea what he was going to say should he even catch her at her desk on a midsummer day as glorious as this one, with the fall semester not scheduled to begin for another six or seven weeks—nor did he find out, because, before he got anywhere near the wide brick path encircling Barton, he noticed around at the back of North Hall, gathered on a shady patch of grass adjacent to a basement stairwell, a group of five college janitors, in custodial staff shirts and trousers of UPS brown, sharing a pizza out of a delivery box and heartily laughing at somebody's joke. The only woman of the five and the focus of her coworkers' lunchtime attention —she who had told the joke or made the wisecrack or done

the teasing and who happened also to be laughing loudest—was
Faunia Farley.

The men appeared to be in their early thirties or thereabouts.
Two were bearded, and one of the bearded ones, sporting a
long ponytail, was particularly broad and oxlike. He was the
only one up on his feet, the better, it seemed, to hover directly
over Faunia as she sat on the ground, her long legs stretched
out before her and her head thrown back in the gaiety of the
moment. Her hair was a surprise to Coleman. It was down. In
his experience, it was unfailingly drawn tightly back through
an elastic band—down only in bed when she removed the band
so as to allow it to fall to her unclothed shoulders.

With the boys. These must be "the boys" she referred to.
One of them was recently divorced, a successless one-time garage mechanic who kept her Chevy running for her and drove
her back and forth from work on the days when the damn
thing wouldn't start no matter what he did, and one of them
wanted to take her to a porn film on the nights his wife was working the late shift at the Blackwell paper box plant, and one of
the boys was so innocent he didn't know what a hermaphrodite
was. When the boys came up in conversation, Coleman listened
without comment, expressing no chagrin over what she had to
say about them, however much he wondered about their interest in her, given the meat of their talk as Faunia reported it.
But as she didn't go endlessly on about them, and as he didn't
encourage her with questions about them, the boys didn't
make the impression on Coleman that they would have had,
say, on Lester Farley. Of course she might herself choose to be
a little less carefree and feed herself less cooperatively into their
fantasies, but even when Coleman was impelled to suggest
that, he easily managed to restrain himself. She could speak as
pointlessly or pointedly as she liked to anyone, and whatever
the consequences, she would have to bear them. She was not
his daughter. She was not even his "girl." She was—what she was.

But watching unseen from where he had ducked back into
the shadowed wall of North Hall, it was not nearly so easy to
take so detached and tolerant a view. Because now he saw not
only what he invariably saw—what attaining so little in life had
done to her—but perhaps why so little had been attained; from

his vantage point no more than fifty feet away, he could observe almost microscopically how, without him to take her cues
from, she took cues instead from the gruffest example around,
the coarsest, the one whose human expectations were the lowest and whose self-conception the shallowest. Since, no matter
how intelligent you may be, Voluptas makes virtually anything
you want to think come true, certain possibilities are never
even framed, let alone vigorously conjectured, and assessing
correctly the qualities of your Voluptas is the last thing you are
equipped to do . . . until, that is, you slip into the shadows
and observe her rolling onto her back on the grass, her knees
bent and falling slightly open, the cheese of the pizza running
down one hand, a Diet Coke brandished in the other, and
laughing her head off—at what? at hermaphroditism?—while
over her looms, in the person of a failed grease monkey, everything that is the antithesis of your own way of life. Another
Farley? Another Les Farley? Maybe nothing so ominous as
that, but more of a substitute for Farley than for him.

A campus scene that would have seemed without significance
had Coleman encountered it on a summer day back when he
was dean—as he undoubtedly had numerous times—a campus
scene that would have seemed back then not merely harmless
but appealingly expressive of the pleasure to be derived from
eating out of doors on a beautiful day was freighted now with
nothing *but* significance. Where neither Nelson Primus nor his
beloved Lisa nor even the cryptic denunciation anonymously
dispatched by Delphine Roux had convinced him of anything,
this scene of no great moment on the lawn back of North Hall
exposed to him at last the underside of his own disgrace.

Lisa. Lisa and those kids of hers. Tiny little Carmen. That's
who came flashing into his thoughts, tiny Carmen, six years
old but, in Lisa's words, like a much younger kid. "She's cute,"
Lisa said, "but she's like a baby." And adorably cute Carmen
was when he saw her: pale, pale brown skin, pitch-black hair
in two stiff braids, eyes unlike any he'd ever seen on another
human being, eyes like coals blue with heat and lit from within,
a child's quick and flexible body, attired neatly in miniaturized
jeans and sneakers, wearing colorful socks and a white tube of
a T-shirt nearly as narrow as a pipe cleaner—a frisky little girl
seemingly attentive to everything, and particularly to him. "This

is my friend Coleman," Lisa said when Carmen came strolling into the room, on her small, scrubbed first-thing-in-the-morning face a slightly amused, self-important mock smile. "Hello, Carmen," Coleman said. "He just wanted to see what we do," Lisa explained. "Okay," said Carmen, agreeably enough, but she studied him no less carefully than he was studying her, seemingly *with* the smile. "We're just gonna do what we always do," said Lisa. "Okay," Carmen said, but now she was trying out on him a rather more serious version of the smile. And when she turned and got to handling the movable plastic letters magnetized to the low little blackboard and Lisa asked her to begin sliding them around to make the words "want," "wet," "wash," and "wipe"—"I always tell you," Lisa was saying, "that you have to look at the first letters. Let's see you read the first letters. Read it with your finger"—Carmen kept periodically swiveling her head, then her whole body, to look at Coleman and stay in touch with him. "Anything is a distraction," Lisa said softly to her father. "Come on, Miss Carmen. Come on, honey. He's invisible." "What's that?" "Invisible," Lisa repeated, "you can't see him." Carmen laughed—"I *can* see him." "Come on. Come on back to me. The first letters. That's it. Good work. But you also have to read the rest of the word too. Right? The first letter—and now the rest of the word. Good—'wash.' What's this one? You know it. You know that one. 'Wipe.' Good." Twenty-five weeks in the program on the day Coleman came to sit in on Reading Recovery, and though Carmen had made progress, it wasn't much. He remembered how she had struggled with the word "your" in the illustrated storybook from which she was reading aloud—scratching with her fingers around her eyes, squeezing and balling up the midriff of her shirt, twisting her legs onto the rung of her kiddie-sized chair, slowly but surely working her behind farther and farther off the seat of the chair—and was still unable to recognize "your" or to sound it out. "This is March, Dad. Twenty-five weeks. It's a long time to be having trouble with 'your.' It's a long time to be confusing 'couldn't' with 'climbed,' but at this point I'll settle for 'your.' It's supposed to be twenty weeks in the program, and out. She's been to kindergarten—she should have learned some basic sight words. But when I showed her a list of words back in September—and by then she was entering first grade—she said, 'What are these?' She didn't even know what words were. And the letters: *h* she didn't know, *j* she didn't know, she confused *u* for *c*. You see how she did that, it's visually similar, but she still has something of the problem twenty-five weeks later. The *m* and the *w*. The *i* and the *l*. The *g* and the *d*. Still problems for her. It's all a problem for her."

"You're pretty dejected about Carmen," he said. "Well, every day for half an hour? That's a lot of instruction. That's a lot of work. She's supposed to read at home, but at home there's a sixteen-year-old sister who just had a baby, and the parents forget or don't care. The parents are immigrants, they're second-language learners, they don't find it easy reading to their children in English, though Carmen never got read to even in Spanish. And this is what I deal with day in and day out. Just seeing if a child can manipulate a book—I give it to them, a book like this one, with a big colorful illustration beneath the title, and I say, 'Show me the front of the book.' Some kids know, but most don't. Print doesn't mean anything to them. And," she said, smiling with exhaustion and nowhere near as enticingly as Carmen, "my kids supposedly aren't learning-disabled. Carmen doesn't look at the words while *I'm* reading. She doesn't care. And that's why you're wiped out at the end of the day. Other teachers have difficult tasks, I know, but at the end of a day of Carmen after Carmen after Carmen, you come home emotionally drained. By then *I* can't read. I can't even get on the phone. I eat something and go to bed. I do like these kids. I love these kids. But it's worse than draining—it's killing."

Faunia was sitting up on the grass now, downing the last of her drink while one of the boys—the youngest, thinnest, most boyish-looking of them, incongruously bearded at just the chin and wearing, with his brown uniform, a red-checkered bandanna and what looked like high-heeled cowboy boots—was collecting all the debris from lunch and stuffing it into a trash sack, and the other three were standing apart, out in the sunshine, each smoking a last cigarette before returning to work.

Faunia was alone. And quiet now. Sitting there gravely with the empty soda can and thinking what? About the two years of waitressing down in Florida when she was sixteen and seventeen, about the retired businessmen who used to come in for lunch without their wives and ask her if she wouldn't like to live in a nice apartment and have nice clothes and a nice new Pinto and charge accounts at all the Bal Harbour clothing shops and at the jewelry store and at the beauty parlor and in exchange do nothing more than be a girlfriend a few nights a week and every once in a while on weekends? Not one, two, three, but four such proposals in just the first year. And then the proposition from the Cuban. She clears a hundred bucks a john and no taxes. For a skinny blonde with big tits, a tall, good-looking kid like her with hustle and ambition and guts, got up in a miniskirt, a halter, and boots, a thousand bucks a night would be nothing. A year, two, and, if by then she wants to, she retires—she can afford to. "And you didn't do it?" Coleman asked. "No. Uh-uh. But don't think I didn't think about it," she said. "All the restaurant shit, those creepy people, the crazy cooks, a menu I can't read, orders I can't write, keeping everything straight in my head—it was no picnic. But if I can't read, I can count. I can add. I can subtract. I can't read words but I know who Shakespeare is. I know who Einstein is. I know who won the Civil War. I'm not stupid. I'm just an illiterate. A fine distinction but there it is. Numbers are something else. Numbers, believe me, I know. Don't think I didn't think it might not be a bad idea at all." But Coleman needed no such instruction. Not only did he think that at seventeen she thought being a hooker might be a good idea, he thought that it was an idea that she had more than simply entertained.

"What do you do with the kid who can't read?" Lisa had asked him in her despair. "It's the key to everything, so you have to do *something*, but doing it is burning me out. Your second year is supposed to be better. Your third year better than that. And this is my fourth." "And it isn't better?" he asked. "It's hard. It's so hard. Each year is *harder*. But if one-on-one tutoring doesn't work, what *do* you do?" Well, what *he* did with the kid who couldn't read was to make her his mistress. What Farley did was to make her his punching bag. What the Cuban did was to make her his whore, or one among them—so Coleman believed more often than not. And for how long his whore? Is that what Faunia was thinking about before getting herself up to head back to North Hall to finish cleaning the corridors? Was she thinking about how long it had all gone on? The mother, the stepfather, the escape from the stepfather, the places in the South, the places in the North, the men, the beatings, the jobs, the marriage, the farm, the herd, the bankruptcy, the children, the two dead children. No wonder half an hour in the sun sharing a pizza with the boys is paradise to her.

"This is my friend Coleman, Faunia. He's just going to watch."

"Okay," Faunia says. She is wearing a green corduroy jumper, fresh white stockings, and shiny black shoes, and is not nearly as jaunty as Carmen—composed, well mannered, permanently a little deflated, a pretty middle-class Caucasian child with long blond hair in butterfly barrettes at either side and, unlike Carmen, showing no interest in him, no curiosity about him, once he has been introduced. "Hello," she mumbles meekly, and goes obediently back to moving the magnetic letters around, pushing together the *w*'s, the *t*'s, the *n*'s, the *s*'s, and, on another part of the blackboard, grouping together all the vowels.

"Use two hands," Lisa tells her, and she does what she is told.

"Which are these?" Lisa asks.

And Faunia reads them. Gets all the letters right.

"Let's take something she knows," Lisa says to her father. "Make 'not,' Faunia."

Faunia does it. Faunia makes "not."

"Good work. Now something she doesn't know. Make 'got.' "

Looks long and hard at the letters, but nothing happens. Faunia makes nothing. Does nothing. Waits. Waits for the next thing to happen. Been waiting for the next thing to happen all her life. It always does.

"I want you to change the first part, Miss Faunia. Come on. You know this. What's the first part of 'got'?"

"*G*." She moves away the *n* and, at the start of the word, substitutes *g*.

"Good work. Now make it say 'pot.' "

She does it. Pot.

"Good. Now read it with your finger."

Faunia moves her finger beneath each letter while distinctly pronouncing its sound. "Puh—ah—tuh."

"She's quick," Coleman says.

"Yes, but that's supposed to be quick."

There are three other children with three other Reading Recovery teachers in other parts of the large room, and so all around him Coleman can hear little voices reading aloud, rising and falling in the same childish pattern regardless of the content, and he hears the other teachers saying, "You know that—*u*, like '*u*mbrella'—*u*, *u*—" and "You know that—*ing*, you know *ing*—" and "You know *I*—good, good work," and when he looks around, he sees that all the other children being taught are Faunia as well. There are alphabet charts everywhere, with pictures of objects to illustrate each of the letters, and there are plastic letters everywhere to pick up in your hand, differently colored so as to help you phonetically form the words a letter at a time, and piled everywhere are simple books that tell the simplest stories: ". . . on Friday we went to the beach. Saturday we went to the airport." " 'Father Bear, is Baby Bear with you?' 'No,' said Father Bear." "In the morning a dog barked at Sara. She was frightened. 'Try to be a brave girl, Sara,' said Mom." In addition to all these books and all these stories and all these Saras and all these dogs and all these bears and all these beaches, there are four teachers, four teachers all for Faunia, and they *still* can't teach her to read at her level.

"She's in first grade," Lisa is telling her father. "We're hoping that if we all four work together with her all day long every day, by the end of the year we can get her up to speed. But it's hard to get her motivated on her own."

"Pretty little girl," Coleman says.

"Yes, you find her pretty? You like that type? Is that your type, Dad, the pretty, slow-at-reading type with the long blond hair and the broken will and the butterfly barrettes?"

"I didn't say that."

"You didn't have to. I've been watching you with her," and she points around the room to where all four Faunias sit quietly before the board, forming and re-forming out of the colorful plastic letters the words "pot" and "got" and "not." "The first time she spelled out 'pot' with her finger, you couldn't take your eyes off the kid. Well, if that turns you on, you should have been here back in September. Back in September she misspelled her first name *and* her second name. Fresh from kindergarten and the only word on the word list she could recognize was 'not.' She didn't understand that print contains a message. She didn't know left page before right page. She didn't know 'Goldilocks and the Three Bears.' 'Do you know "Goldilocks and the Three Bears," Faunia?' 'No.' Which means that her kindergarten experience—because that's what they get there, fairy tales, nursery rhymes—wasn't very good. Today she knows 'Little Red Riding Hood,' but then? Forget it. Oh, if you'd met Faunia last September, fresh from failing at kindergarten, I guarantee you, Dad, she would have driven you wild."

What do you do with the kid who can't read? The kid who is sucking somebody off in a pickup in her driveway while, upstairs, in a tiny apartment over a garage, her small children are supposedly asleep with a space heater burning—two untended children, a kerosene fire, and she's with this guy in his truck. The kid who has been a runaway since age fourteen, on the lam from her inexplicable life for her entire life. The kid who marries, for the stability and the safeguard he'll provide, a combat-crazed veteran who goes for your throat if you so much as turn in your sleep. The kid who is false, the kid who hides herself and lies, the kid who can't read who *can* read, who *pretends* she can't read, takes willingly upon herself this crippling shortcoming all the better to impersonate a member of a subspecies to which she does not belong and need not belong but to which, for every wrong reason, she wants him to believe she belongs. Wants herself to believe she belongs. The kid whose existence became a hallucination at seven and a catastrophe at fourteen and a disaster after that, whose vocation is to be neither a waitress nor a hooker nor a farmer nor a janitor but forever the stepdaughter to a lascivious stepfather and the undefended offspring of a self-obsessed mother, the kid who mistrusts everyone, sees the con in everyone, and yet is protected against nothing, whose capacity to hold on, unintimidated, is enormous and yet whose purchase on life is minute, misfortune's favorite embattled child, the kid to whom everything loathsome that can happen has happened and whose luck shows no sign of changing and yet who excites and arouses him like nobody since Steena, not the most but, morally speaking, the *least* repellent person he knows, the one to whom he feels drawn because of having been aimed for so long in the opposite direction—because of all he has *missed* by going in the opposite direction—and because the underlying feeling of rightness that controlled him formerly is exactly what is propelling him now, the unlikely intimate with whom he shares no less a spiritual than a physical union, who is anything *but* a plaything upon whom he flings his body twice a week in order to sustain his animal nature, who is more to him like a comrade-in-arms than anyone else on earth.

And what do you do with such a kid? You find a pay phone as fast as you can and rectify your idiotic mistake.

He thinks she is thinking about how long it has all gone on, the mother, the stepfather, the escape from the stepfather, the places in the South, the places in the North, the men, the beatings, the jobs, the marriage, the farm, the herd, the bankruptcy, the children, the dead children . . . and maybe she is. Maybe she is even if, alone now on the grass while the boys are smoking and cleaning up from lunch, she thinks she is thinking about crows. She thinks about crows a lot of the time. They're everywhere. They roost in the woods not far from the bed where she sleeps, they're in the pasture when she's out there moving the fence for the cows, and today they are cawing all over the campus, and so instead of thinking of what she is thinking the way Coleman thinks she is thinking it, she is thinking about the crow that used to hang around the store in Seeley Falls when, after the fire and before moving to the farm, she took the furnished room up there to try to hide from Farley, the crow that hung around the parking lot between the post office and the store, the crow that somebody had made into a pet because it was abandoned or because its mother was killed —she never knew what orphaned it. And now it had been abandoned for a second time and had taken to hanging out in that parking lot, where most everybody came and went during the course of the day. This crow created many problems in Seeley Falls because it started dive-bombing people coming into the post office, going after the barrettes in the little girls' hair and so on—as crows will because it is their nature to collect shiny things, bits of glass and stuff like that—and so the postmistress, in consultation with a few interested townsfolk,

decided to take it to the Audubon Society, where it was caged
and only sometimes let out to fly; it couldn't be set free because
in the wild a bird that likes to hang around a parking lot simply
will not fit in. That crow's voice. She remembers it at all hours,
day or night, awake, sleeping, or insomniac. Had a strange
voice. Not like the voice of other crows probably because it
hadn't been raised with other crows. Right after the fire, I used
to go and visit that crow at the Audubon Society, and whenever the visit was over and I would turn to leave, it would call
me back with this voice. Yes, in a cage, but being what it was,
it was better off that way. There were other birds in cages that
people had brought in because they couldn't live in the wild
anymore. There were a couple of little owls. Speckled things
that looked like toys. I used to visit the owls too. And a pigeon
hawk with a piercing cry. Nice birds. And then I moved down
here and, alone as I was, am, I have gotten to know crows like
never before. And them me. Their sense of humor. Is that what
it is? Maybe it's not a sense of humor. But to me it looks like it
is. The way they walk around. The way they tuck their heads.
The way they scream at me if I don't have bread for them.
Faunia, go get the bread. They strut. They boss the other birds
around. On Saturday, after having the conversation with the
redtail hawk down by Cumberland, I came home and I heard
these two crows back in the orchards. I knew something was
up. This alarming crow-calling. Sure enough, saw three birds
—two crows crowing and cawing off this hawk. Maybe the
very one I'd been talking to a few minutes before. Chasing it.
Obviously the redtail was up to no good. But taking on a
hawk? Is that a good idea? It wins them points with the other
crows, but I don't know if I would do that. Can even *two* of
them take on a hawk? Aggressive bastards. Mostly hostile.
Good for them. Saw a photo once—a crow going right up to
an eagle and barking at it. The eagle doesn't give a shit. Doesn't
even see him. But the crow is something. The way it flies.
They're not as pretty as ravens when ravens fly and do those
wonderful, beautiful acrobatics. They've got a big fuselage to
get off the ground and yet they don't need a running start
necessarily. A few steps will do it. I've watched that. It's more
just a huge effort. They make this huge effort and they're up.
When I used to take the kids to eat at Friendly's. Four years

ago. There were millions of them. The Friendly's on East Main
Street in Blackwell. In the late afternoon. Before dark. Millions
of them in the parking lot. The crow convention at Friendly's.
What is it with crows and parking lots? What is that all about?
We'll never know what that's about or anything else. Other
birds are kind of dull next to crows. Yes, bluejays have that
terrific bounce. The trampoline walk. That's good. But crows
can do the bounce *and* the chesty thrust. Most impressive.
Turning their heads from left to right, casing the joint. Oh,
they're hot shit. They're the coolest. The caw. The noisy caw.
Listen. Just listen. Oh, I love it. Staying in touch like that. The
frantic call that means danger. I love that. Rush outside then.
It can be 5 A.M., I don't care. The frantic call, rush outside, and
you can expect the show to begin any minute. The other calls,
I can't say I know what they mean. Maybe nothing. Sometimes
it's a quick call. Sometimes it's throaty. Don't want to confuse
it with the raven's call. Crows mate with crows and ravens with
ravens. It's wonderful that they never get confused. Not to my
knowledge anyway. Everybody who says they're ugly scavenger
birds—and most everybody does—is nuts. I think they're
beautiful. Oh, yes. Very beautiful. Their sleekness. Their shades.
It's so so black in there you can see purple in there. Their
heads. At the start of the beak that sprout of hairs, that mustache thing, those hairs coming forward from the feathers.
Probably has a name. But the name doesn't matter. Never does.
All that matters is that it's there. And nobody knows why. It's
like everything else—just *there*. All their eyes are black. Everybody gets black eyes. Black claws. What is it like flying? Ravens
will do the soaring, crows just seem to go where they're going.
They don't just fly around as far as I can tell. Let the ravens
soar. Let the ravens do the soaring. Let the ravens pile up the
miles and break the records and get the prizes. The crows have
to get from one place to another. They hear that I have bread,
so they're here. They hear somebody down the road two miles
has bread, so they're there. When I throw their bread out to
them, there'll always be one who is the guard and another you
can hear off in the distance, and they're signaling back and
forth just to let everybody know what's going on. It's hard to
believe in everybody's looking out for everybody else, but that's
what it looks like. There's a wonderful story I never forgot that

a friend of mine told me when I was a kid that her mother told her. There were these crows who were so smart that they had figured out how to take these nuts they had that they couldn't break open out to the highway, and they would watch the lights, the traffic lights, and they would know when the cars would take off—they were that intelligent that they knew what was going on with the lights—and they would place the nuts right in front of the tires so they'd be cracked open and as soon as the light would change they'd move down. I believed that back then. Believed everything back then. And now that I know them and nobody else, I believe it again. Me and the crows. That's the ticket. Stick to the crows and you've got it made. I hear they preen each other's feathers. Never seen that. Seen them close together and wonder what they're doing. But never seen them actually doing it. Don't even see them preen their own. But then, I'm next door to the roost, not in it. Wish I were. Would have preferred to be one. Oh, yes, absolutely. No two ways about that. Much prefer to be a crow. They don't have to worry about moving to get away from anybody or anything. They just move. They don't have to pack anything. They just go. When they get smashed by something, that's it, it's over. Tear a wing, it's over. Break a foot, it's over. A much better way than this. Maybe I'll come back as one. What was I before that I came back as *this*? I was a crow! Yes! I was one! And I said, "God, I wish I was that big-titted girl down there," and I got my wish, and now, Christ, do I want to go back to my crow status. My status crow. Good name for a crow. Status. Good name for anything black and big. Goes with the strut. Status. I noticed everything as a kid. I loved birds. Always stuck on crows and hawks and owls. Still see the owls at night, driving home from Coleman's place. I can't help it if I get out of the car to talk to them. Shouldn't. Should drive straight on home before that bastard kills me. What do crows think when they hear the other birds singing? They think it's stupid. It is. Cawing. That's the only thing. It doesn't look good for a bird that struts to sing a sweet little song. No, caw your head off. That's the fucking ticket—cawing your head off and frightened of nothing and in there eating everything that's dead. Gotta get a lot of road kill in a day if you want to fly like that. Don't bother to drag it off but eat it right on the road. Wait until the last minute when a car is coming, and then they get up and go but not so far that they can't hop right back and dig back in soon as it's passed. Eating in the middle of the road. Wonder what happens when the meat goes bad. Maybe it doesn't for them. Maybe that's what it means to be a scavenger. Them and the turkey vultures—that's their job. They take care of all of those things out in the woods and out in the road that we don't want anything to do with. No crow goes hungry in all this world. Never without a meal. If it rots, you don't see the crow run away. If there's death, they're there. Something's dead, they come by and get it. I like that. I like that a lot. Eat that raccoon no matter what. Wait for the truck to come crack open the spine and then go back in there and suck up all the good stuff it takes to lift that beautiful black carcass off the ground. Sure, they have their strange behavior. Like anything else. I've seen them up in those trees, gathered all together, talking all together, and *something's* going on. But what it is I'll never know. There's some powerful arrangement there. But I haven't the faintest idea whether they know what it is themselves. It could be as meaningless as everything else. I'll bet it isn't, though, and that it makes a million fucking times more sense than any fucking thing down here. Or doesn't it? Is it just a lot of stuff that looks like something else but isn't? Maybe it's all just a genetic tic. Or tock. Imagine if the crows were in charge. Would it be the same shit all over again? The thing about them is that they're all practicality. In their flight. In their talk. Even in their color. All that blackness. Nothing but blackness. Maybe I was one and maybe I wasn't. I think I sometimes believe that I already am one. Yes, been believing that on and off for months now. Why not? There are men who are locked up in women's bodies and women who are locked up in men's bodies, so why can't I be a crow locked up in this body? Yeah, and where is the doctor who is going to do what they do to let me out? Where do I go to get the surgery that will let me be what I am? Who do I talk to? Where do I go and what do I do and how the fuck do I get out?

I am a crow. I know it. I know it!

At the student union building, midway down the hill from North Hall, Coleman found a pay phone in the corridor across from the cafeteria where the Elderhostel students were having their lunch. He could see inside, through the double doorway, to the long dining tables where the couples were all mingling happily at lunch.

Jeff wasn't at home—it was about 10 A.M. in L.A., and Coleman got the answering machine, and so he searched his address book for the office number at the university, praying that Jeff wasn't off in class yet. What the father had to say to his eldest son had to be said immediately. The last time he'd called Jeff in a state anything like this was to tell him that Iris had died. "They killed her. They set out to kill me and they killed her." It was what he said to everyone, and not just in those first twenty-four hours. That was the beginning of the disintegration: everything requisitioned by rage. But this is the end of it. The end—there was the news he had for his son. And for himself. The end of the expulsion from the previous life. To be content with something less grandiose than self-banishment and the overwhelming challenge that is to one's strength. To live with one's failure in a modest fashion, organized once again as a rational being and blotting out the blight and the indignation. If unyielding, unyielding quietly. Peacefully. Dignified contemplation—that's the ticket, as Faunia liked to say. To live in a way that does not bring Philoctetes to mind. He does not have to live like a tragic character in his course. That the primal seems a solution is not news—it always does. Everything changes with desire. The answer to all that has been destroyed. But choosing to prolong the scandal by perpetuating the protest? My stupidity everywhere. My derangement everywhere. And the grossest sentimentality. Wistfully remembering back to Steena. Jokingly dancing with Nathan Zuckerman. Confiding in him. Reminiscing with him. Letting him listen. Sharpening the writer's sense of reality. Feeding that great opportunistic maw, a novelist's mind. Whatever catastrophe turns up, he transforms into writing. Catastrophe is cannon fodder for him. But what can *I* transform this into? I am stuck with it. As is. Sans language, shape, structure, meaning—sans the unities, the catharsis, sans everything. More of the untransformed unforeseen. And why would anyone want more? Yet the woman who is Faunia *is* the unforeseen. Intertwined orgasmically with the unforeseen, and convention unendurable. Upright principles unendurable. Contact with her body the only principle. Nothing more important than that. And the stamina of her sneer. Alien to the core. Contact with *that*. The obligation to subject my life to hers and its vagaries. Its vagrancy. Its truancy. Its strangeness. The delectation of this elemental eros. Take the hammer of Faunia to everything outlived, all the exalted justifications, and smash your way to freedom. Freedom from? From the stupid glory of being right. From the ridiculous quest for significance. From the never-ending campaign for legitimacy. The onslaught of freedom at seventy-one, the freedom to leave a lifetime behind—known also as Aschenbachian madness. "And before nightfall"—the final words of *Death in Venice*—"a shocked and respectful world received the news of his decease." No, he does not have to live like a tragic character in *any* course.

"Jeff! It's Dad. It's your father."

"Hi. How's it going?"

"Jeff, I know why I haven't heard from you, why I haven't heard from Michael. Mark I wouldn't expect to hear from—and Lisa hung up on me last time I called."

"She phoned me. She told me."

"Listen, Jeff—my affair with this woman is over."

"Is it? How come?"

He thinks, Because there's no hope for her. Because men have beaten the shit out of her. Because her kids have been killed in a fire. Because she works as a janitor. Because she has no education and says she can't read. Because she's been on the run since she's fourteen. Because she doesn't even ask me, "What are you doing with me?" Because she knows what *everybody* is doing with her. Because she's seen it all and there's no hope.

But all he says to his son is, "Because I don't want to lose my children."

With the gentlest laugh, Jeff said, "Try as you might, you couldn't do it. You certainly aren't able to lose me. I don't believe you were going to lose Mike or Lisa, either. Markie is something else. Markie yearns for something *none* of us can give him. Not just you—none of us. It's all very sad with Markie. But that we were losing *you*? That we've been losing you since Mother died and you resigned from the college? That is something we've all been living with. Dad, nobody has known what to do. Since you went on the warpath with the college, it hasn't been easy to get to you."

"I realize that," said Coleman, "I understand that," but two minutes into the conversation and it was already insufferable to him. His reasonable, supercompetent, easygoing son, the eldest, the coolest head of the lot, speaking calmly about the family problem with the father who *was* the problem was as awful to endure as his irrational youngest son being enraged with him and going nuts. The excessive demand he had made on their sympathy—on the sympathy of his own children! "I understand," Coleman said again, and that he understood made it all the worse.

"I hope nothing too awful happened with her," Jeff said.

"With her? No. I just decided that enough was enough." He was afraid to say more for fear that he might start to say something very different.

"That's good," Jeff said. "I'm terrifically relieved. That there've been no repercussions, if that's what you're saying. That's just great."

Repercussions?

"I don't follow you," Coleman said. "Why repercussions?"

"You're free and clear? You're yourself again? You sound more like yourself than you have for years. That you've called—this is all that matters. I was waiting and I was hoping and now you've called. There's nothing more to be said. You're back. That's all we were worried about."

"I'm lost, Jeff. Fill me in. I'm lost as to what we're going on about here. Repercussions from what?"

Jeff paused before he spoke again, and when he did speak, it was reluctantly. "The abortion. The suicide attempt."

"Faunia?"

"Right."

"Had an abortion? Tried to commit suicide? When?"

"Dad, everyone in Athena knew. That's how it got to us."

"Everyone? Who is everyone?"

"Look, Dad, there are no repercussions—"

"It never happened, my boy, that's why there are no 'repercussions.' *It never happened*. There was no abortion, there was no suicide attempt—not that I know of. And not that she knows of. But just who is this *everyone*? Goddamnit, you hear a story like that, a senseless story like that, why don't you pick up the phone, why don't you come to *me*?"

"Because it isn't my business to come to you. I don't come to a man your age—"

"No, you don't, do you? Instead, whatever you're told about a man my age, however ludicrous, however malicious and absurd, you believe."

"If I made a mistake, I am truly sorry. You're right. Of course you're right. But it's been a long haul for all of us. You've not been that easy to reach now for—"

"Who told this to you?"

"Lisa. Lisa heard it first."

"Who did Lisa hear it from?"

"Several sources. People. Friends."

"I want names. I want to know who this everyone *is*. Which friends?"

"Old friends. Athena friends."

"Her darling childhood friends. The offspring of my colleagues. Who told them, I wonder."

"There was no suicide attempt," Jeff said.

"No, Jeffrey, there wasn't. No abortion that I know of, either."

"Well, fine."

"And if there were? If I *had* impregnated this woman and she'd gone for an abortion and after the abortion had attempted suicide? Suppose, Jeff, she had even succeeded at suicide. Then what? *Then what, Jeff*? Your father's mistress kills herself. Then what? Turn on your father? Your criminal father? No, no, no—let's go back, back up a step, back up to the suicide *attempt*. Oh, I like that. I do wonder who came up with the suicide *attempt*. Is it because of the abortion that she attempts this suicide? Let's get straight this melodrama that Lisa got from her Athena friends. Because she doesn't *want* the abortion? Because the abortion is *imposed* on her? I see. I see the cruelty. A mother who has lost two little children in a fire turns up pregnant by her lover. Ecstasy. A new life. Another chance. A new child to replace the dead ones. But the lover— *no*, says he, and drags her by her hair to the abortionist, and then—of course—having worked his will on her, takes the naked, bleeding body—"

By this time Jeff had hung up.

But by this time Coleman didn't need Jeff to keep on going. He had only to see the Elderhostel couples inside the cafeteria finishing their coffee before returning to class, he had only to hear them in there at their ease and enjoying themselves, the appropriate elderly looking as they should look and sounding as they should sound, for him to think that even the conventional things that he'd done afforded him no relief. Not just having been a professor, not just having been a dean, not just having remained married, through everything, to the same formidable woman, but having a family, having intelligent children —and it all afforded him nothing. If anybody's children should be able to understand this, shouldn't his? All the preschool. All the reading to them. The sets of encyclopedias. The preparation before quizzes. The dialogues at dinner. The endless instruction, from Iris, from him, in the multiform nature of life. The scrutinization of language. All this stuff we did, and then to come back at me with this mentality? After all the schooling and all the books and all the words and all the superior SAT scores, it is insupportable. After all the taking them seriously. When they said something foolish, engaging it seriously. All the attention paid to the development of reason and of mind and of imaginative sympathy. And of skepticism, of well-informed skepticism. Of thinking for oneself. And then to absorb the first rumor? All the education and nothing helps. Nothing can insulate against the lowest level of thought. Not even to ask themselves, "But does that sound like our father? Does that sound like him to me?" Instead, your father is an open-and-shut case. Never allowed to watch TV and you manifest the mentality of a soap opera. Allowed to read nothing but the Greeks or their equivalent and you make life into a Victorian soap opera. Answering your questions. Your every question. Never turning one aside. You ask about your grandparents, you ask who they were and I told you. They died, your grandparents, when I was young. Grandpa when I was in high school, Grandma when I was away in the navy. By the time I got back from the war, the landlord had long ago put everything out on the street. There was nothing left. The landlord told me he couldn't afford to blah blah, there was no rent coming in, and I could have killed the son of a bitch. Photo albums. Letters. Stuff from my childhood, from *their* childhood, all of it, everything, the whole thing, gone. "Where were they born? Where did they live?" They were born in Jersey. The first of their families born here. He was a saloon keeper. I believe that in Russia his father, your great-grandfather, worked in the tavern business. Sold booze to the Russkies. "Do we have aunts and uncles?" My father had a brother who went to California when I was a little kid, and my mother was an only child, like me. After me she couldn't have children—I never knew why that was. The brother, my father's older brother, remained a Silberzweig—he never took the changed name as far as I know. Jack Silberzweig. Born in the old country and so kept the name. When I was shipping out from San Francisco, I looked in all the California phone books to try to locate him. He was on the outs with my father. My father considered him a lazy bum, wanted nothing to do with him, and so nobody was sure what city Uncle Jack lived in. I looked in all the phone books. I was going to tell him that his brother had died. I wanted to meet him. My one living relative on that side. So what if he's a bum? I wanted to meet his children, my cousins, if there were any. I looked under Silberzweig. I looked under Silk. I looked under Silber. Maybe in California he'd become a Silber. I didn't know. And I don't know. I have no idea. And then I stopped looking. When you don't have a family of your own, you concern yourself with these things. Then I had you and I stopped worrying about having an uncle and having cousins . . . Each kid heard the same thing. And the only one it didn't satisfy was Mark. The older boys didn't ask that much, but the twins were insistent. "Were there any twins in the past?" My understanding—I believe I was told this—was that there was either a great- or a great-great-grandfather who was a twin. This was the story he told Iris as well. All of it was invented for Iris. This was the story he told her on Sullivan Street when they first met and the story he stuck to, the original boilerplate. And the only one never satisfied was Mark. "Where did our great-grandparents come from?" Russia. "But what city?" I asked my father and mother, but they never seemed to know for sure. One time it was one place, one time another. There was a whole generation of Jews like that. They never really knew. The old people didn't talk about it much, and the American children weren't that curious, they were het up on being Americans, and so, in my family as in many families, there was a general Jewish geographical amnesia. All I got when I asked, Coleman told them, was the answer "Russia." But Markie said, "Russia is gigantic, Dad. *Where* in Russia?" Markie would not be still. And why? *Why?* There was no answer. Markie wanted the knowledge of who they were and where they came from—all that his father could never give him. And that's why he becomes the Orthodox Jew? That's why he writes the biblical protest poems? That's why Markie hates him so? Impossible. There were the Gittelmans. Gittelman grandparents. Gittelman aunts and uncles. Little Gittelman cousins all over Jersey. Wasn't that enough? How many relatives did he need? There had to be Silks and Silberzweigs too? That made no sense at all as a grievance—it could not be! Yet Coleman wondered anyway, irrational as it might be to associate Markie's brooding anger with his own secret. So long as Markie was at odds with him, he was never able to stop himself from wondering, and never more agonizingly than after Jeff had hung up the phone on him. If the children who carried his origins in their genes and who would pass those origins on to their own children could find it so easy to suspect him of the worst kind of cruelty to Faunia, what explanation could there be? Because he could never tell them about their family? Because he'd owed it to them to tell them? Because to deny them such knowledge was wrong? That made no sense! Retribution was not unconsciously or unknowingly enacted. There was no such quid pro quo. *It could not be.* And yet, after the phone call—leaving the student union, leaving the campus, all the while he was driving in tears back up the mountain—that was exactly what it felt like.

And all the while he was driving home he was remembering the time he'd almost told Iris. It was after the twins were born. The family was now complete. They'd done it—he'd made it. With not a sign of his secret on any of his kids, it was as though he had been *delivered* from his secret. The exuberance that came of having pulled it off brought him to the very brink of giving the whole thing away. Yes, he would present his wife with the greatest gift he possessed: he would tell the mother of his four children who their father really was. He would tell Iris the truth. That was how excited and relieved he was, how solid the earth felt beneath his feet after she had their beautiful twins, and he took Jeff and Mikey to the hospital to see their new brother and sister, and the most frightening apprehension of them all had been eradicated from his life.

But he never did give Iris that gift. He was saved from doing it—or damned to leave it undone—because of the cataclysm that befell a dear friend of hers, her closest associate on the art association board, a pretty, refined amateur watercolorist named Claudia McChesney, whose husband, owner of the county's biggest building firm, turned out to have quite a stunning secret of his own: a second family. For some eight years, Harvey McChesney had been keeping a woman years younger than Claudia, a bookkeeper at a chair factory over near the Taconic by whom he'd had two children, little kids aged four and six, living in a small town just across the Massa-chusetts line in New York State, whom he visited each week, whom he supported, whom he seemed to love, and whom nobody in the McChesneys' Athena household knew anything about until an anonymous phone call—probably from one of Harvey's building-trade rivals—revealed to Claudia and the three adolescent children just what McChesney was up to when he wasn't out on the job. Claudia collapsed that night, came completely apart and tried to slash her wrists, and it was Iris who, beginning at 3 A.M., with the help of a psychiatrist friend, organized the rescue operation that got Claudia in-stalled before dawn in Austin Riggs, the Stockbridge psychiat-ric hospital. And it was Iris who, all the while she was nursing two newborns and mothering two preschool boys, visited the hospital every day, talking to Claudia, steadying her, reassuring her, bringing her potted plants to tend and art books to look at, even combing and braiding Claudia's hair, until, after five weeks—and as much a result of Iris's devotion as of the psychi-atric program—Claudia returned home to begin to take the steps necessary to rid herself of the man who had caused all her misery.

In just days, Iris had got Claudia the name of a divorce lawyer up in Pittsfield and, with all the Silk kids, including the infants, strapped down in the back of the station wagon, she drove her friend to the lawyer's office to be absolutely certain that the separation arrangements were initiated and Claudia's deliverance from McChesney was under way. On the ride home that day, there'd been a lot of bucking up to do, but bucking people up was Iris's specialty, and she saw to it that Claudia's determination to right her life was not washed away by her residual fears.

"What a wretched thing to do to another person," Iris said. "Not the girlfriend. Bad enough, but that happens. And not the little children, not even that—not even the other woman's little boy and girl, painful and brutal as that would be for any wife to discover. No, it's the secret—that's what did it, Coleman. That's why Claudia doesn't want to go on living. 'Where's the intimacy?' That's what gets her crying every time. 'Where is the intimacy,' she says, 'when there is such a secret?' That he could hide this from her, that he *would* have gone on hiding it from her—that's what Claudia's defenseless against, and that's why she still wants to do herself in. She says to me, 'It's like discovering a corpse. Three corpses. Three human bodies hidden under our floor.'" "Yes," Coleman said, "it's like something out of the Greeks. Out of *The Bacchae*." "Worse," Iris said, "because it's not out of *The Bacchae*. It's out of Claudia's life."

When, after almost a year of outpatient therapy, Claudia had a rapprochement with her husband and he moved back into the Athena house and the McChesneys resumed life together as a family—when Harvey agreed to give up the other woman, if not his other children, to whom he swore to remain a responsible father—Claudia seemed no more eager than Iris to keep their friendship alive, and after Claudia resigned from the art association, the women no longer saw each other socially or at any of the organization meetings where Iris was generally kingpin.

Nor did Coleman go ahead—as his triumph dictated when the twins were born—to tell his wife *his* stunning secret. Saved, he thought, from the most childishly sentimental stunt he could ever have perpetrated. Suddenly to have begun to think the way a fool thinks: suddenly to think the best of everything and everyone, to shed entirely one's mistrust, one's caution, one's *self*-mistrust, to think that all one's difficulties have come to an end, that all complications have ceased to be, to forget not only where one is but how one has got there, to surrender the diligence, the discipline, the taking the measure of every last situation . . . As though the battle that is each person's singular battle could somehow be abjured, as though voluntarily one could pick up and leave off being one's self, the characteristic, the immutable self in whose behalf the battle is undertaken in the first place. The last of his children having been born perfectly white had all but driven him to taking what was strongest in him and wisest in him and tearing it to bits. Saved he was by the wisdom that says, "Don't do anything."

But even earlier, after the birth of their first child, he had done something almost equally stupid and sentimental. He was a young classics professor from Adelphi down at the University of Pennsylvania for a three-day conference on *The Iliad*; he had given a paper, he had made some contacts, he'd even been quietly invited by a renowned classicist to apply for a position opening at Princeton, and, on the way home, thinking himself at the pinnacle of existence, instead of heading north on the Jersey Turnpike, to get to Long Island, he had very nearly turned south and made his way down along the back roads of Salem and Cumberland counties to Gouldtown, to his mother's ancestral home where they used to hold the annual family picnic when he was a boy. Yes, then as well, having become a father, he was going to try to give himself the easy pleasure of one of those meaningful feelings that people will go in search of whenever they cease to think. But because he had a son didn't require him to turn south to Gouldtown any more than on that same journey, when he reached north Jersey, his having had this son required him to take the Newark exit and head toward East Orange. There was yet another impulse to be suppressed: the impulse he felt to see his mother, to tell her what had happened and to bring her the boy. The impulse, two years after jettisoning her, and despite Walter's warning, to show *himself* to his mother. No. Absolutely not. And instead he continued straight on home to his white wife and his white child.

And, some four decades later, all the while he was driving home from the college, besieged by recrimination, remembering some of the best moments of his life—the birth of his children, the exhilaration, the all-too-innocent excitement, the wild wavering of his resolve, the relief so great that it nearly *undid* his resolve—he was remembering also the worst night of his life, remembering back to his navy stint and the night he was thrown out of that Norfolk whorehouse, the famous white whorehouse called Oris's. "You're a black nigger, ain't you, boy?" and seconds later the bouncers had hurled him from the open front door, over the stairs to the sidewalk and into the street. The place he was looking for was Lulu's, over on Warwick Avenue—Lulu's, they shouted after him, was where his black ass belonged. His forehead struck the pavement, and yet he got himself up, ran until he saw an alleyway, and there cut away from the street and the Shore Patrol, who were all over the place on a Saturday, swinging their billy clubs. He wound up in the toilet of the only bar he dared to enter looking as battered as he did—a colored bar just a few hundred feet from Hampton Roads and the Newport News ferry (the ferry conveying the sailors to Lulu's) and some ten blocks from Oris's. It was his first colored bar since he was an East Orange schoolkid, back when he and a friend used to run the football pools out of Billy's Twilight Club down on the Newark line. During his first two years of high school, on top of the surreptitious boxing, he would be in and out of Billy's Twilight all through the fall, and it was there that he'd garnered the barroom lore he claimed to have learned—as an East Orange white kid—in a tavern owned by his Jewish old man.

He was remembering how he'd struggled to stanch his cut face and how he'd swabbed vainly away at his white jumper but how the blood dripped steadily down to spatter everything. The seatless bowl was coated with shit, the soggy plank floor awash with piss, the sink, if that thing was a sink, a swillish trough of sputum and puke—so that when the retching began because of the pain in his wrist, he threw up onto the wall he was facing rather than lower his face into all that filth.

It was a hideous, raucous dive, the worst, like no place he had ever seen, the most abominable he could have imagined, but he had to hide somewhere, and so, on a bench as far as he could get from the human wreckage swarming the bar, and in the clutches of all his fears, he tried to sip at a beer, to steady himself and dim the pain and to avoid drawing attention. Not that anyone at the bar had bothered looking his way after he'd bought the beer and disappeared against the wall back of the empty tables: just as at the white cathouse, nobody took him here for anything other than what he was.

He still knew, with the second beer, that he was where he should not be, yet if the Shore Patrol picked him up, if they discovered why he'd been thrown out of Oris's, he was ruined: a court-martial, a conviction, a long stretch at hard labor followed by a dishonorable discharge—and all for having lied to the navy about his race, all for having been stupid enough to step through a door where the only out-and-out Negroes on the premises were either laundering the linens or mopping up the slops.

This was it. He'd serve out his stint, do his time as a white man, and this would be it. Because I can't pull it off, he thought—I don't even want to. He'd never before known real disgrace. He'd never before known what it was to hide from the police. Never before had he bled from taking a blow—in all those rounds of amateur boxing he had not lost a drop of blood or been hurt or damaged in any way. But now the jumper of his whites was as red as a surgical dressing, his pants were soggy with caking blood and, from where he'd landed on his knees in the gutter, they were torn and dark with grime. And his wrist had been injured, maybe even shattered, from when he'd broken the fall with his hand—he couldn't move it or bear to touch it. He drank off the beer and then got another in order to try to deaden the pain.

This was what came of failing to fulfill his father's ideals, of flouting his father's commands, of deserting his dead father altogether. If only he'd done as his father had, as Walter had, everything would be happening another way. But first he had broken the law by lying to get into the navy, and now, out looking for a white woman to fuck, he had plunged into the worst possible disaster. "Let me get through to my discharge. Let me get out. Then I'll never lie again. Just let me finish my time, and that's it!" It was the first he'd spoken to his father since he'd dropped dead in the dining car.

If he kept this up, his life would amount to nothing. How did Coleman know that? Because his father was speaking back to him—the old admonishing authority rumbling up once again from his father's chest, resonant as always with the unequivocal legitimacy of an upright man. If Coleman kept on like this, he'd end up in a ditch with his throat slit. Look at where he was now. Look where he had come to hide. And how? Why? Because of his credo, because of his insolent, arrogant "I am not one of you, I can't bear you, I am not part of your Negro we" credo. The great heroic struggle against their we—and look at what he now looked like! The passionate struggle for precious singularity, his revolt of one against the Negro fate— and just look where the defiant great one had ended up! Is this where you've come, Coleman, to seek the deeper meaning of existence? A world of love, that's what you had, and instead you forsake it for this! The tragic, reckless thing that you've done! And not just to yourself—to us all. To Ernestine. To Walt. To Mother. To me. To me in my grave. To my father in his. What else grandiose are you planning, Coleman Brutus? Whom next are you going to mislead and betray?

Still, he couldn't leave for the street because of his fear of the Shore Patrol, and of the court-martial, and of the brig, and of the dishonorable discharge that would hound him forever. Everything in him was too stirred up for him to do anything but keep on drinking until, of course, he was joined on the bench by a prostitute who was openly of his own race.

When the Shore Patrol found him in the morning, they attributed the bloody wounds and the broken wrist and the befouled, disheveled uniform to his having spent a night in niggertown, another swingin' white dick hot for black poon who—having got himself reamed, steamed, and dry-cleaned (as well as properly tattooed in the bargain)—had been deposited for the scavengers to pick over in that glass-strewn lot back of the ferry slip.

"U.S. Navy" is all the tattoo said, the words, no more than a quarter inch high, inscribed in blue pigment between the blue arms of a blue anchor, itself a couple inches long. A most unostentatious design as military tattoos go and, discreetly positioned just below the joining of the right arm to the shoulder, a tattoo certainly easy enough to hide. But when he remembered how he'd got it, it was the mark evocative not only of the turbulence of the worst night of his life but of all that underlay the turbulence—it was the sign of the whole of his history, of the indivisibility of the heroism and the disgrace. Embedded in that blue tattoo was a true and total image of himself. The ineradicable biography was there, as was the prototype of the ineradicable, a tattoo being the very emblem of what cannot ever be removed. The enormous enterprise was also there. The outside forces were there. The whole chain of the unforeseen, all the dangers of exposure and all the dangers of concealment —even the senselessness of life was there in that stupid little blue tattoo.

His difficulties with Delphine Roux had begun the first semester he was back in the classroom, when one of his students who happened to be a favorite of Professor Roux's went to her, as department chair, to complain about the Euripides plays in Coleman's Greek tragedy course. One play was *Hippolytus*, the other *Alcestis*; the student, Elena Mitnick, found them "degrading to women."

"So what shall I do to accommodate Miss Mitnick? Strike Euripides from my reading list?"

"Not at all. Clearly everything depends on how you teach Euripides."

"And what," he asked, "is the prescribed method these days?" thinking even as he spoke that this was not a debate for which he had the patience or the civility. Besides, confounding Delphine Roux was easier *without* engaging in the debate. Brimming though she was with intellectual self-importance, she was twenty-nine years old and virtually without experience outside schools, new to her job and relatively new both to the college and to the country. He understood from their previous encounters that her attempt to appear to be not merely his superior but a supercilious superior—"Clearly everything depends" and so on—was best repulsed by displaying complete indifference to her judgment. For all that she could not bear him, she also couldn't bear that the academic credentials that so impressed other of her Athena colleagues hadn't yet overwhelmed the ex-dean. Despite herself, she could not escape from being intimidated by the man who, five years earlier, had reluctantly hired her fresh from the Yale graduate school and who, afterward, never denied regretting it, especially when the psychological numbskulls in his department settled on so deeply confused a young woman as their chair.

To this day, she continued to be disquieted by Coleman Silk's presence just to the degree that she wished for him now to be unsettled by her. Something about him always led her back to her childhood and the precocious child's fear that she is being seen through; also to the precocious child's fear that she is not being seen enough. Afraid of being exposed, dying to be seen—there's a dilemma for you. Something about him made her even second-guess her English, with which otherwise she felt wholly at ease. Whenever they were face to face, some-thing made her think that he wanted nothing more than to tie her hands behind her back.

This something was what? The way he had sexually sized her up when she first came to be interviewed in his office, or the way he had failed to sexually size her up? It had been impossible to read his reading of her, and that on a morning when she knew she had maximally deployed all her powers. She had wanted to look terrific and she did, she had wanted to be flu-ent and she was, she had wanted to sound scholarly and she'd succeeded, she was sure. And yet he looked at her as if she were a schoolgirl, Mr. and Mrs. Inconsequential's little nobody child.

Now, perhaps that was because of the plaid kilt—the miniskirt-like kilt might have made him think of a schoolgirl's uniform, especially as the person wearing it was a trim, tiny, dark-haired young woman with a small face that was almost entirely eyes and who weighed, clothes and all, barely a hundred pounds. All she'd intended, with the kilt as with the black cashmere turtleneck, black tights, and high black boots, was neither to desexualize herself by what she chose to wear (the university women she'd met so far in America seemed all too strenuously to be doing just that) nor to appear to be trying to tantalize him. Though he was said to be in his mid-sixties, he didn't look to be any older than her fifty-year-old father; he in fact resembled a junior partner in her father's firm, one of several of her father's engineering associates who'd been eyeing her since she was twelve. When, seated across from the dean, she had crossed her legs and the flap of the kilt had fallen open, she had waited a minute or two before pulling it closed—and pull-ing it closed as perfunctorily as you close a wallet—only be-cause, however young she looked, she *wasn't* a schoolgirl with a schoolgirl's fears and a schoolgirl's primness, caged in by a schoolgirl's rules. She did not wish to leave that impression any more than to give the opposite impression by allowing the flap to remain open and thereby inviting him to imagine that she meant him to gaze throughout the interview at her slim thighs in the black tights. She had tried as best she could, with the choice of clothing as with her manner, to impress upon him the intricate interplay of *all* the forces that came together to make her so interesting at twenty-four.

Even her one piece of jewelry, the large ring she'd placed that morning on the middle finger of her left hand, her sole decorative ornament, had been selected for the sidelight it provided on the intellectual she was, one for whom enjoying the aesthetic surface of life openly, nondefensively, with her appetite and connoisseurship undisguised, was nonetheless subsumed by a lifelong devotion to scholarly endeavor. The ring, an eighteenth-century copy of a Roman signet ring, was a man-sized ring formerly worn by a man. On the oval agate, set horizontally—which was what made the ring so masculinely chunky—was a carving of Danaë receiving Zeus as a shower of gold. In Paris, four years earlier, when Delphine was twenty, she had been given the ring as a love token from the professor to whom it belonged—the one professor whom she'd been unable to resist and with whom she'd had an impassioned affair. Coincidentally, he had been a classicist. The first time they met, in his office, he had seemed so remote, so judging, that she found herself paralyzed with fear until she realized that he was playing the seduction against the grain. Was that what this Dean Silk was up to?

However conspicuous the ring's size, the dean never did ask to see the shower of gold carved in agate, and that, she decided, was just as well. Though the story of how she'd come by the ring testified, if anything, to an audacious adultness, he would have thought the ring a frivolous indulgence, a sign that she *lacked* maturity. Except for the stray hope, she was sure that he was thinking about her along those lines from the moment they'd shaken hands—and she was right. Coleman's take on her was of someone too young for the job, incorporating too many as yet unresolved contradictions, at once a little too grand about herself and, simultaneously, playing at self-importance like a child, an imperfectly self-governed child, quick to respond to the scent of disapproval, with a considerable talent for being wounded, and drawn on, as both child *and* woman, to achievement upon achievement, admirer upon admirer, conquest upon conquest, as much by uncertainty as by confidence. Someone smart for her age, even too smart, but off the mark emotionally and seriously underdeveloped in most other ways.

From her c.v. and from a supplementary autobiographical essay of fifteen pages that accompanied it—which detailed the progress of an intellectual journey begun at age six—he got the picture clearly enough. Her credentials were indeed excellent, but everything about her (including the credentials) struck him as particularly wrong for a little place like Athena. Privileged 16th *arrondissement* childhood on the rue de Longchamp. Monsieur Roux an engineer, owner of a firm employing forty; Madame Roux (née de Walincourt) born with an ancient noble name, provincial aristocracy, wife, mother of three, scholar of medieval French literature, master harpsichordist, scholar of harpsichord literature, papal historian, "etc." And what a telling "etc." that was! Middle child and only daughter Delphine graduated from the Lycée Janson de Sailly, where she studied philosophy and literature, English and German, Latin, French literature: ". . . read the entire body of French literature in a very canonical way." After the Lycée Janson, Lycée Henri IV: ". . . grueling in-depth study of French literature and philosophy, English language and literary history." At twenty, after the Lycée Henri IV, the École Normale Supérieure de Fontenay: ". . . with the élite of French intellectual society . . . only thirty a year selected." Thesis: "Self-Denial in Georges Bataille." Bataille? Not another one. Every ultra-cool Yale graduate student is working on either Mallarmé or Bataille. It isn't difficult to understand what she intends for him to understand, especially as Coleman knows something of Paris from being a young professor with family on a Fulbright one year, and knows something about these ambitious French kids trained in the elite lycées. Extremely well prepared, intellectually well connected, very smart immature young people endowed with the most snobbish French education and vigorously preparing to be envied all their lives, they hang out every Saturday night at the cheap Vietnamese restaurant on rue St. Jacques talking about great things, never any mention of trivialities or small talk—ideas, politics, philosophy only. Even in their spare time, when they are all alone, they think only about the reception of Hegel in twentieth-century French intellectual life. The intellectual must not be frivolous. Life only about thought. Whether brainwashed to be aggressively Marxist or to be aggressively anti-Marxist, they are congenitally appalled by everything American. From this stuff and more she comes to Yale: applies to teach French language to undergraduates and to be incorporated into the Ph.D. program, and, as she notes in her autobiographical essay, she is but one of two from all of France who are accepted. "I arrived at Yale very Cartesian, and there everything was much more pluralistic and polyphonic." Amused by the undergraduates. Where's their intellectual side? Completely shocked by their having fun. Their chaotic, nonideological way of thinking—of living! They've never even seen a Kurosawa film—they don't know *that* much. By the time she was their age, she'd seen all the Kurosawas, all the Tarkovskys, all the Fellinis, all the Antonionis, all the Fassbinders, all the Wertmüllers, all the Satyajit Rays, all the René Clairs, all the Wim Wenderses, all the Truffauts, the Godards, the Chabrols, the Resnaises, the Rohmers, the Renoirs, and all these kids have seen is *Star Wars*. In earnest at Yale she resumes her intellectual mission, taking classes with the most hip professors. A bit lost, however. Confused. Especially by the other graduate students. She is used to being with people who speak the same intellectual language, and these Americans . . . And not everybody finds her that interesting. Expected to come to America and have everyone say, "Oh, my God, she's a *normalienne*." But in America no one appreciates the very special path she was on in France and its enormous prestige. She's not getting the type of recognition she was trained to get as a budding member of the French intellectual elite. She's not even getting the kind of resentment she was trained to get. Finds an adviser and writes her dissertation. Defends it. Is awarded the degree. Gets it extraordinarily rapidly because she had already worked so hard in France. So much schooling and hard work, ready now for the big job at the big school—Princeton, Columbia, Cornell, Chicago—and when she gets nothing, she is crushed. A visiting position at Athena College? Where and what is Athena

College? She turns up her nose. Until her adviser says, "Delphine, in this market, you get your big job from another job. Visiting assistant professor at Athena College? *You* may not have heard of it, but we have. Perfectly decent institution. Perfectly decent job for a first job." Her fellow foreign graduate students tell her that she's too good for Athena College, it would be too déclassé, but her fellow American graduate students, who would kill for a job teaching in the Stop & Shop boiler room, think that her uppityness is characteristically Delphine. Begrudgingly, she applies—and winds up in her minikilt and boots across the desk from Dean Silk. To get the second job, the fancy job, she first needs this Athena job, but for nearly an hour Dean Silk listens to her all but talk her way out of the Athena job. Narrative structure and temporality. The internal contradictions of the work of art. Rousseau hides himself and then his rhetoric gives him away. (A little like her, thinks the dean, in that autobiographical essay.) The critic's voice is as legitimate as the voice of Herodotus. Narratology. The diegetic. The difference between diegesis and mimesis. The bracketed experience. The proleptic quality of the text. Coleman doesn't have to ask what all this means. He knows, in the original Greek meaning, what all the Yale words mean and what all the École Normale Supérieure words mean. Does she? As he's been at it for over three decades, he hasn't time for any of this stuff. He thinks: Why does someone so beautiful want to hide from the human dimension of her experience behind these words? Perhaps just because she is so beautiful. He thinks: So carefully self-appraising and so utterly deluded.

Of course she had the credentials. But to Coleman she embodied the sort of prestigious academic crap that the Athena students needed like a hole in the head but whose appeal to the faculty second-raters would prove irresistible.

At the time he thought that he was being open-minded by hiring her. But more likely it was because she was so goddamn enticing. So lovely. So alluring. And all the more so for looking so daughterly.

Delphine Roux had misread his gaze by thinking, a bit melodramatically—one of the impediments to her adroitness, this impulse not merely to leap to the melodramatic conclusion but to succumb erotically to the melodramatic spell—that what he wanted was to tie her hands behind her back: what he wanted, for every possible reason, was not to have her around. And so he'd hired her. And thus they seriously began not to get on.

And now it was she calling him to her office to be the interviewee. By 1995, the year that Coleman had stepped down from the deanship to return to teaching, the lure of petitely pretty Delphine's all-encompassing chic, with its gaminish intimations of a subterranean sensuality, along with the blandishments of her École Normale sophistication (what Coleman described as "her permanent act of self-inflation"), had appeared to him to have won over just about every wooable fool professor and, not yet out of her twenties—but with an eye perhaps on the deanship that had once been Coleman's—she succeeded to the chair of the smallish department that some dozen years earlier had absorbed, along with the other language departments, the old Classics Department in which Coleman had begun as an instructor. In the new Department of Languages and Literature there was a staff of eleven, one professor in Russian, one in Italian, one in Spanish, one in German, there was Delphine in French and Coleman Silk in classics, and there were five overworked adjuncts, fledgling instructors as well as a few local foreigners, teaching the elementary courses.

"Miss Mitnick's misreading of those two plays," he was telling her, "is so grounded in narrow, parochial ideological concerns that it does not lend itself to correction."

"Then you don't deny what she says—that you didn't try to help her."

"A student who tells me that I speak to her in 'engendered language' is beyond being assisted by me."

"Then," Delphine said lightly, "there's the problem, isn't it?"

He laughed—both spontaneously and for a purpose. "Yes? The English I speak is insufficiently nuanced for a mind as refined as Miss Mitnick's?"

"Coleman, you've been out of the classroom for a very long time."

"And you haven't been out of it ever. My dear," he said, deliberately, and with a deliberately irritating smile, "I've been reading and thinking about these plays all my life."

"But never from Elena's feminist perspective."

"Never even from Moses's Jewish perspective. Never even from the fashionable Nietzschean perspective about perspective."

"Coleman Silk, alone on the planet, has no perspective other than the purely disinterested literary perspective."

"Almost without exception, my dear"—again? why not?—"our students are abysmally ignorant. They've been incredibly badly educated. Their lives are intellectually barren. They arrive knowing nothing and most of them leave knowing nothing. Least of all do they know, when they show up in my class, how to read classical drama. Teaching at Athena, particularly in the 1990s, teaching what is far and away the dumbest generation in American history, is the same as walking up Broadway in Manhattan talking to yourself, except instead of the eighteen people who hear you in the street talking to yourself, they're all in the room. They know, like, *nothing*. After nearly forty years of dealing with such students—and Miss Mitnick is merely typical—I can tell you that a feminist perspective on Euripides is what they *least* need. Providing the most naive of readers with a feminist perspective on Euripides is one of the best ways you could devise to close down their thinking before it's even had a chance to begin to demolish a single one of their brainless 'likes.' I have trouble believing that an educated woman coming from a French academic background like your own believes there *is* a feminist perspective on Euripides that isn't simply foolishness. Have you really been edified in so short a time, or is this just old-fashioned careerism grounded right now in the fear of one's feminist colleagues? Because if it *is* just careerism, it's fine with me. It's human and I understand. But if it's an intellectual commitment to this idiocy, then I am mystified, because you are not an idiot. Because you know better. Because in France surely nobody from the École Normale would dream of taking this stuff seriously. Or would they? To read two plays like *Hippolytus* and *Alcestis*, then to listen to a week of classroom discussion on each, then to have nothing to say about either of them other than that they are 'degrading to women,' isn't a 'perspective,' for Christ's sake—it's mouthwash. It's just the latest mouthwash."

"Elena's a student. She's twenty years old. She's learning."

"Sentimentalizing one's students ill becomes you, my dear. Take them seriously. Elena's not learning. She's parroting. Why she ran directly to you is because it's more than likely you she's parroting."

"That is not true, though if it pleases you to culturally frame me like that, that is okay too, and entirely predictable. If you feel safely superior putting me in that silly frame, so be it, my dear," she delighted now in saying with a smile of her own. "Your treatment of Elena was offensive to her. That was why she ran to me. You frightened her. She was upset."

"Well, I develop irritating personal mannerisms when I am confronting the consequences of my ever having hired someone like you."

"And," she replied, "some of our students develop irritating personal mannerisms when they are confronting fossilized pedagogy. If you persist in teaching literature in the tedious way you are used to, if you insist on the so-called humanist approach to Greek tragedy you've been taking since the 1950s, conflicts like this are going to arise continually."

"Good," he said. "Let them come." And walked out. And then that very next semester when Tracy Cummings ran to Professor Roux, close to tears, barely able to speak, baffled at having learned that, behind her back, Professor Silk had employed a malicious racial epithet to characterize her to her classmates, Delphine decided that asking Coleman to her office to discuss the charge could only be a waste of time. Since she was sure that he would behave no more graciously than he had the last time a female student had complained—and sure from past experience that should she call him in, he would once again condescend to her in his patronizing way, yet another upstart female daring to inquire into his conduct, yet another woman whose concerns he must trivialize should he deign even to address them—she had turned the matter over to the accessible dean of faculty who had succeeded him. From then on she was able to spend her time more usefully with Tracy, steadying, comforting, as good as taking charge of the girl, a parentless black youngster so badly demoralized that, in the first few weeks after the episode, to prevent her from picking up and running away—and running away to nothing—Delphine had gained permission to move her out of the dormitory into a spare room in her own apartment and to take her on, temporarily, as a kind of ward. Though by the end of the academic

year, Coleman Silk, by removing himself from the faculty voluntarily, had essentially confessed to his malice in the spooks
affair, the damage done Tracy proved too debilitating for
someone so uncertain to begin with: unable to concentrate on
her work because of the investigation and frightened of Professor Silk's prejudicing other teachers against her, she had failed
all her courses. Tracy packed up not only to leave the college
but to pull out of town altogether—out of Athena, where
Delphine had been hoping to find her a job and get her tutored
and keep an eye on her till she could get back into school. One
day Tracy took a bus to Oklahoma, to stay with a half-sister in
Tulsa, yet using the Tulsa address, Delphine had been unable
to locate the girl ever again.

And then Delphine heard about Coleman Silk's relationship
with Faunia Farley, which he was doing everything possible to
hide. She couldn't believe it—two years into retirement, seventy-
one years old, and the man was still at it. With no more female
students who dared question his bias for him to intimidate,
with no more young black girls needing nurturing for him to
ridicule, with no more young women professors like herself
threatening his hegemony for him to browbeat and insult,
he had managed to dredge up, from the college's nethermost
reaches, a candidate for subjugation who was the prototype of
female helplessness: a full-fledged battered wife. When Delphine
stopped by the personnel office to learn what she could about
Faunia's background, when she read about the ex-husband and
the horrifying death of the two small children—in a mysterious
fire set, some suspected, *by* the ex-husband—when she read of
the illiteracy that limited Faunia to performing only the most
menial of janitorial tasks, she understood that Coleman Silk
had managed to unearth no less than a misogynist's heart's
desire: in Faunia Farley he had found someone more defenseless even than Elena or Tracy, the perfect woman to crush. For
whoever at Athena had ever dared to affront his preposterous
sense of prerogative, Faunia Farley would now be made to
answer.

And no one to stop him, Delphine thought. No one to stand
in his way.

With the realization that he was beyond the jurisdiction of
the college and therefore restrained by nothing from taking his

revenge on her—on *her*, yes, on her for everything she had done to prevent him from psychologically terrorizing his female students, on her for the role she had willingly played in having him stripped of authority and removed from the classroom—she was unable to contain her outrage. Faunia Farley was his substitute for her. Through Faunia Farley he was striking back at her. Who else's face and name and form does she suggest to you but mine—the mirror image of me, she could suggest to you no one else's. By luring a woman who is, as I am, employed by Athena College, who is, as I am, less than half your age—yet a woman otherwise my opposite in every way—you at once cleverly masquerade and flagrantly disclose just who it is you wish to destroy. You are not so unshrewd as not to know it, and, from your own august station, you are ruthless enough to enjoy it. But neither am I so stupid as not to recognize that it's me, in effigy, you are out to get.

Understanding had come so swiftly, in sentences so spontaneously explosive, that even as she signed her name at the bottom of the letter's second page and addressed an envelope to him in care of general delivery, she was still seething at the thought of the viciousness that could make of this dreadfully disadvantaged woman who had already lost everything a *toy*, that could capriciously turn a suffering human being like Faunia Farley into a plaything only so as to revenge himself on *her*. How could even *he* do this? No, she would not alter by one syllable what she'd written nor would she bother to type it up so as to make it easier for him to read. She refused to vitiate her message where it was graphically demonstrated by the propulsive, driven slant of her script. Let him not underestimate her resolve: nothing was now more important to her than exposing Coleman Silk for what he was.

But twenty minutes later she tore up the letter. And luckily. Luckily. When the unbridled idealism swept over her, she could not always see it as fantasy. Right she was to reprimand so reprehensible a predator. But to imagine saving a woman as far gone as Faunia Farley when she hadn't been able to rescue Tracy? To imagine prevailing against a man who, in his embittered old age, was free now not only of every institutional restraint but—humanist that he was!—of every humane consideration? For her there could be no greater delusion than believing herself a match for Coleman Silk's guile. Even a letter so clearly composed in the white heat of moral repulsion, a letter unmistakably informing him that his secret was out, that he was unmasked, exposed, tracked down, would somehow, in his hands, be twisted into an indictment with which to compromise *her* and, if the opportunity presented itself, to outright ruin her.

He was ruthless and he was paranoid, and whether she liked it or not, there were practical matters to take into account, concerns that might not have impeded her back when she was a Marxist-oriented lycée student whose inability to sanction injustice sometimes, admittedly, overtook common sense. But now she was a college professor, awarded early tenure, already chairperson of her own department, and all but certain of moving on someday to Princeton, to Columbia, to Cornell, to Chicago, perhaps even triumphantly back to Yale. A letter like this, signed by her and passed from hand to hand by Coleman Silk until, inevitably, it found its way to whoever, out of envy, out of resentment, because she was just too damn successful too young, might wish to undermine her . . . Yes, bold as it was, with none of her fury censored out, this letter would be used by him to trivialize her, to contend that she lacked maturity and had no business being *anyone's* superior. He had connections, he knew people still—he could do it. He *would* do it, so falsify her meaning . . .

Quickly she tore the letter into tiny pieces and, at the center of a clean sheet of paper, with a red ballpoint pen of the kind she ordinarily never used for correspondence and in big block letters that no one would recognize as hers, she wrote:

Everyone knows

But that was all. She stopped herself there. Three nights later, minutes after turning out the lights, she got up out of bed and, having come to her senses, went to her desk to crumple up and discard and forget forever the piece of paper beginning "Everyone knows" and instead, leaning over the desk, without even seating herself—fearing that in the time it took to sit down she would again lose her nerve—she wrote in a rush ten more words that would suffice to let him know that exposure was imminent. The envelope was addressed, stamped, the unsigned note sealed up inside it, the desk lamp flicked off, and Delphine, relieved at having decisively settled on the most telling thing to do within the practical limitations of her situation, was back in bed and morally primed to sleep untroubled.

But she had first to subdue everything driving her to get back up and tear open the envelope so as to reread what she'd written, to see if she had said too little or said it too feebly —or said it too stridently. Of course that wasn't her rhetoric. It couldn't be. That's why she'd used it—it was too blatant, too vulgar, far too sloganlike to be traced to her. But for that very reason, it was perhaps misjudged by her and unconvincing. She had to get up to see if she had remembered to disguise her handwriting—to see if, inadvertently, under the spell of the moment, in an angry flourish, she had forgotten herself and signed her name. She had to see if there was any way in which she had unthinkingly revealed who she was. And if she had? She *should* sign her name. Her whole life had been a battle not to be cowed by the Coleman Silks, who use their privilege to overpower everyone else and do exactly as they please. Speaking to men. Speaking *up* to men. Even to much older men. Learning not to be fearful of their presumed authority or their sage pretensions. Figuring out that her intelligence *did* matter. Daring to consider herself their equal. Learning, when she put forward an argument and it didn't work, to overcome the urge to capitulate, learning to summon up the logic and the confidence and the cool to *keep* arguing, no matter what they did or said to shut her up. Learning to take the second step, to sustain the effort instead of collapsing. Learning to argue her point *without backing down*. She didn't have to defer to him, she didn't have to defer to *anyone*. He was no longer the dean who had hired her. Nor was he department chair. She was. Dean Silk was now nothing. She should indeed open that envelope to sign her name. He was nothing. It had all the comfort of a mantra: nothing.

She walked around with the sealed envelope in her purse for weeks, going over her reasons, not only to send it but to go ahead and sign it. He settles on this broken woman who cannot possibly fight back. Who cannot begin to compete with him. Who intellectually does not even exist. He settles on a woman who has never defended herself, who *cannot* defend herself, the weakest woman on this earth to take advantage of, drastically inferior to him in every possible way—and settles on her for the most transparent of antithetical motives: because he considers all women inferior and because he's frightened of any woman with a brain. Because I speak up for myself, because I will not be bullied, because I'm successful, because I'm attractive, because I'm independent-minded, because I have a first-rate education, a first-rate degree . . .

And then, down in New York, where she'd gone one Saturday to see the Jackson Pollock show, she pulled the envelope out of the purse and all but dropped the twelve-word letter, unsigned, into a mailbox in the Port Authority building, the first mailbox she saw after stepping from the Bonanza bus. It was still in her hand when she got on the subway, but once the train started moving she forgot about the letter, stuck it back in her bag, and let the meaningfulness of the subway take hold. She remained amazed and excited by the New York subway. When she was in the Métro in Paris she never thought about it, but the melancholic anguish of the people in the New York subway never failed to restore her belief in the rightness of her having come to America. The New York subway was the symbol of why she'd come—her refusal to shrink from reality.

The Pollock show emotionally so took possession of her that she felt, as she advanced from one stupendous painting to the next, something of that swelling, clamorous feeling that is the mania of lust. When a woman's cell phone suddenly went off while the whole of the chaos of the painting entitled *Number 1A, 1948* was entering wildly into the space that previously that day—previously that *year*—had been nothing more than her body, she was so furious that she turned and exclaimed, "Madam, I'd like to strangle you!"

Then she went to the New York Public Library on Forty-second Street. She always did this in New York. She went to the museums, to the galleries, to concerts, she went to the movies that would never make their way to the one dreadful theater in backwoods Athena, and, in the end, no matter what specific things she'd come to New York to do, she wound up for an hour or so reading whatever book she'd brought with her while sitting in the main reading room of the library.

She reads. She looks around. She observes. She has little

crushes on the men there. In Paris she had seen the movie *Marathon Man* at one of the festivals. (No one knows that at the movies she is a terrible sentimentalist and is often in tears.) In *Marathon Man*, the character, the fake student, hangs out at the New York Public Library and is picked up by Dustin Hoffman, and so it's in that romantic light that she has always thought of the New York Public Library. So far no one has picked her up there, except for a medical student who was too young, too raw, and immediately said the wrong thing. Right off he had said something about her accent, and she could not bear him. A boy who had not lived at all. He made her feel like a grandmother. She had, by his age, been through so many love affairs and so much thinking and rethinking, so many levels of suffering—at twenty, years younger than him, she had already lived her big love story not once but twice. In part she had come to America in *flight* from her love story (and, also, to make her exit as a bit player in the long-running drama—entitled *Etc.*—that was the almost criminally successful life of her mother). But now she is extremely lonely in her plight to find a man to connect with.

Others who try to pick her up sometimes say something acceptable enough, sometimes ironic enough or mischievous enough to be charming, but then—because up close she is more beautiful than they had realized and, for one so petite, a little more arrogant than they may have expected—they get shy and back off. The ones who make eye contact with her are automatically the ones she doesn't like. And the ones who are lost in their books, who are charmingly oblivious and charmingly desirable, are . . . lost in their books. Whom is she looking for? She is looking for the man who is going to recognize *her*. She is looking for the Great Recognizer.

Today she is reading, in French, a book by Julia Kristeva, a treatise as wonderful as any ever written on melancholy, and across at the next table she sees a man reading, of all things, a book in French by Kristeva's husband, Philippe Sollers. Sollers is someone whose playfulness she refuses any longer to take seriously for all that she did at an earlier point in her intellectual development; the playful French writers, unlike the playful Eastern European writers like Kundera, no longer satisfy her . . . but that is not the issue at the New York Public Library.

The issue is the coincidence, a coincidence that is almost sinister. In her craving, restless state, she launches into a thousand speculations about the man who is reading Sollers while she is reading Kristeva and feels the imminence not only of a pickup but of an affair. She knows that this dark-haired man of forty or forty-two has just the kind of gravitas that she cannot find in anyone at Athena. What she is able to surmise from the way he quietly sits and reads makes her increasingly hopeful that something is about to happen.

And something does: a girl comes by to meet him, decidedly a girl, someone younger even than she is, and the two of them go off together, and she gathers up her things and leaves the library and at the first mailbox she sees, she takes the letter from her purse—the letter she's been carrying there for over a month—and she thrusts it into the mailbox with something like the fury with which she told the woman at the Pollock show that she wanted to strangle her. There! It's gone! I did it! Good!

A full five seconds must pass before the magnitude of the blunder overwhelms her and she feels her knees weaken. "Oh, my God!" Even after her having left it unsigned, even after her having employed a vulgar rhetoric not her own, the letter's origins are going to be no mystery to someone as fixated on her as Coleman Silk.

Now he will *never* leave her alone.

4

What Maniac Conceived It?

I SAW Coleman alive only one more time after that July. He himself never told me about the visit to the college or the phone call from the student union to his son Jeff. I learned of his having been on the campus that day because he'd been observed there—inadvertently, from an office window—by his former colleague Herb Keble, who, near the end of his speech at the funeral, alluded to seeing Coleman standing hidden back against the shadowed wall of North Hall, seemingly secreting himself for reasons that Keble only could guess at. I knew about the phone call because Jeff Silk, whom I spoke with after the funeral, mentioned something about it, enough for me to know that the call had gone wildly out of Coleman's control. It was directly from Nelson Primus that I learned of the visit that Coleman had made to the attorney's office earlier on the same day he'd phoned Jeff and that had ended, like the other call, with Coleman lashing out in vituperative disgust. After that, neither Primus nor Jeff Silk ever spoke to Coleman again. Coleman didn't return their calls or mine—turned out he didn't return anyone's—and then it seems he disconnected his answering machine, because soon enough the phone just rang on endlessly when I tried to reach him.

He was there alone in the house, however—he hadn't gone away. I knew he was there because, after a couple of weeks of phoning unsuccessfully, one Saturday evening early in August I drove by after dark to check. Only a few lamps were burning but, sure enough, when I pulled over beside Coleman's hugely branched ancient maples, cut my engine, and sat motionless in the car on the blacktop road down at the bottom of the undulating lawn, there was the dance music coming from the open windows of the black-shuttered, white clapboard house, the evening-long Saturday FM program that took him back to Steena Palsson and the basement room on Sullivan Street right after the war. He is in there now just with Faunia, each of them protecting the other against everyone else—each of them, to

the other, *comprising* everyone else. There they dance, as likely
as not unclothed, beyond the ordeal of the world, in an un-
earthly paradise of earthbound lust where their coupling is the
drama into which they decant all the angry disappointment of
their lives. I remembered something he'd told me Faunia had
said in the afterglow of one of their evenings, when so much
seemed to be passing between them. He'd said to her, "This is
more than sex," and flatly she replied, "No, it's not. You just
forgot what sex is. This is sex. All by itself. Don't fuck it up by
pretending it's something else."

Who are they now? They are the simplest version possible of
themselves. The essence of singularity. Everything painful con-
gealed into passion. They may no longer even regret that things
are not otherwise. They are too well entrenched in disgust for
that. They are out from under everything ever piled on top
of them. Nothing in life tempts them, nothing in life excites
them, nothing in life subdues their hatred of life anything like
this intimacy. Who are these drastically unalike people, so incongruously allied at seventy-one and thirty-four? They are the
disaster to which they are enjoined. To the beat of Tommy
Dorsey's band and the gentle crooning of young Sinatra, dancing their way stark naked right into a violent death. Everyone
on earth does the end differently: this is how the two of them
work it out. There is now no way they will stop themselves in
time. It's done.

I am not alone in listening to the music from the road.

When my calls were not returned, I assumed that Coleman
wished to have nothing more to do with me. Something had
gone wrong, and I assumed, as one does when a friendship ends
abruptly—a new friendship particularly—that I was responsible,
if not for some indiscreet word or deed that had deeply irritated
or offended him, then by being who and what I am. Coleman
had first come to me, remember, because, unrealistically, he
hoped to persuade me to write the book explaining how the
college had killed his wife; permitting this same writer to nose
around in his private life was probably the last thing he now
wanted. I didn't know what to conclude other than that his concealing from me the details of his life with Faunia had, for

whatever reason, come to seem to him far wiser than his continuing to confide in me.

Of course I knew nothing then of the truth of his origins—that, too, I'd learn about conclusively at the funeral—and so I couldn't begin to surmise that the reason we'd never met in the years before Iris's death, the reason that he'd wanted *not* to meet, was because I had myself grown up only a few miles from East Orange and because, having more than a run-of-the-mill familiarity with the region, I might be too knowledgeable or too curious to leave his roots in Jersey unscrutinized. Suppose I turned out to have been one of the Newark Jewish boys in Doc Chizner's after-school boxing classes? The fact is that I *was* one, but not until '46 and '47, by which time Silky was no longer helping Doc teach kids like me the right way to stand and move and throw a punch but was at NYU on the GI Bill.

The fact is that, having befriended me during the time he was writing his draft of *Spooks*, he had indeed taken the risk, and a foolish one at that, of being exposed, nearly six decades on, as East Orange High's Negro valedictorian, the colored kid who'd boxed around Jersey in amateur bouts out of the Morton Street Boys Club before entering the navy as a white man; dropping me in the middle of that summer made sense for every possible reason, even if I had no way of imagining why.

Well, to the last time I saw him. One August Saturday, out of loneliness, I drove over to Tanglewood to hear the open rehearsal of the next day's concert program. A week after having parked down from his house, I was still both missing Coleman and missing the experience of having an intimate friend, and so I thought to make myself a part of that smallish Saturday-morning audience that fills about a quarter of the Music Shed for these rehearsals, an audience of summer folks who are music lovers and of visiting music students, but mainly of elderly tourists, people with hearing aids and people carrying binoculars and people paging through the *New York Times* who'd been bused to the Berkshires for the day.

Maybe it was the oddness born of my being out and about

that did it, the momentary experience of being a sociable creature (or a creature feigning sociability), or maybe it was because of a fleeting notion I had of the elderly congregated together in the audience as embarkees, as deportees, waiting to be floated away on the music's buoyancy from the all-too-tangible enclosure of old age, but on this breezy, sunny Saturday in the last summer of Coleman Silk's life, the Music Shed kept reminding me of the open-sided piers that once extended cavernously out over the Hudson, as though one of those spacious, steel-raftered piers dating from when ocean liners docked in Manhattan had been raised from the water in all its hugeness and rocketed north a hundred and twenty miles, set down intact on the spacious Tanglewood lawn, a perfect landing amid the tall trees and sweeping views of mountainous New England.

As I made my way to a single empty seat that I spotted, one of the few empty seats close to the stage that nobody had as yet designated as reserved by slinging a sweater or a jacket across it, I kept thinking that we were all going somewhere together, had in fact gone and gotten there, leaving everything behind . . . when all we were doing was readying ourselves to hear the Boston Symphony rehearse Rachmaninoff, Prokofiev, and Rimsky-Korsakov. Underfoot at the Music Shed there's a packed brown earth floor that couldn't make it clearer that your chair's aground on terra firma; roosting at the peak of the structure are the birds whose tweeting you hear in the weighty silence between orchestral movements, the swallows and wrens that wing busily in from the woods down the hill and then go zipping off again in a way no bird would have dared cut loose from Noah's floating Ark. We were about a three-hour drive west of the Atlantic, but I couldn't shake this dual sense of both being where I was and of having pushed off, along with the rest of the senior citizens, for a mysterious watery unknown.

Was it merely death that was on my mind in thinking of this debarkation? Death and myself? Death and Coleman? Or was it death and an assemblage of people able still to find pleasure in being bused about like a bunch of campers on a summer outing, and yet, as a palpable human multitude, an entity of sensate flesh and warm red blood, separated from oblivion by the thinnest, most fragile layer of life?

The program that preceded the rehearsal was just ending when I arrived. A lively lecturer dressed in a sport shirt and khaki trousers stood before the empty orchestra chairs introducing the audience to the last of the pieces they'd be hearing—on a tape machine playing for them bits of Rachmaninoff and speaking brightly of "the dark, rhythmic quality" of the *Symphonic Dances*. Only when he'd finished and the audience broke into applause did somebody emerge from the wings to uncover the timpani and begin to set out the sheet music on the music stands. At the far side of the stage, a couple of stagehands appeared carrying the harps, and then the musicians entered, chatting with one another as they drifted on, all of them, like the lecturer, casually dressed for the rehearsal—an oboist in a gray hooded sweatshirt, a couple of bass players wearing faded Levi's, and then the fiddle players, men and women alike outfitted, from the look of it, by Banana Republic. As the conductor was slipping on his glasses—a guest conductor, Sergiu Commissiona, an aged Romanian in a turtleneck shirt, white bush of hair up top, blue espadrilles below—and the childishly courteous audience once again began to applaud, I noticed Coleman and Faunia walking down the aisle, looking for a place close-up to sit.

The musicians, about to undergo their transformation from a bunch of seemingly untroubled vacationers into a powerful, fluid music machine, had already settled in and were tuning up as the couple—the tall, gaunt-faced blond woman and the slender, handsome, gray-haired man not so tall as she and much older, though still walking his light-footed athletic walk —made their way to two empty seats three rows down from me and off to my right some twenty feet.

The piece by Rimsky-Korsakov was a tuneful fairy tale of oboes and flutes whose sweetness the audience found irresistible, and when the orchestra came to the end of their first goround enthusiastic applause again poured forth like an upsurge of innocence from the elderly crowd. The musicians had indeed laid bare the youngest, most innocent of our ideas of life, the indestructible yearning for the way things aren't and can never be. Or so I thought as I turned my gaze toward my former friend and his mistress and found them looking nothing like so unusual or humanly isolated as I'd been coming to envision the pair of them since Coleman had dropped out of sight. They looked nothing like immoderate people, least of all Faunia, whose sculpted Yankee features made me think of a narrow room with windows in it but no door. Nothing about these two seemed at odds with life or on the attack—or on the defensive, either. Perhaps by herself, in this unfamiliar environment, Faunia mightn't have been so at ease as she seemed, but with Coleman at her side, her affinity for the setting appeared no less natural than the affinity for him. They didn't look like a pair of desperadoes sitting there together but rather like a couple who had achieved their own supremely concentrated serenity, who took no notice whatsoever of the feelings and fantasies that their presence might foment anywhere in the world, let alone in Berkshire County.

I wondered if Coleman had coached her beforehand on how he wanted her to behave. I wondered if she'd listen if he had. I wondered if coaching was necessary. I wondered why he'd chosen to bring her to Tanglewood. Simply because he wanted to hear the music? Because he wanted her to hear it and to see the live musicians? Under the auspices of Aphrodite, in the guise of Pygmalion, and in the environs of Tanglewood, was the retired classics professor now bringing recalcitrant, transgressive Faunia to life as a tastefully civilized Galatea? Was Coleman embarked on educating her, on influencing her—embarked on saving her from the tragedy of her strangeness? Was Tanglewood a first big step toward making of their waywardness something less unorthodox? Why so soon? Why at all? Why, when everything they had and were together had evolved out of the subterranean and the clandestinely crude? Why bother to normalize or regularize this alliance, why even attempt to, by going around as a "couple"? Since the publicness will tend only to erode the intensity, is this, in fact, what they truly want? What *he* wants? Was *taming* essential now to their lives, or did their being here have no such meaning? Was this some joke they were playing, an act designed to agitate, a deliberate provocation? Were they smiling to themselves, these carnal beasts, or merely there listening to the music?

Since they didn't get up to stretch or stroll around while the orchestra took a break and a piano was rolled onto the stage —for Prokofiev's Second Piano Concerto—I remained in place as well. There was a bit of a chill inside the shed, more of an autumnal than a summery coolness, though the sunlight, spread brilliantly across the great lawn, was warming those who preferred to listen and enjoy themselves from outside, a mostly younger audience of twentyish couples and mothers holding small children and picnicking families already breaking out the lunch from their hampers. Three rows down from me, Coleman, his head tipped slightly toward hers, was talking to Faunia quietly, seriously, but about what, of course, I did not know.

Because we don't know, do we? *Everyone knows* . . . How what happens the way it does? What underlies the anarchy of the train of events, the uncertainties, the mishaps, the disunity, the shocking irregularities that define human affairs? *Nobody* knows, Professor Roux. "Everyone knows" is the invocation of the cliché and the beginning of the banalization of experience, and it's the solemnity and the sense of authority that people have in voicing the cliché that's so insufferable. What we know is that, in an unclichéd way, nobody knows anything. You *can't* know anything. The things you *know* you don't know. Intention? Motive? Consequence? Meaning? All that we don't know is astonishing. Even more astonishing is what passes for knowing.

As the audience filed back in, I began, cartoonishly, to envisage the fatal malady that, without anyone's recognizing it, was working away inside us, within each and every one of us: to visualize the blood vessels occluding under the baseball caps, the malignancies growing beneath the permed white hair, the organs misfiring, atrophying, shutting down, the hundreds of billions of murderous cells surreptitiously marching this entire audience toward the improbable disaster ahead. I couldn't stop myself. The stupendous decimation that is death sweeping us all away. Orchestra, audience, conductor, technicians, swallows, wrens—think of the numbers for Tanglewood alone just between now and the year 4000. Then multiply that times everything. The ceaseless perishing. What an idea! What maniac conceived it? And yet what a lovely day it is today, a gift of a day, a perfect day lacking nothing in a Massachusetts vacation spot that is itself as harmless and pretty as any on earth.

Then Bronfman appears. Bronfman the brontosaur! Mr. Fortissimo! Enter Bronfman to play Prokofiev at such a pace and with such bravado as to knock my morbidity clear out of the ring. He is conspicuously massive through the upper torso, a force of nature camouflaged in a sweatshirt, somebody who has strolled into the Music Shed out of a circus where he is the strongman and who takes on the piano as a ridiculous challenge to the gargantuan strength he revels in. Yefim Bronfman looks less like the person who is going to play the piano than like the guy who should be moving it. I had never before seen anybody go at a piano like this sturdy little barrel of an unshaven Russian Jew. When he's finished, I thought, they'll have to throw the thing out. He crushes it. He doesn't let that piano conceal a thing. Whatever's in there is going to come out, and come out with its hands in the air. And when it does, everything there out in the open, the last of the last pulsation, he himself gets up and goes, leaving behind him our redemption. With a jaunty wave, he is suddenly gone, and though he takes all his fire off with him like no less a force than Prometheus, our own lives now seem inextinguishable. Nobody is dying, *nobody*—not if Bronfman has anything to say about it!

There was another break in the rehearsal, and when Faunia and Coleman got up this time, to leave the shed, so did I. I waited for them to precede me, not sure how to approach Coleman or—since it seemed that he no longer had any more use for me than for anyone else hereabouts—whether to approach him at all. Yet I did miss him. And what had I done? That yearning for a friend came to the surface just as it had when we'd first met, and once again, because of a magnetism in Coleman, an allure that I could never quite specify, I found no efficient way of putting it down.

I watched from some ten feet behind as they moved in a shuffling cluster of people slowly up the incline of the aisle toward the sunlit lawn, Coleman talking quietly to Faunia again, his hand between her shoulder blades, the palm of his hand against her spine guiding her along as he explained whatever he was now explaining about whatever it was she did not know. Once outside, they set off across the lawn, presumably toward the main gate and the dirt field beyond that was the parking lot, and I made no attempt to follow. When I happened to look back toward the shed, I could see inside, under the lights on the stage, that the eight beautiful bass fiddles were in a neat row where the musicians, before going off to take a break, had left them resting on their sides. Why this too should remind me of the death of all of us I could not fathom. A graveyard of horizontal instruments? Couldn't they more cheerily have put me in mind of a pod of whales?

I was standing on the lawn stretching myself, taking the warmth of the sun on my back for another few seconds before returning to my seat to hear the Rachmaninoff, when I saw them returning—apparently they'd left the vicinity of the shed only to walk the grounds, perhaps for Coleman to show her the views off to the south—and now they were headed back to hear the orchestra conclude its open rehearsal with the *Symphonic Dances*. To learn what I could learn, I decided then to head directly toward them for all that they still looked like people whose business was entirely their own. Waving at Coleman, waving and saying "Hello, there. Coleman, hello," I blocked their way.

"I thought I saw you," Coleman said, and though I didn't believe him, I thought, What better to say to put her at her ease? To put me at my ease. To put himself at his. Without a trace of anything but the easygoing, hard-nosed dean-of-faculty charm, seemingly irritated not at all by my sudden appearance, Coleman said, "Mr. Bronfman's something. I was telling Faunia that he took ten years at least out of that piano."

"I was thinking along those lines myself."

"This is Faunia Farley," he said to me, and to her, "This is Nathan Zuckerman. You two met out at the farm."

Closer to my height than to his. Lean and austere. Little, if anything, to be learned from the eyes. Decidedly uneloquent face. Sensuality? Nil. Nowhere to be seen. Outside the milking parlor, everything alluring shut down. She had managed to make herself so that *she* wasn't even here to be seen. The skill of an animal, whether predator or prey.

She wore faded jeans and a pair of moccasins—as did Coleman—and, with the sleeves rolled up, an old button-down tattersall shirt that I recognized as one of his.

"I've missed you," I said to him. "Maybe I can take you two to dinner some night."

"Good idea. Yes. Let's do that."

Faunia was no longer paying attention. She was looking off into the tops of the trees. They were swaying in the wind, but she was watching them as though they were speaking. I realized then that she was quite lacking in something, and I didn't mean the capacity to attend to small talk. What I meant I would have named if I could. It wasn't intelligence. It wasn't poise. It wasn't decorum or decency—she could pull off that ploy easily enough. It wasn't depth—shallowness wasn't the problem. It wasn't inwardness—one saw that inwardly she was dealing with plenty. It wasn't sanity—she was sane and, in a slightly sheepish way, haughty-seeming as well, superior through the authority of her suffering. Yet a piece of her was decidedly not there.

I noticed a ring on the middle finger of her right hand. The stone was milky white. An opal. I was sure that he had given it to her.

By contrast to Faunia, Coleman was very much of a piece, or appeared so. Glibly so. I knew he had no intention of taking Faunia out to dinner with me or anyone else.

"The Madamaska Inn," I said. "Eat outside. How about it?"

Never had I seen Coleman any more courtly than when he said to me, lying, "The inn—right. We must. We will. But let us take you. Nathan, let's speak," he said, suddenly in a rush and grabbing at Faunia's hand. Motioning with his head toward the Music Shed, he said, "I want Faunia to hear the Rachmaninoff." And they were gone, the lovers, "fled away," as Keats wrote, "into the storm."

In barely a couple of minutes so much had happened, or seemed to have happened—for nothing of any importance had actually occurred—that instead of returning to my seat, I began to wander about, like a sleepwalker at first, aimlessly heading across the lawn dotted with picnickers and halfway around the Music Shed, then doubling back to where the view of the Berkshires at the height of summer is about as good as views get east of the Rockies. I could hear in the distance the Rachmaninoff dances coming from the shed, but otherwise I might have been off on my own, deep in the fold of those green hills.

I sat on the grass, astonished, unable to account for what I was thinking: he has a secret. This man constructed along the most convincing, believable emotional lines, this force with a history as a force, this benignly wily, smoothly charming, seeming totality of a manly man nonetheless has a gigantic secret. How do I reach this conclusion? Why a secret? Because it is there when he's with her. And when he's not with her it's there too —it's the secret that's his magnetism. It's something *not* there that beguiles, and it's what's been drawing me all along, the enigmatic *it* that he holds apart as his and no one else's. He's set himself up like the moon to be only half visible. And I cannot make him fully visible. There is a blank. That's all I can say. They are, together, a *pair* of blanks. There's a blank in her and, despite his air of being someone firmly established, if need be an obstinate and purposeful opponent—the angry faculty giant who quit rather than take their humiliating crap— somewhere there's a blank in him too, a blotting out, an excision, though of what I can't begin to guess . . . can't even know, really, if I am making sense with this hunch or fancifully registering my ignorance of another human being.

Only some three months later, when I learned the secret and began this book—the book he had asked me to write in the first place, but written not necessarily as he wanted it—did I understand the underpinning of the pact between them: he had told her his whole story. Faunia alone knew how Coleman Silk had come about being himself. How do I know she knew? I don't. I couldn't know that either. I can't know. Now that they're dead, nobody can know. For better or worse, I can only do what everyone does who thinks that they know. I imagine. I am forced to imagine. It happens to be what I do for a living. It is my job. It's now all I do.

After Les got out of the VA hospital and hooked up with his support group so as to stay off the booze and not go haywire, the long-range goal set for him by Louie Borrero was for Les to make a pilgrimage to the Wall—if not to the real Wall, the Vietnam Veterans Memorial in Washington, then to the Moving Wall when it arrived in Pittsfield in November. Washington, D.C., was a city Les had sworn he would never set foot in because of his hatred of the government and, since '92, because of his contempt for that draft dodger sleeping in the White House. To get him to travel all the way down to Washington from Massachusetts was probably asking too much anyway: for someone still fresh from the hospital, there would be too much emotion stretched over too many hours of coming and going on the bus.

The way to prepare Les for the Moving Wall was the same way Louie prepared everybody: start off in a Chinese restaurant, get Les to go along with another four or five guys for a Chinese dinner, arrange as many trips as it took—two, three, seven, twelve, fifteen if need be—until he was able to last out one complete dinner, to eat all the courses, from soup to dessert, without sweating through his shirt, without trembling so bad he couldn't hold still enough to spoon his soup, without running outside every five minutes to breathe, without ending up vomiting in the bathroom and hiding inside the locked stall, without, of course, losing it completely and going ballistic with the Chinese waiter.

Louie Borrero had his hundred percent service connection, he'd been off drugs and on his meds now for twelve years, and helping veterans, he said, was how he got his therapy. Thirty-odd years on, there were a lot of Vietnam veterans still out there hurting, and so he spent just about all day every day driving around the state in his van, heading up support groups for veterans and their families, finding them doctors, getting them to AA meetings, listening to all sorts of troubles, domestic, psychiatric, financial, advising on VA problems, and trying to get the guys down to Washington to the Wall.

The Wall was Louie's baby. He organized everything: chartered the buses, arranged for the food, with his gift for gentle camaraderie took personal care of the guys terrified they were going to cry too hard or feel too sick or have a heart attack and die. Beforehand they all backed off by saying more or less the same thing: "No way. I can't go to the Wall. I can't go down there and see so-and-so's name. No way. No how. Can't do it." Les, for one, had told Louie, "I heard about your trip that last time. I heard all about how bad it went. Twenty-five dollars a head for this charter bus. Supposed to include lunch, and the guys all say the lunch was shit—wasn't worth *two* bucks. And that New York guy didn't want to wait around, the driver.

Right, Lou? Wanted to get back early to do a run to Atlantic City? Atlantic City! Fuck that shit, man. Rushin' everything and everybody and then lookin' for a big tip at the end? Not me, Lou. No fuckin' way. If I had to see a couple of guys in tiger suits falling into each other's arms and sobbin', I'd puke."

But Louie knew what a visit could mean. "Les, it's nineteen hundred and ninety-eight. It's the end of the twentieth century, Lester. It's time you started to face this thing. You can't do it all at once, I know that, and nobody is going to ask you to. But it's time to work your program, buddy. The time has *come*. We're not gonna start with the Wall. We're gonna start slow. We're gonna start off with a Chinese restaurant."

But for Les that wasn't starting slow; for Les, just going for the take-out down in Athena, he'd had to wait in the truck while Faunia picked up the food. If he went inside, he'd want to kill the gooks as soon as he saw them. "But they're Chinese," Faunia told him, "not Vietnamese." "Asshole! I don't care *what* the fuck they are! They count as gooks! A gook is a gook!"

As if he hadn't slept badly enough for the last twenty-six years, the week before the visit to the Chinese restaurant he didn't sleep at all. He must have telephoned Louie fifty times telling him he couldn't go, and easily half the calls were placed after 3 A.M. But Louie listened no matter what the hour, let him say everything on his mind, even agreed with him, patiently muttered "Uh-huh . . . uh-huh . . . uh-huh" right on through, but in the end he always shut him down the same way: "You're going to sit there, Les, as best you can. That's all you have to do. Whatever gets going in you, if it's sadness, if it's anger, whatever it is—the hatred, the rage—we're all going to be there with you, and you're going to try to sit there without running or doing anything." "But the *waiter*," Les would say, "how am I going to deal with the fucking waiter? I can't, Lou—I'll fuckin' lose it!" "I'll deal with the waiter. All you have to do is sit." To whatever objection Les raised, including the danger that he might kill the waiter, Louie replied that all he'd have to do was sit. As if that was all it took—sitting—to stop a man from killing his worst enemy.

They were five in Louie's van when they went up to Black-well one evening barely two weeks after Les's release from the hospital. There was the mother-father-brother-leader, Louie, a bald guy, clean-shaven, neatly dressed, wearing freshly pressed clothes and his black Vietnam Vet cap and carrying his cane, and, what with his short stature, sloping shoulders, and high paunch, looking a little like a penguin because of the stiff way he walked on his bad legs. Then there were the big guys who never said much: Chet, the thrice-divorced housepainter who'd been a marine—three different wives scared out of their wits by this brute-sized, opaque, ponytailed lug without any desire ever to speak—and Bobcat, an ex-rifleman who'd lost a foot to a land mine and worked for Midas Muffler. Last, there was an undernourished oddball, a skinny, twitchy asthmatic missing most of his molars, who called himself Swift, having legally changed his name after his discharge, as though his no longer being Joe Brown or Bill Green or whoever he was when he was drafted would cause him, back home, to leap out of bed every morning with joy. Since Vietnam, Swift's health had been close to destroyed by every variety of skin and respiratory and neurological ailment, and now he was being eaten away by an antagonism toward the Gulf War vets that exceeded even Les's disdain. All the way up to Blackwell, with Les already beginning to shake and feel queasy, Swift more than made up for the silence of the big guys. That wheezing voice of his would not stop. "Their biggest problem is they can't go to the beach? They get upset at the beach when they see the sand? Shit. Weekend warriors and all of a sudden they have to see some real action. That's why they're pissed off—all in the reserves, never thought they were going to be called up, and then they get called up. And they didn't do *dick*. They don't know what war *is*. Call that a war? Four-day ground war? How many gooks did *they* kill? They're all upset they didn't take out Saddam Hussein. They got one enemy—Saddam Hussein. Gimme a break. There's nothin' wrong with these guys. They just want money without puttin' in the hard time. A rash. You know how many rashes I got from Agent Orange? I'm not goin' to live to see sixty, and these guys are worryin' about a rash!"

The Chinese restaurant sat up at the north edge of Blackwell, on the highway just beyond the boarded-up paper mill and backing onto the river. The concrete-block building was low and long and pink, with a plate-glass window at the front, and half of it was painted to look like brickwork—pink brickwork.

Years ago it had been a bowling alley. In the big window, the erratically flickering letters of a neon sign meant to look Chinese spelled out "The Harmony Palace."

For Les, the sight of that sign was enough to erase the slightest glimmer of hope. He couldn't do it. He'd never make it. He'd lose it completely.

The monotonousness of repeating those words—and yet the force it took for him to surmount the terror. The river of blood he had to wade through to make it by the smiling gook at the door and take his seat at the table. And the horror—a deranging horror against which there was no protection—of the smiling gook handing him a menu. The outright grotesquerie of the gook pouring him a glass of water. Offering *him* water! The very source of all his suffering could have been that water. That's how crazy it made him feel.

"Okay, Les, you're doin' good. Doin' real good," said Louie. "Just have to take this one course at a time. Real good so far. Now I want you to deal with your menu. That's all. Just the menu. Just open the menu, open it up, and I want you to focus on the soups. The only thing you have to do now is order your soup. That's all you gotta do. If you can't make up your mind, we'll decide for you. They got mighty good wonton soup here."

"Fuckin' waiter," Les said.

"He's not the waiter, Les. His name is Henry. He's the owner. Les, we gotta focus on the soup. Henry, he's here to run his place. To be sure everything is running okay. No more, no less. He doesn't know about all that other stuff. Doesn't know about it, doesn't want to. What about your soup?"

"What are you guys having?" *He* had said that. Les. In the midst of this desperate drama, he, Les, had managed to stand apart from all the turmoil and ask what they were having to eat.

"Wonton," they all said.

"All right. Wonton."

"Okay," Louie said. "Now we're going to order the other stuff. Do we want to share? Would that be too much, Les, or do you want your own thing? Les, what do you want? You want chicken, vegetables, pork? You want lo mein? With the noodles?"

He tried to see if he could do it again. "What are you guys going to have?"

"Well, Les, some of us are having pork, some of us are having beef—"

"I don't care!" And why he didn't care was because this all was happening on some other planet, this pretending that they were ordering Chinese food. This was not what was really happening.

"Double-sautéed pork? Double-sautéed pork for Les. Okay. All you have to do now, Les, is concentrate and Chet'll pour you some tea. Okay? Okay."

"Just keep the fucking waiter away." Because from the corner of his eye he'd spotted some movement.

"Sir, sir—" Louie called to the waiter. "Sir, if you just stay there, we'll come to you with our order. If you wouldn't mind. We'll bring the order to you—you just keep a distance." But the waiter seemed not to understand, and when he again started toward them, clumsily but quickly Louie rose up on his bad legs. "*Sir!* We'll bring the order to *you. To. You.* Right? Right," Louie said, sitting back down again. "Good," he said, "good," nodding at the waiter, who stood stock-still some ten feet away. "That's it, sir. That's perfect."

The Harmony Palace was a dark place with fake plants scattered along the walls and maybe as many as fifty tables spaced in rows down the length of the long dining room. Only a few of them were occupied, and all of those far enough away so that none of the other customers seemed to have noticed the brief disturbance up at the end where the five men were eating. As a precaution, Louie always made certain, coming in, to get Henry to place his party at a table apart from everyone else. He and Henry had been through this before.

"Okay, Les, we got it under control. You can let go of the menu now. Les, let go of the menu. First with your right hand. Now your left hand. There. Chet'll fold it up for you."

The big guys, Chet and Bobcat, had been seated to either side of Les. They were assigned by Louie to be the evening's MPs and knew what to do if Les made a wrong move. Swift sat at the other side of the round table, next to Louie, who directly faced Les, and now, in the helpful tones a father might use with a son he was teaching to ride a bike, Swift said to Les, "I remember the first time I came here. I thought I'd never make it through. You're doin' real good. My first time, I couldn't even read the menu. The letters, they all were swimmin' at me. I thought I was goin' to bust through the window. Two guys, they had to take me out 'cause I couldn't sit still. You're doin' a good job, Les." If Les had been able to notice anything other than how much his hands were now trembling, he would have realized that he'd never before seen Swift not twitching. Swift neither twitching nor bitching. That was why Louie had brought him along—because helping somebody through the Chinese meal seemed to be the thing that Swift did best in this world. Here at The Harmony Palace, as nowhere else, Swift seemed for a while to remember what was what. Here one had only the faintest sense of him as someone crawling through life on his hands and knees. Here, made manifest in this embittered, ailing remnant of a man was a tiny, tattered piece of what had once been courage. "You're doin' a good job, Les. You're doin' all right. You just have to have a little tea," Swift suggested. "Let Chet pour some tea."

"Breathe," Louie said. "That's it. Breathe, Les. If you can't make it after the soup, we'll go. But you have to make it through the first course. If you can't make it through the double-sautéed pork, that's okay. But you have to make it through the soup. Let's make a code word if you have to get out. A code word that you can give me when there's just no two ways about it. How about 'tea leaf' for the code word? That's all you have to say and we're out of here. Tea leaf. If you need it, there it is. But *only* if you need it."

The waiter was poised at a little distance holding the tray with their five bowls of soup. Chet and Bobcat hopped right up and got the soup and brought it to the table.

Now Les just wants to say "tea leaf" and get the fuck out. Why doesn't he? I gotta get out of here. I gotta get out of here.

By repeating to himself "I gotta get out of here," he is able to put himself into a trance and, even without any appetite, to begin to eat his soup. To take down a little of the broth. "I gotta get out of here," and this blocks out the waiter and it blocks out the owner but it does not block out the two women at a wall-side table who are opening pea pods and dropping the shelled peas into a cooking pot. Thirty feet away, and Les can pick up the scent of whatever's the brand of cheap toilet water that they've sprayed behind their four gook ears—it's as pungent to him as the smell of raw earth. With the same phenomenal lifesaving powers that enabled him to detect the unwashed odor of a soundless sniper in the black thickness of a Vietnam jungle, he smells the women and begins to lose it. No one told him there were going to be women here doing that. How long are they going to be doing that? Two young women. Gooks. Why are they sitting there doing that? "I gotta get out of here." But he cannot move because he cannot divert his attention from the women.

"Why are those women doing that?" Les asks Louie. "Why don't they stop doing that? Do they have to keep doing that? Are they gonna keep doing that all night long? Are they gonna keep doing that over and over? Is there a reason? Can somebody tell me the reason? Make them stop doing that."

"Cool it," Louie says.

"I am cool. I just wanna know—are they gonna keep doing that? Can anyone stop them? Is there nobody who can think of a *way*?" His voice rising now, and no easier to stop that happening than to stop those women.

"Les, we're in a restaurant. In a restaurant they prepare beans."

"Peas," Les says. "*Those are peas!*"

"Les, you got your soup and you got your next course coming. The next course: that's the whole world right now. That's everything. That's it. All you got to do next is eat some double-sautéed pork, and that's it."

"I had enough soup."

"Yeah?" Bobcat says. "You're not going to eat that? You done with that?"

Besieged on all sides by the disaster to come—how long can the agony be transformed into *eating?*—Les manages, beneath his breath, to say "Take it."

And that's when the waiter makes his move—purportedly going for the empty plates.

"No!" roars Les, and Louie is on his feet again, and now, looking like the lion tamer in the circus—and with Les taut and ready for the waiter to attack—Louie points the waiter back with his cane.

"You stay there," Louie says to the waiter. "Stay *there*. We bring empty plates to you. You don't come to us."

The women shelling the peas have stopped, and without Les's even getting up and going over and showing them how to stop.

And Henry is in on it now, that's clear. This rangy, thin, smiling Henry, a young guy in jeans and a loud shirt and running shoes who poured the water and is the owner, is staring at Les from the door. Smiling but staring. That man is a menace. He is blocking the exit. Henry has got to go.

"Everything's okay," Louie calls to Henry. "Very good food. Wonderful food. That's why we come back." To the waiter he then says, "Just follow my lead," and then he lowers his cane and sits back down. Chet and Bobcat gather up the empty plates and go over and pile them on the waiter's tray.

"Anybody else?" Louie asks. "Anybody else got a story about his first time?"

"Uh-uh," says Chet while Bobcat sets himself the pleasant task of polishing off Les's soup.

This time, as soon as the waiter comes out of the kitchen carrying the rest of their order, Chet and Bobcat get right up and go over to the dumb fucking gook before he can even begin to forget and start approaching the table again.

And now, it's out there. The food. The agony that is the food. Shrimp beef lo mein. Moo goo gai pan. Beef with peppers. Double-sautéed pork. Ribs. Rice. The agony of the rice. The agony of the steam. The agony of the smells. Everything out there is supposed to save him from death. Link him backward to Les the boy. That is the recurring dream: the unbroken boy on the farm.

"Looks good!"

"Tastes better!"

"You want Chet to put some on your plate, or you want to take for yourself, Les?"

"Not hungry."

"That's all right," Louie says, as Chet begins piling things on Les's plate for him. "You don't have to be hungry. That's not the deal."

"This almost over?" Les says. "I gotta get out of here. I'm not kiddin', guys. I really gotta get out of here. Had enough.

Can't take it. I feel like I'm gonna lose control. I've had enough. You said I could leave. I gotta get out."

"I don't hear the code word, Les," Louie says, "so we're going to keep going."

Now the shakes have set in big-time. He cannot deal with the rice. It falls off the fork, he's shaking so bad.

And, Christ almighty, here comes a waiter with the water. Circling around and coming at Lester from the back, from out of fucking nowhere, another waiter. They are all at once but a split second away from Les yelling "Yahhh!" and going for the waiter's throat, and the water pitcher exploding at his feet.

"Stop!" cries Louie. "Back off!"

The women shelling the peas start screaming.

"He does not need any water!" Shouting, standing on his feet and shouting, with his cane raised over his head, Louie looks to the women like the one who is nuts. But they don't know what nuts is if they think that Louie's nuts. They have no idea.

At other tables some people are standing, and Henry rushes over and talks to them quietly until they are all sitting down. He has explained that those are Vietnam veterans, and whenever they come around, he takes it as a patriotic duty to be hospitable to them and to put up for an hour or two with their problems.

There is absolute quiet in the restaurant from then on. Les picks at a little food and the others eat up everything until the only food left on the table is the stuff on Les's plate.

"You done with that?" Bobcat asks him. "You not gonna eat that?"

This time he can't even manage "take it." Say just those two words, and everybody buried beneath that restaurant floor will come rising up to seek revenge. Say *one* word, and if you weren't there the first time to see what it looked like, you sure as shit will see it now.

Here come the fortune cookies. Usually they love that. Read the fortunes, laugh, drink the tea—who doesn't love that? But Les shouts "Tea leaf!" and takes off, and Louie says to Swift, "Go out with him. Get him, Swiftie. Keep an eye on him. Don't let him out of your sight. We're gonna pay up."

On the way home there is silence: from Bobcat silence because he is laden with food; from Chet silence because he long ago learned through the repetitious punishment of too many brawls that for a man as fucked up as himself, silence is the only way to seem friendly; and from Swift silence too, a bitter and disgruntled silence, because once the flickering neon lights are behind them, so is the memory of himself that he seems to have had at The Harmony Palace. Swift is now busy stoking the pain.

Les is silent because he is sleeping. After the ten days of solid insomnia that led up to this trip, he is finally out.

It's when everybody else has been dropped off and Les and Louie are alone in the van that Louie hears him coming round and says, "Les? Les? You did good, Lester. I saw you sweatin', I thought, Umm-umm-umm, no way he's gonna make it. You should have seen the color you were. I couldn't believe it. I thought the waiter was finished." Louie, who spent his first nights home handcuffed to a radiator in his sister's garage to assure himself he would not kill the brother-in-law who'd kindly taken him in when he was back from the jungle only forty-eight hours, whose waking hours are so organized around all the others' needs that no demonic urge can possibly squeeze back in, who, over a dozen years of being sober and clean, of working the Twelve Steps and religiously taking his meds—for the anxiety his Klonopin, for the depression his Zoloft, for the sizzling ankles and the gnawing knees and the relentlessly aching hips his Salsalate, an anti-inflammatory that half the time does little other than to give him a burning stomach, gas, and the shits—has managed to clear away enough debris to be able to talk civilly again to others and to feel, if not at home, then less crazily aggrieved at having to move inefficiently about for the rest of his life on those pain-ridden legs, at having to try to stand tall on a foundation of sand—happy-go-lucky Louie laughs. "I thought he didn't have a *chance*. But, man," says Louie, "you didn't just make it past the soup, you made it to the fucking fortune cookie. You know how many times it took me to make it to the fortune cookie? Four. Four times, Les. The first time I headed straight for the bathroom and it took them fifteen minutes to get me out. You know what I'm gonna tell my wife? I'm goin' to tell her, 'Les did *okay*. Les did *all right*.'"

But when it came time to return, Les refused. "Isn't it enough that I sat there?" "I want you to eat," Louie said. "I want you to eat the meal. Walk the walk, talk the talk, eat the meal. We got a new goal, Les." "I don't want any more of your goals. I made it through. I didn't kill anyone. Isn't that enough?" But a week later back they drove to The Harmony Palace, same cast of characters, same glass of water, same menus, even the same cheap toilet water scent emitted by the sprayed Asian flesh of the restaurant women and wafting its sweet galvanic way to Les, the telltale scent by which he can track his prey. The second time he eats, the third time he eats *and* orders—though they still won't let the waiter near the table—and the fourth time they let the waiter serve them, and Les eats like a crazy man, eats till he nearly bursts, eats as if he hasn't seen food in a year.

Outside The Harmony Palace, high fives all around. Even Chet is joyous. Chet speaks, Chet *shouts*, "Semper fi!"

"Next time," says Les, while they're driving home and the feeling is heady of being raised from the grave, "next time, Louie, you're gonna go too far. Next time you're gonna want me to *like* it!"

But what is next is facing the Wall. He has to go look at Kenny's name. And this he can't do. It was enough once to look up Kenny's name in the book they've got at the VA. After, he was sick for a week. That was all he could think about. That's all he can think about anyway. Kenny there beside him without his head. Day and night he thinks, Why Kenny, why Chip, why Buddy, why them and not me? Sometimes he thinks that they're the lucky ones. It's over for them. No, no way, no how, is he going to the Wall. That Wall. Absolutely not. Can't do it. Won't do it. That's it.

Dance for me.

They've been together for about six months, and so one night he says, "Come on, dance for me," and in the bedroom he puts on a CD, the Artie Shaw arrangement of "The Man I Love," with Roy Eldridge playing trumpet. Dance for me, he says, loosening the arms that are tight around her and pointing toward the floor at the foot of the bed. And so, undismayed, she gets up from where she's been smelling that smell, the smell that is Coleman unclothed, that smell of sun-baked skin—gets

up from where she's been lying deeply nestled, her face cushioned in his bare side, her teeth, her tongue glazed with his
come, her hand, below his belly, splayed across the crinkled,
buttery tangle of that coiled hair, and, with him keeping an
eagle eye on her—his green gaze unwavering through the dark
fringe of his long lashes, not at all like a depleted old man ready
to faint but like somebody pressed up against a windowpane—
she does it, not coquettishly, not like Steena did in 1948, not
because she's a sweet girl, a sweet young girl dancing for the
pleasure of giving him the pleasure, a sweet young girl who
doesn't know much about what she's doing saying to herself,
"I can give him that—he wants that, and I can do it, and so
here it is." No, not quite the naive and innocent scene of the
bud becoming the flower or the filly becoming the mare. Faunia can do it, all right, but without the budding maturity is
how she does it, without the youthful, misty idealization of
herself and everyone living and dead. He says, "Come on,
dance for me," and, with her easy laugh, she says, "Why not?
I'm generous that way," and she starts moving, smoothing her
skin as though it's a rumpled dress, seeing to it that everything
is where it should be, taut, bony, or rounded as it should be, a
whiff of herself, the evocative vegetal smell coming familiarly
off her fingers as she slides them up from her neck and across
her warm ears and slowly from there over her cheeks to her
lips, and her hair, her graying yellow hair that is damp and
straggly from exertion, she plays with like seaweed, pretends to
herself that it's seaweed, that it's always been seaweed, a great
trickling sweep of seaweed saturated with brine, and what's it
cost her, anyway? What's the big deal? Plunge in. Pour forth. If
this is what he wants, abduct the man, ensnare him. Wouldn't
be the first one.

She's aware when it starts happening: that thing, that connection. She moves, from the floor that is now her stage at the
foot of the bed she moves, alluringly tousled and a little greasy
from the hours before, smeared and anointed from the preceding performance, fair-haired, white-skinned where she isn't
tanned from the farm, scarred in half a dozen places, one knee-
cap abraded like a child's from when she slipped in the barn,
very fine threadlike cuts half healed on both her arms and legs
from the pasture fencing, her hands roughened, reddened, sore

from the fiberglass splinters picked up while rotating the fence, from pulling out and putting in those stakes every week, a petal-shaped, rouge-colored bruise either from the milking parlor or from him precisely at the joining of her throat and torso, another bruise, blue-black at the turn of her unmuscled thigh, spots where she's been bitten and stung, a hair of his, an ampersand of his hair like a dainty grayish mole adhering to her cheek, her mouth open just wide enough to reveal the curve of her teeth, and in no hurry at all to go anywhere because it's the getting there that's the fun. She moves, and now he's seeing her, seeing this elongated body rhythmically moving, this slender body that is so much stronger than it looks and surprisingly so heavy-breasted dipping, dipping, dipping, on the long, straight handles of her legs stooping toward him like a dipper filled to the limit with his liquid. Unresisting, he's stretched across the wavelets of bedsheets, a sinuous swirl of pillows balled together to support his head, his head resting level with the span of her hips, with her belly, with her moving belly, and he's seeing her, every particle, he's seeing her and she knows that he's seeing her. They're connected. She knows he wants her to claim something. He wants me to stand here and move, she thinks, and to claim what is mine. Which is? Him. Him. He's offering me him. Okey-dokey, this is high-voltage stuff but here we go. And so, giving him her down-turned look with the subtlety in it, she moves, she moves, and the formal transfer of power begins. And it's very nice for her, moving like this to that music and the power passing over, knowing that at her slightest command, with the flick of the finger that summons a waiter, he would crawl out of that bed to lick her feet. So soon in the dance, and already she could peel him and eat him like a piece of fruit. It's not all about being beat up and being the janitor and I'm at the college cleaning up other people's shit and I'm at the post office cleaning up other people's shit, and there's a terrible toughness that comes with that, with cleaning up everybody else's waste; if you want to know the truth, it sucks, and don't tell me there aren't better jobs, but I've got it, it's what I do, three jobs, because this car's got about six days left, I've got to buy a cheap car that runs, so three jobs is what I'm doing, and not for the first time, and by the way, the dairy farm is a lot of fucking work, to you it sounds great and to you it looks great, Faunia and the cows, but coming on top of everything else it breaks my fucking hump . . . But now I'm naked in a room with a man, seeing him lying there with his dick and that navy tattoo, and it's calm and he's calm, even getting a charge out of seeing me dance he's so very calm, and he's just had the shit kicked out of him, too. He's lost his wife, he's lost his job, publicly humiliated as a racist professor, and what's a racist professor? It's not that you've just become one. The story is you've been discovered, so it's been your whole life. It's not just that you did one thing wrong once. If you're a racist, then you've always been a racist. Suddenly it's your entire life you've been a racist. That's the stigma and it's not even true, and yet now he's calm. I can do that for him. I can make him calm like this, he can make me calm like this. All I have to do is just keep moving. He says dance for me and I think, Why not? Why not, except that it's going to make him think that I'm going to go along and pretend with him that this is something else. He's going to pretend that the world is ours, and I'm going to let him, and then I'm going to do it too. Still, why not? I can dance . . . but he has to remember. This is only what it is, even if I'm wearing nothing but the opal ring, nothing on me but the ring he gave me. This is standing in front of your lover naked with the lights on and moving. Okay, you're a man, and you're not in your prime, and you've got a life and I'm not part of it, but I know what's here. You come to me as a man. So I come to you. That's a lot. But that's all it is. I'm dancing in front of you naked with the lights on, and you're naked too, and all the other stuff doesn't matter. It's the simplest thing we've ever done—it's *it*. Don't fuck it up by thinking it's more than this. You don't, and I won't. It doesn't *have* to be more than this. You know what? I see you, Coleman.

Then she says it aloud. "You know what? I see you."

"Do you?" he says. "Then now the hell begins."

"You think—if you ever want to know—is there a God? You want to know why am I in this world? What is it about? It's about this. It's about, You're here, and I'll do it for you. It's about not thinking you're someone else somewhere else. You're a woman and you're in bed with your husband, and you're not fucking for fucking, you're not fucking to come, you're fucking because you're in bed with your husband and it's the right thing to do. You're a man and you're with your wife and you're fucking her, but you're thinking you want to be fucking the post office janitor. Okay—you know what? You're with the janitor."

He says softly, with a laugh, "And that proves the existence of God."

"If that doesn't, nothing does."

"Keep dancing," he says.

"When you're dead," she asks, "what does it matter if you didn't marry the right person?"

"It doesn't matter. It doesn't even matter when you're alive. Keep dancing."

"What is it, Coleman? What does matter?"

"This," he said.

"That's my boy," she replies. "Now you're learning."

"Is that what this is—you teaching me?"

"It's about time somebody did. Yes, I'm teaching you. But don't look at me now like I'm good for something other than this. Something more than this. Don't do that. Stay here with me. Don't go. Hold on to this. Don't think about anything else. Stay here with me. I'll do whatever you want. How many times have you had a woman really tell you that and mean it? I will do anything you want. Don't lose it. Don't take it somewhere else, Coleman. This is all we're here to do. Don't think it's about tomorrow. Close all the doors, before and after. All the social ways of thinking, shut 'em down. Everything the wonderful society is asking? The way we're set up socially? 'I should, I should, I should'? Fuck all that. What you're supposed to be, what you're supposed to do, all that, it just kills everything. I can keep dancing, if that's the deal. The secret little moment—if that's the whole deal. That slice you get. That slice out of time. It's no more than that, and I hope you know it."

"Keep dancing."

"This stuff is the important stuff," she says. "If I abandoned thinking that . . ."

"What? Thinking what?"

"I was a whoring little cunt from early on."

"Were you?"

"He always told himself it wasn't him, it was me."

"The stepfather."

"Yes. That's what he told himself. Maybe he was even right. But I had no choice at eight and nine and ten. It was the brutality that was wrong."

"What was it like when you were ten?"

"It was like asking me to pick up the whole house and carry it on my back."

"What was it like when the door opened at night and he came into your room?"

"It's like when you're a child in a war. You ever see those pictures in the paper of kids after they bomb their cities? It's like that. It's as big as a bomb. But no matter how many times I got blown over, I was still standing. That was my downfall: my still standing up. Then I was twelve and thirteen and starting to get tits. I was starting to bleed. Suddenly I was just a body that surrounded my pussy . . . But stick to the dancing. All doors closed, before and after, Coleman. I see you, Coleman. You're not closing the doors. You still have the fantasies of love. You know something? I really need a guy older than you. Who's had all the love-shit kicked out of him totally. You're too young for me, Coleman. Look at you. You're just a little boy falling in love with your piano teacher. You're falling for me, Coleman, and you're much too young for the likes of me. I need a much older man. I think I need a man at least a hundred. Do you have a friend in a wheelchair you can introduce me to? Wheelchairs are okay—I can dance and push. Maybe you have an older brother. Look at you, Coleman. Looking at me with those schoolboy eyes. Please, please, call your older friend. I'll keep dancing, just get him on the phone. I want to talk to him."

And she knows, while she is saying this, that it's this and the dancing that are making him fall in love with her. And it's so easy. I've attracted a lot of men, a lot of pricks, the pricks find me and they come to me, not just any man with a prick, not the ones who don't understand, which is about ninety percent of them, but men, young boys, the ones with the real male thing, the ones like Smoky who really understand it. You can beat yourself up over the things you don't have, but that I've got, even fully dressed, and some guys know it—they know what it is, and that's why they find me, and that's why they come, but this, this, this is taking candy from a baby. Sure—he remembers. How could he not? Once you've tasted it, you remember. My, my. After two hundred and sixty blow jobs and four hundred regular fucks and a hundred and six asshole fucks, the flirtation begins. But that's the way it goes. How many times has anyone in the world ever loved before they fucked? How many times have I loved *after* I fucked? Or is this it, the groundbreaker?

"Do you want to know what I feel like?" she asks him.

"Yes."

"I feel *so* good."

"So," he asks, "who can get out of this alive?"

"I'm with you there, mister. You're right, Coleman. This is going to lead to disaster. Into this at seventy-one? Turned around by this at seventy-one? Uh-uh. We'd better go back to the raw thing."

"Keep dancing," he says, and he hits a button on the bedside Sony and "The Man I Love" track starts up again.

"No. No. I beg you. There's my career as a janitor to think about."

"Don't stop."

" 'Don't stop,' " she repeats. "I've heard those words somewhere before." In fact, rarely has she ever heard the word "stop" *without* "don't." Not from a man. Not much from herself either. "I've always thought 'don't stop' was one word," she says.

"It is. Keep dancing."

"Then don't lose it," she says. "A man and a woman in a room. Naked. We've got all we need. We don't need love. Don't diminish yourself—don't reveal yourself as a sentimental sap. You're dying to do it, but don't. Let's not lose this. Imagine, Coleman, imagine sustaining this."

He's never seen me dance like this, he's never heard me talk like this. Been so long since I talked like this, I'd have thought I'd forgotten how. So very long in hiding. *Nobody's* heard me talk like this. The hawks and the crows sometimes in the woods, but otherwise no one. This is not the usual way I entertain men. This is the most reckless I have ever been. Imagine.

"Imagine," she says, "showing up every day—and this. The

woman who doesn't want to own everything. The woman who doesn't want to own *anything*."

But never had she wanted to own anything more.

"Most women want to own everything," she says. "They want to own your mail. They want to own your future. They want to own your fantasies. 'How dare you want to fuck anybody other than me. *I* should be your fantasy. Why are you watching porn when you have *me* at home?' They want to own who you are, Coleman. But the pleasure isn't owning the person. The pleasure is this. Having another contender in the room with you. Oh, I see you, Coleman. I could give you away my whole life and still have you. Just by dancing. Isn't that true? Am I mistaken? Do you like this, Coleman?"

"What luck," he says, watching, watching. "What incredible luck. Life owed me this."

"Did it now?"

"There's no one like you. Helen of Troy."

"Helen of Nowhere. Helen of Nothing."

"Keep dancing."

"I see you, Coleman. I do see you. Do you want to know what I see?"

"Sure."

"You want to know if I see an old man, don't you? You're afraid I'll see an old man and I'll run. You're afraid that if I see all the differences from a young man, if I see the things that are slack and the things that are gone, you'll lose me. Because you're too old. But you know what I see?"

"What?"

"I see a kid. I see you falling in love the way a kid does. And you mustn't. You mustn't. Know what else I see?"

"Yes."

"Yes, I see it now—I do see an old man. I see an old man dying."

"Tell me."

"You've lost everything."

"You see that?"

"Yes. Everything except me dancing. You want to know what I see?"

"What?"

"You didn't deserve that hand, Coleman. That's what I see. I see that you're furious. And that's the way it's going to end. As a furious old man. And it shouldn't have been. That's what I see: your fury. I see the anger and the shame. I see that you understand as an old man what time is. You don't understand that till near the end. But now you do. And it's frightening. Because you can't do it again. You can't be twenty again. It's not going to come back. And this is how it ended. And what's worse even than the dying, what's worse even than the being dead, are the fucking bastards who did this to you. Took it all away from you. I see that in you, Coleman. I see it because it's something I know about. The fucking bastards who changed everything within the blink of an eye. Took your life and threw it away. Took *your* life, and *they* decided they were going to throw it away. You've come to the right dancing girl. They decide what is garbage, and they decided *you're* garbage. Humiliated and humbled and destroyed a man over an issue everyone knew was bullshit. A pissy little word that meant nothing to them, absolutely nothing at all. And that's infuriating."

"I didn't realize you were paying attention."

She laughs the easy laugh. And dances. Without the idealism, without the idealization, without all the utopianism of the sweet young thing, despite everything she knows reality to be, despite the irreversible futility that is her life, despite all the chaos and callousness, she dances! And speaks as she's never spoken to a man before. Women who fuck like she does aren't supposed to talk like this—at least that's what the men who don't fuck women like her like to think. That's what the *women* who don't fuck like her like to think. That's what everyone likes to think—stupid Faunia. Well, let 'em. My pleasure. "Yes, stupid Faunia has been paying attention," she says. "How else does stupid Faunia get through? Being stupid Faunia—that's my achievement, Coleman, that's me at my most sensible best. Turns out, Coleman, I've been watching *you* dance. How do I know this? Because you're with *me*. Why else would you be with me, if you weren't so fucking enraged? And why would I be with you, if *I* wasn't so fucking enraged? That's what makes for the great fucking, Coleman. The rage that levels everything. So don't lose it."

"Keep dancing."

"Till I drop?" she asks.

"Till you drop," he tells her. "Till the last gasp."

"Whatever you want."

"Where did I find you, Voluptas?" he says. "*How* did I find you? Who are you?" he asks, tapping the button that again starts up "The Man I Love."

"I am whatever you want."

All Coleman was doing was reading her something from the Sunday paper about the president and Monica Lewinsky, when Faunia got up and shouted, "Can't you avoid the fucking seminar? Enough of the seminar! I can't learn! I don't learn! I don't *want* to learn! Stop fucking teaching me—it won't work!" And, in the midst of their breakfast, she ran.

The mistake was to stay there. She didn't go home, and now she hates him. What does she hate most? That he really thinks his suffering is a big deal. He really thinks that what everybody thinks, what everybody says about him at Athena College, is so life-shattering. It's a lot of assholes not liking him—it's not a big deal. And for him this is the most horrible thing that ever happened? Well, it's not a big deal. Two kids suffocating and dying, that's a big deal. Having your stepfather put his fingers up your cunt, that's a big deal. Losing your job as you're about to retire isn't a big deal. That's what she hates about him—the privilegedness of his suffering. He thinks he never had a chance? There's real pain on this earth, and he thinks *he* didn't have a chance? You know when you don't have a chance? When, after the morning milking, he takes that iron pipe and hits you in the head with it. I don't even see it coming—and *he* didn't have a chance! Life owes *him* something!

What it amounts to is that at breakfast she doesn't want to be taught. Poor Monica might not get a good job in New York City? You know what? I don't care. Do you think Monica cares if my back hurts from milking those fucking cows after my day at the college? Sweeping up people's shit at the post office because they can't bother to use the fucking garbage can? Do you think Monica cares about that? She keeps calling the White House, and it must have been just terrible not to have her phone calls returned. And it's over for you? That's terrible too? It never *began* for me. Over before it *began*. Try having an iron pipe knock you down. Last night? It happened. It was nice. It was wonderful. I needed it too. But I still have three jobs. It didn't change anything. That's why you take it when it's happening, because it doesn't change a thing. Tell Mommy her husband puts his fingers in you when he comes in at night—it doesn't change a thing. Maybe now Mommy knows and she's going to help you. But nothing changes anything. We had this night of dancing. But it doesn't change anything. He reads to me about these things in Washington—what, what, what does it change? He reads to me about these escapades in Washington, Bill Clinton getting his dick sucked. How's that going to help me when my car craps out? You really think that this is the important stuff in the world? It's not that important. It's not important *at all*. I had two kids. They're dead. If I don't have the energy this morning to feel bad about Monica and Bill, chalk it up to my two kids, all right? If that's my shortcoming, so be it. I don't have any more left in me for all the great troubles of the world.

The mistake was to stay there. The mistake was to fall under the spell so completely. Even in the wildest thunderstorm, she'd driven home. Even when she was terrified of Farley following behind and forcing her off the road and into the river, she'd driven home. But she stayed. Because of the dancing she stayed, and in the morning she's angry. She's angry at him. It's a great new day, let's see what the paper has to say. After last night he wants to see what the paper has to say? Maybe if they hadn't talked, if they'd just had breakfast and she'd left, staying would have been okay. But to start the seminar. That was just about the worst thing he could have done. What *should* he have done? Given her something to eat and let her go home. But the dancing did its damage. I stayed. I stupidly stayed. Leaving at night—there is nothing more important for a girl like me. I'm not clear about a lot of things, but this I know: staying the next morning, it *means* something. The fantasy of Coleman-and-Faunia. It's the beginning of the indulgence of the fantasy of forever, the tritest fantasy in the world. I have a place to go to, don't I? It isn't the nicest place, but it's a place. Go to it! Fuck until all hours, but then *go*. There was the thunderstorm on Memorial Day, a thunderstorm ripping, pounding, volleying through the hills as though a war had broken out. The surprise attack on the Berkshires. But I got up at three in the morning, got my clothes on, and left. The lightning crackling, the trees splitting, the limbs crashing, the hail raining down like shot on my head, and I left. Whipped by all that wind, I left. The mountain is exploding, and still I left. Just between the house and the car I could have been killed, by a bolt of lightning ignited and killed, but I did not stay—I *left*. But to lie in bed with him all night? The moon big, the whole earth silent, the moon and moonlight everywhere, and I stayed. Even a blind man could have found his way home on a night like that, but I did not go. And I did not sleep. Couldn't. Awake all night. Didn't want to roll anywhere near the guy. Didn't want to touch this man. Didn't know *how*, this man whose asshole I've been licking for months. A leper till daybreak at the edge of the bed watching the shadows of his trees creep across his lawn. He said, "You should stay," but he didn't want me to, and I said, "I think I'll take you up on that," and I did. You could figure on at least one of us staying tough. But no. The two of us yielding to the worst idea ever. What the hookers told her, the whores' great wisdom: "Men don't pay you to sleep with them. They pay you to go home."

But even as she knows all she hates, she knows what she likes. His generosity. So rare for her to be anywhere near anyone's generosity. And the strength that comes from being a man who doesn't swing a pipe at my head. If he pressed me, I'd even have to admit to him that I'm smart. Didn't I do as much last night? He listened to me and so I was smart. He listens to me. He's loyal to me. He doesn't reproach me for anything. He doesn't plot against me in any way. And is that a reason to be so fucking mad? He takes me seriously. That is sincere. That's what he meant by giving me the ring. They stripped him and so he's come to me naked. In his most mortal moment. My days have not been carpeted with men like this. He'd help me buy the car if I let him. He'd help me buy everything if I let him. It's painless with this man. Just the rise and fall of his voice, just *hearing* him, reassures me.

Are these the things you run away from? Is this why you pick a fight like a kid? A total accident that you even met him, your first lucky accident—your *last* lucky accident—and you flare up and run away like a kid? You really want to invite the end? To go back to what it was before him?

But she ran, ran from the house and pulled her car out of the barn and drove across the mountain to visit the crow at the Audubon Society. Five miles on, she swung off the road onto the narrow dirt entryway that twisted and turned for a quarter of a mile until the gray shingled two-story house cozily appeared between the trees, long ago a human habitat but now the society's local headquarters, sitting at the edge of the woods and the nature trails. She pulled onto the gravel drive, bumping right up to the edge of the log barrier, and parked in front of the birch with the sign nailed to it pointing to the herb garden, hers the only car to be seen. She'd made it. She could as easily have driven off the mountainside.

Wind chimes hanging adjacent to the entrance were tinkling in the breeze, glassily, mysteriously, as though, without words, a religious order were welcoming visitors to stay to meditate as well as to look around—as though something small but touching were being venerated here—but the flag hadn't been hoisted up the flagpole yet, and a sign on the door said the place wasn't open on Sundays until 1 P.M. Nonetheless, when she pushed, the door gave way and she stepped beyond the thin morning shadow of the leafless dogwoods and into the hallway, where large sacks heavy with different mixes of bird feed were stacked on the floor, ready for the winter buyers, and across from the sacks, piled up to the window along the opposite wall, were the boxes containing the various bird feeders. In the gift shop, where they sold the feeders along with nature books and survey maps and audiotapes of bird calls and an assortment of animal-inspired trinkets, there were no lights on, but when she turned in the other direction, into the larger exhibit room, home to the scanty collections of stuffed animals and a small assortment of live specimens—turtles, snakes, a few birds in cages—there was one of the staff, a chubby girl of about eighteen or nineteen, who said, "Hi," and didn't make a fuss about the place not yet being open. This far out on the mountain, once the autumn leaves were over, visitors were rare enough on the first of November, and she wasn't about to turn away someone who happened to show up at nine-fifteen in the morning, even this woman who wasn't quite dressed for the outdoors in the middle of fall in the Berkshire Hills but seemed to be wearing, above her gray sweatpants, the top of a man's striped pajamas, and on her feet nothing but backless house slippers, those things called mules. Nor had her long blond hair been brushed or combed as yet. But, all in all, she was more disheveled-looking than dissipated, and so the girl, who was feeding mice to a snake in a box at her feet—holding each mouse out to the snake at the end of a pair of tongs until the snake struck and took it and the infinitely slow process of ingestion began—just said, "Hi," and went back to her Sunday morning duties.

The crow was in the middle cage, an enclosure about the size of a clothes closet, between the cage holding the two saw-whet owls and the cage for the pigeon hawk. There he was. She felt better already.

"Prince. Hey, big guy." And she clicked at him, her tongue against her palate—click, click, click.

She turned to the girl feeding the snake. She hadn't been around in the past when Faunia came to see the crow, and more than likely she was new. Or relatively new. Faunia herself hadn't been to visit the crow for months now, and not at all since she'd begun seeing Coleman. It was a while now since she'd gone looking for ways to leave the human race. She hadn't been a regular visitor here since after the children died, though back then she sometimes stopped by four or five times a week. "He can come out, can't he? He can come just for a minute."

"Sure," the girl said.

"I'd like to have him on my shoulder," Faunia said, and stooped to undo the hook that held shut the glass door of the cage. "Oh, hello, Prince. Oh, Prince. Look at you."

When the door was open, the crow jumped from its perch to the top of the door and sat there with its head craning from side to side.

She laughed softly. "What a great expression. He's checking me out," she called back to the girl. "Look," she said to the crow, and showed the bird her opal ring, Coleman's gift. The ring he'd given her in the car on that August Saturday morning that they'd driven to Tanglewood. "Look. Come over. Come on over," she whispered to the bird, presenting her shoulder.

But the crow rejected the invitation and jumped back into the cage and resumed life on the perch.

"Prince is not in the mood," the girl said.

"Honey?" cooed Faunia. "Come. Come on. It's Faunia. It's your friend. That's a boy. Come on." But the bird wouldn't move.

"If he knows that you want to get him, he won't come down," the girl said, and, using the tongs, picked up another mouse from a tray holding a cluster of dead mice and offered it to the snake that had, at long last, drawn into its mouth, millimeter by millimeter, the whole of the last one. "If he knows you're trying to get him, he usually stays out of reach, but if he thinks you're ignoring him, he'll come down."

They laughed together at the humanish behavior.

"Okay," said Faunia, "I'll leave him alone for a moment." She walked over to where the girl sat feeding the snake. "I love crows. They're my favorite bird. And ravens. I used to live in Seeley Falls, so I know all about Prince. I knew him when he was up there hanging around Higginson's store. He used to steal the little girls' barrettes. Goes right for anything shiny, anything colorful. He was famous for that. There used to be clippings about him from the paper. All about him and the people who raised him after the nest was destroyed and how he hung out like a big shot at the store. Pinned up right there," she said, pointing back to a bulletin board by the entryway to the room. "Where are the clippings?"

"He ripped 'em down."

Faunia burst out laughing, much louder this time than before. "*He* ripped them down?"

"With his beak. Tore 'em up."

"He didn't want anybody to know his background! Ashamed of his own background! Prince!" she called, turning back to face the cage whose door was still wide open. "You're ashamed of your notorious past? Oh, you good boy. You're a good crow."

Now she took notice of one of the several stuffed animals scattered on mounts around the room. "Is that a bobcat there?"

"Yeah," the girl said, waiting patiently for the snake to finish flicking its tongue out at the new dead mouse and grab hold of it.

"Is he from around here?"

"I don't know."

"I've seen them around, up in the hills. Looked just like that one, the one I saw. Probably *is* him." And she laughed again. She wasn't drunk—hadn't even got half her coffee down when she'd run from the house, let alone had a drink—but the laugh sounded like the laugh of someone who'd already had a few. She was just feeling good being here with the snake and the crow and the stuffed bobcat, none of them intent on teaching her a thing. None of them going to read to her from the *New York Times*. None of them going to try to catch her up on the history of the human race over the last three thousand years. She knew all she needed to know about the history of the human race: the ruthless and the defenseless. She didn't need the dates and the names. The ruthless and the defenseless, there's the whole fucking deal. Nobody here was going to try to encourage her to read, because nobody here knew how, with the exception of the girl. That snake certainly didn't know how. It just knew how to eat mice. Slow and easy. Plenty of time.

"What kind of snake is that?"

"A black rat snake."

"Takes the whole thing down."

"Yeah."

"Gets digested in the gut."

"Yeah."

"How many will it eat?"

"That's his seventh mouse. He took that one kind of slow even for him. That might be his last."

"Every day seven?"

"No. Every one or two weeks."

"And is it let out anywhere or is that life?" she said, pointing to the glass case from which the snake had been lifted into the plastic carton where it was fed.

"That's it. In there."

"Good deal," said Faunia, and she turned back to look across the room at the crow, still on its perch inside its cage. "Well, Prince, I'm over here. And you're over there. And I have no interest in you whatsoever. If you don't want to land on my shoulder, I couldn't care less." She pointed to another of the stuffed animals. "What's the guy over there?"

"That's an osprey."

She sized it up—a hard look at the sharp claws—and, again with a biggish laugh, said, "Don't mess with the osprey."

The snake was considering an eighth mouse. "If I could only get my kids to eat seven mice," Faunia said, "I'd be the happiest mother on earth."

The girl smiled and said, "Last Sunday, Prince got out and was flying around. All of the birds we have can't fly. Prince is the only one that can fly. He's pretty fast."

"Oh, I know that," Faunia said.

"I was dumping some water and he made a beeline for the door and went out into the trees. Within minutes there were three or four crows that came. Surrounded him in the tree. And they were going nuts. Harassing him. Hitting him on the back. Screaming. Smacking into him and stuff. They were there within minutes. He doesn't have the right voice. He doesn't know the crow language. They don't like him out there. Eventually he came down to me, because I was out there. They would have killed him."

"That's what comes of being hand-raised," said Faunia. "That's what comes of hanging around all his life with people like us. The human stain," she said, and without revulsion or contempt or condemnation. Not even with sadness. *That's how it is*—in her own dry way, that is all Faunia was telling the girl feeding the snake: we leave a stain, we leave a trail, we leave our imprint. Impurity, cruelty, abuse, error, excrement, semen—there's no other way to be here. Nothing to do with disobedience. Nothing to do with grace or salvation or redemption. It's in everyone. Indwelling. Inherent. Defining. The stain that is there before its mark. Without the sign it is there. The stain so intrinsic it doesn't require a mark. The stain that *precedes* disobedience, that *encompasses* disobedience and perplexes all explanation and understanding. It's why all the cleansing is a joke. A barbaric joke at that. The fantasy of purity is appalling. It's insane. What is the quest to purify, if not *more* impurity? All she was saying about the stain was that it's inescapable. That, naturally, would be Faunia's take on it: the inevitably stained creatures that we are. Reconciled to the horrible, elemental imperfection. She's like the Greeks, like Coleman's Greeks. Like their gods. They're petty. They quarrel. They fight. They hate. They murder. They fuck. All their Zeus ever wants to do is to fuck—goddesses, mortals, heifers, she-bears—and not merely in his own form but, even more excitingly, as himself made manifest as beast. To hugely mount a woman as a bull. To enter her bizarrely as a flailing white swan. There is never enough flesh for the king of the gods or enough perversity. All the craziness desire brings. The dissoluteness. The depravity. The crudest pleasures. And the fury from the all-seeing wife. Not the Hebrew God, infinitely alone, infinitely obscure, mono-maniacally the only god there is, was, and always will be, with nothing better to do than worry about Jews. And not the perfectly desexualized Christian man-god and his uncontami-nated mother and all the guilt and shame that an exquisite unearthliness inspires. Instead the Greek Zeus, entangled in adventure, vividly expressive, capricious, sensual, exuberantly wedded to his own rich existence, anything but alone and anything but hidden. Instead the *divine* stain. A great reality-reflecting religion for Faunia Farley if, through Coleman, she'd known anything about it. As the hubristic fantasy has it, made in the image of God, all right, but not ours—*theirs*. God de-bauched. God corrupted. A god of life if ever there was one. God in the image of *man*.

"Yeah. I suppose that's the tragedy of human beings raising crows," the girl replied, not exactly getting Faunia's drift though not entirely missing it either. "They don't recognize their own species. *He* doesn't. And he should. It's called imprinting," the girl told her. "Prince is really a crow that doesn't know how to be a crow."

Suddenly Prince started cawing, not in a true crow caw but in that caw that he had stumbled on himself and that drove the other crows nuts. The bird was out on top of the door now, practically shrieking.

Smiling temptingly, Faunia turned and said, "I take that as a compliment, Prince."

"He imitates the schoolkids that come here and imitate him," the girl explained. "When the kids on the school trips imitate a crow? That's his impression of the kids. The kids do that. He's invented his own language. From kids."

In a strange voice of her own, Faunia said, "I love that strange voice he invented." And in the meantime she had crossed back to the cage and stood only inches from the door.

She raised her hand, the hand with the ring, and said to the bird, "Here. Here. Look what I brought you to play with." She took the ring off and held it up for him to examine at close range. "He likes my opal ring."

"Usually we give him keys to play with."

"Well, he's moved up in the world. Haven't we all. Here. Three hundred bucks," Faunia said. "Come on, play with it. Don't you know an expensive ring when somebody offers it to you?"

"He'll take it," the girl said. "He'll take it inside with him. He's like a pack rat. He'll take his food and shove it into the cracks in the wall of his cage and pound it in there with his beak."

The crow had now grasped the ring tightly in its beak and was jerkily moving its head from side to side. Then the ring fell to the floor. The bird had dropped it.

Faunia bent down and picked it up and offered it to the crow again. "If you drop it, I'm not going to give it to you. You know that. Three hundred bucks. I'm giving you a ring for three hundred bucks—what are you, a fancy man? If you want it, you have to take it. Right? Okay?"

With his beak he again plucked it from her fingers and firmly took hold of it.

"Thank you," said Faunia. "Take it inside," she whispered so that the girl couldn't hear. "Take it in your cage. Go ahead. It's for you."

But he dropped it again.

"He's very smart," the girl called over to Faunia. "When we play with him, we put a mouse inside a container and close it. And he figures out how to open the container. It's amazing."

Once again Faunia retrieved the ring and offered it, and again the crow took it and dropped it.

"Oh, Prince—that was *deliberate*. It's now a game, is it?"

Caw. Caw. Caw. Caw. Right into her face, the bird exploded with its special noise.

Here Faunia reached up with her hand and began to stroke the head and then, very slowly, to stroke the body downward from the head, and the crow allowed her to do this. "Oh, Prince. Oh, so beautifully shiny. He's *humming* to me," she said, and her voice was rapturous, as though she had at last uncovered the meaning of everything. "He's *humming*." And she began to hum back, "Ewwww . . . ewwww . . . ummmmm," imitating the bird, which was indeed making some sort of lowing sound as it felt the pressure of the hand smoothing its back feathers. Then suddenly, click click, it was clicking its beak. "Oh, that's *good*," whispered Faunia, and then she turned her head to the girl and, with her heartiest of laughs, said, "Is he for sale? That clicking did it. I'll take him." Meanwhile, closer and closer she came to his clicking beak with her own lips, whispering to the bird, "Yes, I'll take you, I'll buy you—"

"He does bite, so watch your eyes," the girl said.

"Oh, I know he bites. I've already had him bite me a couple of times. When we first met he bit me. But he clicks, too. Oh, listen to him click, children."

And she was remembering how hard she had tried to die. Twice. Up in the room in Seeley Falls. The month after the children died, twice tried to kill myself in that room. For all intents and purposes, the first time I did. I know from stories the nurse told me. The stuff on the monitor that defines a heartbeat wasn't even there. Usually lethal, she said. But some girls have all the luck. And I tried so hard. I remember taking the shower, shaving my legs, putting on my best skirt, the long denim skirt. The wraparound. And the blouse from Brattleboro that time, that summer, the embroidered blouse. I remember the gin and the Valium, and dimly remember this powder. I forget the name. Some kind of rat powder, bitter, and I folded it into the butterscotch pudding. Did I turn on the oven? Did I forget to? Did I turn blue? How long did I sleep? When did they decide to break down the door? I still don't know who did that. To me it was ecstatic, getting myself ready. There are times in life worth celebrating. Triumphant times. The occasions for which dressing up was intended. Oh, how I turned myself out. I braided my hair. I did my eyes. Would have made my own mother proud, and that's saying something. Called her just the week before to tell her the kids were dead. First phone call in twenty years. "It's Faunia, Mother." "I don't know anybody by that name. Sorry," and hung up. The bitch. After I ran away, she told everyone, "My husband is strict and Faunia couldn't live by the rules. She could never live by the rules." The classic cover-up. What privileged girl-child

ever ran away because a stepfather was strict? She runs away,
you bitch, because the stepfather isn't strict—because the
stepfather is wayward and won't leave her alone. Anyway, I
dressed myself in the best I owned. No less would do. The
second time I didn't dress up. And that I didn't dress up tells
the whole story. My heart wasn't in it anymore, not after the
first time didn't work. The second time it was sudden and impulsive and joyless. That first time had been so long in coming,
days and nights, all that anticipation. The concoctions. Buying
the powder. Getting prescriptions. But the second time was
hurried. Uninspired. I think I stopped because I couldn't stand
the suffocating. My throat choking, really suffocating, not getting any air, and hurrying to unknot the extension cord. There
wasn't any of that hurried business the first time. It was calm
and peaceful. The kids are gone and there's no one to worry
about and I have all the time in the world. If only I'd done it
right. The pleasure there was in it. Finally where there is none,
there is that last joyous moment, when death should come on
your own angry terms, but you don't feel angry—just elated. I
can't stop thinking about it. All this week. He's reading to me
about Clinton from the *New York Times* and all I'm thinking
about is Dr. Kevorkian and his carbon monoxide machine. Just
inhale deeply. Just suck until there is no more to inhale.

"'They were such beautiful children,' he said. 'You never
expect anything like this to happen to you or your friends. At
least Faunia has the faith that her children are with God now.'"

That's what some jerk-off told the paper. 2 CHILDREN SUF-
FOCATE IN LOCAL HOUSE FIRE. "'Based on the initial investigation,' Sergeant Donaldson said, 'evidence indicates that a
space heater . . .' Residents of the rural road said they became
aware of the fire when the children's mother . . .'"

When the children's mother tore herself free from the cock
she was sucking.

"The father of the children, Lester Farley, emerged from the
hallway moments later, neighbors said."

Ready to kill me once and for all. He didn't. And then I
didn't. Amazing. Amazing how nobody's done it yet to the
dead children's mother.

"No, I didn't, Prince. Couldn't make that work either. And
so," she whispered to the bird, whose lustrous blackness be-

neath her hand was warm and sleek like nothing she had ever fondled, "here we are instead. A crow who really doesn't know how to be a crow, a woman who doesn't really know how to be a woman. We're meant for each other. Marry me. You're my destiny, you ridiculous bird." Then she stepped back and bowed. "Farewell, my Prince."

And the bird responded. With a high-pitched noise that so sounded like "Cool. Cool. Cool," that once again she broke into laughter. When she turned to wave goodbye to the girl, she told her, "Well, that's better than I get from the guys on the street."

And she'd left the ring. Coleman's gift. When the girl wasn't looking, she'd hid it away in the cage. Engaged to a crow. That's the ticket.

"Thank you," called Faunia.

"You're welcome. Have a good one," the girl called after her, and with that, Faunia drove back to Coleman's to finish her breakfast and see what developed with him next. The ring's in the cage. He's got the ring. He's got a three-hundred-dollar ring.

The trip to the Moving Wall up in Pittsfield took place on Veterans Day, when the flag is flown at half-mast and many towns hold parades—and the department stores hold their sales—and vets who feel as Les did are more disgusted with their compatriots, their country, and their government than on any other day of the year. *Now* he was supposed to be in some two-bit parade and march around while a band played and everyone waved the flag? *Now* it was going to make everybody feel good for a minute to be recognizing their Vietnam veterans? How come they spit on him when he came home if they were so eager to see him out there now? How come there were veterans sleeping in the street while that draft dodger was sleeping in the White House? Slick Willie, commander in chief. Son of a bitch. Squeezing that Jew girl's fat tits while the VA budget goes down the drain. Lying about sex? Shit. The goddamn government lies about *everything*. No, the U.S. government had already played enough bad jokes on Lester Farley without adding on the joke of Veterans Day.

And yet there he was, on that day of all days, driving up to

Pittsfield in Louie's van. They were headed for the half-scale replica of the real Wall that for some fifteen years now had been touring the country; from the tenth through the sixteenth of November, it was to be on view in the parking lot of the Ramada Inn under the sponsorship of the Pittsfield VFW. With him was the same crew that had seen him through the trial of the Chinese meal. They weren't going to let him go alone, and they'd been reassuring him of that all along: we'll be there with you, we'll stand by you, we'll be with you 24/7 if we need to be. Louie had gone so far as to say that afterward Les could stay with him and his wife at their house, and, for however long it took, they would look after him. "You won't have to go home alone, Les, not if you don't want to. I don't think you should try. You come stay with me and Tess. Tessie's seen it all. Tessie understands. You don't have to worry about Tessie. When I got back, Tessie became my motivation. My outlook was, How can anyone tell me what to do. I'm going into a rage without any provocation. You know. You know it all, Les. But thank God Tessie steadfastly stood by me. If you want, she'll stand by you."

Louie was a brother to him, the best brother a man could ever hope to have, but because he would not leave him be about going to the Wall, because he was so fucking fanatical about him seeing that wall, Les had all he could do not to take him by the throat and throttle the bastard. Gimpy spic bastard, leave me alone! Stop telling me how it took you ten years to get to the Wall. Stop telling me how it fucking changed your life. Stop telling me how you made peace with Mikey. Stop telling me what Mikey said to you at the Wall. I don't want to know!

And yet they're off, they're on their way, and again Louie is repeating to him, "'It's all right, Louie'—that's what Mikey told me, and that's what Kenny is going to tell you. What he was telling me, Les, is that it was okay, I could get on with my life."

"I can't take it, Lou—turn around."

"Buddy, relax. We're halfway there."

"Turn the fucking thing around!"

"Les, you don't know unless you go. You got to go," said Louie kindly, "and you got to find out."

"I don't *want* to find out!"

"How about you take a little more of your meds? A little Ativan. A little Valium. A little extra won't hurt. Give him some water, Chet."

Once they reached Pittsfield and Louie had parked across the way from the Ramada Inn, it wasn't easy getting Les out of the van. "I'm not doin' it," he said, and so the others stood around outside smoking, letting Les have a little more time for the extra Ativan and Valium to kick in. From the street, Louie kept an eye on him. There were a lot of police cars around and a lot of buses. There was a ceremony going on at the Wall, you could hear somebody speaking over a microphone, some local politician, probably the fifteenth one to sound off that morning. "The people whose names are inscribed on this wall behind me are your relatives, friends, and neighbors. They are Christian, Jew, Muslim, black, white, native people—Americans all. They gave a pledge to defend and protect, and gave their lives to keep that pledge. There is no honor, no ceremony, that can fully express our gratitude and admiration. The following poem was left at this wall a few weeks ago in Ohio, and I'd like to share it with you. 'We remember you, smiling, proud, strong / You told us not to worry / We remember those last hugs and kisses . . .'"

And when that speech was over, there was another to come. ". . . but with this wall of names behind me, and as I look out into the crowd and see the faces of middle-aged men like me, some of them wearing medals and other remnants of a military uniform, and I see slight sadness in their eyes—maybe that's what's left of the thousand-yard stare which we all picked up when we were just brother grunts, infantrymen, ten thousand miles away from home—when I see all this, I am somehow transported back thirty years. This traveling monument's permanent namesake opened on the Mall in Washington on November 13, 1982. It took me roughly about two and a half years to get there. Looking back over that time, I know, like many Vietnam veterans, I stayed away on purpose, because of painful memories that I knew it would conjure up. And so on a Washington evening, when dusk was settling, I went over to the Wall by myself. I left my wife and children at the hotel—we were on our way back from Disney World—and visited, stood alone at its apex, close to where I'm standing right now. And the memories came—a whirlwind of emotions came. I remembered people I grew up with, played ball with, who are on this wall, right here from Pittsfield. I remembered my radio operator, Sal. We met in Vietnam. We played the where-you-from game. Massachusetts. Massachusetts. Whereabouts in Massachusetts? West Springfield he was from. I said I was from Pittsfield. And Sal died a month after I left. I came home in April, and I picked up a local newspaper, and I saw that Sal was not going to meet me in Pittsfield or Springfield for drinks. I remembered other men I served with . . ."

And then there was a band—an army infantry band most likely—playing the "Battle Hymn of the Green Berets," which led Louie to conclude that it was best to wait till the ceremony was completely over before getting Les out of the van. Louie had timed their arrival so they wouldn't have to deal with the speeches or the emotional music, but the program had more than likely started late, and so they were still at it. Looking at his watch, though, seeing it was close to noon, he figured it must be near the end. And, yep—suddenly they were finishing up. The lone bugle playing taps. Just as well. Hard enough to hear taps standing out on the street amid all the empty buses and the cop cars, let alone to be right there, with all the weeping people, dealing with taps *and* the Wall. There was taps, agonizing taps, the last awful note of taps, and then the band was playing "God Bless America," and Louie could hear the people at the Wall singing along—"From the mountains, to the prairies, to the oceans, white with *foam*"—and a moment later it was over.

Inside the van, Les was still shaking, but he didn't appear to be looking behind him all the time and only occasionally was he looking over his head for "the things," and so Louie climbed awkwardly back up inside and sat down next to him, knowing that the whole of Les's life was now the dread of what he was about to find out, and so the thing to do was to get him there and get it done with.

"We're going to send Swift in advance, Les, to find Kenny for you. It's a pretty long wall. Better than you having to go through all those names, Swift and the guys'll go over and locate it in advance. The names are up there on panels in the order of time. They're up there by time, from first guy to last guy. We got Kenny's date, you gave us the date, so it won't take too long now to find him."

"I ain't doin' it."

When Swift came back to the van, he opened the door a crack and said to Louie, "We got Kenny. We found him."

"Okay, this is it, Lester. Suck it up. You're going to walk over there. It's around back of the inn. There are going to be other folks there doing the same thing we're doing. They had an official little ceremony, but that's finished and you don't have to worry about it. No speeches. No bullshit. It's just going to be kids and parents and grandparents and they are all going to be doing the same thing. They're going to be laying wreaths of flowers. They're going to be saying prayers. Mostly they're going to be looking for names. They're going to be talking among themselves like people do, Les. Some of them are going to be crying. That's all that's there. So you know just what's there. You're going to take your time but you're coming with us."

It was unusually warm for November, and approaching the Wall they saw that a lot of the guys were in shirtsleeves and some of the women were wearing shorts. People wearing sunglasses in mid-November but otherwise the flowers, the people, the kids, the grandparents—it was exactly as Louie had described. And the Moving Wall was no surprise: he'd seen it in magazines, on T-shirts, got a glimpse on TV once of the real full-sized D.C. Wall before he quickly switched off the set. Stretched the entire length of the macadam parking lot were all those familiar joined panels, a perpendicular cemetery of dark upright slabs sloping off gradually at either end and stamped in white lettering with all the tightly packed names. The name of each of the dead was about a quarter of the length of a man's little finger. That's what it took to get them all in there, 58,209 people who no longer take walks or go to the movies but who manage to exist, for whatever it is worth, as inscriptions on a portable black aluminum wall supported behind by a frame of two-by-fours in a Massachusetts parking lot back of a Ramada Inn.

The first time Swift had been to the Wall he couldn't get out of the bus, and the others had to drag him off and keep dragging until they got him face to face with it, and afterward he had said, "You can hear the Wall crying." The first time Chet had been to the Wall he'd begun to beat on it with his fists and to scream, "That shouldn't be Billy's name—no, Billy, no!—that there should be my name!" The first time Bobcat had been to the Wall he'd just put out his hand to touch it and then, as though the hand were frozen, could not pull it away —had what the VA doctor called some type of fit. The first time Louie had been to the Wall it didn't take him long to figure out what the deal was and get to the point. "Okay, Mikey," he'd said aloud, "here I am. I'm here," and Mikey, speaking in his own voice, had said right back to him, "It's all right, Lou. It's okay."

Les knew all these stories of what could happen the first time, and now he is there for the first time, and he doesn't feel a thing. Nothing happens. Everyone telling him it's going to be better, you're going to come to terms with it, each time you come back it's going to get better and better until we get you to Washington and you make a tracing at the big wall of Kenny's name, and that, that is going to be the real spiritual healing— this enormous buildup, and nothing happens. Nothing. Swift had heard the Wall crying—Les doesn't hear anything. Doesn't feel anything, doesn't hear anything, doesn't even remember anything. It's like when he saw his two kids dead. This huge lead-in, and nothing. Here he was so afraid he was going to feel too much and he feels nothing, and that is worse. It shows that despite everything, despite Louie and the trips to the Chinese restaurant and the meds and no drinking, he was right all along to believe he was dead. At the Chinese restaurant he felt something, and that temporarily tricked him. But now he knows for sure he's dead because he can't even call up Kenny's memory. He used to be tortured by it, now he can't be connected to it in any way.

Because he's a first-timer, the others are kind of hovering around. They wander off briefly, one at a time, to pay their respects to particular buddies, but there is always someone who stays with him to check him out, and when each guy comes back from being away, he puts an arm around Les and hugs him. They all believe they are right now more attuned to one another than they have ever been before, and they all believe, because Les has the requisite stunned look, that he is having the experience they all wanted him to have. They have no idea that when he turns his gaze up to one of the three American flags flying, along with the black POW/MIA flag, over the parking lot at half-mast, he is not thinking about Kenny or even about Veterans Day but thinking that they are flying all the flags at half-mast in Pittsfield because it has finally been established that Les Farley is dead. It's official: altogether dead and not merely inside. He doesn't tell this to the others. What's the point? The truth is the truth. "Proud of you," Louie whispers to him. "Knew you could do it. I knew this would happen." Swift is saying to him, "If you ever want to talk about it . . ."

A serenity has overcome him now that they all mistake for some therapeutic achievement. The Wall That Heals—that's what the sign says that's out front of the inn, and that is what it does. Finished with standing in front of Kenny's name, they're walking up and down with Les, the whole length of the Wall and back, all of them watching the folks searching for the names, letting Lester take it all in, letting him know that he is where he is doing what he is doing. "This is not a wall to climb, honey," a woman says quietly to a small boy she's gathered back from where he was peering over the low end. "What's the name? What's Steve's last name?" an elderly man is asking his wife as he is combing through one of the panels, counting carefully down with a finger, row by row, from the top. "Right there," they hear a woman say to a tiny tot who can barely walk; with one finger she is touching a name on the Wall. "Right there, sweetie. That's Uncle Johnny." And she crosses herself. "You sure that's line twenty-eight?" a woman says to her husband. "I'm sure." "Well, he's got to be there. Panel four, line twenty-eight. I found him in Washington." "Well, I don't see him. Let me count again." "That's my cousin," a woman is saying. "He opened a bottle of Coke over there, and it exploded. Booby-trapped. Nineteen years old. Behind the lines. He's at peace, please God." There is a veteran in an American Legion cap kneeling before one of the panels, helping out two black ladies dressed in their best church clothes. "What's his name?" he asks the younger of the two. "Bates. James." "Here he is," the vet says. "There he is, Ma," the younger woman says.

Because the Wall is half the size of the Washington Wall, a lot of people are having to kneel down to search for the names and, for the older ones, that makes locating them especially hard. There are flowers wrapped in cellophane lying up against the Wall. There is a handwritten poem on a piece of paper that somebody has taped to the bottom of the Wall. Louie stoops to read the words: "Star light, star bright / First star I see to-night . . ." There are people with red eyes from crying. There are vets with a black Vietnam Vet cap like Louie's, some of them with campaign ribbons pinned to the cap. There's a chubby boy of about ten, his back turned stubbornly to the Wall, saying to a woman, "I don't *wanna* read it." There's a heavily tattooed guy in a First Infantry Division T-shirt—"Big Red One," the T-shirt says—who is clutching himself and wandering around in a daze, having terrible thoughts. Louie stops, takes hold of him, and gives him a hug. They all hug him. They even get Les to hug him. "Two of my high school friends are on there, killed within forty-eight hours of each other," a fellow nearby is saying. "And both of them waked from the same funeral home. That was a sad day at Kingston High." "He was the first one to go to Nam," somebody else is saying, "and the only one of us to not come back. And you know what he'd want there under his name, at the Wall there? Just what he wanted in Nam. I'll tell you exactly: a bottle of Jack Daniel's, a pair of good boots, and pussy hairs baked into a brownie."

There is a group of four guys standing around talking, and when Louie hears them going at it, reminiscing, he stops to listen, and the others wait there with him. The four strangers are all gray-haired men—all of them now with stray gray hair or gray curls or, in one case, a gray ponytail poking out from back of the Vietnam Vet cap.

"You were mechanized when you were there, huh?"

"Yeah. We did a lot of humpin', but sooner or later you knew you'd get back to that fifty."

"We did a lot of walkin'. We walked all over the freakin' Central Highlands. All over them damn mountains."

"Another thing with the mech unit, we were never in the rear. I think out of the whole time I was there, almost eleven months, I went to base camp when I got there and I went on R&R—that was it."

"When the tracks were movin', they knew you were comin', and they knew when you were going to get there, so that B-40 rocket was sittin' there waitin'. He had a lot of time to polish it up and put your name on it."

Suddenly Louie butts in, speaks up. "We're here," he says straight out to the four strangers. "We're *here*, right? We're all here. Let me do names. Let me do names and addresses." And he takes his notepad out of his back pocket and, while leaning on his cane, writes down all their information so he can mail them the newsletter he and Tessie publish and send out, on their own, a couple of times a year.

Then they are passing the empty chairs. They hadn't seen them on the way in, so intent were they on getting Les to the Wall without his falling down or breaking away. At the end of the parking lot, there are forty-one brownish-gray old metal bridge chairs, probably out of some church basement and set up in slightly arced rows, as at a graduation or an award ceremony—three rows of ten, one row of eleven. Great care has been taken to arrange them just so. Taped to the backrest of each chair is somebody's name—above the empty seat, a name, a man's name, printed on a white card. A whole section of chairs off by itself, and, so as to be sure that nobody sits down there, it is roped off on each of the four sides with a sagging loop of intertwined black and purple bunting.

And a wreath is hanging there, a big wreath of carnations, and when Louie, who doesn't miss a thing, stops to count them, he finds, as he suspected, that the carnations number forty-one.

"What's this?" asks Swift.

"It's the guys from Pittsfield that died. It's their empty chairs," Louie says.

"Son of a bitch," Swift says. "What a fuckin' slaughter. Either fight to win or don't fight at all. Son of a fuckin' bitch."

But the afternoon isn't over for them yet. Out on the pavement in front of the Ramada Inn, there is a skinny guy in glasses, wearing a coat much too heavy for the day, who is having a serious problem—shouting at passing strangers, pointing at them, spitting because he's shouting so hard, and there are cops rushing in from the squad cars to try to talk him into calming down before he strikes out at someone or, if he has a gun hidden on him, pulls it out to take a shot. In one hand he holds a bottle of whiskey—that's all he *appears* to have on him. "Look at me!" he shouts. "I'm shit and everybody who looks at me knows I'm shit. Nixon! Nixon! That's who did it to me! That's what did it to me! Nixon sent me to Vietnam!"

Solemn as they are as they pile into the van, each bearing the weight of his remembrances, there is the relief of seeing Les, unlike the guy cracking up on the street, in a state of calm that never before existed for him. Though they are not men given to expressing transcendent sentiments, they feel, in Les's presence, the emotions that can accompany that kind of urge. During the course of the drive home, each of them—except for Les—apprehends to the greatest degree available to him the mystery of being alive and in flux.

He looked serene, but that was a fakeout. He'd made up his mind. Use his vehicle. Take them all out, including himself. Along the river, come right at them, in the same lane, in their lane, round the turn where the river bends.

He's made up his mind. Got nothin' to lose and everything to gain. It isn't a matter of if that happens or if I see this or if I think this I will do it and if I don't I won't. He's made up his mind to the extent that he's no longer thinking. He's on a suicide mission, and inside he is agitated big-time. No words. No thoughts. It's just seeing, hearing, tasting, smelling—it's anger, adrenaline, and it's resignation. We're not in Vietnam. We're beyond Vietnam.

(Taken again in restraints to the Northampton VA a year later, he tries putting into plain English for the psychologist this pure state of something that is nothing. It's all confidential anyway. She's a doc. Medical ethics. Strictly between the two of them. "What were you thinking?" "No thinking." "You had to be thinking something." "Nothing." "At what point did you get in your truck?" "After dark." "Had you had dinner?" "No dinner." "Why did you think you were getting into the truck?" "I knew why." "You knew where you were going." "To get him." "To get who?" "The Jew. The Jew professor." "Why were you going to do that?" "To get him." "Because you had to?" "Because I had to." "Why did you have to?" "Kenny." "You were going to kill him." "Oh yes. All of us." "There was planning, then." "No planning." "You knew what you were doing." "Yes." "But you did not plan it." "No." "Did you think you were back in Vietnam?" "No Vietnam." "Were you having a flashback?" "No flashbacks." "Did you think you were in the jungle?" "No jungle." "Did you think you would feel better?" "No feelings." "Were you thinking about the kids? Was this payback?" "No payback." "Are you sure?" "No payback." "This woman, you tell me, killed your children, 'a blow job,' you told me, 'killed my kids'—weren't you trying to get back at her, to take revenge for that?" "No revenge." "Were you depressed?" "No, no depression." "You were out to kill two people and yourself and you were not angry?" "No, no more anger." "Sir, you got in your truck, you knew where they would be, and you drove into their headlights. And you're trying to tell me you weren't trying to kill them." "I didn't kill them." "Who killed them?" "They killed themselves.")

Just driving. That's all he's doing. Planning and not planning. Knowing and not knowing. The other headlights are coming at him, and then they're gone. No collision? Okay, no collision. Once they swerve off the road, he changes lanes and keeps going. He just keeps driving. Next morning, waiting with the road crew to go out for the day, he hears about it at the town garage. The other guys already know.

There's no collision so, though he has some sense of it, he's got no details, and when he gets home from driving and gets out of the truck he's not sure what happened. Big day for him. November the eleventh. Veterans Day. That morning he goes with Louie—that morning he goes to the Wall, that afternoon he comes home from the Wall, that night he goes out to kill everybody. Did he? Can't know because there's no collision, but still quite a day from a therapeutic point of view. Second half being more therapeutic than the first. Achieves a true serenity now. Now Kenny can speak to him. Firing side by side with Kenny, both of them opened up on fully automatic, when Hector, the team leader, gives the screaming order "Get your stuff and let's get out of here!" and suddenly Kenny is dead.

Quick as that. Up on some hill. Under attack, pulling back—and Kenny's dead. Can't be. His buddy, another farm boy, same background except from Missouri, they were going to do dairy farming together, guy who as a kid of six watched his father die and as a kid of nine watched his mother die, raised after that by an uncle he loved and was always talking about, a successful dairy farmer with a good-sized spread—180 milking cows, twelve machines milking six cows a side in the parlor at a time—and Kenny's head is gone and he's dead.

Looks like Les is communicating with his buddy now. Showed Kenny that Kenny's not forgotten. Kenny wanted him to do it, and he did it. Now he knows that whatever he did—even if he's not sure what it was—he did it for Kenny. Even if he did kill someone and he goes to jail, it doesn't matter—it can't matter because he's dead. This was just one last thing to do for Kenny. Squared it with him. Knows everything is now all right with Kenny.

("I went to the Wall and there was his name and it was silence. Waited and waited and waited. I looked at him, he looked at me. I didn't hear anything, didn't feel anything, and that's the point I knew it wasn't okay with Kenny. That there was more to be done. Didn't know what it was. But he wouldn't have just left me like that. That's why there was no message for me. Because I still had more to do for Kenny. Now? Now it's okay with Kenny. Now he can rest." "And are you still dead?" "What are you, an asswipe? Oh, I can't talk to you, you asswipe! I did it because I *am* dead!")

Next morning, first thing, he hears at the garage that she was with the Jew in a car crash. Everybody figures that she was blowing him and he lost control and they went off the road and through the barrier and over the embankment and front-end-first into the shallows of the river. The Jew lost control of the car.

No, he does not associate this with what happened the night before. He was just out driving, in a different state of mind entirely.

He says, "Yeah? What happened? Who killed her?"

"The Jew killed her. Went off the road."

"She was probably going down on him."

"That's what they say."

That's it. Doesn't feel anything about that either. Still feels nothing. Except his suffering. Why is he suffering so much for what happened to him when she can go on giving blow jobs to old Jews? He's the one who does the suffering, and now she just up and walks away from it all.

Anyway, as he sips his morning coffee at the town garage, looks that way to him.

When everybody gets up to start for the trucks, Les says, "Guess that music won't be coming from that house on Saturday nights anymore."

Though, as sometimes happens, nobody knows what he's talking about, they laugh anyway, and with that, the workday begins.

If she located herself in western Massachusetts, the ad could be traced back to her by colleagues who subscribed to the *New York Review of Books*, particularly if she went on to describe her appearance and list her credentials. Yet if she didn't specify her place of residence, she could wind up with not a single response from anyone within a radius of a hundred, two, even three hundred miles. And since in every ad she'd studied in the *New York Review*, the age given by women exceeded her own by from fifteen to thirty years, how could she go ahead to reveal her correct age—to portray herself correctly altogether—without arousing the suspicion that there was something significant undisclosed by her and wrong with her, a woman claiming to be so young, so attractive, so accomplished who found it necessary to look for a man through a personal ad? If she described herself as "passionate," this might readily be interpreted by the lascivious-minded to be an intentional provocation, to mean "loose" or worse, and letters would come pouring in to her *NYRB* box from the men she wanted nothing to do with. But if she appeared to be a bluestocking for whom sex was of decidedly less importance than her academic, scholarly, and intellectual pursuits, she would be sure to encourage a response from a type who would be all too maidenly for someone as excitable as she could be with an erotic counterpart she could trust. If she presented herself as "pretty," she would be associating herself with a vague catchall category of women, and yet if she described herself, straight out, as "beautiful," if she dared to be truthful enough to evoke the word that had never seemed extravagant to her lovers—who had called her *éblouissante* (as in "*Éblouissante! Tu as un visage de chat*"); dazzling, stunning —or if, for the sake of precision in a text of only thirty or so words, she invoked the resemblance noted by her elders to Leslie Caron who her father always enjoyed making too much of, then anyone other than a megalomaniac might be too intimidated to approach her or refuse to take her seriously as an intellectual. If she wrote, "A photo accompanying the letter would be welcome," or, simply, "Photo, please," it could be misunderstood to imply that she esteemed good looks above intelligence, erudition, and cultural refinement; moreover, any photos she received might be touched up, years old, or altogether spurious. Asking for a photo might even discourage a response from the very men whose interest she was hoping to elicit. Yet if she didn't request a photo, she could wind up traveling all the way to Boston, to New York, or farther, to find herself the dinner companion of someone wholly inappropriate and even distasteful. And distasteful not necessarily because of looks alone. What if he was a liar? What if he was a charlatan? What if he was a psychopath? What if he had AIDS? What if he was violent, vicious, married, or on Medicare? What if he was a weirdo, someone she couldn't get rid of? What if she gave her name and her place of employment to a stalker? Yet, on their first meeting, how could she *withhold* her name? In search of a serious, impassioned love affair leading to marriage and a family, how could an open, honest person start off by lying about something as fundamental as her name? And what about race? Oughtn't she to include the kindly solicitation "Race unimportant"? But it wasn't unimportant; it should be, it ought to be, it well might have been but for the fiasco back in Paris when she was seventeen that convinced her that a man of another race was an unfeasible—because an unknowable —partner.

She was young and adventurous, she didn't *want* to be cautious, and he was from a good family in Brazzaville, the son of a supreme court judge—or so he said—in Paris as an exchange student for a year at Nanterre. Dominique was his name, and she thought of him as a fellow spiritual lover of literature. She'd met him at one of the Milan Kundera lectures. He picked her up there, and outside they were still basking in Kundera's observations on *Madame Bovary*, infected, the both of them, with what Delphine excitedly thought of as "the Kundera disease." Kundera was legitimatized for them by being persecuted as a Czech writer, by being someone who had lost out in Czechoslovakia's great historical struggle to be free. Kundera's playfulness did not appear to be frivolous, not at all. *The Book of Laughter and Forgetting* they loved. There was something trustworthy about him. His Eastern Europeanness. The restless nature of the intellectual. That everything appeared to be difficult for him. Both were won over by Kundera's modesty, the very opposite of superstar demeanor, and both believed in his ethos of thinking and suffering. All that intellectual tribulation —and then there were his looks. Delphine was very taken by the writer's poetically prizefighterish looks, to her an outward sign of everything colliding within.

After the pickup at the Kundera lecture, it was completely a physical experience with Dominique, and she had never had that before. It was completely about her body. She had just connected so much with the Kundera lecture and she had mistaken that connection for the connection she had to Dominique, and it happened all very fast. There was nothing except her body. Dominique didn't understand that she didn't want just sex. She wanted to be something more than a piece of meat on a spit, turned and basted. That's what he did—those were even his words: turning her and basting her. He was interested in nothing else, least of all in literature. Loosen up and shut up—that's his attitude with her, and she somehow gets locked in, and then comes the terrible night she shows up at his room and he is waiting there for her with his friend. It's not that she's now prejudiced, it's just that she realizes she would not have so misjudged a man of her own race. This was her worst failure, and she could never forget it. Redemption had only come with the professor who'd given her his Roman ring. Sex, yes, wonderful sex, but sex with metaphysics. Sex with metaphysics with a man with gravitas who is not vain. Someone like Kundera. That is the plan.

The problem confronting her as she sat alone at the computer long after dark, the only person left in Barton Hall, unable to leave her office, unable to face one more night in her apartment without even a cat for company—the problem was how to include in her ad, no matter how subtly coded, something that essentially said, "Whites only need apply." If it were discovered at Athena that it was she who had specified such an exclusion—no, that would not do for a person ascending so rapidly through the Athena academic hierarchy. Yet she had no choice but to ask for a photograph, even though she knew—knew from trying as hard as she could to think of everything, to be naive about nothing, on the basis of just her brief life as a woman on her own to take into account how men could behave—that there was nothing to stop someone sufficiently sadistic or perverse from sending a photograph designed to mislead *specifically* in the matter of race.

No, it was too risky altogether—as well as beneath her dignity —to place an ad to help her meet a man of the caliber that she'd never find anywhere among the faculty of as dreadfully provincial a place as Athena. She could not do it and she should not do it, and yet all the while she thought of the uncertainties, the outright dangers, of advertising oneself to strangers as a woman in search of a suitable mate, all the while she thought of the reasons why it was inadvisable, as chair of the Department of Languages and Literature, to risk revealing herself to colleagues as something other than a serious teacher and scholar—exposing herself as someone with needs and desires that, though altogether human, could be deliberately misconstrued so as to trivialize her—she was doing it: fresh from e-mailing every member of her department her latest thoughts on the subject of senior theses, trying to compose an ad that adhered to the banal linguistic formula of the standard *New York Review* personal but one that managed as well to present a truthful appraisal of *her* caliber. At it now for over an hour and she was still unable to settle on anything unhumiliating enough to e-mail to the paper even pseudonymously.

Western Mass. 29 yr. old petite, passionate, Parisian professor, equally at home teaching Molière as

Brainy, beautiful Berkshire academic, equally at home cooking médaillons de veau as chairing a humanities dept., seeks

Serious SWF scholar seeks

SWF Yale Ph.D. Parisian-born academic. Petite, scholarly, literature-loving, fashion-conscious brunette seeks

Attractive, serious scholar seeks

SWF Ph.D., French, Mass.-based, seeks

Seeks what? *Anything*, anything other than these Athena men —the wisecracking boys, the feminized old ladies, the timorous, tedious family freaks, the professional dads, all of them so earnest and so emasculated. She is revolted by the fact that they pride themselves on doing half the domestic work. Intolerable. "Yes, I have to go, I have to relieve my wife. I have to do as much diaper changing as she does, you know." She cringes when they brag about their helpfulness. Do it, fine, but don't have the vulgarity to mention it. Why make such a spectacle of yourself as the fifty-fifty husband? Just do it and shut up about it. In this revulsion she is very different from her women colleagues who value these men for their "sensitivity." Is that what overpraising their wives is, "sensitivity"? "Oh, Sara Lee is such an extraordinary this-and-that. She's already published four and a half articles . . ." Mr. Sensitivity always has to mention her glory. Mr. Sensitivity can't talk about some great show at the Metropolitan without having to be sure to preface it, "Sara Lee says . . ." Either they overpraise their wives or they fall dead silent. The husband falls silent and grows more and more depressed, and she has never encountered this in any other country. If Sara Lee is an academic who can't find a job while he, say, is barely holding on to his job, he would rather lose his job than have her think she is getting the bad end of the deal. There would even be a certain pride if the situation were reversed and he was the one who had to stay home while she didn't. A French woman, even a French feminist, would find such a man disgusting. The Frenchwoman is intelligent, she's sexy, she's *truly* independent, and if he talks more than she does, so what, where's the issue? What's the fiery contention all about? Not "Oh, did you notice, she's so dominated by her rude, power-hungry husband." No, the more of a woman she is, the more the Frenchwoman *wants* the man to project his power. Oh, how she had prayed, on arriving at

Athena five years back, that she might meet some marvelous man who projected his power, and instead the bulk of younger male faculty are these domestic, emasculated types, intellectually unstimulating, pedestrian, the overpraising husbands of Sara Lee whom she has deliciously categorized for her correspondents in Paris as "The Diapers."

Then there are "The Hats." The Hats are the "writers in residence," America's incredibly pretentious writers in residence. Probably, at little Athena, she hasn't seen the worst of them, but these two are bad enough. They show up to teach once a week, and they are married and they come on to her, and they are impossible. When can we have lunch, Delphine? Sorry, she thinks, but I am not impressed. The thing she liked about Kundera at his lectures was that he was always slightly shadowy, even slightly shabby sometimes, a great writer *malgré lui*. At least she perceived it that way and that's what she liked in him. But she certainly does not like, cannot *stand*, the American I-am-the-writer type who, when he looks at her, she knows is thinking, With your French confidence and your French fashions and your elitist French education, you are very French indeed, but you are nonetheless the academic and I am the writer—we are not equals.

These writers in residence, as far as she can surmise, spend an enormous amount of time worrying about their headwear. Yes, both the poet *and* the prose writer have an extraordinary hat fetish, and so she categorizes them in her letters as The Hats. One of them is always dressed as Charles Lindbergh, wearing his antique pilot gear, and she cannot understand the relationship between pilot gear and writing, particularly writing in residence. She muses about this in her humorous correspondence to her Paris friends. The other is the floppy-hat type, the unassuming type—which is, of course, so recherché —who spends eight hours at the mirror dressing carelessly. Vain, unreadable, married by now a hundred and eighty-six times, and incredibly self-important. It's not so much hatred she feels for this one as contempt. And yet, deep in the Berkshires starving for romance, she sometimes feels ambivalent about The Hats and wonders if she shouldn't take them seriously as erotic candidates, at least. No, she couldn't, not after what she has written to Paris. She must resist them if only because they try to talk to her with her own vocabulary. Because one of them, the younger, minimally less self-important one, has read Bataille, because he knows just enough Bataille and has read just enough Hegel, she's gone out with him a few times, and never has a man so rapidly de-eroticized himself before her eyes; with every word he spoke—using, as he did, that language of hers that she herself is now somewhat uncertain about—he read himself right out of her life.

Whereas the older types, who are uncool and tweedy, "The Humanists" . . . Well, obliging as she must be at conferences and in publications to write and speak as the profession requires, the humanist is the very part of her own self that she sometimes feels herself betraying, and so she is attracted to them: because they are what they are and always have been and because she knows they think of her as a traitor. Her classes have a following, but they think of that following contemptuously, as a fashionable phenomenon. These older men, The Humanists, the old-fashioned traditionalist humanists who have read everything, the born-again teachers (as *she* thinks of *them*), make her sometimes feel shallow. Her following they laugh at and her scholarship they despise. At faculty meetings they're not afraid to say what they say, and you would think they should be; in class they're not afraid to say what they feel, and, again, you would think they should be; and, as a result, in front of them she crumbles. Since she doesn't herself have that much conviction about all the so-called discourse she picked up in Paris and New Haven, inwardly she crumbles. Only she needs that language to succeed. On her own in America, she needs so much to succeed! And yet everything that it takes to succeed is somehow compromising, and it makes her feel less and less genuine, and dramatizing her predicament as a "Faustian bargain" helps only a little.

At moments she even feels herself betraying Milan Kundera, and so, silently, when she is alone, she will picture him in her mind's eye and speak to him and ask his forgiveness. Kundera's intention in his lectures was to free the intelligence from the French sophistication, to talk about the novel as having something to do with human beings and the *comédie humaine*; his intention was to free his students from the tempting traps of structuralism and formalism and the obsession with modernity, to purge them of the French theory that they had been fed, and listening to him had been an enormous relief, for despite her publications and a growing scholarly reputation, it was always difficult for her to deal with literature through literary theory. There could be such a gigantic gap between what she liked and what she was supposed to admire—between how she was supposed to speak about what she was supposed to admire and how she spoke to herself about the writers she treasured—that her sense of betraying Kundera, though not the most serious problem in her life, would become at times like the shame of betraying a kindly, trusting, absent lover.

The only man she's been out with frequently is, oddly enough, the most conservative person on campus, a divorced man of sixty-five, Arthur Sussman, the Boston University economist who was to have been secretary of the treasury in the second Ford administration. He is a bit stout, a bit stiff, always wearing a suit; he hates affirmative action, he hates Clinton, he comes in from Boston once a week, is paid a fortune, and is thought to make the place, to put little Athena on the academic map. The women in particular are sure she has slept with him, just because he was once powerful. They see them occasionally having lunch together in the cafeteria. He comes to the cafeteria and he looks so excruciatingly bored, until he sees Delphine, and when he asks if he may join her, she says, "How generous of you to endow us with your presence today," or something along those lines. He likes that she mocks him, to a point. Over lunch, they have what Delphine calls "a real conversation." With a thirty-nine-billion-dollar budget surplus, he tells her, the government is giving nothing back to the taxpayer. The people earned it and they should spend it, and they shouldn't have bureaucrats deciding what to do with their money. Over lunch, he explains in detail why Social Security should be given over to private investment analysts. Everybody should invest in their own future, he tells her. Why should anyone trust the government to provide for people's futures when Social Security has been giving you x returns while anybody who had invested in the stock market over the same period of time would now have twice as much, if not more? The backbone of his argument is always personal sovereignty, personal freedom, and what he never understands, Delphine dares to tell the treasury-secretary-who-never-was, is that for most people there isn't enough money to make choices and there isn't enough education to make educated guesses—there isn't enough mastery of the market. His model, as she interprets it for him, is based on a notion of radical personal liberty that, in his thinking, is reduced to a radical sovereignty in the market. The surplus and Social Security—those are the two issues that are bugging him, and they talk about them all the time. He seems to hate Clinton most for proposing the Democratic version of everything he wanted. "Good thing," he tells her, "that little squirt Bob Reich is out of there. He'd have Clinton spending billions of dollars retraining people for jobs they could never occupy. Good thing he left the cabinet. At least they have Bob Rubin there, at least they have one sane guy who knows where the bodies are buried. At least he and Alan kept the interest rates where they had to be. At least he and Alan kept this recovery going . . ."

The one thing she likes about him is that, aside from his gruff insider's take on economic issues, he happens also to know all of Engels and Marx really well. More impressive, he knows intimately their *The German Ideology*, a text she has always found fascinating and loves. When he takes her out to dinner down in Great Barrington, things turn both more romantic and more intellectual than they do at lunch in the cafeteria. Over dinner he likes to speak French with her. One of his conquests years ago was Parisian, and he goes on endlessly about this woman. Delphine does not, however, open her mouth like a fish when he talks about his Parisian affair or about his manifold sentimental attachments before and after. About women he brags constantly, in a very suave way that she doesn't, after a while, find suave at all. She cannot stand the fact that he thinks she's impressed by all his conquests, but she puts up with it, only slightly bored, because otherwise she's glad to be having dinner with an intelligent, assertive, well-read man of the world. When at dinner he takes her hand, she says something to let him know, however subtly, that if he thinks he is going to sleep with her, he is crazy. Sometimes in the parking lot, he pulls her to him by cupping her behind and holding her against him. He says, "I cannot be with you time after time like this without some passion. I can't take out a woman as beautiful as you, talk to her and talk to her and talk to her, and have it end there." "We have a saying in France," she tells him, "which is . . ." "Which is what?" he asks, thinking he may pick up a new *bon mot* in the bargain. Smiling, she says, "I don't know. It'll come to me later," and in this way gently disentangles herself from his surprisingly strong arms. She is gentle with him because it works, and she is gentle with him because she knows he thinks it is a question of age, when in fact it is a question, as she explains to him driving back in his car, of nothing so banal: it is a question of "a frame of mind." "It's about who I am," she tells him, and, if nothing else has done it, that sends him away for two or three months, until he next turns up in the cafeteria, looking to see if she is there. Sometimes he telephones her late at night or in the early hours of the morning. From his Back Bay bed, he wants to talk with her about sex. She says she prefers to talk about Marx, and it takes no more, with this conservative economist, to put a stop to that stuff. And yet the women who don't like her are all sure that because he's powerful she has slept with him. It is incomprehensible to them that, bleak and lonely as her life is, she has no interest in becoming Arthur Sussman's little badge of a mistress. It has also gotten back to her that one of them has called her "so passé, such a parody of Simone de Beauvoir." By which she means that it is her judgment that Beauvoir sold out to Sartre—a very intelligent woman but in the end his slave. For these women, who observe her at lunch with Arthur Sussman and get it all wrong, everything is an issue, everything is an ideological stance, everything is a betrayal—everything's a selling out. Beauvoir sold out, Delphine sold out, et cetera, et cetera. Something about Delphine makes them go green in the face.

Another of her problems. She does not want to alienate these women. Yet she is no less philosophically isolated from them than from the men. Though it would not be prudent for her to tell them so, the women are far more feminist, in the American sense, than she is. It would not be prudent because they are dismissive enough and seem always to know where she stands anyway, always suspecting her motives and aims: she is attractive, young, thin, effortlessly stylish, she has climbed so high so fast she already has the beginnings of a reputation beyond the college, and, like her Paris friends, she doesn't use or need to use all their clichés (the very clichés by which The Diapers are so eagerly emasculated). Only in the anonymous note to Coleman Silk did she adopt their rhetoric, and that was not only accidental, because she was so overwrought, but, in the end, deliberate, to hide her identity. In truth, she is no less emancipated than these Athena feminists are and perhaps even more: she left her own country, daringly left France, she works hard at her job, she works hard at her publications, and she wants to make it; on her own as she is, she *has* to make it. She is utterly alone, unsupported, homeless, decountried—*dépaysée*. In a free state but oftentimes so forlornly *dépaysée*. Ambitious? She happens to be more ambitious than all those staunch go-it-alone feminists put together, but because men are drawn to her, and among them is a man as eminent as Arthur Sussman, and because, for the fun of it, she wears a vintage Chanel jacket with tight jeans, or a slip dress in summer, and because she likes cashmere and leather, the women are resentful. She makes it a point not to be concerned with *their* ghastly clothing, so by what right do they dwell on what they consider recidivist about hers? She knows everything they say in their annoyance with her. They say what the men she begrudgingly respects are saying—that she's a charlatan and illegitimate—and that makes it hurt more. They say, "She is fooling the students." They say, "How can the students not see through this woman?" They say, "Don't they see that she is one of those French male chauvinists in drag?" They say that she got to be the department chair *faute de mieux.* And they make fun of her language. "Well, of course, it's her intertextual charm that's gotten her her following. It's her relationship to phenomenology. She's *such* a phenomenologist ha-ha-ha!" She knows what they are saying to ridicule her, and yet she remembers being in France and being at Yale and *living* for this vocabulary; she believes that to be a good literary critic she *has* to have this vocabulary. She *needs* to know about intertextuality. Does that mean she's a phony? No! It means that she's unclassifiable. In some circles that might be thought of as her mystique! But just be the least bit unclassifiable at a backwoods hellhole like this place, and that annoys everyone. Her being unclassifiable even annoys Arthur Sussman. Why the hell won't she at least have phone sex? Be unclassifiable here, be something they cannot reconcile, and they torment you for it. That being unclassifiable is a part of her *bildungsroman*, that she has always *thrived* on being unclassifiable, nobody at Athena understands.

There is a cabal of three women—a philosophy professor, a sociology professor, and a history professor—who particularly drive her crazy. Full of animosity toward her simply because she is not ploddingly plugged in the way they are. Because she has an air of chic, they feel she hasn't read enough learned journals. Because their American notions of independence differ from her French notions of independence, she is dismissed by them as pandering to powerful males. But what has she ever actually done to arouse their distrust, except perhaps handle the men on the faculty as well as she does? Yes, she'd been at dinner in Great Barrington with Arthur Sussman. Does that mean she didn't consider herself his intellectual equal? There's no question in her mind that she is his equal. She isn't flattered to be out with him—she wants to hear what he has to say about *The German Ideology*. And hadn't she first tried to have lunch with the three of *them*, and could they have been any more condescending? Of course, they don't bother to read her scholarship. None of them reads anything she's written. It's all about perception. All they see is Delphine using what she understands they sarcastically call "her little French aura" on all the tenured men. Yet she is strongly tempted to court the cabal, to tell them in so many words that she doesn't *like* the French aura—if she did, she'd be living in France! And she doesn't own the tenured men—she doesn't own anyone. Why else would she be by herself, the only person at the desk of a Barton Hall office at ten o'clock at night? Hardly a week goes by when she doesn't try and fail with the three who drive her nuts, who baffle her most, but whom she cannot charm, finesse, or engage in any way. "*Les Trois Grâces*" she calls them in her letters to Paris, spelling "*grâces*" maliciously "*grasses*." The Three Greaseballs. At certain parties—parties that Delphine doesn't really want to be at—*Les Trois Grasses* are invariably present. When some big feminist intellectual comes along, Delphine would at least like to be invited, but she never is. She can go to the lecture but she's never asked to the dinner. But the infernal trio who call the shots, they are always there.

In imperfect revolt against her Frenchness (as well as being obsessed with her Frenchness), lifted voluntarily out of her country (if not out of herself), so ensnared by the disapproval of *Les Trois Grasses* as to be endlessly calculating what response might gain her their esteem without further obfuscating her sense of herself and misrepresenting totally the inclinations of the woman she once naturally was, at times destabilized to the point of shame by the discrepancy between how she must deal with literature in order to succeed professionally and why she first came to literature, Delphine, to her astonishment, is all but isolated in America. Decountried, isolated, estranged, confused about everything essential to a life, in a desperate state of bewildered longing and surrounded on all sides by admonishing forces defining her as the enemy. And all because she'd gone eagerly in search of an existence of her own. All because she'd been courageous and refused to take the prescribed view of herself. She seemed to herself to have subverted herself in the altogether admirable effort to *make* herself. There is something very mean about life that it should have done this to her. At its heart, very mean and very vengeful, ordering a fate not according to the laws of logic but to the antagonistic whim of perversity. Dare to give yourself over to your own vitality, and you might as well be in the hands of a hardened criminal. I will go to America and be the author of my life, she says; I will construct myself outside the orthodoxy of my family's given, I will fight *against* the given, impassioned subjectivity carried to the limit, individualism at its best—and she winds up instead in a drama beyond her control. She winds up as the author of nothing. There is the drive to master things, and the thing that is mastered is oneself.

Why should it be so impossible just to know what to do?

Delphine would be entirely isolated if not for the department secretary, Margo Luzzi, a mousy divorcée in her thirties, also lonely, wonderfully competent, shy as can be, who will do anything for Delphine and sometimes eats her sandwich in Delphine's office and who has wound up as the chairperson's only adult woman friend at Athena. Then there are the writers in residence. They appear to like in her exactly what the others hate. But she cannot stand *them*. How did she get *in the middle* like this? And how does she get out? As it does not offer any

solace to dramatize her compromises as a Faustian bargain, so
it isn't all that helpful to think of her in-the-middleness, as she
tries to, as a "Kunderian inner exile."

Seeks. All right then, *seeks*. Do as the students say—Go for it!
Youthful, petite, womanly, attractive, academically successful
SWF French-born scholar, Parisian background, Yale Ph.D.,
Mass.-based, seeks . . . ? And now just lay it on the line. Do
not hide from the truth of what you are and do not hide from
the truth of what you seek. A stunning, brilliant, hyperorgas-
mic woman seeks . . . seeks . . . seeks specifically and un-
compromisingly *what*?
    She wrote now in a rush.
    Mature man with backbone. Unattached. Independent. Witty.
Lively. Defiant. Forthright. Well educated. Satirical spirit.
Charm. Knowledge and love of great books. Well spoken and
straight-speaking. Trimly built. Five eight or nine. Mediter-
ranean complexion. Green eyes preferred. Age unimportant.
But must be intellectual. Graying hair acceptable, even desirable . . .
    And then, and only then, did the mythical man being sum-
moned forth in all earnestness on the screen condense into a
portrait of someone she already knew. Abruptly she stopped
writing. The exercise had been undertaken only as an experiment, to try loosening the grip of inhibition just a little before
she renewed her effort to compose an ad not too diluted by
circumspection. Nonetheless, she was astonished by what she'd
come up with, by *whom* she'd come up with, in her distress
wanting nothing more than to delete those forty-odd useless
words as quickly as possible. And thinking, too, of the many
reasons, including her shame, for her to accept defeat as a
blessing and forgo hope of solving her in-the-middleness by
participating in such an impossibly compromising scheme . . .
Thinking that if she had stayed in France she wouldn't need
this ad, wouldn't need an ad for anything, least of all to find a
man . . . Thinking that coming to America was the bravest
thing she had ever done, but that how brave she couldn't have
known at the time. She just did it as the next step of her ambition, and not a crude ambition either, a dignified ambition, the
ambition to be independent, but now she's left with the con-

sequences. Ambition. Adventure. Glamour. The glamour of going to America. The superiority. The superiority of leaving. Left for the pleasure of one day coming home, having done it, of returning home triumphant. Left because I wanted to come home one day and have them say—what is it that I wanted them to say? "She did it. She did that. And if she did that, she can do anything. A girl who weighs a hundred and four pounds, barely five foot two, twenty years old, on her own, went there on her own with a name that didn't mean anything to anybody, and she did it. Self-made. Nobody knew her. Made herself." And who was it that I wanted to have said it? And if they had, what difference would it make? "Our daughter in America . . ." I wanted them to say, to *have* to say, "She made it on her own in America." Because I could not make a French success, a real success, not with my mother and her shadow over everything—the shadow of her accomplishments but, even worse, of her family, the shadow of the Walincourts, named for the place given to them in the thirteenth century by the king Saint Louis and conforming still to the family ideals as they were *set* in the thirteenth century. How Delphine hated all those families, the pure and ancient aristocracy of the provinces, all of them thinking the same, looking the same, sharing the same stifling values and the same stifling religious obedience. However much ambition they have, however much they push their children, they bring their children up to the same litany of charity, selflessness, discipline, faith, and respect—respect not for the individual (*down* with the individual!) but for the traditions of the family. Superior to intelligence, to creativity, to a deep development of oneself apart from them, superior to *everything*, were the traditions of the stupid Walincourts! It was Delphine's mother who embodied those values, who imposed them on the household, who would have enchained her only daughter to those values from birth to the grave had her daughter been without the strength, from adolescence on, to run from her as far as she could. The Walincourt children of Delphine's generation either fell into absolute conformity or rebelled so gruesomely they were incomprehensible, and Delphine's success was to have done neither. From a background few ever even begin to recover from, Delphine had managed a unique escape. By coming to America, to Yale, to

Athena, she had, in fact, *surpassed* her mother, who couldn't herself have dreamed of leaving France—without Delphine's father and his money, Catherine de Walincourt could hardly dream, at twenty-two, of leaving Picardy for Paris. Because if she left Picardy and the fortress of her family, who would she be? What would her *name* mean? I left because I wanted to have an accomplishment that nobody could mistake, that had nothing to do with them, that was my own . . . Thinking that the reason she can't get an American man isn't that she can't get an American man, it's that she can't understand these men and that she will never understand these men, and the reason she can't understand these men is because she is not fluent. With all her pride in her fluency, with all her *fluency*, she is not fluent! I think I understand them, and I do understand; what I don't understand isn't what they say, it's everything they don't say, everything they're *not* saying. Here she operates at fifty percent of her intelligence, and in Paris she understood every nuance. What's the point of being smart here when, because I am not from here, I am de facto dumb . . . Thinking that the only English she really understands—no, the only *American* she understands—is academic American, which is hardly American, which is why she can't make it *in*, will never make it in, which is why there'll never be a man, why this will never be her home, why her intuitions are wrong and always will be, why the cozy intellectual life she had in Paris as a student will never be hers again, why for the rest of her life she is going to understand eleven percent of this country and zero percent of these men . . . Thinking that all her intellectual advantages have been muted by her being *dépaysée* . . . Thinking that she has lost her peripheral vision, that she sees things that are in front of her but nothing out of the corner of her eye, that what she has here is not the vision of a woman of her intelligence but a flat, a totally frontal vision, the vision of an immigrant or a displaced person, a *misplaced* person . . . Thinking, Why did I leave? Because of my mother's shadow? This is why I gave up everything that was mine, everything that was familiar, everything that had made me a subtle being and not this mess of uncertainty that I've become. Everything that I loved I gave up. People do that when their countries are impossible to live in because the fascists have taken charge but not because of their mother's shadow . . . Thinking, Why did I leave, what have I done, this is impossible. My friends, our talk, my city, the men, all the intelligent men. Confident men I could converse with. Mature men who could understand. Stable, passionate, masculine men. Strong, unintimidated men. Men legitimately and unambiguously men . . . Thinking, Why didn't somebody *stop* me, why didn't somebody *say* something to me? Away from home for less than ten years and it feels like two lifetimes already . . . Thinking that she's Catherine de Walincourt Roux's little daughter still, that she has not changed that by one iota . . . Thinking that being French in Athena may have made her exotic to the natives, but it hasn't made her anything more extraordinary to her mother and it never will . . . Thinking, yes, that's why she left, to elude her mother's fixed-forever overshadowing shadow, and that's what blocks her return, and now she's exactly nowhere, in the middle, neither there nor here . . . Thinking that under her exotic Frenchness she is to herself who she always was, that all the exotic Frenchness has achieved in America is to make of her the consummate miserable misunderstood foreigner . . . Thinking that she's worse even than in the middle —that she's in *exile*, in, of all things, a stupid-making, self-imposed anguishing exile from her mother—Delphine neglects to observe that earlier, at the outset, instead of addressing the ad to the *New York Review of Books*, she had automatically addressed it to the recipients of her previous communication, the recipients of most of her communications—to the ten staff members of the Athena Department of Languages and Literature. She neglects first to observe that mistake and then, in her distracted, turbulent, emotionally taxing state, neglects also to observe that instead of hitting the delete button, she is adding one common-enough tiny error to another common-enough tiny error by hitting the send button instead. And so off, irretrievably off goes the ad in quest of a Coleman Silk duplicate or facsimile, and not to the classified section of the *New York Review of Books* but to every member of her department.

It was past 1 A.M. when the phone rang. She had long ago fled her office—run from her office thinking only to get her passport and flee the country—and it was already several hours

after her regular bedtime, when the phone rang with the news.
So anguished was she by the ad's inadvertently going out as
e-mail that she was still awake and roaming her apartment,
tearing at her hair, sneering in the mirror at her face, bending
her head to the kitchen table to weep into her hands, and, as
though startled out of sleep—the sleep of a heretofore meticulously defended adult life—jumping up to cry aloud, "It did
not happen! I did not do it!" But who had? In the past there
seemed always to be people trying their best to trample her
down, to dispose somehow of the nuisance she was to them,
callous people against whom she had learned the hard way to
protect herself. But tonight there was no one to reproach: her
own hand had delivered the ruinous blow.

Frantic, in a frenzy, she tried to figure out some way, any
way, to prevent the worst from happening, but in her state of
incredulous despair she could envision the inevitability of only
the most cataclysmic trajectory: the hours passing, the dawn
breaking, the doors to Barton Hall opening, her departmental
colleagues each entering his or her office, booting up the computer, and finding there, to savor with their morning coffee,
the e-mail ad for a Coleman Silk duplicate that she'd had no
intention of ever sending. To be read once, twice, three times
over by all the members of her department and then to be
e-mailed down the line to every last instructor, professor, ad-
ministrator, office clerk, and student.

Everyone in her classes will read it. Her secretary will read it.
Before the day is out, the president of the college will have
read it, and the college trustees. And even if she were to claim
that the ad had been meant as a joke, nothing more than an
insider's joke, why would the trustees allow the joke's perpetrator to remain at Athena? Especially after her joke is written up
in the student paper, as it will be. And in the local paper. After
it is picked up by the *French* papers.

Her mother! The humiliation for her mother! And her father!
The disappointment to *him*! All the conformist Walincourt
cousins—the pleasure they will take in her defeat! All the ridiculously conservative uncles and the ridiculously pious aunts,
together keeping intact the narrowness of the past—how this
will please them as they sit snobbishly side by side in church!

But suppose she explained that she had merely been experimenting with the ad as a literary form, alone at the office disinterestedly toying with the personal ad as . . . as utilitarian haiku. Won't help. Too ridiculous. *Nothing* will help. Her mother, her father, her brothers, her friends, her teachers. Yale. *Yale!* News of the scandal will reach everyone she's ever known, and the shame will follow her unflaggingly forever. Where can she even run with her passport? Montreal? Martinique? And earn her living how? No, not in the farthest Francophone outpost will she be allowed to teach once they learn of her ad. The pure, prestigious professional life for which she had done all this planning, all this grueling work, the untainted, irreproachable life of the mind . . . She thought to phone Arthur Sussman. Arthur will figure a way out for her. He can pick up the phone and talk to anyone. He's tough, he's shrewd, in the ways of the world the smartest, most influential American she knows. Powerful people like Arthur, however upright, are not boxed in by the need to always be telling the truth. He'll come up with what it takes to explain everything. He'll figure out just what to do. But when she tells him what has happened, why will he think to help her? All he'll think is that she liked Coleman Silk more than she liked him. His vanity will do his thinking for him and lead him to the stupidest conclusion. He'll think what *everyone* will think: that she is pining for Coleman Silk, that she is dreaming not of Arthur Sussman, let alone of The Diapers or The Hats, but of Coleman Silk. Imagining her in love with Coleman Silk, he'll slam down the phone and never speak to her again.

To recapitulate. To go over what's happened. To try to gain sufficient perspective to do the rational thing. She didn't want to send it. She wrote it, yes, but she was embarrassed to send it and didn't want to send it and she *didn't* send it—yet it *went.* The same with the anonymous letter—she didn't want to send it, carried it to New York with no intention of ever sending it, and *it* went. But what's gone off this time is much, much worse. This time she's so desperate that by twenty after one in the morning the rational thing is to telephone Arthur Sussman regardless of what he thinks. Arthur has to help her. He has to tell her what she can do to undo what she's done. And then, at exactly twenty past one, the phone she holds in her hand to dial Arthur Sussman suddenly begins to ring. Arthur calling *her*!

But it is her secretary. "He's dead," Margo says, crying so hard that Delphine can't be quite sure what she's hearing. "Margo—are you all right?" "He's dead!" "Who is?" "I just heard. Delphine. It's terrible. I'm calling you, I have to, I have to call you. I have to tell you something terrible. Oh, Delphine, it's late, I know it's late—" "No! Not Arthur!" Delphine cries. "Dean Silk!" Margo says. "Is dead?" "A terrible crash. It's too horrible." "What crash? Margo, what has happened? Where? Speak slowly. Start again. What are you telling me?" "In the river. With a woman. In his car. A crash." Margo is by now unable to be at all coherent, while Delphine is so stunned that, later, she does not remember putting down the receiver or rushing in tears to her bed or lying there howling his name.

She put down the receiver, and then she spent the worst hours of her life.

Because of the ad they'll think she liked him? They'll think she *loved* him because of the ad? But what would they think if they saw her now, carrying on like the widow herself? She cannot close her eyes, because when she does she sees *his* eyes, those green staring eyes of his, exploding. She sees the car plunge off the road, and his head is shooting forward, and in the instant of the crash, his eyes explode. "No! No!" But when she opens her eyes to stop seeing his eyes, all she sees is what she's done and the mockery that will ensue. She sees her disgrace with her eyes open and his disintegration with her eyes shut, and throughout the night the pendulum of suffering swings her from one to the other.

She wakes up in the same state of upheaval she was in when she went to sleep. She can't remember why she is shaking. She thinks she is shaking from a nightmare. The nightmare of his eyes exploding. But no, it happened, he's dead. And the ad—*it* happened. Everything has happened, and nothing's to be done. I wanted them to say . . . and now they'll say, "Our daughter in America? We don't talk about her. She no longer exists for us." When she tries to compose herself and settle on a plan of action, no thinking is possible: only the derangement is possible, the spiraling obtuseness that is terror. It is just after 5 A.M.

She closes her eyes to try to sleep and make it all go away, but the instant her eyes are shut, there are *his* eyes. They are staring at her and then they explode.

She is dressing. She is screaming. She is walking out her door and it's barely dawn. No makeup. No jewelry. Just her horrified face. Coleman Silk is dead.

When she reaches the campus there's no one there. Only crows. It's so early the flag hasn't yet been raised. Every morning she looks for it atop North Hall, and every morning, upon seeing it, there is the moment of satisfaction. She left home, she dared to do it—she is in America! There is the contentment with her own courage and the knowledge that it hasn't been easy. But the American flag's not there, and she doesn't see that it's not. She sees nothing but what she must do.

She has a key to Barton Hall and she goes in. She gets to her office. She's done that much. She's hanging on. She's thinking now. Okay. But how does she get into their offices to get at their computers? It's what she should have done last night instead of running away in a panic. To regain her self-possession, to rescue her name, to forestall the disaster of ruining her career, she must continue to think. Thinking has been her whole life. What else has she been trained to do from the time she started school? She leaves her office and walks down the corridor. Her aim is clear now, her thinking decisive. She will just go in and delete it. It is her right to delete it—she sent it. And she did not even do that. It was not intentional. She's not responsible. It just went. But when she tries the handle of each of the doors, they are locked. Next she tries working her keys into the locks, first her key to the building, then the key to her office, but neither works. Of course they don't work. They wouldn't have worked last night and they don't work now. As for thinking, were she able to think like Einstein, thinking will not open these doors.

Back in her own office, she unlocks her files. Looking for what? Her c.v. Why look for her c.v.? It is the end of her c.v. It is the end of our daughter in America. And because it is the end, she pulls all the hanging files out of the drawer and hurls them on the floor. Empties the entire drawer. "We have no daughter in America. We have no daughter. We have only sons." Now she does not try to think that she should think. Instead, she begins throwing things. Whatever is piled on her desk, whatever is decorating her walls—what difference does it make what breaks? She tried and she failed. It is the end of the impeccable résumé and of the veneration of the résumé. "Our daughter in America failed."

She is sobbing when she picks up the phone to call Arthur. He will jump out of bed and drive straight from Boston. In less than three hours he'll be in Athena. By nine o'clock Arthur will be here! But the number she dials is the emergency number on the decal pasted to the phone. And she had no more intention of dialing that number than of sending the two letters. All she had was the very human wish to be saved.

She cannot speak.

"Hello?" says the man at the other end. "Hello? Who is this?"

She barely gets it out. The most irreducible two words in any language. One's name. Irreducible and irreplaceable. All that is her. *Was* her. And now the two most ridiculous words in the world.

"Who? Professor who? I can't understand you, Professor."

"Security?"

"Speak louder, Professor. Yes, yes, this is Campus Security."

"Come here," she says pleadingly, and once again she is in tears. "Right away. Something terrible has happened."

"Professor? Where are you? Professor, what's happened?"

"Barton." She says it again so he can understand. "Barton 121," she tells him. "Professor Roux."

"What is it, Professor?"

"Something terrible."

"Are you all right? What's wrong? What is it? Is somebody there?"

"*I'm* here."

"Is everything all right?"

"Someone broke in."

"Broke in where?"

"My office."

"When? Professor, when?"

"I don't know. In the night. I don't know."

"You okay? Professor? Professor Roux? Are you there? Barton Hall? You sure?"

The hesitation. Trying to think. Am I sure? Am I? "Absolutely," she says, sobbing uncontrollably now. "Hurry, please! Get here immediately, *please!* Someone broke into my office! It's a shambles! It's awful! It's horrible! My things! Someone broke into my computer! Hurry!"

"A break-in? Do you know who it was? Do you know *who* broke in? Was it a student?"

"Dean Silk broke in," she said. "Hurry!"

"Professor—Professor, are you there? Professor Roux, Dean Silk is dead."

"I've heard," she said, "I know, it's awful," and then she screamed, screamed at the horror of all that had happened, screamed at the thought of the very last thing he had ever done, and to her, to *her*—and after that, Delphine's day was a circus.

The astonishing news of Dean Silk's death in a car crash with an Athena college janitor had barely reached the last of the college's classrooms when word began to spread of the pillaging of Delphine Roux's office and the e-mail hoax Dean Silk had attempted to perpetrate only hours before the fatal crash. People were having trouble enough believing all of *this*, when another story, one about the circumstances of the crash, spread from town up to the college, further confounding just about everybody. For all its atrocious details, the story was said to have originated with a reliable source: the brother of the state trooper who had found the bodies. According to his story, the reason the dean lost control of his car was because, from the passenger seat beside him, the Athena woman janitor was satisfying him while he drove. This the police were able to infer from the disposition of his clothing and the position of her body and its location in the vehicle when the wreckage was discovered and pulled from the river.

Most of the faculty, particularly older professors who had known Coleman Silk personally for many years, refused at first to believe this story, and were outraged by the gullibility with which it was being embraced as incontrovertible truth— the cruelty of the insult appalled them. Yet as the day progressed and additional facts emerged about the break-in, and still more came out about Silk's affair with the janitor—reports from numerous people who had seen them sneaking around together—it became increasingly difficult for the elders of the faculty "to remain"—as the local paper noted the next day in its human interest feature—"heartbreakingly in denial."

And when people began to remember how, a couple of years earlier, no one had wanted to believe that he had called two of his black students spooks; when they remembered how after resigning in disgrace he had isolated himself from his former colleagues, how on the rare occasions when he was seen in town he was abrupt to the point of rudeness with whoever happened to run into him; when they remembered that in his vociferous loathing of everything and everyone having to do with Athena he was said to have managed to estrange himself from his own children . . . well, even those who had begun the day dismissing any suggestion that Coleman Silk's life could have come to so hideous a conclusion, the old-timers who found it unendurable to think of a man of his intellectual stature, a charismatic teacher, a dynamic and influential dean, a charming, vigorous man still hale and hearty in his seventies and the father of four grown, wonderful kids, as forsaking everything he'd once valued and sliding so precipitously into the scandalous death of an alienated, bizarre outsider—even those people had to face up to the thoroughgoing transformation that had followed upon the spooks incident and that had not only brought Coleman Silk to his mortifying end but led as well—led inexcusably—to the gruesome death of Faunia Farley, the hapless thirty-four-year-old illiterate whom, as everyone now knew, he had taken in old age as his mistress.

5

The Purifying Ritual

Two funerals.

Faunia's first, up at the cemetery on Battle Mountain, always for me an unnerving place to drive by, creepy even in daylight, with its mysteries of ancient gravestone stillness and motionless time, and rendered all the more ominous by the state forest preserve that abuts what was originally an Indian burial ground—a vast, densely wooded, boulder-strewn wilderness veined with streams glassily cascading from ledge to ledge and inhabited by coyote, bobcat, even black bear, and by foraging deer herds said to abound in huge, precolonial numbers. The women from the dairy farm had purchased Faunia's plot at the very edge of the dark woods and organized the innocent, empty graveside ceremony. The more outgoing of the two, the one who identified herself as Sally, delivered the first of the eulogies, introducing her farming partner and their children, then saying, "We all lived with Faunia up at the farm, and why we're here this morning is why you're here: to celebrate a life."

She spoke in a bright, ringing voice, a smallish, hearty, round-faced woman in a long sack dress, buoyantly determined to keep to a perspective that would cause the least chagrin among the six farm-reared children, each neatly dressed in his or her best clothes, each holding a fistful of flowers to be strewn on the coffin before it was lowered into the ground.

"Which of us," Sally asked, "will ever forget that big, warm laugh of hers? Faunia could have us in stitches as much from the infectiousness of her laugh as from some of the things she could come out with. And she was also, as you know, a deeply spiritual person. A spiritual person," she repeated, "a spiritual seeker—the word to best describe her beliefs is pantheism. Her God was nature, and her worship of nature extended to her love for our little herd of cows, for all cows, really, for that most benevolent of creatures who is the foster mother of the human race. Faunia had an enormous respect for the institution of the family dairy farm. Along with Peg and me and the children, she helped to try to keep the family dairy farm alive in New England as a viable part of our cultural heritage. Her God was everything you see around you at our farm and everything you see around you on Battle Mountain. We chose this resting place for Faunia because it has been sacred ever since the aboriginal peoples bid farewell to their loved ones here. The wonderful stories that Faunia told our kids—about the swallows in the barn and the crows in the fields, about the red-tailed hawks that glide in the sky high above our fields—they were the same kind of stories you might have heard on this very mountaintop before the ecological balance of the Berkshires was first disturbed by the coming of . . .”

The coming of you-know-who. The environmentalist Rousseauism of the rest of the eulogy made it just about impossible for me to stay focused.

The second eulogist was Smoky Hollenbeck, the former Athena athletic star who was supervisor of the physical plant, Faunia’s boss, and—as I knew from Coleman, who’d hired him—was for a time a bit more. It was into Smoky’s Athena harem that Faunia had been conscripted practically from her first day on his custodial staff, and it was from his harem that she had been abruptly dismissed once Les Farley had somehow ferreted out what Smoky was up to with her.

Smoky didn’t speak, like Sally, of Faunia’s pantheistic purity as a natural being; in his capacity as representative of the college, he concentrated on her competence as a housekeeper, beginning with her influence on the undergraduates whose dormitories she cleaned.

“What changed about the students with Faunia being there,” Smoky said, “was that they had a person who, whenever they saw her, greeted them with a smile and a hello and a How are you, and Did you get over your cold, and How are classes going. She would always spend a moment talking and becoming familiar with the students before she began her work. Over time, she was no longer invisible to the students, no longer just a housekeeper, but another person whom they’d developed respect for. They were always more cognizant, as a result of knowing Faunia, of not leaving a mess behind for her to have to pick up. In contrast to that, you may have another housekeeper who never makes eye contact, really keeps a distance from the students, really doesn't care about what the students are doing or want to know what they're doing. Well, that was not Faunia —never. The condition of the student dormitories, I find, is directly related to the relationship of the students and their housekeeper. The number of broken windows that we have to fix, the number of holes in the walls that we have to repair, that are made when students kick 'em, punch 'em, take their frustration out on them . . . whatever the case may be. Graffiti on walls. The full gamut. Well, if it was Faunia's building, you had none of this. You had instead a building that was conducive to good productivity, to learning and living and to feeling a part of the Athena community . . ."

Extremely brilliant performance by this tall, curly-haired, handsome young family man who had been Coleman's predecessor as Faunia's lover. Sensual contact with Smoky's perfect custodial worker was no more imaginable, from what he was telling us, than with Sally's storytelling pantheist. "In the mornings," Smoky said, "she took care of North Hall and the administrative offices there. Though her routine changed slightly from day to day, there were some basic things to be done every single morning, and she did them excellently. Wastepaper baskets were emptied, the rest rooms, of which there are three in that building, were tidied up and cleaned. Damp mopping occurred wherever it was necessary. Vacuuming in high-traffic areas every day, in not-so-high-traffic areas once a week. Dusting usually on a weekly basis. The windows in the front and back door sash were cleaned by Faunia almost on a daily basis, depending on the traffic. Faunia was always very proficient, and she paid a lot of attention to details. There are certain times you can run a vacuum cleaner and there's other times you can't—and there was never once, not once, a complaint on that score about Faunia Farley. Very quickly she figured out the best time for each task to be done with the minimum inconvenience to the work force."

Of the fourteen people, aside from the children, that I counted around the grave, the college contingent appeared to consist only of Smoky and a cluster of Faunia's coworkers, four men from maintenance who were dressed in coats and ties and who stood silently listening to the praise for her work. From what I could make out, the remaining mourners were either friends of Peg and Sally or local people who bought their milk up at the farm and who'd come to know Faunia through visiting there. Cyril Foster, our postmaster and chief of the volunteer fire department, was the only local person I recognized. Cyril knew Faunia from the little village post office where she came twice a week to clean up and where Coleman first saw her.

And there was Faunia's father, a large, elderly man whose presence had been acknowledged by Sally in her eulogy. He was seated in a wheelchair only feet from the coffin, attended by a youngish woman, a Filipino nurse or companion, who stood directly behind him and whose face remained expressionless throughout the service, though he could be seen lowering his forehead into his hands and intermittently succumbing to tears.

There was no one there whom I could identify as the person responsible for the on-line eulogy for Faunia that I'd found the evening before, posted on the Athena fac.discuss news group. The posting was headed:

    From: clytemnestra@houseofatreus.com
    To: fac.discuss
    Subject: death of a faunia
    Date: Thur 12 Nov 1998

I'd come upon it accidentally when, out of curiosity, I was checking the fac.discuss calendar to see if Dean Silk's funeral might show up under coming events. Why this scurrilous posting? Intended as a gag, as a lark? Did it signify no more (or less) than the perverse indulgence of a sadistic whim, or was it a calculated act of treachery? Could it have been posted by Delphine Roux? Another of her unascribable indictments? I didn't think so. There was nothing to be gained by her going any further with her ingenuity than the break-in story, and much to be lost if "clytemnestra@houseofatreus.com" were somehow discovered to be her brainchild. Besides, from the evidence at hand, there was nothing so crafty or contrived about a typical Delphinian intrigue—hers smacked of hasty improvisation, of hysterical pettiness, of the overexcited unthinking of the amateur that produces the kind of wacky act that seems improbable afterward even to its perpetrator: the counterattack that lacks both provocation and the refined calculation of the acidic master, however nasty its consequences may be.

No, this was mischief, more than likely, *prompted* by Delphine's mischief, but more artful, more confident, more professionally demonic by far—a major upgrade of the venom. And what would *it* now inspire? Where would this public stoning stop? Where would this gullibility stop? How can these people be repeating to one another this story told to Security by Delphine Roux—so transparently phony, so obviously a lie, how can any of them believe this thing? And how can any connection to Coleman be proved? It can't be. But they believe it anyway. Screwy as it is—that he broke in there, that he broke open the files, that he broke into her computer, e-mailed her colleagues—they believe it, they want to believe it, they can't wait to repeat it. A story that makes no sense, that is implausible, and yet nobody—certainly not publicly—raises the simplest questions. Why would the man tear apart her office and call attention to the fact that he'd broken in if he wanted to perpetrate a hoax? Why would he compose that particular ad when ninety percent of the people who saw it couldn't possibly think of it as having anything to do with him? Who, other than Delphine Roux, would read that ad and think of him? To do what she claimed he'd done, he would have had to be crazy. But where is the evidence that he was crazy? Where is the history of crazy behavior? Coleman Silk, who single-handedly turned this college around—that man is crazy? Embittered, angry, isolated, yes—but crazy? People in Athena know perfectly well that this is not the case and yet, as in the spooks incident, they willingly act as if they don't. Simply to make the accusation is to prove it. To hear the allegation is to believe it. No motive for the perpetrator is necessary, no logic or rationale is required. Only a label is required. The label is the motive. The label is the evidence. The label is the logic. Why did Coleman Silk do this? Because he is an *x*, because he is a *y*, because he is both. First a racist and now a misogynist. It is too late in the century to call him a Communist, though that is the way it used to be done. A misogynistic act committed by a man who already proved himself capable of a vicious racist comment at the expense of a vulnerable student. That explains everything. That and the craziness.

The Devil of the Little Place—the gossip, the jealousy, the acrimony, the boredom, the lies. No, the provincial poisons do not help. People are bored here, they are envious, their life is as it is and as it will be, and so, without seriously questioning the story, they repeat it—on the phone, in the street, in the cafeteria, in the classroom. They repeat it at home to their husbands and wives. It isn't just that because of the accident there isn't time to prove it's a ridiculous lie—if it weren't for the accident, she wouldn't have been able to tell the lie in the first place. But his death is her good fortune. His death is her salvation. Death intervenes to simplify everything. Every doubt, every misgiving, every uncertainty is swept aside by the greatest belittler of them all, which is death.

Walking alone to my car after Faunia's funeral, I still had no way of knowing who at the college might have had the turn of mind to conjure up the clytemnestra posting—the most diabolical of art forms, the on-line art form, because of its anonymity —nor could I have any idea of what somebody, anybody, might next come up with to disseminate anonymously. All I knew for sure was that the germs of malice were unleashed, and where Coleman's conduct was concerned, there was no absurdity out of which someone wasn't going to try to make indignant sense. An epidemic had broken out in Athena—that's how my thinking went in the immediate aftermath of his death—and what was to contain the epidemic's spreading? It was there. The pathogens were out there. In the ether. In the universal hard drive, everlasting and undeletable, the sign of the viciousness of the human creature.

Everybody was writing *Spooks* now—everybody, as yet, except me.

I am going to ask you to think [the fac.discuss posting began] about things that are not pleasant to think about. Not just about the violent death of an innocent woman of thirty-four, which is awful enough, but of the circumstances particular to the horror and of the man who, almost artistically, contrived those circumstances to complete his cycle of revenge against Athena College and his former colleagues.

Some of you may know that in the hours before Coleman Silk staged this murder-suicide—for that is what this man enacted on the highway by driving off the road and through the guardrail and into the river that night—he had forcefully broken into a faculty office in Barton Hall, ransacked the papers, and sent out as e-mail a communication written purportedly by a faculty member and designed to jeopardize her position. The harm he did to her and to the college was negligible. But informing that childishly spiteful act of burglary and forgery was the same resolve, the same animus, which later in the evening—having been monstrously intensified—inspired him simultaneously to kill himself while murdering in cold blood a college custodial worker whom he had cynically enticed, some months earlier, to service him sexually.

Imagine, if you will, the plight of this woman, a runaway at the age of fourteen, whose education had ended in the second year of high school and who, for the rest of her brief life, was functionally illiterate. Imagine her contending with the wiles of a retired university professor who, in his sixteen years as the most autocratic of faculty deans, wielded more power at Athena than the president of the college. What chance did she have to resist his superior force? And having yielded to him, having found herself enslaved by a perverse manly strength far exceeding her own, what chance could she possibly have had to fathom the vengeful purposes for which her hard-worked body was to be utilized by him, first in life and then in death?

Of all the ruthless men by whom she was successively tyrannized, of all the violent, reckless, ruthless, insatiable men who had tormented, battered, and broken her, there was none whose purpose could have been so twisted by the enmity of the unforgiving as the man who had a score to settle with Athena College and so took one of the college's own upon whom to wreak his vengeance, and in the most palpable manner he could devise. On her flesh. On her limbs. On her genitals. On her womb. The violating abortion into which she was forced by him earlier this year—and which precipitated her attempt at suicide—is only one of who knows how many assaults perpetrated upon the ravaged terrain of her physical being. We know by now of the awful tableau at the murder scene, of the pornographic posture in which he had arranged for Faunia to meet her death, the better to register, in a single, indelible image, her bondage, her subservience (by extension, the bondage and subservience of the college community) to his enraged contempt. We know—we are beginning to know, as the horrifying facts trickle out from the police investigation—that not all the bruise marks on Faunia's mangled body resulted from damage inflicted in the fatal accident, cataclysmic as that was. There were patches of discoloration discovered by the coroner on her buttocks and thighs that had nothing to do with the impact of the crash, contusions that had been administered, some time before the accident, by very different means: either by a blunt instrument or a human fist.

Why? A word so small, and yet large enough to drive us insane. But then a mind as pathologically sinister as Faunia's murderer's is not easy to probe. At the root of the cravings that drove this man, there is an impenetrable darkness that those who are not violent by nature or vengeful by design—those who have made their peace with the restraints imposed by civilization on what is raw and untrammeled in us all—can never know. The heart of human darkness is inexplicable. But that their car accident was no accident, that I do know, as sure as I know that I am united in grief with all who mourn the death of Athena's Faunia Farley, whose oppression began in the earliest days of her innocence and lasted to the instant of her death. That accident was no accident: it was what Coleman Silk yearned to do with all his might. Why? This "why" I can answer and I will answer. So as to annihilate not only the two of them, but, with them, all trace of his history as her ultimate tormentor. It was to prevent Faunia from exposing him for what he was that Coleman Silk took her with him to the bottom of the river.

One is left to imagine just how heinous were the crimes that he was determined to hide.

The next day Coleman was buried beside his wife in the orderly garden of a cemetery across from the level green sea of the college athletic fields, at the foot of the oak grove behind North Hall and its landmark hexagonal clock tower. I couldn't sleep the night before, and when I got up that morning, I was still so agitated over how the accident and its meaning was being systematically distorted and broadcast to the world that I was unable to sit quietly long enough even to drink my coffee. How can one possibly roll back all these lies? Even if you demonstrate something's a lie, in a place like Athena, once it's out there, it stays. Instead of pacing restlessly around the house until it was time to head for the cemetery, I dressed in a tie and jacket and went down to Town Street to hang around there—down to where I could nurse the illusion that there was something to be done with my disgust.

And with my shock. I was not prepared to think of him as dead, let alone to see him buried. Everything else aside, the death in a freak accident of a strong, healthy man already into his seventies had its own awful poignancy—there would at least have been a higher degree of rationality had he been carried off by a heart attack or cancer or a stroke. What's more, I was convinced by then—I was convinced as soon as I heard the news—that it was impossible for the accident to have occurred without the presence somewhere nearby of Les Farley and his pickup truck. Of course nothing that befalls anyone is ever too senseless to have happened, and yet with Les Farley in the picture, with Farley as primary *cause*, wasn't there more than just the wisp of an explanation for the violent extinction, in a single convenient catastrophe, of Farley's despised ex-wife and the enraging lover whom Farley had obsessively staked out?

To me, reaching this conclusion didn't seem at all motivated by a disinclination to accept the inexplicable for what it is—though it seemed precisely that to the state police the morning after Coleman's funeral, when I went to talk to the two officers who'd been first at the scene of the accident and who'd found the bodies. Their examination of the crash vehicle revealed nothing that could corroborate in any way the scenario I was imagining. The information I gave them—about Farley's stalking of Faunia, about his spying on Coleman, about the near-violent confrontation, just beyond the kitchen door, when Farley came roaring at the two of them out of the dark—was all patiently taken down, as were my name, address, and telephone number. I was then thanked for my cooperation, assured that everything would be held in strictest confidence, and told that if it seemed warranted they would be back in touch with me.

They never were.

On the way out, I turned and said, "Can I ask one question? Can I ask about the disposition of the bodies in the car?"

"What do you want to know, sir?" said Officer Balich, the

senior of the two young men, a poker-faced, quietly officious
fellow whose Croatian family, I remembered, used to own the
Madamaska Inn.

"What exactly did you find when you found them? Their
placement. Their posture. The rumor in Athena—"

"No, sir," Balich said, shaking his head, "that was not the
case. None of that's true, sir."

"You know what I'm referring to?"

"I do, sir. This was clearly a case of speeding. You can't take
that curve at that speed. Jeff Gordon couldn't have taken that
curve at that speed. For an old guy with a couple glasses of
wine playing tricks on his brain to drive round that bend like a
hot-rodder—"

"I don't think Coleman Silk ever in his life drove like a hot-
rodder, Officer."

"Well . . . ," Balich said, and put his hands up in the air,
the palms to me, suggesting that, with all due respect, neither
he nor I could possibly know that. "It was the professor who
was behind the wheel, sir."

The moment had arrived when I was expected by Officer
Balich not to insert myself foolishly as an amateur detective,
not to press my contention further, but politely to take my
leave. He had called me sir more than enough times for me to
have no hallucinations about who was running the show, and
so I did leave, and, as I say, that was the end of it.

The day Coleman was to be buried was another unseason-
ably warm, crisply lit November day. With the last of the leaves
having fallen from the trees during the previous week, the hard
bedrock contour of the mountain landscape was now nakedly
exposed by the sunlight, its joints and striations etched in
the fine hatched lines of an old engraving, and as I headed to
Athena for the funeral that morning, a sense of reemergence,
of renewed possibility, was inappropriately aroused in me by the
illuminated roughness of a distant view obscured by foliage since
last spring. The no-nonsense organization of the earth's surface, to be admired and deferred to now for the first time in
months, was a reminder of the terrific abrasive force of the
glacier onslaught that had scoured these mountains on the far
edge of its booming southward slide. Passing just miles from
Coleman's house, it had spat out boulders the size of restaurant

refrigerators the way an automatic pitching machine throws fastball strikes, and when I passed the steep wooded slope that is known locally as "the rock garden" and saw, starkly, undappled by the summer leaves and their gliding shadows, those mammoth rocks all tumbled sideways like a ravaged Stonehenge, crushed together and yet hugely intact, I was once again horrified by the thought of the moment of impact that had separated Coleman and Faunia from their lives in time and catapulted them into the earth's past. They were now as remote as the glaciers. As the creation of the planet. As creation itself.

This was when I decided to go to the state police. That I didn't get out there that day, that very morning, even before the funeral, was in part because, while parking my car across from the green in town, I saw in the window of Pauline's Place, eating his breakfast, Faunia's father—saw him seated at a table with the woman who'd been steering his wheelchair up at the mountain cemetery the day before. I immediately went inside, took the empty table beside theirs, ordered, and, while pretending to read the *Madamaska Weekly Gazette* that someone had left by my chair, caught all I could of their conversation.

They were talking about a diary. Among the things of hers that Sally and Peg had turned over to Faunia's father, there had been Faunia's diary.

"You don't want to read it, Harry. You just don't want to."

"I have to," he said.

"You don't have to," the woman said. "Believe me you don't."

"It can't be more awful than everything else."

"You don't want to read it."

Most people inflate themselves and lie about accomplishments they have only dreamed of achieving; Faunia had lied about failing to reach proficiency at a skill so fundamental that, in a matter of a year or two, it is acquired at least crudely by nearly every schoolchild in the world.

And this I learned before even finishing my juice. The illiteracy had been an act, something she decided her situation demanded. But why? A source of power? Her one and only source of power? But a power purchased at what price? Think about it. Afflicts herself with illiteracy too. Takes it on voluntarily. Not to infantilize herself, however, not to present herself as a dependent kid, but just the opposite: to spotlight the barbaric self befitting the world. Not rejecting learning as a stifling form of propriety but trumping learning by a knowledge that is stronger and prior. She has nothing against reading per se—it's that pretending not to be able to feels right to her. It spices things up. She just cannot get enough of the toxins: of all that you're not supposed to be, to show, to say, to think but that you are and show and say and think whether you like it or not.

"I can't burn it," Faunia's father said. "It's hers. I can't just throw it in the trash."

"Well, I can," the woman said.

"It's not right."

"You have been walking through this mine field all your life. You don't need more."

"It's all that's left of her."

"There's the revolver. That's left of her. There's the bullets, Harry. She left that."

"The way she lived," he said, sounding suddenly at the edge of tears.

"The way she lived is the way she died. It's why she died."

"You've got to give me the diary," he said.

"No. It's bad enough we even came here."

"Destroy it, destroy it, and I just don't know what."

"I'm only doing what is best for you."

"What does she say?"

"It doesn't bear repeating."

"Oh, God," he said.

"Eat. You have to eat something. Those pancakes look good."

"My daughter," he said.

"You did all you could."

"I should have taken her away when she was six years old."

"You didn't know. How could you know what was going to be?"

"I should never have left her with that woman."

"And we should never have come up here," his companion said. "All you have to do now is get sick up here. Then the thing will be complete."

"I want the ashes."

"They should have buried the ashes. In there. With her. I don't know why they didn't."

"I want the ashes, Syl. Those are my grandkids. That's all I've got left to show for everything."

"I've taken care of the ashes."

"No!"

"You didn't need those ashes. You've been through enough. I will not have something happening to you. Those ashes are not coming on the plane."

"What did you *do?*"

"I took care of them," she said. "I was respectful. But they're gone."

"Oh, my God."

"That's over," she told him. "It's all over. You did your duty. You did more than your duty. You don't need any more. Now let's you eat something. I packed the room up. I paid. Now there's just getting you home."

"Oh, you are the best, Sylvia, the very best."

"I don't want you hurt anymore. I will not let them hurt you."

"You are the best."

"Try and eat. Those look real good."

"Want some?"

"No," she said, "I want *you* to eat."

"I can't eat it all."

"Use the syrup. Here, I'll do it, I'll pour it."

I waited for them outside, on the green, and then when I saw the wheelchair coming through the restaurant door, I crossed the street and, as she was wheeling him away from Pauline's Place, I introduced myself, walking alongside him as I spoke. "I live here. I knew your daughter. Only slightly, but I met her several times. I was at the funeral yesterday. I saw you there. I want to express my condolences."

He was a large man with a large frame, much larger than he'd seemed slumped over in the chair at the funeral. He was probably well over six feet, but with the look on his stern, strongly boned face (Faunia's inexpressive face, hers exactly— the thin lips, the steep chin, the sharp aquiline nose, the same blue, deep-set eyes, and above them, framing the pale lashes, that same puff of flesh, that same fullness that had struck me out at the dairy farm as her one exotic marking, her face's only emblem of allure)—with the look of a man sentenced not just to imprisonment in that chair but condemned to some even greater anguish for the rest of his days. Big as he was, or once had been, there was nothing left of him but his fear. I saw that fear at the back of his gaze the instant he looked up to thank me. "You're very kind," he said.

He was probably about my age, but there was evidence of a privileged New England childhood in his speech that dated back to long before either of us was born. I'd recognized it earlier in the restaurant—tethered, by that speech alone, by the patterns of moneyed, quasi-Anglified speech, to the decorous conventions of an entirely other America.

"Are you Faunia's stepmother?" That seemed as good a way as any to get her attention—and to get her perhaps to slow down. I assumed they were on their way back to the College Arms, around the corner from the green.

"This is Sylvia," he said.

"I wonder if you could stop," I said to Sylvia, "so I could talk to him."

"We're catching a plane," she told me.

Since she was so clearly determined to rid him of me then and there, I said—while still keeping pace with the wheelchair —"Coleman Silk was my friend. He did not drive his car off the road. He couldn't have. Not like that. His car was forced off the road. I know who is responsible for the death of your daughter. It wasn't Coleman Silk."

"Stop pushing me. Sylvia, stop pushing a minute."

"No," she said. "This is insane. This is enough."

"It was her ex-husband," I said to him. "It was Farley."

"No," he said weakly, as though I'd shot him. "No—no."

"Sir!" She had stopped, all right, but the hand that wasn't holding tight to the wheelchair had reached up to take me by the lapel. She was short and slight, a young Filipino woman with a small, implacable, pale brown face, and I could see from the dark determination of her fearless eyes that the disorder of human affairs was not allowed to intrude anywhere near what was hers to protect.

"Can't you stop for one moment?" I asked her. "Can't we go over to the green and sit there and talk?"

"The man is not well. You are taxing the strength of a man who is seriously ill."

"But you have a diary belonging to Faunia."

"We do not."

"You have a revolver belonging to Faunia."

"Sir, go away. Sir, leave him alone, I am warning you!" And here she pushed at me—with the hand that had been holding my jacket, she shoved me away.

"She got that gun," I said, "to protect herself against Farley."

Sharply, she replied, "The poor thing."

I didn't know what to do then except to follow them around the corner until they reached the porch of the inn. Faunia's father was weeping openly now.

When she turned to find me still there, she said, "You have done enough damage. Go or I will call the police." There was great ferocity in this tiny person. I understood it: keeping him alive appeared to require no less.

"Don't destroy that diary," I said to her. "There is a record there—"

"Filth! There is a record there of filth!"

"Syl, *Sylvia*—"

"All of them, her, the brother, the mother, the stepfather—the whole bunch of them, trampling on this man his whole life. They have robbed him. They have deceived him. They have humiliated him. His daughter was a criminal. Got pregnant and had a child at sixteen—a child she abandoned to an orphan asylum. A child her father would have raised. She was a common whore. Guns and men and drugs and filth and sex. The money he gave her—what did she do with that money?"

"I don't know. I don't know anything about an orphan asylum. I don't know anything about any money."

"Drugs! She stole it for drugs!"

"I don't know anything about that."

"That whole family—filth! Have some pity, *please!*"

I turned to him. "I want the person responsible for these deaths to be held legally accountable. Coleman Silk did her no harm. He did not kill her. I ask to talk to you for only a minute."

"Let him, Sylvia—"

"*No!* No more letting anyone! You have let them long enough!"

People were collected now on the porch of the inn watching us, and others were watching from the upper windows. Perhaps they were the last of the leafers, out to catch the little left of the autumn blaze. Perhaps they were Athena alumni. There were always a handful visiting the town, middle-aged and elderly graduates checking to see what had disappeared and what remained, thinking the best, the very best, of every last thing that had ever befallen them on these streets in nineteen hundred and whatever. Perhaps they were visitors in town to look at the restored colonial houses, a stretch of them running nearly a mile down both sides of Ward Street and considered by the Athena Historical Society to be, if not so grand as those in Salem, as important as any in the state west of the House of the Seven Gables. These people had not come to sleep in the carefully decorated period bedrooms of the College Arms so as to awaken to a shouting match beneath their windows. In a place as picturesque as South Ward Street and on a day as fine as this, the eruption of such a struggle—a crippled man crying, a tiny Asian woman shouting, a man who, from his appearance, might well have been a college professor seemingly terrifying both of them with what he was saying—was bound to seem both more stupendous and more disgusting than it would have at a big city intersection.

"If I could see the diary—"

"*There is no diary,*" she said, and there was nothing more to be done than to watch her push him up the ramp beside the stairway and through the main door and into the inn.

Back around at Pauline's, I ordered a cup of coffee and, on writing paper the waitress found for me in a drawer beneath the cash register, I wrote this letter:

> I am the man who approached you near the restaurant on Town Street in Athena on the morning after Faunia's funeral. I live on a rural road outside Athena, a few miles from the home of the late Coleman Silk, who, as I explained, was my friend. Through Coleman I met your daughter several times. I sometimes heard him speak about her. Their affair was passionate, but there was no cruelty in it. He mainly played the part of lover with her, but he also knew how to be a friend and a teacher. If she asked for care, I can't believe it was ever withheld. Whatever of Coleman's spirit she may have absorbed could never, never have poisoned her life.

I don't know how much of the malicious gossip surrounding them and the crash you heard in Athena. I hope none. There is, however, a matter of justice to be settled which dwarfs all that stupidity. Two people have been murdered. I know who murdered them. I did not witness the murder but I know it took place. I am absolutely sure of it. But evidence is necessary if I am to be taken seriously by the police or by an attorney. If you possess anything that reveals Faunia's state of mind in recent months or even extending back to her marriage to Farley, I ask you not to destroy it. I am thinking of letters you may have received from her over the years as well as the belongings found in her room after her death that were passed on to you by Sally and Peg.

My telephone number and address are as follows—

That was as far as I got. I intended to wait until they were gone, to phone the College Arms to extract from the desk clerk, with some story or other, the man's name and address, and to send off my letter by overnight mail. I'd go to Sally and Peg for the address if I couldn't get it from the inn. But I would, in fact, do neither the one thing nor the other. Whatever Faunia had left behind in her room had already been discarded or destroyed by Sylvia—the same way my letter would be destroyed when it arrived at its destination. This tiny being whose whole purpose was to keep the past from tormenting him further was never going to allow inside the walls of his home what she would not permit when she'd found herself up against me face to face. Moreover, her course was one that I couldn't dispute. If suffering was passed around in that family like a disease, there was nothing to do but post a sign of the kind they used to hang in the doorways of the contagiously ill when I was a kid, a sign that read QUARANTINE or that presented to the eyes of the uninfected nothing more than a big black capital Q. Little Sylvia was that ominous Q, and there was no way that I was going to get past it.

I tore up what I'd written and walked across town to the funeral.

The service for Coleman had been arranged by his children, and the four of them were there at the door to Rishanger Chapel to greet the mourners as they filed in. The idea to bury him out of Rishanger, the college chapel, was a family decision, the key component of what I realized was a well-planned coup, an attempt to undo their father's self-imposed banishment and to integrate him, in death if not in life, back into the community where he had made his distinguished career.

When I introduced myself, I was instantly taken aside by Lisa, Coleman's daughter, who put her arms around me and in a tearful, whispering voice said, "You were his friend. You were the one friend he had left. You probably saw him last."

"We were friends for a while," I said, but explained nothing about having seen him last several months back, on that August Saturday morning at Tanglewood, and that by then he had deliberately let the brief friendship lapse.

"We lost him," she said.

"I know."

"We lost him," she repeated, and then she cried without attempting to speak.

After a while I said, "I enjoyed him and I admired him. I wish I could have known him longer."

"Why did this happen?"

"I don't know."

"Did he go mad? Was he insane?"

"Absolutely not. No."

"Then how could all this happen?"

When I didn't answer (and how could I, other than by beginning to write this book?), her arms dropped slowly away from me, and while we stood together for a few seconds more, I saw how strong was her resemblance to her father—strong as Faunia's to *her* father. There were the same carved puppetlike features, the same green eyes, the same tawny skin, even a less broad-shouldered version of Coleman's slight athletic build. The visible genetic legacy of the mother, Iris Silk, seemed to reside solely in Lisa's prodigious tangle of dark bushy hair. In photograph after photograph of Iris—photographs I'd seen in family albums Coleman had showed me—the facial features hardly seemed to matter, so strongly did her importance as a person, if not her entire meaning, appear to be concentrated in that assertive, theatrical endowment of hair. With Lisa, the hair appeared to stand more in contrast to her character than—as with her mother—to be issuing from it.

I had the definite impression, in just our few moments together, that the link, now broken, between Lisa and her father would not be gone from her mind for a single day throughout the remainder of her life. One way or another, the idea of him would be fused to every last thing she would ever think about or do or fail to do. The consequences of having loved him so fully as a beloved girl-child, and of having been estranged from him at the time of his death, would never let this woman be.

The three Silk men—Lisa's twin brother, Mark, and the two eldest, Jeffrey and Michael—were not so emotional in greeting me. I saw nothing of Mark's angry intensity as an affronted son, and when, an hour or so later, his sober demeanor gave way at the graveside, it was with the severity of one bereft beyond redemption. Jeff and Michael were obviously the sturdiest Silk children, and in them you clearly saw the physical imprint of the robust mother: if not her hair (both men were by now bald), her height, her solid core of confidence, her open-hearted authority. These were not people who muddled through. That was apparent in just the greeting they extended and the few words they said. When you met Jeff and Michael, especially if they were standing side by side, you'd met your match. Back before I got to know Coleman—back in his heyday, before he began to spin out of control within the ever-narrowing prison of his rage, before the achievements that once particularized him, that *were* him, vanished from his life—you would surely have met your match in him too, which probably explains why a general willingness to compromise the dean was so quick to materialize once he was accused of uttering aloud something racially vicious.

Despite all the rumors circulating in town, the turnout for Coleman far exceeded what I'd been imagining it would be; it certainly exceeded what Coleman could have imagined. The first six or seven rows of pews were already full, and people were still streaming in behind me when I found an empty place midway up from the altar beside someone whom I recognized —from having seen him for the first time the day before—to be Smoky Hollenbeck. Did Smoky understand how close he might have come, only a year earlier, to having a funeral service of his own held here in Rishanger Chapel? Maybe he was attending the service more in gratitude for his own good luck than out of regard for the man who'd been his erotic successor.

On Smoky's other side was a woman I took to be his wife, a pretty blonde of about forty and, if I remembered correctly, an Athena classmate Smoky had married back in the seventies and the mother now of their five children. The Hollenbecks were among the youngest people, aside from Coleman's family, whom I saw in the chapel when I began to look around me. Largely there were Athena elders, college faculty and staff whom Coleman had known for close to forty years before Iris's death and his resignation. What would he think about these old-timers showing up at Rishanger to see him off could he observe them seated before his coffin? Probably something like, "What a wonderful occasion for self-approval. How virtuous they all must feel for not holding against me my contempt for them."

It was strange to think, while seated there with all his colleagues, that people so well educated and professionally civil should have fallen so willingly for the venerable human dream of a situation in which one man can embody evil. Yet there is this need, and it is undying and it is profound.

When the outside door was pulled shut and the Silks took their seats in the front row, I saw that the chapel was almost two-thirds full, three hundred people, maybe more, waiting for this ancient and natural human event to absorb their terror about the end of life. I saw, too, that Mark Silk, alone among his brothers, was wearing a skullcap.

Probably like most everyone else, I was expecting one of Coleman's children to mount the pulpit and speak first. But there was to be only one speaker that morning, and that was Herb Keble, the political scientist hired by Dean Silk as Athena's first black professor. Obviously Keble had been chosen by the family for the reason the family had chosen Rishanger for the service: to rehabilitate their father's name, to push back the Athena calendar and restore to Coleman his former status and prestige. When I recalled the severity with which Jeff and Michael had each taken my hand and acknowledged me by name and told me, "Thank you for coming—it means everything to the family that you're here," and when I imagined that they must have repeated something like that to each individual mourner, among whom there were many people they had known since childhood, I thought, And they don't intend to quit, not until the administration building is rededicated as Coleman Silk Hall.

That the place was nearly full was probably no chance occurrence. They must have been on the phone ever since the crash, mourners being rounded up the way voters used to be herded to the polls when the old Mayor Daley was running Chicago. And how they must have worked over Keble, whom Coleman had especially despised, to induce him voluntarily to proffer himself as the scapegoat for Athena's sins. The more I thought about these Silk boys twisting Keble's arm, intimidating him, shouting at him, denouncing him, perhaps even outright threatening him because of the way he had betrayed their father two years back, the more I liked them—and the more I liked Coleman for having sired two big, firm, smart fellows who were not reluctant to do what had to be done to turn his reputation right side out. These two were going to help put Les Farley away for the rest of his life.

Or so I was able to believe until the next afternoon, just before they left town, when—no less bluntly persuasive with me than I'd imagined them to have been with Keble—they let me know that I was to knock it off: to forget about Les Farley and the circumstances of the accident and about urging any further investigation by the police. They could not have made clearer that their disapproval would be boundless if their father's affair with Faunia Farley were to become the focal point of a courtroom trial instigated by my importuning. Faunia Farley's was a name they never wanted to hear again, least of all in a scandalous trial that would be written up sensationally in the local papers and lodged indelibly in local memory and that would leave Coleman Silk Hall forever a dream.

"She is not the ideal woman to have linked with our father's legacy," Jeffrey told me. "Our mother is," said Michael. "This cheap little cunt has nothing to do with anything." "Nothing," Jeffrey reiterated. It was hard to believe, given the ardor and the resolve, that out in California they were college science professors. You would have thought they ran Twentieth Century Fox.

*

Herb Keble was a slender, very dark man, elderly now, a bit
stiff-gaited, though seemingly in no way stooped or hobbled
by illness, and with something of the earnestness of the black
preacher in both the stern bearing and the ominous, hanging-
judge voice. He had only to say "My name is Herbert Keble"
to cast his spell; he had only, from behind the podium, to stare
silently at Coleman's coffin and then to turn to the congregation and announce who he was to invoke that realm of feeling
associated with the declamation of the holy psalms. He was
austere in the way the edge of a blade is austere—menacing to
you if you don't handle it with the utmost care. Altogether the
man was impressive, in demeanor and appearance both, and
one could see where Coleman might have hired him to break
the color barrier at Athena for something like the same reasons
that Branch Rickey had hired Jackie Robinson to be organized
baseball's first black. Imagining the Silk boys browbeating Herb
Keble into doing their bidding wasn't that easy, at first, not
until you took into account the appeal of self-drama to a personality marked so clearly by the vanity of those authorized to
administer the sacraments. He very much displayed the authority of the second in power to the sovereign.

"My name is Herbert Keble," he began. "I am chairman of
the Political Science Department. In 1996, I was among those
who did not see fit to rise to Coleman's defense when he was
accused of racism—I, who had come to Athena sixteen years
earlier, the very year that Coleman Silk was appointed dean of
faculty; I, who was Dean Silk's first academic appointment.
Much too tardily, I stand before you to censure myself for having failed my friend and patron, and to do what I can—again,
much too tardily—to begin to attempt to right the wrong, the
grievous, the contemptible wrong, that was done to him by
Athena College.

"At the time of the alleged racist incident, I told Coleman, 'I
can't be with you on this.' I said it to him deliberately, though
perhaps not entirely for the opportunistic, careerist, or cowardly reasons that he was so quick to assume to be mine. I
thought then that I could do more for Coleman's cause by
working behind the scenes to defuse the opposition than by

openly allying myself with him in public, and being rendered impotent, as I surely would have been, by that all-purpose, know-nothing weapon of a sobriquet, 'Uncle Tom.' I thought that I could be the voice of reason from within—rather than without—the ranks of those whose outrage over Coleman's alleged racist remark provoked them into unfairly defaming him and the college for what were the failures of two students. I thought that if I was shrewd enough and patient enough I could cool the passions, if not of the most extreme of his adversaries, then of those thoughtful, level-headed members of our local African American community and their white sympathizers, whose antagonism was never really more than reflexive and ephemeral. I thought that, in time—and, I hoped, in less time rather than more—I could initiate a dialogue between Coleman and his accusers that would lead to the promulgation of a statement identifying the nature of the misunderstanding that had given rise to the conflict, and thereby bring this regrettable incident to something like a just conclusion.

"I was wrong. I should never have said to my friend, 'I can't be with you on this.' I should have said, 'I *must* be with you.' I should have worked to oppose his enemies not insidiously and misguidedly from within but forthrightly and honestly from without—from where he could have taken heart at the expression of support instead of being left to nurse the crushing sense of abandonment that festered into the wound that led to his alienation from his colleagues, to his resignation from the college, and from there to the self-destructive isolation which, I am convinced—horrible as believing this is for me—led not too circuitously to his dying as tragically, wastefully, and unnecessarily as he did in that car the other night. I should have spoken up to say what I want to say now in the presence of his former colleagues, associates, and staff, and to say, especially, in the presence of his children, Jeff and Mike, who are here from California, and Mark and Lisa, who are here from New York —and to say, as the senior African American member of the Athena faculty:

"Coleman Silk never once deviated in any way from totally fair conduct in his dealings with each and every one of his students for as long as he served Athena College. Never.

"The alleged misconduct never took place. Never.

"What he was forced to undergo—the accusations, the interviews, the inquiry—remains a blight on the integrity of this institution to this day, and on this day, more than ever. Here, in the New England most identified, historically, with the American individualist's resistance to the coercions of a censorious community—Hawthorne, Melville, and Thoreau come to mind—an American individualist who did not think that the weightiest thing in life were the rules, an American individualist who refused to leave unexamined the orthodoxies of the customary and of the established truth, an American individualist who did not always live in compliance with majority standards of decorum and taste—an American individualist *par excellence* was once again so savagely traduced by friends and neighbors that he lived estranged from them until his death, robbed of his moral authority by their moral stupidity. Yes, it is we, the morally stupid censorious community, who have abased ourselves in having so shamefully besmirched Coleman Silk's good name. I speak particularly of those like myself, who knew from close contact the depth of his commitment to Athena and the purity of his dedication as an educator, and who, out of whatever deluded motive, betrayed him nonetheless. I say it again: we betrayed him. Betrayed Coleman and betrayed Iris.

"Iris's death, the death of Iris Silk, coming in the midst of . . ."

Two seats to my left, Smoky Hollenbeck's wife was in tears, as were several other of the women nearby. Smoky was himself leaning forward, his forehead resting lightly on his two hands, which were entwined at the top of the pew in front of us in a vaguely ecclesiastical manner. I suppose he wanted me or his wife or whoever else might be watching him to believe that the injustice done to Coleman Silk was unendurable to think about. I supposed he was meant to appear to be overcome by compassion, yet knowing what I did about all that he concealed, as a model family man, of the Dionysian substrata of his life, it was an inference hard to swallow.

But, Smoky aside, the attention, the concentration, the *acuity* of the concentration focused on Herb Keble's every word seemed genuine enough for me to imagine that any number of people present would be finding it difficult not to lament what

Coleman Silk had unfairly endured. I wondered, of course, if Keble's rationalization for why he hadn't stood beside Coleman at the time of the spooks incident was of his own devising or one that the Silk boys had come up with so as to enable him to do as they demanded while still saving face. I wondered whether the rationalization could be an accurate description of his motives when he'd said the words that Coleman bitterly repeated to me so many times: "I can't be with you on this."

Why was I unwilling to believe this man? Because, by a certain age, one's mistrust is so exquisitely refined that one is unwilling to believe anybody? Surely, two years back, when he was silent and didn't rise to Coleman's defense, it was for the reason that people are always silent: because it is in their interest to be silent. Expediency is not a motive that is steeped in darkness. Herb Keble was just another one out trying to kosher the record, albeit in a bold, even an interesting way, by taking the guilt upon himself, but the fact remained that he couldn't act when it mattered, and so I thought, on Coleman's behalf, Fuck him.

When Keble came down from the podium and, before returning to his seat, stopped to shake the hands of each of Coleman's children, that simple gesture served only to intensify the almost violent passion aroused by his speech. What would happen next? For a moment there was nothing. Just the silence and the coffin and the emotional intoxication of the crowd. Then Lisa stood up, mounted the few steps to the podium, and, from the lectern, said, "The last movement of Mahler's Third Symphony." That was it. They pulled out all the stops. They played Mahler.

Well, you can't listen to Mahler sometimes. When he picks you up to shake you, he doesn't stop. By the end of it, we were all crying.

Speaking only for myself, I don't think anything could have torn me apart like that other than hearing Steena Palsson's rendition of "The Man I Love" as she'd sung it from the foot of Coleman's Sullivan Street bed in 1948.

The three-block walk to the cemetery was memorable largely for its seemingly not having taken place. One moment we were immobilized by the infinite vulnerability of Mahler's adagio movement, by that simplicity that is not artifice, that is not a strategy, that unfolds, it almost seems, with the accumulated pace of life and with all of life's unwillingness to end . . . one moment we were immobilized by that exquisite juxtaposition of grandeur and intimacy that begins in the quiet, singing, re- strained intensity of the strings and then rises in surges through the massive false ending that leads to the true, the extended, the monumental ending . . . one moment we were immobilized by the swelling, soaring, climaxing, and subsiding of an elegiac orgy that rolls on and on and on with a determined pace that never changes, giving way, then coming back like pain or long- ing that won't disappear . . . one moment we were, at Mahler's mounting insistence, inside the coffin with Coleman, attuned to all the terror of endlessness and to the passionate desire to escape death, and then somehow or other sixty or seventy of us had got ourselves over to the cemetery to watch as he was buried, a simple enough ritual, as sensible a solution to the problem as any ever devised but one that is never entirely comprehensible. You have to see it to believe it each time.

I doubted that most people had been planning to accom- pany the body all the way to the grave. But the Silk children had a flair for drawing out and sustaining pathos, and this, I assumed, was why there were so many of us crowding around as close as we could to the hole that was to be Coleman's eternal home, as though eager almost to crawl in there and take his place, to offer ourselves up as surrogates, as substitutes, as sacrificial offerings, if that would magically allow for the re- sumption of the exemplary life that, by Herb Keble's own ad- mission, had been as good as stolen from Coleman two years back.

Coleman was to be buried beside Iris. The dates on her headstone read 1932–1996. His would read 1926–1998. How direct those numbers are. And how little they connote of what went on.

I heard the Kaddish begin before I realized that somebody there was chanting it. Momentarily I imagined that it must be drifting in from another part of the cemetery, when it was coming from the other side of the grave, where Mark Silk—the youngest son, the angry son, the son who, like his twin sister, bore the strongest resemblance to his father—was standing alone, with the book in his hand and the yarmulke on his head, and chanting in a soft, tear-filled voice the familiar Hebrew prayer.

Yisgadal, v'yiskadash . . .

Most people in America, including myself and probably Mark's siblings, don't know what these words mean, but nearly everyone recognizes the sobering message they bring: a Jew is dead. Another Jew is dead. As though death were not a consequence of life but a consequence of having been a Jew.

When Mark had finished, he shut the book and then, having induced a grim serenity in everyone else, was himself overcome by hysteria. That was how Coleman's funeral ended—with all of us immobilized this time by watching Mark go to pieces, helplessly flailing his arms in the air and, through a wide-open mouth, wailing away. That wild sound of lamentation, older even than the prayer he'd uttered, rose in intensity until, when he saw his sister rushing toward him with arms outstretched, he turned to her his contorted Silk face, and in sheer childlike astonishment cried, "We're never going to see him again!"

I did not think my most generous thought. Generous thoughts were hard to come by that day. I thought, What difference should that make? You weren't that keen on seeing him when he was here.

Mark Silk apparently had imagined that he was going to have his father around to hate forever. To hate and hate and hate and hate, and then perhaps, in his own good time, after the scenes of accusation had reached their crescendo and he had flogged Coleman to within an inch of his life with his knot of filial grievance, to forgive. He thought Coleman was going to stay here till the whole play could be performed, as though he and Coleman had been set down not in life but on the southern hillside of the Athenian acropolis, in an outdoor theater sacred to Dionysus, where, before the eyes of ten thousand spectators, the dramatic unities were once rigorously observed and the great cathartic cycle was enacted annually. The human desire for a beginning, a middle, and an end—and an end appropriate in magnitude to that beginning and middle—is realized nowhere so thoroughly as in the plays that Coleman taught at Athena College. But outside the classical tragedy of the fifth century B.C., the expectation of completion, let alone of a just and perfect consummation, is a foolish illusion for an adult to hold.

People began to drift away. I saw the Hollenbecks move along the path between the gravestones and head toward the nearby street, the husband's arm around his wife's shoulder, shepherding her protectively away. I saw the young lawyer, Nelson Primus, who had represented Coleman during the spooks incident, and with him a pregnant young woman, a woman weeping, who must have been his wife. I saw Mark with his sister, still having to be consoled by her, and I saw Jeff and Michael, who had run this whole operation so expertly, talking quietly to Herb Keble a few yards from where I was standing. I couldn't myself go because of Les Farley. Away from this cemetery he muscled on undisturbed, uncharged with any crime, manufacturing that crude reality all his own, a brute of a being colliding with whomever he liked however he liked for all the inner reasons that justified anything he wanted to do.

Sure, I know there's no completion, no just and perfect consummation, but that didn't mean that, standing just feet from where the coffin rested in its freshly dug pit, I wasn't obstinately thinking that this ending, even if it were construed as having permanently reestablished Coleman's place as an admired figure in the college's history, would not suffice. Too much truth was still concealed.

I meant by this the truth about his death and not the truth that was to come to light a moment or two later. There is truth and then again there is truth. For all that the world is full of people who go around believing they've got you or your neighbor figured out, there really is no bottom to what is not known. The truth about us is endless. As are the lies. Caught between, I thought. Denounced by the high-minded, reviled by the righteous—then exterminated by the criminally crazed. Excommunicated by the saved, the elect, the ever-present evangelists of the mores of the moment, then polished off by a demon of ruthlessness. Both human exigencies found their conjunction in him. The pure and the impure, in all their vehemence, on the move, akin in their common need of the enemy. Whipsawed, I thought. Whipsawed by the inimical teeth of this world. By the antagonism that *is* the world.

One woman, by herself, had remained as close to the open

grave as I was. She was silent and did not look to be crying. She didn't even appear to be quite there—that is to say, in the cemetery, at a funeral. She could have been on a street corner, waiting patiently for the next bus. It was the way she was holding her handbag primly in front of her that made me think of someone who was already prepared to pay her fare, and then to be carried off to wherever she was going. I could tell she wasn't white only by the thrust of her jaw and the cast of her mouth—by something suggestively protrusive shaping the lower half of her face—and, too, by the stiff texture of her hairdo. Her complexion was no darker than a Greek's or a Moroccan's, and perhaps I might not have added one clue to another to matter-of-factly register her as black, if it wasn't that Herb Keble was among the very few who hadn't yet headed for home. Because of her age—sixty-five, maybe seventy—I thought she must be Keble's wife. No wonder, then, that she looked so strangely transfixed. It could not have been easy to listen to her husband publicly cast himself (under the sway of whatever motive) as Athena's scapegoat. I could understand how she would have a lot to think about, and how assimilating it might take more time than the funeral had allowed. Her thoughts had still to be with what he had said back in Rishanger Chapel. *That's* where she was.

I was wrong.

As I turned to leave, she happened to turn too, and so, with only a foot or two between us, we were facing each other.

"My name's Nathan Zuckerman," I said. "I was a friend of Coleman's near the end of his life."

"How do you do," she replied.

"I believe your husband changed everything today."

She did not look at me as if I were mistaken, though I was. Nor did she ignore me, decide to be rid of me, and proceed on her way. Nor did she look as if she didn't know what to do, though that she was in a quandary had to have been so. A friend of Coleman's at the end of his life? Given her true identity, how could she have said nothing more than "I'm not Mrs. Keble" and walked off?

But all she did was to stand there, opposite me, expressionless, so profoundly struck dumb by the day's events and its revelations that *not* to understand who she was to Coleman would, at that moment, have been impossible. It wasn't a re-semblance to Coleman that registered, and registered quickly, in rapid increments, as with a distant star seen through a lens that you've steadily magnified to the correct intensity. What I saw—when, at long last, I did see, see all the way, clear to Coleman's secret—was the facial resemblance to Lisa, who was even more her aunt's niece than she was her father's daughter.

It was from Ernestine—back at my house in the hours after the funeral—that I learned most of what I know about Coleman's growing up in East Orange: about Dr. Fensterman trying to get Coleman to take a dive on his final exams so as to let Bert Fensterman slip in ahead of him as valedictorian; about how Mr. Silk found the East Orange house in 1926, the small frame house that Ernestine still occupied and that was sold to her father "by a couple," Ernestine explained to me, "who were mad at the people next door and so were determined to sell it to colored to spite them." ("See, you can tell the generation I am," she said to me later that day. "I say 'colored' and 'Negro.'") She told me about how her father had lost the optician shop during the Depression, how it took time for him to get over the loss—"I'm not sure," she said, "he ever did"—and how he got a job as a waiter on the dining car and worked for the rail-road for the rest of his life. She talked about how Mr. Silk called English "the language of Chaucer, Shakespeare, and Dickens," and saw to it that the children learned not just to speak prop-erly but to think logically, to classify, to analyze, to describe, to enumerate, to learn not only English but Latin and Greek; how he took them to the New York museums and to see Broadway plays; and how, when he found out about Coleman's secret career as an amateur boxer for the Newark Boys Club, he had told him, in that voice that radiated authority without ever having to be raised, "If I were your father I would say, 'You won last night? Good. Now you can retire undefeated.'" From Ernestine I learned how Doc Chizner, my own boxing instructor during the year I took his after-school class down in Newark, had, earlier, in East Orange, laid claim to young Coleman's talent after Coleman left the Boys Club, how Doc had wanted him to box for the University of Pittsburgh, could have gotten him a scholarship to Pitt as a white boxer, but how

Coleman had enrolled at Howard because that was their father's plan. How their father dropped dead while serving dinner on the train one night, and how Coleman had immediately quit Howard to join the navy, and to join as a white man. How after the navy he moved to Greenwich Village to go to NYU. How he brought that white girl home one Sunday, the pretty girl from Minnesota. How the biscuits burned that day, so preoccupied were they all with not saying the wrong thing. How, luckily for everyone, Walt, who'd begun teaching down in Asbury Park, hadn't been able to drive up for dinner, how things just went along so wonderfully that Coleman could have had nothing to complain about. Ernestine told me how gracious Coleman's mother had been to the girl. Steena. How thoughtful and kind they'd been to Steena—and Steena to them. How hardworking their mother was always, how, after their father died, she had risen, by virtue of merit alone, to become the first colored head nurse on the surgical floor of a Newark hospital. And how she had adored her Coleman, how there was nothing Coleman could do to destroy his mother's love. Even the decision to spend the rest of his life pretending his mother had been somebody else, a mother he'd never had and who had never existed, even that couldn't free Mrs. Silk of him. And after Coleman had come home to tell his mother he was marrying Iris Gittelman and that she would never be mother-in-law to her daughter-in-law or grandmother to her grand-children, when Walt forbade Coleman from ever contacting the family again, how Walt then made it clear to their mother—and employing the same steely authority by which his father had governed them—that she was not to contact Coleman either.

"I know he meant the best," Ernestine said. "Walt thought this was the only way to protect Mother from being hurt. From being hurt by Coleman every time there was a birthday, every time there was a holiday, every time it was Christmas. He be-lieved that if the line of communication remained open, Cole-man was going to break Mother's heart a thousand times over, exactly the way he did it that day. Walt was enraged at Coleman for coming over to East Orange without any preparation, without warning any of us, and to tell an elderly woman, a widow like that, just what the law was going to be. Fletcher, my husband, always had a psychological reason for Walt's doing what he did. But I don't think Fletcher was right. I don't think Walt was ever truly jealous of Coleman's place in Mother's heart. I don't accept that. I think he was insulted and flared up—not just for Mother but for all of us. Walt was the political member of the family; of course he was going to get mad. I myself wasn't mad that way and I never have been, but I can understand Walter. Every year, on Coleman's birthday, I phoned Athena to talk to him. Right down to three days ago. That was his birthday. His seventy-second birthday. I would think that when he got killed, he was driving home from his birthday dinner. I phoned to wish him a happy birthday. There was no answer and so I called the next day. And that's how I found out he was dead. Somebody there at the house picked up the phone and told me. I realize now that it was one of my nephews. I only began calling the house after Coleman's wife died and he left the college and was living alone. Before that, I phoned the office. Never told anybody about it. Didn't see any reason to. Phoned on his birthdays. Phoned when Mother died. Phoned when I got married. Phoned when I had my son. I phoned him when my husband died. We always had a good talk together. He always wanted to hear the news, even about Walter and his promotions. And then each of the times that Iris gave birth, with Jeffrey, with Michael, then with the twins, I got a call from Coleman. He'd call me at school. That was always a great trial for him. He was testing fate with so many kids. Because they were genetically linked to the past he had repudiated, there was always the chance, you see, that they might be a throwback in some distinguishing way. He worried a lot about that. It could have happened—it sometimes does happen. But he went ahead and had them anyway. That was a part of the plan too. The plan to lead a full and regular and productive life. Still, I believe that, in those first years especially, and certainly whenever a new child came along, Coleman suffered for his decision. Nothing ever escaped Coleman's attention, and that held true for his own feelings. He could cut himself away from us, but not from his feelings. And that was most true where the children were concerned. I think he himself came to believe that there was something awful about withholding something so crucial to what a person is, that it

was their birthright to know their genealogy. And there was
something dangerous too. Think of the havoc he could create
in their lives if their children were born recognizably Negro.
So far he has been lucky, and that goes for the two grandchildren out in California. But think of his daughter, who isn't
married yet. Suppose one day she has a white husband, as more
than likely she will, and she gives birth to a Negroid child, as
she can—as she may. How does she explain this? And what will
her husband assume? He will assume that another man fathered
her child. A black man at that. Mr. Zuckerman, it was frighteningly cruel for Coleman not to tell his children. That is not
Walter's judgment—that is mine. If Coleman was intent on
keeping his race his secret, then the price he should have paid
was not to have children. And he knew that. He had to know
that. Instead, he has planted an unexploded bomb. And that
bomb seemed to me always in the background when he talked
about them. Especially when he talked about, not the twin
girl, but the twin boy, Mark, the boy he had all the trouble with.
He said to me that Markie probably hated him for his own
reasons, yet it was as though he had figured out the truth. 'I
got there what I produced,' he said, 'even if for the wrong
reason. Markie doesn't even have the luxury of hating his father
for the real thing. I robbed him,' Coleman said, 'of that part of
his birthright, too.' And I said, 'But he might not have hated
you at all for that, Coleman.' And he said, 'You don't follow
me. Not that he would have hated me for being black. That's
not what I mean by the real thing. I mean that he would have
hated me for never telling him and because he had a right to
know.' And then, because there was so much there to be misunderstood, we just let the subject drop. But it was clear that
he could never forget that there was a lie at the foundation of
his relationship to his children, a terrible lie, and that Markie
had intuited it, somehow understood that the children, who
carried their father's identity in their genes and who would
pass that identity on to their children, at least genetically, and
perhaps even physically, tangibly, never had the complete knowledge of who they are and who they were. This is somewhat in
the nature of speculation, but I sometimes think that Coleman
saw Markie as the punishment for what he had done to his
own mother. Though that," Ernestine added, scrupulously, "is

not something *he* ever said. As for Walter, what I was getting at about Walter is that all he was trying to do was to fill our father's shoes by making sure that Mother's heart would not be broken time and again."

"And was it?" I asked.

"Mr. Zuckerman, there was no repairing it—ever. When she died in the hospital, when she was delirious, do you know what she was saying? She kept calling for the nurse the way the sick patients used to call for her. 'Oh, nurse,' she said, 'oh, nurse—get me to the train. I got a sick baby at home.' Over and over, 'I got a sick baby at home.' Sitting there beside her bed, holding her hand and watching her die, I knew who that sick baby was. So did Walter know. It was Coleman. Whether she would have been better off had Walt not interfered the way he did by banishing Coleman forever like that . . . well, I still hesitate to say. But Walter's special talent as a man is his decisiveness. That was Coleman's as well. Ours is a family of decisive men. Daddy had it, and so did his father, who was a Methodist minister down in Georgia. These men make up their minds, and that's it. Well, there was a price to pay for their decisiveness. One thing is clear, however. And I realized that today. And I wish my parents could know it. We are a family of educators. Beginning with my paternal grandmother. As a young slave girl, taught to read by her mistress, then, after Emancipation, went to what was then called Georgia State Normal and Industrial School for Colored. That's how it began, and that's what we have turned out to be. And that is what I realized when I saw Coleman's children. All but one of them teachers. And all of us—Walt, Coleman, me, all of us teachers as well. My own son is another story. He did not finish college. We had some disagreements, and now he has a significant other, as the expression goes, and we have our disagreement about that. I should tell you that there were no colored teachers in the white Asbury Park school system when Walter arrived there in '47. You have to remember, he was the first. And subsequently their first Negro principal. And subsequently their first Negro superintendent of schools. That tells you something about Walt. There was already a well-established colored community, but it was not till Walter got there in '47 that things began to change. And that decisiveness of his had a lot to do with it.

Even though you're a Newark product, I'm not sure you know that up until 1947, legally, constitutionally separate, segregated education was approved in New Jersey. You had, in most communities, schools for colored children and schools for white children. There was a distinct separation of the races in elementary education in south Jersey. From Trenton, New Brunswick, on down, you had separate schools. And in Princeton. And in Asbury Park. In Asbury Park, when Walter arrived there, there was a school called Bangs Avenue, East or West—one of them was for colored children who lived in that Bangs Avenue neighborhood and the other one was for white children who lived in that neighborhood. Now that was one building, but it was divided into two parts. There was a fence between the two sides of the building, and one side was colored kids and on the other was white kids. Likewise, the teachers on one side were white and the teachers on the other side were colored. The principal was white. In Trenton, in Princeton—and Princeton is not considered south Jersey—there were separate schools up until 1948. Not in East Orange and not in Newark, though at one time, even in Newark there was an elementary school for colored children. That was the early 1900s. But in 1947—and I'm getting to Walter's place in all this, because I want you to understand my brother Walter, I want you to see his relationship to Coleman within the wider picture of what was going on back then. This is years before the civil rights movement. Even what Coleman did, the decision that he made, despite his Negro ancestry, to live as a member of another racial group— that was by no means an uncommon decision before the civil rights movement. There were movies about it. Remember them? One was called *Pinky*, and there was another, with Mel Ferrer, though I can't remember the name of it, but it was popular too. Changing your racial group—there was no civil rights to speak of, no equality, so that was on people's minds, white as well as colored. Maybe more in their minds than happening in reality, but still, it fascinated people in the way they are fascinated by a fairy tale. But then in 1947, the governor called for a constitutional convention to revise the constitution of the state of New Jersey. And that was the beginning of something. One of the constitutional revisions was that there would no longer be separated or segregated National Guard units in New Jersey.

The second part, the second change in the new constitution, said that no longer shall children be forced to pass one school to get to another school in their neighborhood. The wording was something like that. Walter could tell it to you verbatim. Those amendments eliminated segregation in the public schools and in the National Guard. The governor and the boards of education were told to implement that. The state board advised all the local boards of education to set into operation plans to integrate the schools. They suggested first integrating the faculties of the schools and then slowly integrating the schools insofar as pupils were concerned. Now, even before Walt went to Asbury Park, even as a student at Montclair State when he came home from the war, he was one of those who were politically concerned—one of those ex-GIs who were already actively fighting for integration of the schools in New Jersey. Even before the constitutional revision, and after it was revised, certainly, Walter remained among the most active in the fight to integrate the schools."

Her point was that Coleman was *not* one of those ex-GIs fighting for integration and equality and civil rights; in Walt's opinion, he was never fighting for anything other than himself. Silky Silk. That's who he fought as, who he fought for, and that's why Walt could never stand Coleman, even when Coleman was a boy. In it for himself, Walt used to say. In it always for Coleman alone. All he ever wanted was out.

We had finished lunch at my house several hours earlier, but Ernestine's energy showed no signs of abating. Everything whirling inside her brain—and not just as a consequence of Coleman's death but everything about the mystery of him that she had been trying to fathom for the last fifty years—was causing her to speak in a rush that was not necessarily characteristic of the serious small-town schoolteacher she'd been for the whole of her life. She was a very proper-looking woman, seemingly healthy if a bit drawn in the face, whose appetites you couldn't have imagined to be in any way excessive; from her dress and her posture, from the meticulous way she ate her lunch, even from the way she occupied her chair, it was clear that hers was a personality that had no difficulty subjugating itself to social convention and that her inmost reflex in any conflict would be to act automatically as the mediator—entirely the master of the sensible response, by choice more of a listener than a maker of speeches, and yet the aura of excitement surrounding the death of her self-declared white brother, the special significance of the end of a life that to her family had seemed like one long, perverse, willfully arrogant defection, could hardly be reckoned with by ordinary means.

"Mother went to her grave wondering why Coleman did it. 'Lost himself to his own people.' That's how she put it. He wasn't the first in Mother's family. There'd been others. But they were *others*. They weren't Coleman. Coleman never in his life chafed under being a Negro. Not for as long as we knew him. This is true. Being a Negro was just never an issue with him. You'd see Mother sitting in her chair at night, sitting there stock-still, and you knew what she was wondering: could it be this, could it be that? Was it to get away from Daddy? But by the time he did it, Daddy was dead. Mother would propose reasons, but none was ever adequate. Was it because he thought white people were better than us? They had more money than we did, sure—but better? Is that what he believed? We never saw the slightest evidence of that. Now, people grow up and go away and have nothing to do with their families ever again, and they don't have to be colored to act like that. It happens every day all over the world. They hate everything so much they just disappear. But Coleman as a kid was not a hater. The breeziest, most optimistic child you ever wanted to see. Growing up, *I* was more unhappy than Coleman. *Walt* was more unhappy than Coleman. What with all the success he had, with the attention people gave him . . . no, it just never made sense to Mother. The pining never stopped. His photos. His report cards. His track medals. His yearbook. The certificate he got as valedictorian. There were even toys of Coleman's around, toys he'd loved as a small child, and she had all these things and she stared at them the way a mind reader stares into a crystal ball, as if they would unravel everything. Did he ever acknowledge to anyone what he'd done? Did he, Mr. Zuckerman? Did he ever acknowledge it to his wife? To his children?"

"I don't think so," I said. "I'm sure he didn't."

"So he was Coleman all the way. Set out to do it and did it. That was the extraordinary thing about him from the time he was a boy—that he stuck to a plan completely. There was a dogged commitment he could make to his every decision. All the lying that was necessitated by the big lie, to his family, to his colleagues, and he stuck to it right to the end. Even to be buried as a Jew. Oh, Coleman," she said sadly, "*so* determined. Mr. Determined," and in that moment, she was closer to laughter than to tears.

Buried as a Jew, I thought, and, if I was speculating correctly, killed as a Jew. Another of the problems of impersonation.

"If he acknowledged it to anyone," I said, "maybe it was to the woman he died with. To Faunia Farley."

She clearly didn't want to hear about that woman. But because of her sensibleness, she had to ask, "How do you know that?"

"I don't. I don't know anything. It's a thought I have," I said. "It ties into the pact that I sensed was between them—his telling her." By "the pact between them" I meant their mutual recognition that there was no clean way out, but I didn't go on to explain myself, not to Ernestine. "Look, learning this from you today, there's nothing about Coleman I don't have to rethink. I don't know what to think about anything."

"Well then, you're now an honorary member of the Silk family. Aside from Walter, in matters pertaining to Coleman none of us has ever known what to think. Why he did it, why he stuck to it, why Mother had to die the way she did. If Walt hadn't laid down the law," she said, "who knows what would have evolved? Who knows if Coleman wouldn't have told his wife as the years passed and he got further from the decision? Maybe even told his children one day. Maybe have told the world. But Walt froze everything in time. And that is never a good idea. Coleman did this when he was still in his twenties. A firecracker of twenty-seven. But he wasn't going to be twenty-seven forever. It wasn't going to be 1953 forever. People age. Nations age. *Problems* age. Sometimes they age right out of existence. Yet Walt froze it. Of course, if you look at it narrowly, from the point of view simply of social advantage, of course it was advantageous in the well-spoken Negro middle class to do it Coleman's way, as it's advantageous today not to dream of doing it that way. Today, if you're a middle-class intelligent Negro and you want your kids to go to the best schools, and on full scholarship if you need it, you wouldn't dream of saying that you're not colored. That would be the last thing you'd do. White as your skin might be, now it's advantageous *not* to do it, just as then it was advantageous *to* do it. So what is the difference? But can I tell that to Walter? Can I say to him, 'So what really is the difference?' First because of what Coleman did to Mother, and second because in Walter's eyes there was a fight to fight then, and Coleman didn't want to fight it—for those reasons alone, I most certainly cannot. Though don't think that over the years I haven't tried. Because Walter, in fact, is not a harsh man. You want to hear about my brother Walter? In 1944 Walter was a twenty-one-year-old rifleman with a colored infantry company. He was with another soldier from his outfit. They were on a ridge in Belgium overlooking a valley that was cut through by railroad tracks. They saw a German soldier walking east along the tracks. He had a small bag slung over his shoulder and he was whistling. The other soldier with Walter took aim. 'What the hell are you doing?' Walter said to him. 'I'm going to kill him.' '*Why?* Stop! What's he doing? He's walking. He's probably walking home.' Walter had to wrestle the rifle away from this fellow. A kid from South Carolina. They went down the ridge and they stopped the German and they took him prisoner. Turned out he *was* walking home. He had a leave, and the only way he knew to get back to Germany was to follow the railroad tracks east. And it was Walter who saved his life. How many soldiers ever did that? My brother Walter is a determined man who can be hard if he has to be, but he is also a human being. It's *because* he's a human being that he believes that what you do, you do to advance the race. And so I have tried with him, tried sometimes by saying things to Walter that I only half believe myself. Coleman was a part of his time, I tell him. Coleman couldn't wait to go through civil rights to get to his human rights, and so he skipped a step. 'See him historically,' I say to Walt. 'You're a history teacher—see him as a part of something larger.' I've told him, 'Neither of you just submitted to what you were given. *Both* of you are fighters and *both* of you fought. You did battle your way and Coleman did battle his.' But that is a line of reasoning that has never worked with Walter. Nothing has ever worked. That was Coleman's way of becoming a man, I tell him—but he will not buy that. To Walt, that was Coleman's way of *not* becoming a man. 'Sure,' he says to me, 'sure. Your brother is more or less as he would have been, except he would have been black. Except? *Except?* That except would have changed everything.' Walt cannot see Coleman other than the way he always has. And what can I do about that, Mr. Zuckerman? Hate my brother Walt for what he did to Coleman by freezing our family in time like that? Hate my brother Coleman for what he did to Mother, for how he made the poor woman suffer down to the very last day of her life? Because if I'm going to hate my two brothers, why stop there? Why not hate my father for all the things that he did wrong? Why not hate my late husband? I was not married to a saint, I can assure you. I loved my husband, but I have clear vision. And what about my son? There's a boy it would not be at all hard to hate. He goes out of his way to make it easy for you. But the danger with hatred is, once you start in on it, you get a hundred times more than you bargained for. Once you start, you can't stop. I don't know anything harder to control than hating. Easier to kick drinking than to master hate. And that is saying something."

"Did you know before today," I asked her, "why it was that Coleman had resigned from the college?"

"I did not. I thought he'd reached a retirement age."

"He never told you."

"No."

"So you couldn't know what Keble was talking about."

"Not entirely."

So I told her about the spooks business, told her that whole story then, and when I was finished she shook her head and said, straight out, "I don't believe I've ever heard of anything more foolish being perpetrated by an institution of higher learning. It sounds to me more like a hotbed of ignorance. To persecute a college professor, whoever he is, whatever color he might be, to insult him, to dishonor him, to rob him of his authority and his dignity and his prestige for something as stupid and trivial as that. I am my father's daughter, Mr. Zuckerman, the daughter of a father who was a stickler for words, and with every passing day, the words that I hear spoken strike me as less and less of a description of what things really are. Sounds from what you've told

me that anything is possible in a college today. Sounds like the
people there forgot what it is to teach. Sounds like what they do
is something closer to buffoonery. Every time has its reactionary
authorities, and here at Athena they are apparently riding high.
One has to be so terribly frightened of every word one uses?
What ever happened to the First Amendment of the Constitution of the United States of America? In my childhood, as in
yours, it was recommended that each student who graduated
from high school in New Jersey get at graduation two things:
a diploma and a copy of the Constitution. Do you recall that?
You had to take a year of American history and a semester of
economics—as, of course, you have to no longer: 'have to' is just
gone out of the curriculum. At graduation it was traditional in
many of our schools in those days for the principal to hand you
your diploma and somebody else to give you a copy of the Constitution of the United States. So few people today have a reasonably clear understanding of the Constitution of the United States.
But here in America, as far as I can see, it's just getting more
foolish by the hour. All these colleges starting these remedial
programs to teach kids what they should have learned in the
ninth grade. In East Orange High they stopped long ago reading the old classics. They haven't even heard of *Moby-Dick*, much
less read it. Youngsters were coming to me the year I retired,
telling me that for Black History Month they would only read a
biography of a black by a black. What difference, I would ask
them, if it's a black author or it's a white author? I'm impatient
with Black History Month altogether. I liken having a Black
History Month in February and concentrating study on that
to milk that's just about to go sour. You can still drink it, but it
just doesn't taste right. If you're going to study and find out
about Matthew Henson, then it seems to me that you do Matthew Henson when you do other explorers."

"I don't know who Matthew Henson is," I said to Ernestine,
wondering if Coleman had known, if he had wanted to know,
if not wanting to know was one of the reasons he had made his
decision.

"Mr. Zuckerman . . . ," she said, gently enough, but to
shame me nonetheless.

"Mr. Zuckerman was not exposed to Black History Month
as a youngster," I said.

"Who discovered the North Pole?" she asked me.

I suddenly liked her enormously, and the more so the more pedantically teacherish she became. Though for different reasons, I was beginning to like her as much as I had liked her brother. And saw now that if you'd put them side by side, it wouldn't have been at all difficult to tell what Coleman was. *Everyone knows* . . . Oh, stupid, stupid, stupid Delphine Roux. One's truth is known to no one, and frequently—as in Delphine's very own case—to oneself least of all. "I forget whether it was Peary or Cook," I said. "I forget which one got to the North Pole first."

"Well, Henson got there *before* him. When it was reported in the *New York Times*, he was given full credit. But now when they write the history, all you hear about is Peary. It would have been the same sort of thing if Sir Edmund Hillary were said to have gotten to the top of Mount Everest and you didn't hear a word about Tenzing Norgay. My point," said Ernestine, in her element now, all professional correctitude and instruction—and, unlike Coleman, everything her father ever wanted her to be—"my point is, if you have a course on health and whatever, then you do Dr. Charles Drew. You've heard of him?"

"No."

"Shame on you, Mr. Zuckerman. I'll tell you in a minute. But you do Dr. Drew when you have health. You don't put him in February. You understand what I mean?"

"Yes."

"You learn about them when you study explorers and health people and all the other people. But everything there now is black this and black that. I let it wash over me the best I could, but it wasn't easy. Years ago, East Orange High was excellent. Kids coming out of East Orange High, especially out of the honors program, would have their choice of colleges. Oh, don't get me started on this subject. What happened to Coleman with that word 'spooks' is all a part of the same enormous failure. In my parents' day and well into yours and mine, it used to be the person who fell short. Now it's the discipline. Reading the classics is too difficult, therefore it's the classics that are to blame. Today the student asserts his incapacity as a privilege. I can't learn it, so there is something wrong with it. And there is something especially wrong with the bad teacher who wants to teach it. There are no more criteria, Mr. Zucker-man, only opinions. I often wrestle with this question of what everything used to be. What education used to be. What East Orange High used to be. What East Orange used to be. Urban renewal destroyed East Orange, there's no doubt in my mind. They—the city fathers—talked about all the great things that were going to happen because of this urban renewal. It scared the merchants to death and the merchants left, and the more the merchants left, the less business there was. Then 280 and the parkway cut our little town in quarters. The parkway eliminated Jones Street—the center of our colored community the parkway eliminated altogether. Then 280. A devastating intrusion. What that did to that community! Because the high-way had to come through, the nice houses along Oraton Park-way, Elmwood Avenue, Maple Avenue, the state just bought them up and they disappeared overnight. I used to be able to do all my Christmas shopping on Main Street. Well, Main Street and Central Avenue. Central Avenue was called the Fifth Avenue of the Oranges then. You know what we've got today? We've got a ShopRite. And we've got a Dunkin' Donuts. And there was a Domino's Pizza, but they closed. Now they've got another food place. And there's a cleaners. But you can't com-pare quality. It's not the same. In all honesty, I drive up the hill to West Orange to shop. But I didn't then. There was no rea-son to. Every night when we went out to walk the dog, I'd go with my husband, unless the weather was real bad—walk to Central Avenue, which is two blocks, then down Central Ave-nue for four blocks, cross over, then window-shop back, and home. There was a B. Altman. A Russeks. There was a Black, Starr, and Gorham. There was a Bachrach, the photographer. A very nice men's store, Minks, that was Jewish, that was over on Main Street. Two theaters. There was the Hollywood The-ater on Central Avenue. There was the Palace Theater on Main Street. All of life was there in little East Orange . . ."

All of life was there in East Orange. And when? Before. Be-fore urban renewal. Before the classics were abandoned. Before they stopped giving out the Constitution to high school graduates. Before there were remedial classes in the colleges teaching kids what they should have learned in ninth grade. Before Black History Month. Before they built the parkway and brought in 280. Before they persecuted a college professor for saying "spooks" to his class. Before she drove up the hill to West Orange to shop. Before everything changed, including Coleman Silk. That's when it all was different—before. And, she lamented, it will never be the same again, not in East Orange or anywhere else in America.

At four, when I started out of my drive for the College Arms, where she was staying, the afternoon light was ratcheting rapidly down and the day, heavy now with fearsome clouds, had turned into gusty November. That morning they'd buried Coleman—and the morning before buried Faunia—in spring-like weather, but now everything was intent on announcing winter. And winter twelve hundred feet up. Here it comes.

The impulse I had then, to tell Ernestine about the summer day a mere four months earlier when Coleman had driven me out to the dairy farm to watch Faunia do the five o'clock milking in the late afternoon heat—that is, to watch him watching Faunia do the milking—did not require much wisdom to suppress. Whatever was missing from Ernestine's sense of Coleman's life, she was not driven to discover. Intelligent as she was, she hadn't asked a single question about how he had lived out his last months, let alone about what might have caused him to die in the circumstance he did; good and virtuous woman that she was, she preferred not to contemplate the specific details of his destruction. Nor did she wish to inquire into any biographical connection between the injunction to revolt that had severed him from his family in his twenties and the furious determination, some forty years on, with which he had disassociated himself from Athena, as its pariah and renegade. Not that I was sure there was any connection, any circuitry looping the one decision to the other, but we could try to look and see, couldn't we? How did such a man as Coleman come to exist? What is it that he was? Was the idea he had for himself of lesser validity or of greater validity than someone else's idea of what he was supposed to be? Can such things even be known? But the concept of life as something whose purpose is concealed, of custom as something that may not allow for thought, of society as dedicated to a picture of itself that may be badly flawed, of an individual as real apart and beyond the social determinants defining him, which may indeed be what to him seem most *unreal*—in short, every perplexity pumping the human imagination seemed to lie somewhat outside her own unswerving allegiance to a canon of time-honored rules.

"I have not read any of your books," she told me in the car. "I tend to lean toward mysteries these days, and English mysteries. But when I get home, I plan to take out something of yours."

"You haven't told me who Dr. Charles Drew was."

"Dr. Charles Drew," she told me, "discovered how to prevent blood from clotting so it could be banked. Then he was injured in an automobile accident, and the hospital that was nearest would not take colored, and he died by bleeding to death."

That was the whole of our conversation during the twenty minutes it took to drive down the mountain and into town. The torrent of disclosure was over. Ernestine had said all there was to say. With the result that the harshly ironic fate of Dr. Drew took on a significance—a seemingly special relevance to Coleman and *his* harshly ironic fate—that was no less disturbing for being imponderable.

I couldn't imagine anything that could have made Coleman more of a mystery to me than this unmasking. Now that I knew everything, it was as though I knew nothing, and instead of what I'd learned from Ernestine unifying my idea of him, he became not just an unknown but an uncohesive person. In what proportion, to what degree, had his secret determined his daily life and permeated his everyday thinking? Did it alter over the years from being a hot secret to being a cool secret to being a forgotten secret of no importance, something having to do with a dare he'd taken, a wager made to himself way back when? Did he get, from his decision, the adventure he was after, or was the decision in itself the adventure? Was it the misleading that provided his pleasure, the carrying off of the stunt that he liked best, the traveling through life incognito, or had he simply been closing the door to a past, to people, to a whole race that he wanted nothing intimate or official to do with? Was it the social obstruction that he wished to sidestep? Was he merely being another American and, in the great frontier tradition, accepting the democratic invitation to throw your origins overboard if to do so contributes to the pursuit of happiness?

Or was it more than that? Or was it less? How petty were his motives? How pathological? And suppose they were both— what of it? And suppose they weren't—what of *that*? By the time I met him, was the secret merely the tincture barely tinting the coloration of the man's total being or was the totality of his being nothing but a tincture in the shoreless sea of a lifelong secret? Did he ever relax his vigilance, or was it like being a fugitive forever? Did he ever get over the fact that he couldn't get over the fact that he was pulling it off—that he could meet the world with his strength intact after doing what he had done, that he could appear to everyone, as he did appear, to be so easily at home in his own skin? Assume that, yes, at a certain point the balance shifted toward the new life and the other one receded, but did he ever completely get over the fear of exposure and the sense that he was going to be found out? When he had come to me first, crazed with the sudden loss of his wife, the *murder* of his wife as he conceived it, the formidable wife with whom he'd always struggled but to whom his devotion once again became profound in the instant of her death, when he came barging through my door in the clutches of the mad idea that because of her death I should write his book for him, was his lunacy not itself in the nature of a coded confession? Spooks! To be undone by a word that no one even speaks anymore. To hang him on that was, for Coleman, to banalize everything—the elaborate clockwork of his lie, the beautiful calibration of his deceit, *everything*. Spooks! The ridiculous trivialization of this masterly performance that had been his seemingly conventional, singularly subtle life—a life of little, if anything excessive on the surface because all the excess goes into the secret. No wonder the accusation of racism blew him sky high. As though his accomplishment were rooted in nothing but shame. No wonder *all* the accusations blew him sky high. His crime exceeded anything and everything they wanted to lay on him. He said "spooks," he has a girlfriend half his age—it's all kid stuff. Such pathetic, such petty, such ridiculous transgressions, so much high school yammering to a man who, on his trajectory outward, had, among other things, done what he'd had to do to his mother, to go there and, in behalf of his heroic conception of his life, to tell her, "It's over. This love affair is over. You're no longer my mother and never were." Anybody who has the audacity to do that doesn't just want to be white. He wants to be able to do that. It has to do with more than just being blissfully free. It's like the savagery in *The Iliad*, Coleman's favorite book about the ravening spirit of man. Each murder there has its own quality, each a more brutal slaughter than the last.

And yet, after that, he had the system beat. After that, he'd done it: never again lived outside the protection of the walled city that is convention. Or, rather, lived, at the same moment, entirely within and, surreptitiously, entirely beyond, entirely shut out—that was the fullness of his particular life as a created self. Yes, he'd had it beat for so very long, right down to all the kids being born white—and then he didn't. Blindsided by the uncontrollability of something else entirely. The man who decides to forge a distinct historical destiny, who sets out to spring the historical lock, and who does so, brilliantly succeeds at altering his personal lot, only to be ensnared by the history he hadn't quite counted on: the history that isn't yet history, the history that the clock is now ticking off, the history proliferating as I write, accruing a minute at a time and grasped better by the future than it will ever be by us. The we that is inescapable: the present moment, the common lot, the current mood, the mind of one's country, the stranglehold of history that is one's own time. Blindsided by the terrifyingly provisional nature of everything.

When we reached South Ward Street and I parked the car outside the College Arms, I said, "I'd like to meet Walter sometime. I'd like to talk to Walter about Coleman."

"Walter hasn't mentioned Coleman's name since nineteen hundred and fifty-six. He won't talk about Coleman. As white a college as there was in New England, and that's where Coleman made his career. As white a subject as there was in the curriculum, and that's what Coleman chose to teach. To Walter, Coleman is more white than the whites. There is nothing beyond that for him to say."

"Will you tell him Coleman's dead? Will you tell him where you've been?"

"No. Not unless he asks."

"Will you contact Coleman's children?"

"Why would I?" she asked. "It was for Coleman to tell them. It's not up to me."

"Why did you tell me, then?"

"I didn't tell you. You introduced yourself at the cemetery. You said to me, 'You're Coleman's sister.' I said yes. I simply spoke the truth. I'm not the one with something to hide." This was as severe as she had been with me all afternoon—and with Coleman. Till that moment she had balanced herself scrupulously between the ruination of the mother and the outrage of the brother.

Here she drew a wallet out of her handbag. She unfolded the wallet to show me one of the snapshots that were tucked into a plastic sleeve. "My parents," she said. "After World War I. He'd just come back from France."

Two young people in front of a brick stoop, the petite young woman in a large hat and a long summer dress and the tall young man in his full-dress army uniform, with visored cap, leather bandoleer, leather gloves, and high sleek leather boots. They were pale but they were Negroes. How could you tell they were Negroes? By little more than that they had nothing to hide.

"Handsome young fellow. Especially in that outfit," I said. "Could be a cavalry uniform."

"Straight infantry," she said.

"Your mother I can't see as well. Your mother's a bit shaded by the hat."

"One can do only so much to control one's life," Ernestine said, and with that, a summary statement as philosophically potent as any she cared to make, she returned the wallet to her handbag, thanked me for lunch, and, gathering herself almost visibly back into that orderly, ordinary existence that rigorously distanced itself from delusionary thinking, whether white or black or in between, she left the car. Instead of my then heading home, I drove crosstown to the cemetery and, after parking on the street, walked in through the gate, and not quite knowing what was happening, standing in the falling darkness beside the uneven earth mound roughly heaped over Coleman's coffin, I was completely seized by his story, by its end and by its beginning, and, then and there, I began this book.

I began by wondering what it had been like when Coleman

had told Faunia the truth about that beginning—assuming that he ever had; assuming, that is, that he *had* to have. Assuming that what he could not outright say to me on the day he burst in all but shouting, "Write my story, damn you!" and what he could not say to me when he had to abandon (*because of the secret*, I now realized) writing the story himself, he could not in the end resist confessing to her, to the college cleaning woman who'd become his comrade-in-arms, the first and last person since Ellie Magee for whom he could strip down and turn around so as to expose, protruding from his naked back, the mechanical key by which he had wound himself up to set off on his great escapade. Ellie, before her Steena, and finally Faunia. The only woman never to know his secret is the woman he spent his life with, his wife. Why Faunia? As it is a human thing to have a secret, it is also a human thing, sooner or later, to reveal it. Even, as in this case, to a woman who doesn't ask questions, who, you would think, would be quite a gift to a man in possession of just such a secret. But even to her—especially to her. Because her not asking questions isn't because she's dumb or doesn't want to face things; her not asking him questions is, in Coleman's eyes, at one with her devastated dignity.

"I admit that may not be at all correct," I said to my utterly transformed friend, "I admit that none of it may be. But here goes anyway: when you were trying to find out if she'd been a hooker . . . when you were trying to uncover *her* secret . . ." Out there at his grave, where everything he ever was would appear to have been canceled out by the weight and mass of all that dirt if by nothing else, I waited and I waited for him to speak until at last I heard him asking Faunia what was the worst job she'd ever had. Then I waited again, waited some more, until little by little I picked up the sassy vibrations of that straight-out talk that was hers. And that is how all this began: by my standing alone in a darkening graveyard and entering into professional competition with death.

"After the kids, after the fire," I heard her telling him, "I was taking any job I could. I didn't know what I was doing back then. I was in a fog. Well, there was this suicide," Faunia said. "This was up in the woods outside of Blackwell. With a shot-gun. Bird shot. Body was gone. A woman I knew, this boozer,

Sissie, called me to come up and help her. She was going up there to clean the place out. 'I know this is going to sound odd,' Sissie says to me, 'but I know you have a strong stomach and you can handle things. Can you help me do this?' There was a man and woman living there, and their children, and they had an argument, and he went in the other room and blew his brains out. 'I'm going up there to clean it out,' Sissie says, so I went up there with her. I needed the money, and I didn't know what I was doing anyway, so I went. The smell of death. That's what I remember. Metallic. Blood. The smell. It came out only when we started cleaning. You couldn't get the full effect until the warm water hit the blood. This place is a log cabin. Blood on the walls everywhere. Ba-boom, he's all over the walls, all over everything. Once the warm water and disinfectant hit it . . . whew. I had rubber gloves, I had to put on a mask, because even I couldn't take this anymore. Also chunks of bone on the wall, stuck in with the blood. Put the gun in his mouth. Ba-boom. Tendency to get bone and teeth out there too. Seeing it. There it all was. I remember looking at Sissie. I looked at her and she was shaking her head. 'Why the fuck are we doing this for *any* amount of money?' We finished the job as best we could. A hundred dollars an hour. Which I still don't think was enough."

"What would have been the right price?" I heard Coleman asking Faunia.

"A thousand. Burn the fucking place down. There was no right price. Sissie went outside. She couldn't handle it anymore. But me, two little kids dead, maniac Lester following me everywhere, on my case day and night, who cares? I started snooping. Because I can be that way. I wanted to know why the hell this guy had done it. It's always fascinated me. Why people kill themselves. Why there are mass murderers. Death in general. Just fascinating. Looked at the pictures. Looked if there was any happiness there. Looked at the whole place. Until I got to the medicine cabinet. The drugs. The bottles. No happiness *there*. His own little pharmacy. I figure psychiatric drugs. Stuff that should have been taken and hadn't. It was clear that he was trying to get help, but he couldn't do it. He couldn't take the medication."

"How do you know this?" Coleman asked.

"I'm assuming. I don't know. This is my own story. This is my story."

"Maybe he took the stuff and he killed himself anyway."

"Could be," she said. "The blood. Blood sticks. You could not possibly get the blood off the floor. Towel after towel after towel. Still had that color. Eventually it turned more and more a salmon color, but you still couldn't get it out. Like something still alive. Heavy-duty disinfectant—didn't help. Metallic. Sweet. Sickening. I don't gag. Put my mind above it. But I came close."

"How long did it take?" he asked her.

"We were there for about five hours. I was playing amateur detective. He was in his mid-thirties. I don't know what he did. Salesman or something. He was a woodsy-type personality. Mountain type. Big beard. Bushy hair. She was petite. Sweet face. Light skin. Dark hair. Dark eyes. Very mousy. Intimidated. This is only what I'm getting from the pictures. He was the big strong mountain type and she's this little mousy person. I don't know. But I want to know. I was an emancipated minor. Dropped out of school. I could not go to school. Aside from everything else, it was boring. All this real stuff was happening in people's houses. Sure as shit happening in *my* house. How could I go to school and learn what the capital of Nebraska was? I wanted to *know*. I wanted to get out and look around. That's why I went to Florida, and that's how I wound up all over, and that's why I snooped about that house. Just to look around. I wanted to know the worst. What is the worst? You know? She was there at the time he did it. By the time we got there, she was under psychiatric care."

"Is that the worst thing you've ever had to do? The worst work you've ever had to do?"

"Grotesque. Yes. I've seen a lot of stuff. But that thing—it wasn't that it was only grotesque. On the other hand, it was fascinating. I wanted to know why."

She wanted to know what is the worst. Not the best, the worst. By which she meant the truth. What is the truth? So he told it to her. First woman since Ellie to find out. First anyone since Ellie. Because he loved her at that moment, imagining her scrubbing the blood. It was the closest he ever felt to her. Could it be? It was the closest Coleman ever felt to anyone! He loved her. Because that is when you love somebody—when

you see them being game in the face of the worst. Not courageous. Not heroic. Just game. He had no reservations about
her. None. It was beyond thinking or calculating. It was in-
stinctive. A few hours later it might turn out to be a very bad
idea, but at that moment, no. He trusts her—that's what it is.
He trusts her: she scrubbed the blood off the floor. She's not
religious, she's not sanctimonious, she is not deformed by the
fairy tale of purity, whatever other perversions may have disfig-
ured her. She's not interested in judging—she's seen too much
for all that shit. She's not going to run away like Steena, whatever I say. "What would you think," he asked her, "if I told
you I wasn't a white man?"

At first she just looked at him, if stupefied, stupefied for a
split second and no more. Then she started laughing, burst
into the laughter that was her trademark. "What would I think?
I would think you were telling me something that I figured
out a long time ago."

"That isn't so."

"Oh, isn't it? I know what you are. I lived down south. I met
'em all. Sure, I know. Why else could I possibly like you so much?
Because you're a college professor? I'd go out of my mind if
that was you."

"I don't believe you, Faunia."

"Suit yourself," she said. "You done with your inquiry?"

"What inquiry?"

"About the worst job I ever had."

"Sure," he said. And then waited for her inquiry about his
not being white. But it never came. She didn't really seem to
care. And she didn't run away. When he told her the whole
story, she listened all right, but not because she found it incredible or unbelievable or even strange—it certainly wasn't
reprehensible. No. It sounded just like life to her.

In February, I got a call from Ernestine, maybe because it was
Black History Month and she remembered having to identify
for me Matthew Henson and Dr. Charles Drew. Maybe she
was thinking that it was time for her to take up again my education in race, touching particularly on everything that Coleman had cut himself off from, a full-to-the-brimming ready-made
East Orange world, four square miles rich in the most clinging

creaturely detail, the solid, lyrical bedrock of a successful boyhood, all the safeguards, the allegiances, the battles, the legitimacy simply taken for granted, nothing theoretical about it,
nothing specious or illusory about it—all the blissful stuff of a
happy beginning throbbing with excitement and common
sense that her brother Coleman had blotted out.

To my surprise, after telling me that Walter Silk and his wife
would be up from Asbury Park on Sunday, she said that, if I
didn't mind driving to Jersey, I was welcome to come for Sunday dinner. "You wanted to meet Walt. And I thought you might
like to see the house. There are photograph albums. There's
Coleman's room, where Coleman and Walter slept. The twin
beds are still there. It was my boy's room after them, but the
same maple frames are still right there."

I was being invited to see the Family Silk plenty that Coleman jettisoned, as though it were his bondage, in order to live
within a sphere commensurate with his sense of his scale—in
order to become somebody other, somebody who suited him,
and make his destiny by being subjugated by something else.
Jettisoned it all, the whole ramified Negro thing, thinking that
he could not displace it by any other means. So much yearning,
so much plotting and passion and subtlety and dissembling,
all of it feeding the hunger to leave the house and be transformed.

To become a new being. To bifurcate. The drama that underlies America's story, the high drama that is upping and leaving
—and the energy and cruelty that rapturous drive demands.

"I'd like to come," I said.

"I can't guarantee anything," she said. "But you're a grown
man. You can look after yourself."

I laughed. "What are you telling me?"

"Walter may be getting up on eighty, but he is still a large
and roaring furnace. What he says you're not going to like."

"About whites?"

"About Coleman. About the calculating liar. About the heartless son. About the traitor to his race."

"You told him he was dead."

"I decided to. Yes, I told Walter. We're a family. I told him
everything."

A few days later, a photograph arrived in the mail with a

note from Ernestine: "I came upon this and thought of our visit. Please keep it, if you like, as a memento of your friend Coleman Silk." It was a faded black-and-white photograph measuring about four by five inches, a blown-up snapshot, more than likely taken originally in somebody's backyard with a Brownie box camera, of Coleman as the fighting machine that his opponent will find facing him when the bell sounds. He couldn't have been more than fifteen, though with those small carved features that in the man had been so engagingly boyish looking mannishly adult in the boy. He sports, like a pro, the whammy glare, the unwavering gaze of the prowling carnivore, everything eradicated but the appetite for victory and the finesse to destroy. That look is level, issuing straight out of him like a command, even while the sharp little chin is steeply tucked into the skinny shoulder. His gloves are at the ready in the classic position—out in front as though loaded not merely with fists but with all the momentum of his one and a half decades—and each is larger in circumference than his face. One gets the subliminal sense of a kid with three heads. *I am a boxer*, the menacing pose cockily announces, *I don't knock 'em out—I cut 'em up. I outclass 'em till they stop the fight.* Unmistakably the brother she had christened Mr. Determined; indeed, "Mr. Determined," in what must have been Ernestine's girlhood hand, was inscribed in faint blue fountain-pen ink across the back of the picture.

She's something too, I thought, and found a clear plastic frame for the boy boxer and set him on my writing desk. The audacity of that family did not begin and end with Coleman. It's a bold gift, I thought, from a deceptively bold woman. I wondered what she had in mind by inviting me to the house. I wondered what I might have in mind by accepting the invitation. Strange to think that Coleman's sister and I had been taken so by each other's company—though strange only if you remembered that everything about Coleman was ten, twenty, a hundred thousand times stranger.

Ernestine's invitation, Coleman's photograph—this was how I came to set out for East Orange on the first February Sunday after the Senate had voted not to remove Bill Clinton from office, and how I came to be on a remote mountain road that ordinarily I never take on my local back-and-forth driving but that serves as a shortcut from my house to Route 7. And that was how I came to notice, parked at the edge of a wide field I would otherwise have shot right by, the dilapidated gray pickup truck with the POW/MIA bumper sticker that, I was sure, had to be Les Farley's. I saw that pickup, somehow knew it was his, and unable just to keep on going, incapable of recording its presence and continuing on, I braked to a halt. I backed up until my car was in front of his, and, at the side of the road, I parked.

I suppose I was never altogether convinced that I was doing what I was doing—otherwise how could I have done it?—but it was by then nearly three months during which time Coleman Silk's life had become closer to me than my own, and so it was unthinkable that I should be anywhere other than there in the cold, atop that mountain, standing with my gloved hand on the hood of the very vehicle that had come barreling down the wrong side of the road and sent Coleman swerving through the guardrail and, with Faunia beside him, into the river on the evening before his seventy-second birthday. If this was the murder weapon, the murderer couldn't be far away.

When I realized where I was headed—and thought again of how surprising it was to hear from Ernestine, to be asked to meet Walter, to be thinking all day and often into the night about someone I'd known for less than a year and never as the closest of friends—the course of events seemed logical enough. This is what happens when you write books. There's not just something that drives you to find out everything—something begins putting everything in your path. There is suddenly no such thing as a back road that doesn't lead headlong into your obsession.

And so you do what I was doing. Coleman, Coleman, Coleman, you who are now no one now run my existence. Of course you could not write the book. You'd written the book—the book was your life. Writing personally is exposing and concealing at the same time, but with you it could only be concealment and so it would never work. Your book was your life—and your art? Once you set the thing in motion, your art was being a white man. Being, in your brother's words, "more white than the whites." That was your singular act of invention: every day you woke up to be what you had made yourself.

There was hardly any snow left on the ground, only patches of it cobwebbing the stubble of the open field, no trail to follow, so I started bang across to the other side, where there was a thin wall of trees, and through the trees I could see another field, so I kept going until I reached the second field, and I crossed that, and through another, a deeper wall of trees, thick with high evergreens, and there at the other side was the shining eye of a frozen lake, oval and pointed at either end, with snow-freckled brownish hills rising all around it and the mountains, caressable-looking, curving away in the distance. Having walked some five hundred yards from the road, I'd intruded upon—no, trespassed upon; it was almost an unlawful sense that I had . . . I'd trespassed upon a setting as pristine, I would think, as unviolated, as serenely unspoiled, as envelops any inland body of water in New England. It gave you an idea, as such places do—as they're cherished for doing—of what the world was like before the advent of man. The power of nature is sometimes very calming, and this was a calming place, calling a halt to your trivial thinking without, at the same time, overawing you with reminders of the nothingness of a life span and the vastness of extinction. It was all on a scale safely this side of the sublime. A man could absorb the beauty into his being without feeling belittled or permeated by fear.

Almost midway out on the ice there was a solitary figure in brown coveralls and a black cap seated on a low yellow bucket, bending over an ice hole with an abbreviated fishing rod in his gloved hands. I didn't step onto the ice until I saw that he'd looked up and spotted me. I didn't want to come upon him unawares, or in any way look as though I intended to, not if the fisherman really was Les Farley. If this was Les Farley, he wasn't someone you wanted to take by surprise.

Of course I thought about turning back. I thought about heading back to the road, about getting into my car, about proceeding on to Route 7 South and down through Connecticut to 684 and from there onto the Garden State Parkway. I thought about getting a look at Coleman's bedroom. I thought about getting a look at Coleman's brother, who, for what Coleman did, could not stop hating him even after his death. I thought about that and nothing else all the way across the ice to get my look at Coleman's killer. Right up to the point where

I said, "Hi. How's it goin'?" I thought: Steal up on him or don't steal up on him, it makes no difference. You're the enemy either way. On this empty, ice-whitened stage, the *only* enemy.

"The fish biting?" I said.

"Oh, not too good, not too bad." He did no more than glance my way before focusing his attention back on the ice hole, one of twelve or fifteen identical holes cut into rock-hard ice and spread randomly across some forty or so square feet of lake. Most likely the holes had been drilled by the device that was lying just a few steps away from his yellow bucket, which was itself really a seven-gallon detergent pail. The drilling device consisted of a metal shaft about four feet long ending in a wide, cylindrical length of corkscrew blade, a strong, serious boring tool whose imposing bit—rotated by turning the cranked handle at the top—glittered like new in the sunlight. An auger.

"It serves its purpose," he mumbled. "Passes the time."

It was as though I weren't the first but more like the fiftieth person who'd happened out on the ice midway across a lake five hundred yards from a backcountry road in the rural highlands to ask about the fishing. As he wore a black wool watch cap pulled low on his forehead and down over his ears, and as he sported a dark, graying chin beard and a thickish mustache, there was only a narrow band of face on display. If it was remarkable in any way, that was because of its broadness—on the horizontal axis, an open oblong plain of a face. His dark eyebrows were long and thick, his eyes were blue and noticeably widely spaced, while centered above the mustache was the unsprouted, bridgeless nose of a kid. In just this band of himself Farley exposed between the whiskered muzzle and the woolen cap, all kinds of principles were at work, geometric and psychological both, and none seemed congruent with the others.

"Beautiful spot," I said.

"Why I'm here."

"Peaceful."

"Close to God," he said.

"Yes? You feel that?"

Now he shed the outer edge, the coating of his inwardness, shed something of the mood in which I'd caught him, and looked as if he were ready to link up with me as more than just a meaningless distraction. His posture didn't change—still very much fishing rather than gabbing—but at least a little of the antisocial aura was dissipated by a richer, more ruminative voice than I would have expected. Thoughtful, you might even call it, though in a drastically impersonal way.

"It's way up on top of a mountain," he said. "There's no houses anywhere. No dwellings. There's no cottages on the lake." After each declaration, a brooding pause—declarative observation, supercharged silence. It was anybody's guess, at the end of a sentence, whether or not he was finished with you. "Don't have a lot of activity out here. Don't have a lot of noise. Thirty acres of lake about. None of those guys with their power augers. None of their noise and the stink of their gasoline. Seven hundred acres of just open good land and woods. It's just a beautiful area. Just peace and quiet. And clean. It's a clean place. Away from all the hustle and bustle and craziness that goes on." Finally the upward glance to take me in. To assess me. A quick look that was ninety percent opaque and unreadable and ten percent alarmingly transparent. I couldn't see where there was any humor in this man.

"As long as I can keep it secret," he said, "it'll stay the way it is."

"True enough," I said.

"They live in cities. They live in the hustle and bustle of the work routine. The craziness goin' to work. The craziness *at* work. The craziness comin' home from work. The traffic. The congestion. They're caught up in that. I'm out of it."

I hadn't to ask who "they" were. I might live far from any city, might not own a power auger, but I was they, we all were they, everyone but the man hunkered down on this lake jiggling the shortish fishing rod in his hand and talking into a hole in the ice, by choice communicating less with me—as they—than to the frigid water beneath us.

"Maybe a hiker'll come through here, or a cross-country skier, or someone like you. Spots my vehicle, somehow they spot me out here, so they'll come my way, and seems like when you're out on the ice—people like you who don't fish—" and here he looked up to take in again, to divine, gnostically, my unpardonable theyness. "I'm guessin' you don't fish."

"I don't. No. Saw your truck. Just driving around on a beautiful day."

"Well, they're like you," he told me, as though there'd been no uncertainty about me from the time I'd appeared on the shore. "They'll always come over if they see a fisherman, and they're curious, and they'll ask what he caught, you know. So what I'll do . . ." But here the mind appeared to come to a halt, stopped by his thinking, *What am I doing? What the hell am I going on about?* When he started up again, my heart all at once started racing with fear. Now that his fishing has been ruined, I thought, he's decided to have some fun with me. He's into his act now. He's out of the fishing and into being Les and all the many things that is and is not.

"So what I'll do," he resumed, "if I have fish layin' on the ice, I'll do what I did when I saw you. I'll pick all the fish up right away that I caught and I'll put 'em in a plastic bag and put 'em in my bucket, the bucket I'm sittin' on. So now the fish are concealed. And when the people come over and say, 'How are they bitin',' I say, 'Nothin'. I don't think there's anything in here.' I caught maybe thirty fish already. Excellent day. But I'll tell 'em, 'Naw, I'm gettin' ready to leave. I been here two hours and I haven't gotten a bite yet.' Every time they'll just turn around and leave. They'll go somewhere else. And they'll spread the word that that pond up there is no good. That's how secret it is. Maybe I end up tending to be a little dishonest. But this place is like the best-kept secret in the whole world."

"And now I know," I said. I saw that there was no possible way to get him to laugh along conspiratorially at his dissembling with interlopers like myself, no way I was going to get him to ease up by smiling at what he'd said, and so I didn't try. I realized that though nothing may have passed between us of a truly personal nature, by his decision, if not mine, we two were further along than smiling could help. I was in a conversation that, out in this remote, secluded, frozen place, seemed suddenly to be of the greatest importance. "I also know you're sitting on a slew of fish," I said. "In that bucket. How many today?"

"Well, you look like a man who can keep a secret. About thirty, thirty-five fish. Yeah, you look like an upright man. I think I recognize you anyway. Aren't you the author?"

"That I am."

"Sure. I know where you live. Across from the swamp where the heron is. Dumouchel's place. Dumouchel's cabin there."

"Dumouchel's who I bought it from. So tell me, since I'm a man who can keep a secret, why are you sitting right here and not over there? This whole big frozen lake. How'd you choose this one spot to fish?" Even if he really wasn't doing everything he could to keep me there, I seemed on my own to be doing everything I could not to leave.

"Well, you never know," he told me. "You start out where you got 'em the last time. If you caught fish the last time, you always start out at that spot."

"So that solves that. I always wondered." Go now, I thought. That's all the conversation necessary. More than is necessary. But the thought of who he was drew me on. The *fact* of him drew me on. This was not speculation. This was not meditation. This was not that way of thinking that is fiction writing. This was the thing itself. The laws of caution that, outside my work, had ruled my life so strictly for the last five years were suddenly suspended. I couldn't turn back while crossing the ice and now I couldn't turn and flee. It had nothing to do with courage. It had nothing to do with reason or logic. Here he is. That's all it had to do with. That and my fear. In his heavy brown coveralls and his black watch cap and his thick-soled black rubber boots, with his two big hands in a hunter's (or a soldier's) camouflage-colored fingertipless gloves, here is the man who murdered Coleman and Faunia. I'm sure of it. They didn't drive off the road and into the river. Here is the killer. He is the one. How can I go?

"Fish always there?" I asked him. "When you return to your spot from the time before?"

"No, sir. The fish move in schools. Underneath the ice. One day they'll be at the north end of the pond, the next day they might be at the south end of the pond. Maybe sometimes two times in a row they'll be at that same spot. They'll still be there. What they tend to do, the fish tend to school up and they don't move very much, because the water's so cold. They're able to adjust to water temperature, and the water being so cold, they don't move so much and they don't require as much food. But if you get in an area where the fish are schooled up, you will catch a lot of fish. But some days you can go out in the same pond—you can never cover the entire thing—so you might try about five or six different places, drill holes, and never get a hit. Never catch a fish. You just didn't locate the school. And so you just sit here."

"Close to God," I said.

"You got it."

His fluency—because it was the last thing I was expecting —fascinated me, as did the thoroughness with which he was willing to explain the life in a pond when the water's cold. How did he know I was "the author"? Did he also know I was Coleman's friend? Did he also know I was at Faunia's funeral? I supposed there were now as many questions in his mind about me—and my mission here—as there were in mine about him. This great bright arched space, this cold aboveground vault of a mountaintop cradling at its peak a largish oval of fresh water frozen hard as rock, the ancient activity that is the life of a lake, that is the formation of ice, that is the metabolism of fish, all the soundless, ageless forces unyieldingly working away—it is as though we have encountered each other at the top of the world, two hidden brains mistrustfully ticking, mutual hatred and paranoia the only introspection there is anywhere.

"And so what do you think about," I asked, "if you don't get a fish? What do you think about when they're not biting?"

"Tell you what I was just thinking about. I was thinking a lot of things. I was thinking about Slick Willie. I was thinking about our president—his freakin' luck. I was thinkin' about this guy who gets off everything, and I was thinkin' about the guys who didn't get off nothin'. Who didn't dodge the draft and didn't get off. It doesn't seem right."

"Vietnam," I said.

"Yeah. We'd go up in the freakin' helicopters—in my second tour I was a door gunner—and what I was thinking about was this one time we went into North Vietnam to pick up these two pilots. I was sitting out here thinking about that time. Slick Willie. That son of a bitch. Thinkin' about that scumbag son of a bitch gettin' his dick sucked in the Oval Office on the taxpayer's money, and then thinkin' about these two pilots, they were on an air strike over Hanoi harbor, these guys were hit real bad, and we picked up the signal on the radio. We weren't even a rescue helicopter, but we were in the vicinity, and they were giving a mayday that they were goin' to bail out, because they were at the altitude point where if they didn't bail out they were goin' to crash. We weren't even a rescue helicopter—we were a gunship—we were just taking a chance that we could save a couple of lives. We didn't even get permission to get up there, we just went. You act on instinct like that. We just all agreed, two door gunners, the pilot, the copilot, though the chances weren't that good because we had no cover. But we went in anyway—to try to pick 'em up."

He's telling me a war story, I thought. He knows he's doing it. There's a point here that he's going to make. Something he wants me to carry away with me, to the shore, to my car, to the house whose location he knows and wishes me to understand that he knows. To carry away as "the author"? Or as somebody else—somebody who knows a secret of his that is even bigger than the secret of this pond. He wants me to know that not many people have seen what he's seen, been where he's been, done what he's done and, if required to, can do again. He's murdered in Vietnam and he's brought the murderer back with him to the Berkshires, back with him from the country of war, the country of horror, to this completely uncomprehending other place.

The auger out on the ice. The candor of the auger. There could be no more solid embodiment of our hatred than the merciless steel look of that auger out in the middle of nowhere.

"We figure, okay, we're gonna die, we're gonna die. So we went up there and we homed in on their signals, we saw one parachute, and we went down in the clearing, and we picked that guy up with no trouble at all. He jumped right in, we dragged him right in and took off, no opposition whatsoever. So we said to him, 'You have any idea?' and he said, 'Well, he drifted off that way.' So we went up in the air, but by then they knew we were there. We went over a little farther looking for the other parachute, and all freakin' hell broke loose. I'm telling you, it was unbelievable. We never picked up the other guy. The helicopter was gettin' hit like you wouldn't believe it. Ting ping ping boom. Machine guns. Ground fire. We just had to turn around and get the hell out of there as fast as we could. And I remember the guy we picked up started to cry. This is what I'm getting at. He was a navy pilot. They were off the

Forrestal. And he knew the other guy was either killed or captured, and he started to bawl. It was horrible for him. His
buddy. But we couldn't go back. We couldn't risk the chopper
and five guys. We were lucky we got one. So we got back to
our base and we got out and we looked at the chopper and
there were a hundred and fifty-one bullet holes in it. Never hit
a hydraulic line, a fuel line, but the rotors were all pinged up, a
lot of bullets hit the rotors. Bent them a little bit. If they hit
the tail rotor, you go right down, but they didn't. You know
they shot down five thousand helicopters during that war?
Twenty-eight hundred jet fighters we lost. They lost two hundred fifty B-52s in high-altitude bombing over North Vietnam.
But the government'll never tell you that. Not that. They tell you
what they want to tell you. Never Slick Willie who gets caught.
It's the guy who served who gets caught. Over and over. Nope,
doesn't seem right. You know what I was thinking? I was
thinking that if I had a son he'd be out here with me now. Ice
fishin'. That's what I was thinking when you walked out here.
I looked up and I saw someone comin', and I'm sort of day-
dreamin', and I thought, That could be my son. Not you, not
a man like you, but my son."

"Don't you have a son?"

"No."

"Never married?" I asked.

This time he didn't answer me right off. He looked at me,
homed in on me as though I had a signal that was going off
like the two pilots bailing out, but he didn't answer me. Because he knows, I thought. He knows I was at Faunia's funeral.
Somebody told him that "the author" was there. What kind of
author does he think I am? An author who writes books about
crimes like his? An author who writes books about murderers
and murder?

"Doomed," he said finally, staring back into the hole and
jiggling his rod, jerking it with a flick of his wrist a dozen or so
times. "Marriage was doomed. Came back from Vietnam with
too much anger and resentment. Had PTSD. I had what they
call post-traumatic stress disorder. That's what they told me.
When I come back, I didn't want to know anybody. I come
back, I couldn't relate to anything that was going on around
here, as far as civilized living. It's like I was there so long, it was

totally insane. Wearing clean clothes, and people saying hello, and people smiling, and people going to parties, and people driving cars—I couldn't relate to it anymore. I didn't know how to talk to anybody, I didn't know how to say hello to anybody. I withdrew for a long time. I used to get in my car, drive around, go in the woods, walk in the woods—it was the weirdest thing. I withdrew from *myself*. I had no idea what I was going through. My buddies would call me, I wouldn't call back. They were afraid I was going to die in a car accident, they were afraid I was—"

I interrupted. "Why were they afraid you were going to die in a car accident?"

"I was drinking. I was driving around and drinking."

"Did you ever get into a car accident?"

He smiled. Didn't take a pause and stare me down. Didn't give me an especially threatening look. Didn't jump up and go for my throat. Just smiled a little, more good nature in the smile than I could have believed he had in him to show. In a deliberately lighthearted way, he shrugged and said, "Got *me*. I didn't know what I was going through, you *know*? Accident? In an accident? I wouldn't know if I did. I suppose I didn't. You're going through what they call post-traumatic stress disorder. Stuff keeps coming back into your subconscious mind that you're back in Vietnam, that you're back in the army again. I'm not an educated guy. I didn't even know that. People were so pissed at me for this and that, and they didn't even know what I was going through and *I* didn't even know—you know? I don't have educated friends who know these things. I got assholes for friends. Oh, man, I mean real guaranteed hundred percent assholes or double your money back." Again the shrug. Comical? Intended to be comical? No, more a happy-go-lucky strain of sinisterness. "So what can I do?" he asked helplessly.

Conning me. Playing with me. Because he knows I know. Here we are alone up where we are, and I know, and he knows I know. And the auger knows. All ye know and all ye need to know, all inscribed in the spiral of its curving steel blade.

"How'd you find out you had PTSD?"

"A colored girl at the VA. Excuse me. An African American. A very intelligent African American. She's got a master's degree. You got a master's degree?"

"No," I said.

"Well, she's got one, and that's how I found out what I had. Otherwise I still wouldn't know. That's how I started learning about myself, what I was going through. They told me. And not just me. Don't think it was just me. Thousands and thousands of guys were going through what I was going through. Thousands and thousands of guys waking up in the middle of the night back in Vietnam. Thousands and thousands of guys people are calling up and they don't call them back. Thousands and thousands of guys having these real bad dreams. And so I told that to this African American and she understood what it was. Because she had that master's degree, she told me how it was going through my subconscious mind, and that it was the same with thousands and thousands of other guys. The subconscious mind. You can't control it. It's like the government. It *is* the government. It's the government all over again. It gets you to do what you don't want to do. Thousands and thousands of guys getting married and it's doomed, because they have this anger and this resentment about Vietnam in their subconscious mind. She explained all this to me. They just popped me from Vietnam onto a C-141 air force jet to the Philippines, then on a World Airways jet to Travis Air Force Base, then they gave me two hundred dollars to go home. So it took me, like, from the time I left Vietnam to go home, it took about three days. You're back in civilization. And you're doomed. And your wife, even if it's ten years later, she's doomed. She's doomed, and what the hell did she do? Nothin'."

"Still have the PTSD?"

"Well, I still tend to isolate, don't I? What do you think I'm doin' out here?"

"But no more drinking and driving," I heard myself saying. "No more accidents."

"There were never accidents. Don't you listen? I already told you that. Not that I know of."

"And the marriage was doomed."

"Oh yeah. My fault. Hundred percent. She was a lovely woman. Entirely blameless. All me. Always all me. She deserved a helluva lot better than me."

"What happened to her?" I asked.

He shook his head. A sad shrug, a sigh—complete bullshit,

deliberately *transparent* bullshit. "No idea. Ran away, I scared her so. Scared the woman shitless. My heart goes out to her, wherever she may be. Completely blameless person."

"No kids?"

"Nope. No kids. You?" he asked me.

"No."

"Married?"

"No more," I said.

"So, you and me in the same boat. Free as the wind. What kind of books do you write? Whodunits?"

"I wouldn't say that."

"True stories?"

"Sometimes."

"What? Romance?" he asked, smiling. "Not pornography, I hope." He pretended that that was an unwanted idea it vexed him even to entertain. "I sure hope our local author is not up there in Mike Dumouchel's place writing and publishing pornography."

"I write about people like you," I said.

"Is that right?"

"Yes. People like you. Their problems."

"What's the name of one of your books?"

"*The Human Stain*."

"Yeah? Can I get it?"

"It's not out yet. It's not finished yet."

"I'll buy it."

"I'll send you one. What's your name?"

"Les Farley. Yeah, send it. When you finish it, send it care of the town garage. Town Garage. Route 6. Les Farley." Needling me again, sort of needling everyone—himself, his friends, "our local author"—he said, even as he began laughing at the idea, "Me and the guys'll read it." He didn't so much laugh aloud as nibble at the bait of an out-loud laugh, work up to and around the laugh without quite sinking his teeth in. Close to the hook of dangerous merriment, but not close enough to swallow it.

"I hope you will," I said.

I couldn't just turn and go then. Not on that note, not with him shedding ever so slightly a bit more of the emotional incognito, not with the possibility raised of peering a little further into his mind. "What were you like before you went into the service?" I asked him.

"Is this for your book?"

"Yes. Yes." *I* laughed out loud. Without even intending to, with a ridiculous, robust burst of defiance, I said, foolishly, "It's *all* for my book."

And he now laughed with more abandon too. On this loony bin of a lake.

"Were you a gregarious guy, Les?"

"Yeah," he said. "I was."

"With people?"

"Yeah."

"Like to have a good time with them?"

"Yeah. Tons of friends. Fast cars. You know, all that stuff. I worked all the time. But when I wasn't working, yeah."

"And all you Vietnam veterans ice fish?"

"I don't know." The nibbling laughter once again. I thought, It's easier for him to kill somebody than to cut loose with real amusement.

"I started ice fishing," he told me, "not that long ago. After my wife ran away. I rented a little shack, back in the woods, on Dragonfly. Back in the woods, right on the water, Dragonfly Pond, and I always summer fished, all my life, but I was never too interested in ice fishing. I always figure it's too cold out there, you know? So the first winter I lived on the pond, and I wasn't myself that winter—goddamn PTSD—I was watching this ice fisherman walk out there and go out fishing. So I watched this a couple of times, so one day I put on my clothes and took a walk out there and this guy was catching a lot of fish, yellow perch and trout and everything. So I figure, this fishin' is just as good as the summertime, if not better. All you have to do is get the right amount of clothing on and get the right equipment. So I did. I went down and bought an auger, a nice auger"—he points—"jiggin' rod, lures. Hundreds of different kinds of lures you can get. Hundreds of different manufacturers and makes. All various sizes. You drill a hole through the ice, and you drop your favorite lure down there with the bait on it—it's just a hand movement, you just make that jig move up and down, you know. Because it's dark down underneath the ice. Oh, it is dark all right," he told me, and, for the first time in the conversation, he looked at me with not too much but too little opacity in his face, too little deceit, too little duplicity. In his voice there was a chilling resonance when he said, "It's *real* dark." A chilling and astonishing resonance that made everything about Coleman's accident clear. "So any kind of a flash down there," he added, "the fish are attracted to it. I guess they're adaptable to that dark environment."

No, he's not stupid. He's a brute and he's a killer but not so dumb as I thought. It isn't a brain that is missing. Beneath whatever the disguise, it rarely is.

"Because they have to eat," he's explaining to me, scientifically. "They find food down there. And their bodies are able to adapt to that extracold water and their eyes adapt to the dark. They're sensitive to movement. If they see any kind of flashes or they maybe feel the vibrations of your lure moving, they're attracted to it. They know that it's something alive and it might be edible. But if you don't jig it, you'll never get a hit. If I had a son, you see, which is what I was thinkin', I'd be teachin' him how to jig it. I'd be teachin' him how to bait the lure. There's different kinds of baits, you see, most of them are fly larvae or bee larvae that they raise for ice fishin'. And we'd go down to the store, me and Les Junior, and we'd buy 'em at the ice fishin' store. And they come in a little cup, you know. If I had Little Les right now, a son of my own, you know, if I wasn't doomed instead for life with this freakin' PTSD, I'd be out here with him teachin' him all this stuff. I'd teach him how to use the auger." He pointed to the tool, still just out of reach behind him on the ice. "I use a five-inch auger. They come from four inches up to eight inches. I prefer a five-inch hole. It's perfect. I never had a problem yet gettin' a fish through a five-inch hole. Six is a little too big. The reason six is too big, the blades are another inch wider, which doesn't seem like much, but if you look at the five-inch auger—here, let me show you." He got up and went over and he got the auger. Despite the padded coveralls and the boots that added to his bulk as a shortish, stocky man, he moved deftly across the ice, sweeping up the auger in one hand the way you might sweep the bat up off the field while jogging back to the bench after running out a fly ball. He came up to me and raised the auger's long bright bit right up to my face. "Here."

Here. Here was the origin. Here was the essence. Here.

"If you look at the five-inch auger compared to the six-inch auger," he said, "it's a big difference. When you're hand drilling through a foot to eighteen inches of ice, it takes a lot more effort to use a six-inch than a five-inch. With this here I can drill through a foot and a half of ice in about twenty seconds. If the blades are good and sharp. The sharpness is everything. You always gotta keep your blades sharp."

I nodded. "It's cold out here on the ice."

"You better believe it."

"Didn't notice till now. I'm getting cold. My face. It's getting to me. I should be going." And I took my first step backward and away from the thin slush surrounding him and the hole he was fishing.

"Good enough. And you know your ice fishing now, don't you? Maybe you want to write a book about that instead of a whodunit."

Shuffling backward a half-step at a time, I'd retreated toward the shore some four or five feet, but he was still holding the auger up in his one hand, the corkscrew blade raised still to the level where my eyes had been before. Completely bested, I'd begun backing away. "And now you know my secret spot. That too. You know everything," he said. "But you won't tell nobody, will you? It's nice to have a secret spot. You don't tell anybody about 'em. You learn not to say anything."

"It's safe with me," I said.

"There's a brook that comes in down off the mountain, it flows over ledges. Did I tell you that?" he said. "I never traced its source. It's a constant flow of water that comes down into the lake here from there. And there's a spillway on the south side of the lake, which is where the water flows out." He pointed, still with that auger. He was holding it tight in the fingertipless glove of one big hand. "And then there's numerous springs underneath the lake. The water comes up from underneath, so the water constantly turns over. It cleans itself. And fish have to have clean water to survive and get big and healthy. And this place has all of those ingredients. And they're all God-made.

Nothing man had to do with it. That's why it's clean and that's why I come here. If man has to do with it, stay away from it. That's my motto. The motto of a guy with a subconscious mind full of PTSD. Away from man, close to God. So don't you forget to keep this my secret place. The only time a secret gets out, Mr. Zuckerman, is when you tell that secret."

"I hear ya."

"And, hey, Mr. Zuckerman—the book."

"What book?"

"Your book. Send the book."

"You got it," I said, "it's in the mail," and started back across the ice. He was behind me, still holding that auger as slowly I started away. It was a long way. If I even made it, I knew that my five years alone in my house here were over. I knew that if and when I finished the book, I was going to have to go elsewhere to live.

I turned from the shore, once I was safely there, to look back and see if he was going to follow me into the woods after all and to do me in before I ever got my chance to enter Coleman Silk's boyhood house and, like Steena Palsson before me, to sit with his East Orange family as the white guest at Sunday dinner. Just facing him, I could feel the terror of the auger— even with him already seated back on his bucket: the icy white of the lake encircling a tiny spot that was a man, the only human marker in all of nature, like the X of an illiterate's signature on a sheet of paper. There it was, if not the whole story, the whole picture. Only rarely, at the end of our century, does life offer up a vision as pure and peaceful as this one: a solitary man on a bucket, fishing through eighteen inches of ice in a lake that's constantly turning over its water atop an arcadian mountain in America.

CHRONOLOGY

NOTE ON THE TEXTS

NOTES

Chronology

1933   Born Philip Roth on March 19 in Newark, New Jersey, second child of Herman Roth and Bess Finkel. (Bess Finkel, the second child of five, was born in 1904 in Elizabeth, New Jersey, to Philip and Dora Finkel, Jewish immigrants from near Kiev. Herman Roth was born in 1901 in Newark, New Jersey, the middle child of seven born to Sender and Bertha Roth, Jewish immigrants from Polish Galicia. They were married in Newark on February 21, 1926, and shortly afterward opened a small family-run shoe store. Their son Sanford ["Sandy"] was born December 26, 1927. Following the bankruptcy of the shoe store and a briefly held position as city marshal, Herman Roth took a job as agent with the Newark district office of the Metropolitan Life Insurance Company, and would remain with the company until his retirement as district manager in 1966.) Family moves into second-floor flat of two-and-a-half-family house (with five-room apartments on each of the first two floors and a three-room apartment on the top floor) at 81 Summit Avenue in Newark. Summit Avenue was a lower-middle-class residential street in the Weequahic section, a twenty-minute bus ride from commercial downtown Newark and less than a block from Chancellor Avenue School and from Weequahic High School, then considered the state's best academic public high school. These were the two schools that Sandy and Philip attended. Between 1910 and 1920, Weequahic had been developed as a new city neighborhood at the southwest corner of Newark, some three miles from the edge of industrial Newark and from the international shipping facilities at Port Newark on Newark Bay. In the first half of the twentieth century Newark was a prosperous working-class city of approximately 420,000, the majority of its citizens of German, Italian, Slavic, and Irish extraction. Blacks and Jews composed two of the smallest groups in the city. From the 1930s to the 1950s, the Jews lived mainly in the predominantly Jewish Weequahic section.

1938   Philip enters kindergarten at Chancellor Avenue School in January.

1942   Roth family moves to second-floor flat of two-and-a-half-family house at 359 Leslie Street, three blocks west of Summit Avenue, still within the Weequahic neighborhood but nearer to semi-industrial boundary with Irvington.

1946   Philip graduates from elementary school in January, having skipped a year. Brother graduates from high school and chooses to enter U.S. Navy for two years rather than be drafted into the peacetime army.

1947   Family moves to first-floor flat of two-and-a-half-family house at 385 Leslie Street, just a few doors from commercial Chancellor Avenue, the neighborhood's main artery. Philip turns from reading sports fiction by John R. Tunis and adventure fiction by Howard Pease to reading the left-leaning historical novels of Howard Fast.

1948   Brother is discharged from navy and, with the aid of G.I. Bill, enrolls as commercial art student at Pratt Institute, Brooklyn. Philip takes strong interest in politics during the four-way U.S. presidential election in which the Republican Dewey loses to the Democrat Truman despite a segregationist Dixiecrat Party and a left-wing Progressive Party drawing away traditionally Democratic voters.

1950   Graduates from high school in January. Works as stock clerk at S. Klein department store in downtown Newark. Reads Thomas Wolfe; discovers Sherwood Anderson, Ring Lardner, Erskine Caldwell, and Theodore Dreiser. In September enters Newark College of Rutgers as pre-law student while continuing to live at home. (Newark Rutgers was at this time a newly formed college housed in two small converted downtown buildings, one formerly a bank, the other formerly a brewery.)

1951   Still a pre-law student, transfers in September to Bucknell University in Lewisburg, Pennsylvania. Brother graduates from Pratt Institute and moves to New York City to work for advertising agency. Parents move to Moorestown, New Jersey, approximately seventy miles southwest of Newark; father takes job as manager of Metropolitan Life's south Jersey district after having previously managed several north Jersey district offices.

1952   Roth decides to study English literature. With two friends, founds Bucknell literary magazine, *Et Cetera*, and becomes its first editor. Writes first short stories. Strongly influenced in his literary studies by English professor Mildred Martin, under whose tutelage he reads extensively, and with whom he will maintain lifelong friendship.

1954   Is elected to Phi Beta Kappa and graduates from Bucknell magna cum laude in English. Accepts scholarship to study English at the University of Chicago graduate school, beginning in September. Reads Saul Bellow's *The Adventures of Augie March*, and under its influence explores Chicago.

1955   In June receives M.A. with Honors in English. In September, rather than wait to be drafted, enlists in U.S. Army for two years. Suffers spinal injury during basic training at Fort Dix. In November, is assigned to Public Information Office at Walter Reed Army Hospital, Washington, D.C. Begins to write short stories "The Conversion of the Jews" and "Epstein." *Epoch*, a Cornell University literary quarterly, publishes "The Contest for Aaron Gold," which is reprinted in Martha Foley's *Best American Short Stories 1956*.

1956   Is hospitalized in June for complications from spinal injury. After two-month hospital stay receives honorable discharge for medical reasons and a disability pension. In September returns to University of Chicago as instructor in the liberal arts college, teaching freshman composition. Begins course work for Ph.D. but drops out after one term. Meets Ted Solotaroff, who is also a graduate student, and they become friends.

1957   Publishes in *Commentary* "You Can't Tell a Man by the Song He Sings." Writes novella "Goodbye, Columbus." Meets Saul Bellow at University of Chicago when Bellow is a classroom guest of Roth's friend and colleague, the writer Richard Stern. Begins to review movies and television for *The New Republic* after magazine publishes "Positive Thinking on Pennsylvania Avenue," a humor piece satirizing President Eisenhower's religious beliefs.

1958   Publishes "The Conversion of the Jews" and "Epstein" in *The Paris Review*; "Epstein" wins *Paris Review* Aga Khan Prize, presented to Roth in Paris in July. Spends first summer abroad, mainly in Paris. Houghton Mifflin awards Roth the Houghton Mifflin Literary Fellowship to publish the novella and five stories in one volume; George Starbuck, a poet and friend from Chicago, is his editor. Resigns from teaching position at University of Chicago. Moves to two-room basement apartment on Manhattan's Lower East Side. Becomes friendly with *Paris Review* editors George Plimpton and Robert Silvers and *Commentary* editor Martin Greenberg.

1959   Marries Margaret Martinson Williams. Publishes "Defender of the Faith" in *The New Yorker*, causing consternation among Jewish organizations and rabbis who attack magazine and condemn author as anti-Semitic; story collected in *Goodbye, Columbus* and included in *Best American Short Stories 1960* and *Prize Stories 1960: The O. Henry Awards*, where it wins second prize. *Goodbye, Columbus* is published in May. Roth receives Guggenheim fellowship and award from the American Academy of Arts and Letters. *Goodbye, Columbus* gains highly favorable reviews from Bellow, Alfred Kazin, Leslie Fiedler, and Irving Howe; influential rabbis denounce Roth in their sermons as "a self-hating Jew." Roth and wife leave U.S. to spend seven months in Italy, where he works on his first novel, *Letting Go*; he meets William Styron, who is living in Rome and who becomes a lifelong friend. Styron introduces Roth to his publisher, Donald Klopfer of Random House; when George Starbuck leaves Houghton Mifflin, Roth moves to Random House.

1960   *Goodbye, Columbus and Five Short Stories* wins National Book Award. The collection also wins Daroff Award of the Jewish Book Council of America. Roth returns to America to teach at the Writers' Workshop of the University of Iowa, Iowa City. Meets drama professor Howard Stein (later dean of the Columbia University Drama School), who becomes lifelong friend. Continues working on *Letting Go*. Travels in Midwest. Participates in *Esquire* magazine symposium at Stanford University; his speech "Writing American Fiction," published in *Commentary* in March 1961, is widely discussed. After a speaking engagement in Oregon, meets Bernard Malamud, whose fiction he admires.

1962   After two years at Iowa, accepts two-year position as writer-in-residence at Princeton. Separates from Margaret Roth. Moves to New York City and commutes to Princeton classes. (Lives at various Manhattan locations until 1970.) Meets Princeton sociologist Melvin Tumin, a Newark native who becomes a friend. Random House publishes *Letting Go*.

1963   Receives Ford Foundation grant to write plays in affiliation with American Place Theater in New York. Is legally separated from Margaret Roth. Becomes close friend of Aaron Asher, a University of Chicago graduate and editor at Meridian Books, original paperback publisher of *Goodbye, Columbus*. In June takes part in American Jewish Congress symposium in Tel Aviv, Israel, along with American writers Leslie Fiedler, Max Lerner, and literary critic David Boroff. Travels in Israel for a month.

1964   Teaches at State University of New York at Stony Brook, Long Island. Reviews plays by James Baldwin, LeRoi Jones, and Edward Albee for newly founded *New York Review of Books*. Spends a month at Yaddo, writers' retreat in Saratoga Springs, New York, that provides free room and board. (Will work at Yaddo for several months at a time throughout the 1960s.) Meets and establishes friendships there with novelist Alison Lurie and painter Julius Goldstein.

1965   Begins to teach comparative literature at University of Pennsylvania one semester each year more or less annually until the mid-1970s. Meets professor Joel Conarroe, who becomes a close friend. Begins work on *When She Was Good* after abandoning another novel, begun in 1962.

1966   Publishes section of *When She Was Good* in *Harper's*. Is increasingly troubled by Vietnam War and in ensuing years takes part in marches and demonstrations against it.

1967   Publishes *When She Was Good*. Begins work on *Portnoy's Complaint*, of which he publishes excerpts in *Esquire*, *Partisan Review*, and *New American Review*, where Ted Solotaroff is editor.

1968   Margaret Roth dies in an automobile accident. Roth spends two months at Yaddo completing *Portnoy's Complaint*.

1969   *Portnoy's Complaint* published in February. Within weeks becomes number-one fiction best seller and a widely discussed cultural phenomenon. Roth makes no public appearances and retreats for several months to Yaddo. Rents house in Woodstock, New York, and meets the painter Philip Guston, who lives nearby. They remain close friends and see each other regularly until Guston's death in 1980. Renews friendship with Bernard Malamud, who like Roth is serving as a member of The Corporation of Yaddo.

1970   Spends March traveling in Thailand, Burma, Cambodia, and Hong Kong. Begins work on *My Life as a Man* and publishes excerpt in *Modern Occasions.* Is elected to National Institute of Arts and Letters and is its youngest member. Commutes to his classes at University of Pennsylvania and lives mainly in Woodstock until 1972.

1971   Excerpts of *Our Gang*, satire of the Nixon administration, appear in *New York Review of Books* and *Modern Occasions*; the book is published by Random House in the fall. Continues work on *My Life as a Man*; writes *The Breast* and *The Great American Novel.* Begins teaching a Kafka course at University of Pennsylvania.

1972   *The Breast*, first book of three featuring protagonist David Kepesh, published by Holt, Rinehart, Winston, where Aaron Asher is his editor. Roth buys old farmhouse and forty acres in northwest Connecticut, one hundred miles from New York City, and moves there from Woodstock. In May travels to Venice, Vienna, and, for the first time, Prague. Meets his translators there, Luba and Rudolph Pilar, and they describe to him the impact of the political situation on Czech writers. In U.S., arranges to meet exiled Czech editor Antonin Liehm in New York; attends Liehm's weekly classes in Czech history, literature, and film at College of Staten Island, City University of New York. Through friendship with Liehm meets numerous Czech exiles, including film directors Ivan Passer and Jiří Weiss, who become friends. Is elected to the American Academy of Arts and Sciences.

1973   Publishes *The Great American Novel* and the essay "Looking at Kafka" in *New American Review.* Returns to Prague and meets novelists Milan Kundera, Ivan Klíma, Ludvik Vaculik, the poet Miroslav Holub, and other writers blacklisted and persecuted by the Soviet-backed

Communist regime; becomes friendly with Rita Klímová, a blacklisted translator and academic, who will serve as Czechoslovakia's first ambassador to U.S. following the 1989 "Velvet Revolution." (Will make annual spring trips to Prague to visit his writer friends until he is denied an entry visa in 1977.) Writes "Country Report" on Czechoslovakia for American PEN. Proposes paperback series, "Writers from the Other Europe," to Penguin Books USA; becomes general editor of the series, selecting titles, commissioning introductions, and overseeing publication of Eastern European writers relatively unknown to American readers. Beginning in 1974, series publishes fiction by Polish writers Jerzy Andrzejewski, Tadeusz Borowski, Tadeusz Konwicki, Witold Gombrowicz, and Bruno Schulz; Hungarian writers György Konrád and Géza Csáth; Yugoslav writer Danilo Kiš; and Czech writers Bohumil Hrabal, Milan Kundera, and Ludvik Vaculik; series ends in 1989. "Watergate Edition" of *Our Gang* published, which includes a new preface by Roth.

1974   Roth publishes *My Life as a Man*. Visits Budapest as well as Prague and meets Budapest writers through Hungarian PEN and the *Hungarian Quarterly*. In Prague meets Vaclav Havel. Through friend Professor Zdenek Strybyrny, visits and becomes friend of the niece of Franz Kafka, Vera Saudkova, who shows him Kafka family photographs and family belongings; subsequently becomes friendly in London with Marianne Steiner, daughter of Kafka's sister Valli. Also through Strybyrny meets the widow of Jiří Weil; upon his return to America arranges for translation and publication of Weil's novel *Life with a Star* as well as publication of several Weil short stories in *American Poetry Review*, for which he provides an introduction. In Princeton meets Joanna Rostropowicz Clark, wife of friend Blair Clark; she becomes close friend and introduces Roth to contemporary Polish writing and to Polish writers visiting America, including Konwicki and Kazimierz Brandys. Publishes "Imagining Jews" in *New York Review of Books*; essay prompts letter from university professor, editor, writer, and former Jesuit Jack Miles. Correspondence ensues and the two establish a lasting intellectual friendship. In New York, meets teacher, editor, author, and journalist Bernard Avishai; they quickly establish a strong intellectual bond and become lifelong friends.

1975   Aaron Asher leaves Holt and becomes editor in chief at Farrar, Straus and Giroux; Roth moves to FSG with Asher for publication of *Reading Myself and Others*, a collection of interviews and critical essays. Meets British actress Claire Bloom.

1976   Interviews Isaac Bashevis Singer about Bruno Schulz for *New York Times Book Review* article to coincide with publication of Schulz's *Street of Crocodiles* in "Writers from the Other Europe" series. Moves with Claire Bloom to London, where they live six to seven months a year for the next twelve years. Spends the remaining months in Connecticut, where Bloom joins him when she is not acting in films, television, or stage productions. In London resumes an old friendship with British critic A. Alvarez and, a few years later, begins a friendship with American writer Michael Herr (author of *Dispatches*, which Roth admires) and with the American painter R. B. Kitaj. Also meets critic and biographer Hermione Lee, who becomes a friend, as does novelist Edna O'Brien. Begins regular visits to France to see Milan Kundera and another new friend, French writer-critic Alain Finkielkraut. Visits Israel for the first time since 1963 and returns there regularly, keeping a journal that eventually provides ideas and material for novels *The Counterlife* and *Operation Shylock*. Meets the writer Aharon Appelfeld in Jerusalem and they become close friends.

1977   Publishes *The Professor of Desire*, second book of Kepesh trilogy. Beginning in 1977 and continuing over the next few years, writes series of TV dramas for Claire Bloom: adaptations of *The Name-Day Party*, a short story by Chekhov; *Journey into the Whirlwind*, the gulag autobiography of Eugenia Ginzburg; and, with David Plante, *It Isn't Fair*, Plante's memoir of Jean Rhys. At request of Chichester Festival director, modernizes the David Magarshack translation of Chekhov's *The Cherry Orchard* for Claire Bloom's 1981 performance at the festival as Madame Ranyevskaya.

1979   *The Ghost Writer*, first novel featuring novelist Nathan Zuckerman as protagonist, is published in its entirety in *The New Yorker*, then published by Farrar, Straus and Giroux. Bucknell awards Roth his first honorary degree; eventually receives honorary degrees from Amherst,

Brown, Columbia, Dartmouth, Harvard, Pennsylvania, and Rutgers, among others.

1980   *A Philip Roth Reader* published, edited by Martin Green. Milan and Vera Kundera visit Connecticut on first trip to U.S.; Roth introduces Kundera to friend and *New Yorker* editor Veronica Geng, who also becomes Kundera's editor at the magazine. Conversation with Milan Kundera, in London and Connecticut, published in *New York Times Book Review*.

1981   Mother dies of a sudden heart attack in Elizabeth, New Jersey. *Zuckerman Unbound* published.

1982   Corresponds with Judith Thurman after reading her biography of Isak Dinesen, and they begin a friendship.

1983   Roth's physician and Litchfield County neighbor, Dr. C. H. Huvelle, retires from his Connecticut practice and the two become close friends.

1984   *The Anatomy Lesson* published. Aaron Asher leaves FSG and David Rieff becomes Roth's editor; the two soon become close friends. Conversation with Edna O'Brien in London published in *New York Times Book Review*. With BBC director Tristram Powell, adapts *The Ghost Writer* for television drama, featuring Claire Bloom; program is aired in U.S. and U.K. Meets University of Connecticut professor Ross Miller and the two forge strong literary friendship.

1985   *Zuckerman Bound*, a compilation of *The Ghost Writer*, *Zuckerman Unbound*, *The Anatomy Lesson*, with epilogue *The Prague Orgy*, published. Adapts *The Prague Orgy* for a British television production that is never realized.

1986   Spends several days in Turin with Primo Levi. Conversation with Levi published in *New York Times Book Review*, which also asks that Roth write a memoir about Bernard Malamud upon Malamud's death at age seventy-two. *The Counterlife* published; wins National Book Critics Circle Award for fiction that year.

1987   Corresponds with exiled Romanian writer Norman Manea, who is living in Berlin, and encourages him to come to live in U.S.; Manea arrives the next year, and the two become close friends.

1988   *The Facts* published. Travels to Jerusalem for Aharon Ap-
        pelfeld interview, which is published in *New York Times
        Book Review*. In Jerusalem, attends daily the trial of Ivan
        Demjanjuk, the alleged Treblinka guard "Ivan the Terri-
        ble." Returns to America to live year-round. Becomes
        Distinguished Professor of Literature at Hunter College
        of the City University of New York, where he will teach
        one semester each year until 1991.

1989   Father dies of brain tumor after yearlong illness. David
        Rieff leaves Farrar, Straus. For the first time since 1970,
        acquires a literary agent, Andrew Wylie of Wylie, Aitken,
        and Stone. Leaves FSG for Simon and Schuster. Writes a
        memoir of Philip Guston, which is published in *Vanity
        Fair* and subsequently reprinted in Guston catalogs.

1990   Travels to post-Communist Prague for conversation with
        Ivan Klíma, published in *New York Review of Books*. *De-
        ception* published by Simon and Schuster. Roth marries
        Claire Bloom in New York.

1991   *Patrimony* published; wins National Book Critics Circle
        Award for biography. Renews strong friendship with Saul
        Bellow.

1992   Reads from *Patrimony* for nationwide reading tour, ex-
        tending into 1993. Publishes brief profile of Norman
        Manea in *New York Times Book Review*.

1993   *Operation Shylock* published; wins PEN/Faulkner Award
        for fiction. Separates from Claire Bloom. Writes *Dr. Hu-
        velle: A Biographical Sketch*, which he publishes privately
        as a thirty-four-page booklet for local distribution.

1994   Divorces Claire Bloom.

1995   Returns to Houghton Mifflin, where John Sterling is his
        editor. *Sabbath's Theater* is published and wins National
        Book Award for fiction.

1997   John Sterling leaves Houghton Mifflin and Wendy Stroth-
        man becomes Roth's editor. *American Pastoral*, first book
        of the "American Trilogy," is published and wins Pulitzer
        Prize for fiction.

1998   *I Married a Communist*, the second book of the trilogy,
        is published and wins Ambassador Book Award of the
        English-Speaking Union. In October Roth attends three-

day international literary program honoring his work in Aix-en-Provence. In November receives National Medal of Arts at the White House.

2000   Publishes *The Human Stain*, final book of American trilogy, which wins PEN/Faulkner Award in U.S., the W. H. Smith Award in the U.K., and the Prix Medicis for the best foreign book of the year in France. Publishes "Rereading Saul Bellow" in *The New Yorker*.

2001   Publishes *The Dying Animal*, final book of the Kepesh trilogy, and *Shop Talk*, a collection of interviews with and essays on Primo Levi, Aharon Appelfeld, I. B. Singer, Edna O'Brien, Milan Kundera, Ivan Klíma, Philip Guston, Bernard Malamud, and Saul Bellow, and an exchange with Mary McCarthy. Receives highest award of the American Academy of Arts and Letters, the Gold Medal in fiction, given every six years "for the entire work of the recipient," previously awarded to Willa Cather, Edith Wharton, John Dos Passos, William Faulkner, Saul Bellow, and Isaac Bashevis Singer, among others. Is awarded the Edward McDowell Medal; William Styron, chair of the selection committee, remarks at the presentation ceremony that Roth "has caused to be lodged in our collective consciousness a small, select company of human beings who are as arrestingly alive and as fully realized as any in modern fiction."

2002   Wins the National Book Foundation's Medal for Distinguished Contribution to American Letters.

2003   Receives honorary degrees at Harvard University and University of Pennsylvania. Roth's work now appears in 31 languages.

2004   Publishes novel *The Plot Against America*, which becomes a best seller and wins the W. H. Smith Award for best book of the year in the U.K.; Roth is the first writer in the forty-six-year history of the prize to win it twice.

2005   *The Plot Against America* wins the Society of American Historians' James Fenimore Cooper Prize as the outstanding historical novel on an American theme for 2003–04. On October 23, Roth's childhood home at 81 Summit Avenue in Newark is marked with a plaque as a historic landmark and the nearby intersection is named Philip Roth Plaza.

2006   Publishes *Everyman* in May. Becomes fourth recipient of
            PEN's highest writing honor, the PEN/Nabokov Award.
            Receives Power of the Press Award from the New Jersey
            Library Association for Newark *Star-Ledger* eulogy to
            his close friend, Newark librarian and city historian
            Charles Cummings.

2007   Receives PEN/Faulkner Award for *Everyman*, the first
            author to be given the award three times. Wins the inau-
            gural PEN/Saul Bellow Award for Achievement in Ameri-
            can Fiction and Italy's first Grinzane-Masters Award, an
            award dedicated to the grand masters of literature. *Exit
            Ghost* is published.

2008   Roth's seventy-fifth birthday is marked by a celebration of
            his life and work at Columbia University. *Indignation* is
            published.

2009   Honored in program at Queens College, "A 50th An-
            niversary Celebration of the Work of Philip Roth." Re-
            ceives the Charles Cummings Award from the Newark
            Preservation and Landmarks Committee, the sponsor of
            semi-annual tours of "Philip Roth's Newark." Publishes
            The Humbling. Wins the annual literary prize of the Ger-
            man newspaper *Die Welt*.

2010   Receives *Paris Review*'s Hadada Award in April. Publishes
            Nemesis in September.

2011   In March receives the National Humanities Medal at the
            White House. Wins the Man Booker International Prize.

Note on the Texts

This volume contains the three novels of Philip Roth's American Trilogy: *American Pastoral* (1997), *I Married a Communist* (1998), and *The Human Stain* (2000). At the author's request, and because corrections were made to the texts of the novels when brought out in paperback, this volume prints the versions published under Random House's Vintage International imprint.

American Pastoral was published in New York by Houghton Mifflin and in England by Jonathan Cape in 1997. The text printed here is taken from the Vintage paperback edition, published in February 1998.

I Married a Communist was published in New York by Houghton Mifflin and in England by Jonathan Cape in 1998. The Vintage paperback edition, published in November 1999, contains the text of *I Married a Communist* printed here.

The Human Stain was published in New York by Houghton Mifflin and in England by Jonathan Cape in 2000. A limited edition of the novel was brought out that year as well by the Franklin Library. The text printed here of *The Human Stain* is taken from the Vintage paperback edition, published in May 2001.

This volume presents the texts of the original printings chosen for inclusion here, but it does not attempt to reproduce nontextual features of their typographic design. The texts are presented without change, except for the correction of typographical errors. Spelling, punctuation, and capitalization are often expressive features and are not altered, even when inconsistent or irregular. The following is a list of typographical errors corrected, cited by page and line number: 24.25, High; 164.28, anymore; 238.9, Bernadine; 322.26–27, Everyone; 360.27, love'."; 428.26, States; 434.31, Bower's; 529.16, Mendiata; 603.10, Raphael; 812.1, times that; 819.12, Iceland; 855.35, reforming; 911.39, Les,; 918.22, stop.'"; 962.8, had [ ]?; 966.27, Professor?; 970.36, student; 1010.17, Norkay; 1011.29, Russek's; 1033.21, C-41.

Notes

In the notes below, the reference numbers denote page and line of this volume (the line count includes chapter headings). Biblical quotations are keyed to the King James Version. Quotations from Shakespeare are keyed to *The Riverside Shakespeare*, ed. G. Blakemore Evans (Boston: Houghton Mifflin, 1974).

AMERICAN PASTORAL

9.6   Midway]   The battle of Midway, June 3–6, 1942, decisive U.S. naval victory against the Japanese, which allowed the U.S. to take the initiative in the Pacific war.

9.7   Salerno]   The U.S. Fifth Army landed on the Italian mainland at Salerno, September 9, 1943; fierce German counterattacks, September 12–16, were repulsed with the aid of heavy naval gunfire.

9.7   Cherbourg]   French port in Normandy captured by American forces, June 27, 1944.

9.7   the Solomons]   The Solomon Islands in the South Pacific, site of heavy fighting on land, at sea, and in the air, 1942–44, during American offensive against the Japanese that began with landing on Guadalcanal, August 7, 1942.

9.7   the Aleutians]   The Japanese occupied the uninhabited Aleutian islands of Kiska and Attu, June 6–7, 1942. U.S. forces retook Attu, May 11–30, 1943, and the Japanese evacuated Kiska in July.

9.7   Tarawa]   Atoll in the Gilbert Islands in the Pacific, site of battle, November 20–23, 1943, in which approximately one thousand U.S. Marines were killed.

9.21–25   sad, sad day . . . Germany]   The U.S. Eighth Air Force sent 291 bombers on a raid against ball-bearing plants in Schweinfurt, Germany, on October 14, 1943, "Black Thursday." Sixty of the B-17 Flying Fortresses were shot down, and another five crashed over England after running out of fuel.

13.22   shtetl]   Yiddish: small Jewish town in Eastern Europe.

14.26   fleshing]   The second step, after soaking, in the tanning process: the removal of fat, flesh, and excess tissue from an animal skin.

15.23   cordovan leather]   Leather made from horsehide (specifically the tough muscle material under the horse's rump), first manufactured in medieval Córdoba.

16.12   Louis Bamberger]   American Jewish entrepreneur (1855–1944) whose

1054

Newark-based L. Bamberger & Company, founded in 1893, became a major department store chain and the largest retail firm in New Jersey.

16.24   Bernard Baruch] American Jewish financier and philanthropist (1870–1965), advisor to several presidents, including Franklin D. Roosevelt.

18.37   John Lindsay] American politician (1921–2000), mayor of New York, 1966–73, and three-term Republican congressman, 1959–65.

19.24   Hernandez] Hall of Fame first baseman Keith Hernandez (b. 1953), who played for the Mets from 1983 to 1989.

20.12   the era of Carter-Gooden-Hernandez] The mid-1980s success of the Mets, including their 1986 World Series victory, was built on the play of catcher Gary Carter (b. 1954), pitcher Dwight Gooden (b. 1964), and Hernandez, among others.

24.6   Mattingly] New York Yankees first baseman Don Mattingly (b. 1961).

24.11   like a Giacometti] Swiss-born sculptor Alberto Giacometti (1901–1966), best known for his elongated sculptures of human figures.

24.14   Barolo] Red wine produced in Italy's Piedmont area from the Nebbiolo grape; a jeroboam is a 4.5-liter bottle.

26.23   '67 riots] The Newark riots began on the evening of July 12, 1967, spreading from the black Central Ward to other sections of the city. After six days twenty-three people were killed, with 725 injured and 1,500 arrested.

27.10–11   Indianapolis Speedway] Home to the preeminent American auto race, the Indianapolis 500.

27.23   The joint's jumpin'] From "The Joint Is Jumpin'" (1937), music by jazz pianist and composer Thomas "Fats" Waller (1904–1943) and J. C. Johnson (1896–1981), lyrics by Andy Razaf (1895–1973).

28.23   Jamesburg] Juvenile correctional facility in Jamesburg, NJ.

34.35–36   kiss him . . . Gable] Actors Clark Gable (1901–1960) and Lana Turner (1921–1995) were paired romantically in several movies, beginning with *Honky Tonk* (1941).

41.4   war-crimes trials] Tribunals administered by the victorious Allied powers to prosecute war crimes, including those held at Nuremberg, November 1945–October 1946, and Tokyo, May 1946–November 1948.

41.14   GI Bill] Officially called the Servicemen's Readjustment Act (1944), the G.I. Bill guaranteed access to college education and provided tuition funding for veterans.

43.22   yahrzeit candles] Yahrzeit—Yiddish: "year's time." A memorial candle set in a small glass jar is lit on the anniversary of a person's death.

45.5 schmaltz herring] Filleted, mature herring, often pickled in brine.

46.5 *Iolanthe*] Light opera (1882) by W. S. Gilbert (1836–1911) and Arthur Sullivan (1842–1900).

46.6–11 Nat . . . "Mule Train"] Jazz pianist and popular singer Nat "King" Cole (1919–1965); popular singer Frankie Laine (1913–2007), who popularized the novelty "cowboy" song "Mule Train" (1949).

46.23 *rugelach*] A small rolled pastry generally made with a cream cheese dough and filled with raisins, nuts, poppy-seed paste, or jam.

46.38–39 "the savour of the little *madeleine*"] In Marcel Proust's *Du côté de chez Swann* (*Swann's Way*), the first volume of the seven-volume novel *A la recherche du temps perdu* (*In Search of Lost Time*, 1913–27), protagonist Marcel's memory of the past is triggered by the taste of a madeleine.

47.27 *Mechanix Illustrated*] American magazine, 1938–85, featuring instructions for making and fixing things.

47.31–32 Illinois . . . Vaughan] Louisiana-born tenor saxophonist and bandleader Illinois Jacquet (1922–2004), who played with bands led by Lionel Hampton, Cab Calloway, and Count Basie, as well as his own ensembles; pianist and bandleader Buddy Johnson (1915–1977); "The Divine One," jazz singer Sarah Vaughan (1924–1990), who was born and grew up in Newark.

47.33 Mr. B., Billy Eckstine] Billy Eckstine (1914–1993), nicknamed "Mr. B.," a suave ballad singer and swing-era bandleader.

47.34–35 Miss Sepia America Beauty Contest] Beauty pageant for African American women.

48.1 Ellington's "Caravan,"] Composition (1937) written by Juan Tizol (1900–1984) and Duke Ellington (1899–1974), long identified with Ellington's orchestra.

48.13 "race record"] Music-industry term for recordings performed by and primarily marketed to African Americans during the 1920s and 1930s. Major recording companies released blues, gospel, and jazz under labels such as Okeh and Vocalion.

48.22–23 "Miss" Dinah . . . Churchill] Popular rhythm-and-blues singers Dinah Washington (1924–1963) and Savannah Churchill (1920–1974).

48.26–27 Roosevelt Sykes . . . Hunter] Pioneering blues pianist and songwriter Roosevelt Sykes (1906–1983), known as "The Honey Dripper"; rhythm-and-blues pianist, singer, and songwriter Ivory Joe Hunter (1914–1974).

48.30 *Ray*-O-Vacs] New Jersey rhythm-and-blues vocal group, whose biggest hit was "I'll Always Be in Love with You" (1949).

49.8–9 Glenn Miller–Tommy Dorsey] Big band–era bandleaders Glenn Miller (1904–1944) and Tommy Dorsey (1905–1956).

49.13–14   Caldonia . . . Rocks!] From "Caldonia," fast-tempo blues song (1945) written by alto saxophonist, bandleader, and composer Louis Jordan (1908–1975) and recorded by his band, Louis Jordan and His Tympany Five.

49.19   Tillie the Toiler "hot book,"] Pornographic comic based on *Tillie the Toiler*, comic strip (1921–67) created by the American cartoonist Russ Westover (1886–1966) about a flapper who becomes the stenographer for a wealthy industrialist.

50.11   pitching pennies] Children's game in which players pitch coins against a wall, and the player with the coin closest to the wall wins all the others' coins.

52.29   *Red Badge of Courage*] Novel (1895) about the Civil War by Stephen Crane (1871–1900).

54.38   twirlers] Girls who twirl and throw batons into the air at sports games.

55.20–21   *Silver Screen* . . . Man"] Actor George Raft (1895–1980) played gangsters and other tough-guy roles in movies such as *Scarface* (1932) and *The Glass Key* (1935). *Silver Screen* was a fan magazine popular in the 1940s featuring photos of movie stars.

55.29   George S. Kaufman and Moss Hart] From 1934 to 1941, playwrights George S. Kaufman (1889–1961) and Moss Hart (1904–1961) collaborated on numerous Broadway plays, mostly comedies, including the hits *You Can't Take It with You* (1936) and *The Man Who Came to Dinner* (1939).

56.7   *langer loksh*] Yiddish: long noodle; i.e., a tall and skinny person.

56.28   Ebbets Field] Home of the Brooklyn Dodgers baseball team, 1913–57, in the borough's Flatbush section.

57.4–5   Tournament of Roses] A New Year's Day parade in Pasadena, California, with elaborate floats decorated with roses, held in conjunction with a college football bowl game.

57.24   cyclosporin] An immunosuppressant drug used primarily in transplant surgery.

58.15–17   legs . . . *Popeye* comic strip] Skinny character in the *Thimble Theatre* comic strip created by Elzie C. Segar (1894–1938) in 1919; she became the girlfriend of Popeye the Sailor after he was introduced in 1929. The strip was later renamed *Popeye*.

65.4   Waldorf-Astoria] Luxury New York City hotel.

66.4   Rinso . . . Lux] Soap products.

66.25   Ho-Chi-Minhite] Supporter of Vietnamese Communist revolutionary Ho Chi Minh (1890–1969), leader of the Democratic Republic of

Vietnam from its declaration of independence from French rule in 1945 until his death in 1969.

69.40   Willie Mays]   Hall of Fame centerfielder Willie Mays (b. 1931) who played most of his career for the New York and San Francisco Giants baseball teams.

70.25   Princess Grace]   American actress Grace Kelly (1929–1982), star of films such as *Dial M for Murder* (1954) and *Rear Window* (1954), became princess of Monaco when she married Prince Rainier in 1956.

70.39   Che Guevara]   Argentine Marxist revolutionary and guerilla fighter Ernesto "Che" Guevara (1928–1967). A charismatic leader in the Cuban Revolution, he later fought in the Congo and led a failed insurrection in Bolivia, where he was captured and executed on October 9, 1967.

75.5   Spencer Tracy]   American stage and film actor (1900–1967), rough-looking leading man whose starring roles include *20,000 Years in Sing Sing* (1933), *Boys Town* (1938), and *Woman of the Year* (1942).

80.26–27   "Dream . . . do."]   From "Dream" (1945), music and lyrics by Johnny Mercer (1906–1976).

81.2–3   when the Pied Pipers . . . sung]   The Pied Pipers were a popular vocal group that formed among singers on the set of the movie *Alexander's Ragtime Band* (1938) and went on to perform with bandleader Tommy Dorsey. Jo Stafford (1917–2008) sang with the group until she left to begin a successful solo career in 1944; the lead vocalist on their hit recording of "Dream" was Stafford's replacement, June Hutton.

85.23–24   pardonnez-moi . . . que]   French: Excuse me—I thought that. . . .

89.9   4-H Club]   Youth programs focusing on farming and home economics originating in the early twentieth century, called "4-H" (head, heart, hands, and health) by 1912 and soon administered by the U.S. Department of Agriculture in partnership with numerous land-grant universities and municipal offices.

90.13   *Breakfast at Tiffany's*]   Film (1961) based on the novella (1958) by American writer Truman Capote (1924–1984).

90.22   "Moon River"]   Song (1961) featured in *Breakfast at Tiffany's* with music by Henry Mancini (1924–1994) and lyrics by Johnny Mercer.

95.33–34   Senator Case]   Clifford J. Case (1904–1982), liberal Republican U.S. senator from New Jersey, 1955–79.

112.20   Singer]   Established in 1851, Singer & Co. was the principal U.S. manufacturer of commercial sewing machines.

123.6   last of the Mohicans]   I.e., last of a kind, phrase derived from James Fenimore Cooper's novel *The Last of the Mohicans* (1826).

126.15   Bonwit's] Bonwit Teller, high-end department store on Manhattan's Fifth Avenue.

127.32   Legree] Cruel overseer in Harriet Beecher Stowe's novel *Uncle Tom's Cabin* (1852).

134.35–36   "Oh Lydia . . . lady] "Lydia the Tattooed Lady," song with music by Harold Arlen (1905–1986) and words by E. Y. Harburg (1896–1981) in the Marx Brothers' film *At the Circus* (1939), sung by Groucho.

139.28–29   Selective Service . . . ROTC] Selective Service, system established in 1917 for military conscription; ROTC (Reserved Officers' Training Corps), college-based program to commission officers.

139.36–37   Haymarket riots] On May 4, 1886, a crowd assembled in Chicago's Haymarket Square to protest the police shooting of several striking laborers the previous day. A bomb was thrown, shooting ensued, and seven policemen and at least four workers were killed. Although the actual bomb-thrower was not identified, eight anarchists were convicted of conspiracy to commit murder. Four of the defendants were hanged, one committed suicide in prison, and the remaining three were pardoned in 1893 by the newly elected governor, John P. Altgeld, who called their trial unjust.

140.9   Molotov cocktails] Homemade firebombs named after Vyacheslav Molotov (1890–1986), Soviet premier, 1930–41, and foreign minister, 1939–49, 1953–56.

140.18   *Queen Elizabeth*] *Queen Elizabeth 2*, luxury ocean liner and cruise ship.

140.34–35   three explosions . . . townhouse] On March 6, 1970, a bomb blast destroyed a townhouse at 18 West 11th Street in New York's Greenwich Village, when members of Weatherman (later called the Weather Underground), a violent splinter faction of the leftist Students for a Democratic Society (SDS), botched a bomb-making operation reportedly intended for an attack on a military dance at Fort Dix, New Jersey, and possibly on the main administration building at Columbia University. Three of the five Weathermen in the house were killed: Terry Robbins (1947–1970), Theodore Gold (1947–1970), and Diana Oughton (1942–1970). Katherine Boudin (b. 1943) and Cathlyn Wilkerson (b. 1945), the daughter of the townhouse's owners, escaped and immediately went into hiding; both were already wanted for charges related to their involvement in the "Days of Rage," a series of violent demonstrations staged by Weatherman in Chicago in October 1969.

146.22   Diem] Ngo Dinh Diem (1901–1963), first president of South Vietnam, 1955–63. After months of street demonstrations, including the self-immolation of Buddhist monks, Diem was deposed in a military coup and was assassinated on the orders of one of the coup leaders on November 2, 1963.

150.4   Aqua-Lung] Pioneering underwater breathing apparatus invented in 1943 by French naval officer and future oceanic explorer Jacques Cousteau (1910–1997) and French engineer Emile Gagnan (1900–1979).

151.35   one with John Brown]   Abolitionist John Brown (1800–1859) and eighteen of his followers seized the U.S. armory at Harpers Ferry, Virginia (now West Virginia), on October 16, 1859, with the purpose of arming slaves and starting an insurrection. Fifteen people were killed during the raid. Brown was captured, convicted of treason, and hanged on December 2, 1859.

152.19   '67 riots]   See note 26.23.

153.14   Governor Hughes]   Richard J. Hughes (1909–1992), Democratic governor of New Jersey, 1962–70.

154.24–25   LeRoi Jones . . . himself]   In 1967, Newark-born poet, dramatist, and activist LeRoi Jones (b. 1934) changed his name to Imamu Amear Baraka, later altered to Amiri Baraka.

154.38   schvartzes]   Yiddish: blacks.

156.35   Huey Newton's cause]   Huey Newton (1942–1989) cofounded the Black Panther Party for Self-Defense with Bobby Seale (b. 1936) in Oakland in 1966. Newton was arrested for the fatal shooting of Oakland police officer John Frey, Jr. on October 28, 1967. His arrest was regarded as politically motivated by his supporters, who adopted the rallying cry "Free Huey!" Newton was convicted of voluntary manslaughter in September 1968 and sentenced to two to fifteen years in prison. His conviction was overturned in May 1970 and, after two retrials ended in deadlocked juries, the charges were dismissed in December 1971.

156.35   Bobby Seale's cause]   Seale, a cofounder of the Black Panther Party, was indicted in March 1969 along with seven white radicals with conspiring to incite riots during the 1968 Democratic National Convention in Chicago. After the "Chicago Eight" trial began in September 1969, Seale repeatedly disrupted the proceedings to protest the refusal of the judge to grant a delay while his personal attorney recovered from surgery. Judge Julius Hoffman had Seale bound and gagged in the courtroom, then severed his case from the other defendants and sentenced him to four years in prison for contempt of court. The government chose not to retry him on the conspiracy charges, and his contempt conviction was overturned in 1972. Seale was also indicted along with eleven Black Panthers in New Haven, Connecticut, in August 1969 on charges relating to the kidnapping and murder of Alex Rackley, who had been tortured and killed by fellow Panthers who had falsely suspected him of being a police informer. After a lengthy trial the jury deadlocked 11–1 in favor of Seale's acquittal, and the charges against him were dropped in May 1971.

156.35–36   George Jackson's cause]   While incarcerated on armed robbery charges at Soledad state prison near Salinas, California, George Jackson (1941–1971) began to organize inmates based on his reading of Marx, Lenin, and

Frantz Fanon. He and two other black inmates, who became known as the "Soledad Brothers," were accused of murdering a white prison guard on January 16, 1970, in retaliation for the recent shooting deaths of three black prisoners. Jackson published *Soledad Brother: The Prison Letters of George Jackson* in October 1970; his case received worldwide attention and support from leftists. On August 7, 1970, Jackson's seventeen-year-old brother, Jonathan, held at gunpoint a courtroom in the Marin County Civic Center in San Rafael, California; freed and armed three inmates from nearby San Quentin prison; and took the judge, prosecutor, and three jurors hostage in an attempt to free the Soledad Brothers, who had recently been transferred to San Quentin. As the gunmen and hostages were leaving the Civic Center in a van, shooting broke out, and Jackson, two of the freed inmates, and the judge were killed. The guns used in the courtroom seizure had been purchased by Angela Davis, a former philosophy professor at University of California–Los Angeles and an active supporter of the Soledad Brothers Defense Committee. Davis was charged with murder, kidnapping, and conspiracy, and spent nineteen months in jail before being acquitted of all charges in June 1972. George Jackson was shot to death by guards at San Quentin on August 21, 1971, during a failed escape attempt in which three guards and two inmate trustees were killed.

160.37–38   Greystone mental asylum]   Greystone Park Psychiatric Hospital in Morristown, formerly known as the New Jersey State Lunatic Asylum.

160.40–161.2   Lindbergh kidnapping . . . son]   Charles Lindbergh, Jr., the twenty-month-old son of the famous aviator, was abducted from his home in East Amwell, New Jersey, on March 1, 1932. His body was discovered a few months later in Hopewell, a few miles from the Lindbergh estate. Bruno Hauptmann (1899–1936), a German immigrant carpenter, was convicted for the murder and executed on April 3, 1936.

172.24   Steel Pier]   Large amusement pier in Atlantic City.

173.3   "Clair de Lune"]   Third movement of *Suite Bergamasque* (1890; revised 1905) for piano by French composer Claude Debussy (1862–1918).

173.5–6   "Till the End of Time" . . . polonaise]   Popular adaptation of Chopin's "Heroic" Polonaise in A-flat major, op. 53 (1843), by Ted Mossman (1910–1977) with words by Buddy Kaye (1918–2002), a hit recording for singer Perry Como in 1946.

173.20   Bob Russell]   Entertainer (1908–1998) who was master of ceremonies for the Miss America Pageant, 1940–54.

178.32   Best & Co.]   New York department store specializing in women's and children's apparel.

178.33   "New Look"]   A popular style for women introduced in 1947 featuring a full skirt extending to the mid-calf.

179.16–17   song popular that year . . . Heart"]   Jerry Murad's Harmonicats had a huge hit with their 1947 version of "Peg o' My Heart" (1913), originally written for the Ziegfeld Follies by Alfred Bryan (1871–1958) and Fred Fisher (1875–1942).

183.26–27 Mayor "I-am-the-law" Hague] Democratic Party boss Frank Hague (1876–1956) served as mayor of Jersey City, New Jersey, 1917–1947; known for the remark, "I am the law!" made in 1937.

184.9 Brigadoon] Hit Broadway musical (1947) by Alan Jay Lerner (1918–1986) and Frederick Loewe (1901–1987) about a Scottish village that appears for one day every century.

185.18 Admiral "Bull" Halsey's] Elizabeth-born William Frederick Halsey, Jr. (1882–1959), U.S. Navy commander in the South Pacific, October 1942–June 1944, and commander of the U.S. Third Fleet in the North Pacific, June 1944–September 1945.

185.19 Nicholas Murray Butler] Elizabeth-born educator, political advisor, and diplomat (1862–1947), Columbia University president, 1902–45, and winner (with American social reformer Jane Addams) of 1931 Nobel Peace Prize.

186.2 Simmental . . . Hereford] Simmental is one of the oldest breeds of dairy, beef, and draught cattle. Polled Herefords are hornless cows.

187.18 stifle] A knee-like leg joint in four-legged animals.

194.27 DeSoto] American automobile brand manufactured by Chrysler, 1928–61.

195.16 Carmen Miranda] Portuguese-born Brazilian singer and actress (1909–1955), promoted as "The Brazilian Bombshell" and known for her outlandish hats and colorful costumes. She starred on Broadway and in movie musicals such as *Down Argentine Way* (1940) and *The Gang's All Here* (1943).

195.23–24 Peleliu . . . Palaus] Americans forces began their campaign in the Palau Islands in the Pacific with landings on Peleliu, September 15, 1944, meeting fierce resistance from Japanese defenders fighting from fortified caves in steep coral ridges. Organized resistance on Peleliu ended on November 27, 1944, after the Japanese garrison was almost completely annihilated.

197.9 BAR] Browning automatic rifle, American rifle capable of fully automatic fire, used as a light machine gun by army and marine infantry.

197.18 duck] A six-wheeled amphibious truck equipped with a propeller and rudder that could carry twenty-five men or five thousand pounds of cargo.

199.5 slopchute] Down-and-out dive catering to enlisted men.

208.2 Che bellezza] Italian: how beautiful.

214.4 Danny Thomas] Nightclub comedian and television personality (1914–1991).

220.39   tong]   Chinese-American gangs modeled on the secret societies of southern China.

230.40   Mahavira's]   Mahavira ("Great Hero" in Sanskrit), the devotional name for Vardhamana (599–527 BCE), ascetic and spiritual leader who was the last of the twenty-four Jain *tirthankaras* (spiritual teachers); he reformed and systematized earlier Jain monastic practices and beliefs, and helped establish a large, flourishing spiritual movement in the sixth century BCE.

231.23–24   "Lead me not into temptation"]   Cf. Matthew 6:13.

231.40   Montessori school]   School following a method of children's self-directed learning developed by Maria Montessori (1870–1952), Italian physician and educator.

238.6–10   girls in the papers . . . Linda]   Bernardine Dohrn (b. 1942), SDS leader and Weatherman cofounder, was on the FBI's Ten Most Wanted list from 1970 to 1973 on charges related to her involvement in the "Days of Rage" riots in Chicago in October 1969, and remained underground until 1980. Patricia Swinton (b. 1942), coconspirator in several New York bombings during the summer and fall of 1969, was a fugitive until 1975, when she was tried and acquitted of the charges against her. Judith Clark (b. 1949) and Linda Evans (b. 1947) were arrested on charges related to the 1969 Chicago riots; Clark served eighteen months in prison, whereas the charges against Evans were dropped. Cathlyn Wilkerson, see note 140.34–35. Susan Saxe (b. 1950) was placed on the Ten Most Wanted list for the murder of a Boston police officer in a September 1970 bank robbery staged to secure funds for radical activities; a recent Brandeis University graduate, she lived underground until her arrest in 1975 and later pleaded guilty to manslaughter.

238.11–13   police hunt . . . Alpert]   In 1970, Mark Rudd (b. 1947), SDS national secretary and Weatherman cofounder, went underground for seven years to avoid arrest on conspiracy charges related to his role in the 1969 "Days of Rage" riots; he served less than a year in prison after making a plea bargain with federal authorities in 1977. Katherine Boudin, see note 140.34–35; she remained at large until her arrest for her involvement in a 1981 robbery of a Brink's armored car in Nanuet, New York, in which two police officers and a Brink's guard were killed. Jane Alpert (b. 1947) was a coconspirator with Patricia Swinton (see note 238.6–10) in the 1969 New York bombings. Alpert jumped bail after pleading guilty to conspiracy charges in November 1969 and lived as a fugitive before turning herself in to federal authorities in 1974, and served most of a twenty-seven-month sentence before being paroled.

243.24   Marcuse]   German philosopher, political thinker, and political activist Herbert Marcuse (1898–1979), author of *Eros and Civilization* (1955) and *One-Dimensional Man* (1964); his critique of capitalism drew on Marxist and Freudian ideas and was embraced by many on the left in the 1960s.

243.25   Frantz Fanon] French West Indian writer and anticolonialist the-orist (1925–1961), author of *The Wretched of the Earth* (1961).

243.28–37   *It must be . . . tragedy*] From Fanon's essay "Algeria Unveiled" (1959).

251.38–39   Governor's Select Committee on Civil Disorder] Committee chaired by Robert Lilley (1912–1986), president of New Jersey Bell Telephone, to investigate the causes of the Newark riots. After five months of interviews, hearings, and investigation, the commission issued its report in February 1968.

253.3   tuchas] Yiddish: backside.

268.9–10   Senator Weicker . . . House?] Connecticut Republican sena-tor Lowell Weicker (b. 1931) was one of three Republicans on the seven-member Select Committee on Presidential Campaign Activities investigating the Watergate burglary and subsequent cover-up. The committee's nationally televised hearings, May 17–August 7, 1973, were seen by a large audience.

268.10   shnook] Yiddish: a timid and ineffectual person.

268.12   Senator Gurney] Florida Republican senator Edward Gurney (1914–1996), a member of the Watergate Committee.

268.12–13   Typhoid Mary] Mary Mallon (1869–1938), Irish immigrant cook who carried the organism causing typhoid fever without manifesting symptoms of the disease. Vehemently denying that she was infected, Mallon spread the disease to at least fifty-three people (three fatally) while working in New York City and Long Island. After spending 1907–10 in quarantine, she continued to work as a cook and to transmit the disease. In 1915 she was re-turned to quarantine, where she remained for the rest of her life.

268.14   Senator Baker] Tennessee Republican senator Howard Baker (b. 1925), ranking Republican on the Watergate committee.

268.15   Mr. Dash] Samuel Dash (1925–2004), a Democrat, was co–chief counsel with Republican Fred Thompson (b. 1942).

268.20   Kalmbach] Herbert Kalmbach (b. 1921), Richard Nixon's per-sonal attorney, 1968–73.

268.36–37   Ehrlichman . . . staff] John Ehrlichman (1925–1999) served as counsel to President Nixon, 1968–69, and assistant to the president for do-mestic affairs, 1969–73. For his role in the Watergate affair he was convicted of perjury, conspiracy, and obstruction of justice and served eighteen months in prison.

268.39   Tricia] Patricia "Tricia" Nixon (b. 1946), the president's older child.

269.3   Haldeman] H. R. Haldeman (1926–1993), chief of staff in the Nixon White House, 1969–73. For his role in the Watergate affair he served eighteen months in prison for perjury, conspiracy, and obstruction of justice.

269.8   *It Can't Happen Here*]   Satirical political novel (1935) by Sinclair Lewis (1885–1951) about a fascist regime coming to power in America.

270.32   Father Coughlin]   Charles Coughlin (1891–1979), a Catholic priest and popular radio broadcaster during the 1930s who made anti-Semitic and pro-fascist statements in his broadcasts.

270.34–35   Gerald L. K. Smith]   Smith (1898–1976) was a Christian fundamentalist preacher and supporter of extreme right-wing organizations.

270.35   Senator Bilbo]   Theodore G. Bilbo (1877–1947), an advocate for white supremacy, was governor of Mississippi, 1916–20 and 1928–32, and a U.S. senator, 1935–47.

270.37   Mr. Rankin]   John Rankin (1882–1960) served as a congressman from Mississippi, 1921–53, and became notorious for racial demagoguery.

270.37   Mr. Dies and his committee]   Texas congressman Martin Dies (1901–1972) served as chairman, 1938–45, of the House Special Committee to Investigate Un-American Activities, also known as the Dies Committee. The committee's successor was the House Committee on Un-American Activities (HUAC).

270.38–40   J. Parnell Thomas . . . jail]   Stockbroker and politician J. Parnell Thomas (1895–1970), Republican congressman from New Jersey, 1937–50, and chairman of HUAC, 1947–49, pleaded no contest in 1949 to corruption charges involving the use of his congressional office payroll and served nine months in federal prison.

271.2   McCarran . . . Mundt]   Nevada Democratic senator Patrick McCarran (1876–1954), chairman of the Senate Judiciary Committee and the special Senate Internal Security Subcommittee, and cosponsor of the anticommunist Internal Security Act (1950); Indiana Republican senator William E. Jenner (1908–1985), ally of Senator Joseph McCarthy in his anticommunist crusade; South Dakota Republican senator Karl Mundt (1900–1974), sponsor of anticommunist legislation.

271.4   His sidekick Mr. Cohn]   New York attorney Roy Cohn (1927–1986), chief counsel for the Senate Subcommittee on Investigations when it was chaired by McCarthy, 1953–54. McCarthy announced an investigation into alleged Communist infiltration of the army in 1954 after the army refused Cohn's request to grant special privileges to his friend David Schine, a recently drafted private; the subsequent Army-McCarthy hearings addressed Cohn's and McCarthy's conduct in their dealings with the army and caused McCarthy's national influence to wane after his erratic performance during the televised proceedings. Cohn resigned as committee counsel in August 1954 and went into private law practice.

271.8–9   Hearst . . . Pegler]   Reactionary newspaper tycoons William Randolph Hearst (1863–1951), publisher of the *New York Journal-American* and numerous other newspapers nationwide, and Robert H. McCormick (1880–1955), publisher of the *Chicago Tribune*. Westbrook Pegler (1894–1969), columnist known for his right-wing views and vehement criticism of President Roosevelt, Eleanor Roosevelt, and other public figures.

272.2–6   Eugene McCarthy . . . Fulbright]   Senators who became prominent opponents of the Vietnam War: Minnesota Democrat Eugene McCarthy (1916–2005), New York Republican Jacob Javits (1904–1986), Idaho Democrat Frank Church (1924–1984), Oregon Democrat Wayne Morse (1900–1974), Arkansas Democrat J. William Fulbright (1905–1995).

272.8   Tonkin Gulf resolu—]   Resolution passed on August 7, 1964, by both houses of Congress, authorizing the president to "take all necessary measures to repel any armed attack against the forces of the United States and to prevent further aggression" in Southeast Asia. It was submitted to Congress after reports of attacks on August 2 and August 4 on American destroyers in the Gulf of Tonkin by North Vietnamese torpedo boats. Evidence indicates that reports of the August 4 attack were probably the result of false radar contacts caused by tropical weather conditions.

274.7–8   that's the way . . . is]   "And that's the way it is" was the nightly sign-off of Walter Cronkite (1916–2009) when he anchored the *CBS Evening News*, 1962–81.

280.16   *mamzer*]   Yiddish: bastard, literally; a term of endearment.

283.29   Skyway]   The Pulaski Skyway, a cantilever truss bridge opened in 1932 spanning the Hackensack and Passaic rivers. Connecting Newark and Jersey City, the bridge is called a "skyway" because the 3.5-mile roadway rises 135 feet at its highest point.

283.37   WACs]   Members of the Women's Army Corps.

289.22   feed the starving Armenians]   Popular call from international relief agencies to aid survivors of the Armenian genocide after World War I.

295.25   Johnny Appleseed]   John Chapman (c. 1775–1847), legendary frontier folk figure who seeded apple trees in the present-day Midwest.

297.2   Volstead Act]   The National Prohibition Act of 1919, popularly known as the Volstead Act after its sponsor, Minnesota Republican U.S. representative Andrew John Volstead (1860–1947).

311.24   *pisherke*]   Yiddish: one who urinates, literally; squirt, used affectionately with children.

311.27   *shicker*]   Yiddish: a drunk.

312.3   meshugeh]   Yiddish: crazy.

313.23–25   pictures . . . Grounds]   *Dempsey and Firpo* (1924, Whitney Museum of American Art), painting by American artist George Bellows (1882–1925) of the heavyweight boxing match between heavyweight champion Jack Dempsey (1895–1983) and Argentine fighter Luis Angel Firpo (1894–1960) at New York's Polo Grounds on September 14, 1923.

318.13   March on the Pentagon] Antiwar demonstration of fifty thousand people on October 22, 1967.

318.20   yenta] Yiddish: gossip, shrew.

321.32–34   vice president . . . piety] Spiro Agnew (1918–1996), vice president of the United States in the Nixon administration, 1969–73, resigned his office on October 10, 1973, after pleading no contest to a misdemeanor charge of tax evasion. He had been under investigation for bribes solicited while he was Baltimore County executive, 1962–66, and governor of Maryland, 1967–69.

321.38   McGovernites] Supporters of the Democratic Party's candidate for president in 1972, George McGovern (b. 1922), liberal antiwar senator from South Dakota.

322.40   Watts] Six days of large-scale urban rioting beginning August 11, 1965, in the mainly poor black neighborhood of Watts in Los Angeles, California, resulting in the deaths of thirty-four people, with more than 1,000 injured. The Los Angeles police made over 3,400 arrests.

326.32–33   Sir Walter Scott, in one of his classic books] See *Fair Maid of Perth*, ch. 5.

327.4, 10–11   Romeo, Romeo . . . cheek] Cf. *Romeo and Juliet*, II.ii.33 and II.ii.23–25.

341.27–28   William Burroughs . . . Genet] Three notoriously transgressive writers: American novelist, essayist, and performer William S. Burroughs (1914–1997), author of *Naked Lunch* (1959) and *The Soft Machine* (1961); French libertine and philosophical novelist Donatien Alphonse François, Marquis de Sade, author of *120 Days of Sodom* (1785) and *Justine* (1788); French poet, essayist, and novelist Jean Genet (1910–1986), an illegitimate son of a prostitute who was a petty criminal before becoming a writer. He wrote candidly of his homosexuality and life as a hustler in autobiographical novels such as *The Miracle of the Rose* (1946) and *The Thief's Journal* (1949) and was the subject of Jean-Paul Sartre's *Saint Genet: Actor and Martyr* (1952).

374.17   Mickey McDermott] Major League pitcher (1929–2003) for the Boston Red Sox, Washington Senators, and other teams.

374.18   Newcombe] Don Newcombe (b. 1926), Major League pitcher for the Brooklyn and Los Angeles Dodgers and the Cincinnati Reds.

375.21   no kugel, no gefilte fish, no bitter herbs] Foods eaten at Passover.

375.35   U.S. Line] United States Lines, which operated transatlantic passenger ships, including the SS *United States*, its flagship from 1952 to 1969.

376.20   Crillon]   Hôtel de Crillon, luxury hotel in a converted eighteenth-century palace on the Place de la Concorde.

387.11   Leica]   German camera manufacturer, whose 35mm cameras were widely used and admired among mid-twentieth-century photographers.

I MARRIED A COMMUNIST

397.1   I MARRIED A COMMUNIST]   "The author wishes to thank the Newark Public Library and its director, Alex Boyd, for use of its archival resources; to recognize particularly the generosity of the library's city historian, Charles Cummings; to thank New Jersey historian John Cunningham for his guidance; and to acknowledge, as a primary source, *Newark's Little Italy: The Vanished First Ward*, by Michael Immerso (Rutgers University Press, 1997). The name Katrina Van Tassel is taken from 'The Legend of Sleepy Hollow' by Washington Irving" [Roth's note].

401.5–6   17th Airborne Division . . . Bulge]   The U.S. Army's 17th Airborne Division fought against the German offensive in the Ardennes in January 1945.

401.6–8   famous jump . . . war]   Operation Varsity, Allied airborne drop on March 24, 1945, supporting the crossing of the Rhine by British, American, and Canadian ground troops.

404.19   Erlenmeyer flask]   A common type of laboratory glassware that features a flat flared body and a conical neck.

405.13   Representative Walter]   Congressman Francis Walter (1894–1963), Pennsylvania Democrat, chaired the House Committee on Un-American Activities (HUAC), 1955–63.

407.4   Rosenbergs]   Julius Rosenberg (1918–1953) and his wife Ethel Rosenberg (1915–1953), American spies for the Soviet Union, were convicted of espionage and executed on June 19, 1953. Their case was an international cause célèbre.

407.9–10   Wernher von Braun's]   Wernher von Braun (1912–1977), German rocket engineer who designed the V-2 missile for the Nazis during World War II, then immigrated to the United States, where he became a central figure in the American space program.

407.28   Hearst's]   See note 271.8–9.

408.5–6   Cholly Knickerbocker . . . Wilson]   Cholly Knickerbocker, pseudonym of Russian-born Igor Cassini (1915–2002) for his *Journal-American* gossip column; *New York Daily Mirror* gossip columnist Walter Winchell (1897–1972); Ed Sullivan (1901–1974), New York newspaper columnist and host of the long-running television variety show *The Ed Sullivan Show* (called *Toast of the Town* when it premiered in 1948); *New York Post* show business columnist Earl Wilson (1907–1987).

408.6–7   Damon Runyon . . . Hopper]   Journalist and short-story writer Damon Runyon (1880–1946) whose "Runyonesque" tales are typically about raffish New York characters; journalist Bob Considine (1906–1975), author of long-running "On the Line" column and host of a weekly radio program; former actress and feared Hollywood gossip columnist Hedda Hopper (1885–1966).

408.9–10   Sardi's or the Brown Derby]   Sardi's Restaurant in New York's Theater District and Hollywood's Brown Derby were places for famous people to go and be seen.

408.10   Stillman's Gym]   Legendary boxing gym in New York City, where champions such as Jack Dempsey, Joe Louis, and Rocky Marciano trained.

408.11   Racquet Club]   Exclusive men's athletic club on Park Avenue.

408.23   cell between Mitchell's and Ehrlichman's]   Like John Ehrlichman (see note 268.36–37), John Mitchell (1913–1988), attorney general in the Nixon administration, 1969–72, and head of the Nixon reelection campaign in 1972, was convicted of perjury, conspiracy, and obstruction of justice for his role in the Watergate affair. He served nineteen months in prison before his parole in 1979.

408.31–32   hard, gemlike flame]   See the conclusion of Walter Pater, *Studies in the History of the Renaissance* (1873): "To burn always with this hard, gemlike flame, to maintain this ecstasy, is success in life."

410.9–11   Jackson and Velde . . . clergy]   California Republican congressman Donald Jackson (1910–1981), a member of HUAC, accused G. Bromley Oxnam (1891–1963), the Methodist bishop of Washington, D.C., of serving "God on Sunday and the Communist front for the balance of the week" in a 1953 HUAC hearing. Illinois Republican congressman Harold Velde (1910–1985), chairman of HUAC from 1953 to 1955, made public comments that the committee might investigate Communist infiltration of Protestant clergy.

410.29   Tripler's]   F. R. Tripler & Co., established 1886, high-end traditional clothing store on Madison Avenue in New York.

416.34–35   Lincoln's Gettysburg Address . . . Inaugural]   Lincoln's most celebrated speeches, delivered on November 19, 1863, and March 4, 1865, respectively.

417.8   debated . . . Douglas]   Lincoln debated Illinois Democratic U.S. senator Stephen A. Douglas (1813–1861) seven times in 1858 during his unsuccessful campaign to win Douglas's seat.

417.22   Wild Bill Hickok]   James Butler Hickok (1837–1876), frontier gunfighter, scout, soldier, and marshal.

418.12   *The Bob Hope Show*]   Popular radio show, 1937–55 (broadcast under various sponsors' names, then called *The Bob Hope Show* after 1950).

418.25–26   *The Late George Apley* by John P. Marquand]   Stage adaptation (1944) by George S. Kaufman and John P. Marquand (1893–1960) of Marquand's novel *The Late George Apley* (1937), a satire of upper-crust Boston society.

419.15   Cary Grant is Jewish]   Born in Bristol, England, as Archibald Alexander Leach, actor Cary Grant (1904–1986) was rumored to be Jewish on his father's side.

419.29   Religion . . . the people!]   Cf. Karl Marx, *A Contribution to the Critique of Hegel's Philosophy of Right* (1843–44).

422.8   Bob Feller]   Hall of Fame fastball pitcher (1918–2010) for the Cleveland Indians, 1936–56.

422.9–10   Larry Doby . . . League]   Hall of Fame centerfielder Larry Doby (1923–2003) was the first black player to play in the American League; before breaking in to Major League Baseball with the Cleveland Indians in 1947, he played for the Newark Eagles in the Negro Leagues.

422.13–14   Louis knocking out Jersey Joe Walcott]   Heavyweight champion Joe Louis (1914–1981) fought challenger Jersey Joe Walcott (born Arnold Cream; 1914–1994) on December 5, 1947, in a fight widely considered a mismatch in favor of Louis. Walcott knocked Louis down twice in the first four rounds but lost the match by the judges' controversial split decision. Louis won a rematch on June 25, 1948, with a knockout in the eleventh round.

422.26   Leo Durocher]   Baseball manager (1905–1991) of the Brooklyn Dodgers and New York Giants, among other teams.

423.5   Howard Fast]   Left-wing American writer (1914–2003), author of popular historical novels such as *Citizen Tom Paine* (1943) and *Spartacus* (1951). A member of the Communist Party from 1943 to 1956, he served three months in prison for refusing to cooperate with HUAC in 1950 and ran for Congress as a candidate of the American Labor Party in 1952.

424.21   the *Worker*]   *Daily Worker*, founded 1924, newspaper published in New York by the American Communist Party.

424.22–23   Steinbeck . . . Caldwell]   Left-wing American writers who wrote sympathetically about America's economic and social underclass: John Steinbeck (1902–1968), author of *The Grapes of Wrath* (1939); Upton Sinclair (1878–1968), author of *The Jungle* (1906); Jack London (1876–1916), author of *The Call of the Wild* (1903) and *The War of the Classes* (1905); Erskine Caldwell (1903–1987), author of *Tobacco Road* (1932).

424.27   *Common Sense*]   Anti-British pamphlet by Thomas Paine, first published anonymously on January 10, 1776.

427.9–10   Truman Doctrine]   Postwar American commitment to resist the expansion of Soviet influence abroad, formulated early in 1947 to accompany the Truman administration's plan to send aid to Greece and Turkey. In a speech delivered March 12, 1947, Truman declared that the United States would "support free peoples who are resisting attempted subjugation by armed minorities or by outside pressure."

427.10   Marshall Plan] Massive economic aid plan, outlined in 1947, to help rebuild Western European economies and counter Soviet influence.

428.3   Taft-Hartley] The Labor-Management Relations Act (1947), law restricting the activities of labor unions, passed by Congress in 1947 over President Truman's veto.

428.5–6   Mundt-Nixon bill . . . if passed] The bill, passed by the House of Representatives on May 19, 1948, was not taken up by the Senate; its provisions requiring registration of Communists with the attorney general prefigured those of the Internal Security Act of 1950, also known as the McCarran Act, after its sponsor, Nevada Republican senator Pat McCarran (1876–1954).

430.23–26   Why had the CIO . . . Wallace?] Shortly after Henry Wallace announced his Progressive Party candidacy for the presidency in 1948, the executive board of the CIO (Congress of Industrial Organizations) declared that it would officially maintain a nonpartisan position, a stance that effectively rejected Wallace's candidacy in favor of Truman's. The American Communist leadership put pressure on their members to vote for Wallace; the bitter conflict between Communists and anti-communists within the CIO led to the expulsion of eleven member unions by 1950.

431.2–3   "Ol' Man River"] Song written for the musical *Show Boat* (1927), with music by Jerome Kern and lyrics by Oscar Hammerstein II. It was part of Robeson's repertoire after he sang it in the film adaptation (1936) of the show.

431.28–29   appeasing dictators . . . Kai-shek] Autocratic rulers, respectively, of Spain and the Republic of China (Taiwan).

432.31   lend-lease equipment] The Lend-Lease Act, signed into law on March 11, 1941, authorized aid to Great Britain and other nations fighting Germany and Japan.

433.30   Quonset hut] Prefabricated lightweight structure of corrugated steel with a semicircular cross section.

434.31   Bowers's *Young Jefferson*] *The Young Jefferson, 1743–1789* (1945), by journalist, historian, and diplomat Claude Bowers (1878–1958).

434.33   Committees of Correspondence] Committees organized in 1772–73 to coordinate responses to violations of colonial rights.

435.36   Clifford Odets] American playwright and screenwriter (1906–1963) who wrote about proletarian themes in plays such as *Waiting for Lefty* (1935) and *Awake and Sing!* (1935).

435.37 Maxwell Anderson] American playwright and screenwriter (1888–1959), author of *What Price Glory?* (1924), *Both Your Houses* (1933), and *High Tor* (1937).

436.5 WPA] Works Progress Administration (later Works Projects Administration), New Deal program that employed artists and writers.

436.5–6 Whitman . . . roughs] See "Song of Myself" in the 1855 edition of *Leaves of Grass*: "Walt Whitman, an American, one of the roughs, a kosmos."

439.9 rigging gang] Crane and lift operators on a work site.

439.29–30 on the slow bell] Off company time.

439.31–32 hit the bricks] Go on strike.

439.33 blood on the bricks] A violent strike.

441.18 UE] United Electrical, Radio, and Machine Workers of America.

441.27–29 when CIO president . . . membership] See note 430.23–26.

442.4–5 to Iran . . . show] Irving Berlin's musical *This Is the Army* (1942) traveled to Iran to perform for the troops in 1944.

442.22 price controls] Government setting of prices administered by the Office of Price Administration (OPA), 1941–46.

442.22 Smith Act] The Alien Registration Act (1940), called the Smith Act after its sponsor, Democratic Virginia congressman Howard Smith (1883–1976). It required all resident aliens over the age of fourteen to register with the government, and stipulated fines and imprisonment for any person convicted of interfering with the morale of the armed forces or advocating the violent overthrow of the government.

442.23–24 Mississippi's Senator Bilbo] See note 270.35.

443.29 *Looking Backward* by Bellamy] *Looking Backward: 2000–1887* (1888), utopian novel about America in the year 2000 by Boston lawyer Edward Bellamy (1850–1898).

444.33 *Stars and Stripes*] Independent newspaper for the U.S. armed forces, published 1918–19 and revived in 1942.

452.3–4 'twas strange . . . pitiful] *Othello*, I.iii.160–61.

454.14 Meredith] English novelist and poet George Meredith (1828–1909), author of *Modern Love* (1862), *The Egoist* (1879), and *Diana of the Crossways* (1885).

455.24–26 With thee . . . last!] Poem written c. 1860 by Emily Dickinson (1830–1886).

462.14   Longy Zwillman's] Jewish gangster Abner "Longy" Zwillman
(1889–1959) was known as the "Al Capone of New Jersey."

462.22   Bugsy Siegel . . . Luciano] Benjamin "Bugsy" Siegel (1906–1947),
Jewish gangster who played a large role in the development of Las Vegas;
Meyer Lansky (1902–1983), Russian-born Jewish gangster who, along with
Sicilian-born gangster Charles "Lucky" Luciano (1897–1962), helped organize
a national crime syndicate in the 1930s.

462.39–40   like Longy . . . neck] Zwillman was found hanged in his
West Orange home on February 27, 1959, while under investigation by the
U.S. Senate Select Committee on Improper Activities in Labor and Manage-
ment, headed by Frank McClellan; his death was ruled a suicide. He had testi-
fied in 1951 before the Senate's Special Committee to Investigate Crime in
Interstate Commerce, headed by Estes Kefauver.

464.27–28   Good Eating by Duncan Hines] C.f. *Adventures in Good
Eating* (1935) by Duncan Hines (1880–1959).

468.6–7   watching Lemuel Gulliver sleep] In the first book of Jonathan
Swift's satirical novel *Gulliver's Travels* (1726), Lemuel Gulliver is shipwrecked
and swims to the island of Lilliput, where he falls into a deep sleep and is discovered by the island's miniscule inhabitants.

468.17   Paganini] Italian virtuoso violinist and composer Niccolò Paganini (1782–1840).

468.21   Soviet Army Chorus and Band] Ensemble that performed and
recorded Soviet and traditional Russian music, organized by Alexander Vasil-
yevich Alexandrov (1883–1946) in the 1920s.

469.18   rpm switch to 78] Before the introduction in the early 1950s of the
twelve-inch long-playing vinyl record (LP) that revolved at 33⅓ revolutions
per minute (rpms), recordings were available only on ten-inch discs that revolved at 78 rpm.

469.32   Tanglewood] Summer home of the Boston Symphony Orchestra
in Lenox, Massachusetts.

470.12   Bartók] Modernist Hungarian composer Béla Bartók (1881–1945).

479.25–26   Every unhappy . . . way] First line of Leo Tolstoy's novel
Anna Karenina (1877).

484.21   Gutzon Borglum's] American sculptor Gutzon Borglum (1867–
1941), best known for his monumental heads of four American presidents
carved into the face of Mount Rushmore, South Dakota.

485.19   Marshall Plan] See note 427.10.

485.29–31   as Wordsworth . . . Heaven!] From "The French Revolution, as It Appeared to Enthusiasts" (1809), lines 4–5, and *The Prelude* (1850),
book 9, 109–110.

486.15   *Chicago Defender*] African American newspaper, founded in 1905.

487.18   Taft-Hartley] See note 428.3.

488.19   Jack Benny] American entertainer (1894–1974), star of vaudeville and movies and host of the weekly *Jack Benny Program* on radio, 1932–58, and television, 1950–65.

491.3   Royal Crown] A cola soft drink.

491.35   putz] Yiddish: a fool or jerk; literally, penis.

493.28–29 Congressman Dies] See note 270.37.

493.29   Congressman Rankin] See note 270.37.

495.34   the death of Masaryk] Jan Masaryk (1896–1948), foreign minister of Czechoslovakia, 1940–48, was the only non-Communist minister who remained in the government following the Communist seizure of power in February 1948. He was found dead in the courtyard beneath his office in the Foreign Ministry on March 10, 1948. Although the official cause of his death was suicide, it was widely believed that he was murdered under orders of the Communist Party. Jan Masaryk was the son of Tomáš Masaryk (1850–1937), president of Czechoslovakia, 1918–35.

502.2   schmattas] Yiddish: rags; cheap clothing.

503.36   *droit de fille*] French: right of the daughter.

507.33   Piper Cub] Small, lightweight, single-engine aircraft.

508.12–13 playing a harp . . . Marx] Arthur "Harpo" Marx (1893–1964), one of the Marx Brothers, so called because he played the harp.

511.9   *Information Please Almanac*] Almanac first published in 1947, developed out of the popular *Information Please* radio program.

515.7   Sen-Sen] Popular breath freshener.

515.27   Jimmy Durante] American variety entertainer (1893–1980) who sang comic and sentimental songs while accompanying himself on the piano; he was famed for his large nose.

519.40–520.1 Wood . . . Hoover] Democratic Georgia congressman John S. Wood (1885–1968), chairman of HUAC, 1945–46 and 1949–52; J. Edgar Hoover (1895–1972), director of the FBI, 1924–72.

520.3   DAR] Daughters of the American Revolution, a women's professional service organization founded in 1890. Membership is restricted to lineal descendants of patriots of the American Revolution.

520.21–22 when we bomb Frankfurt . . . touched] The German chemical industrial conglomerate I. G. Farben, founded in 1925, worked in close cooperation with the Nazis and used slave labor drawn from concentration camps. It held the patent for Zyklon B, the poison gas used for mass murder at the Auschwitz-Birkenau and Majdanek extermination camps.

523.13   *Eloise and Abelard*] The French theologian Pierre Abélard (1079–1142) fell in love with his pupil Héloïse (1101–1142), and the couple conceived a child together. At the instigation of Héloïse's uncle, Abélard was castrated. The two lovers continued their relationship via letters.

527.31–32   *Make-Believe Ballroom . . . Parade*] *Make-Believe Ballroom*, long-running syndicated radio program based at WNEW in New York, broadcast from a studio made to look and sound like a ballroom. *Your Hit Parade*, popular radio (1935–65) and television (1950–59) program that did a countdown of the week's bestselling records every Saturday evening.

529.16–17   Mendieta . . . Batista] Carlos Mendieta (1873–1960), as provisional president of Cuba, 1934–35, was the puppet of military leader Fulgencio Batista (1901–1973), later the dictator deposed by Fidel Castro in the 1958–59 Cuban Revolution.

530.15–16   Stork Club] On East 53rd Street off Fifth Avenue, the Stork Club, owned and operated by former bootlegger Sherman Billingsley (1900–1966), was New York's preeminent nightclub, 1929–65.

531.16–17   brutal loss . . . Willie] Ten-year-old William Lincoln died on February 20, 1862, probably from typhoid fever.

535.9   poll tax] A fixed tax levied on every person within a jurisdiction. In the South after Reconstruction, the payment of a poll tax was often made a requirement for voting as a means of disfranchising African Americans and, in some cases, poor whites. The ratification of the Twenty-fourth Amendment in 1964 made it unconstitutional to impose poll taxes in federal elections; the levying of poll taxes in state and local elections was deemed a violation of the Fourteenth Amendment's Equal Protection Clause by the U.S. Supreme Court in *Harper v. Virginia Board of Elections* (1966).

536.15   Chesterfield overcoat] Knee-length, velvet-collared men's wool topcoat.

540.1   Rebecca-like . . . *Ivanhoe*] Sir Walter Scott's romantic novel *Ivanhoe* (1820), set in twelfth-century chivalric England, featured a Jewish heroine, Rebecca.

540.8   seder] Celebratory meal served during Passover.

541.4–5   war novels . . . *Lions*] Norman Mailer's *The Naked and the Dead* (1948), based on his experiences as a soldier in the Philippines during World War II; Irwin Shaw's *The Young Lions* (1949), about three young soldiers in Europe during World War II.

543.17   Dreyfus affair] In October 1894, French-Jewish artillery officer

Alfred Dreyfus (1859–1935) was wrongfully arrested on charges of treason and sentenced to life imprisonment. The intense controversy that followed resulted in the case being reopened, and in September 1899 Dreyfus was pardoned by President Émile Loubet. He was fully exonerated by a military commission on July 12, 1906, and one week later publicly decorated with the Légion d'Honneur.

543.30   Lana Turner's] Actress and sex symbol Lana Turner (1921–1995), star of *The Postman Always Rings Twice* (1946).

546.7   Sandhurst] The Royal Military Academy Sandhurst (RMAS) is the British Army's officer-training center.

547.3–4   Nelson Rockefeller . . . Harriman] Republican politician Nelson Rockefeller (1908–1979), governor of New York, 1959–73, and vice president of the United States, 1974–77; industrialist, Democratic politician, and diplomat W. Averell Harriman (1891–1986), governor of New York, 1955–59.

547.31–32   Adler elevated shoes] I.e., elevator shoes, which have built-up insoles under the heels to make the wearer appear taller.

548.12–15   Why dost . . . long] *Richard III*, I.ii.144, 249.

551.8   Itzhak-Perlman] Tel Aviv–born virtuoso violinist and international recording star (b. 1945).

553.34   Fabians] British socialist movement founded in 1884 that favored incremental rather than revolutionary change. Among its early members were George Bernard Shaw, H. G. Wells, and Beatrice and Sidney Webb.

559.13   *Così Fan Tutte*] Mozart's opera (1790), with libretto by Lorenzo da Ponte (1749–1838).

561.18   Modigliani] Italian artist Amedeo Modigliani (1884–1920), who worked in France, best known for his sensuous portraits of women.

563.1   Khrushchev's revelations] On February 25, 1956, Soviet leader Nikita Khrushchev (1894–1971) delivered a speech before a closed session of the Twentieth Congress of the Communist Party of the Soviet Union that was highly critical of his predecessor Josef Stalin and the brutality of his regime.

567.17–20   Browder . . . imperialist] Earl Browder (1891–1973), general secretary of the Communist Party of the United States, 1934–44, and president of the Communist Political Association, 1944–45. His decision to formally dissolve the Party in 1944 was denounced as "revisionist" in the spring of 1945 by Jacques Duclos, a leading French Communist who was widely believed to be expressing the views of the Soviet leadership. The Communist Party of the USA was reconstituted in July 1945, and Browder was expelled from it in 1946.

567.20   Foster] Radical labor leader William Z. Foster (1881–1961),

American Communist Party chairman, 1929–34 and 1945–57, and its candidate for president in 1924, 1928, and 1932.

567.38   Sarah Bernhardt] Celebrated French actress (1844–1923).

570.16   "Twenty Questions"] Popular American parlor game that became a successful radio and television program in the 1940s and 1950s.

570.21–23   what Burton says . . . melancholy] See Robert Burton, *The Anatomy of Melancholy* (1621), part 1, section 1, subsection 5.

572.27–29   151 people . . . *Red Channels*] On June 22, 1950, the editors of the right-wing newsletter *Counterattack* published *Red Channels: The Report of Communist Influence in Radio and Television*. The report named 151 individuals in broadcasting supposedly having ties to Communist activities, who were then blacklisted from working in the entertainment business.

573.8   "fronter"] A person who lends his name to a blacklisted artist so that he may work.

573.35–36   Mr. McCarran's . . . Act] See note 428.5–6.

574.2   old *Herald Tribune*] Daily newspaper, 1924–66, created in 1924 through the merger of the *New York Herald* and *New York Tribune*.

575.3–4   novels . . . Dos Passos] American novelists Thomas Wolfe (1900–1938), author of *Look Homeward, Angel* (1929) and *Of Time and the River* (1935), and John Dos Passos (1896–1970), author of the *U.S.A.* trilogy (1930–36).

575.26–27   fascist . . . Rhee] Korean political leader (1875–1965) and first president of South Korea, 1948–60. His regime was fervently anti-communist.

575.35–37   Truman's attorney general . . . Party] Tom C. Clark (1899–1977), United States attorney general, 1945–49, and an associate justice of the Supreme Court, 1949–67. In 1948, the Justice Department indicted eleven Communist Party leaders under the Smith Act (see note 442.22) for conspiring to overthrow the government; all were convicted, and their defense attorneys received contempt citations. In *Dennis v. United States* (1951) their convictions were upheld by the Supreme Court, with Clark recusing himself because of his prior involvement as attorney general.

577.39   Abbott and Costello] American comedy duo Bud Abbott (1895–1974) and Lou Costello (1906–1959), veterans of burlesque and vaudeville, made thirty-six movies together, starting with *One Night in the Tropics* (1940).

581.8–9   Cape buffalo skull . . . mount] African trophy head with distinctive ram-like horns attached to a bleached-white skull.

588.12   United Mine Workers] American labor union, founded in 1890, that helped secure basic rights for miners such as safer work conditions, the eight-hour workday, and the outlawing of child labor.

588.24   company store]   System where workers were forced to shop exclusively in employer-owned stores and use privately issued scrip rather than U.S. currency.

594.37   Maccabees' struggle]   The second-century BCE Jewish leader Judah Maccabee led a revolt against the repressive king Antiochus IV Epiphanes, the ruler of the Hellenistic Seleucid Empire. After Judah Maccabee's forces drove their enemies out of Jerusalem, the Jewish Temple in the city was rededicated in 165 BCE, an event commemorated by the festival of Chanukah.

598.31   'fifth columnists']   Subversives secretly working for the enemy of their country; traitors.

602.15   Plymouths]   Chrysler Corporation's car brand marketed to the middle class after World War II, comparable to General Motors' Chevrolet brand.

603.10   Rafael Kubelik]   Czech-born conductor (1914–1996) who was appointed conductor of the Chicago Symphony Orchestra in 1950 but left after three years because of criticism from the symphony board for programming too much contemporary music.

604.11–19   Kierkegaard . . . nothing]   Danish philosopher and religious thinker Søren Kierkegaard (1813–1855); his invective against "the public" is part of his essay *The Present Age* (1846).

605.5   Benedetto Croce's]   Italian philosopher, historian, and politician Benedetto Croce (1866–1952), perhaps best known in the English-speaking world for his *Aesthetic as Science of Expression and General Linguistic* (1902).

609.23–25   *For the hardest work . . . rewards*]   Cf. Marx, *Critique of the Gotha Program* (1875): "From each according to his abilities, to each according to his needs." This dictum was already a "famous saying" when cited by the French socialist Jean Joseph Louis Blanc (1811–1882) in *The Organization of Labor* (1841).

612.32–33   Phil Murray's CIO]   See note 430.23–26.

613.28   flash me the V]   "Victory" hand gesture—with the first two fingers extended in a "V" shape—associated with Winston Churchill during World War II.

613.31   Gary Big Mill]   Sprawling United States Steel complex in Gary, Indiana, site of frequent strikes.

615.28   Trotskyites]   Followers of Marxist ideology of Russian revolutionary Leon Trotsky (1879–1940), who was exiled by Stalin and assassinated in Mexico City by an agent of the Soviet secret police (NKVD) on August 20, 1940.

616.13   Eastman]   Max Eastman (1883–1969), American political writer, editor, and poet; editor of the socialist magazines *The Masses*, 1912–17, and *The Liberator*, 1918–22; and translator of Trotsky.

616.13   Lovestone] Jay Lovestone (1897–1990), founder of one branch of what became the Communist Party USA. In 1929 he was expelled from the party for supporting Nikolai Bukharin and became the head of a splinter group commonly known as Lovestonites.

616.13–15   Zinoviev . . . trials] Public show trials were held in Moscow in August 1936, January 1937, and March 1938, during which prominent Soviet Communists were falsely accused of conspiring with the exiled Leon Trotsky to overthrow Josef Stalin and his regime. Among those executed on charges of treason were Grigory Zinoviev (1883–1936), Lev Kamenev (1883–1936), and Nikolai Bukharin (1888–1938).

616.14–15   "the October Revolution"] The Bolsheviks overthrew the Russian Provisional Government led by Alexander Kerensky in a coup d'état on October 25 (November 7, N.S.), 1917.

619.9–10   *Who Owns America?* by James S. Allen] American labor organizer and Marxist theorist James S. Allen (1906–1986) published the tract *Who Owns America?* in 1946.

621.20   aging Montgomery Clift] Montgomery Clift (1920–1966), American stage and movie actor, star of *A Place in the Sun* (1951) and *From Here to Eternity* (1953).

624.40   black Mary Janes] Type of strapped low-heeled shoe or sandal.

625.16–17   famous statue . . . Washington] Two statues of Washington were added to the Washington Square arch (1892) designed by Stanford White (1853–1906): *George Washington as Military Commander* (1916) by Hermon A. MacNeil (1866–1947) and *George Washington as President* by Alexander Stirling Calder (1870–1945).

626.2   Alger Hiss] Alger Hiss (1904–1996) held several positions in the administration of Franklin D. Roosevelt and began working for the State Department in 1936. He was publicly accused in 1948 by Whittaker Chambers (1901–1961), a former Communist, of having been a Soviet intelligence agent. Hiss sued Chambers for slander, and in grand jury testimony denied Chambers's charges that he had transmitted secret documents to the Soviet Union; he was then indicted for perjury, and after two trials was convicted, serving forty-four months of a five-year sentence. He continued to maintain that the charges against him were false.

626.2–3   Rosenbergs] See note 407.4.

634.32   Mary Astor] American actress (1906–1987) whose films include *Dodsworth* (1936), *The Prisoner of Zenda* (1937), and *The Maltese Falcon* (1941).

635.32–33   Town Hall] Venue for lectures, concerts, and dance on West 43rd Street in Manhattan since 1921.

635.39–40   Sol Hurok]   Russian-born concert impresario Solomon Hurok (1888–1974).

636.40   Toscanini]   Arturo Toscanini (1867–1957), Italian conductor of the Metropolitan Opera, La Scala, the New York Philharmonic, and the NBC Symphony Orchestra.

637.2   Phil Spitalny]   Russian-born bandleader (1890–1970), conductor of an all-female orchestra that performed on the radio in the 1930s and 1940s.

637.12   "Tailgunner Joe"]   Senator Joseph McCarthy served in the Marines as an intelligence officer with a dive bomber squadron in the Pacific, 1943–44, and flew eleven combat missions as a gunner-observer (he later falsely claimed to have flown thirty-two missions and was improperly awarded the Distinguished Flying Cross in 1952). McCarthy talked up his wartime experience by referring to himself as "Tailgunner Joe" during his unsuccessful bid for the U.S. Senate in 1944; he also lied about being wounded in combat and was known to feign a limp.

642.2   Scheherazade]   Legendary Persian queen and storyteller in the classic book *The Book of One Thousand and One Nights*.

644.22–24   what Coleridge . . . malignity]   See Coleridge's essay "Notes on Othello" (collected in *Literary Remains*, volume 2): "Iago's soliloquy—the motive-hunting of a motiveless malignity—how awful it is!"

648.11–12   monologue . . . I!]   *Hamlet*, II.ii.550–605.

651.19   *Gangbusters. Your FBI*]   *Gangbusters* (1935–57), American radio drama based on actual police cases; *This Is Your FBI*, radio crime series (1945–53) dramatizing FBI investigations.

651.19–20   Kate Smith singing "God Bless America."]   Singer Kate Smith's (1907–1986) signature song was Irving Berlin's patriotic anthem "God Bless America" (1938).

651.26   AFTRA]   National labor union, American Federation of Television and Radio Artists.

652.36   Westbrook Pegler]   See note 271.8–9.

655.9   Joe Martin . . . chair]   Republican Massachusetts congressman Joseph Martin, Jr. (1884–1968), served as Speaker of the House, 1947–49 and 1953–55.

655.15   Roy Cohn]   See note 271.4.

655.37   C-SPAN at the Nixon funeral]   Nixon's public funeral was held on April 22, 1994, five days after his death, at the Richard Nixon Presidential Library and Museum, Yorba Linda, California, and televised on the Cable-Satellite Public Affairs Network.

656.8   Senator Dole] Kansas Republican senator Bob Dole (b. 1923), the Republican presidential nominee in 1996.

656.26   'The King is in high rage.'] *King Lear*, II.iv.296.

657.1   Billy Graham] Influential Southern Baptist minister (b. 1918), a spiritual advisor to several American presidents.

657.12–13   Governor Pete Wilson] Pete Wilson (b. 1933), Republican governor of California, 1991–99.

657.15   'Doctor' Kissinger] German-born American academic and diplomat Henry Kissinger (b. 1923), national security adviser, 1969–75, secretary of state, 1973–77.

657.19–21   'He was a man . . . again] *Hamlet*, I.ii.187–88.

657.27   court Jew] Originally a description of a select few Jewish bankers who lent money and managed the finances of European royalty.

657.32–33   Foul deeds . . . eyes] *Hamlet*, I.ii.256–57.

657.39   James Baker] Attorney, presidential aide, and diplomat (b. 1930), secretary of the treasury, 1985–88, secretary of state, 1989–92.

657.39–40   Iran-Contra arms dealer Adnan Khashoggi] Saudi arms dealer and businessman Adnan Khashoggi (b. 1935) was involved in the Iran-Contra affair, in which American government officials secretly sold weapons to Iran in an attempt to obtain the release of Americans held hostage in Lebanon. Proceeds from the arms sales were used to illegally funnel supplies and funds to the Contra rebels seeking to overthrow the Sandinista government in Nicaragua.

657.40   Donald Nixon] Donald Nixon (1914–1987), the president's brother.

657.40–658.1   burglar G. Gordon Liddy] G. Gordon Liddy (b. 1930), Nixon aide who with E. Howard Hunt planned the Watergate burglary; he served a four-and-a-half-year prison sentence for his involvement in the break-in.

658.23   Mao's Cultural Revolution] Violent mass movement, initiated by Mao Zedong in 1966, to purge purportedly bourgeois elements of Chinese society.

658.30   Daumier] French artist Honoré Daumier (1808–1870), best known for his political caricatures and satirical tableaux of French social life.

674.9–10   ziconette] Italian gambling game.

675.22–23   You were the guy's Prince Hal] Sir John Falstaff, a disreputable, boisterous knight, befriends England's future king Henry V, Prince Hal, in Shakespeare's *1 Henry IV* and *2 Henry IV*.

678.13–14   Raskolnikov . . . years] In Dostoevsky's *Crime and Punishment* (1866), Raskolnikov, an impoverished student, murders and robs a miserly

pawnbroker; although he rationalizes the murder as an act for the greater social good, he is anguished by having committed the crime.

679.27   And thus . . . revenges] *Twelfth Night*, V.i.376–77.

683.5   *Nation,* the *Reporter,* the *New Republic*] Liberal magazines.

684.25–26   *Confidential*] Scandal and gossip magazine, 1952–78.

686.9   *The Goldbergs*] Serial comedy-drama about a Jewish family in the
Bronx that ran on radio, 1929–46, and television, 1949–56.

686.36   Goneril and Regan] Lear's two ungrateful daughters in *King Lear.*

687.28–29   *The Swiss Family Robinson*] Children's novel (1812), by Johann
David Wyss (1743–1818), about a family's survival of a shipwreck and its
aftermath.

688.12   *J'accuse*] On January 13, 1898, during the Dreyfus affair (see note
543.17), Émile Zola (1840–1902) published "I Accuse," an outraged open letter to the president of the French Republic following the acquittal of Charles-
Ferdinand Esterhazy (1847–1923), the army officer and spy for Germany who
had falsely accused Dreyfus of treason.

THE HUMAN STAIN

701.1   THE HUMAN STAIN] For the limited-edition Franklin Library
version of the novel, Roth contributed a preface (printed here from a manuscript provided by the author): "Ira Ringold, the hero of *I Married a Communist,* is the dark analogue of Swede Levov, the hero of *American Pastoral.* Ira:
the man totally misplaced in society, a bristling, angry Jew, a defiant American,
a turbulent social force with a terrible secret; the Swede: a natural, the man at
ease here, a Jew wholly at peace as a satisfied American citizen, a man with no
secrets at all. Ira: who rushes to radically alter history, society, the class system;
the Swede: who, like most other men, endeavors to secure for himself a life beyond the reach of history's sweep, bound to and by a business, a family, and
the greater society's shared ideals. Ira: the revolutionary spirit undone by the
maddening incursion into his historical struggle of marital and household
mayhem; the Swede: the private man, ahistorical, compliant, utterly content,
crushed by the incursion into his home of the history that isn't quite yet history—destroyed by the present American moment. Coleman Silk is history's
rather different plaything and a third type of hero altogether. The history he
wishes radically to alter is not society's but simply his own. And he succeeds
brilliantly, springing the historical lock of his destiny, boldly remaking his social
being, only to be blindsided by the current mood, by the mind of the country,
by the history that is inescapable: the history that is one's own time."

705.11   Okie] Slang for an Oklahoman.

705.11–12   winds of the Dust Bowl] Term first used in 1935 for drought-stricken regions of Texas, Oklahoma, Kansas, and Colorado that were suffering from severe soil erosion.

705.35–706.3   new Miss America . . . star]   Pop singer and actress Vanessa Williams (b. 1963) first became famous as Miss America 1983, a title she relinquished in July 1984 after the discovery of nude photographs of her and another woman from 1982 and the announcement that they would soon be published in *Penthouse* magazine.

706.4–6   in baseball . . . brown]   In 1998, St. Louis Cardinals first baseman Mark McGwire (b. 1963) and Chicago Cubs rightfielder Sammy Sosa (b. 1968) both broke Roger Maris's single-season record of sixty-one home runs, set in 1961. McGwire finished the season with seventy home runs, Sosa with sixty-six.

706.20   "the persecuting spirit"]   From "The Custom-House," introduction to Hawthorne's *The Scarlet Letter* (1850).

706.23   Senator Lieberman's]   Joseph Lieberman (b. 1942), Connecticut senator (1989–2013) and Democratic vice-presidential candidate (2000), was one of the first Democratic politicians to publicly criticize Bill Clinton after revelations about his affair with Monica Lewinsky were made public.

706.27   William F. Buckley]   William F. Buckley, Jr. (1925–2008), author, editor, host of the public-affairs television program *Firing Line*, and conservative polemicist who founded the magazine *National Review* in 1955.

706.27   Abelard]   See note 523.13.

706.35–38   Khomeini's fatwa . . . incentive]   Iran's Supreme Leader, the Ayatollah Ruholla Khomeini (1900–1989), declared in a 1989 fatwa that British author Salman Rushdie (b. 1947) should be put to death because of alleged blasphemy in his novel *The Satanic Verses* (1988). An Iranian Islamic foundation soon offered a multimillion-dollar bounty to anyone who would kill Rushdie.

707.13   Christo wrapping]   Bulgarian-born artist Christo Vladimirov Javacheff (b. 1935), best known for his outdoor works that typically include draping familiar objects, buildings, or landscapes in fabric.

711.21   c.v.]   Latin: curriculum vitae: an academic or professional résumé.

715.35   strontium 90]   A radioactive isotope of the element strontium that is produced by nuclear fission, strontium 90 is absorbed in human bone and increases the risk of cancer. Concern about the effects of strontium 90, especially in children who were exposed to it by drinking cow's milk, became a focal point of opposition to the atmospheric testing of nuclear weapons in the 1950s and 1960s.

716.21   Art Students League]   Art school founded in 1875.

717.19   Benny Goodman]   Chicago-born clarinetist and bandleader (1909–1986) known as "The King of Swing."

717.26   Vaughn Monroe]   American trumpeter, bandleader, and vocalist (1911–1973) with a buttery baritone sound.

717.34–35   You sigh . . . violins]   "It's Magic" (1947), music by Jule Styne (1905–1994), lyrics by Sammy Cahn (1913–1993).

717.37–38   Helen O'Connell . . . "Green Eyes"]   The American singers Helen O'Connell (1920–1993) and Bob Eberly (1916–1981) sang on the Jimmy Dorsey Orchestra's 1941 hit version of "Green Eyes" (1929), an adaptation of the Spanish song "Aquellos Ojos Verdes."

718.1   Jimmy and Tommy Dorsey]   Jazz reed player and bandleader Jimmy Dorsey (1904–1957), older brother of bandleader Tommy Dorsey (1905–1956).

718.4–5   Dick Haymes . . . Lies.']   Dick Haymes (1918–1980), Argentine actor and pop vocalist of the 1940s and 1950s, had a huge hit in 1948 with "Little White Lies" (1930), song written by Walter Donaldson (1893–1947).

718.12–13   "Everything Happens to Me,"]   Hit song (1941) for Frank Sinatra, words by Tom Adler (1913–1988), music by Matt Dennis (1914–2002).

722.2–3   Gulliver . . . horses]   In book 4 of Jonathan Swift's *Gulliver's Travels* (1726), Lemuel Gulliver encounters the Houyhnhnms, a race of intelligent and virtuous horses. When he returns home he chooses to live with his horses rather than other people.

722.29–30   Nelson Mandela . . . jailers]   In February 1990 Nelson Mandela (b. 1918) was released after spending twenty-seven years in prison for his opposition to the apartheid regime in South Africa. Mandela then helped negotiate a peaceful transition to nonracial majority rule and later became president of South Africa, 1994–99.

724.33   the Reinfelds]   During Prohibition, Polish-born tavern owner Joseph Reinfeld ran a large bootlegging operation out of Newark with Longy Zwillman (see notes 462.14, 462.22); after repeal, he founded the business Reinfeld Distributors but maintained connections with organized crime.

725.29   GI Bill]   See note 41.14.

727.6   "Bewitched, Bothered and Bewildered"]   Hit song from the Rodgers and Hart musical *Pal Joey* (1940).

727.19   Pan]   Greek god of shepherds and flocks, a musician who is also associated with the theater. Often depicted with an enlarged phallus, he is renowned for his sexual prowess.

729.6   La Belle Dame . . . thrall]   John Keats's ballad "La Belle Dame sans Merci" (1819), lines 39–40. The title, which means "The Beautiful Damsel Without Pity," is taken from a 1424 poem by Alain Chartier (c. 1385–1430).

732.35   On top of old Smoky]   From the traditional American folk song "On Top of Old Smoky": "On top of Old Smoky, all covered with snow/ I lost my true lover, for courtin' too slow."

743.37   Balzac]   Prolific French novelist and playwright Honoré de Balzac (1799–1850), author of the Human Comedy cycle of novels.

743.37–38   *The Red and the Black*]   Novel (1830) by French writer Stendhal, pen name of Marie-Henri Beyle (1783–1842).

745.19   "the communications . . . itself"]   From Hawthorne's preface to the 1851 edition of his short-story collection *Twice-Told Tales.*

752.21–22   Aschenbach feverishly watching Tadzio]   Gustave von Aschenbach, dying protagonist of Thomas Mann's novella *Death in Venice* (1912), becomes obsessed with a beautiful young boy named Tadzio.

763.11   Philoctetes]   Greek hero in the Trojan War, the subject of plays by Aeschylus, Sophocles, and Euripides. En route to Troy, because of a festering, foul-smelling foot wound that caused him to swear violently and cry out in pain, he was abandoned on the island of Lemnos at the suggestion of Odysseus, and was marooned there for ten years.

763.12   fulminations of Medea]   In Euripides' *Medea* (431 BCE), Medea takes revenge on her unfaithful husband, Jason, by murdering their two young children.

763.12   madness of Ajax]   Giant Greek warrior, the subject of a play by Sophocles. At the end of the Trojan War, when Achilles' armor is given not to him but to Odysseus, he plots revenge against his fellow Greeks but, driven mad by Athena, slaughters a flock of sheep instead. Remorseful and ashamed of his act, he commits suicide.

763.12–13   the despair of Electra]   In Euripides' *Electra* (413 BCE), Electra urges her brother Orestes to murder their mother, Clytemnestra, in revenge for Clytemnestra's murder of their father, Agamemnon.

763.13   suffering of Prometheus]   In Greek mythology, Prometheus, one of the Titans, was punished for stealing fire from the gods and giving it to mortal men. Zeus had him tied down on Mount Caucasus so that an eagle could feed on his liver, which regenerated itself every day only to be eaten anew.

765.36   VA]   Veterans Administration hospital.

768.39   twenty percent]   Disability payments are based on the severity of a soldier's injuries, calculated on a 1-to-100 scale. Twenty percent disability is a relatively low assessment.

770.4   Thorazine]   Powerful tranquilizer, once used as an antipsychotic medication.

775.29–30   Janis Joplin and Norman O. Brown] American rock 'n' roll singer Janis Joplin (1943–1970), who died from a heroin overdose in 1970; American cultural critic Norman O. Brown (1913–2002), author of *Life Against Death: The Psychoanalytic Meaning of History* (1959).

786.39–40   Golden Gloves] Annual amateur boxing competition held nationally since 1928.

787.30   PAL] Police Athletic League: police-administered welfare organization sponsoring sports leagues and recreational activities for children and teenagers.

788.29–30   at the Knights of Pythias] A hall of the fraternal organization founded in 1864.

790.19   Marc Antony's speech] Speech that begins, "Friends, Romans, countrymen, lend me your ears!": *Julius Caesar*, III.ii.73–252.

791.26   George M. Cohan in *I'd Rather Be Right*] American entertainer George M. Cohan (1878–1942), known for his ebullient singing and dancing, was the star of the Rodgers and Hart musical *I'd Rather Be Right* (1937), with a book by Moss Hart and George S. Kaufman.

794.6–7   Schmeling . . . fight] German heavyweight boxer Max Schmeling (1905–2005) knocked out Joe Louis in the twelfth round at Yankee Stadium, June 19, 1936. Louis won their politically fraught rematch at Yankee Stadium on June 22, 1938, with a knockout in the first round.

796.37   Ray Robinson] "Sugar Ray" Robinson (1921–1989), champion boxer in both welterweight and middleweight divisions.

798.29   labonz] Stomach or gut, in Italian-American slang.

803.28–33   Cowards . . . come] *Julius Caesar*, II.ii.32–37.

804.17–18   What can be avoided . . . gods?] *Julius Caesar*, II.ii.26–27.

805.16   Beware the ides of March] *Julius Caesar*, I.ii.18.

806.22   Phi Beta Kappa] Honor society for liberal arts achievement, founded December 5, 1776, at the College of William and Mary.

806.22   summa cum laude] Latin: with highest honors.

807.7–8   separation center] Place where soldiers are formally discharged from the army.

811.14   Symphony Sid] Sid Torin (1909–1984), "Symphony Sid," preeminent jazz disc jockey whose long career was based mostly in New York.

811.16   "Lady Be Good"] Title song for the George and Ira Gershwin musical (1924), a jazz standard performed by Count Basie (1904–1984) and his ensembles.

811.17–18   Artie Shaw rendition . . . Eldridge] Popular song from the score of *Lady Be Good* performed by clarinetist and bandleader Artie Shaw (1910–2004) and his band, featuring innovative jazz trumpeter Roy Eldridge (1911–1989).

812.19   Beau Jack] American boxer Sidney Walker (1921–2000), twice lightweight champion.

819.14   King Canute] Eleventh-century Viking king of England and Scandinavia.

823.12–13   Kropotkin and Bakunin] Prince Peter Kropotkin (1842–1921) and Mikhail Bakunin (1814–1876), Russian intellectuals and revolutionary anarchists.

823.14   *Freie Arbeiter Stimme*] Yiddish: *The Free Voice of Labor*, principal Yiddish anarchist publication, 1890–1977.

823.33   King Arthur's Court to the Connecticut Yankee] Mark Twain's novel, *A Connecticut Yankee in King Arthur's Court* (1889), is about a practical New England Yankee transported to medieval England.

824.11   "The Karamazov Kids."] The comic strip "Katzenjammer Kids" debuted in a Hearst-owned New York newspaper in 1897 and ran for six decades. It featured the twins Hans and Fritz, who constantly rebelled against authority. "Karamazov" refers to the three troubled Karamazov brothers for which the Dostoevsky novel is named.

826.16–17   *Commentary . . . Review*] *Commentary*, monthly magazine founded in 1945 by the American Jewish Committee; *Midstream*, Zionist monthly founded in 1955; *Partisan Review*, influential quarterly journal known for its serious fiction and literary and political essays, 1934–2003.

835.36   Haddonfield Quakers] After the arrival in 1701 of the Quaker Elizabeth Haddon Estaugh (1680–1762), the town of Haddonfield, New Jersey, was established and became home to a flourishing religious community.

838.12–13   African Methodist Episcopal Church] First African American church indigenous to the United States, founded in Philadelphia by Bishop Richard Allen (1760–1831) in 1816.

838.13–14   Teddy Roosevelt and his Rough Riders] The 1st U.S. Volunteer Cavalry, led by future president Theodore Roosevelt (1858–1919), whose exploits at the Battle of San Juan Hill in Cuba, July 1, 1898, made them national heroes during the Spanish-American War.

840.10   Willey] White House volunteer Kathleen Willey (b. 1946) alleged in 1998 that Bill Clinton sexually assaulted her on November 29, 1993.

840.15   Gennifer Flowers] Actress and singer Gennifer Flowers (b. 1950) claimed during the 1992 presidential election campaign that she had had a twelve-year affair with Bill Clinton. Denying the allegations when they were first made, Clinton testified under oath in 1998 that he had had one sexual encounter with Flowers in 1977.

840.22   Miss Monica] White House intern Monica Lewinsky (b. 1973), whose sexual involvement with Bill Clinton led to his impeachment by the House of Representatives in December 1998.

840.26   Starr] Former federal appellate judge and U.S. solicitor general Kenneth Starr (b. 1946) was appointed in 1994 as independent counsel to continue a federal investigation into possible misconduct by President Bill Clinton and his associates in an Arkansas land deal transacted when he was the state's governor. Starr expanded his investigation into other areas, including a sexual harassment lawsuit against the president by former Arkansas state employee Paula Jones (b. 1967) and Clinton's affair with Monica Lewinsky.

840.28   gang rape . . . hotel] On January 16, 1998, eleven days after she signed an affidavit denying having sexual relations with Clinton, Lewinsky was approached by FBI agents working for Starr's office in the food court of a mall in Arlington, Virginia, and asked to accompany them to the nearby Ritz-Carlton hotel to discuss possible perjury charges against her. She was questioned at the hotel for more than nine hours without her attorney being present.

840.29   talking to Linda Tripp] Linda Tripp (b. 1949) was a coworker of Lewinsky's at the Pentagon's public affairs office after Lewinsky's transfer from the White House in April 1996. At the suggestion of literary agent Lucianne Goldberg, Tripp began making secret recordings of phone calls in which Lewinsky confided details about her relationship with Clinton, which were later given to Starr.

842.11–12   Deep Throat] Investigating the involvement of senior officials in President Nixon's reelection campaign in the Watergate burglaries, *Washington Post* journalist Bob Woodward (b. 1943) met in an underground parking garage with an informant identified only as "Deep Throat" until 2005, when he was revealed to have been FBI associate director Mark Felt (1913–2008).

842.37   Heisman] Award presented annually to the country's outstanding college football player.

844.6   Vince Foster] Attorney (1945–1993) and deputy White House counsel in the first Clinton administration. He was a childhood friend of Bill Clinton's and was a friend and law partner of Hillary Rodham Clinton. Foster committed suicide on July 20, 1993.

844.19   Vernon Jordan] Civil rights leader, attorney, and businessman (b. 1935), a close personal advisor to Clinton.

844.22   California Valley Girls] A term used for vacuous, materialistic girls and young women known for their exaggerated, singsong way of speaking. It originally referred to girls from Southern California's San Fernando Valley, as popularized by Frank Zappa's hit single "Valley Girl" (1982), featuring spoken vocals by his fourteen-year-old daughter, Moon Unit.

845.20   Norman Rockwell Museum] A museum in Stockbridge, Massachusetts, dedicated to the work of the popular illustrator of Americana, Norman Rockwell (1894–1978).

846.10–11   Barbara Walters . . . *NBC*] Barbara Walters (b. 1929), television journalist and interviewer; Joyce Brothers (b. 1927), psychologist and advice columnist; William Bennett (b. 1943), conservative political pundit, author of *The Death of Outrage: Bill Clinton and the Assault on American Ideals* (1998); *Dateline NBC*, weekly television news program that began its long run in 1992.

846.31–32   H. L. Mencken . . . Momism] Journalist and cultural critic H. L. Mencken (1880–1956) railed against the small-mindedness and hypocrisy of the "booboisie"; in the "Common Women" chapter of his *Generation of Vipers* (1942), Philip Wylie (1902–1971) coined the term "Momism" to assail what he saw as the prevalence of domineering, sanctimonious motherhood in America.

847.3   *Babbitt*] Sinclair Lewis's novel *Babbitt* (1922), a satire of American conformity.

847.27–28   the metamorphoses of Malcolm X] Born Malcolm Little, Malcolm X (1925–1965) was imprisoned as a petty criminal and became a member of the black nationalist Nation of Islam, led by Elijah Muhammad (1897–1975). After his release he became a mosque leader and organizer and the most prominent spokesman for Black Muslim separatism. He broke with Elijah Muhammad in March 1964, made a pilgrimage to Mecca and converted to Sunni Islam, expressed solidarity with independence movements in Africa, and founded the Organization of Afro-American Unity in June 1964. He was assassinated in Harlem by members of the Nation of Islam on February 21, 1965.

847.28   the rhetoric of James Baldwin] Novelist, essayist, and public intellectual James Baldwin (1924–1987), author of *Notes of a Native Son* (1955) and *The Fire Next Time* (1963).

847.29   *Amos 'n' Andy*] Popular radio and television comedy featuring the black characters Amos and Andy, which ran from the 1920s through the 1950s.

853.4   Pinto] Popular compact car by Ford, 1970–80, which became notorious for the dangerous location of its gas tank and its tendency to explode in rear-end crashes.

869.14   the Taconic] New York state parkway leading into the Berkshires.

870.19   *The Bacchae*]   Tragedy by Euripides, first performed in 405 BCE.

877.20–21   Danaë . . . gold]   In Greek mythology, disguised as a shower of gold, Zeus impregnated the Greek princess Danaë.

878.14   16th *arrondissement*]   One of the wealthiest of Paris's twenty administrative districts.

878.21   Lycée Janson de Sailly]   One of France's most prestigious preparatory schools, established in 1880.

878.24   Lycée Henri IV]   Elite public secondary school in Paris, the oldest in France.

878.27   École Normale Supérieure de Fontenay]   Specialized school dedicated to advanced studies in the humanities, founded in 1880.

878.29   Georges Bataille]   French philosopher and novelist (1897–1962), author of *L'Érotisme* (1957) and *The Story of the Eye* (1968).

878.31   Mallarmé]   French poet and literary critic Stéphane Mallarmé (1842–1898).

879.17–22   Kurosawa . . . Renoirs]   Japanese director Akira Kurosawa (1910–1998), whose films include *Rashomon* (1950) and *Seven Samurai* (1954); Soviet director Andrei Tarkovsky (1932–1986), whose films include *Andrei Rublev* (1966) and *Solaris* (1972); Italian director Federico Fellini (1920–1993), whose films include *8½* (1963) and *Amarcord* (1973); Italian director Michelangelo Antonioni (1912–2007), whose films include *L'Avventura* (1960) and *Blow-Up* (1966); German director Rainer Werner Fassbinder (1945–1982), whose films include *The Marriage of Maria Braun* (1978) and *Querelle* (1982); Italian director Lina Wertmüller (b. 1928), whose films include *The Seduction of Mimi* (1972) and *Seven Beauties* (1975); Bengali filmmaker Satyajit Ray (1921–1992), best known for his Apu trilogy (1955–59); French filmmaker René Clair (1898–1981), whose films include *Le Million* (1931) and *À nous la liberté* (1931); German film director Wim Wenders (b. 1945), whose films include *Paris, Texas* (1984) and *Wings of Desire* (1987); French filmmaker François Truffaut (1932–1984), whose films include *The 400 Blows* (1959) and *Shoot the Piano Player* (1960); French-Swiss filmmaker Jean-Luc Godard (b. 1930), whose films include *Breathless* (1959) and *Alphaville* (1965); French director Claude Chabrol (1930–2010), whose films include *The Cousins* (1959) and *Le Boucher* (1969); French filmmaker Alain Resnais (b. 1922), whose films include *Hiroshima Mon Amour* (1959) and *Last Year at Marienbad* (1961); French director Eric Rohmer (1920–2010), whose films include *My Night at Maud's* (1969) and *Claire's Knee* (1970); French director Jean Renoir (1894–1979), whose films include *Grand Illusion* (1937) and *The Rules of the Game* (1939).

880.8   Stop & Shop]   New England supermarket chain.

880.18   Herodotus]   Ancient Greek historian (c. 484–425 BCE).

880.18 Narratology] Theory of narrative form that analyzes narrative as analogous to linguistic structures, a term introduced in 1969 by the Bulgarian-born French literary critic Tzetvan Todorov (b. 1939).

880.18–19 The diegetic . . . mimesis] Greek terms contrasting narrative telling and showing, an opposition made by Plato in *The Republic*, book 3, 392D–394D.

882.2 Nietzschean perspective about perspective] See, for example, *On the Genealogy of Morals* (1887) by German philosopher Friedrich Nietzsche (1844–1900): "Let us be on guard against the dangerous old conceptual fiction that posited a 'pure, will-less, painless, timeless knowing subject'. . . . There is *only* a perspective seeing, *only* a perspective 'knowing.'"

888.10 Jackson Pollock show] Large retrospective of American abstract expressionist artist Jackson Pollock (1912–1956) at the Museum of Modern Art, New York, November 1, 1998–February 2, 1999.

889.2–6 *Marathon Man* . . . Hoffman] In the thriller *Marathon Man* (1976), the graduate student Babe Levy, played by Dustin Hoffman (b. 1937), picks up and becomes involved with Elsa Opel, played by Marthe Keller (b. 1945), a woman who lies to him about being Swiss; she is a pawn in an attempt to take possession of a cache of diamonds involving a duplicitous U.S. government operative and a sadistic Nazi dentist.

889.32–33 Julia Kristeva, a treatise . . . melancholy] *Black Sun: Depression and Melancholy* (1987) by the Bulgarian-born French philosopher and feminist literary critic Julia Kristeva (b. 1941).

889.35 Philippe Sollers] Pen name of Philippe Joyaux (b. 1936), French novelist, critic, and editor, cofounder of *Tel Quel*, influential French literary and political journal (1960–82).

889.39 Kundera] Czech novelist Milan Kundera (b. 1929), author of *The Joke* (1967) and *The Book of Laughter and Forgetting* (1979), fled Czechoslovakia in 1975 and immigrated to France.

895.20 Sergiu Commissiona] Romanian violinist and conductor (1928–2005).

896.24–26 Pygmalion . . . Galatea] In Greek myth, Pygmalion creates an ivory sculpture of a beautiful woman known as Galatea, who comes to life.

898.3 Bronfman] Russian-Israeli pianist Yefim Bronfman (b. 1958).

900.29–30 fled . . . storm] "And they are gone: ay, ages ago/These lovers fled away into the storm": John Keats, "The Eve of St. Agnes" (1819), lines 370–71.

902.19 hundred percent service connection] The Veterans Administration assesses the percentage of disability on a hundred-point scale (in increments of ten). One hundred percent service-connected disability is for veterans who are totally disabled.

904.34   Agent Orange]   Defoliant used to destroy forests and crops in South Vietnam during the Vietnam War until 1971. Human health problems linked to exposure to Agent Orange are believed to be caused by dioxin, though the U.S. government has claimed that the amount of the toxin present in the defoliant is too small to be harmful.

912.16   Semper fi!]   Marine Corps motto, shortened from Latin, *semper fidelis*: always faithful.

912.34–35   Artie Shaw . . . trumpet]   See note 811.17–18.

932.22   Kevorkian . . . machine]   Jack Kevorkian (b. 1928), American pathologist and assisted suicide advocate known as "Dr. Death," designed what he called a "Thanatron" (death machine) that allowed patients to administer themselves a lethal dose of drugs. After 1991, when he no longer had access to drugs because his medical license had been revoked, he used a machine that pumped carbon monoxide into a gas mask on the patient's face. From 1990 to 1998, Kevorkian helped 130 people end their lives.

936.13   "Battle Hymn of the Green Berets"]   "The Ballad of the Green Berets" (1966), patriotic popular song written by Robin Moore (1925–2008) and Staff Sergeant Barry Sadler (1940–1989).

939.4   POW/MIA]   Prisoner of War/Missing in Action.

941.2   R&R]   Rest & Recreation; i.e., military leave.

941.4–5   B-40 rocket]   A portable, shoulder-launched, rocket-propelled grenade used by the North Vietnamese army and the Viet Cong.

946.3   *Éblouissante! . . . chat*]   French: Dazzling! You have the face of a cat.

946.6   Leslie Caron]   French actress and dancer Leslie Caron (b. 1931), whose films include *An American in Paris* (1951) and *Gigi* (1958).

946.36   Brazzaville]   Capital of the Republic of the Congo.

946.38   Nanterre]   Established in the 1960s on the outskirts of Paris, Nanterre (Paris West University Nanterre La Défense) is an extension of the Sorbonne.

948.38   SWF]   Single White Female.

950.15–16   *malgré lui*]   French: in spite of himself.

951.38   *comédie humaine*]   French: human comedy, collective title of Balzac's monumental cycle of novels.

952.1   French theory they had been fed]   Term used for works of philosophy, psychoanalysis, cultural criticism, and literary criticism associated with French intellectuals who came to prominence in the 1960s and the 1970s, particularly Jacques Derrida (1930–2004), Jacques Lacan (1901–1981), and Michel Foucault (1926–1984). Yale University was one of the first institutions in America to embrace French theory.

953.10–11   Bob Reich]   Economist Robert Reich (b. 1946), U.S. secretary of labor, 1993–97.

953.13   Bob Rubin]   Robert Rubin (b. 1938), U.S. secretary of the treasury, 1995–99.

953.15   Alan]   Economist Alan Greenspan (b. 1926), chairman of the Federal Reserve, 1987–2006.

953.21   *The German Ideology*]   Book (1845) by Karl Marx and Friedrich Engels.

954.23   Simone de Beauvoir]   French existentialist philosopher, feminist, and prominent public intellectual Simone de Beauvoir (1908–1986), author of *The Second Sex* (1949).

955.28   *faute de mieux*]   French: for the lack of something better.

955.35   intertextuality]   Term coined by Julia Kristeva referring to the way the meaning of texts is affected by other texts.

956.3   *bildungsroman*]   A novel that recounts the development and education of its main character. Goethe's *Wilhelm Meister's Apprenticeship* (1795–96) is a celebrated example of the genre.

972.21   clytemnestra@houseofatreus.com]   The House of Atreus is the tragic family of Greek mythology headed by the patriarch Atreus, the father of Agamemnon, who was murdered by his wife, Clytemnestra.

978.10   Jeff Gordon]   Champion stock car racing driver (b. 1971).

984.11–12   House of the Seven Gables]   Grand old house in Salem, Massachusetts, made famous in Nathaniel Hawthorne's novel *The House of Seven Gables* (1851).

989.8   the old Mayor Daley was running Chicago]   Richard J. Daley (1902–1976), "the Boss," was mayor of Chicago for twenty-one years, dying in office on December 20, 1976. His son, Richard M. Daley (b. 1942), served as mayor from 1989 to 2011.

994.35   Kaddish]   Hebrew mourning prayer.

995.4   *Yisgadal, v'yiskadash*]   In Aramaic, the opening of the Kaddish, Jewish prayer of mourning.

1003.30   *Pinky*]   Film (1949) directed by Elia Kazan about a light-skinned black woman living in the South who can pass for white, starring white actress Jeanne Crain (1925–2003).

1003.30   another, with Mel Ferrer]   *Lost Boundaries* (1949), starring Mel Ferrer (1917–2008), film about a black doctor whose family passed for white while living in New Hampshire.

1009.31   Matthew Henson]   African American explorer Matthew Henson (1866–1955) accompanied Admiral Robert Peary (1856–1920) on his expedition to the North Pole in 1909. His feat went without official recognition until Congress, in 1944, belatedly awarded him a duplicate of the medal given to Peary more than thirty years earlier.

1010.10   Peary or Cook]   American explorer and physician Frederick Cook (1865–1940) falsely claimed to have reached the North Pole on April 21, 1908, a year earlier than his former associate Peary.

1010.15–17   Sir Edmund Hillary . . . Norgay]   On May 29, 1953, New Zealand mountaineer Edmund Hillary (1919–2008) and his Sherpa climbing partner Tenzing Norgay (1914–1986) became the first climbers to reach the summit of Mount Everest, the world's tallest mountain.

1010.21   Dr. Charles Drew]   Surgeon and research scientist (1904–1950) whose research was critical in the development of large-scale blood banks during World War II.

1011.7   urban renewal]   Federal program to redevelop land in high-density areas, also called "slum clearance" because it was primarily employed in impoverished areas.

1011.29–30   B. Altman . . . photographer]   B. Altman, New York department store known for its quality and conservative style; Russeks, a women's clothing store specializing in furs, founded in Brooklyn; Black, Starr and Gorham, jewelry store chain best known for its diamonds; Bachrach Photography, America's oldest photography business.

1022.6   Brownie Box Camera]   Inexpensive and easy-to-use camera introduced by Kodak in 1900.

1032.35–36   All ye know and all ye need to know"]   See John Keats, "Ode on a Grecian Urn" (1819): "Beauty is truth, truth beauty, that is all/Ye know on earth, and all ye need to know."

1033.21   C-141 air force jet]   Four-engine jet transport that saw extensive use by the air force during the Vietnam War.

1033.22   Travis Air Force Base]   Large United States Air Force air base located in Solano County, California, between Sacramento and San Francisco.